Also by Thomas Mann

❖❖❖❖❖❖❖❖❖❖❖❖❖❖❖❖❖❖❖❖❖❖❖❖❖❖❖❖❖❖❖❖❖❖❖❖❖

FICTION

Buddenbrooks

The Magic Mountain

Royal Highness

Stories of Three Decades

Lotte in Weimar

The Tables of the Law

The Transposed Heads

Doctor Faustus

The Holy Sinner

The Black Swan

Confessions of Felix Krull

❖❖❖❖❖❖❖❖❖❖❖❖❖❖❖❖❖❖❖❖❖❖❖❖❖❖❖❖❖❖❖❖❖❖❖❖❖

NON-FICTION

Essays of Three Decades

The Coming Victory of Democracy

❖❖❖❖❖❖❖❖❖❖❖❖❖❖❖❖❖❖❖❖❖❖❖❖❖❖❖❖❖❖❖❖❖❖❖❖❖

JOSEPH AND HIS BROTHERS

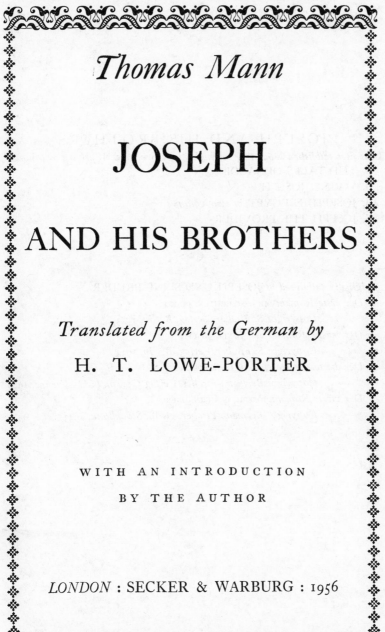

Thomas Mann

JOSEPH

AND HIS BROTHERS

Translated from the German by

H. T. LOWE-PORTER

WITH AN INTRODUCTION

BY THE AUTHOR

LONDON : SECKER & WARBURG : 1956

JOSEPH AND HIS BROTHERS

was first published separately in England by Secker & Warburg as follows:

I. THE TALES OF JACOB
II. YOUNG JOSEPH
III. JOSEPH IN EGYPT *in two volumes*
IV. JOSEPH THE PROVIDER

ॐ

FOREWORD

WHEN I see this pyramidlike piece of work, which differs from its brother monsters at the edge of the Libyan Desert only in the fact that no hecatombs of scourged and panting slaves fell victim to its erection but that it is the product of years of patient labor on the part of *one* man — when I see this formerly quadripartite work united as a proper entity between the two covers of a single volume, I am filled not only with justifiable astonishment at an almost incredible achievement in the art of book-making, but also with memories, with a kind of autobiographical pensiveness.

Long years went into its making — to be exact, counting all interruptions, some of them quite protracted, a total of sixteen: a period of time historically as "weighty with stories" as the stubbornly independent product that grew up within it, weighty in a sense that should have been detrimental to epic equanimity. Is it asking too much of posterity — assuming that we may look forward to any sort of intellectually active posterity — is it asking too much to expect a bit of puzzled surprise that this narrative of seventy thousand calmly flowing lines telling of the primitive occurrences of human life, of love and hate, blessing and curse, fraternal strife and paternal grief, pride and penance, fall and rise, a humorous song of mankind, if one is allowed to call things by name — that this narrative could have come into being in the turbulent circumstances of these years 1926 to 1942, when every day hurled the wildest demands at the heart and the brain? As for me, I yield not to surprise but to gratitude. I am grateful to this work which was my staff and my stay on a path that often led through dark valleys. It was my refuge, my comfort, my home, my symbol of steadfastness, the guarantee of my perseverance in the tempestuous change of things.

The Magic Mountain was completed in Munich in 1924 and was published the same year. Between its conclusion and the day when I found the courage to write the first sentence of the "Descent into Hell," the overture to *Joseph and His Brothers*, this "very deep is the well of the past," there lies a period of no production except the short story *Disorder and Early Sorrow*, improvised for the periodical *Neue Rundschau* on the occasion of my fiftieth birthday. It was one of those active relaxations which I enjoy with a certain degree of regularity after the discharge of a task that I have borne for years. Similarly after *Lotte in Weimar*, *The Transposed Heads*, a metaphysical pleasantry, was created, and after the completion of the Joseph-stories the polemic against Nazism on behalf of human morality called *The Tables of the Law*. Slowly, after that day of the beginning and after inditing the fantastic essay that serves as introduction and reminds one of the base of preparations for a hazardous exploratory expedition, the parts of the mythological novel grew, slowly and with anxious misgivings about all the time and space they demanded. They finally saw the light of day under the title *The Tales of Jacob* — simply because enough manuscript for a substantial volume had accumulated and not because the opus had been planned in several volumes, as a series of novels, or as a "tetralogy." The whole thing, alas, had been planned differently — as always. *Buddenbrooks* had been envisioned as a story of mercantile life of perhaps two hundred and fifty pages and then grew beyond the bounds. *The Magic Mountain*, indeed, was to have been a short story of the size of *Death in Venice*, its grotesque sequel, so to speak. In the case of *Joseph* I had had in mind a triptych of fairly long short stories of religious tinge, the first of which was to be of mythical, Biblical character. The story of Joseph, to be retold in sprightly fashion, was chosen for this purpose. *Habent sua fata libelli* — not only after their publication, but particularly during their genesis. The author knows little about them when he lays hands on them. They have a mind of their own and know what they are doing. The short stories of the Reformation and Counter-Reformation vanished, and for more than a decade and a half I was to remain under the spell of the mythical-Biblical ones. These, as long as the concept remained tenable, were intended as a unified, continuing story, as a single volume that had unfortunately become a little too portly, so that it might be said that only here and now, after years of "disrupted" existence, the story appears in its true form.

Customarily my narrative works are accompanied by essayistic offshoots which may have been stimulated and requested by outside agencies, but which basically serve no other purpose than to strengthen me in the former. The treatises *On the German Republic* and *Goethe and Tolstoy*, to name only these, belong to *The Magic Mountain*, those on *Germany and the Germans*, Dostoyevsky, and Nietzsche to *Doctor Faustus*. It would be tedious to enumerate everything of the nature of such critical capers and marginalia pertaining to and coloured by *Joseph*; they fill volumes and constitute the greater part of the contents of the two English volumes entitled *Order of the Day* and *Essays of Three Decades*. As though the sixty pages of introduction to *The Tales of Jacob* had not sufficed to equip me and put me in the right frame of mind for the journey into the

mythical land, it was followed in the same year, 1926, by the amorous
analysis of Kleist's *Amphitryon*. Moreover, even the casual reader
will find that the mythicizing introductory sentences of my lecture
on Lessing prove that it, too, belongs in this orbit, or let us rather
say, that it has been brought into the orbit by gentle pressure. And
I even interrupted myself with an autonomous narrative when I had
just begun to narrate, in *Mario and the Magician*, a story with strong
political inclinations, dealing with the psychology of Fascism and of
"freedom," with the lack of will of the latter, which puts it at a great
disadvantage with respect to the robust will of its opponent.

It must be remembered that at the time when I began *Joseph* the
internal political postwar tensions in Germany had already become
acute and had a constant disturbing effect on my daily life and
thought. My conscience had been awake in a political sense since the
outbreak of the first World War, which I had been constrained to
recognize as the spectacular finale of the bourgeois era and the
starting-point of incalculable subversions. It availed me little to en-
title the literary product of this consciousness of a turning-point in
the times, and at the same time of a profound crisis in my own life,
Betrachtungen eines Unpolitischen. After that I was ensnared head
and heart in politics, the very thing I had sought to ward off in this
comprehensive book; from then on I was compelled to take a definite
stand. This book, a painful polemic, parts of which make a scandalous
impression today and from which quotations are used for my exposure in post-Hitler Germany and elsewhere, was a boundless, time-
consuming piece of writing of rigorous self-examination and introspection, whose motto: "Compare yourself, recognize what you
are!" should have been supplemented by another: "No one remains
quite what he was when he recognizes himself." I helped my own
development with this work, and after its completion I was prepared
to complement my literary Europeanism, of which the book is full,
with political Europeanism, to accept the European-democratic religion of humanity within my moral horizon, which so far had been
bounded solely by late German romanticism, by Schopenhauer,
Nietzsche, Wagner.

In a recent retrospective review a clever Swiss critic called the
Betrachtungen an "essayistic adventure and cultural novel," a "book
of vanquishment and self-immolation for the sake of the secret demands of growth," and he added that the cathartic function that it
served in my life should also have operated on my German readers.
This is the tragedy. Someone had "taken pains on behalf of Christendom," as Claudel says, and "Christendom" had been too lazy to raise
a finger. When I wrote the last word of the *Betrachtungen* (at the
very latest!) I no longer stood where I had when I wrote the first.
But the Germans still stood there. They had complacently accepted

my culturally conservative polemic and they had regarded it as static rather than dynamic — in other words, they had misunderstood it. Whatever I did from then on: my defence of that poor creature of defeat, the universally sabotaged republic; my opposition to rising nationalism and to all the philosophic endeavours and manœuvres that promoted it, to vitalistic irrationalism; my *Appeal to Reason,* my intercession for Europe and for peace — all these were received at best with a dubious shrug, perhaps accompanied by the puzzled question: "Why does he do these things? Is he angling for a cabinet office?" For the most part, however, my attitude was interpreted as treason and apostasy from a Germany that I saw reeling toward a barbaric people's dictatorship, toward war, toward destruction, taking Europe into the abyss with it, and from this Germany I had salvaged my soul at the eleventh hour.

Thanks to my political activities, I had to do my creative work in those 1920's under the pressure, under the spiritual disturbances and annoyances, of national odium, and the official esteem in which the republic held me made no difference; it only imposed on me the obligation of making all sorts of academic addresses at festive occasions. The unofficial, politically adjuring statements, articles, speeches went their own way. *The Tales of Jacob* were finished and a part of the *Young Joseph* had been written when I made my tour of the Middle East, to Egypt and Palestine, early in 1930. It could hardly be called a trip for the purpose of study; it rather served for verifying on the spot the things of this sphere with which I had been concerned at a distance. At any rate, with my physical eyes I saw the Nile country from the Delta up (or down) to Nubia and the memorable places of the Holy Land, and my impressions were of benefit to the third volume, called *Joseph in Egypt,* part of which was still written in Germany. The essay *Sufferings and Greatness of Richard Wagner* belongs with this volume. Fifty years had passed since the great music-dramatist closed his eyes in Venice, and several cities in various countries had invited me to deliver lectures on his art. I wrote much more than I could hope to deliver orally, and in the abridged form in which I had cast my critical eulogy I read it for the first time on February 10, 1933 before a thoroughly sympathetic audience at the University of Munich. On the following day I set out with a minimum of baggage for Amsterdam, Brussels, and Paris, on the trip from which I was never to return to Germany.

When I left Munich, Hitler was already Chancellor. But it was not until we were vacationing in the Swiss Alps that the major calamities took place: the burning of the Reichstag, the catastrophic victory of the Nazi Party in the election, the establishing of the dictatorship, and the "National Revolution." At the same time a murderous radio and newspaper campaign waged against me for my description of

Wagner made my return home impossible. It meant an interruption of many months in my work on Joseph. A courageous child who had ventured to return to our confiscated house in Munich brought me the manuscript from there to southern France. Here, in loosely provisional circumstances, I was able to resume work on an undertaking that alone vouchsafed the continuity of my life.

Joseph in Egypt was finished at long last and in spite of many lengthy interruptions at Küsnacht on the Lake of Zurich, where we had moved in the autumn of 1933, and it was published in 1936 in Vienna, where the Berlin publishing house with which I was connected had found temporary refuge. This was the time of my ejection from membership in the German State and the revocation of my honorary doctor's degree (now restored), to which I replied to the Dean of the Philosophical Faculty of the University of Bonn in a letter that was translated into many languages. It was, moreover, the time of the founding of the Zurich periodical for free German culture, *Mass und Wert*, of which I was the responsible editor and in which considerable portions of *Lotte in Weimar* appeared, the novel about Goethe on which I had resumed work and which I again regarded as only a brief interlude. I was a member at that time of the Permanent Committee on Letters and Arts appointed by the League of Nations, and before the establishment of the Third Reich I had participated in the meetings of this body in Geneva and in Frankfurt am Main. To a discussion in Nice, which I did not attend in person, I contributed a written memorandum of a political nature that created considerable sensation when it was read and that was later included under the title *Europe Beware* in a collection of essays of the same name (*Achtung, Europa!*). I took part again in the meetings of the committee in Venice and Budapest, and it was at an open session in the Hungarian capital that I undertook to make an extemporaneous speech against the assassins of freedom and on behalf of the need of a militant democracy. It was a statement that offended, almost to the point of bad taste, against the rather academic character of the discussions, which were kept on a noncommittal level, if only out of consideration for the Fascist delegates; but it was received with a demonstration of approval lasting for many minutes on the part of the Hungarian public, and it earned me an enthusiastic embrace from Karel Čapek, the Czech dramatist, who died of a broken heart when the democracies betrayed his country.

As early as 1934 I had made contact with America. The travel diary *Voyage with Don Quixote* was the literary product of my first Atlantic crossing. From then on I crossed the ocean every year and the preponderance of my existence began to shift to the other shore. For America I wrote *On the Coming Victory of Democracy*, a lecture with which I made a tour of fourteen cities in the United States in the winter of 1938. And for an American abridged edition of Schopenhauer I wrote an introduction on this philosopher who had made such a deep impression on me in my youth. It is now included in the collection *Essays of Three Decades.*

Other products of the years of my rotation between Europe and the New World include the two articles on Freud, the second of which served as an anniversary address in Vienna on the occasion of the eightieth birthday of the great scholar; also the second lecture on Wagner, *Richard Wagner and the Ring*, given at the University of Zurich in connection with the gala production of the four operas. All these were interpolations in my work on the novel about Goethe, which in turn was an interpolation in the main epic undertaking, the stories of Joseph. This intercalation of labours, inevitable, it seems, in certain cases of productive economy, is no mean spiritual burden. A major work pauses for the sake of a smaller one, the demands of which were not foreseen and which consume years. Under the pressure of the demands of the day this, too, is set aside, and the author devotes himself to digressive tasks, many of which occupy not weeks but months; it only remains that these in turn should be interrupted by smaller and still smaller improvisations, while at the same time the greater and yet greater concerns must never be lost sight of. And so it comes about that the author must forever carry *the totality* of his work, with all its major and minor ramifications in his head and on his shoulders. Patience alone can help him — an equanimity that, if nature has not endowed him with it, must be wrested from a nervous temperament tending toward despair. Durability, steadfastness, longevity are everything, and all his hope is time. "Give me time, eternal gods," so runs his prayer, "and everything shall be finished."

My establishment in Princeton, New Jersey, took place in 1938 amid the most fearful political conditions — at the moment of "Munich," the capitulation of Democracy to Fascism, the sacrificing of the Czech state and of all political morality to "peace in our time." In profound dejection tinged with indignation I wrote *This Peace*, a bitter indictment of the policies of the Western powers, debased by their fear of Russian socialism. *Lotte in Weimar* was continued in new surroundings in face of impediments incident to acclimatization. But my connection with the university as visiting professor also imposed mild duties on me: public lectures and lectures to advanced students, on Goethe's *Faust* and *Werther*, on Freud, on the history of the European novel, and even on *The Magic Mountain* had to be prepared. I spent the summer of 1939 in Europe, in England, Switzerland, and Holland. On the beach at Noordwijk I wrote the introduction of Tolstoy's *Anna Karenina* at the request of Random House of New York; this, too, was incorporated in the German and English collection of my literary essays.

Surprised in Sweden by the war – if the word "surprise" is appropriate – we had a somewhat distressing, perhaps even perilous trip home, first by air to London and then on the over-crowded S.S. *Washington.* I carried many papers, lecture notes, and books with me, which were the object of tedious inspection at the remote and camouflaged London airport. The inspecting officers were particularly suspicious of a sketch representing the seating arrangement at a dinner that Goethe gave in his house on the Frauenplan in Weimar in honour of the sweetheart of his youth. It was suspected of being of strategic importance, and I had to deliver a condensed lecture on the novel in order to convince the officials of the complete innocence of the paper.

Lotte in Weimar was then nearing completion. In the same year I finished the book in Princeton with the spectral dialogue between Goethe and Lotte in the carriage. Now at last, after an interruption of about five years, I was free to go to work on the final volume of *Joseph and His Brothers.* I was filled with a powerful urge to complete this narrative that I had brought along from Germany and that had survived all vicissitudes; mythical memories, playful parallels, not inappropriate to the topic, increased my inclination. I was standing where Wagner had stood when, after the interpolation of *Tristan* and *Die Meistersinger,* he resumed work on the dramatic epic, the gigantic fairy-tale, *The Ring of the Nibelung.* It is true that my treatment of myth was fundamentally more closely related to the humour of Goethe's "Classical Walpurgis Night" than to the pathos of Wagner; but the unexpected evolution that the story of Joseph had followed was nevertheless somehow secretly determined by the recollection of Wagner's grandiose structure, it had moved in its footsteps. Working with themes invented long before, transforming and elaborating them, carrying them all to a crowning climax, I now had to add a cheerful *"Götterdämmerung"* to my three existing fairy-tale operas. I looked forward to it – and yet I was reluctant to go to work.

It was not because the clay had become dry in the many turbulent years. With tooth and nail I had clung to the old task amid all distractions, and it was alive within me. The reason for my reluctance was simply this: that I feared an anticlimax, a falling off of the fourth volume from the third. The latter, *Joseph in Egypt,* seemed to me unquestionably the artistic zenith of the work, if only on account of the humane vindication that I had undertaken in it, the humanization of the figure of Potiphar's wife, the mournful story of her passionate love of the Canaanite major-domo of her *pro forma* husband. I had no female character in stock to balance the Rachel of the first and second novels, the Mut-em-enet of the third, and it took a long time before I became aware that I had one after all. It was Tamar, the daughter-in-law and seductress of Judah, whom I made into Jacob's pupil, an Astarte-like figure, endowed, at the same time, with features from the Book of Ruth; and in half-humorous style I developed her into the prototype of historical ambition. Through her, who eventually gave her name to an entire section of the novel, a short story in itself, I found the fulfilment of the charms of the remaining material and the final incentive to continue the narrative. Even today I see no exaggeration in the sentence of the text that reads: "She might be called the most amazing figure in this whole story — few will be found to deny it."

Nevertheless I put still one other theme ahead of the resumption of the main task, the Indian legend of *The Transposed Heads*, completed in Princeton. Finally, in Brentwood, California, where I spent the spring and part of the summer of 1940, I found the long-silent lyric tone of the Biblical saga again, and the opening chapters of *Joseph the Provider* were written.

The history of the genesis of this volume, the brightest and cheeriest in mood of them all, is no less agitated, perhaps even more so, than that of the three others, and still fuller of interruptions, to which I always yielded unwillingly and yet with all my heart. It developed amid the terrible tensions of a war upon whose outcome the fate of the world, of Western civilization, in fact of all that I held dear, seemed to depend; of the war that at first showed such ill-boding aspects; into which, after the fall of France, the country of which I was about to become a citizen entered, just as Achilles left his tent after the death of Patroclus; the war into whose service I again and again felt impelled to place my heart and my head and my pen. The war and the world which it promised to create are the subjects of the impromptu essays that belong chronologically to the fourth volume of *Joseph*, things like *This War, The Problem of Freedom,* and others, and I used them as lectures with which I fulfilled my obligations as Fellow of the Library of Congress in Washington. But even in Princeton, before migrating to California after the expiration of my visiting professorship, I had begun to write regular monthly radio messages to Germany at the behest of the British Broadcasting Corporation, the total number of which was to reach fifty-five in the course of the war years. Twenty-eight days of each month were devoted to Joseph, four weeks of liberty and of mythical playfulness — then came a day or two when I was no longer the creative writer but a summoner to battle with all my heart; days when I gave free rein to my hatred of the despoilers of Germany and of Europe, to transfer it later to the spinning disk in a state of agitation that art can never engender but only life and its primal emotions. And then back again to the work of peace and the "Temple Theatre," the humorously exact realization of the unreal by staging and discussion.

The California sky, so like the Egyptian, smiled on my work; to it
the story undoubtedly owes much of its cheerfulness. For while there
were many alarmists who fled the west coast in fear of Japanese attacks, I, on the contrary, utilizing the last moment when building was
still possible, had erected my house in the Santa Monica hills. *Joseph
the Provider* is that part of the work that was written in America
from the first word to the last, and there can be no doubt that it received its share of the spirit of the country. That spirit is reflected not
only in the "success story," which it is by nature and by design, not
only in the occasional, gladly accepted Anglo-Saxon coloration of its
German diction. The spirit of the tale, if anyone is interested in my
mythical opinion, is a spirit untrammelled to the point of abstraction,
whose medium is speech in and of itself, speech in the abstract, which
regards itself as absolute and pays little attention to idiom and to
local linguistic divinities. I have no objection if, for example, the
critics say that the German of the "Prelude in the Upper Circles" in
Joseph the Provider "is really not German any more." Suffice it that
it is speech, and suffice it that the entire opus is fundamentally a work
of speech in whose polyphony sounds of the primitive Orient mingle
with the most modern, with the accents of fictive scientific method,
and that it takes pleasure in changing its linguistic masks as often as
its hero changes his God-masks — the last of which looks remarkably
American. For it is the mask of an American Hermes, a brilliant messenger of shrewdness, whose New Deal is unmistakably reflected in
Joseph's magic administration of national economy.

The year 1942 was drawing to a close when I finished. Under the
last line of *The Magic Mountain*, eighteen years earlier, I had, with
some solemnity, written: *"Finis operis."* What a pleasantly self-
willed, utterly discriminating force is individual style! This time it
prompted me to disguise the finis in the manner of patriarchial story-
tellers, so that the title of the whole work, *Joseph and His Brothers*,
appears prominently as the final word of the last sentence.

Here, then, is the whole work in a single binding, in Helen Lowe-
Porter's admirable translation — an achievement of loyalty and
devotion which this woman would not have been able to accomplish
without faith in the worthiness of her task. May I share this faith?
How will posterity regard this work? Will it soon become a dust-
covered curio for antiquarians, the easy prey of fleeting time? Or
will its pleasantries cheer those who come after us, its pathos touch
them? Or will it perhaps be numbered among the great books? I do
not know and no one can tell me. But as the son of a tradesman I have
a fundamental faith in quality. What is it that has helped many a
product of human hands through the ages, given it strength to resist
the centuries, and restrained mankind in its wildest days from de-
stroying it? Only one thing: quality. The song of Joseph is good,

solid work, done out of that fellow feeling for which mankind has
always been sensitively receptive. A measure of durability is, I think,
inherent in it.

THOMAS MANN

Pacific Palisades, California
February 1948

CONTENTS

THE TALES OF JACOB

III JOSEPH AND BENJAMIN

IV THE DREAMER

V THE JOURNEY TO THE BROTHERS

VI THE STONE BEFORE THE GRAVE

VII HE WHO WAS MANGLED

JOSEPH IN EGYPT

I THE JOURNEY DOWNWARDS

II THE ENTRANCE INTO SHEOL

III THE ARRIVAL

IV THE HIGHEST

V THE MAN OF THE BLESSING

VI THE SMITTEN ONE

VII THE PIT

JOSEPH THE PROVIDER

I THE SECOND PIT

II THE SUMMONS

III THE CRETAN LOGGIA

IV THE TIME OF ENFRANCHISEMENT

CONTENTS

THE TALES OF JACOB

PRELUDE

DESCENT INTO HELL

VERY deep is the well of the past. Should we not call it bottomless?

Bottomless indeed, if — and perhaps only if — the past we mean is the past merely of the life of mankind, that riddling essence of which our own normally unsatisfied and quite abnormally wretched existences form a part; whose mystery, of course, includes our own and is the alpha and omega of all our questions, lending burning immediacy to all we say, and significance to all our striving. For the deeper we sound, the further down into the lower world of the past we probe and press, the more do we find that the earliest foundations of humanity, its history and culture, reveal themselves unfathomable. No matter to what hazardous lengths we let out our line they still withdraw again, and further, into the depths. Again and further are the right words, for the unresearchable plays a kind of mocking game with our researching ardours; it offers apparent holds and goals, behind which, when we have gained them, new reaches of the past still open out — as happens to the coastwise voyager, who finds no end to his journey, for behind each headland of clayey dune he conquers, fresh headlands and new distances lure him on.

Thus there may exist provisional origins, which practically and in fact form the first beginnings of the particular tradition held by a given community, folk or communion of faith; and memory, though sufficiently instructed that the depths have not actually been plumbed, yet nationally may find reassurance in some primitive point of time and, personally and historically speaking, come to rest there.

Young Joseph, for instance, son of Jacob and the lovely, too-soon-departed Rachel; Joseph, living when Kurigalzu the Cassite reigned at Babel, Lord of the Four Regions, King of Sumeria and Akkadia, greatly comfortable to the heart of Bel-Marduk, a ruler both luxurious and stern, the curls of whose beard stood ranged in such perfect rows that they looked like a division of well-furnished shield-bearers; while at Thebes, in the land which Joseph was used to call Mizraim, also Kemt, the Black, His Sanctity the good God, called Amun-is-satisfied, third of this name, the sun's very son, beamed on the horizon

of his palace and blinded the enraptured eyes of his dust-born subjects; when Asshur increased by the might of its gods, and on the
great shore route from Gaza up to the passes of the cedar mountains
the royal caravans went to and fro, bearing gifts in lapis-lazuli and
stamped gold, between the court of the Land of the Rivers and
Pharaoh's court; when in the cities of the Amorites, at Beth Shan,
Ajalon, Ta'anach, Urushalim, they served Astarte, while at Shechem
and Beth-lahma the seven days' wailing went up for the true Son,
the dismembered one, and at Gebal, the City of the Book, El was
adored, who needed no temple or rite; Joseph, then, living in that
district of the land of Canaan which in Egypt is called the Upper
Retenu, in his father's tents at Hebron, shaded by terebinths and
evergreen oaks, a youth famed for his charm and charming especially
by right from his mother, who had been sweet and lovely like to the
moon when it is full and like Ishtar's star when it swims mildly in
the clear sky; but also armed from the father's side with gifts of the
spirit and perhaps in a sense excelling even him; Joseph, lastly and
in conclusion (for the fifth and the sixth time I name his name, and
with gratification, for there is mystery in names, and I will have it
that knowledge of his confers power to invoke that once so living
and conversable personality, albeit now sunk so deep below the marge
of time); Joseph, for his part, regarded a certain town called Uru,
in Southern Babylonia, which in his tongue he called Ur Kashdim,
Ur of the Chaldees, as the beginning of all things — that is, of all that
mattered to him.

Thence, namely, in times long gone by — Joseph was never quite
clear how far back they lay — a brooding and inwardly unquiet man,
with his wife, whom probably out of tenderness he would call his
sister, together with other members of his family, had departed, to
do as the moon did, that was the deity of Ur, to wander and to rove,
because he found it most right and fitting to his unsatisfied, doubting,
yes, tormented state. His removal, which wore an undeniable colour
of contumacy, had been connected with certain structures which
had impressed him as offensive, and which Nimrod the Mighty, then
ruling in Ur, had, if not erected, yet restored and exceedingly increased in height. It was the private conviction of the man from Ur
that Nimrod had done this less in honour of the divine lights of the
firmament to which they were dedicated, than as a bar against dis-
persion and as a sky-soaring monument to his own accumulated
power. From that power the man from Ur had now escaped, by dispersing himself, and with his dependents taking to pilgrimages of
indeterminate length. The tradition handed down to Joseph varied
somewhat as to which had more particularly annoyed the objector:
whether the great moon-citadel of Ur, the turreted temple of the god
Sin, after whom the whole land of Shinar was named, the same word

appearing in his own region, as for instance in the mountain called Sinai; or that towering house of the sun, E-sagila, the temple of Marduk at Babel itself, whose summit Nimrod had exalted to the height of the heavens, and a precise description of which Joseph had received by word of mouth. There had clearly been much else at which the musing man had taken offence, beginning with that very mightiness of Nimrod and going on to certain customs and practices which to others had seemed hallowed and unalienable by long tradition but more and more filled his own soul with doubts. And since it is not good to sit still when one's soul smarts with doubt, he had simply put himself in motion.

He reached Harran, city of the way and moon-city of the north, in the land of Naharain, where he dwelt many years and gathered recruits, receiving them into close relationship with his own. But it was a relationship which spelt unrest and almost nothing else; a soul-unrest which expressed itself in an unrest of body that had little to do with ordinary light-hearted wanderlust and the adventurousness of the free-footed, but was rather the suffering of the hunted and solitary man, whose blood already throbbed with the dark beginnings of oncoming destiny; perhaps the burden of its weight and scope stood in precise relation to his torment and unrest. Thus Harran too, lying as it did within Nimrod's sphere of control, proved but a "station on the way," from which the moon-man eventually set forth again, together with Sarah his sister-wife and all his kin and his and their possessions, to continue as their guide and Mahdi his hegira towards an unknown goal.

So they had reached the west country and the Amurru who dwelt in the land of Canaan, where once the Hittites had been lords; had crossed the country by stages and thrust deep, deep southwards under other suns, into the land of mud, where the water flows the wrong way, unlike the waters of the land of Naharina, and one travelled northwards downstream; where a people stiff with age worshipped its dead, and where for the man of Ur and for his requirements there would have been nothing to seek or to find. Backwards he turned to the westland, the middle land, which lay between Nimrod's domains and the land of mud; and in the southern part, not far from the desert, in a mountainous region, where there was little ploughland, but plenty of grazing for his cattle, he acquired a kind of superficial permanence and dwelt and dealt with the inhabitants on friendly terms.

Tradition has it that his god — that god upon whose image his spirit laboured, highest among all the rest, whom alone to serve he was in pride and love resolved, the God of the ages, for whom he sought a name and found none sufficient, wherefore he gave him the plural, calling him, provisionally, Elohim, the Godhead — Elohim, then, had

made him promises as far-reaching as clearly defined, to the effect
not only that he, the man from Ur, should become a folk in numbers
like the sands of the sea and a blessing unto all peoples, but also that
the land wherein he now dwelt as a stranger, and whither Elohim
had led him out of Chaldæa, should be to him and to his seed in everlasting possession in all its parts — whereby the God of gods had
expressly specified the populations and present inhabitants of the
land, whose "gates" the seed of the man from Ur should possess. In
other words, God had destined these populations to defeat and subjection in the interest of the man from Ur and his seed. But all this
must be accepted with caution, or at least with understanding. We
are dealing with later interpolations deliberately calculated to confirm
as the earliest intentions of the divine political situations which had
first been established by force. As a matter of fact the moon-wanderer's spirit was by no means of a kind likely to receive or to elicit promises of a political nature. There is no evidence that when he left home
he had already thought of the Amurruland as a theatre of his future
activities; and the fact that his wanderings also took him through the
land of tombs and of the blunt-nosed lion maid would seem to point
to the opposite conclusion. But when he left Nimrod's high and mighty
state in his rear, likewise avoiding the greatly estimable kingdom of
the double-crowned king of the oasis, and turned westwards — into a
region, that is, whose shattered public life condemned it to impotence
and servitude — his conduct does not argue the possession of political
vision or of a taste for imperial greatness. What had set him in motion
was unrest of the spirit, a need of God, and if — as there can be no
doubt — dispensations were vouchsafed him, they had reference to
the irradiations of his personal experience of God, which was of a
new kind altogether; and his whole concern from the beginning had
been to win for it sympathy and adherence. He suffered; and when
he compared the measure of his inward distress with that of the great
majority, he drew the conclusion that it was pregnant with the future.
Not in vain, so he heard from the newly beheld God, shall have been
thy torment and thine unrest; for it shall fructify many souls and
make proselytes in numbers like to the sands of the seas; and it shall
give impulse to great expansions of life hidden in it as in a seed; and
in one word, thou shalt be a blessing. A blessing? It is unlikely that
the word gives the true meaning of that which happened to him in
his vision and which corresponded to his temperament and to his
experience of himself. For the word "blessing" carries with it an idea
which but ill describes men of his sort: men, that is, of roving spirit
and discomfortable mind, whose novel conception of the deity is
destined to make its mark upon the future. The life of men with
whom new histories begin can seldom or never be a sheer unclouded
blessing; not this it is which their consciousness of self whispers in

their ears. "And thou shalt be a destiny": such is the purer and more precise meaning of the promise, in whatever language it may have been spoken. And whether that destiny might or might not be a blessing is a question the twofold nature of which is apparent from the fact that it can always and without exception be answered in different ways — though of course it was always answered in the affirmative by the community — continually waxing in numbers and in grace — of those who recognized the true Baal and Adad of the pantheon in the God who had brought out of Chaldæa the man from Ur; that community to the existence of which young Joseph traced back his own spiritual and physical being.

<h2 style="text-align:center">2</h2>

SOMETIMES, indeed, he thought of the moon-wanderer as his own great-grandfather — though such an idea is to be sternly excluded from the realms of the possible. He himself was perfectly aware, on the ground of much and varied instruction, that the position was one of far wider bearings. Not so wide, however, that that mighty man of the earth whose boundary stones, adorned with representations of the signs of the zodiac, the man from Ur had put behind him, had actually been Nimrod, the first king on earth, who had begotten Bel of Shinar. No, for according to the tablets, this had been Hammurabi, the Lawgiver, restorer of those citadels of the sun and moon; and when young Joseph put him on a level with that prehistoric Nimrod, it was by a play of thought which most charmingly becomes his spirit but which would be unbecoming and hence forbidden to ours. The same is true of his occasional confusion of the man from Ur with his father's ancestor and his, who had borne the same or a similar name. Between the boy Joseph and the pilgrimage of his ancestor in the spirit and the flesh there lay, according to the system of chronology which his age and sphere rejoiced in, fully twenty generations, or, roughly speaking, six hundred Babylonian years, a period as long as from our time back into the Gothic Middle Ages — as long, and yet not so long either.

True, we have received our mathematical sidereal time handed down to us from ages long before the man from Ur ever set out on his wanderings, and, in like manner, shall we hand it on to our furthest descendants. But even so, the meaning, weight and fullness of earthly time is not everywhere one and the same. Time has uneven measure, despite all the objectivity of the Chaldæan chronology. Six hundred years at that time and under that sky did not mean what they mean in our western history. They were a more level, silent, speechless reach; time was less effective, her power to bring about change was both weaker and more restricted in its range — though certainly in

those twenty generations she had produced changes and revolutions
of a considerable kind: natural revolutions, even changes in the earth's
surface in Joseph's immediate circle, as we know and as he knew too.
For where, in his day, were Gomorrah, and Sodom, the dwelling-
place of Lot of Harran, who had been received into the spiritual community of the man from Ur; where were those voluptuous cities? Lo,
the leaden alkaline lake lay there where their unchastity had flourished, for the whole region had been swept with a burning fiery flood
of pitch and sulphur, so frightful and apparently so destructive of all
life that Lot's daughters, timely escaped with their father, though he
would have given them up to the lust of the Sodomites instead of
certain important guests whom he harboured, went and lay with
their father, being under the delusion that save themselves there were
none left upon the earth, and out of womanly carefulness for the continuance of the race.

Thus time in its course had left behind it even visible alterations.
There had been times of blessing and times of curse, times of fullness
and times of dearth, wars and campaigns, changing overlords and
new gods. Yet on the whole time then had been more conservatively
minded than time now, the frame of Joseph's life, his ways and habits
of thought were far more like his ancestors' than ours are like the
crusaders'. Memory, resting on oral tradition from generation to
generation, was more direct and confiding, it flowed freer, time was a
more unified and thus a briefer vista; young Joseph cannot be blamed
for vaguely foreshortening it, for sometimes, in a dreamy mood, perhaps by night and moonlight, taking the man from Ur for his father's
grandfather — or even worse. For it must be stated here that in all
probability this man from Ur was not the original and actual man
from Ur. Probably — even to young Joseph, in a preciser hour, and
by broad daylight — this man from Ur had never seen the moon-
citadel of Uru; it had been *his father* who had gone thence northwards, towards Harran in the land of Naharain. And thus it was only
from Harran that this falsely so-called man from Ur, having received
the command from the Lord God, had set out towards the country
of the Amorites, together with that Lot, later settled in Sodom, whom
the tradition of the community vaguely stated to be the son of the
brother of the man from Ur, on the ground, indeed, that he was the
"son of Harran." Now Lot of Sodom was certainly a son of Harran,
since he as well as the Ur-man came from there. But to turn Harran,
the "city of the way," into a brother of the man from Ur, and thus to
make a nephew out of his proselyte Lot, was a kind of dreamy toying
with ideas which, while scarcely permissible in broad daylight, yet
makes it easier to understand why young Joseph fell naturally into
the same kind of game.

He did so in the same good faith as governed, for instance, the

star-worshippers and astrologers at Shinar, in their prognostications
according to the principle of stellar representation, and exchanged
one planet with another, for instance the sun, when it had set, with
Ninurta the planet of war and state, or the planet Marduk with
Scorpio, thereafter blithely calling Scorpio Marduk and Ninurta the
sun. He did so, that is, on practical grounds, for his desire to set a
beginning to the chain of events to which he belonged encountered
the same difficulty that it always does: the fact that everybody has
a father, that nothing comes first and of itself, its own cause, but
that everybody is begotten and points backwards, deeper down into
the depths of beginnings, the bottoms and the abysses of the well of
the past. Joseph knew, of course, that the father of the Ur-man, that is
to say the real man from Uru, must have had a father, who must thus
have really been the beginning of his own personal history, and so on,
back to Abel, son of Adam, the ancestor of those who dwell in tents
and keep sheep. Thus even the exodus from Shinar afforded him only
one particular and conditioned beginning; he was well instructed,
by song and saga, how it went on further and further into the general,
through many histories, back to Adapa or Adama, the first man, who,
indeed, according to a lying Babylonian saga, which Joseph more or
less knew by heart, had been the son of Ea, god of wisdom and the
water depths, and had served the gods as baker and cup-bearer — but
of whom Joseph had better and more inspired knowledge; back to
the garden in the East wherein had stood the two trees, the tree of
life and the unchaste tree of death; back to the beginning, the origin
of the world and the heavens and the earthly universe out of confusion and chaos, by the might of the Word, which moved above the
face of the deep and was God. But this, too, was it not only a conditioned and particular beginning of things? For there had already
been forms of existence which looked up to the Creator in admiration
and amaze: sons of God, angels of the starry firmament, about whom
Joseph himself knew some odd and even funny stories, and also rebellious demons. These must have had their origin in some past æon
of the world, which had grown old and sunk and become raw material — and had even this been the very first beginning?

Here young Joseph's brain began to reel, just as ours does when
we lean over the edge of the well; and despite some small inexacti-
tudes which his pretty and well-favoured little head permitted itself
but which are unsuitable for us, we may feel close to him and almost
contemporary, in respect to those deep backwards and abysms of
time into which so long ago he already gazed. He was a human being
like ourselves, thus he must appear to us, and despite his earliness in
time just as remote as we, mathematically speaking, from the beginnings of humanity (not to speak of the beginnings of things in general), for they do in actual fact lie deep down in the darkness at the

bottom of the abyss, and we, in our researches, must either stop at the conditioned and apparent beginnings, confusing them with the real beginning, in the same way that Joseph confused the man from Ur on the one hand with his father, and on the other with Joseph's own great-grandfather; or else we must keep on being lured from one time-coulisse to the next, backwards and backwards into the immeasurable.

3

I HAVE said that Joseph knew by heart some pretty Babylonian verses which originally came from a written tradition of great extent and full of lying wisdom. He had learned them from travellers who touched at Hebron, with whom he had held speech, in his conversable way, and from his tutor, old Eliezer, a freedman of his father, not to be confused (as Joseph sometimes confused him, and even the old man himself probably enjoyed doing) with that Eliezer who was the oldest servant of the original wanderer and who once had wooed the daughter of Bethuel for Isaac at the well. Now we know these verses and legends; we have texts of them, written on tablets found at Nineveh, in the palace of Asshurbanipal, king of the universe, son of Assarhaddon, son of Sennacherib; some of them, preserved in graceful cuneiform characters on greyish-yellow clay, are our earliest documented source for the Great Flood in which the Lord wiped out the first human race on account of its corruption, and which played such an important rôle in Joseph's own personal tradition. Literally speaking, this source itself is not an original one; these crumbling tablets bear transcriptions made by learned slaves only some six hundred years before our era, at the command of Asshurbanipal, a sovereign much addicted to the written word and the established view, an "exceeding wise one," in the Babylonian phrase, and by a zealous accumulator of the fruits of exceeding wisdom. Indeed they were copied from an original a good thousand years older, from the time, that is, of the Lawgiver and the moon-wanderer; which was about as easy, or as hard, for Asshurbanipal's tablet-writers to read and to understand as for us to-day a manuscript of the time of Charlemagne. Written in a quite obsolete and undeveloped hand, a hieratic document, it must have been hard to decipher; whether its significance was wholly honoured in the copy remains matter for doubt.

And then, this original: it was not actually an original; not *the* original, when you come to look at it. It was itself a copy of a document out of God knows what distant time; upon which, then, though without precisely knowing where, one might rest, as upon a true original, if it were not itself provided with glosses and additions by the hand of the scribe, who thought thus to make more comprehensible an original text lying again who knows how far back in time; though what they probably did was further to transmogrify the original wisdom of his text. And thus I might go on — if I were not convinced that my readers already understand what I mean when I speak of coulisses and abysses.

The Egyptians expressed it in a phrase which Joseph knew and himself used on occasion. For although none of the sons of Ham were tolerated in Jacob's tents, because of their ancestor the shamer of his sire, who had turned black all over, also because Jacob entertained religious doubts on the score of the morals of Mizraim; yet the eager-minded lad had often mingled with Egyptians, in the towns, in Kirjath Arba as well as in Shechem, and had picked up this and that of the tongue in which he was later to bear such brilliant witness. The Egyptians then, speaking of something that had high and indefinite antiquity, would say: "It comes from the days of Set." By whom, of course, they meant one of their gods, the wily brother of their Marduk or Tammuz, whom they called Osiris, the Martyr, because Set had first lured him into a sarcophagus and cast it into the river, and afterwards torn him to pieces like a wild beast and killed him entirely, so that Osiris, the Sacrifice, now ruled as lord of the dead and everlasting king of the lower world. "From the days of Set"; the people of Egypt had many uses for the phrase, for with them the origins of everything went back in undemonstrable ways into that darkness.

At the edge of the Libyan desert, near Memphis, hewn out of the rock, crouched the colossus and hybrid, fifty-three metres high; lion and maid, with a maiden's breasts and the beard of a man, and on its headcloth the kingly serpent rearing itself. The huge paws of its cat's body stretched out before it, its nose was blunted by the tooth of time. It had always crouched there, always with its nose blunted by time; and of an age when its nose had not been blunted, or when it had not crouched there, there was no memory at all. Thothmes the Fourth, Golden Hawk and Strong Bull, King of Upper and of Lower Egypt, beloved of the goddess of truth and belonging to the eighteenth dynasty which was also the dynasty of Amun-is-satisfied, by reason of a command received in a dream before he mounted the throne, had had the colossal statue dug out of the sands of the desert, where it lay in great part drifted over and covered up. But some fifteen hundred years before that, King Cheops of the fourth dynasty — the same, by the bye, who built the great pyramid for his own tomb and made sacrifice to the sphinx — had found it half in ruins; and of any time when it had not been known, or even known with a whole nose, there was no knowledge at all.

Was it Set who himself hewed out of the stone that fabulous beast, in which later generations saw an image of the sun-god, calling it Horus in the mount of light? It was possible, of course, for Set, as likewise Osiris the Sacrifice, had probably not always been a god, but sometime or other a man, and indeed a king over Egypt. The statement is often made that a certain Menes or Horus-Menes some six thousand years before our era founded the first Egyptian dynasty, and everything before that is "pre-dynastic"; he, Menes, having first united the two countries, the upper and the lower, the papyrus and the lily, the red and the white crown, and ruled as first king over Egypt, the history of which began with his reign. Of this statement probably every word is false; to the penetrating eye King Menes turns out to be nothing but a coulisse. Egyptian priests told Herodotus that the written history of their country went back eleven thousand, three hundred and forty years before his era, which means for us about fourteen thousand years; a reckoning which is calculated to rob King Menes' figure of all its primitiveness. The history of Egypt alternates between periods of discord and impotence and periods of brilliance and power; epochs of diverse rulers or none at all and epochs of strongly concentrated power; it becomes increasingly clear that these epochs alternated too often to make it likely that King Menes was the earliest ruler over a unified realm. The discords which he healed had followed upon earlier unification and that upon still earlier disruption. How many times the "older," "earlier," "again" are to be repeated we cannot tell; but only that the first unification took place under dynastic deities, whose sons presumably were that Set and Osiris; the sacrifice, murder and dismemberment of the latter being legendary references to quarrels over the succession, which at that time was determined by stratagem and crime. That was a past of a profound, mythical and theological character, even to the point of becoming spiritualized and ghostlike; it became present, it became the object of religious reverence in the shape of certain animals — falcons and jackals — honoured in the ancient capitals, Buto and Nekheb; in these the souls of those beings of primitive time were supposed to be mysteriously preserved.

4

"FROM the days of Set" — young Joseph relished the phrase, and I share his enjoyment; for like the Egyptians, I find it most applicable, and to nearly everything in life. Wherever I look, I think of the words: and the origin of all things, when I come to search for it, pales away into the days of Set.

At the time when our story begins — an arbitrary beginning, it is true, but we must begin somewhere, and fix a point behind which we do not go, otherwise we too shall land in the days of Set — at this time young Joseph already kept the flocks with his brethren, though only under rather privileged conditions; which is to say that when it

pleased him so to do, he watched as they did his father's sheep, goats
and kine on the plains of Shechem and Hebron. What sort of animals
were these, and wherein different from ours? In nothing at all. They
were the very same peaceful and familiar beasts, at the same stage of
development as those we know. The whole history of cattle-breeding
— for instance of the domestic ox from the wild buffalo — lay even in
young Joseph's day so far back in the past that "far" is a feeble word
to use in such a connection. It has been shown that the ox was bred
in the stone age, before the use of metal tools, that is before the bronze
age; this boy of the Amurruland, Joseph, with his Egyptian and
Babylonian culture, was almost as remote from those dim times as we
ourselves are.

As for the wild sheep from which Jacob's flocks — and ours — were
bred, we are told that it is extinct. It died out "long ago." It must have
been completely domesticated "in the days of Set." And the breeding of the horse, the ass, the goat and the pig — out of that wild boar
which mangled Tammuz, the young shepherd — all that was accomplished in the same remote and misty past. Our historical records go
back some seven thousand years — during which time no wild animal
was still in process of domestication. There is no tradition nor any
memory of such events.

If we look at the cultivation of wild grasses and their development
into cereals, the story is the same. Our species of grain, our barley,
oats, rye, maize and wheat — they are the very ones which nourished
the youthful Joseph — have been cultivated so long that no botanist
can trace the beginning of the process, nor any people boast of having
been the first to initiate it. We are told that in the stone age there
were five varieties of wheat and three of barley. As for the cultivation
of the vine from its wild beginnings — an incomparable achievement,
humanly speaking, whatever else one may think about it — tradition,
echoing hollowly up from the depths of the past, ascribes it to Noah,
the one upright man, survivor of the flood, the same whom the Baby-
lonians called Utnapishtim and also Atrachasis, the exceeding wise
one, who imparted to Gilgamesh, his late grandchild, hero of the
legends written on the tablets, the story of the beginning of things.
This upright man, then, as Joseph likewise knew, was the first to
plant vineyards — nor did Joseph consider it such a very upright deed.
Why could he not have planted something useful: fig trees, for instance, or olives? But no, he chose to plant the vine, and was drunk
therefrom, and in his drunkenness was mocked and shamed of his
manhood. But when Joseph imagined all that to have happened not
so very long ago, that miracle of the grape, perhaps some dozen of
generations before his "great-grandfather," his ideas of time showed
themselves to be hazy indeed; the past which he so lightly invoked
being actually matter of remote and primeval distances. Having said

thus much, it only remains to add — however much we may pale at
the thought — that those distances themselves must have lain very
late in time, compared with the remoteness of the beginning of the
human race, for them to have produced a civilization capable of that
high emprise, the cultivation of the vine.

Where then do they lie in time, the beginnings of human civilization? How old is it? I put the question with reference to young Joseph, whose stage of development, though remote from ours, did not
essentially differ from it, aside from those less precise habits of
thought of his, at which we may benevolently smile. We have only
to enquire, to conjure up a whole vista of time-coulisses opening out
infinitely, as in mockery. When we ourselves speak of antiquity we
mostly mean the Græco-Roman world — which, relatively speaking,
is of a brand new modernity. Going back to the so-called "primitive
population" of Greece, the Pelasgians, we are told that before they
settled in the islands, the latter were inhabited by the *actual* primitive
population, a race which preceded the Phœnicians in the domination
of the sea — a fact which reduces to the merest time-coulisse the
Phœnician claim to have been the first seafaring folk. But science is
increasingly unfavourable to all these theories; more and more it inclines to the hypothesis and the conviction that these "barbarians"
were colonists from Atlantis, the lost continent beyond the pillars
of Hercules, which in times gone by united Europe with America.
But whether this was the earliest region of the earth to be populated
by human beings is very doubtful, so doubtful as to be unlikely; it is
much more probable that the early history of civilization, including
that of Noah, the exceeding wise one, is to be connected with regions
of the earth's surface much older in point of time and already long
before fallen to decay.

But these are foothills whereupon we may not wander, and only
vaguely indicate by that before-quoted Egyptian phrase; the peoples
of the east behaved with a piety equal to their wisdom when they
ascribed to the gods their first knowledge of a civilized life. The red-
hued folk of Mizraim saw in Osiris the Martyr the benefactor who
had first given them laws and taught them to cultivate the soil; being
prevented finally by the plotting of the crafty Set, who attacked
him like a wild boar. As for the Chinese, they consider the founder
of their empire to have been an imperial half-god named Fu-hsi, who
introduced cattle into China and taught the priceless art of writing.
This personage apparently did not consider the Chinese, at that time
— some two thousand, eight hundred and fifty-two years before our
era — to be ripe for astronomical instruction; for according to their
annals they received it only about thirteen hundred years later, from
the great foreign emperor, Tai-Ko-Fokee; whereas the astrologers
of Shinar were already several hundred years earlier instructed in

the signs of the zodiac; and we are told that a man who accompanied Alexander of Macedon to Babylon sent to Aristotle Chaldæan astronomical records scratched on baked clay, whose antiquity would be to-day four thousand, one hundred and sixty years. That is easily possible, for it seems likely that observation of the heavens and astronomical calculations were made in Atlantis, whose disappearance, according to Solon, dated nine thousand years before that worthy's own time; from which it follows that man attained to skill in these lofty arts some eleven and a half thousand years before our era.

It is clear that the art of writing is not younger than this, and very possibly much older. I speak of it in particular because Joseph entertained such a lively fondness for the art, and unlike his brothers early perfected himself in it; being instructed at first by Eliezer, in the Babylonian as well as in the Phœnician and Hittite scripts. He had a genuine weakness for the god or idol whom in the East they called Nabu, the writer of history, and in Tyre and Sidon Taut; in both places recognizing him as the inventor of letters and the chronicler of the beginnings of things: the Egyptian god Thoth of Hermopolis, the letter-writer of the gods and the patron of science, whose office was regarded in those parts as higher than all others; that sincere, solicitous and reasonable god, who was sometimes a white-haired ape, of pleasing appearance, sometimes wore an ibis head, and likewise had certain tender and spiritual affiliations with the moon which were quite to young Joseph's taste. These predilections the youth would not have dared confess to his father Jacob, who set his face sternly against all such coquetting with idols, being even stricter in his attitude than were certain very high places themselves to which his austerity was dedicated. For Joseph's history proves that such little departures on his part into the impermissible were not visited very severely, at least not in the long run.

As for the art of writing, with reference to its misty origins it would be proper to paraphrase the Egyptian expression and say that it came "from the days of Thoth." The written roll is represented in the oldest Egyptian art, and we know a papyrus which belonged to Horus-Send, a king of the second dynasty, six thousand years before our era, and which even then was supposed to be so old that it was said Sendi had inherited it from Set. When Sneferu and that Cheops reigned, sons of the sun, of the fourth dynasty, and the pyramids of Gizeh were built, knowledge of writing was so usual amongst the lower classes that we to-day can read the simple inscriptions scratched by artisans on the great building blocks. But it need not surprise us that such knowledge was common property in that distant time, when we recall the priestly account of the age of the written history of Egypt.

If, then, the days of an established language of signs are so unnumbered, where shall we seek for the beginnings of oral speech? The oldest, the primeval language, we are told, is Indo-Germanic, Indo-European, Sanscrit. But we may be sure that that is a beginning as hasty as any other; and that there existed a still older mother-tongue which included the roots of the Aryan as well as the Semitic and Hamitic tongues. Probably it was spoken on Atlantis — that land which is the last far and faint coulisse still dimly visible to our eyes, but which itself can scarcely be the original home of articulate man.

5

CERTAIN discoveries have caused the experts in the history of the earth to estimate the age of the human species at about five hundred thousand years. It is a scant reckoning, when we consider, first, how science to-day teaches that man in his character as animal is the oldest of all mammals and was already in the latter dawn of life existing upon this earth in various zoological modes, amphibious and reptilian, before any cerebral development took place; and second, what endless and boundless expanses of time must have been at his disposal, to turn the crouching, dream-wandering, marsupial type, with unseparated fingers, and a sort of flickering pre-reason as his guide, such as man must have been before the time of Noah-Utnapishtim, the exceeding wise, into the inventor of bow and arrow, the fire-maker, the welder of meteoric iron, the cultivator of corn and wine, the breeder of domestic cattle — in a word, into the shrewd, skilful and in every essential respect modern human being which appears before us at the earliest grey dawn of history. A priest at the temple of Sais explained to Solon the Greek myth of Phæton through a human experiencing of some deviation in the course of the bodies which move round the earth in space, resulting in a devastating conflagration on the earth. Certainly it becomes clearer and clearer that the dream memory of man, formless but shaping itself ever anew after the manner of sagas, reaches back to catastrophes of vast antiquity, the tradition of which, fed by recurrent but lesser similar events, established itself among various peoples and produced that formation of coulisses which forever lures and leads onwards the traveller in time.

Those verses which Joseph had heard and learned by heart related among other things the story of the Great Flood. He would in any case have known this story even if he had not learned of it in the Babylonian tongue and version, for it existed in his western country and especially among his own people, although not in quite the same form, but with details differing from those in the version current in the land of the rivers; just at this very time, indeed, it was in process of establishing itself in a variant upon the eastern form. Joseph well knew the tale: how all that was flesh, the beasts of the field not excepted, had corrupted most indescribably His way upon the earth; yes, the earth herself practised whoredom and deceivingly brought forth oats where wheat had been sown — and all this despite the warnings of Noah; so that the Lord and Creator, who saw His very angels involved in this abomination, at length after a last trial of patience, of a hundred and twenty years, could no longer bear it and be responsible for it, but must let the judgment of the flood prevail. And now He, in His majestic good-nature (which the angels in no wise shared), left open a little back door for life to escape by, in the shape of a chest, pitched and caulked, into which Noah went up with the animals. Joseph knew that too and knew the day on which the creatures entered the ark; it had been the tenth of the month Marcheswan, and on the seventeenth the fountains of the great deep were broken up, at the time of the spring thawing, when Sirius rises in the daytime and the fountains of water begin to swell. It was on this day, then — Joseph had it from old Eliezer. But how often had this day come round since then? He did not consider that, nor did old Eliezer; and here begin the foreshortenings, the confusions and the deceptive vistas which dominate the tradition.

Heaven knows when there happened that overwhelming encroachment of the Euphrates, a river at all times tending to irregular courses and sudden spate; or that startling irruption of the Persian Gulf into the solid land as the result of tornado and earthquake; that catastrophe which did not precisely create the tradition of the deluge, but gave it its final nourishment, revivified it with a horrible aspect of life and reality and now stood to all later generations as *the* Deluge. Perhaps the most recent catastrophe had not been so very long ago; and the nearer it was, the more fascinating becomes the question whether, and how, the generation which had personal experience of it succeeded in confusing their present affliction with the subject of the tradition, in other words with *the* Deluge. It came to pass, and that it did so need cause us to feel neither surprise nor contempt. The event consisted less in that something past repeated itself, than in that it became present. But that it could acquire presentness rested upon the fact that the circumstances which brought it about were at all times present. The ways of the flesh are perennially corrupt, and may be so in all god-fearingness. For do men know whether they do well or ill before God and whether that which seems to them good is not to the Heavenly One an abomination? Men in their folly know not God nor the decrees of the lower world; at any time forbearance can show itself exhausted, and judgment come into force; and there is probably always a warning voice, a knowledgeable Atrachasis who knows how to interpret signs and by taking wise precautions is one among ten thousand to escape destruction. Not without having first confided to the earth the tablets of knowledge, as the seed-corn of future wisdom, so that when the waters subside, everything can begin afresh from the written seed. "At any time": therein lies the mystery. For the mystery is timeless, but the form of timelessness is the now and the here.

The Deluge, then, had its theatre on the Euphrates River, but also in China. Round the year 1300 before our era there was a frightful flood in the Hoang-Ho after which the course of the river was regulated; it was a repetition of the great flood of some thousand and fifty years before, whose Noah had been the fifth Emperor, Yao, and which, chronologically speaking, was far from having been the true and original Deluge, since the tradition of the latter is common to both peoples. Just as the Babylonian account, known to Joseph, was only a reproduction of earlier and earlier accounts, so the flood itself is to be referred back to older and older prototypes; one is convinced of being on solid ground at last, when one fixes, as the original original, upon the sinking of the land Atlantis beneath the waves of the ocean — knowledge of which dread event penetrated into all the lands of the earth, previously populated from that same Atlantis, and fixed itself as a movable tradition forever in the minds of men. But it is only an apparent stop and temporary goal. According to a Chaldæan computation, a period of thirty-nine thousand, one hundred and eighty years lay between the Deluge and the first historical dynasty of the kingdom of the two rivers. It follows that the sinking of Atlantis, occurring only nine thousand years before Solon, a very recent catastrophe indeed, historically considered, certainly cannot have been *the* Deluge. It too was only a repetition, the becoming-present of something profoundly past, a frightful refresher to the memory, and the original story is to be referred back at least to that incalculable point of time when the island continent called "Lemuria," in its turn only a remnant of the old Gondwana continent, sank beneath the waves of the Indian Ocean.

What concerns us here is not calculable time. Rather it is time's abrogation and dissolution in the alternation of tradition and prophecy, which lends to the phrase "once upon a time" its double sense of past and future and therewith its burden of potential present. Here the idea of reincarnation has its roots. The kings of Babel and the two Egypts, that curly-bearded Kurigalzu as well as Horus in the palace at Thebes, called Amun-is-satisfied, and all their predecessors and successors, *were* manifestations in the flesh of the sun god, that is to say the myth became in them a *mysterium*, and there was no distinction left between being and meaning. It was not until three thousand years later that men began disputing as to whether the Eucharist "was" or only "signified" the body of the Sacrifice; but even such highly supererogatory discussions as these cannot alter the fact that the essence of the mystery is and remains the timeless present. Such is the meaning of ritual, of the feast. Every Christmas the world-saving Babe is born anew and lies in the cradle, destined to suffer, to die and to arise again. And when Joseph, in midsummer, at Shechem or at Beth-Lahma, at the feast of the weeping women, the feast of the burning of lamps, the feast of Tammuz, amid much wailing of flutes and joyful shoutings relived in the explicit present the murder of the lamented Son, the youthful god, Osiris-Adonis, and his resurrection, there was occurring that phenomenon, the dissolution of time in mystery, which is of interest for us here because it makes logically unobjectionable a method of thought which quite simply recognized a deluge in every visitation by water.

6

PARALLEL with the story of the Flood is the tale of the Great Tower. Common property like the other, it possessed local presentness in many places, and affords quite as good material for dreamy speculation and the formation of time-coulisses. For instance, it is as certain as it is excusable that Joseph confused the Great Tower itself with the temple of the sun at Babel, the so-called E-sagila or House of the Lifting of the Head. The Wanderer from Ur had doubtless done the same in his time, and it was certainly so considered not only in Joseph's sphere but above all in the land of Shinar itself. To all the Chaldæans, E-sagila, the ancient and enormous terraced tower, built, according to their belief, by Bel, the Creator, with the help of the black men whom he created expressly for the purpose, and restored and completed by Hammurabi, the Lawgiver; the Tower, seven stories high, of whose brilliantly enamelled splendours Joseph had a lively mental picture; to all the Chaldæans E-sagila signified the present embodiment of an abstract idea handed down from far-away antiquity; the Tower, the sky-soaring structure erected by human hands. In Joseph's particular milieu the legend of the Tower possessed other and more far-reaching associations, which did not, precisely speaking, belong to it, such as the idea of the dispersal. This is explainable only by the moon-man's own personal attitude, his taking umbrage and going hence; for the people of Shinar had no such associations whatever with the Midgals or citadels of their cities, but rather the contrary, seeing that Hammurabi, the Lawgiver, had expressly caused it to be written that he had made their summits high in order to "bring together again" the scattered and dispersing people under the sway of "him who was sent." But the moon-man was thereby affronted in his notions of the deity, and in the face of Nimrod's royal policy of concentration had dispersed himself and his; and thus in Joseph's home the past, made present in the shape of E-sagila, had become tinctured with the future and with prophecy;

a judgment hung over the towering spite-monument of Nimrod's royal arrogance, not one brick was to remain upon another, and the builders thereof would be brought to confusion and scattered by the Lord God of Hosts. Thus old Eliezer taught the son of Jacob, and preserved thereby the double meaning of the "once upon a time," its mingled legend and prophecy, whose product was the timeless present, the Tower of the Chaldæans.

To Joseph its story was the story of the Great Tower itself. But it is plain that after all E-sagila is only a time-coulisse upon our endless path toward the original Tower. One time-coulisse, like many another. Mizraim's people, too, looked upon the tower as present, in the form of King Cheops' amazing desert tomb. And in lands of whose existence neither Joseph nor old Eliezer had the faintest notion, in Central America, that is, the people had likewise their tower or their image of a tower, the great pyramid of Cholula, the ruins of which are of a size and pretentiousness calculated to have aroused great anger and envy in the breast of King Cheops. The people of Cholula have always denied that they were the authors of this mighty structure. They declared it to be the work of giants, strangers from the east, they said, a superior race who, filled with drunken longing for the sun, had reared it up in their ardour, out of clay and asphalt, in order to draw near to the worshipped planet. There is much support for the theory that these progressive foreigners were colonists from Atlantis, and it appears that these sun-worshippers and astrologers incarnate always made it their first care, wherever they went, to set up mighty watch-towers, before the faces of the astonished natives, modelled upon the high towers of their native land, and in particular upon the lofty mountain of the gods of which Plato speaks. In Atlantis, then, we may seek the prototype of the Great Tower. In any case we cannot follow its history further, but must here bring to an end our researches upon this extraordinary theme.

7

BUT where was Paradise — the "garden in the East"? The place of happiness and repose, the home of man, where he ate of the tree of evil and was driven forth or actually drove himself forth and dispersed himself? Young Joseph knew this as well as he knew about the flood, and from the same source. It made him smile a little when he heard dwellers in the Syrian desert say that the great oasis of Damascus was Paradise, for that nothing more paradisial could be dreamed of than the way it lay among fruit orchards and charmingly watered gardens nestled between majestic mountain range and spreading seas of meadow, full of bustling folk of all races and the commerce of rich wares. And for politeness' sake he shrugged his shoulders only inwardly when men of Mizraim asserted that Egypt had been the earliest home of man, being as it was the centre and navel of the world. The curly-bearded folk of Shinar, of course, they too believed that their kingly city, called by them the "gateway of God" and "bond between heaven and earth" (*Bab-ilu, markas samê u ur-sitim*: the boy Joseph could repeat the words glibly after them), in other words, that Babel was the sacred centre of the earth. But in this matter of the world-navel Joseph had better and more precise information, drawn from the personal experience of his good and solemn and brooding father, who, when a young man on his way from "Seven Springs," the home of his family, to his uncle at Harran in the land of Naharain, had quite unexpectedly and unconsciously come upon the real world-navel, the hill-town of Luz, with its sacred stone circle, which he had then renamed Beth-el, the House of God, because, fleeing from Esau, he had there been vouchsafed that greatest and most solemn revelation of his whole life. On that height, where Jacob had set up his stone pillow for a mark and anointed it with oil, there henceforth was for Joseph and his people the centre of the world, the umbilical cord between heaven and earth. Yet not there lay Paradise; rather in the region of the beginnings and of the home — somewhere thereabouts, in Joseph's childish conviction, which was, moreover, a conviction widely held, whence the man of the moon city had once set out, in Lower Shinar, where the river drained away and the moist soil between its branches even yet abounded in luscious fruit-bearing trees.

Theologians have long favoured the theory that Eden was situated somewhere in southern Babylonia and Adam's body formed of Babylonian soil. Yet this is only one more of the coulisse effects with which we are already so familiar; another illustration of the process of localization and back-reference — only that here it is of a kind extraordinary beyond all comparison, alluring us out beyond the earthly in the most literal sense and the most comprehensive way; only that here the bottom of the well which is human history displays its whole, its immeasurable depth, or rather its bottomlessness, to which neither the conception of depth nor of darkness is any longer applicable, and we must introduce the conflicting idea of light and height; of those bright heights, that is, down from which the Fall could take place, the story of which is indissolubly bound up with our soul-memories of the garden of happiness.

The traditional description of Paradise is in one respect exact. There went out, it says, from Eden a river to water the garden, and from thence it was parted and came into four heads: the Pison, Gihon, Euphrates and Hiddekel. The Pison, it goes on to say, is also called the Ganges; it flows about all India and brings with it gold. The Gihon is the Nile, the greatest river of the world, that encompasseth the whole of Ethiopia. But Hiddekel, the arrow-swift river, is the Tigris, which flows towards the east of Assyria. This last is not disputed. But the identity of the Pison and the Gihon with the Ganges and the Nile is denied with considerable authority. These are thought to be rather the Araxes which flows into the Caspian Sea, and the Halys which flows into the Black Sea; and accordingly the site of Paradise would still be in the Babylonian sphere of interest, but not in Babylon itself, rather in the Armenian Alpine country north of the Mesopotamian plain, where the two rivers in question have their sources close together.

The theory seems reasonably acceptable. For if, as the most regarded tradition has it, the "Phrat," or Euphrates, rose in Paradise, then Paradise cannot be situated at the mouth of that river. But even while, with this fact in mind, we award the palm to Armenia, we have done no more than take the step to the next-following fact; in other words, we have come only one more coulisse further on.

God, so old Eliezer had instructed Joseph, gave the world four quarters: morning, evening, noon and midnight guarded at the seat of the Most High by four sacred beasts and four guardian angels, which watch over this fixed condition with unchanging eyes. Did not the pyramids of Lower Egypt exactly face with their four sides, covered with shining cement, the four quarters of the earth? And thus the arrangement of the rivers of Paradise was conceived. They are to be thought of in their course as four serpents, the tips of whose tails touch, whose mouths lie far asunder, so that they go out from each other towards the four quarters of the heavens. This now is an obvious transference. It is a geography transferred to a site in Near Asia, but familiar to us in another place, now lost; namely, in Atlantis, where, according to Plato's narrative and description, these same four streams went out from the mount of the gods towering up in the middle, and in the same way, that is, at right angles, to the four quarters of the earth. All learned strife as to the geographical meaning of the four head waters and as to the site of the garden itself has been shown to be idle and received its quietus, through the tracing backwards of the paradise-idea, from which it appears that the latter obtained in many places, founded on the popular memory of a lost land, where a wise and progressive humanity passed happy years in a frame of things as beneficent as it was blest. We have here an unmistakable contamination of the tradition of an actual paradise with the legend of a golden age of humanity. Memory seems to go back to that land of the Hesperides, where, if reports say truth, a great people pursued a wise and pious course under conditions never since so favourable. But no, the Garden of Eden it was not; it was not that site of the original home and of the Fall; it is only a coulisse and an apparent goal upon our paradise-seeking pilgrimage in time and space;

and our archæology of the earth's surface seeks for Adam, the first man, in times and places whose decline and fall took place before the population of Atlantis.

What a deluded pilgrimage, what an onward-luring hoax! For even if it were possible, or excusable, however misleading, to identify as Paradise the land of the golden apples, where the four great rivers flowed, how could we, even with the best will in the world to self-deception, hold with such an idea, in view of the Lemurian world which is our next and furthest time-coulisse; a scene wherein the tortured larva of the human being — our lovely and well-favoured young Joseph would have refused with pardonable irritation to recognize himself in the picture — endured the nightmare of fear and lust which made up his life, in desperate conflict with scaly mountains of flesh in the shape of flying lizards and giant newts? That was no garden of Eden, it was Hell. Or rather, it was the first accursed state after the Fall. Not here, not at the beginning of time and space was the fruit plucked from the tree of desire and death, plucked and tasted. That comes first. We have sounded the well of time to its depths, and not yet reached our goal: the history of man is older than the material world which is the work of his will, older than life, which rests upon his will.

8

A VERY ancient tradition of human thought, based upon man's truest knowledge of himself and going back to exceeding early days whence it has become incorporated into the succession of religions, prophecies and doctrines of the East, into Avesta, Islam, Manichæanism, Gnosticism and Hellenism, deals with the figure of the first or first completely human man, the Hebraic *Adam qadmon;* conceived as a youthful being made out of pure light, formed before the beginning of the world as prototype and abstract of humanity. To this conception others have attached themselves, varying to some extent, yet in essentials the same. Thus, and accordingly, primitive man was at his very beginning God's chosen champion in the struggle against that evil which penetrated into the new creation; yet harm befell him, he was fettered by demons, imprisoned in the flesh, estranged from his origins, and only freed from the darkness of earthly and fleshly existence by a second emissary of the deity, who in some mysterious way was the same as himself, his own higher self, and restored to the world of light, leaving behind him, however, some portions of his light, which then were utilized for the creation of the material world and earthly creatures. Amazing tales, these, wherein the religious element of redemption is faintly visible behind the cosmogonic frame. For we are told that the original human Son of God contained in His body of light the seven metals to which the seven planets correspond and out of which the world is formed. Again it is said that this human light-essence, issuing from the paternal primitive source, descended through the seven planetary spheres and the lord of each partook of his essence. But then looking down he perceived his image mirrored in matter, became enamoured of it, went down unto it and thus fell in bondage to lower nature. All which explains man's double self, an indissoluble combination of godlike attributes and free essence with sore enslavement to the baser world.

In this narcissistic picture, so full of tragic charm, the meaning of the tradition begins to clarify itself; the clarification is complete at the point where the descent of the Child of God from His world of light into the world of nature loses the character of mere obedient pursuance of a higher order, hence guiltless, and becomes an independent and voluntary motion of longing, by that token guilty. And at the same time we can begin to unravel the meaning of that "second emissary" who, identical in a higher sense with the light-man, comes to free him from his involvement with the darkness and to lead him home. For the doctrine now proceeds to divide the world into the three personal elements of matter, soul and spirit, among whom, and between whom and the Deity there is woven the romance, whose real protagonist is the soul of mankind, adventurous and in adventure creative, a mythus, which, complete by reason of its combination of oldest record and newest prophecy, gives us clear leading as to the true site of Paradise and upon the story of the Fall.

It is stated that the soul, which is to say the primevally human, was, like matter, one of the principles laid down from the beginning, and that it possessed life but no knowledge. It had, in fact, so little that, though dwelling in the nearness of God, in a lofty sphere of happiness and peace, it let itself be disturbed and confused by the inclination — in a literal sense, implying direction — towards still formless matter, avid to mingle with this and evoke forms upon which it could compass physical desires. But the yearning and pain of its passion did not diminish after the soul had let itself be betrayed to a descent from its home; they were heightened even to torment by the circumstance that matter sluggishly and obstinately preferred to remain in its original formless state, would hear nothing of taking on form to please the soul, and set up all imaginable opposition to being so formed. But now God intervened; seeing nothing for it, probably, in such a posture of affairs, but to come to the aid of the soul, His errant concomitance. He supported the soul as it wrestled in love with refractory matter. He created the world; that is to say, by way of assisting the primitive human being He brought forth solid and permanent forms, in order that the soul might gratify physical desires upon these and engender man. But immediately afterwards, in pursuance of a considered plan, He did something else. He sent, such literally are the words of the source upon which I am drawing, He sent out of the substance of His divinity spirit to man in this world, that it might rouse from its slumber the soul in the frame of man, and show it, by the Father's command, that this world was not its place, and that its sensual and passional enterprise had been a sin, as a consequence of which the creation of the world was to be regarded. What in truth the spirit ever strives to make clear to the human soul imprisoned in matter, the constant theme of its admonitions, is precisely this: that the creation of the world came about only by reason of its folly in mingling with matter, and that once it parted therefrom the world of form would no longer have any existence. To rouse the soul to this view is the task of the reasonable spirit; all its hoping and striving are directed to the end that the passionate soul, once aware of the whole situation, will at length reacknowledge its home on high, strike out of its consciousness the lower world and strive to regain once more that lofty sphere of peace and happiness. In the very moment when that happens the lower world will be absolved; matter will win back her own sluggish will, being released from the bonds of form to rejoice once more, as she ever did and ever shall, in formlessness, and be happy in her own way.

Thus far the doctrine and the romance of the soul. And here, beyond a doubt, we have come to the very last "backward," reached the remotest human past, fixed upon Paradise and tracked down the story of the Fall, of knowledge and of death, to its pure and original form. The original human soul is the oldest thing, more correctly *an* oldest thing, for it has always been, before time and before form, just as God has always been and likewise matter. As for the intelligent spirit, in whom we recognize the "second emissary" entrusted with the task of leading the soul back home; although in some undefined way closely related to it, yet it is after all not quite the same, for it is younger: a missionary sent by God for the soul's instruction and release, and thus for accomplishing the dissolution of the world of form. If in some of its phases the dogma asserts or allegorically indicates the higher oneness of soul and spirit, it probably does so on good ground; this, however, does not exclude the conception that the human soul is originally conceived as being God's champion against the evil in the world, and the rôle ascribed to it very like the one which falls to the spirit sent to effect its own release. Certainly the reason why the dogma fails to explain this matter clearly is that it has not achieved a complete portrayal of the rôle played by the spirit in the romance of the soul; obviously the tradition requires filling out on this point.

In this world of form and death conceived out of the marriage of soul and matter, the task of the spirit is clearly outlined and unequivocal. Its mission consists in awakening the soul, in its self-forgetful involvement with form and death, to the memory of its higher origin; to convince it that its relation with matter is a mistaken one, and finally to make it yearn for its original source with ever stronger yearning, until one day it frees itself wholly from pain and desire and wings away homewards. And therewith straightway the end of the world is come, death done away and matter restored to her ancient freedom. But as it will sometimes happen that an ambassador from one kingdom to another and hostile one, if he stay there for long, will fall a prey to corruption, from his own country's point of view, gliding unconsciously over to the other's habits of thought and favouring its interests, settling down and adapting himself and taking on colour, until at last he becomes unavailable as a representative of his own world; this or something like it must be the experience of the spirit in its mission. The longer it stops below, the longer it plies its diplomatic activities, the more they suffer from an inward breach, not to be concealed from the higher sphere, and in all probability leading to its recall, were the problem of a substitute easier to solve than it seems is the case.

There is no doubt that its rôle as slayer and grave-digger of the world begins to trouble the spirit in the long run. For its point of view alters, being coloured by its sojourn below; while being, in its own mind, sent to dismiss death out of the world, it finds itself on the contrary regarded as the deathly principle, as that which brings death into the world. It is, in fact, a matter of the point of view, the angle of approach. One may look at it one way, or the other. Only one needs to know one's own proper attitude, that to which one is obligated from home; otherwise there is bound to occur the phenomenon which I objectively characterized as corruption, and one is alienated from one's natural duties. And here appears a certain weakness in the spirit's character: he does not enjoy his reputation as the principle of death and the destroyer of form — though he did largely bring it upon himself, out of his great impulse towards judgment, even when directed against himself — and it becomes a point of honour with him to get rid of it. Not that he would willfully betray his mission. Rather against his intention, under pressure, out of that impulse and from a stimulus which one might describe as an unsanctioned infatuation for the soul and its passional activities, the words of his own mouth betray him; they speak in favour of the soul and its enterprise, and by a kind of sympathetic refinement upon his own pure motives, utter themselves on the side of life and form. It is an open question, whether such a traitorous or near-traitorous attitude does the spirit any good, and whether he cannot help serving, even by that very conduct, the purpose for which he was sent, namely the dissolution of the material world by the releasing of the soul from it; or whether he does not know all this, and only thus conducts himself because he is at bottom certain that he may permit himself so much. At all events, this shrewd, self-denying identification of his own will with that of the soul explains the allegorical tendency of the tale, according to which the "second emissary" is another self of that light-man who was sent out to do battle with evil. Yes, it is possible that this part of the tale conceals a prophetic allusion to certain mysterious decrees of God, which were considered by the teachers and preachers as too holy and inscrutable to be uttered.

9

WE can, objectively considered, speak of a "Fall" of the soul of the primeval light-man, only by over-emphasizing the moral factor. The soul, certainly, has sinned against itself, frivolously sacrificing its original blissful and peaceful state — but not against God in the sense of offending any prohibition of His in its passional enterprise, for such a prohibition, at least according to the doctrine we have received, was not issued. True, pious tradition has handed down to us the command of God to the first man, not to eat of the tree of the "knowledge of good and evil"; but we must remember that we are here dealing with a secondary and already earthly event, and with human beings who had with God's own creative aid been generated out of the knowledge of matter by the soul; if God really set them this test, He undoubtedly knew beforehand how it would turn out, and the only obscurity lies in the question, why He did not refrain from issuing a prohibition which, being disobeyed, would simply add to the malicious joy of His angelic host, whose attitude towards man was already most unfavourable. But the expression "good and evil" is a recognized and admitted gloss upon the text, and what we are really dealing with is knowledge, which has as its consequence not the ability to distinguish between good and evil, but rather death itself; so that we need scarcely doubt that the "prohibition" too is a well-meant but not very pertinent addition of the same kind.

Everything speaks for such an explanation; but principally the fact that God was not incensed at the yearning behaviour of the soul, did not expel it nor add any punishment to the measure of suffering which it voluntarily drew upon itself and which indeed was outweighed by the might of its desire. It is even clear that He was seized if not by understanding at least by pity, when He saw the passion of the soul. Unsummoned and straightway He came to its aid, and took a hand personally in the struggles of the soul to know matter in love, by making the world of form and death issue from it, that the soul might take its pleasure thereupon; and certainly this was an attitude of God in which pity and understanding are scarcely to be distinguished from one another.

Of sin in the sense of an offence to God and His expressed will we can scarcely speak in this connection, especially when we consider the peculiar immediacy of God's relation with the being which sprang from this mingling of soul and matter: this human being of whom the angels were unmistakably and with good reason jealous from the very first. It made a profound impression on Joseph, when old Eliezer told him of these matters, speaking of them just as we read them to-day in the Hebrew commentaries upon early history. Had not God, they say, held His tongue and wisely kept silence upon the fact that not only righteous but also evil things would proceed from man, the creation of man would certainly not have been permitted by the "kingdom of the stern." The words give us an extraordinary insight into the situation. They show, above all, that "sternness" was not so much the property of God Himself as of His entourage, upon whom He seems to have been dependent, in a certain, if of course not decisive way, for He preferred not to tell them what was going on, out of fear lest they make Him difficulties, and only revealed some things and kept others to Himself. But does not this indicate that He was interested in the creation of the world, rather than that He opposed it? So that if the soul was not directly provoked and encouraged by God to its enterprise, at least it did not act against His will, but only against the angels' — and their somewhat less than friendly attitude towards man is clear from the beginning. The creation by God of that living world of good and evil, the interest He displayed in it, appeared to them in the light of a majestic caprice; it piqued them, indeed, for they saw in it, probably with some justice, a certain disgust with their own psalm-chanting purity. Astonished and reproachful questions, such as: "What is man, O Lord, that Thou art mindful of him?" are forever on their lips; and God answers indulgently, benevolently, evasively, sometimes with irritation and in a sense distinctly mortifying to their pride. The fall of Shemmæl, a very great prince among the angels, having twelve pairs of wings whereas the seraphim and sacred beasts had only six apiece, is not very easy to explain, but its immediate cause must have been these dissensions; so old Eliezer taught — the lad drank it in with strained attention. It had always been Shemmæl who stirred up the other angels against man, or rather against God's sympathy for him, and when one day God commanded the heavenly hosts to fall down before Adam, on account of his understanding and because he could call all things by their names, they did indeed comply with the order, some scowlingly, others with ill-concealed smiles — all but Shemmæl, who did not do it. He declared, with a candour born of his wrathfulness, that it was ridiculous for beings created of the effulgence of glory to bow down before those made out of the dust of the earth. And thereupon took place his fall — Eliezer described it by

saying that it looked from a distance like a falling star. The other
angels must have been well frightened by this event, which caused
them to behave ever afterwards with great discretion on the subject
of man; but it is plain that whenever sinfulness got the upper hand
on earth, as in Sodom and Gomorrah and at the time of the Flood,
there was rejoicing among the angels and corresponding embarrassment to the Creator, who found His hand forced to scourge the of-
fenders, though less of His own desire than under moral pressure
from the heavenly host. But let us now consider once more, in the
light of the foregoing, the matter of the "second emissary" of the
spirit, and whether he is really sent to effect the dissolution of the material world by setting free the soul and bringing it back home.

It is possible to argue that this is not God's meaning, and that the
spirit was not, in fact, sent down expressly after the soul in order to
act the part of grave-digger to the world of forms created by it with
God's connivance. The mystery is perhaps a different one, residing in
that part of the doctrine which says that the "second emissary" was
no other than the first light-man sent out anew against evil. We have
long known that these mysteries deal very freely with the tenses, and
may quite readily use the past with reference to the future. It is possible that the saying, soul and spirit *were* one, really means that they
are sometime to become one. This seems the more tenable in that the
spirit is of its nature and essentially the principle of the future, and
represents the It will be, It is to be; whereas the goodness of the
form-bound soul has reference to the past and the holy It was. It remains controversial, which is life and which death; since both, the
soul involved with nature and the spirit detached from the world,
the principle of the past and the principle of the future, claim, each
in its own way, to be the water of life, and each accuses the other of
dealings with death. Neither quite wrongly, since neither nature
without spirit nor spirit without nature can truly be called life. But
the mystery, and the unexpressed hope of God, lie in their union, in
the genuine penetration of the spirit into the world of the soul, in the
inter-penetration of both principles, in a hallowing of the one through
the other which should bring about a present humanity blessed with
blessing from heaven above and from the depths beneath.

Such then might be considered the ultimate meaning and hidden
potentiality of the doctrine — though even so there must linger a
strong element of doubt whether the bearing of the spirit, self-
betraying and subservient as we have described it to be, out of all too
sensitive reluctance to be considered the principle of death, is calculated to lead to the goal in view. Let him lend all his wit to the
dumb passion of the soul; let him celebrate the grave, hail the past
as life's unique source, and confess himself the malicious zealot and
murderously life-enslaving will; whatever he says he remains that

which he is, the warning emissary, the principle of contradiction, umbrage and dispersal, which stirs up emotions of disquiet and exceptional wretchedness in the breast of one single man among the blithely agreeing and accepting host, drives him forth out of the gates of the past and the known into the uncertain and the adventurous, and makes him like unto the stone which, by detaching itself and rolling, is destined to set up an ever-increasing rolling and sequence of events, of which no man can see the end.

10

In such wise are formed those beginnings, those time-coulisses of the past, where memory may pause and find a hold whereon to base its personal history — as Joseph did on Ur, the city, and his forefather's exodus therefrom. It was a tradition of spiritual unrest; he had it in his blood, the world about him and his own life were conditioned by it, and he paid it the tribute of recognition when he recited aloud those verses from the tablets which ran:

> Why ordainest thou unrest to my son Gilgamesh,
> Gavest him a heart that knoweth not repose?

Disquiet, questioning, hearkening and seeking, wrestling for God, a bitterly sceptical labouring over the true and the just, the whence and the whither, his own name, his own nature, the true meaning of the Highest — how all that, bequeathed down the generations from the man from Ur, found expression in Jacob's look, in his lofty brow and the peering, careworn gaze of his brown eyes; and how confidingly Joseph loved this nature, of which his own was aware as a nobility and a distinction and which, precisely as a consciousness of higher concerns and anxieties, lent to his father's person all the dignity, reserve and solemnity which made it so impressive. Unrest and dignity — that is the sign of the spirit; and with childishly unabashed fondness Joseph recognized the seal of tradition upon his father's brow, so different from that upon his own, which was so much blither and freer, coming as it chiefly did from his lovely mother's side, and making him the conversable, social, communicable being he pre-eminently was. But why should he have felt abashed before that brooding and careworn father, knowing himself so greatly beloved? The habitual knowledge that he was loved and preferred conditioned and coloured his being; it was decisive likewise for his attitude towards the Highest, to Whom, in his fancy, he ascribed a form, so far as was permissible, precisely like Jacob's. A higher replica of his father, by Whom, Joseph was naïvely convinced, he was beloved even as he was beloved of his father. For the moment, and still afar off, I should like to characterize as "bridelike" his relation to Adon the heavenly. For Joseph knew that there were Babylonian women, sacred to Ishtar or to Mylitta, unwedded but consecrated to pious devotion, who dwelt in cells within the temple, and were called "pure" or "holy," also "brides of God," "*enitu.*" Something of this feeling was in Joseph's own nature: a sense of consecration, an austere bond, and with it a flow of fantasy which may have been the decisive ingredient in his mental inheritance, and which will give us to think when we are down below in the depths beside him.

On the other hand, despite all his own devotion, he did not quite follow or accept the form it had taken in his father's case: the care, the anxiousness, the unrest, which were expressed in Jacob's unconquerable dislike of a settled existence such as would have befitted his dignity, and in his temporary, improvised, half-nomad mode of life. He too, without any doubt, was beloved, cherished and preferred of God — for if Joseph was that, surely it was on his father's account! The God Shaddai had made his father rich in Mesopotamia, rich in cattle and multifarious possessions; moving among his troop of sons, his train of women, his servants and his flocks, he might have been a prince among the princes of the land, and that he was, not only in outward seeming but also by the power of the spirit, as "*nabi,*" which is: the prophesier; as a wise man, full of knowledge of God, "exceeding wise," as one of the spiritual leaders and elders upon whom the inheritance of the Chaldæan had come, and who had at times been thought of as his lineal descendants. No one approached Jacob save in the most respectful and ceremonious way; in dealings and trade one called him "my lord" and spoke of oneself in humble and contemptuous terms. Why did he not live with his family, as a property-owner in one of the cities, in Hebron itself, Urusalim or Shechem, in a house built of stone and wood, beneath which he could bury his dead? Why did he live like an Ishmaelite or Bedouin, in tents outside the town, in the open country, not even in sight of the citadel of Kirjath Arba; beside the well, the caves, the oaks and the terebinths, in a camp which might be struck at any time — as though he might not stop and take root with the others, as though from hour to hour he must be awaiting the word which should make him take down huts and stalls, load poles, blankets and skins on the pack-camels, and be off? Joseph knew why, of course. Thus it must be, because one served a God whose nature was not repose and abiding comfort, but a God of designs for the future, in whose will inscrutable, great, far-reaching things were in process of becoming, who, with His brooding will and His world-planning, was Himself only in process of becoming, and thus was a God of unrest, a God of cares, who must be sought for, for whom one must at all times keep oneself free, mobile and in readiness.

In a word, it was the spirit, he that dignified and then again he that debased, who forbade Jacob to live a settled life in towns; and if little Joseph sometimes regretted the fact, having a taste for pomp and worldly circumstance, we must accept this trait of his character and let others make up for it. As for me, who now draw my narrative to a close, to plunge, voluntarily, into limitless adventure (the word "plunge" being used advisedly), I will not conceal my native and comprehensive understanding of the old man's restless unease and dislike of any fixed habitation. For do I not know the feeling? To me too has not unrest been ordained, have not I too been endowed with a heart which knoweth not repose? The story-teller's star — is it not the moon, lord of the road, the wanderer, who moves in his stations, one after another, freeing himself from each? For the story-teller makes many a station, roving and relating, but pauses only tent-wise, awaiting further directions, and soon feels his heart beating high, partly with desire, partly too from fear and anguish of the flesh, but in any case as a sign that he must take the road, towards fresh adventures which are to be painstakingly lived through, down to their remotest details, according to the restless spirit's will.

Already we are well under way, we have left far behind us the station where we briefly paused, we have forgotten it, and as is the fashion of travellers have begun to look across the distance at the world we are now to enter, in order that we may not feel too strange and awkward when we arrive. Has the journey already lasted too long? No wonder, for this time it is a descent into hell! Deep, deep down it goes, we pale as we leave the light of day and descend into the unsounded depths of the past.

Why do I turn pale, why does my heart beat high — not only since I set out, but even since the first command to do so — and not only with eagerness but still more with physical fear? Is not the past the story-teller's element and native air, does he not take to it as a fish to water? Agreed. But reasoning like this will not avail to make my heart cease throbbing with fear and curiosity, probably because the past by which I am well accustomed to let myself be carried far and far away is quite another from the past into which I now shudderingly descend: the past of life, the dead-and-gone world, to which my own life shall more and more profoundly belong, of which its beginnings are already a fairly deep part. To die: that means actually to lose sight of time, to travel beyond it, to exchange for it eternity and presentness and therewith for the first time, life. For the essence of life is presentness, and only in a mythical sense does its mystery appear in the time-forms of past and future. They are the way, so to speak, in which life reveals itself to the folk; the mystery belongs to the initiate. Let the folk be taught that the soul wanders. But the wise know that this teaching is only the garment of the mystery of the eternal presentness of the soul, and that all life belongs to it, so soon as death shall have broken its solitary prison cell. I taste of death and knowledge when, as story-teller, I adventure into the past; hence my eagerness, hence my fear and pallor. But eagerness has the upper hand, and I do not deny that it is of the flesh, for its theme is the first and last of all our questioning and speaking and all our necessity; the nature of man. That it is which we shall seek out in the underworld and death, as Ishtar there sought Tammuz and Isis Osiris, to find it where it lies and is, in the past.

For it *is*, always *is*, however much we may say It was. Thus speaks the myth, which is only the garment of the mystery. But the holiday garment of the mystery is the feast, the recurrent feast which bestrides the tenses and makes the has-been and the to-be present to the popular sense. What wonder then, that on the day of the feast humanity is in a ferment and conducts itself with licensed abandon? For in it life and death meet and know each other. Feast of story-telling, thou art the festal garment of life's mystery, for thou conjurest up timelessness in the mind of the folk, and invokest the myth that it may be relived in the actual present. Feast of death, descent into hell, thou art verily a feast and a revelling of the soul of the flesh, which not for nothing clings to the past and the graves and the solemn It was. But may the spirit too be with thee and enter into thee, that thou mayest be blest with a blessing from heaven above and from the depths beneath.

Down, then, and no quaking! But are we going at one fell swoop into the bottomlessness of the well? No, not at all. Not much more than three thousand years deep — and what is that, compared with the bottom? At that stage men do not wear horn armour and eyes in their foreheads and do battle with flying newts. They are men like ourselves — aside from that measure of dreamy indefiniteness in their habits of thought which we have agreed to consider pardonable. So the homekeeping man talks to himself when he sets out on a journey, and then, when the matter becomes serious, gets fever and palpitations none the less. Am I really, he asks himself, going to the ends of the earth and away from the realms of the everyday? No, not at all; I am only going there and thither, where many people have been before, only a day or so away from home. And thus we too speak, with reference to the country which awaits us. Is it the land of nowhere, the country of the moon, so different from aught that ever was on sea or land that we clutch our heads in sheer bewilderment? No, it is a country such as we have often seen, a Mediterranean land, not exactly like home, rather dusty and stony, but certainly not fantastic, and above it move the familiar stars. There it lies, mountain and valley, cities and roads and vineclad slopes, with a turbid river darting arrowy among the green thickets; there it lies stretched out in the past, like meadows and streams in a fairy tale. Perhaps you closed your eyes, on the journey down; open them now! We have arrived. See how the moonlight-sharpened shadows lie across the peaceful, rolling landscape! Feel the mild spring freshness of the summer-starry night!

Chapter I

BY THE WELL

ISHTAR

It was beyond the hills north of Hebron, a little east of the Jerusalem road, in the month Adah; a spring evening, so brightly moonlit that one could have seen to read, and the leaves of the single tree there standing, an ancient and mighty terebinth, short-trunked, with strong and spreading branches, stood out fine and sharp against the light, beside their clusters of blossom — highly distinct, yet shimmering in a web of moonlight. This beautiful tree was sacred. In more than one way enlightenment was to be had within its shadow: from the mouth of man, for whoever through personal experience had aught to communicate of the divine would gather hearers together under its branches; but likewise in more inspired manner. For persons who slept leaning their heads against the trunk had repeatedly been vouchsafed dispensations and commands in a dream; and at the offering of burnt sacrifices, the frequency of which was witnessed by the stone slaughtering table, where a low fire burned on the blackened slab, the behaviour of the smoke, the flight of birds, or even a sign from heaven itself had often, in the course of the years, proved that a peculiar efficacy lay in these pious doings at the foot of the tree.

There were other trees nearby, if none so venerable as this single one; even other terebinths, as well as leafy fig trees and evergreen oaks; these last sent out bare roots along the trodden ground, and their foliage, pallid in the moonlight, between needle and leaf, looked like thorny fans. Behind the trees, southwards toward the hill that shut off the town, and even mounting up its slope, stood houses and cattle-byres, whence the hollow lowing of a bullock, the snort of a camel or the anguished onset of the asses' bray sounded sometimes across the silence of the night. Now, toward midnight, the prospect was vacant; the moon, three-quarters full and shining high in the sky, lighted first the space round the oracle-tree, which was enclosed by an extended mossy wall made of two courses of roughly-hewn square stone and looked like a terrace with a low parapet; and then revealed the level land beyond stretching away to the billowing hills that

closed the horizon. It was a region populous with olive trees and
tamarisk thickets, traversed by many paths; in the distance it turned
to treeless pastureland, where the light from a shepherd's camp fire
glimmered here and there. Cyclamens bloomed along the parapet,
their lilac and rose-colour bleached by the moonlight; white crocus
and red anemone sprang among grass and moss at the base of the trees.
Flowery and spicy scents were on the air, mingled with odours of
wood-smoke and dung and moist exhalations from the trees.

The sky was glorious. A broad band of light encircled the moon;
her lustre in all its mildness was so strong that it almost hurt the eyes,
and star-seed seemed to have been scattered, flung as it were with open
hand across the firmament, here sparsely, there thick and rich in
ordered patterns of twinkling light. In the south-west, Sirius-Ninurta
stood out, a clear and living blue-white fire, a ray-darting gem; he
formed a group with Procyon, standing higher and further south in
the Little Dog. Marduk the king had soon after sunset taken the field
and would shine on all night; he might have rivalled Sirius, had not
the moon diminished the brightness of his rays. Nergal was there, not
far from the zenith, a little south-east: the seven-named foe, the
Elamite, portending plague and death — we call him Mars. But earlier
than he, Saturn, the just and constant, had risen above the horizon and
was glittering southwards in the meridian. And familiar Orion, with
his splendid red star, a huntsman girded and armed, was declining
towards the west. In the west too, only further south, Columba hovered; Regulus in Leo beckoned from on high, the Great Bear likewise
had climbed to the top of the sky; while red-yellow Arcturus in
Boötes still stood low in the north-east, and the yellow light of Capella
and the constellation of Auriga had already sunk deep toward evening
and midnight. But lovelier than all these, fierier than any portent or
the whole host of the Kokabim, was Ishtar, sister, mother and wife,
Astarte the queen, following the sun and low in the west. She glowed
silvery and sent out fugitive rays, she glittered in points of fire and a
tall flame stood up from her like the tip of a spear.

THE FABLE AND THE FLESH

THERE were eyes here well-skilled in the observation and interpretation of all this — dark eyes lifted up to receive the whole of this manifold shining. They sought the causeway of the zodiac, the fixed ridge
that ordered the billows of the sky, where the guardians of time kept
watch; that sacred order of signs which had begun to appear in quick
succession after the brief twilight of these latitudes; and first the Bull,
for when these eyes were on earth, the sun stood at the beginning
of spring in the sign of the Ram, and thus with the sun that sign went
down into the depths. They smiled, those knowing eyes, at the Twins,

as they declined at evening from the zenith; one glance to eastwards showed them the Ear in the Virgin's hand. But always as though irresistibly drawn they returned to the quarter of the sky where the moon showed her gleaming silver shield and dazzled them by the pure mild lustre of her light.

They were the eyes of a youth, who sat by the margin of a well near the sacred tree. The watery depths were enclosed by a masonry wall, with a stone arch above; the youth's bare feet rested upon broken steps that led up to the mouth all round, and both feet and step were wet from the pouring of water. In a drier spot lay his upper garment, yellow with a wide rust-red border, and his neats-leather sandals, which were almost shoes, having flexible sides wherein to thrust feet and ankles. The lad had lowered his shirt of coarse bleached linen and tied the sleeves about his hips; the brown skin of his body glistened oily in the moonlight; the torso seemed rather full and heavy in proportion to the childish head, and the high square shoulders looked Egyptian. He had washed in the very cold water from the well, showering himself again and again with the pail and dipper — a process which was both a pious duty and a much-enjoyed refreshment after the burdensome heat of the day. Then he had suppled his limbs with scented olive oil from a salve-box of opaque iridescent glass that stood beside him, but had not removed the light myrtle wreath from his hair nor the amulet that hung round his neck from a bronzed lace, and contained a little packet stitched with root fibres of strong protective virtue.

He seemed now to be performing his devotions, his face upturned to the moonlight which shone full upon it, his elbows upon his hips but the forearms held out, palms extended; thus he sat, weaving to and fro, and words or sounds came from his lips, half spoken, half sung. He wore a ring of blue faïence on his left hand, and both finger- and toe-nails showed traces of brick-red henna dye. Probably his vanity had led him to put it on, in order to dazzle the eyes of the women on the housetops, when last he had attended a feast in the town. But he needed no cosmetics and might have confided only in his own pretty face which God had given him, whose childish oval was charming indeed, particularly the gentle look in the black, some-what slanting eyes. Beautiful people are prone to heighten the gifts of nature and to "dress the part," probably in obedience to their pleasing rôle and with a sense of performing service for gifts received. It is quite possible to interpret their conduct as an act of piety and so justify it; whereas for the ugly to deck themselves out is folly of a sadder kind. But even beauty is never perfect, and by that very reason clings to vanity and makes a self-imposed ideal of what she lacks — another error, since her secret power lies in the very attractiveness of the incomplete.

This youth by the well — saga and story have woven a halo of legendary loveliness about his head, at which, seeing him now in the flesh, we may have cause to wonder — even though the moon is on his side and lends her soft enchantment to dazzle our judgment. Yes, what all, as the days multiplied, was not said and sung, in apocrypha and pseudepigrapha, in praise of his outward man — praise at which seeing him we might incline to smile! That his countenance shamed the splendour of the moon and sun is the least that was said. Literally it was written, that he was fain to wear a veil about his head and face that the hearts of the people might not melt with the fire of earthly longing for his god-given beauty; and again, that those who saw him without the veil, "deep-sunk in blissful contemplation," had no longer recognized the youth. Oriental legend does not hesitate to declare that half the available supply of beauty in the world fell to this one youth and the rest of mankind divided the other half. A Persian poet of the highest authority goes further still: he draws a fantastic picture of a single goldpiece of six half-ounces' weight, in which all the beauty of the earth was melted down, five of which then, so the poet rapturously sings, fell to the paragon, the incomparable.

A reputation like that, arrogant and immeasurable because it no longer reckons on being checked, has a bewildering and contagious effect; it is an actual hindrance to objective observation of the facts. There are many instances of the influence of such exaggeration by common consent, which then blinds the individual judgment and makes it willingly or even fanatically subservient to the prevailing view. Some twenty years before the time of which I now speak, a certain man, closely related, as you shall hear, to the youth by the well, bred sheep and sold them in the district of Harran in the land of Mesopotamia, said sheep having such a reputation that people would pay fantastic prices for them, although it was plain to any eye that they were not fairy sheep but quite normal and natural ones, although of excellent breeding and quality. Such is the power of our human need to stand with the majority! But though we must not be influenced in this matter by reports which we find ourselves in a position to confront with reality, yet let us not err in the other direction with excess of tendency to carp. For the posthumous enthusiasm which threatens our judgment cannot have arisen out of nothing at all; it must have been rooted in reality, the tribute must have been paid in good part to the person when he was still alive. But to sympathize on æsthetic grounds we must adjust ourselves to the dark Arabian taste then and there current, and certainly from that point of view the youth must have been so beautiful, and so well-favoured, that at first glance he could really have been taken for a god.

Let me then pay heed to my words, and without either weak compliance or hypercritical airs venture the statement that the face of the youthful moon-worshipper by the well was lovely even in its defects. For instance, the nostrils of his rather short and very straight nose were really too thick; but the fact itself made them look dilated and imparted liveliness, passion and a fleeting pride to the face and set off the friendly expression of the eyes. The curling lips suggested a proud sensuality which I would not censure, since it might be deceptive, and moreover in that time and place would be accounted a virtue. But I am justified in finding the space between mouth and nose too full and arched — or I should be, rather, had it not been counterbalanced by a peculiarly charming contour of the corners of the mouth, from which, only by laying the lips together, without the least muscular tension, there ensued the serenest smile. The forehead above the thick and well-drawn brows was tranquil below, above it ran into bays beneath heavy black hair which was confined by a light-coloured leather thong as well as by the myrtle wreath. The hair fell like a bag in the neck behind, leaving the ears free — and with the ears all would have been well, but that the lobes had been made rather long and fleshy by the silver rings worn since early childhood.

Was the youth praying, then? Surely his pose was too easy for that, he should have been erect on his feet. The lifted hands and murmured singsong seemed more like a self-absorbed game, a soft dialogue with the planet which he addressed. He rocked and prattled:

"Abu — Hammu — Aoth — Abaoth — Abiram — Haam — mi — wa — am."

In this improvisation were mingled all sorts of remote allusions and associations: Babylonian pet names for the moon, as Abu (father) and Hammu (uncle); Abram, the name of his own supposed ancestor, but also as a variant and extension upon it, transmitted by venerable tradition, the legendary name of Hammurabi the Lawgiver, "My uncle is sublime," syllables whose meaning pursued the father-thought through the realms of primitive oriental religion, star-worship and family tradition, and made stammering efforts to express the new thing coming into being, so passionately cherished, debated and fostered in the minds of his nearest kin.

"Yao — Aoth — Abaoth —" he chanted. "Yahu, Yahu. Ya — a — we — ilu, Ya — a — um — ilu —" rocking and swaying with hands uplifted wagging his head and smiling up at the radiant moon. But other manifestations, strange and almost uncanny, began to creep into the posturings of the solitary figure. He seemed intoxicated by his own lyric ritual, whatever it was, rapt into a growing unconsciousness that was not quite normal. He had not given much voice to his song, probably had not much to give, for it was still undeveloped, a sharp, half childish organ, lacking fullness and resonance. But now he had lost it quite, it gave way with a gasp and his "Yahu, Yahu," was a mere panting whisper that issued from lungs empty for want of an intake of breath. At the same moment the body changed shape, the chest fell in, the abdominal muscle began a peculiar rotatory motion, neck and shoulders stretched upwards and writhed, the hands shook, the muscles of the upper arm stood out like tendons, and in a flash the black eyes turned inwards, till only the whites glittered unwholesomely in the moonlight.

I must remark here that no one could have anticipated from the youth's bearing a seizure of this kind. His attack, or whatever one might call it, would have surprised and perturbed an onlooker, it was so obviously out of tune with so attractive, not to say dandified an exterior, and with a personality which immediately impressed everyone by its air of friendly and understanding courtesy. If his behaviour was to be taken seriously, then the question was, who was responsible for the soul welfare of this young posturant, since it seemed, if not actually in danger, at least to be acting in obedience to a call. On the other hand, if it were but whim and child-play, even then it remained questionable — and that it was something of the sort at least seemed likely enough, judging from the subsequent behaviour of the moon-struck youth.

THE FATHER

FROM the homestead in the direction of the hill his name was called: "Joseph! Joseph!" twice or thrice, each time a little nearer at hand. At the third time he heard the call, or at least showed that he had heard it, and there came an immediate change in his bearing, while he muttered: "Here I am." His eyes returned to normal, he let fall his arms, his head drooped and a shamefaced smile played over his features. It was his father's voice that called: mild, a little plaintive, as always charged with feeling. Presently it came from close at hand, repeating, though he had already seen his son by the well: "Joseph, where art thou?"

His garments were long; also moonlight, for all its apparent and fantastic clarity, tends to deceive; thus Jacob — or as he signed himself, Yaakow ben Yitzchak — looked majestically, almost superhumanly tall as he stood there between the well and the oracle-tree, closer to the latter, so that the leaf-shadow patterned his mantle. His figure — consciously or unconsciously — looked even more impressive by reason of his posture, for he was leaning upon a long staff which he grasped so high that one arm was raised above his head and the sleeve of his mantle or upper garment fell back from hand and forearm. The garment, a wool and cotton mixture in narrow pale-coloured stripes, hung down in large folds; the hand above his head was that of an old man, and it had a copper band round the wrist. The

twin brother of Esau, favoured before him, was then sixty-seven
years old. His beard though not heavy was long and broad; it ran up
into the hair on his temples and fell from his cheeks and down upon
his breast at the same width, in sparse strands that were uncurled and
unrestrained and shimmered silver in the moonlight, with his thin
lips showing through them. Deep furrows ran down into the beard
from the nostrils of the sharp-ridged nose. His brow was half covered
by a hooded shawl of dark-coloured Canaanite-woven cloth, which
lay in folds on the chest and was tossed back over the shoulder; beneath it his eyes — little eyes, brown, bright, with pouches of soft
skin beneath them, eyes grown weary with age and only keen from
the keenness of the soul within — peered anxiously after the boy at
the well. The position of his arm drew up the mantle to expose an
undergarment of dyed goat's-wool hanging down to the tips of the
cloth shoes; it hung in long fringing folds, so unevenly as to look like
several garments coming out one beneath the other. Thus the old
man's dress was heavy and multifarious, an arbitrary combination of
various styles; elements from the civilizations of the orient mingling
with those belonging rather to the desert world of the Bedouins and
Ishmaelites.

Quite sensibly Joseph did not answer to the last call; the question
was already answered, since Jacob saw his son. He contented himself
with a smile that parted the full lips and showed the glistening teeth,
set rather far apart and white as teeth can only be in a dark face. He
accompanied the smile with easy gestures of welcome. He put up his
hands in the posture with which he had saluted the moon, nodded his
head and made a little smacking sound with his tongue expressive of
surprise and pleasure. Then he brought one hand to his forehead and
let it glide downwards in a smooth and elegant motion; next laid
both hands on his heart, closing his eyes and inclining his head; lastly
he gestured outwards several times toward the old man, with hands
still laid one over the other, always returning them to the position
over the heart, in token, as it were, that it awaited the father's coming. Again he pointed with both index fingers to his eyes, to his knees,
head and feet, falling back at intervals on the first position of greeting
and worship with arms and hands. It was a pretty game, played with
all the rules prescribed by good breeding, but he brought to it a personal art and charm as well — the expression of a courteous and ingratiating nature — and no little real feeling besides. It was a panto-
mime — which the accompanying smile relieved of formality — of
filial submission before the master and progenitor, the head of the
tribe; but also it was enlivened by very genuine pleasure in the opportunity thus afforded of paying homage. Joseph well knew that his
father had not always played the dignified and heroic rôle in life.
His loftiness of speech and bearing had sometimes been badly served

by the gentleness and timidity of his soul; he had known hours of depression, of retreat, of pallid fear, situations in which one who loved him would not gladly imagine him, though precisely they had been most transparently bearers of the blessing. So that if Joseph's smile was not quite free from flattery or from triumphant self-consciousness, yet it was in good part called up by pleasure at the sight of his father, by the waxing beauty of the moonlit night and the advantageously regal posture of the old man as he leaned on his staff; in Joseph's childish satisfaction at the scene there was involved much feeling for pure effect without respect to any deeper cause.

Jacob paused where he was. Perhaps he could see his son's appreciation and was willing to prolong it. His voice — I called it emotional because it always vibrated with inward stress — sounded again, half questioning, half asserting.

"It is my child sitting there by the well?"

The question was a strange one, it sounded uncertain and absentminded, or as though the speaker found something surprising and unfitting in the fact of one so young sitting by any well — as though the conceptions child and well did not go together in the mind. What it in truth expressed was Jacob's concern lest Joseph, whom the father saw as much younger than he actually was, might fall into the well.

The boy's smile widened, so that more of the separated teeth came into view; he nodded without answering. But his expression changed at Jacob's next words, which had a sterner ring: "Cover thy nakedness," he commanded.

Joseph, his arms curved above his head, looked down with whimsical consternation at his body, and then quickly untied his sleeves and drew the linen garment over his shoulders. It seemed as though the old man had kept at a distance because his son was naked, for he now drew near. He leaned in earnest on the long staff he held, lifting it and setting it down at each step, for he limped, and had done so for the past twelve years; in fact ever since a certain adventure which had befallen him on a journey, under painful circumstances, at a time of great stress, he had halted on one thigh.

THE MAN JEBSHE

Not much time had elapsed since the two last met. As usual, Joseph had taken the evening meal in his father's myrrh- and musk-scented tent, together with such of his brothers as were at home — the rest were tending other flocks in the country further to the north, near a hill city and shrine overlooked by the mountains Ebal and Garizim, and called Shechem, or Sychem, the neck, also probably Mabara or the pass. Jacob had religious affiliations with the people of Shechem. True, the deity to whom they prayed was a variant of the Syrian shepherd and beautiful lord, Adonis and that Tammuz, the lovely youth whom the boar mangled, whom down in the Southland they called Osiris, the Sacrifice; but as early as the time of Abram and the priest-king Melchizedek, this divine personality had taken on a particular cast of thought which had endowed him with the name of El Elyon, Baal-Berith, the name, that is, of the Most High God, the Lord of hosts, the creator and possessor of heaven and earth. Such a conception seemed right and good to Jacob, who was accordingly inclined to see in the mangled son of Shechem the true and most high God, the God of Abraham, and in the Shechemites brothers in the bond of faith, particularly since oral tradition from generation to generation reported that the original wanderer, in a learned conversation with Melchizedek the magistrate of Sodom, had called his God El Elyon and thus put him on a par with the Baal and Adon of Melchizedek. Jacob himself, his inheritor in the faith, had years before, after his return from Mesopotamia, when he set up his camp before the city of Shechem, erected an altar to this god. Also he had sunk a well and purchased pasture rights with good silver shekels.

Later there had arisen grievous misunderstandings between the people of Shechem and Jacob's people, with frightful consequences for the city. But peace had been restored and relations resumed, and a part of Jacob's flocks grazed on Shechem's ground and some of his sons and shepherds were always absent from his countenance to look after these flocks.

But two of Leah's sons had partaken of the meal with their father as well as Joseph; the raw-boned Issachar, and Zebulun, who cared nothing for the calling of a shepherd, neither desired to be a husbandman, but longed with a single longing for a sailor's life. For ever since he had been at Askalon on the sea he thought nothing finer than such a life, and drew many a long bow about strange adventures and uncanny hybrid creatures who lived across the water, to be visited by men whose life was on the seas — human beings with the heads of bulls or lions, two-headed and two-faced men, possessing at once a human countenance and that of a shepherd dog, so that they spoke and barked by turns; people with feet like sponges and other suchlike abnormalities. Then there had been Bilhah's son, the agile Naphtali, and Zilpah's two: the forthright Gad, and Asher, who as usual had taken the best pieces for himself while saying yea to all that was said. As for Joseph's own brother, the child Benjamin, he still lived in the women's quarters, being too young to share in a guest-meal, such as this evening's supper had been.

There was a man named Jebshe, who said he came from Ta'anach and talked as they ate of the fish-ponds and flocks of doves in the temple there; he had been already some days on the way, with a brick which the lord of Ta'anach, Ashirat-Yashur, called by courtesy king, had inscribed on all four sides with messages for his "brother" the prince of Gaza, named Riphath-Baal, to the effect that he wished for Riphath-Baal every pleasure in life and that all the more important deities might work together for his welfare and that of his house and his children; but that he, Ashirat-Yashur, could not send him the wood and the money which the other with more or less right demanded of him, partly that he had not got it and partly that he had a pressing need of it himself, but was sending instead by the man Jebshe an uncommonly efficacious clay image of his personal protectress and that of Ta'anach, namely the goddess Ashera, that it might bring him blessing and help him to pass over the difficulty about the money and wood; this Jebshe then, who wore a pointed beard and was wrapped from head to foot in coloured woollens, had come to break bread with Jacob, to hear his views, and to get a night's lodgement before continuing his journey seawards. And Jacob had extended hospitality, only letting the messenger know that he was not to approach him with the image of Astarte — a female figure in trousers, crowned and veiled, holding her tiny breasts with both hands — but to keep it remote from his sight. Otherwise he had welcomed the man without prejudice, mindful of a tale that was handed down about Abraham, who had once furiously hounded a grey-haired idolater out into the wilderness, but had been rebuked by the Lord for his lack of forbearance and fetched the foolish old man back again.

Served by two slaves in freshly washed linen smocks, old Modai and young Mahalaleel, they had squatted on cushions round the carpet mat (for Jacob held fast to the custom of his fathers and would not hear of sitting on chairs like fashionable folk in towns who aped the manners of the great kingdoms to the west and south) and partaken of the evening meal: olives, a roasted kid with the good bread *Kemach*, and afterwards a compote of plums and raisins served in copper bowls, and Syrian wine in cups of coloured glass. And between host and guest a discreet conversation went on, listened to by Joseph at least, with all his ears, upon themes public and private, the earthly and the divine, and even branching out into the political. Upon the family circumstances of the man Jebshe and his official relation to Ashirat-Yashur, the lord of the city; upon the journey he had made so far, by way of the plain of Yezreel and the upland, beginning at the pass on the watershed at Esel, which Jebshe thought to continue to the land of the Philistines on a camel which he would purchase next day in Hebron; upon the local prices of cattle and crops; upon the cult of the blossoming rod, the "finger" as it was called of Ashera of Ta'anach, her oracle, through which she had communicated her permission to send one of her images, to be called "Ashera of the Way," on a journey to rejoice the heart of Riphath-Baal of Gaza; upon her feast-day, which had recently been celebrated

by untrammelled dancing and inordinate consumption of fish, likewise by the changing of clothes between men and women, in token
of the man-woman character or double sex of Ashera, as taught by
her priests. Here Jacob stroked his beard and interposed with searching and subtle questions: as, how was the realm of Ta'anach now protected, its tutelary deity being gone a journey; and how was the understanding to deal with the matter of the travelling image and the
relation it bore to the goddess, and whether she did not suffer a sensible diminution of her power by this removal of some part of her essence? To which the man Jebshe had replied that it was not likely,
were this the case, that Ashera's finger would have consented to the
journey; and that the priests taught that the entire power of the divinity resided in each of her images, each being alike efficacious. Further, Jacob had mildly pointed out that if it were really true that
Ashirta was male and female, Baal and Baalat at once, mother of the
gods and king of heaven, then must one reverence her not only as
equal to Ishtar, whom one heard of in Shinar, and Isis, a deity of the
impure Egyptians, but also as equal to Shamush, Shalim, Addu, Adon,
Lahma or Damu, in short the most high god and lord of the world;
and the conclusion one came to was that we were dealing with El
Elyon, the God of Abraham, Father and Creator, whom one could
not send on journeys because he was always and everywhere, and
whom one could not honour in the eating of fish, but only by walking before him in purity and being reverent in his sight. But these remarks of Jacob did not meet with much understanding in the man
Jebshe. Rather the other declared that as the sun always worked out
of a certain sign and appeared in the same, as it lent its light to the
planets so that each in his own way influenced the destinies of mankind, so likewise did the divine parcel itself out and transmute itself
into the various godheads, among whom the god-goddess Ashirat was
well-known to be the especial representative of the divine power in
the sense of the fruitfulness of all vegetation and the annual resurrection of nature out of the bondage of the lower world, in that each
year she made a blossoming stalk out of a dry one, and on such an
occasion a somewhat immoderate eating and dancing were surely in
place, and even a more wholesale liberty and license bound up with
the feast of the blossoming stalk, since purity was an attribute only of
the sun and the primitive undivided god-head, not at all of its terrestrial manifestations, and the reason had to make a sharp distinction
between the pure and the holy, he himself being aware that there was
no necessary connection between the two. Whereat Jacob, with the
utmost deliberation: he had no desire to injure anyone, least of all
the guest upon his hearthstone and the bosom friend and messenger
of a great king, in respect of the convictions emplanted in him by
parents and scribes. But the sun itself was but a work of El Elyon's

hand, as such godlike indeed but not god; the understanding had to
make this distinction. Indeed, it was in contravention to this fact and
would call down the anger and jealousy of the Lord if one were to
worship one or other of his works instead of himself, and the guest
Jebshe had out of his own mouth characterized the gods of the country as idols, another name for which he, the speaker, would out of
charity and politeness refrain from giving. And if that god, who had
created the sun and the fixed and moving stars as well as the earth itself, was the highest god, so he was also the only one, and thus it would
be better to have no talk of another, since one could then only characterize him with the name which Jacob had suppressed, precisely on
the ground that the name and symbol "highest god" was to be understood and reverenced as equal to "only god." Upon this point then,
whether these two ideas were the same or different, there had ensued
a long discussion, of which the host could never weary, and which,
had it rested with him, would have gone on the half or even the whole
of the night. But Jebshe had brought the conversation round to
events in the world at large, to trade and traffic, about which as the
friend and relative of a Canaanite city prince he knew more than
most: as, that the plague was raging in Cyprus, which he called
Alashia, and had killed off a great many men but not all, though the
ruler of the island had so reported to the Pharaoh of the lower country, as an excuse for the almost total cessation of the copper tribute;
that the king of the country of the Hittites, called Subbiluliuma,
could command such military strength that he threatened to overpower King Tushratta of Mitanni and take away his gods, although
Tushratta was the brother-in-law of the great ruling house of
Thebes; that the Cassite of Babel had begun to tremble before the
priest-prince of Assyria, who was striving to withdraw his power
from the kingdom of the Lawgiver and to found a separate state on
the river Tigris; that Pharaoh had greatly enriched the priesthood of
his god Amun with Syrian tribute money and built this god a new
temple with a thousand columns and doors with money from the
same source, but that the source was soon going to dry up, not only
because the Bedouins were pillaging the cities there, but because the
Hittite troops were coming down from the north to dispute the overlordship of the Ammonites in Canaan and not a few of the Amorite
princes were making common cause with the foreigner against Ammon. Here Jebshe had winked one eye, probably to indicate, as
among friends, that Ashirat-Yashur was of those who were pursuing
this prudent diplomatic course. But his host's interest in the conversation had sensibly diminished since it ceased to centre round the
deity; it began to languish, and they rose from the cushions: Jebshe
to make sure that no harm had come to Astarte of the Way and then
to retire, Jacob to make the round of the camp, leaning on his staff, to

give an eye to the cattle-byres and the women's quarters. As for his sons, Joseph had parted from the other five at the door of the tent, though he had evidently meant to remain with them, until the forthright Gad remarked:

"Away with thee, little fop and harlot, we need thee not!"

To which Joseph, after a brief pause to order his thoughts, had responded:

"Thou'rt like a wooden beam, Gad, over which the plane hath not passed, and like a butting goat in the flock. If I repeat thy words to our father he will rebuke thee; if I bring them to the ears of Reuben our brother he will chastise thee in his righteousness. But be it as thou sayst, go ye to the right and I will go left, or the other way round. For I love you all, but alas, I am an abomination in your sight, and to-day especially, because our father gave me of the kid from his dish and smiled upon me. Therefore be it so, that there be no cause for your anger and ye fall not unaware into sinning. Farewell."

To all which Gad listened over his shoulder, with a contemptuous expression, yet curious to hear what the creature would think of to say this time. Then he made a coarse gesture and went off with the others, Joseph by himself.

He had taken a pleasant little evening stroll — in so far as there could be any talk of pleasure, that is, for Gad's coarseness had cast him into a depression which his own skill at repartee only partly assuaged. He had sauntered eastward, uphill, where the slope was easiest, and soon reached the crest, which commanded a view towards the south, so that he could look down on his left into the valley and the town lying white in the moonlight, at its thick wall with four-square corner towers and gates, at the columned court of the palace and the bulk of the temple, surrounded by a broad terrace. He liked to look at the town, in which so many people dwelt. And from this point too he could have seen signs of the burial place of his people, the double cave which Abraham had solemnly bought aforetime of the Hittite man, where rested the bones of his ancestors, the Babylonian first mother and later heads of the tribe. The pediments of the stone gate towers of the double rock grave were plain to be seen at the left by the surrounding wall; and feelings of piety, whose source is death, mingled in his breast with the lively sympathy aroused there at the sight of the populous city. Then he had turned back to the well, where he washed, refreshed, and anointed himself and then performed with the moon that somewhat decadent ritual of wooing at which his ever-anxious father had surprised him.

THE INFORMER

THE OLD man stood beside him now, and passing his staff over into
his left hand, laid the right on Joseph's head and gazed with penetrating old eyes into the youth's lovely black ones; who first looked
up at him, his lips parting in a smile that showed again the gleaming
enamel of his separated teeth, then dropped his eyes, partly in simple reverence, but also from a flickering sense of guilt that rose from
his father's command to cover himself. Truly it was not alone the
pleasant coolness of the evening air that had made him slow to resume his garment; and he suspected his father of reading his mind
and the impulses that had led to his addressing his half-nude observances to the moon. It was true that he had found it sweet and of
good omen to display his young body to her, with whom he felt
himself connected through his horoscope and by all sorts of intuitions and imaginings; convinced that she must take pleasure in it, and
of set purpose to charm her — or the powers above in general — and
prejudice them in his favour. The sensation of cool brightness that
touched his shoulders with the evening air had confirmed to him
the success of his childish enterprise — which we must not consider
shameless, because it was really tantamount to a sacrifice of shame.
We must remember that the rite of circumcision, taken over as
outward practice from the Egyptians, had in Joseph's family and
tribe long ago acquired a peculiar mystic significance. It was the
marriage commanded and appointed by God between man and the
deity, performed upon that part of the flesh which seemed to form
the focus of his being, and upon which every physical vow was
taken. Many a man bore the name of God on his organ of generation, or wrote it there before he possessed a woman. The bond of
faith with God was sexual in its nature, and thus, contracted with a
jealous creator and lord, insistent upon sole possession, it inflicted
upon the human male a kind of civilizing weakening into the female.
The bloody sacrifice of circumcision has more than a physical connection with emasculation. The sanctifying of the flesh signified both
being made chaste and the offering up of chastity as a sacrifice; in
other words, a female significance. Joseph, moreover, as he knew
himself, and as everybody told him, was both beautiful and well-
favoured — a condition which certainly embraces a consciousness of
femininity; and "beautiful" was an adjective always and by everybody
used to describe the moon, in particular the full, unshrouded and
unclouded moon, a moon-word, in short, belonging by rights to the
heavenly sphere and only applicable by transference among men;
so that in Joseph's mind the idea beautiful and the idea nude flowed

together and were interchangeable almost at will, and it seemed to him the part both of wisdom and piety to respond to the unshrouded loveliness of the planet with his own, that the pleasure and admiration might be mutual.

How much connection there was between these vague sentiments and a certain degeneracy betrayed in his behaviour, I should not like to say. At all events, the sentiments had their origin in the primitive meaning of a ritual uncovering which was still customary and often practised before his eyes; just for that very reason it was that he felt a vague sense of shame in his father's presence and correction. For he both loved and feared the old man's spiritual side, and was aware that he repudiated as sinful a good share of the thought-world to which Joseph clung, if only in fancy and child's play; putting it behind him as pre-Abramite, applying to it his swiftest and most frightful condemnation, the word "idolatrous." The youth prepared himself for an express and downright admonition in this sense. But Jacob, from among the cares that as always weighed him down in connection with this son of his, produced a different one. He began:

"Verily it had been better did my child sleep now, after his devotions, in the shelter of the house. Unwillingly I behold him alone in the oncoming night, beneath the stars which shine alike upon the good and the evil doer. Why has he not kept with the sons of Leah, or gone whither the sons of Bilhah went?"

He was well aware why Joseph, once again, had not gone with them, and Joseph knew that only Jacob's distress over the long-standing situation could have driven him to the question. He answered, with his lips stuck out:

"My brethren and I discussed the matter and resolved it in peace."

Jacob went on:

"It may come about that the lion of the desert, and he who had his dwelling in the cane-brake of the outlet, where it flows into the salt sea, comes when he is hungry and falls upon the flocks, when he thirst after blood and seek his prey. It is five days since Almodad the shepherd lay before me on his belly and confessed that a ravening beast had struck down two ewes in the night and dragged one away to devour it. Almodad was pure in my sight without an oath, for he showed to me the one ewe in her blood so that it was plain to the understanding that the lion had stolen the other, and so the loss came upon my own head."

"It is little loss," said Joseph wheedlingly, "verily it is as nothing compared with the riches the Lord hath vouchsafed out of His love to my lord in Mesopotamia."

Jacob bowed his head, letting it droop a little toward the right shoulder, in token that he did not vaunt himself over the blessing, though even so it had scarcely been effective without some shrewd assistance on his own part. He answered:

"To whom much is given from him can much be taken away. The Lord hath made me silver, yet can He make me clay and poor as the potsherds on the dungheap; for His spirit is mighty and we know not the ways of His righteousness. Silver hath a pale light," he went on, keeping his eyes away from the moon, to which Joseph straightway sent up a sideways glance. "Silver is affliction, and the bitterest fear of the fearful is the folly of those for whom his heart is heavy."

The boy looked entreatingly at him and made a caressing and soothing gesture.

Jacob did not let him finish; he went on:

"It was where the shepherds keep their flocks, a hundred or two hundred paces from here, that the lion crept up and stole the ewe lambs away from their dam. But my child sits alone by the well at night, naked and without a weapon, careless and forgetful of the father-heart. Art thou made for danger and armed for strife? Art thou like Simeon and Levi, thy brothers, may God keep them, who fall upon the enemy with clamour, sword in hand, and who burned the city of the Amorites? Or art thou like Esau, thy uncle, at Seir in the deserts of the south — a hunter and man of the field, red of skin and hairy like a he-goat? No, thou art gentle and a dweller in tents, for thou art flesh of my flesh, and when Esau came to the ford with four hundred men and my soul knew not the issue before the Lord, I put the handmaids and their children, thy brothers, foremost, and Leah with her children after, and lo, thee I put hindermost, with Rachel, thy mother. . . ."

His eyes had already filled with tears. He could not name, dry-eyed, the name of her whom he had loved beyond all else, although it was eight years since God had so incomprehensibly taken her from him; his voice, always full of feeling, faltered and broke.

The boy stretched out his arms to his father, then carried the clasped hands to his lips.

"How idly troubleth itself," he said in tender reproach, "the heart of my father and dear lord! And how extravagant is his concern! When our guest wished us good health and went to see after his precious image," he smiled maliciously to please Jacob, and added, "which seemed to me poor and impotent indeed and worthless as coarse earthenware in the market —"

"Thou sawest it?" broke in Jacob. Even this vexed and misgave him.

"I besought the guest to show it me before the evening meal," answered Joseph, curling his lip and shrugging his shoulder. "It is mediocre work and feebleness stands written on its brow. . . . As the talk between thee and thy guest came to an end, I went out with my brothers; but one of Leah's maid's sons, I think it was Gad, whose manner is blunt and downright, told me not to set my feet in his steps nor the steps of the others, and somewhat bruised me in my soul for he called me not by my name but with false and evil ones to which I do not listen gladly. . . ."

He had launched into his tale without thinking and against his own will, for he was aware of a certain tendency in himself; it detracted from his own self-satisfaction, and he honourably desired to conquer it, in fact had already struggled with it the moment before. He could never check his need to communicate his thoughts, and it here operated in a vicious circle with the bad relations to his brethren; by estranging him from them and thus driving him closer to his father, there was created for him an intermediate position which lent itself easily to tale-bearing. And the tale-bearing in its turn increased the estrangement and so on, so that one could not say with whom the wrong had begun, and at least the oldest ones among his brothers could hardly catch sight of Rachel's son without making a face. But the original source was no doubt Jacob's love for this son of his — an actual fact with which one would not wish to reproach the too-much-feeling man. Feeling, however, of its own nature inclines to unrestraint and an enervating cult of itself; it will not be hidden, it knows no reserves, it behaves so as to draw attention upon itself, it flies in the face of the world that the world may be driven to take notice. Such is the intemperance of the feelingful; and Jacob was encouraged in his by the tradition handed down in his tribe, of God's own intemperateness and majestic caprice in matters of sympathy and preference. El Elyon's way of preferring this and that one, without, or at least over and above, merit on their part, was very highhanded, hard to understand and humanly speaking often unjust; it was a fixed and lofty state of feeling which was not to be interpreted but simply to be honoured with fear and ecstasy, in the dust; and Jacob, himself a conscious — if also a humble and fearful — object of one among these predilections, imitated his God in that he wantonly insisted upon his own and gave them free rein.

The soft unrestraint of the man of feeling was Joseph's heritage from his father. Later I shall have to tell of his powerlessness to set limits to his fullness; of the lack of tact which brought him into extreme danger. At nine years old, still quite a child, it had been he who complained to his father of Reuben, a good if impetuous youth, who seeing that Jacob, after Rachel's death, had made his bed with Bilhah the maid, and taken her for his favourite, while Leah crouched neglected and red-eyed, in her tent, had torn his

father's cot from the new place and mishandled it with curses. It
was a rash act, committed out of offended filial pride, committed for
Leah's sake and early rued. The bed might have been quietly set up
again, Jacob needed to hear naught of the occurrence. But Joseph
had seen and had nothing better to do than to tell the father. And it
was since that time that Jacob, himself the first-born not in the way
of nature, but only nominally and legally, conceived the plan of
divesting Reuben of his right, depriving him of the blessing, to confer
it not on Simeon, Leah's second, the next in order, but with the
most arbitrary exercise of authority, on Joseph.

His brethren did the youth wrong in saying that his prattle was
deliberately directing the parental resolve towards such a goal. It
was the simple truth that he could not keep still. But that he could
not hold his tongue even after he knew of the plan and his brothers'
accusation was harder to forgive and was like fuel to the flames of
their suspicion.

It is not generally known how Reuben's "sporting" with Bilhah
came to Jacob's ears. That was a much worse affair than the one with
the bed; it had happened before they settled at Hebron, at a place between Hebron and Beth-el. Reuben, then twenty-one, in the full
tide of his strength and instincts, had not been able to refrain from
his father's wife — the very same Bilhah toward whom he cherished
so bitter a grudge because she had dispossessed Leah, his mother.
He had spied upon her in the bath, first by chance, then for the
pleasure of humiliating her without her knowledge — until desire
took the upper hand. A rash and sensual passion for Bilhah's mature
and artfully preserved charms — for her still firm breasts and soft
belly — had seized on the hardy youth, and was not to be stilled by
any of the maids, any yielding and submissive Shechemite slave. He
slipped in to his father's concubine and present favourite, he took
her unawares, and if he did her no violence, yet the woman, who
before Jacob did but tremble, was seduced by the overmastering
pride of his youthful virility.

Joseph, lounging idly about the camp, if not precisely with intent
to spy, had learned enough of this scene of passion to make simple
and zealous report to the father that Reuben had "sported" and
"laughed" with Bilhah. The words conveyed less than he really
knew, yet in the local parlance they insinuated everything. Jacob
turned pale and gasped. Not many minutes after the boy had told
all his tale, Bilhah lay whimpering before the master, tearing with
her nails those breasts which Reuben had thrown in confusion, now
for ever bespotted and untouchable by her lawful lord. The evil
doer lay there too, girt only in sackcloth, in token of his abasement
and surrender, with his hands lifted up above his dishevelled and
dust-strewn head, in utter abandonment, letting pass over him the

formal fury of his father's wrath. Jacob called him Ham, the shamer of his sire, the dragon of the prime, Behemoth and shameless hippopotamus — the last with reference to an Egyptian legend that this animal has the devastating habit of killing its father and mating with its mother by violence. That was to assume that Bilhah, because he himself slept with her, was really Reuben's mother; in his words of thunder rumbled the sinister old idea that Reuben, by lying with his mother, had betrayed his wish to be lord over all — and Jacob met the assumption by making him lord over nothing. He stretched forth his arm and took away from the groaning sinner his firstborn rights — took them indeed only unto himself, without for the moment bestowing the title further; so that from then on the matter was undecided, save as the majestic partiality of the father's heart took the place for the time being of legal fact.

It was remarkable that Reuben bore the boy Joseph no grudge, but of all the brothers behaved most forbearingly towards him. Justly enough, he did not attribute the boy's behaviour to pure malice, but in his heart gave him right for cherishing the honour of so loving a father and making known to him events the shocking character of which Reuben was far from denying. Conscious of his own frailty, Reuben was good-natured and just. In his person rather ill-favoured, though of great strength like all of Leah's sons, having his mother's stupid eyes, with the constitutionally suppurating lids, on which he spent much ointment to little end, he was more accessible than the others to Joseph's admitted charms; was dumbly moved by them and could feel it right that that inheritance from the wandering fathers of his race, the blessing and the election, should fall upon the lad rather than upon him or any other of the twelve. However sorely smitten by the parental wishes and designs concerning the blessing of the firstborn, he consented to them with his mind.

Joseph had known very well what he was about when he threatened with Reuben's wrath the son of Zilpah, who, moreover, in his downrightness, was by no means the worst of the lot. For Reuben had often — even if contemptuously — stood up for Joseph, often protected him with the strength of his arm and rebuked the brothers when, enraged at his tattling ways, they were provoked to fall foul of him. For the simpleton learned nothing from the early and serious occurrences with Reuben; made no amendment through the latter's magnanimity and as he grew up became a more dangerous eavesdropper and talebearer than he had been as a child. Dangerous to himself too, and in particular, for the rôle he had taught himself to play daily heightened both his observation and his isolated state; prejudiced his happiness, drew down upon him a hatred which it was not in the power of his nature to bear and gave him every ground to fear his brothers — the which then supplied fresh temptation to flatter the father and secure himself against them — all this despite oft-taken resolves to let his tongue refrain from poison and thus to heal his relations with the ten, of whom none was actually a scoundrel, and with whom he felt a secret and sacred bond on the score of the number of the signs of the zodiac, whose circle he and his little brother helped to complete.

In vain. Whenever Simeon and Levi, always swift in anger, had brawled with strange shepherds or even with people in the town and brought shame upon the tribe; whenever Judah, a proud and afflicted man, whom Ishtar plagued, so that he found cause for tears in matters where others found cause for laughing, had become secretly involved with the daughters of the countryside, displeasingly to Jacob; whenever one among the brothers had sinned before the only and most high God by privily burning incense to an idol, thus imperilling the fruitfulness of the flocks and threatening to bring down pox or scab or staggers upon them; or whenever the sons, either at home or at Shechem, had tried to make a little extra profit from the sale of the fallow cattle and quietly to divide it among themselves — the father heard of it from his favourite child. He even heard things without truth or reason, and was prone to believe them for the sake of Joseph's beautiful eyes. The lad asserted that some of the brothers had repeatedly cut steaks from the flesh of living sheep and rams and eaten them, and that this had been done by the sons of the two concubines, but to excess by Asher, who was in fact a good deal of a glutton. This appetite of Asher was the only evidence in support of a charge which on its face looked incredible and which could never have been established against the four. Objectively speaking, it was a slander; from Joseph's point of view, perhaps, it did not quite deserve that name. He may have dreamed it; or more precisely, had let himself dream it, at some time when he deserved and was expecting a beating, in order to seek shelter behind it with his father, and afterwards could or would not distinguish between truth and barefaced lie. In this instance, of course, the fury of the brothers found more than usually extravagant vent. They declared their innocence of the charge, with such vehemence as almost to render them suspect, as almost to make one think some small grain of truth lay at the bottom of it. We are usually bitterest over accusations which are false, of course — and yet perhaps not utterly without ground after all.

THE NAME

JACOB was about to start up at mention of the evil names which Gad had applied to Joseph, and which the old man was at once ready to regard as a culpable disrespect to his holiest feelings. But Joseph had such a charming way and plausible tongue, he knew so well how to speak with sudden vivacity, to pacify and pass on, that Jacob's anger died down before it had mounted, and he could do nothing but gaze with a rapt smile into the speaker's black and somewhat slanting eyes, narrowed by guile unspeakably sweet.

"It was nothing," he heard his son say, in the thin sharp voice which he loved because it had much of Rachel's quality in it. "I spoke to him like a brother for his rudeness, and he took the reproof with mildness, so it shall be counted to him as a virtue that we parted kindly. I went to the top of the hill to look down upon the town and Ephron's double house; I purified myself here with washing and prayer; as for the lion with which my father thought to frighten me, the ravager of the lower world, the breed of the black moon, he came not out of the thicket of the Jardên" (he pronounced the words with other vowels than ours, forming the r on the palate indeed, but not rolling it, and giving the e an open sound), "but found his evening meal in the gulleys and the cliffs, and the eyes of thy child have not seen him, neither near nor far off."

He called himself child because he knew that the reminder of his babyhood was especially moving to the father. He went on:

"But if he had come, with lashing tail, and roared after his prey, like the voice of the chanting seraphim, yet thy child would have been little affrighted or not at all before his rage. For of a certainty he had sought again the lambs, robber that he is, if Almodad had not driven him off with fire and clattering, and would wisely have avoided the child of man. For knoweth not my father that the beasts fear and avoid man, for that God gave him the spirit of understanding and taught him the orders into which the single things fall; doth he not know how Shemmæl shrieked when the man of earth knew how to name the creation as though he were its master and framer, and how all the fiery servants of the Lord were amazed and cast down their eyes, because they may know how to cry Holy, holy, holy in part choruses, but have absolutely no understanding of upper and lower orders? And the beasts too they are ashamed and put the tail between their legs because we know them and have power over their names and can thus render powerless the roaring might of the single one, by naming him. If now he had come, with long slinking tread, with his hateful nose, mewing and spitting, terror would not have robbed me of my senses, nor made me pale before his riddle. 'Is thy name Blood-thirst?' I would have asked of him, making merry at his expense. 'Or Springing Murder?' But then I would have sat upright and cried out: 'Lion! Lo, Lion art thou, by nature and species, and thy riddle lieth bare before me, so that I speak it out and with a laugh it is plain.' And he would have blinked before the name and gone meekly away before the word, powerless to answer unto me. For he is quite unlearned and knows nought of writing tools. . . ."

He went on punning, which he loved at all times to do, but did so now as with the previous boasting, in order to divert his father. It was a constant gratification to him that the word *sefer* — book, also writing tools — played upon his own name; for in contrast to all his brothers, not one of whom could write, he loved occupation with the stilus, and displayed so much skill that he might have served as scribal apprentice at one of the places where documents were kept, Kirjath Sefer or Gebal, if Jacob could conceivably have consented to such a career.

"If," he went on, "the father would come here and sit down in ease and comfort beside the son at the well, for instance here upon its rim, while the book-learned child slipped down to sit at his feet, it would be well and charmingly done. For then he would entertain his master and lord, telling him a little fable of names and naming which he has learnt and knows how to recite with good effect. For it was at the time of the generations of the flood that the angel Senhazai saw upon the earth a damsel named Ishchara, and was enamoured of her beauty so that he said: 'Hear me!' But she answered and said: 'There will be no thought of hearing thee, unless thou first teach me the true and unfeigned name of God, by the might of which thou springest up in pronouncing it.' Then the messenger, Senhazai, in his folly taught her the true name, and out of his burning desire that she should hearken unto him. But hardly did Ishchara see herself in the possession of it, what thinkest my father that she did, but out of a clear sky snap her fingers in the face of the importunate messenger! This is the climax of the story — but alas, I see that the father hearkeneth not, but that his ears are sealed up by his thoughts, and he is in deep musing."

And truly Jacob was not listening, but "mused." It was a vastly expressive musing, in the truest sense of the word, it was the highest degree of emotionally absorbed absence of mind, for less he did not do. When he mused it had to be a proper musing, recognizable at a hundred paces, so that not alone it was evident to everybody that Jacob was plunged in a muse, but everybody then first found out what a proper musing really was, and was seized with awe at state and picture: the old man leaning on his staff which he grasped with both hands, the head bowed over the arm; the deep, dreamy bitterness of the lips in the silver beard; the old brown eyes, boring and burrowing into the depths of memory and thought — eyes whose gaze was cast up so much from below that it almost got caught in the overhanging brows. . . . Men of feeling are expressive, for expression comes from the need of bringing to proof the feelings that well up unsilenced and unrestrained; it springs from a lofty and sensitive nature, in which shyness and austerity, high-mindedness and sensuality, straightforwardness and pose all appear on the stage in one single dignified rôle; producing in the beholder a sense of respect together with a slight inclination to smile. Jacob was very expressive — to Joseph's great joy, for he loved his father's high-pitched emotional key and took pride in it; but it troubled and agitated others who had daily business with him, and in particular his other sons, who in every disagreement between him and them feared nothing so much as just his power of expression. Thus Reuben, when after the wretched affair with Bilhah he had to confront his father. Fear and awe before the high-flung phrase were deeper and darker then than they are now; but under such a visitation then as now the ordinary man would feel like expressing his superstitious avoidance in some such words as our "God forbid." But Jacob's power of expression, the vibration in his voice, the elevation of his language, the solemnity of his nature in general, were linked with a disposition and tendency which was likewise the reason why one so often saw him powerfully and picturesquely musing. He so inclined to association of thought, that it characterized and controlled his whole inner life, and in such thoughts his whole nature almost literally exhausted itself. Wherever he went, his soul was played upon by chords and correspondences, diverted and led away into far-reaching considerations which mingled past and to come in the present moment, and made his gaze blurred and broken as in deep introspection. It was almost painful, but by no means peculiar to him alone, for many people suffer from it in varying degrees; it might almost be said that in Jacob's world intellectual value and significance — the words taken in their most actual sense — depending upon the copious flow of mythical association of ideas and their power to permeate the moment. But why had it sounded so strange, so strained and charged with meaning when the old man in his broken sentence had given voice to his fear that Joseph might fall into the well? Because Jacob could not think of those depths without connecting them in his thought, to their enrichment and consecration, with the idea of the lower world and the kingdom of the dead — that idea which played an important part, not indeed in his religious convictions, but probably in the depths of his soul and in the power of his imagination: that primitive mythical inheritance of all peoples, the conception of the underworld, the realm of Osiris the dismembered one, where he ruled, the place of Namtar, the god of plagues, the kingdom of terrors, whence came all evil spirits and pestilences. It was the world whereinto the constellations descended at their setting, to rise again at the appointed hour, whereas no mortal who trod the path to this abode ever found the way back again. It was the place of filth and excrement, but also of gold and riches; the womb in which one buried the seed corn,

out of which it sprouted again as nourishing grain; the land of the
black moon, of winter and the parching summer, whither Tammuz
the shepherd in his spring sank down and would sink each year,
when the boar killed him, and all creation ceased and the weeping
world lay sere, until Ishtar, goddess and mother, made pilgrimage to
hell to seek him, broke the dust-covered bolts of his prison, and mid
laughter and rejoicing, brought forth the beautiful and beloved out
of the pit and the grave, to reign over the new season and the fresh-
flowering fields.

Why then should Jacob's voice not shake with emotion and his
question wake strange, significant echoes, since to him — not with
his mind but with his feeling — the mouth of the well was an entrance
to the lower world, so that the mere word called up all this and
yet more within him? A man of dull and untrained sense, void of
imagination, could utter it and have only the most immediate and
practical reaction. As for Jacob, it imparted dignity and solemn
spirituality to his whole being, made it expressive to the point of
painfulness. The effect upon the erring Reuben, when Jacob hurled
at him the opprobrious name of Ham, is impossible to measure. For
Jacob was not the man to use such an epithet in the sense of a mere
pale allusion. His spirit had frightful power to dissolve the present
in the past, to bring back into force the consummated event, and his,
Jacob's, personal identity with Noah, the father who was spied
upon, reviled and dishonoured at the hand of his son. And Reuben
too knew beforehand that it would be so and that he would quite
literally lie as Ham before Noah — that was why his flesh had crept
when he went in.

The old man's present mood of deep and manifest musing was
due to memories called up by his son's prattle about names and naming: remote and anxious memories that weighed on his spirit like a
dream, of the old days, when in actual bodily fear he had awaited
the meeting with the brother from the plains, whom he had cheated
and who was doubtless still thirsting for revenge; and then, aspiring
so fervently after the power of the spirit, had wrestled for the sake of
the name with the strange man who had fallen upon him. A frightful, heavy, highly sensual dream, yet with a certain wild sweetness;
no light and fleeting vision that passes and is gone, but a dream of
such physical warmth, so dense with actuality, that it left a double
legacy of life behind it as the tide leaves the fruits of the sea on the
strand at the ebb: the breaking of Jacob's hip, the hollow of the
thigh, from which he halted ever since the unknown had put it out
of joint in wrestling; and then the name — but not the stranger's
name, for that had been denied up to the last, until the dawn, until
it was almost too late, however Jacob demanded it of him, hot and
panting and with resistless strength — not the stranger's name but

Jacob's own other and second name, the surname, which the strange
man left him in the struggle, that he might let him go before the sun
rose and save him from the painful danger of being late: the title
of honour which since that time had been bestowed upon Jacob
when one would flatter him and make him smile — Israel, "God doeth
battle." . . . Again he saw the ford of Jabbok before him, where
he had remained alone in the shrubbery, having sent on ahead his
sons and his women and the flocks and herds which he had set apart
as a present for his brother Esau to find favour in his eyes, saw the
unquiet and cloudy night, when he, unquiet as the sky, had roved
about between two efforts after slumber, still shaken from the encounter with Rachel's father — which by God's help had gone off
well and the father been successfully overreached — but already in
torment before the approach of yet another whom he had defrauded
and betrayed. How he had exhorted the Elohim in prayer, and fairly
conjured Him to stand by him! He saw the man too, with whom so
unwittingly he had been involved in a life-and-death struggle; for
the moon had suddenly glared out of the cloud and he has seen him
breast to breast: the wide-apart, unwinking ox-eyes, the face and
shoulders glistening like polished stone; and in his heart he felt again
the fury of desire with which in agonized whispers he had demanded
the Name. . . . How strong he had been! With the desperate
strength of a dream, and enduring with unsuspected reserves of
power in the depth of his soul! He had held out all night, until the
dawn, until he had seen that the man would be too late and the latter
had prayed him Let me go! Neither had prevailed over the other —
but did not that mean the victory was Jacob's, he being no extraordinary man, but a man from hereabouts, and of the seed of
mankind? Yet it seemed as though the wide-eyed one had doubted
that. The painful thrust and grip upon the thigh had seemed like an
examination. Perhaps it was meant to find out whether there was a
socket there, whether it was movable and not, like the strange man's
own, fixed and not adapted to sitting down. And then the man had
known how to turn the thing so that he did not utter his own name,
but gave Jacob another in place of it. He could hear in his musing —
as clearly as then with his mortal ears — the man's high and brazen
voice, speaking to him: "Thy name shall henceforth be called Israel,"
whereupon he had loosened his arms and let the owner of the strange
voice go, so that there was still some hope he might arrive in
time. . . .

THE MONKEY LAND OF EGYPT

THE STATELY old man's way of coming out of his reverie was no less
expressive than his absorption in it. With a deep sigh, with weighty

dignity, he straightened up and shook it from him and with lifted head looked about him widely in space as one who wakes; plainly collecting himself and finding his way back to the present. He seemed not to have heard Joseph's suggestion that he sit down at his side; the lad realized to his embarrassment that this was no moment for historiettes, however pleasing. The old man had still things to say of serious import; the lion had not been his sole concern, for Joseph had given cause for others, and his father spared him nothing. He heard:

"There is a country far to the south, the land of Hagar the maid, called Ham's country, or the Black, the monkey land of Egypt. For its people are black of soul, though red of face, they come old out of the womb, their nurslings are like little old men, and in their cradles lisp of death. I have heard that they carried the manhood of their god, three ells long, through their streets with playing of lutes and trumpets, and cohabit with painted corpses in the graves. They are all swollen with conceit, lustful and melancholy. They clothe themselves after the curse that lighted on Ham, who was to go naked with his shame exposed; for their garments are linen thin as spider-web, which covers their nakedness without hiding it — and on this they pride themselves, saying that they wear woven air. For they have no shame of their flesh and neither word nor understanding for that which is sin. The bellies of their dead they stop with spices, and on the place of the heart they lay as is most fit the image of a dung beetle. They are rich and lustful like the folk of Sodom and Gomorrah. It pleasureth them to make their beds together and to exchange their wives one with another, and when a woman goeth in the street and seeth a young man after whom she lusteth, so lieth she with him. They are like the beasts, and they bow down to beasts in the innermost of their ancient temples; and I have heard that a virgin, and whom no man had known until that time, let herself be covered before all the people in the temple by a ram named Banebdedu. Doth my son approve these ways?"

Joseph saw to what offending of his these words had reference, and his head and lower lip hung down like a chidden child's. But a smile hid behind his expression of half-pouting repentance, for he was aware that Jacob's description of the customs of Mizraim was full of prejudice, exaggeration and easy generalities. He waited in humility, but seeing his father insisted on an answer, he lifted up his eyes appealingly, seeking in the old man's face the first sign of a smile, trying to lure one out by cautious overtures, by alternate advance and retreat, by gravity and gaiety in turn.

"If these be indeed the ways of Mizraim, my dear lord, then God forbid that this ignorant child of thine should call them good. But indeed to me it seemeth that the skill of those old dung beetles in

weaving linen so that it is like air for fineness, might speak for them
provisionally, on the other side. And in that they have no shame of
their flesh it might be said to their excusing by one ready in indulgence that they are mostly spare of habit and lean in body, fat flesh
having more occasion to feel shame than dry, and indeed. . . ."

But now it was Jacob's turn to be serious. He interposed on a
voice wherein impatient chiding strove with tenderness:

"Thou speakest as a child! Thou knowest how to set thy words
together and thy speech is beguiling like a camel dealer's when he
would bargain to his profit — but its sense is utterly childish. I would
not believe that thou meckest my anxiety, that maketh me to tremble
lest thou displease our God and stir up His anger against thee and
Abraham's seed. Mine eyes have seen how thou sattest naked beneath
the moon, as though the Highest had not given us in our hearts the
knowledge of sin, and as though the nights of spring were not cool
upon these heights after the heat of the day, so that an evil flux
might fall upon thee overnight and fever take away thy sense before
cockcrow. Therefore will I that thou puttest straightway thy upper
garment about thee, according to the religion of the children of
Shem. For it is woollen and a wind goeth from Gilead. And I will
that thou shouldest grieve me not, for mine eyes have seen more
than this, and I am in great fear that they saw thee kiss thy hand at
the stars. . . ."

"By no means!" cried Joseph aghast. He had sprung up from the
margin of the well to put on the knee-length brown and yellow
smock which his father had taken and held out to him; but the sudden movement and erect posture seemed to express his repudiation
of the old man's charge, which must be refuted at all costs — and
with all means. Let us take careful note, for everything here was
highly significant. Jacob's habit of thinking in many layers and involved associations was shown in the way he included three reproaches in one: lack of care for the health, lack of modesty, and
religious backsliding. The last was the deepest and worst layer of
the combined anxieties, and Joseph, his arms in the sleeves of his
smock, the opening of which, in his excitement, he could not find,
took on the battle as he did his garment, as if to illustrate the importance in his eyes of denying a course of conduct which at the
same time he went about most cunningly to justify.

"Never! By no means!" he asseverated, while his beautiful and
well-favoured head found its way through the opening in the smock.
And with intent to convince still more by the choiceness of his
phrases, he added:

"My father's mind is, I assure him, most grievously darkened by
error."

He twitched his shoulders to settle his smock and pulled it down

with both hands, snatched the dishevelled myrtle wreath from his
head and cast it aside, then began without looking to pull at the
strings that tied the garment below the neck. "Kiss my hand? I
know nothing of it; how could I think of committing so evil a deed?
Let my dear lord but consider my failings, he will see that they do
not tally. I gazed upwards, certainly, that is the truth. I saw the light
shining, the splendid rays streaming, and mine eyes, wounded by
the fiery darts of the sun, bathed in the mild radiance of the frame
of the night. For thus sayeth the song, and passeth from mouth to
mouth among men:

> "Thee, Sin, made He to shine. The times to establish,
> The changes of season, to night thee He wedded
> And with splendour He crowned thy high consummation."

He chanted the words, standing one step higher than his father,
with upraised hands; at each half verse he bent his body, first to one
side and then to the other.

"*Shapattu*," said he. "That is the day of the solemn consummation,
the day of beauty. It is not far off, by one or two morrows it will
be here. Yet not even on the holy Sabbath day would it occur to me
to send the time-decider even the smallest and most secret kiss, for
it is not said that it shines by its own light, but that He made it to
shine and gave it the crown. . . ."

"Who?" asked Jacob in a low voice. "Who made it to shine?"

"Marduk-Bel," cried Joseph rashly, but followed up the word
by a long drawn out "Eh-h-h!" and an expiatory headshake. He
went on:

"As they call him in the tales. But it is — as my lord needs not to
learn from his foolish child — the Lord of all Gods, stronger than the
Anunnaki and Baals of all the peoples, the God of Abraham, who
slew the dragon and created the threefold world. When He turns
away in His wrath He turns not his face again, and when He is
wroth no other god goeth up against His fury. Magnanimous is He,
and all-wise, sinners and blasphemers are a stench unto His nostrils,
but to him who went up out of the land of Ur unto him He hath
inclined and made a bond with him that he will be the God of him
and his seed. And His blessing is come upon Jacob, my lord, to
whom also the beautiful name and title of Israel belong, and who is a
great harbinger of the Lord and full of insight and far from so ill
instructing his children that they would take it on themselves to
throw kisses to the stars, since such should appertain unto the Lord
alone, always supposing it were fitting to throw kisses to Him,
whereas that is so little the case that one might almost say it were
better by comparison to throw them to the bright stars. But

though this might be said, yet do I not say it, and if I have even
carried a finger to my mouth in the way of hand-kissing, then may
I never carry it there again, rather let me starve. And indeed I will
eat no more but rather choose to hunger, if my father doth not at
once sit down comfortably on the ledge beside his son. For my
lord standeth much too long upon his feet, seeing that he hath a
holy weakness of his thigh, come by in so high and strange a way,
as is well known unto all —"

He ventured to step down to the old man and cautiously put an
arm about his shoulder, convinced that he had charmed and soothed
him by his prattle; and Jacob, who had stood plunged in meditation
on the divine, fingering the little cylindrical seal which hung down
on his breast, yielded to the gentle pressure, put his foot upon the
step and let himself down on the margin of the well, resting his staff
in the hollow of his arm, smoothing his garment and in his turn
looking up at the moon, as it lighted his aging majesty and mirrored
itself in the shrewd and anxious chestnut-brown eyes. Joseph sat
down at his feet, by way of completing the picture he had already
drawn. He felt his father's hand upon his hair, moving slowly to and
fro in a stroking movement of which the old man was probably
unconscious, and in a lower voice he went on:

"Behold, it is lovely and pleasant thus, and I could sit through all
the watches of the night, as indeed I have often longed to do. My
lord gazeth up into the countenance of his Lord, and I in my turn
with the liveliest pleasure into his, that I behold as a countenance of
a god and that is illuminated by the reflected light. But hast thou not
seen the face of my hairy uncle Esau like the face of the moon, when
all unhoped he met thee so gentle and brotherly by the ford, as thou
hast reported unto me? But that too was but a mild reflection on
his hot and hairy face, the reflection of thy countenance which is
like the moon's to look upon and the shepherd Abel's, whose sacrifice was pleasing unto the Lord, and not like Cain's and Esau's,
whose faces are like the ploughed field when the sun breaks it up
and like the clod when it gathers size from the drought. Yea, thou
art Abel, the moon and the shepherd, and all thine we are shepherds
and people of the sheep, not people of the sun, the husbandmen,
like the peasants who sweat behind the plough and behind the ox
of the plough, and pray to the Baal of their land. But we look up to
the Lord of the way, the Wanderer, who rises there in garment of
shining white. But tell me," he went on, hardly stopping to draw
breath, "did not Abraham our father depart in anger from Ur in
Chaldæa and leave behind him in his wrath the moon citadel of his
city because the Lawgiver mightily exalted his god Marduk, who
is the burning fiery sun, and set him up above all the gods of Shinar,

to the vexation of the people of Sin? And tell me likewise do not his people out there call him Shem, when they would exalt him — the the same as Noah's son was called, whose children are black but comely, as Rachel was, and abide at Elam, Asshur, Arpaxad, Lud and Edom? Listen and hear, for a thought cometh unto thy child: was not the wife of Abraham called Sahar, which is the moon? For lo, I will make thee a little reckoning: seven times fifty days are the days of the year, and four over. But in every month are four days when men do not see the moon. Let my Lord take away then, if it please him, those three times twelve from those three hundred and fifty-four, leaving three hundred and eighteen days of the visible moon. Now there were three hundred and eighteen trained servants, born in Abram's own house, with whom Abram smote the kings of the East and pursued them beyond Damascus and brought again his brother Lot out of the hand of Chedorlaomer, the Elamite. Lo, so hath Abiram our father loved the moon, and so sacred to him was its shining that he counted his servants for the battle precisely according to the days of its giving light. Then supposing I had kissed my hand three hundred and eighteen times, whereas I did so not even once, would that have been so great a sinning?"

THE TESTING

"Thou art shrewd," said Jacob, and the hand that had stood still during the reckoning began to move again, less absently, over Joseph's head, "thou art shrewd, Yashub, my son. Thy head is outwardly beautiful, and well-favoured, as Mami's was" (he used the pet name which Joseph had given Rachel, the earthly and familiar name of Ishtar, of Babylonian origin), "and within it is godly and wise. So lively was mine too when I counted no more than thy years, but it is weary from the events, not only from the new but from the old which have come upon us, and which give it cause to ponder. And from the troubles, and the inheritance, for the words of the Lord are not clear. For His countenance may be mild to look upon but also it is like the burning fiery brand, and it destroyed Sodom with fire, and man goeth through the fire of the Lord to purify himself. The devouring flame is He, that consumeth the feast of the first of the flock at the feast of the equinox, outside of the tent, when it grows dark and we sit within with trembling and eat of the lamb, whose blood stains the door-posts, because the Avenger passeth over. . . ."

He broke off, and his hand slipped down from Joseph's head. The lad looked up, and saw that his father's face was covered with his hands and that he was shaking.

"What hath come to my lord?" he cried, dismayed, and flinging himself round he put up his hands to his father's hands without daring to touch them. He had to wait, and to speak again. Only with hesitation did Jacob change his posture. When he uncovered his face it looked lined and consumed with grief and the woeful eyes stared past the boy into space.

"I thought upon the Lord with trembling," he said, and his lips seemed scarcely able to move. "It was as though my hand were the hand of Abraham and lay upon Yitzchak's head. And as though His voice went out upon me, and His command. . . ."

"His command?" Joseph asked, challenging him with a quick, birdlike motion of the head.

"The command and the precept, thou knowest it, since thou knowest the tales," answered Jacob in a resigned tone, sitting bowed over with his forehead against the hand that held the staff. "And I hearkened; for is He less than Melech, the Bull-king of Baalim to whom they bring the firstborn of men in their need and in secret feast give the child into his arms? And shall He not demand from His own what Melech demands from those who believe on him? Then demanded He it and I heard His voice and spoke: Behold, here I am! And my heart stood still and my breath went from me. . . . And I saddled an ass early in the morning and took thee with me. For thou wast Isaac, my late-born and first-born, and the Lord smiled upon us when thou wast announced, and wast my one and all, and upon thy head lay all the future. And now He demanded thee of me, as was His right but contrary to the future. Then I clave wood for the burnt offering and laid it upon the ass and set the child thereon, and rose up with two young men three days distant from Beersheba far down towards Edom and the land of Muzri and towards Horeb His mountain. And when I saw the mountain of the Lord from afar and the peak of the mountain, I sent the ass back with the young men and took the fire in my hand and a knife, and we went alone. And when thou spakest to me and said: 'My father,' then I could not say 'Here am I, my son,' but instead moaned in my throat. And when thou in thy voice saidest: 'Behold the fire and the wood, but where is the lamb for a burnt offering?' then could I not answer as I should that the Lord would provide himself a lamb, for I was sick within me, so that I could have spat out my soul with tears, and moaned again so that thou lookest at me as thou wentest beside me. And when we came to the place I builded an altar of stone and laid the wood in order and bound the child and laid him upon it. And took the knife with my left hand and covered thy two eyes. And when I drew the knife and the edge of the knife against thy throat, lo, then I did deny the Lord, and my arm fell from my shoulder, and the knife fell down, and I fell down upon my face on the ground and bit the earth and the grass of the earth and struck at it with my feet and my fists and cried: 'Slay him, slay him, Thou, O Lord and Destroyer, for he is my one and only, and I am not Abraham and my soul fails before Thee.' And as I thrust about me and shrieked, lo, thunder rolled from the place along the heaven far and wide. And I had the child and had the Lord no more, for I could not do it for Him, no, no, no, I could not," he groaned, and shook his head against the hand on the staff.

"At the last moment," asked Joseph with lifted brows, "did thy soul give way? For in the next," he went on, as his father only turned his head a little without speaking, "in the very next would have sounded the voice and called unto thee: 'Lay not thine hand upon the lad, neither do thou anything unto him,' and thou wouldest have seen the ram in the thicket."

"I did not know," said the old man, "for I was as Abraham and the tale had not yet been told."

"Ah, but saidest thou not thou hast cried out 'I am not Abraham!' " responded Joseph, smiling. "But if thou wast not he, then wast thou Jacob my father, and the tale was old and thou knewest the issue. And also it was not the boy Yitzchak whom thou boundedst and wouldst slay," he added, with the same airy movement of the head. "But that is the profit of these later days, that we know already the course in which the world rolls on, and the tales in which it is fulfilled and which were founded by the fathers. So mightest thou have trusted in the voice and the ram."

"Thy words are full of wit but not of wisdom," countered the old man, forgetting in the argument his previous pain. "For firstly, if I was Jacob and not Abraham, then was it uncertain whether it would fall out as before, and I could not know if the Lord would not let it come to pass to the end, whereas once he had stayed his hand. But secondly, what had my strength been before the Lord, had it come to me out of foreknowledge of the angel and the ram and not rather from my great submission and the faith that God can make the future go through the fire unsinged and spring the bolts of death and is Lord of the resurrection? But thirdly, hath then God tried me? No, he hath tried Abraham, who was steadfast. But I have tried myself with the trial of Abram and my soul hath refused, for my love was stronger than my faith and I could not," he lamented afresh and leaned his head against his staff — giving himself again to grief now that he had justified his understanding.

"Surely I have uttered much folly," said Joseph humbly. "My lack of wisdom is greater beyond doubt than that of many sheep, and a camel is like to Noah in prudence compared with this senseless child of thine. Doubtless my answer to thy just rebuke will be no more enlightened, but to this foolish one it seemeth that thou wast neither Abram nor Jacob, but — awful to utter — that thou wast the

Lord, who tried Jacob with the trial of Abram, and thou hadst the wisdom of the Lord and knewest what trial He was minded to lay upon Jacob, namely that one which He was not minded to let Abram endure to the end. For He spoke to him: 'I am Melech, the Bull god of Baalim. Bring me thy firstborn!' But when Abram hasted to bring him, then spake the Lord, 'Am I Melech the Bull king? No, for I am the God of Abraham, whose face is not like the ploughed field when the sun breaks it up, but rather like the face of the moon, and that which I commanded I did not command that thou mightest fulfil, but that thou mightest learn that thou shouldst not do it because it is an abomination in My sight, and moreover, lo, here is a ram.' My father then did but divert himself with trying whether he could do that which the Lord forbade unto Abraham, and now he grieveth because he found that he could never do it."

"Like an angel," said Jacob, as he rose, shaking his head in the greatness of his emotion, "like an angel near to the throne of God so speakest thou, Jehosiph, my child of God. Would that Mami could hear thee. She would clap her hands, and her eyes, which are thy eyes, would shine with laughter. But only half of the truth is in thy words, the other half remaineth in mine, for I shewed myself weak in self-confidence. But thy part of the truth hast thou adorned with the ornament of graciousness and anointed it with the oil of wit, so that it was a delight to the understanding and a balsam unto my heart. How cometh it now that the words of my child are a stream full of wisdom and fall blithely over the rocks of truth and drop plashing into the heart, making it leap for joy?"

OF OIL, WINE, AND FIGS

"Thus it is then," Joseph replied. "Wit is of the nature of a messenger to and fro, and of a go-between 'twixt sun and moon and 'twixt the power of Shamash and of Sin over men's bodies and understandings. Such was the teaching of Eliezer, thy man of wisdom, when he taught me the knowledge of the stars and their conjunctions and their power over the hour according to their aspects. And when he put the hour-hand of my birth in Harran in Mesopotamia, at midday in the month of Tammuz, when Shamash stood in mid-heaven and in the sign of the Twins and in the East the sign of the Virgin was rising." He pointed to the constellations, one of which was declining westwards, the other just coming up in the eastern sky, and went on: "That is a sign of Nabu, may it please my father to know, a sign of Thoth the writer of tablets, a light and versatile god, as which he speaketh between things for their good and promoteth intercourse. And the sun too, standing in a sign of Nabu, was lord of the hour, and was in conjunction with the moon, fa-

vourable to him according to the learning of priests and interpreters,
for his wisdom receiveth mildness therefrom and his heart clemency.
But Nabu, the go-between, was in opposition to Nergal, the fox and
mischief-maker, giving hardness to his dominion and stamping it
with the seal of fate. Ishtar as well — whose part is moderation and
sweetness, love and mercy — who culminated at that hour, and was
in good aspect to Sin and Nabu. She too was in the sign of the Bull,
and instructed it to give tranquillity and abiding valour and shaped
the understanding for delight. But likewise, so said Eliezer, she had
a trine aspect of Nergal in Capricorn, whereat Eliezer rejoiced, for
her sweetness would not be savourless but like honey spiced with
the herbs of the field. The moon stood in the sigh of Cancer, its own
sign, and all indicators stood, if not in their own, at least in benefic
signs. But if Nabu, the judicious, is united with the powerfully
placed moon, then will the man go far in the earth. And if, as at that
hour, the sun hath a trine aspect to Ninurta, warrior and huntsman,
that is a sign of a share in the events of the kingdoms of the earth
and the administration of authority. Indeed it had been no evil
nativity, if the folly of thy ill-begotten child bring not all to naught."

"H'm," said the old man, looking aside as he lightly smoothed the
lad's hair. "It resteth with the Lord who ruleth the stars. But what
He sheweth with them cannot mean the same each time. Wert thou
the son of the great and of a man of power in the world, then might
one read that thou shouldest partake of government and authority.
But since thou art a shepherd and a shepherd's son, then it is clear to
the understanding that it must mean something of a lesser import.
But what of wit as a messenger to and fro?"

"I am returning to that now," quoth Joseph, "and guiding my
thoughts in that direction. For my father's blessing was his birth with
the sun in the zenith with its aspect to Marduk in Libra and Ninurta
in the eleventh sign, and added to that the aspect between two paternal indicators, the king and the warrior exchanged with each other.
That is a powerful blessing. But my lord knoweth how powerful
likewise was the maternal too and the blessing of the moon, from the
powerful configurations of Sin and Ishtar. There, then, was probably
the understanding that was displayed, for instance in the opposition
of Nabu to Nergal, from the ruling writer of tablets and the hard
light of the retrograde blackguard in Capricorn, displayed that he
might play the go-between 'twixt paternal and maternal inheritance,
keep the balance between father- and mother-power, and blithely
reconcile the blessing of the day with the blessing of the night. . . ."

He broke off with a somewhat wry smile, which Jacob, sitting
above and behind him, did not see. The father said:

"The old man Eliezer hath much experience and hath gathered together wisdom and as it were hath read the stones of the time before

the flood. And he hath taught thee manifold truths and values from the beginnings, the origins and relations of things, and much that is of use to be used in the world. But of many a thing can it not be said with certainty whether it is to be counted with the true and useful, and my heart is swayed by doubt whether he did well to show thee the arts of the star-gazers and magicians of Shinar. For indeed I hold the head of my son to be worthy all wisdom, but I knew not that our fathers had read in the stars or that God had commanded Adam to do so, and I am careful and in doubt whether it may not come close to worship of the stars and perhaps it may be an abomination before the Lord and a doubtful and devilish middle-thing between worship and idolatry." He shook his head anxiously, attacked at his most vulnerable point between distress over the right course and brooding affliction over God's unclarity.

"Much is in doubt," answered Joseph — if what he said may be called an answer. "For instance, is it the night that conceals the day, or the day the night? For it would be important to distinguish this, and often in field and hut have I considered it, hoping, if I could decide, to draw from the decision conclusions as to the virtue of the blessing of the sun and of the moon, as well as of the beauty of the father- and the mother-inheritance. For my little mother, whose cheeks smelt of rose-leaves, went down into the night in childbed with my brother who still dwells in the women's tents, and dying she gave him the name Ben-oni, and it is well known that at On in the land of Egypt, Osiris has his place, who is the king of the under-world. But thou calledst the boy Ben-jamin, as much as to say the son of the true and favourite wife, and that is a beautiful name. Yet not always do I obey thee, but sometimes name my brother Ben-oni, and he heareth it gladly, for he knoweth that Mami, at the moment when she parted, would have it so. She is now gone into the night and loveth us from out of it, the little one and me, and her blessing is the blessing of the moon and the depths. Doth my lord not know of the two trees in the garden of the world? From the one cometh oil, with which they anoint the kings of the earth that they may live. From the other come forth figs, green and rosy and full of sweet seeds, and whoever eats of them shall die. Out of its broad leaves Adam and Eve made themselves aprons to hide their shame, since knowledge became their portion beneath the full moon of the summer equinox, when he passeth through his marriage point to decline and die. Oil and wine are sacred to the sun, and well for him whose brow drippeth with oil and his eyes are drunken with the shining of red wine! For his words will be a brightness and a laughing and a consolation to the peoples, and will shew them the ram in the thicket for a sacrifice unto the Lord instead of the firstborn son, so that they are healed of tormenting fear. But the sweet fruit of the fig is sacred to the

moon, and well for him whom the little mother nourisheth out of
the night with its flesh. For he will grow as though beside a stream,
and his soul have roots whence the streams arise, and his word be
made flesh and living as a body of earth, and with him shall be the
spirit of prophecy. . . ."

How was he speaking? In a whisper. It was as it had been before
his father found him, it was not quite canny. His shoulders shook, his
hands trembled on his knees, he smiled, his eyeballs rolled inwards to
show the whites. Jacob saw it not, but he had listened. He bent towards the child, lifting his hands above his head protectingly yet not
touching it. But then he laid his left hand on Joseph's hair, and at the
touch the boy at once relaxed; at the same time with the other he
sought his son's right hand that lay on his knee, and he said, with deliberate homeliness of speech:

"Hearken, Yashub, my son, to what I will ask thee, since my heart
misgiveth me for the cattle and for the prospering of the flocks. The
early rains were comforting, and they fell before winter came on,
with no bursting of the cloud to flood the meadows and fill only the
wells of the unsettled, rather a gentle drizzling doing good unto the
fields. But winter was dry, and the sea would not send the air of its
mildness, rather came the wind from desert and plain, and the heavens were clear, a delight to the eye but care unto the heart. Woe unto
us if the latter rains delay and come not for there would be no harvest for the husbandman and the sowing of the farmer would be vain,
and the grass would wither before its time so that the cattle found
nought to eat and the udders of the kine would hang down empty.
Let then my child say what he thinketh of wind and weather and
what hope may be ours, and what is in his mind concerning the latter
rains, whether they will set in betimes."

He bent lower over his son, turning his head aside to listen above
him.

"Thou listest," said Joseph at once without seeing, "and thy child
listeth too, both without and within, and bringeth to thy listening
knowledge and the word. For there is a dropping in mine ear from
the branches and a sound of trickling over the plains, although the
moon's shining is overbright and a wind goeth from Gilead. For these
sounds are not yet in time but near to time, and my nose smelleth
them out securely, that, before the moon of Nisan hath declined another quarter, the eatrh will be pregnant from the male water of the
sky and will smoke and steam with delight, for I can smell it, and the
pastures will be full of sheep and the meadows of the stream stand
thick with corn, so that we shall exult and sing aloud. I listed and
learned that in the beginning the earth was watered by the river Tawi
that went out from Babel and watered it once in forty years. But then
the Lord decreed that it should be watered from heaven, for four

reasons, of which one was, that all eyes should look upwards. So look we up in thanks to the heavens and the throne, where are all the contrivances of the weather and all the chambers of the tempests and the whirlwinds, as I saw them in a dream when I slumbered yesterday beneath the tree of wisdom. For a cherub named Jophiel led me thither in his kindness by the hand, that I might look about me and take cognizance. And I saw the caves full of steam, whose towers were of fire, and I saw the busyness of the workers, and heard them saying each to the other: 'Orders have gone forth with respect to the firmament and the cloudy heavens. For lo, there is a drought in the western land and the plains and meadows of the upland are parched. There shall be taken measures that rain shall fall early upon the country of the Amorites, the Ammonites and Perizzites, the Midianites, Hivites and Jebusites, but in especial upon the district of Hebron upon the height of the watershed, where my very son Jacob, whose name shall be called Israel, pastures his countless flocks.' This I dreamed with such a liveliness that it must not be mocked, and since moreover I lay under the tree, my lord may rest assured and joyful that all will be well in the matter of the rains."

"Praised be Elohim," said the old man. "But even so will we choose out cattle for the burnt offerings and hold a feast before Him and burn the entrails with incense and honey, that it may come to pass as thou sayest. For I am fearful lest the townspeople and the countryfolk may bring all to nought, in that they deal after their own fashion, to the honour of Baalat and with a feast of pairing, with cymbals and shouting, for the sake of the fruitfulness. It is good that my child is blest with visions — which come from his being the firstborn of my true and dearest wife. Also unto me was much revealed in my youth — and what I saw as I came from Beersheba, and against my will and without my knowledge fell upon the place and the entrance — that may be set against this which has been shown to thee. I love thee for what thou hast said to reassure me in respect of the moisture, but say it not abroad, that thou dreamest under the tree, say it not to the children of Leah and speak it not to the sons of the maids, for that they might be angry at thy gift."

"I swear it and put my hand beneath my thigh," responded Joseph, "thy word is a seal unto my mouth. I know well that I am a prattler, but when reason commands I can master my tongue, so much the easier that my humble visions are not worthy of mention compared with that which was vouchsafed my lord at the place of Luz, when the messengers went up and down from the earth to the gates, and Elohim was revealed to him."

DUET

"Ah, my dear father and most dear lord," said he, turning round
with a happy smile to embrace his parent with one arm — which delighted no little the good old man. "How glorious it is, that the Lord
loveth us and hath desire unto us, and the smoke of our sacrifice is a
pleasure in His nostrils! For though Abel had not time to beget children, being slain upon the fields by Cain, for the sake of their sister
Nœmah, yet are we of the breed of Abel the tent-dweller and from
the tribe of Isaac, the younger, to whom fell the blessing. And therefore have we both reason and dreams and they are a great delight the
one and the other. For it is of great worth to possess knowledge and
tongues so that one knoweth how to speak and to answer and to name
all things by their names. And equally it is of great worth to be an
innocent before the Lord, so that one may strike unawares upon the
place which is the bond between heaven and earth, and in sleep be
seized of counsel and know how to interpret dreams and visions,
that they give knowledge what may happen from moon to moon.
Thus was it with Noah, wisest of all men, to whom the Lord gave
foreknowledge of the flood that he might save his life. And thus was
it with Enoch the son of Jared, who was of unblemished life and
washed himself in living water. That was Hanoch the boy, knowest
thou of him, for I know well how it was with him and how God's
love to Abel and Yitzchak was lukewarm in comparison to His love to
him. For Hanoch was wise and pious and had read in the secret tablets, and set himself apart from men and the Lord took him hence so
that he was no more seen. And made him an angel in His sight, Metatron the great scribe and prince of the world. . . ."

He stopped and went pale. His breath had grown shorter and
shorter, and now he hid his face on his father's breast, who received
it gladly, speaking into the silvery airs above it:

"Well know I of Hanoch, who was of the first tribe of men, son
of Jared, who was son of Mahalaleel, who was son of Cainan, who
was son of Enos, who was son of Seth, who was son of Adam. Such
was Hanoch's birth and tribe back to the beginnings. But the son of
his son's son was Noah, the second first man, and he begot Shem,
whose children are black but comely, of whom Eber came in the
fourth remove, so that he was the father of all the children of Eber
and of all the Hebrews, and our father. . . ."

This was all well-known fact, there was nothing new in what he
said. Every member of the tribe and race had the succession at his
tongue's end from early childhood, and the old man was only taking
occasion to repeat it and bear witness to it in conversation. Joseph
understood that the talk was now to turn "fine"; that they were now

to indulge in "fine language" — in other words, in conversation which no longer served the purpose of a practical exchange of ideas or of intellectual discussion, but consisted in the mere relation and utterance of matters well known to both speakers: in recollection, confirmation, and edification, a kind of spoken antiphony, such as the shepherds in the fields exchanged round their evening fires, beginning: "Knowest thou? Well I know." He sat up and chimed in:

"And lo, from Eber came Peleg, and begot Serug, whose son was Nahor, the father of Terah, Hosannah! Who begot Abram at Ur in Chaldæa and departed with Abram his son and his son's wife Sarah, like the moon, and who was unfruitful, and with Lot the son of his brother's son. And took them and led them out of Ur and died at Harran. And then befell the command of the Lord to Abram that he go on further with the souls which he had won for the Lord across the plain and across the river Euphrates on the road that runs between Shinar and Amurruland."

"Well I know," said Jacob, taking up the tale afresh. "It was the country which the Lord would show him. For Abram was the friend of God, and with his spirit he had in truth discovered the highest god among the gods. And came towards Damascus and begat Eliezer there with a maidservant. Then went he on through the land with his people who were the people of God, and with his spirit he consecrated anew the places of worship of the people of the land and the altars and circles of stone and instructed the people under the trees and taught them the coming of the time of the blessing, so that he had increase out of the neighbourhood and the Egyptian maiden came to him, Hagar, the mother of Ishmael. And came towards Shechem."

"That know I as thou knowest it," chanted Joseph, "for our forefather came upwards out of the valley and came towards the place that is known of all, and which Jacob found and builded to Yahu, the Highest, an altar table between Bethel and the refuge Ai. And went thence southwards to the Negeb, and that is here, where the mountains run down towards Edom. Then went he entirely down and into the filthy land of Egypt and the country of Amenemhet the king, and there he became silver and gilden that he was very rich in treasures and flocks. And went up again towards the Negeb, and there parted from Lot."

"And knowest thou wherefore?" Jacob feigned to inquire. "For that Lot too was very heavy with sheep and cattle and huts and the land was not able to bear them both. But lo, then, how mild was the father, for there was strife between the herdsmen over the pasturage, and then it was not as it is with the robbers of the deserts who come and slay the people whose wells and pastures they covet, but he spoke to Lot, his brother's son: 'Let there be no strife, I pray thee, between thine and mine! Is not the whole land before thee? Separate thyself, I pray thee, from me, so that one go right and the other left, without anger.' Then Lot chose and journeyed east and beheld all the plain of Jordan."

"Thus was it in truth," began Joseph in his turn. "And Abram dwelled by Hebron the city of the four, and made holy the tree that giveth us shade and dreams and was a refuge to the wanderer and a shelter to the shelterless. He gave water to the thirsty and brought the strayed upon their way, and defended from robbers. And took neither reward nor pay, but lived to worship his god El Elyon, the Lord of the House, the merciful Father."

"Thou sayest rightly," Jacob intoned. "And it happened that the Lord made a covenant with Abraham, as he was sacrificing at sunset. For he took an heifer, a she-goat and a ram, all of three years' age, and a turtle-dove and a young pigeon. And cut into pieces all that had four feet and separated the halves and put a bird on each side and left open the way of the covenant between the parts, and looked after the eagles which swoop down upon the pieces. Then fell there a sleep upon him that was not as other sleep, and a horror of great darkness fell upon him. For the Lord spoke to him in sleep and shewed him the far spaces of the world and the kingdom that went out out of the seed of his spirit and spread itself out, out of the carefulness and truth of his spirit, and great things of which the princes of the empires knew nothing nor the kings of Babel, Asshur, Elam, and the land of the Hittites. And passed through in the night like a burning fiery flame upon the way of the covenant between the pieces of the sacrifice."

"All that thou knowest beyond praise," Joseph lifted his voice anew, "yet know I more. For that is the inheritance of Abram, that came upon the heads, upon Isaac and upon Jacob my lord: the promise and the covenant. And it was not so with all the children of Eber and was not given unto the Ammonites, the Moabites and the Edomites, but he alone was of the seed chosen of the Lord, and in whom he chose himself the firstborn, not according to the flesh and the womb, but according to the spirit. And it was the mild and the wise that He chose."

"Yea, thou sayest it as it was," uttered Jacob. "For what happened unto Abram and Lot, that they parted, that happened again and the peoples went asunder. For in Lot's pastures those he had begotten of his own flesh remained not together, Moab and Ammon, rather the latter adhered to the desert and to the life of the desert. But in the pastures of Isaac Esau did not remain, but went forth with wives, sons and daughters and all the souls of his house and with goods and cattle into another land, and became Edom on the mountains of Seir. And what did not become Edom, that was Israel, and is a peculiar

people, unlike to the wanderers from the land of Sinai and ragged
robbers from the land of Arabaia, but also unlike the peasants of the
fields and the town-dwellers in the citadels, but instead shepherds
and lords and free men, who drive their herds by stages and keep
their wells and are mindful of the Lord."

"And the Lord is mindful of us and our peculiarity," cried Joseph, flinging back his head and stretching out his arms in his father's
arm. "The heart of the child is full of jubilation in the arms of the
father, it is enraptured of the known and drunken with edification
exchanged. Knowest thou the sweetest dream of all, that I dream
many thousand times? It is the dream of childhood and of the blessing. For to the child of God will much be vouchsafed, that which he
undertaketh will prosper, he will find favour in the eyes of all and
kings shall praise him. Lo, I have lust to sing unto the Lord of Hosts
with a fluent tongue, ready as the writer's stilus. For they sent to me
according to their hate and have laid snares about my feet, they
digged a pit before my feet and thrust me alive into the grave so
that the darkness became my dwelling. But I cried His name out of
the darkness of the pit, and He healed me and snatched me away out
of the underworld. He made me great among strangers and a strange
people knelt to me upon their faces. The sons of strangers spoke flattering words unto me, for without me they would perish. . . ."

His breast heaved. Jacob looked at him wide-eyed.

"Joseph, what seest thou?" he asked in disquiet. "My child's words
are full of persuasion, but they speak not to the understanding. For
what meaneth he by saying that folk of a strange land will serve him
upon their faces?"

"That was only making speeches," answered Joseph, "to say something great unto my lord. And the moon — the moon is bewitching
to the senses."

"Keep thy heart and thy senses and be wise," said Jacob impressively. "So will it be with thee as thou hast said, that thou wilt find
favour in all eyes. And I purpose to give thee that over which thy
heart will rejoice and that will be fitting unto thee. For God hath
poured out grace upon thy lips and I pray that He make thee holy
forever, my lamb!"

The moon, shining with a light so pure as to transform matter into
essence, had continued as they talked to hold her path up the sky,
the constellations changed their places after the laws of their hour.
The night spread a web of peace, of mystery and of the future far
and wide. The old man sat a while yet with Rachel's son at the edge
of the well. He called him "Damu" — little child — and "Dumuzi"
— the true son; names which the people of Shinar gave to Tammuz.
Also he called him Nezer, a word from the Canaanitish language,
meaning shoot and blossoming twig, and caressed him. As they sought

the dwelling-place, he besought him not to vaunt himself before his
brothers and not to tell the sons of Leah nor those of the maids that
he had sat so long with the father in familiar talk — and that too Joseph promised. But even the next day he told them not only this but
prattled recklessly of his dream about the weather, and it vexed them
the more when the dream was fulfilled, for the latter rains came down
in grateful abundance.

Chapter II

JACOB AND ESAU

LUNAR SYNTAX

IN the "fine language" which we have heard, the evening antiphony between Jacob and his volatile favourite at the well, the old man had mentioned Eliezer, who was borne to their forefather by a slave woman during the family's sojourn at Damascus. Nothing is clearer than that Jacob's words could not have referred to the learned old man of that name, himself the manumitted son of a slave woman, and probably Jacob's own half-brother, who lived in Jacob's camp, with two sons named Damasek and Elinos, and used to instruct Joseph in much useful and much superfluous knowledge under the tree of wisdom. It is clear as daylight that the man Jacob meant was the Eliezer whose firstborn son Abram, the wanderer from Ur, or Harran, had long been obliged to regard as his heir, until first Ishmael, and then — fantastically enough, though it had ceased to be with Sarah after the manner of women and Abram himself was so old that you might say he had lived a hundred years — Yitzchak, or Isaac, the true son, saw the light of day. But daylight is one thing and moonlight another, and it was moonlight that had presided over the bestowing of all that superfluous knowledge. Things look differently under the moon and under the sun, and it might be the clearness of the moon which would appeal to the spirit as the truer clarity. Therefore let us agree and admit among ourselves that when Jacob spoke of Eliezer he did mean his own steward and first servant — him too, that is; both at once, and not only both but *the* Eliezer altogether; for since the time of the oldest Eliezer, Eliezer the freedman had often been in existence in the camp of the head of the tribe, and often had sons named Damasek and Elinos.

And Jacob might be certain that his view of this matter would also be the view of Joseph — who was far enough from distinguishing clearly between his old mentor and the original Eliezer, and had the less reason to do so, in that the old man himself did not, who in referring to himself as often as not had in mind Eliezer the servant of Abraham. For instance he had more than once told Joseph the tale

of how he, among the kin of the family in Mesopotamia, had wooed
Rebecca, the daughter of Bethuel and Laban's sister, for Isaac; told
it down to the smallest detail, down to the little moons and crescents
that tinkled on the necks of his ten dromedaries, and the precise value
of the nose rings, arm bands, festal garments and spices which had
been the dowry of the maiden Rebecca — just as though it had been
his own experience. He could not say enough about Rebecca's gentleness and charm, on that evening when she had let down her pitcher
upon her hand at the well by the city of Nahor, and held it for the
thirsty man to drink. Particularly he treasured it in his memory that
she had called him lord. He told of the good breeding and propriety
with which she had sprung from her camel and veiled herself at the
first sight of Isaac, who had gone into the field to meditate upon the
death of his mother. Joseph listened with a pleasure in no way marred
by Eliezer's syntactical idiosyncrasies, and certainly not by the fact
that the old man's ego was not quite clearly demarcated, that it
opened at the back, as it were, and overflowed into spheres external
to his own individuality both in space and in time; embodying in his
own experience events which, remembered and related in the clear
light of day, ought actually to have been put into the third person.
But then, just what do we mean by actually? And is man's ego a
thing imprisoned in itself and sternly shut up in its boundaries of
flesh and time? Do not many of the elements which make it up belong to a world before it and outside of it? The notion that each person is himself and can be no other, is that anything more than a convention, which arbitrarily leaves out of account all the transitions
which bind the individual consciousness to the general? The conception of individuality belongs after all to the same category of conceptions as that of unity and entirety, the whole and the all; and in
the days of which I am writing the distinction between spirit in general and individual spirit possessed not nearly so much power over
the mind as in our world of to-day which we have left behind us to
tell of the other. It is highly significant that in those days there were
no words for conceptions dealing with personality and individuality,
other than such external ones as confession, religion.

WHO JACOB WAS

It is entirely in this connection that I am led to tell the tale of the
origin of Abram's riches. When he came into Lower Egypt — it must
have been under the twelfth dynasty — he was by no means so full
of this world's goods as when he parted from Lot. His extraordinary
increase came about in this wise:

From the first he had cherished the profoundest mistrust of the
morals of the people; rightly or wrongly, he considered them to be

a marsh and a quagmire, like one of the mouths of the river Nile. He was fearful with respect to Sarah his wife, who was with him and very beautiful to look upon. He was affrighted at the lust of the people, who would surely covet Sarah straightway and kill him in order to take her to themselves; and the tradition has come down that when they came into the country he commanded her in that sense, out of fear for his own safety, and told her to speak of herself as his sister, in order that the shameless people should not leer at her; this she might do, without actually uttering falsehood, for it was the custom, especially in the land of Egypt, to use the word "sister" in referring to the beloved. And moreover Sarai was a sister of Lot, whom Abram was used to regard as his nephew and brother; so that he might think of her as his niece and give her the name of sister in the usual extended sense — which he accordingly did, for the purpose of misleading the stranger and protecting himself. What he expected came to pass — and more. Sarai's dusky loveliness was marked by high and low, news of it reached even to the throne of the ruler of the land, and the hot-eyed oriental was taken from her "brother's" side — not by force or robbery but for a high price — purchased of him, that is, she being found worthy of admission to the choice society of Pharaoh's house of women. Thither she was conveyed, and her "brother" — whom one does not understand to have been in the least affronted by the arrangement, rather in the common view was considered a lucky fellow — was not only allowed to remain in her nearness, but was loaded down with favours, presents and benefits from the court, which he calmly accepted, so that he was presently very rich in sheep, oxen, he-asses, men-servants, and maid-servants, she-asses and camels. But meanwhile, though hidden from the ears of the common people, an extraordinary scandal had taken place at court. Amenemhet (or Senusret, it is not easy to be quite certain which conqueror of Nubia it was who was just then bestowing upon both countries the blessing of his overlordship), His Majesty then, a deity in the flower of his youth, was stricken with impotence — not once but repeatedly — when he was about to taste the novelty; it seems, moreover, that his entire court were stricken likewise — the highest dignitaries and administrators of the realm — with this same mortifying, and — when one takes into consideration the higher cosmic significance of the gift of virility — calamitous visitation. It was clear that something had gone wrong, that there was some mistake, possibly an evil spell or the opposition of higher powers. The brother of the Jewess was brought before the throne, questioned and pressed and confessed the truth. The conduct of His Sanctity was reasonable and dignified beyond all praise. "What is this," he asks, "that thou hast done unto me? Why hast thou exposed me to unpleasantness through thy double speaking?" And without a thought of depriving

Abraham of any of the presents which he had so freely heaped upon
him, he hands his wife over to him and tells them to go their ways in
the name of the gods, giving the party safe conduct to the borders
of the kingdom. Thus the father, not only in possession of an undefiled Sarah, but also so very much richer than before in worldly
goods, might flatter himself that the simple shepherd had turned a
very successful trick. One likes to think that he counted from the
beginning on God being able in one way or another to prevent the
defilement of Sarah; that he had pocketed all the gifts in this definite
conviction, and felt certain that his method of going at the work
would result in dealing the lustful Egyptian one in the eye. For only
thus is his conduct — the denial of his marriage and the sacrifice of
Sarah — set in the proper light and seen for the masterly performance which it really was.

This is the tale; for whose truth tradition expressly vouches, by
repeating it a second time, when the scene is not Egypt but the land
of the Philistines and the capital city of Gerar, at the court of King
Abimelech — whither the Chaldæan had come from Hebron with
Sarai — and where everything fell out precisely as before, from Abraham's command to his wife, to the lucky outcome of the stratagem.
This repetition of a narrative by way of emphasizing its truth is unusual, without being very startling. It is far more remarkable that,
according to tradition — the evidence for which, of course, in written form comes from a later time, but must have always existed *as*
tradition and thus goes back to the statements and utterances of the
fathers themselves — the selfsame experience, told for the third time,
is ascribed to Isaac; from which it follows that he had committed it
to memory as his experience — or the same as his. For Isaac too (some
time after the birth of his twins) on account of a dearth of corn
came into the land of the Philistines and the court at Gerar with his
lovely and clever wife. He too, on the same ground as Abraham
Sarai, gave out that Rebecca was his sister — not quite falsely, since
she was the daughter of his cousin Bethuel — and the story goes on to
say that in this case King Abimelech "looked out at a window" —
that is, as a secret spy and eavesdropper — and saw Isaac "sporting"
with Rebecca, his wife, and was as shocked and disillusioned as only
a lover can be, when he learns that the object of his desires, whom he
has supposed to be free, is in firm possession by another man. His
words betray him, for Yitzchak, on being questioned, told the truth,
whereupon the Philistine cried out reproachfully: "What is this that
thou hast done unto us? For one of the people might lightly have lien
with thy wife and thou shouldst have brought guiltiness upon us!"
The phrase "one of the people" is unmistakable. But the end of it
was that the pair found themselves under the peculiar and personal
protection of the god-fearing if luxurious king, and that under this

protection Isaac increased in the land of the Philistines just as Abraham had once done either there or in Egypt, and grew so heavy with flocks and herds that it was finally too much even for the Philistines and they discreetly got rid of him.

Assuming that the scene of Abraham's adventure was Gerar, then it is not credible that the Abimelech of Yitzchak's adventure was the same as he who found himself prevented from defiling the purity of Sarah's married state. The characters are distinguished; Sarah's princely lover simply took her into his harem without more ado, whereas Isaac's Abimelech behaved with much more caution and reserve, so that we could only imagine them to be the same person on the assumption that the king's more careful behaviour in the case of Rebecca was due to his having grown much older since Sarah's day, also to his being already warned by what had happened the other time. But what interests us here is the personality not of Abimelech but of Isaac, and the question of his relation to the story about the women. And even with this we are concerned only indirectly, and on account of the further question of who Jacob was: that Jacob, that is, whom we have heard talking with his little son, Joseph, Yashub or Jehosiph, in the moonlight.

Let us weigh the possibilities. Either Yitzchak did himself in Gerar undergo with slight variations the same experience that had befallen his father either there or in Egypt, and in this case we have a phenomenon which might be called imitation or succession: a conception, that is, which envisages the task of the individual person as the filling out in present time and again making flesh certain given forms, a mythical frame that was established by the fathers. Or else Rebecca's husband did not have the experience "himself," not in the narrower fleshly limits of his ego, but regarded it, as it were, as belonging to his life-history, and handed it down as such to his descendants, because he distinguished less sharply between the I and the not-I than we — with how little justification has been already shown — are in the habit of doing (or were in the habit of doing until we embarked upon this narrative). For him the life of the individual was more superficially separated from that of the tribe, birth and death represented a less radical shock to existence; in short he had the attitude of the latter Eliezer, to which we have already referred, when he related to Joseph in the first person stories about the original Eliezer, and displayed the phenomenon of the open identity, which accompanies that of imitation or succession and alternately with it determines the consciousness of self.

I do not conceal from myself the difficulty of writing about people who do not precisely know who they are. But also I make no question of the necessity of reckoning with these vacillating states of consciousness, and if the Isaac who relived Abraham's Egyptian adventure took himself for the Isaac whom the original wanderer would have offered up, the fact affords me no ground for the conviction that he did not deceive himself, and that the sacrifice-temptation did not in fact belong to the scheme and recur repeatedly. The Chaldæan wanderer was the father of the Isaac whom he would slay; but though it is impossible that this Isaac was the father of Joseph's father whom we have seen by the well, yet it is quite conceivable that the Isaac who either imitated Abraham's simple shepherd's game or else wove it into his own personal life confused himself, at least in part, with the Isaac who so narrowly escaped slaughter, although actually he was a much later Isaac and generations removed from the original Abraham. Indeed it is evident — so evident that a simple statement carries conviction, without need of proof — that the history of Joseph's ancestors, as transmitted by tradition, is a pious abbreviation of the original facts, that is of the succession of generations which must have filled up the centuries between the Jacob whom we have met and the original Abraham. Again, just as Abraham's house-steward and natural son, Eliezer, must often have recurred in the flesh since the day when he wooed Rebecca for his young master, must often have wooed a Rebecca across the Euphrates, and now, in the person of Joseph's mentor, rejoiced once more in the light of day; just so since then had many an Abraham, Isaac and Jacob beheld the birth of day out of the night, without having any exaggeratedly precise ideas about time and the flesh, without making any very clear distinctions between their present and the present of aforetime, or delimiting their own individualities with reference to the individualities of earlier Abrahams, Isaacs and Jacobs.

These names were handed on from generation to generation — if the word be accurate or comprehensive enough to apply to the community in which they recurred. For it was a community whose growth was not that of a family tree, but rather of a group of trees, resting as it did moreover in good part upon the propagation of the faith and the winning of souls. The tribal headship of the original Abraham must be understood as largely spiritual; whether Joseph was actually related to him in the flesh, whether he was indeed his forefather, and in such a direct line as is assumed, is open to question. Open to question it was even for themselves; though the twilight of their own and the general consciousness permitted them to question it in a hazy and vaguely pious way, taking words for actuality and actuality more than half for a word. They could call Abraham the Chaldæan their grandfather and great-grandfather, more or less in the spirit in which he himself called Lot of Harran his "brother" and Sarah his "sister" — that too being both true and untrue at once.

But not even in a dream could the people of El Elyon assert that their community possessed racial purity. Babylonian and Sumerian — that is, not entirely Semitic — stock had been crossed with seed from the desert of Arabia; from Gerar, Muzriland, Egypt itself other elements had come in — for instance in the person of the slave woman Hagar, who had been found not unworthy to share the bed of the head of the tribe and whose son in turn had married an Egyptian — and it has always been too well known for me to waste more words upon it here, what vexation Rebecca suffered hourly from the Hittite wives of her Esau, daughters of a stock whose progenitor was not Shem, and which had come into Syria sometime or other out of Asia Minor, and the Ural-Altai region. Many a branch dropped off by the way. We know that Abraham begot children after the death of Sarah, having taken to wife Keturah, a Canaanite woman; not too nice a choice, considering his objection to the marriage of Isaac with a Canaanite. One of Keturah's sons was Midian, whose descendants dwelt south of Edom-Seir, Esau's country, at the edge of the Arabian desert, like the children of Ishmael before Egypt. For Abraham gave all that he had unto Isaac, the true son, and put the children of the concubines off with gifts and shoved them away eastwards where they quite lost touch with El Elyon, if they had really ever had it, and worshipped their own gods. But godly was the bond of continual effort wreaked from generation to generation upon the idea of God; and in all the admixture of blood it united the spiritual community, which — among the other Hebrews, the sons of Moab, Ammon and Edom — particularly assumed this name unto itself, and precisely at the time to which we have arrived, began to associate it with another name, the name of Israel, which was destined to affect the common history.

For the name and title which Jacob had wrested for himself had not been an invention of his strange adversary. Israel, God fighteth, had always been the name of a warlike robber tribe of the desert, of highly primitive manners and customs; small groups of these people had, at the time of the changing of pastures, driven their flocks among the settlements of the cornland, had exchanged their purely nomadic existence for a more or less settled state, and by conversion and agreement had become part of Abraham's communion of faith. Back in the wilderness their god had been a fire-breathing and storm-breeding warrior named Yahu, a troublesome sort of hobgoblin, with more demonic than godlike traits, spiteful, tyrannical and incalculable. His dusky people, though proud of his prowess, went in terror of their lives, ever seeking by means of spells and blood rites to harness their harebrained divinity and lead him into ways profitable to themselves. Yahu might without any clear provocation fall by night upon a man whom he had every reason to treat with favour, and kill him; but also he might be moved to abandon his purpose if the man's wife

made haste to circumcise her son with a stone knife and touch the
devil's genitals with the foreskin, at the same time incanting a mystic
formula, the rendering of which into any kind of sensible English has
so far encountered unsurmountable difficulties, but which had power
to soothe the demon and turn away his wrath. All this by way of giving an idéa of what Yahu was like. For there was reserved for this
sinister deity, entirely unknown to the civilized world, an extraordinary theological career, merely by dint of the fact that some of
his followers had penetrated into the sphere of influence occupied
by Abraham's thoughts about God. Thus drawn into the orbit of
the wanderer's spiritual speculations, these shepherd folk not only
strengthened the physical basis of the Chaldæan's religious tradition,
but also contributed elements of their own devastating deity to nourish the conception of the divine essence which was struggling towards realization through the spirit of mankind; to which indeed
Osiris of the East, Tammuz, as well as Adonai, the mutilated son and
shepherd of Melchizedek and his Shechemites, had also given colour
and substance. The very name Yahu, once a war-cry — we have just
heard it chanted by certain lovely lips — in the form in which the
god's dusky worshippers brought it out of the desert, as well as in
abbreviations and variants which made it conform to the Canaanite
dialect, was among the words used to make experiments in the inexpressible. For ages there had existed a village called Be-ti-ya, the
house of Ya, that is to say Beth-el, or house of God; and there is evidence for the fact that before the days of the Lawgiver, there were
Amurru people who had immigrated into Shinar and brought their
names with them, among them a name for God, which was Ya-we.
Yes, the original Abraham had given to the tree by the shrine of
"Seven Springs" the name of Ya-we el-Olam, which is to say, Ya-we
is the god of all the ages. But the name which Yahu's Bedouin warriors gave themselves was to become the name of Abraham's spiritual
seed, and the distinctive badge of a purer and higher Hebraism, precisely because Jacob had had it whispered to him, in that pregnant
night by Jabbok ford.

ELIPHAZ

For people like Simeon and Levi, Leah's stout sons, it was a matter
for private mirth that just this bold and lawless-sounding title was
what their father had as it were wrung from the heavenly powers.
For Jacob was no fighter. He would never have been the man to do
what the original Abraham did, when eastern hirelings, the merce-
nary troops of Elam and Shinar and Larsa and beyond the Tigris,
harried the land of the Jordan on account of tribute overdue, plundered the cities and took away Lot of Sodom and his goods. For

Abraham, with bold and loyal resolution, got together a few hundred of servants born in his own house, together with neighbours of near faith, people of El-Berith the most high god, set out with them by forced marches from Hebron, overtook the retiring Elamites and Gojim, and brought such confusion to their rear that he freed many of the prisoners, among them his brother Lot, and carried back in triumph much of the stolen goods. No, that would have been no place for Jacob, he would not have stood up to it, he admitted as much to himself when Joseph began to tell the oft-told tale. He "could not do it" — as little as, by his own confession, he could have done to his son what the Lord demanded of him. He would have left it to Simeon and Levi to free Lot. But if these two had instituted a massacre among the moon-worshippers and set up that hair-raising yell which they had at their command on such occasions, he would have veiled his countenance and said: "My soul may not come in your counsel!" For that soul was soft and fearful, abhorring the use of force, trembling lest force be its portion; mindful of many occasions on which its virile courage had known defeat. But no violence was ever done by these memories to the dignity or solemnity of the soul; for always and regularly in such states of physical depression there came a ray of light, an influx of the spirit, a powerfully consoling and freshly confirmatory revelation of grace, so that it might lift its head, secure in the knowledge that it had wrestled and overcome out of its own undefeated depths.

There was the case of the encounter with Eliphaz, Esau's splendid son. Eliphaz had been borne to Esau by one of his Hittite or Canaanite women, worshippers of Baal, whom he had early brought home to Beersheba, and of whom Rebecca, Bethuel's daughter, used to say: "It is a vexation to me to live among the daughters of Heth." Jacob was no longer certain which one of them Eliphaz called his mother, probably it was Adah, daughter of Elon. At all events, this thirteen-year-old grandson of Yitzchak was an uncommonly winning youth; simple in spirit but brave, generous and high-thinking, upright in body and mind, and holding his dispossessed father, Esau, in great love and respect. In more than one way life was made hard to him, in the involved nature of the family relations and in matters of faith. For no less than three creeds laid hold on his soul: the god of his grandparents, El Elyon, the Baalim of the mother's side, and a lowering, arrow-shooting deity named Kusakh, honoured by the mountain folk in the south, the Seirim or people of Edom, with whom Esau had early had relations, and to whom he later went over altogether. The great affliction and powerless rage of the shaggy man over the event, instigated by Rebecca, which had come to pass in the tent where his grandfather sat in darkness on account of his sore eyes, an event which drove Jacob out of house and home and into foreign lands, had been a frightful blow to the lad Eliphaz. The hatred he conceived for his young uncle, who had received the blessing under false pretences, had a galling intensity beyond his years and almost mortal. At home, under the eye of the watchful Rebecca, nothing could be done against the thief of the blessing. But when he learned that Jacob had escaped, Eliphaz rushed to Esau and urged him to set out after the traitor to slay him.

Esau had fled to the desert; he was too much crushed, too much weakened by bitter weeping over his lower-worldly fate, to be equal to the deed. He wept because it was in his nature, because that was his rôle in life. His way of looking at things, and at himself, was conditioned by inborn habits of thought, which held him in bondage, as they do all the world, and the character of which had been fixed by the cosmic images of the circling year. By his father's blessing Jacob had definitely become the man of the full and "beautiful" moon, and Esau the man of the dark one, that is, the man of the sun, or of the lower world; and in the lower world one wept, although, quite possibly, one became very rich in treasure. When later he entirely cast in his lot with the people of the mountains on the south and with their god, he did it because it seemed fitting, for one thought of the south as the lower world, as one did of the wilderness into which Ishmael, the corresponding brother of Isaac, had been driven out. But long before this time, long before the receiving of the curse, Esau had, from Beersheba, established relations with the people of Seir; from which we gather that blessing and curse alike had only been a confirmation of established facts, and that Esau's character, his rôle upon earth, had long ago been fixed and he long ago perfectly aware that this was so. He had become a hunter, a rover of the steppes, in contrast to Jacob, who was a tent-dweller and shepherd of the moon; become so certainly according to his nature, on the basis of his strongly masculine disposition. But it would be a mistake and do small justice to the traditional and established mythology in which his character was rooted, to suppose that his calling alone had imbued him with the feeling and the consciousness of himself and his rôle as the sun-scorched son of the lower world. On the contrary — at least quite as much on the contrary — he had chosen the calling because of its suitability; that is, out of obedience to the programme and knowledge of the myth. Regarding in a cultural light his relation to Jacob — and that Esau, despite all his shagginess, was always ready to do — it was nothing else than the return and the reliving, the rendering into timeless presentness of the relation between Cain and Abel, in which Esau took the part of Cain; to begin with in his capacity as elder brother, which indeed was honoured by the newer world order, but also probably feeling and knowing that since the times of the matriarchy the deepest preference of the human heart is for the younger

and the youngest. If we are to take as representing an actual occurrence the story of the mess of pottage (it may be a later addition designed to justify the deception, and Jacob still might easily have believed in its truth) then Esau's apparent folly is explainable on the
ground of these sentiments; he may have been so ready to surrender
his rights as the firstborn because he hoped to win for himself in exchange at least the sympathies which are traditionally accorded to
the younger.

In short, the shaggy Esau wept, and showed himself definitely disinclined to any enterprise of pursuit and revenge. He had no desire
to kill his Abel-brother and thus to accentuate the parallel on which
the parents had played from the beginning. But when Eliphaz implored or rather hotly demanded that he himself might pursue and
slay the bearer of the blessing, Esau made no objection, but nodded
his permission amid tears. For the nephew to kill the uncle would
mean for him a pleasing break with a wretched tradition and the establishment of a new historical foundation which should serve as a
pattern to later Eliphazes and relieve him, Esau, at last from the rôle
of Cain.

So Eliphaz got together a few of his father's people, five or six,
who usually accompanied him on his expeditions to the land of
Edom; armed them from the household stock with long cane lances,
tipped with equally long, sharp points above their gay tufts of hair,
and abstracted some camels from Yitzchak's stables in the grey of
the dawn. Before it broke, Jacob, riding on a camel between two
mounted slaves and well provided, thanks to Rebecca, with food and
presents, had the avenging troop close at his heels.

All his life long Jacob never forgot the fright he got when he understood the significance of the approaching riders. When he first
caught sight of them he flattered himself that Yitzchak had had too
early wind of his departure and sent to summon him back. But when
he recognized Esau's son, he saw the whole state of affairs and shook
in his shoes. A life-and-death race began; the dromedaries grunting
as they strode with their long necks stretched straight out, all the
little moons and tassels flying. But Eliphaz and his men were riding
lighter than Jacob, who saw his lead melting moment by moment;
when he was overtaken by the first flying lances he gave signal of
surrender, dismounted with his men and awaited his pursuer with
face in the dust and hands over his head.

What happened then had touched Jacob's pride and honour more
sorely than anything else in all his life; it was calculated to undermine and would have undermined forever the dignity and self-confidence of another man. He was obliged — if he wanted to live, and
that he did at all costs; not, we must remember, out of common cow-
ardice but because he was consecrated, because the promise and the

blessing handed down from Abraham lay upon him — to try to soften by entreaties the heart of this lad, his nephew, so much younger than himself and so much lower in station, who in the heat of his anger already and more than once had lifted the sword above his head; to reach him through self-abasement and tears and flatteries, through whining appeals to his magnanimity, with a thousand pleas and excuses; in a word by thoroughly demonstrating the fact that it was not worth Eliphaz's while to turn his sword against such a grovelling suppliant. He did it. He kissed the lad's feet like one frenzied, he flung whole handfuls of dust in the air to fall back upon his head; his tongue ran without stint — imploring, conjuring, in a fluency urged on by fear, designed and calculated to daze the boy's astonished senses and prevent him from the rash commission of a fatal deed.

Had he intended the deception? Had he urged it, was it his idea? Might his entrails be consumed in sacrifice, if that were even remotely the truth. It was the mother and aunt who had conceived and willed the whole, in the weakness of her excessive and undeserved love for him, and he, Jacob, had done his utmost against the plan, telling her how great was the danger that Isaac might discover all, and curse not only him but the all too ingenious Rebecca as well. Eliphaz must know how desperately he had urged upon her his position in the eyes of the noble firstborn son, even if the plan should succeed. Not blithely, not lightly and audaciously, but with fear and trembling had he entered, bearing the wine and savoury meat, with the skins on his hands and his neck, arrayed in Esau's festal garment, into the beloved father's and grandfather's tent. The sweat had run down his joints for fear, his voice had died in his throat when Isaac asked him who he was, and touched him, and smelt him — but Eliphaz's aunt had even remembered to anoint him with the scent of the flowers of the field. He a deceiver? He was much more a victim of the guile of womankind, Adam, tempted by Eve, the friend of the serpent! Let Eliphaz his life long — and might he live several hundred years and longer! — beware of the advice of woman and avoid by wisdom the snare of her deceitfulness! He, Jacob, was entangled therein, and was destroyed. He the bearer of a blessing? But how could it be said that his father had blessed him — a mistaken blessing like that, bestowed against the wish and will of the recipient? Had it any worth or weight? Could it avail? (He was perfectly well aware that a blessing was a blessing, having its full value and efficacy, and only asked to confuse Eliphaz's mind.) And again, had he, Jacob, taken advantage by word or deed of the error, spreading himself in the house and crowding out Esau, his rightful superior? Not in the least — quite the contrary. He willingly left the field to his brother, Rebecca herself had remorsefully urged him forth, he was going out into the unknown, never to return, into exile, into the underworld, and his part would be weeping for evermore! Let Eliphaz slay him with the edge of his sword — he, the cock pigeon with the bright pinions, the young mountain bull in all his pride, the beautiful buck antelope! But since the Lord had said to Noah that he would require the blood that was shed of man, and since to-day it was no longer as it had been in the days of Cain and Abel, but there were laws in the land, the violation of which might become highly dangerous to Eliphaz's noble young person — all that on account of his uncle if he were slain; whereas if he were set down and made nought of, sent empty forth to wander in a land where he would be a stranger and a servant, then might the heart of Eliphaz be heavy with joy and his mother blest among the daughters of Heth, for that he had held back his hand from the shedding of blood and turned away his soul from wrong-doing. . . .

Thus Jacob rattled on, pouring out pleas in the urgency of his fear until young Eliphaz was amazed and his head fairly swam. He had expected to find a defiant thief, instead here was repentant sinner whose humility seemed fully to re-establish his father's lost dignity. Eliphaz was a good-natured soul, like his father. A warm rush of magnanimity replaced the fire of anger in his soul, and he cried out that he would spare his uncle's life — whereat Jacob wept for joy, covering with kisses Eliphaz's hands and feet and the hem of his garment; slight disgust and some little embarrassment came to mingle with loftier sentiments in the breast of the youth. He felt angered at his own wavering, and harshly told his uncle that all the valuables must go back, everything that Rebecca had given him, it belonged to Esau, the injured party. Jacob tried to soften the decision, but Eliphaz simply shouted at him to be quiet, and had him plucked so thoroughly that nothing was left but his life. All the gold and silver vessels, the jars of finest oil and wine, the neck and arm bands of malachite and cornelian, the incense, the sweetmeats made of honey, all the embroidered and woven stuffs which Rebecca had packed in his saddle-bags — it all had to be disgorged. Even the two slaves who had stolen from the court, one of them now bleeding from a lance wound in the shoulder, had to turn back with the animals they led; and then Jacob with nothing but a couple of earthen water jugs at his saddle-bow, might continue his dark way eastwards — who can say in what a frame of mind?

HIS HEAD LIFTED UP

He had saved his life, his precious, covenanted life, for God and the future — what were gold and cornelian to set against that? For life is all; and young Eliphaz had been even more brilliantly swindled than his parent — but at what a price! Above and beyond the valuables, it had meant the loss of the man's whole honour; for how could one be more shamed than Jacob was, having bowed his head in the dust before a stripling, whining, his face smeared with dust and tears? And then? What had happened straightway after the degradation?

Almost immediately, at most a few hours later, by starlight, he reached the town of Luz, lying on one of the terraced and vineclad slopes of that undulating countryside; a place unfamiliar to him, as indeed was all the region. A few square houses huddled together at half the height of the path-marked hill; an inward voice exhorting him to take shelter here for the night, he guided his camel up the road — the beast was still frightened and unruly from the late lamentable episode, and he felt ashamed before it. He watered the animal at the fountain outside the wall, and washed the traces of his shame from his own face — whereby he felt his heart sensibly lightened. Yet in his beggared state he avoided asking hospitality of the people of Luz, but led his camel, now his sole possession, uphill beyond the settlement and as far as the flattened summit, the sight of which made him poignantly regret that he had not reached it sooner — for the place had a stone circle — a Gilgal — which marked it as a sanctuary, and here young Eliphaz, the highway robber, durst not have touched him.

In the centre of the Gilgal a peculiar stone was set upright, coalblack and cone-shaped — obviously fallen from heaven, and possessing heavenly powers. Its form suggested the organ of generation, therefore Jacob piously saluted it with lifted eyes and hands and felt greatly strengthened thereby. Here he would spend the night, to the rising of the day. He chose for a head-rest one of the stones of the circle, and addressing it: "Come," he said, "faithful old stone, lift up for a night the head of the persecuted." He spread his headcloth upon it and lay down with his head toward the phallic emissary from the skies; blinked a little at the stars and fell asleep.

Then it was high matters came to pass; then truly, toward midnight, after some hours of profound slumber, his head was lifted up from every ignominy, even to the countenance of the Most High, wherein mingled all of the royal and of the divine which his soul had ever compassed in its imaginings; which that soul then, humbled, yet smiling privily in its abasement, erected for its own strengthening and consolation in the space of its dream. . . . Yet he dreamed himself not away from the place. For in his dream, too, he lay there with his head propped up and slept. But his eyelids were pervious to a plenitude of brilliant light. He saw through them: saw Babel, saw the navel cord of heaven and earth, the stair up to the palace of the Lord, the wide and fiery unnumbered steps, beset with astral watchers, whose mighty slope led up to the uppermost temple and dwellingplace of the Most High. They were not stone nor wood, nor any earthly substance; they seemed of molten bronze and built of the

stuff that is of the stars; and their starry brilliance lost itself in measureless breadth upon the earth and mounted upwards so high and
wide and blinding as to be unbearable to the open· eye, so that one
saw them through the lids alone. Winged creatures, half man, half
beast, cherubim, cows with crowns and virgins' faces, their pinions
folded, stood motionless on both sides and gazed straight ahead of
them; their striding legs, first forward and then back, left spaces that
were filled in with bronze tablets inscribed with holy writings. Bull-
gods with bands of pearl across the brow and earlocks that hung
down as long as the fringe-shaped beards ending in rows of curls,
crouched with their heads turned outwards so that they gazed at the
sleeper with quiet, long-lashed eyes; with these alternated lionlike
forms that sat upon their tails, their arching chests covered with fiery
manes. They seemed to hiss from square wide-open jaws, the hairs
stood out fiercely beneath their flat noses. But the whole width of
the stair, between these animals, was alive with messengers and servants pacing up and down in measured tread, like a slow movement of
a dance, as in joyous conformity to heaven's law. The lower half of
their bodies was shrouded in garments covered with pointed script,
their bosoms seemed too soft for those of youths, too flat for those of
maidens. With arms uplifted they bore basins on their heads, or else
a tablet in the crook of one arm, pointing at it with the finger of the
other hand; but many played on harps and flutes, or struck on lutes
and drums; behind them stood singers, who filled all space with high,
metallic, sibilant voices and kept time with clapping hands. Thus the
whole breadth of this stair between the worlds was one mighty wave
of harmonious sound, downwards and upwards as far as the narrow
flaming fiery arch that was the gateway of the palace with pillars and
lofty pinnacles. The pillars were of golden bricks, from which pro-
jected scaly beasts with forefeet of leopards and behind the feet of
eagles; and the jambs of the fiery gate on either side had the feet of
bulls, and crowns with fourfold horns, and eyes of precious stones,
and curled beards bound up in clusters on their cheeks. But in front
stood the golden seat of the kingly power and the golden footstool,
and behind it a man with bow and quiver, who held a long-handled
fan over the mitre crown of the Power. And it was adorned with a
drapery woven out of moonlight and had fringes of tiny flames. And
the arms of God were full of the nerves of power, and in one hand he
held the sign of life and in the other a drinking vessel. His beard was
blue and held together with bronze bands, and beneath his high-
arched brows his countenance was awful in stern benignity. Before
him was another man with a wide band round his head, like to a vizier
and a servant closest to the throne, who looked into the Face of the
Power and motioned with his open hand towards Jacob sleeping on
the earth. Then the Lord inclined His head and stood up on His sin-

ewy foot and the servant hasted to stoop and take away the footstool
that the Lord might stand. And God stood up before the throne and
held out towards Jacob the sign of life and breathed in the air into
his lungs so that his breast rose high. And the splendour of His voice
accorded with the psaltery and the star-music of those that moved up
and down upon the stair, and was taken up into mild and mighty harmony. But He spake: "I am! I am the Lord of Abraham and the Lord
of Isaac and thy Lord. My eye looks upon thee, Jacob, with far-seeing favour, for I will make thy seed unnumbered as the dust of the
earth, and thou shalt be to Me blessed before all and keep the gates of
thine enemies. And behold I am with thee and will keep thee in all
places whither thou goest, and bring thee again rich unto this land
where thou sleepest, and never forsake thee. I am and I will!" Thus
thundered in harmony the voice of the King, and Jacob awaked.

What a dream and a vision had that been, what a lifting up of the
head! Jacob wept for joy, laughing the while at the thought of Eliphaz, as he walked about under the stars, within the circle of stones,
and saw that one whereon his head had rested while he gazed. What
place is this, he thought, upon which I am fallen by chance? He was
cold from the freshness of the night, and shivered to his depths from
excitement as he spoke: "Surely it is right that I so shiver! For the
people of Luz know naught of this place, though indeed they have
made a sanctuary here and a Gilgal, yet surely they know as little as
I knew that it is a place of the presence and the gate of splendour,
and a bond between heaven and earth." Later he slept again, a few
hours of deep and prideful sleep, full of privy laughter, but at dawn
he arose and went down to Luz, and sought the bazaar. For he had
in the folds of his girdle a seal ring with a deep blue lazuli stone,
which the servants of Eliphaz had missed in their search. This he sold
for a price, for dry food to eat and two jars of oil — which latter he
particularly needed for a purpose which he had in mind and conceived to be his duty. Before he went on eastwards and towards the
river Naharina, he climbed the hill once more to the place of his
dream, lifted up the stone against which he had slept, set it erect as
a monument, and poured oil lavishly upon it, saying: "Beth-el, Beth-el
shall be the name of this place and not Luz, for it is a house of the
presence, and God, the King, hath revealed Himself here to His humble servant and strengthened his heart above all measure. For surely
it was beyond bounds and an exaggeration, that which He called out
to me amid the music of the harps, that my seed should be countless
as the dust, and my name be high in honour. But if He will be with
me, as He promised, and keep me in this way that I go and will give
me bread to eat and raiment to put on, so that I come again to my
father's house in peace, then shall the Lord be my God, and I will give
Him a tenth of all that He giveth me. And if all this be fulfilled, with

which He hath so boundlessly strengthened my heart, then shall this stone which I have set up for a pillar be God's house, wherein nourishment shall be brought to Him without end, and moreover strong-smelling incense burned for His nostrils. This is my vow and my promise against the other promise, and may God the King now do as seemeth to Him in His interest."

ESAU

THUS, then, had it been with Eliphaz, the splendid youth, who after all was but a poor stripling compared with Jacob, whom he had humbled as a sacrifice to his pride. For Jacob, thanks to resources of spiritual strength unknown to Eliphaz, had triumphed with ease over such humiliations as a boy could force upon him, and it was precisely out of the depth of the abasement that the revelation had come. And how had it been with the father — had his experience differed from that of the son? I mean in that meeting with Esau to which we have heard Jacob refer. In this case the exaltation and strengthening had come first, at Pen-iel, in that night of fear, when he had wrestled for the name that made Simeon and Levi smile. And in possession of the Name, already triumphant, he had gone to meet his brother, armed beforehand against any humiliation which might prove unavoidable; armed as well against the indignity of his own fear of an encounter that was to display once more to the full the unlikeness between the twin brothers.

He had himself, convinced that the situation was no longer tenable and must be cleared up, sent messages to his brother; but he could not tell in what spirit Esau was approaching. He knew through spies that his brother had put himself at the head of four hundred men; which might be interpreted as an honour due to the meek and flattering messages he had sent, or equally might represent an actual danger. He had made his preparations. His nearest and dearest, Rachel and her five-year-old son, he had hidden behind the laden camels, and laid Dinah, his daughter by Leah, as dead in a coffin, where she nearly smothered; the other children he had ranged with their mothers, the concubines and their offspring in the lead. He had the herdsmen draw up the present of cattle, the two hundred he-goats and she-goats, the same number of rams and ewes, the thirty camel mares in suck, the forty cows and ten bull-calves, the twenty she-asses with their foals; all these he arranged in echelon, and had them driven in single herds with space between each two, so that Esau might ask of each in turn and learn that they were for him, a present from his servant Jacob. Thus it came to pass. And though when Esau left the mountains of Seir to meet the returned wanderer, his mood may still have been very vacillating, unclear even to himself, by the time he once more after the lapse of twenty-five years met his brother face to face, his spirits were of the highest.

However much Jacob may have set himself to effect it, he found this blitheness quite out of place; no sooner had he grasped the fact that for the moment at least he had nothing to fear, than he found it hard to conceal his disgust at Esau's brainless good-heartedness. Never did he forget the scene of his brother's approach. Rebecca's twin sons were at this time fifty-five years old: the sweet-smelling grass and the prickly plant, as they had been known in all the countryside between Hebron and Beersheba. But the sweet-smelling grass, the smooth man, Jacob, had never behaved very youthful, a tent-dweller, thoughtful and timid, he had shown himself even as a boy. And now he was a ripe man, with much experience, heavy with goods that had accrued unto him, preoccupied in spirit, bearing with dignity the weight of events. And on the other hand Esau, though like his brother grey-haired, seemed still to be as of yore, the same feckless insignificant child of nature, always either wailing in grief or bursting with animal spirits; nor did he look to have altered in face — for in fact most of the changes we see in our boyhood companions consist in their having grown beards and added a wrinkle or so to a physiognomy which remains as boyish as ever!

What Jacob first heard of the oncoming Esau was the sound of the pipes — the well-remembered high and hollow trilling on a bundle of reeds of different lengths, held together by crosswise bands. It was an instrument beloved of the dwellers in the mountains of Seir, and perhaps invented by them; Esau had early acquired one and taught his thick lips to draw out therefrom most pleasing music. Jacob knew of old and hated the foolish and abandoned tunefulness of the sounds, the irresponsible tra la la that was native to the underworld of the south — scorn rose in his soul as his ears caught the first notes. And Esau was dancing. His pipe at his lips, his bow at his back, a flutter of goatskin round his loins, but otherwise no clothing, for he was so hairy that he really did not need it, and the fleece hung down in reddish grizzled tangles from his shoulders; with his pointed ears, and his nose lying flat on his upper lip, he danced and sprang across the open meadow towards his brother and his brother's train; blowing, becking, laughing and weeping, until Jacob, between shame and scorn, and pity and disgust, could only think to himself something like "For Heaven's sake!"

At all events he got down from his beast, as fast as his swollen thigh permitted, and holding up his garment hastened to drag himself towards the musical goat and on the way to give all the evidence of submission and self-abasement which he had set himself to perform — they came much easier to his self-esteem after the triumph of the night before. Some seven times he flung himself down, despite his pain, with the palms of his hands above his bent head, and thus he arrived at Esau's feet, and pressed his forehead to them, while his hands reached up to his brother's fleecy knees, and his lips repeated the words which despite the blessing and the curse were to put the whole situation in a light completely favourable to Esau and thus to disarm and reconcile him: "My lord! Thy servant!" But Esau's attitude was not only one of appeasement, it was actually friendly and tender beyond all expectation — even, most likely, his own. For his feeling upon having news of his brother's return had been merely a vague and general excitement, which even up to just before the meeting might quite as easily have turned to rage as to tenderness. He seized Jacob up from the dust, pressed him with audible sobs to his hairy bosom, and kissed him with loud smacks on lips and cheeks — the caresses were almost more than Jacob could stand. Yet he wept himself — partly because, his fears proving groundless, the tension was relaxed, partly out of his own nervous sensibility, but largely in general, over life, and time, and the destiny of human kind. "O my brother, my brother!" babbled Esau, between his kisses. "All is forgotten, all the knavishness of aforetime, all!" So painfully explicit a forgiveness was calculated to dry Jacob's tears at once rather than to make them flow more freely, and Esau passed on to speak of things of moment, leaving, however, to the last, the question which interested him most, namely the meaning of the herds that had been driven up in advance of Jacob's party. And first, with lifted brows, he enquired about the women and children on the camels behind his brother. These then dismounted and advanced to be presented: first the concubines with their four children bowed before the hairy one, then Leah with her six, and last the sweet-eyed Rachel, with Joseph, was fetched up from the rear. As each name was mentioned Esau gave a little flourish on his pipes, praised the women's bosoms and the sturdiness of the offspring. He commented loudly upon Leah's weak eyesight and gave her an Edomite herb balsam for her chronically inflamed lids, at which she kissed the tips of his toes and thanked him with rage in her heart.

Even the outward forms of the reconciliation made some difficulty: both brothers tried to speak in the language of their common childhood, but found it hard. Esau spoke the harsh dialect of Seir, which differed from his native tongue by the addition of Midianitic words and elements from the desert of Sinai; whereas Jacob had learned in Naharina to speak Akkadian. They helped each other out with gestures, but Esau found words for his curiosity in the matter of the far herds, and his offhand manner of receiving the splendid present, when Jacob indicated that by its means he hoped to find favour in his brother's eyes, showed that he was not without a knowledge of good breeding. He affected a blithe indifference to property and riches and all suchlike burdens. "By no means, O my brother!" he cried out. "It were exceeding folly! Take it and keep it, I return it thee back, I have no need of it to forget the disgraceful old tale and to forgive it. I have come to terms with my lot and am content. Dost thou imagine that we of the lower world go about all our days with our tails between our legs? That were to believe most mistakenly, praise be to God. We do not swagger, indeed, or roll our eyes, because of the blessing on our head, but in our own way we are of good cheer. To us too it is sweet to lie with a woman, we too cherish love for the children we breed. Thinkest thou the curse I owe thee, rascally brother that I love, made me a scurvy beggar and starveling in Edom? Not so! For there I am a lord, and great among the sons of Seir. I have more wine than water, abundance of honey, oil and fruits, and wheat and barley more than I can eat. My underlings bring me fowls, they send me bread and flesh meat every day, and game ready prepared for the meal, and venison that they hunt in the wild with their dogs and also that I myself kill; and milk dishes have I to make me lie awake half the night with belching. Presents? Flocks and herds as sin-offering and eyewash, to make me forget the ancient filthy wrong done upon me by the woman and by thee? Fie upon it, fie" — here he gave a flourish on his pipes. "What need of presents betwixt thee and me? For the heart is all, and I have forgiven and forgotten the ancient baseness nor think any more how thou mockedst me and my hairiness before our father with skins upon thy thigh and thy wrist, thou rascal, so that I laugh even in my old age as I remember it, though then I wept bloody tears and sent after thee Eliphaz, and made thee to grow pale with fear, thou woman's man!"

And he embraced his brother afresh and smeared kisses all over his face, Jacob simply enduring without showing any response. For he was disgusted to his very core with Esau's words, finding them brainless and lewd and utterly painful, and thinking of nothing save how to get free with utmost despatch of this strangelike relative — only not without having regulated the situation and quit him once more for the birthright with tribute paid down on the spot, for of course Esau only wanted to be urged. So there was further exchange of courtesies, more self-abasements, more pressing offers — until at last when Esau let himself be persuaded to take the gift from his brother's hand and be grateful for it, the poor devil's heart was really won over and he was far more sincerely reconciled with Jacob than Jacob by any means found it in his heart to be with him.

"And now, my brother," Esau cried, "not another thought of that shabby old affair! For came we not out of the same womb, thou and I, one after the other, and as good as at the same time? For thou heldest my ankle as thou knowest, and I the stronger dragged

thee behind me into the light of day. We had fought with each
other in the womb, forsooth, and outside it too — but let there be
an end to all that! Let us live brotherly with one another and like
twins before the Lord, and dip the hand in the same dish and depart
not each from the side of the other for the rest of our lives! Up,
then, and let us take our journey toward Seir and let us dwell together."

"Thanks very much," was Jacob's thought to himself. "Go to
Edom, shall I, and be a piping he-goat like thee and live forever
with thee, thou fool? But that is not the meaning of God nor of
my soul. All that thou speakest is but empty and idle words in my
ear, for that which happened between us will not be buried, thou
thyself bringest it into every word that thou utterest, while thinking in thy feeble wits it can be forgiven and forgotten." Aloud
he said:

"The words of my lord are an enchantment, and each one singly
has hearkened to the inmost wishes of his servant's heart. But my
lord seeth that with me are my half-grown children, likewise little
ones of five like this one here named Jehosiph, a weakling on a
journey. And then, alas, a dead child in the coffin, whom it were impious to harry over stock and stone; not to speak of my sucking
calves and lambs. All these would die were I to hasten. Let my lord,
I pray thee, pass over before his servant; and I will lead on softly,
according as the cattle that go before me and the children are able
to endure, until I come unto my lord at Seir to dwell fondly together."

It was a polite refusal, and Esau, rather gloweringly, understood it
as such. He made, indeed, another trial, suggesting to his brother
that he should leave some of his people with him to lead the train
and to cover its rear. But Jacob thanked him and said there was no
need, if only he found grace in the sight of his lord — so that the
emptiness of his words stood revealed. Esau shrugged his shaggy
shoulders, turned his back on the fine and false one, and went hence
into his mountains with cattle and train. Jacob, behind him, lingered
a little, then at the first turning took another way and disappeared.

Chapter III

THE STORY OF DINAH

THE LITTLE MAID

SINCE he came next to Shechem, it is here in place to tell the tale of the grievous complications that ensued from his sojourn there — and to tell them, moreover, as they really came to pass, with some correction of those little adornments and improvements which crept in later into the "fine language" beginning with "Knowest thou? Well I know," and were then handed down to posterity as the history of the seed and of the world. For if I unfold the story of the evil and in the end bloody doings of that time, a story inscribed in Jacob's lined and weary old lineaments along with other events that made up the burden of his ancient memories, it is because it forms part of the man's spiritual history, the character of his soul; and because nothing is better calculated than his attitude in this episode to explain why Simeon and Levi secretly poked each other in the ribs when their father made use of the title and honour bestowed upon him by divine grace.

The hapless heroine of the adventure at Shechem was Dinah, Jacob's only daughter, who was born of Leah at the beginning of her second period of fruitfulness; at the beginning and not at the end, and thus before Issachar and Zebulun, and not after them, as later tradition would have it. This tradition must be wrong; for according to it Dinah would have been still unripe and physically too young for the misfortune which befell her; she would have been still a mere child. Actually she was four years older than Joseph, which would make her nine at the time of Jacob's arrival at Shechem and thirteen at the time of the catastrophe. Two important years older, that is, than the tradition would have her, for in those two years she flowered, became a woman, and as attractive as it was given to any child of Leah to be, yes, for a brief space more attractive than might have been expected from this strong but unlovely stock. She was a true child of the Mesopotamian steppe, where no living summer follows the early-burgeoning and flowery spring; for even in May all the enchanting loveliness is burnt black as a coal by a pitiless sun. Such were Dinah's natural parts; to which events added their share to make of her before her time a weary and a wasted woman. As for her place in the list of Jacob's descendants, it is of no great importance what the scribes have set down. It was haste, or indifference, that guided their pens, when they simply entered her name at the end of the list of Leah's children instead of in its right place — they would not interrupt the tale of sons by anything at once so petty and so annoying as a girl's name — it did not matter about a girl. There was not much to choose between actual barrenness and the birth of a female; and Dinah's name in the place where it belongs forms as it were a transition between Leah's brief period of sterility and the ensuing period of fruitfulness which began in earnest and properly with the advent of Issachar. Every schoolboy knows to-day that Jacob had twelve sons, some even know their names by heart — whereas large circles of the population are unaware that the unhappy little Dinah ever existed, and when she is mentioned display surprise. But she was dear to Jacob — as dear as a child of the unchosen one could be; he hid her from Esau in a coffin, and when her time came, his heart bled for her.

BESET

ISRAEL, then, the blessed of the Lord, with all his goods and possessions, his flocks, of which the sheep alone were five and a half thousand head, with his women and their increase, with male and female slaves, shepherds and drovers, with asses and goats and pack- and riding-camels; in good spirits at having left behind the heat of the river valley and the dangers from the wild boars and leopards hidden in its poplar and willow thickets — Jacob, the father, found himself in a moderately mountainous region, where rushing streams watered the blooming and fruitful valleys, and barley was growing wild. In one such valley he happened upon the city of Shechem, a pleasant place, shaded by the rock Garizim. It was centuries old, with a ring wall of unmortised blocks of stone, enclosing two cities, a lower one to the south-west, an upper to the north-east. The upper one was so called because it stood upon an artificial mound five double ells in height, but likewise in a figurative sense, because it consisted almost entirely of the palace of Hamor, prince of the city, together with the square massif of the temple of Baal-Berith. These two towering structures were the first things to meet the eyes of Jacob and his train as they entered the valley and approached the eastern gate. Shechem had some fifteen hundred inhabitants, not counting the twenty men who formed the Egyptian garrison, and whose commander, an officer in the heyday of youth, came from the Delta region and was set here for the sole purpose of collecting each year certain bars of gold in ring form, from the hands of Hamor, but indirectly from the large merchants of the lower city. This gold had then to take its way down to the city of Amun, and its failure to arrive would have been attended by great personal inconvenience to the young Weser-ke-bastet, such being the name of the captain.

One can imagine the mixed feelings with which the people of Shechem regarded the approach of that straggling train, having been informed of it by the guards on the walls and by homecoming citizens. Who could tell whether it was for good or evil the wanderers came? And if the latter, the people of Shechem had already enough experience of wars and plundering expeditions on their own side to make them feel misgivings for the safety of their city despite the thick wall that went round it. These were not martial spirits, but rather peaceful, trading, comfortable souls; Hamor, the prince, was a peevish old man with painfully enlarged joints, and his son, Sichem, a pampered young gentleman, an elegant drone who lay upon rugs and ate sweetmeats. Under such conditions the reliance of the population upon the soldierly valour of the occupying garrison would have been warm and joyous, had there been any ground whatsoever for such confidence to rest upon. But this little troop of men under a falcon standard decorated with peacock feathers, though it called itself the division "refulgent as the solar disk," did not awaken any hopes of reliance in the hour of need — and least of all their captain, the aforementioned Weser-ke-bastet, who had as good as nothing of the soldier about him. He was a bosom friend of young Sichem, and he had himself two passions in life: flowers and cats. He came from the city of Pi-beseth in Lower Egypt, and in fact was known to the Shechemites simply as Beset. The local divinity of his city was the cat-headed goddess, Bastet; and Beset's devotion to the feline species knew no bounds. Wherever he went he was surrounded by these animals — not only living ones of all colours and ages, but dead ones as well; for several mummies stood against the walls of his quarters, and he wept as he laid before them offerings of mice and milk. With this softness of disposition went his love of flowers; as a counterpose to masculine traits it might have been thought of as a pleasing charactersitic, but in the absence of these it did not inspire confidence. He went about always wearing a wide collar of fresh flowers, and however humble the article of his daily use, all must have fresh garlands — in short, the whole thing was absurd. His clothing was entirely civilian: a white batiste skirt through which the loincloth was visible, swathings round his arms and waist — no one had ever seen him in a cuirass or armed with anything more warlike than a little cane. Simply on the score of a certain skill at writing he had been made an officer.

As to his men, about whom he troubled himself hardly at all, they had forever on their lips in polished sentences praises of the warlike deeds of an early king of their country. Thothmes the Third, and of the Egyptian army, who in seven campaigns under his leadership had conquered the whole land to the Euphrates river. But for themselves, they revealed their prowess chiefly in the destruction of roast goose and beer; on other occasions, as for instance an outbreak of fire or an attack by Bedouins upon the outlying villages belonging to the town, they had shown themselves arrant cowards — and particularly the born Egyptians among them, for there were also some yellow Libyans and a few Moors from Nubia. Sometimes they would show themselves in the narrow lanes of Shechem, with their wooden shields, their lances, sickles and three-cornered leather aprons, and run in crouching quickstep as though in flight, through the press of donkeys and camel-riders, of melon- and water-sellers and peddlers before the bazaar, and the citizens would make faces at them behind their backs. As for the rest, these warriors of Pharaoh amused themselves with games of "How many fingers?" or "Who hit you?" and songs about the hardships of the soldier's life, particularly of those who were condemned to live in this miserable Amunland, instead of flourishing on the shores of the many-barked life-giver and beneath the gaily coloured columns of No, the city of cities, the city incomparable, No Amun, the city of God. That they cared no more for the fate or the protection of Shechem than a grain of corn admits of no doubt whatever.

THE ADMONISHING

BUT the good citizens of Shechem would have felt even worse had they heard the conversation which the older sons of the head of the tribe were having among themselves as they came on: discussion of plans concerning Shechem all too nearly, which these dusty but energetic young people were concocting among themselves before bringing them to the ears of their father — who indeed, when he heard them, vetoed them decisively. Ruben, or Reuben, as the eldest was really named, was then seventeen, Simeon and Levi counted sixteen and fifteen years, Bilhah's Dan, a sly and ingenious youth, was likewise fifteen, and the swift, slim Naphtali of like age with the strong but brooding Judah, namely fourteen. These were the sons of Jacob who took part in the conspiracy; Gad and Asher, eleven and twelve, though already sturdy youths and mentally ripe, had no share at this time, nor, of course, the three youngest sons.

What were they discussing? Well, it was the same theme as gave the Shechemites food for discussion inside the wall. These were stout fellows who put their heads together outside: burnt nearly black with Naharina's sun, their hair stiff with grease, clad in shaggy belted smocks. Shepherds and sons of the steppe they were, running almost wild since infancy; ready with bow and knife, used to encounters with lions and wild bulls and also to wholesale brawling with strange herdsmen over pasture rights. Very little of Jacob's mild and pensive piety had come down to them — their concerns were strictly practical, their minds full of the youthful spirit of defiance which forever looks for insults and seeks out quarrels. They were arrogantly proud of their race, though knowing naught of the spiritual nobility upon which its true greatness rested. It was long since they had been under a roof or had settled habitation, and their attitude towards the inhabitants of the fertile land they were now entering was that of nomads conscious of superior freedom and audacity, and occupied with visions of booty. It was Dan who first, out of the corner of his mouth, made the suggestion that they should take Shechem by guile and plunder it. Reuben, a high-minded lad but prey to rash enthusiasms, was quickly won, while Simeon and Levi, biggest brawlers of the lot, danced and shouted in their zeal to begin. The younger ones came in out of pride at being asked.

The idea was, after all, not so fantastic. It had happened before, that towns in the region had been besieged by desert marauders, Kabiri or Bedouins, and even temporarily occupied; it was not precisely an everyday occurrence, yet not a rare one. Tradition, however, the sources of which are not the cities but the Kabiri, the Ibrim in the narrower sense of the word, the ben Yisrael, keeps silence with the best conscience in the world, and convinced of the permissibility of such epic purifications of reality, upon the fact that a settlement with Shechem by force of arms was always contemplated by those in Jacob's camp, and was only delayed for a few years by the opposition of the head of the tribe — delayed, that is, until the tragic events in connection with Dinah.

In any case, Jacob opposed and his opposition was majestic and impregnable. His mood at the time was a particularly lofty one, the combined product of his traditional culture, the singular importance of his soul-life, and his inclination to far-reaching associations of ideas. In his solemn musings, the course of his life for the past twenty-five years appeared to him in the light of his relation to the cosmos, as a symbol of the circle: as an up and down of ascension, descent into hell and resurrection, as an exceedingly happy fulfilment of the mystical schema of growth. Journeying from Beersheba, he had arrived at Beth-el, the place of the great vision of the ladder — that was the ascension. Thence into the valleys of the underworld, where he had had to serve twice seven years, sweating and freezing; afterwards growing very rich by outwitting a sly and silly devil called Laban — Jacob's associational habit of thought drove him to see in his Meso-

potamian father-in-law a black moon-demon and evil dragon, who
had betrayed him and whom he had then consummately betrayed
and plundered and in particular freed from his spell his Ishtar, the
sweet-eyed Rachel — breaking the bolts of the lower world and
mounting with her and all his riches, his heart bursting with godly
laughter, out of the lower world and journeying towards Shechem.
The vale of Shechem had no need to be so full of blossom as it actually was, for Jacob's eyes to greet it as a new spring and station of
renewal on the course of his life; thoughts of Abraham standing in
this very place did their part towards filling him with tender and
reverent feeling as he drew near. His sons, perchance, might dwell
upon Abraham's warlike deeds, his bold assault upon the armies of
the East, and how he had blunted the teeth of the star-gazers, but he,
Jacob, was thinking of his forefather's friendship with Milchizedek,
high priest of Shechem; of the blessing he had from him, the sympathy and recognition he had paid to Abraham's god. And thus the
reception which Jacob gave his older sons when tentatively and in
almost poetic language they hinted at their unseemly intentions, was
of the most unfavourable.

"Depart from me," he cried, "and straightway! Sons of Leah and
of Bilhah, shame upon your heads! Are we thieves of the desert, who
come like grasshoppers over the land and like a plague from God and
devour the husbandman's harvest? Are we rabble and a nameless
tribe, sons of nobody, whose only choice is to beg or to steal? Was
not Abraham a prince among the princes of the land and a brother
of mighty powers? If ye set yourselves with dripping swords against
the lords of the cities and live among wars and alarms, how then shall
ye pasture our lambs on hostile ground and our goats among hills
that resound with hatred? Away, fools! Submit yourselves! Look to
the flocks, and see that the three-week-olds take to their fodder that
the milk of the mothers may be saved. Go gather camel's-hair that we
may have frieze for the garments of slaves and under-shepherds, for
now is the time of shedding. Go, I say, and try the cords of the tents
and the eyelets of the tent roofs that nothing be rotted and a mischance come about and pull down the house of Israel about our
heads. But know ye, that I now gird myself up and go forth and enter the gate of the city and speak in peace and wisdom with the people and with Hamor their shepherd, that we may make covenant
with them, lawfully and in writing, and have land of them and trade
to our profit and to the harm of none."

THE COMPACT

So it came to pass. Jacob had set up his camp not far from the city
near a group of ancient terebinth and mulberry trees, which seemed

to him sacred, in a rolling stretch of meadow and ploughland out of
which the rock Garizim arose, bare above but fertile below; in the
distance one saw the bald cliffs of Mount Ebal. From here he sent
three men to Shechem with presents for Hamor the shepherd: a basket of pigeons, bread made of pressed fruits, a lamp shaped like a
duck and some beautiful jars painted with fish and birds. And he sent
word that Jacob, the mighty traveller, would treat with the heads of
the city under the gate concerning sojourn and rights. In Shechem
they were relieved and delighted. The hour of meeting was appointed, and when it arrived Hamor the gouty man came out of the
east gate with his household train and Sichem his son, a fidgety
youth, and also Weser-ke-bastet came in a fresh garland of flowers,
out of curiosity, accompanied by several cats. And Yaakow ben
Yitzchak in all his dignity placed himself on the other side, attended
by his oldest servant, Eliezer, and his older sons, upon whom he had
enjoined perfect courtesy for the occasion; and so they met under
the city gate and held speech together, there and before it, for the
gate was a heavy structure, projecting both outside and inside in
hall-shaped bays and the inside was the market square and place of
judgment, and a press of people had come hither behind the heads
of council, to look on and listen at the business, which proceeded
with all due and proper forms and got to the heart of the matter only
with difficulty, so that the sitting lasted six hours and the merchants
in the market place drove a thriving business. After the first salutations the two groups sat down opposite each other on camp stools,
mats and carpets, and refreshments were handed: spiced wine and
curds with honey. For a long time the conversation was confined to
the health of the heads and their families; then passed to the state of
communications on both sides of the "outlet," and thence to matters
even more remote. But by slow degrees, reluctantly and with shoul-
der-shruggings, they got round to the object of the meeting, casu-
ally at first, each side seeming to dissuade the other from talking of it,
and treating it with contempt on grounds of their higher humanity,
precisely because it was the one and only topic of discussion and the
actual reason for the meeting. For after all it is just this indulgence
in the superfluous, this submission to artificial hierarchies, and the unashamed wasting of time on their account, which differentiates the
civilized from the natural and makes up the sum of human values.

The impression which Jacob's personality made upon the inhabitants was of the best. They realized — if not at first sight, then after
only a little conversation — whom they had before them. This was a
man of God and prince of men, aristocrat by his possession of gifts
of the spirit, in virtue of which likewise his person was ennobled. It
was the working of that same nobility which had been from time immemorial the mark of the successor or reincarnation of Abraham in

the eyes of the people; quite independently of birth, basing itself
upon form and spirit, it had conferred upon this race the gift of spiritual leadership. The moving mildness and profundity of Jacob's
gaze, his consummate propriety, his fastidious gestures, the quaver
in his voice, his cultured and florid speech, moving in strophe and
antistrophe, rhythmical thought and mythical allusion, so charmed
them all, in particular the gouty Hamor, that early in the proceedings he stood up and crossed over to kiss the sheikh, amid loud applause from the populace in the inner hall. The stranger's actual business, which as they all knew had to do with permanent and legal
settlement among them, that was indeed a matter of some difficulty
for the head of the city; since if it became known higher up that he,
Hamor, was parcelling out the country to the Kabirites, it might get
him into trouble in his old age. But reassured by an exchange of looks
with the head of the garrison, who was as much taken with Jacob as
was Hamor himself, he opened the negotiations with a sweeping
courtesy and the too sweeping proposal that Jacob should quite simply take land and rights as a present — following it up with a thumping price: a hundred silver shekels for twelve and a half acres of
cornland; and adding in expectation of much tough haggling to ensue, that money had no meaning between such a purchaser and himself. But Jacob did not bargain. He was moved in his soul, exalted by
thoughts of recurrence, duplication and the past made present. He
was Abraham, come from the east, buying from Ephron the ploughed
land and the field of the double cave for a burying place. Had the
Founder haggled over the price with the head of Hebron and with
the children of Heth? The centuries were as though they were not.
What had been was again. The wealthy Abraham, the wealthy Jacob, out of the east, they struck bargains in dignity, without more
ado. Chaldæan slaves brought up the weighing scales and the stone
weights, old Eliezer advanced with an earthen jar full of ring silver;
Hamor's clerks rushed up, squatted down and began to write out the
articles of peace and agreement according to justice and the law. The
money was weighed out for ploughland and pasture, legal and sacred
the contract, accursed might he be who broke the bond. Jacob's people became duly accredited citizens of Shechem. They might go in
and out at will through the city gates. They might go abroad through
the land and trade in it. Shechem's sons might take their daughters
to wife and the daughters of Shechem their sons as husbands. It was
established by law — and he who opposed it should be bare of honour for his whole life long. Likewise the trees should be his on the
fields Jacob had bought, and who brought it in question was an enemy to the law. In witness whereof Weser-ke-bastet pressed his seal
ring with the scarab into the clay, Hamor his stone and Jacob the
cylindrical seal that hung round his neck. So it was done. They ex-

changed kisses and flatteries. And thus it was that Jacob settled in the land of Canaan and near the city of Shechem.

JACOB DWELLS BEFORE SHECHEM

"Knowest thou?" "Well I know it." But when Israel's shepherds later gathered round their fires and exchanged "fine language" they were far enough from knowing it well. They suppressed some of the facts and rearranged others all for the sake of the story and with perfectly clear consciences. They said nothing at all of the wry faces that were made by the sons of Jacob, particularly by Simeon and Levi, even while the contract was being drawn up; and they would have it that the bargain was signed after the affair between Sichem and Dinah had already begun — and begun, in fact, quite otherwise than as they "knew" it. They would have it that a certain condition made to Sichem with reference to the daughter of Jacob had actually been part of the compact — whereas that condition had been quite another matter and had come up at quite another time than the time and the connection they pretended to "know" so well. Let me explain. The contract was the beginning. Without it the settlement at Shechem could not have taken place nor the other events have followed on. They had lived in their tents before the city, at the entrance to the valley, for almost four years before the complications ensued. They planted their wheat in the fields and their barley on the loam of the fields, they gathered the fruit of their olive trees, pastured their flocks and traded with them in the countryside; they dug a well where they had settled, fourteen ells deep and very wide, and lined it with masonry, Jacob's well. But why such a deep and wide well — when the whole valley abounded in springs and the city possessed a well before its gate, what need had the children of Israel to dig themselves one? Good, and they did not need it at first, they did not dig it at once when they had settled down, but somewhat later, when it became clear that it was a necessity of existence for them, the Ibrim, to be independent in the matter of a water supply and to have on their own ground a source that would not run dry even in the greatest drought. The compact had been made and the brotherhood sealed; and whoever misconstrued it, his entrails should be the price. But it had been made and sealed by the chiefs, even though with the applause of the populace; and in the eyes of the people of Shechem, the people of Jacob still remained strangers and wanderers — not such very agreeable or harmless ones either, rather vain and dictatorial, indeed, boasting of their superior spirituality, and at the same time capable of looking after their own interest in the wool and cattle trade in a way that made one's self-esteem suffer in comparison. In other words, the brotherhood did not go very deep.

There were certain shallow spots, one of these being in respect of the water supply: it had not been explicitly mentioned in the contract, and before very long the Hebrews were refused the use of the available sources. Hence the great well, the well of Jacob, the existence of which is a witness to the fact that even before the more serious troubles things stood between the seed of Israel and the people of Shechem much as they were in the habit of standing between nomad Kabirites and the settled owners of the land, and not at all as they should have stood in virtue of the contract signed before the gate of the city.

Jacob knew this, and did not know it; that is to say, he looked the other way, and directed his mild gaze upon everyday things and spiritual matters. At that time his sweet-eyed Rachel was still with him, whom he had so toilsomely wooed and so hardly won and rescued and brought to the land of his fathers; his one true and beloved wife, delight of his eyes, a balm to his heart and refreshment to his senses. Joseph, her offspring, the one true son, grew apace, being at that charming age between childhood and boyhood, and turning, indeed, into so lovely, clever, bewitching and beguiling a lad that the father's heart swelled with pride at sight of him, and the older sons had already begun to exchange glances over the follies their father committed in his doting on the sharp-tongued brat. Moreover, Jacob was often away on journeys. He got into touch with those of the faith in city and country, visited the spots sacred to the God of Abraham in the valleys and on the heights, and in many a discussion expounded the essence of the Only and Most High. It is certain that he first of all went southwards to embrace his father, from whom he had been separated for a lifetime, and to confirm himself in a blessing by which he had so obviously profited. For Yitzchak was still living, a very old man and long since wholly blind, whereas Rebecca years before had descended into the kingdom of the shades. Her death had been the cause of Isaac removing the place of his burnt offering from the tree Yahwe el Olam at Beersheba to the oracle-terebinth by Hebron, in the immediate neighbourhood of the "double cave," where he had buried his cousin's daughter and sister-bride, and where after a little while he too, Yitzchak, the rescued sacrifice, after long and eventful life would be laid to rest and be mourned by his sons Jacob and Esau. But that was later, when Jacob came down broken in spirit after Rachel's death, with her infant slayer, the newborn Ben-oni, Ben-jamin.

THE VINTAGE

Four times the wheat and barley were green and golden on Shechem fields, four times the anemones in the valley blossomed and died, and eight times the people of Jacob had held sheep-shearing; for the fleece of his spotted yearlings grew again in the turning of a hand, and he had a rich yield of wool from them twice a year, in Sivan as well as in the autumn month of Tisri. Then the feast of the vintage was held in the city and on the vineclad terraces of Garizim, at the full moon of the autumn equinox, when the year renewed itself. Everywhere was shouting, processions were on every hand and harvest offerings in town and valley; for they had plucked the grapes with singing, and trodden them with naked feet in the stone wine-press, and their legs were purple to the thighs and the sweet blood flowed through a trough into the vat and they kneeled down with laughter and let it run into their jars and wineskins to ferment. And when the wine was racked there began the seven-day feast, and they sacrificed a tenth of the firstlings of cattle and sheep, of corn, oil, and must, feasted and drank. They brought to Adonai, the great god, lesser gods for attendants in his house, and himself they carried in his ship in procession on their shoulders, with drums and cymbals, and bore him through all the land, to bless anew the fields and the vineyards. But in the midst of the feast, on the third day, they held music and dancing before the city and the castle and in the presence of all who cared to come thither. Women and children not excepted. Old Hamor was carried out in a chair, and the fidgety Sichem, also in a chair with a train of women and eunuchs; officials, merchants, and smaller folk were there; and Jacob came from his tents with wives and sons and servants, and they all sat down together where the music was and the dancing should be performed. This was beneath the olive trees in a broad part of the valley made by the falling away of the sacred mount, where it stood up rocky on top and smiling below; in the gorges of the mount of cursing goats were clambering in search of dry grass. The afternoon was warm and blue, the waning light kind to all men and things; gilding the figures of the dancers who, with embroidered bands about their heads and hips and metallic dust in their lashes, their eyes lengthened out by painting the corners, postured with rolling bellies before the musicians, turning their heads away from the tambours on which they played. The musicians squatted and struck their lutes and lyres and filled the air with the high whining of their pipes. Those behind the musicians beat time with their hands, and others sang, squeezing their throats with their hands to make a plaintive sound. There were men dancers as well, bearded and naked, with the tails of animals bound round them; they leaped like goats, and tried to catch the maidens who escaped them by sudden swerving of their lithe young forms. There was playing at ball, at which the females were very clever, folding their arms while keeping several balls in the air at a time, or while one of them perched herself on another's hip. Great was the satisfaction of town-dwellers and tent-dwellers, and if Jacob did not care for the hubbub and the drumming still he put a good face on it for the sake of the people and even courteously beat time with his hand now and then.

And now it was that Sichem, the son of the castle, saw Dinah, the daughter of the Ibrim, when she was thirteen years old, and first looked on her with longing and could never cease to desire her. She sat with her mother, Leah, on their mat near the musicians, opposite Sichem's seat, and he looked at her and could not turn away his dazzled eyes. She was not beautiful, no child of Leah's was; but the charm of youth went out from her, and she drew him with a clinging sweetness like the threads of date honey until Sichem was like the fly in the honey-pot, who draws up his sticky legs to see if he can get free if he wishes, does not seriously wish, for the honey is so sweet, yet is frightened to death seeing that he cannot, however much he tries; so it was with Sichem, who squirmed about on his little camp stool and was covered with blushes. She had a dark little face with fringes of black hair under the head-cloth, and long, narrow eyes of sticky black and a fatal sweetness; they kept going cross-eyed under the gaze of the sore-smitten youth. Her nose had wide nostrils, with a gold ring swinging from the partition between them; the mouth was a red cavity, with wide and painfully twisted lips, and as good as no chin. Her ungirdled smock of blue and red wool covered only one shoulder, and the bare one was extremely charming, in its slenderness, loveliness itself; matters were not improved when she raised her arm to put her hand to the back of her head, exposing to Sichem's gaze the damp curls in the little arm-pit, and the delicate small breasts standing out firm under shift and smock. Very damaging too was the effect of the little dark feet with copper anklets, and rings of soft gold on all the toes save the big ones. But almost worst of all were the little golden-brown hands with painted nails, the fingers covered with rings as well; she played with them in her lap, looking wise and childlike at once, and when Sichem thought of how these hands might caress him at their nuptials, his head swam and he gasped for breath.

But it was of the nuptials, the wedding night, he thought at once, and thought of nothing else. To speak with Dinah herself and pay court to her otherwise than with his eyes was forbidden him by custom. But even on the way home, and after they had reached the castle, he dinned in his father's ears that he could not live, that he would fade away and die without the Kabirite girl, and that the old man must go out and buy her for his couch, otherwise his life was a matter of days. What was there for the gouty Hamor to do save to be carried by two men and taken to Jacob's house of skins, to bow before him, to call him brother and with much circumlocution speak to him of the heart's desire of Sichem, his son, offering rich morning-presents in the hope that Dinah's father might consent to the match? Jacob was surprised and dismayed. He was embarrassed by conflicting feelings. From a worldly point of view he had ambitions towards establishing relations with a princely house of the land — they would be useful to him and to his seed. And he was moved too by memories of distant days, of his own wooing of Rachel from the devil Laban, and how Laban had put him off, exploited and betrayed him. Now he himself was in the rôle of Laban, it was his daughter on whom a youth cast eyes of desire, and he was not minded to behave as Laban had done. On the other hand he had lively doubts of the propriety of such a union. As for Dinah, he had never taken much notice of the little minx, all his affection being centred on the captivating Joseph; nor had he ever received from on high any guidance regarding her. Still, she was his only daughter, the wooing of Sichem enhanced her value in his eyes, and he bethought him that he must take care not to throw away this hitherto unprized possession. Had not Abraham made Eliezer put his hand beneath his thigh to swear that he would choose no wife for Yitzchak, the chosen son, from the daughters of Canaan, among whom he lived, but would find him one from their own seed, and among their kindred in the east? And had not Yitzchak passed on the prohibition, saying to himself, the chosen one: "Thou shalt not take a wife of the daughters of Canaan"? Dinah was but a girl, and a child of the unchosen to boot, and it was probably not so important as in the case of the bearer of the blessing how she should be bestowed in marriage. Yet it was also written that one should keep the vows made before the Lord.

THE CONDITION

JACOB sent for all his sons down to Zebulun and called them to council; they all sat before Hamor, lifting their hands and shaking their heads. The eldest among them, who set the key for the rest, were not the men to take up the idea as though they had no thought of anything better. They were at one in saying that the matter must be taken under advisement. Dinah, their sister, daughter of Leah, this priceless and lovely creature, only just ripened? And to be given to Sichem, the son of Hamor? Certainly such a matter required the maturest consideration, and they asked for time to think. They were prompted in this by their commercial instinct in general; but Simeon and Levi had other, ulterior ideas, and cherished certain vague hopes. For they had never given up their former plan, and though the refusal of the water rights had never brought it to fruition, they thought that it might be forwarded by this wooing of Sichem.

Three days' time for consideration. Hamor was borne away, rather testy. But at the end of the time it was Sichem who came riding into

camp on a white ass; his father had told him to attend to the affair
himself, as indeed was most fitting to the impatience of his desire. He
did not bargain nor disguise the feelings of his heart, he made no
concealment of the fact that he was consumed by a fire of longing
for Dinah the maid. "Ask what you like," said he, "make bold your
demands in presents and morning gifts. For I am Sichem, son of the
castle, I am splendid in the house of my father, and Baal is my witness
that I will grant you your demands." So then they told him the condition that they had fixed among themselves which must be fulfilled
before any further discussion.

We must pay close attention to the order of events, for it was not
that later recorded in the "fine language." According to it, Sichem
had at once and straightway committed the evil deed and called
down the stratagem and the violence of the brothers upon his head.
But in actual fact, he only resolved upon deeds after Jacob's people
had put themselves in the wrong towards him, and he saw himself
fobbed off if not cheated. They told him that first of all he must be
circumcised. It was indispensable. For such as they were, and according to their beliefs, it would be a scandal and abomination to give
their daughter and sister to an uncircumcised man. It was the brothers who had suggested this stipulation to the father, and Jacob, satisfied to have gained a little time by it, found nothing in principle to
object to, although something wondering at his sons' sudden piety.

Sichem laughed aloud, and begged pardon, covering his mouth
with his hand. "Is that all?" cried he. Was that all they required? But,
my lords! When he was ready to give one eye, or his right hand to
possess Dinah, what to him was the loss of anything so insignificant
as his foreskin? By Sutekh, there was no difficulty here, not the smallest! His friend Beset was circumcised, and thought nothing of it.
Not one of Sichem's little sisters in his house of delights would take
the least offence at the loss! It was as good as done — it should be performed by the hand of one of the priests of the temple of the Highest, a man skilled in healing. Directly he was whole he would come
again. And he ran off, beckoning to his slaves to follow with the ass.

A week later he was back, scarcely healed, still inconvenienced by
his sacrifice, but radiating confidence; he found the head of the family away on a journey. Jacob avoided the meeting and let his sons act
for him. He found himself pushed after all into the rôle of the devil
Laban, and preferred to play it *in absentia*. Poor Sichem told the sons
that their condition was fulfilled; it had been no such trifling matter
as he had thought but bothersome enough; however, now it was
done, and the sweet reward earned. And what did the brothers say?
Done, yes, they answered him. Yes, perhaps, they would willingly
think so. But done in the wrong spirit, without understanding, superficially — and quite meaningless. It was done, perhaps. But done

simply for the sake of the female Dinah, not at all in the sense of marriage with "Him." And it was highly probable that it had been done with a metal knife, not with a stone one as was indispensable — this alone made the whole thing most questionable. And moreover, Sichem the son of the castle had already a chief wife and sister, the only true wife, Rehuab the Hivite woman; Dinah, daughter of Jacob, would be only one of his concubines. It was not to be thought of.

Sichem fidgeted. How could they tell, he cried, in what spirit and understanding he had fulfilled the unpleasant condition? And as for the business of the stone knife, that they were bound to have told him beforehand. But as for being a concubine! The king of Mitanni himself had sent his daughter, named Gulichipa, with pomp and retinue, to marry Pharaoh, not to be the queen of the country, for the goddess Teia was that, but as a second wife; and if King Shutarna himself —

Yes, said the brothers, that was very well for Shutarna and Gulichipa. But this was a matter of Dinah, daughter of Jacob, a prince of God and of the seed of Abraham; and that she could not become a concubine to Sichem of the castle would be plain to his understanding directly he consulted it.

And this Sichem was to take as their final word?

They lifted their shoulders and spread out their hands. Could they possibly appease him with a present — two or three muttons, perhaps? . . .

Then there was an end of his patience. He had paid for his ardour with a good deal of vexation. The temple priest had not proved nearly so competent as he had pretended, and his awkwardness had resulted in much swelling, pain and inflammation for Hamor's son. And this was the result! He gave vent to a curse, the burden of which was the consignment of the sons of Jacob to the weightlessness of light and air — which they tried to ward off with quick and practised motions — and rushed away. Four days later Dinah disappeared.

THE ABDUCTION

"KNOWEST thou of it?" Again we must give heed to the sequence of events. Sichem was a spoilt and rickety youth, not brought up to relinquish easily any sensual gratification he had set his heart on. But that is not to say that we must take literally those fairy tales of the shepherds which put him in the worst possible light. The reason why the story was graven so deeply in Jacob's careworn face was precisely that he himself, however much he desired to tell it, and to believe it, in its softened and improved form, knew very well even as he did so who it was had the first thoughts of violence and pillage, who had planned the affair from the start, and that Hamor's son had

not stolen Dinah at all, in the beginning, but wooed her honourably,
and only when he had been cheated felt himself justified in making
his happiness the basis of further negotiations. Dinah was gone,
stolen, carried off. In broad daylight, in the open field, in sight of her
own people, men from the castle had stolen upon her as she played
with her lambs; they had put a cloth over her mouth, flung her upon
a camel and were far upon the way to the city before the men of
Israel could mount to ride after. Gone she was, shut up in Sichem's
house of delights, surrounded by all sorts of unknown and urban
amenities; and Sichem held in haste his much-desired nuptials, against
which she made no particular resistance. She was an insignificant
thing, very yielding, without judgment or power of resistance. Whatever happened to her, provided it was vigorous and unequivocal, she
took as natural and right: And Sichem did her no violence, quite the
contrary; and the rest of the little sisters, including the first wife,
Rehumah, were most friendly.

But the brothers — particularly Simeon and Levi! Their rage
seemed to know no bounds, and Jacob, bewildered and distressed,
had to bear the brunt of it. Dishonoured, violated, villainously seduced, their sister, their little black pigeon, their only one, and of
Abraham's seed! They broke their ornaments, rent their clothing, put
on sackcloth, tore their hair and beards, howled aloud and gashed
their faces and bodies with knives until they were terrible to look
upon. They flung themselves on their bellies, struck the ground with
their fists and swore never to eat food nor to void it before they had
torn Dinah from the lustful Sodomites and made like the desert the
place of her shame. Revenge, revenge! Assault, murder, bloodshed,
torture, were all the words they knew. Jacob was profoundly agitated and cast down; painfully aware that he had behaved like Laban
after all, and well knowing too that the brothers were now in sight
of what had been their goal all the time. He had hard work to keep
them even temporarily in leash without laying himself open to the
reproach that he was lacking in pride and fatherly feeling. He took
part to some extent in their manifestations of grief and rage, putting
on a soiled garment and somewhat dishevelling his hair; but at the
same time he was pointing out to them that there was not much good
in tearing Dinah by force from the castle as it would settle nothing
and give rise to the fresh question of what they were to do with the
shamed and ravished creature. Now that she was actually in Sichem's
hands, no wise person could want her back; it would be the part of
wisdom to moderate their grief and wait a little — and also such a
line of conduct seemed to be suggested by the liver of a sheep he had
slaughtered in the emergency. The way things stood between the
city and the seed of Abraham on the basis of their covenant, Sichem
would doubtless be heard from himself before long; he would make

new proposals and open up possibilities of putting a better, if not an actually gratifying face on the ugly affair.

And behold, to Jacob's own astonishment they assented and agreed to wait for the messenger. Their sudden composure disquieted Jacob almost more than their former raging — what was behind it? He watched them with misgiving, but was not a party to their counsels, and heard indeed of their new decision hardly sooner than did the messenger of Sichem, who, just as Jacob had expected, appeared after a few days, bearing a letter written in Babylonian upon several potsherds. It was polite in form and in content no less friendly and ingratiating. It said:

To Jacob, son of Yitzchak, prince of God, my lord and father, whom I love and upon whose love I set the greatest store. Sichem, son of Hamor, speaks, thy son-in-law who loves thee; heir of the castle, whom the populace exalt with shoutings. I am well. Mayest though likewise be of good health. And may thy wives and thy sons and the people of thy house, thy cattle, sheep and goats and all that is thine rejoice in the highest degree of well-being! Behold Hamor my father hath at one time made with thee, my other father, a covenant of friendship and sealed it, and there hath been between us and you a close friendship for four cycles, during which time it was my constant thought that the gods might keep it so and not otherwise, that as we are now friendly one with another, by commandment of my god Baal and thy god Él Elyon who are almost one and the same god, differing from each other only in trifles, so might it remain to all eternity and through countless years of jubilee, in respect to the cordiality of our friendship.

But when mine eyes beheld thy daughter, Dinah, child of Leah the daughter of Laban, I desired most fervently that our friendship might not suffer as to its infinite duration but also be increased in kind even a millionfold. For thy daughter is like a young palm tree by the waters and as a pomegranate blossom in the garden, and for her sake my heart quivereth with desire, so that I knew that without her my breath would be of no worth. Then as thou knowest, Hamor, prince of the city, whom the people acclaim, came out to speak with his brother and to take counsel with my brothers, thy sons, and he returned comforted. And when I myself came, to woo Dinah, thy daughter, and to beseech you for breath unto my nostrils, then you spoke and said Friend, before Dinah can be thine thou must be circumcised in thy flesh for otherwise it were an abomination before our god. And lo, I gave no offence to the heart of my father and my brothers for I was friendly and I said: I will do according to your will. For I rejoiced beyond all bounds and sought Yawoh, the writer in the book of God, to do unto me that which you had said, and I suffered pain under his hands and afterwards, so that mine eyes ran over with tears, and all this for the sake of Dinah. But when I came again, lo, it was of no avail. Then came unto me Dinah thy child, the condition being fulfilled, and I knew her upon my bed to my highest delight and to hers no little as she hath told me with her own lips. But that there might not therefore be discord between thy god and my god, let my father straightway fix the price and the conditions of my marriage with Dinah, who is so sweet unto my heart, that a great feast may be held at Shechem in the castle and we may all celebrate the wedding with laughter and with song. For Hamor, my father, will stamp three hundred scarabs with my name and the name of Dinah, my spouse, in memory of this day and of the everlasting friendship between Shechem and Israel. Given in the castle on the twenty-fifth day of the month of the harvest home. Peace and good health to the receiver.

MODEL AND COPY

This was the letter. Jacob and his sons withdrew to study it, and when he looked at them they told him what they had agreed to do in this situation, and he wondered greatly but could not on principle dissent from their proposal. For the fulfilment of the new condition would not only be a spiritual triumph of real importance, it would also constitute repentance and compensation for the past misdeed. So when they sat again in the presence of the letter-bearers he left the word to Dinah's offended brethren, and it was Dan who played the spokesman and announced the decision. They were, he said, rich by the grace of God and set no great store by the amount of the dowry for Dinah, their sister, whom Sichem had justly compared with a palm tree and a fragrant pomegranate blossom. Hamor and Sichem might decide as seemed to them commensurate with their dignity. But Dinah had not "come" to Sichem, as he had been pleased to express it, she had been stolen, and an entirely new situation had thus been created, which the brothers were not prepared to accept without more said. They would therefore lay down the prior condition, that just as Sichem had himself most commendably submitted to be circumcised, all the male citizens of Shechem must now do the same, greybeards, men and boys, all that had the name of a male in Shechem, on the third day reckoned from the present day, and with stone knives. When that was done, then the wedding feast might be held in good sooth at Shechem and celebrated amid laughter and shoutings.

The condition seemed rather extravagant, at the same time it would be easy of compliance, and the messengers at once expressed their opinion that Hamor, their lord, would not be behindhand in what was needful. But they were hardly gone before Jacob felt on a sud-

den the deepest misgiving surge up within him concerning the meaning and intent of the apparently godly stipulation — so that he quaked
in his very entrails, and was fain to call back the messengers. For he
did not believe that the brethren had forgotten their ancient cravings, nor ever abandoned their revenge for Dinah's seduction and
dishonour, and when he considered their late sudden complaisance in
the light of this new demand, and recalled the look on their savagely
gashed faces when Dan spoke of the tumult of the wedding feast,
then he marvelled at his own stupidity in not comprehending their
dark designs the moment they had uttered them.

What had put him off was his own pleasure in repetition and recurrence. He had thought of Abraham: how at the Lord's command
and in obedience to the covenant he and his whole house with him,
Ishmael and all the servants, born in the house or bought with money
of any stranger, everything that bore the name of a man-child was
circumcised in the flesh of his foreskin. And he had realized that the
sons' stipulation was based on this history; yes, they had certainly
got their idea from it — but how did they think to carry it out? He
repeated the story to himself; how that on the third day, when his
wound was hot, the Lord came to Abraham to see how he fared.
And stood before the house, where Eliezer did not see him. But
Abram saw him and asked him in. But when the Lord saw him un-
bind and bind up his wound, he said: "It is not meet that I should
stand here." So delicately had God demeaned Himself in the presence of Abraham's holy and sacred suffering. And now the brethren
— what forbearance had they in mind to display to the ailing citizens of Shechem, on the third day, when the wound smarted? This
kind of recurrence made Jacob shiver, and he shivered again at the
look on their faces when the message came from the castle that the
condition was readily accepted, and that the general sacrifice would
be consummated on the third day of the given term, counting from
yesterday. More than once he almost lifted his hands to implore them.
But he was afraid of their outraged fraternal feeling, their just right
to revenge; he saw that conduct which once he might have with
overwhelming solemnity interdicted now received from circumstances strong elements of justification. He was even, he discovered,
conscious of a little private gratitude towards them for not bringing
him into their plot, for keeping him aloof and innocent, so that he
need know or suspect nothing unless he liked, but could simply let
happen what was to happen. Had not God the Lord, at Beth-el, cried
out to the sound of the harps that he, Jacob, would possess gates,
even the gates of his enemies; and might that not mean that regardless of his own personal love of peace, it was written in the stars that
conquests, wars and plunderings should accompany his course? Horror, unrest, and a secret pride in the craft and virility of his own seed,

kept him from slumber. Nor did he sleep at all in that night of terrors, the third night after the expiry of the given term, when he lay in his tent, wrapped in his mantle, and his horror-struck ear caught from afar the noise of armed conflict.

I have come to the end of this faithful depiction of the interlude at Shechem which later was the occasion of so much extenuating fable, saga and fine writing — extenuating in favour of Israel, with reference to the sequence of events which led up to the extremity if not to the extremity itself — for that gave no ground for extenuation, and indeed the saga dwells in pride and vain-boasting upon its uttermost frightful detail. Thanks to their disgraceful stratagem the people of Jacob, though far outnumbered, being only fifty men all told, had an easy victory over the Shechemites. The wall was almost bare of watchers, when they noiselessly and easily mounted it with cords and scaling-ladders; once inside they threw off all disguise and hurled themselves upon the startled inhabitants in a furious onslaught with which the latter, in their maimed state, were little calculated to deal. For every man child in Shechem, whether old or young, suffered from fever and was busy unbinding and binding up his wound, not excepting the greater part of the garrison. Whereas the Ibrim were sound of limb, and their spirits unitedly enflamed by the cries of "Dinah!" which they shouted ever and anon at their bloody work; they raged like lions, they were here, there, and everywhere at once, and from the first moment the souls of the citizens perceived them as an oncoming and inescapable calamity, so that they offered little or no resistance. Simeon and Levi, the instigators of the plot, were the most frightful of all; they practised a battle-cry like the roaring of a bull, making the inwards of the hearer to quake, and possessing its victim with that fear of God which makes him seek refuge from death in flight alone, and never by any chance in battle. "Woe, alas!" they all cried. "These are not men, this is Sutekh come among us! Baal the glorious is in all their members!" And as they fled they were struck down with the naked club. Literally with fire and sword the Hebrews worked their will: from city, castle and temple went up clouds of smoke, the streets and houses swam in blood. Only the physically strong were taken prisoner, the rest were strangled; and if horrors were perpetrated upon the dead we must remember in extenuation that the doers were no less involved than their victims in the mythological implications of their deeds. For they envisaged in the struggle a war of dragons, the victory of Marduk over Tiâmat the dragon of Chaos, symbolically represented by the many mutilations and cuttings-off of "show" members which followed the slaying. The whole execution lasted hardly two hours; at its end Sichem the son of the castle, shamefully disfigured, stuck head down in the waste-pipe of his own latrine; and the body of

Weser-ke-bastet with its draggled garland, lay bleeding in the street, having suffered a deprivation which the eye of his ancestral religion would have viewed as more serious than death. Old Hamor had simply died of fright. Dinah, the blameless, insignificant cause of so much desolation, was restored to her family.

The pillage went on for a long time. That old wish dream of the brethren came to pass: they comforted their souls with rapine, a brilliant haul; the very considerable riches of the city came into the hands of the victors, and their return home at the end of the last watch of the night, with their prisoners in chains, with high-piled loads of golden sacrificial jugs and basins, sacks full of rings, hoops, buckles, girdles and necklaces, with fine household gear in silver, amber, faience, alabaster, cornelian and ivory, to say nothing of the crops and stores, the flax, oil, flour and wine, resembled a triumph. Jacob did not leave his tent when they came. He had occupied great part of his wakefulness that night in making a sin-offering to the imageless god, under the sacred trees near his camp: the blood of a milk lamb had flowed upon the stone and the fat been burnt with fragrant drugs and spices. But now, when his sons entered his tent all glowing, swollen with pride, bringing with them the sister they had so horribly rescued, he lay shrouded upon his face and for long would not be moved to look either at her or his bloodthirsty sons. "Away," he cried with a gesture of repulsion. "Fools and accursed ones!" They stood defiantly, pursing their lips. "Should we," asked one of them, "let him deal with our sister as with a whore? Lo, we have washen our hearts clean. Here is Leah's child. She is seven and seventy times avenged." He kept silent and would not uncover his head, then they said: "If our lord would deign to look upon the things which are outside. There is much more to come, for we left men to bring up the townsmen's flocks from the fields and lead them to the tents of Israel." Then he sprang up and lifted his clenched fists above their heads so that they shrank back. "Accursed be your anger," he cried out with all his strength, "that it is so violent and ye so stiff-necked in your rage. For ye have troubled me to make me to stink among the inhabitants of the land like an ass that is troubled by flies! When they gather themselves together against me, what then? I being a few in number they will slay me, and my house, and the blessing of Abraham will be lost, which ye should continue into the centuries, and that which has been founded will be broken. Ye bloodthirsty ones! For ye go to avenge your hurts and to make us rich for the moment, and are too feeble in your heads to think of the future, the covenant and the promise!"

They only stood there pursing their lips. They knew nothing else but to repeat: "Shall they then deal with our sister as with an harlot?" "Yes," he screamed, beside himself, to their horror. "Rather that, than endanger our lives and the blessing. Hast thou conceived?" he went on to Dinah, where she cowered miserably on the ground. "How can I know?" she wailed. "The child shall not live," he said with decision, and she wailed afresh. More quietly he spoke: "Israel will set forth with all that is his, and remove with all his flocks and possessions which ye have taken with the sword for Dinah's sake. For it is not meet for him to remain in the place of this abomination. I have had a vision in the night and the Lord spake to me in a dream: 'Take up thy route towards Beth-el!' Away! And put our goods together."

The vision and the command had actually been vouchsafed to him, when after the sacrifice by night, while his sons were pillaging the city, he had fallen into a doze in his tent. It was a reasonable vision and after his own heart, for Luz, the place of sanctuary, which he knew so well, had under these circumstances great attraction; if he went thither it was as though he had taken flight to the feet of God the King. Fugitives from Shechem, escaped from that bloody marriage feast, were indeed on their way towards the neighbouring cities to tell the tale. And likewise just at this time certain letters, written by the various heads and shepherds of the cities of Canaan and Amor, had reached the city of Amun, in order to be laid before Horus in the palace, the sacred majesty of Amenhotep the Third; most unfortunately, indeed, because this deity was at the time suffering from an attack of nerves due to an abscess in his tooth, such as often afflicted him; also he was preoccupied with the erection of a marvellous forecourt for the Amun temple of the southern quarter of the city, and the building of his own tomb on the western side, so that he simply had no ear at all for any disquieting news from the wretched Ammon country, to the effect that "the cities of the king are lost" and "the land of the Pharaohs is fallen to the Kabirites, who have plundered all the countries of the king," for so it was written in the letters of the shepherds and chiefs. These documents accordingly — which had moreover sounded rather comic at court on account of their faulty mastery of the Babylonian tongue — found their way into the archives without producing in the mind of Pharaoh any resolve to take steps against the robbers. So that here again Jacob's people might boast of their good fortune. Likewise the nearby cities had been put in awe by the extraordinary savagery of the attack, and made no head against the perpetrators; thus Jacob, the father, having undertaken a general purification, having collected the numerous idols which in these four years had found their way into his camp, and buried them with his own hands under the sacred trees, might set himself in leisurely motion with all his goods and chattels, and leaving in his rear that place of horror, over which the vultures were circling, go jogging off toward Beth-el on made roads.

Dinah and her mother Leah were mounted on the same strong and intelligent camel. They rode in baskets slung under a canopy on both sides of the animal's hump; Dinah let down the shade and rode for the most part in darkness. She was with child. When her time came, the infant she brought into the world was exposed, by the stern command of her menfolk. She herself pined and withered long before her time. When she was fifteen her poor little face looked like an old woman's.

Chapter IV

THE FLIGHT

THE PRIMORDIAL BLEATING

THESE are grievous tales. And Jacob the father was weighty with them, stately and bowed down as by his manifold possessions: by the latest and only just happened as well as by the old and ancient — by stories and by history too.

History is that which has happened and that which goes on happening in time. But also it is the stratified record upon which we set our feet, the ground beneath us; and the deeper the roots of our being go down into the layers that lie below and beyond the fleshly confines of our ego, yet at the same time feed and condition it — so that in our moments of less precision we may speak of them in the first person and as though they were part of our flesh-and-blood experience — the heavier is our life with thought, the weightier is the soul of our flesh.

When Jacob came again to Hebron, called also the "town of four"; when he returned to the tree of wisdom, planted and blessed by Abram — whether *the* Abiram, or another, unknown one — and entered once more his father's house, after having meantime suffered that sorest blow, of which I shall speak in due course; Isaac declined and died, being a very old man and blind, a grey-haired old man bearing that ancestral name, Yitzchak, son of Abram; and in the dread hour before his death he spoke to Jacob and to the others who were by, in high and awe-inspiring tones, very darkly and oracularly, of "himself" as the rescued sacrifice, and of the blood of the ram, which was to be thought of as his very own blood, the true son's, poured out in sin-offering for all. Yes, just before the end he essayed with remarkable success to bleat like a sheep and his bloodless face took on an astounding likeness to the countenance of that animal — or rather, they were conscious all at once that the likeness had always been there, to an extent that they were all horrified and made haste to fall upon their faces in order not to see how the son became a ram; while he began again to speak, calling the ram father and god. "A god shall they slay," he babbled, in ancient and poetic language, and went on, with his head bent back, his eyes wide open and fixed, and his fingers spread out, to say that they should all hold a sacrificial meal with the flesh and the blood of the slain ram as he and Abram had once done, the father and son, for whom the god-and-father beast had intervened. "Lo, it was slain," they heard him rattle in his throat; he went babbling and rambling on, they not daring to look at him, "the father and the beast instead of the man and the son, and we ate. But verily I say to you there shall be slain the man and the son instead of the beast and in the place of God and ye shall eat." Then he bleated again, in a most lifelike manner, and then he died.

They remained some time upon their faces after he stopped speaking, uncertain whether he were really dead and would not speak and bleat again. It was with them all as though their entrails turned over within them and the undermost came uppermost so that they could have brought it all up; for the words and bearing of the dying man had about them something aboriginally indecent; something grisly, yet primevally, pre-religiously sacred, which lay beneath all the civilized layers in the most unregarded, forgotten and ultra-personal depths of their souls and had been turned uppermost by the death of Yitzchak, with nauseating effect: an obscene apparition out of the far-away and deep-down past of the animal that was God, namely the ram, the god-ancestor of the race, from which it came down, and whose divine and tribal blood they had once in that unspeakable aforetime poured out and consumed, in order to strengthen the bond between the tribe and the beast-god. That was before He came, the God from far away, Elohim, the God from beyond and above, God of the wilderness and God of the moon peak, who had chosen them, severed the connection between them and their primitive nature, married them with the ring of circumcision and established a new beginning of God in time. Hence it was they were sick at sight of Yitzchak's ramlike face and his bleating — Jacob himself had felt sick. But also he had felt mightily exalted when he presided over the burying. Barefoot and dust-strewn, with shorn head, he had attended to the rites, the wailings and the sacrificial vessels for offerings to the dead: he and Esau the pipe-playing goat, who had come from his goat-mountain to help bury his father in the double tomb, and with tear-wet beard to add his childishly unrestrained howls to the "Hoi-adon" of the male and female singers. Together they sewed up Yitzchak in a ram-skin, with his knees under his chin, and thus they gave him to time to devour, to time which devours his children that they may not set themselves over him, but must choke them up again to live in the same old stories as the same children. (For the giant cannot tell by touching it that the artful mother has only given him a thing like a stone, wrapped up in a skin, and not the child.) "Woe, alas, for the lord!" That had often been cried over Yitzchak the

rescued sacrifice and many a time and oft had he lived again in his
tales, telling them in the first person, as was right, partly because his
ego faded out and back into the archetype, partly because what had
been had now become the present in his flesh and might have repeated itself conformably to the foundation. In this sense had Jacob
and the rest heard and understood it when dying he spoke again of
the averted sacrifice; heard as it were with a double ear yet understood in a single sense — just as we, in fact, hear with two ears and
see with two eyes, yet grasp the thing heard and seen as one. Moreover Yitzchak was a very old man talking about a little boy who had
been near being killed; whether the child had once been himself or
an earlier one was scarcely pertinent, since in any case the remote
little almost-sacrifice could not have been stranger or more utterly
outside of himself than the boy which Yitzchak had once been.

THE RED ONE

DEEP-SUNK in musing, yet mightily uplifted, was the soul of Jacob in
these days when he with his brother Esau buried their father; for all
past events stood up in him and became present to his spirit, as they
had once become present again in the flesh according to the archetype; and to him it was as though the ground beneath his feet were
transparent, consisting of crystal layers going down and down without any bottom and lighted up by lamps which burned between the
layers. But he walked above them among the experiences of his
proper flesh, Jacob, present in time, and gazed at Esau, who likewise
walked again with him according to his archetype and was Edom,
the Red.

Such a characterization of Esau's personality is doubtless unobjectionable; yet doubtless in a certain sense and unobjectionable only in
a qualified one. For the clearness of it is like that of the moonlight,
an illusory and deceptive clearness, in which we of to-day can
scarcely move with the bearing of pensive simplicity which characterized the persons of our story. I have related how Esau, the red-
skinned, had even in his youth and while still at Beersheba, established
relations with the land of Edom, the people of the goat mountains
and the wooded ranges of Seir; how he cultivated these relations
and later entirely identified himself with them; went over root and
branch, with his Canaanitish wives, Aholibamah and Bashemath, and
their sons and daughters, to them and to their god Kusakh. The goat
people, then, were already in existence, and had been for no one
knows how long, before Joseph's uncle Esau went over to them, and
the tradition, later embodied in the chronicle and fabricated in the
course of generations of "fine language," which refers to him as the
"father of the Edomites," and original goat of the goat people, is

really nothing but moonshine. For Esau was not the father of Edom, not this Esau, but personally, however much he might be so considered in the story and even in a manner of speaking by himself. The Edomites were in existence long before Joseph's uncle — I refer thus to Esau because it is much safer to fix his identity in terms of the descending rather than of the ascending generations. They were immeasurably older than he; for that Bela, son of Beor, who is mentioned in the tables as the first king in Edom, is no more certainly the first king than Menes was certainly the first king of Egypt — and Menes' kingship is notoriously a case of time-coulisse. So that our present Esau was certainly not the father of the Edomites in any exact sense; and when it was expressly sung of him "He is Edom" but not, for instance, "he was Edom," the present tense is not a matter of chance, and the phrase is better understood as referring to a timeless and extra-personal generalization. Historically and also individually the original goat of the goat tribe was a remotely older Esau, in whose footsteps the present Esau trod. And it is well to add that the footsteps were right well-marked ones and often trodden in; probably — to put a point on it — they were not even the footsteps of him of whom the story might with justice assert that "He was Edom."

And here indeed our tale issues into mysteries, and our signposts are lost in the endlessness of the past, where every origin betrays itself as but an apparent halt and inconclusive goal, mysterious by its very nature — since that has to do not with distance but with the sphere. For distance in a straight line has no mystery. The mystery is in the sphere. But the sphere consists in correspondence and redintegration; it is a doubled half that becomes one, that is made by joining an upper and a lower half, a heavenly and an earthly hemisphere, which complement each other in a whole, in such a manner that what is above is also below; and what happens in the earthly repeats itself in the heavenly sphere and contrariwise. This complementary interchange of two halves which together form a whole and a closed sphere is equivalent to actual change — that is, to revolution. The sphere rolls — that lies in the nature of spheres. Bottom is soon top and top bottom, in so far as one can speak of top and bottom in such a connection. Not only do the heavenly and the earthly recognize themselves in each other, but, thanks to the revolution of the sphere, the heavenly can turn into the earthly, the earthly into the heavenly, from which it is clear that gods can become men and on the other hand men can become gods again.

All this is as true as it is true that Osiris the dismembered martyr was once a man, namely a king over Egypt, but became a god, though with a constant inclination to become a man again; indeed the phenomenon is plainly seen in the form of existence of all the Egyptian

kings, all of them being god as man. But the question as to what
Osiris was in the beginning, whether god or man, remains unanswered, since there is no beginning in the rolling sphere. The same is
true of his brother, Set, who, as I said some while back, was his murderer and dismembered him. This evil-doer was said to have an ass's
head and to be of warlike mien, a huntsman to boot, who taught the
kings of Egypt how to shoot with the bow, at Karnak near the Amun
city. By others he was called Typhon and he had early been assimilated to the burning desert wind Chamsin, the burning sun, fire itself,
and became Baal Hammon or the god of fire and was called among the
Phœnicians Moloch or Melech, the bull king of Baal, who with his
fire consumes the children and the firstborn, and to whom Abram
had been tempted to offer Isaac. What proof is there that Typhon-
Set, the red huntsman, was first and last at home in the skies and
none other than Nergal, the seven-named foe, Mars, the red, the fire
planet? With equal right might it be asserted that he was in the beginning and at the end a man, Set, brother of Osiris the king, whom
he thrust down from his throne and murdered, and that he only afterwards became a god and a planet, always prepared indeed to become
a man again, according to the revolving of the sphere. He is both,
and neither first: planet-god and man, by turns, in one. And therefore
no time-form is meet for him but the timeless present, which is resolved in the revolution of the sphere — and rightly is it always said
of him, "He is the Red."

But if Set the archer corresponds in the alternation of earth and
heaven with Nergal-Mars, the fiery planet, it is clear that the same
relation exists between the murdered Osiris and the royal planet
Marduk, to whom those black eyes looked up from the edge of the
well and whose god is called Jupiter-Zeus. Of him is told that he cut
off with a sickle the manhood of his father, Chronos, that giant
deity who devoured his children and would have done the same to
Zeus but for the artfulness of his mother. Zeus deposed his father and
made himself king in his place. This is a piece of information useful
to those who in the search for truth are not minded to stop halfway.
For it clearly means that Set, or Typhon, was not the first king-mur-
derer, that Osiris himself had a murder to thank for his throne, and
that what he had done as Typhon was done to him as king. This, in
other words, is part of the mystery of the sphere; that thanks to the
revolution the unity and identity of the person may go hand in hand
with a change of rôle. He is Typhon, so long as he is at the stage of
plotting murder; after the deed he is king, in the full majesty of success, and the rôle and character of Typhon fall to another. It has
been thought by many that it was the red Typhon and not Zeus,
who cut off Chronos' manhood and dethroned him. But argument is
idle, for what we are dealing with is only the same thing in revolu-

tion: Zeus is Typhon before he conquers. But the father-son relation revolves too, it is not always the son slaying the father, for at any moment the rôle of sacrifice may fall to the son, who then is slain by the father; in other words, Typhon-Zeus by Chronos. The original Abram probably knew all this when he set out to sacrifice his only begotten son to Moloch the red. Obviously he took the melancholy view that he must base himself on the story and carry out the tradition. God, however, prevented him.

There was a time when Esau, Joseph's uncle, was constantly with his own uncle Ishmael, Isaac's cast-off half-brother; visited him with surprising frequency in his wilderness underworld and laid plots with him, the shocking nature of which we shall learn hereafter. The companionship was, of course, not due to chance, and if one speak of the red one one must also speak of Ishmael as well. His mother was named Hagar, the wanderer — a name calculated to get her sent into the wilderness at once that it might be fulfilled. But the immediate occasion of her expulsion was Ishmael, whose underworldly characteristics had always been much too prominent to make it likely that he could permanently retain the favour of the gods of the upper earth. It was written of him that he was a "mocker." Not in the sense of being loose-mouthed — that alone would not have disqualified him for the upper spheres. No, in his case "mocking" is to be interpreted as "sporting"; Abram having happened to see "through the window" Ishmael disporting himself in an underworldly manner with Isaac his younger half-brother — which was by no means without its dangers for Yitzchak, the trueborn son, Ishmael having a beauty like to the sunset on the desert plain. Therefore the future father of many sons was alarmed and found the time was come for taking a decisive step. The relations between Sarah and Hagar had always been bad; Hagar had flaunted her maternity in the face of the barren woman, and once already had been obliged to flee before the jealous wrath of Sarah, who was constantly scheming to bring about the expulsion of the Egyptian and her offspring, not least because of the unsettled and contentious matter of the inheritance. Between the elder son of the concubine and the younger son of the true wife, the question arose whether Ishmael ought not to inherit jointly with Yitzchak or even before him — a state of affairs intolerable to Sarah's jealous mother-love, and unpleasant likewise to Abraham. What he had seen brought down the scale; he presented the supercilious Hagar with her son, some bread and a bottle of water, and sent her away never to return. What else could he have done? Should Yitzchak, the saved sin-offering, fall victim after all to the fiery Typhon?

Let me make the matter plain. It sounds most injurious to Ishmael — but was only fair. For the injuriousness lay in himself; that he walked in ways that were not quite everyday, that he was himself not an everyday person, is undeniable. His very name sounds symbolic to us; significant too is the fact that he became a very fine archer in the wilderness — it made an impression upon the wise men who have compared him with a wild ass, the beast Typhon-Set, the murderer, the wicked brother of Osiris. Yes, he is the bad man, he is the Red, and Abraham did well to drive him out, and to protect his favourite, who had received the blessing, from the snares of the fiery and the unrighteous. When Isaac begot sons of his wife's body, the red man came again, to relive his history beside Jacob, the smooth man; the sweet-smelling grass and the prickly plant, Esau the red-skinned, whom teachers and seers rail at more violently than his commonplace earthly person really merits. They call him serpent and Satan, and swine as well, the wild pig, in allusion to the boar which tore in pieces the shepherd and lord in the glades of Lebanon. Yes, in their instructed anger they call him a strange god, so that nobody can be deceived by his commonplace person as to what he actually is in the revolution of the sphere.

It revolves, and often they are father and son, the unequal, the red man and the bearer of the blessing, and the son unmans the father or the father slays the son. But often again — and nobody knows what they were at first — they are brothers, like Set and Osiris, Cain and Abel, Shem and Ham. And it may be that there are threes forming both pairs in the flesh: the father-son pair on one hand, the brother pair on the other. For Ishmael, the wild ass, stands between Abram and Isaac. To one he is the son with the sickle, to the other the red brother. Did Ishmael then desire to unman Abram? Certainly he did. For he was in act to beguile Isaac into underworldly love, and if Isaac had not begotten upon his wife's body, Jacob had never been born nor his twelve sons, and what then would have become of the promise of unnumbered seed — and of Abram's name, which signifies "father of many"? But now they moved again in the presentness of their own flesh, as Jacob and Esau; and even Esau, simpleton as he was, understood his own position; how much the more then Jacob, the instructed and pondering man?

OF ISAAC'S BLINDNESS

THE DIM and blurring gaze of Jacob's wise brown eyes, with their somewhat weary expression, rested upon the huntsman his twin as the latter helped him to bury their father, and all the events of the past rose up again in him and became the brooding present: their childhood, and how the long-awaited decision had at last been made, with the curse and the blessing and all that these involved. He mused dry-eyed, only now and again his breast heaved with the heaviness of his thoughts, and he gave an inward gasp. But Esau blubbered and howled throughout — though all in all he had little for which to be grateful to the old man they were sewing up; for nothing indeed, save the curse which was all that was left for him after the giving away of the blessing — to the father's sore grief, as Esau remained convinced; for it was a necessity to him, this conviction, and therefore he craved to hear it again and again, even out of his own mouth. Ten times while they worked, snuffling and wiping his nose he said amidst wailings, "Thou, Yekew, wast beloved of the woman, but my father loved me, and ate with satisfaction of my venison. 'Hairy-skin,' said he, 'my firstborn, it is savoury to me, that which thou hast killed and prepared for my eating by the blazing fire. Yea, and I will eat of it and thank thee for thy skill, and thou shalt remain my firstborn all thy days, and I will remember thee.' Thus and not otherwise spake he an hundred times and a thousand. But the woman loved thee and spoke to thee: 'Little Yekew, my chosen one!' And the gods know that in the mother's love one lies softer than in the father's. So have I found it."

Jacob was silent. And Esau went on between his sobs, and saying that which his soul had need to hear: "And ah, how wrathful was the old man when I came after thee and brought what I had prepared that he might be strengthened for the blessing and he understood that it was not Esau who had come before! He was wroth beyond all measure and cried out again and again: 'Who then was the huntsman, who was he? For now he has the blessing for I had strengthened myself to give it. Esau, my Esau, what remaineth us to do?'"

Jacob was silent.

"Be not so silent, smooth man!" cried Esau. "Thou sittest in thy self-seeking silence and givest it out still silent for mild forbearance, until it maketh my gall to rise. Have I not right, that the old man loved me and was angry beyond all measure?"

"Thou sayest it," answered Jacob, and Esau had to be content. But that he said it did not make it more true than it was, did not make it less involved; it still remained half-truth and equivocal, and that Jacob first kept silent and then answered in monosyllables was not due to dissembling or spite but to his feeling of helplessness before the complicated nature of the whole affair, which could not be got at in Esau's way, with wailings and exclaimings, natural as they were and fitting to Esau's character — the self-deceiving and extenuating emotions of the survivor, who tries to put in the best light the relations that existed between him and the deceased. It might be true that Isaac had been angry when Esau appeared, after Jacob had been there. For the old man might have feared that some stranger had been with him in the darkness, some villain who was no relation at all and made off with the blessing — which would certainly have been regarded as a catastrophe. But whether he would have been so enraged, and so sincerely enraged, if he had known that it was Jacob who preceded Esau, was a question not so easily answered as Esau's heart was fain to answer it. It was at bottom the same question as the other one, whether the love of the parents had actually been divided between the sons on the simple lines laid down by Esau: with "red-skinned" on the one side and "little Yekew" on the other. Jacob found some ground for doubt on the subject, but felt it unfitting to bring the same to the notice of his weeping brother.

Often, when the younger lad nestled at his mother's side, she had told him how hard it had been to carry the brothers in the months before they were born; how she had dragged herself about, mis-shapen and clumsy on her overburdened feet, while in her womb the two would not have peace but strove together over precedence. She said that he, Jacob, was actually the firstborn, in the eyes of Isaac's God, but that Esau had claimed the right with such violence that Jacob had courteously retired before him — very likely in the secret conviction that not much attention is paid between twins to the small difference in age, that it was not actually decisive, and that only out-side and in the course of time would the true firstborn be made mani-fest, the smoke of whose sacrifice would rise to the nostrils of the Most High. Rebecca's account seemed probable. Yes, Jacob certainly might have behaved like that, he himself seemed to recall doing it. But what the mother's tale betrayed was precisely this: that Esau's defiant little bid for priority had never been taken seriously by the parents, and the expectation of the blessing had for long hung in the balance between the brothers, even up to their early manhood and the fatal day; so that Esau might complain of a decision made against him, but not of an arbitrary injustice. For a long time, especially in the eyes of the father, his actual priority had weighed heavily enough to overcome any disinclination to Esau's character — and by char-acter I mean his physical as well as his mental and moral parts — but the time came when it did so no more. Red-haired he had been from the beginning, all over his body, like the fell of a bezoar, and equipped with a full set of teeth. These were uncanny manifestations, but Isaac set himself to welcome and interpret them in the most favourable sense. He wanted to stick to the elder-born and was himself the author and for long years the champion of the idea to which Esau clung, that Esau was his son and Jacob the mother's. He spoke to the fair-skinned and toothless infant and admonished his own soul, for about the small person was a sort of mild radiance, he had a wise and friendly little smile — whereas the other wrinkled up his face and squalled intolerably; but the smooth one was obviously delicate, there was not much hope of him, while the hairy one seemed made of heroic stuff and would certainly go far. Such-like phrases the father used every day, quoting old saws mechanically, though his voice

sometimes trembled with inward irritation; for Esau wounded Rebecca's breast with his untimely little teeth, so that they became
enflamed and young Jacob had to be fed on diluted goats' milk. "He
will be a hero," was what Isaac said to that, "and he is my son and
my firstborn. But the smooth one is thine, daughter of Bethuel, heart
of my heart!" For he called her so in this connection, and said that
the gentle child was her son and the rough one his. Which then did
he prefer? Esau. So it was stated later in the shepherds' songs and was
known at the time in all the region roundabout. Yitzchak loves Esau,
Rebecca Jacob, such was the view fostered by Yitzchak and supported by his own words — a little myth within a much larger and
more significant one, but contradicting the larger one to such extent
that it finally brought about Yitzchak's blindness.

We are to understand this statement in the light of the fact that
the fusion of soul and body is far more profound, the soul something
much more physical and the body much more malleable by the soul,
than has at times been thought. Isaac was blind, or as good as blind,
when he died, there is no denying it. But when his twins were small
his eyesight was not nearly so poor, and if by the time they were
young men it had grown very much worse, that was due to the fact
that he had neglected it for years; had humoured it by disuse, and
excused it on the ground of his tendency to conjunctivitis — an ailment very prevalent in his circle, Leah and several of her sons suffering from it all their lives. But the real ground was distaste. Is it possible for a man to become blind, or as nearly blind as Yitzchak was
in his old age, because he does not like to see, because seeing is a
torture to him, because he feels better in a darkness where certain
things can happen *which must happen?* I do not assert that such a
cause would have such a result; but only that the causes were present.

Esau was precocious, like an animal. When still a mere boy he
married several times, daughters of Canaan, Hittite women, Hivites,
as we know: first Judith and Adah, then Aholibamah and Bashemath.
He lodged his wives in his father's tents, was fruitful with them and
allowed them and their brood to practise their ancestral nature- and
idol-worship under the eye of his parents, the more unconcernedly
that he himself lacked all feeling for his father's lofty inheritance,
had struck up a hunting friendship with the people of Seir in the
south and openly paid homage to the tempestuous Kusakh. And as
the song later had it and it still stands in the chronicle, this was a
grief of mind to Isaac and Rebecca; to both of them, but of course
far more to Yitzchak than to his sister-bride, although Rebecca gave
vent to her irritation and Isaac was silent. He was silent, and when he
spoke his words were: "Mine is the red one. The firstborn is he, and
I hold him dear." But Isaac, the bearer of the blessing and custodian
of the God-idea which Abram had won, whom his brothers in the

faith regarded as the son and reincarnation of the Chaldæan, Isaac
suffered sore by reason of what he saw or must close his eyes to in
order not to see it, and suffered from his own weakness which prevented him from making an end of the difficulty by sending Esau
into the wilderness, as had actually been done with Ishmael, his beautiful wild uncle. The little inner myth prevented him, Esau's actual
priority of birth, which still bore heavily on the vexed question as to
which of the twins was the chosen one; thus he complained of his
eyes, how they ran, and of the burning of the lids, and that he saw
dimly, like the dying moon, that the light hurt him — and he sought
the darkness. Shall we say that he became blind in order not to witness the idol-worship of his daughters-in-law? Ah, that was the least
among all that offended his sight, that made him long for blindness —
because only so could that happen which must happen.

For the older the boys grew the clearer to a seeing eye grew the
lines of the "great myth" which despite all the father's principles
made the "little myth" more and more forced and untenable; the
clearer it became *who they both were*, in whose footsteps they
walked, on whose story they were founded, the red man and the
smooth man, the huntsman and the dweller in tents. How could Isaac,
who with Ishmael the wild ass had formed the brother pair; who
himself had not been Cain but Abel, not Ham but Shem, not Set but
Osiris, not Ishmael but Isaac the trueborn son — how could he, with
seeing eyes, have supported the claim that he preferred Esau? So his
eyes failed him, like the dying moon, and he lay in darkness that he
might be betrayed, together with Esau, his eldest son.

THE GREAT HOAXING

BUT actually nobody was deceived, not even Esau. For if I am ven-
turing here to write about people who did not always know precisely
who they were — Esau himself not being of the clearest on the subject and sometimes taking himself for the original goat of the Seir
people and mentioning him in the first person — yet this occasional
lack of clarity had to do only with the individual and the time-condi-
tioned, and was precisely the consequence of the fact that everybody
knew, perfectly well outside of time, and mythically and typically
speaking, who the individual was, and so did Esau, of whom it has
not been idly said that he was in his way as pious a man as Jacob. He
wept and raved, of course, after the betrayal, and was more murderously minded against his favoured brother than Ishmael had been
against his — indeed, it is true that he discussed with Ishmael an attack upon Isaac as well as upon Jacob. But he did all that because it
was the rôle he had to play; he knew and accepted the fact that all
events are a fulfilment, and that what had happened had happened

because it must, according to the archetype. That is to say, it was
not the first time, it was ceremonially and in conformity to pattern,
it had acquired presentness as in a recurrent feast and come round as
feasts do. For Esau, Joseph's uncle, was not the father of Edom.

Therefore when the hour came, the brothers being almost thirty,
when Yitzchak out of the darkness of his tent sent the slave who
served him — a youth lacking one ear, it having been cut off on account of his light-headedness and manifold shortcomings, greatly to
his amendment — to stand before Esau where he worked with the
hands in the ploughed field, to fold his arms across his black chest,
and announce: "The master hath need of my lord," Esau stood like
one rooted to the ground, and his ruddy face paled under the sweat
that covered it. He murmured the formula of compliance: "Here am
I." But in his soul he thought "Now is the time!" and that soul was
full of pride and dread and solemn unrest of mind.

Then he left the sunny field and went in unto his father who lay
in the half-light with two little damp pledgets on his eyes; made an
obeisance and said: "My lord hath summoned me."

Isaac answered rather querulously:

"That is the voice of my son, Esau. Is it thou, Esau? I have called
thee, for the hour is at hand. Come near to me, my eldest son, that I
may be sure of thee."

And Esau knelt in his goatskin apron beside the couch and raised
up his eyes to the little pledgets as though he would bore through
them into his father's eyes, while Isaac felt his shoulders and arms
and breast, saying:

"Yea, these are thy fells and Esau's red fleece, I see them with my
hands, which for good or evil have learned right well to fill the place
of my declining eyes. Hearken now, my son, and open thine ears and
receive the words of thy sightless father, for the hour is come. Behold, now I am old, I know not the day of my death and as my eyes
have long since failed, so it may be that I shall soon fail utterly and
disappear into the darkness so that my life is night and no more seen.
Therefore, that I die not before I hand on the blessing and give the
power from me and the inheritance, let it be now as it hath been: go
hence, my son, and take thy weapons, thy quiver and bow, with
which thou art mighty before the Lord, and go about in the plain
and the field and take me venison. And make me savoury meat such
as I love, cooked in sour milk by a bright fire and well seasoned, and
bring it to me that I may eat and be strengthened that I may bless
thee before I die, with seeing hands. This is my will, now go."

"It is already done," murmured Esau perfunctorily, yet remained
upon his knees and only bowed his head low so that the blind eyes
stared over it into space.

"Art thou still there?" asked Isaac. "A moment I thought thou wast already gone, and was not surprised, for the father is accustomed to have all performed quickly in love and fear according to his wish."

"It is already done," repeated Esau and went out. But after he had lifted the skin at the door of the tent he let it fall and came back, knelt again by the couch and spoke with breaking voice:

"My father!"

"What then!" asked Isaac, raising his brows above the pledgets. "It is well," he said then; "go, my son, for the hour is come, that is great for thee and for us all. Go, hunt and cook, that I may bless thee."

And Esau went out, with his head high, and stood before the tent, in the hour of his pride, and in a loud voice announced to all within hearing his impending honour. For events do not happen all at once, they happen point for point, they develop according to pattern, and it would be false to call a narrative entirely sad because the end is so. A tale with a lamentable close has yet its stages and times of honour, and it is right to regard these not from the point of view of the end, but rather in their own light, for while they are the present they have equal strength with the presentness of the conclusion. Thus Esau was proud in his hour and cried out with a ringing voice:

"Hear, ye people of the court, children of Abram and who burn sacrifice to Ya, hear ye, too, ye who sacrifice to Baal, wives of Esau and your seed, the fruit of my loins! Esau's hour is come. The lord will bless his son to-day. Isaac sendeth me forth to the fields that with the bow I may find him savoury meat to strengthen him for my sake. Fall down!"

And while those at hand who heard him fell upon their faces, Esau saw a maid running so that her breasts danced up and down.

That was the maid who shortwindedly announced to Rebecca what Esau had said in his boasting. And again the maid, quite breathless from running, came to Jacob, who was tending the sheep in company with a crop-eared dog named Tam, and leaning sunk in thought, on a long staff with a crook at the top. She gasped with her forehead bent to the grass: "The mistress!" Jacob looked at her and after a pause of some length answered very low: "Here am I." For in the pause he had thought in his soul: "The hour is come!" And his heart was full of pride and awe.

He gave his staff to Tam to watch and went in to Rebecca, who was awaiting him impatiently.

Rebecca, the successor of Sarah, was a matron with gold earrings, stately and strong-boned, with large features that still possessed much of the beauty once so alluring to Abimelech of Gerar. The gaze of her black eyes was shrewd and steadfast beneath arched brows that were evenly accentuated with pencilling and showed between them the two perpendicular folds of an energetic character. Her nose was well formed and masculine, with a pronounced hook and distended nostrils. Her voice was deep and resonant, and there was a line of little black hairs on her upper lip. Her black and silver locks were parted in the middle and came down upon her forehead, veiled by the brown headcloth which hung far down her back but left uncovered the fine shape of her noble shoulders and arms — these were in colour an amber-brown and the years had had as yet no power to touch them. She wore an ungirdled garment of figured wool, reaching down to her ankles. Her small, veined hands had just now been busy at the loom set up in the middle of the floor, correcting the women who squatted there using their fingers and wooden pegs to urge the flaxen woof through the warp. But she had stopped their work and sent them away, and was waiting for her son inside her own tent — the mistress's tent, hung with skins and mats. She moved swiftly towards Jacob as he respectfully entered.

"Yekew, my son," said she softly and low, and drew his upraised hands to her breast. "The time has come. The master would bless thee."

"Me would he bless?" asked Jacob, losing colour. "Me, and not Esau?"

"Thee in him," said she impatiently. "It is not a time for quibbling. Speak not nor seek to reason, but do as it is commanded thee, that no wrong may happen and no error come to pass."

"What is the command of my little mother from whom I have my life, as at the time when I was still within her?" Jacob asked.

"Hearken," she said. "He hath ordered him to slay and make him a savoury meat to strengthen him for the blessing. That canst thou do quicker and better than he. Go then to the flock, take two kids, kill them and bring them. Of the best parts I will make for the father a meal such that he will leave none for thee. Away!"

Jacob began to tremble, he did not cease to tremble unto the end. At times he had the greatest trouble to control the chattering of his teeth. He said:

"Merciful mother of men! As the word of a goddess is thy word to me, yet what thou sayest is more dangerous than can be told. Esau is hairy all over and thy child is smooth with but little exception. If now our lord lay hold upon me and feel my smoothness, how shall I stand before him? As though I would deceive him, surely, and I should have instead of his blessing his curse straightway upon my head."

"Art again at thy hair-splitting?" she hectored him. "Upon me be the curse. I will see to it. Away and fetch the kids. A mistake is in act to be made."

He ran. He hastened to the slope near the tents, where the goats were pastured, seized two of the young kids as they gambolled about their mother, and cut their throats, calling to the goatherd that they were for the mistress. He let their blood run out before the lord, flung them over his shoulder by the hind legs and went home, his heart thumping. The little heads hung down behind, with their small curling horns and cleft snouts, their eyes glazing — so early sacrificed, to so great an end. Rebecca stood waiting. She nodded.

"Quick," said she. "All is ready."

There was a hearth built of stones under her roof, and a fire burnt under the brazen pot and all the gear was there for the cooking. His mother took the kids and began hastily to skin and cut them up. She moved about the blazing hearth, large and capable, fork in hand, stirred and seasoned, and during all this there was silence between the two. But while the dish was cooking Jacob saw how she took out of her clothes-press garments which lay there folded, shirt and smock: Esau's festal garments, which she kept for him, as Jacob remembered, going pale again. Then he saw her cut up into strips and pieces with the knife the skins of the kids, which were wet inside and sticky with blood, and he shuddered at the sight. But Rebecca bade him take off the long smock with half-sleeves which was at that time his daily wear, and drew over his smooth and shivering arms the short shift and then the fine coat of blue and red wool, which left one shoulder bare. Then she said "Come!" And while her lips moved in murmured words and the frown stood out on her brow she put on him the pieces of skin everywhere where he was bare and smooth, on neck and arms, on his shanks and on the backs of his hands and bound them fast with thread, although they were sticky and clung of themselves, most unpleasantly.

She murmured:

"I cover the child, I cover the youth, changed be the child, changed the youth, by the skin, by the fell."

And again:

"I cover the child, I cozen the lord, the lord shall touch, the father shall eat, the brothers of the deep shall be made to serve thee."

Then with her own hands she washed his feet, as she had done when he was small; took anointing oil that smelt of the fields and the fragrance of the fields, which was Esau's oil, and anointed his head and his newly washen feet, and as she did so muttered through her clenched teeth:

"I anoint the child, I anoint the stone, the blind shall eat; at thy feet, at thy feet must fall the brethren of the deeps!"

Then she said: "It is finished"; he stood up, clumsy and altered by his strange disguise, with his arms and legs stuck stiffly out, and his teeth a-chatter. Meanwhile she dished up the savoury meat, with wheaten bread and golden-clear oil to dip it in, and a jug of wine;

gave the whole into his hands and said: "Now go thy ways!"

And Jacob went, laden with the meal, awkward and straddling in his fear lest the hatefully sticky skins slip awry under the cords. His heart beat hard, his face was screwed up, and his eyes were on the ground. Many of the household saw him as he passed through the court, held up their hands and wagged their heads; they clucked with their tongues and kissed their finger-tips, and said: "Lo, the master!" He came before his father's tent, put his mouth to the curtain and spoke:

"Here am I, my father. May thy servant lift his foot to enter unto thee?"

Out of the depths of the tent came Isaac's fretful voice:

"But who art thou? Art thou not a thief and the son of a thief, that thou comest before my tent and sayest it is I? For anyone can say I, but all depends upon who sayeth it."

Jacob answered, and his teeth did not chatter, because he clenched them: "It is thy son who hath said I, for I have hunted and killed for thee to eat."

"Well and good," answered Isaac then. "Come thy ways in."

Then Jacob entered into the twilight of the tent, at the back of which ran a covered clay ledge, and Yitzchak lay upon it, wrapped in his mantle and his head elevated upon a headrest with a bronze half-ring, and with the pledgets over his eyes. He asked again:

"Who art thou then?"

And Jacob answered, in a failing voice:

"I am Esau, the hairy, thy elder son, and I have done as thou hast commanded. Sit up then, my father, and strengthen thy soul, for here is the meat."

But Isaac did not yet sit up. He asked:

"How so soon hast thou found game and so quickly brought it within the range of thy bow?"

"The Lord thy God, he hath given me good hunting," answered Jacob, and his voice died away on some of the syllables. However, he had said "thy" God, speaking for Esau, whose god was not the God of Isaac.

"But how is it then with me?" asked Isaac again. "For thy voice is uncertain, Esau, my eldest son; yet it sounds to me like the voice of Jacob."

Then Jacob knew not what to say for fear, and stood quaking. But Isaac spoke with mildness:

"Yet often are the voices of brothers alike, and words come with the same sounds out of their mouths. Come hither, that I may feel thee with my seeing hands, whether thou art Esau my eldest son or no."

Jacob obeyed. He set down his burdens, came close and offered himself to be felt. And when he was near he saw that his father had bound the pledgets to his head with a cord that they should not fall off when he sat up, just as Rebecca had secured upon himself the hateful skins.

Isaac felt about a little in the air with his fingers spread out before he touched Jacob. Then the lean white hands found him out and felt him, over his neck and arms where no garment was, on the backs of his hands and down his legs, everywhere touching the skins of the kids.

"Yea," said he, "these are thy hairy limbs and Esau's red fleeces, I see them with my seeing hands and must be convinced. The voice is the voice of Jacob, but the hands are the hands of Esau. Art thou then my very son Esau?"

And he said: "Thou seest and sayest it."

"Then give me to eat," said Isaac and he sat up, with his mantle hanging down over his knees. And Jacob took the dish and crouched down at his father's feet and held out the meat. But first Isaac bent over with his hands on Jacob's skin-covered hands and smelt of the dish.

"It is good," he said. "Thou hast prepared it well. It is in sour cream, as I have commanded, and there is in it cardamom and thyme and somewhat of caraway." And he named the names of other things that were therein which he discerned by his sense of smell. So he nodded and fell to and ate of the dish.

He ate it all, it took a long time.

"Hast thou bread likewise, Esau, my son?" he asked as he chewed.

"Wheaten cakes and oil, of a surety," answered Jacob.

He broke off some of the bread, dipped it in the oil and brought it to his father's mouth. The old man chewed and took more meat, stroking his beard and nodding his satisfaction, while Jacob looked up in his face and watched him while he ate. It was very thin and transparent, this face, with fine hollows in the cheeks, and a sparse grey beard springing from them, a thin high nose with delicate nostrils, whose bridge was like the blade of a knife. Despite the pledgets on the eyes it looked so spiritual, so well-nigh holy, as to make the meal and the chewing appear unfitting. Jacob was almost ashamed to watch the old man while he ate — as though he must feel ashamed to be watched. But it may be that the pledgets protected him, at all events he chewed away very comfortably, his thin jaw moving up and down under the scanty beard, and as only the best parts of the kids were in the dish, he ate it all.

"Give me to drink," he said then. And Jacob hastened to fetch the wine jug and hold it himself to the thirsty lips, Isaac's hands grasping it over his son's hairy ones. But as Jacob came thus close to his father the old man smelled the nard in his hair and the fragrance of the

flowers of the field in his garments; he turned away from the jug
to say:

"Truly it is strangely deceiving, how my son's festal garments
smell sweet, like the fields and the meadows in the spring of the year
when the Lord hath sown them far and wide with blossoms for our
delight."

And with two thin finger-tips he lifted one pledget a very little
and said:

"And thou art then verily Esau, my oldest son?"

Jacob laughed in desperation and asked in his turn:

"Who then else?"

"Then it is good," spake Isaac and took a long draught, so that his
Adam's apple went up and down under the beard. Then he commanded that water be poured over his hands. But when Jacob had
done this and dried his hands, the father said:

"So let it be."

And mightily strengthened by the food and drink, flushed of face,
he laid his hands upon the trembling and crouching Jacob, to bless
him with all his strength, and as his soul was strong from the meal he
had taken, so were his words full of all the power and richness of the
earth. Its fatness gave he him, and its voluptuousness like to a female's,
and thereto the dew and the male water of the sky, gave him the fullness of the ploughland, tree and vine, and the rank fruitfulness of the
flocks and a double shearing in each year. He laid upon him the covenant, and gave him to bear the promise and the inheritance of that
which had been founded throughout time. His words were high-
sounding and flowed like a stream. He gave him the victory in the
battle of the hemispheres, the light and the dark, and victory over the
dragon of the waste; he called him the beautiful moon and bringer
of the equinox, with laughter and the renewal of the year. He used
the fixed phrase which Rebecca had muttered: the primitive phrase
which was so old that it was already a mystery; it did not precisely
fit the case, for here the brothers were only two. But Isaac uttered it
solemnly above his head: the children of his mother shall serve the
bearer of the blessing, and all his brothers shall fall down at his
anointed feet. Then he cried out three times the name of God, and
said: "So be it and so may it come to pass!" and released Jacob out of
his hands.

Jacob rushed away to his mother. But shortly afterwards Esau
came home with a young wild goat which he had shot — and matters
became both comic and tragic.

Jacob saw with his own eyes nothing of that which followed, nor
had he any desire to, and kept himself hidden. But he knew all from
hearsay, and remembered it as well as though he had been present.

Esau came back still in the same high mood, knowing nothing, of course, of what had happened in the meantime, for he had not reached that stage in the tale. Puffed up with pride and self-esteem, with his bow in his hairy fist and the buck over his shoulder, he marched in triumph, throwing out his legs, and beaming darkly in all directions to see if his splendour and preferment were being observed. Still at some distance he began to boast again, so loud and vaingloriously that it was both comic and painful for all who heard. And those who had seen Jacob go in unto the master in his skins and come out again all put their heads together, and likewise those who had not seen it. Only Esau's women and children drew not near, though he summoned them repeatedly to come and witness his greatness and his pride.

The household ran together and laughed to see him throw out his legs and made a circle round him to see and hear what he did. For he began to skin his buck, as he continued to boast; dressed and cut it up, made a fire with kindlings, hung a kettle over it and shouted out commands to the laughing watchers to bring him this and that of which he had need for the feast.

"Ha, ha," he cried, and "Ho, ho! Ye godly gapers! Fetch me the great cook's fork! And bring me sour milk of the sheep for he savours it best seethed in sheep's milk. And bring me salt from the salt mine, good-for-nothings and idlers: coriander and garlic, mint and mustard to tickle his palate, for I would cram him so that the strength breaks out at his pores. And bring me good *solet* bread to eat with the dish and oil pounded from olives, and strain the wine, ye sluggards and slumberers, so that no yeast come in the jug, or may the white ass trample you! Run and fetch. For it is the feast of the feeding and the blessing of Isaac, Esau's feast, the feast of the hero and son, whom the lord hath sent to make him a meal, and whom he will bless within his tent in this hour!"

Thus he went on, with mouth and hand, with ha, ha! and ho, ho! and bombast and braggadocio, with windy boasting of his father's preference and the great day come to the red skin; so that the folk of the household bent double and writhed with laughter and wept and held their sides. He went off with his dish, holding it high before him like the tabernacle, and throwing out his legs and prancing up to his father's tent; and they shrieked aloud, clapping and stamping their feet — and then were suddenly still. For Esau, at the door of the tent, was saying:

"Here am I, my father. Let my father arise and eat of his son's venison that thy soul may bless me. Is it his will that I come in?"

Isaac's voice came forth:

"Who is it that sayest I and will come in to the blind man?"

"Esau, thy hairy-skin," answered he, "hath hunted and cooked for the strengthening, as thou commandest."

"Thou fool and robber!" the voice said. "Why speakest thou false-hood in my sight? For Esau, my eldest, he was here long since and gave me to eat and drink, and I have blessed him."

Then Esau was so startled that he almost let everything fall and he gave such a jump that he spilled the sour cream sauce all over him. His auditors roared with laughter. They wagged their heads feebly and wiped the water out of their eyes and shook it off. But Esau rushed into the tent, without more asking, and there came a silence, while those outside covered their mouths with their hands and thrust their elbows into each other's ribs. But presently came a roar from inside, a perfectly incredible roar, and Esau burst out again, no longer red, but purple in the face, with uplifted arms. "Curse it, curse it, curse it," he shrieked, at the top of his lungs — words we might use to-day on occasion of some trifling vexation. But at that time, and from the lips of Esau the shaggy, it was a new cry, full of the origi-nal meaning, for he himself had really been cursed, instead of blessed, solemnly betrayed and made a mock of like no one before him, in the eyes of the people. "Curse it," he shrieked. "Betrayed, betrayed, be-trayed!" And he sat himself down on the ground and howled with his tongue hanging out, his tears rolled down the size of hazel nuts, while the crowd stood round and laughed until they cried at this tremen-dous sell, the story of the hoaxing of Esau the red.

JACOB MUST JOURNEY

THEN came the flight, Jacob's escape from house and camp, planned and carried out by his resolute and stouthearted mother, who sent her darling away content never to see him again if only he possessed the blessing and might carry it through the years. She was too wise and far-seeing not to know what must be the issue of that solemn betrayal; but she assumed the burden deliberately, as she had de-liberately laid it upon her son, and offered up her heart.

She did so silently; even in the necessary conversation with Isaac not a word was said of the real posture of affairs; they avoided actualities. But nothing escaped her. It lay in the nature of things that Esau would brood in his bewildered soul over plans of revenge, and seek to upset what she had done. But also she knew how he went about to play the rôle of Cain. She learned that he had got in touch with Ishmael, the man of the wilderness, the darkly beautiful youth who had been cast forth. They plotted together — nothing could be more natural. They were of the same disadvantaged breed — the brother of Isaac, the brother of Jacob; they walked in the same footsteps, they were unlovely, shut out; of course they would draw together. In reality, matters were even worse than Rebecca had foreseen, for Esau's murderous thoughts were directed not only

towards Jacob but towards Isaac as well. She heard that he had
proposed to Ishmael to murder the blind man, after which he, Esau,
would take upon himself the smooth man. He shrank from the deed
of Cain, shrank from becoming more, and more clearly, himself
through committing it. Thus the suggestion that the uncle give him
courage by acting first. But Ishmael made difficulties, and that gave
his sister-in-law time to turn round. He did not care for the idea.
Memories of the feeling he had once cherished towards his more
delicate brother, which must then have been made the pretext for
his expulsion, made it hard for him, he said, to raise his hand against
Isaac. Esau would better do that himself; then he, Ishmael, would
plant an arrow so neatly in the back of Jacob's neck that it would
stick out through his throat in front and the favourite would straightway measure his length on the ground.

It was like Ishmael to make these proposals. They were something
new, whereas Esau had only the traditional fratricide in mind. He
did not understand the other's meaning, and thought he was talking
at random. Father-murder did not come within his range of ideas,
it had never happened, there was not such a thing, the proposal was
without practical value, it was absurd. It might come to pass that a
man cut off his father's manhood, with a sickle, as had been done
to Noah; but to kill him — the idea was sheer moonshine. Ishmael
laughed at his nephew's open-mouthed incomprehension. He knew
that the idea was far from being moonshine; that it had in fact quite
a venerable actuality and was perhaps the beginning of all things;
that Esau contented himself with stopping short too soon, with beginning too late, when he thought such a thing had never come to
pass. He told him so, and more. He said things that, when he heard
them for the first time, made Esau run away in horror with his fleeces
standing on end. He recommended him, after killing his father, to
eat abundantly of the flesh, in order to incorporate into himself the
Abram-blessing; and to that end he must not cook Isaac's body but
eat from it raw with bones and blood — whereat Esau ran away a
second time.

He came back, of course; but it took some time for them to ap-
portion their rôles in the murder drama, and that gave mother Rebecca time to act. She told Isaac nothing of what his near relatives
were plotting against him. Husband and wife confined their conversations to Jacob, and not in the sense that he was threatened by
danger — though even Isaac must have been aware of that. Their
talk had no reference to the deception or the wrath of Esau — about
that they were altogether silent. They merely said that Jacob must
go a journey to Mesopotamia, in search of his Aramaic kin, for if
he stopped here there was danger of him making an unfortunate
marriage — he too! It was on this plane the parents came to an under-

standing. If Jacob took a wife from the daughters of the land, said Rebecca, a Hittite woman, who would be like Esau's wives, and commit the abomination of idol-worship, what, she asked Isaac in all seriousness, would life be worth to her? Isaac nodded, and on this ground agreed with her that Jacob must go away for a while. For a while. So she told Jacob too and she meant it seriously, at least she hoped it would be so. She knew Esau, he was a harebrained, light-headed creature, he would forget. He was bent on bloodshed just now, but his mind could be distracted. She knew that while he was with Ishmael in the wilderness he had lost his head over Ishmael's daughter, Mahalath, and considered marriage with her. Perhaps even now his mind was beginning to dwell on this more peaceful concern rather than on thoughts of revenge. When he seemed to have calmed down and abandoned all such ideas, then Jacob would receive a message from her and return home to her bosom. For the present, her brother Laban, the son of Bethuel, living seventeen days' journey from here, in the country of Naharaim, would receive him with open arms. So the flight was resolved upon and Jacob privily got ready for the journey towards Aram. Rebecca did not weep. But she held him long to her in the early dawn, stroked his cheeks, hung charms round his and his camels' necks, embraced him again and thought in her heart that if her god or another so willed it she might perhaps never see him again. So it turned out. But Rebecca had no regrets, either then or later.

JACOB MUST WEEP

WE know what happened to the traveller on the first day out — his shame, and his great exaltation. But the exaltation was inward, a great soul-vision, whereas the disgrace was actual and physical, like the journey, which he then had to continue in its sign and as its victim: alone, that is, and a beggar. The way was long, and he was not Eliezer, to whom the land "came to meet him" as he went. He thought a great deal about the old man. Abram's messenger and head servant, who had resembled his forefather in face, according to all accounts, and who had come this way on his great errand, to fetch Rebecca for Isaac. But he had travelled in state as was fitting, with his ten camels and all goodly gear of his master's providing, with necessities and with superfluities, as Jacob himself had been before the accursed meeting with Eliphaz. Why had God the King seen fit to do this to him? Why had he punished him with such wretchedness and hardship? For that the matter was one of punishment, of retribution and compensation for Esau's sake, he did not doubt; and upon his hard and heavy journey he pondered much upon the nature of the Lord, who had certainly willed and brought about what had happened yet punished him, Jacob, for it, making him pay for Esau's tears — if only for form's sake, as it were, and with benevolent partiality. For all his burden, however heavy — was it fair payment for the advantage he had over his permanently disadvantaged brother? The mere question made Jacob laugh in his beard — the beard which had grown on his journey, that darkened the more his lean brown face, glistening with sweat beneath the damp and dirty headcloth.

It was high summer, the month Ab, hopelessly hot and dry. The dust lay finger-thick on trees and shrubbery. Jacob swayed loosely on the ridge of his lean uncomfortable camel, whose great knowing eyes were infested round with flies and grew ever wearier and more melancholy; when he passed other travellers he veiled his face. Or he eased the animal by leading it on the bridle, walking beside it on one of the parallel paths that made up the road, his feet deep in a dust of powdered stone. He slept in the open — in the field, at the foot of a tree in an olive orchard, beside the wall of a village, as it happened, lying close to his beast for warmth; for the nights were often perishingly cold, and he was used to houses and sensitive, so that he often caught cold and coughed like a consumptive on the hottest day. The cough was troublesome, it hindered him in earning his living; for of course he had to get his bread by relating to all and sundry the story of his distresses and the reason why he, the son of such a family, was journeying in poverty. He told his tale in the villages, in the market squares, by the well outside the wall, where he was permitted to wash himself and water his beast. Men and boys, and women with jugs stood round and listened to his tale, which was broken by coughing but otherwise well and vividly told. He gave his name, celebrated his origins, described in detail the lordly life he led in his own home and the rich meals he sat down to. Then went on to draw a picture of the loving liberality with which he, the firstborn son of the house, had been equipped for the journey to Harran in the land of Aram, eastwards and northwards, beyond the river Prath, where dwelt certain kin of his, whose repute among the inhabitants of the land was not matter for wonder, seeing how many thousands of sheep and goats they possessed. He had been sent to them, and the reason of his sending was partly business, but partly a religious mission of far-reaching importance. He dwelt in detail on the gifts and tokens he had had in his pack, the adornments of his camels, the weapons for securing his princely safety, the dainties for him and his train; and his sensation-hungry auditors, though well aware that a man can draw a long bow, unanimously refrained from making any distinction between the true and the well invented, and stood with eyes and mouths open wide as they listened. In such state he had left home; but alas, certain districts of the land were infested with bandits. They were quite young but uncommonly bold. As he passed with his caravan through a ravine, they had with their great numbers cut off his advance and his rear, also any possibility of escaping sideways; and a battle had ensued, more thrilling than anything of the kind in the memory of man — Jacob painted it in detail, thrust for thrust and blow for blow. The ravine had been filled with bodies of men and beasts, he himself had laid low seven times seven young robbers and each one of his men a smaller number. But alas, the superior numbers of the foe had told in the end, one after another his own people had fallen round him, and after many hours of fighting, he, the sole survivor, had voided the field.

Why, asked a woman, had they not killed him too?

They had tried to. The robber captain, youngest and most insolent of the band, had lifted his sword for the mortal blow, but Jacob in his great need had called upon his God and the name of the God of his fathers; with the result that the bloodthirsty youth's sword had been shattered in mid-air into seven times seventy pieces. And the detestable creature's senses were so dazed, and he so sorely smitten with fright, that he and his men had fled away, taking with them, however, all Jacob's possessions, and he was left naked. Naked then he had steadfastly pursued his course, for at his goal there awaited him only balsam for his wounds, milk and honey, and clothing of purple and fine linen. But till then, alas, he had nought, no place to lay his head, nothing to still the pangs of hunger in his belly, for it was empty these many days.

He struck his breast, and his hearers at the booths where they sold meat and drink did likewise, for they were affected by his story and found it shameful that such things could come to pass and the highways be so unsafe. In their country, they said, there were guards on the road, one every two hours' journey. Then they gave the afflicted man to eat: cakes and dumplings, cucumbers, garlic and dates, sometimes even a pair of pigeons or a duck, and they put down hay and even grain for his beast to give it strength to proceed on its way.

Thus he went on, moving towards the course of the Jordan, into hollow Syria, the gorge of the Orontes and the foot of Mount Lebanon; but his progress was slow, for he had to earn his bread. He visited the temples in the cities, talked with the priests about the divine essence, and made a good impression on them with wise and well-informed words, so that they let him strengthen and provide himself from the store chambers of the god. He saw upon his travels much that was beautiful and sacred; saw the Lordly Mountain of the furthest north sparkle as with fiery precious stones, and prayed to it; saw regions watered by the snow from the mountains, where the tall trunks of the swaying date palms were like the scaly tails of dragons where the landscape was dark with groves of cedar and sycamore, and there were trees with clusters of sweet fruit like bread. He saw crowded cities, and Damascus lying among fruit orchards and enchanted gardens. There he saw a sundial. And from there, in fear and repulsion, he saw the desert. It was red, as it should be, stretching eastwards in a dull red haze, a sea of impurity, the playground of evil spirits, the lower world. Yes, this now fell to Jacob's lot: God sent him into the desert, because he had been the cause of Esau's loud and bitter wailing; it was God's will. His path, which had led on Beth-el's height to so comforting an ascent, had now attained its westernmost point, where it descended into the infernal regions of the world, and who knew what danger of dragons awaited him there? He wept a little, as he swayed into the wastes on the hump of his beast. Ahead of him a jackal was running, dirty-yellow, with pointed ears, his tail sticking out stiffly behind, a sorry god-beast, an offensive mask. He ran before the rider, sometimes letting him come so near that Jacob could scent his pungent smell; turned his dog's head to look at the rider out of hateful little eyes, then trotted on, with his abrupt laugh. Jacob was far too well versed in such matters not to recognize in him the opener of the way, the everlasting guide into the kingdom of the dead. He would have been surprised not to see him, and wept afresh as he followed on into those drear and barren stretches of the borderland between Syria and Naharina, among loose boulders and desolate rock, through stony fields and plains of clay and sand, burnt-out steppe and dry tamarisk thicket. He was fairly clear as to his route, the way his first forefather had once taken in reverse direction, the son of Terah, coming to the place whither Jacob now strove, sent westwards, as he now eastwards. The thought of Abram somewhat consoled him in his loneliness; moreover the road was not without all trace of human beings and their concerns. Here and there was a clay tower, that one might climb, first to look round, but also if one were in danger from wild beasts. And now and then there was even a well. But best of all there were signposts, stakes and stones set up with inscriptions, guided by which night travel was possible, provided there was even a little moonlight — they had doubtless served Abram upon his journeyings. Jacob praised God for the good deeds of civilization, and followed Nimrod's signposts towards the river Prath, that is to say towards the point he had in mind, which was the right one: where the Very Broad issued from the mountain gorges through which it burst from the north, and subsided in the plain. O wonderful hour, when Jacob stood at last in the mud among the reeds and let his poor beast drink from the yellow flood! A bridge of boats crossed it, and on the other side lay a town; but it was not the dwelling of the moon god, not the city of the way and Nahor's city. That was still far off across the eastern plain, which he had yet to cross by the help of the signposts, under the burning fiery sun of Ab. Seventeen days? Ah, it became much more for Jacob, needing as he did to keep on relating his bloodthirsty tale — he knew not how many times, he had ceased to count, and only knew that the earth by no means sprang to meet him, but rather the contrary, doing all it could to keep withdrawing the goal from his weary march. But he never forgot — he spoke of it even on his death-bed — how it was suddenly there, all in a moment, when he least expected it and thought it far away; he had reached it, or as good as reached it; after all, it did come to meet him, together with the best and dearest of all it had to give — that which Jacob then had one day, after his long, long sojourn, to take away with him.

JACOB COMES TO LABAN

ONE day, toward evening, as the sun was sinking behind him in the sallow mists and the shadow of rider and beast was like a tower on the plain; on this late afternoon, when the air would not cool but was a breathless heat under the brazen dome of heaven, so that it quivered above the dry grass and seemed about to burst into flame; when Jacob's tongue was parched in his throat for he had had no water since the day before and went rocking along with his mind in a daze — he saw between two hills that made a gateway into a rolling stretch of country a moving point far off in the plain; and his eye, keen despite his fatigue, recognized it at once as a flock of sheep with shepherds and dogs, gathered round a well. He jumped for joy and breathed a thankful sigh to Yah the Most High God; but his only clear thought was "Water, water!" and he cried out the word from his parching throat, clucking to his beast, that seemed to know the joyful news, for it summoned its powers, stretched its neck, dilated its nostrils, and lengthened its stride.

Soon he was so near that he could see the coloured markings on the sheep, the faces of the herdsmen under their shady hats, the hair on their breasts and the bands on their arms. The dogs growled and were on the defensive, preventing the sheep from scattering; but the men quieted them with a word, for they had no fear of a single rider, and also they saw that he greeted them courteously even from afar. There were four or five men, Jacob remembered, with perhaps two hundred sheep, of a large, thick-tailed breed, as his trained eye quickly noted. They were squatting idly round the well, which was still covered with a round stone. They all carried slings and one of them a lute. Jacob spoke to them at once, calling them brothers and with his hand to his forehead, saying to them at random that their god was great, although he was not certain which one they acknowledged. But to that as well as to whatever else he said they only shook their heads, or rather wagged them from side to side, indicating their regret by clucking with their tongues. But one of them turned out to have a silver disk on his breast with his name on it — Jerubbaal — and to be a native of Amurruland, as he said. His speech was not quite like Jacob's, but sufficiently so that they understood each other and Jerubbaal the shepherd could act as interpreter and translate what Jacob said into the *ummu-ummu* language of the others. They conveyed their thanks for his acknowledgment of the power of their god, invited him to sit down in their circle, and introduced themselves by their names, which were Bullutu, Shamash-Lamassi, Dog of Ea, and so on. He did not leave them to ask his own name and origins but hastened to give them, with a passing but embittered reference to the mischance which had reduced him to such poverty, and implored them above all else to give him water for his parching tongue. They handed him a leathern bottle, the water was already lukewarm, but he gulped it down rejoicing. His camel, however, had to wait; the sheep too seemed waiting to be watered, yet the stone lay over the mouth of the well and nobody rolled it away.

Whence came his brothers, Jacob asked.

"Harran, Harran," they answered. "Bel-Harran, lord of the way. Great, great — the greatest."

"One of the greatest, at least," said Jacob guardedly. "But I am bound for Harran. Is it far?"

Not far at all. The town lay on the other side of the nearby slope. They could reach it with their flocks in an hour.

"Praise be to God!" Jacob cried. "Then am I at the end, after more than seventeen days' journeying. Scarcely can I believe it." And he asked them if they knew Laban, son of Bethuel, son of Nahor, since they were from Harran.

They knew him well. He dwelt not in the city, but only a half-hour from here. They were waiting for his sheep.

Was he in good health?

Very good. Why?

"Because I have heard of him," Jacob said. "Do you pluck your sheep or shear them?"

They all answered with scorn that of course they sheared them. Did they pluck them where he came from?

Oh, no, he answered. They were far enough on, in Beersheba and the region round, to have shears.

They came back to Laban, saying that they were waiting for Rachel, his daughter.

As to that, he cried, he had greatly longed to enquire — about the waiting, that was. "For ye sit here round the covered well like watchmen, instead of rolling away the stone that your flocks may drink. Why then? True, it is yet early to drive them home, but ye could move the stone and water your lord's sheep instead of lounging here, even though ye must still wait for the wench, Laban's daughter, whatever her name is."

He spoke with authority, like a man who is more than a servant, even though he called them brothers. For the water had strengthened him in body and mind and he felt his superiority.

They talked together — *ummu, ummu,* and then told him through Jerubbaal that what they did was regular and in order, and a matter of courtesy. They might not roll away the stone and water and go home before Rachel came with the sheep which she tended for her father. For all the flocks had to be gathered together and driven home at the same time, and if Rachel reached the well before them she too waited until they came and rolled away the stone.

"Ye say sooth," Jacob laughed. "For she is but a maiden and it needeth the arms of men to roll away the lid." But they answered that was all the same, why she waited, in any case she did so, and they did the same.

"Good," said Jacob then. "Ye are belike in the right, and for you it would not be right any other way. But I am sad that my camel must thirst so long. How said ye that the maiden's name is? Rachel?" he repeated. "Jerubbaal, say what that meaneth in our tongue. Hath she then yeaned, the ewe, for whom we wait so long?"

Oh no, they said, she was as pure as the spring lilies in the field and undefiled like the petals of the garden rose in the dewy morning, and had never known the arms of man. She was twelve years old.

It was plain that they respected her, and unconsciously Jacob did the same. He smiled and drew a long breath, for the thought of meeting with his uncle's child made his heart contract a little with pleasurable curiosity. He chatted a while longer with the shepherds, through Jerubbaal: about the local prices for sheep, and how much wool one got for five minas, and how many selas of corn their masters allowed them in the month. Until one of them said: "She cometh." Jacob had just begun to beguile the time with his robber story, but he broke off and turned to look where the shepherd pointed. Thus first he beheld her, his heart's destiny, his soul's bride, for whose lovely eyes he was to serve fourteen years, the mother sheep of his lamb.

Rachel was walking in the midst of her flock; it huddled close about her, and a dog with lolling tongue ran at the margin of the woolly flood. She raised her staff, the shepherd's crook, the top of which consisted of a metal sickle or knife, by way of greeting the group; putting her head on one side and smiling — so that Jacob, while she was still at a distance, saw for the first time her shining white teeth, with the spaces between them. As she came up she overtook the animals round her and walked in front, parting them with her crook. "Here am I," said she; like a short-sighted person she contracted her eyes, but then lifted her brows in surprise and delight as she added: "Lo, a stranger!" She must have seen long before, if her short-sightedness was not unusually bad, Jacob's figure and the riding-camel, but she had given no sign at first.

The shepherds round the well kept silence and held back from the meeting of the young master and mistress. Jerubbaal too seemed to feel that they were already in touch; he gazed in the air, munching grain. Jacob greeted Rachel with upraised hands, while her dog barked round them. She gave a quick word of reply to his salute, and the two stood there, soberly, side by side, in the bright slanting rays of the late afternoon sun, among the tumbling sheep, enveloped in their warm and friendly steam, under the wide pale sky.

Laban's daughter was slender — as one could see despite the shapelessness of her garment, a yellow smock or pinafore with a red border patterned in black moons. It hung free and comfortably from throat to hem, showing the little bare feet, but fitted round the shoulders displaying their appealing fineness and tenderness, and it had sleeves reaching halfway down the upper arm. Her black hair was tumbled rather than curled, and almost short, at least shorter than Jacob had ever seen it on women at home; only two braids, curling at the ends, hung across her cheeks and down upon her shoulders. She played with one of them as she stood and looked. What a sweet face! Who shall describe its magic? Who shall decipher the sum of those sweet and happy dispensations of providence, out of which life, groping among inherited stores, adds the one unique thing to make up the charm of the human face? It is a charm balanced on a razor's edge, it hangs, as one may say, on a hair; so that if one tiny trait were altered, the smallest muscle differently placed, though but little were changed yet the heart's delight, the whole little miracle, would be lacking. Rachel was beautiful and well-favoured, and both at once in such an arch and gentle way that one saw — Jacob saw, as she looked at him — how spirit and will-power, wisdom and courage in their feminine counterparts, were the effective source of all this loveliness, so expressive her whole person was of open-eyed readiness for life. She looked towards him, one hand fingering her braid, the other grasping the staff that rose above her head, and measured the young man, gaunt from his journey, in dusty, faded and tattered garments, with the brown and bearded, sweat-marked face that was not the face of a hireling. As she looked, the nostrils — perhaps too thick — of her little nose seemed to dilate drolly, and her upper lip, which stuck out somewhat beyond the lower, to shape with it in the corners of her mouth, all by itself and with no tension of the muscles, that lovely thing, a tranquil smile. But loveliest and best of all was the look, peculiarly sweetened and transfigured by her short-sightedness, in her black, perhaps just faintly slanting eyes, that look which, with no exaggeration, nature had endowed with the uttermost of charm that she can give a human face — a deep, liquid, speaking, melting, friendly night, at once serious and playful, and such as Jacob never before in all his life had seen or thought to see.

"Down, Marduka!" she cried, stooping to reprove the noisy dog. And then she asked, as Jacob could guess without understanding:

"Whence cometh my lord?"

He pointed westwards over his shoulder and said Amurru.

She turned towards Jerubbaal and laughing beckoned him with a motion of her chin.

"So far?" said she, in words and gestures. And then she asked in more detail, saying that the west was wide, and naming two or three of its cities.

"Beersheba," Jacob answered.

She started and repeated the word, and her mouth, which he had already begun to love, shaped the name of Isaac.

His face twitched, his mild eyes ran over. He did not know Laban's people and would not have been eager for contact with them. He was an outlaw, stolen to the lower world, not here of his own will, and felt not much cause for soft emotion. But his nerves gave way; under the strain of the journey they had gone soft. He was at his goal, and this maiden, with eyes so darkly sweet, uttered his far-off father's name and was his mother's brother's child.

"Rachel," said he, with a sob, and put out his arms to her, his hands trembling. "May I kiss thee?"

"How canst thou claim such a right?" she asked, and retreated in smiling dismay. She gave no sign of suspecting anything, just as before she had not seemed to mark the presence of a stranger.

But with one arm still stretched out towards her he pointed to his own breast.

"Jacob, Jacob," he said. "I. Yitzchak's son, Rebecca's son, Laban, thou, I, child of mother, child of brother. . . ."

She gave a little cry. She put one hand on his breast and so held him away from her as together they reckoned up the kinship between them, laughing, but with tears in both their eyes. They cried out names, nodded their heads, making out the genealogical tree by signs to each other, putting their forefingers together, crossing them, or laying the left across the tip of the right.

"Laban — Rebecca," cried she. "Bethuel, son of Nahor and Milka! Thy grandfather and mine!"

"Terah," cried he. "Abram — Isaac, Nahor — Bethuel! Abram — forefather, thine and mine."

"Laban — Adina," cried she. "Leah and Rachel! Sisters, cousins, thine!"

They nodded to each other over and over, amid tears, while they came to the conclusion as to the blood relationship between them, through both his parents and through her father. She gave him her cheeks and he kissed her solemnly. Three dogs sprang at them baying, as the creatures do when men, for good or evil, lay hands on each other. The shepherds applauded rhythmically, singing in high head-tones: *"Lu, lu, lu!"* So he kissed her, first on one cheek then on the other. He forbade his senses to perceive more of her femininity than just the softness of her cheeks, he kissed her reverently; but the friendly darkness of her eyes had bewitched him already, and he felt favoured to have received her kiss at once. Many a one must look longingly, desire and serve, before there would be incredibly vouchsafed to him that which had fallen at once as it were into Jacob's lap, because he was the cousin from afar.

When he let her go she laughed, rubbing with her palm the cheek his rough beard had tickled, and cried:

"Quick, Jerubbaal! Shamash, Bullutu! Roll away the stone that the sheep may drink, and see that they drink, yours and mine, and water my cousin Jacob's camel and be swift and skilful, ye men, that I may run to Laban, my father, and tell him that Jacob is come, his sister's son. He is on the meadows not far from here and will come running in haste and joy to embrace him. Make haste, and follow after me, for I will run whip and spurs. . . ."

Jacob got the sense of what she said by tone and gesture, even some of the words. Already, for her lovely eyes, he began to learn the speech of her land. And when she had begun to run, he stopped the men and cried so that she might hear:

"Halt, brothers, away from the stone, for that is Jacob's work. Ye have guarded it like good watchmen, but now I will roll it away from the well for Rachel my cousin, I alone. For not yet hath the journey drawn away all the strength from my man's arms, and it is fitting that I lend their strength to the daughter of Laban and roll the stone, that the blackness may be taken from the moon and the round of the waters and become beautiful."

So they made way for him, and with all his strength he rolled the stone away, though it was not the work of one man, yet by his strength alone he put the heavy stone on one side though his arms were not of the strongest. The cattle pressed forwards and there was a many-toned baaing of sheep, goats, and lambs — and Jacob's camel grunted as it got to its feet. The men drew up the living water and poured it in the troughs. With Jacob they kept watch over the watering, drove away those that had drunk, and made way for the thirsty, and when all were sated, they put the stone again over the hole, covered it with earth and grass that the place might not be known and uninvited folk make use of the well, and they drove home all the sheep together, Laban's as well as their master's; and Jacob towered up on his camel in the midst of the press.

THE CLOD

PRESENTLY came running a man in a cap with a neck-shield; he suddenly stopped short. It was Laban, Bethuel's son. On such occasions he always came running, had done so a few decades, a swift generation ago, when he had found Eliezer, the wooer, with his ten camels and his train at the well, and said to him: "Come in, thou blessed of the Lord!" But now a grey-beard he ran again, Rachel having told him that Jacob was here from Beersheba, no servant, but the grandson of Abram, his sister's son. But if he stood still and let the other come to him, that was because he had seen no gold clasp on Rachel's forehead nor any bracelets such as Rebecca had had; and because he saw that the stranger came not at the head of a well-furnished caravan, but obviously quite alone, mounted on a lean and mangy beast. Therefore he would make no concessions nor go too far to meet the supposed nephew; but remained standing with his arms folded, full of mistrust, as Jacob approached.

Jacob but too well understood, ashamed and embarrassed as he was by the evil conscience of his poverty and need. Ah, he came not as a rich ambassador, delighting the household with costly presents from his saddlebags, and urged to stop one day or ten. A fugitive and houseless man he came, with empty hands, sent away from home, begging for shelter — he had good reason for a humble bearing. But he recognized his man at once and knew what stripe it was who stood before him, and that it would not do to humble himself too much. Therefore he made no especial haste to dismount from his beast, but advanced towards Laban with all the dignity of his seed, greeting him with propriety, and saying:

"My father and brother! Rebecca thy sister hath sent me, to tell thee she hath bid me to live a while under thy roof; I greet thee in her name, and in the name of Yitzchak, her lord and mine, further in the name of our common forefathers; and I call on Abram's god to protect the health of thee, thy wife and thy children."

"And thee likewise," said Laban, having understood the drift of Jacob's words. "And art thou then in truth Rebecca's son?"

"Truly am I," the other answered. "Yitzchak's firstborn am I, thou sayest it. And I recommend to thee not to be misled by my lack of attendance nor my clothing, rotted by the sun. My lips shall explain all these things to thee at a fitting time, and thou shalt see that if I have nothing save that which is all-important, at the least I have that, and that if thou callest me 'Blessed of the Lord,' thou choosest thy words aright."

"Then I embrace thee," said Laban dourly, after Jerubbaal the shepherd had translated all this into their *ummu-ummu* speech. He laid his arms across Jacob's shoulders, bent first right and then left and kissed the air on either side. Jacob's immediate impressions of this uncle of his were most equivocal. He had a couple of bad lines between the eyes, and one of the eyes was almost shut and blinked, though at the same time he seemed to see more with it than with the other. And on that side there was a distinctly underworldly twist to the mouth, a paralytic droop of the corner, under the grizzled beard, which looked like a sour smile and affected Jacob with misgiving. Laban was stout, with grey hair that stuck out behind under the neck-shield; he wore a knee-length smock with a knife and a whip thrust into the girdle, and narrow sleeves that left free the sinewy forearms, covered with grizzled hair like his muscular thighs and wide, moist hands. They were the hands of a having man, Jacob saw, whose thoughts ran in the dark and narrow circle of earthly possessions — a perfect clod. Yet in the face this uncle might almost have been good-looking, with heavy, well-marked brows that were still quite black, a strong thick nose making one line with the forehead and full lips showing in his beard. Rachel had her eyes from him — as Jacob noted with the mingled recognition, emotion and jealousy with which one traces the earthly source and natural history of traits possessed by a beloved being. The knowledge is agreeable, in so far as it gives us a sense of penetrating the mysteries and discovering the intimate origins of something we love; yet in another way it is unpleasant, and our feeling towards the immediate predecessor and ancestor of such traits is a curious mixture of awe and disgust.

Laban said:

"Welcome, then, and follow me, stranger, since thou sayest, and I am fain to believe, that thou art my nephew. In the past we had room for Eliezer, straw and fodder for his ten camels, and that shall we also have for thee and thy one beast, for more thou seemest not to have. Gifts hath thy mother not sent then, gold, garments, spices or the like?"

"Verily she did, and in abundance, be assured," answered Jacob. "That I have none of these things now shall be explained when I have washed my feet and had somewhat to eat."

He deliberately took a high tone to sustain his dignity before the clod and the latter marvelled at the combination of so much poverty with so much pride. They spoke no more till they reached Laban's farm, where the strange shepherds left them to go on towards the town, while Jacob helped the master to fold the sheep, in mud pens that had wattles on top as a protection against beasts of prey. Three women were watching them from the house-top, one of them Rachel, the others Laban's wife and elder daughter, Leah, who squinted. The house and indeed the whole steading — for besides the dwelling-house there were other reed huts and storehouses shaped like bee-hives — made a marked impression upon Jacob the tent-dweller; but he had seen in the towns he had passed through much finer houses and was not minded to betray any admiration. Indeed he began carping at once: had a word of contempt for the wooden ladder which led up to the roof outside and said they ought to build a brick stair; also the whole house ought to be whitewashed and lattices put on the ground-floor windows.

"There is a stair up from the court," Laban said. "My house is good enough for me."

"Say not so," answered Jacob. "If man be easily content, so is God for him, and withdraweth the hand of blessing. How many sheep hath my uncle?"

"Eighty," replied his host.

"And goats?"

"Some thirty."

"No oxen?"

Laban made an irritated gesture with his beard in the direction of one of the mud and straw huts, indicating the cattle-stalls, but gave no figures.

"There must be more," said Jacob. "More of every kind of beast." Laban flung him a sour glance; but behind the sourness was lively speculation. They turned towards the house.

THE EVENING MEAL

SEVERAL poplar trees overtopped the dwelling-place, one of them barked down its whole length by lightning. The house was a rude structure of modest dimensions, built of crumbling clay bricks; but the airiness of the upper part gave it a certain architectural charm, for the roof rested only at the corners and in the middle of the sides upon masonry, and for the rest upon wooden pillars. The top was covered with earth and provided with several little straw huts. The picture would be clearer if I spoke of a cluster of roofs; for the whole house formed a square surrounding a small court in the centre. A few steps of trodden clay led up to the palm-wood door.

Two or three domestic slaves were working in the court as uncle and nephew crossed it, a potter and a baker who was slapping his barley dough at the outer wall of his little oven. A maid in a loincloth was fetching water from the nearest watercourse, called the Bel-canal, which in its turn flowed from another, the Ellil-canal. Laban watered his unhedged barley and sesame fields from the Bel-canal; it belonged to a merchant in the town, who had had it dug and charged an oppressive tribute of oil, corn and wine for its use. Beyond the ploughed fields the open country rolled away to the horizon, on which rose the terraced tower of the moon-temple of Harran.

The women had come down from the roof and awaited their guest in the ante-room which one entered through the house door; a great mortar for grinding corn was fixed in the centre of its clay floor. Adina, Laban's wife, was an insignificant-looking matron, with a headcloth hanging down over the close-fitting cap that covered her hair, a necklace of gaily coloured stones and a facial expression which was like her husband's in its joylessness save that the look round the mouth was less sour than bitter. She had no sons, a fact that perhaps went far to explain Laban's gloom. Jacob later learned that they had had a son early in their married life, and sacrificed him when the house was built, burying him alive in an earthen jar, with lamps and basins, in the foundations of the building, by way of invoking the blessings of prosperity upon the house and farm. But the sacrifice had brought no particular benefit, and thereafter Adina had not proved capable of bearing sons.

As for Leah, she was certainly not less well built, in fact she was larger and more imposing than Rachel. But she was a good example of the strange abatement of value a fine figure suffers when it has an ugly face on top. She had extraordinarily thick ash-blond hair, covered with a little cap and hanging in a great knot in her neck. But her green-grey eyes squinted dejectedly down her long red nose, and the lids were sore and red; red too were her hands, and she tried to hide them, as indeed she hid her squint too by dropping her eyelids with a sort of shamefaced dignity. There we have it, thought Jacob as he looked at the sisters: the pale moon and the bright. Yet he spoke to Leah and not to Rachel, as they crossed the little paved court, in the centre of which an altar was set up. But she only gave a deprecating little cluck, like the shepherds in the field, and seemed to be waiting for the interpreter, whose Canaanitish name she mentioned several times: a domestic called Abdcheba, the same whom they had seen baking cakes in the outer court. For when they had climbed the brick stair leading up to the roof, and reached the open room where the meal was taken, he brought water for Jacob's feet and hands, and announced that he was born in a village belonging to the lords of Jerusalem, because of his parents' poverty had been sold into slavery for the fixed price of twenty shekels—a sum which apparently conditioned the modest opinion he had of himself—and since then had many times changed hands. He was short, grey-haired and hollow-chested, but he had a ready tongue; whatever Jacob uttered he at once translated into the native idiom and returned the answer with equal fluency.

It was a long, narrow room in which they sat down, a pleasant, airy spot. Between the pillars that supported the roof one looked out on one side over the darkening fields, on the other into the peaceful quadrangle of the inner court, which was hung with coloured awnings and had a pebbled pavement and a wooden gallery running round it. Evening was coming on. The maid in the loincloth apron, who had brought the water, now fetched fire from the hearth and lighted three earthenware lamps that stood upon tripods. Then she and Abdcheba brought in the meal: a pot of thick porridge, prepared with oil of sesame ("*Poppasu, poppasu!*" shouted Rachel in childish glee, licking her lips comically and clapping her hands); warm cakes of barley flour, radishes, cucumbers, sprouts of the cabbage palm, and for beverages goats' milk and water from the canal, a supply of which hung in a great earthenware amphora on one of the pillars. There were also two large earthenware chests on the outer wall of the room, full of various copper basins, milk vessels, goblets and a hand-mill. The family sat or perched irregularly about the low leather-covered dais which served as a table: Laban and his wife reclined side by side on a couch, the daughters sat with their legs curled under them on bundles of reed with cushions atop; and Jacob had a backless chair of gaily painted earthenware, with a footstool to match. There were two cowshorn spoons for the *poppasu*, which were used in turn, each person after using filling his spoon from the dish and passing it on to the next. Jacob sat next to Rachel, and filled the spoon so full each time for her that it made her laugh. Leah saw it, and her squint became positively painful.

Little was said during the meal, and that little had reference to the food. Adina would say to Laban:

"Eat, my husband, all is thine!"

Or to Jacob:

"Come, stranger, refresh thy weariness with food!"

Or one of the parents would say to one of the daughters:

"I see, thou takest all for thyself and leavest the others naught. Bridle thy greediness, else the witch Labartu will turn thy inwards over and make thee to vomit."

Even such trifles as these Abdcheba failed not to translate for Jacob's benefit; and the latter began to take his share in the conversation, saying to Laban in the strange tongue:

"Eat, father and brother, all is thine!"

Or to Rachel:

"Come, sister, eat and rejoice thy heart."

Abdcheba and the maid in the apron ate at the same time as the others, interrupting their meal to serve; suddenly squatting down to munch a radish or to take turns in drinking goats' milk out of a bowl. The maid, whose name was Iltani, kept brushing the crumbs from her hanging breasts with the tips of her fingers.

When the meal was finished Laban called for liquor for himself and the guest. Abdcheba dragged up a skin of beer, made from fermented grain, and two beakers were filled, with straws to drink from as there were many wheat kernels floating on top. The women retired, after Laban had perfunctorily laid his hand upon the head of each. They took leave of Jacob for the night, and as Rachel did so, Jacob gazed once more into the friendly darkness of her eyes and saw the whiteness of her teeth, with the spaces between, as she said laughing:

"Much, much *poppasu*, spoon full up!"

"Abraham, forefather, thine, mine!" he answered as in explanation, repeating the gesture of laying one forefinger across the tip of the other. They nodded again as they had in the field, while the mother's face wore its bitter smile, Leah looked down her nose and the father blinked, with his usual wry and gloomy expression. Then uncle and nephew were alone in the airy upper room, only Abdcheba squatted beside them on the floor, puffing from his exertions during the meal, and kept his eyes fixed on the lips of each in turn.

JACOB AND LABAN STRIKE A BARGAIN

"Speak now, guest," said the master of the house, after drinking, "and unfold to me the particulars of thy life."

So Jacob related to him all things in detail as they had fallen out and according to the facts. At most he somewhat glozed over the precise circumstances of the encounter with Eliphaz; though even here, since his poverty and nakedness were eloquent enough, he gave honour to the truth. From time to time, in convenient sections, he interrupted his tale and gestured towards Abdcheba, who then translated. Laban drank a great deal of beer during the process, listening dourly and sometimes nodding his head. Jacob spoke with objectivity. He did not characterize as either good or evil the late happenings between him, Esau and their parents; he merely narrated, freely and god-fearingly, for he could afford to let everything rest upon the one great, decisive fact before which his present nakedness paled into insignificance; that he, and none other, was the bearer of the blessing.

Laban listened, blinking furiously. He had sucked so industriously upon his straw that his face was like the late and waning moon when it rises red and threatening on the horizon, and his belly was swollen so that he unloosed his girdle, let down his coat from his shoulders and sat in his shirt, with his muscular arms crossed on the half-naked grizzled breast. He sat humped upon his bed and put questions, the questions of a practical and practised business man, about this blessing of which his interlocutor boasted; he, Laban, was not prepared to swallow it whole. He had his doubts. The blessing was not wholly innocent, he felt. Jacob had brought it out clearly enough, that Esau was definitely the man of the curse and he himself the man of the blessing. But considering how the blessing had been acquired, he, Laban, felt that some curse was bound up with it, which must make itself felt in the end. Everybody knew how the gods were. They were all alike, the local ones, with whom Laban naturally kept in good odour, as well as the vague and unnamed ones belonging to Isaac's people, whom likewise he conditionally recognized. The gods willed and compelled human acts; but the guilt therefor was man's. The possession upon which Jacob rested his case was weighted with guilt; the question was, who was the guilty party. Jacob assured him of his own innocence. He himself, he said, had scarcely done anything, he had merely let happen what had to happen, and even that with great personal compunctions. The guiltiest party was the energetic Rebecca, who had arranged everything. "Upon me be the curse, my son," she had said; meaning, of course, in case the father had seen through the deception. But her words expressed her relation to the whole affair, the responsibility she had taken upon herself, and her maternal acceptance of her son's innocence.

"Yes, maternal," said Laban. The drink made him breathe heavily through his mouth and his body sagged forward and sideways. He pulled himself up, then sagged over on the other side. "Maternal. The way mothers are, and parents. And the way the gods are." Parents and gods displayed their partiality in the same questionable way. Their blessing was power and its source was power, for love too, and in particular love, was sheer power, and gods and parents blessed their favourites, out of love for them, with a life of power, made them powerful in good and evil. That was the way of it and that was the blessing. On my head the curse — that was only talk, a mother's prattle, ignoring the fact that love was power and blessing power and life power and that was all there was to it. But after all, Rebecca was only a female, and Jacob was the bearer of a blessing in whose possession guilt was involved. "Upon thee will the guilt be visited," said Laban, thick-tongued, pointing with his heavy hand and arm, at his nephew. "Thou hast betrayed, and thou shalt be betrayed — Abdcheba, stir thy chaps and tell him all that, thou villain. I bought thee for twenty shekels and if thou sleepest instead of interpreting, I will leave thee a week buried to the upper lip in the earth, thou gowk."

"Hold, and shame upon thee," said Jacob, and spat upon the ground. "Doth my father and brother curse me? What then hast thou in thy head? Am I not thy flesh and blood?"

"That art thou," answered Laban. "So far as that goes. Thou hast told me of Rebecca and Isaac, and Esau the red, and thou art Jacob, my sister's son, as thou hast proven. I embrace thee. But the case must be thought of in the light of all thy words, and the consequences drawn for thee and me according to the laws of trade and husbandry. I am convinced of the truth of thy reports, yet have I no ground to praise thy sincerity, since to explain thy state thou haddest no recourse but truth. And it tallies not with thy first statement, that Rebecca sent thee to me to pay me a respect. For it was rather for the sake of thy not abiding at home, where thy life was in danger from Esau because of thine and thy mother's deed, which I deny not was crowned with much success yet did it make thee for the time a naked beggar. Thou camest to me not of thy free will, but because thou hadst else no place to lay thy head. Thou wast given to me, and therefrom follows the consequence; thou art not guest but servant in my house."

"My uncle speaks with justice, yet not mingling with it the salt of love," said Jacob.

"Words," said Laban. "I speak with the natural harshness that governs the life of trade, and by it I am accustomed to govern my actions. The bankers in Harran are two brothers, sons of Isullanu; they can demand of me what they will because I have pressing need of their water and that they know, so they demand as it pleaseth them, and if I cannot comply then they will sell me and my possessions and their gains. No man can afford to be a fool. Thou art sent me, and I will use thee. I am not rich enough, nor bear a blessing, that I should indulge myself in charity and keep open house for all the homeless. Of pairs of arms to labour for me I have but his here, who hath no more strength than a toad, and Iltani the maid, who hath the brains of a chicken and of a cackling hen; for the potter is a journeyman and I have contracted with him for only ten days, and when it is the time of harvest or of shearing I know not whence the workers will come, for I cannot pay them. For long hath it been unfitting that Rachel my daughter keepeth the sheep and suffereth heat by day and frost by night. That shalt thou do for lodgment and herbs and nothing more, for thou knowest not whither to go and art not a man to write conditions. This is the state of the matter."

"Gladly will I tend the sheep for thy child Rachel's sake," said Jacob, "and serve for her that her life may be soft. I was born a shepherd, and I can breed the sheep and have understanding of all things. I had it never in mind to play the idler and be a useless mouth to thee; but since I hear that it is for Rachel, thy child, and that I can replace her strength with the strength of my man's arms, I am twice glad to serve."

"Stands it so?" asked Laban, shooting a glance across at him and blinking hard, while the corner of his mouth went down. "Good," said he. "For well or ill, thou must, for the conditions of the business life compel thee. But if thou dost so gladly, that is an advantage to thee without being a harm to me. And tomorrow we shall make the contract."

"Seest thou?" said Jacob. "It can come to pass that there are advantages which advantage both sides and make soft the natural harshnesses: that wouldst thou not have believed. Thou wouldst not mingle with thy justice the salt of love, so have I given thee of mine; naked and nothing as I stand at this moment before thee."

"Words, words," Laban finished for him. "We will write down the contract and seal it, that all may be in order and no one may assail it lest he behave illegally. Go, now, for I am sleepy, and bloated with beer. Put out the lamps, toad," said he to Abdcheba; stretched himself out on the bed, covered himself with his coat and fell asleep with his mouth open and awry. Jacob might sleep where he would. He mounted to the roof, laid himself down on a coverlet under the awning of a straw hut, and thought of Rachel's eyes until sleep kissed his own.

Chapter V

SERVING LABAN

HOW LONG DID JACOB STAY WITH LABAN?

THIS was the beginning of Jacob's sojourn in Laban's country and in the land of Aram Naharaim, which in his private thinking he called Kurnugia: at first because it was from the beginning the lower world for him, whither for a while he had once wandered; but afterwards because in the course of years this stream-circumscribed land proved that it could hold its man fast; it turned out to be literally and actually the land whence one never more returned. For what does one mean by never more? One means, at least approximately, until the ego no longer retains its form and its condition, is no longer itself. A return after five and twenty years no longer concerns the ego which, when it departed, thought to return in half a year or at most in three and take up its life where it was interrupted. To return thus is for that ego to return "never more." Twenty-five years are not an interval, they are life itself, they are, if they occur in a man's young years, life's kernel and core; and if Jacob lived a long time after his return, and passed through his highest and his hardest times — for he was precisely reckoned a hundred and six years old when, once more a dweller in that lower world, he solemnly departed this life — yet one may say that he dreamed the dream which was his life down yonder in Laban's house, in the land of Aram. For there he loved, he married, and there four women bore him his children down to the youngest, twelve in number; there he grew heavy with increase and stately with possessions. But the youth who had set forth never returned, it was a grey-haired man of fifty-five, a roving eastern sheikh, who returned to the west as a foreign land, and moved towards Shechem.

That Jacob sojourned twenty-five years with Laban is demonstrably true, and the certain result of any unbiassed investigation. Song and story display a looseness of thought more excusable in them than it would be in ourselves. They would have it that Jacob spent twenty years in all with Laban: fourteen and then six. They adhere to the view that he had demanded his freedom of Laban for several years before he broke the dusty bolt and fled; but that Laban had never yielded, always binding him over under new conditions for a longer space. The time when this happened is fixed by the phrase "when Rachel had borne Joseph." But when did that happen? If only fourteen years had passed, then in these fourteen, or precisely speaking in the last seven of them, all twelve children including Dinah and Joseph, and only excepting Benjamin, must have been born. This would not be impossible, in itself, considering that four women were in activity, according to the order of birth ordained by God; but the fact was otherwise. For the sweet-toothed Asher, five years older than Joseph, was born after the end of the second seven years, that is in the eighth year of wedlock; and a detailed consideration will show that Joseph could not have been born less than two years after the birth of the sea-loving Zebulun, namely in the thirteenth year of wedlock and the twentieth of the sojourn at Harran. How could it be otherwise? For he was a child of Jacob's old age; Jacob must have been at least fifty years old when his darling was born and in consequence must have already spent twenty years with Laban. But of these twenty, only twice seven, or fourteen years were years of actual service; so that between them and the time of giving notice and signing the new contract lie a further six years not covered by contract, a quiet passage of time which, from the point of view of Jacob's ultimate riches, must be reckoned with the last five, during which another contract obtained. For though these years may afford the best and most convincing explanation of the man's extraordinary increase, yet after all they are not space enough in which to accumulate a fortune the magnitude of which has been celebrated in song and story. Granted that much exaggeration had crept in; for instance, the statement that Jacob had two hundred thousand sheep is obviously impossible to believe. But there must have been many thousand, to say nothing of his other cattle, his slaves, his gold and silver; Laban's words, when he overtook his son-in-law on the flight, that he might restore what he had "stolen" by day and "stolen" by night, would not have a shadow of justification, they would be meaningless, if Jacob's riches had been founded merely on the last contract with Laban; if he had not already, in the aforementioned interval, done much business for himself and laid the foundations of his later fortunes.

Twenty-five years; to Jacob they passed like a dream, as life passes for the living; in desire and attainment, in expectation, disillusion, fulfilment — a succession of days which he does not count, each of which gives what it has to give, and in waiting and striving, patience and impatience, retreat one by one into the past, and melt into larger units, into months, years and decades, each of which, in the end, is like a single day. It is a question, whether monotony or organized variation makes the time pass more swiftly; in any case it is a matter of the passage of time: the living creature urges forwards, he strives to put time behind him, he strives, at bottom, towards death, thinking that he is striving towards the various goals and turning-points of his life. And though time for him is articulated and divided into epochs, in another sense it is uniform because it is *his* time, moving on always under the constant sign of his own ego; so that for him the passage of time and of life are always attended by two favouring powers, uniformity and articulation.

In the end it is an arbitrary business, this dividing up of time — not greatly different from drawing lines in water. One can draw them so, or again so, and even as one draws the water flows together again into uniformity. We have divided the five times five years of Jacob's sojourn at Harran into twenty and five, and again into fourteen and six and five; but he might himself have divided them into the first seven years, then the thirteen in which the children were coming, and then the five final ones which completed the term just as the five intercalated days complete the twelve times thirty of the solar year. He might so reckon — or even otherwise. At all events, there were twenty-five years in all; uniform not only because they were Jacob's years, but because in all outward circumstances they were just alike, and any variation they showed in the point of view was not sufficient to stem the flow of their uniformity.

JACOB AND LABAN CONFIRM THEIR BARGAIN

AN ARTICULATION, a sort of epoch in Jacob's sojourn, came about through the fact that the contract which he signed with Laban on the day after his arrival was voided after only a single month and replaced by another much more binding one. The uncle had taken immediate steps to give legal sanction to Jacob's position in his house, as he had conceived it in his dry and materialistic communings over his beer. They set off early from the steading and betook themselves on asses to the town of Harran: Laban, Jacob and the slave Abdcheba, the last-named having to serve as witness before the notary or officer of the law. This officer had his seat set up in a court where there was a great press of people, all come hither to execute or to contest contracts: buyers and sellers, lessors and lessees, couples to be married and to be divorced — the justice and his two clerks who squatted beside him had their hands full to satisfy the claims of the town and country population, and Laban and his people had to wait a long time until it was the turn of their after all insignificant and quickly despatched affair. Laban had first to find a bystander — several stood about in hope of such windfalls — and to pay him with corn and oil, to act as second witness. This man then, with Abdcheba, became guaranty for the contract, and both sealed to it by pressing their thumbnails into the convex reverse of the clay tablet. Laban possessed a cylindrical seal; Jacob had forfeited his and so sealed with the hem of his garment. Thus they attested the simple text scratched down by one of the scribes to the mechanical dictation of the judge: Laban, sheepbreeder, took this and this man from Amurruland, being homeless, son of this and this man, as hired servant until further notice; said man obliging himself to devote his powers of body and mind in the service of Laban's house and business, with no other pay than the satisfaction of his bodily needs: qualification, appeal, complaint, there were none. Whoever might, contrary to law, in future impugn this contract and seek to challenge it, his suit should be no suit, and he should be fined, five minas of silver. That was all. Laban had to pay the charges, and did so with a couple of copper plaques which he threw grumbling on to the scales. But actually it was cheap at the price, to bind Jacob over on such terms, for he set more store by the blessing than he had been willing to confess, and it would be to underestimate his business sagacity to assume that he was not aware of the good bargain he had made. He was a depressing man and unpleasing in the sight of the gods; without confidence in his own star and hence unsuccessful so far in his undertakings. He did not for a moment fail to recognize that he could do excellently well with a blessing-bearing man as a partner.

Thus after the contract was signed he was in good spirits, for him, and indulged in a little shopping, buying food, stuffs and small equipment; and challenging his companions to express their admiration of the city and its noisy traffic. The thickness of the walls and bastions and the beauty of the well-watered gardens surrounding them, where garlands of vine hung between the date palms; the sacred splendours of E-hulhul, the walled temple, whose courts had gates plated with silver and guarded by bronze bulls; the loftiness of the tower, rising in graduated steps on its immense mound, surrounded by ramparts — a monstrosity erected of tiles in seven different colours, the top being azure blue, so that the shrine and temporary quarters of the god, where his marriage bed was set up, melted into the brilliant blue of the upper air. But Jacob had only Hum and Ha to say to these sights. The urban did not speak to him, he loved neither the bustle and tumult nor the exaggerated gorgeousness of the buildings, which gave themselves the airs of the eternal, but in his view were destined to destruction within a term which in God's sight was very trifling indeed — and that no matter how cleverly the brick mountain was drained and protected by bitumen and reed mats. He was homesick for the meadows of Beersheba; but by contrast with the pretentious splendours of the town, which oppressed his shepherd's soul, he could almost think of Laban's farm as home, where there waited for him a pair of black eyes in whose expression he had read utter readiness; with which, he felt, important matters were to be discussed. He thought of her, as he absently regarded these doomed and presumptuous structures: of her and of his God, who had promised to keep his feet in strange places and to lead him rich home, the God of Abram, for whom he felt jealous as he looked at Bel-Harran's house and court, this fortress of an idolatrous faith, guarded by bronze griffins and wild bulls, in whose inmost cell, sparkling with precious stones and built of gilded cedar beams, the bearded statue of the idol stood on a silver pedestal and received the smoke and incense and adoration of a regally developed ritual. Whereas Jacob's God, whom he felt was greater than all others, even to being the only God, possessed no house at all upon earth, and was worshipped in simplicity under trees and on heights of ground. Doubtless He would not have it otherwise, and Jacob felt proud that He had scorned and despised such earthly and urban splendours, because they would not have done Him enough honour. But in his pride there mingled some suspicion that even his God would have liked to live in an enamelled house with beams of cedar and adorned with carbuncles, which of course would have to be seven times finer than the house of the moon-idol, and only resigned it because His people were not yet powerful enough to build it for Him. "Only wait," Jacob thought, "and boast your uttermost of the splendours of your high lord Bel! Me hath my God at Beth-el promised to make rich those who believe in Him; and when we are rich, we will build to Him a house of pure gold and sapphire, rock crystal and jasper, within and without, so that the houses of all your gods and goddesses shall pale before it. Awful is the past and the present mighty for that it is present to the eye. But greatest and holiest is beyond doubt the future, and consoling to the oppressed heart of him to whom it is promised."

OF JACOB'S EXPECTANCY

LATE as it was when uncle and nephew returned from the town, Laban insisted on putting the tablet with the contract into the chamber in the cellar of his house, which served for the deposit of such documents. Jacob went with him, each with a lighted lamp in his hand. The chamber lay beneath the floor of the left-hand room, opposite the gallery where they had taken yesterday's meal; it was a sort of archive, combined with a chapel and a burial place, for Bethuel's bones reposed here in the centre in an earthen chest, surrounded by vessels and food offerings and tripods with pans for the burning — and somewhere here too, deeper down or within a side wall, must be the jar with the remains of Laban's sacrificed little son. There was a niche at the back of the cellar with a square brick altar before it,

and along the sides ran low narrow benches; on the right-hand one
lay various tablets, receipts, accounts and contracts, put here for safe
keeping. But on the opposite bench stood some ten or twelve little
gods, curious to behold, some with high caps and the faces of bearded
children, others bald and beardless, with skirts like scales and bare
upper parts, holding their hands folded peacefully under their chins.
Others had coarsely modelled garments falling in folds, the plump
toes sticking out beneath. These were Laban's household gods and
little soothsayers, his teraphim, in whom he reposed great confidence
and was wont to consult them upon every occasion of moment. They
protected the house, he explained to Jacob; they were fairly reliable
weather prophets, advised him in matters of buying and selling, indicated the direction in which a lost sheep might have strayed, and
so on.

Jacob did not relish the bones, the receipt tablets nor the idols,
and was glad when they had reascended the ladder that led down to
their domains through a hole in the floor, and he could go to sleep.
Laban had worshipped before Bethuel's coffin, changing the water
which was there for the refreshment of the deceased — "poured out
water" to him — and made his obeisances to the teraphim; it only
lacked that he should have worshipped the documents. Worship of
the dead and adoration of idols were alike repugnant to Jacob; he was
depressed by the confusion and lack of clarity that reigned in this
house in religious matters — one would have expected a much more
enlightened attitude in Laban, who after all was Rebecca's brother
and the grandnephew of Abram. He was not without knowledge of
the religious tradition of his relatives in the west, but so much local
observance mingled with his original convictions that it formed now
their main content, to which the Abramitic contribution was only
subsidiary. Seated though he was at the very source and fount of the
spiritual history of his tribe — and perhaps because he had remained
seated there — he regarded himself entirely as a subject of Babel and
adherent to its state religion, speaking to Jacob of Ya-Elohim, "the
god of thy fathers," and mixing him up quite ridiculously with Marduk, the god of Shinar. That upset Jacob, he had expected a more
enlightened culture, as his father and mother had obviously done too,
and particularly on Rachel's account he was disquieted, for of course
her beautiful and well-favoured little head must suffer from equal
confusion — he took every occasion from then on to influence her in
the direction of the true and just God. For from the first day, indeed
from the moment he had seen her at the fountain, he thought of her
as his bride; and it is probably not too much to say that she too, in
the little cry which escaped her when she was convinced of his cou-
sinship, acknowledged him as her bridegroom.

Marriage between relatives was at that time, for excellent reasons, quite the usual thing. It was the only proper, sensible and respectable arrangement — we know how poor Esau damaged his position by his eccentric marriages. It was no personal crotchet of Abram's which caused him to insist that Yitzchak "the true son" should take a wife only from his race and his father's house, that is from Nahor's house at Harran, in order that one might know what one was getting. In coming to this house of marriageable daughters, Jacob was treading in the footsteps of Isaac — or more precisely in Eliezer's — and the idea of marriage was for him, as well as for Isaac and Rebecca, bound up with the visit; as indeed it would also have been for Laban, had the man of business been able at once to recognize a son-in-law in this fugitive and beggar. Laban, like any other father, would have found dangerous and repugnant the idea of giving his daughters into a strange and unknown race — to sell them, as he would have put it, abroad. Far wiser and more fitting it was for them to remain, as married women, within the bosom of the tribe; and a cousin on the father's side being available, he — that is to say, Jacob — was the natural and foreordained husband for them. Which meant, not only for one of them but for both. Such was the tacit general assumption in Laban's house when Jacob came — and certainly it was Rachel's. She it was who had first greeted the newcomer, and she understood her rôle on this earth quite well enough to know that she was beautiful and well-favoured, whereas Leah had "tender" eyes — yet in that open-hearted measuring gaze she had given Jacob at the well, she was by no means thinking of herself alone. Life would have it that the coming of their cousin made rivals of the sisters and playmates; but not in regard to the decisive question of whom he would choose; it might indeed rest with her to use her greater attractiveness to the advantage of them both. No, it would be later that a question would arise: the question as to which of them would make a better, more capable, fruitful and beloved wife to the cousin-husband — a matter in which she had no advantage, and which did not depend on a more or less ephemeral power of attraction.

Such was the attitude in Laban's house, and only Jacob himself — and this was the cause of much misunderstanding — looked at things differently. For in the first place, though he knew that besides the lawful wife one could have concubines and slaves, who bore one half-legitimate children, he was not aware, and did not learn for a long time, that in this region, and particularly in Harran and roundabout, marriage with two equally legitimate wives was not only frequent, but in well-to-do families even customary. And in the second place his heart and senses were too full of Rachel's charms even to spend a thought upon the somewhat older, more mature and ill-favoured sister. Even when he spoke to her out of politeness he was not thinking of her, and she knew it and smiled bitterly, shrouding in dignity the pain at her heart and drooping her eyelids to hide her squint. Laban saw it too and was jealous for his eldest born, rejoicing for her neglected sake that he had reduced the cousin-suitor to the legal status of a hired slave.

JACOB MAKES A DISCOVERY

As often as he could, Jacob came to speech with Rachel; but that was seldom enough, for both were busy during the day; and in particular Jacob found himself in the position of a man whose heart is filled with a single matter which he would fain make the sole concern of his days, yet is compelled to hard labour precisely for the sake of his love, and in that labour must even forget his love, and thus again do violence to it. For a man of feeling, such as Jacob was, that is hard indeed. For he would gladly have rested in feeling and made it his life, yet might not, but must play the man precisely in honour of his feeling — since if he did not, how should he else have honoured it? Of course, they were really one and the same, his love for Rachel and his work for Laban; for if he did not succeed in this, how should he in the other? Laban must be convinced of the full value of his nephew's claim, and be eager to attach him to himself. In a word, Jacob must not put to shame the blessing of Isaac; for it was the part of a man to do his utmost not to make a shame of the blessing, but rather to bring to honour the feeling of his heart.

In the beginning, the meadow where he watched his uncle's sheep was not far, not more than an hour from his uncle's house. He went thither every morning with food in his shepherd's pouch, a sling in his belt and armed with the long crook, and stopped there all day, with the dog Marduka. This had the advantage that he could sleep at home; driving his flock in at sunset and putting his best foot foremost all the evening. He was glad of this, for otherwise his shepherding would have left him little chance to convince Laban that he had taken a blessing into his household with the runaway nephew. Not a lamb was missing when at folding time he let the flocks pass under his crook into the pen beneath Laban's eyes; he taught the young lambs to feed so early that he saved Laban much in milk and curds; and by dint of skill and devotion he cured one of the two he-goats, a fine breeder, of the pox. But Laban took all these achievements as the service due from a capable shepherd and expressed no gratitude, either then or when Jacob, soon after he entered upon his tasks, fitted the ground-floor windows with pretty lattices. He refused to pay for whitewash for the walls and Jacob had to give up the idea of marking his advent with so signal an improvement to the appearance of the steading. He was at his wit's end how to testify to the blessing; but the inward tension produced by all his ardent desires and searchings

may have prepared him for revelations and made him the instrument
of an event of far-reaching importance, which all his life long he
thought back upon with joy.

He found water near Laban's cornfield, living water, a subterranean spring; found it — as he well knew — by the Lord's help, though
the miracle was attended by somewhat offensive manifestations,
which were apparently a concession of His pure essence to the local
spirit and the ideas current in the region. Jacob had just been talking
with the lovely Rachel outside of the house, and his language had
been as frank as it was gallant. He had told her that her charm was
like to that of the Egyptian Hathor, or of Isis, or the beauty of a
young heifer. The light of her womanliness shone round her, he poetically said; she was like a mother nourishing with humid warmth
the good seed, and to have her for wife and to beget sons of her was
his dearest desire. She listened with a chaste and noble charm. The
cousin and bridegroom had come, she had proven him with her eyes,
and loved him with all her youthful readiness for love. With her head
between his hands he asked her whether she too would rejoice to
give him children, she had nodded, and the sweet black eyes had
brimmed with tears, and he had kissed these tears from her eyes,
their moisture was still on his lips. In the twilight, between daylight
and moonlight, he had gone out to the meadows; suddenly he felt his
feet held and pulled back, while a strange twitching ran from his
shoulder to his toes, like a flash of lightning. Straining his eyes, he
saw close in front of him a most strange figure. It had the body of a
fish, glistening silvery-slippery in the moonlight and the daylight, and
its head was a fish's head. But beneath that, and covered by it as by
a cap, was a human face with a ringleted beard, and the creature likewise had human feet growing out of its fish-tail and a little pair of
arms. It was stooping down and seeming to draw something from
the ground in a pail, which it held with both its hands, to pour it out
and draw it full again, and again. Then it tripped a few steps sideways on its little feet and glided into the earth; at least it vanished.

Jacob understood at once that the shape was Ea-Oannes, god of
the water depths, lord of the middle earth and of the oceans above
the deeps, to whom the people hereabouts ascribed their possession of
almost all they knew that was worth knowing, considering him very
great, as great as Ellil, Sin, Shamash and Nabu. Jacob, of course,
knew that he was not so great in comparison with the highest, known
of Abram, in the first place for the reason that he had a shape, and
even an absurd one. He knew that if Ea had appeared to him to show
him something, it could only be at the instigation of Ya, the one and
only, Isaac's God, who abode with him. But what this lesser god had
indicated to him by his gestures was none the less of great importance
in itself, and also in all its issues and ramifications, and he pulled him-

self together and ran to the court to fetch tools, and roused up
Abdcheba the twenty-shekel man to help him, and dug half the night,
slept for an hour, and then went on digging, until to his distress he
had to drive out the sheep and leave his labours for the whole day. He
could neither stand nor lie nor sit that day while he pastured Laban's
flock.

It was still some time to the beginning of the winter rains and the
resumption of field-work. Everything was burnt up, Laban paid no
further attention to the fields, but worked in the court, so that he did
not come to where Jacob was, and knew nothing of the activities
which the latter resumed that evening and continued by the light of
the rising moon until Ishtar appeared. He dug at several points within
a small circumference, and went deep down through clay and stone, in
the sweat of his brow. But when the eastern sky grew bright, before ever the sun had pushed its rim over the horizon, lo, the water
gushed up, the spring spirted forth in great force, it leaped up three
spans high inside the hole and began to fill the hastily dug and shape-
less ditch; it sprinkled the earth roundabout, and its waters tasted like
the treasures of the lower world.

Then Jacob prayed; yet even as he prayed he ran to find Laban.
When he saw him from afar, he went more slowly; came up and
greeted him and said with bated breath:

"I have found water."

"What sayest thou?" asked Laban, the corner of his mouth going
down.

"A spring from beneath the earth," was Jacob's reply. "I have dug
it between the court and the field; it gusheth up the height of an ell."

"Thou'rt possessed."

"No. The Lord my God showed me, according to my father's
blessing. Let my uncle come and see."

Laban ran, as he had run at the announcement of Eliezer's coming,
the rich wooer. Long before Jacob, who followed more slowly, he
was at the ditch, gazing.

"That is running water," he said, with some emotion.

"Thou sayest it," Jacob agreed.

"How hast thou done this?"

"I had faith and dug."

"This water," said Laban, without lifting his eyes from the ditch,
"I can lead on my field in an open channel and water it."

"It will be very good," responded Jacob.

"I can," Laban went on, "say to Isullanu's sons at Harran that I renounce the contract which I have with them, for that I have no more
need of their water."

"Such a thought had passed likewise through my mind," said Jacob. "Moreover, thou canst dig a pond and wall it in, and plant a gar-

den with date palms and all kinds of fruit trees, as figs, pomegranates
and mulberries. If thou thinkest well, thou canst plant likewise pistachio trees, pears and almonds, and put in a few strawberry trees; and
thou wilt have from the dates the flesh, the sap and the kernel, and
the pith of the palm for food, the leaves for woven work, the ribs for
many household uses, the bast for weaving and rope-making, and the
wood for building."

Laban said nothing. He did not embrace the bearer of the blessing,
nor fall down before him. He said nothing; he stood, turned on his
heel and went. Jacob, too, departed, sought and found Rachel, who
sat milking in a stall. He told her all, and how that now they might
in all likelihood have children together. They took each other by the
hands and danced about and sang: "Hallelu-Ya!"

JACOB SUES FOR RACHEL

WHEN Jacob had been a month with Laban he came before his master
and said that now Esau's wrath must be sensibly abated, he, Jacob,
had somewhat he must say.

"Hear me, before thou speakest," responded Laban, "for I had in
mind to speak unto thee. Lo, now, thou art a month in my service
and we have made offerings together on the roof, by the new moon,
the half moon, the full moon and the day of vanishing. In this time
have I taken, besides thee, three hired servants, for a term, whom I
pay according to the law. For water hath been found, not without
thy aid, and we have begun to wall in the spring and lay the runnels
of bricks. And we have measured off the pond that is to be dug, and
if we shall plant a garden, there is much labour and the strength of
many arms required, thine, and theirs whom I have hired, whom I
feed and clothe and reward with each five selas of corn daily. Until
now thou hast served me without reward, out of kinship and love,
according to our contract. But, lo, we will make a new contract, for
it is no longer right, before gods and men, that the strange servants
should be rewarded and thou, because thou art my nephew, serve
me for naught. Tell me, therefore, what shall thy wages be? For I
will give thee what I give the others, and somewhat more if thou
wilt seal to sojourn with me for as many years as the week hath days,
and as one counts, until the ploughland lie fallow and the earth rest,
that man neither sows nor reaps. Thus shalt thou serve me seven
years for the reward which thou demandest."

Such was the speech of Laban and the course his thoughts took;
plausible speech, clothing plausible thoughts. But the thoughts — and
not only the words — of the earth-bound man are only a garment
and a gloze for his inner hopes and desires, which he clothes in
plausible form, so that he is prone to lie even before he speaks, and

his words have such an honest ring, because it is the thoughts that are false and not they. Laban was downright horrified to hear that Jacob wished to go, for since the finding of the spring he had known that Jacob was in truth a bearer of blessings, a man with a lucky hand; and that he must do his uttermost to bind him to him, for thus his affairs would prosper from the blessing which the other bore with him wheresoever he came. The finding of the spring was a mighty blessing, so full of consequence that it was only one of its boons, not the greatest, that it freed Laban from his heavy tribute to Isullanu's sons. They had made all sorts of excuses, declaring that without their water Laban could never have planted his field, and therefore whether he used it or not he owed the oil, the corn and the wool, he, and like-wise his posterity, for evermore. But the judge feared the gods and declined in Laban's favour — which Laban was inclined to interpret as another manifestation of Jacob's God. And now there was much under way and in progress, much undertaken, for which the blessing was requisite for its prosperity and success. The economic relation between the two was altered in the nephew's favour. Laban felt he needed him; Jacob was well aware of the fact, and could bring pres-sure by his threat of leaving, which Laban's practical sense was pre-pared to take into account. Thus, even before Jacob had applied it, Laban anticipated the pressure by acknowledging that the conditions of Jacob's servitude were unworthy of him, and taking the words out of his mouth by his fair proposals. Jacob knew, nobody better, that he could not dream of leaving, that the circumstances were by no means ripe; he rejoiced that his uncle conceded that the nephew had the whip hand, and felt grateful to him for meeting him halfway, though well knowing that the offer was prompted not by love, but by self-interest. He even felt grateful to him for the interest which bound the other to him; for man is so constituted that the friendliness which is the outward expression of the interest will often elicit a loving response. But more than all, Jacob loved Laban for the sake of that which he had to give, and for what he thought to demand of him, for it was greater than much corn and many shekels. He said:

"My father and brother, if thou wilt that I shall stay here and re-turn not to Esau, even though he be now appeased, but serve thee, then give me Rachel thy child to wife, and let her be my meed. For in beauty she is like to a young heifer, and she looks upon me with kindness. We have spoken together and have said to each other that we would have children together after our likeness. Give her, then, to me, and I am thine."

Laban was not at all surprised. I have already said that he had begun by thinking of Jacob as a wooer, and only on account of Jacob's plight had the thought slipped into the background of his mind. It was not strange that his nephew, now that his position had so greatly improved, should bring up the idea, and also it was not unpleasing to the clod to realize — as he did at once — that the tactical advantage passed thereby once more into his hands. For Jacob, in confessing that he loved Rachel, put himself again, as it were, in Laban's power, and weakened the pressure of his threat to leave. But what annoyed the father was that Jacob spoke of Rachel, only of her, and passed over Leah entirely. He answered:

"So I should give you Rachel?"

"Yes, Rachel. She, too, would have it so."

"Not Leah, my elder child?"

"No. She is not quite so dear unto my heart."

"She is the elder, and the next to woo."

"Truly, she is somewhat older. She is likewise of fine figure and bearing, despite some small defects, or just on account of them; and she would probably be fruitful in bearing me children, such as I desire. But my heart hangs upon Rachel, thy younger child, for she is to me like Hathor and Isis; she is radiant in womanly charm, like Ishtar, and her sweet eyes follow me whithersoever I go. Lo, an hour since my lips were wet with tears which she had shed for me. Give her to me, then, and I will labour for thee."

"Certainly it is better I should give her to thee than to a stranger," Laban said. "But shall I, then, give Leah, my elder, to a stranger, or shall she wither without a husband? Take first Leah; take both!"

"Thou art of a kindly heart," said Jacob, "but let it not affront thine ears if I say that Leah speaks not to my man's desires, but on the contrary, and my service hath to do with Rachel alone."

Then Laban looked at him a while with his afflicted and drooping eye and said gruffly:

"As thou wilt. Then seal unto me that thou wilt sojourn seven years with me and serve me for this reward."

"Seven times seven," Jacob cried. "A jubilee, in the name of the Lord. When shall the wedding be?"

"After seven years," answered Laban.

We can imagine the start Jacob gave.

"What," he cried, "I should serve thee for Rachel seven years, and before thou givest her to me?"

"How else?" responded Laban, as though in astonishment. "I should be a fool to give her to thee at once, that ye might be up and off, when it pleased thee, do what I would. Or where is the purchase price and the dowry and the fitting morning presents thou wilt give me that I may bind them to the bride's girdle and they remain unto me according to the law, in case thou drawest back from the marriage? Hast thou them by thee, the minas of silver and the other matters, or where are they? Thou art as poor as a field mouse, and poorer. And so let it be signed and sealed before the judge that I sell thee the wench for seven years that thou wilt serve, and the payment will be when it has been earned. And we will lay the tablet below with the other tablets, and entrust it to the charge of the teraphim."

"A hard-hearted uncle," ejaculated Jacob, "hath the Lord given to me!"

"Words!" was Laban's reply. "I am as hard as the situation permits me to be, and if it require, then I shall be softer. But thou wilt have the wench to wife — go, then, without her, or else serve."

"I will serve," Jacob said.

OF THE LONG WAITING

THUS passed the prelude; the first and preliminary period of Jacob's long sojourn with Laban; it was only one month, and at its end the new contract, with its fixed and far-away terminus, came into force. It was a contract of marriage as well as a contract of service, a mixture of the two, such as the *mashkim*, or presiding judge, had probably not had often come before him, though something similar probably now and again, and which he recognized as a matter susceptible of legal treatment, and also, with the consent of both parties, legally binding. The contract was written out in duplicate, and then discussed with both sides, in order to clear up any doubtful points, and the words of both set down, so that there was clear and apparent proof that they had agreed. This man had said to that man: Give me thy daughter to wife, and the other man had answered: What wilt thou give for her? And the other man had had nothing. Then the above-mentioned man had said: Seeing that thou canst pay no dowry nor any presents to hang at the bride's girdle at the betrothal, thou shalt serve me for as many years as the week hath days. And that shall be the price which thou payest, and the bride shall be thine for the nuptials after the end of the term, together with a mina of silver and a maid, which I will give as dowry, but so that the price of the maid shall be reckoned as two-thirds of the mina of silver and the other third be paid in metal or the fruits of the fields. Then said the other man: So be it. In the name of the king, so be it. Each side took one of the contracts. Whoever shall set himself up against it, in that he behaveth unlawfully, there shall no good come unto him for it.

The agreement was sensible, the judge found it fair, and from the business side, Jacob himself had not much to complain of. If he owed his uncle a mina of silver at sixty shekels, seven years' labour would not suffice to pay the debt, for the average wage for a labourer was seven shekels a year, and seven of them would not make up the sum. He felt profoundly that the economic point of view was a very deceptive one; that if there were a just scale, a God's scale, as it were, the side with the seven years would have made the side with the shekels fly up into the air. But after all, he would spend these years in Rachel's company, and thus love's sacrifice would be mingled with much joy; besides which, beginning with the signing of the contract, she would be legally betrothed and sealed to him, so that no other man could approach her without being as guilty as though he had led away a married woman. Seven years! Seven years they must wait for each other, these children of brother and sister. They would be at a quite different time of life, before they might bring forth sons to each other, and that was a bitter condition, which proceeded either from Laban's cruelty or his lack of imagination, and displayed him, in short, once more, and in the most glaring light, as a man without heart or imagination. Another grievance was his extraordinary greed and his tendency to overreach even his nearest and dearest, for instance, in the clause in the contract which referred to the dowry, the parental morning gift, which was such a bad bargain for poor Jacob, particularly as the problematical maid was valued at at least twice the sum asked for a fair average slave either in these parts or in the west. But there was no helping this offensive feature, nor any other, of the situation. The time when he could drive a better bargain would come, Jacob realized; he felt in his soul the promise of good business and a secret power and capacity which was certainly greater than any resident in the bosom of this underworldly devil of a father-in-law of his, Laban, the man of Aram, whose eyes had become lovely in Rachel his child. As for the seven years, they were even now in the process of being lived down. It would have been easier to sleep them away; but not only because that was not possible, but because it seemed better on the whole to look after them actively, Jacob suppressed the thought in his mind.

This he did, and so, too, should the narrator, and not imagine that he can pass over and obliterate the time with a little sentence like "Seven years went by." It is the story-teller's way to say things like that; and yet no one should let the words, if they must be spoken, pass his lips lightly, nor otherwise than heavy with meaning and hesitant with reverence for life, so that the hearer, too, feels them heavy with meaning, and he marvels how they can pass, those years the end of which one can see only with the understanding but not with the soul; and even pass as though they had been seven days. For such is the tradition: that the seven years, before which Jacob had at first quailed with fear, passed by like days; and the tradition must ultimately go back to his own words, must be, as they say, authentic, and also most illuminating. What we have here is certainly no "seven-sleeper" enchantment, nor, indeed, any other kind, save that of time itself, whose larger units pass as do the smaller ones, neither slow nor fast, but simply pass. A day has four-and-twenty hours; quite a fair amount of time, with room in it for much life and many thousand heartbeats. Still, from one morning to another so many of them pass, what with sleeping and waking, one way and another; you do not know how, and just as little do you know how seven days pass, a week, the unit a mere four of which suffices the moon to go through all her phases. Jacob did not say that seven years went as fast as days; he would not have made a comparison so derogatory to the value of one day of life. And the day, too, does not go "fast," but it goes, with its times of day, its morning, midday, afternoon and evening, one among others; and so likewise does the year, with its seasons, from spring to spring, in the same unqualifiable way, one among others. Thus it was Jacob said that seven years passed, to him, like days.

It is idle to say that a year consists not only of its seasons, the succession of spring, green grazing and sheep-shearing, harvest and summer heat, first rains and new planting, snow and frosty nights, and round again to the rosy blossoms of the tamarisk. That is only the frame of the year; the year itself is a filigree of life, heavy with events, an ocean to drink up. Such a filigree of thinking, feeling, acting, and happening the day is likewise, and the hour, on a smaller scale, if you like; but distinctions of size among time units are very little absolute, and their relative yardstick is the measure of ourselves, our feeling, our adaptation, or the lack of it. Seven days may under some circumstances be harder to swallow, a more daring adventure in time, than seven years. But what do we mean by daring? For whether one plunge hot-blooded or shivering into time's stream, there lives not a soul who is not forced to surrender to it. And nothing more is needed. For it carries us away, tears us along with it, without our marking, and if we look back, lo, the point where we stepped in is "far back," it is, for instance, seven years away, years that have passed like days. No, we cannot even express or distinguish the manner in which man gives himself to time, whether gladly or with misgiving; for the necessity dominates such distinctions and makes them void. No one says that Jacob undertook and entered upon his seven years with joy, for only after they had passed might he beget children with Rachel. But that was a trouble of the mind which was greatly assuaged by the contrary workings of his vitality, which conditioned his relation to time and time's relation to him. For Jacob was to live into his hundred-and-sixth year, and though his spirit knew it not, yet his body knew it, and the soul of his flesh; and thus seven years to him, while not so little as seven years in the sight of God, were yet not nearly so much to him as to one who should live but fifty or sixty years; thus his soul could more tranquilly envisage the waiting-time. And finally, for our general comfort be it said, that it was not pure waiting which he had to bear, for that would have been too long. Pure waiting is torture; no one could bear to sit seven years, or seven days, or walk up and down and wait, as one can do for perhaps an hour. In the large and larger time units that cannot happen, because the waiting gets longer and thinner, and at the same time more densely occupied with mere living, so that for long stretches of time it falls victim to sheer forgetfulness; that is to say, it withdraws into the depth of the soul and is no longer consciously present. Thus a half hour of pure and mere waiting is more frightful and a crueller test of patience than a waiting that is put into a life of seven years. What we await close at hand affects us, precisely because of its nearness, as a much keener and more immediate stimulus than if it were far off; it transforms our patience into nerve- and muscle-consuming impatience, it makes us morbid; we literally do not know what to do with our limbs, while a long-term waiting leaves us in peace; it not only permits, but forces us to think of other things, and do other things, for we must live. Such is the origin of the surprising truth, that no matter with what degree of longing we wait, we do it not with more difficulty, but with more ease, the more distant in time lies the goal of our hopes.

These consoling reflections — which simply amount to the statement that nature and the soul have ways of helping themselves out — proved particularly true in Jacob's case. He served, ostensibly, as Laban's shepherd; and a shepherd, we know, has much idle time. Hours on end, whole half-days long, his lot is spacious contemplation, and if he is waiting for something, his waiting is not enveloped in much activity. But here was the virtue of long-sight waiting; for it was by no means the case that Jacob could not sit nor stand nor lie, but ran about the plain with his head between his hands. Rather his soul was tranquil, if also a little sad, and waiting formed not the treble, but the ground-bass of his life. Of course he thought much of Rachel, and their children to be, when he was far from her, with the dog Marduka; as he lay propped on his elbows with his cheeks in his hands, or with his hands folded in the back of his neck, one leg supported on the other knee, in the shade of rocks or shrubbery; or leaning on his staff in the wide plain with his sheep grazing round him. And not alone of her, but of God, and all the tales he knew, the near and far, his flight and wandering, of Eliphaz, and the proud vision of Beth-el; of the feast of the cursing of Esau; of Yitzchak the blind, of Abram, of the tower, the flood, of Adapa or Adama, in the garden of paradise . . . which reminded him of the garden which he had helped his clod of a father-in-law to plant, through his blessing, and which had meant such increase of prosperity to the man.

I may say that in the first year of the contract, Jacob did not, or not often, keep the sheep. Either Abdcheba, the twenty-shekel man, or one of Laban's daughters did it, and Jacob devoted himself, by his uncle's wish and command, to the works that arose out of his discovery: the laying of the water system and the building of the pond, for which he utilized a natural hollow in the ground, evened it out with the spades, walled it round and hardened the floor with stone cement. At last the garden was in being — Laban laid great stress on having this new enterprise carried out with the aid of the blessing-bearing hands, for he was now quite convinced that the blessing, so shrewdly obtained, was indeed efficacious, and flattered himself at his own cunning in enlisting it to the interest of his own business. Certainly it was plain and clear that Rebecca's son brought good luck, almost against his will; that his mere presence could set in vigorous motion enterprises which had seemed destined to drag and to founder. What a prosperous bustle there was in Laban's court and in his fields, what digging, hammering, ploughing and planting! Laban had borrowed money to enlarge his business, and to make the necessary purchases. Isullanu's sons at Harran had advanced it him, despite their loss of the lawsuit over the water. For they were cool and practical heads, personally quite unemotional, the loss of the suit seemed to them no ground at all for refusing to do business with the man who had won it; it was precisely the advantage by means of which he had won it that now made him look like a good investment in their eyes. They lent him money without a thought. But so it is in business, and Laban was not at all surprised. He needed the bank's money, if only to pay and feed the three new servants, who were the property of a lender in the city. Jacob directed the work of these, sometimes giving a helping hand, and overseeing the whole. For it goes without saying that his position in the house, even without any agreement on the subject, was not in the least like that of these crop-headed hirelings and slaves, who wore the name of their owner written in indelible dye in the right hand. The seven-year contract, down below among the teraphim, was far from putting him into their category. He was the nephew of the house, the betrothed of its daughter, and he was lord of the water-sources to boot and engineer and head gardener — all this Laban conceded to him and knew very well why he did so.

Also he knew why he entrusted Jacob with the larger part of the buying of tools, material, seeds and plants needed for the new operations, upon which the borrowed money was laid out. He confided in his nephew's lucky hand — and with right; for it always turned out to his advantage and he got better material than when he dealt himself, being sour of visage and lacking in the blessing. But Jacob profited too, and this period saw the slender beginnings of the prosperity which was to assume such large proportions. For he conceived his dealings in the city and with business associates scattered throughout the country not in the fixed and rigid sense that he was Laban's authorized middle-man and agent, but as though he were commissioner and factor, and such a very good, experienced, sociable and conversable one that he could always put aside a smaller or greater private gain in cash or goods; and was soon the owner of a little flock of sheeps and goats — even before he had begun to tend Laban's sheep. God the King had cried out to the sound of the harps that Jacob should return with riches to Yitzchak's house, and that was at once a promise and a command, the latter in so far as such promises can hardly be expected to be fulfilled without human co-operation. Should he prove God the King a liar and bring his words to shame out of sheer carelessness and unlimited consideration towards an uncle who himself dealt with affairs in the most grimly practical manner and yet failed to draw any advantage from them? Jacob was not even tempted to make such a blunder. Let nobody think that he cheated Laban and secretly overreached him. No, for Laban was in general aware of what Jacob did; as to details, he drew down the corner of his mouth and deliberately shut his eyes. For the man saw that things almost always turned out to better advantage than when he kept them in his own two heavy fists; also he had some reason to feel afraid of Jacob and to connive at what he did. For Jacob was very sensitive, and required to be dealt gently with, out of consideration for the blessing. He said so quite openly, and warned Laban once for all in plain words: "If my lord check me and set me to rights in every small matter that falleth to my advantage in his service, and if he looketh askance when not he alone hath some advantage from his servant's wisdom, then quencheth he my heart in my breast and the blessing in my body, so that his affairs no longer prosper in my hands. For the Lord my God spoke in a dream to the man Belanu, from whom I have bought seed-corn for thee, that thou needest for the enlarging of thy fields, and He said: 'It is Jacob, bearer of the blessing, with whom thou dealest, and I guide his head and his feet. Therefore have a care that thou reckon the five cor which he will buy from thee for five shekels, with two hundred and fifty selas the cor, and not two hundred and forty, or thirty, as thou mightest reckon with Laban, else I will deal with thee. Jacob will give thee nine selas of oil instead of a shekel and five minas of wool instead of another, besides a good mutton of the value of a shekel and a half, and for the rest a lamb of his flock. All that will he pay for thee for thy five cor of seed-corn instead of five shekels, besides much friendly words and looks so that thou wilt have pleasant trading with thy purchaser. But if thou makest him worse prices, then beware. For I will come amongst thy flocks and strike them with pestilence and I will visit thy wife with barrenness, and the children thou already hast with blindness and folly, and thou shalt learn to know Me.' Then did Belanu fear the Lord my God, and did as he had been commanded, so that I had the barley cheaper than another person, and much more cheaply than my uncle. For let him try himself and

see if he could have made a deal with nine selas of oil for a shekel
and five minas of wool for another, when in the market one gets
twelve selas and more and six minas of wool, not reckoning in the
exchange. And for the other shekel and a half hadst thou not given
at least three lambs or a pig and a lamb? Therefore I took two lambs
from thy flock and marked them with my mark and they are now
mine. But what is that between thee and me? Am I not the bridegroom of thy child and through her is not what is mine likewise
thine? If thou wilt that the blessing profit thee and I serve thee with
wisdom and out of a willing heart, then must a reward and promise
spur me on, else my soul weary in thy service and my blessing come
not to profit thy works."

"Thou mayest keep the sheep," said Laban; and thus it was between
them several times, until Laban preferred to say nothing and let
Jacob do as he would. For he was unwilling that his nephew should
weary in well-doing, and so had to give way. But he was glad when
the water system was finished, the pond filled, the garden planted
and the field enlarged, and he could send Jacob out with the sheep,
away from the court, first near at hand, then further away, so that
for weeks and months at a time he came not under Laban's roof, but
set up his own light shelter against sun and rain, out on the plain, near
a spring, and made pens of clay and wattle and a temporary tower
for refuge and look-out. There he lived, on scanty fare, with his
crook and his sling, and with the dog Marduka guarded the scattered
herds and yielded himself to time; talking to Marduka, who pretended to understand him and in part did so, watered his beasts and
penned them evenings in the folds; suffered heat and cold, and got
but little sleep, for the wolves howled at night after the lambs, and
sometimes even a lion crept upon them, and Jacob had to make the
noise of twenty men with rattle and shouting, to drive the robber
away.

OF LABAN'S INCREASE

WHEN he drove home the sheep, a day's journey or so, to give accounting to the master of flock and yearlings, and let the sheep pass
under his staff, he saw Rachel, who was waiting too, and they withdrew hand in hand and spoke together long over their lot, how they
must wait for so long upon one another and might have no children
together, and they consoled each other by turns. Yet chiefly it was
Rachel who needed consolation, for the time was longer and the
waiting bore harder upon her soul, since she was not to become one
hundred and six years old, but only forty-one, so that seven years
were more than twice as much of her life as they were of his. And so
her tears welled up from the depth of her soul, when they stood apart

together, and the sweet black eyes ran over with copious tears as she mourned:

"Ah, Jacob, thou cousin from afar, who art promised unto me, how the heart of thy little Rachel is sore within her in the impatience of her soul! For lo, the moons change and time passeth by, and it is both a pain and a gladness; for I shall soon be fourteen and I must be nineteen before the harps and drums can sound for us and we withdraw into the bridal chamber, and I am before thee as is before God the spotless one in the upper temple, and thou speakest: 'Like to the fruit of the garden will I make fruitful this woman.' All that is still so far away, according to our father's will, who hath sold me to thee, that I shall no longer be as I am when it comes, and who can tell if before that time a demon might not touch me, that I be seized with an illness and even the roots of my tongue be attacked and human help be vain? And if I recover from the touching, perhaps it might make me lose all my hair and blemish my skin with spots and yellowness, so that my friend knoweth me no more. All this I fear unspeakably, and cannot sleep and throw off my covers and wander through house and courtyard while my parents sleep, and grieve over the time, that it passeth and passeth not, for it is borne in upon me that I shall be fruitful unto thee, and by the time that I am nineteen we could have had six sons, or even eight some of them being twins, and I weep for very longing of the time."

Then Jacob took her head between his hands and kissed her beneath her two eyes, Laban's eyes, transformed in her to beauty, kissed away her tears so that his lips were wet, and said:

"Ah, dear, good, wise and clever little mother-sheep, be of good cheer! Lo, these thy tears I take with me to the field, they go with my loneliness as pledge and token that thou art mine, my very own, and in patience and impatience thou waitest for me as I for thee. For I love thee, and the darkness of thine eyes is dear beyond all else to me, and the warmth of thy head against mine moves me to my soul. Thy hair is like to the goats in the herd, for its darkness and silkiness, like to the goats of the mount of Gilead; thy teeth are as white as a bright light, and thy cheeks make me to think of the softness of peaches. Thy mouth is like young figs when they redden on the bough; and when I close them in a kiss, so is the breath of thy nostrils like the fragrance of apples. Thou art surpassingly beautiful and well-favoured, but thou wilt be so still more when thou art nineteen, and thy breasts will be like clusters of dates and clusters of grapes. For thou art pure of blood, my beloved, and no sickness can touch thee, and no demon seize thee; thy Lord my God, who led me to thee and kept thee for me, will have thee in His safe keeping. And as for me, my love and my tenderness for thee is unfaltering, it is as a flame which the rain of many years cannot quench. I think of thee when I lie in the shadow of the rock or of the bushes or stand leaning on my staff; when I go to seek the strayed sheep or tend the sick ones or bear the weary lamb in my arms, when I confront the lion and when I water my flocks. In all that I do I think of thee and I slay the time. For it passes unceasingly in all that I do and have to do, and God lets it not stand one moment still, whether I rest or run. Thou and I, we wait not upon emptiness and vacancy, but we know well our hour and our hour knoweth us and it cometh to meet us. And thus it is in some ways not evil that there is still time between us and it, for when it is come we shall go hence into the land whither our forefather went, and it will be well if I am then heavier with possessions, that the promise of my God may be fulfilled, that He should lead me back with riches into Yitzchak's house. For thine eyes are to me like the eyes of Ishtar, goddess of marriage, when she said unto Gilgamesh: 'Thy goats shall bear twofold and thy ewes twins.' Yes, though we may not yet embrace and be fruitful, our sheep are for us, and bear twofold for our sake that I may make prosperity for Laban and for me and become heavy before the Lord before we go hence."

Thus he consoled her, and the fineness of his feeling found the right words, speaking of the sheep and their, as it were, vicarious fruitfulness. For truly it was as though the local goddess of fertility, in bonds and prevented against human fruitfulness, freed herself and made good her loss in the beasts of the field, and especially in Laban's flocks which Jacob tended. They throve as no others, and manifested the blessing as never before, so that Laban might rejoice that he had taken Jacob for his servant, for his gain was great; and he was greatly astonished at this fruitfulness, when he came out riding upon an ox, one or two days' journey, to see after the increase of the flocks. But he said nought, either for good or for evil, not in evil either, for the most ordinary shrewdness bade him deal cannily with such a breeder and man of the blessing, if ever in trade he should take his own advantage now and then as he had said openly that he would. It would have been unwise to combat the principle even if it had been applied wholesale; for such a man is sensitive and one must not offend the blessing in his body.

The truth is that Jacob was far more in his element as sheep-breeder than he had been as overseer of the operations in court and garden. He was shepherd by birth and breeding, a moon-man, not a sun-man and farmer. The life on the meadows, however much drudgery and even danger it held, was after his nature and his heart, it was a contemplative life and it had dignity, it left him leisure to think of God and Rachel. And he loved the sheep, loved them in his senses and with his spirit, he was drawn to them in his deep and gentle musings. He loved their warmth, loved their way of life, now scattered abroad, now huddled close together, and the idyllic many-voiced chorus of bleating beneath the wide vault of heaven. He loved their characteristic look, solemn and withdrawn, their level ears, their wide glassy eyes, with the wool growing down upon the base of the flat nose; loved the strong and stately head of the ram and the finer, more delicate shape of the ewe, and the innocent face of the young lamb. He loved the matted, curly, precious wool, borne patiently about on their backs, the ever-renewing fleece, which twice in the year, in spring and autumn, he and Laban and the slaves washed on their backs, then sheared it off. And his interest gave him mastery in the art of breeding, the tendance and careful regulation of the rutting and lambing times; for he had knowledge of breeds and single sheep, and of physical characteristics and grades of wool to apply in his work — though I should not ascribe entirely to these the remarkable results which he achieved. For it was not only that he improved the quality of the wool and the flesh, but also under his hands the fertility of the flocks increased beyond all known measure. There was not one barren ewe in his folds, they all bore, they bore twofold and threefold, they were still bearing at eight years old, the time of their rutting was two months and they carried the lambs only four, their lambs matured and propagated within the year, and strange herdsmen asserted that in Jacob's flocks the wethers rutted at the full moon. That was a jest, or a superstition, but it shows Jacob's extraordinary success in this field, and suggests that it went beyond mere knowledge of the shepherd's craft. Shall we invoke the local goddess of fertility to explain these half-envious comments? As for me, I think the explanation rather lies in the state of mind of the shepherd. He was an impatient lover. He might not yet be fruitful with his Rachel; and just as often in the history of the world a damming-up of desires and powers has found its outlet in deeds of the spirit; so here, by a similar process of transference, they found expression in sympathy and care for the life entrusted to the sufferer.

The tradition, which forms the learned commentary to an original text, which in its turn represents a late and literary version of the antiphonal songs and recitatives of the shepherds, has extraordinary things to relate of Jacob's lucky transactions. In its enthusiasm it is guilty of exaggerations, from which we must not too sternly detract lest in our endeavour to clarify we distort the tale afresh. The exaggeration is perhaps not so much in the later glosses and comments as in the original events themselves, or rather in the human beings concerned, for we know how men are prone to overstress the value of something which it has become the fashion to admire and to covet. Thus it was with the tales of Jacob's successes. The report of their unique excellence spread abroad among the breeders of the neighbourhood — I leave on one side the question of how much they were

blinded by the blessing. In any case, everybody was possessed with
the desire to have even one of Jacob's sheep. They made it an affair
of honour. They came from far to trade with him, and if when they
got there they discovered that it was after all a question of ordinary
and not supernatural sheep, they forced themselves to find them
miraculous, on account of the fashion; a sheep whose teeth were obviously falling out and which therefore was at least six years old, they
would buy for a yearling or a tup on his bare say-so. It was said that
he had traded a sheep for a camel, an ass for a slave, male or female,
and though certainly nothing like such bargains were the rule or
practice, yet they might happen in trade — even with reference to
the slaves such reports might not be entirely without foundation.
For Jacob ultimately needed helpers in his work, undershepherds,
whom he hired from other dealers, and whose price might be reckoned against the value of wool, curds, fells, sinews or live animals.
In the course of time he appointed some of these shepherds independent overseers over the meadows and the care of the sheep, and
made a fixed bargain with them: six-and-sixty or seventy lambs a
year for every hundred sheep, a sela of curds for the same number
or a mina and a half of wool for each sheep — profits which accrued
to Laban, of course, but as they passed through Jacob's hands left a
little something behind, if only because he knew so well how to
employ it to make more.

Were these the only blessings which Jacob's management secured
for our loutish Laban? No — provided we assume that there was an
actual connection between the nephew's presence and the greatest
blessing of all that the man had to be grateful for. And I think we
may assume it, whether we interpret the fact in a mystical sense or
only according to the dictates of reason. If I were here a mere inventor of tales, and conceived my contract with the public as an
obligation to fabricate stories which should have a pleasing though
ephemeral convincingness, what I have to tell would certainly expose
me to the reproach of drawing too long a bow, and presuming far
too much upon a credulity which after all has its limits. Luckily, such
is not my rôle. I rest upon the traditional facts, which are not less
sound because some of them ring as though they were newly minted.
Thus I am in the position to state what I have to tell in an assured
and tranquil tone that in the face of all doubts and reproaches carries
conviction.

In a word, then, Laban, the son of Bethuel, became a father again
during Jacob's first seven years — and the father of sons. Recompense
was vouchsafed to the man, along with increasing prosperity, for
the unrewarded and rejected sacrifice, the little son in the jar down
below. Not single recompense, but threefold. Three times, in the
third, fourth and fifth years of Jacob's sojourn, Adina, Laban's wife,

that insignificant woman, was expectant; the very groans were proud
with which she brooded over what she had conceived; wearing round
her neck the symbol of her state, a hollow stone with a smaller one
like a clapper inside it, and between prayers and howlings she was
brought to bed in Laban's house and in his presence, kneeling on two
bricks, to make space for the child before the gateway of her body.
One midwife held her arms behind, another crouched in front of
her to watch the gate. Despite Adina's age all three births were successful and without danger to herself. They had brought many times
food offerings to Nergal the red: beer, wheaten bread and even sheep,
so that he being appeased his fourteen disease-bearing slaves might
not mingle in the matter. And thus it was that in none of the three
cases did the inwards of the labouring woman turn over, or the witch
Labartu close the gateway of her body. She bore three sturdy boys,
and their vociferous claims turned Laban's dull house into a very
cradle of life. One was called Beor, one Alub and one Muras. And
after these three successive pregnancies and births Adina not only
suffered no harm but actually looked younger and less insignificant,
and adorned herself assiduously with head bands, girdles and necklaces that Laban bought for her at Harran in the city.

Laban's heart was as glad as it was given his heart to be. He beamed
— as well as he could — the drooping corner of his mouth looked less
sour and more like a smug and even scornful smile. Taken all together, his increase of business and heightened prosperity, added to
the lucky renewal of fruitfulness to his loins, and the merciful relaxation of the curse which had so long darkened his household in consequence of that unlucky speculation in the spiritual, justified all the
self-complacency the man could have felt. He had no doubt that the
birth of his sons, like all the rest of his good fortune, was intimately
bound up with Jacob's presence and partnership, with the blessing
of Yitzchak; he would have been wrong indeed to doubt it. The better spirits of the wedded pair, in particular of Laban, in respect of
the good business his nephew brought him, might have stimulated
their conjugal activity enough to open the sluices of fruitfulness — in
one way or the other Jacob's influence was to be presumed. But that
did not prevent Laban from feeling personal pride. After all, it was
himself who had been clever enough to attach the blessing-bearer to
his house — the fugitive and beggar from whom prosperity obviously
went forth wherever he came and even whether he would or no.
Indeed, from the very moderate joy manifested by Jacob at the births
of Beor, Alub and Muras, Laban deduced that he had very likely
not wished for them at all.

"Tell me, now, my nephew and my son-in-law," Laban might say,
when he came out to the fields riding on an ox, to visit the flocks, or
when Jacob in his turn brought them home for inspection, "tell me

whether I am not worthy of praise, and whether the gods smile upon Laban or no, when they rouse up to me sons in my old age and my wife Adina is big with them and brings them to birth, who before was so plain to look upon?"

"Verily," answered Jacob, "thou hast cause to rejoice, and yet the matter is not greatly marvellous in the sight of the Lord. Abram was one hundred years old when he begot Yitzchak, and it is well known that it was no longer with Sarah after the manner of women."

"Thou hast a dry way," said Laban, "of setting great things at nought and diminishing a man's joy."

"It is little fitting of us," responded Jacob with coolness, "to make too much of good fortune in which we may ascribe great share to our own labours."

Chapter VI

THE SISTERS

THE UNCLEAN BEAST

As the seven years drew on to their end, and the time approached when Jacob should know Rachel, he found he scarcely realized the truth, yet rejoiced beyond measure, and his heart beat mightily when he thought upon the hour. For Rachel was now nineteen years old and had waited for him in the purity of her blood, invulnerable through it to evil spirits and sickness which might have snatched her from her bridegroom; so that she was indeed, in respect to her bloom and beauty, all that Jacob had so tenderly prophesied: lovely to look at beyond all the daughters of the land, with her full and yet delicate form, the soft braids of her hair, the thick nostrils of her little nose, the sweet, short-sighted gaze of her slanting eyes and the friendly night that rested in their depths; lovely above all in the smiling way the upper lip lay upon the lower, and shaped the inexpressible charm of the corner of her mouth. Yes, lovely was she beyond all others; but if I say, as Jacob always said to himself, that she was lovely most of all before Leah, that does not mean that Leah was uglier than any other maiden, but merely that she was the nearest object of comparison, and suffered most of all next to Rachel. For it is quite possible to imagine a man less enslaved than Jacob to that single point of view, who might have preferred the elder daughter, despite the stupid gaze and the "tenderness" of her blue eyes, and the trick she had, both proud and bitter, of dropping the lids over their squinting stare. For Leah's rich blond hair hung knotted in her neck, and she had the figure of a fruitful woman, ripe for motherhood. Much might be said in praise of Rachel, that she did not vaunt her own charms above her sister's, or take undue advantage of her lovely little face, the image and likeness of the full moon, as Leah's might be of the waning one. Rachel was not so untaught as not to reverence the latter in right of its condition, and indeed at the bottom of her heart she disapproved of Jacob, that he so utterly rejected the thought of her sister and turned the brightness of his sole regard upon her — even though she could not quite put out of her heart all feminine satisfaction in his preference.

The nuptial feast was set for the full moon of the summer solstice; and Rachel too confessed that she longed for the coming of the festal day. Yet in the weeks just before she had been sad, weeping silently on Jacob's shoulder and against his cheek, answering his anxious query only by a painful smile and a quick head-shake that dashed the tears from her eyes. What weighed upon her heart? Jacob did not know — yet often he himself felt sad as well. Was she mourning over her maidenhead, since now the time of her blossoming drew to an end, when she should become a fruit-bearing tree? Such is the sadness inseparable from life yet not from joy, and Jacob knew it too. For the day of high marriage is the day of death and a feast of the solstice; the moon climbs to her height and from then on turns her face again to the sun, into which she will sink. Jacob was to know her whom he loved, and begin to die. For from then on he would not stand alone, living for himself and as lord of the world; he would be dissolved into his sons and in his person belong to death. Yet he would love them, they who became the bearers of his divided and diverse lives, because it was himself which consciously he had poured into Rachel's womb.

At this time he had a dream, which he remembered long on account of its strange mood of peaceful sadness. He dreamed it on a warm night of Tammuz, in the meadows by his flocks, when the moon's sickle stood facing left in the sky, which at its fullness should usher in the marriage feast. But in the dream he was still upon his flight from home, or another flight, driven once more to ride into the red waste; and as before a jackal trotted before him, prick-eared, dog-headed, with tail held stiffly out behind him, looked round and laughed. It was a repetition of reality, yet the same reality; recurring to work itself out, since the first time it had been left incomplete.

He was riding among loose boulders and dry shrubbery — naught else grew. The evil one wound among rock and bushes, appearing, disappearing, looking round. Once, when he had vanished, Jacob blinked; when he looked again, the creature sat in front of him on a stone, and was an animal still as to the head, the usual dog's head with sharp upstanding ears and a projecting snout whose mouth ran right round to them; but his body was human down to the slightly dusty toes, and pleasant to look on, like the body of a slender youth. He sat on the piece of rock in a careless posture; one leg was drawn up, and he leaned with his elbow upon that thigh so that a fold came across his abdomen; the other was stretched out before him sidewise, the ankle on the ground. This limb, the delicate knee, the long, fine-sinewed, slightly curving leg, was a most pleasant sight. But a fell, the colour of yellow clay, began on the slender shoulders, the upper

back and breast of the god, merging into the dog's head with the
wide jaws and crafty little eyes, which suited the body so ill, was so
painful a humiliation of it, that one could only say how lovely, without it, that body might have been. As Jacob rode up he got a strong
whiff of the pungent odour which, sad to say, the boy-jackal exhaled.
And how sad and strange at once it was to see the figure open its wide
jaws and address itself to speech in a labouring, throaty voice:

"*Ap-uat, Ap-uat.*"

"It hath no need, son of Osiris, that thou troublest thyself," Jacob
said. "Thou art Anubis, guide and opener of the way, as well I know.
And I had marvelled not to meet thee here."

"It was a blunder," said the god.

"What meanest thou?" asked Jacob.

"They were in error," the other said, in his difficult speech, "they
who begot me, the lord of the west and my mother, Nephthys."

"I am sad to hear it," said Jacob, "but relate to me how it fell out."

"She should not have been my mother," responded the youth, gradually learning to manage his jaws in speech. "She was the wrong
one. The darkness was to blame. She is a cow, it is all one to her. She
wears the disk of the sun between her horns, in sign that now and
again the sun goes in unto her to beget with her the young day; but
the bearing of so many radiant sons has made no abatement in her
dull indifference."

"I seek to understand," Jacob said, "that that might be a danger."

"Very dangerous," agreed the other, nodding. "Blindly, in all the
good-natured warmth of her cowishness she embraces all that comes
to her, and dully passive lets it come to pass, though it happen only
on account of the dark."

"That is an evil," said Jacob. "But which had been the right one,
then, if Nephthys were not she?"

"Dost thou not know?" asked the jackal youth.

"I cannot precisely distinguish," Jacob answered, "between that
which thou tellest me and that which I know of myself."

"If thou knowest it not," the other responded, "then I could not
tell thee. In the beginning — not quite in the beginning, but nearly
so, there were Geb and Nut. The earth god and the heaven goddess.
They had four children: Osiris, Set, Isis and Nephthys. But Isis was
the sister-bride of Osiris and Nephthys of Set the red."

"So much is clear," said Jacob. "And then these four did not keep
the arrangement clearly enough in mind?"

"Alas, no," responded Anubis, "two of them did not. What wouldst
thou, for we are feckless beings, heedless and distracted from birth
onwards. Carefulness and foresight are base earthly characteristics,
whereas what all has not carefreeness been the cause of in this life?"

"It is but too true," Jacob confirmed. "One must take care. For to speak openly, it dependeth on the fact that ye are all idols. God knoweth always what He willeth and doth. He promiseth and keepeth to His word. He setteth up a bond and is true unto eternity."

"What god?" asked Anubis. But Jacob answered him:

"Thou feignest. When earth and heaven mingle, then indeed come forth heroes and great kings, but no god, neither four nor one. Geb and Nut, thou hast thyself said it, were not quite the beginning. Whence came they?"

"Out of Tefnut, the Great Mother," came the prompt reply from the stone.

"Good, thou sayest it because I know it," Jacob went on in his dream. "But was Tefnut the beginning? Whence came Tefnut?"

"The secret, the unbegotten one, whose name is Nun, he called her," responded Anubis.

"I asked thee not his name," said Jacob. "But now thou beginnest to speak sensibly, boy-dog. I had no intent to reason with thee. After all, thou art an idol. Relate to me of thy parents' error."

"The darkness was to blame," repeated the evil-smelling one. "And he that carrieth the scourge and the shepherd's crook, he was carefree and distraught. And in his majesty he sought for Isis, his sisterbride, and by mistake he came in the night upon Nephthys, sister of the red one. Thus she received that great god, thinking he was her bridegroom, and they were both enfolded in the utter unconcern of the night of love."

"Can such things come to pass?" cried Jacob.

"With ease," answered the other. "For in its unconcern night knoweth the truth, and in her eyes the lively prepossessions of the daylight are as naught. For one woman's body is like another's, good to love, good to beget upon. Only the countenance distinguishes one from another and is the cause of our choosing one and not another. For the countenance is of the day, full of living fancies, but before the night, that knows the truth, it is as nothing."

"Thou speakest crudely and without feeling," said Jacob, greatly disquiet. "One may have ground to speak thus when one hath a head like to thine and a face which one must cover up only to be able to say that thy leg is pretty and well-favoured as it lies stretched out before thee."

Anubis looked down, drew his leg in beside the other one and put his hands between his knees.

"Leave me out," said he. "I shall one day be rid of my head too. Wouldst thou hear the rest of the tale?"

"What happened?" asked Jacob.

"In that night," went on the other, "the lord Osiris was for Nephthys like Set the red her lord, and she for Osiris like to the lady Isis. For he was on begetting bent and she on conceiving, and to the night naught else was of importance. And they delighted one another in begetting and conceiving, for thinking to love each other they could but beget. Then was that goddess pregnant with me, whereas it should have been Isis the true wife."

"Sad," Jacob said.

"When morning came, they parted in great haste; yet might all have been well, had not the god left behind with Nephthys the lotus garland that he wears; Set the red found it and roared aloud. Since that time he seeketh Osiris' life."

"As thou tellest it, so I know it," said Jacob. "Then came the affair with the chest, into which the red one lured his brother, and slew him by its means, so that Osiris, the dead lord, swam downstream into the sea in the sealed-up chest."

"And Set became king of all his lands and sat upon the throne of Geb," concluded Anubis. "But it is not that upon which I would dwell, or which gives this dream of thine its point. For the red one was not for long king of the lands, for Isis gave birth to the youth Horus, who slew him. And lo, as Isis went searching and bewailing through the world, after her lost and murdered lord, and cried unceasingly: 'Come into thy house, come into thy house, beloved, O beautiful child, come into thy house!' there stood beside her Nephthys, wife of his murderer, whom the slain god had in his error embraced, and went beside her whither she went, and they agreed together in their grief and mourned together: 'O thou, whose heart beats no more, O lord of beauty, thee I would fain behold!' "

"That was sad and friendly," said Jacob.

"And that," responded the other from his stone, "is the meaning of the dream. For who else was with her and aided her in her search, her roving and her wailing, then as well as later, when Set found the discovered and rehidden corpse and cut it up into fourteen pieces, which then Isis must seek anew? Who but I, Anubis, son of the unlawful wife, fruit of the murdered one, who was ever at Isis' side in her erring and seeking, and as she wandered she laid her arm about my neck that she might lean upon me, and we lamented together: 'Where art thou, thou left arm of my beautiful God, where shoulderblade and foot of his right side, where art thou, lovely head, and holy sex, which it seemeth is irreparably lost so that we are fain to replace it with an image made of sycamore wood?' "

"Thou speakest obscenely," said Jacob, "and like to the deathgod of the two countries." But Anubis replied:

"And thou, where thou standest, shouldst have more understanding for such matters, for thou art a bridegroom, and shalt beget and die. For in the sex is death and in death sex, that is the miracle of the grave chamber, and sex teareth the bonds of death and standeth up against death, as it happened to the lord, Osiris, above whom Anubis

hovered as a female vulture and made his seed flow out of the dead
and cohabited with him even as she mourned."

"It is best now that I should awake," thought Jacob. And even as
he still thought to see the god swing himself up from the stone and
vanish, so that movement and vanishing were the same, he found
himself lying under the starry night beside the sheep-pens. His dream
of Anubis the jackal soon faded, it returned into his simple recollection of the experience of his journey and he remembered it, after a
while, only thus. But a faint melancholy, pleasant to feel, lingered
still a while in his soul, in that Nephthys, wrongfully embraced, had
yet sought and mourned with Isis, and the bereaved one been cherished and supported by the wrongly begot.

THE WEDDING

AT this time Laban and Jacob often took counsel together over the
approaching event and the nuptial celebrations, and how Laban in
general thought to hold the feast; and Jacob learned that his father-
in-law had ambitious plans and meant to celebrate regardless of
expense.

"It will cost me," Laban said, "a pretty penny, for there are now
many more mouths and I must feed them. But I shall not rue it, for
lo, trade is not at all bad, rather fairly favourable in these times,
thanks to many circumstances among which we should mention the
blessing of Isaac. Therefore it is I can pay for more labour in the
court, and have bought two maids in addition to that lazy Iltani, and
they are quite seemly wenches, named Zilpah and Bilhah. And on the
wedding days I will give these to my two daughters, Zilpah to Leah
my eldest and to the second Bilhah. And at the marriage will the maid
be thine, and I will give her thee as dowry and her price shall be reckoned as two-thirds of the mina of silver, according to our contract."

"I embrace thee in thanks," said Jacob, shrugging his shoulders.

"But that is the least of it," went on Laban. "For all the feast will
be at my sole charge, and I will invite people on the sabbath from
far and near and have musicians who shall play and dance, and I will
lay two bullocks and four sheep upon their backs, and comfort the
guests with drink until they see all things double. All that will be a
heavy charge but I will bear it and not pull a long face for is it not
my daughter's wedding? And besides I have in mind to make the
bride a gift, that she may wear it and it will rejoice her heart. I
bought it long ago of a traveller, and it cost much money, and I have
kept it in the chest: a veil, for the bride to shroud herself in, that she
may be holy unto Ishtar and a consecrated one, whose veil also thou
shalt lift. It may have belonged to a king's daughter in times past, being the maiden garment of a daughter of princes, so artfully is it

embroidered throughout with manifold symbols of Ishtar and Tammuz, but she, the spotless one, shall veil her head in it. For immaculate is she and shall be like one of the *enitu*, like to the bride of heaven, whom each year at the feast of Ishtar, the priests at Babel lead up to God before all the people up the steps of the stairs and through the seven gates, and take from her some piece of her garment and her ornaments at every gate, and at the last gate her shame, and they lead the holy maid naked into the uppermost bedchamber of the tower E-temenanki. There she receives the god upon the bed in the darkness of the night and exceedingly great is the mystery."

"H'm," said Jacob. For Laban opened wide his eyes and spread out his fingers at the sides of his head and put on an air of sanctimoniousness that in his nephew's view suited him not at all. Laban continued:

"Of course, it is very fine and lovely when the bridegroom hath a house and court of his own, or is held in great esteem in the house of his parents, whence he cometh in great pomp to fetch the bride and to lead her in procession by land or by water to his own place, and his inheritance. But thou as thou knowest art but a fugitive and homeless man, fallen out with thine own, and sittest with me as my son-in-law, and I make no complaint. There will be no bridal procession by land or water, and you will sojourn here after the feast and the nuptial night; but when I have come between you and touched your foreheads, then we shall do as is the custom of our land in these cases and lead you with singing round the court and into the bridal chamber. Thou shalt sit there upon the bed with a flower in thy hand, and await the bride. For her too, the spotless one, shall we lead round about the court with torches and singing, and at the door of the chamber we put out the torches, and I lead the devoted one in unto thee, and leave you, that thou mayest hand her the flower in the darkness."

"Is that the custom and lawful?" asked Jacob.

"Far and wide, thou sayest it," replied Laban.

"Then will I also approve it," responded Jacob. "And I assume that there will likewise be a torch burning, or a little lamp with a wick, that I may see my bride when I hand her the flower and also afterwards."

"Be silent," cried Laban. "Would I might know what thou hast in thy mind, with thy unchaste speaking, to speak so before the father, to whom it is moreover painful and bitter to lead his child in unto a man that he may uncover her and sleep with her. At least in my presence hold thy lewd tongue and restrain within thyself thy overgreat lustfulness. For hast thou not hands to see, and must thou also swallow up the spotless one with thine eyes to sharpen thy lust upon her shame and her maiden trembling? Have respect before the mystery of the high tower!"

"Pardon!" said Jacob, "and forgive me. I have not meant it so unchastely in my thoughts as it soundeth in thy mouth. Gladly would I have looked upon my bride with my eyes. But since it is far and wide the custom to do as thou sayest, I will be satisfied for the time."

Thus the day of the fullness of splendour came on, and the nuptial feast, and in the house of Laban, the prosperous breeder of sheep, and in his court, there was a slaughtering and a seething and roasting and brewing, so that everything steamed and all was bustle and noise, and all eyes watered from the smoke of the fires that burned under pots and ovens. For Laban was saving of charcoal and heated almost altogether with thorns and dung. And the master and mistress and all that were in the house, including Jacob, hurried on the work and the servants, to make hospitality for so many and to prepare the banquet; for the wedding would last seven days and for all that time the supplies must be inexhaustible, of cakes and buns and fish bread, of thick soups and plantains and milk dishes, of beer and fruit juices and strong waters, not to mention the roasted mutton and joints of beef — else shame and mockery would be the portion of the household. And as they worked they sang songs to Uduntamku the fat, the god of the belly, the presiding deity of feasting, they all sang and composed them, Laban, Adina, Jacob and Leah, Iltani the idle and Bilhah and Zilpah the daughters' maids, Abdcheba the twenty-shekel man, and the latest-acquired slaves. Laban's sons in their little shirts ran boisterously among the press, slipped on the blood from the slaughtering and befouled themselves, so that their father wrung their ears and they howled like jackals. Only Rachel sat still and idle in the house — for she might not see the bridegroom now nor he his bride — and examined the costly veil, her father's present, which she should wear at the feast. It was splendid to see, a magnificent specimen of the arts of weaving and embroidering: it seemed an unmerited piece of good fortune that such a thing should have found its way into Laban's house and his chest; the man who let it go so cheap must have been greatly pressed by circumstances.

It was large and broad, a garment and over-garment, with wide sleeves to put one's arms in at will; so cut that a piece of it could either be drawn over the head to cover it or else wound about the head and shoulders, or else left to hang down the back. And the maiden garment weighed uncertainly in the hand, for it was heavy and light at once, and of unequal weight in different places. The background was of the palest blue, woven thin and fine as a breath of air, a misty nothing, to be squeezed together in one hand, and yet weighted heavily everywhere by the embroidered pictures which covered it with brilliant, glittering colours, carried out in close, fine work, in gold and silver and bronze, and every imaginable shade: white, purple, rose and olive, likewise black and white, all blended together like paintings in bright enamel. And such clever pictures and designs! Here was Ishtar-Mami, in various shapes, a tiny nude figure, pressing milk out of her breast with both hands, the sun and moon on either side. Everywhere the five-pointed star was repeated in varying colours, signifying god; the dove, the bird of the mother-goddess of love, was woven most often in silver thread. Gilgamesh, the hero, two-thirds god and one-third man, was displayed strangling a lion in the bend of his arm. One recognized the human scorpion pair who at the ends of the earth guarded the gate through which the sun goes down to the lower world. One distinguished various animals, sometime paramours of Ishtar and transformed by her — a wolf, a bat, the same who had once been Isullanu, the gardener. But Tammuz, the shepherd, was represented by a brilliant bird, the first partner of her lust, to whom she had decreed weeping year for year; and there was not lacking the fire-breathing bull of heaven, whom Anubis sent against Gilgamesh because of Ishtar's baffled longing and perfervid plaints. The garment slipped through Rachel's hands: she saw a man and woman sitting at both sides of a tree, stretching up their hands to the fruit, while a snake rose up behind the woman's back. And again there was embroidered a sacred tree, with two bearded angels on either side, touching it with scaly masculine cones to make it bear; while above the tree of life the female emblem hovered surrounded by sun, moon and stars. And likewise there were sayings woven into the veil, in broad-pointed signs, lying down or standing straight or slanting. Rachel made out: "I have put off my coat, how shall I put it on?"

She sat and played with the bright-coloured weave, the splendid garment and veil; she wrapped it round her and turned herself about in it, she found new ways to drape its picture-book transparency. Thus she beguiled the time while she waited and the others prepared the feast. Sometimes she had visits from Leah, her sister, who also tried the beauties of the veil upon her own person and afterwards they sat together, and caressed each other, with tears. Why did they weep? They alone knew — though I might go so far as to say that they had different reasons.

When Jacob sat and mused, with swimming gaze, and all the tales that had written themselves in the lines of his face and weighed down his life with their dignified burden came back and were present in his mind, as they had been on the day when he and his red-haired twin had buried their father; then there was one day, and one story, which possessed beyond all others this power of presentness, having inflicted upon him a defeat so devastating to his senses and so humiliating to his feeling that his soul for long could not shake it off, and

only regained faith in itself with the advent of a feeling that was like
a rebirth and resurrection of those shamed and shattered ones. Present, I say, before all, was the story of his wedding day.

They had all, the people of Laban, washed their heads and limbs
in the water of the blessed pond, had anointed and curled themselves
to their taste, put on their festal garments and burned much fragrant
oil, to receive the incoming guests with a sweet savour. And they
came, on foot, on the backs of asses, in carts drawn by bullocks and
mules, men alone, men with women, even with children, if they could
not be left at home: the peasants and cattle-breeders of the neighbourhood, likewise anointed and curled and clad in festal garments;
people like Laban, of the same heavy-handed tribe, with the same
prosaic habits of thought. They saluted, hand to forehead, made en-
quiry into the health of all and sundry, and then settled down in
house and court, round cook-pots and shaded tables. Water having
been poured over their hands and feet, they smacked their lips and
fell to upon the lengthy meal, amid loud invocations in praise of
Shamash and of Laban, father of the bride and giver of the feast. The
banquet was laid in the outer court of the steading, between the storehouses, as well as in the inner court round the altar, on the roof of
the house and in the wooden galleries; and round the altar were
grouped the musicians hired from Harran — they played on harps,
drums and cymbals and likewise danced. The day was windy, the
evening still more so. Clouds glided across the moon, hiding her altogether from time to time, a bad omen to many of those present
though they did not expressly say so. They were simple folk, and
made no distinction between complete darkening and a cloud passing
over her face. A sultry wind went sighing through the steading, got
caught in the chimney of the storehouses, made the tall poplars creak
and groan, and whirling among the savours of the feast, the odours
of the anointed guests and the fumes of the cookery, mingled them
all together in gusts of vapour, and seemed to try to snatch the flames
from the tripods where nard-grass and *budulhu*-gum were burning.
Jacob, when he recalled his wedding day, always recognized in his
nostrils that wind-driven mingling of spices and sweat and roasted
meats.

He sat with the family among the feasting guests in the upper
room, where seven years before he had first broken bread with his
stranger kin; sat with the master, his fruitful wife and their daughters
at a table heaped up with dessert and dainties of various sorts, sweet
breads and dates, cucumbers and garlic, and pledged the guests who
lifted their glasses to him and Laban. Rachel, his bride, whom soon he
should receive for his own, sat beside him, and he kissed from time
to time the seam of her veil that enveloped her in its heavy picture-
folds. She did not lift it to eat or drink; it seemed the consecrated

one's hunger had been satisfied earlier. She sat quiet and silent, only bending meekly her shrouded head when he kissed her veil. Jacob too sat silent and dreamy, with a flower in his hand, a blossoming twig of myrtle from Laban's well-watered garden. He had drunk beer and date wine and his senses were somewhat clouded; his soul could neither free itself for thought nor rouse itself to observation, but was heavy inside his anointed body, and his body was his soul. Gladly would he have thought, gladly comprehended how his god had brought all this to pass; how he had brought the beloved in the way of the fugitive, the human creature whom he had but needed to behold for his heart to elect her and love her for all time and eternity — beyond itself, and in the children whom his love would beget. He tried to rejoice in his victory over time, that hard time of waiting, laid upon him, it seemed, in penance for Esau's undoing and his bitter weeping; to lay it at the feet of God the Lord, in thanks and praise, this triumph, for that it was His; God through him and his not unachieving patience having enforced the time, that seven-headed monster, as once the dragon of chaos, so that what had been but inward wish and waiting was now the present, and Rachel sat beside him in the veil, which in a little while he would be permitted to lift. He tried to partake of this joy in his soul. But with joy it is as with the waiting for it; the longer one waits, the less it is pure joy, the more it is filled with practical activities and living needs. And when it comes, that joy so actively awaited, it is not of the stuff of the divine, but has become bodily present and has material weight, like all life. For the life of the body is never pure bliss, but a mixture, in part unpleasant, and if joy becomes the life of the body the soul does also, and is no longer anything else but the body, with the oil-soaked pores, whose affair that once distant bliss has now become.

Jacob sat, and spanned his thighs, and thought of his sex, whose property this joy had now become, and which very soon might and must approve itself mightily in the holy darkness of the nuptial chamber. For his joy was marriage joy and a feast of Ishtar; it was celebrated with over-eating and drunkenness, wreathed about with the odours of spices — whereas once it had been God's affair and rested in his hand. And as once Jacob had been pained over the waiting, and forced to forget it in life and action, so now he was pained for the sake of God, who was the Lord of life and all the longed-for future, yet, when the hour came to pass, must yield his dominion to the special idols of the physical, in whose sign it stood. And therefore Jacob kissed the little nude figure of Ishtar, lifting the hem of Rachel's veil as she sat beside him, immaculate sacrifice to procreation.

Laban sat opposite, leaning forward with his heavy arm on the table and looking steadfastly at his son-in-law.

"Rejoice, my son and my sister's son, for thy hour is at hand and

the day of rewarding, and thou shalt be paid the reward according
to law and contract for the seven years that thou hast laboured for
my house and my business to the reasonable satisfaction of its head.
And the reward is neither goods nor gold but a tender maiden, my
daughter, whom thy heart desireth, and thou shalt have her after thy
heart's desire, and she shall be submissive to thee in thy arms. I marvel how thy heart may be beating, for the hour is big for thee, truly
an hour of life like to be thy greatest hour, great as the hour when in
thy father's tent thou wonnest the blessing, as thou hast told me, thou
crafty one and son of a crafty woman!"

Jacob did not hear.

But Laban mocked at him with gross words before the guests:

"Tell me, then, son-in-law, hear me and answer how dost feel?
Dost thou quake before the bliss of embracing thy bride? Hast thou
not fear as once in that matter of the blessing, when thou wentest in
to thy father with thy knees shaking? Didst thou not say the sweat
ran down thy thighs for dread and thy voice stuck in thy throat even
when thou wouldst win the blessing away from Esau the accursed?
Thou happy man, pray that joy take not away thy manliness in the
moment when thou needest it most — else the bride might take it ill!"

They all roared with laughter in the upper room, and once more
Jacob smiled and kissed the picture of Ishtar to whom God had given
the hour. But Laban got heavily to his feet, swaying somewhat, and
said:

"Come then, for it is midnight, come up to me and I will put you
together."

The crowd pressed close to see Jacob and Rachel kneel down on
the paved floor before the bride's father, and to hear how Jacob answered to the questions according to custom. For Laban asked him
whether this woman should be his wedded wife and he her husband,
and if he willed to give her the flower — to which he answered yes.
Asked whether he was well-born, whether he would make rich this
woman and fruitful her womb; Jacob answered that he was the son
of the great and would fill her lap with silver and gold and make fruitful this woman like the fruit of the garden. Then Laban touched both
their foreheads, and stepped between them and laid his hands upon
them. Then he told them to stand up and embrace each other and
that then they were wed. And he led the dedicated one back to her
mother, but the nephew he took by the hand and led him in front of
the guests, who crowded after, beginning to sing. They passed down
the brick staircase into the paved court and the musicians left their
stand and walked before them. Next came boys with torches and
after them children in short smocks with censers hanging between
chains. Jacob, led by Laban, walked in the sweet-smelling cloud, with
the white blossoming myrtle twig in his right hand. He did not join

in the traditional songs that swelled up as they marched, and only
hummed a little when Laban nudged him and told him to open his
mouth. But Laban sang in a heavy bass and knew all the songs by
heart; they were sentimental and amorous ditties about loving couples in general, on the verge of their nuptials, and how on both sides
they can scarcely wait. They told of the procession, coming out of
the wilderness like pillars of smoke, perfumed with myrrh and frankincense; and of the bridegroom walking, with the crown wherewith
his mother crowned him on the day of his espousals. All this was
about the procession in which they were actually moving, but the
allusions did not fit Jacob; his mother was far away, he was a fugitive, and he was not leading his beloved into his mother's house and
into the chamber of her who had borne him. Just for that reason, it
seemed, Laban sang the more lustily, honouring the pattern in the
face of all present lacks, that Jacob might feel how different it was.
And then the bridegroom spoke, in the song, and the bride gave
ardent answer and they sang in turn long rapturous speeches of mutual praise and longing. Their bed was freshly prepared in the pan-
elled chamber; they pointed one another the way thither, promising
the greatest pleasure in the union of their nard-scented loveliness. For
his left hand would be under her head and his right hand embrace
her, and sweeter than wine from the hills would be their mutual love.
Thus they told one another in song, each painting in intoxicated language the other's loveliness. And finally they charged the company
to stir not up nor awake from voluptuous slumber either bride or
bridegroom until they pleased. They implored the people in song,
by the roes and by the hinds of the field, and the company took up
the words as they paced and sang them with great heartiness; even
the incense-bearing boys sang lustily if without precise understanding. And so they marched, in the windy, moon-darkened night, round
Laban's steading, once and twice, and came before the house and before the house door of palm-wood, and Laban pressed through, with
the musicians in the lead, and came to the bed-chamber on the ground
floor, that likewise had a door, and Laban led in Jacob by the hand.
He made light with the torches, that Jacob might see into the room
and make out the position of table and bed. Then he wished him
blessings on his manhood and turned back to the company that
crowded about the doorway. They went away, singing as they went,
and Jacob was alone.

After long decades, and in his great age, and even on his dying bed,
where he still spoke solemnly of it, Jacob remembered naught more
clearly than how he had stood alone in the darkness of the bridal
chamber, where it blew, and was draughty, for the night wind burst
through the window-openings under the roof and out again through
the openings on the side toward the court, getting caught in the car-

pets and hangings with which, as Jacob had seen by the torchlight, they had adorned the walls, and making a great flapping and clapping. It was the room above the archive and grave chamber, with the teraphim and the receipts. Jacob could feel through the thin carpet they had put down the ring of the little trap door by which one went down. And he had seen the bed and he went towards it with his hands out. It was the best bed in the house, one of three; Laban and Adina had sat on it at that first meal seven years ago: a sofa on metal-covered feet, with a round headrest of polished bronze. They had put covers on the wooden frame, with linen over them, Jacob could feel it, and there were pillows against the headrest. But it was a narrow bed. On the table beside it stood beer and a little food. There were two tabourets in the room, also covered with stuff, and lamp-stands at the bed's head, but there was no oil in the lamps.

Jacob tried the lamps and discovered their emptiness, as he stood in the wind and the darkness while the train was fetching the bride and filling house and court with the noise of their singing and the trampling of their feet. He sat down on the bed and listened, the flower in his hand. The procession was leaving the house again, with the harps and cymbals at its head, bringing Rachel, his beloved, to whom all his heart belonged, and she walked there in her veil. Laban led her by the hand as he had done Jacob; perhaps Adina was there too, and the music of the wedding songs rose and died away. At last he heard the words:

"My beloved is mine, he is altogether mine;
  I am a garden enclosed, full of pleasant fruits and full of the odours
    of the finest spices.
  Come, O beloved into thy garden!
  Eat of thy pleasant fruits, take unto thee the refreshment of their
    juices!"

The feet of those who sang were before the door, and the door opened a little so that snatches of the song and the music came through, and then the veiled one was in the room, ushered by Laban, who closed the door quickly and they were alone in the darkness.

"Is it thou, Rachel?" Jacob asked after a little while, during which he had waited for those outside to move away from the door. He asks as one says: "Have you returned from your journey?" when the traveller stands there in the flesh and it cannot be otherwise than that he has returned, so that the question is nonsense, only asked that the voice may be heard and the traveller does not answer but can only laugh. But Jacob heard that she bent her head, he knew it from the faint rustling and rattling of the light-heavy veil.

"Thou beloved, little one, my dove, and apple of my eye, heart of my heart," he said fervently. "It is so dark . . . and bloweth. . . . I am sitting here upon the bed, if thou hast not seen it, straight into the room and then somewhat to the right. Come, then, but strike not against the table else a bruise will come upon thy tender skin and also thou wouldst knock over the beer. I am not thirsty for beer, I am only thirsty for thee, my pomegranate. How good that they have brought thee to me and that I sit here no longer alone in the wind. Comest thou now? Gladly would I come to meet thee, but that probably I may not, for it is by law and custom that I hand thee the flower while sitting, and though no one seeth us, yet we will hold to that which is prescribed, that we may be well and truly wedded as we have steadfastly desired through so many years of waiting."

The thought overcame him, his voice broke. Memories of the time when in patience and in impatience he had arisen for the sake of this hour, laid hold on him mightily and moved him to the depths; and the thought that she had waited with him and now on her side saw herself at the goal of her desires stirred the tenderest emotions of his heart. Such is love, when it is complete: feeling and lust together, tenderness and desire; and while feeling made the tears gush out of Jacob's eyes, at the same time he felt the tension of his manhood.

"Here art thou," he said, "thou hast found me in the darkness, as I found thee after more than seventeen days' journey and thou camest on among the sheep and spoke: 'Behold, a stranger!' Then we chose each other among men and I have served for thee seven years and the time lies at our feet. My doe and my dove, here is the flower. Thou seest it and findest it not, and therefore I will guide thy hand to the twig that thou mayest take it, and I give it to thee and thus we are one. But thy hand I keep, since I so love it, and I love the bones of thy wrist, so well known unto me that I know it again in the darkness, and thy hand is to me like thyself, and like thy whole body, but that is like to a sheaf of wheat garlanded with roses. My sister, my love, let thyself down to me and sit by my side and I will move that there may be space for two and would be for three if needful. Yet how good is God, that He lets us be two alone together, thee by me and me by thee! For I love only thee, for the sake of thy face that I cannot now see but saw a thousand times and kissed for very love, for it is thy loveliness that crowns thy body as with roses, and when I think that thou art Rachel, with whom I have often been, yet never thus, and who waited for me and likewise now waiteth for me, and upon my tenderness, then a bliss cometh upon me stronger than I am, so that it overcometh me. A darkness enfoldeth us, thicker than thy veil which enfoldeth thee, thou purest one, and darkness is bound upon our eyes so that they see naught beyond themselves and are blind. But it is only they, thanks be to God, and not one of our other

senses. For we hear each other when we speak, and the darkness cannot part us more. Tell me, my soul, thou too art enraptured by the
greatness of this hour?"

"I am thine in bliss, dear lord," she softly said.

"That might have been Leah who spoke, thy older sister," he answered. "Not according to the sense, of course, but in the way of
speaking. The voices of sisters are alike, indeed, and words come from
their mouths with the same sound. For the same father begot them,
upon the same mother, and they are a little distinguished in time and
move with separate movement, yet are one in the womb of their origin. Lo, I am afraid, a little, at my own blind words, for I had lightly
said that the darkness hath no power over our speech, yet I feel after
all that it presseth hard upon my words and sinketh into them so
that I fear somewhat before them. Let us be glad of the distinction,
that thou art Rachel and I Jacob, and not for instance Esau, my red
brother! My forefathers and I, at night beside the flocks, have pondered much upon the person of God, who He is, and our children
and our children's children will follow us in our musings. But I at this
hour will say and make clear my words, that the darkness may roll
back away from them: 'God is the distinction!' And therefore now
I lift thy veil, beloved, that I may see thee with seeing hands; and I
lay it carefully upon this chair that is here, for it is priceless with
pictures and shall be handed down through generations, and be worn
by beloved ones without number. Lo, here is thy hair, black but
comely, I know it so well, I know the fragrance of it, I carry it to my
lips and what power hath darkness over it? It cannot come in between my lips and thy hair. Here are thine eyes, smiling night in
the night, and their tender sockets and the soft places beneath them
where so many a time I have kissed away the impatient tears, and
my lips were wet from them. Here are thy cheeks, soft as down and
the costliest wool of goats from strange lands. Here thy shoulders,
which feel to mine hands larger than I see them in the day, and here
thine arms, and here — "

He ceased. As his seeing hands left her face and found her body
and the skin of her body, Ishtar pierced them both to the marrow,
the bull of heaven breathed and its breath was as the breath of both
that mingled. And all that windy night did Jacob find the child of
Laban a glorious mate, great in delights and mighty to conceive, and
she received him many times and again and again, so that they counted
no more but the shepherds answered one another that it was nine
times.

Later he slept on the ground beside her, for the bed was narrow
and he gave her room and comfort for her rest, sleeping himself
crouching beside the bed, with his cheek against her hand that hung
over the edge. The morning dawned. Dim red and hushed it stood

before the windows, and slowly filled with light the bridal chamber. It was Jacob who first awaked, from the daylight between his lids, and from the stillness; for until deep into the night the feasting had continued, with much laughter and noise in house and court, and only toward morning, when the bridal pair already slept, had quiet descended. And also he was uncomfortable — though how joyfully — and waked the easier. He stirred and felt her hand, remembering everything and turned his mouth to kiss it. Then raised his head to see his dear one in her slumbers. With eyes heavy and sticky from sleep, still unwilling to focus, he looked at her. And it was Leah.

He dropped his eyes and shook his head with a smile. "Ah," thought he, while even then a chill crept round his heart and into the pit of his stomach, "what madness, what a morning-after mockery! Darkness was hung before mine eyes, and now that they are unblinded they see false things. Are then sisters so mysteriously alike, and show it in their sleep, though no likeness shows itself in their features? Let me look again!"

But he did not look, because he feared to, and what he said to himself was only a panic-struck gabbling. He had seen that she was blonde, and her nose somewhat red. He rubbed his eyes with his knuckles and forced himself to look. It was Leah who lay and slept.

The thoughts tumbled over each other in his head. How came Leah here, and where was Rachel, whom they had brought in unto him and whom he had known this night? He staggered backwards away from the bed into the middle of the room and stood there in his shirt, his fists to his cheeks. "Leah!" he screamed, in a strangled voice. She sat up at once. She blinked, smiled, and dropped her eyelids as he had so often seen her do. One shoulder and breast were bare; they were white and beautiful.

"Jacob, my husband," she said, "let it be so, according to the father's will. For he would have it so and so arranged it, and the gods shall give me that to make thee thank both him and them."

"Leah," he stammered, and he pointed to his throat, his breast and his brow, "since when is it thou?"

"Always it was I," she answered, "and I was thine this night ever since I entered in the veil. And always I was tender towards thee and ready as Rachel, since I saw thee from the roof; and have I not proved it to thee the whole of this night? For say thyself if I have not served thee as well as any woman could, and been strong in desire! And certain am I in my inwards that I have conceived from thee, and it shall be a son, strong and brave, and we shall call his name Reuben."

Then Jacob cast back and bethought himself how he had taken her for Rachel this night, and he went to the wall and laid his arm along it and his forehead on his arm and wept bitterly.

Thus for some while he stood, torn by his emotions, and each time the thought returned, how he had believed and had known her, how all his joy had been delusion and the hour of fulfilment turned to shame, for which he had served and conquered the time, it was with him as though his stomach and his brain turned over within him, and he despaired with his whole soul. But Leah knew no more to say, and only wept likewise, from time to time, as she had done the day before with Rachel. For she saw how little it had been she who had again and again received him, and only the thought that she would now in all probability have a fine son named Reuben came to strengthen her heart.

Then he left her and rushed out of the chamber. He had almost stumbled over the sleepers that lay everywhere outside in house and court, in the disorder from the feast, on covers and mats or on the bare ground, sleeping off their debauch. "Laban!" he cried, and stepped over forms that emitted surly grunts, stretched out and snored again. "Laban!" he repeated more quietly, for torment and bitterness and the fierce demand for a reckoning did not slay in him all consideration for these sleepers in the early morning after the heavy feasting. "Laban! where art thou?" And came before the master's chamber, where he lay with Adina his wife, knocked and cried: "Laban, come forth!"

"What, what!" answered Laban from within. "Who is it calleth me in the early dawn, after I have been sleeping?"

"It is I. Thou must come out!" Jacob cried.

"Oh, indeed," said Laban. "So it is my son-in-law that calleth, and sayeth I, like a child, as though one could tell from that alone who he is, but I know the voice and will come forth to hear what he hath to tell to me in the dawning, though just then I was enjoying my best sleep." And came forth in his shift, with rumpled hair, and blinking.

"I was asleep," he repeated. "Such a deep sleep and doing me so much good. How comes it thou thyself sleepest not or dost according to thy new state?"

"It is Leah," said Jacob, with trembling lips.

"Of a surety," replied Laban, "and callest thou me in the grey dawn out of beneficent slumber after heavy drinking to tell me what I know as well as thou?"

"Thou monster, thou tiger, thou devilish man!" cried Jacob beside himself. "I tell thee not that thou mayest know it, but to show thee I know it and to bring thee to accounting in my torment."

"Take care of thy voice above all then," said Laban, "that thou lowerest it considerably: that I counsel thee, if thou lettest not thyself be counselled by the plain circumstances. For not enough that I am thy uncle and father-in-law, and thy master to boot, whom it beseemeth not to breathe upon with cries of murder, but also house and court lie full of sleeping guests, as thou seest, who in a few hours

will go out with me to the hunt and take their pleasure in the wild
and in the reedy places of the swamps, where we will set snares for
birds, the partridge and the bustard, or slay a wild boar, that we may
pour out a tribute of liquor to him. Thereto my guests strengthen
themselves in slumber, and I mar it not, and in the evening the drinking bout shall go on. But thou, when on the fifth day thou issuest
out of the bride's chamber, shalt join with us in the pleasures of the
chase."

"No pleasures can there be for me in the chase," answered Jacob,
"and my poor senses do not set that way, which thou hast confused
and brought to shame so that they cry out from earth to heaven. For
thou hast deceived me beyond all bounds, with cruelty and shamelessness, and hast privily brought in Leah to me, thy elder daughter,
in the place of Rachel for whom I have served thee. How shall I
then deal with thee and with me?"

"Hearken now," said Laban, "there are words which thou hadst
best not take upon thy tongue and shouldst shame thyself to utter
them aloud; for in Amurruland there sits as I know a shaggy-haired
man who weeps and tears his fleece and seeks after thy life, and he
it is might well speak of deception. It is unpleasant when a man must
blush for another man because he blusheth not for himself, and thus
standeth it at the moment between thee and me because of thy
ill-chosen words. Sayst thou I have betrayed thee? In what respect?
Have I brought in unto thee a bride who was no longer unspotted
and unworthy to mount the seven stairs into the arms of the god?
Or have I brought thee one deformed and incapable in body or who
cried out at the hurt thou gavest her, and was not willing and serviceable to thee in thy lust? Is it after this fashion I have betrayed
thee?"

"No," Jacob said, "not after such a fashion. Leah is great in conceiving. But thou hast gone behind me and duped me, and made it so
that I did not see and took Leah for Rachel throughout the night, and
I have given to the wrong one my soul and all the best of my
strength, so that it repenteth me beyond my power to utter. This,
thou wolf-man, hast thou done unto me."

"And thou callest it betraying and shamelessly likenest me to wild
beasts and evil spirits because I held with the custom and as a righteous man did not presume to reject that which is sacred and traditional? I know not how such things are in Amurruland or in the country of king Gog, but in our land we give not the younger before the
elder; that would be to smite tradition in the face, and I am a respectable man and law-abiding. Thus did I what I did, and dealt wisely
against thy unreason and like a father who knoweth what is owing
to his children. For thou hast bluntly affronted my love to my eldest
born, saying to me 'Leah speaketh not unto my manly desires.' And

therefore hast thou not deserved a correction and called down upon
thee an admonishment? For now thou hast seen whether she speaketh
to thy manly desires or no!"

"I have seen nothing at all," Jacob cried. "It was Rachel whom I
embraced."

"Yes, so the dawning hath proven," answered Laban mockingly;
"but the truth is that Rachel, my little one, hath nothing whereover
to complain. For the reality was Leah's but the intent was Rachel's.
And now have I also taught thee the intent for Leah, and whichsoever
thou embracest in the future there will be the reality as well as the
intent."

"Wilt thou then give me Rachel?" Jacob asked.

"Of a surety," answered Laban. "If thou wilt have her and pay me
the legal price, thou shalt have her."

But Jacob cried:

"I have served thee for Rachel seven years!"

"Thou hast," responded Laban with dignity and solemnity, "served
me for a child. Wilt thou now have the second, as would be agreeable unto me, then must thou pay again."

Jacob was silent.

After a little he said: "I will obtain the buying price and see to it
that I contribute the dowry. I will borrow a mina of silver from
people with whom I deal in trade, and I will likewise pay for presents
to hang on the bride's girdle; for some possessions have naturally,
and without my will, cleaved unto me in this long time, and I am of
more substance than when I first wooed for Rachel."

"Again thou speakest without any delicacy," answered Laban, with
a smug shake of the head, "and foolishly bringest things to speech
which it were better to bury in thy bosom; thou shouldst rather be
glad if others also keep silent and dwell not upon them to rebuke thee
for them, instead of shouting them aloud and making it so that a man
must be ashamed for thee since thou art not for thyself. I will hear
nothing of unexpected possessions and provocations of that sort. I
will have no silver of thee as dowry and no gear, from whomever it
be, as presents for the bride, but rather shalt thou serve me for the
second child as long as for the first."

"Wolf-man!" cried Jacob, hardly restraining himself. "And thou
wilt give me Rachel only after another seven years?"

"Who hath said so?" countered Laban, superiorly. "Who hath even
so much as suggested such a thing? Thou alone pratest without any
reason and in thy haste comparest me to a werewolf; for I am a
father and I will not that my child pine after the man until he is old.
Go thou now to thy right place and keep thy week and thine honour.
Then shall the second be given thee in all stillness, and thou shalt
serve me as her husband other seven years."

Jacob hung his head and was silent.

"Thou art silent," Laban said, "and canst not bring it over thyself to fall at my feet. Truly I am curious, whether I shall yet succeed to awaken thy heart to thankfulness. That I stand here in the dawning in my shift, disturbed out of my most needful slumber and deal with thee, it seems is not enough to engender in thee such a feeling. I have not mentioned yet that with the second child thou receivest likewise the second maid which I bought. For to Leah I give Zilpah as dowry, and to Rachel Bilhah, and two-thirds of the mina of silver that I give thee shall be reckoned in. Thus thou hast four wives overnight and a women's house like the king of Babel, thou that sattest so lately barren and forlorn."

Jacob still kept silence.

"Thou cruel man," he said at last, with a sigh. "Thou knowest not what thou hast done unto me; thou knowest and thinkest not on it, I must believe, nor can have any imagining of it in thy iron heart. I have squandered my soul and all the best of me upon the wrong woman this night, and that crusheth my heart together at thought of the right one for whom it was meant and I shall have to do with Leah all the week, and when my flesh is weary for I am only human, and it is sated and my soul all too drowsy for high feelings, then shall I be given the right one, Rachel, my treasure. And thou thinkest it is good so. But that can never be made good, which thou hast done to me and to Rachel thy child, and even unto Leah, who sitteth there upon her bed in tears because I had her not in my mind."

"Dost thou mean," Laban asked, "that after the marriage week with Leah thou wilt have no more manhood left to make fruitful the second?"

"Not that, may God forbid," answered Jacob.

"All the rest is whimseys and moonshine," concluded Laban. "Art satisfied with our new contract, and shall it be so or no between me and thee?"

"Yea, it shall be so," said Jacob, and went back to Leah.

OF GOD'S JEALOUSY

Such, then, are the tales of Jacob, written in the mien of the grey-haired man, as they passed before his swimming gaze, that got entangled in his eyebrows, when he fell into his solemn musing, either alone or with other people — and his look gave them a start, so that they nudged each other and whispered: "Hush, Jacob is thinking of his stories!" Many of them I have already told and put in their proper light, even some which lie further ahead in point of time, such as Jacob's return to the west and the events thereafter; but seventeen years rich with incidents and episodes remain to be filled in, of these the most important being Jacob's double wedding with Leah and Rachel, and the birth of Reuben.

But Reuben was Leah's and not Rachel's; Leah bore to Jacob his first son, who later trifled away his birthright, being like water for instability, it was not Rachel who conceived and bore him, the bride of Jacob's affection did not present to her lord this child, nor, according to the will of God, Simeon, Levi, Dan or Judah, or any of the ten ending with Zebulun; although at the end of the wedding feast, after Jacob had left Leah on the fifth day and somewhat refreshed himself by going bird-shooting with the company, Rachel was brought in unto him — upon which event I will not further dwell. For I have already told how Jacob received Rachel; as the result of Laban's chicanery he first received her in Leah, and it was in fact a double wedding that was held, the marriage with two sisters, one of whom he actually married but the other in intent — and in this sense what do we mean by actually? For from this point of view Reuben was after all Rachel's son, conceived by union with her. And yet she that was so ready and willing went empty away, and Leah rounded apace, and folded her hands in contentment over her burden, with her head meekly on one side and her lids dropped to hide her squint.

She was delivered on the bricks, and displayed great talent, it was a matter of a couple of hours, perfect child's play. Reuben shot out like a stream of water, and when Jacob, being hastily summoned, came in from the field, for it was the time of the sesame harvest, the infant was already bathed, rubbed off with salt and wrapped up in swaddling bands. He put his hand upon him, and in the presence of all the household he said: "My son." Laban made a congratulatory speech. He adjured Jacob to be as untiring as himself, to add a new name three years running to his credit — and the newly delivered cried out joyfully from her bed across the court: Twelve years running, without pause, she would be fruitful. Rachel heard it.

Rachel could not be got to leave the cradle, it hung from the ceiling by cords, so that Leah could guide it with her hand. Rachel sat at the other side and looked at the child. When it cried she got up and gave it to her sister, who put it to her swelling, milk-veined breast; looked on greedily as it suckled, growing red and steamy with satisfaction; and watching pressed her hands against her own delicate bosom.

"Poor little one," Leah would say to her. "Fret not thyself, thy turn will come. And thy prospects are far better than mine, for it is thee upon whom the master's eyes are turned, and for once that he cometh to me there are four or six times that he is with thee, then how canst thou fail?"

But whatever the prospects for Rachel, it was Leah, by God's will, in whom they were fulfilled; for scarcely was she about than she was again expectant, and went carrying Reuben upon her back and Simeon in her belly; and felt hardly sick as he began to wax, and found it no matter for sighing that he made her greatly misshapen; but was sturdy and of good cheer up till the end, and worked in Laban's fruit-garden until her hour came and her face changed and she gave order for the bricks to be set up. Then came forth Simeon with the greatest ease, and sneezed. He was admired of all, and most by Rachel, and what anguish it gave her to admire him! For the matter stood a little differently this time, indeed: consciously and undeceived Jacob had begot him upon Leah, he was hers entirely and beyond a doubt.

And Rachel — how was it with the little one? How blithely and earnestly she had looked in her cousin's eyes, with what courage and loving readiness for life! How confidently she had hoped and felt that she would bring forth to him children in both their likenesses, even sometimes twins! And now she went empty away, while Leah rocked her second born. How came this about?

The letter of the tradition is all we have, when we seek to explain this melancholy fact. Briefly it says: "And when the Lord saw that Leah was hated he opened her womb, but Rachel was barren." Just for that reason. It is an attempt at explanation, as good as another, a hypothesis, for we have no direct and authentic utterance of El Shaddai as to the meaning of this decree and doubtless one never existed. It would be proper, however, to reject the interpretation if I knew a better one; but since I do not, I prefer to consider this one as essentially correct.

The kernel of it is that God's dispensation was not primarily directed against Rachel, nor in Leah's favour. Rather it constituted a discipline and an admonishment for Jacob himself, who, that is, was therein instructed that the soft and sentimental sovereignty he permitted to his feelings, the arrogance with which he cherished and promulgated them, were looked upon by Elohim with much disfavour — notwithstanding that this very tendency to selection, and unbridled indulgence in arbitrary favouritism, this pride of feeling which would not submit itself to judgment but rather required all the world to take it at its own valuation, might be referred back to a higher prototype, of which it was in fact the mortal counterpart. Do I say although? Precisely because Jacob's glorification of his feelings was a duplicate of the other, it was punished. Anyone undertaking to speak on this point must take heed to his words; but even after the most scrupulous examination of the words I have quoted, there is no doubt that the motive power of the measure was God's jealousy of a privilege which, as He sought to make clear by this humiliation of Jacob's feeling, he regarded as his sole prerogative. I may be blamed for this interpretation, and it will hardly escape the objection that so petty and passionate a motive as jealousy is inapplicable as an explanation of divine decrees. But those who feel the offensiveness of the interpretation are free to regard the decree as a relic, spiritually unabsorbed, of earlier and less disciplined stages in the development of the divine essence — primitive manifestations, upon which I have earlier sought to cast some light: I mentioned, for instance, the facial type of Yahu, warrior and weather control, lord of a swarthy troop of sons of the desert who called themselves his soldiers, which displayed harsh and violent traits as distinct from any holy ones whatever.

The bond of God with the human spirit active in Abram was a bond for the purpose of mutual sanctification, a bond in which human and divine necessity were so mingled that one can scarcely say from which side, human or divine, the original impulse went out; but a bond, in any case, the existence of which betrays that the sanctification of God and that of man represent a dual process in which both are most intimately "bound up." Else, one might ask, why a bond? God's command to men: "Be holy, even as I am holy!" already assumes the sanctification of God in man; it really means "Let me become sanctified in thee and be thou also sanctified." In other words, the purification of God from the gloomy and violent deity into the sanctified one includes if we work it backwards that of man too, in whom it is consummated by God's urgent wish. This inward link, however, between the two situations, and the facts that God only attains His true dignity by the aid of the human spirit, and that man, on the other hand, only becomes worthy by contemplation of the actuality of God and its reference to Himself — precisely this highly connubial combination and reciprocity of relations, sealed in the flesh, and vouched for by the ring of circumcision, makes it understandable that precisely jealousy, as a survival of God's passionate and unsanctified stage, has remained longest with Him, either as jealousy of idols or perhaps of His prior right and prerogative of extravagant feeling — which is at bottom the same thing.

For what was that uncontrolled feeling of one human being for another, which Jacob permitted himself for Rachel, and later, perhaps even intensifiedly, for her firstborn, but idolatry? Jacob's experiences with Laban may still, in part, be rightly understood as a just retribution for Esau's sufferings and fate, as a squaring of accounts with him in whose favour the balance had inequitably been weighed down. But on the other hand when one considers Rachel's sad destiny, and after that remembers all that young Joseph had to bear, so that it was only by exceeding shrewdness and adroitness in his dealings with God and man that he managed to give things a turn to the good at last, one feels convinced beyond the shadow of a doubt that what we are dealing with is jealousy of the purest water and in

the most literal sense; not merely general and with respect to a prerogative, but highly personal jealousy of the objects of the idolatrous
feeling by which it was roused to an avenging rage — in a word, with
passion. We may call it a primitive survival, if we will; the fact remains that only in passion does the turbulent word of "the living
God" rightly test and fulfil itself. After we have heard the whole
story we shall realize that Joseph, however much his weaknesses injured him, possessed more understanding for this livingness of God,
and knew better how to take skilful cognizance of it, than his father
who begot him.

OF RACHEL'S DISTRACTION

LITTLE Rachel, of course, knew nothing of all this. She hung on
Jacob's neck and said to him: "Give me children, else I die." He
answered: "Little pigeon, of what avail is all this? For thine impatience maketh thy husband likewise to feel impatient, and I should
not have thought that I could ever have such a feeling against thee
in my heart. Truly it hath no reason that thou shouldst hang about
me with prayers and tears. Am I in God's stead, who hath withheld
from thee the fruit of thy womb?"

He put it off on God, by way of saying that the fault was not his,
and that he had given ample evidence that he was not to blame —
for was he not fruitful in Leah? To advise the younger sister to turn
her prayers to God was the same as to say that the trouble lay at her
door, in which, as in the vibration of his voice, he betrayed his impatience. It was natural that he should be irritated, for it was silly of
Rachel to implore him for something for which he himself felt equal
longing without making his disappointed hopes a reproach to her.
Still, one must needs make excuses for the poor child, for if she remained barren, she had the worse end of it. She was friendliness itself,
but it was more than her woman's nature could bear and not feel
jealous of her sister; and envy is a solvent to the emotions in which
much else besides admiration unfortunately comes to the surface, and
the reaction simply cannot be the best in the world. It could not but
undermine the sisterly feeling between the two — in fact it already did
so. Leah's maternal status outweighed the advantage of her infertile
co-wife, whose appearance was so much that of a virgin that the
other must have been a hypocrite to be able to betray in her manner
no trace of any consciousness of her superior worth. In the accepted
and thoughtless phrase, the wife who had blessed her husband with
children was the "beloved," the other the "unloved" wife; a terminol-
ogy hateful to Rachel's ears, and utterly false to boot; it was only
human that she could not be content with the fact, but must bring
it to speech and utter it. It unfortunately came to this, that she would

refer, with flashing eyes and paling cheek, to Jacob's never concealed preference and his more frequent visits at night — a sore point
with Leah, of course, who, when it was touched upon, could only
answer with a shrug that at least they did her no good. Thus sisterly
tenderness was at an end, and Jacob stood embarrassed between
the two.

Laban looked gloomily on. He rejoiced that the daughter whom
Jacob had scorned should now come to honour; but he suffered for
Rachel, and also he began to fear for his shekels. The law-giver had
set down in writing that if one wife went childless the father-in-law
must return the money, for such a marriage was only a mistake.
Laban hoped that Jacob had not understood this, but he might learn
it any day, and when there was no more hope for Rachel, Laban or
his sons might be faced with the prospect of paying Jacob in cash for
his seven years' service. The thought lay heavy in Laban's belly.

Therefore, when in the third year of her marriage Leah was again
expectant, being big this time with the boy Levi, and on Rachel's
side there was no stirring whatever, it was Laban who came forward
with the suggestion that there were certain measures which might
be taken; in fact he demanded that something be done and introduced
into the conversation the name of Bilhah, saying that Jacob might
lie with her that she might bear upon Rachel's knees. It would be a
mistake to suppose that Rachel had suggested, must less advocated,
this after all rather obvious resource. Her feelings with regard to it
were much too mixed for her to do more than simply acquiesce. But
it is true that she was on close and friendly terms with Bilhah, her
maid, an attractive little thing, before whose charms Leah had later to
abandon the field entirely; and her craving to possess the dignity of
motherhood drove out all the natural disinclination she must have
felt for acting as once her stern father had acted, and introducing
with her own hands a substitute into Jacob's bed.

Actually the affair was done the other way round: she led Jacob
by the hand to Bilhah, who had scented herself beyond all limits and
whose little head was swimming with bliss; having given the child a
sisterly kiss and said to her: "Since it must be so, sweetheart, I am
glad that it is thou. Be mother of thousands!" The exaggeration was
simply an expression of her wish that Bilhah might be receptive in
her mistress' place — which the child straightway was, announcing
the success of the manœuvre to her mistress, that the latter might tell
her husband and parents. Bilhah bore the increase of her body in the
ensuing months with little less stateliness than Leah hers, and Rachel,
who was full of tenderness for the child from now on, and often put
her ear and her caressing hands to Bilhah's rounding form, could
read in the eyes of all observers the increased respect which her
sacrifice earned for her.

Poor Rachel! Was she happy? By means of a recognized resource in such cases, she had to a certain extent weakened the force of the divine decree. But her yearning heart was confused by the fact that her merit was waxing in a stranger's body. It was a half-merit, a half-joy, a half-self-deception, sanctioned by tradition since needs must, but without flesh and blood confirmation in Rachel herself; the very children would be only half-real, the sons whom Bilhah would raise up to her and to the husband whom she so fruitlessly loved. Rachel's had been the pleasure, another's would be the pain. That was convenient, but it was a sham and an abomination as well — not in her thoughts, for they consented to the law and the custom; but to her straightforward and valiant little heart. In these days she wore a bewildered smile.

But she performed, piously and joyfully, all that was granted and prescribed for her to do. Bilhah gave birth upon her knees, as the custom demanded. She embraced her from behind with her arms, and hours long she shared in the labour, the shrieking and the groans, midwife and parturient in one. It was not an easy birth, Bilhah laboured for a full four and twenty hours, and at the end Rachel was almost as worn out as the mother after the flesh — and that was a gratification to her soul.

Thus came into the world that scion of Jacob who was named Dan, only a few weeks after the birth of Leah's Levi, in the third year of marriage. But in the fourth year, when Leah was delivered of him whom she named Judah (praise God), Bilhah and Rachel with their united powers presented to the husband their second son, and called his name Naphtali, for it seemed to them that he would be a wrestler. Thus Rachel had, in the name of God, two sons. And after this there were for the time no more.

THE DUDAIM

JACOB had spent the first years of his marriage almost entirely in Laban's court, leaving to the under shepherds and hirelings the care of the flocks in the meadows, though he visited them from time to time, took a muster of their charges, and received the increase in animals and goods, which belonged to Laban, and yet not all, sometimes not even the larger share. For a good deal outside and even in the courtyard, where Jacob had erected several new buildings to store his goods, already belonged to Laban's son-in-law; so that in time one might have spoken of the intermingling of two flourishing businesses, and a sufficiently complicated calculation of interests, which Jacob obviously oversaw and controlled, but which had long since got beyond Laban's power to disentangle, though he would never have admitted as much — partly because of fear to expose his lack of understanding, partly because of the old anxiety lest he vex the blessing in the body of his overseer by meddling and criticizing in his affairs. Things were going too well to risk that; he must wink at any irregularities he saw, and in truth by now he scarcely dared to open his mouth in matters of business — so obvious and overwhelming was the evidence that Jacob was indeed the very child of his God. Six sons and "water-pourers" he had raised up to himself in four years, double that which Laban had been able to do in the near neighbourhood of the blessing. His respect, if secret, knew no bounds, the only abatement of it was due to Rachel's barrenness. One must give the man his head, and only be grateful that it seemed not to occur to him to break off and set out on his wanderings.

The thought of return, of a resurrection from this pit and underworld that was Laban's country had actually never been remote from Jacob's thoughts — as little now after twelve years as it was after twenty-four. But he took his time, in the organic consciousness that he had time to take (for he was to live to a hundred and six) and had got out of the habit of connecting the idea of leaving with the time when Esau's wrath might be supposed to have died down. Furthermore a certain rooting of his life in the soil of Naharina had necessarily come about; for he had lived through much in this spot, and the things a man goes through in a place are like roots which he sinks into the ground. But in the main Jacob's reasoning was that he had not yet taken enough advantage from his sojourn, was not yet heavy enough in goods. The underworld afforded two kinds of things: filth and gold. He had made acquaintance with the filth: in the shape of the cruel waiting and the even crueller deception with which the demon Laban had rent his soul in twain on the bridal night. And he had begun to lade himself with the riches — but not enough, not in abundance; whatever there was to take he must pack, and Laban must still bleed gold. They were not yet quits, the man must be even more thoroughly cheated — not for the sake of Jacob's revenge but simply because it was fitting that the biter should be bit — though our Jacob had not as yet seen the effective means of carrying out the decree.

All that put him off, and his business occupied him. He was now much abroad in field and steppe, absorbed in breeding and trading on his own and Laban's account; which might be, among others, a reason for the check in the flow of blessings in the shape of progeny; although his wives and their children, as well as Laban's growing sons, were often with him at the sheep-pens, and lived there in tents and huts. Rachel had now become jealous of Bilhah, by whose help she had achieved sons of her own; she no longer suppressed her feeling, but forbade intercourse between master and maid, both of them readily bowing to her command. She herself remained barren into the fifth, then into the sixth year — or forever, as it unhappily seemed; also Leah's body lay fallow — very much to her vexation, but it simply rested one year and then two, so that she said to Jacob:

"I know not what it can mean nor what sort of disgrace I am visited with that I am now empty and useless. If thou haddest only me it would not happen nor had I remained two years unblest. But my sister is all unto our lord, and taketh my husband from me, so that hardly can I help cursing her although I love her. Perhaps this strife it is that weakeneth my blood so that I bear no fruit and thy God thinketh no more of me. But what was pleasing unto Rachel pleaseth me too; take then Zilpah, my maid, and lie with her that she may bear upon my lap, and I shall have sons through her. If then I am already unworthy before thee, yet I will still have children in any case, for they are like balm upon the wounds which thy coldness makes."

Jacob scarcely denied her grievance. He told her that she too had worth in his eyes, but his words bore the stamp of indifferent polite-ness. In this he was blameworthy; could he not bring himself to show a little kindly feeling towards this woman, even though he had suf-fered so sorely through her means? Must every kind word he gave her seem to him like treachery towards his own cherished feelings? The day would come when he should bitterly repent the arrogance of his heart, but that day was still far off, and before it came his feeling was still to be vouchsafed its highest triumph.

Leah had probably made the suggestion about Zilpah for form's sake, as another way of hinting that Jacob should pay her more frequent visits. But the loftiness of Jacob's feeling made him ignore or fail to see the point; he simply said that he was willing to avail himself of Zilpah's aid in breaking the dam in the stream of progeny. Rachel, of course, could not refuse her consent, especially after the high-bosomed Zilpah, who had a certain likeness to Leah and never found much favour in Jacob's eyes, came humbly and begged per-mission of the favourite. Then Leah's maid, in meekness and slavish compliance, received the master, conceived, and gave birth on the knees of her mistress, who helped her to groan. In the seventh year of marriage, the fourteenth of Jacob's sojourn, she bore Gad and commended him to fortune; likewise in the eighth and fifteenth the sweet-toothed Asher. Jacob had now eight sons.

At this time, near the birth of Asher, occurred the episode of the *dudaim.* It was Reuben who had the luck to find them — he was eight at the time, a swarthy, muscular lad, with inflamed eyelids. He already shared in the work of the early harvest, for which Laban and Jacob had come from the shearing, and which made the household labourers and hired hands to pant. Laban, the sheep-breeder, who when Jacob first came had sowed nothing but one sesame field, now after the coming of the water planted barley and millet, and above all wheat. His wheat field, enclosed in a clay wall and scored with irrigation ditches, was his most important one. It was six acres in extent, undulating over a shallow rise of ground, and its loam was rich and strong. If Laban let it lie fallow from time to time, as he never failed to do according to the time-honoured rule, it bore more than thirtyfold.

This year was a year of blessing. The pious labour of planting, of the plough and the scattering hand, of the hoe, the harrow and the water-pail, had been rewarded from on high. Before the ears formed, Laban's cattle had had rich green pasturage; no gazelle had pilfered the fruit nor had locusts covered the land nor floods wrenched it away. The harvest stood rich in Ijar and Jacob, although known to be no farmer, this time gave evidence of the blessing in this sphere as well, and by deed and word brought about a thicker sowing than usual; with the result that though the kernels were somewhat fewer in the ear, yet the whole yield was larger — enough larger, that Laban, as Jacob tried to make clear to him with figures, reaped an advantage, even though a fixed share fell to his son-in-law.

They were all working in the fields, even Zilpah, who gave suck to Gad and Asher in the intervals of work; only the daughters of the house, Leah and Rachel, had remained home to prepare the meal. The harvesters swung their scythes among the corn, their bodies glistening with sweat, singing hymns as they worked; they wore sun-shields made of reed, and aprons of sheep-skin round their loins. Others cut straw or bound the sheaves, loaded them upon asses and ox-carts, which bore the blessing to the threshing-floor, where it was threshed by oxen, winnowed, sifted and stacked. The boy Reuben had shown himself a man among the labourers; now in the golden afternoon his arms were tired, and he sauntered away to the margin of the field. There, by the clay wall, he found the mandrake.

It needed a sharp eye, and a trained one, to have seen it. The coarse oval leaves showed only a little above the soil, invisible to any but an instructed gaze. It was by its berries, the *dudaim* themselves, dark-coloured and about the size of hazel nuts, that Reuben knew what was underneath, in the earth. He laughed, and praised God. He seized his knife, drew a circle round and dug until the root hung only by slender threads. Then he uttered a two-worded charm for his own protection and pulled out the root with a quick jerk. He had thought that it would shriek, but nothing happened. And yet it was a proper and well-shapen little sprite that he held by the topknot; white like flesh, with two legs; the size of a child's hand, bearded and covered all over with fibrous hairs. It was a kobold, fit to make you laugh with amazement. The boy knew its properties;

they were many and useful, but in particular, Reuben knew, they
were good for women. Therefore he thought at once of Leah, his
mother, and ran home to fetch it her.

Leah was delighted. She praised and complimented her eldest,
gave him a fistful of dates, and warned him not to boast of the
matter before father and grandfather. "Silence is no sin," she said,
and it was not necessary that everybody should know what they
had in the house; it was enough if all should reap the benefit.
"I will bide the time," she finished, "and get from it all that it has
to give. Thanks, Reuben, my eldest-born, son of the first wife,
thanks that thou hast had her in mind. There are others that think
not of her. From them hast thou thy lucky hand. Go now thy ways."

Thus she dismissed him and thought to keep the treasure for herself. But Rachel, her sister, had been watching and seen all; who
was it later used to peep about just so, and then prattle to his own
undoing? It was in her flesh and blood, along with her many charms,
and she passed it on to her offspring. She said to Leah:

"What hath our son brought to thee?"

"My son," said Leah, "hath brought me nothing, or the merest
trifle. Wast thou by chance hereabouts? For he brought me a
beetle in his childishness and a bright-coloured stone."

"He hath brought thee a little earth mannikin, with the leaves and
the fruit," Rachel said.

"Yes, he brought me that too," responded Leah. "Here it is. See
how plump and stocky it is. My son found it for me."

"Ah, yes," cried Rachel, "thou'rt right, it is firm and fleshy, and
hath many *dudaim*, full of seed." She had folded her hands against
her pretty cheek, almost she had stretched them out in entreaty.
She asked:

"What wilt thou make of it?"

"Put a little shirt on him, of course," answered Leah, "after I
have washed and anointed him and lay him in a basket and wait for
him to bring blessing on the house. He will frighten the demons of
the air, that none of them enters into a man or into a beast in the
stall. He will foretell the weather and find out things that are hidden for the present or that lie in the future. It will make a man
proof against weapons if I put it in his clothing, and will bring him
gain in trade and grant him judgment before the judge even though
he be in the wrong."

"How thou pratest!" said Rachel. "Know I not myself it is good
for all that? But what else wilt thou do?"

"I will cut off the top of the berries and make a brew that putteth
to sleep him that smelleth thereat, and if he smell longer he shall
lose his tongue. It is a strong infusion, my child, and who taketh

of it too much be it man or woman shall die the death, but a little is good against snakebite, and if one must be cut in his flesh it is to him as though it were the flesh of another.

"But all that is as nothing," Rachel cried, "and of what thou hast above all in thy mind, of that speakest thou not. Ah, dearest little sister, and dear Leah," she cried, beginning to wheedle her, and to beg with her hands as a child does, "little vein of my eye, thou stateliest among daughters! Give me, I pray thee, of thy son's mandrake, that I may be fruitful, for my discontent at my lack consumes my life, and I have such shame of mine own unworthiness! Seest thou, my doe, my golden-haired among the swarthy, thou knowest the virtue of the brew, and how it can bewitch men, and is like the dew of heaven upon the barrenness of women, that they may blessedly conceive and give birth with ease! Thou hast in all six sons, and I but two, which are not mine, what then are the *dudaim* to thee? Give them me, my little wild she-ass, if not all then a morsel therefrom, that I may bless thee and fall at thy feet, for my desire is like a burning fever!"

But Leah pressed the mandrake to her breast and looked at her sister with threatening, squinting eyes.

"What sauciness is this?" asked she. "Cometh here the favourite and hath peeped and spied and will have my *dudaim*? Is it a small matter that thou takest my husband, daily and hourly, and wouldst thou take away my son's mandrake also? It is beyond all shame."

"Must thou speak so hatefully," responded Rachel, "and canst not speak otherwise even though thou wouldst? Put me not beside myself by thus wrenching the truth, for I would be tender with thee for the sake of our childhood days. Sayest thou I have taken from thee Jacob, our husband? Thou thyself hast taken him from me, in that holy night when thou didest secretly with him, instead of me, and in his blindness he poured into thee Reuben, whom I myself should have received. And he would be now my son, if all had gone well, and would have brought me the stalk and the root, and if thou hadst asked of me I would have given thee."

"How thou talkest!" Leah replied. "So thou wouldst have received my son? Why then hast thou not since that time conceived and wilt make spells and do magic in thy need! Well I know thou wouldst have given me nothing. For hast thou ever when Jacob flattered thee and would take thee to him, said unto him, 'Remember my sister too!' No, thou hast but pined and languished, and given him thy bosoms that he might play with them and thought of naught at all but thy philandering. Now comest thou and beggest, saying: 'I would have given thee.'"

"Ah, how hateful!" answered Rachel again. "It is all ugly and hateful, what thine own nature driveth thee to say, and I suffer

under it, yet for thyself I suffer more than all. For it is a curse to
have power to utter naught but ugliness when one opens one's
mouth! That I sent not Jacob to thee when he would come unto
me, was by no means because I grudged him to thee, may his gods
and the gods of our father be my witness! But I am now unfruitful
into the ninth year of our marriage, and I am in despair, and every
night that he chooseth me I hope ardently for the blessing and risk
not to neglect it. But thou, who mayest easily neglect it now and
again, what purposest thou to do? Thou wilt bewitch him with the
dudaim, and give me not of them, so that he may forget me and
thou mayest have all and I nothing. For I had his love and thou
hadst the fruit, so there was a kind of justice. But now thou will have
all, the love and the fruit, and I shall eat dust. So thinkest thou of thy
sister."

And she sat down upon the ground and wept aloud.

"I take now my son's mannikin and go hence," said Leah coldly.

Then Rachel sprang up, forgot her tears and cried out in an imploring whisper:

"Do not so, for God's sake, but stay and hearken. He would be
with me this night, he hath spoken of it this morning when he left
me. 'Sweetest one,' he said, 'thanks for this time. To-day the wheat
shall be cut, but after the heat of the day I will come, beloved, and
bathe me in the mildness of thy light that is like the moon's.' Ah, how
he speaketh, our husband! For his words are like pictures and full
of solemnity. Do we not both love him? But for to-night will I
leave him to thee for the sake of the *dudaim*. Expressly will I leave
him to thee, if thou wilt give me of them, and hide myself away, and
thou shalt tell him: 'Rachel will not, she hath no taste for this night
for billing and cooing. And thou shalt sleep with me, such were her
words.'"

Leah went red and pale.

"Is it sooth," she said, hesitating, "and wilt thou sell him to me
for the *dudaim* of my son, that I may say to him 'To-night thou art
mine'?"

Rachel answered: "Thou sayest."

Then Leah gave her the mandrake, leaves and root and all together, gave it her hastily in her hand, and whispered with heaving
breast:

"Take it, go, let thyself not be seen!"

But she herself, as evening came and the people came from the
field, went to meet Jacob and said:

"To-night thou shalt lie with me; for our son found a tortoise and
Rachel begged it of me at this price."

Jacob answered:

"So I am of the worth of a tortoise and a tabbied box made from

the shell? I have no memory of being so resolved to sleep this night
with Rachel! so hath she bought the certain with the unsure, and I
give her praise. But if ye have so agreed, so let it be. For a man shall
not set himself against women's counsel nor kick against their resolved decisions."

Chapter VII

RACHEL

THE OIL GAZING

IT was the little minx Dinah who was thus conceived — an ill-fated child. But through her Leah's womb was opened anew, after a pause of four years the sturdy creature came again into action. In the tenth year of wedlock she bore Issachar, the bony ass, in the eleventh Zebulun, who would not be a shepherd. Poor Rachel! She had the *dudaim*, and Leah bore the fruit. God would have it so, and for yet a while; until His will changed or rather reached a new stage, until a further segment of His scheme became plain in time and Jacob, the man of the blessing, was vouchsafed a joy fuller of life and more pregnant with suffering than his time-imprisoned human sense gave him to understand when he received it. Laban, the clod, had very likely been right when he said, in his sluggishness over the beer, that blessing was strength and life strength and nothing else. For it is vain superstition to think that the life of men of blessing is nothing but happiness and shallow well-being. For the blessing is in truth only the basis of their existence, gleaming goldenly through a plenitude of affliction and trial.

In the twelfth year of marriage, the nineteenth of Jacob's sojourn, no child was born. But in the thirteenth and twentieth, Rachel became expectant.

What a turn that was, what a new beginning! We may fancy the anxious, incredulous rejoicing, and Jacob's weak-kneed exaltation. She was then thirty-one years old, no one still thought that God meant thus at last to smile upon her. In Jacob's eyes she was Sarah, to whom the threefold man announced a son against all the laws of probability; he called her by the name of that early mother, as he sat at her feet and gazed through adoring tears into her pale and twitching face which to him seemed lovelier than ever. But their fruit, the long withheld, at length conceived, the child which had by inscrutable providence so many years been denied to their hopeful longings, it he called, while she was carrying it, by the primitive, archaic name of a youthful god scarcely any longer officially recognized, though beloved among the people: Dumuzi, the true son. Leah heard it. She had borne him six true sons and an equally true daughter.

But she had understood without that. Quite plainly and openly she told her four eldest sons, at that time from ten to thirteen years old, as good as grown, sturdy, competent, manly youths, withal rather ill-favoured and all of them with a tendency to inflamed eyelids:

"Sons of Jacob and Leah, we are undone. If she bear him a son — and as the gods see my heart I wish her joy and health — then the master will look no more at us, neither you nor the little ones, nor the children of the maids, and me least of all, were I ten times the first wife. For that I am, and sevenfold have his God and my father's gods blessed me with motherhood. But she is the favourite, therefore is she likewise the first and the only one, so proud is his feeling, and he calleth her son, who hath not yet seen the light, Dumuzi, ye have heard it. Dumuzi! It is like a knife in my breast and a blow in my face and like a weal is it in the face of each of you, yet must we endure it. For so it is my sons. We must be strong, I and ye, and hold our hearts in both our hands that they burst not against the injustice. We must love and honour our master though we were in future worthless in his eye, and he will look through us as though we were air. And her too I will love, and will enforce my heart that it may not curse her. For it is tender toward the little sister, and mindful of our childhood days; but with violence it longeth to curse the favourite, her who shall bear Dumuzi, and so divided are my feelings for her that I am ill and sick of it in my very body and no longer know myself."

Reuben, Simeon, Levi and Judah caressed her awkwardly. Her red eyes were brooding and she gnawed her under lip. It was then it began. Then that stirred in Reuben's heart the beginning of that sudden angry deed which he was to commit for Leah's sake, and which would be the beginning of the end of his first-born rights. Then that was planted in the brothers' breasts that seed of hatred against the life which was as yet only a seed; the sowing begun of a harvest of unnamable anguish for Jacob, the man of the blessing. Did it then have to be so? Could not peace and blithe good feeling have reigned among the tribe of Jacob, and events have taken a mild and even course of mutual toleration? Alas, no, if that which happened had to happen, and if the fact that it happened is evidence that it must and was to happen. Very much happens in the world; and as we cannot wish that it might rather have peacefully remained unhappened, we may not curse the passions which are its instrument; for without passion and guilt nothing could proceed.

The great notice that was taken of Rachel's condition was in itself monstrous to Leah and a vexation to her spirit, her own healthy pregnancies having passed with no attention from anyone. But Rachel, through hers, became as it were consecrated — a conception of which of course Jacob was the author, but which infected everybody in the house, from Laban down to the meanest of the stable hands. They all moved about her on tiptoe, and spoke to her only in soft commiserating voices, with head inclined and hands describing curves as though to caress the air about her person. All that lacked was the strewing of palm branches and the laying of carpets that her foot might not strike against a stone. Palely smiling she accepted all the adulation, less out of self-love than for the sake of the fruit of Jacob with which she had at last been blessed and in honour of Dumuzi, the genuine son. But who can tell the difference between meekness and arrogance, in one endowed with the blessing?

Behung with amulets she sat, forbidden to lift hand in house or court, garden or field. Jacob forbade it. He wept if she did not eat or could not keep down what she had eaten, for she sickened from week to week, and it was greatly feared that she was afflicted by some evil spirit of the air. Adina, her mother, plied her with bandages and application of ointments made after some old recipe, whose effect should be twofold: naturally emollient and healing, as well as a charm and protection against evil. She ground up night-shade, garden cress, dog's-tongue, and the root of the plant of Namtar, lord of the sixty diseases, mixed the powder with pure and expressly consecrated oil, and massaged the expecting one round the navel, with an upward motion, muttering as she did so, in a meaningless and mumbled jargon:

"Bad Utukku, bad Alu, go away; bad death spirit, Labartu, Lamashtu, heart disease, gripes, head pains, toothache, Asakku, harmful Namtaru, go away, out of the house, by heaven and earth I conjure you!"

In the fifth month Laban insisted that Rachel be taken to a priest-seer at the temple of Sin, E-hulhul, at Harran, that her future and the child's might be foretold. Jacob held to his principles, giving his voice against it and refusing his co-operation; but that was outwardly. Inwardly he was as eager as the others to hear the prophecy and the first to desire that no time should be lost. Moreover, the prophet in question, the old seer and temple incumbent, Rimanni-Bel — Bel-have-mercy-upon-me — a son and grandson of prophets, was a very popular and experienced soothsayer and oil gazer, who, according to the consensus of opinion, was a master of the art and had a constant stream of visitors. Jacob refused, naturally, to appear before him as a petitioner and sacrifice to the moon, but he was much too curious to hear whatever might be said, from any point of view, of Rachel's condition, not to give way circumspectly to the parents' wishes.

Thus they set forth, Laban and Adina, on the way to Harran, holding on both sides the bridle of the ass upon which the pale and pregnant woman sat; they led it with care that it might not stumble and shake her, and they dragged behind them the sheep for the sacrifice. Jacob waved them good-bye; he stopped at home, not to afflict his eyes with the pompous abominations of E-hulhul, nor vex his spirit with the sight of the house beside it, where lived the temple prostitutes and love-boys, whose embraces could be hired for the honour of the idol and the payment of a round sum of money. Thus, without personal contamination, he awaited the verdict of the son of seers, the prophecy of the gazing, which the others brought back with them. Clearly it had given them to think. He listened silently to their account of their experience in the temple precincts and before the face of Rimanni-Bel the oil gazer, or Rimut, as he was called for short. "Just call me Rimut," he had said in his mildness. "For indeed I am called Rimanni-Bel, that Sin may have mercy upon me; but I am myself full of mercy for those who in their need and their doubt learn to sacrifice, and therefore shall ye say simply 'Mercy' when ye speak to me, it is shorter and it suits my looks." And then he asked what needful things they had brought with them, and examined the spotlessness of the offering and directed them to buy such and such spices for the burnt-offering at a booth in the main court.

A charming man, this Rimanni-Bel, or Rimut, in his white linen garments and cone-shaped linen cap; already old, but of lithe figure not misshapen by corpulence, with a white beard, a bulbous red nose and twinkling eyes which made one feel merry when one looked at them. "I am well-shapen," he said, "unblemished without and within, like the sacrificial animal when it is well-favoured, and the sheep when there is naught to say against it. I am of the right height and girth, and my leg is crooked neither out nor in, nor have I lost a single tooth, nor am afflicted with disease of the scrotum nor do I squint. Only my nose is somewhat red, as ye can see, yet out of cheerfulness and mirth, and no other cause, for I am as sober as the purest water. I could come naked before God, as it was once the custom, as we read and are told. Now we stand before Him in white linen, and in this too I rejoice, for it is pure and sober likewise and conformable to my soul. I cherish no envy of my brethren, the exorcizing priests, who do their incanting in a red garment with a mantle, enveloped in terrifying splendour in order to throw into a fright all the demons and lurkers and sprites of the air. They too are useful and necessary and worthy of their hire, but Rimanni-Bel (that is me) would not be one of them, nor one of the priests who do the washing and anointing, nor a possesed nor yet a wailing priest, not one of those whose manhood Ishtar hath changed into the female, however holy it may be. I bear none of them the least grudge, my own skin fits me too well, nor should I care to practise any other kind of soothsaying than just the oil gazing, for it is far and away the most sensible, the clearest and the best. Just between ourselves, in the augury from inspection of the liver and the oracle of the arrow a good deal of arbitrary choice cometh in, and also the interpretation of dreams and transports is not without sources of error, so that often I have privily to smile. But as for you, father and mother and pregnant child, ye have taken the right road and knocked on the right door. For I am descended from Enmeduranki, who was king of Sippar before the flood, sage and guardian of the art entrusted to him by the great gods, to look upon oil on water and to recognize, according to the behaviour of the oil, what shall come to pass. From him I am descended in a direct line from father to son, and the tradition is unbroken, for always the father made the son whom he loved to swear upon tablet and writing tool of Shamash and Adad and had him learn the work 'When the son of the seers' down to Rimut, the blithe and blameless (and that is me). And I receive of the sheep, that ye may know beforehand, the hinder part, the fell and a pot of broth, further the sinews and the half of the entrails according to the tables and according to the array. The loins, the right leg and a goodly roasting piece the god receiveth; and what is left we servers of the temple have at the temple meal. Are ye satisfied?"

Thus Rimut, the son of seers. And they had sacrificed upon the roof that was sprinkled with holy water, and had carried up four jugs of wine and twelve loaves of bread as well as porridge made of curds and honey up to the table of the lord, and had strewn salt. Then they had strewn spices upon the stands for the incense and slaughtered the sheep; the offrant held it, the priest slew it, and due offering was made. Very charming it had been to see the old man, Rimut, in the blamelessness of his limbs, perform the final dance before the altar and leap disposedly. Laban and his spouse could not say enough in praise to Jacob, who listened in silence and concealed impatience for the verdict.

Yes, the verdict, the judgment of the oil — it had been rather dark and equivocal, one was not much wiser having it than before; it sounded both auspicious and threatening, but thus perhaps must the future sound if it speak at all; and it had spoken, at least they had heard a humming, as though through shut teeth. Rimanni-Bel had taken the cedar staff and the bowl, had prayed and sung and poured oil on water as well as water on oil, and observed the pictures made with the oil, with his head on one side. Two rings had come out of the oil, one large and one small, indicating that Rachel, the sheep-breeder's daughter, would probably bear a son. Out of the oil when shaken a ring had come on the east and had remained; the woman in travail would recover her health. Out of the oil when shaken a bubble had come: her protecting deity would stand by her in her hour of need, for it would be hard. The creature would escape out of its need, for the oil had sunk and risen when water was poured in, it had divided and joined again; thus the creature, though after sore suffering, would become whole. But since the oil, when water was poured, had gone down and then come up again and clung round the edge of the bowl, so indeed the ailing would arise, but the healthy belong to death. "But not the boy!" Jacob could not refrain from crying out. No, for the child there seemed to be a reverse process, according to the oil — but just here the matter became unclear to human understanding. The child would go down into the pit yet still live, it would be like the seed-corn that bears no fruit, save it die. This, Rimut assured them, was unquestionably the meaning of the oil in parting when he poured in water and then joining again and glistening peculiarly on the side towards the sun, for this sig-nified the lifting up of the head from death. It was not very clear, the soothsayer had said, he himself did not understand it, he would not pretend to be wiser than he was; but whatever it meant it was reliable. But with respect to the woman: she would not see, accord-ing to the testing and the countertesting, the star of her son when it stood at its highest; let her then beware of the number two. For it was in any case an unlucky number, but in especial for the daughter of the sheep-breeder, and according to the oil she should undertake no journey in the figure two, else she would be like an army that reacheth not the head of the field.

Thus the speech and the muttering — Jacob heard it and nodded his head, at the same time shrugging his shoulders. What was to be said to it? It was of some weight, having reference to Rachel and her child, but after all one must rely on oneself and leave to the future to make what it would out of its mutterings. Destiny and the future kept to themselves a free hand. Much might happen and not happen, and it would always be possible to make it fit the prophecy after-wards and say: "So that was what it meant." Jacob mused for several hours over the nature of oracles in general, and talked about it to Laban, who was not receptive. Was an oracle by its nature the reve-lation of a future in which nothing could be altered, or was it like an admonishment to caution and a warning to human beings to do their part, that a threatened misfortune might not happen? That presupposed that the destiny and the decree were not fixed, that it was given to men to alter them. But if this were the case, then the future did not lie outside of man, but within him, and how then could one read it? Moreover it had often happened that the misfortune that had been announced had been prevented by appropriate measures, or even without these measures could not have happened — which reduced both destiny and warning to a mockery and the sport of demons. The oil had said that Rachel would, after hard labour, be delivered of a son. But if she were neglected while in labour, if no incantations were said, the necessary anointings not carried out, how then would destiny act to bring about the fulfilment of its prophecy? But then was it not sinful to try to bring in a good end contrary to destiny?

Laban had no use for such quibbling. It was ill-considered, he said, tortuous, over-refined and carping. The future was the future; that was to say, it was not yet and so was not fixed, but it would one day be, and then it would be so and so; thus it was in a certain way fixed, that is according to its property as future, and that was all there was to say about it. Yet judgments about it were enlightening and edifying to the heart, and these soothsayers were hired and paid to dispense them, and they studied for years, under the protection of the king of the Four Regions at Babel-Sippar on both sides of the river Euphrates, favourite of Shamash and beloved of Marduk — the king of Sumeria and Akkadia, who dwelt there in a palace whose foundations were fathoms deep and in a throne-room of unnamable splendours. Therefore Jacob was not to carp.

Jacob had already fallen silent. Against Nimrod of Babel he cherished in his heart a profound suspicion inherited from the original wanderer. It did not make the pronouncement he had heard any the holier that Laban invoked that mightiness in its favour, or that his father-in-law would never lift a finger without taking a soothsayer's advice. Laban had paid for the judgment with a sheep and all sorts of edibles for the moon idol, and just on this account would be bound to rely on what he heard. Jacob, who had not paid, took a more detached view; but he on his side was pleased to have heard something without paying for it, and as for the future, at least in one point it was already settled: whether Rachel's child was a boy or a girl. The decision had already been made, in her womb — only one could not see it. There was such a thing, then, as a fixed future, and it was strengthening to the faith, after all, that Rimanni-Bel's oil had pointed to a boy. And also Jacob was grateful for the practical advice which the prophet had given, for as a priest and temple incumbent he had some knowledge of healing and had not been sparing (though there seemed to be a contradiction here, as between his two characters, since no healing could be any good against the future) of advice and counsel for the accouchement; mingling charms and invocations with medical prescriptions in a most edifying manner.

It went hard with little Rachel. Long before her hour — that came so near to being her last one — the treatments began: she had to drink bad-tasting draughts, for instance a great deal of oil in which was pounded up a stone efficacious in pregnancies; she had to wear poultices of bitumen, swine's fat, fish and herbs, yes, whole pieces of unclean animals which like the poultices were bound upon her body with cords. When she slept a kid-offering was always at her head, that the greedy demons might take it and leave her alone. Near her by day and night there stood a clay doll in the image of the swamp-born Lamashtu, in its mouth the heart of a suckling pig, which was meant to lure away the demons from the body of the pregnant one into the image; every three days one smashed it with a sword and buried it in the corner of the wall, meanwhile taking care not to look behind one. The sword was thrust in a brazier of burning coals, which Rachel had to have beside her, although the season was already very warm and they were near the month of Tammuz. Her bed was surrounded by a little wall of pap, and the three heaps of grain in her chamber were likewise put there by direction of Rimanni-Bel. When the first pains began they hastened to smear the sides of the bed with the blood of a sucking pig and the house door with plaster and bitumen.

THE BIRTH

It was summer; the month of Tammuz, master of the herds, the mangled one, was already advanced some days. Since the great moment when he knew that his true and most beloved wife was expectant, Jacob had never stirred from her side; he had shared with his own hands in her care and treatment, renewing the bandages and ointments, and even once smashing and burying the image of Lamashtu: treatments and practices which were not commanded by the god of his fathers, but, above and beyond all the idols and soothsayers, might come from him after all, and in any case were the only ones there were to follow. Rachel — pale and wasted, heavy only in the body, where her fruit insensate and pitiless sucked up all her strength and her juices to its own advantage — would often carry his hand to where he might feel the muffled movements; and he would speak to Dumuzi through the fleshly veil and tell him to take heart and come forth into the daylight, but in so doing to take care how he climbed over the hills that the dear shepherdess might anguish as little as possible. And now, when she gave a wry little smile and said shortwindedly that she felt it near, he fell into great excitement, called her parents and the maids, told them to make ready the bricks, and bustled aimlessly to and fro, his heart great with supplications.

No praise could be too great for the readiness and courage which Rachel displayed. Valiantly, joyously, resolved to bear and to endure greatly, she entered upon the work of nature. And this not for the sake of increased outward respect nor because she would now no longer be the childless and unloved wife of the popular phrase; but out of a much deeper, a more physical sense of honour — for not only human society has its sense of honour, the flesh knows one too and a better one, as Rachel learned when scatheless and for honour's sake she became a mother through Bilhah. The smile she wore when her trial began was other than that bewildered one which the painful conscience of her flesh had then painted upon her face. The lovely short-sighted eyes alight with happiness rested in Jacob's eyes, to whom she should now bear a child in honour; this was the hour to which in open-eyed readiness for life she had looked forward when the stranger, the cousin from afar, had first stood before her in the fields.

Poor Rachel! So glad she was, so full of good will for the work of nature — and nature showed her so little good will in turn, made it so hard for the brave sufferer! Impatient for motherhood as she had been, sincerely convinced of her gift and aptitude, Rachel was probably in the flesh much less made for maternity than Leah the unloved; so that the sword of death hovered over her when she was brought to bed, and even at the second time it fell upon and slew her. Can nature so strive against herself, so mock the confidence and proud desire which she herself has emplanted in the heart? It seems so. For Rachel's joyousness was not acceptable, her trust was given the lie — such was the lot that fell to her ready and willing heart. Seven years had she and Jacob waited in hope, and then for thirteen more been incomprehensibly disappointed. And now, when nature had at last and finally granted the longed-for boon, she asked a harsher price than Leah, Zilpah and Bilhah together had paid for all their maternal honours. Thirty-six hours, from midnight to mid-day and again through a whole night to the next middle-day the frightful labour went on, and had it lasted even an hour or a half-hour more it would have left her breathless. Even at the beginning Jacob grieved to see her disappointment, for she had dreamed of a swift, triumphant finish and now nothing stirred. The first indications proved deceptive; long pauses supervened after the early pains, empty, silent and fruitless hours, in which she did not suffer, but felt weary and ashamed. Often she said to Leah: "With thee, sister, it was another matter," and Leah had to admit, with a quick glance at her husband, that this was so. Then anguish would seize upon the sufferer, crueller and longer each time, yet when it passed, seemed to have been all in vain. She went from bricks to bed and from bed to bricks; the hours, the night watches, the times of the day came and went; she blushed and groaned for her unableness. Rachel shrieked not when her pains took her and would not let her go; she bit her teeth together and obstinately did her part; she would not frighten her lord, whose soft heart she well knew, and who in the pauses of exhaustion kissed her hands and feet in the distraction of his soul. Her fortitude helped not at all, it was rejected. And after it was exhausted she shrieked indeed, wild and frenziedly, so that one would not have known her for the little Rachel. For at this time — the second morning had then come — she was no longer in her senses, one could tell it by the hideous howling, for the voice was no longer hers, it was the demons yelling, and the sucking pig's heart had had no power to lure them away from her body into the puppet.

They were unavailing pangs, that merely held the precious sufferer in a gripe of relentless torture, so that the shrieking mask that was her face went blue and her fingers clutched the air. Jacob ran through house and court, knocking against everything, since he had his thumbs in his ears and his eight other fingers before his eyes. He called on God — no longer for a son, he had no longer any thought of him, but only that Rachel might have a peaceful death and lie quiet and released from these hellish torments. Laban and Adina, whose draughts and anointings and strokings had borne no fruit, in deep dejection muttered invocations and amid the shrieks chanted prayers to Sin the moon-god, reminding him how once he had sustained a cow in labour, and might now so untie the knots of this woman's body and aid the pangs of the sufferer. Leah stood bolt upright in a corner of the room, her arms at her sides, hands lifted at the wrists, and gazed silently with her squinting blue eyes at this life-and-death struggle of Jacob's beloved.

And then came forth out of Rachel a final shriek, the last furious demonic yell, such as one cannot twice shriek without dying and not twice hear without losing one's mind — and then Laban's wife had something else to do than chant about Sin's cow, for Jacob's son had issued forth, his eleventh and his first, issued out of the dark and bleeding womb of life — *Dumuzi-absu*, true son of the abyss. It was Bilhah, mother of Dan and Naphtali, who came running, white-faced and laughing, out to the court whither Jacob had rushed, and with flattering tongue announced to the master that unto us a child is born, and unto us a son is given and that Rachel liveth; and trembling in every limb, he dragged himself to the bed, fell down beside it and wept. She was covered with sweat, transfigured as by the hand of death, and she was singing in breathless exhaustion. The gateway of her body was torn, she had bitten through her tongue, and she was weary unto death. Such was the reward of her joyful readiness.

She had no strength to turn her head, nor to smile, but she stroked his brow as he knelt beside her, and her eyes went towards the hanging cradle in sign that he should see the child was alive and lay his

hand upon his son. The infant had been bathed, it had stopped scream-
ing, it was swaddled and slept. It had smooth black hair upon its little
head that in issuing had torn the mother; long lashes and tiny hands
with well-shaped nails. It was not then beautiful — one cannot speak
of beauty in so young a child. And yet Jacob saw as he had not seen
in Leah's children nor observed in the sons of the maids, saw at first
glance, what filled his heart, the longer he looked, full to overflowing, with reverent rapture. There was about this newborn babe
something ineffable, a clear-shining loveliness, equability, sympathy,
divine charm, of which Jacob, if not to understand, yet thought to
recognize the essence. He laid his hand on the child and said: "My
son." But as he touched it, it opened its eyes, which then were blue and
reflected the radiance of its birthday sun shining high in the heavens;
with its tiny, strangely complete little hand it laid hold on Jacob's
finger, holding it in a gentle clasp as it fell asleep. Rachel, the mother,
slept too, a profound slumber. But Jacob stood there bent, a prisoner
to his tender feeling, and gazed upon the brightness of his little son,
perhaps an hour, until it nestled and whimpered for its food, and
Jacob lifted it over.

They called the boy Joseph, which being interpreted means increase — as when we name our sons Augustus. His whole name, with
God, was Joseph-el, or Josiphya; but liking to think that the first
syllable also had reference to the most high they spoke to him as
Jehosiph.

RING-STRAKED AND SPOTTED

AND now that Rachel had borne Joseph, Jacob was in a high and
feeling mood, speaking only in a voice that trembled with emotion;
and the self-satisfaction he showed was really culpable. The babe had
been born at about midday, and the sign of the virgin had risen in
the east; Jacob knew that it corresponded to Ishtar, the planetary
revelation of divine femininity, and he insisted on seeing in Rachel,
the mother, a heavenly virgin and mother-goddess, a Hathor and
Isis with the child at her breast; while his son was a marvel and
anointed one, whose appearance was bound up with a season of
blessing and rejoicing, and who would be nourished there in the
strength of Yahu. He stands convicted of arrogance and lack of
proportion. Mother and child are of course holy; but the most rudi-
mentary regard for certain sensibilities should have prevented Jacob
from making them into an image, in the most offensive sense of the
word, and of little Rachel an astral divine maid. He knew, of course,
that she was not a virgin, in the everyday meaning of the word —
what sort of arrangement would that have been! When he used the
word it was only in a mythical and astrological sense. But he insisted upon the allegory with far too evident delight, tears of self-

indulgence standing in his eyes. And since he was actually a shepherd and the beloved of his heart was named Rachel, a ewe, what
more natural, or even more charming, than that he should call her
babe "the lamb." But the tone in which he spoke of the lamb that
had come forth out of the virgin was by no means jesting; rather
it seemed to claim for the little rascal in the hammock the sanctity
of the immaculate firstling and sacrifice of the flock. All the wild
beasts, he said in his fervour, would attack the lamb, but it would
conquer them all, and peace would come over all the earth and upon
angels and men. And he called his son a branch and a shoot from
the tenderest root, connecting it in his over-poetic soul with the
image of the spring of the world and the beginning of that time of
blessing in which the heavenly youth would strike down the mighty
with the staff of his mouth.

These were all emotional exaggerations. But yet in Jacob's mind
the coming of the blessing-time had, in so far as it was a matter of
his own personal time, a very practical meaning. It meant the blessing of riches. Jacob was convinced that the birth of a son to the
true wife was guaranty that his business affairs, however much or
little they had secretly profited while he had been serving Laban,
would now take a steep and decisive upward trend; that the filthy
underworld would after this unreservedly bestow all the treasures
of gold which it possessed. With the thought, indeed, was bound up
a higher one, from the realm of feeling: he envisaged his return,
treasure-laden, to the upper world and the land of his fathers. Yes,
the coming of Jehosiph was like a turning-point in the course of his
life, which ought strictly speaking to have coincided with his departure out of Laban's kingdom. But that could not be, it was in
itself not advisable. Rachel could not travel; the recovery from so
frightful a childbirth was slow and difficult and left her pale and
weak; nor was the exhausting Eliezer journey of more than seventeen
days to be thought of for the infant. It is surprising, it is almost ridiculous, to see how lightly these matters are sometimes decided and
dismissed. Thus we are told that Jacob spent fourteen years with
Laban, seven and seven; at the end of which Joseph was born and
then he departed for home. And we are told expressly that at the
meeting with Esau at the ford of Jabbok, Joseph came near and
Rachel, and they bowed themselves. But how could a babe at the
breast draw near and bow? At that time Joseph was five years old,
and these five years it was that Jacob still lived with Laban after the
twenty, and indeed under a new contract. He could not leave, but
he could behave as though he meant to go at once, and thus put
pressure on the clod Laban, for he could be got at in no other way
than by exploiting the stark necessities of business life.

So then Jacob spoke with Laban and said:

"Let my father and uncle graciously incline his ear unto my words."

"Before thou speakest," Laban hastily broke in, "rather hearken unto me, for I have that which is pressing to say. We can no longer go on as we are, and I cannot for long endure the absence of legal regulation in the affairs of men. Thou hast served me seven and again seven years for thy wives according to our contract which is laid up below with the teraphim. But since some years now, I think since six, contract and document are out of date, and there is no law any more, only use and routine, so that no one any longer understandeth where he is. Thus is our life become like a house that is built without any level, and is, to speak openly, like the life of beasts. I see clearly, for the gods have given me eyes, that thou comest for a reckoning, since thou hast served me without conditions or contracted reward, for thou hast stored up all kinds of goods and possessions which I will not count, since now they are thine, and when my sons Beor, Alub and Muras have made long faces over them, lo, I have rebuked them. For it is a labour worthy of its hire, yet must it be governed. Therefore let us now go and make a new contract for another seven years and thou wilt find me ready to treat with any condition which thou art minded to make."

"It cannot be," Jacob said, shaking his head. "Alas, my uncle wasteth his precious words, and need not have wasted them had he first listened to me. For I speak not to Laban in the matter of new contracts but in the matter of leave and permission to depart. Twenty years have I served thee, and thou thyself must needs bear witness how I have performed my service, for I myself may not for the sake of seemliness take the words in my mouth which alone are fitting to use. Yet it would be fitting that thou shouldest use them."

"I deny it not," said Laban; "that thou hast served me well and without reproach cometh not here to speech."

"And am grown old and grey in thy service, without need," Jacob went on, "for Esau's anger is long since spent and the ground therefore that I have left my home. The childlike nature of my brother the huntsman retaineth no longer any memory of the ancient tales. Years since might I have gone at any hour into mine own land, but I did it not. And why did I it not? To give the ground therefor there are but words to use and the using of them would not be seemly for me since their quality is praise. But now Rachel, the heavenly maid, in whom thou art grown lovely, hath borne me Dumuzi, Joseph, my son and hers. Him will I take, with my other children, sons of Leah and of the maids, and mount and ride that I come into my land and my place and at length take thought for my own house as I have so long done only for thine."

"That I would regret, in the truest sense of the word," answered Laban, "and what I can do that I will, that it may not come to pass. Let my son and nephew speak freely and unfeignedly what he demandeth in the way of new conditions, and I swear to him by Anu and Ellil that he will find me well inclined towards any reasonable demand."

"I know not what thou wouldst find reasonable," Jacob said, "considering what were thy possessions when I came hither and how they have extended under my hand, so that even Adina, thy wife, was drawn into the circle of growth and with unhoped-for vigour brought thee three sons in thy grey old age. Thou couldest have spoken, yet wouldst thou not speak, therefore will I also be silent and go."

"Speak and thou wilt remain," responded Laban.

Then Jacob named his condition, saying what he would have as the price of his staying another year or so. Laban had expected much, but not this. In the first moment he was staggered, and his mind wrestled with the problem first of understanding the demand and then of giving the needful counterstroke.

It was the famous story of the speckled and spotted sheep, told a thousand times by fireside and fountain, a thousand times celebrated in strophe and antistrophe in honour of Jacob, the shepherd, and as a master-stroke of ingenuity and shrewdness — this story, of which Jacob himself, in his old age, as he sat musing, could not think without a smile that curled the thin lips through his beard. In a word, Jacob asked for the pied sheep and goats, the speckled black and white; not the ones already born — we must understand the matter aright — but the speckled and spotted ones which should be dropped in future from Laban's flocks; they should be his hire and be added to the possessions which he had for long stored up and accumulated in his uncle's service. It was a matter of dividing between master and man the sheep which were bred from now on though not precisely in equal halves, for the larger half were white and the smaller pied, so that Jacob's request was in the nature of selection. Yet both well knew that the pied were fat and fruitful more than the white, and Laban said so at once, with mingled anger and respect for his nephew's cleverness and audacity.

"*Thou* thinkest of things!" he exclaimed. "A man might be stricken in sight and hearing at thy demands. So thou wouldst have the speckled, the excellent fat ones? Not that I have as yet said no, for I gave thee free to ask, and I keep to my word. If this be thy condition and thou persistest in it, otherwise thou wilt go hence and tear away my daughters from my heart, Leah and Rachel, thy wives, that in my old age I behold them no more, then be it as thou wilt. Yet must I frankly admit that the matter goeth to my heart."

And Laban sat down as though he were taken with a palsy.

"Hearken," said Jacob. "I see that my condition smiteth thee sore, and is little to thy liking. But since thou art own brother of my mother, and hath begotten Rachel, the starry virgin and my true and most beloved wife, so I will condition my condition that it may be less frightful to thee. Let us then pass through all thy flock to-day, removing from thence all the speckled and spotted and all the brown ones among the sheep, and put them aside from the white, so that the ones know nothing of the others. And after that what is dropped speckled, that is my hire. Art thou satisfied?"

Laban sat and blinked.

"Three days' journey," he suddenly cried out. "Three days' journey shall be set between the white and the pied, and there shall be separate breeding and tending between them, so that the ones know naught of the others, for so I will have it. And so it shall be sealed at Harran before the judge and laid by below with the teraphim and it is my absolute condition."

"It is harsh for me," said Jacob. "Yea, it is harsh and oppressive. Yet from the beginning have I been aware that my uncle thinketh with sternness, strictly and unbendingly in business matters. And therefore I accept."

"Thou dost well," Laban answered, "for never should I have departed from it. But hearken and tell me, which herd thinkest thou to pasture and to let pass under thy staff for thine own person? The speckled or the white?"

"It is lawful and natural," Jacob said, "that each shall guard his own, from which he shall have the profit; I will take then the pied ones."

"Not so," cried Laban then. "By no means. Thou hast made thy demand and it is a mighty one. But now it is my turn and I will ask what seemeth to me the least and cheapest for the honour of the business. Thou agreest with me anew in this contract. But if thou art my servant then the interest of the business demandeth that thou guardest the sheep that shall profit me, the white ones, not the ones that shall drop for thee, the parti-coloured ones. Beor, Alub and Meras, my sons, whom Adina so proudly bore in her old age, they shall tend the parti-coloured sheep."

"H'm," Jacob said. "So be that also, I will not obstinately set up my will against thine, thou knowest my mildness."

Thus the bargain was struck, and Laban knew not the rôle he played, nor how he was being fooled to the top of his bent. He was too slow-witted to see the point. He wanted above all to cling to the blessing, and reckoned that its effect would be strong enough to outweigh the natural superiority of the speckled sheep. He knew that the white flock, from which, after the parting of the herds, pied

yearlings were not to be expected, would propagate more freely under Jacob's care than would the coloured ones under the faithful but
heavy hands of his sons. Clod that he was! He reckoned, indeed, on
the blessing, but without enough foresight to imagine the issue of
Jacob's shrewdness and inventive spirit, to say nothing of even
dreaming of the plan which stood in the background of his son-in-
law's demand and concessions: the sagacious reasoning, based upon
extended previous experiment, which was at the bottom of it all.

For we must not think that it was only after the bargain was struck
and with intent to turn it to his advantage, that Jacob hit upon the
deep device by means of which he bred his sheep ring-straked and
speckled. The idea had originally been without thought of gain, a
play of imagination, and tested in a scientific spirit. The bargain
with Laban had to do only with its application. It went back to the
time before Jacob's marriage, when he had been an expectant lover,
and his interest in breeding had been keenest and warmest; had originated, in fact, out of sympathetic divination and emotional inspiration. One can really not praise enough the intuition which showed
him how to make nature confess one of her most miraculous secrets,
and to confirm his discovery by experiment. He discovered the phenomenon of shock in pregnancy. He found out that when the female
was in heat the sight of the parti-coloured animal affected the lamb
which she then dropped, so that a parti-coloured animal was the result. I must emphasize the fact that his curiosity was entirely abstract;
that the pleasure was entirely intellectual, with which he set down a
record of the successes he achieved. Instinct taught him, however, to
conceal from Laban and from everybody else this insight he had
gained into sympathetic magic; but the thought of turning his knowledge to his own profit was a secondary one, and only crystallized
when he came to drive the new bargain with his father-in-law.

To the shepherds, in their songs, the result was everything, the
apparatus of a very clever piece of over-reaching. How Jacob had
snapped his fingers at Laban's precautions and systematically robbed
him of his own; how he had taken rods of green poplar and of the
hazel tree, and "pilled white strakes" in them and set them before
the flocks in the gutters when they came to drink, where they were
accustomed to copulate; how the flocks conceived before the rods
and brought forth lambs and kids, ring-straked, speckled and spotted
although they themselves were white; and how Jacob had done this
especially at the spring running, whereas the later and less productive
animals might be Laban's; all this the shepherds said and sang to the
accompaniment of their lutes, and held their sides with laughter over
the priceless trick. For they had not Jacob's piety nor his knowledge
of mythology, and did not know the sense of duty which guided his
action: first that he might be helpful to God the King in carrying

out His promise of riches, and secondly because that devil Laban had
to be deceived, who had deceived him in the darkness with the stately
but dog-headed Leah, because the saying had to be fulfilled which
said that one did not leave the underworld save laden with the treasures which lay there so richly spread forth among the filth.

Thus, then, it was: there were three flocks, the white, tended by
Jacob, the brown and parti-coloured, watched over by Laban's sons,
and Jacob's own flock, accumulated in the course of trade during
these years, tended by his own servants and under-shepherds, to
which from time to time were added the coloured yearlings dropped
by the parti-coloured herd and the bewitched white one. And it was
after this fashion that the man grew so heavy with possessions that
it was the talk and the admiration of the whole region — the number
of cattle, and maidservants, and menservants, and camels and asses,
the man called his own. In the end he was much richer than Laban,
the clod, or than all the owners of businesses who had been invited
to his wedding.

HOW THEY STOLE

AH, how Jacob remembered — how deeply, how clearly! Everyone
realized it, who saw him standing sunk in solemn musing, and everyone took care to check his own manifestations in reverence for this
many-layered burden of life and history. For the situation of Jacob
the rich man had become precarious — God Himself, El, the highest,
had perceived that the blessing was become out of sheer size unwieldy, and given him corresponding instruction in a dream. It came
to his notice, in other words, and was only too easy to believe, that
his brothers-in-law, Laban's heirs, had a certain disposition towards
him, expressed in grumblings repeated by the under-shepherds and
servants, who heard them from his cousins' people at chance meetings in the courtyard. The fact that they had a ring of truth did not
make them less disquieting. This man, Jacob, a distant cousin of ours,
so he says, came hither before our time, a beggar and a fugitive, with
naught but his skin; and our father in his goodness sheltered and cherished this good-for-nothing for the sake of the gods. And now, lo,
the turn that things have taken before our face and eyes! He had fed
himself on our flesh and blood and taken our father's goods unto
himself, and is waxed fat and rich so that it is a stench in the nostrils
of the gods, for it is robbery in their sight and defraudeth the heirs of
Laban. It is time that something be done to re-establish justice in one
way or another in the name of the gods of the country, Anu, Ellil
and Marduk, not to forget Bel Harran, to whom we pray after the
custom of our fathers, whereas our sisters, alas, the wives of this
stranger, hold in part with his God and the Lord of his tribe, who
teacheth him to make magic that the spring lambs are dropped speck-

led and our father's property passeth to him according to a vile contract which they made. But we shall see who is to prove stronger on this ground and in these plains, when time proveth all: the gods of the country, who have dwelt here for ages, or his god, who has no house but Beth-el, and that is naught but a stone on top of a hill. For it might be that something would happen to the man, on the side of justice, and that a lion might tear him in pieces in the fields, which would not be a lie, for we are like lions in our wrath; Laban, our father, indeed is too faithful to his contract and feareth it where it lieth below with the little gods of our house. But one might say to him that it was a lion and he will be satisfied. Indeed this robber from the west hath strong sons, two of whom, Simeon and Levi, can roar that it maketh one to quake. But to us too have the gods given bronze in our arms, though we are children of an old man, and we could strike unexpectedly, without notice, at night when he sleepeth and say it was the lion — the father would believe it easily.

Thus Laban's sons talked among themselves, talk not intended for Jacob's ear, but brought to him by the under-shepherds and servants whom he hired. He shook his head over it, full of objective disapproval, for without the blessing of Isaac, he reflected, these youths would have no breath of life in their nostrils — to it was owing all of Laban's prosperity, and they ought to feel shame at plotting thus against him who was in truth the source of their being. But aside from this he felt disquiet, and from that hour onwards he tried to read Laban's countenance and learn how it stood with the master of the house in the matter; whether he would be disposed to believe that it was a wild beast who had killed Jacob, if his sons said so. He searched the man's face when he came out upon his ox to see after the breeding, and found that he must search again; rode himself to the steading to discuss the shearing and studied the heavy face anew. And behold, it was no more towards him as it had been the day before and the day before that; it did not respond to his searching gaze, the features seemed to sag and not one time did the man raise his eyes to Jacob, but they were averted and downcast as he discussed the most necessary matters with his son-in-law; so that after this second reading it was clear and certain to Jacob that not only would the man believe in the ravening beast, but he would thank it in his heart.

Then Jacob knew enough and he heard God's voice in a dream as soon as he fell asleep, and it said: "See that thou goest hence," and urged him: "Pack up all that thou hast, and rather to-day than to-morrow, and take thy wives and thy children and all that has grown unto thee through Me in all this time, and roll away heavily homewards in the direction of the Mount of Gilead, and I will be with thee."

The command was in general terms; consideration and arrangement of the details were the part of man, and in silence, cautiously, Jacob began to set in motion his flight out of the underworld. And first he sent for his wives where he was in the fields, Leah and Rachel, daughters of the house, to consider with them and be assured of their attachment. As for the concubines it was not a matter of their consenting for they would obey.

"Thus is it," he said to them when all three squatted before his tent together, "and so and so. Your later brethren seek after my life for the sake of my goods, which are yours and the inheritance of our children. And when I search in your father's face to learn if he would shield me from their evil counsel, I find that he looketh not at me, as he did yesterday and the day before, but rather not at all, letting the one half of his face hang down as though he were stricken nor will the other half know anything of me. But how is this? For I have served him with all my powers. Three times seven and four years long, but he hath betrayed me and made my hire according as he would, and saying it is the harshness of the life of trade. But the God at Beth-el, the God of my father, hath not permitted him to do me any harm, rather hath He turned all things in my favour. And when it was said: the pied yearlings shall be thy hire, lo the rams leaped and the whole herd bare speckled, so that your father's possessions were turned from him to me. Therefore shall I now die, and it shall be said a lion hath eaten him. But the Lord at Beth-el to whom I have anointed the stone, he will that I should live and grow old, and therefore He hath commanded me in a dream to take what is mine and go secretly across the water into the land of my fathers. I have spoken. Speak ye now."

It proved that the women were with one voice of the opinion of God — how should they be otherwise? Poor Laban! Probably he would have lost even if it had been anything like a choice that was set before them, as was hardly the case. They were Jacob's. Their purchase price had been paid in fourteen years. Under normal circumstances their master and purchaser would long ago have taken them from the house of their fathers into the bosom of his own tribe. They had been the mothers of eight of his children even before nature at length acted, and Jacob made finally fruitful the earliest wooed and rightful bride. Should they let him go, with the sons and with Dinah, Leah's daughter, in order to hang upon their own father? Should he flee alone with the riches which his God had turned aside from their father to him and their children? Or should they betray the plan to their father and brothers that he might be lost indeed? All impossible. Each one more impossible than the rest. And besides they loved him, yes, they had vied in love for him since the day of his coming, and no moment had ever been better than this for each to be more devoted than the other. They clung to him on both sides and spoke both at once:

"I am thine! How the other feeleth, I know not and ask not. But I am thine, where thou art and whither thou goest. Stealest thou away, then steal me with thee and all that Abraham's God hath given thee, and may Nabu, the guide and the god of thieves, be with us!"

"Thank you," Jacob replied. "Thanks to you both equally. The third day from to-day Laban cometh out to the shearing of his flock. Thereafter he journeyeth three days' journey, to shear his speckled sheep, with Beor, Alub and Muras. And when he is gone I will gather together my flocks which are in the midst between here and there, the herds which God hath given me, and the sixth day from now, when Laban is far off, we shall all draw off heavy laden and go towards the river Prath and towards Gilead. Go, for I love you both almost alike. But thou, Rachel, apple of my eye, have a care for the lamb of the virgin, Jehosiph, the true son, that the journey may not be hard for him, and look that thou provide warm coverings for the cold nights, for the shoot is tender as the stock from which it sprung with so much anguish and pain. Go, then, and do according to my words."

Thus, and in yet more detail, was the flight appointed, on which Jacob in his old age looked back with the same mixed feelings of excitement and cunning. But he was always moved to remember, and talked about it to the day of his death, what Rachel, the little one, had done in her sweet simplicity and slyness. She did it quite alone, no one else knew, and not until afterwards did she confess it to Jacob; not to burden his conscience with her act, that he might swear with a pure heart before Laban. And what was it she did? Since they were stealing away, and all the world stood in the sign of Nabu, so stole she likewise. When Laban was gone to the shearing, and all was quiet in the house, she descended through the trap door into the grave-chamber, where the receipts were, took Laban's little house gods, the teraphim, one after the other, by their bearded and their feminine little heads, stuck them under her arm and in her girdle, held a pair in her hand and slipped back unseen into the women's quarters, to cover up the images among the household goods and take them upon the thievish journey. In truth there was much confusion in her little head — it was precisely that which moved Jacob so, when he heard of it, with emotion and concern. For according to her confession she was won over through her love of him to his God the Highest and Only One, and had abjured her childhood's gods. Yet in her secret heart she was still partly idolater, at least she thought it better to be on the safe side. At all events, she took away Laban's soothsayers and counsellors that they might not give him knowledge of the fugitives route, and kept them as protection against pursuit, which in the local view was one of their virtues. She knew how Laban leaned upon these little men and these little Ishtar women, how highly he treasured them; yet she stole them from him for Jacob's sake. No wonder Jacob kissed her moist-eyed, when she confessed the deed, and only reproved her quite mildly and incidentally for her muddle-headedness and because she had made him to forswear himself with a bodily oath before Laban, when the latter had overtaken them; for he had blindly staked all their lives that the gods were not under his roof.

THE PURSUIT

THE TERAPHIM did not in this instance display their efficacy as protectors — perhaps because they did not want to turn against their lawful owners. That Yitzchak's son had fled, with his wives and their maids and their eleven offspring and all their goods, and of course gone westwards, Laban learned on the third day; he had scarcely reached the place where the speckled and pied sheep were to be sheared when he heard it from the servants and watchers who had in fact expected a better reward than they got for their loyalty, for Laban all but beat them. The furious man hurried home, where he discovered the theft of the idols and thence took up the pursuit, with his sons and a band of armed men.

Yes, it was just like twenty-five years before, on Jacob's journey hither, when he had had Eliphaz at his heels; again he saw himself pursued, more formidably even than before, because this time the pursuing forces could move far lighter than this long train of cattle, pack-animals and ox-carts, crawling along like a worm in the dust. In the alarm he felt when the spies and listeners in his rear announced the approach of Laban, there was mixed a sort of mental gratification at the correspondence and the symmetry. Seven days, so it is stated, did Laban need to overtake his son-in-law; Jacob had the desert, the worst part of the journey, behind him, he had already reached the wooded heights of the mount of Gilead, whence he had only to descend into the valley of the Jordan, where it flows into the Sea of Lot or the Salt Sea — when his start was used up and he had to face the meeting and the explanation.

The scene, the unchanging landscape, river, sea and misty mountain range are silent witness and sworn warrant for the truth of these stories which made Jacob's thoughts so weighty and his mien so awe-inspiring when he mused. I relate them in detail, circumstantially, as they can be proven to have happened here, in abiding harmony with mountain and valley. Here it was, it all fits, I myself went down into the depths and looked from the western shore of the evil-tasting sea of Lot, saw all with my own eyes, and that it is in order and agrees one part with another. Yes, these bluish heights in the east, beyond the lye, are Moab and Ammon, the lands of the children of Lot who were thrust out, whom his daughters bare to him. Far off to the south, beyond the sea, glimmers Edom, Seir, the goatland, whence Esau rushed wildly off to meet his brother and met him at Jabbok. And the Mount of Gilead, where Laban overtook his son-in-law, and its local relation to the Jabbok river whither Jacob afterwards came. It is all quite right. The name of Gilead, on the eastern side of the Jordan, was probably used by extension much further north, as far as the river Warmuk, which unites its rushing waters with the Jordan not far from the sea of Chinnereth of Gennesareth. But more precisely the name applies to the heights which extend westward and eastward on both shores of the Jabbok, and from them one goes down to its thickets and the ford which Jacob chose for his train. But he stopped behind for the night and experienced that remarkable adventure which made him limp somewhat in his walk forever after. How clear it is, moreover, that since here the entry followed into the hot *ghor* of the stream, he did not at once turn off with his weary train of human beings and animals actually into his own native district but went straight through westwards into the vale of Shechem at the foot of Gerizim and Ebal, where he hoped to come to rest. Yes, it all agrees in itself and bears evidence in the long run to the truth of the shepherds' songs.

It will forever remain unclear how the clodlike Laban felt in his mind during his hot and panting pursuit; for his bearing when he reached his goal was indeed a most pleasant surprise to Jacob, whose mind later revelled in its beautiful correspondence with Esau's unhoped-for mildness at their meeting. Yes, Laban's state of mind had been obviously just as confused as the red one's. He snorted with rage, and took up arms against the fugitive; but afterwards more mildly characterized Jacob's conduct as folly, and during the conversation with his nephew admitted that a god, the god of his sister, had visited him in a dream and threatened him on his life not to speak otherwise than friendly with his son-in-law. That might all be, since it would be quite enough for Laban to hear of Abram's and Nahor's god in order to ascribe to him just as actual an existence as to Ishtar or Adad, even though he did not reckon him among his own. But whether he, though not of the faith, did actually see and hear Yeho, the one and only, in his dream, remains doubtful. Teachers and commentators have confessed themselves baffled, and it is more likely that he clothed in the garment of a vision certain feelings and fears which came over him on the way, certain considerations which made themselves felt in the silence of his soul. Jacob would be no wiser than he in the matter, but would acquiesce in that way of putting it. Twenty-five years had taught Laban that he had to do with a man of blessing;

his rage is comprehensible, considering that by his departure Jacob was removing the blessing for whose sake Laban had sacrificed so much; but no less comprehensible is it that his first intention of confronting Jacob in force was on the way weakened by his misgivings. There could be no objection to Jacob having taken the daughters of Laban with him. Jacob had bought them, they were his, body and soul, and Laban himself had once upon a time jeered at the beggar who had nowhither to lead them in the wedding procession from the house of their parents. Times were changed indeed, for now the gods had granted this man to plunder him, Laban! In setting out in pursuit, he had not consciously the intention of taking away the plunder by force of arms, but was vaguely urged to soften the blow of losing all that had passed out of his hands into Jacob's by at least parting friends with the lucky thief — it would certainly be better for him if he did so. There was only one matter which still enraged him and which he would certainly push to a settlement: the theft of the teraphim. This was the clear and definite motive among all the vague ones which urged him on: he must have back his household gods — and if the reader has conceived in his heart the smallest stirring of sympathy for the Chaldæan man of business and keeper of contracts, he may feel a little pang over the reflection that Laban never did get them back!

The meeting of the fugitive and the pursuer took place quite quietly, with a strange lack of unpleasantness; considering Laban's mood when he set out one would have expected a clash. Night fell upon Gilead, and Jacob had just made his camp on the damp plateau, pegged out the camels, and herded the sheep and goats together to keep warm, when Laban silently came on like a shadow, set up his tent nearby, and disappeared into it for the night without more ado.

But he left it early and went with heavy tread to Jacob's, before which the other somewhat aimlessly awaited him. They touched forehead and breast and sat down together.

"It rejoiceth my soul," so Jacob began the somewhat delicate interview, "to behold once more my father and uncle. May the hardships of travel not have availed to lessen his bodily well-being!"

"I am strong beyond my years," Laban replied. "Surely thou knewest it, to have laid upon me this journey."

"How so?" Jacob asked.

"How so?" Laban repeated. "Man, bethink thyself what thou hast done to me, stealing away like a thief from me and our contract, and robbing me of my daughters as by the sword. For in my way of looking at things thou shouldest always have remained with me, according to the contract, which hath cost me blood, but yet I have held to it as is thought right in our land. But if thou sufferest it not but covetedst so vehemently to go, why then hast thou not opened thy mouth and spoken like a son? Even so late might we have made good what at the right moment thy circumstances prevented thee in, and have accompanied thee in state with harps and cymbals by land or by water according to the custom. But what hast thou done? Must thou then always steal by day and by night and hast thou no heart in thy body and no bowels of feeling that thou hast not granted to my old age to kiss my children for the last time? But I will tell thee what thou hast done, thou hast dealt with great folly, such is the word that occurs to me to describe thy dealings. And if I would, and if yesternight a voice had not come to me in a dream, and it was it may be the voice of thy God, and counselled me not to meddle with thee, thou canst believe me that my sons and my servants have enough iron in their arms to make thee pay for thy folly in stealing away like a thief!"

"Yea," Jacob replied, "what is true must remain so, and the sons of my master are boars and young lions and would long since have done to me after their kind, if not in the day, then at night when I lay asleep, for thou wouldst willingly have believed that it was a ravening beast, and greatly have bewept me. Askest thou why I have gone away in silence and made no speeches? Should I then not have feared before thee that thou wouldst not agree but would have taken away from me my wives thy daughters or at least have laid upon me new conditions for the permission to depart and have wrested from me my goods and possessions? For my uncle is hard and his god is the ruthless law of business dealings."

"And why hast thou stolen my gods from me?" cried Laban suddenly, and the angry veins stood out finger-thick on his brow.

Jacob was speechless, and he said as much. But at bottom his soul was lightened that Laban put himself in the wrong by such a mad assertion — it counted in his favour.

"Gods?" repeated he, in amazement. "The teraphim? Thou meanest that I have taken thy images from the chamber? But that is the greatest matter for laughter that I have heard in my life. Take thy reason to thy aid, man, and consider with what thou reproachest me! What worth or value could they have for me, thy idols, the clay images, that I should make myself guilty for the sake of them? For I know that they were turned upon the wheel and dried in the sun like to other household gear, and have no power enough to make a slave brat's nose stop running when it hath a cold. But as thou seemest to have lost them, it were better not to praise them too highly before thee."

Laban responded:

"That is all only false and cunning of thee, to do as though thou settest no value upon them, that I may believe thou hast them not. But no man can ascribe so little worth to the teraphim as not to steal them gladly, that is impossible. And since they are no longer where they were, then it must be that thou hast them."

"Hearken now unto me," said Jacob. "It is very good that thou art here and hast not found it hasty to steal after me so many days in this matter; for it must be made plain to the uttermost, I, the accused, demand it. My camp is open unto thee. Go thou through, where thou wilt and search. Turn everything out without fear and according to thy pleasure; I give thee a free hand. With whomsoever thou findest thy gods let him not live; whether it be by me or by my seed, let him be slain here straightway before all eyes, and let it happen by fire, by the sword or by burial as thou choosest. Begin thy search here with me and search carefully, for I insist that the matter be done thoroughly."

His heart was light because he could put off everything on the teraphim, so that there should be no talk save of them, and he would be able to play the injured party at the end. He did not dream how slippery the ground was beneath his feet and how he measured himself against death. For his innocent Rachel was the guilty one; but by her great shrewdness, with the utmost skill and resolution, she came off scatheless from the folly that she had done.

For Laban answered and said: "So let it be then," and getting up eagerly he began to make search of the camp for his images. We know exactly the course it took: at first he was very zealous and thorough, but as the hours went by in vain hunting he grew tired and disheartened. The sun got very hot and though he was without an upper garment, in a shirt open at the throat and with his sleeves rolled up, the sweat rolled down under his cap and his face got so red that one might have feared an apoplexy for the stout, elderly man — and all on account of the teraphim! Had Rachel no heart at all for her father that she could let him be so tortured and mock him with so straight a face? We must remember the power of suggestion and communication that went out from Jacob's significant personality and his spiritual conceptions upon all those about him, especially upon those who loved him. By the power of his spirit and his self-will Rachel herself played a divine part, that of the virgin of the skies and mother of the blessing-bringing boy; she was the more inclined to see the rest of the world, her father included, through Jacob's eyes and to acquiesce in his appointed rôle therein. For her as for her beloved, Laban was a betraying devil and demon of the black moon, who at length himself suffered betrayal, in grander style than his own; and Rachel never blinked an eye at the sight, for it was a pious, significant and predestined event which here went forward, in which even Laban played his part with more or less awareness and consent. She had as little sympathy with Laban as Isaac's people with Esau at the time of the great hoax.

Laban had come up at night and gone to Jacob early next morning, no doubt to demand of him that which she had with her. The father had got up from the interview and begun to search — this was reported to her by the little maid she had sent to spy, who in her haste held up her skirt between her teeth to run the faster so that she was quite bare in front. "Laban is hunting," she announced in a loud whisper. Then Rachel made haste and took the teraphim, which were wrapped in a cloth, and carried them out in front of her black tent, where Leah's riding camel and her own were picketed, highly bred animals possessing a grotesque beauty, with wise little serpents' heads on top of their swaying necks, and feet like cushions, so that they did not sink in the sand. They lay on straw which the servants had strewn plentifully for them, arrogantly chewing the cud. Rachel thrust her stolen gods among their straw, buried them entirely in it and sat down on the place she had disturbed, in front of the animals, so that they looked over her shoulder as they chewed. Thus she awaited Laban.

He, as we know, had begun looking in Jacob's tent, turning his son-in-law's gear upside down, shaking the rugs, pulling the mattress from the stretcher bed, turning over shirts, mantles and woollen covers; upsetting the box that held Jacob's game, which he loved to play with Rachel, the evil eye, so that five of the little stone figures were broken. His shoulders twitching with rage he had gone thence into Leah's place and then into Zilpah's and Bilhah's, sparing none of their women's matters in his search, trembling so that he stuck himself with their pins and smeared his beard with the green dye which they used to lengthen the corners of their eyes; so clumsy was he made by his eagerness and his consciousness that to be ridiculous was his rôle in life.

So he came to where Rachel sat, and spoke:

"Greeting and good health, my daughter. Thou hadst not thought to see me."

"May I see thee in health," she responded. "My father seeketh?"

"I seek stolen goods," said Laban, "throughout all your huts and herds."

"An evil matter," she nodded, and the two camels looked over her shoulder with sly and arrogant smiles. "Why doth not Jacob, my husband, help thee in thy search?"

"He would find nothing," answered Laban. "I must hunt alone and broil myself in this scorching sun on Gilead's mount."

"Yes, yes, a grievous matter," she said again. "There is my dwelling. Look about within it, if thou must, and deemest it fit. But take care of my pots and spoons, already thy beard is somewhat green."

Laban stooped and went in. He soon came out again to Rachel and the camels, saying nothing, but sighing.

"Were there no stolen goods within?" she asked.

"Not to my eye," he answered.

"Then they must be elsewhere," said he. "Of a surety my lord hath wondered why I stand not up before him as would be respectful and mannerly. It is only that I feel myself somewhat unfit, and am hindered in the freedom of my movement."

"How then unfit?" Laban desired to know. "Art thou then hot and cold by turns?"

"Not so, I am only indisposed," she answered.

"But wherein?" he asked once more. "Hast thou a bad tooth or a boil?"

"Indeed, my lord, it is naught but the custom of women that is upon me, and I have my periods," she answered, while the camels smiled more mockingly and arrogantly than before over her shoulder.

"Naught else?" said Laban. "It counteth not, rather I am even glad for thee, that thou art not pregnant, for thou hast little gift for child-bearing. Blessings on thee! I must search my goods."

With which he left her and hunted until the afternoon, when the sun was declining and he was almost worn out. Then he came back to Jacob, tired, dirty and undone, with hanging head.

"Well, and where were the images?" Jacob asked.

"Nowhere, it seemeth," the other replied, lifted his arms and let them fall.

"It seemeth," Jacob sneered — for now he knew where he stood and that he could say what he liked. "Sayest thou seemeth to me, and yet wilt not take it for proof of my guiltlessness, that thou hast nothing found after ten hours' search, turning my camp upside down and rooting about in thy rage to slay me or one of mine? All my gear thou hast tumbled; certainly I gave thee free permission, but that thou hast done it was surely lacking in tact. And what hast thou found of thine own? Lay it down before me and accuse me before thy people and mine and let the public voice choose between us! And how hast thou befouled and overheated thyself, and all to destroy me! And what is my trespass? I was young when I came unto thee and I am now of ripe years, even though as I hope long life may still be vouchsafed unto me. So much time have I spent in thy service and have been unto thee a head-servant such as the world hath not seen; so much my anger letteth me not to say, though my shame should shut it up within me. I have found water, so that thou wast free of Isullanu's sons and couldst throw off the yoke of the bankers, and thou hast blossomed like the rose in the valley of Sharon and stood in fruit like to the date palm in the low-lying plains of Jericho. Thy goats have dropped twofold and thy sheep twins. And may I be struck down if ever I have eaten a ram of thy flock, for I have cropped grass with the gazelles and drunk at the watering place of the cattle. Thus have I lived for thee and served thee fourteen years for thy daughters and six years for nothing, and again nothing and five for the outcasts of thy flocks. And in the day the heat consumed me, and I have shivered with the frost at night in the plains, and for carefulness my sleep departed from mine eyes. But if any mischance touched the flocks, or a lion stole upon them, then might I not swear to my own guiltlessness, but I must pay for the loss, and thou diddest as though I stole from thee day and night. And thou hast changed my wages according to thine own will and put Leah off upon me when I thought to embrace my rightful bride, and that shame I shall feel in my limbs the rest of my life. And except the God of my father, the almighty God, had been with me, surely thou hadst now sent me empty away. But God would not that His blessing be mocked. Never hath He spoke with a stranger, but to thee He spake for my sake and rebuked thee yesternight, that thou shouldst not deal with me other than in friendly wise. And shall I call that speaking friendly when thou comest and ravest that I have stolen thy gods? But since thou findest them not despite thy much search, then must the loss be only apparent."

Laban sighed, and was silent.

"Thou art so shrewd, and so false," he said, wearily, "and I can make no head against thee, nor should any one try since thou wilt but set him in the wrong. But when I look about me, I am as in a dream. All that I see is mine, daughters, children, flocks and waggons and beasts and men, they are mine, but they have passed over into thy hands I know not how, and thou takest away all before mine eyes, till I am as in a dream. But lo, I am peaceably minded and I would make a covenant with thee, that we may part in peace and I may not be consumed all the days of my life on thy account."

"That is good to hear," Jacob answered, "and better than when thou speakest of 'seemeth' and suchlike complainings. For what thou sayest is after mine own heart, for behold thou didst beget for me the maid, the mother of my son, in whom thou art become lovely, and it were despicable that the fruit of Laban should be strange in my sight. Only that it might be less hard for thee have I stolen away and taken mine own with me, but that we should part in friendliness is dear to my heart, that I may then think of thee in a peaceful mind. And I will set up a stone — shall I? — for I do it with willing heart. And four of my servants and four of thine shall make a cairn for a meal and a pledge, that we may eat in the sight of God and make a covenant before Him. Art thou content?"

"Thou sayest it," quoth Laban, "for truly I see naught else."

Then Jacob went and set up a fine tall stone straight upright, that God might be in their midst; but eight men heaped up the heap of stones for the covenant out of all kinds of rubble and small boulders and they sat down upon it together and ate a dish of mutton with the whole fat of the tail in the midst of the dish. But Jacob let Laban eat almost all the tail fat and only tasted of it. So they ate together in the open air and made the contract together over the heap between them with eye and hand. Laban swore by his daughters, for he did not know what else; Jacob had to swear by the God of his fathers and the fear of Isaac, that he would not mistreat his wives nor take any others but them: the stone-heap and the meal were witness. Laban did not concern himself greatly over his daughters, but pitched upon them out of yearning to conclude matters with the man of blessing, in order to get some sleep.

He spent that night also on the mountain with his daughters. Next morning he embraced them, said a last blessing over them and turned his face homewards. But Jacob gave a sigh of relief and another followed of anxiety over new cares. For, sayeth the proverb, if a man have outrun a lion, he is like to meet a bear. Next came the red man.

BENONI

Two women were expectant in Jacob's train, when after the grievous happenings at Shechem he went down towards Beth-el and thence onwards in the direction of Kirjath-Arba and Isaac's house; two who have a place in history, that is, for among the slave women one does not distinguish — there might have been several, we cannot tell. Pregnant was Dinah, that unhappy child; she was pregnant from Sichem, the unblest, and over her fruit there hung a harsh decree, and she rode shrouded from view. And pregnant was Rachel.

What joy! But moderate your exultation, remember and be still. For Rachel died. God would have it so. The sweet thief, she who had met Jacob at the fountain, looking with fearless childlike gaze from among Laban's sheep, she was brought to bed again upon this journey and survived it not, even as the first time she had hardly done so; her breath went from her and she died. The tragedy of Rachel is the tragedy of valour rejected.

One has barely courage to enter into Jacob's feelings at this time, when the life of this heart's bride was quenched and she went hence as a sacrifice to his twelfth son; one is reluctant to imagine how his reason was struck down, and the soft self-will of his emotions trodden deep into the dust. "Lord," he cried, as he watched her die, "what dost Thou?" Well might he so cry. But the perilous thing was, alarming even to contemplate, that he did not surrender his wilfulness, his arbitrary indulgence of feeling, when Rachel died, nor bury it with her in that hastily dug grave by the wayside; but as though he would give notice to the Almighty that He might expect to gain nothing by cruelty, he transferred it, in all its arrogant luxuriousness, to Rachel's firstborn, the beautiful nine-year-old lad, Joseph, loving him with a twofold and altogether provocative preference, and thus offering another exposed side for fate to strike at. One wonders whether the feelingful man actually and consciously despised a life of peace and repose, knowingly challenged destiny and wished for nothing else than to live among alarms and with a sword hanging over him. Such arrogance is obviously an accompaniment to excess of feeling, for such excess presupposes readiness for pain, and everybody knows that nothing is more unthinking than love. The contradiction in nature which here obtains is precisely this: that they are soft souls who choose this life, not formed to bear that which they have drawn upon themselves; whereas they who could have borne it never think of exposing themselves, and thus nothing can happen to them.

Rachel had counted thirty-two years when in devoted agony she had given birth to Joseph; thirty-seven when Jacob broke the dusty bolts and took her away. She was forty-one when she became again expectant, and in that state must depart from Shechem on their journey. It is I who say it, for with her and among her people it was not the practice to make such reckonings. She would have had to think a long time to be able to say, even approximately, how old she was — it was in general not an important question. In the eastern world the chronological awareness of the occidental is almost unknown; it is much simpler there to leave time and life to themselves and the darkness, not subjecting them to systems of measuring and counting; a man is so little prepared for a question concerning his personal age that the questioner may be surprised by a shoulder-shrug and an answer that wavers among whole decades: forty or seventy, perhaps! Jacob too was very unclear over his own age, and did not mind it. Certain periods spent in Laban's service were, it is true, precisely reckoned, but others not; moreover he did not know, and did not care, how old he was when he came. As for Rachel's age, the abiding present of their loving companionship prevented him from noting the natural changes which time, whether watched and reckoned or no, must effect in her beautiful and well-favoured person, changing the charming young girl into the ripe woman. For him, as usually happens, Rachel was still the bride of the well, who with him had endured the seven years of waiting while he kissed the impatient tears from her eyes; he saw her with longsighted eyes, as a blurring of the picture his gaze had first drunk in, the essentials of which could never have been touched by time, the friendly night of the eyes, the short-sighted habit of drawing them together, the too-thick nostrils and the little nose, the formation of the corners of the mouth, her touching smile, that very special way in which the lips lay against each other, which was reproduced in the idolized boy — but above all the archness, gentleness, stout-heartedness that lay in her character, the expression of clear-eyed readiness for life, which even at the well, at the first glance, had made Jacob's heart to swell in his bosom, and which came out so clearly again in the camp at Shechem when she told him of her condition.

"May He add children," that was the meaning of the name which, weary almost unto death, she had given to her firstborn. And now that another one was to be added she had no fear, she gloried in once more enduring all that she had before endured, for the sake of her wifely honour and for the increase. And here a strange organic forgetfulness of women probably came to her aid; for many a woman who in childbed swears never to know her husband again, that she may never repeat those pangs, is pregnant again within the year, for the memory of the pains escapes the sex in the strangest way. Jacob, on the other hand, had by no means forgotten the hell he had endured, and revolted from the thought that after nine years' lying fallow Rachel's body should again be subjected to that paroxysm. For her credit's sake he rejoiced, also because now the number of his sons would be raised to the temple of the zodiac — that was a fascinating thought. Yet again, it disturbed him to think that a younger successor was making bold to follow the declared favourite; for the youngest always tends to be the favourite, and already he was conscious of something like jealousy for Joseph's sake, that mingled in his parental expectation and made him from the first not particularly glad over Rachel's state — as though, indeed, a presentiment hovered over him.

It was still the time of the winter rains in Chislev, when she told him. The tragedy of Dinah was still far in the future. He surrounded the expectant mother as before with all his love and care. He held her head in despair when she was sick, and cried out on his God as he saw her dwindle and grow pale, and only that part of her wax where the gross and natural selfishness of the fruit displayed its unconscious cruelty. The thing in the womb was bent on growing; pitilessly and heeding naught else it drew sap and strength into itself at the expense of her who bore it, it fed upon her unthinking either for good or for evil; and if it had known how to express its notion of the state of affairs — or even had had one — it would have said that the mother was only a means to its own activity, nothing but the tower of its strength and nourishment; she would be left behind, a useless husk or shell, after it had issued forth, which was the centre and significance of the whole proceeding. Of course it could not say anything like that nor even think such things; yet unmistakably such was its meaning, and Rachel smiled and assented. Not always is motherhood so utterly synonymous as this with sacrifice — it should not be. But in Rachel nature showed herself of this mind, had done

so clearly in the case of Joseph though not quite so openly and ter-
rifyingly to Jacob as now.

His bitterness against his eldest sons, those refractory Dioscorides,
for the deed of Shechem, was largely on Rachel's account. It would
never have occurred to him to set out upon a journey with that
fragile and pregnant woman, in whom now only her fruit was strong.
But now these mad youths had forced it upon him with their notions
of honour and of revenge. Precisely now these insensate creatures
had had to strike down men in their rage and maim cattle in sheer
love of mischief! They were Leah's children, like Dinah in whose
cause they raged. What did they care for the ailing state of their
father's true and favoured wife or their father's concern on her
account? Never had one such thought crossed their reckless minds.
But now it was come to this, they must all away. It was already eight
moons and more since Rachel had told him: eight counted moons and
Rachel-moons, while she grew and diminished, while the child in her
grew and she declined. The round year had begun in blossom anew,
they were in Ellul, the sixth month, midsummer heat. It was not a
time to travel, but no choice was left. Rachel must mount. He chose
an ass, an intelligent beast — so as not to expose her to the rocking
motion of the camel. She sat far back on the animal, where the motion
was least, and two donkey-boys led it, on pain of a beating if they
let it stumble against a stone. So they set out with the flocks. Their
goal was Hebron, whither the larger part of the caravan should
proceed at once; but for himself, his wives and a certain retinue Jacob
proposed a brief sojourn at Beth-el, where he should find sanctuary
against pursuit and attack, and where he would gladly rest once more
in memory of that night of exaltation and the dream of the ascending
stair.

This was Jacob's mistake. He had two passions in life: God and
Rachel. Here they came in conflict; and yielding to the spiritual he
brought down disaster upon the earthly one. He might have gone
straight to Kirjath-Arba, reaching it in four or five days of steady
travel. If Rachel had died there, at least she need not have gone
hence, helpless and wretched, like a beggar by the wayside. But he
paused for several days with her at Luz, at Beth-el on the hilltop,
where once he had slept so poorly and dreamed so high. For now too
he was in danger and extremity and was minded to have his head
lifted up again from on high and hear the utterance of mighty
things. The Gilgal was undisturbed, with the blackish stone in the
centre. Jacob showed it to his people, and pointed out the spot where
he had slept and been found worthy of his extravagant vision. But
the stone which had lifted up his head, and which he had anointed,
was no longer there — and this vexed him. He set up another, sprin-
kling it with oil; and spent the whole day in various sorts of devo-

tions, libations and burnt offerings, with which he took the most careful pains, for he was minded to make this spot, which he recognized as a Place of the Presence, far beyond what local significance attached to it, worthy and fitting for worship; and to build not only an earthen hearth, where nourishment for Yah might ascend in smoke, but also to hew an altar out of the rock that crowned the hilltop, with steps leading up to a platform in which there should be hollowed out a basin for libations with little troughs for them to run off. That took some trouble, and Jacob gave much time to directing the work. His people looked on, and listened to his orders; likewise folk came up out of curiosity from the town of Luz and lying or squatting filled the free space before the altar and watched the proceedings of this roving priest and seer, with thoughtful faces and murmured exchange of opinions. There was nothing strikingly new in what they saw, though it was clear to them that this dignified stranger was bent on interpreting the usual in an unusual and even irregular sense. For instance, he pointed out the horns at the four corners of his sacrificial table and told them that they were not moon horns, not the bull horns of Marduk-Bel, but the horns of rams. This was a surprise, they discussed it among themselves. When he addressed the Lord as Adonai, they supposed for a long time that he meant the lovely one who had been mangled and had arisen; but later they were convinced that he referred to somebody else. The name of El they did not hear. That He was called Israel was a mistake, that was the name of the man himself, personally, and the name of the sect whose shepherd he was. Then for a while it was thought that he himself was the god of the rams' horns or gave out so to be; but that was set right later. One might not make a picture of God, for though He had a body He had no form, He was fire and cloud. Some of them accepted that, others rejected it. In any case it was plain that the man Jacob's thoughts about his God were highly significant, even though a sort of anxiety, or actually pain, was visible in his wise and solemn presence. He looked wonderful up there, when he slew the kid with his own hand, let the blood run down and smeared with it the horns which were not moon horns. Likewise wine and oil were richly poured out before the Unknown, and bread brought — the stranger must be rich — a fact which spoke in his favour as well as in his God's. He burnt the best pieces of the kid, the smoke whereof smelt sweet of *samim* and *besamim;* from the rest a meal was prepared, and it was partly to be able to partake of this, if also because the wanderer's personality had won them over, that several of the townsfolk declared their readiness to sacrifice to the God of Israel, though only as subsidiary to their own inherited worship. In the course of these proceedings and advances, most of the natives had been bewitched by the incredible beauty of Joseph the youngest son of Jacob. They kissed their finger-tips when he appeared, clapped their hands above their heads, feasted their eyes and almost burst with laughter when with ingratiating shamelessness he called himself the favourite of his parents, on the ground of his mental and bodily charms; enjoying his childish conceit with that pedagogic irresponsibility which characterizes our relation to other people's children.

Jacob spent in retirement the later hours of this day, preparing himself for the revelations which might be vouchsafed him in the night. And they came to pass, though not with the overwhelming vividness of that early experience. A voice — great, abstract, vague and elevating — spoke to him: of fruitfulness and the future, and of the fleshly bond with Abram, and most impressively of all of the name which the sleeper had wrested with strength and anguish at Jabbok, and which he forcibly confirmed to him, as it were forbidding him his old and original one and blotting it out and giving authority to the new. It filled the listener's heart with a stirring sense of new beginnings, as though a cut had been made and the old fell away and time and the world stood renewed. So much did all this express itself in his manner next day that he was avoided of all. In his deep absorption he seemed to have forgotten Rachel's state, and nobody made bold to remind him, least of all the sufferer herself, who in her affectionate modesty subordinated to his musing her own great need of going on. At last he gave the order.

From the Mount of Olives near Jebus, also called Urushalim, where a Hittite man named Putichepa administered the government and took the taxes in the name of the Egyptian Amun, one might have looked down — and very likely did so — upon the little train of tiny figures winding down from Beth-el through broad, rolling country that lay parched in the summer heat; it passed by Jebus on its left and took its way south towards the house of Lahma or Beth-Lahma. Jacob might well have wished to turn in at Jebus, to enquire of the priests about the sun-god Shalim, a local deity here in the west, after whom the town took its second name. For it stirred him to hear talk even about false and foreign deities, and contributed to his inward labours upon the image of the one and only God. But the story of Shechem and what his sons had done to the garrison and Beset their captain, might very easily have come to the ears of Amun's deputy, the shepherd Putichepa; it seemed wiser to the traveller to practise discretion. On the other hand, at Beth-Lahma, the house of bread, he could discuss with the incense burners of the Lahma the origin of this manifestation of the arisen and the nourisher, in whose cult even Abram in his time had shown a friendly interest as in a possibly related faith. He rejoiced to see the town greeting him from its site. It was late afternoon. The western sun, sinking beneath a bluish wall of storm-cloud, sent down broad rays and bands of light across the mountainous landscape, so that the little hill-settlement glistened white in its radiance. Dust and stone were kindled by the soft and solemn brightness; it filled Jacob's heart with a proud and pious sense of the divine. On their right, behind a wall of loose stone, ran violet-tinted vineyards, while small fruit orchards filled in the spaces between the rubble on their left. The distant ranges paled to shadow in a sort of translucent glimmering. A very ancient, mostly hollow mulberry tree bent athwart the road, its trunk supported by a pile of stones. They were just passing it, when Rachel slipped from her ass in a faint.

Hours before the pains had begun, at first slight, but she had not liked to disquiet Jacob and interrupt the journey, and had said nothing. Now on a sudden her agony was so great, so rending, that it deprived of her senses the frail receptacle of the sturdy fruit. Jacob's tall, splendidly caparisoned dromedary came to its knees unbidden, to let its rider dismount. He cried to an old slave Gutah, a woman from beyond the Tigris, learned in women's matters, who had aided many a labour in Laban's house before now. They laid the sufferer under the mulberry tree and dragged up mattresses. Perhaps it was the aromatic herbs they gave her to smell, it may have been fresh pains, that brought her round. She promised not to faint again.

"I will be alert and I will labour, from now on," she gasped. "For I would hasten and not make the train to tarry, my dear lord. Alas, that it hath come upon me now, so near the goal! But one chooseth not one's time."

"It mattereth not, my dove," answered Jacob softly. And involuntarily he murmured an invocation, such as at Naharin one sent up to Ea in time of need: "You have made us, may then illness, swamp fever, ague and all misfortune be far from us." And the midwife repeated other such sayings, and hung about the sufferer a well-tried charm of her own in addition to those she already wore; as the pains came on again in fury, she talked to Rachel in her broken Babylonian tongue:

"Be consoled, thou fruitful one, and endure the rage of the attack. For thou shalt have this son likewise to the other one, so much in my wisdom I can see, and thine eye shall not run out ere thou beholdest him, for the child is quick indeed."

Quick indeed it was, that centre and significance of the whole, and decidedly it thought its hour to have come; it strove towards the light, it sought to throw off the maternal husk. It gave birth to itself, as it were, rudely storming the narrow womb, without help from her who had so blissfully received the seed and nourished it in her body, but was powerless, despite so much sincere good will to bring it forth. It was of no avail that the old woman prattled instructions and arranged her limbs, showed her how to breathe, to hold her chin and her knees. The next spasm of anguish destroyed all ordered effort; under the sore punishment she flung herself about regardless, streaming cold sweat, and biting her blue lips. "Oh, oh," she screamed, and called in turn upon the gods of Babel and Jacob's God. Night came on, the moon's silver boat swam up above the hills, and waking from a fainting fit she said:

"Rachel will die."

All those about her cried out — Leah, the maids and all the other women, and flung up their arms in prayer. Then the monotonous murmur rose again and louder than before, like a swarm of bees, with which almost unbroken they had accompanied Rachel's labour. Jacob, holding her head in his arms and hearing her despair, only managed after a long pause to utter dully: "What sayest thou?"

She shook her head, with an effort after a smile. There came a pause, while the attacker seemed to take counsel with himself in his hole. The midwife half approved this pause, and thought it might last some time; and Jacob suggested that they employ the interval to make a light stretcher and carry Rachel to Beth-lahma to the inn. But Rachel would not have it so.

"Here it hath begun," she said, stiff-lipped, "here let it end. Who knoweth if there be room for us at the inn? The midwife is wrong, for lo, I shall begin again, Jacob my husband, to bring thee our second son."

Poor wretch, there could be no hope of her helping, she knew it even when she spoke the words. What in her heart she thought, and knew, she had already said; and again, in the course of the night, between two periods of martyrdom, she let her knowledge and her secret thought be seen again, as with stiff lips, already swollen from the weakness of her heart, she spoke of the name they should give their second child. She enquired of Jacob what he thought, and he answered:

"Lo, he is the son of the one and true wife, and he shall be called Benjamin."

"No," said she, "be not angry, for my thought is better, and Benoni shall his new life be called. So shalt thou name the new lord whom I bring thee, and he shall be in memory of Mami, who made him beautiful in thine and in her image."

Jacob's skill in far-flung spiritual associations made him understand her almost without pausing to reflect. Mami, or the wise Ma-ma was a folk-name for Ishtar, mother of the gods and shaper of men, of whom it was said that she made the male and the female babe lovely after her image; Rachel in her mother-wit and weakness mingled the person of the divine creatress and her own motherhood, the more readily that Joseph oftentimes called her Mami. But for the initiated, whose thought took the right way, Ben-oni meant Son of the Dead. Yet she no longer knew that she had betrayed herself, already, and took this way to make Jacob understand the truth in time, that he might not feel too sore a shock and lose his reason.

"Benjamin, Benjamin," he wept and said. "Not Ben-oni." And then it was that he directed upwards into the silvery light of those worlds above their heads, almost as a confession that he understood, his question: "Lord, what dost Thou?"

To such questions there is no answer. Yet it is the glory of the human spirit that in this silence it does not depart from God, but rather learns to grasp the majesty of the ungraspable and to thrive thereon. Beside him the Chaldæan women and slaves chanted their litanies and invocations, thinking to bind to human wishes the unreasoning powers. But Jacob had never yet so clearly understood as in this hour, why all that was false, and why Abram had left Ur to escape it. The vision vouchsafed him into this immensity was full of horror but also of power; his labour upon the godhead, which always betrayed itself in his care-worn mien, made in this awful night a progress not unconnected with Rachel's agonies. And quite in the spirit of her love it was, that Jacob, her husband, should draw spiritual advantage from her dying.

The child came into the world towards the end of the last night watch, when the heavens were palely brightening with the dawn. The old woman had to wrench it by force from the poor womb, for it was choking. Rachel could shriek no more, she had fainted. Much blood came, such a loss that the pulse in her wrist throbbed no longer, but flickered thinly. She lived another hour. But she saw the living child, and smiled. When they brought her Joseph, she did not know him.

The last time she opened her eyes was when the east had begun to redden and the morning shone in her face. She looked up in Jacob's face that bent over her, her lids contracted a little and she said indistinctly:

"Ah, behold, a stranger! Why, then, should I let thee kiss me? Is it because thou art the cousin from afar off and we are both the children of one forefather? Then kiss me . . . and the shepherds by the well rejoice, saying 'Lu, lu, lu!' "

He kissed her, trembling, for the last time. She said again:

"Lo, thou rollest away the stone for me, Jacob my lover, with the strength of thy man's arms. Roll it now away from the grave, and lay therein the child of Laban, for I leave thee to go hence. How all burdens have been taken from me, childbearing, lifebearing, and it is the night. Jacob, my husband, forgive me that I was unfruitful and brought thee but two sons, but yet two, Jehosiph, the blessed, and the little one, the son of death. And ah, I am sore to go from them.

And from thee too, Jacob, I am sore to part, for we were the right ones for each other. And now thou must muse alone and learn without Rachel who God is. Learn, then, and farewell. And forgive too," she breathed, "that I stole the teraphim." Then death passed over her countenance and put out its light.

The humming of the exorcists ceased at a sign from Jacob's hand. They all fell upon their faces. But he sat, her head still in his arms, and his tears fell silently and unquenchably upon her breast. After a while they asked him if they should not now make a bier and carry the dead to Beth-Lahma or Hebron to bury her.

"No," he said, "here hath it begun, here it shall end. Where He hath done it, there shall she lie. Dig a grave and hollow it out by the wall. Take fine linen from the pack to shroud her, and choose a stone, at once for the grave and to her memory. Then Israel will go onwards, without Rachel and with the child."

While they dug, the women loosed their hair and bared their breasts, and mixed dust with water to defile themselves for the mourning, and sang to the music of the flute the lament, Woe for our sister, smiting their foreheads and striking their breasts. But Jacob held Rachel's head until they took her from him.

When the earth had closed above the beloved, on the spot where God had taken her, by the wayside, Israel passed on, and made a stage at Migdal Eder, an ancient tower. There Reuben sinned with Bilhah, the concubine, and was cursed.

YOUNG JOSEPH

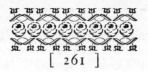

Chapter I

THOTH

OF BEAUTY

THE STORY goes on to tell how Joseph, being seventeen years old, was feeding the flock with his brethren; and the lad was with the sons of Bilhah and with the sons of Zilpah, his father's wives. That is correct; and we have instances of the fact which the saga further states: namely, that Joseph brought unto their father their evil report. It would not be hard to find a point of view from which Joseph could be regarded as an unlicked cub. It was the brothers' point of view. I do not share it; or, rather, I might entertain it for a moment, but I would give it up. For Joseph was more. The passages I have quoted, however, require explanation, each in turn, that the lie of the land may be clear, and that which has shrunk away into the past may be expanded again into its true proportions and presentness.

Joseph was seventeen years old, and in the eyes of all who saw him the most beautiful among the children of men. I confess that I do not care for talk about beauty. The word and the idea are alike tiresome. For beauty is a conception as pallid as it is lofty — a pedant's dream. There are supposed to be laws of beauty. But a law addresses itself to the understanding and not to the emotions — for these do not brook the understanding's control. Hence the vapidness of perfect beauty, which leaves nothing to be forgiven. For the emotions need something to forgive, else they turn away in sheer boredom. Nobody but the schoolmaster, with his love of the accepted and formalized, can pay so much honour to mere perfection as to wax enthusiastic over it, and to that kind of enthusiasm it is hard to ascribe much depth. A law is outwardly binding and edifying, but inward compulsion is a matter not of law but of magic. Beauty is a magic worked upon the emotions — as such always half illusory, very vacillating and ephemeral in its effect. Set an ugly head upon a beautiful body, and the body itself is no longer beautiful in any sense which can touch the emotions — except perhaps in the dark, and then delusion comes in. And, indeed, how much delusion, trickery, and deceit are involved in this matter! The world is full of stories about youths dis-

guised as women, turning men's heads; of girls in doublet and hose,
awaking the passions of their own sex. And in every case, when the
fraud is discovered, the emotions subside, because the beauty no
longer serves a practical end. Perhaps, even, human beauty, in its effect upon the feelings, is nothing at all but the magic of sex, sex itself
become visible; so that one might better speak of a complete man, a
perfectly feminine woman, than of a beautiful one. Only by dint of
a victory over self can one woman, or one man, speak of another as
beautiful. Cases in which emotional effectiveness triumphs over obvious unpracticality are rare, though of course they occur and can
be proved. What comes into play here is the moment of youth; that
is to say, a magic which the emotions are prone to confuse with
beauty. So that youth, if it is not marred by all-too-disturbing flaws,
affects the beholder as beauty, and is even so affected itself, as its
smile unmistakably betrays. For it possesses charm, a phenomenon
which of its very nature for ever hovers between the masculine and
the feminine. A youth of seventeen is not beautiful in the sense of
perfect masculinity. Nor yet in the sense of fruitless femininity — that
would be worst of all. But so much we must admit: that beauty in
the guise of youth must always both inwardly and outwardly incline toward the feminine. That is its essence, that conditions the
tenderness between it and the world; that is betrayed by its smile. At
seventeen, it is true, one can be more lovely than woman or man,
lovely like woman and man, lovely in both ways and in all — "beautiful and well-favoured" to a pitch that makes both men and women
fall head over heels in love.

So was it with Rachel's son, and so it is that we are told that he
was the most well-favoured among the children of men. That was
exaggerated praise, since there were and are hosts of his like. Since
the time when man no longer lived in the deep or crawled on his
belly, but had travelled some way toward the bodily image of God,
many a youth of seventeen has displayed to admiring eyes quite as
slender legs and narrow hips, quite such a well-shaped throat and
golden-brown skin. Many a youth has seemed neither too tall nor too
short, but precisely the right height; many have known how to stand
and to walk in a way that is half divine, many have found the exquisite mean between delicacy and strength of form. And it is not
extraordinary either that upon such a body there should sit not a
dog's head but a very winning human one, smiling to boot with a
smile that is half divine. That happens every day. But in Joseph's
world and in his circle his was the person and his the presence which
practised the magic of beauty upon the emotions of the beholder. It
was generally felt that upon his lips — which, save when they moved
to speak or smile, were certainly too full — the Eternal had poured
out grace. True, there was an opposition party, here and there was

ill-will against him. But it proved nothing, and one cannot even say that it did not share the prevailing opinion. For much goes to show that the brethren's hatred for Joseph was nothing but the reverse side of the universal adoration.

THE SHEPHERD

So much for Joseph's beauty, and his seventeen years. That he kept the flocks with his brothers — that is, with the children of Zilpah and Bilhah — is a statement which likewise calls for explanation, qualification, and expansion.

Jacob, the man of the blessing, was a stranger in the land, a *ger*, as they said, a tolerated and respected guest. Not because he had dwelt so long out of his own land, but by nature, rank, and inheritance, as son of his fathers, who also had been *gerim*. He had not become an established citizen and member of the ruling class in the city; not therein lay the dignity he possessed. It had its source in wisdom and riches, both together, and in the impressiveness of his person and bearing. But not in his manner of life; for that was lax, though quite legal, and characterized by what one might call a regular irregularity. He lived in tents before the walls of Hebron as once he had dwelt before Shechem's gates, and might one day set out again to seek other springs and pasture-lands. And yet he was no Bedouin, with the mark of Cain upon his brow, the sign of vagrancy and rapine, a terror and an abomination to town-dwellers and peasants alike — that not at all. His God was like the other Baals of the land in their deadly enmity against Amalek, as he had many times proved by arming his people that they might help the dwellers in Hebron and the cattle-keeping peasantry to thrust back the oncoming hordes from the deserts of the south — camel-breeding folk bent on plunder, their faces painted with their tribal signs. Yet Jacob himself was no peasant — quite expressly and consciously not. It would not have harmonized with his religious feelings, which were so different from those of the sunburnt tillers of the soil. Moreover, as *ger* and guest he had no right to the ownership of land, save only his dwelling-places. He rented a little plough-land, now here, now there; sometimes smooth and level, sometimes steep and rocky, with rich soil between the stones, where corn and barley might sprout. It was worked by his sons and slaves. Joseph too sometimes played sower and reaper as well as shepherd — as everybody knows. But this casual kind of farming had little meaning in Jacob's life. He practised it half-heartedly, as evidence of some sort of permanence. For his life's true riches and substance lay in his teeming movable property, the flocks. He exchanged all they produced for plentiful supplies of corn and oil, figs, pomegranates, honey, even silver and gold; and the possession of them determined his relation to townsfolk and country-folk — a relation carefully regulated and qualified by many contracts which gave him civic standing despite the anomalous character of the life he led.

And for the sake of his flocks he required good business relations with the inhabitants, the tradesmen in the town and the peasants who worked for or rented of them. If Jacob wanted any settled life at all, if he did not wish to be thought of as a nomad who had broken into others' land and laid it waste, he needed to have fixed and friendly contracts with the people of Baal, stipulating that he might drive his flocks into the stubble and let them rove and crop over the fallow land. For the moment, indeed, there was less of this up here in the hills. There had been a long and blessed season of peace; the highways were full of coming and going, the land-exploiting town-dweller grew fat on the caravan trade, on payments for warehousing, lading, and convoy for goods that came from the land of Marduk via Damascus, along the road east of the Jordan, through that district to the sea and thence to the land of mud — or the other way round. And the town-dweller accumulated land, farming it by the labour of slaves or debtors; its produce enriched him, aside from the profits he made on his business. Thus, even as the sons of Ishullanu did to Laban, he got the peasants under his thumb by making them loans. Cultivation and settlement rapidly increased, they encroached upon the grass-land, and it came about that as once the meadows of Sodom could not support both Lot and Abram together, so now the land could no longer support Jacob. He had to divide his flocks. It was arranged that the larger part should be sent to pasture five days' journey to the north, in that well-watered vale of Shechem where he had been before. Thither went in the main the sons of Leah, from Reuben down to Zebulun, while only the four of Bilhah and Zilpah and the two of Rachel lived with their father. So that it was as with pictures of the signs of the zodiac, of which six only are visible to the eye at a time — an image or parable to which Joseph never tired of referring. The six at Shechem did, it is important to say, return when it was harvest time at Hebron, and more hands were needed. But mostly they were four or five days distant, an equally important fact, which explains the saying that Joseph was with the sons of the maids.

But Joseph did not work every day with the brethren in meadow and field. We must not take his labours too seriously. Not always did he tend the flocks or turn up the plough-land for the winter sowing when it was soft from the rains. Rather he only worked now and then, when he thought of it or felt like it. Jacob his father granted him much free time for labours of a higher kind, of which I shall presently speak. But when he did work with the brethren, in what character was it: as helper, or as overseer? The brothers never knew.

They would order him about as the youngest, and roughly enough; but he did little work and behaved not as though he belonged with them, one among the sons of his father, but as the father's representative and emissary, set there to spy. The result was that they disliked having him, and yet were vexed when he took a notion to stop at home.

LESSONS

WHEN that happened he sat with old Eliezer beneath the tree of God, the great terebinth beside the well, occupied in the pursuit of knowledge.

People said of old Eliezer that he was like Abraham in the face. Actually they could not know this, for none of them had seen the Chaldæan, nor had any picture or likeness of him come down the ages. The assertion could only be an indirect way of saying that Eliezer's features helped them when they tried to conjure an image of the original wanderer and friend of God. This was not so much because they were large and stately, like his whole figure and bearing, but rather because there was something about them of the tranquilly generalized and divinely inexpressive, which made it easy to transfer them to a venerable unknown of past time. Eliezer was a little older than Jacob, and dressed like him, in garments which were partly Bedouin, partly in the fashion of the people of Shinar, with looped and fringed draperies and a scarf-like girdle wherein his writing-materials were stuck. His forehead, so far as the head-cloth left it free, was serene and unwrinkled. The still dark eyebrows ran in a flat, narrow curve from the broad and shallow base of the nose to the temples. Beneath them the formation of the eyes was such that the almost lashless upper and lower lids, heavy and as it were swollen, looked like lips, between which the black eyeballs rounded out. The nose, thin-nostrilled and flat-boned, drooped down to the narrow moustache which ran from the corners of the mouth and lay upon the yellowish beard. Below it hung the even red line of the lower lip. The cheeks, with a thousand little wrinkles in their yellow skin, stood out above the line of the beard; and this line, where cheek and beard met, was so extraordinarily even as to suggest that the beard was fastened behind the ears and could be taken off. Or, rather, the whole face suggested a mask, with Eliezer's own underneath. Joseph remembered thinking so as a child.

There were current all sorts of absurd stories about Eliezer himself and his origins, with which I will deal further on. For the present it is enough to say that he was Jacob's house steward and eldest slave, could read and write, and was acting as Joseph's teacher.

"Tell me, son of the true wife," he might address the lad, as they sat together in the shade of the tree of enlightenment, "for what three reasons did God create man last, after the beasts and all growing things?"

To which Joseph would make answer:

"God created man last, firstly lest someone might say he had holpen at the rest of the work; secondly, for the humbling of man, that he must needs say to himself: 'The blowfly was born before me'; but thirdly, that he might sit down straightway to the meal, as the guest for whom all things had been made ready."

Whereto Eliezer would respond with satisfaction: "Thou sayest," and Joseph would laugh.

But that was the least of it; it was only one instance of all the exercises in quick wit and memory, the countless little sayings and snatches of ancient time in which the boy must become versed. Eliezer had begun this teaching in Joseph's tender childhood, and Joseph had long known how to enchant his hearers with his graceful repetitions, though they were silly enough about him even without that.

Thus at the well he had tried to divert his father with his fable of the names and naming, how the damsel Ishchara demanded the name of God from the lustful messenger; and how no sooner had she learned the true and rightful one than she had called it out and vaulted upwards, thus bringing to scorn the importunate Senhazai. And how the Lord had received her in great favour on high, saying unto her: "Thou hast escaped from the snare of sin and therefore will We give thee thy place in the heavens." And how that was the origin of the constellation of the Virgin. But Senhazai, alas, had had to stop down below in the dust, until that day when Jacob, son of Yitzchak, dreamed by Bethel his dream of the ladder leading up to heaven. Only upon that ladder had Senhazai been able to mount once more, deeply humiliated that he could do so only in a human being's dream.

We can scarcely call this learning. No, for it was only half true — an adornment, merely, to the mind, though calculated to discipline it for the reception of austere and sacred truths. Thus Joseph learned of Eliezer about the universe, the heavenly one: ideally composed of the upper heaven, the heavenly earth of the zodiac, and the southern ocean of the heavens. And about the earthly universe as well, which precisely corresponded, being likewise in three parts, the skyey heaven, the kingdom of the earth, and the earthly ocean. This last, so he learned, ran round the earth's disk in a band, but was also beneath it, and at the time of the Great Flood might break through all the cracks and mingle its waters with those of the downrushing heavenly sea. But the earthly kingdom was just like the firm-trodden earth to look at, and the heavenly earth up above was like a mountainous country with two peaks, the sun and the moon, Horeb and Sinai,

Sun and moon, together with five other moving stars, made up the seven which is the number of the planets and bearers of the command, which went round the dam of the zodiac in seven circles of differing circumference; so that this was like the seven-tiered tower whose rings of terraces led up to the highest heaven of the north and the Almighty's seat. Yes, there sat God, and His holy mount glittered as with fiery precious stones — just as Mount Hermon in the north glittered in his snows above the land. As he talked, Eliezer pointed to the gleaming white height in the distance, visible from everywhere and so also from the tree of enlightenment; and Joseph distinguished not between earthly and heavenly.

He learned the wonder and the mystery of numbers: sixty, twelve, seven, four, and three; the divineness residing in measure, and how everything agreed and corresponded, so that one could only wonder at and adore the greatness of the harmony.

Twelve were the stations of the zodiac; they formed the stations of the great circle, and were the twelve months of thirty days each. But the small circuit corresponded to the great; for it too was divided into twelve sections; thus there was a space of time sixty times as great as the course of the sun, and that was the double hour. It was the month of the day, and proved just as significantly divisible. For the diameter of the sun's course was contained in the course of the sun as visible at the equinox, precisely as many times as the year had days: namely, three hundred and sixty times; and on just these days the rising of the sun, from the moment when its upper rim appeared over the horizon to that when it stood full and clear, lasted the sixtieth part of a double hour. That then, was the double minute; and as the great circle was formed out of summer and winter, out of day and night the small one, so from the twelve double hours came twelve single ones, for the day and for the night, and sixty single minutes for each hour of the day and night.

What order, harmony, and satisfaction in all that!

But mark once more, Dumuzi, son of the true wife! Make thy senses clear, calm, and alert!

Seven was the number of the moving stars and bearers of the command, and to each belonged a day. But seven was also and especially the moon's number, which marks a path for its brothers the gods there in the sky; for the number of its quarters are seven days each. Sun and moon were two, like everything else in the world and like yes and no. Thus one might group the planets as two and five — and how rightly too, considering the five! For that number had a wonderful relation with twelve, seeing that five times twelve make the sixty already shown to be sacred; but even more wonderful with seven, for five and seven made twelve. And that was not all. For by such division and grouping one got a five-day planetary week, of which seventy-two came in the year. But five was the number by which one must multiply the two-and-seventy to arrive at the glorious three hundred and sixty — and this was at once the sum of the days in the year and the result of that division of the sun's course by the longest line which could be drawn upon the disk.

How wonderful that was!

On the other hand, one might group the planets into three and four, upon the highest authority from both sides. For three was the number of the rulers of the zodiac, sun, moon, and Ishtar. Moreover it was the world-number, it determined both above and below the constitution of the universe. Again, four was the number of the quarters of the earth, to which corresponded the times of day; likewise it was the number of the parts into which the sun's course fell, each presided over by a planet; also the number of the moon and Ishtar, each of which displayed four phases. But if you multiplied four by three, what did you get? You got twelve!

Joseph laughed. But Eliezer lifted up his hands and spoke: "Adonai!"

And how did it come that if you divided the days of the moon by the days of its quarters — namely, four — you got again the seven-day week? That was the work of His finger!

With all this young Joseph, under his elder's watchful eye, played as with a game, amusing and profitable at once. He perceived that God had given man understanding, in order that he might deal with these sacred matters and make them more consistent: man, then, had had to make the three hundred and sixty-five days match up with the solar year by intercalating five days at the end. They were hard and evil days, days of dragons and cursings and wintry nights; only when they were over did spring appear and the blessing once more prevail. Here the number five appeared in intolerable aspect. But thirteen was also bad — and why? Because the twelve moon months had only three hundred and fifty-four days, and from time to time extra days had to be shoved in, which corresponded to the thirteenth sign of the zodiac, the raven. Its remainder character stamped the thirteen as an unlucky number — just as the raven was a bird of ill omen. Therefore it was that Benoni-Benjamin had wellnigh died, when he went through the gates of birth as through the narrow pass between the peaks of the high mountains of the world, and was almost overcome in the struggle against the powers of the underworld — all because he was Jacob's thirteenth child. But Dinah had been accepted as a sacrifice in his stead, and Dinah perished.

It was well to see into the absolute and penetrate into the nature of the mind of God. For His wonder-working with numbers was not quite without flaws, and man had to have wits enough to adjust it. But the adjustment was attended with misfortune and cursings, and even the number twelve, otherwise such a fine number, became ominous, for it had to be added to the three hundred and fifty-four days of the moon year to bring them up to the three hundred and sixty-six days of the lunar-solar year. But if one took three hundred and sixty-five days as the right number, then there was always lacking, according to Joseph's reckoning, a quarter of a day; and this amounted in the course of time to fourteen hundred and sixty quarters, or an entire year. That was the period of the dog-star; and Joseph's conception of time and space now became superhuman, it passed on from the little circles to more and more mammoth ones which circled far round them, to closed years of awe-inspiring extent. The day itself was a little year, with its times and seasons, its summer daylight and winter night, and the days were closed into a great circle. But it was great only relatively speaking, and one thousand, four hundred and sixty of them closed to comprise the year of the dog-star. The world, however, consisted of the overpowering course and cycle of the greatest — or even then perhaps not quite finally the greatest — years of all, of which each had its own summer and winter. Winter came when all the constellations were in the sign of Aquarius or Pisces; summer when they were in the sign of the lion or the crab. Every winter began with a flood, every summer with a fire; so that all the great circles and world-revolutions had their definite beginning and end within which they were comprised. Each of them contained four hundred and thirty-two thousand years and each precisely repeated all those before it, since the constellations returned to the same position and must reproduce the same effects in great and in small. Hence it was that the world-revolutions were called "renewals of life," also of course "repetitions of the past" and "everlasting recurrence." Likewise their name was Olam, "the æon"; but God was the Lord of the Ages, El Olam, He living throughout the ages, Hai Olam, and He it was who had given to man *olam* in his heart; that is to say, the capacity of thinking in æons and thus in some sense the mastery of them.

This was knowledge of the most majestic; Joseph received it in the grand style. But how much else did Eliezer not know: mysteries which made of knowledge a pleasure at once great and flattering, precisely because it was mysterious, the property on earth of only a small number of highly discreet and exceeding clever folk in temple and lodge, and not shared by the masses of mankind. For instance Eliezer knew and taught to Joseph that the Babylonian double ell was the length of the pendulum which made sixty double oscillations in a double minute. Joseph, prattler that he was, repeated this to no one; for it displayed once more the sacredness of the number sixty, which, multiplied by the excellent number six, produced the most sacred of all, three hundred and sixty.

He learned the measures of length and distance, deducing them both from his own pace and from the course of the sun. This, Eliezer assured him, was not presumptuous, since man was a little universe, in all things corresponding to the great one. And thus the sacred numbers of the planetary cycle played their rôle in the whole structure of measure and in time which became space.

It became volume, and thereby it became weight. Joseph learned the weights and money values of gold, silver, and copper, according to Babylonian and Phœnician, the royal and the common usage. He practised himself in business calculations, learned how to exchange copper for silver, and an ox for such measures of oil, wine, and grain as corresponded to its value in metal. In all this he was so quick-witted that Jacob, as he listened sometimes, made a clucking sound with his tongue and exclaimed:

"Like an angel art thou! Like a very angel of Araboth."

Again Joseph learned the most important of the human ailments and their treatment; he learned about the human body, which likewise conformed to the cosmic trinity and was comprised of solids, liquids, and gases. He learned to associate the parts of the body with the signs of the zodiac and the planets; to understand how it was that kidney fat was more precious than all others, in that the organ which it surrounded was connected with the organ of procreation and was the seat of the vital energies; to recognize in the liver the seat of the emotions; and to get by heart a system of instruction written out in sections on a clay model, from which it appeared that the entrails were a mirror of the future and a source of dependable omens. Next he learned about the peoples of the earth.

There were seventy of these, or more probably seventy-two, since that was the number of the five-day planetary weeks. Some of them had quite extraordinary customs and religious practices. This was true in particular of the barbarians of the furthest north, who dwelt in the land of Magog, far beyond the heights of Mount Hermon and also beyond the country of Hanigalbat, north of Taurus. But the extreme west, called Tarshish, was frightful too; thither men who knew not fear had come from Sidon, having sailed the length of the "Great Green" for uncounted days. And people of Sidon and Gebal had penetrated as far as Chittim, that is to say Sicily, bent on trade and distance, and had there founded settlements. They had indeed done much to make known the ends of the earth. Not for Eliezer's use and behoof, that he might have wherewith to teach; but because they felt the urge to visit distant parts and cry up their purple stuffs and skilled embroideries to the inhabitants thereof. There were winds that bore one effortlessly to Cyprus or Alashia and Dodanim or Rhodes. And thence without too grave perils of the deep they would be borne on to Muzriland or Egypt, whence a trade wind would take

their ship back home. But the people of Egypt themselves had subdued Kush and opened up to knowledge the lands of the Negroes
further south up the Nile. They had boldly taken ship and had discovered the incense-lands furthest south on the Red Sea, Punt, the
kingdom of the Phœnix. In the furthermost south of all lay Ophir,
the land of gold, according to all accounts. As for the east, there
was a king in Elam, whom no one yet had been able to ask whether
he could see further than his own domains in that quarter of the
heavens. Probably not.

All this is only an extract from the information imparted by Eliezer to Joseph as they sat under the tree of wisdom. The lad wrote it
down under the elder's direction and read it aloud to himself, with
his head on one side, until he knew it by heart. The reading and writing were of course the basis and the accompaniment to all else; otherwise it would have been naught but a whispering and hearsay
among men and then died away. So Joseph had to squat very erect
under the tree, his knees apart, holding in his lap the writing-tools,
the clay tablet on which he made wedge-shaped signs with a style;
the leaves made of reeds pressed together; or the smoothed piece of
sheep- or goatskin on which he made rows of pot-hooks with a reed
chewed or sharpened to a point and dipped into the red or the black
part of his paint-saucer. Sometimes he wrote the ordinary writing of
the country, in order to practise himself in the language of his time
and surroundings, also to learn to write business letters and statements in cleanly fashion, as the Phœnicians did. But at other times he
wrote the writing of God, the official and sacred script of Babel, the
script of the law, the doctrine, and the sagas; for these he used the
style and tablet. Eliezer possessed many beautiful models: writings
about the stars, hymns to moon and sun, chronological tables, weather
records, even tax lists, as well as fragments of the great versified fables of primitive time. None of these were true, yet they were
clothed in words so bold and impressive as to make them seem real
to the mind of the reader. They were about the creation of the world
and man; about Marduk's fight with the dragon, Ishtar's elevation
from servitude to royal dominion, and her journey into hell; about
the herb of birth and the water of life, the astonishing things that
happened to Adapa, Etana, and that Gilgamesh whose body was divine flesh and who yet did not manage to achieve immortality. All
this Joseph read with his index finger, writing it down in the prescribed posture, erect, with only his eyelids dropped. He wrote down
and read about Etana's friendship with the eagle, who bore him upwards towards Anu's heaven; so high, in fact, that the earth beneath
them looked like a cake, and the sea like a bread-basket. But when
both had disappeared, fear had seized upon Etana, and he had plunged
down into the depths, together with the eagle — a most mortifying

issue. Joseph hoped that he would, in like case, have borne himself better than the hero Etana. But better than this story he liked that of the man of the forest, Engidu, and how the woman of the city of Uruk converted him to civilization. She taught the brute beast to eat and drink in seemly fashion, to anoint himself and wear clothes, in short to be like a man and a dweller in cities. Joseph found all this fascinating. It was capital, how the harlot taught the man, after having made him sensitive to refinement by seven days and seven nights of love. He recited the lines, the language of Babel falling in obscure splendour from his lips; Eliezer kissed the hem of his pupil's robe and cried out:

"Hail to thee, son of the lovely one! Thy progress is brilliant; soon thou wilt be the Mazkir of a prince, and the admonisher of some great king. Remember me, when thou comest into thy kindom!"

And then Joseph would swagger out to his brethren in the field or plain, to play at working under them. But they, showing their teeth, would say:

"Look, there he cometh swaggering, the inky-fingered fool, and hath been reading stones of the time before the Flood. Perhaps now he will graciously milk the goats; but perhaps he hath come only to spy and see whether we cut out pieces from a sheep for our cook-pot. Lay it only in our hands, he should not go empty away, but we should beat him — as now we dare not, for fear of Jacob."

OF BODY AND SOUL

IF we consider not the details but the general bearing of the bad relations between Joseph and his brothers, as they grew with the years; not the daily vexations and misunderstandings but the fundamental causes of the trouble, these would be found to lie in envy and in arrogance. The most justice-loving would find it hard to decide which fault, or personally speaking which sinner, the single one or the troop who made ever more threatening their common cause against him, was the chief source of the trouble. Strict justice and the upright desire to put aside any temptation to partisanship might perhaps lead one to consider arrogance as the primary evil and source of mischief. But on the other hand he will in very justice be driven to confess that not often in the world has there been so much occasion for arrogance — and indeed for envy — as here.

It is seldom indeed that beauty and wisdom are combined upon this earth. Rightly or wrongly, we are accustomed to think of learning as ugly, and charm as mindless — and, indeed, as is fitting for the possessor of charm, mindless with a good conscience. For what need has charm of letters, mind, or wisdom, when it even runs a risk of being warped and destroyed if it possess them? The typical bridging over, however, of the gulf between mind and beauty, the union of both excellences in a single being, appears as the release of a tension, which one is used to think of as based upon the natural and human and makes one quite involuntarily think of the divine. The unprejudiced eye must look with rapture upon such a manifestation of godlike ease and absence of strain; while it can only give rise to feelings of bitterness in those who have reason to find themselves injured or eclipsed by its light.

So it was here. That delighted acceptance which certain sights find at once in the human heart and which we are accustomed objectively to call their beauty was invariable in the case of Rachel's firstborn son; whether or no we could now subscribe with such enthusiasm, everybody then found him so well-favoured that his charms early became proverbial over the countryside. And not only so, but they added unto themselves the arts of the intellect, which they absorbed with the greatest readiness and then recoined, stamped with their own seal; so that there seemed no longer any contradiction, and almost no difference between the two. I said that the harmonizing of the conflict must have seemed to result in the divine; a sentence that needs interpretation. The two elements were not resolved *into* the divine — for Joseph was a human being, and a very erring one to boot, with far too good an understanding not to recognize the fact. No, but they were resolved *in* the divine; that is to say, in the moon.

I have already described a scene which was very typical of the relations, physical and mental, which Joseph cherished with that wonder-working star. It was behind his father's back of course, who, as he came up, made haste to rebuke his son for baring himself in flirtation with the naked splendour there above. But in the youth's mind the thought of the moon was associated with more than the mere idea of beauty. It had just as close connection with the conception of wisdom and of letters. For the moon was the heavenly image of Thoth, the white ape and inventor of signs, the speaker and writer of the gods, recorder of their words and protecting deity of all those who write. Thus it was the combined magic of beauty and of learning, together and as a unity, which had ravished his soul and given its peculiar meaning to his solitary worship. As a cult it was vague, confused, and prone to degenerate — calculated to alarm the careful father — but just on that ground intoxicating, because mental and physical emotions were therein so enchantingly mixed.

Beyond a doubt every human being holds and cherishes, more or less consciously, some conception, some treasured idea, which forms the source of his secret passion, and by which his vital sense of life is nourished and sustained. For Joseph this precious idea was the cohabitation of body and spirit, beauty and wisdom, and the reciprocally strengthening consciousness of both. Chaldæan travellers and slaves had related to him how when Bel purposed to create mankind he had had his head cut off, his blood had mingled with the earth, and out of those blood-besprent clods life had been created. He did not believe the tale; but if he wished to feel aware of his own existence and know a mysterious sense of rejoicing in it, he would recall that blood-boltered mingling of the earthy with the divine and be conscious of peculiar bliss in being of such substance. He would be smilingly mindful that the consciousness of the body and of beauty must be improved and strengthened through the consciousness of the mind and spirit, as well as the other way round.

What he believed was that the spirit of God, whom the people of Shinar called *"Mummu,"* brooded upon the face of chaos and had created the world by the might of the Word. What a marvel! he thought: the world had arisen by the might of the free and external Word; and even today, let a thing be ever so present, it was in actual fact only actually present when man has given it life in words and called it by name. So did his pretty and well-favoured little head convince itself of the importance and wisdom of the Word.

But all these teachings and tendencies, indulged by Jacob on grounds yet to be mentioned, served only the more to estrange Joseph from the sons of Leah and of the maids. It set him apart; and this in itself bore the seeds of arrogance and mistrust. It goes against my grain to say that the brothers, those first-born males of Jacob's seed whose names everybody knows by heart, were in the main very ordinary fellows. To two of them at least, the complicated and suffering Jehudah and the fundamentally decent Reuben, the characterization does scant justice. In the first place, one could not speak of beauty in connection with any of them; neither of those who were near Joseph's age nor those who were well on in the twenties at this time — though they were stout fellows, particularly Leah's brood, and rejoiced in physical strength and agility, most of all Reuben, but also Simeon, Levi, and Jehudah. As for wisdom and the word, not one among them but would have prided himself on his complete ignorance and contempt of such talents. Bilhah's Naphtali, indeed, was known from his youth up for his gift of the gab. But the popular standards in this matter were modest, and the sum total of Naphtali's powers amounted to a shallow glibness without foundation in any higher things. All the brethren, in short, were — as Joseph too should have been in order to fit into their society — shepherds, and farmers on the side. In both which capacities, of course, they were very much worth while, and felt, as was natural, great resentment toward their younger brother, who imagined, with his father's connivance, that he might be farmer and shepherd too, but only incidentally, his real occupations being those of scribe and reader of tablets. Later on they had a name for Joseph, which expressed to the full the height of their hatred: the "dreamer of dreams." But at this time they mock-ingly called him Noah, Utnapishtim, the exceeding wise one, the reader of stones from before the Flood. He, on his side, retorted with "dogs'-heads" and "people who know not good from evil," calling them these to their faces, protected only by their fear of Jacob, for otherwise they would have beaten him black and blue. That would have been painful to see; yet his beauty must not blind us to the fact that his retort was no better than their mockery. Worse, even; for what use is wisdom if it cannot shield us from the sin of arrogance?

But Jacob the father — how did he stand to all this? He was not a scholar. Of course, in addition to his south-Canaanitish dialect he spoke Babylonian, perhaps even better. But he had no Egyptian, probably because, as we have seen, he mistrusted and condemned everything that came from that country. It stood to him as the home of immorality and feudal abuse. The service of the state, which obviously conditioned all things in that country, offended his hereditary sense of independence and personal responsibility; while the cult of animals and of the dead which flourished there was to him folly and abomination, the latter even more than the former. For all that worship of the under-earth, which began even with the earth, even with the seed-corn which fruitfully rotted therein, was to him synonymous with lewdness. He called the land of mud down there not Kemt or Mizraim, but Sheol, hell, the kingdom of the dead. His disgust, on grounds both ethical and intellectual, extended to the exaggerated respect which, as he had heard, was paid there to letters. He, personally, could not do much more in that line than sign his name to contracts — and even so he mostly stamped it. All the rest he left to Eliezer, his eldest servant, and was justified in so doing, for the skill of our servants is as our own, and in any case Jacob's weight and dignity rested not upon such, being essentially personal, native, and freely arising. They were based upon the power of his feeling and experience, upon a fullness of shrewd and signifi-cant anecdote, upon the natural spirituality which radiated from him and was perceptible to everybody, upon the preponderant per-sonality of a gifted man who dreamed bold dreams and had immedi-ate relations with God; a man, in short, who need not trouble about book-knowledge. It would be idle to compare Jacob with Eliezer — certainly the idea of doing so would never have occurred to the latter. But, after all, would Eliezer ever have dreamed the dream of the ladder, or with God's help have made discoveries in the natural kingdom such as the part played by sympathetic magic in the breed-ing of the streaked yeanlings? No, never.

But then why did Jacob approve of Joseph's education and look with a favouring eye upon teachings the danger of which to the lad and to his relations with his brethren could not have escaped him?

He had two reasons, both of which sprang from his love of Joseph: one of them was ambitious in its nature, the other had to do with his care for the disciplining of the boy's character. Leah, the unloved wife, had of course known whereof she spoke when she had said to herself and the sons of her body, at the time of Joseph's birth, that they would now all be as nothing in Jacob's eyes, and light as air. Since the day when the child of the true wife, Dumuzi, the only scion and son of the virgin, had been vouchsafed to him, Jacob had thought of nothing else but to set this late comer before the early ones, to place him at their head and make him, who was only Rachel's first-born, the first-born of them all. His anger when Reuben had so forgotten himself with Bilhah had been real enough; but also ulterior in its nature, and his expression of it somewhat calculated. Joseph had not known, or had only been half conscious; but when in childish malice he had repeated to his father what he had seen, Jacob's first thought had been: "Now I can curse my eldest-born and the place will be free for the little one." But he was conscious of the thought and also he was afraid of the anger of the sons who came after Reuben. Thus he had not dared to take advantage at once of the opportunity to set Joseph in the ill-doer's room. He held off, waiting and as it were keeping warm the place for the little one. For of course what we are dealing with here is the blessing of Abraham, which Jacob owned, which he had received in Esau's stead from his blind father, and which now he had in mind to hand on in a way which was not aboveboard, but underhanded. If he could possibly manage it, this great good should be Joseph's; who was quite obviously, both in flesh and in spirit, more fitted to receive it than the heavy-handed and light-headed Reuben. He would clutch at any means to make clear to others, even to the brethren, Joseph's higher gifts — for instance, learning. The times had changed. Up till now the spiritual heirs of Abraham had not needed this good gift. Jacob himself had not suffered from its lack. But who knew if in the future it might not be perhaps not necessary, yet useful and desirable that the bearer of the blessing should also be a scholar and learned. Whether great or small, it was an advantage, and Joseph could never have too much of anything that would set him before the brothers.

This was one ground of Jacob's consent. The other lay deeper in the father's careful heart; it had to do with the boy's salvation and religious sanity. We have seen how Jacob, in that scene by the well, had cautiously questioned his son about the coming rainfall — holding as it were his hand protectingly over him the while. He had not liked to ask. Only his great need for information on this all-important subject had made him turn to advantage a mood in his son which none the less it disquieted him to see, though he was not without admiration for it.

He was aware of Joseph's tendency to states approaching the ecstatic; to half-pretended, undeveloped, but at times genuinely prophetic seizures. His attitude toward these, as a parent, fluctuated, impressed as he was by the equivocal mixture of evil and holiness in such tendencies. The brethren — dear me, none of them showed any faintest sign of belonging to the elect; they did not look in the least like seers or sufferers. One need lose no sleep over them! Ecstasies, whether for good or for evil, were not in their line; it did in a certain way fall in with Jacob's hopes that Joseph differed from them in these matters: you could interpret the fact as a distinction which, along with the others, made the choice a convincing one.

None the less, Jacob was not quite at ease over what he had seen. There were people about — God forbid that Joseph should become one of these! — holy innocents, slaverers, possessed of spirits, who earned their bread by foaming at the mouth and delivering prophecies. Human oracles who went about babbling or were visited by the inquiring in caves and earned food and money for jobs of finding lost articles or prophesying lucky days. Jacob, on religious grounds, loved them not at all, but then, nobody did, though all took care not to offend them. They were dirty, with crazed and disordered ways; children ran after them shouting out: "*Aulasaulalakaula*" — in imitation of their babbling. They wounded and mutilated themselves, ate polluted food, went about with a yoke on their necks or a pair of horns on their heads; sometimes they went naked. That was like them: the horns as well as the nakedness. It was not hard to know the source of their behaviour: the filthiness of the worship of Baal, the ritual whoredom, the fertility magic and orgiastic sacrifices at the feet of Melech the Bull King. That was no mystery; everybody knew the ideas and their associations. But the people round about Jacob knew it with a sort of matter-of-fact respect which was quite different from the sensitiveness of Jacob's spiritual tradition. He had nothing against a reasonable oracle, say of the arrow or by lot, to find out the favourable time for a business transaction; and he probably took note of the way birds flew or smoke blew at a sacrifice. But where god-given understanding went to pieces and rank frenzy took its place, then began that which he called "a foolishness" — which was in his mouth a strong word, strong enough to express the extreme of disapproval. It was "Canaan"; it was all that which had to do with the sinister story of the grandfather in his tent, and who should go naked, with his manhood bared, whoring after the Baals of the land. Exposing oneself, round singing, intemperate feasting, official unchastity with the temple women, cult of Sheol — yes, and *aulasaulalakaula* and wild epileptic prophesyings — it all went together, it was all one, and it was "a foolishness" in Jacob's eyes. It tortured him to think that Joseph's childish tendency to roll his eyes and

dream dreams could have any connection with this impure region
of the soul. Jacob too, as we know, was a dreamer — but in all
honour! He had seen in his dream God the King and His angels,
and to the surging music of the harps he had received from Him
the most heartening promises. But certainly such a lifting up of the
head from affliction and outward humiliation was distinguished by
reason, measure, and spiritual integrity from every sort of evil-
working magic. Alas, that such honourable gifts and blessings of the
fathers could dwindle down to elegant corruption in their unstable
sons! It was charming to see the parent in the guise of the son, but
alarming and suspect to see him dwindling down. At least there was
consolation in the thought that Joseph was still so young; he would
lose his instability, become more solid and robust, and ripen to sobriety in godlike understanding. But it did not escape Jacob's sharp
eye that the lad's proneness to a suspicious kind of seizure had to
do with nakedness, so with abandonment, so with Baal and Sheol,
with death magic and under-earthly unreason; and here then was
the ground of Jacob's approving the influence of the man of letters
upon his beloved son. It was good to have Joseph learn something,
good that he practised himself under informed guidance in the word
and in the art of writing. He, Jacob, had not needed this; his wildest
dreams had all been modest and honourable. But Joseph's, the old
man felt, might need to be disciplined by application of reason and
exactitude. Thus there might come a blessing to the steadying of his
unstable youth, and then he would bear no resemblance at all to
horned and naked vagrants and epileptics.

So Jacob considered within himself. Certain dark elements in the
composition of his beloved seemed to him to need release and clarification in the intellectual. Thus we see that he, in his considering way,
came to Joseph's own boyish conclusion, that the awareness of the
body must be corrected and justified by the awareness of the mind.

Chapter II

ABRAHAM

OF THE OLDEST SERVANT

ABRAM may actually have resembled Eliezer — and again, perhaps, he may have looked quite different. He may have been lean, puny, twitching with restlessness, and bitten by the tooth of care; the assertion that Eliezer, Joseph's teacher, looked like the moon-wanderer certainly had nothing to do with the person of the learned head servant as now manifest in the flesh. People spoke in the present, but they referred to the past, and transferred the one to the other. Eliezer, they said, "resembled" Abram in the face; the tradition might easily be justified in view of the one-time wooer's birth and origin. For presumably he was Abram's son. Indeed, some would have it that Eliezer was the servant whom Nimrod of Babel had given to Abram when he was obliged to let him go; but this was improbable to the point of impossibility. For Abraham never came into personal touch with the great power in whose reign his exodus from Shinar had taken place; the latter had never troubled his head about him. The conflict which had driven Jacob's spiritual forefather from the land had been a silent and internal one; and all the accounts of personal contact between him and the lawgiver, of his martyrdom, his languishing in prison, of a trial by fire in a lime-kiln — all these tales, of which we can dwell only upon such as Eliezer told to Joseph, were either a random combination of legend or were handed down from the most distant past and crystallized upon a past much nearer; that is to say, only six hundred years old. Abram's king, who in his time restored the towers and made them taller, had not been called Nimrod, for that was only a regal and dynastic title, but Amraphel or Hammurabi, and the real Nimrod had been the father of that Bel of Babel of whom it was said that he had built tower and city and who became a god-king, after he had been a man-king, like the Egyptian Osiris. The figure of the original Nimrod thus belongs to times before Osiris; from which one can guess at the historical gap which divided him from Abram's Nimrod; or, rather, one at least becomes aware of its immeasurable nature. As for the events supposed to have taken place during his reign: for instance, how the birth of a boy very dangerous to his power was foretold to him by his star-gazers; whereat he had resolved upon a general slaughter of innocents; how a boy named Abram escaped from the massacre and was brought up in a cave by an angel, who fed him on milk and honey from his finger-tips, and so forth — all these of course have no discoverable historical foundation. In short, the figure of Nimrod the king is much like that of Edom, the Red: it is a presentness, through which shine ever older pasts, losing themselves in the divine, which in its turn issued out of the human in still profounder deeps of time. The day will come when we shall feel that the same was true of Abram. But for the moment we shall do well to stick to Eliezer.

Eliezer, then, was not given to Abram by "Nimrod" as a present. We must regard that as a fable. Rather, in all probability he had been Abram's natural son, begot upon a slave woman and born probably at Damascus during the stay of Abraham's people in that flourishing city. Abram had later given him his freedom, and his rank in the family was somewhat lower than that of Ishmael, son of Hagar. As for Eliezer's sons, Damasek and Elinos, the Chaldæan had long regarded the former as his heir in default of legitimate ones; until first Ishmael and then Yitzchak the true son were born. But Eliezer retained his place and importance among the people of Abraham; and his had been the honour of going to Naharina to woo a bride for Isaac, the rescued sacrifice.

Often and with relish, as we know, he related to Joseph the tale of this journey — yes, I am betrayed perhaps all too willingly into writing here simply the word "he," although quite aware that according to our habits of thought it was certainly not Abram's Eliezer who was speaking to Joseph. What leads me astray is the natural way in which he used the first person when he spoke of the bridal journey, and his pupil's silent acquiescence in this lunar syntax of his. Joseph smiled indeed, but he nodded as well, and whether the smile implied any criticism, the nod any suggestion of courteous forbearance, one cannot tell. Personally I prefer to believe in his smile rather than in his nod; I incline to think that Joseph's attitude toward Eliezer's manner of speech was clearer-eyed than was that of Jacob's worthy half-brother.

We are justified of reason for thus referring to Eliezer, for that was what he was. Isaac, the true son, before he became blind, had been a man of strong desires, who had by no means confined his attentions to Bethuel's daughter. The circumstance that she like Sarah remained long unfruitful must have determined him betimes to seek an heir elsewhere; for years before Jacob and Esau were born he had had a son from a beautiful slave; which son was named Eliezer and had later received his freedom. It was, in fact, traditional that such a

son should receive his freedom and should be called Eliezer. One
might find Yitzchak's conduct the more excusable on the ground that
there had to be an Eliezer. There always had been one in the courtyards of Abraham's spiritual family, where he played the rôle of
house steward and head servant and was, whenever possible, sent as
a proxy wooer for the son of the true wife. Regularly, also, had the
head of the family given him a wife, from whom he had two sons;
namely, Damasek and Elinos. In short, he was an institution, like
Nimrod of Babel; and when he and young Joseph sat at the lesson
hour in the leafy shade of the tree of wisdom, beside the well, and
the boy, his arms clasped round his knees, gazed into the face of the
old teacher who "looked like Abraham" and knew how to say "I" in
so ample and majestic a way, strange thoughts and feelings must have
floated through that young mind. His lovely and well-favoured eyes
were fixed on the figure of the narrator; but he looked through him
into an endless perspective of Eliezer-figures, who all said "I" through
the mouth of the present manifestation. They sat in the twilight
shades of the great tree; but behind Eliezer the sun-drenched air
quivered in the heat, and the succession of identities lost itself not
in darkness but in light. . . . . .

The sphere rolls; never can it be certainly known where a story
has its original home, whether in heaven or on earth. The truth is
best served by the statement that it takes place simultaneously and
concordantly both here and there, and only to our eyes does it appear
that it came down and went up again. The story comes down, as a
god becomes a man, it becomes earthly, becomes bourgeois, so to
say. A good instance of what I mean is afforded by a favourite boast
of Jacob's seed: the so-called battle of the kings; namely, how Abram
defeated the army out of the East in order to set free his "brother"
Lot. Later learned editors and commentators state as their opinion
that Abram followed the kings, defeated and drove them beyond
Damascus, not with three hundred and eighteen men, as Joseph knew
the tale, but quite alone with his boy Eliezer; and the stars had fought
for them so that they conquered and routed the foe. It happened
that Eliezer himself told Joseph the story in this form also — the lad
was familiar with the variants. Everybody can see, however, that
told like this the story loses the earthly and therewith the heroic
character given it in the saga and assumes another instead. When one
hears it, it is — Joseph too had this impression — as though two gods,
master and servant, had fought and conquered superior numbers of
giants or inferior Elohim. And this can only mean that the event is
reconverted, in the interest of truth and justice, to its heavenly form,
and re-established therein. But should we on this account deny its
earthly one? On the contrary, we might even say that the truth and
reality which clothed it in heaven go to prove the same qualities on

earth. For what is above comes down; but what is beneath would not know how to happen and could not, so to speak, occur on its own account, without its heavenly image and counterpart. In Abram became flesh that which had previously been celestial; he based on the divine, he supported himself upon it, when he victoriously scattered the robbers from beyond the Euphrates.

Again, had not, for instance, the account of Eliezer's journey to woo Rebecca its own story on which it was founded and on which its hero and narrator might found himself, as he lived and told the tale? This too the old man sometimes metamorphosed in a singular way, and in such a form has it been cherished and handed down to us. It is said, namely, that Eliezer, when Abram sent him wooing for Isaac to Mesopotamia, covered the journey from Beersheba to Harran, a journey which takes twenty days or at the very least seventeen, in three days, and that the earth "sprang to meet him." We can only understand this figuratively, since the earth never runs or springs toward anybody; yet it seems to do so to him who moves across it with great ease and as though on winged feet. Moreover, the commentators pass over the fact that the journey was made, as usual, with caravan, with beast and pack; they do not speak of the ten camels. Rather the light which they cast upon the story tends to suggest that Abram's messenger and natural son covered the distance alone and with wings to his feet; with such celerity, indeed, that winged feet would not be enough, he would need wings on his hat as well! . . . To come to the point, we must conclude that the account of Eliezer's earthly and fleshly journey is an earthly tradition based upon a heavenly one. Thus it came that in telling the tale to Joseph he confused not only the language but also the matter of the story somewhat, and said the earth had "sprung to meet him."

Yes, when the young pupil's musing gaze rested upon the present fleshly Eliezer-manifestation, the perspective of his personality lost itself not in darkness but in light. And this was true not only of Eliezer's identity but of other people's as well — it is easy to surmise whose. And here, as a sort of advance light upon Joseph's history, let me say that those impressions were the most real and enduring, which he got from his hours with old Eliezer. Children are not inattentive when their masters say they are. They are only attending to other, perhaps more important things than those which the severely practical master is commending to their attention. Joseph, however absent he might seem, was more observant than the most observant child — in fact probably much more so than was good for him.

HOW ABRAHAM FOUND GOD

In the above, I have in some sense been putting Eliezer's master, Abraham, in the same category as the eldest servant. What did Eliezer know of Abraham? Much, and of various kinds. He spoke of him as it were with a double tongue, sometimes thus and then again quite differently. At one time the Chaldæan had been simply the man who had found God, whereat the latter had kissed His fingers in joy and cried: "Up to now no man hath called Me Lord and Highest, so now shall I be called!" The discovery had cost much labour and even pain; Forefather had tortured himself no little. And indeed his pains and performances had been conditioned and compelled by a conception quite peculiar to him: the conception that it was highly important whom or what thing man should serve. That made an impression on Joseph; he grasped it at once, particularly the part about taking things seriously. For in order to give any sort of importance or significance to things — or any one thing — one had to, before God and man, take them seriously. Forefather had beyond a doubt taken seriously the question as to whom man should serve; and had given it a remarkable answer, to wit: one should serve the Highest alone. Remarkable indeed. For the answer revealed a self-assertiveness which might be called excessive and arrogant. The man might have said to himself: "What am I and of what avail, or the human being in me? What mattereth it which little god or idol or minor deity I serve?" He would have had an easier time. But instead he said: "I, Abram, and humanity within me, must serve the Highest and naught else." And that was the beginning of it all (as it pleased Joseph to hear).

It began with Abram thinking that to mother earth alone was due service and worship, for that she brought forth fruits and preserved life. But he observed that she needed rain from heaven. So he gazed up into the skies, saw the sun in all its glory, possessed with the powers of blessing and cursing; and was on the point of deciding for it. But then it set, and he was convinced that it could not be the highest. So he looked at the moon and the stars — at these with particular expectation and hope. It may have been the first cause of his vexation and his desire to wander, that his love for the moon, the deity of Uru and Harran, had been offended by the exaggerated official honours paid to the sun-principle, Shamash-Bel-Marduk, by Nimrod of Babel, these being an offence to Sin, the shepherd of the stars. Perhaps it was duplicity on God's part, born of desire to glorify Himself in Abiram and through him to make His name great, that stirred up in the moon-wanderer, through his love of the moon, that first conflict and unrest, employed them to His own ends, and made them the secret spring of all Abram's later acts. For when the morning star rose, both shepherd and sheep disappeared, and Abram concluded. "No, neither are they gods worthy of me." His soul was greatly troubled and he thought: "High as they are, had they not above themselves a guide and lord, how could the one set, the other rise? It would be unfitting for me, a man, to serve them and not rather Him who commands over them." And Abraham's thought lay so painfully close to the truth that it touched the Lord God to His innermost and He said to Himself: "I will anoint thee with the oil of gladness more than all thy fellows."

Thus out of impulse toward the Highest had Abraham discovered God; had by teaching and by taking thought shaped Him further and bodied Him forth and therewith done a great good deed to all concerned: to God, to himself, and to those whose souls he won by his teaching. To God, in that he made ready the way of realization of Him in the mind of man; to himself and to the proselytes especially, in that he laid hold upon the manifold and the anguishingly uncertain and converted it into the single, the definite, and the reassuring, of whom everything came, both good and evil — the sudden and frightful as well as the blessed usual, and to whom in any case we had to cling. Abraham had gathered together the powers into one power and called them the Lord — exclusively and once for all. It was not as for a feast-day, when one sung praises and heaped all power and honour upon the head of one god, Marduk or Anu or Shamash — only to do the same to another god on the next day or in the next temple. "Thou art the Only and the Highest, without Thee is no judgment given, no decision made; no god in heaven or on earth can oppose Thee, Thou art lifted up above them all!" How many times had that not been said and sung out of ephemeral devotion in Nimrod's kingdom! Abram found and declared that it could and might with truth be said and sung only to One, who was always the same, who was utterly the known, because everything came from Him, and who thus made all things known after their source. The men among whom he grew up anguished themselves sore not to fail this source in prayers and thanksgivings. If they were doing penance in some calamity, they set at the head of their prayer a whole list of invocations to their deities; painstakingly they called upon each single god whose name they chanced to know, that the particular one who had sent the affliction — they could not tell which it was — might not be left out. But Abraham knew which it was, and taught his people. It was always and only He, the Highest and Uttermost, who alone could be the true God of mankind; who unfailingly answered man's cry for help and his song of praise.

Joseph, young as he was, well understood the boldness and strength of mind which expressed themselves in first Forefather's thoughts of

God — though many there had been to shrink back in horror from the teaching. Whether Abram had been tall and goodly to look on in his old age like Eliezer, or whether he had been little, lean, and bent of stature, at least he had had the courage, the consummate courage, which was needed to concentrate all the manifold properties of the divine, all blessing and all affliction, upon the one and only God; to take his stand there and to cling solely and undividedly to the Most High. Lot himself, white with fear, had said to Abraham:

"But if thy God forsake thee, then art thou forsaken indeed!"

To which Abraham had answered:

"It is true, thou sayest it. Then can there be no forsakenness in heaven or upon earth like to mine in extent — it is consummate. But bethink thee, that if I appease Him and He is my shield, nothing can lack me and I shall possess the gates of mine enemies!"

Whereupon Lot had strengthened himself and spoken:

"Then will I be thy brother!"

Yes, Abram had known how to communicate his exaltation of spirit. He was named Abiram; that is to say: "my father is exalted," or also, probably just as correctly, "father of the exalted." For in a way Abraham was God's father. He had perceived Him and thought Him into being. The mighty properties which he ascribed to Him were probably God's original possession, Abraham was not their creator. But was he not so after all, in a certain sense, when he recognized them, preached them, and by thinking made them real? The mighty properties of God were indeed something objective, existing outside of Abraham; but at the same time they were also in him and of him. The power of his own soul was at certain moments scarcely distinguishable from them; it interlaced and melted consciously into one with Him, and such was the origin of the bond which then the Lord struck with Abraham. True, it was only the outward confirmation of an inward fact; but it was also the origin of the peculiar character of Abram's fear of God. For since the greatness of God was something frightfully objective outside of him, yet at the same time coincided to a certain extent with the greatness of his own soul and was a product of it, so was this fear of God somewhat more than fear in the regular sense of the word: it was not alone trembling and quaking, but also and at the same time the existence of a bond, a familiarity and friendship. In fact Forefather had sometimes had a way of going about with God, which must have aroused the amazement of heaven and earth, if one did not take into consideration the extraordinary involutions of the relationship. For instance the familiar way in which he had addressed the Lord at the destruction of Sodom and Amorra was not far from insolence, considering the awful greatness and power of God. But, after all, who should be offended, if God were not? And God was not. "Hearken, O Lord," had Abram said then, "it must be one way or the other, but not both. If thou wilt have a world, then thou canst not demand justice, but if thou settest store by justice, then it is all over with the world. Thou wouldst hold the cord by both ends: wouldst have a world and in it justice. But if thou dost not mitigate thy demands, the world cannot exist." He had even accused the Lord of double-dealing, and upbraided him: once he had revoked the flood of water, but now he would invoke the flood of fire. But God, who probably could not have dealt otherwise with the cities after what had happened or almost happened to His messengers at Sodom, had taken all that Abram said in good part or at all events not ill; for He had enveloped Himself in a benevolent silence.

This silence was the expression of a tremendous fact, which had to do with the outward side of God as well as with the inward greatness of Abraham, whose own actual creation it probably was: the fact that the contradiction in terms of a world which should be living and at the same time just resided in God's greatness itself; that He, the living God, was not good, or only good among other attributes, including evil, and that accordingly His essence included evil and was therewith sacrosanct; was sanctity itself and demanded sanctity.

Oh, wonder! He it was who had dashed in pieces Tiamat, and cloven the dragon of chaos; the exultant cry with which at the creation the gods had greeted Marduk and which the people of Abram's country repeated every New Year's day, belonged by rights to Him, the God of Abram. From Him issued order and joyous confidence. It was His work that the early and the late rains fell at their appointed time. He had set bounds to the monstrous sea, the residue of the original flood, the home of leviathan, that in its most awful turbulence it could not pass beyond them. He made the sun to rise in its creative power to the zenith and at evening begin its journey to hell; likewise the moon to measure time by her ever recurrent change of quarters. He made the stars to shine, likewise ordered them to form pictures; and He ruled the lives of men and beasts, nourishing them according to the seasons. From places where no man had been the snow fell and watered the earth, whose disk he had fixed upon the flood of waters, so that it never or only very seldom swayed or shook. How much of blessing, of goodness, and of benefit was there in all this!

But as a man who conquers an enemy, by the victory adds unto himself the properties of the conquered, so God, it would seem, when He clave the monster of chaos, embodied in Himself its essence and perhaps only thereby grew to the full height of His living majesty. The struggle between light and darkness, good and evil, blessing and fruitfulness upon this earth was not, as the people of Nimrod believed, the continuation of that war which Marduk waged against Tiamat. Neither the darkness, the evil and the unknown terror, the earthquake, the crackling lightning, the plague of grasshoppers darkening the sun, the seven evil winds, the dust Abubu, the serpents and the hornets — none of these but were from God, and if He was called the Lord of the pestilence, it was because He was alike its sender and its physician. He was not the Good, but the All. And He was holy! Holy not because of goodness, but of life and excess of life; holy in majesty and terror, sinister, dangerous, and deadly, so that an omission, an error, the smallest negligence in one's bearing to Him, might have frightful consequences. He was holy; but He demanded holiness too, and that He demanded it by His mere being gave the Holy One greater significance than that of mere awfulness. The discretion which he enjoined became piety, and God's living majesty the measure of life, the source of the sense of guilt, the fear of God, and the walking before Him in holiness and righteousness.

God was present, and Abraham walked before Him, consecrated in his soul by that outward nearness of His. They were two, an I and a Thou, both of whom said "I" and to the other "Thou." It is true that Abraham composed the properties of God, with the help of his own greatness of soul — without which He would not have known how to compose them or name them, so that they would have remained in darkness. But after all God remained a powerful Thou, saying "I," independent of Abraham and independent of the world. He was in the fire but was not the fire — wherefore it would have been very wrong to worship fire. God had created the world, in which such tremendous things happened as the storm wind or leviathan. This had to be considered in order properly to measure His own outward greatness, or, if not to measure it, at least to conceive it. He must be much greater than all His works, and just as necessarily outside of His works. *Makom* he was called, space, because He was the space in which the world existed; but the world was not the space in which He existed. He was also in Abraham, who recognized Him by virtue of his own power. And it was just this that strengthened and fulfilled Abraham's sense of his own ego; which was not at all minded to be lost in God, to become one with Him and be no more Abraham, but rather held itself stoutly upright in face of Him — at a great distance, certainly, for Abraham was but a man, and made of clay — but bound up with Him through knowledge and consecrated by the high essence and presence of the Deity. It was on this basis that God had made His compact with Abraham, that covenant so full of promise for both sides; of which God was so jealous that He would be honoured entirely alone by His worshippers without the flicker of an eyelash toward those other gods of whom the world was full. For here was the important fact: through Abram and his bond something was come into the world that had never been there before and which the peoples did not know — the accursed possibility that the bond might be broken, that one might fall away from God.

Much besides did Forefather know of God — but not in the sense in which others knew of their gods. There were no stories about God. That was indeed perhaps the most remarkable thing: the courage with which Abram represented and expressed God's essence from the first, without more ado, simply in that he said "God." God had not proceeded, had not been born, from any woman. There was also beside Him on the throne no woman, no Ishtar, Baalat, mother of God. How could there be? One had only to use one's common sense to understand that, considering the nature of God, it was not a possible conception. God had planted the tree of knowledge and of death in Eden, and man had eaten of it. Birth and death were of man, but not of God; He saw no divine female at His side, because He needed not to know woman, but was Baal and Baalat at one and the same time. Neither had He children. For the angels were not so, nor Sabaoth who served Him, nor yet those giants whom some angels had begotten upon the daughters of men, led astray by sight of their lewdness. He was alone; such was the mark of His greatness. The wifeless and childless condition of God might perhaps explain His great jealousy concerning His bond with man; however that may be, it certainly explains the fact that He has no history and that there is nothing to tell of Him.

Yet even so, one may only take all this in a qualified sense; referring it to the past, but not to the future — if indeed we may speak of the future in this sense at all. For God did after all have a story; but it referred to the future, a future so glorious for Him that His present, splendid as it always was, could not compare with it. And that very discrepancy between the present and the future lent to God's sacred majesty and greatness a shadow of strain and suspense, of suffering and unfulfilled promise, which we must frankly recognize in order to understand the jealous nature of His covenant with man.

There would come a day, the latest and last, which alone would bring about the fulfillment of God. This day was end and beginning, destruction and new birth. The world, this first or perhaps not first world, would be dispersed in ultimate catastrophe; chaos, primeval silence would reign once more. Then God would begin His work anew and more wonderfully than before — being Lord of destruction, as Lord of creation. Out of chaos and confusion, out of slime and darkness His word would call up a new cosmos; louder than ever before would ring the jubilations of the onlooking angels; for the renewed world would exceed the other in every respect, and in it God would triumph over all His foes!

So it would be: at the end of days God would be king, king of kings, king over men and gods. But then, was He not that already, even now? Of course He was, in all quietness and in the consciousness of Abram. Yet even so, not everywhere recognized and admitted, and thus not entirely realized. The realization of God's great and boundless kingship was reserved for that first and last day, for the day of destruction and resurrection; when out of the bonds wherein it still lay, His absolute splendour would rise up before the eyes of all. No Nimrod would exalt himself against God, with shameless terraced towers; no human knee would bow save before Him, no human mouth give to another praise. God, as in truth from Everlasting, now actually would be lord and king over all other gods as well. In the blare of ten thousand trumpets directed slantwise at the skies, in the singing and thundering of the flames, in a hailstorm of lightnings, He, clothed in majesty and terrors, would pace away to His throne across a world praying with forehead in the dust, to take possession in sight of all and for ever of a reality which was His truth.

Oh, day of God's apotheosis, day of the Promise, expectation, and fulfillment! It would, be it remarked, embrace the apotheosis of Abraham, whose name thenceforward would be a word of blessing, with which the races of mankind would greet each other. That was the Promise. But this resounding day lay not in the present, but in the uttermost future; and until then was a time of waiting; this it was that brought lines of suffering into the countenance of God of today, which were the mark of the to-be and of the not-yet-accomplished. God lay in bonds, God suffered; God was held in prison. That mitigated His exaltedness; all the suffering might adore Him and He consoled those who were not great but small in the world; it gave them to feel scorn in their hearts against all that were even as Nimrod was, and against the shamelessness of vaunting greatness. No, God had no stories like Egyptian Osiris, the sacrifice, the mutilated, the buried and arisen one, or like Adonis-Tammuz, for whom the flutes wailed in the gorges; Tammuz, lord of the sheepfold, whose side Ninib the boar did tear and he went down into prison, and rose again. Far be it from us, and forbidden, to think that God was associated with the nature-myths — nature, withering in affliction, freezing in anguish, that she might be renewed according to the promise, in laughter and billows of flowers; with the seed-corn, that decayed in darkness and in the prison of the earth, that it might arise and sprout; with dying and sex; with the corrupt worship of Melech-Baal and his ritual at Tyre, where men offered their semen to the God of abominations in base-begotten folly and deathly shamelessness. God forbid that He could have had any dealing with such affairs! But He lay in bonds and was a God of waiting upon the future; and that made a certain likeness between Him and those other suffering godheads. Therefore it was that Abram at Shechem talked long with Melchisedek, who alone might enter the temple of the Baal of the Covenant and El

Elyon, over the question whether and up to what point any likeness of essence subsisted between Adon and Abraham's God. But God had kissed His finger-tips and cried, to the private resentment of the angels: "It is unbelievable, what knowledge of Me is possessed by this son of earth! Have I not begun to make Myself known through his means? Verily, I will anoint him!"

THE MASTER OF THE MESSENGER

In such wise, and so simply, had Eliezer painted Abraham to Joseph with his words. But unconsciously his tongue forked in speaking and talked of him quite otherwise as well. Always it was Abram, the man from Uru, or more correctly from Harran, of whom the forked tongue spoke — calling him the great-grandfather of Joseph. Both of them, young and old, were quite aware that, unless by moonlight, Abram was not the man, that unquiet subject of Amraphel of Shinar; likewise that no man's great-grandfather lived twenty generations before him! Yet this was a trifling inexactitude compared with others at which they had to wink; for that Abraham of whom the tongue now spoke, changefully and inconsistently, was not he, either, who had lived then and shaken the dust of Shinar from his feet; but rather a different figure perceptible far behind the other, visible through him, as it were, so that the lad's gaze faltered and grew dim in this perspective just as it had in the one called Eliezer — an ever brighter vista, of course, for it is light that shines through.

Then came into view all the stories which belonged to that half of the sphere in which master and servant, not with three hundred and eighteen men, but alone save for the help of supernatural powers, drove the foe beyond Damascus; and in which the ground had sprung towards Eliezer the messenger; the story of Abraham's birth foretold by prophecy; of the massacre of innocents on his account; of his childhood in a cave and how the angel fed him while his mother sought him round about. All that bore the mark of truth: somewhere and somehow it was true. Mothers always wander and search; they have many names, but they wander about the fields and seek the poor child that has been led away into the underworld, murdered or muti-lated. This time she was called Emathla, also probably Emtelai — names in which Eliezer probably indulged his fantasy; for they were better suited to the angel than to the mother — the latter, indeed, in an effort at verisimilitude on the part of the forked tongue, may also have had the form of a goat. Joseph found it all very dreamlike; his eyes changed their expression as he listened and heard that the mother of the Chaldæans was called Emtelai; for the name quite plainly sig-nifies "mother of my elevated one," or, in other words, "mother of God."

Should the good Eliezer have been reproved for talking like that? No. Stories come down as a god becomes man; they civilize themselves as it were and become earthly, without thereby ceasing to take place on high and to be narratable in their celestial form. For instance, the old man sometimes referred to the sons of that Keturah whom Abram in his old age took for a concubine: Medan, Midian, and Jokshan, that is, Zimran, Ishbak and whatever their names were. These sons had "glittered like lightning" and Abram had built for them and their mother a brazen city, so high that the sun never shone inside it, and it was lighted by precious stones. His listener would have had to be much duller than he was not to see that this brazen city signified the underworld, as whose queen, in this version, Keturah accordingly appeared. An unassailable conception! Keturah was indeed simply a Canaanitish woman whom Abram in his old age honoured by his couch; but likewise she was the mother of a whole series of Arabian progenitors and lords of the desert, as Hagar the Egyptian had been mother of Ishmael; and when Eliezer said of the sons that they glittered like lightning, that meant nothing else than seeing them with both eyes instead of with one, in token of the simultaneous and the unity of the doubled: that is, as homeless Bedouin chiefs, and as sons and princes of the underworld, like Ishmael, the wrongful son.

Then there were other moments in which the old man spoke in strange accents of Sarah, Forefather's wife. He called her "daughter of the unmanned" and "Heaven's queen"; adding that she had given birth to a spear, and that it was quite proper that she had originally been called Sarai — namely, heroine — and only been toned down by God to Sarah — that is to say, lady. A like thing had happened to Sarah's brother-husband: for he was reduced from Abram, which means "the exalted father" and "father of the exalted," to Abraham, which is to say "the father of many," of a swarming posterity, spiritual and physical. But had he therefore ceased to be Abram? By no means. It was only that the sphere rolled; and the subtle tongue, forking between Abram and Abraham, spoke of him now so and then again so.

Nimrod the father of the land had sought to devour him, but he had been snatched away, fed in a cave by a goat-angel, and when he was grown up had played so shrewd a game with the greedy king and his idolatrous majesty that one might even say that the latter came to "feel the sickle." He had suffered much before achieving his position. He had been held captive — it was heartening to hear how he had employed his imprisonment to make proselytes and to convert the keepers of the dungeon to the Most High God. He was sentenced to be sacrificed to Typhon; in other words, to be burned; had been put in the lime-kiln or — Eliezer's versions varied — had mounted the stake. This last sounded genuine to Joseph, for he knew that even in his time in many cities a feast of the stake was celebrated. And are there ever feasts without an idea at bottom — feasts without a root, unreal feasts? Do people, at New Year's, on the day of creation, perform in pious mummery things which they have sucked out of themselves or out of an angel's fingers and which never really happened? Man does not think himself out. He is of course exceeding clever, since he ate of the tree, and is not far from being a god. But with all his cleverness how should he be able to find something which is not there? Yes, there must have been some truth in the story of the stake.

According to Eliezer, Abraham had founded the city of Damascus and had been its first king. A specious utterance; but towns are not in the habit of being founded by men, nor do the beings which one calls their first kings wear human countenances. Hebron itself, called Kirjath Arba, outside which they were sitting, had not been built by human hands, but by the giant Arba or Arbaal, at least so ran the legend. Eliezer, on the other hand, stuck to it that Abram had founded Hebron as well. That may have been no contradiction to the popular idea, nor should have been so. Forefather must himself have been of a giant's greatness; that was already clear from the fact that according to Eliezer he had taken steps a mile long.

What wonder, then, that to Joseph, in dreamy moods, the figure of his forefather, the founder of cities, merged to the distant view in that of Bel of Babel, who built the tower and the city and who became a god after he too had once been a man and been buried in the Baal-tomb? With Abraham it seemed to be the other way round. But again what does that mean, in such a connection? Who will say what Abram had been at first and where the stories are originally at home, whether above or below? They are the present of the revolving sphere, the unity of the dual, the image that resolves the riddle of time.

Chapter III

JOSEPH AND BENJAMIN

THE GROVE OF ADONIS

HALF an hour distant from Jacob's straggling settlement, his tented huts, his stalls, penfolds, and barns, there was a gully filled with myrtle bushes of strong, sturdy growth, a sort of miniature grove, of which the folk of Hebron thought as sacred to Ashtar — or even more to her son, brother, and spouse, Tammuz-Adonai. The air within it, though hot in summer, had a pleasant bitter tang, and the thicket was not impenetrable, but pierced by numerous crooked openings which one might take for paths. Choosing one at random and making for the lowest part of the glade, one came upon a free space made by grubbing up the bushes. It had a shrine. A four-sided stone pyramid somewhat above a man's height, with procreation symbols stamped upon it, a Massebe, itself probably a symbol of procreation, was erected in the middle of the clearing. At its base lay offerings, in the shape of clay vessels filled with earth, from which pale greenish sprouts were springing. Also more complicated artistic efforts, such as wooden laths fastened together in a square and covered with canvas, upon which a clumsy human figure stood out. The women who presented these had drawn the figure with mould upon the linen, sown it with seed, and trimmed the sprouts to even growth, so that the figure showed in relief against its background.

To this spot Joseph came often with his brother Benjamin, now eight years old. Benjamin had begun to outgrow the tendance of womenfolk and liked to try to keep up with his elder brother's pace. He was a chubby-cheeked child, no longer running about naked, but clad in a short-sleeved, knee-length garment of rust red or dark blue, with an embroidered hem. He had beautiful grey eyes, which he would lift to his elder's with utter trustfulness; and thick, shining hair, which covered his head like a metal helmet from the middle of his forehead down to the nape of the neck, with bays for the ears. These were small and firm, like his nose and his short-fingered hands, one of which he would slip into his brother's as they

walked together. He had a confiding nature, Rachel's friendly spirit
was in him. Yet his whole little person was weighed down by a certain melancholy and shyness. He knew that for which all unbe-
knownst he had been responsible, knew the hour and the manner
of his mother's death; and the tragic and guiltless guilt which he
bore about with him was enhanced by Jacob's bearing toward this
son of his. It was not untender, rather it was marked by a painful
reserve, the father avoiding instead of seeking his son's gaze; yet
from time to time he would press his youngest-born long and fervently to his heart, call him Benoni, and whisper in his ear of Rachel
his mother.

Thus when the little one grew too old to cling to the women's
skirts, he could have no natural, unembarrassed intercourse with his
father, and hung the more upon his brother, whom he in every way
admired. Joseph might be smiled at by all he met, yet in a certain
way he stood isolated and could therefore feel grateful for the small
brother's loyalty. He too felt deeply the natural bond and made of
this nearest of kin his friend and intimate, despite the difference in
age, to an extent which was almost more of a burden than a pride or
happiness to Benjamin. This clever and fascinating Jossef — for so
Benoni pronounced it — told him so much that he could not take in!
His very eagerness to do so deepened the shadow which lay upon
the pathetic little mother-slayer.

Hand in hand they left Jacob's olive orchard on the hill, where
the sons of the maids were plucking and pressing. These latter had in
fact sent Joseph away, after he had gone to Jacob, where he sat in
the cattle-yard with Eliezer standing before him giving account,
and reported that the fruit on almost all the trees had been allowed
to get too ripe and would not yield the best oil; also that in his opinion the brothers were using too much violence in crushing them in
the mill. Dan, Naphtali, Gad, and Asher had accordingly been reproved, and thereupon with outstretched arms and mouths open on
one side ordered Joseph to take himself off. Joseph had called Benjamin and said to him:

"Come, let us go to our place."

On the way he said: "I said 'on almost all the trees.' Well, that was
an exaggeration, such as one uses in speaking. I admit that it would
have been more exact to say 'on some of them.' I climbed myself
into the old one with three trunks, the one with the wall round it,
and plucked the fruit and tossed it into a cloth, whereas the brethren,
alas, were using sticks and stones; and with my own eyes I saw that
on that tree at least the fruit had got too ripe — of the others I will
say nothing. But they behave as though I were simply lying, and as
though one could get really fine oil by mangling the precious gifts
with stones. Could I look on and not complain?"

"No," Benjamin answered, "thou knowest better than they, and thou art obliged to go to the father that he may know too. I am glad thou hast quarrelled with them, little Jossef, for now thou hast called me to come with thee."

"And now, my noble Beni," said Joseph, "let us take a jump and fly over this little wall; one, two, three — "

"Yes," responded Benjamin, "it is good, but keep fast hold on me. Together it is more fun and also safer so for my little self."

They ran, jumped, and went on again. Benjamin's hand would get hot and wet as Joseph held it in his own; then the elder would take it by the wrist and flap it in the air that the breeze might dry it. This so amused the little one that he always laughed until he stumbled and fell.

When they came to the myrtle glade and the sacred grove they had to separate and walk one behind the other in the narrow paths. They took endless pleasure striking about in this labyrinth, finding a winding opening which would permit them to pass for a certain distance, where they would stick fast; or, twisting and turning, up-hill and down, they might find a way on, only to issue at last in a cul-de-sac. They fought their way, talking and laughing, shielding their faces from scratches and blows. Joseph as he went broke twigs from the bushes, blossoming white with spring, and took a store of them for the wreaths he loved to wear in his hair. Benjamin had wanted to do the same; he had gathered twigs and begged his brother to make a wreath for him too. But he soon saw that Joseph did not care to have his little brother adorned with myrtle green. He did not say so straight out, but he wanted to keep the decoration for himself. Benoni knew that some kind of idea was behind the reserve; he had seen that Joseph often had such secret thoughts, which he did not confide — especially not to him, the little brother. But Benoni sus-pected that the jealousy about the myrtle garland had to do with the inherited first-bornship and blessing, which, as everybody knew, was in the father's mind hovering above Joseph's head.

"Never mind, little brother," Joseph might say, kissing the other on his cool little helmet of hair. "At home I will make thee a wreath of oak leaves or bright thistles, or a garland of mountain ash with its scarlet pearls. What dost thou say, is it not far finer? What wouldst thou of the myrtle? It doth not suit thee. One must needs choose the right sort of adornment."

Whereto answered Benjamin:

"Clearly thou art right, I see it well, Josephja, Yaschup, my own Jehosiph. Thou art wise above all others, and what thou sayest, that could I never say. But when thou speakest, then I see and agree so that thy thoughts become mine and I am as wise as thou makest me. I see that each must make his choice and that not all adornments would suit everyone. And I see that thou wouldst stop there and leave me as wise as I was before. But wert thou to go on and tell thy brother things more clearly, thou wouldst see I would follow thee; thou wouldst not be disappointed in thy little brother."

Joseph was silent.

"So much have I heard people say," Benjamin went on, "that the myrtle meaneth youth and beauty; that is what big people say. If I say it, it maketh us both to laugh, for how could we say that the words fit me? Young I am, indeed, or rather small, not so much young as dwarfish. Young art thou, and lovely, so that the world is full of the report of thy beauty. But I, I am more a matter for jesting than for wonderment. When I look at my limbs I see that they come short as respects the rest of me; and I have a fat little paunch as one who still taketh his mother's milk and my cheeks puff out as though filled with wind, to say naught of the hair of my head, which is like to a cap of an otter's fell. So then if the myrtle suiteth to youth and beauty and standeth therefor, then verily it suiteth to thee and not to me, and it were a fault in me to assume it. I know well that one can err and do oneself harm in such matters. Seest thou, quite of myself and before thou speakest, I understand much; yet of course not all, and thou must aid my understanding."

"Brave little man," said Joseph, and laid his arm about him, "I love thy otter cap, thy little paunch, and thy chubby cheeks, and thou are my dearest and only true brother and flesh of my flesh, for out of the same abyss came we both, which is called *absu*, but for us is Mami, the sweet one, for whom Jacob served. Come and let us go down to the stone and rest."

"Right gladly," answered Benjamin. "Let us look at the frames and the pots which the women have put there, like to a little garden, and thou shalt explain to me the meaning of the stone, for that I love to hear. Because, at least," he went on as they followed the sloping path, "after all, Mami died of me, and half of my name meaneth 'son of death'; at least in that sense might the myrtle become me too, since I have heard folk say that it might also be a tiring of death."

"Yea," said Joseph, "there is lamenting in the world for youth and loveliness, for that Ashera maketh to weep and bringeth to destruction those whom she loveth. That must be why the myrtle is a tree of death, and a garland for the same. Therefore likewise hath it that sharp and bitter smell, as thou canst tell from the twig in thy hand. For it is the adornment of the whole sacrifice, set apart for one set apart, and destined for the predestined. Dedicated youth, that is the name of the whole sacrifice. But the myrtle worn in the hair, that is the herb touch-me-not."

"Thou hast taken away thine arm from about me," Benjamin remarked, "and lettest thy little brother walk alone."

"Here is mine arm again," cried Joseph. "Thou art my true and own little brother, and at home I will make thee a wreath of every colour of the rainbow of all the flowers of the field, so that he that seeth thee shall laugh for joy. Shall that be a bargain twixt thee and me?"

"It is sweet and good of thee," said Benjamin. "Lend me thy coat that I may kiss the seam of it with my lips."

He was thinking: "Plainly it is the inheritance and the blessing he hath in his mind. Yet it moveth me anew and strangely that he maketh reference to the whole sacrifice and to the herb touch-me-not. It may be that he thinketh of Isaac when he speaketh of the whole sacrifice and of the one set apart. Certain he meaneth me to understand that myrtle is the sacrificial garland, and that disquieteth my mind."

Aloud he said: "When thou speakest as now, thou art doubly beautiful; in my folly I cannot tell whether the scent of the myrtle cometh from thy words or from the trees. But lo, here is the shrine. And the gifts are more than when we were last here: two gods in frames and two sprouting vessels have been added. There have been women here. They have put little gardens in front of the grotto; I would look at them. But the stone is untouched, not rolled away from the grave. Is now the Lord within, His beauteous form, or whither hath He gone?"

He referred to a rocky hollow framed in shrubbery, carved out of the hill-side; not high, but as deep as the height of a man, and partially closed with a stone at its mouth. This hollow served the women of Hebron for the ritual of the feast.

"Nay," answered Joseph to his brother's question, "the figure is not here, nor is it to be seen throughout the year. It lieth preserved in the temple at Kirjath Arba and is brought forth only at the feast of the solstice, when the sun beginneth to decline and the light to go down to the lower world, and the women do with it according to their custom."

"They entomb it there in the cave?" Benjamin inquired. He had asked thus on the first occasion and Joseph had instructed him; since then he had often pretended forgetfulness, in order to hear the story anew and have Joseph tell him of Adonai, shepherd and lord, the murdered one, for whom arose lamentation throughout the world. For then he listened as it were to the thoughts in between Joseph's words, to the tone and the rhythm of his speech; for he was vaguely possessed by the idea that so he might come upon his brother's secret thoughts, in solution in his words as salt is in solution in the sea.

"Nay, the burying cometh later," answered Joseph. "For first they seek Him." He was sitting on the base of the shrine of Ashtaroth, a rough-hewn pyramid of blackish stone, the surface of which looked as though it were broken out into tiny pustules. Already he was busy weaving the myrtle wreath, and the fine tendons stood out as they moved on the backs of his hands.

Benjamin looked at him from the side. Cheeks and chin showed a dusky smoothness, they betrayed that Joseph already shaved. He used a mixture of oil and potash, and a stone knife. If he were to let his beard grow, what then? It might be that it would have changed him a good deal. Quite possibly he had not as yet much beard; yet even so what would have become of his beauty, that especial beauty of his seventeen years? He might just as well wear a dog's head on his shoulders — the difference could not have been much greater. Certainly we must agree that beauty is a very perishable good. "They seek Him," Joseph went on, "for He is noble and He is lost. Some of them have hidden the figure in the shrubbery, but they search with the others, they know where it is and know it not, they purposely bemuse themselves. And they all lament as they move about in the searching, they lament in chorus and singly: 'Where art thou, O my adored god, my spouse and my son, my bright shepherd-bird? I long for Thee. What hath befallen Thee, in the grove, in the green meadow, in the world?'"

"But they know," put in Benjamin, "that the Lord is dead and mangled?"

"Not yet," Joseph responded. "That is the feast. They know it because the figure hath been discovered before, yet know it not because the hour to discover it again is not yet come. In the feast each hour hath its knowledge, and each of the women is the goddess, seeking what she hath not yet found."

"But then they find the Lord?"

"Thou sayest it. He lieth in the bushes, and His side is torn. They rush to Him, they fling up their arms and shriek."

"Thou hast seen and heard it?"

"Thou knowest I have already twice seen and heard it; but I had thy promise not to tell our father. Hast thou kept silence?"

"Indeed have I," Benjamin assured him. "Shall I offend our father? I have enough offended him with my very life."

"And when the feast cometh round, I will go again," said Joseph. "At the moment we are equally distant from the last and the next. The solstice cometh with the next pressing of the oil. It is a wonderful feast. There lieth the Lord, stretched out in the shrubbery, and His wound gapeth wide."

"How doth He look?"

"As I described Him to thee. Of beautiful form, carven of olive wood, with wax and glass, for His eyeballs are of black glass and they have eyelashes."

"He is young?"

"I have told thee already He is young and beautiful. The grain of the yellow wood looketh like to veins upon His body, His locks are black, and His loincloth embroidered in divers colours with pearls and glass paste and purple fringes."

"What hath He in His hair?"

"Nought at all," answered Joseph shortly. "His lips and nails and the marks on His body are made of wax and likewise the frightful wound of Ninib's teeth is marked with red wax. It bleedeth."

"Thou sayest the laments of the women are very great when they find Him?"

"They are very great. At first they were but mourning of the loss, but now beginneth the mourning of the finding, and that is incomparably louder. There is the wailing of the flutes for dead Tammuz; for the flute-players sit here on the spot and blow with all their might upon little flutes, so that their sobbing maketh the bones to quake. And the women let down their hair and give free vent to gesture as they lament over the corpse: 'O my spouse and my child!' For each of them is as the goddess, and each laments: 'None loved Thee more than I!' "

"Joseph, I cannot forbear to weep. For I am so small, the death of the Lord is almost too great a pain for me and rendeth me within. Why was it the young and lovely one had to be mangled, in the grove, in the green field, and in the world and be lamented with such anguish?"

"That canst thou not yet understand," Joseph said. "He is the sufferer and is the sacrifice. He descendeth into the abyss that He may rise again and be glorified. Abram knew that of a surety, when he raised the knife against his true-born son. But when the knife fell, there was a ram in the place. Thus it is that when we sacrifice a ram or a lamb, we hang about him a seal with the image of a man, as a sign that it representeth the man. But this mystery of the substitute is greater than that: it comprehends the whole stellar position of man, god, and beast and is the mystery of substitution. Man offereth the son in the beast; so too the son offereth himself in the beast. Ninib is not accursed, for it standeth written: 'A god shall they slay,' and the meaning of the beast is the meaning of the son, who knoweth his hour as he doth in the feast, and knoweth moreover when he shall overset the dwelling of death and come forth out of the hollow."

"Ah," said the little one, "if only it were now, and the feast of joy were beginning! Do they lay the Lord in the grave and in the hollow there?"

Joseph, at his weaving work, rocked lightly from his hips as he hummed:

" 'In the time of the feast of Tammuz play upon the flute of lazuli,
And upon the ring of cornelian play thou likewise.'

"With wailing and lamenting," he said, "they bear it hither to the
stone. And the flute-players play ever louder so that their wailing
pierceth the heart. I saw the women busy over the form of the corpse
in their laps. They washed it with water and anointed it with oil of
nard, so that the face of the Lord and His mangled body glistened in
the light. Then wrapped they it in bands of wool and linen, shrouded
it in purple cloths, and laid it upon a bier here at the stone, lamenting unceasingly the while to the sound of the pipes:

'Woe, alas, for Tammuz!
Alas for my beloved son, my spring and my light!
Adon! Adonai!
We sit down with tears,
For Thou art dead, my God, my spouse, my child.
Thou art a tamarisk, which in its bed hath drunk no water,
Whose tips in the field brought forth no shoot.
A sprig art Thou, not planted in the stream,
A shoot whose roots have been torn out,
An herb that in the garden hath drunk no water.
Alas, my Damu, my child, my light!
None hath loved Thee more than I!' "

"All the words of the wailing thou knowest, then?"
"I know them," Joseph said.
"And they go near to thy heart too, so it seemeth to me," added
Benoni. "For as thou sangest, it was to me twice or thrice as though
the words would pierce thy heart too from within, even though
thou well knowest the women do as they have learned and that the
son is not Adonai, the God of Jacob and Abram."

"He is the son and the beloved," said Joseph, "and He is the sacrifice. But what sayest thou? For it hath not touched me. I am not
small and puling like to thee."

"Nay, for thou art young and beautiful," said Benjamin meekly.
"And so thy garland is ready, which thou reservest to thyself. I see
thou hast made it higher and wider in front than behind, like a crown,
that it may display thy skill. I am rejoiced that thou wearest it, instead of the wreath of the rowan which thou wilt weave for me.
But the beautiful God lieth now four days upon the bier?"

"Thou sayest, and hath held it in thy memory," Joseph answered.
"Thy understanding waxeth and will soon be round and full, that one
may speak with thee of all things without exception. He lieth exposed until the fourth day, and daily the townsfolk come out from

the town, with their musicians, and beat their breasts at sight of Him and wail:

> 'O Duzi, my Lord, how long liest Thou there?
> O Lord of the sheepfold, how long liest Thou powerless there?
> I will eat no bread, I will drink no water,
> For dead is youth and dead is Tammuz!'

And in the temple and in the dwellings they send up the same lament. But on the fourth day they come and lay Him in the coffer."

"In a box?"

"One must call it a coffer. 'Box' would be just as good a word, only not admissible here. 'Coffer' is the word that has always been used. The Lord fitteth exactly into it, it is made to measure, out of wood painted scarlet and black, and could not fit better. So soon as He is within they shut down the lid and put pitch all round the edge, and then they entomb Him there in the hollow place with weeping, roll the stone to the mouth, and return home from the grave."

"And then doth the weeping cease?"

"Thou hast forgotten. They lament in temple and dwelling the space of two and a half days. But on the third day, at dusk, beginneth the feast of lamps."

"That I loved. Then they light a few lamps?"

"Lamps without number they light, everywhere," Joseph said, "as many as they have, round about the houses under the sky as well as on the ways hither and here upon the spot and among the bushes — everywhere are burning lamps. They come to the grave and again they lament, the most bitter lamenting of all; never wailed the flutes so piercingly to the lament 'O Duzi, how long liest Thou there?' Never have the women so beaten their breasts as in this affliction. Their bruises will last long. But at midnight all is still."

Benjamin clutched his brother's arm.

"And the stillness is very sudden?" he asked.

"They all stand without motion or sound. The stillness is long. Then from afar cometh the sound of a voice, a single voice, swelling loud and joyous: 'Tammuz liveth! The Lord is risen! He hath overthrown the abode of the shadow of death. Great is the Lord!'"

"Ah, what a word is that, my Joseph! I knew that it would come at the time of the feast, but yet the words pierce me to my marrow as though I had never heard them before. Who is it that calleth?

"It is a maiden, of delicate countenance, chosen and named anew each year. Her parents are proud and held in high honour on account of it. She who bringeth the tidings cometh walking, a lute in her hands, and she striketh it and singeth:

'Tammuz liveth, Adon is arisen!
Great is He, great, the Lord is great.
His eye, that was closed in death, He hath opened it.
His mouth, that was closed in death, He hath opened it.
His feet, that were fettered, walk,
Flowers and leaves they strew beneath His feet.
Great is the Lord, Adonai is great!'

But as the maiden cometh and singeth, they all rush to the grave.
They roll away the stone, and lo, the coffer is empty."

"Where is the mangled one?"

"He is no more there. The grave hath had no power to hold Him,
for lo, now three days are past. He is risen."

"Oh! But how, then, Joseph, arisen? Forgive me, chubby-cheeked
urchin that I am, if I ask thy meaning. Pray deceive not thy mother's
son. For thou hast told me more than once that the lovely image is
kept in the temple from year to year. Then what meaning hath here
'arisen'?"

"Little foolish one," responded Joseph, "thy understanding still
lacketh much, however it increaseth. It still resembleth a little bark
gliding across the sea of the sky. Do I not tell thee of the feast as it
occurreth hour by hour, and do not likewise the folk deceive themselves, knowing what is to come, yet honouring what is? For they all
know that the image is kept in the temple, and yet is Tammuz arisen.
I almost think thou meanest that because the image is not God, God
is not the image. But God forfend that it should be so! For the image is
the instrument of the present and of the feast. But Tammuz, the
Lord, is Lord of the feast."

So saying he set the finished crown on his head.

Benjamin looked at him large-eyed.

"God of our fathers," cried he admiringly, "how the myrtle crown
becometh thee, this that thou hast made before my eyes with thy
skilful fingers! Only thee it becometh; and when I think how it
would look upon my otter cap, then I see what a mistake it would be
not to keep it for thyself. But go on and tell me truly: when the
townsfolk have found coffer and grave empty, then, I suppose, they
go home with inward joy and peace unto their homes."

"Then beginneth the rejoicing," Joseph corrected him, "and the
feast of joy bursteth out. 'Empty, empty, empty,' cry they all; 'the
grave is empty, Adon is risen.' They kiss the maiden and cry: 'The
Lord is great.' Then they kiss one another in turn and cry: 'Glorified is Tammuz!' Then they hold round dances and whirl about the
monument of Ashtaroth in the lamplight. And also in the lamplit
town is naught but joy and merrymaking, feasting and drinking,
while the air resoundeth with the crying of the glad tidings. Even

next day they greet each other with exchange of kisses and the greeting: 'He is risen!'"

"Yes," Benjamin said, "so it is, and so hast thou told it to me. I had but forgotten it and thought they went quietly homewards. That is then the glorious feast, in each hour as it proceedeth. And the Lord hath had His head lifted up for this year, yet He knoweth the hour when Ninib will slay Him again in the greenwood."

"Not 'again,'" Joseph instructed him. "It is always the one and the only time."

"As thou thinkest, dear brother, so it is. My words were unripe, they were the language of a little urchin. The one and the first time always, for He is the Lord of the feast. But after all, when one considereth, there must have once been the first time in order that the feast should be at all; it must have been that Tammuz died and the lovely one was mangled — or must it not?"

"When Ishtar vanisheth from heaven and descendeth to awaken her son, that is the event."

"Oh, yes, that is the heavenly event. But how in the world below? Thou speakest of the event; but tell me then the story."

"They say," answered Joseph, "there was a king at Gebal, at the foot of the snow mountains, who had a daughter fair of face; and Nana, that is Ashtaroth, smote him with a madness of desire for her, so that he lusted after his own flesh and blood, and knew his daughter."

As he spoke, Joseph pointed behind him to the signs cut into the monument by which they sat.

"As she was now pregnant," he went on, "and the king saw that he would be the father of his grandchild, confusion seized upon him, rage and remorse, and he roused himself up to kill her. But the gods, well knowing that Ashrath had done this, changed the pregnant woman into a tree."

"What kind of a tree?"

"A tree or a bush," said Joseph with some irritation. "Or a bush as large as a tree. I was not there, and I cannot tell thee the shape of the king's nose, nor what sort of ear-rings the nurse of his daughter wore. If thou wilt hear, then listen, and throw me not thy ill-considered questions, like stones into a hedge."

"But if thou chideth me I shall weep," Benjamin complained, "and then must thou console me. Therefore do not chide, but only believe I want naught more than to hearken."

"In ten months," Joseph went on with his narrative, "the tree opened and revealed itself after this space of time, and lo, it was the lad Adonai who came forth. And Ashera, who had done all this, saw him and yielded him to no one. Therefore she kept him in the kingdom of the lower world, with Queen Ereshkigal. But she too, the queen, would yield him to no one, and said: 'Never will I give him up, for this is the land of nevermore-return.'"

"Why then did these queens yield him to no one?"

"To no one, neither to each other. Thou askest all and will know all. But if one hath the power of inference, then one needeth to say but one thing, and the rest proceedeth from it. Adon was the son of the fair one, and Nana herself had a hand in his begetting — from which it followeth that he was born to be occasion for envy. Thus when the queen of the air appeared in the lower realms to ask for him, Queen Ereshkigal was affrighted in the depths of her soul and clenched her teeth. She spoke to the gate-keeper: 'Deal with her according to custom.' And thus Astarte the queen had to pass through the seven gates, leaving behind at each a piece of her garments in the gate-keeper's hands: head-cloth, draperies, girdle, and clasps, and at the last door the loincloth, so that she came naked before Queen Ereshkigal to ask for Tammuz. Then these mistresses made claws of their fingers and flew at each other."

"They flew at each other with their nails?"

"Yes, one wound the other's hair round her hand and plucked at it, so great was their jealousy. But then Queen Ereshkigal had Queen Astarte locked in the lower regions with sixty locks and afflicted her with sixty diseases, so that the earth in vain awaited her return, and the shoots were imprisoned in the earth as the blossoms on the tree. At night the field grew white, for it bore salt. No grass sprung up nor any grain grew. The bull no longer covered the cow, nor the ass the she-ass, nor man woman. The womb was closed. Life, forsaken by desire, lay numb in affliction."

"Ah, Josephja, let us get on to the other hours of the tale and speak no more of this. I cannot hear that the ass no longer crouched over the she-ass and that the earth was leprous with salt. I shall weep, and thou will be troubled with me."

"And God's messenger wept too, when he saw it," said Joseph, "and showed it weeping to the Lord of hosts. And He said: 'It is not good that the blossoms should be imprisoned on the tree. I will throw Myself into the breach.' And He intervened between the queens Ashtaroth and Ereshkigal and arranged that Adonai should spend a third of the year in the lower regions, a third on earth, and a third where he himself chose. Then Ishtar led back her beloved to the upper earth."

"But where did the shoot of the tree stay in the third part of the year?"

"That is hard to tell. In various places. There was much jealousy of him and many machinations of envy. Ashtaroth loved him, but more than one god led him astray and yielded him to no one."

"Gods made in man's image, and made like me?" asked Benjamin.

"Made like thee — it is a phrase which everybody would understand," answered Joseph. "But with gods and half-gods the thing is not so clear. For many call Tammuz not master but mistress, not lord but lady. By which they mean Nana the goddess, but at the same time the god who is with her, or even they mean him instead of her — for, indeed, is Ishtar a wife? I have seen pictures of her and she had a beard. So why do I not say: 'I saw pictures of him'? Jacob, our father, imagineth no picture. No doubt that is the wisest way. But we must speak, and often the clumsiness of our speech doth not serve the truth. Is Ishtar the morning star?"

"Yea, and the evening star as well."

"So she is both. And I saw written upon a stone about her: 'At evening a woman, in the morning a man.' How could one make an image of that — and what sort of words should one choose to express the truth? I saw an image of God, showing the water of Egypt that waters the fields, and its breast was half a woman's and half a man's. Perhaps Tammuz was a maiden and became a youth only in death."

"Hath death then the power to alter nature?"

"The dead is God. He is Tammuz the shepherd, who is called Adonis here, but Osiris in the underworld. There he hath twisted mustaches, even if he was a woman when alive."

"Mami's cheeks, so thou hast told me, were very soft, and smelled like a rose-leaf when one kissed her. I will have no bearded image of her! If thou requirest it of me, I shall be rude and not comply."

"Foolish child," answered Joseph laughing, "I require it not from thee. I am only telling thee of the people of the lower land and their ideas concerning things not readily understood."

"My chubby cheeks are soft and tender too," Benjamin remarked, and felt his cheeks with both his little palms. "That cometh because I am not yet even what one could call young, but only a little urchin. But thou art young. And therefore keepest thou thy face clean of beard until thou art a man."

"Yea, I keep myself clean," answered Joseph. "And thou art clean. Thou hast cheeks soft as were Mami's, tender as though thou wast still an angel of the Most High God, the Lord, who hath betrothed Himself to our seed and to whom the same is betrothed in the flesh through the bond of Abraham. For He is to us a bridegroom by the shedding of blood, full of ardour, and Israel the bride. But then is Israel a bride or a bridegroom? That is not readily understood, and one may make no image of it, for after all he is a bridegroom, circumcised for the bride, dedicate and set apart. If I try to make a mental picture of Elohim, He looks like my father, who loveth me more than he doth our fellows. But I know that it is Mami whom he loveth in me, because I am living while she is dead — and liveth now in another nature. I and the mother are one. But Jacob, when he looketh on me, thinketh of Rachel, just as the people hereabouts think of Nana when they call Tammuz the queen."

"I think of Mami, too, when I am tender with thee, Josephja, dear Jehosiph," Benjamin cried, and flung his arms about Joseph. "Behold, that is the substitute and the representation. For our soft-cheeked mother went down to death for the sake of my life, and the little urchin is an orphan and ill-doer even from the first. But thou art to me like her; thou leadest me by the hand to the grove, into the greenwood, into the wide world, thou tellest me of the feast of God in all its hours as they pass, and makest me garlands as she would have done — even though of course thou wilt not grant me the wear of every sort of green, but keepest something for thyself alone. Woe, alas, that it had to come over her with such sharpness by the way, so that she had to die! Would she had been like the tree that sprang up and opened out so conveniently and sent forth a shoot! What sort of tree saidst thou it was? My memory is as short as my legs and my little finger."

"Come, let us go now," Joseph said.

THE DREAM OF HEAVEN

AT that time the brothers had not yet begun to call him "The Dreamer"; that came a little later. At present they named him Utnapishtim, and Reader of Stones, and the mildness of these epithets, intended to give offence, shows the poverty of the brothers' imagination. They would gladly have called him worse if they could have thought of it, and so they were glad when they could take up the "Dreamer of Dreams," as having a little more edge. But that day was not yet come. His prattle to his father about the dream concerning the winter rains had not been enough to make them take notice of his presumption: moreover, up till now he had not talked in their presence of his dreams, though he had had them for a long time. The tallest of them he never did tell, either to them or to his father; it was the relatively modest ones which he repeated, to his own undoing. But to Benjamin he told all; in their private hours he told his little brother even the most shameless ones, which otherwise he had the good sense to suppress. It goes without saying that the little urchin listened with all his ears and heard with the utmost gratification, and that he never tired of asking to hear. But even so, weighed down as he already was by such mysterious doings as that of the myrtle garland, he never was able to get rid of a feeling of unease and anxiety

as he listened, though he ascribed it to his own youngness and tried
to overcome it. Unfortunately there was far too good ground for the
feeling; probably nobody could have helped having some concern,
in view of the rank egotism of the dream that follows, which Benjamin, and Benjamin alone, got to hear more than once. Precisely the
circumstance that he was the only hearer oppressed the child no little, however much he recognized the necessity and felt honoured by
the fact.

Joseph told his dream for the most part with his eyes closed, in a
voice now dying away, now suddenly swelling forth, with his fists
held clenched on his chest, plainly in a state of great emotion, though
he warned his hearer not to be carried away, but to listen quietly.

"Thou must not be startled," he said, "nor cry out; thou must neither weep nor laugh, else will I not speak."

"How should I?" Benjamin would answer each time. "I may be
but a little urchin, but I am no simpleton. I know well what I shall
do. So long as I feel quiet, I will forget that it is a dream, that I may
enjoy it to the full. But so soon as I am frightened or feel myself getting hot and cold, then I will tell myself that it is all a dream which
thou art telling me. And that will cool my mood, that I make no
disturbance."

"I dreamed," Joseph began, "that I was in the fields with the flocks
and was alone among the sheep that pastured on the slope where I lay.
I lay on my belly with a straw in my mouth, and had my feet sticking
in the air, and my thoughts were as carefree as my limbs. Then it
happened that a shadow fell upon me and the spot where I lay, as of
a cloud which darkened the sun; and therewith was a mighty rustling
in the air above, and when I looked up, lo, it was an eagle which
hovered over me with outspread wings, a huge bird, large as an ox,
and with the horns of an ox on its head. This it was which overshadowed me. And there was all about me a great and violent roaring of
wind, for it came straight over me, seized me by the hips with its talons, and snatched me up from the earth with flapping pinions, from
out of the middle of my father's flocks."

"Oh, wonder!" interjected Benjamin. "I do not mean that I should
have been afraid; but didst thou not cry out: 'Help, help'?"

"That did I not," said Joseph, "for three reasons: for first there was
nobody there on the wide fields to hear me; second, my breath failed,
so that I could not have cried out had I wished; and, thirdly, I did
not wish, for there was instead a great joy within me, as of something
long awaited and hoped for. The eagle held me by my hips from behind and held me before him with his claws, his head above mine,
while my legs hung down into the great wind of our flight. Sometimes he bent down his head to mine and looked at me with his steely
eye. Then spoke he from his bronze beak: 'Do I hold thee well, my

child, and not clutch thee too firmly with my resistless talons? I am
taking great pains not to do so, to do no injury to thy flesh, for were
I to hurt thee, then woe is me.' I asked: 'Who art thou?' He answered: 'I am the angel Amphiel, to whom this shape hath been given
for this present purpose. For thy sojourn, my child, is not upon
earth; thou shalt be transported; such is the decree.' "

" 'But why?' I asked.

" 'Be silent,' said the uprushing eagle, 'and keep thy tongue from
questioning, as all the heavenly hosts are bound to do. For it is the
decree of overwhelming favour, and there is no tongue-glibness
availeth against it; if thou speakest and talkest, the decree cometh
down heavy-handed; let no one blister his tongue by speaking monstrous words.' So then I held my peace at his words and was silent.
But my heart was full of fearsome joy."

"I am glad thou sittest beside me, in proof that it was all a dream,"
Benjamin said. "But hadst thou then no sadness, to be mounting from
the earth on the wings of eagles, and hadst thou no pain at all to be
leaving us, even for instance thy little one here?"

"I was leaving you not," Joseph answered. "I was taken from you
and could not help it; but it seemed to me also that I had expected it.
It is true in a dream too that one hath not all the happenings before
one at once, but only one thing, and with me that was the fearful joy
in my heart. So great was it, and so great what happened to me, that
it may be the things thou speakest of looked small by comparison."

"I am not angry with thee," Benjamin said; "I only look at thee
amazed."

"Thanks, dear little Beni. And thou must remember that the ascent
perhaps blotted out memory, for upward I went, without pause, in
the eagle's talons, and after two double hours he said to me: 'Look
down, my friend, on land and sea. What hath become of them?' And
lo, the land had become like a mountain in size and the sea like a river
of water. And then after another two double hours the eagle said
again: 'Look down, my friend, and see what hath become of ocean
and shore.' And the land was become like to a plantation, and the sea
like a gardener's ditch. But after two double hours again, when Amphiel the eagle bade me look down, lo and behold, there was the land
like a flat cake and the sea the size of a bread-basket. After I saw this
I was swept upwards again another double hour and then he said:
'Look down, my friend, and see that they have vanished, the land
and the sea.' And they were vanished, but I was not afraid.

"Through Shejakim, the cloudy heavens, the eagle rose with me,
and his pinions dripped with wet. There were golden gleams in the
grey and white, for already on the cloudy islets about us stood single
angels and members of the heavenly host, all clad in golden armour.

These held one hand to their foreheads and peered after us, and animals crouched upon cushions and I saw them lift their noses and sniff the breeze of our upward flight.

"Through Rakia, the starry heaven, we rose; then came a thousand-fold harmonious thunder in mine ear and all about us were stars and planets, in their musical numbers, and angels stood upon fiery footstools here and there, with tablets full of numbers in their hands, and pointed with their fingers the way to those oncoming mightily, for they might not turn round. And they cried to each other: 'Blessed be the glory of the Lord where it resideth!' But when we passed they were silent and cast down their eyes.

"In the midst of my joy I was afraid and I asked the eagle: 'Whither then and how high wilt thou bear me?' He answered: 'Endlessly high, into the highest height of the north of the world, my child. For so it hath been decreed, that I should bring thee straightway and without delay unto the uttermost height and breadth of Araboth, where are the storehouses of life, peace and blessedness, and unto the highest vault, into the midst of the great palace. There is the chariot and there the seat of glory, which from now on thou shalt daily serve, and shalt stand before Him and have power over the keys, to open and to close the halls of Araboth — and whatever else One hath in mind concerning thee.' I said: 'If then I am elected and chosen out among mortals, then so let it be. For indeed it cometh to me not quite without my expectation.'

"Then saw I a fortress, most awe-inspiring, built of ice-crystal, the battlements manned with warriors, whose wings covered their bodies down to their feet, and their legs stood straight, but their feet were round feet, as one might say, and they shone like polished bronze. And lo, two such stood together, resting their arms on their snaky swords, bold of countenance and with prideful furrows on their brows. The eagle said: 'They are Aza and Azael, two of the seraphim.' Then heard I how Aza spake to Azael: 'Five and sixty thousand miles have I smelt out his coming. But tell me, what is the smell of one born of woman and what the worth of one grown from the white drop of semen, that he may come up to the highest height of the heavens and take service amongst us?' And Azael, in alarm, closed his lips with his finger. But Aza said: 'Not so, I will fly with thee before the face of the One and Only and will dare to speak; for I am an angel of the lightning, and my words are free.' And the two of them flew behind us.

"And through whatever heavens the eagle bore me by my hips, and through whatever ranks of hosts and swarms of fiery ministrants, all singing praises, their song was silenced on the instant as we flew past; and of the children of the upper air some attached themselves to us, so that we were soon accompanied by hosts of the winged before and behind, and I heard the rustling of their wings like the rushing of mighty waters.

"Oh, Benjamin, believe me! I saw the seven halls of Zebul, built in fire, and seven hosts of angels stood there, and seven fiery altars. There ruled the highest prince, named 'Who is like God?' in all the splendour of priestly vestments and made fiery sacrifice and caused columns of smoke to rise on the altar of the burnt sacrifice.

"I know not the sum of the double hours nor can bring to mind the number of the miles, until we reached the heights of Araboth and the seventh terrace and set foot upon its earth, which was so soft and light that it did good to the sole of my foot all through my body even to mine eyes, that I was like to weep. The children of light passed on before and behind us, leading and following. And one took me by the hand and led me, a strong angel, naked to the waist, in a golden skirt to the ankle-bones, with arm-bands and necklace and a round helmet resting on his hair, and the points of his pinions touching his ankles. He was heavy-lidded and fleshy-nosed, and his red mouth smiled as I looked upon him, but he did not turn his head towards me.

"I lifted up mine eyes in my dream and I saw, far on into endless space, light glittering upon arms and pinions, as of countless hosts encamped about their standard and singing full-throated praise and war; it all swam about me in the colours of milk and gold and roses. I saw wheels revolving, frightful in height and round; they glowed like turquoise and one wheel went into the other, four together, and they turned not when they went. And their rings were full of eyes round about them.

"But in the midst was a mountain, sparkling with fiery stones, and upon it a palace built out of the light of sapphires, and thither we went attended by hosts before and behind. Its halls were full of messengers, guards, and keepers. We entered into the pillared hall in the centre, and its end and depth were not to be seen, for they led me in along the length of it, and cherubim stood on both sides in front of the columns and between them, each with six wings and all covered with eyes. Thus we passed between them, I know not how far, towards the throne of the Most High. And the air was jostling with the cries of those among the columns and of those who stood in hosts about the throne: 'Holy, holy, holy, Lord God of Sabaoth, heaven and earth are full of the majesty of thy glory.' The throng about the throne, however, was of seraphim, which with two wings covered their feet and with two their faces, but they peered a little through the feathers. And he who led me said to me: 'Cover also thy countenance, for it is fitting.' Then I put my hands before my face, but I peered out somewhat too between my fingers."

"Joseph," cried Benjamin, "for God's love, tell me didst thou see the countenance of the Universal?"

"I saw Him sitting in sapphire light upon the throne, formed like a man and created in his image, in majesty well known unto us. For His beard and the hair on His temples flowed down shining, and there were furrows in His cheek, good and deep. The flesh under His eyes was soft and weary-looking, and the eyes, not very large, but brown and bright, peered at me as though in concern as I came up."

Benjamin said: "It giveth me a picture of Jacob our father looking at thee."

"It was the father of the world," Joseph responded, "and I fell upon my face. Then I heard the voice of One speaking and saying to me: 'Child of man, stand upon thy feet. For from now onwards shalt thou stand before My throne as *metatron* and child of God, and I will give thee power over the keys, to open and to close my Araboth, and thou shalt be set as commander over all the hosts, for the Lord hath pleasure in thee.' Then through the hosts of angels there went a rustling and a roaring like the sound of a great army.

"But now, behold, there came forth Aza and Azael, whom I had heard speaking together. And the seraph Aza said: 'Lord of all the worlds, who is this one that cometh to these upper regions, to take his service amongst us?' And Azael added, and covered his face with his two wings to lessen the force of his words: 'Hath he not been begot of the white drop of semen and from the race of those who drink up injustice like water?' And I saw the countenance of the Lord cloud over with ill-will, and his words were proud and imperious as He answered and said: 'What are you, that you speak in the midst of My speaking? For I favour whom I favour and give grace to those to whom I give grace. Truly, sooner than you all will I make him prince and lord in the heights of heaven.'

"And again there went throughout the throng that wave of sound, and it was as though the wave retreated and went back. The cherubim beat their wings and all the children of heaven made the echoes ring with crying: 'Glory be to the Lord where He resideth!'

"But the King went still further in His language and said: 'Upon him do I lay My hand and bless him with three hundred and five and sixty thousand blessings and make him great and exalted. For I will make him a throne, like to Mine own, with a tapestry over it wove out of pure brilliance, light, glory, and splendour. It I will set at the entrance to the seventh terrace, and seat him on it, for I will magnify him beyond all words. There shall go a cry before him from heaven to heaven; have a care and take it to heart: Henoch, My servant, have I named prince and mighty over all the princes of My kingdom and over all the children of light save at most the eight powerful and awful ones who are named with the name of God after the name of the King. And every angel that hath a plea to Me shall go first before him and speak with him. But every word which he speaketh to you in My name you shall heed and obey, for the princes of wisdom and reason stand at his side. Such the cry that shall go out before him. Give Me the robe and the crown.'

"And the Lord threw over me a priceless garment with all sorts of light woven into it, and arrayed me therein. And took a heavy ring with forty-nine stones of unspeakable brilliance. This with His own hands he set upon my head in addition to the robe, before the face of the whole heavenly host, and named me by my title: 'Yahu, the lit-tle one, the immanent prince.' For indeed He went very far.

"Then again the wave of the angels swept and shrank backwards and all the sons of heaven bowed themselves and likewise the princes among the angels, the mighty and great ones, the lions of God, greater than all the hosts, who have their service before the throne; furthermore the angels of fire, of hail, of lightning, of wind, of anger and wrath, of storm, snow, and rain, of day and of night, of the moon and the planets, who guide the destinies of the world with their hands — all these trembled too and covered their faces as though blinded.

"But the Lord stood up from His throne and carried things to the uttermost, and went on to declare and to say: 'Lo there was in the valley a tender shoot of the cedar tree; this have I transplanted upon a lofty mountain-top, and made of it a tree within which the birds can dwell. And among the hosts he was the youngest in days, moons, and years; this youth made I greater than all other created beings, simply out of My incalculable will and predilection. I made him over-seer over all the treasures of the halls of Araboth, and over all the treasures of life preserved in the heights of heaven. And it was more-over his office to bind the garlands round the heads of the sacred beasts, to adorn the wheels of splendour mightily, to clothe the cher-ubim in magnificence, to make to shine the firebolts of heaven and enfold the seraphim in pride. Each morning he put My throne to rights, when I would mount My seat to sit in it and hold review in all the height of My power. I garbed him in a priceless garment full of pride and glory. With a heavy crown I crowned his head and I gave him of the majesty, the pomp and magnificence of My throne. And My one sorrow is that I could not make higher his throne than Mine own and his splendour greater than Mine, for it is infinite. But his name was the Little God.'

"Upon this pronouncement came a mighty clap of thunder, and all the angels fell upon their faces. But the while the Lord so singled me out for joy, my flesh was on fire, my veins glowed bright, my bones were like a fire of juniper-wood, the casting up of my lashes like a lightning-flash, my eyeballs rolled like balls of fire, the hair of my head was a lambent flame, my limbs were fiery pinions, and I awaked."

"I tremble in my whole body," said Benjamin, "from thy dream, Joseph, for it is beyond all bounds. Thou too tremblest somewhat, I should think, and art thyself somewhat pale. I can see that, for the places in thy face that are dark and shiny from the razor stand out very plainly."

"Absurd," said Joseph. "Shall I tremble at my own dream?"

"And wast thou then eternally glorified in those heights and thoughtest no more of thine own, for example of thy little one here?" asked Benjamin.

"Thou canst despite all thy simplicity imagine," responded Joseph, "that I was a little bewildered with all that arbitrary grace and favour and had not much time to think back. But I am convinced that in a little while I should have thought of you all and had you come after me and be exalted by my side, the father, the women, the brothers, and thou. That would be but a trifle, with all the power that I possessed. But hearken now, Benjamin, and be warned. In thee I confide everything, because thou art ripe to hear and understand. Thou must not prattle to our father or to the brethren concerning my dream which I have told thee, for they might put upon it a bad construction."

"Not for my life," Benjamin responded. "That were a mortal evil. All too easily thou forgettest the difference between an urchin and a simpleton, although it is an important one. Not even in a dream will it occur to me to prattle, not even a syllable of all that hath come to thee in sleep. But thou thyself, Joseph, if I may say so, thou must be even more careful; do for my sake, my dearest brother. For it is easy for me not to forget, out of gratefulness for thy confidence. But it doth not prevent thee, who hast thyself dreamed and art fuller of it than I, to whom thou hast only lent of the splendour and brilliance of thy dream. Therefore think of thy little one, when it itcheth thee to relate in how much gladness the Lord chose thee out and exalted thee. I for my part find it fitting and I am angry with Aza and Azael that they spoke against it. But it might cloud the father's mind with care, as such things are wont to do, and the brothers would spit and spew out their disapproval and make thee to suffer in their envy and jealousy. For they are all louts in the sight of the Lord, and that we both well know."

Chapter IV

THE DREAMER

THE COAT OF MANY COLOURS

NOT for the harvesting, as had been expected, but as early as the night of the spring full moon, the sons of Leah came tumbling heels over head back to Hebron from the plains of Shechem. They came, ostensibly, to eat the Passover lamb with their father and with him to observe the moon; but actually because they had heard an exciting piece of news, affecting all of them. They came to convince themselves, on the spot, of its truth, with their very own eyes, and to see if anything about it could be changed. The thing was so startling and portentous that the sons of the maids had found it of the first importance to select one of their number to make the four-day journey from Hebron to Shechem to fetch news. Of course it was the nimble Naphtali who had been chosen. At bottom, actually, it did not matter who went, or how fast. For Naphtali rode on an ass, as another would have done; whether a longer or shorter pair of legs hung down on either side the beast was of no importance. In any case the journey took four days. But it was with Naphtali, son of Bilhah, that the idea of celerity was bound up. The rôle of messenger was his traditionally; and as his tongue was as nimble as his legs, there was perhaps some sense in the idea that he would, at least in the last moment, give the brothers the benefit of what he had learned a little quicker than anyone else.

What was it had happened? Jacob had made a present to Joseph.

That was nothing new. The father in wilful indulgence of his feeling toward his son, his lamb, his scion, his heavenly youth and son of a virgin — or whatever other appellations might occur to him — had always made him gifts and tender remembrances: sweetmeats, pretty bits of pottery and stones, purple laces, scarabs, and what not. Seeing them in his careless possession, the brethren would scowl. They would feel their rights curtailed and be aggrieved. To such fundamental and almost intentionally emphasized injustice they had had plenty of opportunity to accustom themselves. But this particular gift was so startling in its nature, one could not but fear that the act was decisive. It appeared to mean a slap in the face for them all.

Here is what happened. It was tenting weather, the latter rains had come on. Jacob had withdrawn himself in the afternoon into his house of hair, that secure and complete protection against the blessing-bringing downpour: a woven felt of black goats' hair, stretched over nine stout poles and fastened by strong ropes to pegs driven into the ground. It was the largest tent in the rather scattered settlement. Jacob lived in it alone, being a rich man and setting store by being able to give the women their separate dwelling. It was divided from front to back by a curtain hanging to the middle posts. One of the rooms served as private storeroom and supply chamber: camel saddles and pockets, unused carpets rolled or folded, hand-mills, and other gear lay about and there were skins hung up, full of grain, butter, drinking-water, and palm wine made of soaked dates.

The other half was the dwelling of the bearer of the blessing; the conveniences it displayed were in strong contrast to the half-Bedouin kind of life to which he clung. Jacob needed ease. He disliked the effeminacy of city life, but that did not prevent him from wanting certain comforts when he withdrew from the world into himself for meditation and laboured upon his thoughts of God. Open in front to the height of a man, the chamber was warmly carpeted with felt and over that with gaily coloured rugs; some of these also hung upon the walls. A cedar-wood bedstead with covers and cushions and bronze feet stood in the background. Several earthen lamps with ornamental bases and shallow bowls with short snouts for the wick were always burning here, for it would have been unfitting and poverty-stricken for the bearer of the blessing to sleep in the dark; they were even lighted in the daytime, that they might lend no sinister meaning to the phrase: "Jacob's lamp is out." Painted jugs with handles stood on the flat top of a sycamore coffer, the sides of which were decorated with intaglio in blue glaze. Another tall-legged coffer, carved and written over with texts, had a vaulted lid. There did not lack a glowing brazier in the corner, for Jacob was inclined to chilliness. Low stools were everywhere, less as seats than as places whereon to lay things: on one stood a small incense-burner, shaped like a tower, out of whose little window-openings came clouds of smoke scented with cinnamon, styrax, and galbanum. On another was a valuable specimen of Phœnician art, which only a well-to-do person could possess: a flat gold basin on a dainty stand. When you pressed the bottom with your hand, it showed a female figure playing on a lute.

Jacob and Joseph were sitting on cushions by a low tabouret at the entrance to the tent, playing a game with pieces spread out on the engraved bronze surface. He had summoned his son to play the game at which Rachel once had been his companion. Outside the rain plashed down on stones and shrubbery and olive trees, the blessing of God's moisture upon the corn of the valley, that it might bear up under the summer's heat until the harvest time. The wind lightly rattled the wooden rings on the roof, to which the tent ropes were fastened.

Joseph let his father win the game. He had purposely got into the field of the "evil eye" and put himself at a disadvantage; thus Jacob, though playing with his attention greatly distraught, had to his pleasurable surprise finally won the game. He admitted his absence of mind and said the victory was his more by good luck than good management.

"Hadst thou not been defeated in time, my child," he said, "I must have been so; for my thoughts wandered and I made many blunders, whereas thou hast drawn cleverly and never failed to make good thy mischances. Thy way of playing reminds me of Mami's, she used so often to put me in the corner. Even her way of biting her little finger as she considered, and certain little stratagems she loved, thou hast and I am moved by them as I play."

"All that is as nothing," Joseph answered, stretching himself, putting his head back, one arm out sideways and the other bent to his shoulder. "The issue speaketh against me. If my dear father won even with his thoughts distracted, how would it have gone with the child if he had had his full attention upon the game? The end would have come quickly."

Jacob smiled. "My experience," he said, "is longer and my school the best, for as a boy I played with Yitzchak, thy grandfather upon my side, and after that often with Laban, thy grandfather on the side of my beloved, in the land of Naharain, beyond the water; he too played with great deliberation."

Jacob too, more than once, had let Laban and Yitzchak win, when he was wanting to put them in a good mood; but it never occurred to him that Joseph might have done the same.

"It is true," he went on, "that I played badly today. More than once a thought came over me that made me forget the position of the pieces. What I was thinking had to do with the approaching feast and the night of sacrifice, when after sunset we slaughter the sheep and dip the sprig of hyssop into the blood to strike it upon the two side posts, that the Avenger may pass over. For it is the night of the Passover, and the substitution of the sacrifice, in token that the firstling is slain in expiation for man and beast whom it lusteth him to slay. Upon all this I fell a-musing, for lo, a man will do much and know not what he doth. Yet were he to know and think about it, it might be that his entrails would turn over within him and he would be sick to his very bottom, as it hath happened to me many a time in my life, and the first time was when I heard that Laban, at Shinar beyond the river Prath, had slain his first-born little son as a sacrifice and buried it in a jar in the foundations to bring good fortune to his house. But dost thou think it brought him blessing? No, but harm, hindrance, and adversity; and had I not come and given a little life to house and business, it would all have foundered in misery. Never again would he have been fruitful with his wife Adina. And yet Laban would not have walled up his little son had such a deed not brought his forbears blessing in earlier times."

"Thou sayest it," Joseph responded. He had folded his hands at the back of his neck. "And it is clear to me, from thy words, how this came to pass. Laban behaved according to outworn custom, and thereby committed serious blunders. For the outworn is repulsive to the Lord; He is already beyond it and wisheth us to be so too, and He rejecteth and curseth it. Therefore, if Laban had understood himself and the times, he would have slaughtered instead of his son a goat or a kid and struck the blood upon the posts and threshold; then would he have been glad and his incense would have mounted up to heaven."

"Again," said Jacob, "thou sayest it and takest the thoughts and the words out of my mouth. For the Avenger lusteth not alone after the beast, but also after the blood of man; and we appease his desire not only in respect to the flocks through the blood on the doorposts, but also by the sacrificial meal, which we eat and devour in haste by night that nothing of the roast meat may remain over by the morning. But when we think of it, what sort of roast meat is that, and doth the lamb atone only for the flock when we slay it? What should we slay and eat, if we were mad like Laban, and what was slain and eaten in more indecent times? Do we know what we do in the feast, when we slay and eat, and would not our very inwards come uppermost if we thought of it, so that we vomited?"

"Let us slay and let us eat," said Joseph, lightly, in a high-pitched voice, rocking himself in his hands at the back of his neck. "The feast and the feasting are both good, and if they are also salvation, then let us joyfully save ourselves from being obscene, by dint of understanding the Lord and the times in which we are. Lo, there is a tree," he cried, and pointed with outstretched arm into the tent, as though a tree actually stood there, "splendid in trunk and crown, planted by the fathers for the delight of those coming after. Its tips move and sparkle in the wind, its roots cleave to the kingdom of the earth, in darkness, in the dust, and among the stones. But doth the blithe tip know overmuch of the dirt-encrusted root? No, for it hath come out beyond it with the Lord, swayeth in the air, and thinketh not thereupon. So, in my view, is it with the tradition and the indecency. But if we want to have the pious tradition taste well in our mouths, by all means let us leave the underneath things quietly underneath."

"Thy parable is charming," Jacob said, nodding. He stroked his beard, holding it at one side and letting it glide through the hollow of his hand. "Thy words are witty and well invented. But even so, we must still meditate, still stoop under the cares and the unrest which were Abraham's portion and must be ours for ever and ever, that we may free ourselves according to the Lord's will; and it may be are already free of that from which He would release us: namely, care. But say, who is the Avenger and what is his passing over? Doth not the moon, on the night of the feast, go full and beauteous through the pass which is the northernmost point and zenith of his way, where he himself turneth in his fullness? But the northernmost point is Nergal's, the murderer; the night is his, Sin ruleth for him, Sin is Nergal at the time of this feast, and the Avenger, who passeth over and whom we appease, he is the Red One."

"That is clear," Joseph said. "We hardly think of it, but so he is."

"Such was the unrest," went on Jacob, "that was distracting me as we played. For it is the stars that determine this feast for us, the moon and the Red One; and on that night they change places. But shall we then throw kisses to the stars and celebrate their histories? Must we not rather distress ourselves over the Lord and the time, whether we do truly and in fact understand them and not transgress against both, considering that we continue out of sheer idle habit in the ritual indecency from which He would win us? Sometimes I seriously ask myself if I ought not to call the people together under the tree of wisdom, that they might hear my misgivings and hearken to my cares in the matter of the feast Pesach."

"My dear father," said Joseph, as he bent over and laid his hand on the old man's beside the board which registered his defeat, "is much too precise in his interpretations; I must pray him not to let himself be moved to undue haste and so to destruction. If thy child may regard himself as having been asked, then he would advise that the feast be spared and not too hotly attacked on account of its legends, instead of which perchance another might come up, which then thou wouldst relate at the roast meal: for instance the saving of Isaac, which would be very suitable. Or else we wait on time, whether God might not for once glorify Himself in us by a great redemption and deliverance; which then we would make the basis of the feast and its legend, and sing songs of rejoicing. Have I, in my folly, spoken consolingly?"

"Thy words," responded Jacob, "are like balsam: very sage and comforting, which is what I mean by balsamic. For thou spokest for the custom and yet at the same time for the future, and that shall be reckoned to thy honour. And spokest at the same time for an abiding, which is at the same time a station on the way; and thereover my soul smileth at thine, Joseph-el, thou shoot of the tenderest tree. Let me kiss thee!"

And across the board he took Joseph's lovely head between his hands and kissed him, rejoicing in his son from the depths of his heart.

"If only I knew," Joseph said, "whence wisdom cometh to me at this hour, or the small sagacity I have to meet the shrewdness of my lord in his speech! Thou saidst that thy thoughts wandered during our game; then, to be frank, so did mine. They kept slipping aside from the pieces, and the Elohim alone know how I managed to keep going on so long."

"Whither then, my child, went thy thoughts?"

"Ah," answered the youth, "thou canst easily guess. A word of thine itcheth in mine ear day and night; a word which my father spoke of late to me by the fountain, and which hath robbed me of peace, so that curiosity plagueth me wherever I go, for it was a word of promise."

"What said I, then, and what promise gave I to thee?"

"Oh, thou knowest — I can tell by thy face thou knowest! Thou haddest in mind, so saidst thou — well, canst thou guess now? — 'I purpose to give thee somewhat to make thy heart rejoice, and which will be fitting unto thee.' Thus word for word didst thou speak. I remember it only too well, it keepeth on tickling me in my ear. What then did my little father mean with this promise of his?"

Jacob reddened, and Joseph saw it. It was a slight rosy flush, which ran up into the grey hair on his cheeks, and his eyes clouded over in mild confusion.

"It was nothing, nothing at all," he said defensively. "My child is indulging in vain imaginings. What I said was mere chance, uttered without purpose or significance. Have I not given thee various things, as my heart prompteth me? Thus, then, was the meaning of what I said, that I might give thee something some day, at a fitting hour...."

"Nay and indeed," Joseph cried, sprang up and embraced his father. "This wise and good man who sitteth here cannot speak without meaning — that would be unheard of. As though I had not seen plain and clear as he spoke, that he spoke not emptily, but had a plain thing in his mind's eye, beautiful and definite, not just anything at all, but some particular and splendid thing which he thought of for me. But not only hast thou thought of, thou hast spoken and promised. May I not know what is mine and what awaiteth me? Dost thou think I could find rest or give thee any peace until I knew?"

"How thou teasest me," said Jacob, hard-pressed. "Shake me not so, and take away thy hands from the lobes of mine ears, that I

may not look like a child in thy hands. Thou wouldst know — well,
why shouldst thou not know? I will tell thee, I will admit that I did
have one clear thing in my mind, and not anything indefinite.
Hearken then, and stand down upon the ground. Hast thou heard of
Rachel's *ketonet passim?*"

"A garment of Mami's? Something she wore? Oh, I understand:
thou wilt make me from her robe . . ."

"Hearken, Jehosiph! Thou dost not understand. Let me tell thee.
When I had served seven years for Rachel and the time approached
when I should receive her in the Lord, Laban spoke to me: 'I will
give thee a veil, wherein the bride may veil herself and dedicate herself to Nana and be a consecrated one. Long ago,' he said, 'I bought
the *haik* from a pilgrim and preserved it in the chest, for it is precious.
It is supposed to have belonged to a king's daughter in times past and
been the maiden garment of a princess, a thing easy to believe, so
skilfully is it embroidered everywhere with all sorts of emblems of
idols. But she shall veil her head in it and be as one of the *enitu* and
like to the bride of heaven in the tower Etemenanki.' In some such
words spoke the devil Laban to me. And lied not in these words
which he spake, for Rachel received the garment and was a splendour
incomparable in it as we sat at the wedding feast and I kissed the
image of Ishtar. But when I handed the bride the flower and lifted
her veil that I might see her with my seeing hands, lo, it was Leah,
whom the devil had craftily brought into the bedchamber, so that I
was happy only in my imagination, but not in the fact. All which
maketh one to lose one's reason to think upon, so I pass it over.
But at the time I was glowing in the sun of my fancied bliss, and I
folded the sacred weave and laid it upon a chair and to the bride
I said: 'We shall hand it down through the generations, and countless
blissful brides shall wear it.' "

"And did Mami too wear the wrap at her time?"

"It is no wrap, it is a sumptuousness, a piece of material to be used
as one will, ankle-length, with sleeves, and one can put it on as suiteth
one's taste and one's looks. Mami? Yea, she wore it and kept it; when
she went away, when we broke the dusty bolts and swindled that
devil Laban, she faithfully packed it up and took it with her. Always
it went where we went, and as Laban preserved it for years in his
chest, so have we done."

Joseph's eyes darted about through the tent and rested on the
coffers. He asked:

"Is it close to us?"

"Not far off."

"And my lord will give it me?"

"I have designed it for the child."

"Designed and promised."

"But for later, not this very minute," cried Jacob in his distress. "Be reasonable, child, and let it stop for the moment at the promise. Lo, things are in the balance, and the Lord hath not yet pronounced upon them in my heart. Thy brother Reuben fell away and I was driven to take from him his right as first-born. Is it then thy turn next, that I should give thee the right to array thee in the *ketonet*? One might say no, for after Reuben came Judah and then Simeon and Levi. One might answer yes, for after Leah's first-born fell and was cursed, then came the turn of Rachel's first-born. But all that is doubtful and unclear. We must wait and let the signs make it plain to our understanding. But if I garb thee in the *ketonet*, then might the brethren falsely interpret it in the sense of the blessing and the choice and rise up in jealousy against thee and against me."

"Against thee?" asked Joseph, in great astonishment. "I almost think that my ears deceive me. Art thou not our father and our lord? If they murmur, canst thou not rise up and overwhelm them with thy words and say unto them: 'I choose whom I choose and show favour to whom I show favour? Who are ye that ye oppose me? Sooner than any of you will I clothe him in the garment and with his mother's *ketonet passim*.' But I think not that mine ears deceive me, they are young and keen. And especially when my dear father speaketh I prick them up. Saidest thou once to the bride: 'Countless ones among beloveds shall wear it?' Or saidest thou not? Tell me, then! Who, saidest thou, shouldst wear it?"

"Be quiet, tempter. Leave me, and coax me not, that thy folly may not overflow and fall upon mine own head."

"Dear father — let me see it!"

"See it? Well, seeing is not having. But seeing is wanting to have. Be reasonable."

"Shall I not see what is mine and promised unto me? Shall we make a bargain? I will sit here and not stir from the spot. Then thou goest and showest me the festal garment, holding it up before thee as the merchants in the bazaar at Hebron display their wares and drape the cloth upon themselves before the eyes of him who coveteth it. But he is poor and cannot buy. So then the merchant putteth it away again."

"So be it, in the name of the Lord," said Jacob. "Although an on-looker would think thou tookest liberties with me. Stop where thou art. Squat upon thy heels, put thy hands behind thee. Then shalt thou see that which perhaps, under certain circumstances, might be thine."

"What is mine already," Joseph cried, "only that I may not yet enjoy it."

He rubbed his eyes with his knuckles, to see the better. Jacob went over to the round-topped coffer, slipped the bolt, and flung back the lid. On top were woollen things, mantles, covers, skirts, head-cloths, smocks, which he dropped, folded, on the floor in a pile. He found the veil where he knew that it lay, took it, turned round, and spread out the folds.

The lad stared in amaze. He drew a long breath through his open, laughing mouth. The metal embroideries glittered in the lamplight. The flashing silver and gold blotted out at times the quieter colours as the old man held it up in his unsteady arms: the purple, white, olive-green, rose-colour, and black of the emblems and images, the stars, doves, trees, gods, angels, men, and beasts, lustrous against the bluish mist of the background.

"Ye heavenly lights!" Joseph burst out. "How beautiful! O dearest father merchant, what showest thou to thy customer, there under thy arch? There is Gilgamesh, with the lion in the bend of his arm, I recognize him from here. And there is a man fighting with a griffin and swinging a club. Wait, wait! Ye heavenly hosts, what animals are here! I see the paramours of the goddess — bat, steed, wolf, and bright-coloured bird. Let me look — ah, let me look! I cannot make out, I cannot distinguish. And my eyes burn from staring across such a distance. Is that the scorpion-human pair, with the prickly tails? It seemeth so, but I cannot be certain, though mine eyes water with staring. One moment, merchant, while I hitch a little nearer, still with my hands behind my back. But oh, ye Elohim, how it groweth in beauty as I come nearer it! And all becometh clear. What are the bearded spirits doing at the tree? They are fructifying it. . . . And what is it that is written here? 'I have put off my coat; how shall I put it on?' Wonderful! Always Nana, with sun, moon, and dove. Ah, I *must* stand up! Merchant, I *must* get up, else I cannot see the top: the date palm, out of which a goddess stretcheth her arms with food and drink. I may touch it, may I not? There is no charge, I hope, if I lift it up, ever so carefully, in my hand, to feel its weight and its mixture of lightness and heaviness. . . . Merchant, I am poor, I cannot buy. Merchant, give it to me! Thou hast so many wares — give me the veil! Or be so kind to lend it me, that I show myself to the people to the honour of thy shop. No, thou wilt not — thou art adamant? Or waverest thou, perhaps, a tiny bit, and despite all thy severity wouldst like to see me in it? No, I am wrong, thou swayest a little only from the holding up and spreading out. Thou hast strained thyself much too long already. Give it to me. How doth one wear it, how put it on? Like this — or like this? Or this way? How do I please thee? Am I the gay shepherd-bird in the many-coloured coat? Mami's raiment — how doth it become her son?"

He looked, of course, like a young god. The effect he produced was only to be expected, and his eagerness to bring it about did anything but strengthen Jacob's resistance. We shall do well to recognize at once the irresistible guile by which he had finessed the garment out of Jacob's hands into his own. And this was scarcely done when the thing was on his back — put there by two or three deft and assured motions which themselves evinced great skill in the art of dressing. How well it set him off! It covered his head and wrapped his shoulders, the silver doves glittered and the gay embroideries glowed, it fell in folds about his youthful form and made him look taller than he really was. But not only so. For the festal garment became his face to such an extent that nobody who saw him could have disputed the popular verdict upon his charms. It made him so lovely and so well-favoured that the phenomenon was actually no longer quite earthly; in fact it bordered on the supernatural. Worst of all, the likeness to his mother — her look, her forehead and brows, the shape of her mouth — had never stood out so clearly as in this dress; poor Jacob was so smitten by it that his eyes overflowed, and he thought nothing else than that he was beholding Rachel in Laban's house, on the day of the fulfilment.

It was the mother-goddess who stood there before him smiling, in the boy's lovely guise, and asked:

"I have put on my coat — shall I take it off?"

"No, no, keep it, keep it!" the father said. The young god rushed away. Jacob lifted his brow and his hands, and his lips moved in prayer.

THE NIMBLE RUNNER

THE EXCITEMENT was tremendous. The first to see Joseph in his coat of many colours was Benjamin; but Benjamin was not alone. Joseph found him in the women's tent, with the concubines. He entered their quarters in his new finery and said: "Greeting to you all. I have just come by chance to look in on my little brother. Lo, thou art here, my Beni; I only wanted to ask how you all are. So you are combing flax? And Turturra is helping? Do any of you know the whereabouts of old Eliezer?"

"Turturra" meant "little one" — Joseph often called his brother by this Babylonian pet name. And Turturra was already giving vent to long-drawn-out cries of admiration. Bilhah and Zilpah chimed in. He wore his robe with a careless air, drawn up and thrust through the girdle of his smock.

"What are you all chirping about and making eyes like cart-wheels? Oh, you mean my garment, Mami's veil *ketonet*? I am wearing it for a while, Israel having made me a present of it a few minutes ago."

"Joseph-el, thou sweetest lord, son of the favourite," cried Zilpah. "Hath Jacob then given thee the coat of many colours, in which he first received Leah my mistress? He hath done wisely and justly indeed, for the heart melteth within one at the sight so that one could

not imagine another wearing it. One of those now on a journey perhaps, the offspring of Leah, from whom Jacob lifted it for the first
time? Or my Gad or Asher, born on Leah's lap? The very idea maketh
one to smile, albeit ruefully."

"Joseph-ja, loveliest one!" Bilhah cried. "Nothing more beautiful
can be conceived than thy looks in this robe! One is tempted to pros-
trate oneself at the sight; and especially I, who am only a handmaid,
though sister and favourite to Rachel thy mother, to whom by the
power of Jacob I bore thy elder brothers Dan and Naphtali. They
too will fall down before thee or be like to it, when they see the
youth in their mother's wedding garment. Go then swiftly and show
thyself to them unawares, while they are yet all innocence and dream
not that our lord hath chosen thee. Likewise thou shouldst go across
country and show thyself to Leah's six red-eyed sons, that thou
mayest hear their exulting shouts and their hosannas may strike upon
thine ear."

It is almost incredible, but Joseph did not notice the thick layer
of bitterness and spite which coated the women's words. His self-
absorption, his blissful though none the less reprehensible self-confidence made him deaf and unresponsive to any warning. He sucked
up the honey of their words, quite convinced that he deserved it all.
It never occurred to him to look beneath the surface. But precisely
therein lay the blame. Indifference to the inner life of other human
beings, ignorance of their feelings, display an entirely warped attitude toward real life, they give rise to a certain blindness. Since the
days of Adam and Eve, since the time when one became two, nobody
has been able to live without wanting to put himself in his neighbour's
place and explore his situation, even while trying to see it objectively.
Imagination, the art of divining the emotional life of others — in
other words, sympathy — is not only commendable inasmuch as it
breaks down the limitations of the ego; it is always an indispensable
means of self-preservation. But of these rules Joseph knew nothing.
His blissful self-confidence was like that of a spoilt child; it persuaded
him, despite all evidence to the contrary, that everyone loved him,
even more than themselves, and that therefore he needed to take no
thought of them. To pardon such conduct as his on the score of his
beautiful eyes would be weakness indeed.

But with Benjamin the thing was different. Here for once complete whole-heartedness was in place. He cried out:

"Jehosiph, thou heavenly one! Not as in our waking life but as in
a dream it seemeth; and the Lord hath wrapped thee in a garment
of splendour, woven full of coloured lights and hath put upon thee
a mantle full of pride and glory. It must ravish the soul of a little
urchin like me. Go not, I pray thee, to the sons of Bilhah, and leave

the sons of Zilpah yet in ignorance a little. Stay by thy little brother, that I may admire thee the more and look my fill!"

All that Joseph might take at its face value; it rang true. Even so, he might draw a warning from his little brother's simple words. For we cannot help feeling that Benjamin was afraid of the meeting of the brothers and wanted at least to delay it. Joseph himself possessed enough instinct, if not enough insight, not to appear straightway before the children of the maids in his new garment. With the exception of a few underlings, who saw him in passing and outdid themselves in adulation, hand-kissings, and obvious envy, the only person who beheld him that day was Eliezer. The old man fell into a prolonged nodding, which might be taken for approval, but equally for a sort of general contemplation of mankind and his destiny. He then, with an abstracted and godlike mien, began to enlarge upon his so-called recollections, those which the sight of the garment called up in him. How, that is, he, Eliezer, had once as wooer in Isaac's stead brought Rebecca up out of Harran's underworld, and when they had reached the upper regions and the bridegroom was approaching, had shrouded her in the veil. And for what reason? That Isaac might know her. For how should he have known her and lifted her veil unless she had veiled herself beforehand? Eliezer's countenance, as he talked, was so unmoved that it looked like a false face, which you could perhaps take off and show another one beneath it. "A marvellous thing, my child," said he, "hath Israel given thee; for in the veil is life and death. But death is in life, and life in death, and he who hath learned this truth hath penetrated the mysteries. The sister-mother-bride had to unveil herself and stand naked at the seventh gate of hell and in the face of death. But when she returned again to the light she veiled herself, in token of life. Lo, the seed-corn, how it sinketh to earth and dieth, that it may arise again for the harvest time. For the sickle lieth already close to the blade — the sickle which waxeth in the darkness of the moon as young life, yet is it death and taketh the manhood of the father that it may assume new lordship over the world; and from the harvest of the sickle rolleth the fruit of life and death. Thus the veil signifieth life after the unveiling in death, and therewith already possesseth knowledge and death, since after all in knowledge is procreation and life. A great thing hath the father given thee, he hath given light and life when he veiled thee with the veil which thy mother had to leave behind her in death. Therefore cherish it, my child, that no one rend it from thee and that death may not know thee."

"Thanks, Eliezer," answered Joseph. "Many thanks, wise old servant, who in Abram's train struck down the kings and toward whom the earth did spring! How weightily thou speakest of all these mingled things, of veil and sickle and seed-corn; rightly too, since these things are related and are one in God, though to our eyes they are embroidered many-fold upon the veil. But now, as for me, I will take off my coat and cover me with it upon my couch, that I may sleep beneath it as sleepeth the earth beneath the world-mantle of the stars."

Thus he did. And thus they found him sleeping, the children of the maids, when, instructed by their mothers, they entered the tent which he shared with them. The four brothers, Dan, Asher, Gad, and Naphtali, stood at his bedside, and the youngest, Asher the sweet-tooth, barely twenty-two, held the lamp to lighten his sleeping face and the gay robe that covered him.

"Behold," he said, "there hast thou it! It is precisely and no other than what the women said, when they told us that the coxcomb had shown himself to them in his mother's *ketonet passim.* He hath spread it out and sleepeth beneath it the sleep of the just, with a sancti-monious expression on his face. Is there any more doubt? Our father, poor man, hath given it him, beguiled thereto with honeyed words. Oh, for shame! For we feel equally angered over this abomination that hath come to pass; and it is Asher who taketh our combined anger into his mouth and spitteth it out over the head of this offence that here sleepeth — may it give him at the very least bad dreams!"

He greatly loved, this Asher, to be of one mind and heart with his fellows and to strengthen his sense of unity by expressing it in words which should do full justice to the common opinion; this gave him a feeling of warmth and comfort even in the midst of his rage, and the characteristic harmonized with his humid lips and eyes and his love of eating. He went on:

"So I have cut pieces out of live rams and sheep and eaten them, have I? He told that to our dear, good, credulous father, who then gave him the *ketonet* as a reward for his lying. And so with each of us: he hath charged each one of us with some fault, and now lieth there under the garment gained by his falsity and the evil reputation he hath given to us. So then, brethren, let us stick together and be of one mind in our wrath, and let me name him by some name that shall ease all our hearts — such as 'thou — puppy'!"

He had wanted to call him, quite simply, "thou dog"; but at the last minute a fear of Jacob made him soften the epithet.

It was Dan who spoke next. He was seven-and-twenty, the same age as Leah's Simeon. He wore a tight-fitting embroidered smock; had no moustaches, but a pointed beard, and his prominent eyes lay close together at the root of a crooked nose. "It may be," said he, "that I am called snake and adder, forsooth, because I am said to be somewhat malicious. But what is that compared with him who lieth here? He is a monster in the guise of a lovely youth. Cursed be that lying shape, which maketh the folk to ogle and gape and bewitcheth our father utterly! I would I knew the charm which could force him to reveal his true form!"

Then Gaddiel took his turn, a sturdy fellow, a year older than Asher, with an expression of rude honesty. He wore a sugar-loaf cap and had a military air, due to the baldric round his short coat, and the breast-plates he had sewn upon it. His red and sinewy arms, with their stubby and equally sinewy hands, stuck out from the short sleeves of his coat. "Let me advise thee, Asher," he said, "to take heed to thy lamp, that thou lettest no oil drip down, to awaken the sleeper with its smart. For if he awake, he shall feel my fist straightway in his jaw, and it will swell till he seem to have a lump of flour in it, and so remain till nine days from tomorrow, as sure as my name is Gad. For I am hot with rage and sick to death at sight of him and of the coat beneath which he sleepeth, the price of his shameless betrayal of our father. I am no coward; but something, I know not what, rumbleth in my belly and admonisheth me out of my entrails. Here we stand, we brethren, and there lieth he — the rascal, the coxcomb, the puppy, the turner of heads — and he hath the coat. Are we to bow down before him? I keep hearing those words 'bow down' as though some cursed insect kept buzzing them in mine ear. Therefore it is that my hand itcheth to be at his ear; that would be the right treatment for him and would satisfy the hatred in my belly."

The straightforward Gad had uttered much profounder things than any that Asher — despite all the latter's need to consolidate opinion and achieve unity through the spoken word — had even tried to reach. For Asher's one thought was to call out affection and produce solidarity by expressing only what was simple and easy to grasp. Gad took more trouble. He struggled to get at the things that tormented and frightened them all, things which lay far beneath the simple emotions of envy and rage. He wrestled to find words for obscure memories, anxieties, apprehensions; for some shadowy train of associations which should combine the essence of manifold conceptions — such as first-born, deception, exchange, world-dominion, brother-vassalage — and which, while not properly recognizable as either past or future, as legend or as prediction, yet perversely evoked the words "bow down," "they shall bow before thee." The others felt greatly, even inexplicably challenged by the power of Gad's words. Especially the long, lean, stoop-shouldered Naphtali, who was already shifting from one foot to the other, so greatly had Gad's words made him tingle in all his limbs with eagerness to be off. He had the instinct of a carrier-pigeon, and his calves had for long been fairly twitching and his body shaken. His imagination was completely controlled by the conceptions of space and separation. He regarded space as his most familiar enemy, and himself as the appointed means of its conquest. In other words, he felt it his mission to even out those differences in men's knowledge which were effected by distance. When anything happened in the place where he was, he immediately connected it in his mind with some distant spot where nothing of it was yet known. And to be in such a state of so to say vegetable unconsciousness was intolerable in Naphtali's eyes; it made him quiver with the urgency of striding out with his legs and of loosening his tongue to set things right; in order wherever possible to equalize the sum of man's information by spreading it from where it existed to regions still disgracefully ignorant. The place in point at present was that where the rest of the brethren were; straightway, and before any of the others, he thought of it. They were in ignorance, they knew naught, thanks to the deplorable working of space and distance, but they must learn speedily. In his mind Naphtali was already running.

"Listen and hearken, brethren, children and friends," he began, in his quick, soft voice. "We are standing here and see with our eyes what has happened, we are on the spot. But at this very moment in the vale of Shechem the red-eyed brothers are sitting about the fire, chatting of this and that and the other, of anything save the fact that Jacob hath exalted Joseph's head, to their own undoing. For they know it not, and however loud their shame crieth aloud, theirs and ours, they hear it not. But shall we then content ourselves with the advantage we have, saying: 'They are distant and thus foolish, for to be distant is to be foolish,' and let it go at that? No, for we must tell them, that it may be there as it is here and that they may not go on living as though it were not. Send me, send me! I will speed to them across country and give them word that shall lighten their darkness and make them to shriek aloud. But to thee, hastening back again, will I announce how they shrieked."

The others were of the same mind. The red-eyed brethren must hear the truth. Indeed it almost touched them more closely than it did the present four. Naphtali knew the road. They would tell their father that he had gone on pressing business. He scarcely slept for impatience and saddled his ass before dawn; when Joseph awaked under his world-mantle he was already far off, and knowledge well on its way to the distant brethren. Nine days later, exactly on the day of the full moon, they all returned to Hebron, together with the messenger — Reuben, Simeon, Levi, Judah, Issachar, and Zebulun — and peered dourly about them. Naphtali said that the twins — Simeon and Levi, so called because they were only a year apart — had roared like bulls on hearing the news.

OF REUBEN'S ALARM

JOSEPH did have enough sense and understanding not to appear at once before his brothers in the coat, though he had the greatest desire to do so. A faint doubt whether they really did love him so much more than themselves that they would have no other feeling than pure joy at his elevation made him lay aside the garment for the time and greet them in his everyday clothes.

"Greetings, dear sons of Leah, brothers and strong men," he addressed them. "Welcome to our father's house. A few of you at least I will kiss."

And he went among them and kissed three or four on the shoulder, they standing like images and not touching him at all, save Reuben, now a man of twenty-nine years. Without any particular change of feature he lifted one heavy hand when he felt Joseph's kiss on his shoulder, and stroked the lad's hair lightly, almost furtively. He was tall and heavy and wore a skin apron, with leather straps wound round his powerful legs. His face was red, clean-shaven, fleshy, and muscular; it had a pugnacious expression, yet the rather blunt profile suggested both dignity and self-consciousness. His low brow was darkened by a mop of curly black hair. Jehudah, the next elder son, but three years younger than Reuben, was quite as tall, but walked with a stoop and showed traces of suffering about his nostrils and lips. He wore a cloak, in which he wrapped his hands, and a close-fitting cap from which a shock of red-brown hair streamed out like a mane Red-brown too was the heavy, pointed beard and the narrow, drooping moustaches that covered the thick red lips. These last spoke of sensuality, but the nose, finely shaped and delicately arched, which drooped over them, suggested some gift of the spirit; while the eyes, large and prominent and heavy-lidded, like a stag's, had a melancholy cast. Like several of his brothers and half-brothers, Judah was already a married man. Reuben, for instance, had wooed a daughter of the soil and with her raised up several children to Abram's god, among them the lads Hanoch and Pallu, whom Jacob sometimes trotted on his knees. Simeon had married a maid of Shechem, named Bunah, carried off as booty when they had sacked the town; Levi a worshipper of Yahu, who passed for a grandchild of Eber; Naphtali a young female whose origin Jacob somewhat arbitrarily derived from Nahor, brother of the Chaldæan; and Dan quite simply a Moabite woman. It would not have been possible to compass marriages entirely irreproachable from the religious point of view; and in Judah's case Jacob had perforce to be satisfied with any which might bring the youth some tranquillizing and steadying influence, for his sex life had from the first been marked by disorder and suffering. His relations with the love-goddess kept him strained and unsatisfied, he writhed beneath her lash and was her unsubmissive slave — hence the deep conflict in his soul and the lack of unity in his character. His intercourse with the consecrate and the whores in the temples of Ishtar brought him into contact with the follies and abominations of the worship of Baal and the shamelessness of Canaan; and nobody, not even Jacob himself, could find that more repugnant than did Judah, he being of a religious temperament, seeking a pure and reasoned worship and from the bottom of his heart abominating Sheol and the follies and mysteries with which the folk defiled themselves. Moreover he felt he had good reason to think well of himself; for since the stumbling of Reuben and the night when the twins had plundered Shechem, there was something to be said for the view that Judah, the fourth son, was next in line for the blessing and the bearer of the promise. Of course, these things were not said among the brethren, no claims being put forward save in the form of their common ill-will against Rachel's son.

Through one of his shepherds, named Hirah, from the village of Adullam, Judah had got to know a Canaanite man called Shuah, and Shuah's daughter found favour in his eyes. He married her, with Jacob's consent. Up to now she had borne him two sons, whom he brought up in the fear of God. But just as Ishmael had resembled Hagar, so these sons were like their mother and not like their father. At least Judah thought and said so, saying that they were an evil generation, children of Canaan, of the bad breed of Baal, Sheol, and Melech, though it was possible that the trouble was not all of Shuah's daughter's making. She was now pregnant with a third child, and Judah already looked forward with misgivings to its appearance. In short, the shadow of melancholy lay in Judah's eyes, but that did not make him better-natured nor lead him to stroke Joseph's hair, as Reuben had done. He said:

"Well, writing-man, is it seemly of thee to come thus before thy elders, in an ordinary smock full of ink-spots, they having been long away and now are returned home? Carest thou so little to please us, when thou art so ready to curry favour among common folk with fine garments? We hear thou hast fine and dazzling raiment in thy chest, worthy of a prince's son. Wouldst thou insult us by being so niggardly with it at our homecoming?"

Next spoke Simeon and Levi, the twins, leaning upon their heavy cudgels; their eyes were hot, their tattooed breasts glistened with oil, their whole bodies were marked with scars. They burst out together into a short bellowing laugh. Said one: "Since when do wantons walk about unveiled?" And the other: "How long since have the temple whores ceased to cover their eyes?" He spoke unmindful of Judah, who started at the words.

"Oh, thou meanest my picture robe?" questioned Joseph. "Hath our brother Naphtali told thee on the way how your father Jacob hath had his heart moved toward me? But in thy goodness forgive my lack" — and he made the most charming obeisance before them all, with his arms crossed. "It is hard," said he, "to hit upon the right thing in doing and in leaving undone, and whatever he doth a man falleth into sin. I thought, in my folly: shall I spread myself before my elders? No, for I should come before them in humility, so that they take no umbrage at my arrogance, but love me instead. And lo, I have done foolishly, for I hear that I should have made myself fine in your honour. But believe me, on the evening of the roast meal, when you have washen yourselves and put on feast-day garments, I will sit on Jacob's right hand in my *ketonet* and you shall see our father's son in all his glory. Shall it be a promise?"

Again the savage twins gave a roar of laughter. And the others bored deep into his eyes trying to distinguish between simplicity and impudence in what he had said, and not succeeding.

"A golden promise!" said Zebulun. He was the youngest, and tried to look like a Phœnician. His beard was trimmed to a round shape and he had a mop of short curls. His upper garment was patterned in gay colours and ran over one shoulder and under the other, showing the undershirt. His mind was set on the sea, so that he had liefer not been a shepherd. "A delicious promise, like a sacrificial cake of fine meal made with honey — a promise which I should like to thrust back down thy throat that thou mightst choke upon it!"

"Come, come, Zebulun, these are but coarse jests," Joseph replied, casting down his eyes and smiling as though embarrassed. "Hast thou heard them from the galley-slaves at Gaza and Ascalon?"

"He hath called my brother Zebulun a drunken galley-slave," said Issachar, twenty-one years old, tall and heavy-limbed, nicknamed "the bony ass." "Reuben, thou hast heard, and thou must take it up, if not with thy fist, as I could wish, yet with such words as shall make him remember."

"Thy words are inexact, Issachar," Reuben replied, in the high, effeminate voice which men of his powerful build may sometimes have. "He hath not called him that, but merely asked if he heard the words from such a one. It was pert enough as it was."

"I understood him to say that he would like to choke me with the sacrificial cake," put in Joseph, "which would have been blasphemous to boot, as well as very unfriendly. But if he did not say that or mean it, then of course I will take back what I said too."

"And now," concluded Reuben, "let us go our ways, that our coming together may not end in tauntings and misunderstanding."

They separated, the ten and the one. But Reuben followed Joseph and called him by name. He stood before him, just they two alone, Reuben on his leather-bound legs like heavy columns, and Joseph gazing up with polite attention into the hard-fleshed face, which expressed both embarrassment and dignity, since he was conscious both of his strength and of his proneness to err. His eyes, with their inflamed lids, were close to Joseph's; they lost themselves in Joseph's face or rather they stopped at it and returned into themselves. He kept kneading his brother's shoulder with his powerful right hand, as he was wont to do when he talked with anyone.

"Thou keepest the robe, young one?" asked he, moving his lips, but scarcely opening his mouth.

"Yes, Reuben, my lord, I will keep it," answered Joseph, "for Israel hath given it me, when he was merry from play."

"Did he defeat thy men?" Reuben asked. "Thou playest shrewdly and discreetly, for thou art practised by Eliezer in all sorts of mental exercise, which can stand thee in good stead in a game. Doth he often win?"

"Now and again," Joseph said, showing his teeth.

"When thou wilt?"

"It doth not depend on me alone," replied the other evasively.

"Yes, yes, so is it," thought Reuben to himself, and his gaze grew even more brooding. "That is the deceitfulness of the blessing-bearer, and his way of deceiving. He must hide his light under a bushel, that it light him not to his harm, and the others must boast of more light than they have in order to keep up with him." He looked at his half-brother. "Rachel's child," he thought, "what charm he hath! The people are right to smile upon him. He is precisely tall enough and casteth up his lovely eyes at me and mocketh within himself, of that I am certain, as I stand here before him like a tower, disproportioned, tall and unwieldy, with this loutish body of mine, the veins of it fairly bursting with strength, so that I forgot myself like a young bull with Bilhah, not even looking to see if we were alone. Then with innocent malice Joseph goeth and telleth Jacob and I am undone. For he is wise as the serpent and gentle as the dove, and thus one should be. Malicious in his innocence and innocent in his malice, so that innocence becometh a danger and malice a sign of grace, and these are the unmistakable marks of the blessing, and one could do naught against it, even if one would, and one would not at all, for there is God. With a single blow I could stretch him out upon the earth so that he rose not again. The strength that overcame Bilhah were enough for that, and the thief of my first-born right should feel it as a man, even as Bilhah felt it as a woman. But what would that avail me? Abel would lie slain, and I should be he whom I understand not, that is Cain. For how can one act against his conviction

and open-eyed strike down the pleasing one, because one is oneself
unpleasing? I will deal not against mine own conviction, I will be fair
and just, as is more conformable to my soul. I shall betray it in nothing. I am Reuben, my veins full of strength, Leah's first-born, Jacob's
eldest son, and head of the twelve. I will make no lovesick faces at
him, nor humble myself before his charms. It was silly of me even
to have stroked his hair, silly and weak. I will lay no hand upon
him, one way or the other. I stand before him like a tower, clumsy
if you like, but in dignity."

The muscles of Reuben's face were drawn as he asked: "Thou hast
wheedled the coat out of him, hast thou not?"

"He promised it me of late," answered Joseph, "and when I reminded him of the promise, he gave it to me out of the coffer and
said: 'Keep it, keep it.'"

"Ah, so thou hast reminded him and begged him for it. He gave
it thee against his will, tempted by thine. Knowest thou that it is
against God to misuse the power that is given thee so that he willeth
unjustly and doth what he regretteth?"

"What power have I over Jacob?"

"Thou liest in asking. For thou hast over him Rachel's power."

"Then have I not stolen it."

"Nor earned it."

"The Lord saith: 'I favour whom I favour.'"

"Thou'rt impudent," Reuben said, with drawn brows, shaking
him slowly to and fro as he held him by the shoulder. "It is said of
me that I am unstable as water and that sin is not far from me. But
what is far from me is impenitent frivolity like unto thine. Thou
boasteth of thy God and fleerest at the heart that lieth in thine hand.
Dost thou know that thou hast brought the old man into anguish
and stress by beguiling him of the coat?"

"Into what sort of stress, big Reuben mine?"

"I know already thou liest, since thou askest. Hast thou then such
joy in being able to do this? In stress over thee, who art his dearest
without desert, according to the wish of his heart that is so proud
and yet so soft. He was blessed before Esau, his twin; yet hath he
not suffered enough, in that Rachel died a furlong from Ephron, and
in the matter of Dinah his child, and even through me — which I
mention myself, seeing that thou wast about to remind me?"

"Not so, big Reuben. For I had not in mind that day when thou
didst sport with Bilhah so that thou wast to the father in his wrath
like to a hippopotamus."

"Hold thy tongue! How canst thou mention it, when I took it
out of thy mouth and said it before thee? Always thou thinkest of
new sorts of lies, saying thou thinkest not thereupon when thou
expressly spakest of it. Is it that which thou learnest from the tablets

of stone and connest when thou and Eliezer study the wisdom of the temple? Thy lips move, I know not how, having been carved in this wise by the Creator, and thy teeth glisten between them. But the words that come forth are naught but insolence. Have a care, have a care, my young one," he said, and held him so that Joseph rocked to and fro on heels and toes. "Have I not saved thee ten times out of the hands of the brethren and from the wrath of those who trod Shechem under their feet for the sake of the ravished one — ten times and more, when they would have given thee a good pummelling for telling tales to the father about 'cutting pieces from the living flesh' and more of the same sort? And for that thou wouldst go and beguile our father of the coat, while we are pasturing far away, and wouldst in thy folly defy the wrath of nine brothers if not ten? Tell me who thou art, and how much is thine arrogance, that thou makest thyself different from us all and walkest as one set apart? Fearest thou not that thy conceit will draw down about thee the dark clouds out of which the lightning striketh? Hast thou no gratitude at all for those who mean kindly by thee, that thou causest them anguish? Thou'rt as one who climbeth high in rotting branches and laugheth at those who stand beneath and call to him in fear lest the branch break and he fall and his bowels gush out."

"Put me down upon the ground, Reuben, and hearken to what I say. For I am grateful that thou speakest a word for me against the brethren's ill-will. And I am grateful too that thou holdest me thus and shakest me about, both together. But now set me upon my feet that I may speak. I cannot collect my thoughts being so shaken about. But now, standing here upon my feet, I will collect them, and sure am I that thou wilt in thy justice grant me right. I have not got the coat by stealth or stealing. For he promised it to me by the well, and ever since I have known of his purpose to give it to me, to keep. But as I saw him, our gentle-hearted father, somewhat at odds with his own will, I held to what he had said and easily got him to give it to me — give, I say, and not present, for mine it was before he gave it me."

"How so thine?"

"Thou askest? I will answer. For who was it from whom Jacob first lifted the veil and made a promise concerning it at that hour?"

"It was Leah."

"Yes, actually, it was. But in deeper truth it was Rachel. Leah was only arrayed in it, but Rachel was the owner of the robe, and she kept it to her death, a furlong from Ephron. But since she died, where is she now?"

"Where the earth is her portion."

"Yes, actually again. But in very truth it is otherwise. Knowest

thou not that it is in the power of death to change the sex, and that
Rachel still liveth for Jacob though in another form?"

Reuben started back.

"I and my mother are one," Joseph said. "Knowest thou not that
Mami's garment is likewise her son's and that they wear it by turns,
one in the other's place? Name her and thou namest me. Name what
belonged to her and thou namest what is mine. Well then, whose is
the veil?"

He had stood there quite simply and modestly as he spoke, his
eyes cast down. But when he had done he suddenly directed his
wide-open gaze upwards upon his brother's face. Not as though he
wanted to force his view aggressively upon the other, but rather as
though he were silently offering his soul to be looked into; as though
he were receiving the astonished and blinking stare of Leah's red-
eyed son deep into the unfathomableness of his own gaze.

The tower shook. Big Reuben shuddered. What did the lad mean,
what was he trying to express, what was the origin of it all? Reuben
had taunted him with his arrogance — and now he was sorry, for
he had had his answer. He had asked in his wrath who the lad
thought that he was — ah, would that he had not done so! For now
he had heard, heard so riddlingly that it made him shiver all the
way down his back, long as it was. Was it chance that had shaped the
words in the boy's mouth? Had he meant to play upon the divine
and make use of it to justify his own duplicity, or . . . or — and
this *or* gave rise in the very marrow of Reuben's being to the same
horror of which Brother Gaddiel had complained as they stood at
Joseph's bedside. Only it was stronger in Reuben, a profounder
shock, and it was accompanied by a sort of admiration, a gentle,
even tender amazement and terror.

We must try to understand Reuben. He was not the man to be
unique in misconstruing the significance of the question as to who
one was, in whose footsteps one walked, to what past one's present
had reference, in order to give it reality. Joseph had given evidence
— in so monstrously presumptuous a way as to make Reuben shudder.
But the magic of the word, whereby the uppermost was turned
undermost, an unforced and flexible and perfectly genuine use of
language to work enchantment, brought before Reuben's eyes in
brilliant clarity the footsteps in which his younger brother walked.
He did not go so far at this moment to think of Joseph as a veiled
god-goddess; that we must not suppose. But yet his love was not
very far from becoming belief.

"Child, child," said he, in that piping voice out of his powerful
body, "spare thine own soul, spare thy father, spare the light thou
walkest in! Put it under a bushel, that it may not light thee unto thine

undoing." He took three backward steps, with drooping head, then
turned and walked away.

But at the evening meal Joseph wore the coat. The brothers sat
there like graven images. Jacob was full of fears.

THE SHEAVES

WHEN these things had happened, and after many days, it came about
that they were cutting the wheat in the vale of Shechem; it was the
time of the harvest and of joyous and sweating labour up till the
day of the first fruits, when they made offering of leavened bread
of the new wheaten flour, seven weeks after the spring full moon.
For the late rains had been plenteous, but the hatches of the sky
were early closed, the waters ran off, and the land dried. Marduk-Bel,
the sun, the triumphant, drunk with his victory over the dripping
leviathan, ruled flaming in the heavens and sent up golden spears into
the blue. Even at the turn between the second and the third months
so great was the ardour of his sovereignty that there might have
been fears for the sowing but that a wind sprang up, the welcome
approach of which was first scented by Zebulun, sixth son of Leah,
who said:

"My nose is pleasantly assailed by this wind, for it bringeth moisture from afar and beareth on its wings the refreshing dew. Lo, now,
as I always say, what great good cometh from the sea! Better it were
to dwell by the edge of the green vast and close to Sidon, rather than
to tend the sheep, which pleaseth me but little. For upon the wave
and on the shapen plank one can reach folk who wear tails, and a
lighted horn upon their foreheads. Or to such as have ears so great
as to cover the whole body, and others whose forms are covered
with grass. A man from the port of Khadati told me of all this."

Naphtali agreed with him. It would be good to exchange news
with those grass-grown folk; for most likely neither they nor the
ear-lapped nor the tailed creatures had the least notion what went
on in the world. But the others dissented and would hear nothing
of the sea, even though it brought the moisture-bearing wind. Those
were subterranean regions, full of monsters of the prime; Zebulun
might just as well express admiration for the desert. Simeon and Levi
expressed themselves with peculiar force, in this sense; they were
crude but religious, and at bottom they did not much care for the
shepherd's life, preferring something more exciting, though they
stuck to this one for the sake of the succession.

The harvesting, beginning with the reaping of the barley, was a
welcome change for them all; they sweated blithely in their hopes
of profit, as one does at this season; even their relations with Joseph
sensibly improved, as he worked by their side cutting and binding —

until by his irresponsible chatter he ruined everything again and reduced them to extremes. All which I shall relate in due course. As for Jacob, these seasonal joys touched him but little, though all the district yielded to them with gusto, his own sons swinking in the midst of the sweating peasantry. Rather he had a dampening effect upon the gaiety, even without appearing on the field, which he seldom did. This time he came once, by way of exception and at the request of Joseph, who had his own reasons for making it. But on the whole Jacob troubled little about the sowing and mowing, carrying on his bit of farming as it were without looking at it and only out of prudence, not inclination. Nay, he felt not only indifference but even disinclination to the whole sphere, the religious hostility of the moon shepherd toward the duty which the sunburnt farmer paid the earth. The harvest time was even, in a certain sense, an embarrassment to him, in the sense that it made him draw profit from the cult of fertility which the children of the country paid from spring to spring to the sun-gods and love-women of their temples — a cult abhorrent to his soul. He was rather ashamed of drawing profit from it, and closed his lips tightly when he heard the thanksgiving hymns of the workers bringing home their sheaves.

After the barley harvest he ordered the wheat to be cut for the provisioning of his own people; and as every pair of arms was needed, Eliezer having also taken on a few hired hands for the harvest weeks, Joseph's studies with the latter were interrupted, and he too, in his own exalted person laboured from early morn to dewy eve in the fields. He attacked the bearded grain with the sickle, gathering the stalks together with his right hand; he bound the sheaves with straw and helped the brethren and the hands to load them on carts or hang them on asses to be brought to the threshing-floor. We must recognize that he did all this gladly and willingly, not looking upon it as an imposition, and in simple modesty; but it is also true that his attitude toward the work was in flat contradiction to certain revelations of his inward life, which he permitted himself precisely at this very time. In any case it would have been easy for him to get Jacob's permission not to appear on the field, yet he never thought of doing so. Partly because he liked the work, but even more because it brought him into contact with the brethren, and he felt pride and pleasure in working among them, helping them, hearing them call him by name; all that was literally true. Labour upon a common task improved relations between him and them, it uplifted his heart, it made him happy. However inconsistent all this may seem, it was the truth; the seeming contradictions cannot do away with the fact that he loved his brothers; that, however senseless and even deluded it may seem, he counted on their love and expected some advantage from it — for the unhappy lad little imagined how much he asked.

The field work tired him very much, and he often took short naps; was asleep, indeed, at the midday hour which found all the sons of Jacob, save Benjamin, gathered to rest and eat, beneath a brown awning stretched over crooked poles. They had broken bread and talked, squatting on their heels. Each of them wore for all clothing a leather apron; their bodies were burnt by the ardour of the sun, which blazed down between fleecy clouds upon the half-harvested field. Here and there, the sickle had made breaches in the golden host, leaving patches of stubble dotted with leaning sheaves and bounded by low walls of rubble which served to divide Jacob's land from that of the peasants. At a little distance stood the hill which served his people for a threshing-floor; laden asses were on their way thither and men were on top, using pitchforks to separate the stalks and toss them down before the oxen.

Joseph then, likewise in his working apron, his skin glowing from the sun, was asleep in a squatting posture, with his head on his arm. When he lay down, he had in all simplicity begged Issachar, the bony ass, who sat next to him, to lend him one of his knees to prop up his head. But Issachar had inquired whether he would not also like him to scratch his head and to keep off the flies; and then curtly bade him to be his own pillow. Joseph had laughed and taken it in good part, resigning himself to sleep without the desired prop. He found it elsewhere, as we shall see. But for the moment nobody was paying him any attention, only Reuben glanced now and again at the sleeper's face, as it lay turned toward him. It was not in repose; the forehead was drawn, the lips twitched, and the partly open mouth moved as though to speak.

Meanwhile the brethren had been discussing the pros and cons of a new sort of implement which had come into use of late, the thresh-ing-table. It was drawn by oxen and had pointed stones on the under side, which tore the ears. It was undeniable that it saved time. But some of them said that the winnowing afterwards was harder work than if the grain had been thoroughly trodden out by means of oxen. Also they spoke of a threshing-cart used by many of the peasants; it ran on rollers and was fitted with sharp iron plates. At that point Joseph roused and sat up.

"I have had a dream," he said, looking round upon the brethren and smiling as though in surprise.

They turned away their heads and went on talking.

"I have had a dream," he repeated, and rubbed his hands across his brows as though still dazed, smiling pleasantly as he gazed into space; "such a vivid and wonderful dream!"

"What is that to us?" retorted Dan, suddenly turning his promi-nent eyes upon Joseph. "Better is it to sleep without dreams, if thou needs must sleep, for dreams, so they say, are not refreshing."

"Would you like to hear my dream?" asked Joseph.

Nobody answered. One of them — it was Jehudah — went on with their discussion in a tone which was itself a proper reply to such a question.

"It is needful," he said, in a clear, detached voice, "to keep the iron blades very sharp, as otherwise they do not cut but crush and the grain cometh not fully out of the ear. But consider if we can rely upon the labourers, especially the hired hands, to sharpen them regularly. And then, if the little wheels, on the other hand, are very sharp, they cut the grain and so cometh it that the meal . . ."

Joseph listened awhile to the talk passing over his head. But finally he interrupted and said:

"Forgive me, brothers, but I feel drawn to tell you this dream which I have had. It was not a long dream, but so real and marvellous that I desire not to keep it to myself, but from my heart I yearn to put it before each of your eyes, that ye may laugh for joy and slap your thighs."

"Hearken," said Judah, and shook his head. "What aileth thee that thou troublest us with matters that concern us not? For what do we care about thine inward workings or the ferment of thy dreams or what riseth from thy belly to thy head after eating? It is not seemly to speak of it, and it concerneth us not at all; therefore be quiet!"

"But it doth concern you," Joseph eagerly cried. "It concerneth you all, for you all come into it and so do I; and my dream is so full of meaning and marvel that you might well sit with your heads in your hands and think of naught else for three days long."

"Shall he tell us it then, in few words, without more ado, so that we may know it?" Asher asked. People with a sweet tooth are often very inquisitive — and indeed they were all curious and liked well to hear stories told, and the fact and fable, the legend, dream, song, and story of primitive time.

"Very good, then," Joseph said with satisfaction, "if you like, I will tell you my vision, which is worth hearing on account of its meaning alone. For the dreamer shall not interpret his dream, but another shall do it for him. If any of you dream and ask me, I will tell him the meaning; it costeth me naught, for the Lord giveth it to me for the asking. But with mine own it is different."

"Dost thou call that a few words?" asked Gad.

"Listen, then," Joseph began. But at the last moment Reuben would have prevented him. He had been watching the owner of the veil all this time, and his mind misgave him.

"Joseph," said he, "I know not thy dream, for I lay not with thee in thy sleep, there thou wast alone. But meseemeth it were better each one should be alone with his own dreams and thou shouldst keep thy dream to thyself, that we may all go to work."

"We were at work," Joseph snatched up his words, "for upon the field saw I us all together, us sons of Jacob, and we were harvesting the grain."

"Marvellous," cried Naphtali. "That is a dream like to an unreal vision, forsooth, and thy dreams are remote from us, and very fantastic and high-coloured indeed!"

"But it was not our own field," went on Joseph, "it was the field of another, very strange to us. But we spoke not of it. We laboured together without speech and bound the sheaves after cutting the stalks."

"That is a great dream before the Lord," said Zebulun. "A vision incomparable. For of course, thou dolt, we should have bound first and cut afterwards. Must we hear it all, even to the end?"

Some of the brethren had already got up, shrugging their shoulders and making ready to leave.

"Yea, hear it up till the end," cried Joseph, lifting his hands. "For now cometh the marvel: each of us was binding a sheaf and we were twelve, for Benjamin too was with us in the field and bound his little sheaf with you in a circle."

"Do not talk rubbish," ordered Gad. "Why 'with you' in a circle, when thou meanest 'with us'?"

"Not so, Gaddiel, for my meaning is far otherwise. For ye made up the circle, the eleven of you, and were binding, but I stood in the centre of the circle and bound my sheaf."

He paused and looked into their faces. They had all lifted their brows and tipped back their necks so that the Adam's apple stood out as their heads swayed slightly. Misgiving, amazement, mockery, and warning were expressed in all their attitudes. They were waiting.

"Hearken now how it fell out and how wonderful was my dream," said Joseph again. "When we had bound our sheaves, each one his own, we left them and went away, not speaking and as though we had nothing more to do there. But we had gone only twenty paces or so together when lo, Reuben turned round to look and motioned backward with his hand to the place where we had been. Yea, Reuben, it was thou. We all stood and looked, shading our eyes. And behold, my sheaf arose there in the middle and also stood upright, and your sheaves stood round about and made obeisance to my sheaf. And mine stood upright."

There was a long silence.

"Is that all?" asked Gad, breaking the silence, in a low, curt voice.

"Yea, for after that I awaked," replied Joseph, rather crestfallen. His dream had disappointed him in the telling, though in the dreaming it had been strange and gratifying and even a little frightening, especially the part about Reuben pointing silently behind them. However, the narration had sounded meagre, even foolish; in Joseph's

opinion it could not have impressed any of his hearers, and his view
was confirmed by Gad's words: "Is that all?" He was ashamed of
himself.

Silence had fallen again, broken by Gad with an oath, so suppressed
that only the first syllables were anything but a whisper.

Joseph lifted his head, he took heart. It would seem that his dream,
even as he had told it, was not without any effect upon his hearers.
"Is that all?" had been crushing, but the oath was full of encouragement. It meant all sorts of things, it meant no little, it meant: "What
the devil!" and that sort of thing. He looked into their faces. They
were all pale, and vertical folds stood between their brows — altogether they made a singular impression indeed, as when one gnaws
his under lip, or his nostrils go in and out like gills, as many of theirs
did. Their breath came fast and uneven, so that it sounded like an
irregular, tenfold snorting. And all this went on under the awning
where they sat, and if regarded as the effect of his narrative might
well have made young Joseph feel disturbed.

And so it did, to a certain extent, but in a way that made the scene
seem to him like a continuation of his dream, having, for all its actuality, the same extraordinary character of uncanny joy and joyful
uncanniness. True, the effect upon the brethren was not very happy,
but it was obviously much stronger than Joseph had dared to hope;
so that he was evenly balanced between the sinking feeling he had
at sight of them and gratification that his tale had after all not
missed fire.

He felt no different when — after the lip-biting and the snorting
had gone on for some while — Jehudah burst out in a hoarse, throaty
voice:

"A more disgusting piece of nonsense have I never heard in all
the days of my life!" For such words could only be an expression,
not very happy indeed, of Jehudah's amaze.

Then came another pause, filled with pallid silence and gnawing
of lips.

Then: "Thou brat! Thou jackanapes! Thou poison toad! Thou
stinking fart," roared Simeon and Levi both at once. They could not
even speak in turn and make a sort of couplet as they usually did, but
all mixed up together, with crimson faces and veins standing out on
their foreheads. Actually they displayed the phenomenon reported
of them at the time of the plundering of Shechem; for the hair on
their chests rose up and bristled like porcupine quills as they roared
with one voice:

"Thou peacock, thou swaggering puppy, thou blackguardly fool!
What care we what thou hast dreamed and what seen behind thine
eyelids, thou shameless, thou thorn in our flesh and stone of stumbling to our feet, thou stench in our nostrils — that we should inter-

pret it unto thee? 'Bow down, bow down' — ah, the falsehood and vanity of what thou dreamest and forcest us honest men to hear! So our sheaves stand in a circle and flop down before thee, but thine standeth upright? It turneth the stomach as nothing I have before heard in this world. Thou foul, thou filthy sink of abominations, so thou wouldst play the master and lord with us by filching the *ketonet* behind the backs of thy elders! Thou trickster and thief of the birthright! But we will teach thee all about standing and bowing down, and will show thee thy masters, and thou wilt name to us thy name and wilt perceive thine own shameless lies!"

Thus bellowed the twins. And when they had done roaring, all the ten left the shadow of the awning and went out on the field, still red and pale, still gnawing their lips. But Reuben, as he went out, said to Joseph: "There hast thou it, my lad." Joseph still sat awhile, pondering, upset and cast down because the brethren did not believe in his dream. For this was the thing he had grasped of all they had said, that they did not believe him — had not the twins several times used word like "lies" and "vanity"? He asked himself, sadly, what he could do to prove to them that he had not said a word too much, but only quite honestly related what he had dreamed in their very presence. If they only believed him, he thought, their violent humour would abate; for surely he had shown brotherly good feeling in telling them what God had revealed to him in a dream, that they might likewise rejoice and with him discuss the significance of the matter? It was impossible that they should take umbrage at his confidence in them and the bond between them, which had been the whole ground of his revealing God's mind concerning him. True, the dream displayed him exalted over them; but that they, to whom he had always, in one sense, looked up, could find that fact intolerable would have been such a disappointment to him that he simply could not have thought of it. At all events, he perceived that the harmony between them was destroyed for the day; he did not go back to the field, but went home and found his little brother. To him he confided that he had told the brethren an altogether modest dream, comparatively speaking, the content being such and such. But that the brethren had not believed it and the twins had been furious — although by comparison with the eagle dream, of which he had not mentioned a single syllable, this one was modesty itself.

Turturra was glad that nothing had been said of that monstrous dream, and for his part displayed such delight over the dream of the sheaves that it entirely made up to Joseph for the fact that it had missed fire with the elder brethren. The little one jumped and laughed at the thought of his own small sheaf bowing down with the rest — it so precisely corresponded to his feelings.

THE COUNCIL

MEANWHILE the ten stood on the meadow in the light of the setting
sun and took council together in anger and in fear, leaning on their
tools. At first they had silently acquiesced in the interpretation given
by Simeon and Levi to the dream — namely, that the little liar had
made up the whole thing himself. Indeed, they preferred this interpretation, for it fortified their own inward position. It had been Judah
who had wanted to explore all the possibilities; and he it was who
pointed out that Joseph might actually have so dreamed as he reported himself to have done and not drawn a long bow at all. After
that they all explicitly reckoned with the possibility and thereupon
subdivided it into two: namely, that the dream, if actually so dreamed,
had indeed come from God — this they naturally regarded as the
greatest conceivable catastrophe; or, contrariwise, that it had nothing
to do with God, but had originated entirely in the insufferable vanity of Joseph, which, overweeningly nourished by the gift of the
ketonet, had given rise to these visions. Reuben's contribution to the
discussion was that if the dream came from God, then there was
nothing for it but to pray — to God, of course, not to Joseph. But
if, on the other hand, it had been born of conceit, they they could
afford to shrug their shoulders over it and leave the dreamer to his
folly. In the end he reverted to the probability that the lad had
childishly made up the dream and deserved a beating for the same.

Big Reuben, in short, proposed that Joseph be beaten for telling
lies. At the same time, he recommended that they all shrug their
shoulders — which proves that he was not very serious about the
thrashing, for you cannot thrash with any conviction while shoulder-
shrugging. And from this one might deduce that Reuben wished
to believe in the second interpretation in order to discount the first
and distract the minds of the brethren from thinking of it. Reuben,
in short, was afraid that belief in the theory that God had sent the
dream would not at all incline the brethren to humility and self-
restraint, but rather to conduct infinitely more drastic than mere
thrashing. They were not at all prepared, he felt, to view the matter
objectively and let their attitude be governed according as Joseph
had dreamed out of sheer conceit or had really had a revelation of
God's plans for him. For their words seemed to show that in the
latter case they did not find his conduct one whit the less worthy
of vituperation. If the dream really came from God and was a token
of great preferment, then of course there was nothing to say against
God — as little as there was to say against Jacob for his honourable
weakness. With them the whole point was Joseph. If God had
actually preferred him over them and made their sheaves flop down

before his, it was because God too had been made a fool of, even as Jacob, and by the same means: namely, the double-dealing by which he supplanted them in the father's affections. God was great, He was holy and irresponsible — but Joseph was a viper. It is clear — and Reuben saw it too — that their notion of Joseph's relation to God perfectly agreed with his own view; they considered it the same as his relation to their father. Indeed, it had to be so, for proper hate is only generated on a basis of some common belief.

Reuben was afraid of this train of thought. Therefore he did not try to defend Joseph by persuading the brethren that God sent him the dream. Rather he wanted to convince them that the lad had humbugged them and ought to suffer for it — while shrugging their shoulders. But he was, in reality, as little capable as the others of shrugging his shoulders. For even more, perhaps, than they, Reuben knew in the pit of his stomach the sinking sensation to which the downright Gad had first referred and of which now not only the four sons of the maids but all the ten were painfully aware. It was a horror springing from mythical and prophetic associations wrapped about such ideas as bartered birthrights, world-domination, and fraternal submission; Reuben suffered in his soul more even than the others on the score of them; except that they did not put him in a fury of rage against the lad who was the source of his oppression, but only gave rise to unnamable emotions toward the innocent babble of the chosen one, as well as an overpowering sense of surrender in the face of destiny.

"It would have been the last straw if he had said: 'bow down,'" Gaddiel said through his clenched teeth.

"He said 'made obeisance,'" remarked the bony Issachar, who loved a quiet life and for its sake was willing to make sacrifices. If he dissociated himself at all for the brethren on this occasion it was because of this pacific leaning of his.

"I know," answered Gad. "But he may only have said that to play a trick, and anyhow, it is just as disgusting either way."

"Not quite," Dan answered; he was a stickler by nature and never failed to stickle conformably to his nature. "To make obeisance is not quite so much as to bow down. We have to admit that it is really less."

"Why do we?" yelled Simeon and Levi, determined to bear witness to their savage stupidity, let the occasion be foul or fair.

Dan and some of the others, including Reuben, insisted that to make obeisance was rather less than to bow down. The former might happen not out of inner conviction but as an empty and formal gesture. One made obeisance only on occasion, whereas bowing down was a constant attitude of the heart which honestly took cognizance of facts as they were; and thus, as Reuben explained, one might make obeisance out of caution and shrewdness, without really

bowing down, or, on the other hand, might actually bow down and
yet be too proud to make the gesture of obeisance. Jehudah disagreed.
He did not think that the position could be sustained, for that they
were dealing with a dream, in which making obeisance was only the
picture representation of the attitude for which Reuben would reserve the words "bow down." At this point young Zebulun interpolated that they were now doing the very thing to which Joseph
had shamelessly invited them and which all of them had refused to
consider: namely, they were blithely engaged in interpreting his
shameful dream. The comment was so exasperating that it broke up
the meeting, amid shouts from Simeon and Levi that it was all stuff
and nonsense and that one neither bowed down nor made obeisance
before such insults, but only took steps to get rid of the author of
them, as had been their course at Shechem. Thus the council came
to an end without other result than unappeased bitterness.

SUN, MOON, AND STARS

AND Joseph? He had no notion, of course, of the torment which his
dream was causing to the brethren, but thought of nothing else than
that they had not believed him and of how he could carry conviction — conviction in two directions, both as to the actuality and the
truth of his dream. How should he best bring this about? Insistently
he asked himself the question, and later was surprised that he had not
known the answer, but had to be given it or rather that it had given
itself to him. That is to say, he had another dream, or rather he had
the same dream, only in a form so much more splendid that the confirmation was more impressive than if he had dreamed exactly the
same dream the second time. He was sleeping under the open starry
sky, on the threshing-floor, where he and some of the brothers and
hands often spent the night at harvest time, to guard the grain which
had not yet been threshed and put into the pits. Very likely — though
this is in no sense an explanation of the source of dreams — the character of his had been influenced by the starry heavens spanned above
him, also by the companionship in sleep of those whom he wished to
convince. Still another element was introduced by the content of
his day, the fact that he had spent hours receiving instruction upon
the last things from old Eliezer under the tree of wisdom: upon
world-judgment and blessing-time, the final triumph of God over
all the powers to which the peoples had so long sent up the smoke
of incense; upon the triumph of the Saviour over the pagan kings, the
planetary powers and gods of the zodiac, whom He was to subdue
and cast down, shut up in the underworld, and mount above them
to a universal and glorious world-dominion. Of all this Joseph
dreamed; but in such confusion that he childishly substituted his

own person for that of the eschatological god-hero, and beheld or rather perceived himself, the boy Joseph, as the actual sovereign and ruler of the whole world as it revolved through the zodiac. He perceived, I say, rather than beheld this, for it would be impossible to reduce such a dream to an ordered narrative, and in repeating it he had to put it into the simplest and shortest words in order to express the feelings it gave him rather than to narrate it as a series of events. All which did not help to make it more acceptable to the hearer.

He began to be concerned over the form and manner of his communication, directly he roused from his dream and sat up in joyful possession of such striking confirmation of the earlier vision. His concern had to do with the question whether the brethren would give him a chance to tell them another dream – it seemed unlikely. Even the first time it had been a toss-up whether they would not refuse their attention or simply get up and leave the tent before he was done. A second opportunity appeared to him the more unlikely in that they had not seemed to derive unmixed pleasure from the first.

It behoved him to find some means to enforce them; and even as he lay upon the threshing-floor Joseph conceived how this might be done. In the morning he went to his father, as he usually did, since Jacob desired to see him at the beginning of each day, to look into his son's eyes, assure himself of his well-being, and give him his blessing for the day.

Joseph said: "A right good morning to thee, my father and lord! Lo, here is a new day born of the night and methinketh it will be a hot one. One followeth another like to a string of pearls, and life is joyous to this child of thine, especially at this season, when we bring in the harvest. It is lovely upon the meadow, whether we toil or whether we rest; and men grow to understanding of each other in common tasks."

"What thou sayest is pleasant unto mine ears," Jacob replied. "So it goeth well with you all on the field and the threshing-floor and you come together in the Lord, the brethren and thou?"

"Excellently well," answered the lad. "Aside from small differences of opinion such as each day of necessity bringeth forth, and the division of the world displayeth them, everything is in the best of order. For honest words, even though they may be rude, help to clear up error, and then harmony ruleth once more. I wish that our father might but witness it. For thou art never there, and often do we regret it together."

"I do not love the field work."

"It is natural. And yet what a pity that the workers get no sight of the master and no feeling that his eye is upon them, especially the hired hands, upon whom is no reliance. My brother Jehudah complained to me only lately that they do not sharpen the little wheels on the threshing-cart, so that they crush the grain instead of cutting it. But thus it is when the master's eye lacketh."

"I must admit the justice of thy reproach."

"Reproach! May God preserve my tongue from such! It is but a request, proffered by thy offspring in the name of the eleven. And nobody suggesteth that thou shouldst share our labours, the service of the soil, the work of Baal. But only our midday rest, when the sun is high in the heaven and we break bread in the shade and talk among ourselves, we sons of the one and the four, and one or another may relate some jest or dream that he hath had. Often we nudge each other with our elbows and say how fine it would be to see our father's head in the midst of the circle."

"Ah, well, I will come, for once in a way."

"Hurrah! Come then today and rejoice the hearts of thy sons. The work neareth its end, there is no time to lose. So it shall be today, then? I will say naught to the red-eyed ones, nor blab it out to the sons of the maids, for it shall come to them as a surprise. But thy child will hug to himself in secret the knowledge to whom they owe it and who hath so cunningly and loyally schemed to bring it about."

Such, then, was Joseph's device. It so came about that midday of that very day found Jacob sitting under the awning on the field, after he had inspected the grain-pits and the threshing-floor and tested with his thumb the sharpness of the little wheels. The ten were amazed. For the last few days the dreamer had not shared their noontide rest; now he was here again, with his head in his father's lap. Naturally, he ought to be here, if the father was; but what was it that had brought the old man, so suddenly? They sat stiff and silent, all decently covered out of respect to Jacob's views. The latter was surprised to find none of the hearty good feeling which according to Joseph's account reigned at the harvesting. Perhaps its absence was due to respect for the father and master. Even Joseph had not much to say. He was afraid, even though he lay in his father's lap and had the protection and the hearing for his tale which that implied. He was, indeed, troubled by his dream and the results which might flow from it. He could say in a sentence all there was to say, there would be nothing left. If Gad were to ask: "Is that all?" he would be a beaten man. Of course, the briefness of his tale had the advantage that it would all be out at once, before anyone could stop him. But the large lines and scant ornament might be the very things which would defeat his purpose.

He almost let slip his chance, in the end, for they were all so bored that they were tempted to break up early. Even the signs of departure were not enough to conquer his misgivings, and perhaps nothing at all would have happened if Jacob had not helped him out by saying genially:

"I hear you tell each other stories at the rest hour — recite and so on — did I not?" They stared in bewilderment.

"Yes, yes," Joseph cried, starting up, "funny stories and dreams. Sometimes we are full of them. Do we know anything new?" he asked brazenly, looking round the circle.

They kept on staring at him and saying nothing.

"But I do," said he, and sat up on Jacob's lap with an absorbed look. "There is a dream, which I dreamed last night on the threshing-floor; father and brethren, ye should hear and be amazed. I dreamed," he went on — and then stopped. There was a curious writhing of the limbs, a spasmodic lifting of the neck and shoulders, a twisting of the arms. His head drooped, the smile upon his lips seemed to deprecate and extenuate the sudden whiteness of his eyes. "I dreamed," he repeated, in a sort of gasp, "and I saw in my dream, this I saw: I saw the sun, the moon, and the eleven *kokabim* waiting upon me. They came and bowed down before me."

Nobody stirred. Jacob, the father, kept his eyes severely cast down. It was very still; but in the stillness came an evil, mysterious, and yet distinct sound. It was the gnashing of the brethren's teeth. Most of them kept their lips closed, but Simeon and Levi showed their teeth as they gnashed. Jacob heard the gnashing. It is hard to say whether Joseph grasped its significance. He was smiling quietly and dreamily to himself, with his head on one side. It was out, let them do what they chose about it. Sun, moon, and stars, eleven in number, had attended him. Let them look to it. Jacob looked timidly round the circle. It was as he expected: ten pairs of eyes were fixed wildly and importunately upon him. He summoned up his powers. And sitting at the boy's back he addressed him, as harshly as he could:

"Jehosiph! What sort of dream is this thou hast dreamed, and how couldst thou dream so unsavoury a thing and tell it unto us? Shall I and thy mother and thy brethren come and worship thee? Thy mother is dead and therewith beginneth the crackbrainedness, but is far from ending it. Shame upon thee! By all human reckoning, this stuff thou hast served up to us is so preposterous that it might just as well have been nothing but *aulas-aulalakaula* and done just as much good. I am grieved in my soul that thou, with full seventeen years, and despite all the enlightenment of the written word and reason which thou hast enjoyed by my permission through instruction from my servant Eliezer, hast made no greater progress in the understanding of the divine than to allow thyself to dream that which dishonoureth thee and to play the buffoon before thy father and brethren. Let this be the punishment meted out to thee. I would punish thee more severely and perhaps pull thy hair till thou didst cry out for pain, were not thy prattle too childish for riper minds to take note of it or the man settled in years be tempted to repay thee with great harshness. Fare thee well, sons of Leah! And greetings after the meal, sons of Zilpah and Bilhah!"

Saying which he stood up, behind Joseph, and went hence. The reproof had cost him much to utter; he only hoped that it had satisfied the brethren. If any real anger had spoken in it, that could be only on the score that the lad had not told the dream to him alone, instead of being so mad as to make the brethren witness of the telling. Had he done it of set purpose to cause the father embarrassment, Jacob thought, he could not have found a better device. That he would certainly tell him when they were alone, since he could not have done it now; probably he understood how shrewdly the lad had used the brothers as protection against himself, and himself as protection against the brothers. For he even suppressed a smile in his beard, as he went homewards, over the cleverness of this double-dealing. He certainly felt the irritation he had expressed on the score of the boy's soul, as well as the anxiety over his tendency to dreams and prophetic spasms; but both anger and anxiety were swallowed up in the yearning, half-credulous satisfaction which filled him when he thought of Joseph's presumptuous dreams. Quite absurdly, he prayed God that the dream might have come from Him — which was utter nonsense, seeing how highly unlikely it was that He had had anything to do with it. And tears of sheer tenderness came into his eyes at the thought that his son's innocent prattle might represent, though vaguely and uncomprehendingly, actual premonitions of future greatness. Ah, poor weak father-heart! He might well have been angry to hear that he and the brethren would come to bow down before the good-for-nothing — that was perplexing for him to hear, for did he not adore him?

As for the brethren, hardly was Jacob gone than they flung as one man into the open, but after a few paces out into the meadow stood still together and took stormy council. Big Reuben spoke, he told them what was to be done. Away! That was the thing. Unanimous departure from the paternal hearth, voluntary banishment. That, Reuben said, would be dignified and impressive behaviour and the only possible answer to such detestable treatment. Away from Joseph, was what he had in mind, in order that no disaster might befall the lad. Of course he did not express his feelings, but put his advice entirely in the light of a reproach and a protest.

That very evening they came before Jacob and told him they were going. A place where such dreams were told, without other risk than at worst of getting one's hair pulled, was no place for them; they had nothing to lose by leaving it. They had helped mightily with the harvesting, now they would go to Shechem: not only the six, but also the four, in fact all ten. For the meadows of Shechem were fat and fertile, and there, in unchanged if also in unrewarded loyalty, they would pasture their father's flocks, and the camp at Hebron should know them no more, now that it was become a place of such high dreaming. They made obeisance and bowed down, they said (suiting the action to the words), in taking reverent leave of their father and lord. They needed not to fear that their going would give him pain, since it was well known that Jacob would give ten for one.

Jacob bowed his head. Did he begin to fear lest the ascendancy of the emotions which, basing on an exalted model, he permitted himself, was being taken amiss in the high place of its origin?

Chapter V

THE JOURNEY TO THE BROTHERS

THE CHALLENGE

WE have been told how Jacob bowed his head when he heard the embittered brethren announce their departure from his hearth. From then on he lifted it but seldom. It was now the season of parching heat; at no other time in the year did the sun's rays so cruelly scorch the land, for the moment of its waning was at hand. This was the solstice, the season in which the true wife had presented Joseph to Jacob, in the month of Tammuz. Yet even so Jacob's spirit was wont to suffer beneath the blackened desolation of this quarter of the circle; that he suffered now might be explained in the same way. But no. The true ground of his depression was the unanimous departure of his sons. I should be saying too much if I asserted that this had given Jacob great pain. In his heart he truly did "give ten for one"; yet it was quite another matter to reckon with the objective fact, to realize that the brothers' notice to quit was decisive; and that he, Jacob, would be left with two sons instead of twelve, a tree lopped of its branches. It was a blow to his dignity, first of all; but also it put him in an embarrassing position before his God, and he inquired of himself how much these actions of his went counter to the plans of the Lord of the Promise, and how great was the accounting he had invited upon his own head. For He that ruled future things, had He not taken care that not all matters should go after Jacob's heart and he be fruitful in Rachel alone? Yes, He had made him fruitful against his own will, and even those unwanted sons from the unloved wife were themselves the fruit of the blessing and bearers of destinies unknown. Jacob was well aware that his elevation of Joseph was a piece of arbitrary self-indulgence, which might easily come to clash with the vast designs of God and so reveal itself as culpable presumption. Indeed, it seemed already to have done so; for though Joseph's folly may have been the immediate occasion of the catastrophe, and though Jacob had suffered in chiding him, yet the father well knew who it was who must pay for this folly, before God and man. In contending with Joseph he contended with himself. The boy had been only the medium of whatever mischief had been done; the real culprit was Jacob's own loving heart. It had not availed to hide it from himself; for God knew it, and one hid not himself before God. For the truth was, therein lay the inheritance of Abram, it meant no more than that one did not give false evidence in matters known to God.

Such were the mental struggles, in the time after the grain harvest, which slowly shaped Jacob's decisions. He had conceived evil in his heart; now that heart must conquer its weakness by seeing to it that the spoilt darling who had been the medium of the harm should also be the medium of the healing. He would treat the lad with a little severity, would lay a responsibility upon him by way of doing penance himself.

Seeing him at a distance he summoned him rather peremptorily: "Joseph!"

"Here am I," answered the boy, and was beside him at once. He was glad to be called, for since the departure of the brothers his father had spoken to him but little. Besides, that last meeting with the brethren had left him, even in his folly, with a feeling of discomfortable anxiety.

"Hearken," said Jacob. Some obscure motive made him feign absent-mindedness; he blinked repeatedly and drew his beard through his hand. "Tell me if I am right in thinking that thy elder brothers are grazing the sheep together in the vale of Shechem?"

"Yes, of a surety," responded Joseph; "for it seemeth to me too, if my memory erreth not, they desired to go together to Shechem to tend thy flocks, on account of the fat meadows there and because this valley will not hold all of thine."

"So it is," confirmed Jacob, "and it is for this reason that I called thee. For I hear naught of the sons of Leah, and of the sons of the maids all knowledge is hidden from me. It is not known to me how it standeth in the meadows of Shechem; whether Yitzchak's blessing was upon the summer lambing or whether my herds are afflicted with swelling and with liver fluke. For my children thy brothers, I know naught of them nor hear whether they exercise our pasture rights in peace, in that district where, as I mind me, serious things once came to pass. It giveth me to think; and in such thoughts I resolved to send thee to them to greet them from me."

"Here am I," cried Joseph again. He flashed his white teeth at his father, hopped up and down, and stamped with his heels, on fire to be off.

"When I consider," went on Jacob, "that thou enterest into the eighteenth year of thy age, methinks it is time to put thy manhood to some sterner test than thou hast known. And therefore I am resolved to stir thee up to this mission; that thou leavest me for thy brothers, for some short space; to inquire of them concerning all that of which I am ignorant, and to return to me, with God's help, after ten or nine days and tell me what thou hast learned."

"Verily, here am I," cried Joseph again, enraptured with the idea. "My father's words are golden and silver. I will make a journey across the land, I will visit the brethren and look after things in the vale of Shechem, and all that will be the greatest pleasure. Could I have wished for my heart's desire, it would not have been other than this."

Jacob said: "Thou dost not go to look after things. Thy brethren are men enough to do that themselves and need not a child. Moreover, that is not the sense in which I send thee. Rather shalt thou bow before them with all seemliness and the forms of courtesy and speak thus: 'I am come some days' journey to greet you and ask after your well-being, from my own desire as well as at my father's bidding, for our wishes in this matter are one.' "

"Give me Parosh to ride; he is long-legged and hard, very strong-boned, and like to my brother Issachar."

"It speaketh for thy manliness," answered Jacob after a pause, "that thou rejoicest over thy mission and regardest it not as strange to go away from me for a number of days, so that the moon shall change from a sickle to a half-round before I see thee again. But say to thy brethren: 'The father willed it.' "

"Shall I have Parosh?"

"I am indeed minded not to deal with thee softly, but according to thy age. Yet the ass Parosh I will not give thee, for he is balky, and his intelligence doth not keep pace with his fire. A much better choice is white Hulda, a friendly and careful beast, also smart to look at; when thou journeyest abroad thou shalt ride her. But that thou mayst know that I expect somewhat of thee, and that the brothers may know it too, it is my command that thou makest the journey alone, from here to the meadows of Shechem. For I will give thee no servant along with thee nor let Eliezer ride at thy side. Thou shalt travel independently and shalt tell the brethren: 'Alone I come, upon a white ass, to visit you, according to our father's will.' Then may it be that thou needest not to ride back alone, but that the brethren may journey with thee, some or all. At least such is my second purpose in this order."

"That I will contrive," promised Joseph; "I make myself bail to bring them back to thee; indeed, I will be guarantee therefor and say to thee I come not again unless to bring them to thee."

Thus Joseph pranced about his father, prattling away heedlessly and giving praise to Yah that he was to travel by himself and see the world. He ran off to Benjamin and to Eliezer the old man to tell them all. Jacob, looking after him, nodded his head. For he perceived that if one could speak of a challenge, it was directed toward himself and nobody else. But was he not doing rightly and acting as his inward

responsibility for Joseph bade him act? He would not see the lad for
several days; it seemed to him sufficient penance; and he refused to
speculate as to what the upper spheres would have considered due
severity. He reckoned with a failure of Joseph's mission; that is, he
realized that the latter might return without the brethren. That they
might return without him was so frightful a thought that his conscious mind did not even deal with the possibility. But since things
always turn out otherwise than as one had thought, we might forestall destiny by our fears and apprehensions as with an exorcism; and
therefore fate paralyses our imagination, that it may deal its crushing
blows unhampered by our preventive spells.

The needful preparations for Joseph's journey put Jacob in mind
of his own past and of that fateful day when Rebecca got him ready
and he left, after the transfer of the blessing which she had conceived
and carried through. And his soul was full of the solemn emotions of
recurrence. Certainly the comparison was far-fetched enough. For
his was by no means the heroic part which Rebecca had played when
she deliberately sacrificed her own heart, assumed responsibility for
the rectifying deceit, and then, fully conscious that she would probably never see him again, sent away the beloved son into a strange
land. The theme admitted of some variations. True, Joseph too was
leaving home on account of his outraged brethren's wrath; yet he
was not flying from the wrath; Jacob was sending him as it were into
Esau's arms. It was the scene by Jabbok ford which Jacob had in
mind and whose recurrence he was so eager to bring about: the outward humiliation, the outward reconciliation which was inwardly so
full of reservations; the smoothing over of obvious discords, the
achievement of apparent harmony. How different from all that was
Rebecca's resolute assumption of the guilt! Jacob's aim in sending
Joseph was the impossible one of putting things back where they
were; but since it was already plain that that could not be done, the
result would simply be a resumption of the game, in which the pieces
were Jacob's weakness, Joseph's blind conceit, and the brothers'
deadly grudge, and which would have led, in all probability, to the
same result.

But it held so far good, that the favourite was being sent a journey
on account of fraternal discord; and Jacob conformed to the pattern
by fixing the time of Joseph's departure for the earliest dawn, before
sunrise, it having been so in his own case. But when the parting took
place, Jacob — or rather Rebecca, for he was playing the mother's
rôle — held the traveller in long embrace, murmuring blessings against
his cheek; took an amulet from his own neck and hung it round the
boy's, pressed him to his heart again and again, and all in all behaved
as though Joseph were to be gone for years or for ever, seventeen
days or more distant Naharain-wards, into the unknown, whereas

instead, amply supplied with provisions, he was setting out, to his
own great joy, on safe roads and to travel no farther than to Shechem.
Which shows that a man can behave out of all proportion, as measured by his own knowledge; while from the point of view of the
still unknown destiny his conduct may turn out to have been only too
suitable. There may even lie some consolation therein, when we
learn the real state of the case. Thus men should never take leave of
each other lightly; for then, should the worst happen, they can say
to themselves: "At least I did press him to my heart!"

Father and son took leave in the dawning, standing at the stirrup
of white Hulda, who was laden down with good things and adorned
with glass beads and bright worsted flowers. The leave-taking, of
course, was only the last of the many counsels, admonitions, warnings which had gone before. Jacob had instructed the boy in his
route and the well-known stages on it, just in his mother's way; had
warned him of the dangers of overheating and sudden cold; given
him the names of folk and brethren in the faith in the various villages
at which the traveller might spend the night; and sternly forbade
him, when he touched at the city of Urusalim and saw at Baal's temple the dwellings of those consecrate to Ashera, who lived and moved
and had their being in her, to permit himself the smallest speech with
them. Above all he enjoined him to behave with particular courtesy
toward the brethren. It could do no harm, he remarked, were Joseph to fling himself down seven times before them, addressing them
frequently as lords, when they would in all likelihood resolve to dip
their hand at once in the bowl with him and not to go from his side
for the rest of their lives.

Much of all this Rebecca-Jacob repeated afresh in the grey morning, before he allowed the youth to fling his leg over his ass, chirrup
to it, and ride off northwards. Jacob even went a piece alongside the
lively Hulda, as she curvetted in the high spirits of the dawn. But he
could not keep it up long, and stopped with an absurdly heavy heart.
One last gleam of Joseph's teeth as the lad looked laughing back and
waved his hand; then his son's figure was hidden by a turn in the
road. Joseph had ridden away, he saw him no more.

JOSEPH JOURNEYS TOWARD SHECHEM

THE BOY, no longer under the father's eye, but pleasantly absorbed
in his own well-being, sitting far back on the crupper of his beast,
with his slim brown legs stretched out and his body leaning gallantly
backwards, trotted in the tender light of the morning sun through
hilly country, on the road to Bethlahma. He felt entirely in harmony
with the whole situation as he saw it, viewed with amused and indulgent forbearance the long-drawn-out character of Jacob's farewell,

and felt not a whit weighed down by the consciousness that at this first separation he had snapped his fingers at the parental concern.

Jacob, certainly, had expended himself in instruction and advice, forgetting neither precept nor warning. One thing only had he neglected; by reason of a singular and not quite innocent lapse of memory he had refrained from cautioning the boy on a certain matter, upon a certain subject, or object; nor did it again occur to his mind's eye until so horribly made present to his material sight. It was the *ketonet;* he had not told Joseph to leave it at home and Joseph had slyly and silently taken advantage of the lapse. He had it with him. He was so on fire to show himself to the great world in the garment that he had literally trembled lest the father at the last minute might think to forbid it. It is quite possible that he would in this case have lied to the old man, saying that the sacred embroidery lay in the chest, whereas in reality it was packed among his luggage. The milk-white Hulda was a charming beast, a three-year-old, wise and sweet-tempered, if also inclined to the harmless and engaging tricks which will sometimes betray the individuality of the dumb brute. She had eloquent velvet ears and a droll fuzzy forelock hanging down to the great soft, playful eyes, the corners of which were too prone to gather flies. From Hulda's back various supplies and requisites for the journey were hung on both sides: the goatskin full of sour thin milk to slake the thirst; and many-coloured baskets and earthen pots with oatmeal and fruit cakes, parched corn, salt olives, cucumbers, roast onions, and fresh cheeses. All this and more, designed for the refreshment of the traveller himself and for presents to his brothers, the father carefully inspected; only one thing he failed to examine, an object which since time immemorial had formed the most indispensable luggage on a journey: a circular piece of leather, sewn round the edge with metal rings, which served the traveller as table-cloth and as table too. It was a Bedouin invention, particularly in use by desert folk; they ran a string through the rings and hung it up as a bag for the journey. Joseph had done this too; and with thievish joy he had thrust the *ketonet* into this leather bag.

Since he had inherited it, he reasoned, since it was his own, why not show himself in it on his travels? The neighbourhood folk on road and field recognized him and joyfully called him by name. But after some hours' travel no one would know him; it would be well to show them, and not alone by the wealth of his provisioning, that a fine gentleman was riding by. And thus, the more so that the sun was rising too, he soon drew out the splendid garment and put it on in his own way, to protect his head; so that the myrtle garland which he wore rested not upon his hair, but upon the veil that framed his face.

On this first day he did not reach the shrine, to honour which had been another reason for wearing the *ketonet*. Jacob had admonished him with tears, also his own desire urged him, to stop there for sacrifice and prayer. It was only a furlong from Bethlahma, where he spent the night with a man of Jacob's acquaintance, a carpenter, who believed in God. Early on the second morning, after parting from his host, his wife, and their friends, he reached the spot. Hulda waited under the crutched mulberry tree while Joseph, arrayed in the bridal finery, performed his prayers and poured his libations at the stone which had been erected by the way — the memorial for God, who, seeing it, might be reminded of what He had once done at this place.

The stillness of the morning lay upon the vineyards and the rocky plots of ground; there was as yet no movement upon the Urusalim road. A little wind played carelessly in the shining foliage of the tree. The landscape was still; and silently the shrine where Jacob once had laid the child of Laban to rest received the oblations and prayers of her son. He put water by the stone, and raisin bread; kissed the ground, beneath which a life so ready and willing had gone down; and stood up again, to murmur formulas of veneration with lifted hands, and the eyes and lips which he had from the departed. Nothing answered from the depths. The past kept silence, folded in forgetfulness, unable to feel. Such of it as had survived and was here present was himself, who wore her bridal gown and turned her very eyes toward heaven. Why could the maternal spirit, residing still in his own flesh and blood, not have warned him against his fate? Alas, it could not speak, being held in bonds by childish folly and self-indulgence.

Joseph went on his way in great good cheer, upon made roads and along mountain paths. It was the smoothest journey in the world, its pleasantness unmarred by any mishap or unforeseen incident. Not that the earth exactly sprang to meet him. Rather it spread itself charmingly before his eyes and bade him welcome through the eyes and mouths of people whithersoever he came. He was strange to all, but his type is extraordinarily popular in these regions, and not alone by virtue of the veil did his appearance meet with favour and applause from all who saw him, especially the women. They sat suckling their babes, by the garish sunlit village walls, made of loose baked loam and dung; and the comfort afforded them by the suckling was heightened by the sight of the charming and well-favoured youth who rode past.

"Health to thee, thou sight for sore eyne!" they called to him. "Blessed be she who bore thee, heart's darling!"

"And to you all health," responded Joseph, flashing his teeth. "May your sons have dominion over many!"

"Thousand thanks," they called after him. "May Ashtar favour

thee. Thou art like to one of her gazelles." For they all swore by
Ashera and thought of naught but her service.

Many, again thanks to the veil, but also on the ground of his lavish
provisioning, actually took him for a god and were inclined to worship him. Still this was only in the countryside, not in the walled
towns such as Beth Shemesh, Kirjath Ajin, Kerem Baalat, or the like,
by whose ponds and city gates he chatted with the people, a crowd
of whom often gathered round him. He astonished and delighted
them by his urban culture, speaking of the magic numbers of God,
of the wonders of the pendulum, and of the peoples of the globe. He
told them too, in order to flatter them, of the harlot of Uruk, who
civilized the man of the forest; and in all that he said he displayed
such a charming sense of form and language that they thought
amongst themselves: he might well be the *mazkir* of a city prince
and a great king's admonisher!

He dazzled them by the knowledge of tongues which he had
gleaned with old Eliezer's help; speaking Hittite at the city gate with
a man from Hatti, Mittannian with one from the north, and a few
words of Egyptian with a cattle-dealer from the delta. It was not
much that he knew; but a clever man speaks better with ten words
than a fool with a hundred, and he knew how to create, if not in his
interlocutor, at least in the crowd, the impression of wonderful
polyglot facility. For a woman who had had a horrible dream he interpreted her dream for her at the fountain. She dreamed that her
little son, a three-year-old boy, had suddenly grown larger than herself and wore a beard. That meant, he told her, rolling the whites of
his eyes into view, that her son would soon leave her and she would
indeed see him again, but only after many years, as a grown man,
with a beard. . . . . As the woman was very poor and would quite
possibly be forced to sell her son into slavery, the interpretation had
a certain probability in itself, and all the folk marvelled at so much
beauty and wisdom embodied in the young traveller.

He always had many invitations and might have been a guest for
days at a time. But he did not pause longer than human courtesy
required, following as well as might be his father's directions for
the journey. Of the three nights which separated his four days of
travel, he spent the second in a house as the guest of a silversmith,
named Abisai, who had once visited Jacob and who, while not exclusively adhering to the God of Abraham, yet paid Him homage and
excused the fact that he made idols of the moon metal by saying that
after all he had to live. That Joseph granted him as a man of the
world, and slept under his roof. The third of the brief spans of darkness he passed in the open, in a fig grove where he made his bed; for
he had rested in the heat of the day and thus reached his third station
so late that he hesitated to enter the town. The same thing happened

the last night, as he neared his goal. For he had slept again under trees in the daytime, overcome by the power of the sun, and taken the road again only toward evening. Thus the second night watch had come on as he reached the narrow valley of Shechem. And from this moment on, in the measure that his journey had been easy and pleasant, by so much did it now seem altogether bewitched and bedevilled. He entered the valley and by the light of the moon that swam, a slender bark in the skies, beheld the walled town with citadel and temple lying on the slope of Garizim; and thereafter nothing went right, but everything wrong and wry to the extreme; Joseph, indeed, was tempted to connect the change in his fortunes with the person of the man who met him in the night before Shechem and made himself his companion for the last stage of his journey, leading up to the greatest change of all.

THE MAN ON THE FIELD

WE are told that "he was wandering in the field." But what is the meaning of that? Had his father expected too much of him, and did young Joseph order his affairs so badly that he went astray and wandered lost? By no means. Wandering is not necessarily going astray, and if one seeks what is not there, he does not need to stray in order not to find it. Joseph had as a boy spent several years in the vale of Shechem; the neighbourhood was not strange to him, even though his familiarity with it had the quality of dreams, and likewise it was night, with an ineffectual moon. He did not stray, he sought; and since he did not find, his seeking became a straying in space. In the darkness and stillness, leading his beast by the bridle, he wandered about among rolling stretches of meadow and plough-land, above which the mountain brooded darkly in the starlight, and he thought: "Where may the brothers be?" He came upon sheepfolds, of course, where the sheep slept standing; but whether these were Jacob's sheep was unknown, and there were no human creatures, the stillness being intense.

Then he heard a voice and perceived that he was addressed by a man whose approaching step he had not heard, but who nevertheless had overtaken him and was now by his side. If he had come toward Joseph the lad would have spoken; as it was, the stranger got in first, and said:

"Whom seekest thou?"

He did not ask: "What seekest thou here?" but simply: "Whom seekest thou?" and it may be that just this way of asking conditioned Joseph's rather childish and thoughtless answer. The lad was tired and confused, and his joy at meeting a human being in this accursed night walk was so great that he made the man, just because he was a man, the object of a simple and uncalled-for confidence. He said:

"I am seeking for my brethren. Tell me, dear man, I pray thee, where they graze."

The dear man took no offence at the simplicity of this request. He seemed to be in a position to disregard it and forbore to say to Joseph that his request was somewhat vague. He answered:

"They are not here, nor yet even in this neighbourhood."

Joseph looked at him in bewilderment as they went. He saw him quite clearly. This was not yet a man in the full meaning of the word, being only a few years older than Joseph; but taller, really tall; wearing a sleeveless linen tunic drawn loosely through a girdle, thus freeing the knees, and a little mantle flung back over the shoulder. His head, resting upon a somewhat thick neck, seemed small by comparison; his brown hair made an oblique wave that partly covered the forehead down to the eyebrows. His nose was large, straight, and firmly modelled, the space between it and the small red mouth very narrow, but the depression beneath so soft yet so pronounced that the chin jutted out like a full round fruit. He turned his head rather affectedly on his shoulder and looked across it at Joseph. His eyes were not unlovely, but half-shut, with weary, half-dazed expression, as of one politely forbearing to yawn. His arms were round, but white and rather weak. He wore sandals and carried a stick which he had obviously cut for a staff.

"Not here, then," repeated the boy. "How can that be? They said so definitely that they were all going together to Shechem when they left home. Dost thou know them, then?"

"A little," answered his companion. "As much as is needful. Oh no, very familiar with them I am not, indeed no. Why dost thou seek them?"

"Because my father sent me to them, to greet them and to see whether things go well with them."

"Indeed! Then thou art a messenger. Even as I. I often make journeys on foot with my staff. But also I am a guide."

"A guide?"

"Yes, truly. I guide travellers and open the ways for them; that is my business and therefore I spoke to thee as I saw that thou wast seeking as thou wentest."

"Thou seemest to know that my brethren are not here. But dost thou know where they are?"

"I think so."

"Then tell me."

"Art thou then so eager to see them?"

"Certainly I am eager for my goal, and that is my brethren, to whom my father hath sent me."

"Well, then, I will name it to thee, thy goal. When I came by this place the last time on my ways, a few days ago, I heard thy brethren say: 'Up, we will go to Dothan with a part of the sheep, for a change.'"

"To Dothan?"

"Why not to Dothan? It occurred to them and they did it. There is sweet pasturage in the valley of Dothan, and the people of the settlement on their hill are good for trade, they buy sinews, milk, and wool. Why art thou surprised?"

"Surprised I am not, for there is no matter for it. But it is an evil star. I was so certain I should find the brethren here."

"Thou art not much used to having things go against thy will? Thou seemest a mother's boy to me."

"I have no mother," replied Joseph in some annoyance.

"Nor I," said the stranger. "Perhaps a father's boy?"

"No matter for that," responded Joseph. "Rather advise me, what shall I do now?"

"Very simple. Thou goest to Dothan."

"But it is night and we are tired, Hulda and I. To Dothan, for so much I know already, is more than a furlong from here. With easy going it is a day's journey."

"Or a night's. Since thou sleepest under the trees by day, thou must take the night to reach thy goal."

"How dost thou know that I slept under the trees?"

"Asking thy pardon, I saw. I came past on my staff where thou layest, and left thee behind. Then found I thee here."

"I do not know the way to Dothan, especially by night," Joseph complained. "The father hath not described it to me."

"Rejoice then," said the other, "that I found thee. I am a guide and will lead thee, if thou wilt. I will open to thee the road to Dothan without price, since I must go thither myself; I will take thee the shortest way if thou wilt. We can take turns riding on thy ass. A pretty beast," said he, and looked at Hulda with his half-open eyes, whose gaze expressed a negligence and contempt out of harmony with his words. "Pretty as thyself. But its pasterns are too weak."

"Hulda," Joseph said, "is next to Parosh the best ass in Israel's stables. No one thinketh that her pasterns are weak."

The stranger made a wry face. "Thou wouldst do better," he said, "not to contradict me. It is foolish in more than one way, first because thou art in my care that thou mayest find thy brothers, and second because I am older than thou. These two reasons will be clear to thee. When I say thy ass hath frail pasterns, then they are frail; there is no occasion for thee to defend them as though thou hadst made the ass, when thou canst only step before him and name

him. And while we are talking about names, I should also like to beg
thee not to call the good Jacob Israel in my hearing. It is unfitting
and annoyeth me. Give him his proper name and leave these high-
flown titles alone."

Pleasant the man was not. He continued to speak across his own
shoulder with a weary politeness which seemed every minute about
to pass into an incomprehensible irritation. This inclination to ill
temper seemed to contradict his ready offer to help a complete
stranger; indeed, it took away half the effect, since he appeared to
be helpful against his own will. Perhaps he only wanted a lift to
Dothan. For he mounted the ass as they set out, and Joseph walked
alongside, chafing under the man's ill-will over the name of Israel.
He said:

"It is his title of honour which he got at Jabbok ford after his
victory."

"I find it absurd," the other retorted, "that thou talkest of victory,
where there can be no talk of anything of the sort! A proper victory, from which one cometh off halting all the rest of one's life,
carrying off, indeed, a name, but not that of him with whom he
wrestled! Moreover," he said suddenly, making his eyeballs roll
round in a circle in the most extraordinary way, "pay no heed to
me, but call thy father Israel if it please thee. It hath its justification, and my opposition was mere caprice. Likewise I note that I
am sitting upon thy ass," he added, making his eyeballs perform the
circuit once again. "If thou preferrest I will get off so that thou
canst mount."

A singular man. He appeared to regret his former unfriendliness;
yet even the repentance seemed no deeper or more spontaneous than
his readiness to help. Joseph on the other hand was friendly by nature, and held with the principle that one best meets strangeness with
increase of friendliness. He answered:

"Since thou guidest me and openest out of kindness the way to
my brethren, thou hast a right to my animal. Sit still, I pray thee,
and we shall change anon. Thou hast walked the whole day, whereas
I could ride."

"Many thanks," said the youth. "Thy words are indeed no more
than becoming, but still I thank thee kindly. I have been temporarily
robbed of certain facilities for travel," he added, and shrugged his
shoulders. "Do missions and messages make thee pleasure?" he next
inquired.

"I rejoiced when the father called me," answered Joseph. "Who
then sendeth thee?"

"Thou mayest understand that many messengers go to and fro
between the great lords east and south through this land," responded
the other. "Who actually sendeth thee, that thou dost not know at

all; the commission goes through many mouths and it helps thee little to follow it to its source; in any case thou must take to the road. At present I have a letter to deliver in Dothan," said he, "which I carry in my girdle. But I can see in the future that I must also play the guard."

"The guard?"

"Yes, I am liable, for instance, to be commanded to watch over a well or some shrine or other, of which there is question. Messenger, guide, guard — all these I must play as they come, according to the taskmaster's will. Whether it give one pleasure and whether one actually feel made for the task is another matter, which I put aside. Likewise will I not inquire whether one has understanding for the ideas which give rise to these missions. No, I prefer to leave such questions open; only saying, as between ourselves, that there is much incomprehensible urgency about the matter. Dost thou love mankind?"

He put the question abruptly; yet it did not come to Joseph as a surprise, since the stranger's whole bearing displayed an arrogant displeasure with the human species, and a disinclination to go about his business among men. Joseph answered:

"We usually smile at each other, mankind and I."

"Yes, because thou art known to be beautiful and well-favoured," said his guide. "Wherefore they smile at thee and thou smilest back, in order to strengthen them in their folly. Thou wouldst do better to show them a gloomy mien and say: 'What would you with your smiling? These hairs will fall out, alas, and these now white teeth as well; these eyes are only a jelly of blood and water; they will dissolve away and this whole hollow charm of the flesh will shrivel and shamefully decay.' It would be decent for thee to sober them, by the remembrance of what they know already, though they let themselves be beguiled by the servile smile of the present moment. Such creatures as thou are naught but a fleeting and dissembling gloss upon the horror of all flesh beneath the surface. I do not say that even this skin and husk is the most appetizing in the world, with its steaming pores and sweat-glands; but scratch it ever so little and the salt scarlet brew comes out, while the deeper one goes, the worse it gets; it is sheer guts and stink. The beautiful and well-favoured should be beautiful and well-favoured through and through, solid and fine-grained and not filled up with dirt and jelly."

"Then," said Joseph, "you must stick to graven and carven images, for instance to the beautiful god which the women hide in the shrubbery and seek lamenting that they may bury him in the pit. He is beautiful through and through, of solid olive-wood, not gory and steaming. But they wish him to look as though he were not solid, but bleeding from the tusk of the boar; they paint upon him red wounds and deceive themselves so that they may weep over his dear life lost. So it is: either life is deception, or beauty. Thou canst not find both united in truth."

"Fie," said the guide, puckering his round chin and looking down over his shoulder with half-closed eyes at his companion.

"No," he added after a pause, "say what thou wilt, it is an ugly breed, that drinketh unrighteousness like water and has long since merited another flood, this time without an ark."

"Thou art most likely just, in the matter of the unrighteousness," Joseph responded. "But consider that everything cometh in pairs in the world, part and counterpart, to the end that one may distinguish between them; and if the one were not next the other, then they both were not. Without life were no death, without riches no poverty, and if we made an end of stupidity, who could speak of cleverness? But thus is it with purity and impurity, so much is clear. The unclean beast speakest to the clean one: 'Give thanks to me, for if I were not, then how shouldst thou know that thou art pure, and who would call thee so?' And the evil man to the just: 'Fall at my feet, for without me where were thine advantage?'"

"Thou hast said it," answered the stranger. "For it is just that which I mistrust from my soul, this dual world; I do not understand the necessity for a breed whose purity can be spoken of only comparatively and in retrospect. Yet one hath always to be mindful of him, there are always plans regarding him, goodness knows how far-reaching, and this and that to be brought about respecting his puny little future — just as now, for instance, I must see that thou comest to thy right goal, thou bag of wind! It maketh me to weep with boredom."

"The vexatious creature, why then does he show me the way, if it is such a burden to him?" Joseph thought. "It is stupid to play the agreeable and then to sulk. It is clear he has only been thinking of the ride. He might get off too; we were going to take turns. He talks just like a man," he thought, and smiled to himself over the way people have of criticizing their own kind and excepting themselves, so that the man sits in judgement over mankind as though he were not one of them. Then he said:

"Yea, thou talkest of humanity and sittest in judgement, saying of what bad stuff it is composed. But there was a time when even to the children of God themselves man seemed not so evil, since they went in unto his daughters, and giants and mighty men were conceived."

The guide turned his head in his affected way toward the shoulder farther from Joseph.

"Thou knowest all the little stories, I see," he answered with a titter. "For thy years thou'rt informed in events, that I must say.

For my part, be it said, I consider the tale to be idle gossip. But if it be true, then let me tell thee why it was that the children of light so behaved to the daughters of Cain. They did so from excess of contempt, yes, verily. Knowest thou why destruction came upon the daughters of Cain? They went with uncovered shame and mated like cattle. Their whoredom so mocked all bounds that man as it were could not look at it without being tempted — I know not if thou understandest that. They went to all extremes, they threw their garments on the ground and went forth without them. If they had not known shame, it might have answered and the sight of them would not have got into the bones of the children of light. But they well knew shame, they were, on religious grounds, very chaste indeed, and their lust consisted precisely therein, that they would tread shame underfoot — can such a thing be borne? The man had intercourse with mother and daughter and brother's wife openly and on the streets, and they had altogether one thought in mind: the frightful enjoyment of wounded shame. Must that not seize upon the members of the children of light? They were tempted by their scorn — canst thou not understand that? The last shred of respect was gone from them for this breed, who were set under their noses, as though there were not enough already in the world, and whom they should have respected on grounds of higher necessity. They found that man simply existed for unchastity, and their contempt took the form of lasciviousness. If thou canst not understand all that, thou art but a calf."

"I can understand it if I try," replied Joseph. "But how dost thou come to know it?"

"Ask thy old Eliezer, too, whence cometh what he teacheth thee. I know as much of the events too, perhaps even more, moving to and fro in the world as I do, as messenger, guide, and guard; I come to hear the most various things. I can assure thee that the flood only came at last because it appeared that the contempt of the children of light for mankind had taken the form of desire. That turned the scale; otherwise it would perhaps never have happened. I need only add that the children of light were of fixed purpose to bring on the flood. But unfortunately there was the ark, and man came in again by the back door."

"Let us be glad of that," said Joseph. "Otherwise we should not be here chatting on the way to Dothan and *taking turns* to ride according to our agreement."

"Thou art right," replied the other, and again rolled his eyes round. "I forget everything chattering. Of course I must lead thee and guard thee that thou comest to thy brethren. But who is more important, the watcher or the watched? Not without some bitterness must I answer: the watched is more important, for for him is the watcher there, and not the other way about. Therefore I will now dismount and thou shalt ride, and I walk beside thee in the dust."

"I can stand that too," said Joseph, as he mounted. "It is after all pure chance that thou canst ride even a part of the time and not go all the way in the dust."

So they went on under the stars by the pale moonlight, northwards from Shechem toward Dothan through broad and narrow valleys, over steep hills, clothed in forests of cedar and acacia, past sleeping villages. Joseph too slept by the hour as he sat on the ass, and the guide walked in the dust. But awaking out of such slumber — it was already dawn — he missed a little basket of pressed fruit and another of roast onions from the ass's load and noted reluctantly that the folds of his guide's girdle were correspondingly fuller. The man stole! It was a painful discovery and showed how little ground he had had to except himself when he criticized the race of mankind. Joseph said never a word; indeed, he himself in their conversation had defended the evil for the sake of its opposite. Moreover, the man was a guide and thus dedicate to Nabu, the lord of the westernmost point in the cycle, leading down into the underworldly half of the world — a servant, that is, of the god of thieves. One might assume that he had performed a pious and symbolic act when he stole from his sleeping charge. For all these reasons Joseph said naught of his discovery, but reverenced the dishonesty of the man, in the guise of religious duty. Yet it was painful to learn that the guide had stolen, out and out. The fact might be a fresh explanation of his willingness to play the guide; in any case it impressed Joseph unfavourably and cast him down.

But something much worse than the theft happened soon enough. The sun had come up behind field and wood and Dothan's green hill was already in sight; it lay diagonally on their right in the morning sunshine, with the village on its top. Joseph, sitting on the ass while the thief held the bridle, was looking thither; there was a jerk and a fall, and it had happened. Hulda had gone into a hole with her forefoot, had fallen, and could not get up again. She had broken her pastern. They both examined it.

"Broken," said the guide, shortly. "What a fix! Have I not said to thee the pasterns were weak?"

"Thou shouldst not rejoice even if thou art right; the words should not come in thy mouth. Thou wast leading her and wast not careful, so that she stepped into the hole."

"I was not careful and thou complainest of me? But so it is with human beings; they must have someone to blame when things go wrong, even though it was prophesied beforehand."

"It is also the way of mankind to have wilfully foreseen misfor-

tune and to make a petty triumph of it. Be glad that I complain of
thee only for heedlessness, I might have accused thee of other things
as well. If thou hadst not advised me to ride by night, then we
should not have overtired Hulda and a wise beast like her would
never have stumbled."

"Dost thou think the pastern will be made good again by thy
lamentings?"

"No," Joseph said. "That I do not. But that brings me back to
the question: what shall I do? I cannot after all leave my beast lying
here with all the load of provisions which I was to present to the
brethren in Jacob's name. There remaineth much though I have
eaten some and more has been got rid of in other ways. Shall
Hulda die helpless here and the beasts of the fields eat my goods?
I am near to weep from vexation."

"And who knows again what to do but I?" responded the stranger.
"Did I not say that I can play the watchman, when need is? Go then,
for I will sit here and watch thy beast, and the provisions, and
frighten off birds and other thieves. Whether I am born for such a
task is another matter which we need not talk of here. Enough, I
will sit and guard thy ass until thou hast gone to the brethren and
come back with them or a couple of servants to fetch the goods
and look after the beast to see if it is to be cured or killed."

"Thanks," said Joseph, "so let us do. I can see thou art just like
a man; thou hast thy good sides and of the others we will not speak.
I will make all haste and return again with help."

"I will await thee. Thou canst not go wrong: round the hill and
then back into the valley behind it five hundred paces through scrub
and clover — there wilt thou find thy brethren, near a well where
there is no water. If thou needest aught from thy ass bethink thee
now. Not a head-cloth to shield thee from the sun?"

"Thou'rt right," cried Joseph. "The mischance hath robbed me
of my head. That will I not leave here," said he, and drew the *ketonet*
out of the beringed leather bag, "nor in thy care either, whatever
good side thou showest. For I will take it with me afoot into the
vale of Dothan, that I may arrive in splendour even if not on white
Hulda as Jacob would have wished. I will put it on at once and before thine eyes — so — and so — and thus, and thus. How dost thou
like it? Am I not a gay shepherd-bird in my coat of many colours?
Mami's veil, how doth it become her son?"

OF LAMECH AND HIS HURT

MEANWHILE Leah's sons and those of the maids sat, all ten, behind
the hill at the bottom of the valley round a burnt-out fire where they

had cooked their morning mess; they stared into the ashes. They had all risen betimes from their striped tents set up at some distance in the shrubbery; had risen singly, but all very early, some even before dawn; for their sleep had relished them little. They had got, in fact, but little refreshment from it since they had left Hebron; indeed, they had exchanged the pastures of Sechem for the vale of Dothan out of no other than the desolate hope that it might refresh them better elsewhere.

They had gone grumbling to the well, stumbling with stiff joints over the matted and twisted roots of gorse. It was a well of fresh water near the place where the flocks were scattered over the field; for the well close at hand was dry at this time of year. They had drunk, washed themselves, and prayed, looked after the lambs, and then assembled at the eating-place in the shade of a group of red-trunked, branching pines. The view from here took in the level country dotted with single trees and shrubbery, the hill with the village of Dothan on top, the distant flocks of sheep, and the low mountains in the background. The sun was already well up. The air was full of scents of sun-warmed grass, of fennel, thyme, and other field odours beloved of sheep.

The sons of Jacob sat in a circle upon their haunches, in their midst the dying brushwood fire with the pot atop. They had long since finished eating and sat there idle and red-eyed, their bodies sated, but their souls gnawed by a hunger and dry thirst to which they could not have given a name, but which spoiled their sleep and made their food like ashes to them. A thorn was in their flesh, in the flesh of each one. It could not be pulled out, it festered, tortured, and consumed. They felt slack, and most of them had headache. When they tried to clench their fists they could not. These men who once, to do vengeance for Dinah, had bathed Shechem in blood, asked themselves if they were the men for like deeds today; and they answered no, they were no longer those men. The gnawing worm of their grievance, the festering thorn, the hunger in their inwards unnerved and unmanned them. Simeon and Levi, that savage pair, suffered especially from their shameful state. One of them poked dully with his crook in the dying embers. The other, Simeon, swaying his body to and fro, began a half-muttered singsong, in which some of the rest joined one after another. It was an ancient ditty, a fragment of some half-forgotten ballad or epic, from times far remote:

And Lamech the hero took unto him two wives,
The name of the one was Adah and the name of the other was Zillah.
Adah and Zillah, hear my voice;
Ye wives of Lamech, hearken unto my speech!
For I have slain a man to my wounding

And a young man to my hurt.
If Cain shall be avenged sevenfold,
Truly Lamech seven and seventyfold.

That was all they knew, it was without beginning or ending. So
they stopped there; yet hung on the sound, as it died away, seeing
in their mind's eye Lamech the hero, how he came up armed and
glowing with pride from his deed and told his women, as they bowed
before him, how that he had washen his heart clean. They saw the
young man laid low and lying in the blood-stained grass, the almost
guiltless sin-offering for Lamech's frantically sensitive honour. The
plain word "man" was softened to the tenderer "young man" in the
next line, and in the sacredness of his suffering and death might well
have roused emotions of pity at least in the hearts of Adah and Zillah,
being women. Even so, they could only have enhanced their adoration of Lamech's implacable and incorruptible virility and unquenchable thirst for revenge, these being the ringing theme of the ancient
saga.

"Lamech he was called," said Leah's Levi, thrusting his charred
stick into the fire till it broke. "Does it please you all? I ask that
because it pleaseth me well and even very well. That was a man, a
blade, a lion-heart, a fellow of the ancient mould; there are no more
of his like. He lives only in a song, which we sing to refresh ourselves with thoughts of the past. With his heart washed clean he
might come before his wives; and if he visited his strength upon
them, one after the other, then they knew what manner of man they
received, and trembled with desire. Dost thou come so before
Shuah's daughter, Judah, or thou, Dan, before the Moabitess? Tell
me what has become of the breed since then, that it begets only the
prudent and pious, but no true men?"

Reuben answered him: —

"I will tell thee what takest man's revenge out of his hand and
bringeth it about that we are grown unlike to Lamech, the hero. It is
twofold: Babel's law and the jealousy of God, both of which say:
'Vengeance is mine.' For revenge must be taken from the man, otherwise it breeds furiously on, rank as the swamp, and the world is full
of blood. For what was Lamech's end? Thou dost not know, for
the song telleth it not. But the youth whom he slew had a son or a
brother, who struck Lamech down, that the earth received his blood
likewise. Then one out of Lamech's loins slew Lamech's murderer
out of revenge, and thus it went on, until neither of Lamech's seed
nor of the seed of the slain youth was there any left, but the earth
might close its maw, for it was sated. But it is not good so, it is a
weedy growth of revenge and groweth by no rule. Hence it was,
when Cain slew Abel, God set His mark upon him, that he belonged

to Him and spoke: 'Whosoever slayeth Cain, vengeance shall be taken on him sevenfold.' But Babel decreed that man should humble himself to judgement for blood-guilt and not revel in revenge."

Thereto Gad, son of Zilpah, in all his directness:

"Yea, so speakest thou, Reuben, with thy thin voice which cometh out of thy mighty body, and however often one heareth it one is surprised. Had I thy limbs I would not speak like thee and defend the revolution of time and its changes, which unman heroes and breed no more lion-hearts in the world. Where is the pride of thy body, that thou speakest with thin voice and wilt put thy vengeance into God's hands or submit it to judgement? Shamest not thou thyself before Lamech, who spoke: 'This is a thing between three, between me, and him who offended me, and the earth?' Cain said to Abel: 'Will God console me when Noemah our sweet sister taketh thy gifts and smileth upon thee; or will the judgement decide to whom she belongeth, thee or me? I am the first-born, and so is she mine. Thou art her twin, so is she thine. That God decideth not, nor the judgement of Nimrod. Let us go out upon the field that we may decide it!' And they decided it together; and as I sit here, named Gaddiel, whom Zilpah bore upon Leah's lap, I am for Cain."

"And I, for my part," said Jehudah, "would no more be the young lion as I am called of the people if I were not for Cain and still more for Lamech. He thought well of himself, on my word, and thought not meanly of his pride. 'Seven times?' quoth he. 'Bah! I am Lamech. Seven and seventy times will I be avenged, and there lieth he, the lout, for the sake of my hurt!'"

"What sort of hurt may that have been?" asked Issachar, the bony ass, "and wherein may the pitiful youth have fallen under the mighty Lamech's displeasure, that he left it neither to God nor to Nimrod to avenge, but took vengeance abundantly with his own hand?"

"That no man now knoweth," responded his half-brother Naphtali, Bilhah's son. "The nature of the youth's insolence is unknown and what it was which Lamech washed off in his blood, that is lost to the world's memory. Still I have it from hearsay that men in our time swallow shame much more loathsome than that which Lamech suffered. They swallow it, the craven creatures, so we hear, and go away elsewhither, and sit them down; and in their belly the shame fermenteth and consumeth, that they care neither to eat nor to sleep; and if Lamech whom they admire should see them he would give them a kick behind, for they are worth no more."

He spoke with glib and spitefully fluent tongue, and his face was distorted. The twins groaned and tried to clench their fists but could not. Zebulun said:

"There were Adah and Zillah the wives of Lamech; and Adah is to blame, as I shall show you. For she bore Jabal, the father of such as dwell in tents and of such as have cattle, the ancestor of Abram, of Yitzchak and Jacob our gentle father. Therefrom have we our trouble and our destruction, and are no more men, as thou sayst, brother Levi, but cautious and pious, and as though castrate with the sickle, which may God forbid. Yes, were we huntsmen or even seafarers, all would be changed. But with Jabal, Adah's son, came love of tents into the world, the shepherd nature and Abram's dreams of God, and all that hath weakened us so that we tremble to do our worthy father a hurt, and big Reuben sayeth: 'Vengeance belongeth unto God.' But can one rely by means of abominable dreams upon God and upon His justice when He is a party in the strife and Himself instils arrogance into the good-for-nothing youth? For what can we do against the dreams?" he cried out, his voice cracking in his anguish, "if they are from God and it is ordained that we should bow?"

"But something we might do against the dreamer of the dreams!" shrieked Gad, likewise with heaving chest; and Asher added: "So that the dreams were without a master and no longer knew how to come true!"

"That," replied Reuben, "would likewise have meant setting oneself against God. For it were all one, to set oneself against the dreamer or against God, provided the dreams were from Him." He spoke in the past tense, saying not "would mean" but "would have meant," in token that the question was solved.

It was Dan who spoke after him. He said:

"Hearken, brethren, and give heed to my words, for Dan is called snake and adder, and on account of a certain subtlety he availeth as judge. It is surely true and Reuben is right. If we punish the dreamer, so that the dreams become masterless and powerless, we thereby expose ourselves to the wrath of the self-willed and invoke upon us the vengeance of the unjust. There is no gainsaying it. But so," saith Dan, "we must run the risk, for there is naught imaginable that could be worse or even as bad as the fulfilling of the dream. For in any case self-will will have lost, let it rage and storm as it will, and the dreams shall seek their dreamer in vain. We must act, for only the accomplished deed instructeth. Hath not Jacob too suffered this and that for his deceitfulness and found Laban's service no matter for laughter on account of Esau's bitter tears? Yet he hath endured, for he carried off the main advantage, that is the blessing; it was put aside and in safety, and no God, whoever he was, could have done aught against him however much he would. One must endure tears and revenge for the sake of the good, for what is put aside and in safety, that cometh not again. . . ."

Here his speech, which had begun so subtly, began to wander. But

Reuben answered; and it was strange to see that man, strong like a tree in strength, turn pale and white:

"Thou has spoken, Dan, and mayst now be silent. For we have gone thence and departed from the father's hearth. And our annoyance is afar from us and in safety, and in safety we sit at Dothan, five days distant, and all that is an accomplished deed."

And then, after all these speeches, they let their heads droop low, almost between their knees, which stood up high as they squatted on their haunches; and there they crouched round the ashes of their fire, like ten sheaves of misery.

JOSEPH IS THROWN INTO THE PIT

Now it happened that Asher, Zilpah's son, with curiosity unquenched even by affliction, peered out over his knees so that his eyes roved across the plain. And afar off in the morning light he saw something glitter like a flash of silver, which disappeared and came again, sometimes in a single flash, sometimes two or more close together.

Asher jogged his brother Gad as they sat next each other, pointed out the will-o'-the-wisp, and asked him what it meant. They shaded their eyes to look and gestured their surprise; the others saw and heard, and those who sat with their backs to the plain turned round to gaze, following the direction of Asher's eyes; until at last all the brothers had lifted their heads and peered out together at a shimmering figure which was moving toward them.

"One cometh, all shining," Judah spoke. But after they had waited awhile for the figure to come nearer, Dan answered:

"It is not a man, it is a boy."

And with one accord their sunburnt faces all went ashen as Reuben's had done a little time before, and their hearts beat with a wild and rapid rhythm, like drums, so that a hollow concerted drumming noise arose in the breathless stillness.

Joseph came on across the plain, directly toward them, in his coat of many colours, and his garland resting on his veiled head.

They did not believe it. They sat with their thumbs in their cheeks, fingers before their mouths, elbows on their knees, and stared out over their fists with starting eyes at the approaching illusion. They hoped they were dreaming, yet feared to find it so. Some of them, even, in a confusion of fear and hope, refused to believe their eyes when the oncoming figure smiled and spoke, and there was no more doubt.

"Yea, verily, and greetings to you all," he said in his very voice, and came close up to them. "It is indeed I. I am come for our father's sake on Hulda, the she-ass, to look after things with you and to —" he stopped, disconcerted. They sat without word or stir and stared, a sinister group, like men bewitched. But as they so sat — although there was no sunrise and no sunset which might have painted their faces, yet these grew red as the twisted trunks of the trees at their backs, red as the desert, dark red as the star in the sky, and their eyes looked as though blood would spurt out. He stepped back. There arose and swelled a thunderous roar, that bull's roar of the twins, which made one's inwards to quake; and with a long-drawn shriek as from tortured gullets, a furiously exultant yell of rage and hate and sudden release, they all ten sprang up as one man and flung themselves savagely upon him.

They fell upon him as the pack of hungry wolves falls upon the prey; their blood-blinded lust knew no pause or consideration, it was as though they would tear him into fourteen pieces at least. Rending, tearing apart, tearing off — upon that they were bent, to their very marrow. "Down, down, down!" they panted with one voice; it was the *ketonet* they meant, the picture-robe, the veil. It must come off, and that was not so easy, for it was wound about him and fastened at head and shoulder; and they were too many for the deed. They got in each other's way; one thrust another away from the victim as he flew and fell and bounded among them. The blows meant for him showered upon themselves — though he indeed received a plenty as well. His nose bled almost at once, and one eye was closed with a great blue weal.

But the confusion served Reuben's ends, as he towered among them shrieking: "Down, down," with the rest. He used the immemorial tactics of those who wish to control a savage mob and keep a grip upon the course of events: he took part with apparent zeal in the fray, in order to prevent the worst from coming to pass. He dealt out blows while feigning to receive them, all the while cuffing and pushing those nearest Joseph, protecting him as best he might when they were about to strike him and tear off his robe. He aimed particularly at Levi, on account of the crook in his hands, blundering against it as often as he could. But despite all Reuben's manœuvres, Joseph was served worse than the petted youth could ever have dreamed possible. He reeled half-dazed, with his head drawn down between his shoulders, and his elbows spread against the hail-storm of brutality, descending out of a blue sky, which horribly seemed not to care where it struck, but beat down upon him, cutting into very little pieces his trust, his whole notion of the world, his conviction that everybody must love him more than themselves, as though it were a law of nature.

"Brothers," he stammered, with the blood streaming down his chin from his nose and his bruised lips, "what are you — " A rude blow, which Reuben failed to fend off, knocked the words from his mouth. Another, landing in the pit of the stomach, between the ribs, made

him collapse and disappear beneath the pack. I cannot deny, rather
I must emphatically say, that this uprising of the sons of Jacob, however much justice they had on their side, was a most shameful relapse
into savagery. They sank below the level of the human and availed
themselves of their teeth, being otherwise busy with their hands, to
tear his mother's garment from the body of the bleeding, reeling lad.
They were not dumb at the work, they said other things besides
"Down, down, down!" They were like labourers pulling and heaving and with monotonous cries subduing themselves to the common
task; bringing up broken words out of the depths of their hate to feed
their rage and stave off thought. "Bow down, bow down, thou sayest?" "Look after things, wilt thou, thou thorn in the flesh, thou lingering sickness! There for thy dreams!" And their unhappy victim?

To him the most horrible and incredible thing of all was what
happened to the *ketonet*. That was worse, crueller, even, than all
this howling horror about him. Desperately he tried to protect the
garment and keep the remnants and ruins of it still upon him. Several
times he cried out: "My coat! My coat!" and even after he stood
naked, still begged them like a girl to spare it. Yes, he was naked, for
the violence of the brothers' onslaught not only carried off the veil,
but shift, loincloth, and myrtle wreath lay in tatters beside it on the
moss; while blows rained down upon his naked flesh and he sought as
best he could to ward them off with his arms. "Bow down, bow
down! Take that for thy dreams!" Big Reuben did what he could to
keep them off by behaving as though the others prevented him from
coming at the victim and dealing his blows. "Thou thorn in the flesh,
thou lingering sickness!" he cried out with the rest. But also he cried
out something else, which occurred to him on the spur of the moment; cried it loud and repeatedly, in order that they might all hear
it and be guided in their blind rage: "Bind him, bind him! Tie his
hands and feet!" It was a new suggestion, invented in haste to a good
end: namely, to set a definite goal to this otherwise incalculable business and introduce a breathing-space, in the which big Reuben, as
he feverishly prayed, might avert the worst. They would not strike
Joseph while they were busy binding him; and when he lay bound,
that would be a temporary gratification, a stage at which they might
stand off and consider what next. Such was Reuben's hasty calculation. And thus with desperate zeal he proposed his expedient, as
though he were indicating the one and only useful and reasonable
plan and as though anyone was a fool who did not hearken to it.
"There — that for thy dreams!" he shrieked. "Bind him — bind him!
You fools! What a senseless revenge! Instead of hitting me, bind
him. Is there no rope?" he cried once more with all his strength.

Yes, Gaddiel for one wore a length round his waist; and he took
it off. As their heads were empty, there was room in them for Reu-

ben's words. They bound the naked lad, bound his arms and legs with one long piece of cord, trussed him up properly while he moaned and groaned; and Reuben assisted zealously at the work. When it was done, he stepped back and wiped off his sweat with a gasp, as if he had worked harder than any.

The others stood there, their lust for battle slaked for the present; panting, inactive, dazed. Before them lay Rachel's son, in grievous state. He lay on his bound arms, with the back of his head buried in the grass, his knees drawn up stiffly, his ribs going in and out, all bludgeoned. Moss and dirt clung to his body, it was slobbered with the foam of his brothers' fury, and across it ran in winding streams the red juice which gushes out of beauty when its surface is marred. His undamaged eye now gazed terror-struck at his murderers, now closed spasmodically in a reflex action against fresh violence.

The evil-doers stood getting their wind; they exaggerated their breathlessness in order to cover the lack of counsel, of which, as reason returned, they were slowly aware. They, like Reuben, wiped off their sweat with the backs of their hands; they puffed out their lips and made faces expressive of justified revenge, as who should say: "Whatever we have done, can any reproach us for it?" They said the same in words. They panted out words justifying themselves in each other's eyes or before any court in the world: "Cuckoo! Thorn in the flesh! But we have shown him, we have cast him out!" "Could one credit it? Cometh here – here before us, in his coat – before our eyes – to look after things – but we've looked after them – so he'll not forget it!" – and all the while there was stirring within them a horror and shuddering, which all their words were meant to quiet. And if the horror and shuddering were looked at nearly, it would turn out to be – the thought of Jacob.

Great God, what had they done with the father's lamb – to what state had they brought the youthful heir of the departed Rachel? How would the master of words behave when he knew or learned it, how would they stand before him and what would happen to them? Reuben thought of Bilhah. Simeon and Levi thought of Shechem and of Jacob's wrath and now he had come down upon them when they returned from their heroic deeds. Naphtali, Naphtali especially, found it a present consolation that Jacob was five days away and entirely unsuspecting. Yes, for the first time Naphtali realized as a blessing the power of space, which separates and spares. But they all realized that the blessing could not be preserved. Jacob must presently hear all. When Joseph came again before his eyes, the storm of emotion, the rolling thunder of his words, the flashing lightning of his curses – the brethren could not escape nor yet endure them. Grown men as they were, they were frightened like children, possessed with the fear of the curse in itself, and in all its meaning and consequence. Cursed they would be, one and all, because they had raised their hand against the lamb; and now the young hypocrite would definitely be exalted above them as the chosen heir. They would actually have themselves to thank for the fulfilment of those shameful dreams; precisely that which God willed would have been brought about by this accomplished fact. They perceived that big Reuben had made fools of them with his advice. Here they stood, and there lay the thief of the blessing; pretty well punished indeed, and bound — but was that really an accomplished fact? It would be different if Joseph never did come before his father's eyes again; if something final and conclusive happened to him. The calamity and the lamentation would be even greater, of course — too great to think on. But — somehow or other — it would pass. Stopping half-way, even so they were guilty. If they went on, they needed not to be. All this went through their heads as they stood — through Reuben's too. He could not help recognizing the situation. He had brought the brawl to a halt with a shrewdness which came from his heart. But his reason told him that too much had happened for it to stop there. That more had to happen, and yet on no account and at no price must happen — this it was which made him giddy. Big Reuben's sinewy features had never before worn that baffled, sullen look.

Each moment he feared they would voice the inevitable — and he had no answer. Then they voiced it, and he heard. One of them said it — no matter who, since they must all be thinking the same thing: "He must away."

"Away," nodded Reuben with grim confirmation. "Thou sayest it. But thou sayest not where."

"Away altogether," answered the voice. "He must go down to the pit and be no more. Long time he ought not to have been; now certainly he must be no more."

"I agree," responded Reuben with bitter scorn. "And then come we before Jacob, his father, without him. 'Where is the boy?' he will ask. 'He is no more,' we answer. But if he ask: 'Why is he no more,' then we answer: 'We have killed him.'"

They were silent.

"No," said Dan, "not so. Brothers, hear me, I am called serpent and adder, and a certain subtlety is not to be denied me. Thus will we do. We will put him in the pit, down in the dry well here, half choked, in which is no water. There lieth he in safety and put away, and will see what his dreams bring him to. But before Jacob we must lie and speak with assurance: 'We have not seen him and know not whether he still is or is not. If not, then in any case a ravening beast hath devoured him, oh woe, alas!' We must add 'Oh woe' for the sake of the lie."

"Be quiet," said Naphtali, "he lieth close at hand and heareth us."

"No matter," answered Dan. "He will tell no one. That he heareth it is one reason more that he may not go from here; even before that he could not, but now everything goeth together. We can speak as we like before him, for he is already as good as dead."

A cry came from Joseph, he wailed out of his breast stretched taut under his bonds on which the tender red nipples stood out. He wept.

"Can you hear it and not pity?" Reuben asked.

"Of what avail is that, Reuben?" answered him Judah, "and what talkest thou of pity, though the rest of us may feel it as well as thou? Doth his weeping in this hour blot it out that he hath been a shameless toad all his days and stank to heaven and hath supplanted us with the father with most shameless guile? Doth pity avail against necessity and is it a good reason why he should go from hence and tell all? What good to talk of pity, even if it be felt? Hath he not already heard how we shall lie before Jacob? That is enough to end his life, that he hath heard it; and whether with or without pity Dan spoke the truth: he is as good as dead."

"Thou art right," said Reuben then. "Let us throw him in the pit."

Again Joseph wailed piteously.

"But he still weepeth," one of them reminded them.

"Must he then not even weep?" cried Reuben. "Let him go weeping into the pit; what more can you ask?"

I would fain pass over what was said next, for it would shock our modern taste and however delicately put would place the brothers or some of them in an exceedingly bad light. The truth is that Simeon and Levi, as well as the downright Gad, offered to make an end of the lad without more ado. The twins wanted to do it with their staves, hitting out with the full strength of their arms, as Cain had done, until he was no more. But Gad asked to be given the job of cutting his throat quickly with the knife, as Jacob had once done with the kid whose skin he needed for the forged blessing. That these suggestions were made is undeniable; but I am not anxious that the reader be finally disgusted with the sons of Jacob, therefore I will not put their thoughts into precise words. They uttered them because those things had to be said; because, so to speak, they lay in the nature of the business. Besides, it was only natural that those best suited to the rôle were they who expressed their readiness and so conformed to their myth on earth: namely, the savage twins and the stout Gad.

But Reuben opposed. It is known that he opposed, and would not have it happen to Joseph as it had to Abel or to the kid. "To that I will not agree," he said, protesting in his character as Leah's eldest, which despite fall and curse entitled him to a voice. The boy was as good as dead, they had said so themselves. He was only sobbing a little still, it would suffice to throw him into the pit. Let them look at him and say whether that was still Joseph the dreamer. He was already unrecognizable from the punishment, in which he, Reuben, had taken part, and would have done more had he not been struck from all sides. But what had happened had been just a happening, it was not an act, not a deed, you could not call it so. It had come about, indeed, through them, but they had not done it, it had simply happened to them. Now, however, they were deliberately proposing, of set purpose, to commit a crime and raise their hands against the boy; they were about to spill their father's blood, whereas up to now it had only flowed. And that was a world-wide difference, it was all the difference between an act and an occurrence; and if they did not see that, then they were short in their understanding. Were they, he asked, appointed judges of life and death, to judge in their own matter and then carry out the blood-decree as well? No, there should be no shedding of blood, he would not stand for it. What remained to them to do, after what had occurred, was to put the boy into the pit and leave the rest to happen.

Thus big Reuben, but nobody believed that he was deceiving himself or that he was so stoutly convinced of the hard and fast difference between happening and doing. Or that he did not see that putting Joseph in the pit would be the same as killing him. After a while Jehudah asked him what it would avail to kill the boy and conceal his blood; the question told Reuben nothing new. For all along we have looked into Reuben's heart and seen that his great desire was to gain time. He could not have said for what; simply time to feed the hope that he might save Joseph out of the brethren's hands and somehow bring him back to his father. It was his fear of Jacob which actuated him, as well as his crabbed and shamefaced love of the culprit; they drove him to conceal his thoughts and meditate treason against the clan — for it can be called nothing else. Moreover, Reuben the unstable had manifold sins to atone for in Jacob's eyes, on account of Bilhah. What if he brought Joseph safe home? Would not then the ancient wrong be more than made good, the curse lifted and his first-born-ship be restored? I do not assume to understand all Reuben's thoughts and actions, nor would I minimize the motives of his deeds. But need it belittle them to guess that in his secret heart he hoped both to save and to vanquish Rachel's son?

In any case his words met with scarcely any opposition from the brothers. They were willing to refrain and to let events decide. Probably they would have preferred that the "happenings" should have continued and led in one blind thrust to the goal they sought. But to continue deliberately and to shed blood, to "act" now that a pause for reflection had intervened — nobody wanted to do that, not even the twins, however savage, nor yet Gaddiel, no matter how stoutly he spoke. They were all glad, indeed, that their offer about bludgeons and knives had not been taken up, but that Reuben's authority should prevail again: first the tying-up, now the pit.

"Into the pit," was the word. They seized the cord which bound Joseph, caught hold here and there, and dragged the poor wretch across the field toward the pit at the edge of the pasture-land. Some dragged in front, some tugged at the sides, the rest ran behind. Reuben did not run, but moved with a long stride at the tail of the convoy; when a stone lay in the way, a gnarled root or stump or a prickly shrub, he lifted the poor soul that he might not suffer needless pain.

So it was off with Joseph to the pit, with a heigh and a ho, for as they went, a fury of merriment seized upon the brethren, the animal spirits of men working in unison. They laughed and joked and shouted nonsense to each other; as that this was a sheaf which had been well bound and now should bow itself into the pit, into the well, into the depths. In all this they were venting the relief they felt at not being impelled to follow the pattern represented by Abel and the kid. Besides, it drowned the sound of Joseph's prayers and lamentations: "Brothers! Have pity!" he mumbled with his bruised mouth. "What is it you do? Stop, stop! Woe, alas, what will befall me?"

His moans helped him not at all; on they went at a trot, through bush and grass, a long way across country to a mossy slope. Here some steep, broken steps led down to a walled-in bottom, paved with cracked flags. The air was cool, and oak scrub and fig trees grew out of the ruined walls. They dragged Joseph down the steps, he struggling desperately in their arms and against his bonds, for he shuddered at the thought of the well that was there and of the hole of the well, but even more at the broken, mossy well-stone that lay on the flags and was meant to lie over the top. But let him struggle and weep as he might, his unclosed eye directed in horror into the blackness of the well, they hoisted him to the brink with a heave and a ho and tipped him in, to fall who knew how far!

It was far enough, though not an abyss, not a bottomless pit. Such wells often reach a hundred feet and more down, but this one had been long out of use and choked with earth and broken stone — perhaps on account of old quarrels about the place. It was no more than five or six fathoms deep if that. Certainly too much to climb out of with bound limbs. But he fell with as much care for life and limb as he could, braking here and there with feet and elbows round the wall, and moderating his fall to a slipping which landed him fairly sound among the rubbish at the bottom, to the discomfiture of all sorts of beetles, wood-lice, and other crawling things. While he was collecting himself, the brethren did the rest, shouting as they lifted the stone at the top and heaved it into place. It was heavy — not one

man's work to roll it on top of the pit; so they all laid hold and shared
in the task. For the ancient stone, all green with moss and full five
foot round, was sprung into two halves; and when they had rolled
each into place the two did not meet, but yawned; and through the
uneven gap some light fell into the hole. Joseph looked up at it with
his one eye as he lay huddled anyhow, naked and exposed, in the
depths.

JOSEPH CRIES OUT OF THE PIT

THEIR task being done, the brothers sat down on the steps of the
well-chamber to rest; some drew bread and cheese out of their girdles
and ate. Levi, religious in all his savagery, gave them to remember indeed that one should not eat at the shedding of blood, but they answered him that what they had done was to avoid bloodshed. Upon
which, Levi ate too.

They ruminated as they chewed. For the moment their thoughts
were occupied with sensations which, though of little importance,
yet altogether possessed them: their hands and arms, that is, bore the
memory of the contact with Joseph's bare skin, as they dragged him
to his doom. No matter how ungentle the contact had been, now
that it was all over, it gave them a retrospective feeling of tenderness
which was very strong, however little they understood what it meant.
Nobody gave expression to it by so much as a syllable; and what
they said concerned only the fact that Joseph was now safely out of
the way, together with his dreams, and that they were greatly lightened thereby.

"Now he is no more," said they. That was that; now they could
sleep; they could sleep in peace, they repeated, the more emphatically the more uncertain they felt about it. It might be true with
regard to the dreamer who was gone and could tell the father nothing. But the thought failed to soothe, for it reminded them of the
father waiting in vain for Joseph's home-coming — eternally in vain.
Such a picture, however much security it contained, noways invited
to slumber. For all the ten, including the savage twins, it was a picture full of horror. Their childish fear of Jacob and of the tenderness
and power of his soul was clear and lively. True, Joseph would never
be able to accuse them. But they had bought their security by means
of an offence against their father's emotions, which it terrified them
to realize. What they had done to Joseph had its cause in jealousy;
but we all know what feeling it is that suffers this distortion. It seems
little convincing, looking at the slick brutality of the twins, to ascribe
any such feeling to them; and precisely on this ground it is that I do
not make any positive statements. There are cases where only half-
words will serve.

So they mused and blinked as they chewed, feeling on hands and arms the memory of the softness of Joseph's flesh. Their reflections were not light, and they were further weighted by the weeping and begging that rose faintly out of the pit. After the fall he had so far gathered himself together as to realize the need of crying out, and he implored them from below:

"Brothers, where are you? Ah, go not away, leave me not alone in the pit. It is so earthy and so horrible. Brothers, have pity and save me still out of the night of this pit where I perish. I am your brother Joseph. Brothers, hide not your ears from my sighs and cryings, for you do falsely to me. Reuben, where art thou? Reuben, I cry thy name from below in the pit. You have all misunderstood, you have misunderstood, dear brothers, so help me still and save my life. I came to you on our father's account five days' journey on Hulda the white ass, to bring you presents, ears of corn and fruit cakes. Ah, how it hath all gone wrong! The man is to blame that it went wrong, the man who led me. Brothers in Jacob, hearken and understand me, I came not to you to see how things were, for I am but a child. I came to bow before you with decorum and the forms of courtesy and to ask after your welfare, that you should return home to our father. Brothers! the dreams . . . was I so unmannerly as to relate my dreams? Believe me, I have only told quite modest dreams by comparison with what I could have, but not this was it I wanted to say. Oh, oh, my bones, my sinews right and left, and all my limbs! I thirst, brothers, the child thirsteth, for he hath lost much blood, and all through a mistake. Are ye yet there? Am I already quite forsaken? Reuben, let me hear thy voice. Tell them that I will say nothing if they will but spare my life. Brothers, I know you think you must leave me in the pit; otherwise I would tell. But by the God of Abraham, God of Isaac, God of Jacob, by the heads of your mothers and by Rachel's head, my little mother's, I swear that I will not tell for ever and ever, if you let me out of the pit but this one time."

"He would tell, of a certainty, if not today, then tomorrow," muttered Judah between his teeth; and there was none who did not share this view, Reuben not excepted, however much it might conflict with his wavering hopes and plans. But so much the more must he keep these secret and assert the contrary; therefore he hollowed his hands about his mouth and called:

"If thou art not quiet we will throw down stones upon thee that shall kill thee entirely, for we will hear no more of thee, thou art sped."

When Joseph heard this and recognized Reuben's voice, he was terrified and ceased to speak and they might sit undisturbed and taste their fear of Jacob. Of course, if they had meant to prolong their self-imposed exile and live in lasting discord with their father, then they need not have troubled themselves over the agony of waiting and long despair which was hovering over Jacob's head. But the truth was exactly the opposite. The casting away of Joseph could serve one only purpose: that of removing the obstacle between them and the father's heart. Upon that they were childishly bent. The trouble was that they had been driven to extremes in order to win this soft but mighty heart for their own. This was the point of view under which they at all times saw the affair. Not punishment of Joseph's presumption, they were of one mind in thinking, nor yet revenge, nor even, in the first instance, the obliteration of the dreams, was their main concern. What they thought of was how to smooth their path to their father's heart. This now was done, and they would return — without Joseph, as they had set out. Where was he? He had been sent after them. And thus sent, to those who by their departure had demonstrated that they could not stand him, their return without him would look very suspicious. Certainly Jacob would have an awful right to question them. They might shrug their shoulders in reply. Were they their brother's keepers? Of course not; but the answer would not satisfy Jacob's piercing, mistrustful gaze which he would direct upon them relentlessly, while they continued to be witnesses of his tortured expectancy and of the prolonged despair which in the nature of things must be its only issue. It was a penance before which they quailed. On the other hand, were they to stop away until all hope had died and waiting had given way to the knowledge that Joseph would never return? That would last long, for the stout-hearted can bear long suspense, and besides in the meantime the question might easily answer itself and become a curse for them all. No, it was clear that they must once and for all establish the fact that Joseph would not come back; that alone could clear their skirts. Their minds were all busy with these thoughts, but snake-and-adder Dan brought to them speech. He combined his own earlier idea of telling the old man that a wild beast had killed Joseph with Gad's reminder of the kid which Jacob had killed to obtain the blessing; and he said:

"Hear me, brothers, for I have power to judge and I know what we should do. For we shall take a beast of the flock and cut its throat and let the blood run out. But in the blood of the beast we shall dip the accursed thing, the coat of many colours, Rachel's bridal garment that lieth all in rags. Bring we it before Jacob and say to him: 'This have we found on the ground, torn and covered with blood. Is it not thy son's garment?' Then may he draw his conclusion from the state of the garment, and it will be as when a shepherd showeth to the master the remains of the sheep that a lion hath slain; thus is he cleansed and needeth not to swear himself free from guilt."

"Hush," muttered Judah, shuddering. "For he can hear what you say under the stone and can understand what we shall do."

"What harm in that?" Dan retorted. "Shall I whisper and mutter for his sake? It hath naught to do with his life; it is our affair, but no longer his. Thou forgettest that he is as good as dead and done for. When he hath understood that and also this that I now say with my natural voice, then everything is settled. Never have we been able to speak freely and without caution when he was amongst us, for we well knew that he would tell the father and then we had to pay. But now at last we have him amongst us as our brother, whom we trust and he may hear everything we say — it maketh me to feel that I should like to throw a kiss to him there in the pit. But what think you all of my idea?"

They were about to speak; but Joseph lifted up his voice once more, imploring them from the pit not to do it.

"Brothers," he cried, "do not that with the beast and the robe, treat not the father so, for he will not survive it. Ah, I beg you not for myself, for body and soul are broken in me and I lie in the grave. But spare our father and bring him not the bloody garment — it would kill him. Ah, hadst thou heard how he warned me in anxiousness about the lion, when he found me alone by night, and now it will be that a lion hath eaten me. Had you seen the care with which he prepared me for the journey and I indifferently endured his concern! Woe is me, it is most likely unwise that I speak to you of his love of me, but what shall I do, dear brothers, and how counsel myself that I do not vex you? Why after all is my life involved with his, that I cannot adjure you to spare his without begging for my own? Ah, dear brothers, hear my weeping and do no violence to his suffering by showing him the bloody robe, for his gentle soul will bear it not and he will be stricken to the earth."

"Nay," Reuben said, "that is more than I can stand, it is unbearable." He stood up. "Let us move farther away, if you like; one cannot talk with him wailing, nor think for his crying out of the depths. Come to the huts." He said it angrily, they might think he had gone pale with rage. But actually his pallor was due to his having agreed in his heart with what the boy had said. He, too, realized that Jacob, at sight of the robe, would literally be struck to the earth. But more than that, Joseph's words had impressed it upon Reuben that the lad, in his hour of need, was mindful of their father and pleaded with the brethren on his behalf and for himself only for the father's sake. But was he perhaps pretending as of old? No, no, this time it was different. This was another Joseph who cried out from beneath the stone from the one whom he once had shaken by the shoulder to awaken him from vanity and folly. What the shaking had not achieved the fall into the pit had done: Joseph was aroused, he pleaded for the father-heart, he mocked no more, but felt distress and remorse. The discovery strengthened big Reuben's vacillating purpose, while at the same time it made him more acutely sensitive of its helpless and hopeless character.

Thence his pallor, as he got up and suggested to them all to go with him away from the place where Joseph was buried. They followed him, they went from thence, to gather up the rags of the veil on the spot of the beating, to bring them to the tents and there to take counsel over Dan's idea. So Joseph was left alone.

IN THE PIT

His soul was anguished to remain alone in the grave; for some time he wailed after the brothers and implored them not to leave him. Yet he scarcely knew what he cried out; his actual thoughts were not with these mechanical and superficial prayers and lamentations but far below them, while lower down again were others yet more real, like their undertones and ground-basses, so that the whole was like a moving music, perpendicularly composed, which his spirit was occupied in conducting on all three levels. This preoccupation was what caused him to commit the blunder of telling the brethren that he had only told them comparatively modest dreams, considering those others which he had also dreamed. No one in his right senses could even for a moment think that the remark was calculated to soften their hearts; but an absent and preoccupied mind might have done so, and thus was it with Joseph.

Much had gone on within him, even since that astonishing and horrible moment when the brethren fell upon him like wolves and he had looked into their faces distorted by fury and hate, out of the eye which they had not closed at once with their fists. Their faces had been very near to him while they with nails and teeth tore the picture-robe from his body — frightfully near; and the hatred which he had read therein had been the greatest torture and the main cause of the horror he felt at the onslaught. Certainly he had quaked with fear and wept for pain under their blows; but fear and pain were quite permeated with the pity he felt for the torturing hatred which he read in the mask-like faces, dripping with sweat, that rose and fell and were thrust into his own. But pity for a pain the source of which we must recognize to be ourselves comes close to being remorse. Reuben's intuition had been quite right: this time Joseph had been so rudely shaken that his eyes were opened and he saw what he had done — and that he had done it. While he was flung hither and thither among their raging fists, while his robe was torn off, while he lay bound, and during his penitential journey to the well-house, amid all his daze of horror his thoughts had never once stood still. They had not paused upon the frightful present, but sped back over a past in which all this, hidden to his blissful self-conceit though partly and presumptuously known to it, had been preparing itself the while.

My God, the brothers! To what had he brought them? For he did understand that he had brought them to this: through manifold and great mistakes which he had committed in the assumption that everybody loved him more than themselves — this assumption which he believed and yet did not actually quite believe, but according to which he had always acted and which had brought him — as he now clearly and distinctly recognized — to the pit. In the brothers' distorted and sweating masks he had read clearly with his one eye that the premise had gone beyond human power and over a long period had strained their souls and given them great suffering, until now at last the final issue had been reached in this end, so frightful for him and doubtless for them too.

Alas, poor brothers! What must they have borne before in desperation they laid hold on the father's lamb and actually threw it into the pit! Into what a state had they thereby brought themselves — to say nothing of his own, which was hopeless, as he shudderingly confessed himself. It was not credible that he would hold his tongue if he were restored to his father. He could never make them believe it, he could not believe it. And so they must leave him in the grave, to perish there; there was nothing else for it. This he saw; yet wonderful to say, horror at his own impending fate left him room in his soul for pity for his murderers. We know this to be true. Joseph was quite aware, he admitted it to himself openly and honourably as he sat at the bottom of the well, that the unashamed presumption which had been the guiding principle of his life had been a game in which he himself had not seriously believed nor could have done; that, for one thing, he ought never to have told his brothers his dreams. It had been impossibly and incredibly tactless. He even realized that he had actually known this all the time — and yet he had done it. Why? That he did not know. Apparently, that he might be destroyed. But at the bottom of his heart Joseph did not believe it. Privately he was convinced that God looked further than the pit, that He had far-reaching things in mind as usual and had His eye upon some distant purpose, in the service of which he, Joseph, had been made to drive the brethren to the uttermost. They were being sacrificed to the future, and he suffered for them, however badly things went with himself. They would send their father the robe, unhappy men, after they had dipped it in the blood of the kid in lieu of his own; and Jacob would be struck to the earth. At the thought Joseph was moved to start up, to protect his father from the sight — with the only result of course that he felt shooting pains through and through him, sank back in his bonds against the stones of the well, and began once more to weep.

He had an agony of leisure in which to weep, to feel anguish, remorse, and pity; and despairing of his life, yet in his inmost being to believe in the wise and healing future purposes of God. For, frightful as it is to think of it, he was to remain three days in the pit, three days and nights in his bonds, naked and exposed, in dirt and earth mould, among crawling worms, without bite or sup, without consolation or any reasonable hope of ever reaching the light again. I, who tell it, must take care that I paint it as it was, that I make clear what it meant for Jacob's little son, who had never imagined that fate could be so harsh: how dismally the hours passed, till his scrap of daylight died in the crack between the stones and a pitying star sent down its diamond ray into the grave; how the pale dawn twice came, abode, and went again; how he constantly peered up in the twilight at the round walls of his house to see whether there were footholds in the broken wall, or crevices made by pushing roots — but his bonds, and the stone well-cover, each by itself and certainly together, quenched every hope in the bud; how he twisted himself about in the cords to find an easier posture, which quickly became even worse than the other; how thirst and hunger tortured him and the emptiness of his stomach gave him burning sensations in his back; how like the sheep he soiled himself with his own filth and therein nestled and shivered till his teeth chattered. I am greatly concerned to give a lively and exact picture of this all-embracing unpleasantness; at the same time I must be careful to cling to reality and not let my imagination get the upper hand and lose itself in empty emotion. Reality is sober — precisely in its character as reality. At grips with the actual and undeniable, driven to an understanding with it, reality insists upon our suiting ourselves to the circumstances and adapting us without loss of time. We are easily persuaded to call a situation unbearable. Our easily aroused humanity protests indignantly, and that probably does the sufferer good; but it becomes a little absurd in the face of the *really* intolerable. The sympathetic friend's relation to this reality, which is of course not his own, is an unreal and sentimental one. He commits an error of the imagination, for the sufferer, thanks to his suffering, is in a different category. What do we really mean by the unbearable, when there is nothing to be done but bear it so long as we are in our senses?

But young Joseph had not been entirely and clearly in his senses for a long time; not since the moment when the brethren had turned into wolves before his eyes. The storm which then broke over him had numbed him very much, effecting those palliations which the unbearable needs in order to be borne. The beatings he had received had dulled his feeling, as had that unbelievable conveyance into the well. His situation was certainly desperate, but at least it had put a period to those frightful shocks and produced a sort of equilibrium.

However objectionable his present state, it had the advantage of security. Buried in the womb of the earth he needed not to fear further
violence and had time to pursue his labouring thoughts — for these at
times almost made him forget his physical sufferings and dangers.
And his security (if we may use the word with reference to almost
certain death — but why not, since death is at all times certain and yet
we feel secure), his feeling of security then, inclined him to sleep.
His exhaustion was so great that it outweighed all else. He fell asleep
and through long stretches of time knew little or nothing of himself.
When he roused, his astonishment at the refreshment which the sleep
had brought (for food and sleep can for a while replace each other)
mingled with a fresh sense of horror that he was still in the pit and
still in misery. Even in sleep he did not entirely lose the sense of
misery; but its worst rigours did, as it were, manage to relax a little.
The bonds were hard, the cramped position still endured; but even
they began to relax, on the second and third days the cords had given
way a little and yielded to the needs of the poor tortured limbs. I say
all this, once more, to confront our sympathy with the solid reality
of facts. But on the other hand, if I add that Joseph was of course
growing weaker all the time, it will serve to keep our pity from quite
dying out, even though I must add that his very weakness was an
amelioration to his sufferings. From this point of view one might
almost say that the longer his stay in the pit lasted, the more tolerable
it was; so that by the end he was scarcely aware of his own misery.

But his thoughts worked on and on, the body almost forgotten. It
was as though, in the piece of music which we have imagined them
to represent, those undertones and basses at the bottom came out
stronger and stronger, thanks to that dreamy weakness of his, until
at last they almost drowned out the overtones. So long as the brethren
were near, the fear of death had been apparent, as expressed in his
urgent entreaties and wailings. But now they were gone and the cries
had died away, why was it that Joseph did not shout in hopes of a
chance rescue? Because he quite forgot to, absorbed as he was in
far other trains of thought, having to do with his abrupt downfall,
with the past and its errors, perhaps ordained by God, but not on
that account less heavy and grievous.

The garment which the brothers had torn off his body — partly
with their teeth, shocking to say — played a prominent rôle in his reflections. That he ought not to have spread himself in it before them,
nor made his ownership visible to their eyes; above all things that he
ought not to have appeared before them in it here and now came over
him so forcibly that he could have beat himself on the head but for
his bonds. He did so in spirit; but even so he had to confess to himself
the futility and curious hypocrisy of the gesture; for now he saw that
he had always understood the whole thing and yet had so behaved.

With amazement he contemplated the riddle of self-destructive arrogance presented to him by his own extraordinary behaviour. His wits could not cope with the riddle successfully — nor can anyone's. Perhaps because so much of the incalculable is implicit therein, so much that is contrary to reason and even perhaps holy. How he had trembled lest Jacob discover the *ketonet* in the bag — trembled, that is, before his own salvation! He had deceived his father, taken advantage of the old man's failing memory, and packed the *ketonet;* but not because he had disagreed with the father as to the effect which the sight of the veil would have upon the brothers. He had understood perfectly and had packed it none the less. How could he have done so? Again, since he had not forgotten to take care for his own destruction, why had Jacob forgotten to prevent it? Another puzzle. Joseph's desire to smuggle the coat could not have been stronger than the father's loving concern that he should leave it at home. Why had not love and anxiety been strong enough to remind the old man and so to foil Joseph's plan? Joseph had succeeded in beguiling away the rich garment from Jacob's tent; it was partly the effect of the game, partly because Jacob wanted the child to have the robe, quite as much as the latter desired it. The consequences followed promptly. Together they had brought the lamp to the pit, and now Jacob would be struck to earth.

But after that he might well bethink him of the mistakes of the past, common to them all — just as Joseph was now doing. The boy was honest with himself: he admitted that he had forsworn himself when he said he would say nothing to Jacob if the brothers released him. The promise had been born of fear; Joseph knew that if the old state of things were restored — which with some part of his being he ardently desired — he must unavoidably tell all, and the brethren would suffer the consequences. Restoration was out of the question; but even if it were not, he was in a way at one with the brethren in not wishing for it. He could almost have returned the kiss which Dan had wanted to throw to him in the pit, so much did he feel that for the first time he was really among them as their brother and might hear all that they said; might even hear that about the blood of the kid which should pass for his blood; it did not matter, since he was as good as dead and buried already.

A strong impression had been made upon Joseph by what Dan had said: that they might say what they liked before Joseph, since every word they uttered only heightened the impossibility of his return home, and that it was good to utter them, since each one bound him more firmly to the lower world and made of him more and more a ghost before whom one shudders. Joseph saw in such words the counterpart and inversion of the rôle which he had played so far in life, that of needing to heed nobody because all the world loved him more than they did themselves. For it was come to this, that no one heeded him at all! The thought conditioned those undertones and basses of his composition, and the weaker he became, the more did they sonorously predominate over the overtones.

But they had begun to play even earlier; at the moment when the undreamed-of became reality; when his provocative conduct had called down punishment and he was tossed to and fro like a toy amongst the brethren and they had torn the picture-robe with their nails and teeth. From that moment on, then, they had been vocal; in the midst of that hail of horrifying blows his ear had in good part hearkened to them. It would be wrong to suppose that under such deadly serious circumstances Joseph had stopped playing and dreaming — if one may still speak of his activity as playing and dreaming, in this connection. He was a true son of Jacob, the man of thoughts and dreams and mystical lore, who always understood what happened to him, who in all earthly events looked up to the stars and always linked his life to God's. Granted that Joseph's way of dignifying his life by attaching it to the higher law and reality was not the same as Jacob's, less spiritual, more shrewdly calculating; yet he seriously held that a life and activity without the hall-mark of higher reality, which does not base upon the traditionally sacred and support itself thereupon, nor is able to mirror itself in anything heavenly and recognize itself therein, is no life or activity at all. He was convinced that nothing in the lower world would know how to happen or be thought of without its starry prototype and counterpart; and the great certainty guiding his life was belief in the unity of the dual, in the fact of the revolving sphere, the exchangeability of above and below, one turning into the other, and gods becoming men and men gods. Not for nothing was he the pupil of old Eliezer, who knew how to say "I" in such an ample way that Joseph's eyes grew dim with musing as he beheld him. The transparency of being, the characteristic recurrence of the prototype — this fundamental creed was in his flesh and blood too, and all spiritual dignity and significance seemed to him bound up with awareness of it. That was as it should be. What was after all not quite as it should be, but seemed more like a degenerate deviation from the significant and admirable type, was Joseph's inclination to draw advantage from the general prepossession in his favour and consciously to impose himself upon those about him.

From the first moment on he was aware of all this. Incredible as it may seem, in the thick of the turmoil, in the acutest moment of fear and danger of death, he had kept his mental eye open to realities. Not that fear and danger grew less thereby; but he actually experienced a sort of joy as well; the pleasure of enlightenment, almost like the relief which laughter brings, had illuminated the dark terror in his soul.

"My coat!" he had cried out in the anguish of his concern; "tear it not, I pray you." Yes, they had rent it in pieces and torn it off him, that was his mother's robe and that belonged also to her son, so that they wore it by turns and became one, and god and goddess by its means. Mercilessly had the brethren unveiled him. As love unveils the bride in the bedchamber, thus had their fury done to him, and they had known him naked, so that his frame quivered with the deathly shame. In his mind thoughts of unveiling and of death dwelt close together — how could he then have helped holding the rags of the garment round him in his fright, begging them to tear it not? Yet no more could he have helped being filled with the joy of understanding, coming to him through association of thought, through the conviction of repetition and realization. No danger of the flesh and the soul could prevent the concentration of his spirit upon the wealth of allusion by which the event proclaimed itself as higher reality, as a transparency of the ancient pattern, as the uppermost turning undermost; in short, as written in the stars. And his concentration was very natural, as the allusions all had to do with being and selfhood, with the vista of his ego which he had opened to Reuben a little time ago to the latter's amaze and which now was growing brighter and brighter. He had wept and wailed when big Reuben had given his voice that they should throw him into the pit; yet at the same time his reason had laughed as at a joke, the word used was so laden with allusions: "*Bor*" the brothers had said. And the monosyllable was capable of various interpretations. It meant not only well, but prison; not only prison, but the underworld, the kingdom of the dead; so that prison and the underworld were one and the same thought, one being only a word for the other. Again, the well, in its property as entrance to the underworld, likewise the round stone which covered it, signified death; for the stone covered the round opening as the shadow covers the dark moon. In Joseph's mind the primeval prototype of the death of the planet peeped through the present event: the dead moon, which is invisible for three days until its new birth, means the death of the gods of light, who must for a time descend to the underworld. When the horror happened and the brothers hoisted him onto the edge of the well and on the margin of the pit, so that he must descend below the daylight with all the caution he could muster — then his quick mind had clearly understood the allegory of the star which one evening is a woman and in the morning a man and which sinks into the well of the abyss as evening star.

It was the abyss into which the true son descends, he who is one with the mother and wears the robe by turns with her. It was the nether-earthly sheepfold, Etura, the kingdom of the dead, where the son becomes the lord, the shepherd, the sacrifice, the mangled god. Mangled? They had torn only his lips and his skin here and there, but the robe they had torn off and rent with nails and teeth, those red murderers and conspirators, his brothers, and they would dip it in the blood of a kid, which should pass for his blood, and they would bring it before the father. God demanded from the father the sacrifice of the son, for the soft-hearted one, who shuddering had confessed that he "could not do it." Poor man, he would have to do it, and it was like God that He paid little heed to what man thinks he can do.

Here Joseph wept in his transparent misery, presided over by his understanding. He wept over poor Jacob, who would have to summon his endurance, and over the brethren's confidence in his death. He wept for weakness and giddiness from the exhalations of the well; but the more lamentable his situation became in the course of the seventy-two hours which he spent here below, the more clearly the undertones of his thoughts came out, the more deceptively his present mirrored itself in its heavenly prototype; so that by the end he no longer distinguished the heavenly from the earthly at all and in the dreamy self-satisfaction of death saw only the unity of the double. We may with justice regard that as a device of nature to tide him over the unbearable. For the natural hope, to which life clings up to the last, needs a reasonable justification; and Joseph found it in this identification. Indeed it extended beyond his life, his hope that he would not finally perish but somehow be saved out of the pit. For, literally speaking, he gave himself up for dead. There was the brethren's confidence, there was the bloody robe, which Jacob should receive. The pit was deep; and return to his former life was inconceivable — a thought as monstrous as that the evening star might return out of the abyss wherein it was sunk, and the shadow be withdrawn from the dark moon, that it should again be full. But the conception of the death of the planet, the darkening and setting of the sun, whose habitation becomes the lower world, included likewise the idea of reappearance, new light, resurrection. And therein Joseph's natural hope that he might live justified itself by faith. It was not a hope that he might return out of the grave into his former life; yet by its means the grave was defeated. Joseph cherished it not only for itself and for its own sake but for the poor old man at home, whom he had brought down into the pit together with himself and who would be stricken to the earth. It would probably be after the son's death that Jacob would receive the bloody robe. But if only the father could have faith beyond death according to the ancient hope, then, thought Joseph in the grave, the blood of the beast would be taken as once it had been, for the blood of the son.

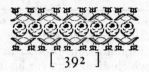

Chapter VI

THE STONE BEFORE THE GRAVE

THE ISHMAELITES

MEN came from Gilead, from the East and beyond the river; rocking along on their camels, four or five, with a few extra pack-animals laden with wares; and with slaves and camel-boys bringing their number up to eight or ten. They were travelling merchants, at home neither here nor in the place whence they came; strange men, very brown of face and hands, with felt circlets round their head-cloths, each wrapped in a burnous with diagonal stripes; they had sharp eyes, showing the whites as they rolled them observantly round. One of their number, who rode at the head of the train, was of dignified age; a thick-lipped boy in a white cotton garment led his animal on a long rein, while the master sat in the high saddle, his head consideringly on one side, with his hands, wrapped in his mantle, resting on the saddle-bow. It was clear that he was the head of the party. The others were his nephew, son-in-law, and sons.

What manner of men were these? That can be told in general, and also with some precision. They lived in the south of the Edom-Seir country, at the edge of the Arabian desert, on the Egyptian side. Their domain, which was a passage and crossing into the land of mud, was called Mizraim, another name for Egypt. But it was also called Muzri; in another dialect Mosar, or even Midian, after the son of Abram and Keturah. It was a colony of the people of Ma'in, farther south, near the land of incense, who traded between Arabia and the kingdom of beasts and of the dead; they had fixed market in western Canaan and the land of the two rivers and at Muzri, went to and fro with wares between the peoples, and convoyed all the state and royal caravans between one country and another.

In other words, our travellers were Ma'onites from Ma'in, or Minæans, called Midianites. But since one scarcely distinguished between Medan and Midian, Abraham's sons by his desert concubine Keturah, they might be called Medanim as well as Midianites — it made no difference to them. Even if you gave them the generic name of all desert folk, taking not Keturah but Hagar the Egyptian as their foremother and simply called them Ishmaelites, they had no objection either. It was of no importance to them what people called them and who they were; the main point for them was that they existed and could trade to and fro on the trade routes. Indeed there was some reason to call the old man and his companions Ishmaelites; for as men of Muzri they were half Egyptian, as had been the fiery and beautiful youth named Ishmael. You might, loosely speaking, say that they were descended from him.

This was no royal or state caravan coming on from the East — by no means. They were private travellers, bound on their own business, and without ostentation. They had been marketing their wares on the hither side of the Jordan, at the fairs which were held on feast-days. They sold Egyptian linens, coarse and fine, also pretty glass trifles of various kinds, taking in exchange, with a good profit to themselves, all sorts of sweetmeats, balsams, incense, and gums. And if on this side of the river they managed to acquire some of the native products, such as honey and mustard, a camel-load of pistachios and almonds, they would be well content. As for their route, they were as yet undecided: whether to follow the road running north and south which ran along the crest of the mountain and would take them by way of Urusalim and Hebron to Gaza by the sea, or whether they would do better first to keep to the north and east and then by way of the Megiddo plain reach the coast and follow along it to their country, which was a passage and a crossing into the land of Egypt.

It was past midday when they entered the valley, the old man in the lead, the others behind him in a row. They intended to see whether the people of Dothan were holding a fair where they could do business. They let their animals pace along on low ground which fell away into a mossy slope. And their quick eyes spied below them the ruined steps and the masonry among the thickets. The old man, crooking his neck, saw it first; he pointed it out to the others, made them stop, and sent down the youth in the cap to spy out the place; for travellers such as these are explorers and inquisitive by nature and must see all there is to see.

The boy was not gone long; he simply jumped down and sprang up again and announced with his thick lips that a covered well was below.

"If it be covered and hidden," said the old man shrewdly, "then it will be worth looking into. The people of the land hereabouts are jealous and stingy; I think it is possible that the well hath water of unusual coolness and freshness — we can use it and take our vessels full; I see nobody who could hinder us; moreover, why are we called Ishmaelites if we may not take what we can in defiance of their jealousy? Take a skin and some bottles and let us go down."

They did as he bade them, for he was their leader. They made
their animals lie down, untied the vessels, and climbed down into the
well-chamber: uncle, nephew, son-in-law, and sons, with some of the
slaves. They soon saw that the well had no bucket and no windlass.
But that was no matter, they would let down a leather bottle and fill
it with the jealously guarded water. The old man sat down on a fallen
quarrystone, settled his clothing, and motioned with his dark-skinned
hand that they should roll away the stone from the hole. The stone
was broken in two.

"This well," the old man said, "is covered indeed, and hidden, but
also it is in a very bad state. The children of the land seem jealous,
but likewise heedless. Meanwhile I will cherish no doubts of the
goodness of the water; that would be premature. Good, one-half of
the stone is rolled aside. Seize me now the other with your young
arms and lay it down beside its moss-grown sister on the flags. So!
Doth now the round of the water within laugh in its purity and is
the mirror clear?"

They stood close to the well, on the low ledge that ran round it,
and bent over the depths.

"The well is dry," said the son-in-law, still looking without turning his head toward the old man. As he said it they all pricked up
their ears. A wailing rose out of the depths.

"It cannot be that the wailing cometh out of this hole," said the
old man. "I trust not my ears. Let us be still and silent and hearken if
perchance we may hear it again."

It wailed once more.

"Now am I forced to trust my ears," the elder said; he stood up
and mounted the step, shoving those aside with his arms who were
in his way, and in his turn looked into the depths.

The others waited courteously for his verdict; but his sight was
already dim and he saw naught.

"Dost thou see anything, Mibsam, my son-in-law?" he asked.

The son-in-law permitted himself to answer: "I see a white thing
on the ground, that moveth and seemeth like a being, and a living
thing."

Kedar and Kedma, the sons, confirmed his words.

"It is amazing," said the old man. "I confide in your sharp eyes and
will call to see if it will answer. Halloo!" he called down the well in
his ancient high-pitched voice. "Who or what is it moaneth in this
well? Is thy place native to thee or wouldst thou be elsewhere?"

They listened. There was a little pause. Then they heard faint and
far away:

"Mother! Save thy son!"

At once they were all excitement.

"Up! No delay!" the elder cried. "Bring a rope, that we may

throw it down and draw the creature up to daylight, for plainly that
abode is not native to him. Here is no mother," he shouted down,
"but we are pious people up here who desire to save thee if it is thy
wish. See now," he turned to his men, "what one may come upon on
a journey! But this is more extraordinary than aught I have met between the two rivers. Was it not shrewdly done, to spy out this
hidden and covered well? And was it not I who proposed it? Men of
small courage might falter or take to their heels; I can see in your
faces that the thought has entered your minds; for it is uncanny to
be spoken to thus, out of the depths; and it is very possible that that
which speaketh is the genius of the abandoned well or some spirit of
the abyss. But we must look at the matter on its practical side and
meet the situation with all our energy; for the wailing from below
indicateth extreme need. Where is the rope?" He bent and called
into the pit: "Canst thou seize a rope which we will throw and tie it
round thee that we may draw thee up?"

Again there was a pause before answer came. Faintly it sounded:
"I lie in bonds."

The old man had put his hands to his ears, but the others had to repeat to him what the voice had said.

"You hear," he said then. "In bonds it lieth. It both heighteneth
his need and maketh harder our task. One of you must go down into
the hole to loose the creature's bonds. Where is the rope? We have
it. Mibsam, my son-in-law, I appoint thee to go down. Thou shalt be
well attached to the rope and it shall be like an arm which we stretch
down into the depths and draw it up again with the bundle in it.
So soon as thou hast it fast, thou must call out and with our united
powers we shall draw thee and our booty up to us again."

Mibsam declared himself ready, for good or for ill. He was a young
man with a short face, a rather long, flat nose, and prominent eyes
whose whites gleamed in the darkness of his face. He took the head-
cloth from his curly hair, laid off his burnous, and lifted his arms to
let himself be wound round with the rope. It was no hempen rope,
but a cord of Egyptian papyrus, wonderfully softened, pounded, and
smoothed, practically unbreakable. He knew its quality well, for the
men carried several bales of it, to sell.

Soon son-in-law was tied and harnessed, ready to swing down.
They all took part in winding him up; Epher, the old man's nephew,
the sons, and the slaves. Then Mibsam sat down on the edge of the
well, let go his hold, and dropped into the empty depths, while those
at the rope braced their legs and passed it in little jerks through their
hands. It soon slackened; Mibsam was on the ground. They could
relax their legs and go to peer into the well. They could just hear
his voice speaking to the creature down there, panting as he lifted
him to attach the rope. "Haul up," he cried then. They hauled away

on the double burden, shouting in unison, while the old man stood by directing them with gestures. Up came the son-in-law above the ruin, bearing in his arms the inhabitant of the well.

Great was the amazement of the merchants when they saw the fettered boy. They lifted eyes and hands to heaven, shook their heads, and clacked with their tongues. They rested their hands on their knees to look at their prize as he sat on the step leaning against the well, with hanging head, in his bonds, spreading abroad a mouldy air. He wore an amulet on a bronze cord round his neck and a ring with a lucky stone on his finger, but nothing else at all. His wounds were closed over and nearly healed by this time and the bump on his eye so far reduced that he could open it. Now and then he did, though mostly he had kept both eyes shut. Now, however, he feebly lifted the long-lashed lids and looked upwards pathetically but with interest at his rescuers. He even smiled over their astonishment.

"Merciful mother of God!" the old man said. "What have we fished up out of the depths? Is he not like the spirit of the abandoned well, miserable, wretched, and half dead, when the water receded and left him stranded? But let us abide by the common-sense side of the affair and the needs of this creature we have found. For from the practical point of view he seems to me to be a boy of good quality, if not of the best, and fallen into bad luck I know not how. Look well at these eyelashes and the delicate growth of the limbs, however befouled they are and stinking from the pit. Kedar and Kedma, shame upon you for holding your noses, for sometimes he openeth his eyes. Loose him first from his fetters, cut them through. Now bring milk to refresh him. Wilt thy tongue obey thee, my son, to make us know who thou art?"

Joseph might have found words, despite his feebleness. But he had no wish to speak, nor any thought of uncovering the family quarrel to these Ishmaelites — it was no affair of theirs. Therefore he only looked dyingly at the old man and smiled piteously as with his freed hand he made a gesture of negation before his lips. He received milk and drank it out of a pot which a slave held for him, for his arms were lame from the bonds. He drank so greedily that a good part of the milk dribbled out of his mouth again directly he had done, as though he were a suckling. When the old man, upon this, asked him how long he had been in the pit, he stretched out three fingers in sign that it had been three days, which the Minæans found very significant and thrilling in view of the three dark days of the moon. When they asked how he got into the pit — in other words, who had thrown him in — he confined his answer to a gesture and motioned with his forehead upwards, so that one could not tell whether men had done so to him or heavenly powers been in play. But when they asked him again who he was, he whispered: "Your servant," and collapsed; so that they were none the wiser.

"Our servant," repeated the elder. "Well, in so far as he is a foundling and without us would not have had breath for his nostrils. I know not what you think, but so much I see, there is a mystery here, for many such there are in the world, as sometimes on journeys one discovereth to one's great amaze. Naught remaineth to us to do but to take this creature with us, for here can we not leave him, nor yet here build huts until he get his strength. I find," he added, "that this lad from the well toucheth my heart in some way, I know not how. For it is not pity alone nor the mystery about him. But about every human being there is an encircling ring, which is not his own flesh, but yet of his flesh, and light or dark as the case may be. Old experienced eyes perceive it better than young heedless ones, who look indeed, but do not see. Now as I look fixedly at this foundling his aura seemeth to me strikingly light and I conceive that he is the sort of find which one doth not throw away."

"I can read tablets and write cuneiform," said Joseph, lifting himself a little. Then he fell back again.

"You hear?" asked the elder, after he had had Joseph's words repeated to him. "He can write and is well brought up. Then is he worth finding, as I said, and not made to be left lying. We will take him with us, for, thanks to my inspiration which led me to look into the well, nobody can say us nay or call us robbers because we exercise a finder's right and do not trouble overmuch to ask after those who threw away or heedlessly lost what we have found. If the owners turn up we have a right to a reward and ransom, and it looketh as though we shall make something either way. Come, put this mantle upon him, for he came naked and foul out of the depth as from the body of his mother and is as it were twice born."

The old man pointed to the mantle which son-in-law Mibsam had thrown down; its owner grumbled against handing it over to the boy from the well, that he might pollute it. But grumbling was of no avail; he yielded to the old man's will, and two slaves bore the child in the mantle to the camels, where he was mounted with Kedma, one of the sons, a youth with severe and regular features and a lofty carriage of the head, so that he looked down upon all things underneath drooping lids. Round his head, atop the white head-cloth, he wore a black felt ring. At the old man's bidding Kedma took Joseph before him on the saddle, and the train got under way, taking the road to Dothan, for it might be market day there.

ALL this time the sons of Jacob were very ill at ease. They were in no wise happier than when the thorn had sat in their flesh and they had stumbled about in the broom hot with their shame. Now the thorn had been pulled out, but the wound was unhealed. It kept on rankling, as though the thorn had been a poisoned one. They had washed out their shame, but it would be too much to say that their sleep tasted better than before. They did not say so, they kept quiet about it.

In fact, in these days they were silent altogether; spoke only when necessary and then grudgingly and between their teeth. They did not meet each other's eyes, but looked anywhere and everywhere, only not in one another's faces when they had to speak. The result was that nobody felt settled about any arrangement, since bargains struck only by word of mouth and not also with the eyes always seem to lack validity. But they did not even care, apparently, whether they were valid or not. Sometimes one or other let fall comments like "All very well —" or "So far, so good," or even "If that were all," which were but gloomy allusions to the thing which stood in the background of all their thoughts and which, not being settled, but very far from it, made worthless every word they uttered.

However, this would have to come to an end some time and some-how, however long, lingering, and disgusting the process: that slow perishing and dying down in the depths, though nobody could proph-esy how long it would take. On the one hand they would have liked to hasten the process, on the other they would gladly have slowed it down, on the chance of some less ugly termination — though they could not imagine what that should be. I have repeatedly warned my readers against taking these sons of Jacob for particularly hardened ruffians and withdrawing all sympathy from them. Even the most partisan weakness for Joseph (a centuries-old weakness from which I strive to be free) should remember that such a judgement would be very one-sided, and that Joseph himself would not concur in it. For the truth is that they had all of them stumbled unawares into the mess they were in, and would much rather be quit of it. More than once in these dreadful days they wished that they had finished with the business at once, and grumbled at Reuben, who had prevented them. But these dismal regrets were only a consequence of the tight place they were in. They felt put in a corner and checkmated; in a situation such as life will often confront us with, and for which a game of chess furnishes a good analogy.

Big Reuben was by no means alone in the wish to save Rachel's child alive out of the grave. Indeed, hardly one among the brethren

but would start up every few hours under the spur of such a wish.
But then would come the question: was it possible? Alas, no, it was
not; the hasty resolve died down, being defeated by the relentless
claims of reason. Suppose they were to rescue the dreamer just in
time to save him — what could they do with him? It was a blank wall,
there was no way out; he must stop where he was. They had not
only thrown him in; in every other way as well they had consigned
him to the tomb and taken every precaution against his rising from
it. He was logically dead; their part was to do nothing but wait until he was actually so: an unnerving programme and without a time
limit. For these poor souls knew nothing of three days. On the contrary, they knew of people who got lost in the desert and spent
seven, yes, twice seven days without food or drink before they were
found. It was good to know this, for it gave some room for hope.
And it was dreadful to know it, since the hope was a mad and impossible one. Not often have men been in such a tight place; to think
only of Joseph's sufferings in these three days would be to give way
to prejudice in his favour.

These tormented souls were sitting one afternoon beneath the red-
trunked trees, on the spot where they had beaten Joseph and where,
a little earlier, they had talked of Lamech, that primitive hero, and
blushed in their shame that they were not as he. Only eight of them
were there; Naphtali the runner was about somewhere in the neighbourhood seeking to hear new things and report them from place to
place; and Reuben had been missing since early morning. He had
mumbled something about going up to Dothan to buy spiced wine
and breadfruit in exchange for some of their own wares. The others
had approved of Reuben's going, on account of what he would bring
back; they were unwontedly eager to comfort themselves and blur
their understandings with some of the myrrh wine which was made
at Dothan.

But the real truth was that Reuben had left them being bent on
quite other activity and had only told them about the wine to make
them approve his going. Tossing sleepless the night before, big Reuben's resolve had come to maturity: he would deceive the brethren
and save the boy. Three days he had held out and left Jacob's lamb
to perish in the well. He could endure no more — God grant it was
not too late. He would steal away and with his own hand free him
whom they had consigned to the grave. He would take him by the
hand and lead him back to their father and speak to him: "I am unstable as water, and sin is not far from me. But lo, here I have flowed to
good purpose, for I bring thee thy lamb, which they would have rent.
Is my sin thereby blotted out, and am I again the first-born?"

Reuben tossed no longer, but lay open-eyed and motionless the
rest of the night and made detailed plans for the rescue and the flight.

It would not be too easy: the boy was bound hand and foot and would be very weak. He would not be able to grasp the rope which Reuben would throw to him; a cord would not do, there must be a strong hook on it, to catch the knotted rope, in order to haul up the prize. Perhaps a web of cords would be better, a net to take his fish in. Or even a board among the cords, on which the boy, clumsy in his bonds as he was, could sit and be drawn up over the edge. Reuben went over all the necessary preparations and equipment, including his own clothes, which he would have ready for the naked lad; he chose in his mind the stout ass which he would drive to Dothan with wool and cheeses, and then ride, with the boy before him and in the shelter of darkness, the five days' journey to Hebron, to the father. Big Reuben's heart was full of eager joy, only dampened somewhat by the fear lest Joseph might not survive until dark of the third day. When he took leave of his brethren that morning, he had ado to speak and act with the dour ill-temper which had become their settled mood.

THE SALE

Eight of them, then, sat beneath the spreading branches of the pines and gazed gloomily into space in the direction whence the shining had come and that wandering will-o'-the-wisp that had so dazed their senses and lured them to their present pass. As they looked they saw their brother Naphtali, Bilhah's son, come running among the shrubbery on their right. He came on with great leaps of his long sinewy legs, and they could tell even at this distance that he was bringing them news. They cared but little for it, however.

"Brothers, children, friends," he unfolded, "I bring you news: a train of Ishmaelites is riding from Gilead, their noses directed hitherwards, and must soon be here and pass by three stones' cast from where you sit. They seem friendly heathen, with bales of goods, and trade with them would be possible if we were to call to them."

They hearkened, then turned their heads listlessly away.

"It is so far good," said one. "Good, Naphtali, we thank thee for thy news."

"If that were all," another added, sighing. Then they were quiet, tortured with irritation and feeling no desire for trade.

Yet after a while they became restless, fidgeted to and fro, and stared about them. And when Jehudah — for it was he — lifted up his voice and addressed them, they all started and turned toward him: "Speak, Judah, for we hearken." And Judah spoke:

"Sons of Jacob, I have somewhat to ask you, and it is this: of what profit is it to us that we slay our brother and hide his blood? I answer for you all: no profit whatever. It was utterly weak and contemptible that we threw him in the pit and persuaded ourselves that his blood was spared thereby, that we might eat by the well; for to shed it we were all afraid. But do I blame our fear? Nay, yet I blame that we lied to ourselves over it and made distinctions like doing and happening, hiding ourselves behind them, yet standing naked and bare, for that they are but wind. We lusted to be like Lamech in the song and slay the young man for our hurt. But our customs are not those of the ancient time and of heroic mould. Somewhat we must yield to the present; and lo, instead of killing the youth we could only let him die. Fie upon us, for it was but a bastard thought, begot of the ancient saga and the modern customs! Therefore I say to you, since we did not know how to do like unto Lamech and had to yield somewhat to the conditions as they exist, let us then be honest to conform to them altogether and let us sell our brother to these Ishmaelites."

A stone fell from all their hearts, for Judah had spoken after their thoughts. Now were their eyes entirely open, which indeed had already begun to blink at the light as they considered the news brought by Naphtali. Here was the way, simple and clear, out of their impasse. It was the way of Naphtali's Ishmaelites, coming God knew whence and passing into the immensity, the misty distance whence there was as little return as from the grave. They could not have lifted up the boy, however much they had wished — and suddenly now they could; for he should be delivered to these oncoming ones of the desert, and with them should depart out of sight and knowledge as the falling star and its trail quench in nothingness together. Even Simeon and Levi, seeing that heroic methods were out of fashion, found nothing to object to in the plan.

They all broke out together in eager, low-toned haste, saying: "Yea, yea, yea, yea! Thou sayest it, Judah, thou hast spoken most excellently. To the Ishmaelites; sell him, sell him, for that is the way out; thus are we freed and our troubles at an end. Bring Joseph here; up, and raise him out of the well, for they are coming, and it is still conceivable that he liveth. A man may live twelve or fourteen days, so experience teacheth. Some to the well straightway, while the others . . ."

But lo, even as they spoke, here came the Ishmaelites. The foremost appeared three stones' throw away, an old man with his hands wrapped in his mantle, and his camel led by a boy. Behind him in single file came the others, riders, pack-camels, and drovers — no very stately train; these traders seemed not to be very rich, two even sat on one camel. They moved like shadows tranquilly across the scene, their eye directed upon Dothan's hill.

It was too late to fetch Joseph. Too late for the moment. But Jehudah was firmly resolved, and the others as well, not to lose the opportunity, but to clutch it by the forelock and attach the boy to these Ishmaelites that they should take him out of sight and sound and so set the brethren free, for the situation was no longer endurable. The ancestor of these travellers — had he not been sent by Abraham, with Hagar into the desert, because he had "sported" in an underworldly manner with Isaac, the son of the true wife? With Ishmael's sons should Joseph be put off into the desert — the situation had roots; it had been once, and it recurred. New, if you like, a really original contribution, was the idea of the sale. But even so it has for thousands of years been booked too high on the debit side of the brethren's account. To sell a man, to sell one's own brother! But after all it is sentimental to judge without soberly taking into account the customs of the time and the country, which deprive the sale of almost all its unique and dubious character. A needy man sold his sons — and surely the brethren were in sore need! Fathers sold their daughters in marriage — the eight now sitting here would never have drawn breath or been sitting there at all if Jacob had not bought their mothers from Laban with fourteen years' toil.

It was a bit awkward, after all, that the merchandise was not at hand, but stored, so to speak, in a pit in the field. But it could be fetched at the right moment, and the first thing was to accost the strangers and try if they had desire to buy.

Therefore the eight set their hands to their lips and cried out abroad:

"Halloo, men and strangers, whence come ye and whither go? Stay a little. For here are shade-trees and folk with whom to talk."

The sound travelled across and found hearing from the merchants. They turned their eyes from the hill of Dothan and their heads toward those who called. The leader nodded, gestured, and turned aside to visit these natives, who had got up and greeted the travellers, putting their fingers under their eyes in token that they were glad to see the guests. The brethren touched brow and breast to indicate that here as there all was in readiness to receive them. The boys ran, flourishing their switches, among the camels and making clucking sounds to induce them to kneel and lie down. The riders dismounted, went through the formalities of greeting, and sat down together. The brothers remained where they were, with the strangers opposite. The old man held the middle place, right and left of him the row of his companions, sons, nephew, and son-in-law. The retinue kept farther back. But between it and the heads of the party, behind the strangers, and in a space directly between the master and one of his sons, sat a figure with a cloak drawn over his head and before his face so that only a gap of forehead showed.

Why were the brothers impelled, during the preliminary exchange of courtesies, to keep looking at the shrouded figure in the second row? The question answers itself. The silence of the isolated figure involuntarily drew all eyes upon it — everyone would have done as the brethren did, for who wraps himself up to the eyes in fine weather as though a dust-spirit were approaching? The brothers were not at their ease, they were distracted. Not on account of that solitary figure — it best knew why it shunned the light, and might keep the knowledge to itself. No, it was because the merchandise they had to sell ought to be fetched, and it would have been well if some of them, two or three, had got up and gone to take it from where it was kept and somewhat freshen it up before offering it for sale, as they had arranged in whispers to do, while the company was approaching. Why did they not go? Probably because it had not been decided who should go. But they might have decided among themselves. Perhaps they feared to seem rude. But they could have made some excuse. Dan, Zebulun, Issachar, for instance — what held them glued to their places, staring distracted at the figure in the space behind the merchant and his son?

Each side gave account of itself, with phrases in which boasting and self-depreciation were equally balanced. Jehudah stated that he and his were simple shepherd folk, scum of the earth, compared with the lords sitting before them, and sons of an exceeding rich man in the south, a real king of the flocks, and prince of God. Some of his countless possessions were pastured in this valley, a small part only, though more than the eye could take in. The rest were at Hebron, and there too the country was too small to hold them. With whom, then, had they, in their unworthiness, to do?

The old man answered to all this that if one were to turn away his eyes from so much splendour and cast them upon himself and his troupe, one would see scarcely anything, first because their eyes had been dazzled, but secondly because there was not much to see. They were, indeed, sons of the great kingdom of Ma'on in the continent of Arabia, and dwelt in the land of Mozar or Midian. Thus they were Midianites, or, if you liked, Medanites, or, more simply still, Ishmaelites. It mattered not how they were called, since they were too worthless to merit a name. They had equipped caravans which more than once had gone to the ends of the earth; they traded to and fro amongst kingdoms, convoying treasures worth a king's ransom: the gold of Ophir and the balsams of Punt. From the kings they asked royal prices, but amongst friends they were cheap. Their camels were laden with sheets of milk-white tragacanth, of exquisite fracture, such as had never been seen in this valley, and frankincense which would tempt the noses of the gods, so that no one once smelling it would smell any other. So much for the insignificance of the guests.

The brothers kissed their finger-tips and sketched a contact between the earth and their foreheads.

"This land of Mosar, or Ma'inland," Jehudah inquired, "is it very far away indeed, in dim and misty distance?"

"Very far in space and thus also in time, certainly," the old man agreed.

"Seventeen days distant?" asked Jehudah.

"Seven times seventeen," responded the elder. Even at that its remoteness was only approximately indicated. In motion as in rest — for rest, too, belongs to travel — one must patiently leave it to time to overcome space. Some time or other, in the end unexpectedly time would bring that about.

Then one might say, Judah ventured to think, that these regions of their destination lay beyond our ken, God knew how far in immeasurable space?

One might so express oneself, assented the old man, if one had never traversed the distance in question and was not used to league himself with time against space, but rather to take no advantage of time for that end. If one was at home in that distance, one naturally thought about it in less fantastic terms.

He and his, Judah said, were shepherds and not travelling merchants. But if he might say so, the latter were not unique in their understanding of the patient pact with time against space. Shepherds too were travellers, they had to seek new pastures and wells and to rove and wander even as the lord of the road, in this respect being unlike the peasant of the fields, the settled sons of Baal. Their father, the king of the flocks, dwelt, as he had said, five days' journey southwards, and this distance, however insignificant compared with a stretch of seven times seventeen days, they had often traversed to and fro, so that they knew by heart every boundary stone, well, and tree that was in it, and nothing on the way surprised them. As for travel and the conquest of space: of course they could not compete with merchants from the dim and remote distance; yet even as boys they had come from the land of the rivers in the far East, where once their father had laid the foundation of his riches, and come into this land, and dwelt in the vale of Shechem, where indeed their father had built a well fourteen ells deep and very broad because the children of the city had been jealous over the existing water-supply.

"May they be punished unto the fourth generation!" said the old man. It was lucky that the children of the land had not also seized on the well of the speaker's father and zealously filled it up so that it would have become dry, he added.

Two could play at that game, responded the nine. They had in the end been able to leave the Shechemites with a bitter taste in their mouths!

Were they then, the old man asked, such mighty heroes, so cruel and implacable in their wrath?

Shepherds they were, was the answer; accustomed to bear arms, to battle with bandits and beasts of prey, and not to give ground in disputes over pasture and well. But as for distance, and stout-heartedness on the way, Judah went on, after the old man had paid homage to their virility, their ancestor seemed to have had wandering in the blood. He came from Ur, in the land of the Chaldees and had migrated into these valleys, which he had measured across and across, unable to settle down. If one reckoned up all his wanderings, the sum would probably come to seven times seventeen days. But once he had sent his oldest servant on a journey with ten camels toward Naharaim, that was Shinar, to woo a bride for his miraculous late-born and rescued son, and the servant had fared so briskly that it was scarce exaggeration to say that the earth had sprung to meet him. And at a well in the field he had found the bride and recognized her because that she gave him water with her own hand and had also given his ten camels to drink. All this travelling and conquest of space had been in their family — not to speak of its father and lord, who already as a doughty youth had left home and gone into Chaldæa, some seventeen days and more. There he had come on a well . . . .

"Pardon," said the old man, as he stretched his hand out of his cloak and stopped the speech. "Pardon, my good friend and shepherd, if thy elder servant make some comment on thy words. When I list to thee and hear thee tell of thy tribe and its history, it seemeth to me that in it the well hath played a rôle as important as all your experience in moving and wandering."

"How so?" asked Judah, and stiffened his back. All the brothers did the same.

"Thus," replied the elder. "Thou speakest and every second the word 'well' striketh on mine ear. You change well and pasture. You have the wells of the country by heart. Your father hath built a well very deep and broad. Your grandfather's oldest slave wooed at the well. Your father too as it seems. Mine ears are buzzing with all these wells."

"My lord merchant," answered Judah, standing very stiff and erect, "meaneth to say that my words are monotonous and droning. That is grievous to hear. We brothers are herdsmen, not spinners of tales by the we— not lie-mongers of the market-place, who have learned it and do it after their art, for hire. We speak and tell as we think, without artifice or skill. But indeed I would ask how one could tell of the life of man, for instance the life of shepherds, and not talk of travel and therewith of wells, without which there cannot be any coming and going. . . ."

"Very true," the old man interrupted. "My friend, the son of the king of the flocks, answereth me most aptly. What a part doth not the well play in the life of man, and how many tales and sayings are bound up with them, even in the mind of your ancient servant; whether they hold standing or living water, or are dry and choked with refuse! But indeed mine hearing, which is somewhat dull from age, had not been so receptive for the word were it not for a strange matter we have encountered on our travels, which I reckon amongst the most astonishing within my memory. I trust that of your good-ness you will give me advice and enlighten me concerning it."

The brothers started bolt upright once more; their backs were quite hollow, their eyes stared unwinkingly.

"Is there not perchance," asked the old man, "in the country here-abouts where you pasture, a child missing, so that it cannot be found at its home, but hath been stolen or carried away or indeed devoured by a lion or other beast of prey, because it hath not come home for three days?"

"No," answered the brethren. Not that they knew of.

"Then who is this?" said the old man. He reached behind him and jerked Joseph's mantle from off his head. There he sat, behind and between the men, in a nest of falling folds, his eyes modestly cast down. His face looked rather as it had on the day in the field when he sat in his father's lap and related his shameless dream of the stars. At least it reminded the brethren of that.

Several of them had leaped to their feet on recognizing the figure, but they all sat down again at once.

"Oh, thou meanest him," said Dan, seeing that it was time for him to display his snake- and adder-like gifts, "when thou spakest of the well and of lost people? Nobody else? Well, thou hast made a great find. That is a slave, a nobody's son, a villein of the lowest sort, a dog whom we have had to punish for continual theft, for lying, blasphemy, brawling, impenitence, whoredom, and all heaped-up sins against virtue. For young as he is, he is a standing sink of iniquity. Thou hast found him and taken him out of the pit where we put him for his instruction, the gallows-bird? Lo, thou hast been before us, for his punishment was out at this hour and we were about to grant him his life, if perchance he might have profited from the chastise-ment."

Thus Bilhah's son in all his subtlety. What he said had the boldness of desperation, for there sat Joseph and could open his mouth if he would. But it seemed that his brothers might still have confidence in him, thanks to his thoughts while in the pit, for in fact Joseph said no word, but sat with mild eyes cast down and behaved like a lamb that before the shearers is dumb.

The old Midianite said "Oh" and "Ah," wagging his head, as his eyes roved to and fro between the culprit and his judges. The wag-ging gradually became a shaking, for something about the tale rang false, and the old man would gladly have asked his foundling the rights of the matter; but tact forbade. Therefore he said:

"What do I hear, what do I hear? Such a rogue is he, on whom we had pity and helped him out of the pit in his extremity? For this I must say, you carried your discipline to the last notch. When we found him, he was already so weak that he could not swallow the milk we gave him. If you set any store by him, you have delayed full long with your rescue; though of course he may not be worth saving, being, as you say, uncommonly full of misdemeanours, as is shown, indeed, by the harshness of the punishment."

Then Dan bit his lip, for he saw that he had said too much. He had spoken incautiously, even if Joseph's silence could be depended upon; a poke in the ribs from Judah apprised him of the fact. Dan had only thought of explaining to the Ishmaelites why they had treated the boy so cruelly. Judah, however, was thinking of the sale, and the two points of view were hard to reconcile. They were being forced to cry down their merchandise in the ears of the purchaser — it went against all sense, it had never happened to the sons of Jacob, and they were exceedingly ashamed. Apparently in this business of Joseph they got out of one tight place only to fall into another.

Judah undertook to rescue their business honour out of this pass. He said: "Well, well, all honour to the truth: the measure of the punishment may have gone beyond the offence and perhaps is misleading as to the worth of the chattel — but let that pass. We sons of the king of the flocks are somewhat harsh and hasty masters; stern, mayhap over-stern in anger against moral lapses, a little hard-handed and ruthless in our decisions. The misdeeds of this young scapegrace here, if taken singly, were not too considerable; only the sum and the repetition of them gave us to think and decided us on the sharpness of the punishment. Its very excess showeth how highly we valued the slave and what care we took to preserve his worth. For his skill and understanding are remarkable; and as he now sits there with his sins purged by our severity, he is a valuable possession. All this I say and set down in the interest of truth," Judah concluded.

Dan blushed not a little for his misplaced subtlety, yet rejoiced that Leah's son had been so clever in getting out of the trap.

"H'm, h'm," croaked the old man, looking to and fro between Joseph and his brothers, shaking his head the while. "A clever rogue, indeed, as you say. What is the young dog's name?"

"He hath no name," replied Dan. "What should his name be? He has had no name at all up to now, for we said already that he is a nobody's son, a bastard and wild shoot begot in the swamps; he hath no tribe. We simply whistle or shout to call him, or say 'Come hither.' "

"H'm, h'm," went the old man again. "So, a bad stock and wild is this culprit of yours. Strange, strange! How surprising is the truth at times! It is against reason and politeness, and yet one wondereth. When we took him out of his prison, this rush-born rascal told us he could read written, and write himself. Was he lying?"

"Not quite that," answered Judah. "We said already that he hath an understanding worthy of mention and is of no common dexterity. He can keep a list and books about jugs of oil and bales of wool. If he said no more, he kept his tongue clear of false witness."

"May it be at all times avoided," responded the elder. "For truth is god and king, and Neb-ma-rê is its name. One must bow before it, no matter what its sound. Can my lords and the lords of the swamp boy read and write?" asked he, with narrowed eyes.

"We consider that a slave's business," answered Judah shortly.

"That it sometimes is," granted the old man. "But also gods write the name of kings on trees, and great is Thoth. Possibly he hath himself sharpened the rushes and instructed him; may the ibis-headed one not set down the jest against me! But true it is: all ranks of men are governed. Only the scribe is not, for he governeth himself and needeth not to drudge. There are countries where this child of the calamus would be set over you and the sweat of your brows. For lo, I can imagine — and my imagination doth not entirely desert me, if I choose to put the case, in jest — that he were the lord and you his slaves. See," he went on, "I am a merchant, and a skilled one, believe me; for I have grown old in appraising things and the value of them; so that it is not easy to fool me when I have stuff between thumb and forefinger, as to whether it be of worth, and whether the weave is coarse or fine or of medium quality. All that I can tell between my fingers; and my old head too is bent askew with the old habit of testing, so that no one can sell me poor for good. See now, the youth is fine in grain and fibre, if also worn from hard usage. I put my head on one side and rub my fingers and I can tell. I speak not of his skill, his understanding and dexterity in writing, but of the stuff and the texture — and there I am a judge. Therefore I make bold to jest and say: My reason would not stand still were I to hear that the 'Come hither' was the master and you his servants. But ye tell me truly it is the other way round."

"Of a certainty," replied the brethren, and stiffened their backs again.

The old man was silent.

"Well," he said after a while, and again he narrowed his eyes, "since he is your slave, sell me the boy!"

In this way he put them to the test. Something in the affair was dark to him, and he made the offer suddenly and at random, slyly curious as to its effect.

"Take him as a gift," murmured Judah mechanically. And when the Midianite had shown that his head and heart were receptive to the flourish of speech, the other went on:

"Though it is against fairness that we should have had trouble with the boy and, having purged him from moral offence, should give you to inherit the fruit of our discipline! But since you have a mind to him, then make your offer."

"Do you, on the contrary, make your own price," said the old man. "For not otherwise will I consider it."

And now began the bargaining and the haggling over Joseph, and persisted unabated five hours long, until sunset and late in the day. Thirty silver pieces Judah demanded in the name of the brethren. The Minæan replied that he must be jesting. One might smile at the joke, but naught else would come of it. Was he to pay in moon metal for a mere son of the swamps and nameless "Come hither," who, on their own evidence, suffered from great moral weakness? (This was the retort upon Dan's over-zealous crying down of the merchandise by justifying the severity of the penance.) The old man made full use of the blunder to cheapen the price. But he too had made a mistake, in rubbing his fingers and boasting of his knowledge of quality, for thus he committed himself to his high valuation of the goods by texture and weave — and that was to the advantage of the sellers. Judah took him at his word and on his honour as a judge of quality, crying up the lad's superior fineness as though he and his had never cherished the smallest ill-will against it, nor on account of it had thrown the object of their competition into the well. In the heat of the bargaining they forgot all shame; yes, Judah did not hesitate to say that a youth so fine that he could be master of them all and they his slaves should not be flung away under thirty pieces of silver! He behaved as though he were quite infatuated with the article of sale, saying that five-and-twenty silver pieces was the very lowest sum, with which he went over and kissed the mute and blinking Joseph on the cheek and exclaimed that not even for fifty shekels could he or would he part with such a treasure of cleverness and charm!

But the old man did not let himself be led away in suchwise; and his position was the stronger, seeing that he was fairly sure that the brothers were bent on being rid of the boy at any price. It was easy to find this out, by feigning to break off the chaffering. Fifteen silver shekels, namely according to the lighter Babylonian weight, were what he had offered; but when the brethren, by urging upon him his own words, had made him go up to twenty Phœnician shekels, he stopped there and would not be screwed up any further. It was in his power to say that he had found the boy in utter danger of death and to assert a finder's right to ransom money. So that he was showing very high business standards in not subtracting anything from the purchase price but rather in being prepared to pay the good round sum of twenty shekels Phœnician. If that were not worth their while, then he would withdraw the offer and would hear no more talk about this lad of the swamps who could wield the reed.

So the bargain was struck: twenty silver pieces, weighed out according to custom. The brethren slew a lamb of the flock beneath the trees in honour of the guests, let the blood run out, and fanned their fire to roast the flesh, that they might lift their hands and eat together in confirmation, and to celebrate the bargain. Joseph too received a piece from his new master, the Minæan. And as he ate, he saw how the brethren took occasion privily to take the tattered festal garment and stain it all over in the blood of the sacrifice. Before his eyes and unashamed they had done this, confiding in his silence. And he ate of the lamb whose blood was to stand for his own.

The meal and the strengthening were in place, for the chaffering was very far from being finished. The large lines had been laid down when the price was fixed. But now began, so to speak, the retail trading; namely, the laying out of the sum in goods. For we need not think, no matter how often we have heard it, that the brothers, when they sold Joseph, received this price from the Ishmaelites in ringing coin paid out of the bag into their hands. The old man never dreamed of paying in silver, to say nothing of currency. He had his own reasons. For who carries such a weight of metal about with him on journeys? Moreover, what buyer would not prefer to liquidate his debt in articles of value, since thereby he assumes the part of the seller, and every article thus sold becomes itself an opportunity for profit? One and a half shekels of silver, in silver pieces, the Minæan weighed out to the shepherds on the delicate scale he carried at his girdle. The rest of the sum would be made up by the merchandise in his packs. They unloaded the camels and spread out their wares in the grass: incense and fine-fractured gums from beyond the river and all sorts of other delightful and useful objects: razors and knives of copper and flint, lamps, ointment-spoons, canes with inlaid work, blue glass beads, oil of resin, and sandals — a whole bazaar of notions that lay before the buyers' covetous eyes. Up to the sum of eighteen and a half silver pieces they might pocket what they chose for their own. Each object now began to be haggled over, as though it were an end in itself. The evening came on, long before they got to the end and Joseph had been sold for a little silver, a great many knives, bits of scented gum, lamps, and walking-sticks.

Then the Ishmaelites packed up again and made their adieux. They had taken time for the deal, sparing not the hours. So now they must make time spatially fruitful again and had in mind to travel another stretch in the night before they encamped. The brothers did not

urge them to stop. But they advised them concerning their journey
and the roads to take.

"Above all," they said, "avoid going inland or along the watershed
to Hebron — it is inadvisable, let our friends be warned. The roads
are rough, the animals will stumble, and vagabonds are lurking everywhere. Go farther along the plain and turn into the road that leads
down through the hills along the foot of the orchards to the borders
of the country. Thus you will be safe and can ride always on the
pleasant sea-sand seven times seventeen days or as far as you like; it
is a pleasure to travel by the sea, one never tires of it, and it is on all
accounts most sensible."

The merchants promised, as they took their leave. The camels got
up beneath them, and Joseph, the bartered slave, was mounted with
Kedma, the old man's son. His eyelids drooped as they had done the
whole time, even when he ate of the lamb. And the brothers, too,
stood with downcast eyes as the train disappeared in the quickly falling twilight. Then they took a long breath and breathed it out again:
"Now is he gone and is no more!"

REUBEN COMES TO THE PIT

BUT in the falling dusk and in the whispering evening that drew on,
lighted by great stars, Reuben, Leah's son, was driving his laden ass
from Dothan along sequestered paths toward the grave of Joseph, that
he might fulfil the plans he had made the night before in anguish and
in love.

In his broad, powerful breast his heart throbbed strongly; for
though he was big, he was soft and excitable, and he feared the brethren, that they might seek him and prevent the work of rescue, which
was to be likewise the instrument of his atonement and reinstatement.
His muscular face was pale in the darkness, and his great legs like columns in their bands trod the ground noiselessly. He spoke no word
to his ass, but grimly prodded the phlegmatic beast in the flesh of its
rump to make it get on. One thing Reuben feared above all: that the
stillness of death might prevail in the well when he came up and
softly called his brother's name. That Joseph might not have kept
soul and body together, but be gone beyond reach, and all preparations be vain, including the ladder which the ropemakers of Dothan
had made under his eye.

For Reuben had, after much thought, decided on the ladder. It
would do for various contingencies: Joseph could climb up on it if
his strength held out; or, if it did not, he might seat himself between
the treads and be drawn up to the daylight by Reuben's muscular
arms, which had once enfolded Bilhah and would surely be strong
enough to draw up Jacob's lamb out of the depths. He had a coat to

cover Joseph's nakedness, and food for five days hung from the animal's flanks — for five days' time would be needed for the flight from
his brothers, whom Reuben would thus betray and bring to grief.
He bowed his head and owned as much to himself as he stole by
night to the grave. This much evil big Reuben would do in order to
do good. For that it was good and necessary to save Joseph, of that
he had no doubts at all, and if the good and the evil mingled in his
deed, it could not be helped. Life was like that. But Reuben also had
faith that he could turn evil into good. Once he had put himself right
with the father and was again the first-born son, he could hope to
rescue the brethren too and hack a way for them out of their impasse.
His word would avail much, and he would give it on their side, in
asking all to share the guilt, including even the father himself, that
there might come a great insight and mutual pardon, and righteousness might prevail for ever.

Thus Reuben sought to still his throbbing heart and to console
himself for his mixed motives, which were turbid and involved like
everything in life. But now he had come to the slope and the wall,
where he stopped to see that he was not being watched. Then he
took rope and coat and descended on tiptoe to the broken steps and
penetrated through the fig-tree scrub into the well-chamber.

The stars shone down on the broken flags, but there was no moon,
and Reuben walked warily, drawing a deep breath as he went down,
for his excitement had winded him and he needed breath for the call
he was to cry down into the depths. "Joseph, art thou alive?" With
what a passionate joy would he hear the answer, with what heartsinking the lack of it! And then the call died unuttered, or changed
into a hoarse cry of fear. For he was not alone down here. Someone
was sitting there in the starlight.

How could that be? Someone sat there beside the well, and it was
uncovered. The two halves of the lid lay one on top of the other
on the flags, and the figure sat on them in a short mantle, leaning on
his staff, and looked at Reuben sleepily, saying not a word.

Big Reuben's legs felt shaky from his stumbling. He was so dazed
that for a moment he thought he saw Joseph before him, Joseph who
had died and now, a spirit, sat beside his tomb. But this unlovable
presence was not at all like Rachel's son: even Joseph's ghost would
surely not have been so uncommon tall; nor would he have had such
a thick neck and little head on top. But then why was the stone
rolled away from the well? Reuben was utterly puzzled. He stammered:

"Who art thou?"

"One of many," coolly answered the seated figure. He raised his
chin and well-shaped mouth so that they looked particularly plastic. "I am nothing startling, be not afraid. But whom seekest thou?"

"Whom I seek?" repeated Reuben, put out by the unexpected encounter. "First of all I will hear what thou dost in this place."

"Oh, so thou wouldst know that? I am the last to imagine that there is anything here to seek. I am set to guard this well, therefore I sit here and watch. If thou imaginest that I have particular pleasure or sit here for the fun of the thing, then thou mistakest. I act according to duty and to carry out orders — it easeth many a vexed question to do so."

Curiously enough Reuben's anger at the presence of the stranger was somewhat appeased by these words. It was so unwelcome and annoying to find anyone on the spot that he was glad to hear that the man was not here by his own wish. It made a sort of bond between them.

"But who hath placed thee here?" he asked, somewhat mollified. "Was it the people of the place?"

"Of the place, yes. Whence such an order cometh, we shall let that pass. It is commonly transmitted through many mouths and there is small use in following it back to its source, for one must stand guard in any case."

"Stand guard by an empty well!" cried Reuben, his voice choking.

"Empty, certainly," the watcher replied.

"An uncovered one," Reuben amended, and pointed with trembling finger at the well-hole. "Who hath rolled away the stone from the well? Was it thou, perchance?"

The man smiled and looked down at his arms in the sleeveless linen garment; they were round, but weak. He was right, these were no arms to roll the lid either on or off.

"Neither on nor off have I rolled the stone," said the stranger, smiling again and shaking his head. "The one thou knowest, the other thou seest. Others have toiled and moiled, and I should not be needing to sit here and watch, were the stone still in its place. But who can say where is the true place of such a stone? Sometimes it is on the hole, but must not the lid be rolled away if refreshment is to come out of the well?"

"What sayest thou?" cried Reuben, tortured by his impatience. "I think thou prattlest, stealing my costly time with thy nonsense. How shall a dry well give refreshment, wherein is naught but dust and mould?"

"That dependeth," the seated one replied, pursing his lips, his little head laid on one side, "what one had previously confided to the dust and what one sank into its womb. If it were life, then will life and refreshment come out again a hundredfold. A kernel of wheat for instance. . . ."

"Thou fellow," Reuben interrupted him in a trembling voice, and the ladder and the mantle for Joseph shook in his hands, "it is intolerable that thou sittest there speaking of the rudiments of things as one knoweth them by heart and as the child is taught in its mother's lap. I charge thee — "

"Thou art right impatient," said the stranger. "Permit me to say that thou remindest me of a rushing stream. Thou shouldst learn patience and to await; for these are the rudiments of things and must be understood by all, for he who cannot abide nor have patience findeth nothing, either here or anywhere. For all fulfilment is a slow matter. It may begin and may cast this way and that and appear as the temporary present both in heaven and on earth, when as yet it is but a trial and a promise. Thus will fulfilment roll along but slowly, like the stone when it is heavy and hard to roll from the tomb. Yet must one roll and push until it be really rolled away, though meanwhile I myself sit here only as a trial and a promise."

"Sit here then no longer," Reuben cried out. "Dost thou understand? I would pack thee off and have thee vanish that I may be alone with this well, which is my affair more than thine; up, this minute, or I will help thee find thy legs. Canst thou not see, spindle-arms, thou who canst not roll but only sit there and gape, that God hath made me strong as a bear and I am provided with a knotted rope to serve various ends? Up and away, or I will fly at thy throat."

"Touch me not," said the stranger, and stretched out his long round arm toward the angry man. "Bethink thee that I am of this place and thou wilt have them about thine ears if thou layest hand on me. Have I not told thee that I am set here? Vanish of course I could and with ease, but not at thy behest and in neglect of my duty, which telleth me to sit here for practice and watch. Comest thou with thy fine coat and thy trumpery cords and markst not at all how absurd thou art in coming thus to an empty well — as thou sayest thyself!"

"Empty as a well," explained Reuben impetuously, "empty of water!"

"Empty altogether," answered the watchman. "The grave is empty, now that you are here."

But Reuben held in no longer; he rushed to the well, leaned over, and cried, low but urgently, into the depths:

"Joseph, Joseph, art alive and hast yet strength?"

The man on the stone shook his head and smiled pityingly. He even copied Reuben's voice, calling and clucking with his tongue. Then he said: "Comest here to talk into an empty hole? What unreason! Here is no boy, far and wide. If one was once there, then the place did not hold him. Cease thou to make a fool of thyself with thy gear and thy crying into the void!"

Reuben stood there still bent over the gulf out of which no word answered him.

"Horrible!" he cried. "He is dead or gone. What shall I do? Reuben, what wilt thou do now?"

And all his pain, his disappointment, his despair burst out of him.

"Joseph!" he cried out. "I would save thee and help thee out of the pit with my arms. Here is the ladder, here is the coat for thy body. Where art thou? Thy door is open. Thou art lost. I am lost. Where shall I go, since thou art gone, stolen and dead? — Thou fellow, thou man of the place," he cried, in an abandonment of suffering, "sit not there dumb, on these stones which the thieves have rolled away, but advise and help me. A boy was here; Joseph, my brother, Rachel's child. His brethren and I, we put him here three days ago in punishment for his arrogance. But his father waiteth for him — with what infinite waiting cannot be told; and if they say to him that a lion hath torn the lamb, he will be struck to earth. Therefore I am come with cord and coat, to draw up the boy out of the well and bring him to the father, for he must have him back! I am the oldest. How shall I come before the father's face if the boy returneth not, and where shall I go? Tell me, help me, who hath rolled away the stone and where has Joseph gone?"

"Seest thou?" said the stranger. "Thou camest to the well-house, thou wast incensed at my presence and vexed because I sat upon the stone; but now thou comest to me for comfort and advice. And thou dost quite rightly; perhaps it is thou on whose account I am set here near the grave, that I should sink one or other seed-corn in thy understanding and it might germinate there. The boy is no longer here, that thou seest. His dwelling standeth open, it has not held him, thou wilt see him no more. But someone there must be to cherish the seed of expectation, and since it was thou who camest to save the brother, thou shalt be the one."

"What shall I await, if Joseph is gone, stolen and dead?"

"I know not what thou understandest by dead and what by living. Thou hast laughed at the childish elements of things, but yet I may remind thee of the grain of corn when it lieth in the grave, and ask thee how thou thinkest of it in reference to life and death. For these are after all only words. For it is so that the corn falling into the earth and dying bringeth forth much fruit."

"Words, only words," cried Reuben, and wrung his hands. "They are only words thou givest me. Is Joseph dead or living? That it is which I must know."

"Manifestly he is dead," responded the watchman. "Thou and the others laid him to rest, as I hear, and since then he hath been stolen or perhaps torn by wild beasts; there is naught for it but to tell the father and make it manifest to him that he may accustom his heart to the truth. And yet, after all, it remaineth always equivocal; for it is not made to get used to, but rather hides always the seed of expectation. Men do much to penetrate the secret by ritual ways. I saw a youth descend into the grave in garland and festal garment, and above him they slaughtered a beast of the flock, whose blood they let run down, that it ran all over him and he received it with all his limbs and senses. So when he ascended again he was divine and had won life — at least for some time to come; for he had to go again into the grave, for the life of mankind cometh to an end several times, and each time cometh the grave and the rebirth, and many times must he be, until at length he finally is."

"Ah, the wreath and the festal garment," moaned Reuben and buried his face in his hands, "they lie torn and the boy is gone naked into the grave."

"Yes, and therefore thou comest hither with thy coat," responded the watchman, "and will clothe him anew. That can God do too. He can clothe anew the naked, and better than thou. Therefore I counsel thee: go home and take thy coat with thee. God can even throw a cloak over him who is clothed; after all, perhaps it was not so serious with the uncovering of this boy of thine. I would, if thou permittest, sink a seed-corn of thought into thy understanding: I would tell thee that all this is but a play and a feast, like that of the youth sprinkled with blood, a beginning only and attempt toward fulfilment; a present which is not to be taken quite seriously, but is only a jest and an allusion, a symbol, so that we might nudge each other and wink while we behold it. For perhaps this pit was only a grave created by the lesser cycle, and your brother still very much in becoming and by no means already become, as this whole story is in becoming and not already become. Receive this, I pray thee, into the womb of thy understanding and let it quietly die therein and germinate. But if it bear fruit, then give of it to thy father for his comforting."

"My father, my father!" Reuben cried. "Speak not to me of him. How shall I come before the father without the child?"

"Look up," said the watchman. For it had become clearer in the well-house, and the bark of the moon had just swum up above their heads, its darker part faintly visible in the depths of the sky. "Look at it, how it goeth and shineth and maketh the way plain for its brethren. Such allegories happen in heaven and on earth without end. He whose mind is open, and he knoweth how to read them, he abideth in expectation. But the night advanceth apace, and who need not sit and play watchman, he would do well to lie down, wrapped in his coat, with knees comfortably drawn up, that he may rise again in the morning. Go, my friend! Here, at least, thou hast nothing to seek, and as for me I shall not disappear at thy bidding."

Then Reuben turned away shaking his head, and with heavy heart and lagging feet climbed the steps and the slope up to where he had left his animal. Almost the whole way thence to the brethren's huts he did not cease to shake his bewildered head, in desperation half, and half in dumbfounded reflection. He hardly distinguished the one from the other, but he shook his head.

THE OATH

So he came to the huts and roused the nine, snatched the early sleep from their eyes, and spoke with trembling lips:

"The boy is gone. Where shall I go?"

"Thou?" they asked. "Thou speakest as though he had been only thy brother, when after all he was as much ours. Where shall we all go? That is the question. And what meanest thou by 'gone'?"

"Gone — that is, stolen, disappeared, torn in pieces, dead," Reuben shrieked. "Lost to the father, in any case. The pit is empty."

"Wast thou at the pit?" they asked. "To what end?"

"To the end of finding out," he said wrathfully. "That is still allowed, I should think, to the first-born. Shall what we have done give us peace and not harass us? Yea, I desired to see after the boy, and now I tell you that he is gone and that we must ask ourselves whither we shall go."

"To call thyself the first-born," they answered, "is somewhat bold, as we may remind thee simply by uttering the name of Bilhah. There was danger that the rights of the first-born would fall to the dreamer; but now it is the twins who come next; and Dan too could put in his claim, for he was born in the same year as Levi."

But they had seen the ass with ladder and coat — Reuben had not even tried to hide them — and easily put this and that together. So then big Reuben had meant to steal a march on them and rescue Joseph; he had intended to exalt his own head and to put them in a hole. Very fine. They exchanged meaningful glances. But if that was the way of it, their glances said, then they owed Reuben no explanation of what they had done in the meantime. Unfaith for unfaith. Reuben needed to hear nothing, of the Ishmaelites nor how at that moment they were bearing Joseph out of sight and hearing. If he knew, he might follow after them. Therefore the brethren were silent, shrugged their shoulders at his news, and feigned indifference.

"Gone is gone," they said, "no matter whether it signifieth stolen, vanished, torn to pieces, betrayed, or sold; we would snap our fingers at it, were it worth a snap. Was it not our longing and our just desire that he might cease to be? And now it has been vouchsafed us, the pit is empty."

But he wondered that they took this surprising and monstrous news so coldly; peered into their eyes and shook his head.

"And the father!" he cried, in sudden passion, flinging up his arms.

"That hath been settled and arranged," they said, "by the clever-

ness of Dan. For the father shall not be let to wait and doubt, but it
shall be clean and clear to him and graspable with his hands, that
Dumuzi is no more and his pampered darling no longer remaineth.
But we shall be united before him by means of the sign. See what we
have got ready while thou wentest thine own ways."

And they fetched out the remnants of the garment, which was
stiff with half-dried blood.

"Is it his blood?" Reuben cried with his high voice out of his
mighty body, and shuddered frightfully. . . . For a moment he
thought not otherwise than that they had been beforehand with him
at the pit and killed Joseph.

They smiled at one another.

"What all dost thou not dream and spin!" they said. "But it hath
been done according to our agreement, and a beast of the flock hath
given his blood in sign that Joseph is gone. The garment bring we
now before the father and let it be his affair to explain it as he must,
for there is nothing left than that a lion surprised him in the field
and tore him to pieces."

Reuben sat, his huge knees in front of him, and rubbed his fists in
his eye-sockets.

"Unhappy!" he groaned. "Unhappy wretches that we are! You
prattle light-heartedly of the future, yet see it not and know it not.
For unclear and pale it lieth in the distance and you lack the power
in your heads to bring it near, and for even the twinkling of an eye-
lid to live in the hour when it hath become real. Otherwise you
would shudder and would wish rather that lightning would strike
you down in time or that you were sunk in water with a millstone
round your necks where it is deepest than that you should bring in
the dish and serve up the soup that you have brewed. But I have lain
before him when I did evilly and he cursed me and I know the fire
of his soul when it is angry. And I can see, as though it were happening, the frightful wrestlings of his soul in its affliction. *That* shall we
bring before the father and let it speak to him! Ye praters and bab-
blers! Yea, he will interpret it! But who will dare to look at him when
he interpreteth it, and who will bear it when he uttereth his soul?
For God created it large and tender and taught it how to reveal itself
with overwhelming power. Ye see nothing and imagine nothing with
clearness that hath not yet happened; therefore you prattle cheer-
fully of the future and know no fears. But I am afraid," he cried
out, and stood up before them strong like a bear, like a tower, with
arms outstretched. "Where shall I go when he interpreteth it?"

The nine sat there each one quite intimidated, looking down at his
lap.

"Very good," responded Judah softly. "Here is nobody who spit-
eth thee on account of thy fear, Reuben, son of thy mother; for like-

wise it is brave to confess thy fear. And if thou thinkest we are blithe and gay round heart and kidneys and know naught of the fear of Jacob, then thou mistaketh. But what good is it to regret what has happened and what avail to boggle at the inevitable? Joseph is out of the world, and this coat witnesseth the truth. A sign is milder than words. Therefore we shall bring the sign before Jacob and are dispensed of words."

"Must we then," asked Asher, Zilpah's son, and licked his lips after his habit, "must we then, since we speak of carrying the robe, all of us at once bring the sign to Jacob and all of us be there when he interpreteth it? Rather let one go delicately ahead with the garment and bring it to him; but we others come afterwards and get there only when he hath already interpreted it to himself. It seemeth to me milder so. I propose Naphtali, the runner, for bearer and messenger. Or let us draw lots to see who shall bear it."

"Draw lots," cried Naphtali in haste. "I am for drawing lots, for I too imagine the future when I speak of it and I freely confess my fear."

"Listen, men," said Dan. "Now I will be the judge and free you all. For from me cometh the plan and I can shape it in my mind like wet earth and potter's clay. I will improve it; for we shall not bring Jacob the robe, neither one nor all of us. To strangers will we give it, somebody whom we shall hire, people of the place and the neighbourhood, receptive to good words and a little wool and a few curds. We will impress on him what he shall say to Jacob: thus and thus; and 'This found we in the field near Dothan and came upon it in the desert by chance. Look at it closer, father and lord, whether it is not indeed the garment of thy son.' Thus shall they speak, and when they have said, let them go away. But we will tarry a few days before we follow, until he has fully interpreted to himself the sign and knows that he has lost one and gained ten. Are ye satisfied?"

"It is well," they said, "or at least is worth talking about. Therefore let us accept it, for anything that is a practical plan, in a case like this, must be considered good."

They all accepted it, even Reuben, although he had laughed bitterly when Dan spoke of ten whom Jacob was winning for one. But they kept on sitting before the huts under the stars and continued to take counsel, for they were somewhat uncertain of each other. The nine looked at Reuben, who had obviously intended to steal the lad and cheat them; and they were afraid before him. But he looked at the nine who had remained so strangely unmoved at the news that the pit was empty, and did not know what he should think.

"A frightful oath," said Levi, rude but pious, who liked to arrange religious ceremonies and had knowledge of them; "we must swear a frightful oath, that none of us ever tell Jacob or anyone a single little word of what hath happened here and what we did with the dreamer; not by a sign or a flicker of an eyelash, so long as he shall live."

"Thou sayest it, that we must," agreed Asher. "And this oath must bind us ten together and make us into a league so that we are like one body and one silence, as though we were not single persons, one here and one there, but one man who presseth his lips together and openeth them not, even in death, but dieth, his mouth shut together over his secret. One can stifle and slay an event by silence, which one rolleth over it like a stone. Then the breath goeth out of it for lack of air and light, and the event ceaseth to have happened. Believe me, so dieth much that has happened, if the silence over it is unbroken; for without the breath of words can naught exist. We must keep silence as one man; then will this story be as it had not been; and thereto Levi's frightful oath may help us — for it shall make us a bond."

They agreed to this, no one of them being willing to rely upon himself for his silence, but preferring to share in a mighty common bond, which should shelter him from his weakness. Therefore Levi, Leah's son, devised frightful formulas for the oath; they drew so close together that their noses rubbed and their breath mingled, put their hands in a pile, and with one voice called on the Highest, El Elyon, God of Abraham, Yitzchak, and Jacob. Neither did they forget the several Baals of the land, known unto them: Anu of Uruk, Ellil of Nippur, and Bel Harran, Sin, the moon; but named them as compurgators and swore with one voice, mouth almost on mouth, that he who did not keep silence about "it" or who did even with nod, wink, or sign betray it or glance at it, such a one should turn whore, and the daughter of Sin, mistress of womenkind, should take from him the bow, that is his manhood, that he should be like a mule, but more rightly said a whore, who took her hire upon the street. One land should drive him into the other, so that he should not know where to lay his whorish head and should neither live nor die, but life and death should spit him to one another in disgust his life long.

Thus the oath. When they had sworn it they were easier and steadier, for this was a mighty insurance. But when they broke up the counsel and went each one to his sleep, one said to another (it was Issachar said it to Zebulun):

"I have an envy, and my envy is of Turturra, the little one, Benjamin, our youngest at home, for that he knoweth nothing of all this and remaineth outside this matter and this oath. He is fortunate and I envy him. Thou too?"

"I too, indeed," answered Zebulun.

But Reuben for his part was trying to remember the words of the irritating youth of the place, who had sat on the well-stone. It was not easy to remember them, for they had been vague and full of twilight, more idle than real words and hard to reproduce. Yet in Reuben's deepest understanding a seed did remain behind, which knew naught of itself, as the seed of life knoweth naught of itself in the body of the mother, but the mother knoweth of it. It was the seed of expectation which Reuben cherished, and nourished it secretly, sleeping and waking, till he was a greyhaired man, through as many years as Jacob had served for the devil Laban.

Chapter VII

HE WHO WAS MANGLED

JACOB MOURNS FOR JOSEPH

Is a sign more merciful than words? That is a moot question. Judah argued from the point of view of the bringer of bad tidings who prefers the sign because it saves him the trouble of words. But for him who receives it? In the strength of his ignorance he can put the word aside; he can tread it underfoot as a lie and an abominable fabrication and consign it to perdition as unutterable rubbish. He can roar with laughter born of solid conviction — before it dawns on the poor wretch that the matter is not to be got rid of that way. The word penetrates but slowly. At first it is incredible, its sense not to be grasped or realized. You are still free to remain in your ignorance by retorting upon the messenger the confusion which his message would set up in your own heart and brain, and to denounce him roundly as wrong in the head. "What is that you say?" you may ask him. "Are you not well? Come, let me look after you, have a little something to drink, then you will feel better and talk at least so that a body can take in what you say." It is not very pleasant for the messenger, but he pities you and knows himself master of the situation; he is kind, and slowly his look of mingled reason and compassion casts doubt into your soul. You cannot sustain that look, you understand that it is impossible to hold to that allocation of rôles to which you cling as a means of self-preservation; and at length you perceive that it is you who need to take a little drink from him.

It is the word which permits of this slow rear-guard action against the forces of truth. With a sign nothing of the sort is possible. No temporizing fiction avails against its heaped-up cruelty. It is unmistakable, it does not need to be realized, because it is real. It is palpable, it scorns to spare by being only gradually effective. It leaves no possible way of escape. It forces you to conceive in your own head the idea which, if presented in words, you would brush aside as madness; it drives you to the conclusion that either you are mad or it is true. Directness and indirectness are differently mingled in the word and the sign; it is hard to tell which is the more brutally immediate. The sign is mute — not out of gentleness, however, but only because it needs not to speak to be understood, being the thing itself. Without a word it lays you low.

And Jacob, truly, according to all expectation, was, at sight of the coat of many colours, stricken to the earth. This is an assured fact. But nobody saw just what happened; for the two wretched men of Dothan who had undertaken, in consideration of a fixed amount of wool and curds, to play the rôle of finders, had taken to their heels as soon as they had made their little speech, not waiting to see what would be its effect. They gave the blood-stiffened rags into the hands of Jacob the man of God and left him standing there before his tent of skins; they slunk away, first taking very long steps and then bursting into a run as they got farther off. No one knows how long he stood there looking down at that little, which, as his understanding slowly forced him to comprehend, was all there was left in the world of Joseph. Then, indeed, he had fallen, and women passing came and found him lying there; the wives of his sons they were, the Shechemite Bunah, Simeon's spouse, also Levi's, the so-called grandchild of Eber. These lifted him in alarm and brought him within his tent. They knew at once, from what he held in his hands, the cause of his attack.

It was no common faint in which he lay, but a sort of rigor, that gripped every muscle and fibre of his body, turning it to stone, so that one could not bend a joint without breaking it. It is a rare phenomenon, but does sometimes occur, as a reaction to some extraordinary stress; it is like a spasm of resistance, a desperate, defiant insensibility called up to meet something which the system cannot bear. It will last some hours, slowly capitulating before the relentless onslaught of reality and suffering, against which there is no help.

Men-servants and women-servants, surrounding him on all sides, watched fearfully the spectacle of this pillar of salt slowly melting before their eyes into the limp receptivity of abject suffering. He had still no voice and could only whisper his answer — as it were his admission — to the long-since-departed messengers: "Yes, it is my son's coat." But then suddenly he cried out, in a voice which rose to a shriek under the spur of his despair: "A beast of prey hath preyed upon Joseph; an evil beast hath rent him in pieces." And as though his own words put him in mind of what was now to be done, he began tearing his clothes.

It was high summer, his clothing was light and offered little resistance. He put all his strength into the work, but it took some time, because of the uncannily silent thoroughness with which he did it. The onlookers saw with horror, and with futile gestures designed to prevent the extravagance, that he did not stop at the upper garment, as they expected; no, he went on apparently of fell design to strip off every rag he had on, throw the several pieces from him, and stand there stark naked. Considering the known delicacy of the man's feelings, that aversion to exposure of the flesh which everybody respected in him, the sight was so unnatural and debasing that nobody could bear it. With one accord, wailing and protesting, the onlookers turned away and went hence.

There is only one right and proper word for the feeling which was at the bottom of their action: shame. But one must understand it in its ultimate and often forgotten sense, as a monosyllabic description of the horror we feel when the primitive breaks through the layers of civilization, at the surface of which it is only active in a much softened and allegorical form. We must regard the tearing of the upper garments in heavy sorrow as being of such a nature; it is the civilized and domesticated form of the original or primitive custom of shedding all the clothes, shedding every covering and adornment considered as the badge of human dignity now destroyed and ruined by the extremity of human woe. It is the abasement of man to mere creature. So it was with Jacob. In the depth of his grief he went back to the original meaning, from the allegory to the crude thing itself and to the horrible reality. He did what "one does not do" — and that, rightly considered, is the source of all horror. For therein the undermost comes uppermost. If, for instance, it had occurred to him to give utterance to the abandonment of his misery by bleating like a ram, his people could not have felt more nauseated than they did.

They fled, then, out of shame. But we may question whether they so best served the pathetic old man; whether he was not gratifying his deepest desire in this crass exhibition of utter woe and whether it was quite so gratifying to him to be left alone with it. He was not, however, actually alone; for what he did needed no human witness to serve its end and aim, which was to stir up feelings of horror. At Whom, or, to be exact, against Whom, his action was directed; in Whom it was designed to stir up feelings of horror; before Whose eyes he was trying to bring this manifestation of a return to the original state of nature — all this the desperate father knew only too well. His people came to know it too, especially Eliezer, "Abraham's oldest servant." He took particular interest in it, that strange institution of an old man who knew how to use the first person singular in so truly singular a way, and to meet whom the earth had advanced by bounds.

He, too, was pierced to the heart by the sight of the token and by the frightful news that Joseph, his lovely and so intelligent pupil, had fallen victim to a mischance on his journey and been made the prey of a ravening beast. But his curiously impersonal character, his peculiarly extensive consciousness of his own individuality, enabled him to receive the blow with a certain composure; also, his natural concern for Jacob, the man of sorrows, left him small leisure to dwell upon his own pain. It was Eliezer who brought food to Jacob, though the latter refused for days to touch it; who enforced him to seek his couch by night and then did not stir from beside it. By day, Jacob had taken up his station on a heap of potsherds and ashes in a remote and shadeless corner of the settlement. There he sat, naked, with the pieces of the coat in his hands, his hair, beard, and shoulders strewn with ashes. From time to time he scraped himself with a potsherd from the heap, in token that he was afflicted with sores and boils. All of which was purely symbolic behaviour (for he had none), and the scraping was part of the demonstration, directed to the same address as the rest.

Certainly the sight of this pitiful figure, so absorbed in its penance, was touching enough, even without the symbolic representation of impurity. Everybody save the eldest servant avoided in awe and embarrassment the scene of this exposure. Jacob's body was no longer that of the slender yet sturdy young man who had wrestled unde-feated with the ox-eyed stranger by Jabbok ford and lived out that windy night with the unchosen bride. Nor was it that of him who late begot Joseph upon the true wife. Some seventy years, not pre-cisely counted and reckoned, but "counting" to good effect in the objective sense, had since passed over his head and marked him with the touching if unattractive mis-shapenness of old age; and this it was that made his naked state so painful to see. Youth displays itself freely and joyously, with a good conscience based on its own beauty. Age shrouds itself in modesty and dignity — and well knows why. This breast, with its growth of white hairs on a skin reddened by the sun, and its shape, as a man's does in age, approaching to a woman's; these nerveless arms and spent thighs, the folds of the re-laxed abdomen — all this was no sight for anybody save old Eliezer, who took it with composure and made no objection, so little minded was he to put obstacles in the way of his master's demonstration.

He was even less likely to prevent Jacob in the performance of the other rites, which did not go beyond what was customary in heavy sorrow: particularly the sojourn on the dust-heap, the re-peated sprinkling of ashes, which then mingled with his sweat and his tears. These were only proper. Eliezer was merely concerned to erect a temporary shelter over the place of penance, that the sun of Tam-muz might not turn the penance into torture. Even in its shade Jacob's woebegone face was suffused with bright crimson from the heat and his affliction; his jaw hung down, his eyes rolled up-wards ever and anon out of the unfathomable deeps of his suffering.

And he remarked all this himself, as soft and self-examining natures do, being concerned with their own condition and convinced that it receives too little notice by going unmentioned.

"Crimson and swollen," he said, his voice trembling, "is my countenance from weeping. For deep-bowed in my affliction I sit me down to weep, and my face is wet with the tears that flow down it."

The words, as one could tell, were not original with him. For Noah, according to the legend, was supposed to have said some such thing, and Jacob made it his own. And indeed it is good, it is convenient and consoling, that from the suffering of our ancestors we inherit right and suitable words in which to clothe our own, which then fit it as though they were made for it; so that they give us ease in so far as words can give ease from pain, and unite our own sorrow with that which has been and will always be. Certainly Jacob could do his grief no greater honour than to set it on a level with the great flood and apply to it words which were coined for that catastrophe.

At all events, he spoke and lamented much in his despair, in words already coined or only half-coined. And over and over again came the wailing cry: "Joseph is rent, is rent in pieces" — which may easily have been already in existence, but lost nothing of its impressiveness by the fact. No, that they had, however much they may have been used before.

"The lamb and the mother ewe are slain," intoned Jacob; he rocked to and fro and wept most bitterly. "First the mother and now the lamb as well. The mother ewe hath forsaken the lamb, when it was only a furlong to the inn; and now the lamb too hath strayed and is lost. Ah, no, ah, no, ah, no! Woe, alas! It is too much. Wailing ariseth above the beloved son. Over the young shoot whose roots are torn out, over my hopes that are rooted up like to a sapling. Woe, alas, my Damu, my child! His dwelling is become the underworld. Bread will I not eat, water will I not drink. Joseph is rent, is rent in pieces. . . ."

From time to time Eliezer wiped his master's face with a cloth wet in water. He also took part in the lamentations, in so far as they kept to the prescribed formulas, and paid honour to all that abides through change, by joining in the half-sung, half-murmured cry of "Woe, alas!" or "He is rent, he is rent!" Indeed, the whole courtyard resounded for hours; Jacob's people would have done the same even though their mourning had been less sincere than it really was. "*Hoi achi! Hoi Adon!* Alas for our brother! Woe, alas for our Lord!" Jacob and Eliezer could hear the chorus from where they were; and the servants in their turn could hear the rejection, not quite literally meant, of food and drink, for that the herb was withered in the desert wind and the sapling was torn out by the root.

Customs are useful: the regulation of both our joy and our grief in prescribed channels, that they may not flow in every direction and end in excess and confusion, but keep to a settled bed ready to receive them. Jacob, too, felt the blessing and usefulness of conforming to tradition; but the grandson of Abraham was far too individual a nature, he had far too lively a sense of his own personality in relation to the general, to be able to confine himself to formulas. He spoke and lamented in his own words as well, Eliezer attending and wiping his face from time to time and throwing in a word of soothing confirmation or of correction and warning.

"What I have feared," Jacob broke out, in a voice diminished, heightened in pitch, and sometimes half choked by anguish, "what I have feared is come upon me, and that which gave me concern is come to pass. Canst thou understand that, Eliezer? Canst thou grasp it? No, no, no, no one can understand it, when that which one has feared actually cometh to pass. Had I had no concern nor thought, if it had burst upon me unsuspecting, then I would believe it. I would say unto my heart: 'Thou tookest no heed, hadst no care to avoid the evil by foreseeing it.' A surprise is believable. But that that which hath been foreboded cometh, and shrinketh not from coming, that is an abomination in mine eyes, and with it I come not to terms."

"There is nothing hard and fast in these matters," responded Eliezer.

"No, not before the law. But for man's feelings, which likewise have their reason and their limits. For why was fear given to men, and foresight, but that he might therewith conjure evil and take away from fate betimes the power of thinking. It may be angry, but is also ashamed and sayeth to itself: 'Are they still my thoughts? They are the thoughts of man, I like them no more.' But what shall become of man if forethought no longer avail and he feareth in vain; that is, he feareth with reason? Or how shall a man live if he can no longer rely on things turning out differently from what he thought?"

"God is free," Eliezer said.

Jacob closed his lips. He took up again the potsherd he had dropped and began again to scrape his symbolic sores. For the moment he did not continue the subject. He went on:

"How have I feared and anguished lest a wild beast from the thicket one day fall upon my child and do him a harm; and cared not at all that I was a laughing-stock among my people for my solicitude, nor minded when they said of me: 'Lo, how the old dotard playeth at being nurse!' And was ridiculous like a man who sayeth always: 'I am ill, I am ill unto death,' yet looketh healthy and doth not die, and nobody taketh it seriously and in the end not he himself. But when they find him dead and are remorseful that they laughed, and say: 'Lo, he had right in what he said,' can it do the man any good that they are ashamed? No, for he is dead. And would rather have been a fool before them and before himself than to be justified in so unpalatable a way. Here I sit in the dust, my face red and swollen from weeping, and ashes and tears course down it. Can I rejoice in my tears, because it hath come to pass? No, because it hath come to pass. Dead am I indeed, for dead is Joseph, Joseph is rent, is rent in pieces.

"Lo, Eliezer, take and see: the robe, the remnant of the picture-garment. I lifted it from off the dearest and true bride in the bridal chamber and I handed to her the blossom of my soul. But then it proved to be the unchosen one, through Laban's deceit, and my soul was outraged and intolerably torn for a long time — until the right one in horrible pain brought me the boy, Dumuzi, my all; now he too is rent and is slain, who was the delight of my eyes. Can that be explained? Is it acceptable, is it acceptable, this demand? No, no, no, no, I covet to live no more. I would my soul were bare space and these bones given over to death."

"Israel, sin not."

"Ah, Eliezer, teach thou me to fear God and to adore His over-whelming power. He hath Himself royally paid for name and bless-ing and Esau's bitter tears; paid mightily. He setteth the price accord-ing to His arbitrary will and is moved by strange considerations. He hath not dealt with me after my knowledge of what is too much for me. He taketh what He judgeth I can pay, knowing better than I what my soul is able. Can I argue with Him from like to like? I sit here in these ashes and scrape myself, what will He more? My lips speak: what the Lord doth is well done. Let Him keep to my lips. What I think in my heart is my affair."

"But He readeth likewise the heart."

"That is not my fault. He it was, and not I, who so arranged that He seeth also the heart. He would have done better to leave men a refuge before the overwhelming, that man might grumble a little against the unacceptable and think his thoughts about the justice of things. His refuge was this heart, and his pleasant tent. Came He to visit, it was finely adorned, and swept with a broom, and the seat of honour was prepared for Him. Now is nothing but ashes therein, mingled with tears, with filth and misery. Let Him avoid my heart, that He not defile Himself, and let Him keep to my lips."

"But yet thou shouldest not sin, Yakow ben Yitzchak."

"Thresh not words, old man, they are but empty straw. Espouse my cause, and not God's; for He is overgreat and laugheth at thy con-cern, while I am but a storehouse of wailing. Speak not to me from the outside in, but speak to me out of thy soul, nothing else can I bear. Knowest thou and hast understood that Joseph is gone and re-turneth not to me, never and nevermore? Only when thou thinkest thereon canst thou speak to me out of thy soul and thresh no empty straw. Out of my own mouth I laid upon him the journey and said:

'Go toward Shechem and bow before thy brethren that they may
come home and Israel not stand here like a tree without its boughs.'
This task laid I upon him and upon me, chastening us both somewhat
rudely, for he should travel alone without a servant. I recognized
his folly for my folly and concealed not from myself what God
would. But God dissembled from me what He knew, for He inspired
me to command the child: 'Go hither'; and hid Himself away from
me with His knowledge and His savage design. Such is the faith of
the Almighty God, and thus repayeth He the truth with truth."

"Have a care at least to thy lips, son of the true wife."

"My lips are made to me so that I can spew out what I cannot
bear. Speak not from outside, Eliezer, but from within. What is God
thinking of, that He layeth on me that from which my eyes turn
inwards and I lose my senses because it is what I cannot bear? Have
I then the strength of stone and is my flesh of bronze? If only He
had made me of bronze in His wisdom — but as I am, it is naught
for me. My child, my Damu! The Lord hath given him, the Lord
hath taken him away — would He had not given him at first or that I
myself had not come out of my mother's womb; would there were
nothing at all! What shall one think, Eliezer, and whither turn and
twist in his need? If I were not, then should I know naught, and all
would be naught. But even as I am, it is better that Joseph is gone
than that he had never been; for so I still have what remaineth to me,
and that is my mourning for him. Ah, God hath taken care that one
cannot be against Him and must say yes, even while one sayeth no.
Yea, He had given him to my old age, His name be praised. He had
moulded him with His hands and made him lovely. Like milk had
He milked him and built his bony structure, had drawn over it skin
and flesh and poured out grace upon him so that he took me by the
ear-lobes and laughed: 'Dearest Father, give it to me!' And I gave
it him, for I was not of bronze or stone. When I called him to the
journey and gave him the command, he cried: 'Here am I,' and
kicked up his heels — when I think upon it my tears pour out like
water. For it was even as though I had laid wood upon him for the
burnt sacrifice and taken him by the hand and myself carried fire
and knife. Oh, Eliezer, I have confessed before God and openly admitted in all humility that I should not have been able. Thinkest
thou He might graciously have accepted by submission and had pity
of my confession? No, but He breathed fire out of His nostrils and
spake: 'What thou canst not do shall be done; whether or no thou
art able to give it, I will take it.' That is God.

"Behold and see: here is the coat and the rags of the coat stiff with
blood. That is the blood of his veins, which the ravening beast rent,
and it rent his flesh. Oh, horror, horror! Oh, sin of God! Oh, wild,
blind, reasonless misdeed! Too much had I laid upon him, Eliezer,

too much for the child. He went astray upon the field and wandered
lost in the waste — then came the hideous monster upon him and
struck him down and devoured, unheeding his anguish. Mayhap he
called upon me, or upon the mother, who died when he was small.
No one heard him, God saw that it should be so. Thinkest thou it
was a lion who struck him down, or a great boar that fell upon him
with standing bristles and buried his tusks in him? . . ."

He shuddered, and plunged into a brooding silence. Inevitably
the word "boar" set up in him trains of thought which lifted the
horrible single event now wringing his heart and placed it in the
upper regions, among the primitive and symbolic, in the timeless and
ever revolving sphere; set it, as it were, under the stars. The boar, the
raging swine of swine, that was Seth, the God-murderer, it was the
Red. It was Esau, whom he, Jacob, as a variant upon the pattern, had
known how to mollify, by weeping at Eliphaz's feet; but who in the
true and primeval pattern had cut up his brother and himself might
occur here below as cut up and divided into ten pieces. And at the
thought a surmise struggled to rise into Jacob's consciousness; a sort
of traditional suspicion lying in the deeper layers of his mind, where
he had dwelt ever since he saw the blood-stained tatters of the coat.
It was a sinister conjecture as to the identity of the boar who had
torn Joseph. But it fell back again before it reached the surface — in
fact he himself helped to push it down. Strange though it may seem,
he recoiled from knowledge of such a nature, he would have none
of it, because it would have made him recognize the upper in the
lower; because his suspicion would have been directed against itself.
He was courageous, he loved the truth, he had recognized his responsibility for Joseph's act; and he had summoned strength to send
him upon the journey. But he was not brave enough, despite all his
love of truth, to face the thought of the brothers' guilt, because that
would have driven him to a consciousness of his own. Surely he may
be pardoned for this. He could not have endured — and therefore
his whole being rejected in agony — the bitter thought that he himself had been the chief boar, and that his foolish doting, born of his
own pride and self-indulgence, had been the instrument which had
brought the lad to his death. And yet the unbearableness of his suffering consisted precisely in this suppressed suspicion. And his need
to manifest his wretchedness in the most striking way before God
should be referred to the same source.

For to Jacob God was the important thing, He was behind everything; upon Him were Jacob's weeping, brooding, desperate eyes
directed. Lion or boar, it was God who had willed, had allowed — in
a word, had done the frightful thing; and he felt a certain recognizable satisfaction in that his despair raised him up to a height where
he might actually expostulate with God, despite the contradiction

of his outward debasement in nakedness and in ashes. Indeed, without the debasement there could have been no expostulating. Jacob scraped his wretchedness — and in exchange he spoke freely and guarded not his lips.

"That is God," he repeated, with visible shuddering. "The Lord hath not asked me, Eliezer, nor set before me the test, saying: 'Offer Me up the son whom thou lovest.' Perhaps I should have been strong beyond my humble expectation and should have taken the child to Moriah despite his question where then was the sheep for the burnt offering; perhaps I could have heard it without falling in a faint and been able to lift the knife over Isaac and had faith in the ram — it would have depended on the test! But not so, not so, Eliezer. He did not even vouchsafe me the test. But lured the child from my heart by dint of my honest admission that I was not guiltless of the brother-strife, and led him astray, that the lion should fall upon him, and a wild boar strike its tusks in his flesh and root its snout in his entrails. For this beast, I may tell thee, devoureth everything. It even brought of Joseph to his lair, for the little swine, his children. Can one understand and accept that? No, it is insupportable. I spew it out as a bird the feathers. There it lieth. May God do with it what He will, for it is naught for me."

"Bethink thyself, Israel."

"No, I am without the power, my steward. God hath snatched my senses from me, now let Him hear my words. He is my creator, I know full well. He hath milked me like milk and let me curdle like cheese, I admit it. But how is it with Him, and where would He be without us, the fathers and me? Is He short of memory? Hath He forgotten the trouble and labour of man on His account? And how Abram found Him and thought Him forth, so that He might kiss His finger and cry: 'At last am I called Lord and Highest!' I ask: hath He forgotten the bond, that He gnasheth with His teeth against me and behaveth as though I were His foe? Where is my transgression and my misdeed? Let Him show me! Have I burned incense to the Baals of the land and thrown kisses to the stars? There was no vice in me, and my prayer was pure. Why must I endure violence instead of justice? Let Him in His wilfulness shatter me straightway and throw me in the pit, for that were a trifle to Him, even without right, and I covet not greatly to live if I must suffer violence. Doth He then mock the spirit of man, that He arrogantly destroyeth both good and evil? But then where would He be Himself without the spirit of man? Eliezer, the covenant is broken! Ask me not why, for I should have to answer thee sadly. God hath not held the pace — dost thou understand me? For God and man chose each other and made a compact whereby they might really become, the one in the other, what they are, and be holy one in the other.

But when man hath grown fine-grained and tender-hearted in God, with disciplined soul, and God then inviteth him to an abomination of desolation which he can in no wise stomach but must spew it out and say: 'It is nothing for me'; then, Eliezer, one must conclude that God hath not kept pace in the work of sanctification, but hath halted behind and is still a sorcerer."

Eliezer was of course aghast to hear such words; he prayed to the Lord to have mercy upon his master, whose affliction had brought him beside himself; at the same time he did not spare Jacob in his reproaches.

"Thy words are beyond all bounds," he said; "I cannot hear them, for they drag down the majesty of God against all warrant. That say I unto thee, who with Abram, thanks to God's help, struck down the kings from the East and toward whom the earth sprang on the bridal journey. For thou hast called God a hateful sorcerer and settest thyself up against Him as fine and tender; but it is thy words out of which the desert howls, and in thy great pain thou makest a mock of pity, for thou beliest Him and lettest thyself down with the frightfullest licence of thy tongue. Dost thou decree upon wrong and right and sit in judgement upon Him who made not only the behemoth, whose tail stretcheth like a cedar, and leviathan, whose teeth are dreadful to see and whose scales are like to brazen shields; but likewise Orion, the seven-starred constellation, the dawn, hornets, snakes, and the dust-abubu? Did He not give to thee Yitzchak's blessing before Esau, who was somewhat older, and gloriously confirmed the promise to thee at Beth-el in the vision of the ladder? To all that thou consentedst, and found no objection therein on the score of the fine and tender human spirit, for it was all after thy liking. Hath He not made thee rich and fat in the house of Laban and moved the dusty bolts to open, that thou camest away with child and chattel, and Laban was like a lamb before thee on the Mount of Gilead? But now, when a misfortune is fallen on thee, a very heavy one, that no one denieth, then thou art defiant, my master, and kickest out like a balky ass and wouldst upset everything in the most reckless way and say: 'God hath not kept pace in sanctification.' Art thou then free of sin, being flesh, and is it so certain that thou hadst practised righteousness thy life long? Canst thou understand that which is far above thy understanding, and fathom the riddle of life and ride over it roughshod with thy human words and say: 'It is naught for me, and I am holier than God'? Truly, these things should I not need to hear, O son of the true wife!"

"Yea, thou sayest, Eliezer," answered Jacob to that, with dismal irony. "Truth is in thy mouth, and well thou knowest it. Thou hast eaten up wisdom with a spoon and sweatest it out of all thy pores. It is truly edifying how thou chidest me and forgettest not to bring in how thou hast holpen Abram to strike down the kings, that which is out and out impossible; for in the eye of reason thou art born of a slave girl at Damascus and hast seen Abram with thine eyes as little as I myself! Lo, how I in my misery make free with thy wisdom! Pure was I, but God hath drenched me over and over in filth, and such as thou art find it reasonable, for knowing naught of pious palliation they let the truth go naked. I even herewith express my doubt that the earth sprung toward thee. And now it is all out!"

"Jacob, Jacob, what dost thou? Thou destroyest the world in the arrogance of thine affliction, thou smitest it in pieces and throwest them on the head of the admonisher. For I would not say upon whose head thou throwest them, strictly speaking. Art thou the first accosted by sorrow, and may nothing go against thee but thou puffest out thy belly with blasphemy and rebellest and runnest against God like a bull? Dost thou think that on thine account the mountains are moved and water runneth uphill? Verily I think that thou wilt burst of malice here on this spot, since thou callest God godless and the Most High unjust!"

"Silence, Eliezer. Speak not of me so amiss, for I am bruised with mine affliction and cannot bear it. Is it God hath had to give away His son, so that He came before swine and before the grice of the swine in his lair, or is it I? Why then speakest thou for Him, taking His part and not mine? Hast thou any understanding of what I say? Nay, naught at all dost thou understand, and wilt speak for God. Ah, thou God's-defender, thou wilt receive thy reward and be counted high in His sight for that thou hast stood up for Him and shrewdly praised His deeds, He being God! But I tell thee He will fall upon thee! For thou wilt praise Him falsely, deceiving Him as one deceiveth a man, and wilt secretly flatter Him. Thou hypocrite, He will have none of this way of serving His cause and waiting upon Him with fawning, when what He hath done to me shrieketh to heaven, in that He hath thrown Joseph to the swine. For what thou sayest I too could say, and thou knowest I am not duller of sense than thou. But I speak to Him otherwise, and even so am nearer to Him than thou! For one must defend God against His defenders, and protect Him against those who would protect Him. Thinkest thou He is a man, even of overwhelming power, and it is His side thou must espouse against me, a worm? When thou callest Him eternally great, thou utterest merely wind, if thou knowest not that God is still above God, still everlastingly above Himself, and will punish from above, where He is my healing and my reliance and where thou art not, if thou regardest thyself as between Him and me!"

"We are altogether evil flesh and prone to sin," responded Eliezer quietly. "Each of us must deal with God according to his understanding and to the height he can reach, for no one can reach His height. Most likely we have both greatly sinned in our speech. But come now, my dear master, enter thy house, for here is enough of the violence of sorrow. Thy face is quite swollen from the heat on this pile of shards, and thou art too tender and fine for such a height of affliction."

"From weeping," said Jacob, "from weeping for the beloved is my face crimson and swollen." But he allowed himself to be led into the tent, being not further interested in the dust-heap, in stark nakedness and scraping his imaginary sores, they having served his turn to the end that he might expostulate his fill with God.

THE TEMPTATIONS OF JACOB

Now at least he put on a sackcloth, after the first three days, and his life was a little less distracted by grief; so that the sons when they arrived did not find him in the deepest depth of his affliction. But as yet they had not come; it was their wives who mourned and lamented, supported his head and consoled him, those at least who dwelt with him; for Judah's child of Shuah was not there. Likewise Zilpah and Bilhah and little Benjamin, to whom he clung and with whom he sobbed. He could not love the little one in the least as he loved Joseph, and when he looked at him his gaze was full of gloom, because Benjamin had cost him Rachel. But now he pressed the child passionately to his heart, calling him Benoni for his mother's sake, and swore to him that he would never under any circumstances send him on a journey; neither alone nor even with escort. Always, however big he got, and even as a married man, he should stop here under the father's eye, cherished and protected, and not take a step from the safest roads, for there was no confidence in the world, in nothing and in nobody.

Benjamin accepted the assurance, though with a heavy heart. He remembered his excursions with Joseph to the grove of Adonis; and the thought that the dear and lovely one would never again run and jump with him, nor even fan his little hand when it sweated; that he would never again relate his great dreams of heaven and make proud the heart of the little urchin with confidence in his understanding — all that wrung bitter tears from his eyes. But at bottom he was not capable of realizing what they told him of Joseph, that he would never come back, that he would never be with him again and was dead; he did not believe it despite the horrible evidence, which never left the father's hand. Our natural incapacity to believe in death is the denial of a denial and thus an affirmation. It is helpless belief, for all belief is helpless, and its helplessness is its strength. As for Benjamin, he clothed his unquenchable belief in the idea that Joseph had been snatched away. "He will come back," he asseverated, caress-

ing the old man. "Or he will have us come to him." Jacob for his part
was no child, but weighed down with the stories life had told him.
He had drunk too deep of the bitter-tasting reality of death to have
anything but a melancholy smile for Benoni's consolations. But he
too, at bottom, was utterly unable to affirm the denial of life; and
his efforts to avoid doing so, to get round the necessity of coming
to terms with both reality and impossibility, with this inhuman contradiction, were of such an extravagant nature that in our day we
should be forced to speak of mental derangement. His household
would not have gone so far, but Eliezer was in sore straits with the
desperate plans and speculations that Jacob revolved.

We are told that when he was spoken to, his sole answer was: "I
will go down into the grave unto my son mourning." It was, then
and afterwards, generally understood that he wished not longer to
live, but simply to die and to unite himself in death with his son —
partly in view of his lament that it was all too bitter and hard that
he had to lay down his grey head in death for such a grief. He meant
it so to be understood. But Eliezer came to hear otherwise and in
greater detail. However mad it may sound, Jacob's mind was dwelling
on the possibility of descending into the pit — in other words to the
kingdom of the dead — and fetching Joseph back.

The idea was the more senseless in that it was not the father but
the mother-bride who set out to free the true son from his prison
in the lower world and return him to the upper one desolated for
lack of him. But Jacob's wandering wits led him to make the most
fantastic analogies; moreover he had long since a tendency to deal
freely with sex. He had never known how to make a clear distinction
between Rachel's eyes and Joseph's. They were really the same,
really those from which he had kissed away the impatient tears —
now since Rachel's death they had become indistinguishable; the beloved beings themselves flowed together to a double-sexed picture
which was the object of his yearning. And like everything else that
was of the upper sphere, this yearning too was male-female — supra-
sexual. But as it was Jacob's yearning and he its, so Jacob partook of
this nature — a conclusion which he had long since accepted with his
emotions. Since Rachel's death he had been to Joseph mother and
father both. He had taken over the maternal rôle to such an extent
that it conditioned the nature of his love for Joseph; the identification of Joseph with Rachel had its counterpart in his own identification with the departed as well. But a double object can only be completely loved with a double love. It invokes the masculine in so far as
it is feminine, the feminine in so far as it is masculine. A father-feeling
which sees in its object at once the son and the beloved; in which
there mingles a tenderness which is proper to the love of the mother
for the son, is indeed masculine in so far as it has to do with the

beloved in the son, but maternal in so far as it is love to the son. This dual nature of his love made possible to Jacob the mad projects with which he burdened the ears of Eliezer concerning the bringing back of Joseph to life by conforming to the mythical pattern.

"I will go down," he asseverated, "to my son. Look at me, Eliezer — is not the shape of my breast grown somewhat feminine? In my years nature probably seeks a balance. Women get beards and men bosoms. I will find my way into the land without return, tomorrow I will set out. Why lookest thou doubtfully at me? May it not be possible? One must go always westward, and cross the Chubu river, then one cometh to the seven gates. Nay, doubt not, doubt not. No one loved him more than I. I will be as his mother. I will find him and go down with him to the lowest depth whence springeth the water of life. I will sprinkle him and will loose the dusty bolts for his return. Have I not once already done so? Am I not a master of the arts of outwitting and of flight? I will get the better of the mistress below there as I did once of Laban, and they too shall deal with me with fair words. Why must I see that thou shakest thy head?"

"Ah, dear master, I enter as far as I can into thine aspirations and grant that in the beginning all would go according to thy thoughts. But at the latest at the seventh gate it must and would be revealed that thou art not the mother."

"Of a certainty," responded Jacob, and could not in all his extremity quite suppress a gratified smile. "That is inevitable. It would become plain that I did not suckle but begot him. . . . Eliezer," said he, for his thoughts had suddenly taken a turn from the mother-bride to the phallic, "I will beget him anew. Might that not be possible, to beget him again, just as he was, very Joseph, and thus to lead him back from below? Am I not after all still here, from whom he came; should he then be lost? So long as I live, can I not give him up for lost! I will awaken him anew and by begetting re-establish his image on earth!"

"But Rachel is no more here, who shared in the begetting, and ye two must unite if very Joseph is to spring from you. But even if she lived and you begot again, yet would it not be the hour nor the horoscope which summoned Joseph into being. Not him would you call up, neither Benjamin, but a third whom no eye yet hath seen. For naught happeneth twice and all that is here is only itself, as it were, for ever."

"But then it may not die and be lost, Eliezer. That is impossible. If everything is only for once and hath its like neither next to nor after him, and no great cycle bringeth it round again, then can it not be destroyed and thrown to the pigs; that I cannot accept. True it is that Rachel was necessary to Joseph's begetting, and that the hour too must coincide. But of this I was aware and knowingly have I challenged thy reply. For the begetter is only the tool of creating; it is blind, and knows not what it doth. When we begot Joseph, the true wife and I, we begot not him, but a something — anything — and that it became Joseph was the work of God. Begetting is not creating. It only plungeth life into life, in blind lust: but He createth. Oh, that my life might plunge into death and know it, that I might beget upon it and awaken to life Joseph, as he was! Toward that goal is my musing directed; that is my meaning when I say: 'I will go down.' Might I beget backwards into the past and into the hour that was Joseph's hour! Why shakest thou thy head so misgivingly? That I cannot do it I know myself, but that I wish it, over that shouldst thou not shake thy head, for God hath so ordered it that I am here and Joseph not, which is a shrieking contradiction and rendeth my heart. Knowst thou what that is, a heart rent in twain? No, thou but prattlest when thou sayest it, meaning only that my case is sad. But my heart is literally torn so that I am forced to think against reason and must brood upon the impossible."

"I shake my head, master, for pity, because of thy defiance of that which thou wouldst call a contradiction; namely, that thou art and thy son no more. For therein is precisely thy sorrow, which thou manifestest to a high degree and hast performed for three days long upon the heap of shards. But now it would be better for thee to give thyself gradually into God's counsel, which sayeth that thou shouldst summon up thy heart and speak no longer of such disjointed thoughts as that of begetting Joseph anew. How were that possible? When thou begottest him thou knewest him not. For man begetteth only what he doth not know. But would he beget consciously and knowing, his art would be creation and he in his presumption would be thinking of himself as God."

"Well, Eliezer, and what then? Must man then not presume, and would he be still man if he did not at all times itch to be like God? Thou forgettest," said Jacob in a whisper, approaching his mouth to Eliezer's ear, "that I have secret knowledge of procreation more than most men, and well know the means and ways of blurring the distinction between begetting and creating, and how to let somewhat of creation flow into the begetting, as Laban learned when I made the white ewes conceive over the peeled wands and they cast speckled in my favour. Seek me a woman, Eliezer, who resembleth Rachel in eyes and limbs, there must be such. I will beget with her, mine eyes firmly and consciously directed upon Joseph's image, which I know so well. Then will she bear him again to me from the dead."

"Thy words," replied Eliezer, just as softly, "make me to shudder, and I would not willingly have heard them. For it seemeth to me they come not only out of the depths of thy lamenting, but even from deeper still. Weighted with years thou art besides, and it is not proper thou shouldst think of begetting any more, to say nothing of such begetting as has a tinge of creating and should at no time be thought of."

"Mistake me not, Eliezer. I am an old man, yet full of virility and not at all like the angels, as I am well aware. I should like well to beget. — To be sure," he added after a pause, "my vital powers are for the time cast down by grief over Joseph, so that because of my affliction I might not be able to beget, whereas truly I would wish to precisely on account of it. Therein canst thou see in me the contradictions which rend me, which God hath brought about."

"I can see that thy affliction is set as guard and protection against great sacrilege."

Jacob pondered.

"Then," he said, close to his servant's ear, as before, "one must deceive the watchman and play him a trick, which may easily happen, as he is the obstacle and the motive both at once. For it must be possible, Eliezer, to make a man without begetting him, if one is prevented by suffering and grief! Hath then God begotten man in the womb of woman? No, for there was none, and it is an offence to think of such a thing. Rather He made him as He would, with His hands, out of clay, and breathed the living breath in his nostrils, that he might walk. Nay, Eliezer, but listen and let thyself be won. If we were to make a figure out of clay and a thing formed of earth, like an image, three ells long and with all its limbs, as God thought of and envisaged them when He conceived man in the spirit and made him after His image. God saw and made man, Adam, for He is the creator. But I see Joseph, the single creature, as I know him, and I will awake him much more eagerly even than when I conceived him and did not know him. And it would lie before us, Eliezer, the figure, and stretch itself in human length on the ground, the face turned toward heaven; we, however, should stand at its feet and look into its face of clay. Ah, my oldest servant, my heart beats high and fast, for how if we did it?"

"If we did what, master? What new and strange thing doth thine anguish conceive?"

"Do I yet know already, my elder servant, and can I tell thee? But let thyself be won and help me to that which I do not yet rightly know! And if we went round the figure once and seven times, I to the right and thou to the left, and laid a little leaf in its dead mouth, a little leaf with God's name. . . . I would kneel down and enclose in my arms the clay and kiss it as I could kiss it, from the bottom of my heart. . . . There!" he shrieked aloud. "Eliezer, lo! The body turneth red, red as fire, it gloweth, it scorcheth me, but I let it not down, I hold it fast in my arms and kiss it again. Then is it extinguished and water floweth into the clayey body, it swelleth and gusheth with water, and lo, hair springeth up on his head, and nails sprout on fingers and toes. Then I kiss him for the third time and blow into him my breath which is God's breath; and fire, water, and breath of air, these three bring it about that the fourth, the earth, waketh to life and in deep amaze openeth its eyes to me the awaker and speaketh: 'Abba, dear Father. . . .'"

"All that maketh me to shudder," said Eliezer, and indeed he was trembling slightly, "for it is as though thou hadst won me over for these new and mysterious doings and that the *golem* liveth before mine eyes. Truly my life is a burden to me and thou makest a strange return that I am constant to thy couch of affliction and loyally support thy head, whilst thou speakest of wonder-making and images, and so enforcest me that I see all with thine eyes, whether I would or no."

And Eliezer was glad of the brethren when they returned, but they were not so.

ACQUAINTANCE WITH GRIEF

THEY came the seventh day after Jacob had received the sign, they too with sackcloth round their loins, and their hair full of ashes. They were sick at heart, and none of them understood how they could ever have persuaded themselves that all would be well and the father's heart would return again to them, if only the spoiled brat were out of the way. Long ago they had discarded the hope and wondered that they could ever have entertained it. On their journey thither they confessed, haltingly, to each other and to themselves, that putting Joseph away had in no wise altered their father's attitude to them.

They were pretty well aware how Jacob was taking it, and how he felt about them; they understood in what uneasy discomfort their lives would henceforth be led. Deep within the father, obscurely and perhaps not quite consciously, he thought of them as the murderers of the boy. Perhaps he did not believe that they had slain their brother with their own hands. Somehow the beast had done it for them, taking away the blood-deed and doing according to their wish, so that in his eyes they might be guiltless and unassailable and yet the more despicable murderers. In reality, of course, it was just the other way round: they were guilty, indeed, but were no murderers. However, they could not tell the father that; to clear themselves of the blood-guilt they must have confessed their guilt, which would have meant forswearing their oath and their bond. Though indeed they had moments when they found the oath as futile as everything else.

In short, no comfort could be expected, none at all — they could see that perfectly well. A bad conscience is bad enough; but a bad conscience with a grievance is almost worse; for it makes sullen confusion in the soul, it is both foolish and anguishing and cuts a sorry figure. Thus then they would stand before Jacob all their life long, the ten, and there would be no relief. For he suspected them and they learned to know what that means: a mistrust and suspicion, one man mistrusting himself in that he mistrusts another and the other in himself, so others cannot have the repose he cannot find himself, but must peer and pry and taunt and plague himself by plaguing others — for that is the nature of suspicion and incurable mistrust.

All this they perceived in the first moment when they stood before Jacob — they read it all in the look which he directed toward them, as he raised himself a little from the arm on which he lay. That gaze, reddened by weeping, melancholy and piercing at once, anxious and mistrustful, tried to penetrate their hearts, yet knowing it could not; it held them long before fitting words came: the unanswerable, already answered, empty, senseless, fruitless, pathetic query:

"Where is Joseph?"

They stood with hanging heads before that impossible question: those sorry figures, those sinners with a grievance. They saw that he would spare them nothing, but make all things as hard as he could. When he knew of their approach, he might have risen to receive them; but — though a week had passed since he had received the sign — he lay there, with his face on his arm, and only raised it after a good space of time. And his look conveyed the question which in the abandonment of his grief he insisted on asking them. He deliberately made use of affliction in order to lie thus before them and ask his question, so that it might sound like an outburst of anguish. They saw through all that. Men saw through each other in that distant day as well as in this.

They answered, wryly (Jehudah spoke for the rest):

"We know, dear lord, what pain and deep mourning hath afflicted thee."

"Me?" he asked. "Not you also?"

"Us too of course," they replied. "Of us we would wish not to speak."

"Why not?"

"Out of reverence."

A lamentable exchange of words. They shuddered to think that it would be so from now on.

"Joseph is no more here," he said.

"Alas!" they responded.

"I gave him up to the journey," he said again, "and he exulted in it. I told him to go to Shechem that he might bow before you and incline your hearts to return. Did he do so?"

"Alas, the tragic thing befell," they replied, "that he did not get

so far as to reach us. Before he could do so, the wild beast had struck
him down. For we were pasturing no longer in the vale of Shechem,
but in the valley of Dothan. So the boy went astray and was struck
down. We saw him no more with our eyes since the day when he
announced to you and us in the field what he had dreamed."

"The dreams," said Jacob, "which he dreamed, they were then a
vexation to you, heavy and great, so that you bore a grudge to him in
your hearts?"

"Something of a grudge," they answered. "A grudge indeed, yet
in measure. We saw that his dreams gave thee vexation, for that you
chid him and indeed even threatened to pull his hair. Therefore we
too were angry with him to some extent. Now, alas, hath the cruel
beast worried him far more than was thy intent."

"It hath rent him," said Jacob, and wept. "Why say you worried,
for it rent and devoured him? To say worried instead of rent, it is a
scorn and a mocking and sounds like gladness."

"Out of bitter affliction," they answered, "it might happen that one
said worried for torn — or even to spare the afflicted."

"That is true," he said. "You are right in what you say and I must
be content. But if Joseph could not incline your hearts, why then
are ye returned?"

"To mourn with you."

"Then mourn," responded Jacob. And they sat down with him to
join in a lament: "How long liest thou there?" and as they did so,
Jehudah supported his father's head on his knee and dried his tears.
But after a little while Jacob interrupted the lamentations and said:

"I do not care to have thee support my head, Judah, and dry my
tears. The twins shall do it."

The offended Judah gave over his father's head to the twins and
they held it awhile as they lamented, until Jacob said again:

"I know not why, but it is unpleasant to me that Simeon and Levi
should do me this service. Reuben shall do it."

Hugely insulted, the twins gave over the head to Reuben, who held
it in his turn, until Jacob said once more: "It suiteth and comforteth
me not that Reuben holdeth my head and drieth my brow. Dan
shall do it."

But things went no better with Dan, he had to pass on the head to
Naphtali, of whom Jacob tired even more quickly, and chose Gad
for the next in turn. Thus it went on through Asher and Issachar to
Zebulun, Jacob saying each time something to the same effect:

"I feel it vaguely displeasing that he should hold my head; another
shall do it."

Until all of them had been affronted and put aside — then he said:
"We will cease to mourn."

So they just sat silent round him with dropped jaws. For they understood that he partly thought of them as Joseph's murderers, which indeed they partly were, and if not wholly, then it was only by chance. They were mightily aggrieved that he took the part for the whole, and hardened their hearts.

Thus, they thought, would their lives be spent from now on: sinners suffering under a misunderstanding which they could never wholly explain. This was what they got for putting Joseph away. Jacob's eyes rested upon them. Those bright, brown, tear-inflamed eyes with the enlarged glands beneath them, those troubled eyes that were wont to be turned inward in musings upon the nature of God; now they were bent upon his sons, always upon them whenever they themselves were not looking: brooding and spying in incurable misgiving and turning aside when one met their gaze. As they were eating, he began:

"But if a man hath hired an ox or an ass and there cometh a stroke, or a god striketh the beast so that it is dead, then shall the man swear and purge himself from guilt, before he can be free from suspicion."

Their hands felt cold; for they understood what Jacob's words pointed at.

"Swear?" they grumbled, their hearts sinking. "He must swear when nobody seeth how it went with the beast and there is no blood and no wounding such as the lion doth or any beast of prey. But if there be blood or traces, who shall molest the hireling? It is the affair of the owner."

"Is so the way of it?"

"So it standeth written."

"But it standeth written: if a shepherd pasture the owner's sheep, and a lion killeth among the fold, then the shepherd shall swear an oath to clear himself, and the damage shall be the owner's. Then how standeth it with me? Shall not the hired shepherd also swear if it seem clear and certain that the lion hath killed?"

"Yes and no," they answered, and their feet too were cold by now. "More no than yes, if it please thee. For if it is a sheepfold on which the lion falleth, then he draggeth his prey out away and no one seeth, and it must be sworn. But if the shepherd can produce the slain and bring forth some mangled remnant, then shall he not be made to swear."

"You might all be judges, so well you know the law. But if the sheep were the judge's and were of value to him, but to the shepherd of none — is it not enough that it was not his and of no worth to him, to force him to swear?"

"Not ever yet in the world was that enough to force an oath."

"But if the shepherd hated the sheep?" he asked, and looked at them with wild and frightened eyes. Wildly, fearfully, with heartsinking they countered the gaze. It eased their pain that his eyes

roved from one to the other so that none of them had to bear that
mistrustful look for long at a time.

"Can one hate a sheep?" they asked, and their faces were cold
and sweaty. "That does not happen in the world, there can be no
law concerning it, and it cometh not into consideration. But we are
no hired shepherds; rather the sons of the king of shepherds, and
if we lose a sheep, so is it our loss as well as his, and all in all there
can be no talk of judging or of a compulsory oath, in any case."

Such idle, cowardly, wretched talk! Must it go on like that for
always? Then were it better that the brethren should go away again,
to Shechem, Dothan, or elsewhere, since it was proven that their stay
here without Joseph was as impossible as it had been with him.

But did they go? Not at all, they stopped, and if one of them went
his own ways, he soon came back. Their evil consciences had need
of his suspicion, his suspicion of their evil consciences. They were
bound to one another in God and in Joseph; in the beginning they
suffered greatly in living together; yet they accepted it as penance,
Jacob and his sons. For these knew what they had done, and if they
knew they were guilty, Jacob knew that he was too.

But time passed and habit was re-formed. Habit wiped the peering
mistrust out of Jacob's eyes; habit made vague in the minds of the
ten brothers what they had actually done. Gradually they lost sight
of the distinction between doing and happening. It had happened that
Joseph was lost — the question how slowly retreated behind the fact
as father and sons adjusted themselves to it. He was not here; that
was the fixed fact upon which they all came to rest. The ten knew
that he had not been murdered, as Jacob thought. But even this difference in knowledge lost meaning in the end, for to them as to him
Joseph was a shadow, wandering far outside any sphere of human
knowledge in the land of no-return. In this idea father and sons were
at one. The poor old man from whom God had snatched his treasure
of feeling, so that no sweet spring could bloom any more in his heart,
but only parching summer and the barrenness of winter reigned
therein and he was really as "stiff" as at the beginning, in his seizure,
did not cease to bewail his lamb; and when he wept they did so with
him, for their hatred was taken from them, until in the end they
could not clearly remember how it was the fool had so angered them.
They could even mourn him, too; for they knew him to be safe in
the shadow, and in absence, and buried outside the circle of their
life — and Jacob did so too.

He relinquished the idea of "going down" as mother and fetching
Joseph back; he no longer distressed anyone with wild plans of begetting him anew or shaping him out of clay and playing the part
of God. Life and love are beautiful; but death has also its good side,
hiding and preserving the beloved in the past and in absence; so that

where once there were care and fear there is now perfect calm. Where was Joseph? In Abraham's bosom. With God, who had "taken him to Himself." Or whatever other words one finds for that last absence — all of them chosen to express gently and finally, if somewhat hollowly and bleakly, the ultimate security of all.

Death, after having restored, preserves. What had Jacob done to restore Joseph, since he had been dismembered? Death itself had seen to that, and quickly. Death had recomposed a whole out of fourteen pieces (or even more), recomposed it in laughing beauty, and thus preserved him more sweetly and better than the people of the evil land of Egypt preserved their dead with bandages and spices: inviolate, unchanged, unchangeable, that dear, vain, brilliant, wheedling youth of seventeen, who had sat on white Hulda and ridden away.

Unchanged, unchangeable; needing no more carefulness, yet ever seventeen however much the years might increase since he rode away and the years of the living increase with him.

So was Joseph for Jacob; and so how shall any say that death has not its good side, however chill and hollow it may be? Jacob adapted himself to it. He looked back with chagrin upon his bickering and arguing with God in the first flowering of his grief, and no longer found it reactionary, but splendid and worthy of reverence instead, that God had not crushed him out of hand, but rather in silent forbearance had let him give rein to the intemperance of his misery.

Ah, good old man! Didst thou divine what amazing favour still lay behind the silence of thy dread and wonderful God, and with what incredible rapture thy soul was still to be shaken, according to His word? When thou wast young in the flesh, thou didst once awake at dawn to find thy dearest bliss turned to illusion and trickery. Very old must thou become before thou learnest that naught but illusion and trickery was thy sorest anguish likewise.

JOSEPH IN EGYPT

Chapter I

THE JOURNEY DOWNWARDS

OF THE SILENCE OF THE DEAD

"WHERE are you taking me?" Joseph asked Kedema, one of the old man's sons, as they were setting up the sleeping-huts, in the rolling, moonlit lowland at the foot of the mountains called Fruitlands.

Kedema looked him up and down.

"Thou'rt a good one!" said he, and shook his head in token that he did not mean good at all but various other things such as pert or queer or simple. "Where are we taking thee? But are we taking thee anywhither? No, not at all. Thou art by chance with us, because our father hath purchased thee from harsh masters, and thou goest with us whither-ever we go. But taking thee that cannot be called."

"No? Then not," responded Joseph. "I only meant: whither doth God lead me, in that I go with you?"

"Thou art and remainest a funny fellow," countered the Ma'onite, "and thou hast a way of putting thyself in the centre of things till one knoweth not whether to wonder or be put out. Thinkest thou, thou 'Come-hither,' that we are a-journeying in order that thou mayest arrive somewhither where thy God will have thee to come?"

"Not that do I think," Joseph replied. "For I know that you, my masters, journey whither you will and on your own affairs and of a certainty no question of mine meaneth any wrong to your dignity or power. But lo, the world hath many centres, one for each created being, and about each one it lieth in its own circle. Thou standest but half an ell from me, yet about thee lieth a universe whose centre I am not but thou art. Therefore both are true, according as one speaketh from thy centre or from mine. And I, on the other hand, stand in the centre of mine. For our universes are not far from each other so that they do not touch; rather hath God pushed them and interwoven them deep into each other, so that you Ishmaelites do indeed journey quite independently and according to your own ends, whither you will, but besides that you are the means and tool, in our interwovenness, that I arrive at my goal. Therefore I ask whither you are leading me."

"Well, well!" said Kedema, and kept looking him up and down, his face turned away from the peg he was driving. "All that thou thinkest out and thy tongue runs on like a lizard's tongue. I will tell the old man my father how thou — son of a dog as thou art — takest leave to riddle and stick thy nose into such high wisdom as that thou hast a universe to thyself and we are destined for thy guardians. Take care, I'll tell him!"

"Do so," responded Joseph, "it will do no harm. It will make thy father careful not to sell me too cheap to the first comer, if he thinketh of making trade with me."

"Are we chattering here," asked Kedema, "or are we setting up a hut?" And he motioned him to lend a hand. But as they worked he said:

"Thou askest too much, when thou wilt know from me whither we journey. I would have naught against telling thee, if I knew. But it is the old man my father's business, he keepeth all in his own head how it will go and afterwards we see how it cometh to pass. So much is clear, that we keep on, as the shepherds thy harsh masters counselled us, and go not into the interior but are bound toward the level shore; there shall we travel day by day and come into the land of the Philistines, the cities of the seafaring traders and the pirate strongholds. Perhaps thou wilt be sold there somewhere to the galleys."

"That would I not have," said Joseph.

"No use to wish. All will be as the old man hath thought, and whither we journey at the end, that he himself perhaps knoweth not. But he would like us to think that he knoweth all quite precisely, beforehand, and so we all act as though we thought so — Epher, Mibsam, Kedar, and I. . . . I tell thee this because we happen to be setting up the huts here together; otherwise I have no reason to say it to thee. I could wish the old man would not exchange thee too soon for purple and cedar oil but that thou wouldst remain here with us for a spell that one might hear more from thee about the universes of men and their interwovenness."

"As thou wilt," answered Joseph. "You are my masters and have bought me for twenty silver pieces, including my tongue and my wits. They are at your service; and to that about the universe of the individual I can add something about God's not quite flawless wonder-working with numbers, so that man must improve His calculations; and further about the pendulum, the year of the dog star, and the renewal of life —"

"But not now," Kedema said. "The huts must absolutely be set up now for the old man my father is tired, and so am I. I fear that I could not follow thy tongue any more for today. Art thou still ailing from thy fast and are thy limbs still sore where thou wast bound with cords?"

"Scarcely at all," responded Joseph. "After all it was only three days that I spent in the pit, and your oil with which I might anoint myself has done my limbs great good. I am now whole, and nothing detracteth from the value and usefulness of thy slave."

He had, in fact, had opportunity to cleanse and anoint himself, had received from his masters a loincloth and for cooler hours a rumpled white hooded cape such as the thick-lipped camel-boy wore. Probably the expression "to feel as one new-born" may have fitted him more precisely than it has any human being since the creation of the world — for had he not actually been born again? It was a deep cleavage and abyss that divided his present from his past, it was the grave. Since he had died young his vital forces reassembled themselves quickly and easily beyond it; but that did not prevent him from distinguishing sharply between his present existence and that earlier one which had ended in the grave, nor from considering himself not the old Joseph but a new one. If to be dead and perished means to be quite inseparably bound to a state which permits no looking back, no gesture, no smallest resumption of relations with his previous life; if it means to be vanished speechless from that former life without leave or thinkable possibility of breaking the silence with any whatsoever sign — then Joseph was dead; and the oil with which he might anoint himself after cleansing from the dust of the grave had been no other than that which one gives the dead into the grave for his anointing in another life.

I stress this point, for it seems to me urgent to defend Joseph, now and later, from a reproach which has often historically been levelled against him. For certainly a reproach lies in the query: why, after escaping from the pit, had he not bent all his strength to get in touch with Jacob in his pitiable state, to let him know that he still lived? The opportunity must early have presented itself; yes, as time passed it would surely have been more and more possible for the son to send to that father in his error some word of the truth. Proportionally strange, even offensive must it seem that he did nothing of the kind.

But the reproach confuses the outwardly with the inwardly possible, and leaves out of consideration the three black days which preceded the rising of Joseph. They had driven him, amid severest anguish, to an insight into the deadly error of his former life and to a renunciation of it; they had taught him to accept his brothers' conviction of his death. His resolve and purpose not to betray their belief was the firmer because it was not voluntary but as involuntary and logically necessary as the silence of the dead. A dead man is silent about his love, not out of lovelessness but necessity; and not in cruel wise was Joseph silent to his father. Indeed it became very hard on him, and the longer it lasted the harder it grew, that we may believe; not easier than on the dead lies the earth which covers him.

Pity for the old man who he well knew had loved him more than himself, whom he too loved with grateful, natural love, and together with whom he had brought himself down to the grave tempted him sore and would have made him glad to act contrary to his better sense. But there is something strange about a pain felt by others for our own fate. Our sympathy with it is of a peculiar kind, distinctly harder and colder than that we feel with a stranger sorrow. Joseph had passed through frightfulness, he had received cruel instruction; and it eased for him his compassion for Jacob, yes, the consciousness of their common burden made his father's woe seem somehow in the nature of things. His bond to death prevented him from cancelling the bloody sign which the other must have received. Jacob, he knew, could not fail to take the blood of the kid for his son's blood; and that this must be so worked upon Joseph until it practically obliterated the distinction between "This is my blood" and "This represents my blood." Jacob held him for dead; and since he did so irrevocably, unalterably — then was Joseph dead or was he not?

He was. The proof lay in the compulsion to keep silence to the father. The kingdom of the dead received him — or rather would receive him; for he soon learned that he was still on the way thither, being led in that direction by the Midianites who had bought him.

TO THE MASTER

"Thou'rt to come to the master," a boy named Ba'almahar said one evening to Joseph as the latter was busy baking pancakes on hot stones. They were now some days distant from Mount Kirmil, having come along the sandy shore close to the open sea. Joseph had asserted that he made uncommonly good pancakes. And actually by God's help he succeeded in making excellent ones, though he had never made or been asked to make them before. They had camped at sunset at the foot of the rushy and grassy line of dunes which had for days monotonously accompanied their course on the land side. It had been very hot; now mildness descended from a paling sky. The beach extended, violet-hued. The retreating sea rustled silkily, sending broad, shallow waves to the wet margin of the shore, where they were gilded with red-gold splendour by the scarlet rays of the parting sun. The camels rested beside their pegs. Not far from the shore a clumsy freight boat, worked by two men and seemingly laden with wood, was being towed southwards by a sailing-ship propelled by oars. The sail-boat had a short mast and a long yard, many cables, and an animal's head on the prow high above the water.

"To the master," repeated the camel-boy. "He summons thee through my mouth. He is sitting on the mat in his tent and he says thou art to come before him. I was passing and he called me by my name, Ba'almahar, and spake: 'Send to me him lately bought, that son of the swamps, that "Come-hither" out of the depths, I would question him.'"

"Aha!" thought Joseph, "Kedema hath told him about the universes, that is very well." "Yes," said he, "he expressed himself thus because he knew not how otherwise to make thee comprehend whom he meant. He must speak to thee, my good fellow, according to thy understanding."

"Indeed," retorted the other, "what else should he have said? For wanting to see me, he would say: 'Send to me Ba'almahar.' For that is my name. But with thee it is harder, for to thee one can but whistle."

"I suppose he would see thee always," said Joseph, "though thou art but a scaldhead! Go now. Thanks for thy message."

"What thinkest thou?" cried Ba'almahar. "Thou must come straightway with me, that I bring thee before him, for if thou comest not I shall suffer."

"But first," answered Joseph, "I must just finish this pancake before I go. I will take it with me, that the master may try my excellent baking. Be quiet and wait." And with the slave emitting cries of impatience he baked the pancake brown, then rose from his squatting posture and said: "I come."

Ba'almahar accompanied him to the old man, who sat contemplatively on his mat in the low entrance of his travelling tent.

"To hear is to obey," said Joseph, saluting. The old man, gazing into the fading glow of eve, nodded and then lifted one of his hands from his lap with a sidewise wave in sign that Ba'almahar should disappear.

"I hear," he began, "that thou hast said thou art the navel of the world."

Joseph shook his head with a smile.

"What could that mean," answered he, "and what may I have chanced to utter and turn-a-phrase that they have so bungled it to my lord's ears? Let me see. Yea, truly, I said that it hath many centres, the world, as many as there are men on earth to say 'I say.' For each a centre."

"That is the same in the end," said the old man. "It is true, then, that thou didst give tongue to such a folly. Never have I heard the like, in all my wanderings, and I see too well thou art a blasphemer and ill-doer, just as thy former masters said. What should we be coming to if every gawk and gaby in all the tribes were to consider himself the centre of the world wherever he standeth? And what should we do with so many centres? When thou wast in the well, whither thou camest, as I now see, only too justifiably, was then this well the sacred centre of the world?"

"God hallowed it," answered Joseph, "in that He kept an eye on it and let me not be destroyed therein but sent you by that way that you might save me."

" 'So that'?" questioned the merchant, "or 'in order that'?"

" 'So that,' and 'in order that,' " responded Joseph, "both, or as one will."

"Thou art a prattler. Up to now there was at least question whether Babel was the centre of the world and its tower or perhaps the city of Abdu on the river Hapi, where he lieth buried, the First of the West. Thou multipliest the question. To what god belongest thou?"

"God the Lord."

"Adon, then, and thou lamentest the going down of the sun. To that I agree, it is at least a statement worthy of a hearing, and better than if one were to say: 'I am a centre,' as though he were gone mad. What hast thou there in thy hand?"

"A pancake, which I baked for my lord. I can make uncommonly good pancakes."

"Uncommon? Let me see."

And the old man took the cake out of Joseph's hand, turned it about, and then bit a piece off with his side teeth, for he had none in front. The pancake was as good as could be and not better; but the old man gave judgment:

"It is very good. I will not say uncommonly, since thou hast said it first; thou shouldst have left it to me. But good it is. Capital, indeed," he added, as he chewed. "I commission thee to bake them often."

"It shall be done."

"Is it true or not, that thou canst write and keep a record of stocks?"

"With ease," answered Joseph. "I can write human and divine writing, with reed or graver, at will."

"Who taught thee?"

"He did who was set over the house. A wise steward."

"How many times goeth seven into seventy-seven?"

"But twice, as written. But in sense I must take the seven first once, then twice, then eight times to reach seventy-seven, for seven, fourteen, and fifty-six make it up. One, two, and eight are, however, eleven and thus I have it: eleven times doth seven go into seventy-seven."

"So quickly findest thou a hidden number?"

"Quickly or not at all."

"Thou hast probably learned from practice. But suppose I have a piece of meadow that is three times as large as the field of my neighbour Dagantakala, but he buyeth a yoke of land in addition and now mine is only twice as large as his. How many yoke have both fields?"

"Together?" asked Joseph and reckoned.

"No, each one."

"Hast thou a neighbour named Dagantakala?"

"I only call so the owner of the second field in my sum."

"I see and understand. Dagantakala — that must be a man from the country of Pelesheth to judge by the name, from the land of the Philistines, whither we seem to be going down according to the decree of thy mind. There is no such person; but he is named Dagantakala and he tills in contentment his little ploughland, now increased to three yoke, incapable of envy of my lord and his six yoke, since after all he hath increased from two to three yoke and besides, because he doth not exist at all nor yet the ploughland which all together maketh up nine yoke — that is the joke of it. There is only my lord and his busy brain."

The old man blinked uncertainly, for he did not quite see that Joseph had already solved the problem.

"Well?" asked he. . . . "Ah, yes, yes. Thou hast said already and I scarce marked it, so hast thou woven and fabled it into thy prattle that I almost failed to hear it. It is right, six, two, and three, those are the figures. They were concealed and hidden — how then hast thou so quickly brought them out while prattling?"

"One must fix the unknown quantity clearly in one's eye, then the concealments fall away and it becometh known."

"I must laugh," the old man said, "because thou madest the answer run all in together so and made nothing of it when thou gavest it. I really must laugh heartily at that." And so he did, with his toothless mouth, his head on one side, and shaking it to boot. Then he grew serious again and blinked with eyes yet moist.

"Now hearken, Come-hither," said he, "and answer honestly and in accordance with the truth. Tell me, art thou really a slave and a nobody's son, a rascal and under-servant of the basest sort, heavily punished for heaped-up crimes and moral transgressions as the shepherds said?"

Joseph veiled his eyes and rounded his lips in a way he had, making the under one protrude.

"My lord," said he, "hath given me unknown problems to try me, and not given me the answer at once, for then there would be no trial. Since now God trieth thee with riddles — wilt thou have the answer at once and shall the questioner answer for the asked? So doth it not go in the world. Hast thou not drawn me out of the grave where I had fouled myself like a sheep with its own filth? What sort of under-servant must I then be and how gross my moral breach! I have moved the double and triple to and fro in my brain and weighed their relations until I saw the solution. Reckon thou too, if thou wilt, to and fro between punishment, guilt and baseness and of a certainty thou wilt come from the two to the three."

"My example was in words and bore the answer in itself. Figures are clear and final. But who giveth me warrant that life too can be solved like them, not deceiving the known about the unknown? For many things speak here against a clear conclusion."

"Then one must take that into consideration: if life cannot be solved like figures, on the other hand it is spread before thee so that thou seest it with thine eyes."

"Whence hast thou the precious stone on thy finger?"

"Perhaps the base servant stole it," suggested Joseph.

"Perhaps. But thou must know whence thou hadst it."

"I have had it so long that I no longer remember when I did not have it."

"So then thou hast brought it with thee out of the swamps and reeds where thou wast conceived? For thou art truly a son of the swamps and child of the rushes?"

"I am the child of the well, out of which my lord drew me and brought me up with milk."

"Hast thou known no mother but the well?"

"Yes," said Joseph. "I did know a sweeter mother. Her cheek smelt like the rose-leaf."

"Thou seest. And hath she not named thee with a name?"

"I have lost it, my lord, for I have lost my life. I may not know my name as I may not know my life, which they thrust into the grave."

"Tell me thy transgression, which brought thy life down to the grave."

"It was culpable," answered Joseph, "and is named confidence. Criminal confidence and blind, unreasoning presumption, that is its name. For it is blind and deadly to test men beyond their strength and require of them what they neither will hear nor can. Before such love and respect their gall runneth over and they become like ravening beasts. Not to know this, or not to want to know it, is fatal. But I did not know or I flung it to the winds, so that I did not hold my tongue and told them my dreams, in order that they might marvel at me. But 'in order that' and 'so that' are sometimes two different things and go not together. The 'In order that' did not come to pass and the 'So that' was called the grave."

"Thy presumption," said the old man, "with which thou madest men mad, that was of course arrogance and pride, I can well believe it, and it doth not surprise me in one who sayeth: 'I am navel and centre of the world.' But I am much travelled between the rivers that take different courses, the one from south to north, the other the other way, and I know that many a mystery obtaineth in the apparently so manifest world, and behind loud rumour the hidden things pursue their silent way. Yea, often it hath seemed to me as though the world is full of such loud rumours to the end that it may better hide the hidden beneath them and out-talk the secrets that lie behind men and things. Much I came on without looking, much thrust itself on me unsought. Yet I heeded not, for I am not so curious that I must get to the bottom of everything, rather it sufficeth me to know that mystery encompasseth the garrulous world. I am a doubter as I sit here; not because I believed nothing, rather because I hold everything for possible. Such am I, an old man. I know of fables and happenings which count not as probable and yet come to pass. I know of one, come from the nobility and of lofty rank, wherein he clothed himself with royal linen and anointed himself with the oil of gladness, who was driven into desert and misery — "

Here the merchant interrupted himself and blinked for the necessary and given conclusion of his speech, the continuation which was now due, without his having thought in advance that it would be due, put him in thoughtful mood. There are deeply chamferred trains of thought out of which one does not escape, once in them; associations cut and dried from old time, which fit into each other like rings in a chain, so that he who has said A cannot help saying B or at least thinking it; and like links in a chain they are, too, in that in them the earthly and heavenly are so interlocked one into the other that one passes willy-nilly, and whether speaking or silent, from one to the other. True it is that man for the most part thinks in set phrases and fixed formulas; not such as he himself searches out but as he remembers the traditional. Even as the old man spoke of one driven from high estate into darkness and misery, he had fallen into a pattern. And to continue with the pattern was inevitably to arrive at the resurrection of the abased to be the saviour of man and bringer of the new time; and thus the old man paused, in silent perplexity.

But more than mild perplexity it was not — only the decent and reverent restraint of the self-respecting practical man before the metaphysical or the sacred. If it became more — a sort of disquiet, a deeper dismay, yes, an alarm, if only passing and half unconscious — that could only be due to the encounter between the old man's blinking gaze and the eyes of the youth standing before him. Hardly did it even deserve the name of encounter — not so much; for Joseph's eyes did not "encounter" the other's gaze, did not actually respond to it or return it. They only received it, only offered themselves, in silence and candour, to be looked at: a mystery, equivocal, intriguing, obscure. Others before now had blinked and been startled as they tried to pierce this mute provocation to its depths, as now the old Ishmaelite tried, in face of the question: what had he done, what not quite canny business had he been about when he bargained with the shepherds for his possession?

But after all, that and nothing else had been the subject of the whole conversation; and when it suddenly showed signs of shifting into the unearthly and fabulous, the old man had to tell himself that many things on this earth could be regarded in the same uncanny light; it was for a sensible man to make distinctions and to shift back again as soon as possible to the practical side.

He cleared his throat to facilitate the process.

"H'm," said he. "All in all, thy master is travelled and full of experience between the rivers and hath knowledge of affairs. He needeth not to be instructed therein by thee, child of the swamps and son of the well. I have bought thy body and what thou displayest of dexterity, but not thy heart, that I could force it to reveal thy thoughts. Not only is it unnecessary that I should urge thee, it is not even advisable and might be to my harm. I have found thee and given thee again the breath of life; but to buy thee was not my purpose; for I did not even know thou wast for sale. I thought of no advantage save perhaps a finder's reward or a ransom, as might be. However, it came to a bargain for thy person, and I made a test. I said: 'Sell him to me,' and the test seemed decisive to me and it was so decided, for the shepherd men entered into it. I have won thee by hard and prolonged bargaining, for they were stubborn. Twenty shekels of silver according to weight, as is customary, have I weighed out for thee and have not remained in their debt. How is it with the price and how do I stand? It is a medium price, not too good, not too bad. I could lower it, on account of the errors which, as they said, brought thee to the pit. According to thy parts I could sell thee higher than I bought thee and enrich myself at will. What should I gain from prying into thy antecedents and perhaps learning that it standeth with thee the gods know how, so that thou wast not at all for sale and art not, so that I have lost mine own, or if I sell thee again it is a wrong and a trade with stolen goods? Go to, I will know naught of thy affairs nor their details, that I may remain innocent and in the right. It is enough that I suspect that they are something out of the common and belong to things which I am doubter enough to consider possible. Go, I have already talked longer with thee than needful and it is time for sleep. But bake such pancakes often, they are right good, if yet not so out of the common. Further I command thee that thou procure from Mibsam, my son-in-law, writing tools, sheets, reed, and ink, and make for me in common writing a list of the wares we are carrying, each after its kind: the balsams, salves, knives, spoons, canes, and lamps, as well as the footgear, the burning-oils, and the glass-paste, according to count and weight; the items in black, the weight and quantity in red, without blunder or blot, and shalt bring me the list within three days. Is it understood?"

"Commanded is as good as done," said Joseph.

"Then go."

"Peace and sweetness to thy slumbers," spoke Joseph. "May blithe and easy dreams be woven from time to time among them."

The Minoan smiled. And he followed Joseph with his thoughts.

TALK BY NIGHT

THREE days they had gone on by the margin of the sea and it was evening once more and time of rest in the tents, and as they rested, it looked just as it had three days before; it might have been the same place. As the old man sat on his mat at the door of his tent, Joseph appeared before him, with pancakes and a written scroll in his hands.

"The least of his slaves," he said, "bringeth to the master according to his commands."

The Midianite put the bake-stuff to one side; the list he unrolled, and studied the script with his head on one side. He did so well pleased.

"No blots," said he, "and that is well. But one can tell likewise that the signs are drawn with pleasure and a sense of beauty and are an adornment. It is to be hoped that the content agrees, so that it is not only decorative but also practical. It is a pleasure to see one's own so cleanly set down and the various items listed in order. The goods themselves are greasy or they are sticky with gum; the merchant does not willingly soil his hands, he deals with them as they are written. They are there, but they are also here; clean, not stinking, easy to see. A list like this is like the Ka or the spiritual body of things, alongside the real. Good, then, Come-hither, thou knowest how to write and canst also reckon somewhat, as I saw. And in thy station it lacketh thee not for readiness of speech, for it hath pleased me, the way thou gavest thy lord good-night three days past. What were thy words again?"

"I know them no more," replied Joseph. "But it may be that I wished peace to thy slumbers."

"No, it was pleasanter than that. But no matter; likely there will come more occasion for such a phrase. But what I could say is this: when I have naught more important to think of, then at the third and fourth remove I think of thee. Thy lot may be hard, since in any case thou hast seen better days and now thou servest the travelling merchant as baker and clerk. Since, then, I purpose to dispose of thee, and innocent of the knowledge of thy origins to enrich myself further as much as I can, I will see to it that I look out for thee."

"That is most gracious."

"I will bring thee to a house that I know, where I have sometimes done a service to mine own and its advantage; a well-kept house, a house of honour and distinction. It is a blessing, I say to thee, to belong to such a house, be it only as the least of servants, and if there be one wherein a servant may display the finer gifts it is this. If thou hast fortune and I bring thee to this house, then is thy lot as favoured as in view of thy guilt and culpableness it could possibly fall."

"And to whom belongeth the house?"

"Yea, to whom? To a man — and a man he is, or rather a lord. A great among the great, gilded with gold of favour, a man good, stern, and holy, for whom his grave waits in the West, a shepherd of men, the living image of a god. Fan-bearer on the right hand of the king is his title, but dost thou think he beareth the fan? No, the man leaves that to others, he himself is too exalted for it, he only beareth the title. Thinkest thou I know the man, the gift of the sun? No, for I am a worm before him, he seeth me not at all, and also I saw him but once from afar in his garden on a lofty seat, as he stretched forth his hand to command, and I made myself small that he take not offence at me and be distracted from his commanding, for how could I answer for it? But the upper high steward of his house I know from face to face and word to word, who is over the stores and domestics and tradesmen and governeth all. He loveth me and greeteth me in blithe words when he seeth me and sayeth: 'Well, old man, so we see thee again and thou comest with thy pack before our house to overreach us?' That he sayeth in sheer jest, thou perceivest, thinking to flatter the merchant by calling him a cheat and we chuckle together. To him will I show thee and propose thee and if he be in good mood and can use a young slave for the house, so art thou provided for."

"What king is that," asked Joseph, "whose golden rewards the master beareth?"

He wanted to learn whither he was being taken, and where the house lay for which the old man destined him; but it was not this alone made him ask. He did not know it; but his thinking and asking were controlled by traditions which worked hither from the beginnings and the times of the forefathers. Abraham spoke out of him; he who in his arrogance toward man held the view that he could serve the Highest and Him alone, and whose thinking and doing had excluded with contempt all lower and lesser gods to address itself to the Most High. The grandson's voice was pitched in a lower, more worldly key; yet the question was Abraham's question. Joseph heard with indifference of the house steward, on whom after all, according to the old man, his immediate fate depended. For the Midianite he felt contempt because he knew only the steward and not even the nobleman to whom the house belonged. But even about the latter he troubled himself little. Above him was a higher, a highest, of whom the old man spoke; and he was a king. Toward him alone and urgently went Joseph's thoughts and the speech of his tongue, unaware that it was guided not by chance or choice but by inheritance and tradition.

"What king?" repeated the old man. "Neb-mat-Re-Amun-hotpe-Nimmuria," he said in liturgical accents as though repeating a prayer.

Joseph was startled. He had stood there, his arms folded across his back, but now he quickly released them and seized his cheeks in both palms.

"That is Pharaoh!" he cried. How could he not have understood? The name which the old man chanted was known to the ends of the earth and to the stranger people of whom Eliezer had taught him, to Tarshish and Kittim, to Ophir and Elam closing in the east. How could it have been meaningless to the instructed Joseph? Some names of the title pronounced by the Midianite: "Lord of truth is Re," "Amun is satisfied," were incomprehensible; but the Syrian addition "Nimmuria" ("He goes to his fate") must have enlightened him. There were many kings and shepherds, every town had one, and Joseph had stood quietly as he put his question expecting to hear the name of some ruler of a fortified city by the sea, some Zurat, Ribaddi, Abdasherat, or Aziru. He had not been prepared to interpret the title in its most splendid and regal sense, in the most godlike and glorious significance which the word commands. Written inside a longish, upstanding annulet, guarded by falcon wings spread over it by the sun itself, it stood last of a glorious row of such names, losing themselves in the mist of the past, each similarly ringed and each illustrious. With each was associated the history of victorious campaigns, of far-extended boundary-stones and buildings world-famous for their magnificence; so that this last name itself connoted such a heritage of awe, such enhancement of the single life, as justified any homage and made quite comprehensible the involuntary start which Joseph gave. But did nothing else stir in him save the respectful awe which anyone else would have felt in his place? Yes: there were other, and opposed feelings, whose source lay as deep as that question, about the Highest: and with these he involuntarily began to control the first ones. Scorn and derision at the shameless mighty of this earth; private rebellion, in God's name, against Nimrod's assembled powers — such sentiments as these it was, which made him at length take his hands from his face and repeat his cry in the tone of a simple statement: "That is Pharaoh."

"Certainly," said the old man. "That is the Great House that hath made great the house to which I will bring thee and will offer thee to my friend the overseer to try thy fortune."

"Then wilt thou lead me down to Mizraim into the land of mud?" asked Joseph and felt his heart beat.

The old man, his head bent on one shoulder, gave it a shake.

"The question is like thee again. I know already from Kedema, my son, that out of childish conceit thou imaginest we lead thee hither or thither, though in truth we are taking our way where we take it, even without thee, and thou only comest thither where our way leadeth us. I do not travel to Egypt that I may bring thee thither, but because I have business there which will enrich me: I will buy things there which they are skilful in producing and are much sought after, such as glazed collars, camp-stools with pretty little legs, head-rests, draught-boards, chess-boards, and pleated linen aprons. These I will buy in the workshops and in the bazaars as cheap as the gods of the land will let me and take them back over the mountains of Canaan, the Retenu and Amor, into Mitanniland on the Euphrates and to the country of King Hattusil, where they have an eye for them and will spend money recklessly. Thou speakest of the 'land of mud' as though it were a land of filth, baked out of excrement like a bird's nest and like an uncleaned stall. And yet it is the land whither to travel again I am resolved and where I shall perhaps be able to leave thee; the finest land in all the round of earth, with such exquisite customs that thou wilt seem to thyself like an ox before whom one plays the lute. Thou, wretched Amu, wilt make great eyes when thou seest the country beside the river of God, which is called there 'the lands' because it is two lands, and double-crowned, but Mempi, the house of Ptah, holds the balance between them. There range unthinkably vast spaces that antechamber the desert; there crouches the lion in the head-cloth, Hor-im-akhet, created before time, the mystery of the ages, at whose breast the king fell asleep, the child of Thoth, and in dreams had his head lifted up with most exalted promise. Thine eyes will stand out of thy head when thou seest the marvels and all the splendour and choiceness of the land that is called Kemt, because it is black with fruitfulness, not red like the poverty-stricken desert. But from what is it fruitful? Because of the river of God and from that alone. For it hath its rain and its fructifying semen not in heaven but on earth and it is the god, Hapi, the Strong Bull, who spreads himself out above it and stands over it full of blessing the space of a season, leaving behind the blackness of his power, wherein one may sow and harvest a hundredfold fruit. But thou speakest as though it were a dunghill."

Joseph hung his head. He had learned that he was on his way to the kingdom of the dead; for the habit of regarding Egypt as the underworld, and its inhabitants as a people of Sheol, was born with him, and never had he heard otherwise, especially from Jacob. So then he was to be sold into the melancholy nether world, the brothers had sold him down thither, the well had been its appropriate entrance. It was very sad, he could have wept. Yet joy in the appropriateness balanced the sadness, his view that he was dead and the blood of the beast had been in truth his blood being so neatly confirmed by the old man's disclosures. He had to smile — however near to tears on his own and Jacob's account. Precisely down thither should he go, into the land which was the object of his father's pronounced aversion, Hagar's home, the monkey-land of Egypt! He recalled the prejudiced description with which Jacob had sought to make this land intolerable to his son, regarding it, without any acutal knowledge, in the light of his own hostile and horrified principles, as the seat of worship of the past, of dalliance with death, of insensibility to sin. Joseph had always been inclined to a blithe mistrust of the justice of the picture, to that sympathetic curiosity which is regularly the consequence of parental moralizing and warning. If the good, worthy, and didactic man had known that his lamb was travelling Egyptwards, to the land of Ham, the bare, as he called it, because it was black on account of the black fruitful soil, which its god gave it! The confusion of thought was right indicative of the pious prejudice of his judgment, Joseph said to himself with a smile.

But the bond between son and father was not one of opposites alone. True, it was a diabolic joke that he should be travelling toward the utterly taboo; it was a youthful triumph thus to coquet with the moral terrors of the underworld. Yet with it, in his blood, was a mute resolve which must have gladdened the father's heart: the resolve of the child of Abram not to let his eyes run over at sight of the elegance and the marvels so praised by the Ishmaelite; quite definitely not to admire too warmly the splendid civilization which awaited him. A deep and native spirit of mockery drew down the corners of his mouth at the mere thought of that elegance; and his contempt was to be a shield and buckler against the timidity which results from too great reverence.

He asked, looking up: "Is the house to which thou wilt bring me at Mempi, the dwelling of Ptah?"

"Oh, no," the old man replied, "we must go farther up, that is down, I mean up the river, out of the land of the serpent into the land of the vulture. Thou askest in thy simplicity; for when I said to thee that the master of the house is fan-bearer on the king's right hand, of course that means he must be where His Majesty the good god is, and whose house is at Wese, the city of Amun."

Joseph learned much that evening by the sea, hosts of information thronged upon him. So he was going to No, No-Amun, the city of cities and talk of the world, a subject of conversation amongst the remotest populations, where rumour said that it had a hundred gates and more than a hundred thousand inhabitants. Would Joseph's eyes then not run over, after all, when they caught sight of the metropolis? He saw that he must firmly resolve beforehand not to fall prey to vacant admiration. He stuck out his lips disdainfully. But despite his efforts to compose his features, to the honour of his own God, he could not quite escape a certain embarrassment. For he felt somewhat afraid of No, more particularly the name of Amun alarmed him: that mighty name, intimidating to everybody and having a domineering ring even in regions strange to the god. Trepidation seized him at the thought of entering the throne of the god's cult and seat of his power. The sovereign of Egypt, ruler of the two lands, king of the gods, that was Amun. Joseph knew it well, and confusion dwelt in the thought of that unique power. Amun was the Highest — if indeed only in the eyes of the children of Egypt. It seemed it would be useful to speak of Amun and practise himself in talk of him. He said:

"Wese's lord in his chapel and in his bark, that is one of the more exalted gods hereabouts?"

"The more exalted?" answered the old man. "Truly thou speakest not better than thy understanding. What thinkest thou that Pharaoh hath set before him of bread and cake, beer, wine, and geese, for his consuming? That is a god without compare, I tell thee; what treasures he calleth his own, movable and immovable, my breath would give out would I tell the tale of them, and the number of his scribes who administer all is like to the stars."

"Wonderful," said Joseph. "A very important god indeed according to all thou relatest. Only I asked, to be precise, not about his importance but about his nobility."

"Bow down before him," advised the old man, "since thou wilt live in Egypt, and make not too many distinctions between important and noble, as though one could not stand for the other and both were not all the same. For Amun's are all the ships of the seas and rivers, and the rivers and seas are his. He is the sea and the land. He is also Tor-Neter, the cedar mountain, whose trunks grow for a barge called Amun's-Front-is-Mighty. In Pharaoh's shape he goeth in unto his first and true wife and begets Hor in the palace. He is Baal in all his members, doth that impress thee? He is the sun, Amun-Re is his name — doth that satisfy thy demands as to nobility, or not quite?"

"But I heard," Joseph said, "he is a ram in the darkness of the innermost chamber."

"I heard, I heard. . . . As thou hast understood, so speakest thou and not a doit better. Amun is a ram, just as Bastet in the land of the Delta is a cat, and the great writer of Schmun an ibis and an ape. For they are sacred in their animals and the animals sacred in them. Thou must learn much if thou wilt live in the land and wilt live before him, be it only as the lowest of his youthful slaves. How wilt thou see the god if not in the beast? The three are one: god, man, and beast. For if the divine wed with the beast, then it is the man, as Pharaoh when he is at the feast puts on a beast's tail, according to ancient custom. And if on the other hand the beast wed with the man, then it is a god, and the divine is not otherwise to be regarded and understood than in such a marriage; thus you see Heqet, the great midwife, like a toad on the wall, to judge from her head, and Anpu, the Opener of the Way, dog-headed. Lo, in the beast man and god find themselves, and the beast is the sacred place of their meeting and their union, sacred and honourable in its nature as such. And very worthy of honour among feasts is that one in which the ram cohabits with the pure virgin in the city of Djedet."

"I have heard of it," Joseph said. "Doth my lord approve of the practice?"

"I?" asked the Ma'onite. "Leave an old man in peace! We are travelling merchants, middlemen, at home everywhere and nowhere, and for us the word holdeth good: 'Nourish thou my belly, I honour thy customs.' Heed it in the world, for it will behove thee too."

"Never," answered Joseph, "will I in Egypt in the house of the fanbearer say a word against the honour of the feast of the covering. But between thee and me, let me point out that in this word 'honourable' lieth a snare for the unwary. For easily doth man hold the old for honourable, simply because it is old, and imagineth they are the same. But the catch is that sometimes we do reverence to the old when it is simply worn out and rotted with age. Then its honourableness is but seeming, and is in fact an abomination and indecency before the Lord. Just between you and me, the presentation of the human virgin at Djedet seems more like an indecency."

"How wilt thou distinguish? And where should we be if every booby were to set himself up as the navel of the world and as a judge of what is sacred and what merely old, what still worthy of reverence and what an abomination? Soon there would be nothing sacred! I do not believe that thou wilt hold thy tongue and hide thy impious thoughts. For it is peculiar to such thoughts as thou hast that they must be uttered — I know that."

"In thy presence, my lord, it is easy to learn to hold age and honour as the same."

"Flatter me not with sweet words, for I am but a travelling merchant. Heed rather my warning, that thou run not up against the children of Egypt and speak to thy undoing. For certainly thou canst not keep thy thoughts; therefore must thou take care that thy thoughts are fitting, and not only thy words. Certainly nothing is more holy than the union of god, man, and beast in the sacrifice. Reckon to and fro between these three with reference to the sacrifice and they are resolved therein. For in the sacrifice are all three and each represents the other. And therefore Amun moves as sacrificial ram in the darkness of the furthermost chamber."

"I know not rightly how I feel, my lord and purchaser, reverend merchant. It is so dark, while thou instructest me, and scattered sparkles of light trickle down like dust of precious stones from the stars. I must rub my eyes, pardon me for doing it, for I am dazed, and as thou sittest before me on thy mat, it is to me as though it were the head of a green frog that thou wearest, and as though thou squattest there wise and wide and comfortable, like a toad."

"Seest thou that thou canst not hold thy thoughts, however offensive they may be? Why wilt thou and wouldst thou see a toad in me?"

"My eyes ask not if it is my will. Just like a squatting toad thou seemest to me under the stars. For thou wast Heqet, the great midwife, when the well bore me, and thou didst lift me from my mother."

"Ah, chatterer! That was no great nurse that helped thee to the light. Heqet, the she-frog, is called great because she was by at the second birth and resurrection of the mangled one, when the lower world fell to him, but to Hor the upper, according to the belief of the children of Egypt, and Osiris became the First of the West, king and judge of the dead."

"I like that. So then if one is going toward the west, one must at least become the first of those there. But instruct me, my lord: Is then Osiris, the sacrifice, so great in the eyes of the children of Kemt that Heqet became a great frog because she was midwife at his rebirth?"

"He is great entirely."

"Great above the greatness of Amun?"

"Amun is great by reason of his kingdom, his renown affrights stranger peoples so that they cut their cedars for him. But Osiris, the mangled one, is great in the love of the people, all the people from Djanet in the Delta up to Heb, the elephant island. There is not one among all, from the coughing pack-slave of the quarry, who liveth millionfold, to Pharaoh, who liveth once and singly and worshippeth himself in his temple — I say to thee there is not one who did not know and love him and wish to find his grave in Abdu his city, at the grave of the mangled one, were it possible. And since it is not possible, yet they all hang fervently on him, trusting in the hope of becoming like him at their hour and to live for ever."

"To be like God?"

"To be as the god and to be like him; that is, one with him, so that the dead man is Osiris and so is called."

"What all thou sayest! But spare me, my lord, in thy teaching and help my poor understanding as thou helpedst me out of the womb of the well. For it is not for everyone's understanding, that which thou wilt teach me here in the night by the slumbering sea, of the beliefs of the children of Mizraim. Shall I then understand that it

would be in the power of death to change nature and for the dead
to be a god with the beard of a god?"

"Yes, that is the confident belief of all the folk of the land and
they all as one love it so fervently from Zoan to Elephantine for that
they have had to wrest it for themselves in prolonged struggle."

"They have wrested the belief for themselves in prolonged struggle and held out for it until the dawn?"

"They have brought it to pass. For in the beginning and originally
it was only Pharaoh, he alone, Hor in the Palace, who when he died
came to Osiris and became one with him so that he was like a god
and lived for ever. But all those who cough, as they drag the heavy
statues, all the brick-makers, the pot-drillers, those behind the plough
and those in the mines, they have not rested and have struggled till
they achieved it and made it good, so that they too now at their hour
become Osiris and are called Osiris-Khnumhotpe, Osiris Rekh-mi-re
after their death, and live for ever."

"Again it pleaseth me, that which thou sayest. Thou hast chidden
me for the view that every child of earth hath his own universe about
him for himself alone and is the centre thereof. But in one way or the
other it seemeth to me the children of Egypt shared the view, since
each would be Osiris after his death, as in the beginning only Pharoah, and have brought it to pass."

"That is and remaineth foolishly spoken. For not the child of earth
is the centre point, Khnumhotpe or Rekh-mi-re, but rather their
faith and confident belief; they are all one in that, up the water and
down, from the Delta to the sixth rapid: the belief in Osiris and his
resurrection. For thou must know: not only one single time hath
this very great god died and risen; rather he doth it ever anew in
even ebb and flow before the eyes of the children of Kemt — he goeth
down and cometh forth again mightily to stand as blessing over the
land, Hapi, the Strong Bull, the river of God. Countest thou the days
of the winter time, when the river is small, there are two-and-seventy
of them and they are the two-and-seventy who were forsworn with
Set, the wicked ass, and brought the king to his coffin. But at his
hour he goeth forth, the growing, swelling, flooding, the increasing,
the lord of bread, who begetteth all good things and maketh all life,
by name Provider of the Land. They slaughter the oxen before him;
but seest thou then that god and sacrifice are one, for he himself is a
bull and an ox before them on earth and in his house: Hapi, the
black, with the sign of the moon on his flank. But when he dieth he
is preserved with balsam and swaddled and put away and is called
Osiris-Hapi."

"Lo then!" exclaimed Joseph, "hath he also brought it about, like
Khnumhotpe and Rekh-mi-re, that he becometh Osiris when he
dieth?"

"I think thou mockest?" queried the old man. "I see thee little in the glimmering night, but I hear thee and it seemeth to me very much as though thou mockest. I tell thee, mock not in the land whither I am taking thee because simply I am travelling that way, and presume not in thy folly against the beliefs of its children, thinking that thou knowest better with thy Adon, rather adapt thyself piously to its customs; otherwise thou wilt be grievously disappointed. I have taught thee somewhat and initiated thee, and turned a few phrases with thee this evening to my amusement and to pass the time; for I am already old, and sometimes sleep faileth me. I had no other ground to speak with thee. Thou mayest say good-night now, that I may try to sleep. But pay heed to thy phrases."

"Commanded is as good as done," replied Joseph. "But how should I mock, since my lord hath so graciously instructed me this evening that I may hold out and not come to grief in the land of Egypt, and hath taught the culprit things of which I, in my lowliness, dreamed not, so new are they to me and not to be understanded of all. Might I know how I could thank thee I would. But since I know not, I will do something yet this evening for my benefactor, do that which I would not do, and answer a question before I leave thee, which thou askedst me. I will tell thee my name."

"Wilt thou do that?" asked the old man. "Do so or rather do not so; I have not urged thee to it, for I am old and cautious and would rather not know what are thy connections, because I must take care not to involve myself therein and be guilty of wrong-doing through the knowledge."

"Not at all," Joseph replied. "Thou runnest no such danger. But at least thou must know how to call the slave, if thou wilt pass him on into this house of blessing in the city of Amun."

"Then what is thy name?"

"Usarsiph," answered Joseph.

The old man was silent. Though only a distance of respect was between them, they were aware of each other but as shadows.

"It is well, Usarsiph," spoke the old man after a while. "Thou hast named me thy name. Take thy leave now, for with the sunrise we shall set forth."

"Farewell," Joseph saluted him in the dark. "May night cradle thee in softest arms and thy head slumber on her breast as thy childish head on thy mother's heart."

THE TEMPTATION

AFTER Joseph had told the Ishmaelite his name in death and had shown him how he wished to be called in the land of the dead, they all passed on down for some days, several and many, with the greatest placidity and in entire indifference to the time, which some day, as they were aware, by adding to itself, would have done with space, and this the more securely if one did not trouble about it at all but left it to time quietly and unobservably to heap up its progress to large quantities the while one lived on and only held in the direction of the goal.

Their direction was given them by the sea, which spread endlessly away on the right of their sandy route, under a sky fading into mystic distance; now in silver-shot blue calm, now hurling great waves aglitter with foam like strong bulls roaring against the peopled coast. And in the sea the sun went down, the changing-unchangeable, the Eye of God, sometimes a clear-glowing and solitary orb, which made as it sank a gleaming path across the endless water to the shore and to passers-by who worshipped as they went; but sometimes too in the heart of a splendour of gold and rose, that worked still more adoring conviction in the soul of the worshipper. But his soul might sometimes be saddened too or oppressed by fears, when the deity enveloped himself in threatening mists or clouds suffused with lurid light. He rose, however, not on an open horizon but behind the heights and hills that hid the view on their left. Between shore and mountains spread the immediate inland, with cultivated fields, wells scattered through the rolling expanse, and orchards adorning the terraced hills. Often our travellers took their way through it, at a distance from the sea and some half a hundred ells above its glassy surface; passing through the federation of fortified hill-cities. Gaza in the south, Khadati, the strong citadel, was head of the league.

The walled white cities, fringed with palm, crowned the hill-tops, the mother cities, refuge of the inhabitants of the land, the citadels of Sarnim. And on the level ground before the village and at its heart, the square before the gate of the crowded city with its temples, the Midianites spread out their wares and offered to the people of Ekron, of Jabne, of Asdod, their merchandise from beyond the Jordan. Joseph performed the office of clerk. He sat and set down with his brush countless petty transactions with the hard-bargaining children of Dagon; fishermen and boatmen, tradefolk and mercenaries from the citadels, in their copper armour. Usarsiph, the literate young slave, laboured to pleasure his good master. The heart of the young chattel beat higher day by day — not hard to guess why. He was not formed to drift content with sensuous impressions alone, but must make a mental picture of the place where he was and its relation to other places. He knew that he was taking, in leisurely, time-consuming fashion, a parallel route, some field-lengths farther west and in reverse direction, the same journey which he had covered riding on poor Hulda to meet his brothers. He was going toward, if also past, his home; soon the point must be reached where he had covered the distance and was separated from the paternal hearth by a space not more than half the length of the whole journey. Somewhere not far from Asdod it would be: seat of Dagon the fish-god whom they worshipped hereabouts; a busy settlement, two hours from the coast and connected with it by a road crowded with people, ox-carts, and teams of horses, all making terrific din. The coast road down to Gaza, as Joseph knew, curved more and more westwards, so that the distance from the mountainous interior increased with each day they travelled; he also knew that they would be passing by noon under the heights of Hebron.

Therefore it was his heart beat so anxiously as temptation knocked; here, and on the slow road beyond to Askalona, the rocky citadel. He knew the contours of the countryside: they were entering Sephala, the lowland, running along the coast. But his Rachel-eyes sought out and dwelt pensively on the mountain ranges, which looked down on the east and formed the second, higher, valley-furrowed level of the land of the Philistines. Behind again and ever steeper the world rose toward the east and into the highlands above sea-level, rougher, harsher ground, to pastures unpeopled by the lowland palm, and upland meadows on whose short grass grazed sheep, grazed Jacob's sheep. . . . Could it be? Up there Jacob was sitting, despairing, dissolved in tears, in God-sent, God-suffering agony, in his hands the blood-spotted sign of Joseph's death and mangling — while down here, under his feet, from one city of the Philistines to the next, marched Joseph, the stolen one, dumb, making no sign, past his own place with strangers, down to Sheol, into the house of bondage and of death. How near lay the thought of flight! How the urge to it pulled and tugged at his limbs, how his thoughts worked in him to half-resolves and even to visions of their tempestuous realization. They came, these visions, especially at evening, when he had bade the good old man his owner good-night, for that he had daily to do, it was one of his duties, he had to wish the Ishmaelite pleasant dreams at the day's end and always in choice and varied phrases, otherwise the old man would say he knew that one already. Especially then in the darkness when they lay camped before a city of the Philistines and his companions were wrapped in slumber, the boy who had been ravished away was ravished anew by longings to be off up the orchard-clad hills, in the dark, on over heights and gullies, eight miles and furlongs of ground, for more it probably was not, and Joseph would easily find the right direction as he climbed — on into the mountain land, into Jacob's arms, to dry his father's tears with the words "Here am I!" and once again to be his darling.

But did he carry all this out and flee? We know that he did not. He reconsidered —sometimes just on the verge; put away temptation, gave up the idea, stopped where he was. When all was said and done, it was at the moment more sensible. Flight in itself meant great perils; he might perish, might fall among robbers and murderers, be devoured by wild beasts. Yet it is not doing justice to his renunciation to attribute it to our human tendency to indolence instead of action. In his career we know that Joseph renounced a physical act far sweeter than a wild escape over the mountains would have been. No, the renunciation which in both cases followed on the violent temptation came from a point of view quite peculiar to Joseph. Put into words, it was something like this: "How could I commit such a folly and sin against God?" In other words, he had insight into the mad and sinful error that would lie in escape: the clear and intelligent perception that it would have been a clumsy blunder to try to destroy God's plan through flight. For Joseph was penetrated by the certainty that he had not been snatched away to no purpose, that rather the planning intelligence which had rent him away from the old and led him into the new had plans for him in one or another way; and to kick against the pricks, to shrink from the affliction, would have been a great sin and error — these being one and the same in Joseph's eyes. The conception of sin as blunder, as clumsy offence against God's wisdom, was right native to him, and life so far had extraordinarily strengthened him therein. He had made mistakes enough — he learned that in the pit. But now he had escaped from the pit and was obviously being taken away according to plan; so the mistakes committed up to now might be considered as lying in the plan itself, as purposeful and God-guided in all their blindness. But any more of them — as now for instance escape — would be very distinctly evil; it would literally mean to wish to be wiser than God — which according to Joseph's shrewd insight was quite simply the height of folly.

The darling of his father once again? Ah, no, for he was always that; but now it would be so in a new sense — one he had always longed for and dreamed of. Now, since the experience of the pit, it was his to live in a new and higher state of being chosen and preferred in the sense and the bitter savour of the myrtle wreath, which was set apart for the set-apart and reserved for the reserved. The torn garland, the adornment of the whole sacrifice, he wore it anew — no longer in prophetic play but in very truth and in the spirit. Should he now for the sake of the blind urge of the flesh betake himself to his own? So foolhardy, so lacking in all divine wisdom Joseph was not — in the last moment he was not so blind as to fling away the advantage of his state. Did he know, or did he not, the feast in all its hours? The centre of the present and of the feast, was he or was he not? The garland in his hair, should he run from the feast to be once more with his brothers a shepherd of the flocks? The temptation was strong in his flesh, but weak in his spirit. Joseph resisted.

He went on with his owners, on past Jacob and out of his neighbourhood — Usarsiph the swamp-born, Joseph-em-heb, to speak Egyptian, which is to say: Joseph in the Feast.

A MEETING

SEVENTEEN days? No, it was a journey of seven times seventeen — not
in actual number, but in the sense of a very long time indeed; and at
the end of it nobody knew how much of its length was due to the
Midianites' tarrying progress and how much to the extent of the
ground they covered. They went through a populous, busy, fruitful
land, crowned with olive orchards and palms, set thick with walnut
and fig trees, planted with corn, watered from deep springs where
camels and oxen gathered. Little royal fortresses lay sometimes in
the open fields, called stations, with walls and battle-towers; bowmen
stood on their battlements and charioteers drove snorting steeds forth
from their gates. The Ishmaelites did not hesitate to enter into trade,
even with the soldiers of the kings. Villages, farms, and Migdal settlements everywhere invited them to stop, and they lingered for
weeks without a thought. Before they reached the spot where the
low land along the coast rose to the abruptly towering rocky wall on
whose top lay Ascalon, summer was already waning.

Sacred and strong was Ascalon. The four-square stones of its ring
walls, which ran down to the sea in a half-circle and included the
harbour, seemed borne up by giants, its temple of Dagon was square
and full of courts, very lovely its grove and the pond of its grove,
abounding in fish, and its dwelling of Ashtaroth was renowned as
older than any shrine of Baalat. A spicy sort of little onion grew wild
in the sand here under the palms. Derketo vouchsafed them, the lady
of Ascalon, and one could sell them abroad. The old man had them
gathered into sacks and wrote thereon in Egyptian characters: "Finest Ascalon onions."

Thence they went on among gnarled olive groves in whose shadow
flocks were pastured, and by the time they had reached Gaza, called
Khadati, they were certainly come very far. Almost within the Egyptian sphere of influence. For in times past Pharaoh had come up from
Egypt with wagons and foot-soldiers, to thrust through the barren
lands of Zahi, Amor, and the Retenu to the ends of the earth that his
gigantic image might be graven deep above the temple walls, holding
clutched in his left hand the topknots of five barbarians at once and
with his right swinging his club over their dazzled heads. And in such
enterprises Gaza had always been the first stage. Nowadays in its
reeking streets one saw many Egyptians. Joseph observed them attentively. They were broad-shouldered, white-clad, and high-nosed.
Excellent wine grew here very cheap on the coast and far inland on

the way to Beersheba. The old man traded for numerous jugs, two camel-loads of them, and labelled the jugs: "Thrice-excellent wine from Khadati."

But however much ground they had covered to reach the strong-walled city of Gaza, the worst part of the journey still lay before them, compared to which the leisurely progress through the land of Philistia had been but child's play. For beyond Gaza to the south, where a sandy road ran along the coast toward the Brook of Egypt, the world, as the Ishmaelites well knew, having covered the ground several times, was inhospitable in the extreme. Between them and the rich plains where flowed the branches of the Nile there extended a melancholy underworld, a frightful expanse, nine days in breadth, accursed and perilous, the dreaded desert, where could be no loiter-ing, rather it was imperative to cross it as fast as possible and get it behind one. Gaza therefore was the last halting-place before Mizraim, and the old man, Joseph's master, was in no hurry to leave it. There would be far too much time hereafter to hurry, he said. He lingered at Gaza for several days, partly to make careful preparations for the desert journey; provision for water, the engaging of a special guide and opener of the way. Actually, weapons were needed to protect the train against roving bands and robber dwellers in the desert. Our old man, however, made no such provision. Firstly because he in his wisdom thought it useless. Either, he said, one had luck and escaped the marauders — then one needed no weapons — or else one did not; and then however many of them one killed, enough were left to steal one bare. The merchant, he said, must trust to luck, not to spears and crossbows, they were not for him.

But in the second place the guide whom he had engaged, at the gateway where they congregated for engagements, expressly reas-sured him about the roving bands and said he would need no arms under his conveyance, he was a perfect guide and opened the safest way through the dreaded region, so that it would be quite absurd to secure his services and then carry arms to boot. How Joseph started, pleased and incredulous at once, when he recognized in the man who came in the dawning to the little caravan and put himself at its head the officious and annoying youth who had guided him from Shechem to Dothan, so short and so crowded a time before!

He it was beyond a doubt, although he was changed by the bur-nous he wore. The small head and swelling throat, the red mouth and round fruity chin, and especially the weariness of his gaze and the peculiarly affected posture were unmistakable. Joseph was amazed to see or think to see the guide wink at him, shutting one eye with an otherwise wholly immovable face. It seemed at once to recall their former acquaintance and to suggest discretion on the score of it. That reassured Joseph a good deal; for this meeting led further back into

his former existence than he wanted the eye of the Ishmaelite to penetrate, and he interpreted the wink as a sign that the man understood.

Yet he sorely wanted to exchange a word with him, and when the
little troop, amid the ringing of camel-bells and the songs of the drivers, had left the green country behind them and faced the parching
desert before, Joseph asked the old man, behind whom he rode, if he
might once and for all make certain from the guide that he was quite
sure of his task.

"Art thou afeard?" asked the merchant.

"For all of us," responded Joseph. "But I now ride for the first
time into the accursed land and I am near to tears."

"Ask him, then."

So Joseph guided his beast abreast of the foremost animal and said
to the guide:

"I am the mouthpiece of our master. He would know if thou art
certain of thy road."

The youth looked at him in his old way over his shoulder with
half-opened eyes.

"Thou shouldest be able from thy experience to reassure him," he
answered.

"Hush!" whispered Joseph. "How comest thou here?"

"And thou?" was the answer.

"Yes, of course. Not a word to the Ishmaelites that I went to my
brethren," whispered Joseph.

"Have no fear," the other answered as softly; and therewith the
matter was closed for the time.

But as they pressed farther into the desert, a day and then another
day — the sun had set sombrely behind dead mountain chains, and
hosts of cloud, grey in the centre and with a sunset glow at the rim,
covered the sky above a waxen-yellow sandy plain, while far and
wide in front of them were visible scattered hummocks with tufts of
withered grass — there was a chance to speak again unobserved with
the man. Some of the troop were camped about one of the tussocks
of grass on which they had kindled a brushwood fire against the sudden cold; among them the guide, who for the most part associated little either with masters or servants, scorned exchange of talk, and
only spoke briefly with the old man from day to day about the route.
Joseph finished his tasks, wished the old man a good night's rest, and
then mingled with the group by the fire. He lay down near the guide
and waited till the monosyllabic exchange among them died down
and they were falling visibly into a doze. Then he gave his neighbour
a little nudge and said:

"Hearken: I am sorry that I could not keep my word that time and
had to leave thee in the lurch as thou waitedst for me."

The man only looked at him idly over his shoulder and stared again into the embers.

"So, thou couldst not?" he answered. "Well, let me tell thee, so faithless a chap as thou I have never seen in all the world. I might have sat guarding thy ass seven jubilees long, if it had depended on thee, who came not again as thou hadst promised. I am surprised that I will speak with thee again at all, I am surprised at myself."

"But I am explaining, as thou hearest," murmured Joseph, "and I have truly an excuse, that knowest thou not. Things turned out other than I had thought, and went as I could not have guessed. I could not return to thee, however much I wished."

"Yes, yes, yes. Idle talk. Seven jubilee years might I have sat and waited for thee. . . ."

"But thou hast not sat seven jubilee years for me, but hast gone thy way when thou sawest I was not coming. Exaggerate not the trouble which I unwillingly made for thee; tell me rather what became of Hulda after I left."

"Hulda? Who is Hulda?"

" 'Who' is a little too much," said Joseph. "I am asking thee news of Hulda, the ass that carried us, my white ass out of my father's stall."

"Ass, ass, white ass for a journey!" mocked the guide in a murmur. "Thou hast a way of speaking of thine own, so tenderly that one may guess at thy self-love. Such people behave then so faithlessly — "

"Not so," Joseph contradicted him. "I speak not tenderly of Hulda on my own account, but on hers, she was so friendly and careful a beast, entrusted to me by my father; when I think of her mane on her forehead, and the way it hung down in curls to her eyes, my heart melteth within me. I have not ceased to feel troubled about her since I lost her, and even asked after her fate in moments and long hours which for my own fate were not lacking in perils. Thou must know that since I came to Shechem ill luck hath not ceased to follow me and heavy oppression hath been my lot."

"Impossible," said the man, "and unbelievable. Oppression? My understanding standeth still and I am stoutly convinced I have not heard aright. But thou wentest after all to thy brethren? And with all the folk thou hast passed thou hast not ceased to exchange smiles, for thou art beautiful and well favoured as a carven image and hast dear life to boot! Whence came then thy ill luck? I ask myself and am not answered."

"None the less it is so," replied Joseph. "And through it all, I tell thee, not a moment have I ceased to think of the fate of poor Hulda."

"Good," said the guide, "very good." And Joseph recognized that curious movement of the eyeballs which he had noted before: a rapid squinting and rolling right round. "Good, then, young slave Usarsiph, thou speakest and I hear. One might think indeed that it were idle to waste so many words on an ass, for what sort of rôle doth an ass play in thy larger concerns and of what importance could it be in them? Yet I think it possible that thy care shall be reckoned to thee for a virtue, that thou thoughtest of the little creature in thine own need."

"Then what became of her?"

"Of the beast? Verily, it is somewhat annoying for the likes of us to have to play the part of ass-herd for nothing and be asked to give account of what happened besides. One would like to know why one should. But set thy heart at rest. My impression is that the creature's pastern was not so bad as we thought in our first dismay. It seems it was sprained, and not broken — that is, apparently broken and actually only sprained, dost thou understand? Waiting for thee I had only too much time to tend it, and when at last I lost my patience thy Hulda too was so far along that she could amble, even though mainly on three legs. I rode on her myself as far as Dothan and put her in a house there where I had often done a good turn to advantage both sides. It is the first in the place, belonging to a farmer, where she will be as well off as in the stall of thy father, the so-called Israel."

"Is that true?" cried Joseph, low and rejoicingly. "Who would have thought it? So she got up and could walk and thou hast cared for her so that she is well off?"

"Very well," confirmed the other. "She can count herself lucky that I took her to the farmer's house and her lot has fallen well for her."

"In other words," Joseph said, "thou hast sold her in Dothan. And the price?"

"Thou askest after the price?"

"Yea, herewith."

"I have paid myself for my guidance and my service as watchman."

"So. Well, I will not inquire the amount. And all the good eatables that hung round the saddle?"

"Is it really true that thou thinkest of those tidbits among thy larger concerns and findest that they have comparative importance?"

"Not so much; but they were there."

"With them too I have reimbursed myself."

"Indeed," Joseph said, "thou hadst early begun to repay thyself behind my back, by which I mean certain quantities of onions and fruit-bread. But never mind, perhaps it was well meant and I will always and everywhere extol the good side thou showest. That thou gottest Hulda once more on her legs and madest her full in the land, for that I reckon my thanks are due, and I thank the good fortune that made me meet thee unexpectedly to learn it."

"Yea, have I again to guide thee, thou windbag, that thou mayest come to thy goal," replied the man. "Whether it be so fitting and proper for me, I do ask myself that, in passing; yet in vain, for no one else payeth any heed."

"Now thou art vexing again," responded Joseph, "just as in the night on the way to Dothan when thou unasked didst help me to find my brethren and did it with such ill grace. Well, this time I need not reproach myself for molesting thee; for thou hast bargained with the Ishmaelites to guide them through the desert and I am only among them by chance."

"It mattereth not if I guide thee or thy Ishmaelites."

"Say not that to the Ishmaelites, for they keep themselves on their dignity and self-independence and do not like to hear that in a way they journey that I may come hither where God will have me."

The guide was silent and dropped his chin into his mantle. Did his eyes roll round again after their wont? Very like, but the darkness prevented one from telling.

"Who liketh to hear that he is a tool?" said he with a certain effort. "And particularly who would hear it from a brat like thee? Coming from thee, young slave Usarsiph, it is shameless, but on the other hand that is just what I say, that it cometh to the same thing and even so it might be the Ishmaelites who are coming with thee, and it is really thou to whom I must open the way — it is all one. Moreover, I had a well to watch down there, to say nothing of the ass."

"A well?"

"I always had to reckon with such a job, as far as the well was concerned. It was the emptiest hole I ever saw, could not be emptier; and the more absurd was its emptiness, by that measure may be judged the dignity and fitness of my task. Yet perhaps it was the very emptiness that was the important thing about this well."

"Was the stone rolled away?"

"Of course. I sat on it; and I remained sitting however much the man wanted me to go."

"What man?"

"Why, he who in his folly came secretly to the well. A man of towering stature, with legs like the pillars of a temple, and inside this husk a poor thin voice."

"Reuben!" cried Joseph, almost forgetful of caution.

"Call him as thou wilt, it was a blundering tower of a man. Came back there with his rope and his coat to such a proper empty hole."

"He wanted to save me!" Joseph affirmed.

"As thou wilt," said the guide and yawned like a woman, putting his hand affectedly before his mouth and giving a dainty little sigh. "He too played his rôle," he added. His voice was indistinct, for he had tucked his chin and mouth farther into his mantle and seemed to want to go to sleep. Joseph heard him still muttering disconnectedly and irritably: "Trifling and folly — words of a young brat. . . ."

There was nothing more pertinent to be got out of him. Even in their further journey Joseph did not succeed in getting more speech with his guard and guide.

THE FORT OF THEL

DAY by day they plodded patiently through the bad lands, to the sound of the bell on the leading camel, from well-station to well-station, until nine days had passed; and they counted themselves lucky. The guide had not boasted when he said he knew his business. He did not lose his way nor get off the road even when it passed through wild mountain country where there was no good going, but merely a confusion of frightful sandstone boulders, grotesque shapes and towering masses, that glistened blackly, more like bronze than stone. Their sombre gleam suggested a tall city built of iron. The guide held on his road all day long, even when there could be no talk of a road in any upper-worldly sense at all. For it was like a country of the damned, like the illimitable floor of the sea, shutting them in with corpse-coloured sand up to the hot bleached horizon, and they rode over mounds of dune with ridges ruffled by the wind into unpleasant sharp-edged patterns. Across the plain the heat vibrations looked as though near to bursting into tongues of flame, and sand whirled in the air so that the men wrapped their heads before this evil dance of death and tried not to look, but rode blindly on to get past these horrors.

Bleached skeletons often lay by the way, the ribs and thigh-bones of a camel and the parched limbs of a human being stood up out of the waxen-coloured dust. They looked at it dazed and kept on trying to hope. Two half-days long, from midday to evening, a pillar of fire went on before and seemed to guide them. They well knew the nature of the phenomenon, but their attitude toward it was not conditioned by their knowledge. These fiery pillars were, as they were aware, small cyclones in which the whirling dust was turned flame-coloured by the sun. But to each other they said with due awe: "A pillar of fire leadeth us on." If the sign were suddenly to collapse before their eyes it would be frightful; for in all probability a dust abubu would follow. But the pillar did not collapse, only changed its shape like a jinnee and slowly flickered away on the north-east wind, which prevailed throughout the nine days. Their good luck banned the south wind that it was quiet and could not parch their water-skins and drink away the moisture on which their lives depended. But on the ninth day they were already out of danger, escaped from the horrors of the desert, and could count themselves fortunate; for the region now before them was colonized and administered by Egypt. Bastions, breastworks, and watch-towers by the wells extended for some distance into the desert, with little companies of soldiery, Nubian bowmen wearing ostrich feathers in their hair, and Libyan axe-bearers with Egyptian captains, who called out harshly to the oncomers and questioned them whence they came and whither they went.

The old man had a shrewd and cheery way of talking with the military to put beyond doubt the innocence of his designs; and of giving them little presents out of his pack, knives, lamps, and Ascalon onions to win their goodwill. So they passed well pleased through all the formalities from watch to watch; for it was much better to be exchanging jokes with the guards than to be going through the brazen city and across the bleached sea-floor. Our travellers, however, knew that only the preliminaries were over with the passing of these frontier stations and that they had still to prove their harmlessness and their innocence of any designs against civilized society. The real test would come at the mighty and ineluctable barrier which the old man called the sovereign's wall, which had been built ages before across the neck of land between the Great and Little Bitter Lakes, as a protection against the savages of Shosu and the sand-dwellers who thought to drive their cattle upon Pharaoh's soil.

From the rising ground where they halted at sunset they overlooked these menacing precautions and arrogant measures of defence. The old man had succeeded several times, by dint of his harmless garrulity, in passing them in both directions; wherefore he did not now fear them all too much. Tranquilly he lifted his hand and pointed them out to his train: a long marching wall, notched with battlements, broken by towers and running behind canals which connected a chain of lakes great and small. Somewhere about the middle a bridge crossed the water, but at this point, on either side of the passage, rose the sternest barriers of all: castellated forts enclosed in their own ring walls, two-storeyed, massive and tall, whose sides and ajutments rose in ingenious broken lines to the parapets to make them yet more secure against siege. They bristled with square battlemented towers, bastions, sally-ports, and ledges for defence on all sides; narrower structures had grated windows. This was the fort of Thel, the powerful offensive and defensive structure set up by the refined and fortunate and vulnerable land of Egypt against the poverty and rapine of the East. The old man named it to his followers by name and was not afraid before it. But yet he said so much about it, asserting how easy it would be for his utter harmlessness to get past once more, that one might have thought he was talking to keep his courage up.

"Did I tell you I have a letter from a business friend at Gilead across the Jordan," he said, "to his business friend in Djanet, also called Zoan, which was built seven years after Hebron? Well, I have; and you will see, it will open for us gate and door. The great thing is to have a document to show and that the people of Egypt have in their turn to write something and send it somewhere to be copied down again and keep the record. For without something written you do not get through; but if you can show a potsherd or a roll and document, then they brighten up. They say, of course, that Amun is the highest, or Osiris, the Eye Enthroned; but I know better, at bottom it is Thoth, the writer. Believe me, if only Hor-waz comes on the wall, the young officer-clerk who is an old friend of mine, and I can get speech with him, then there will be no trouble at all and we can pass. Once we are inside, nobody tests our innocence again and we can go freely through all the districts up the river as far as we like. Let us set up huts here and pass the night, for my friend Hor-waz will not come on the wall any more today. But tomorrow before we go thither and beg for entrance at the fort of Thel we must wash ourselves and dust the desert from our garments and wipe it out of our ears and scratch it out from our nails that we seem to them like men and not like sand-rabbits; also you young ones must pour oil on your hair and paint your eyes and make yourselves look wanton; for to them misery is suspect and lack of elegance an abomination."

Thus the old man, and they did after his words, stopped where they were for the night and made themselves beautiful in the morning as well as they could after so long a journey through the waste. During these preparations, however, they were surprised to find that their guide, whom the old man had hired at Gaza and who had guided them so safely, proved to be no more among them, without anyone being able to say when he had gone: whether back in the night or while they were adorning themselves for Thel. Anyhow, when they looked round for him he was no more there, though the bell-camel was, on which he had ridden; nor had the guide collected his pay from the old man.

That was no cause for lamenting, but only for surprise, since they no longer needed a guide, and the man had been a distant creature at best, and chary of speech. They wondered awhile, and the old man's satisfaction over the saving of money was diminished by his lack of understanding and the disquiet caused by unfinished business. He concluded that the man would turn up again some time to get his pay. Joseph thought it possible that the guide had privately taken to himself goods instead of pay and instigated an examination of the stock; but it proved him in the wrong. It was Joseph who wondered the most, especially over the inconsistency in the character of his acquaintance and the indifference in money matters which seemed not to fit with the covetous nature. For services voluntarily offered he had paid himself extravagantly. Now it seemed he heedlessly let

slip a covenanted wage. But Joseph could not talk with the Ishmaelites about these discrepancies, and words that are not uttered are
soon forgotten. They all had other things to think of besides the
guide and his caprices; for when they had washed their ears and
painted their eyes they advanced toward the water and the sovereign's wall and came before midday to Thel, the fort on the bridge.

Ah, it was even more alarming from near by than at a distance,
double and unassailable by force, with its irregular line of walls, towers, and defence platforms, the battlements filled all round with warriors of the heights, clad in jerkins with shields of hide on their backs,
who stood with lances folded in their fists and on their fists their
chins, looking down right contemptuously on the little caravan as it
approached. Officers were there in half-long wigs and white shirts,
with leather stomachers in front over their skirts, and little canes in
their hands; they moved to and fro behind the men. The latter paid
no heed to the advancing train; but the foremost posts raised their
arms, curved a hand round their mouths, their lances lying in the
hollow of their arms, and cried out:

"Back! Turn back! Fort of Thel! No passage. We will shoot!"

"Pay no heed," said the old man. "Only be quiet. It is not half so
bad as it looks. Let us give evidence of peace by advancing slowly
but undisturbed. Have I not the letter of my business friend? We
shall get through."

Accordingly they moved straight up to the gap in the walls where
the entrance was, and behind it the great bronze gate which led to
the bridge. Here they indicated by signs their peaceful intentions.
In the wall above the gate, graven deep in the masonry and painted in
glaring colours, was a huge figure of a bare-necked vulture with pinions spread, the ring of the cartouche in its claws. Right and left of
it out of the brick structure sprang a pair of stone cobras on sockets,
four feet high, with spread hoods, erected on their bellies, horrible
to see, the symbol of defence.

"Turn round!" cried the watch on the wall above the outer gate,
above the vulture. "Fort of Thel! Back, sand-rabbits, into the desert!
Here is no road."

"You mistake, Egyptian warriors," answered them the old man
from his camel, among his group of retainers. "Just here is the entrance and not elsewhere. For where else could it be in this bottle-
neck? We are well-informed people, who come not to the wrong
quarter but know exactly where one enters into the land, for we have
already been across your bridge and back again."

"Yes, back!" cried those above. "Always back and nothing but
back with you into the desert, that is the order. No rabble shall be
let into the land."

"To whom say you that?" countered the old man. "To me who

not only know it well but also expressly approve it? I hate rabble and sand-rabbits as much as you and praise you highly in that you prevent them from profaning your land. But look well at us and study our faces. Do we look like thieves and vagrants and rabble from Sinai? Do our looks awake the idea that we want to spy out the land with evil intent? Or where are our flocks that we thought to drive on Pharaoh's pasture-lands? Nothing like that cometh in question even for a moment. We are Minæans from Ma'on, travelling traders, proud of our degree; and bring from abroad attractive wares which we would offer you, and would sell them in exchange with the children of Kemt, that we may carry in turn the gifts of Jeor, which here is called Harri, to the ends of the world. For it is the season of trade and barter and we travellers are its servants and priests."

"Fine priests! Dust-covered priests! All that is a lie!" the soldiers shouted back.

But the old man did not lose courage, he only shook his head forbearingly.

"As if I did not know," he remarked aside to his people; "they always do this on principle, and make difficulties till one would be glad to turn round and go away. But I have never turned back and I will get through this time too."

"Hearken, ye stout brown warriors of Pharaoh," he called up again. "Gladly speak I here with you, for your words are blithe. But actually would I speak with one who is the youthful commander of the troops, Hor-waz, who let me in the last time. Call him, if you will be so good, to the wall. I will show him the letter which I am bearing to Zoan. A letter!" he repeated. "A written letter, a document. Thoth, Djehuti, the ape!"

He smiled as he called out the words.

And indeed it often happens, in speaking to those who are not known to us as individuals but representatives of some well-known nation, that we thus half tease, half flatter them by invoking some phrase or symbol by which they are labelled in popular fancy. The soldiers on the wall laughed too. Perhaps they were simply amused at the obsession of every foreigner, that all Egyptians were quite daft about writing and the written word. At the same time they were probably impressed with the old man's knowledge of the name of one of their leaders. For they consulted among themselves and then called down to the Ishmaelites that the troop leader Hor-waz was away on duty in the town of Sent and would not be back for three days.

"What a pity!" said the old man. "How badly it falls out, ye Egyptian warriors! Three black days, three new-moon days without Hor-waz, our friend! That means waiting. We will wait here, dear warriors, till his return. Only call him, if you will, to the wall at once on his return from Sent, with the news that the famous Minæans from Ma'on are on the spot and bring written papers."

And actually they set up their tents in the sand before the fort of Thel and remained three days awaiting the lieutenant, keeping on good terms with the people on the wall, some of whom came down to them to see their wares and drive bargains. Their numbers were increased by another party of travellers who came from the south, probably from Sinai, along the Bitter Lakes. They too would enter into Egypt. They were a right ragged crew and little polished by civilization. They waited with the Ishmaelites, and when the hour came and Hor-waz was back, all the applicants were let in through the wall into the court in front of the bridge gate. Here they had again to wait a few hours until the young officer came springing on spindling legs down the stair and stood on the lower step. With him were two men, one of whom had his writing tools, the other a standard with a ram's head. Hor-waz beckoned the petitioners to advance.

His head was covered with a light brown wig cut straight on the forehead and lying smooth as glass as far as the ears; behind them it consisted of tiny curls that fell down on his shoulders. The mailed doublet he wore, with an order in the shape of a bronze fly, went ill with the delicate folds of the snow-white, short-sleeved linen garment that showed underneath it, and not better with the snowy pleated skirt that hung diagonally to the hollow of his knee behind.

The travellers greeted him with circumstance; yet not more courteously — however poor they were in his eyes — than he returned their greetings. It was a foppish politeness. He arched his back like a cat, throwing back his head with a sickly-sweet smile, kissed the air, as it were, with his pursed lips, and raised toward them out of his pleated sleeve a very thin brown arm adorned at the wrist with a bangle. He did it so simply and easily that only for a brief moment did he give this picture of a graceful, fastidious, and over-expressive pose. It went as it came. But one realized — at least Joseph did — that it had nothing to do with them but proceeded from his own self-respect and his reverence for the civilization he represented. Hor-waz had the face of an elderly child, short, with a pug nose, the eyes lengthened by cosmetics, and sharp furrows graven at the sides of his still pursed and laughing mouth.

"Who are you?" he asked in rapid Egyptian. "Men of wretchedness in such great numbers, who would enter the country?"

With the word "wretchedness" he did not mean exactly a criticism; he meant simply foreigners. But in the "great numbers" he included both groups of travellers, making no difference between the Midianites and the people from Sinai, who indeed cast themselves on the ground before his feet.

"There are too many of you," he went on reproachfully. "Every day come some from here or there, from the land of God or the mountains of Shu, and want to set foot inside; if daily is saying too much, then almost daily. Day before yesterday I let some come in from the land of Upi and the mount User, for they had letters. I am a scribe of the great gate, who renders reports upon the affairs of the lands, well and good for him who sees it. My responsibility is great. Whence come ye and what would ye? Do ye design good things or not so good or even quite evil, so that you must either be driven back or else pale your cheeks in death? Come ye from Kadesh and Dubakhi or from the city of Her? Let your leader speak. If from the port of Sur, that wretched spot is known to me, to which water is brought in boats. We know foreigners too well in all conscience, for we have conquered them and taken their tribute. . . . Above all, know ye how to live? I mean, have ye to eat and can be at your own cost so that ye come not as burden on the state or be driven to steal? But if the first be the case, where then is the evidence and the written guarantee that ye know how to live? Have ye letters to a citizen of the country? Then out with them. Else there is naught but turning back."

The old man aproached him with studied mildness. "You are here as Pharaoh," he said, "and if I fear not the influence you wield and stammer not in amazement before your authority, it is only because I stand not for the first time before you and have already known your kindness, O wise lieutenant!"

And he recalled to him, about such a time it had been, perhaps two years ago, or four, that he, the Minæan merchant, trod the gate for the last time and for the first was passed by the troop leader Hor-waz on the ground of the purity of his intentions. Hor-waz seemed faintly to recollect; to remember the little beard and drooping head of this old man, who spoke Egyptian as though he were a human being. He listened amicably as the other answered to the questions put, that not merely had he no evil designs, not merely fair ones, but quite definitely the best; that he was come across Jordan on a business trip, through the land of Pelesheth and through the desert; and with his followers well knew how to live and to pay, as the valuable wares on the backs of his pack-animals bore witness. But as to his connections in the country: here was a letter — and he unrolled before the lieutenant the piece of polished goatskin on which the business friend at Gilead had written some phrases of recommendation in Canaanitish script to the business friend at Djanet in the Delta.

Hor-waz's slim fingers — all ten of them, indeed — reached with a fastidious gesture for the document. He could not gather much from it, but so much he saw from his own visa in the corner, that this parchment had already lain before him.

"You bring me always the same letter, old friend," said he. "That will not do, you cannot come in on it for ever. This paper crackles with age, I would see it no more; it is out of date, you must show something new."

The old man retorted that his connections were not limited to the man in Djanet. They extended, he said, as far as Thebes itself, the city of Amun, whither he had it in mind to go, to a house of honour and distinction, with whose overseer, called Mont-kaw, son of Ah-mose, he had been on terms of close acquaintance for many years, and often been permitted to supply him with foreign goods. The house, however, belonged to one great above the great, Petepre, fan-bearer on Pharoah's right hand. This mention of a connection with the court, however second-hand, obviously made an impression on the young officer.

"By the king's life!" said he. "According to that you would amount to something, and if you lie not with your Asiatic mouth, that would indeed alter the matter. Have you nothing written concerning your connection with this Mont-kaw, son of Ahmose, who is set over the house of the fan-bearer? Nothing at all? What a pity, for that would have simplified matters no little! But still, you know this name to tell me, and your peaceable countenance gives your words a satisfactory warrant of good faith."

He beckoned for his writing materials and the attendant hastened to hand him the sharpened rush and the wooden tablet on whose smooth clay surface the lieutenant was used to scribble notes. Hor-waz dipped the rush in an inkwell of the palette held by the soldier next to him, shook off a few drops, carried his writing hand in a wide curve to the surface, and wrote down the old man's record as it was repeated to him. He wrote standing beside the standard, the tablet on his arm, bent slightly forward, with his mouth pursed, squinting a little — charming, self-satisfied, and with obvious enjoyment.

"Pass!" he said, handed back tablet and pen, saluted again in his absurdly fastidious way, and sprang up the stair by which he had come. The Sinai sheik, with the dishevelled beard, who had spent the whole time on his face, was not interrogated at all. Hor-waz had included him and his among the old man's train, and the information, written out on beautiful paper and sent to the officials at Thebes, would be most incomplete. But there would be no wailing in Egypt on that account nor would any confusion come to the land. To the Ishmaelites the main point was that the soldiers of Thel pushed back the bronze wings of the gate that gave access to the floating bridge, across which they might move with beasts and burdens and enter the plains of Hapi.

Least among them, noted by none and named by no name in Hor-waz's official protocol, Joseph, son of Jacob, came into Egypt.

Chapter II

THE ENTRANCE INTO SHEOL

WHAT part of it did he see first? That we know with some precision; the circumstances show it. The route which the Ishmaelites took him was dictated to them in more than one way, and by the lie of the land besides: it is as certain as it is ever little commented on that the part of Egypt to which Joseph first came was one which is known and even famous, not because of the rôle it played in the history of Egypt but on account of its connection with the story of Jacob and his family. It was the land of Goshen. It was called Gosen or Goshen, indifferently, according to the speaker's enunciation, and belonged to the district of Arabia, the twentieth of the land of Uto the serpent, that is to say, Lower Egypt. It lay in the eastern part of the Delta, wherefore Joseph and his guides entered it so soon as they had left the salt inland seas and frontier fortifications behind. There was certainly nothing great or remarkable about it — Joseph did not find himself in any danger of losing his head or being hampered by awe at the importunate marvels of Mizraim.

Wild geese flew across a mild, dull, rainy sky above the monotonous marshland, threaded with ditches and dikes, out of which here and there rose a single blackthorn or a mulberry-fig-tree. The travellers went on causeways, following the watercourses where long-legged birds, storks and ibises, stood in the cane-brake that choked the streams. Whole villages mirrored the cone-shaped clay roofs of their storehouses and the shade of their doum-palms' fan-shaped leaves in the green duck-ponds beside them. They were not different to the eye from villages in the homeland and not a very rewarding sight after a journey of seven times seventeen days. It was simple earth-land that Joseph saw, without any surprising features; it was not even the "granary" of the well-known phrase. For what he saw was simply grassland and pasture-land far and wide, though, to be sure, the pasturage was lush and well watered — and the son of shepherds looked with interest at it. Many flocks grazed over it, cattle white and red, either hornless or with upstanding lyre-shaped horns; there were sheep too; their shepherds had made shelters from the drizzling rain by stretching papyrus mats above their crooks, and squatted underneath with their jackal-eared dogs.

The cattle, the old man instructed his followers, were mostly not from these parts. They came from far upstream and belonged to the landowners and the overseers of the temple stables in regions where there was hardly anything but arable land and the cattle would have had to feed on the clover-fields. So at the right time of year the herds were sent down into the fenny districts of northern Lower Egypt to batten on the meadows made luxuriant by these very fresh-water canals along which our little train was now passing. They led it straight to Per-sopd, the original holy city of the district. For there the ditch branched off from the Delta arm of Hapi and connected the river with the Bitter Lakes. These, as the old man knew, were in turn united by a canal with the Sea of the Red Earth, otherwise the Red Sea; so that one could pass straight on through from the Nile and sail from the city of Amun to the incense land of Punt, as had once the bold ships of Hatshepsut, the woman who had been Pharaoh and worn the beard of Osiris.

As they went on, the old man continued to prattle about all these traditional matters, in his shrewd and easy-going way. But Joseph listened uncomfortably and had no ear at all for the doings of Hatshepsut, that woman whose sex had been changed by the dignity of the kingship so that she had worn the beard. Shall I be saying too much if I set down how his fancy flung an airy bridge between the gay meadows here and his kin at home, his father and little Benjamin? Surely not — even though his thinking may not have been of the same kind as ours, but played about a few dream-motifs which formed, as it were, the musical fabric of his mental life. One of these had always been closely related to the thoughts of being "snatched away" and "lifted up": the motif of being "followed after." Then there was another, contradictory one, in his changeful play of thought, which concerned Jacob's dislike of the country whither he was snatched. He harmonized the two contrapuntally, by telling himself that this peacefully primeval pasture-land here might indeed be already Egypt but after all was not the real Egypt, therefore not utterly abhorrent; and that it might appeal to Jacob, the king of many flocks who found it hard to sustain them at home. He looked at the grazing herds sent hither by Upper Egyptian proprietors to feed on the fat of the land, and had a lively feeling that the motif of being "snatched away" needed completion by that of being "lifted up," before the flocks of the lords of the upper river would make way for other flocks in the land of Goshen; in other words, before the motif of being "followed after" could come in. He weighed afresh his conviction and strengthened himself mightily in it, that if one were indeed going to the West, at least one must become the first of those who were there.

For the present, however, he went with his masters along the flat, clayey margin of the beneficent watercourse dotted here and there with spindling palms. On the smooth water a flotilla of boats was slowly gliding eastward with monstrously tall sails on swaying masts. By this route they could not miss the holy city Per-sopdu, which, when they reached it, proved to be a huddled settlement surrounded by disproportionately high walls with but little life inside them. For almost the whole population consisted of the presiding "field judge" and "privy bearer of the king's command," who bore the good Syrian title of Rabisu, together with his officials and the shorn priesthood of the regional god Sopd, called "Scourge of the Dwellers of Sinai." Among the rest of the inhabitants the coloured Asiatic dress and the language of Amor and Zahi were much more in evidence than the white Egyptian garb and the Egyptian tongue. The narrow streets of Per-sopd smelt so strong of carnations or clove-pinks that at first it was pleasant and then painful: for this was the incense most favoured of Sopdu in his temple, and every offering reeked of it. This Sopdu was so old, so ancient a god that his own priests and prophets, who wore lynx-skins on their backs and went about with their eyes cast down, no longer knew for a certainty whether his head was that of a pig or a hippopotamus.

He was a god rejected and obscure; embittered thereby, to judge from the mood and language of his priests. For a long time now he had not been the scourge of the dwellers in Sinai. His image — only hand-high — stood in the remotest part of his primitive and very clumsy temple, whose courts and antechambers were adorned with extremely ungainly seated images of the early Pharaoh who had built the temple. The foremost gatehouse, with its buttressed, picture-covered walls, had little niches in each of which stood a gilded flag-pole flying a gay pennant; but all this strove in vain to give blitheness to the house of Sopd. It was poorly endowed, the treasuries and storehouses round the main court stood empty, and not many people waited on Sopdu with offerings — only the Egyptian inhabitants and none from elsewhere; and there was no feast of general observance to draw zealous pilgrims down-river and within the crumbling walls of Per-sopd.

The Ishmaelites, as a business gesture, laid on the offertory in the square hall a few nosegays which they found for sale in the open court, also a duck spiced with cloves. They talked to the shiny-pated priests with long fingernails and for ever downcast gaze; and from them heard, in heavy accents, of the fallen state of their aboriginal lord and his city. They complained of the times, which brought great injustice with them and heaped all the power, splendour, and precedence in one side of the balance of the lands — namely, in the southern or upper part, since when it was that Wese had grown so great; whereas originally they had piously weighed down the northern or lower land of the Delta, as was right and just. For in the good old times, when Mempi had been the brilliant city of kings, the Delta region had been the real and true Egypt, and the upper parts, including Thebes, had ranked almost with the wretched Kush and the Negro countries. Then the south had been poor in culture and enlightenment, as well as in beauty of life. From the ancient north these blessings had spread fruitfully southwards up the river. Here were the sources of knowledge, civilization, and prosperity; here the most venerable gods of the land had had their birth, as, for instance, Sopd, the Lord of the East in his chapel, whom now a wrong adjustment of the balance had put quite in the shade. For Theban Amun, up there near the Negro lands, set itself up today as a judge of what was to be considered Egyptian and what not — convinced that its name spelled Egypt and Egypt Thebes. A little time ago, said the embittered "temple-treaders," people of the west living near the Libyans had even sent to Amun and represented to him that it seemed to them they were Libyans too and not Egyptians; for they lived outside the Delta and agreed in nothing the children of Egypt, either in service of the gods or otherwise: they loved, so they said, the flesh of cows and wanted freedom to eat it as did the Libyans, whose like they were. But Amun had answered and reproved them: there could be no talk of the flesh of cows, for all that land was Egypt which was fertilized by the Nile, up and down stream, and all were Egyptians who dwelt this side of the city of elephants and drank from the river.

Thus Amun's judgment; the priests of the lord Sopdu lifted their long-nailed hands as they strove to make clear to the Ishmaelites the arrogance of it. Why then, they scornfully asked, this side of Shab and the first cataract? Just because Thebes lay this side? If Sopd, their lord, down here in the north, in the first and genuine land of Egypt, were to declare that everything was Egyptian that drank from the river, it would be a broad and high-minded thing to say. But when Amun said it, a god who, to speak mildly, stood under suspicion of Nubian origin and of being originally a god of the wretched Kush; who had achieved primacy in the mind of the peoples only by arbitrarily putting himself on a par with Atum Re — then there was something lacking in his broad-mindedness and you could not call it high-minded at all.

In short, the prophets of Sopd suffered from jealousy and peevishness at the eclipse of their god through time and events. And the Ishmaelites, the old man at their head, humoured them like the good

men of business that they were. Also they increased their offerings
with sundry loaves of bread and jugs of beer and showed the neglected Sopd all due attention before they went on to Per-Bastet
close by.

THE CITY OF CATS

AND HERE it smelt so strong of catnip that it almost turned a stranger's stomach. For the odour is offensive to everybody, save only to
the sacred animal of Bastet, namely the cat, which is well known to
love it. Numerous specimens of the animal were kept in Bastet's
shrine, the city's mighty core; black, white, and coloured, they
frisked with the stealthy and persistent charm of their species among
the worshippers in the court and were flattered with offerings of the
hateful herb. But cats were everywhere in Per-Bastet — in all the private houses as well — and the smell of valerian pervaded everything;
it even flavoured the food and lingered in men's garments, so that
when they went as far as On and Mempi they were greeted with
laughter and the words: "You come from Per-Bastet, don't you?"
     The laughter had not to do with the smell alone, but with the cat-
city itself and its associations, which were matter enough for mirth.
For Per-Bastet, unlike Per-Sopd — which it exceeded in size and population — had a reputation for gaiety. It even looked jolly, although
lying so deep in the ancient Delta, its jollity being of a primitive,
coarse-fibred kind which made all Egypt laugh whenever it thought
of it. This city — also therein unlike the shrine of Sopd — had a feast
of general observance; its citizens boasted that "millions," that is certainly tens of thousands of people, came down-river by land or water
to attend it. Even on the way thither they got very jolly; the women
especially, equipped with rattles, behaved with roguish abandon, according to all accounts; and words and gestures of a decidedly primitive character were flung across from the decks of their boats to the
villages on the shore. The men too were jolly; they whistled, sang,
and clapped; and all of the visitors held great press of popular meetings in Per-Bastet, camping in tents for a three days' feast, with sacrifices, dances, and mummery to the dull rolling of drums; with a
fair, story-telling, juggling, snake-charming, and more grape wine
than was drunk otherwise in Per-Bastet in all the rest of the year.
We are told that the mood of the people so passed over into the
primitive that they even flagellated themselves, or rather beat themselves till it hurt with a sort of thorny club, amid general bawling.
And this bawling was an inseparable feature of the primitive feast;
indeed, it was what made people laugh when they thought of Bastet,
for it sounded just like the nocturnal caterwauling of the female at
the visit of the male cat.
     With all these matters, then, the inhabitants regaled the strangers

and boasted of the profitable crowds which enlivened once every year an otherwise uneventful life. The old man, on business grounds, regretted that he had not come at the right time of year for the feast. His young slave Usarsiph listened to the narration with apparently respectful eyes, nodded politely, and thought of Jacob. Of him he thought, and of the templeless God of his fathers, as he stood at the highest part of the city and looked down through its middle depth where two tree-shaded branches of water embraced the sacred peninsula, into the dwelling of the female idol, enclosed in towering walls. The main building lay inside a hedge of old sycamore trees; its pylons were thick with images, its courts were shaded by awnings, and the roofs of its colourful halls were borne by columns whose capitals imitated the open and closed calyxes of the byblus reed. It lay there, spacious and extended, accessible by the stone-paved road from the east, by which he had come in the Ishmaelite train. He continued to think when later he entered the temple halls and looked at the pictures graven on the walls and painted deep red and sky-blue: Pharaoh burning incense before the cat goddess, among incredibly clear inscriptions of eyes, mouths, arrows, beetles, and birds; while red-brown deities, with tails, wearing loincloths and brilliant arm-bands and collars, high crowns on their animal heads and the cross-ring of the symbol of life on their hands, laid a friendly touch on the shoulders of their earthly son.

Joseph, a tiny figure among giants, gazed up at all this with calm young eyes. Young he was, and it was weighty with age. Yet he was aware that he opposed it with his youth not only according to the measure of his years but in a larger sense; he stiffened his back against the weight of the ages; and when he thought of the ancient crying by night with which the folk at the feast filled the courts of Bastet he gave his shoulders a twitch.

EDIFYING ON

How well we know the route by which the "snatched away" was taken! — up or down according as you choose to put it. For, like so much else here, the up and the down were confusing. For Joseph — probably for Abram too — the road to Egypt went down; but in Egypt it went up — that is, against the river, which flowed from the south, so that as you went southwards you went, not down, but up. It seemed like a deliberate confusion, like a game in which one turns a blindfold person two or three times round till his head whirls and he no longer knows hind from fore. And not only with direction but also with time and the calendar things were confusing down here below.

It was in the twenty-eighth year of the reign of Pharaoh; and, as

we should say, in the middle of December. The people of Kemt said
and wrote the "first month of the flood," called Thoth, as Joseph
learnt with pleasure, or Djehuti, as they called the moon-friendly
ape. But nature and the calendar did not agree: the current year almost always conflicted with reality; only at enormous distances of
time did the New Year's Day of the calendar coincide with the natural one, when the dog-star appeared again in the morning sky and the
waters began to rise. In short, between the conception of a year and
the seasons of nature confusion reigned. Even practically there could
be no sense in saying that they were now at the beginning of the
flood season; the river had so abated as almost to be back in its old
bed; the land had emerged, the sowing had been largely finished, the
crops were up. Indeed, the journey of the Ishmaelites had been so leisurely that half a year had passed since Joseph, at the time of the summer solstice, had gone down to the pit.

    Somewhat dazed, then, as to time and space, he moved on in his
stations — and which were they? We know precisely; the circumstances show us. For his guides, the Ishmaelites — who still gave themselves plenty of time, or rather, after their old wont, troubled about
time not at all, only taking care that their slow progress kept more or
less the right direction — went with him along the branch from Per-
Bastet south to the point where it flowed into the river at the apex of
the triangle of the Delta. And so they came to golden On, lying at the
apex, a most extraordinary city, the house of the Sun, the largest place
which Joseph had ever seen. It seemed to his dazzled eyes to be built
chiefly of gold.

    But thence they would some day reach Mempi, likewise called
Menfe, time-honoured one-time royal city, whose dead did not need
to take the water journey, as it lay already on the western bank.
This they knew beforehand about Mempi. And from that point they
meant to travel no farther by land but to charter a boat and sail to
Pharaoh's city, No-Amun. Thus the old man had planned, according to whose planning everything proceeded, and so they went on
for the present, with halts for trade, along the bank of the Jeor, here
called Harri. The stream had gone brown in its bed, and lay in isolated pools on the fields, which were beginning to green, as far on
both sides, between desert and desert, as the fertile land extended.

    Where the bank was steep, men were drawing up water in leather
bottles at well-curbs, with a lump of clay at the other end of the
sweep to serve as balance. Drawing up the muddy seminal fluid from
the river and pouring it into channels that it might flow down into
the ditches below and prosper the corn against the coming of Pharaoh's scribes. For this was the Egyptian house of bondage so frowned
upon by Jacob; the tax-gatherers were accompanied by Nubian lic-
tors carrying palm rods.

The Ishmaelites did business among the labourers in the villages, trading their lamps and resin for necklaces, head-rests, and the linen which the peasant women made out of field flax and turned over to the tax-gatherers. They talked with the people and they saw the land of Egypt. Joseph saw it too and breathed in its vital air as they took their trading way. It was strange enough; the customs, beliefs, and forms of the country were sharp-flavoured like the taste of its spices. Yet we must not conclude that what he thus took in with mind and senses was utterly foreign and unheard-of to him. His fatherland — if we take in that sense the region of the Jordan, the mountains and the mountainous country where he grew up — was a region of passage and transit. On the south accordingly it took character from Egyptian influence, on the east from the Babylonian sphere. Pharaoh's campaigns had passed through and left behind garrisons, governors, and buildings. Joseph had seen Egyptians and the clothes they wore; the look of Egyptian temples was not strange to him; all in all he was not only the child of his mountains but the child of a larger territorial unit, that of the eastern Mediterranean, within which nothing could impress him as quite outlandish or absurd. Still more, he was a child of his age, that time now submerged in which he lived and moved, into which we have gone down to him as Ishtar went down to her son. Time and space worked together to create a unity and community in the physical and the mental world. So that probably the one actual novelty which Joseph perceived on his travels was just this: that he and his were not alone in the world, not quite unique; that much of the thinking and doing of the fathers, their outlook and their anxious speculation anent the nature of God, had not been altogether a peculiar personal advantage of theirs, but rather it was a property of the unifying time and space — aside of course from considerable differences in the amount of the blessing and their adroitness in the use of it.

When for instance Abram had argued so long and ardently with Melchisedec about the degree of unity which subsisted between his own Adon and El Elyon, the Shechemite god of the league of Baal, their discussion had been quite typical of their world and time; as regards not only the problem they discussed but also the importance they attached and the feeling they brought to its discussion. At the very time when Joseph came to Egypt the priests of On, the city of Atum-Re-Horakhte, the sun lord, had just made a pronouncement on the relation of their sacred bull Merwer to the Dweller on the Horizon, designating it a "repeating birth" — a formulation in which the idea of proximity and identity came more or less into its own. Wherefore also it occupied the thoughts of all Egypt and even at court had made a lively impression. Everybody talked about it, great and small; the Ishmaelites could not exchange five deben of labdanum against a corresponding quantity of beer or a good bullock hide without hearing mentioned in the preliminaries to the bargain the capital new definition of the relation of Merwer to Atum-Re and being asked what the strangers thought of it. The questioner could reckon, if not on their agreement, at least on their interest; they came indeed from afar, but not from outside his unit of space; though, above all, it was the time they had in common which made them listen with a certain excitement to the new thing.

On, then, the dwelling of the sun, the dwelling, that is, of him who in the morning is Kheper, at midday Re, and Atum in the evening; who opens his eyes and the light arises, who closes his eyes and darkness comes; of him who had named to Eset his daughter his name; On in the land of Egypt, thousands of years the same, lay on our travellers' southward route. Over it glittered the gilded four-sided top of the enormous obelisk of highly polished granite, which stood on the projecting foundation before the great temple of the sun. Here was the alabaster table of Re-Horakhte, covered with lotus-crowned wine-jugs, laden with cakes, dishes of honey, birds, and all sorts of vegetable produce. And here the "treaders" of the sanctuary, in stiffly starched kilts, panther-skins on their backs with the tails dangling, were burning incense before that very bull Merwer: the great bull, the "repeating birth" of the god, with a brazen neck just behind the lyre-shaped horns, and powerful hanging testicles. This at least was a city such as Joseph had never seen; different not only from the cities of the rest of the world, but also from the other cities of Egypt. Its very temple — with the adjacent lofty-built "Ship of the Sun" made of gilded bricks — was also entirely different in ground-plan and appearance from other Egyptian temples. The whole city glittered and glistened with gold, like the sun; in such wise that all its citizens had permanently enflamed and weeping eyes and strangers mostly drew hood or mantle over their heads against the glare. The roofs of its ring wall were gold, golden rays quivered and darted everywhere from the tips of the phallic sun-lances with which they were lined — all these golden symbols of the sun in the shape of beasts, all these lions, sphinxes, goats, bulls, eagles, falcons, and sparrow-hawks. And it was not enough that even the poorest house, built of bricks made of Nile mud, bore a gilt symbol of the sun — a winged disk, a hooked wheel or wagon, an eye, an axe, or a scarab, or showed on its roof a golden ball or apple. For the dwelling-houses, granaries, and buildings in the outlying villages of Greater On were the same: each reflected the rays of the sun in some such emblem — a copper shield, a snaky spiral, a gilt beaker or shepherd's crook; for this was the domain of the sun and precinct of the blinking.

A city to make one blink was On, the thousand-year-old. Yet not only in outward appearance; it was so in its inward kind and spirit as

well. Age-old doctrinal wisdom was here at home, as the stranger perceived at once — it came in through his pores, one might say. But it
was a doctrinal wisdom solely and simply concerning the measure-
ment and structure of bodies conceived as in three-dimensional space,
and the surfaces bounding them; bounded by equal angles, meeting
in sharp edges that came together at a point which although it existed had no extension and occupied no space — and more mysteries
of the kind. All this interest in abstract figure which prevailed at On,
the sense for the theories of space, characterized this ancient city
and obviously had to do with its local cult, the worship of the day-
star. It betrayed itself even in the structure of the place. Situated just
at the apex of the triangular region of the diverging river-mouths, it
formed with its houses and streets an equilateral triangle, whose tip
— ideally and also more or less in fact — coincided with the apex of
the Delta; and on this very spot there reared itself from a mammoth
rhomboidal base the four-sided obelisk of flame-coloured granite,
covered with gold at the top where its surfaces met in a point. Daily
it kindled in the first gleam of the rising sun; and with its surrounding courtyards it formed the culmination of the temple precincts,
which extended as far as the middle of the triangular city.

The temple gate was hung with banners and gave access to passages
painted with the most delightful representations of the seasonal activities on the land and their fruits. In front of the gate was an open
square planted with trees; and here the Ishmaelites spent nearly the
whole day, for all the weak-eyed people of On came hither to do business and strangers from other parts as well. The servants of the god
came out to the market too, their eyes running with much gazing
into the sun; with heads reflecting it on their shiny surfaces, and wearing only the short aboriginal kilt and priest's garland. They mixed
with the people and had nothing against conversing with such as
would learn from their wisdom. It appeared indeed that they were
kept here to that end and only waited to be asked to testify for their
venerable cult and the ancient learning which their temple possessed.
Our old man, Joseph's master, availed himself freely of the unspoken
but obvious willingness and conversed at length with the sun-in-
structed teachers on the square; Joseph at his side listened too.

The power of thinking on God and the gift of giving laws to the
faith were, they said, hereditary in their order. They had possessed
for ages a faculty of religious insight. They, or rather their forerun-
ners in the sevice, had first divided up and measured time and contrived the calendar; all which, as well as that fruitful understanding
for abstract figure, was connected with the nature of the god at the
opening of whose eye the day began. Up to that time men had just
lived on in blind timelessness, without measure or mark. But He, who
made the hours — from which then the days were born — had through

his wise men opened the people's eyes. That they — that is to say, their forbears — had discovered the sun-dial, went without saying. The tradition was not so clear with regard to the apparatus that measured the hours of the night, the water-clock. But probably it was made through the circumstance that Sobk, the crocodile-shaped water-god from Ombo, like so many other objects of veneration was, when one fixed it with one's watering eyes, nothing but Re under another name and in token bore the serpent and the disk.

That sort of general survey, in fact, was the special line and learning of these shiny-pated priests. They were, by their own account, very strong at generalization and at equating any and every regional and local protecting deity with Atum-Re-Horakhte of On — a complex himself and representing a constellation of originally single numina. To make out of many one: that was their preferred activity, yes, according to them there were at bottom only two great gods: one the living, that was Hor in the Mount of Light, Atum-Re; and one the dead, Osiris, the Eye Enthroned. But the eye also was Atum-Re, it was the disk of the sun; and so to the penetrating mind Usir was lord of the nightly bark into which, as everybody knew, Re mounted after his setting, to travel from west to east and to light the underworld. In other words, even these two great gods were at bottom one and the same. But if the shrewdness of such a general survey was admirable, not less so was the art these teachers displayed of avoiding offence; for in the midst of their assimilating activities they took care to leave intact the actual multiplicity of the gods of Egypt.

This they achieved by means of their science of the triangle. Were their hearers, asked the teachers of On, at all versed in the nature of this glorious symbol? To its width, they said, corresponded the deities many-named and many-shaped, invoked of the people, served by the priests in all the cities of the lands. But above its rose and strove to a meeting the two legs of the beautiful figure, and the unique space which they bounded might be called "the space of conspectus," distinguished by the fact that it narrowed as it went up and the hypothetical bases drawn through it became shorter and shorter until they had a very narrow extension and finally none at all. For the legs met in a point, and this terminus and point of intersection, beneath which all the varying widths of the symbol remained equilateral — that was the lord of their temple, that was Atum-Re.

Thus the theory of the triangle, the beautiful figure of the conspectus. The priests of Atum plumed themselves no little on it. They had, they said, made a school with it; conspectus and comparison were going on everywhere. But only in a clumsy and uninstructed way, not in the right spirit — without intelligence, crudely and by force. Amun, for instance, the "Rich in Bulls," at Thebes in Upper Egypt, had had himself made equal to Re by his prophets and would now be called Amun-Re in his shrine. All very well, but not in the sense of the triangle and reconciliation; rather in the sense that Amun had conquered Re, had consumed him and lived in him — as though Re, so to speak, had had to name him his name! That was a brutal misuse of the doctrine, a narrow-minded effrontery quite contrary to the meaning of the triangle. Atum-Re for his part was not called the "Horizon-Dweller" for nothing; his horizon was wide and all-embracing, and all-embracing was the triangular field of his con-spectus. Yes, he was world-wide, and world-friendly the nature of this ancient god; long ago it had matured into blitheness and benevo-lence. He was ready, so said the shiny-pated priests, to find himself not alone in the changeful shapes which the people worshipped in the regions and cities of Kemt. No, for he was also complaisantly inclined to come to terms of a far-reaching and general kind with the sun-gods of other peoples. How different from young Amun in Thebes, who lacked every speculative faculty and whose horizon was in fact so narrow that he not only knew and realized nothing but the land of Egypt, but even here had no thought but to consume and incorporate instead of giving free rein — in all of which, so to speak, he saw no farther than his own nose.

But, said the blear-eyed ones, they would not dwell upon conflict with young Amun at Thebes; conflict was not the nature or affair of their god, but rather complaisance and harmony. He loved the stran-ger as himself, and thus they his priests delighted in converse with strangers — namely, with the old man and his companions. Whatever gods they served and whatever name they called them, they might without disloyalty and with good heart approach the alabaster table of Horakhte and offer doves, bread, fruit, and flowers, according to their power. One glance at the mild and smiling countenance of the fatherly head priest, as he sat on a golden chair at the foot of the great obelisk, a golden cap on his bald pate with its aureole of white hair, the white robe flowing wide about him, a winged sun's disk at his back, and presided with benignity over the offerings — a single such glance would convince the strangers that in offering to Atum-Re they offered to their own domestic gods, to whom satisfaction was given within the triangle.

The servants of the sun embraced and kissed the old man and his companions, including Joseph, one after the other, in the name of the fatherly great prophet. Then they turned to other visitors to the market, to make further propaganda for Atum-Re, lord of the far horizon. But the Ishmaelites departed, very pleasantly impressed, from On at the apex of the triangle, and bent their steps farther down — or up — into the land of Egypt.

JOSEPH AT THE PYRAMIDS

The Nile rolled its slow course along between flat reedy banks, where many a palm tree still stood half-submerged and mirrored its trunk in the subsiding flood. There were plots of land in the blessing-zone between desert and desert where the corn and barley were already green; on others cattle and sheep were being driven by white-aproned brown bearers across the level land, that they might tread the seed into the soft moist earth. Vultures and white falcons peered and hovered under a clearing, sunny sky; they swooped down toward villages half-hidden by towering date-palms with crowns of fan-shaped leaves. There were many such settlements along the irrigation canals; their dung-roofed dwellings had walls made out of Nile mud and buttressed like pylons. And everything bore the stamp of the characteristic, all-pervadnig spirit of the land of Egypt: its forms and its gods conditioned the picture of men and things. Heretofore, and in his own country, Joseph had only seen it in single manifestations, as for instance some characteristic building. Here it confronted him in all its typicality and in great and small.

At the village landing-places naked children were playing among farm-yard fowl; shelters made of poles and withies stood along the bank, and people returning from their necessary occasions came poling along the canal and landed from their high-backed osier barks. The river, dotted with sails, divided the land into two parts from north to south; but everywhere the fertilizing watercourses ran east and west and made it into islands like oases of fan-shaped green. You walked on the road as on a causeway among ditches, reservoirs, and groves. Thus the Ishmaelites passed on southwards, amid all the people of the land, riding on asses, driving loaded wagons drawn by oxen and donkeys, or going on foot, apron-wearers carrying ducks and fish on yokes to market. A lean, reddish, flat-bellied folk, square-shouldered, inoffensive in bearing, ready to laugh. They had thin-boned faces with projecting jaws; little noses broad at the end, and childish cheeks; a rush blossom in their mouths, behind one ear, or stuck in the much-washed apron, which had a diagonal hem and was higher back than front. Their hair fell smooth over the brow and was cut off straight under the ear-lobes. Joseph liked these wayfarers. Considering what they were — people of Sheol and the land of the dead — they were pleasant to look at, and they laughed as they shouted greetings to the Shabirite dromedary-riders, for anything foreign to them was a joke. Joseph tried his tongue on their speech by himself and trained himself by listening, that he might soon be able to talk readily with them in their own idiom.

The land of Egypt was narrow at this point, the strip of fertility

small. To the east, on their left, the arid Arabian ranges ran close by,
matched by the sandhills of Libya on the west, their deathly desolation masked in purple loveliness as the sun sank behind them. But
at the edge of the desert, in front of this chain and near the greening
fields, the travellers saw straight ahead of them a symmetrical and
very singular elevation, composed of triangular surfaces, whose huge
planes met in sharp corners and ran together to a point at the top.
These were mountains not created by nature but made by the hand of
man; they were the world-famous erections — the old man pointed
them out to Joseph as they went — the monuments of Khufu, Khef-
ren, and other kings of the early time, built through decades by the
sweat of hundreds of thousands of slaves coughing under the lash;
built out of granite blocks weighing millions of tons which they
dug in the Arabian quarries and dragged to the river, ferried over,
and, groaning, sledged to the border of Libya, where they hoisted
them with some kind of incredible lifting apparatus and piled them
into pointed mountains. Men fell and died, their tongues hanging
out with their superhuman effort on the blazing desert — all in order that Khufu, the king and god, might lie far beneath them, shut
off by a tiny chamber from the perpetual weight of millions of tons
of heavy stone, a little twig of mimosa on his heart.

It was no work for human beings that the children of Kemt had
there performed. And yet it was the work of the same little folk who
trotted and poled along the causeways; the work of their bleeding
hands, lean muscles, and panting lungs — won from the human, if surpassing the human, because Khufu was a god-king, the son of the
sun. But the sun which struck down and consumed the builders might
be satisfied with the superhuman human achievement — Ra-hotep,
the satisfied sun. For in their abstract form they represented him,
they were his pictographic symbols; these great piles of death and
resurrection stood there sun-monument and sun-tomb at once; and
their vast triangular surfaces, polished and glittering from base to
apex, lay piously adjusted to the four quarters of the heavens.

Joseph looked up wide-eyed at these three-dimensional tomb-
mountains, heaped up by slave-labour in the Egyptian house of
bondage so misprized by Jacob. As he looked he listened to the old
man, who expended himself in tales of King Khufu. Even today sinister tales of that superhuman master builder were on the lips of the
people. These thousand years and more the folk of Kemt had preserved a grudge against the memory of that evil-doer who had got
from them the impossible for that he had been a bad and self-seeking
god and closed all the temples that no one should steal time from him
with sacrifices. And he had kept all the people harnessed in toil for
the building of his marvellous tomb and for thirty years had not
granted even one little hour for their own life. Ten years, that is, had

they to drag and chisel and on top of that build for twice ten, expending every ounce of strength they had and more besides. For reckoning all their strength together it would not have been quite enough to build the pyramid. The necessary remainder had come to them from the divinity of King Khufu, but they had not been glad. The building had cost great treasures; and when the treasure of that majestic godhead had been exhausted, he exposed his own daughter in the palace and gave of her body to every man who paid the price. By such means he replenished his treasury.

So went the legends, the old man said. It is quite possible that they were for the most part fairy-tales and falsehoods, which were told these thousands of years after Khufu's death. But so much was clear, that the people were even now more terrified than grateful to him for wringing out of them their utmost and more, and insisting on the impossible.

As our travellers came nearer, the peaks stood up separate in the sand, and they saw that the surfaces of the triangles were damaged, their polished planes had begun to crumble. Desolation reigned between the giant tombs, as each by itself, and all too massive for time to have done more than nibble at their surfaces, they stood there on the shelving rubble and sand of the desert plain. They alone had come off victorious in the frightful struggle with time, which had long since destroyed and buried the splendours with which piety had once filled the spaces between their mammoth forms. Temples of the dead had once leaned against their sides, where services in honour of those dead in the sun had been set up "for ever"; covered passages thick with pictures had once led thence and broad-based gates on the eastern side near the fertile zone had once formed the entrance to the closed passages which led into the enchanted kingdom of immortality. All of this Joseph in his day saw no more and did not even know that not seeing was actually a no-more-seeing, a beholding of destruction. He came on them early of course by comparison with his relation to us. But from another point of view he was late and green indeed; his gaze encountered this great rubbish-heap of death, this bald survival of a mathematic of giants, as one's foot will stub against a pile of rubble. Astonishment and awe did move him, of course, at sight of these triangular domes; but the frightful endurance which made them, forsaken of their time, stand here, survivals into God's present day, gave them among their other aspects something awesome and accursed in his eyes; he thought of the Tower.

Then there was that riddle in the head-cloth, Hor-im-akhet, the great sphinx, which lay somewhere hereabouts residual, flat on the sands which were drifted over so as almost to cover it. Pharaoh's predecessor, Thutmose IV, had rescued it out of them, obedient to the promise-dream which he dreamed when he took his midday nap.

That was not so long ago; but the sand was already mounting again about the enormous creature, which had lain there so long that no man could say when and how it had come out of the rock — drifts of sand slanted up to its breast and hid one of the paws. The other paw, still free, was the size of three houses. At the breast of this mountain the son of the king, like a doll compared to the immense god-beast, had lain asleep while his servants at some distance guarded his hunting-wagon. And high above the manikin rose the inscrutable head, with the stiff neckcloth, the immortal brow, the eroded nose which lent it a somewhat roguish air, the rocky vault of its upper lip, the wide mouth which seemed to be shaping a sort of calm and primitive and senusal smile. The clear, wide-open, intelligent eyes, intoxicated from deep draughts of time, gazed eastwards as they had ever done.

And thus it lay there now, the immemorial Chimera, in a present whose distance and difference from times of yore were doubtless negligible in its eyes; and gazed steadfastly, sensually, unchangeably away eastwards above the heads of Joseph and his owners. An inscribed tablet more than a man's height leaned against its breast, and the Minæans read it with refreshment and strengthening of the heart. For this recent stone afforded a firm basis of time; it was like a narrow platform which gave a foothold above the abyss; it was the commemorative tablet which Pharaoh Thutmose had erected here in memory of his dream and the moving of the sand. The old man read the text and the pronouncement to his people: how the prince, lying in the shadow of the monster, was overcome by sleep at the hour when the sun was at its height and saw in his dream the majesty of this glorious god, his father, Harmakhis-Khepere-Atum-Re, who spoke fatherly to him and called him his dear son. "It is already a long time in years," he said, "that my countenance is directed upon thee and my heart the same. I will give thee, Thutmose, the royal sovereignty, the crowns of the two lands shalt thou wear upon the throne of Geb, and to thee shall the earth after its length and breadth belong with all that the radiant eye of the all-lord shineth upon. The treasure of Egypt and the great tribute of the people shall be thine. But meanwhile the sands of the desert where I lie weigh heavy upon me, all worthy of adoration as I stand. My justified wish groweth out of this weight. I doubt not that thou wilt accede to it as soon as thou canst. For I know thou art my son and my deliverer. But I will be with thee." When Thutmose awoke — so the story went — he still knew the words of the god and kept them in mind until the hour of his elevation. And in that very hour his command went forth that they should at once remove the sand which rested heavy on Harmakhis, the great sphinx, at Mempi in the desert.

Thus the tale. And Joseph, who listened as the old man his master read it, took care to add not even one little word. For he heeded the old man's warning to hold his tongue in this land of Egypt, and wished to show that in case of need one could conceal even such thoughts as he had. But in secret he was vexed on Jacob's account at this dream of the promise, and in his vexation found it arid and meagre. Pharoah, so he thought, made altogether too much of his tablet. What after all had he been promised? Nothing more than that which had been his destiny from birth; that at a certain hour he would become king and reign over the two lands. This definite prospect the god had confirmed to him, in case, that is, Pharoah rescued his image from the sands that threatened it. And here one saw the folly of making to oneself an image. The image fell into danger from the sand, and the god into such a pass as to implore: "Save me, my son!" And to enter into a bond wherein he promised in exchange for a petty benefaction something that would most likely happen anyhow. Joseph found that offensive. It had been a different and higher bond that God the Lord had concluded with the fathers, likewise out of need, yet mutual need: that they should save each other out of the sands of the desert and become holy the one in the other. In any case, the king's son had become king at his hour, but the desert sand had already encroached again upon the image to a considerable extent. For such passing relief probably only a redundant return-gift was in place, thought Joseph. He expressed his thought to Kedema, the old man's son, when they were alone; and Kedema was amazed at such a critical spirit.

But let Joseph carp as he would and mock out of respect to Jacob, yet the sight of the sphinx made on him in one way or another more impression than all he had hitherto seen in the land of Egypt. It set his young blood in an unrest, against which mockery did not avail and which did not let him sleep. Night had fallen while they lingered by these great things of the desert; and so they set up their tents that they might sleep and go on to Mempi in the morning. But Joseph, who had already lain down in the hut with Kedema, his bedfellow, strolled out once more under the stars. He heard in the distance jackals howling as he approached the giant idol, to look at it quite by himself, without witnesses, in the brightness of the night and question its uncanny vastness.

For uncanny it was, that monster of old time, in its regal rock headdress, and uncanny not only for its size or even for the darkness of its origins. How did the riddle run? Ah, it ran not at all, it lay there, or crouched, consisting but in the silence, that rapt-drunken silence in which the monster gazed out with its wide wild eyes above the questioning and questioned. And its want of nose had an effect as when a man sets his cap crooked over one ear. Yes, if this had been a riddle like the good old man's about his neighbour Dagantakala's plot of land — then, however the numbers were hidden and concealed, one might have shifted the unknown quantity hither and thither and weighed the proportions so as not only to find the answer but to enjoy the game and be arrogant at one's own skill. But this riddle was nothing but silence, and its was the arrogance, to judge from its nose; and if it had a human head it was nothing for such as he, let him be ever so clear-headed.

To begin with: what sex was it, male or female? The people called it Hor in the Mountain of Light and took it for an image of the sun lord, as Thutmose had done not long before. But that was a modern interpretation, it had not always obtained, and even if it were the sun lord who manifested himself in the recumbent figure — that proved nothing as to its sex. As it lay there, one could not tell. Suppose it got up, would it then have majestic dangling testicles like Merwer at On — or would it reveal itself as female, as a lion virgin? There was no answer. For if at some time or other it had produced itself forth out of the rock, it had been as an artist makes a lying picture, or actually not makes but represents it, so that what was not visible was not there; and let a hundred masons come with hammer and chisel to question the monster of its sex, there would be no answer still.

It was a sphinx, in other words a mystery and a riddle — and certainly a savage one, with lion's paws, thirsting after young blood, dangerous to the child of God and a snare to the descendants of the promise. Alas for the tablet of the king's son! At this rocky breast, between the claws of the dragon-woman, one dreamed no promise-dreams — or at least very meagre ones came to pass. It had nothing to do with promise; wide-eyed and cruel, with time-gnawn nose, fixed in vacant immobility, it gazed across at its river, and its menacing riddle was not of such a kind. It endured drunkenly on into the future, but that future was wild and dead for that it was mere endurance and false eternity, bare of expectancy.

Joseph stood there and tried his heart upon the voluptuously smiling majesty of that endurance. He stood quite close . . . would not the monster lift its paw from the sand and snatch the youth to its breast? He armed his heart and thought of Jacob. Curiosity is a shallow-rooted weed; it is but youth triumphing in freedom. Eye to eye with the forbidden, one knows the sonhood of the spirit and holds with the father.

Joseph stood long under the stars before the giant riddle, leaning on one leg, his elbow in one hand, his chin in the other. When he lay again with Kedema in the hut, he dreamed of the sphinx, that it said to him: "I love thee. Come to me and name me thy name, of whatever sex I am!" But he answered: "How shall I commit such a deed and sin against God?"

THE HOUSE OF THE SWADDLED ONE

THEY had gone along the western bank, the one on their right as they faced south and the right one in any case. For they needed not to cross over to reach Mempi the great, which itself lay in the west — the hugest sheepfold of men that Rachel's first-born had ever seen. Above it towered the heights where stone was quarried and where the city buried its dead.

Bewilderingly ancient was Mempi, and venerable in so far as the two ideas coincide. Meni, the first king, he who stood at the beginning of all memories and dynasties, had fortified the city to keep out the subjugated lower land. The mighty dwelling of Ptah, built out of eternal stone, was Meni's work; accordingly it had stood here much longer than the pyramids — had stood here since days behind which no man could look.

But there was no rigidity nor torpor here; the primitive and ancient presented itself in Mempi's image as a scene of bustling life and alert modernity; a city of more than a hundred thousand souls and composed in its great extent of many variously named quarters — a confusion of narrow winding streets going uphill and down, all sloping toward their centres, where waste water ran in a drain. They reeked and seethed with trade and traffic, and hordes of grubbing and garrulous little men. There were the smiling quarters of the rich, where villas with beautiful gates lay enclosed in lovely gardens; there were green temple precincts, where pennants fluttered and halls bright with delicate colour were mirrored in sacred pools. There were sphinx-avenues fifty ells broad, and tree-bordered drives on which the wagons of the great rolled along, drawn by fiery steeds crowned with bunches of feathers. They were heralded by panting runners who cried out: "Abrek!" "Take thy heart to thyself!" "Take care."

Yes, "Abrek!" Joseph too might well say it to himself and take heed to his heart so as not to fall victim to idle admiration before all that elegance and distinction. For this was Mempi or Menfe, as the people said here, pertly abbreviating the name from Men-nefru-Mire, which signified "The beauty of Mire abides." Mire was a king of the sixth dynasty, who in his time had extended the temple fortress about his royal quarters and built close by the pyramid wherein his beauty was to abide. It had actually been the tomb that had been called Men-nefru-Mire; but the whole city overlapping had taken over the name of the burial place: Menfe, the balance of the lands, the royal city of the dead.

How strange it was that the name Menfe was an impertinent abbreviation for a place of tombs! The idea occupied Joseph's mind a good deal. It was these little people thronging the narrow streets, with the gutters in the middle, who had run it all together like that; these lean-ribbed dwellers in the crowded poorer quarters of the town. In one such quarter was the caravanserai where the Ishmaelites lodged. It was crammed with strange specimens of the human race, Syrian, Libyan, Nubian, Mitannic, and even Cretan; its dirty brick court was full of the bleating of animals and the squealing and whining of blind beggars playing on musical instruments. If Joseph issued forth, the street scene was like that in the cities of the homeland as well, only Egyptian and much magnified. On either side of the gutter barbers were shaving their customers, and cobblers pulling straps with their teeth. Potters turned their whirling vessels and shaped them with practised and earthy hands, singing the while songs to Khnum the creator, goat-headed lord of the wheel. Coffin-makers planed coffins in human shape with chin-beards; drunken men staggered out of noisy pot-houses and were jeered at and mocked by little boys whose youth-locks still hung over their ears. What hordes of people! They all wore the same linen apron and the same haircut; had the same square shoulders and thin arms and lifted their brows in one and the same naïve and unabashed way. They looked quite capable of shortening the pomp and circumstance of death into the brisk and sprightly "Menfe." Joseph, when he heard it, recalled the feelings that possessed him when once, from his hill-top home, he looked down on Hebron, the burial-place of his ancestors, and piety, whose source is death, had mingled in his heart with the appeal made by the sight of the bustling town. A complex and delightful mixture, and one peculiarly his own. He felt its mysterious fitness in the light of the double blessing whose child he was. And also in the light of the jesting spirit which might be regarded as the link and messenger between them. To this latter, then, corresponded the popular name for the city of the dead; as a message from the jesting spirit; he felt his heart warm toward its inventors, those lean-ribbed little people along the gutters. He wanted to joke with them in their own tongue, to laugh and lift his eyebrows with their unconcern — that would not be hard.

Likewise he saw with sympathy that their love of the jest did not come from numbers alone, nor did it direct itself entirely outwards. The people of Menfe were making fun of themselves when they laughed about what their city once had been and was no longer. And their joke was an expression of the same sullenness which Joseph had felt in Per-Sopd when he listened to the bitter carping of the temple priests. It was the mood of the outmoded and the superseded; but here it turned into a mockery which misdoubted all the world, including itself. For the fact was, Menfe, the balance of the lands, thick-walled, had been the royal city at the time of the pyramid-builders. Menfe had been world-famous for endless years, and Thebes, in the upper southlands had not been known at all. But after the accursed epoch of confusion and foreign domination, it was from Thebes that liberation came, and reunion under the now ruling dynasty of the sun. It was Wese that now wore the double crown and bore the sceptre; while Menfe, though bursting with population and no smaller than before, was a former queen, the grave of her own greatness, a capital whose name was an impudently abbreviated name of death.

Not that Ptah, in his chapel, was a god rejected and impoverished, like Sopd in the east. No, great was his name among the regions, and rich in foundations, lands, and cattle was the god in human shape. So much was plain, from the treasuries, granaries, stalls, and hay-ricks included in the complex of his temples. The lord Ptah was seen of no one — for even when he made a progress in his bark and visited one or other local divinity, his little image was hidden behind golden curtains and only the priests who performed his service knew his face. He dwelt in his house, together with his wife, called Sakhmet or the Mighty, who was depicted lion-headed on the temple walls and who was said to love war, and their son Nefertem, whose name signified "the beautiful," but who was even more obscure than Ptah the human-formed and Sakhmet the grim. He was the son, more one knew not, nor did Joseph learn more by questioning than this: that Nefertem the son wore a lotus blossom on his head. It was even as-serted that he himself was nothing else than a blue-water-lily. This vagueness, however, did not prevent the son from being the most popular person of the Triad of Menfe. Since all that was certain about him was his preference for the sky-blue lotus, that became the essence of his being, and thus his dwelling was always richly adorned with bunches of that beautiful flower. The Ishmaelites did not hesitate to honour his popularity, in the way of trade, by bring-ing him offerings of the blue lotus.

Never had Joseph been so much among forbidden things as here, those things to which his tradition referred when it said: "Thou shalt make to thyself no graven image." For Ptah was the god who created works of art, the protector of masons and craftsmen, of whom it was said that the plans of his heart were realized and his thoughts carried out. Ptah's great dwelling was nothing but pictures; full of images his house and the courts thereof. Hewn out of the hardest, or out of lime and sandstone, wood and copper, the thoughts of Ptah peopled his halls; columns thick with shining scenes, resting on bases like millstones, elephant-like, and crowned with capitals like bun-dles of reeds, rose up to the gold-dusted beams. Statues were every-where, standing, sitting, striding, embraced on thrones with their diminutive children: single images of kings with caplike crowns and crooked staves, the pleated front piece of their kilts spread out on their laps; head-cloths with wings falling on the shoulders, on the front of which their ears stood out. These broad-shouldered, narrow-hipped lords of the earth had tender breasts, their hands lay flat on their thighs, their mien was high and grave. And their muscular upper arms were held by the clumsy little fingers of a tutelary goddess, while a falcon spread its wings in the nape of their necks. King Mire, who had made the city great, paced on his staff, a figure in copper, with his disproportionately small son at his side. He was fleshy of nose and lips; and like the other images was reluctant to lift from the ground the sole of his rear foot, but trod on both soles, standing in his walk and walking in his stance. They trod on sturdy legs, with heads erect, away from the stone pilasters at the back of their pedestals, and let their arms hang down from their square shoulders. In their clenched fists they held short, cylindrical pegs. Or they were represented as scribes, legs tucked under them, hands busy with the work spread out in their laps, looking out over it with shrewd eyes. Sometimes there was a man and wife, sitting beside each other with knees together, with their skin, hair, and garments painted in the most natural colours, so that they were like the living dead. Often Ptah's artists had made them eyes to frighten the beholder — not out of the material of their faces, but separately put in: a little black stone set in vitreous paste, with a little silver peg inside that which caught the light and glittered until one felt impelled to escape that flashing gaze and hid one's face in one's hands.

Such were the thoughts of Ptah. For ever fixed and rigid they dwelt there in his house, along with him, the lion mother, and the lotus son. He himself appeared in his human shape a hundred times over, in his chapel shrine, not an inch on whose walls but was covered with the magic of art. Yes, certainly in human shape, yet oddly doll-like and as it were in abstract form, a side view, with one leg and one long eye; his head covered with a close-fitting cap, on his chin the artificially attached wedge of the kingly beard. His whole figure was curiously undeveloped, sketched in outline as were his fists, which held the staff of power before him. He seemed to be sheathed in a close, formless upper garment, or rather, quite frankly, he looked swaddled and embalmed. . . . What was it about the lord Ptah? How did it stand with him? Did the ancient great city deserve its name, not only on account of the pyramids after which it was called, and not only because its glory was of the past, but further and finally, even solely, as the house of the lord Ptah? Joseph had understood whither he was bound when his purchasers led him down into Egypt, the land of Jacob's misprison. He had fully recognized that in consequence of his own estate he belonged thither and that the forbidden was not forbid to him, but even oddly appropriate. Indeed, he had not betimes given himself a name which should characterize him as native-born? And yet he had constantly felt a grudge against his new surroundings, in the sense of his father, and always he itched to try the children of the land with questions about their gods and about the land of Egypt itself, that they might betray it to him who knew and also themselves when they seemed not to know it rightly.

So was it with master baker Bata of Menfe, whom they met at the Apis-sacrifice in the temple of Ptah.

For besides the formless one, the lioness, the obscure son, and the concrete thoughts of Ptah, there abode in the temple Hapi, the great bull, the "repeating birth" of the lord, begot by a light-ray from the sky upon a cow which afterwards never bore again; and his testicles dangled as massive as those of Merwer at On. He lived behind bronze doors at the back of a roofless columned hall where wainscotings filled with magnificent stone-work ran between the pillars and fine mouldings at half their height. A dense crowd thronged the flag-paven court, when Hapi was brought forward by his servants some paces out of the lamplit twilight of his chapel stall that the people might see that the god lived and bring him offerings.

Joseph with his owners witnessed one such ceremony: it was an extraordinary abomination and an amusing one as well, thanks to the good nature of the folk of Menfe, men and women and sprawling children. They were excited by the festival and their expectation of the god; chattered and laughed, "kissed" (as they said for ate) sycamore figs and onions; water dripped from the corners of their mouths from the watermelon slices they ate; and they chaffered with the hucksters who lined the court selling consecrated bread, sacrificial fowl, frankincense, honey, and flowers.

A fat-bellied man in bast sandals stood next the Ishmaelites, and as the crowd squeezed them together, they spoke with each other. He wore a knee-length apron skirt of coarse linen with a three-cornered turnover; about his arms and rump he had wound all sorts of ribbons in which he tied knots with pious intent. His hair lay short and smooth on his round pate, he had a good-natured face, and his glassy protruding eyeballs protruded still more when his well-formed shaven mouth moved as he talked. He measured the old man and his company from one side for a long time before he addressed them and questioned them, curious of their strangeness, whence they came and whither they went. He himself was a baker, he explained; that is, he did not bake with his own hands and stuck not his head in the oven, but employed half a dozen journeymen and distributors who carried his excellent rolls and crescents in baskets on their heads through the city. Woe to these if they did not take pains to wave their arms above their wares so that the birds of the air did not pounce down and steal out of the basket! The bread-carrier to whom this happened "got a lesson," as master baker Bata expressed himself.

That was his name. Also he possessed some ground outside the city where he grew the corn he baked. But it was not enough, for his business was considerable and he had to buy as well. Today he had come out to see the god, which was profitable in so far that it was not profitable to omit it. His wife, meanwhile, was visiting the Great Mother in the Eset-house and taking her flowers, being especially affected to that goddess; while he, Bata, got more satisfaction from coming here. And as for them, the baker asked, they were visiting the country for their business interests?

That was it, the old man responded. And they were, so to speak, at their goal, in that they were at Menfe, mighty in gates, rich in dwellings and enduring monuments; and might just as well now turn around again.

"Thanks very much," said the master baker. The could, but probably they would not; for like everybody else they would more likely regard this old hole as a stage where to set their feet that they might pass on to the splendours of Amun. They would be the first to do otherwise, the first travellers whose goal was not Weset, the brand-new, Pharaoh's city — might he live, thrive, and be healthy! — where men and treasure streamed together and where Menfe's weather-beaten name was good enough to be used for titles by Pharoah's courtiers and head eunuchs; for instance the head baker of the god, he who had oversight over the palace baking, was called Prince of Menfe, and perhaps with some justice. At least so much was true, that at Menfe fine cakes in the shape of cows and snakes were carried round and sold when the Amun-city was still content to bolt down roasted corn.

The old man replied that, well, yes, they would probably go to Weset after a considerable sojourn at Menfe: to cast an eye and see how far it had come on since then in the refinements of life and the development of bakestuffs.

He was interrupted by a roll of drums; the rear gate opened and the god was led into the court, only a few paces forward from the open doors. The excitement of the crowd was great. "Hapi! Hapi!" they shrieked, as they hopped on one leg, and whom the crush permitted threw himself on his face and kissed the earth. Many backs were so bent, the air was full of the throaty mewing of the sound with which the hundredfold utterance of the god's name began. It was likewise the name of the river, which had made the land and which preserved it. It was the name of the sun-bull, the abstract of all the powers of fertility, on which these people knew themselves to depend, the name of the continued existence of land and folk, the name of life. They were deeply moved, light and garrulous though they might be, for their adoration was compact of all the hope and anxiousness with which narrowly conditioned existence fills the

breast. They thought of the flood, which must not be an ell too high
or too low if the land was to survive; of the industry of their wives
and the health of their children; of their own body and its functions subject to reverses, which gave them comfort and pleasure
when all went well but caused hard suffering when they gave out,
and which must be safeguarded by magic against magic. They
thought of the enemies of the land, south, east, and west; of Pharaoh,
whom also they called the "Strong Bull" and who they knew was
cherished and preserved in the palace at Thebes just as Hapi here,
for that he protected them and formed in his transitory person the
bridge between them and him on whom all depended. "Hapi! Hapi!"
they cried in anxious jubilation, oppressed by the sense of their narrowly conditioned, precarious lives. Hopefully they stared at the
square forehead of the beast-god, the brazen horns, the compact
neck-line, without a curve from back to skull; at his sex organs, the
pledge of fruitfulness. "Security!" was what they meant by their
cry. "Protection and permanence!" "Up Egypt!"

Vastly beautiful was Ptah's "repeating birth." And no wonder;
for experts spent years searching for the finest specimen between the
marshes of the Delta and the Elephant Isle. He was black; and his
blackness set off in great, not to say godlike splendour the scarlet
shabracke on his back. A bald-headed servitor, in an apron of pleated
gold stuff which left the naval free in front and reached behind
half-way up the back, held him on either side by a gold cord. The
one on the right hand lifted the cover a little before the eyes of the
people to display the white spot on Hapi's flank, in which one was
supposed to recognize the sign of the crescent moon. A priest, down
whose back hung a leopard-fell together with the claws and tail,
came and made obeisance. Then he stood with one leg before the
other and held out the incense vessel on a pole toward the bull, who
lowered his head, sniffed, and blew out his thick moist nostrils as
the smoke tickled them. He sneezed mightily; the crowd redoubled
its acclaim and hopped still more joyously on one leg. Harp-players
knelt, with their faces turned heavenwards, sang and played, while
behind them other singers clapped out the time, during the offering
of the incense. There were women too, temple maidens with unbound hair. One of them always naked and with a girdle for all
covering above the swelling hips; the second in a long garment, fine
like a veil, that stood open in front and likewise showed all her youth.
Pacing the scene in dance, they shook sistra and tambourines above
their heads, stretching and lifting their legs astonishingly high from
the hips. A priest-reader sitting at the feet of the bull with his face
to the crowd began to chant a text out of his roll, nodding his head
in time, while the people joined in the refrain: "Hapi is Ptah. Hapi
is Re. Hapi is Hor, the son of Eset!" After that appeared another

priest, bald-headed and of haughty mien, obviously of high rank
for he was escorted by bearers holding feather fans and wore a wide
batiste apron held on with shoulder-straps. He came on in a sort of
dextrous crawl, one leg far out behind him, the other, balanced on
its toes, tucked up beneath. He carried a gold basin of herbs and
spices, holding it up to the god with both arms outstretched.

Hapi paid no heed. He was used to all these ceremonial offerings;
to an existence of stately boredom which, thanks to a certain bodily
constitution, was become his melancholy lot in life. He stood there
straddle-legged, and looked loweringly with his little bloodshot
bull-eyes out over the ministrant's head at the populace, skipping
and hopping, one hand on their breasts, the other stretched toward
him, as they cried out his holy name. They were so glad to see him
held with golden strands, in the safe custody of the temple, hemmed
round by ministering guardians. He was their god and their prisoner.
And it was his imprisonment, the security it afforded them, that
gave rise to their exultation and made them jump about; and perhaps he looked so lowering and evilly upon them because he realized
that despite all the honours and ceremony they did not mean so well
by him after all.

Master-baker Bata did not jump about, on account of his corpulence. But he joined in the responses with a powerful voice and repeatedly saluted the god, prostrating himself and raising his arm,
visibly pleased by the spectacle.

"The sight of him does one good," he declared to his neighbour.
"It strengthens the spirits and restores one's confidence in life. My
experience is that I need to eat nothing more the whole day when
I have seen Hapi, for it is like a hearty meal of beef in all my limbs.
I am full and sleepy; I take a nap and awake as one new-born. He is
a very great god, the living representative of Ptah. You must know
that his grave awaits him in the West, the command hath gone out
that in death he shall be swaddled and embalmed in the most costly
manner with good resin and bands of royal linen and laid to rest
in the city of the dead according to custom in the eternal house of
the god-bull. So it is commanded," he said, "and so it will be. Already two Usar-Hapis rest in stone coffins in their eternal home in
the West."

The old man gave a glance at Joseph which the latter took as
encouragement to test the man with a question. He said:

"Ask the man to explain to you why he says that Usar-Hapi's
eternal home awaits him in the West; because it is not the West
where it waits, but Menfe, city of the living, itself lies on the west
bank, and no dead ferries across the water."

"This youth," the old man turned to the baker, "asks thus and
thus. Will you give him answer?"

"I spoke as they speak," responded the Egyptian, "and took no thought of the phrase, and so do we all. The West, that is the city of the dead, according to our speech. But it is true that Menfe's dead travel not across the river as elsewhere, but the city of the living lies also and already in the West. According to reason your youth is right with his objection. But according to our speech I spoke correctly."

"Ask him this too," said Joseph. "If Hapi, the beautiful bull, is the living Ptah for the living, what then is Ptah in his chapel?"

"Ptah is great," answered the baker.

"Tell him I do not doubt that," Joseph replied. "But Hapi is called Usar-Hapi when he has died; and again Ptah in his bark is Usir and called in human form because the figure has the form with the chin-beard, on which the joiners work, and he seems swaddled. What is he then?"

"Instruct your youth," said the baker to the old man, "that the priest enters daily to Ptah and opens his mouth with a powerful instrument that he may eat and drink, and renews daily for him the paint of life upon his cheeks. That is the service and the cherishing."

"And now I would ask, with all due politeness," Joseph continued, "what about the dead before his burial, when Anpu stands behind him, and wherein for instance the service may consist which the priest practises on the mummy?"

"Does he not even know that, your youth?" answered the baker. "It is plain that he is a sand-dweller, wholly foreign and a new-comer in the land. The service, so I would have him told, consists in the so-called opening of the mouth, above all. It is called that because the priest therewith opens the mouth with a special staff that the god may eat and drink again and enjoy the edible offerings. Therefore is it that the priest of the dead, in sign that the dead like Usir will live again, puts the blush of rouge on the mummy for a consolation to the hearts of the mourners."

"I hear with gratitude," Joseph said. "This then is the difference between the service of the gods and that of the dead. But now ask the lord Bata wherewithal one builds in the land of Egypt."

"Your youth," answered the baker, "is good to look upon but somewhat stupid. We build for the living with Nile bricks. But the abodes of the dead as well as the temples are of everlasting stone."

"I hear," Joseph answered again, "with many thanks. But if of two things the same holds, then they are like and one may interchange them unreproved. The graves of Egypt are temples, but the temples —"

"Are houses of God," finished the baker.

"You have said it. The dead of Egypt are gods; and your gods — what are they?"

"The gods are great," replied Bata the baker. "I feel it in the fullness and fatigue which steal over me now I have seen Hapi. I will go home and lay myself down to the sleep of new birth. Also my wife will have come back from waiting on the Great Mother. Be healthy, ye strangers. Rejoice and rest in peace!"

With that he went. But the old man said to Joseph:

"The man was worn out with God; thou shouldest not have pressed him through my mouth with petty questionings."

"But must not," the other justified himself, "thy slave inform himself that he may find himself with understanding of life in Egypt, where thou wilt leave him and he will abide? Strange and novel enough is everything here for the youth. For the children of Egypt worship in tombs, whether they be called temples or eternal dwellings; but we at home worship after the custom of our fathers beneath the green trees. Shall not one laugh and ponder at thought of these children? They call Hapi the living form of Ptah, and such, it seems to me, Ptah can use, as he himself is certainly embalmed and is a corpse. But they rest not until they have also wrapped up the living form and made out of it an Osiris and god-mummy; until then there is something wrong about it. But I like Menfe itself, whose dead need not to travel across the water because it already lies in the West — this great city so full of people, who so blithely make a nickname of its solemn form. It is a pity that the house of blessing before which you will bring me, Petepre the fan-bearer's house, lieth not at Menfe, for it pleaseth me among the cities of Egypt."

"Thou art much too unripe," the old man answered him, "to distinguish what is good for thee. But I know, and procure it for thee like a father. For such I evidently am to thee, assuming that thy mother is the grave. Tomorrow early we take ship and sail nine days long through the land of Egypt, southwards up the river, that we may set our feet on the shining shore of Weset-per-Amur the royal city."

Chapter III

THE ARRIVAL

RIVER JOURNEY

"Shining in Swiftness" was the name of the boat on which the Ishmaelites embarked with their animals, after providing themselves from the booths at the landing-place with food for nine days' travel. The name was written on both sides of its goose-head prow. And the empty boat was characteristic of the country, for it was the clumsiest freighter to be found anywhere on Menfe's landing-places; with a bellying hold built for cargo space, latticed wooden weatherboards, a cabin consisting only of a mat-covered shelter opening forward, and a tiny but very heavy rudder fastened perpendicularly to a pole at the stern.

The pilot was named Thot-nofer. He was a man from the north, in ear-rings, with white hair on head and breast. The old man had made his acquaintance at the hostel and covenanted with him for a cheap passage. Thot-nofer's ship carried lumber, one bale of royal and one of coarse linen, papyrus, neatskins, ship's rope, twenty sacks of lentils, and thirty casks of dried fish. "Shining in Swiftness" also had on board the portrait statue of a rich burgher of Thebes, standing quite forward at the peak, done up in slats and sacking. It was for the "good house" — in other words, for the grave — of the man who had ordered it, west of the river. It would be set up as issuing from an imitation door to behold his everlasting goods and the representations of his daily life painted on the walls. To be sure, the eyes by which he might do this were not yet set, the figure was not yet coloured with the tints of life, and the stick was lacking that should go through the fist extended along the slantwise front of his projecting skirt. But its model had set store by having at least his double chin and his thick legs executed in the rough under the eyes of Ptah and by the hand of Ptah's artists; the last touches might be given in some workshop in Thebes, the city of the dead.

At midday the crew untied the ship from the pile and raised the patched brown sail, which at once filled with the strong north wind. The pilot sitting on the slanting beak in the stern of the boat began to operate the rudder with the perpendicular lever; a man at the goose-head in the prow tested the channel with a pole; while Thot-nofer, the ship-master, propitiated the gods by burning in front of the cabin some of the resin with which the Ishmaelites had paid their fares. Thus the boat bearing Joseph moved upstream, curving fore and aft and cutting the water only with the middle of her keel; while the old man, sitting with his party on the lumber piled behind the cabin, extended himself in observations on the wisdom of life; how almost always the advantages so equalized and cancelled each other that the result was a moderate perfection, not too good and not too bad. Thus one travelled upstream against the current; but on the other hand the wind came regularly from the north and swelled the sail to advantage so that the two contrary forces resulted in mod-erate progress. Of course, it was all very fine, sailing downstream, for one could let oneself be borne by it. But it was easy for the boat to get out of hand, it might go crosswise of the stream and give no end of trouble with the steering to avoid accidents. Thus in life the advantages were always balanced by the disadvantages and vice versa, and the result, mathematically, might seem to be nil; but in practice it was a wise balance and an average felicity; in view of which neither jubilation nor cursing but real satisfaction was in place. For perfection consisted not in one-sided heaping up of ad-vantages until life became impossible on the other. Rather it con-sisted in the mutual cancellation of disadvantage and advantage, and the result was called contentment.

So the old man, with uplifted finger and head on one side. His people listened open-mouthed, but exchanged abashed and sulky looks, as ordinary people do when listening unwillingly to the claims of the higher life. Nor did Joseph give more than half an ear to the old man's prosing; for he was rejoicing in the new experience of the water journey, the fresh wind, the melodious chuckling of the waves against the bow, the gentle rocking and gliding on the wide river, whose tide came sparkling toward him as once to Eliezer the earth, upon his travels. The shore afforded a changing succession of gay or luxuriant or sacred scenes; pillared halls often stood on the banks, sometimes with palm groves before them, but just as often stone roads built by men, belonging to the temples of the city. Villages glided past, with high dove-cotes and green orchards; and again gay and splendid cities with spires glittering golden to the sun, and pennanted gates. Pairs of statues of enormous size sat stately and rigid with their hands on their knees and gazed from the bank across the river and the land, into the desert. Sometimes it was all quite close, and then far away; for they moved at times in the centre of a river whose waters had widened to a lake; or again wound in curves be-hind which new scenes of Egypt unfolded. But life on the sacred river itself, the great highway of Egypt, was hugely diverting. How many sails, fine and coarse, swelled in the wind, how many rudders stemmed themselves in its flood! The carrying air was full of voices: the jokes and halloos of sailors, the warning cries of the polesmen at the prow as the boat approached eddies and sandbanks; the chanting calls of seamen on the cabin roofs to sailors and pilots below. Common boats like Thot-nofer's there were in hordes; but also fine slender barks met and hailed "Shining in Swiftness" or overtook her. They were painted blue, with a short mast and a broad dove-coloured sail, which bellied in a charming swell; their beaks were shaped like the lotus flower and they had dainty pavilions instead of a rude board cabin. The temple barks had purple sails and large pictures painted on the side; the private yachts of the great and mighty boasted twelve oarsmen on a side, and on the deck a pillared pleasure-house with the owner's luggage and chariot stowed on the roof. Its walls were formed by splendid carpets, and in it sat the lordly owner, hands in his lap, fixed, as it were congealed, in beauty and richness and looking neither right nor left. They even met a funeral procession of three ships fastened together, and on the rear one, a white bark without rudder or sail, the bright-coloured Osiris, head to the prow, lay amongst his mourners, on a lion-footed bier.

Yes, there was much to see, on river and shore. Joseph, on whom the joys of a water journey had never smiled before, on such a one as this now found the days pass like hours. He was to grow used indeed to this kind of travel and to this very stretch between Amun's house and grave-jesting Menfe! Very like these mighty ones in their carpet-hung chapels he himself would one day sit, with the prescribed and stately immobility which he would have to learn because the common folk expected it from gods and great ones. For he was to bear himself so shrewdly and prove himself so skilled in his dealings with God as to become the first among those of the West and entitled to sit there looking neither right nor left. This was reserved for him. But meanwhile he looked right and left all he could round about in the land and the life of the land, to take it into his spirit and senses, always mindful lest his curiosity should express itself in amazement and futility instead of keeping a certain due and blithe reserve for the father's sake.

Thus the evening and morning were another day and so the days increased. Menfe lay behind them, and the day when they sailed hence. The sun sank down, the desert distance turned violet-blue; the Arabian sky on their left gave back a softened glow from the extravagant orange of the western, Libyan sky. Where they found themselves at nightfall they tied up and slept, to float on next day. The wind favoured them, with exception of the days when it fell. Then they had to row, and the slave Usarsiph, also the younger

Ishmaelites, helped at the oars; for the boat had no large crew, and Thot-nofer was anxious not to lose time, for he had promised to deliver the statue by a certain date. They were in fact not greatly delayed; for when the wind blew, it filled the sails the fuller, and thus advantage and disadvantage were resolved in satisfaction. On the ninth evening they saw some jagged heights rising rosy and translucent in the distance. They looked like red corundum, and very beautiful, though, as everyone knew, they were barren and accursed like all the mountains of Egypt. The pilot and the old man recognized them as Amun's mountains, the heights of No; and when they had slept and sailed again and even taken in sheer impatience to the oars — at last they saw it, it came nearer, Pharaoh's famous city, glittering with gold, greeting their eyes with shimmering rainbow colours. They entered it while still on the boat and without going on shore, for the river became a splendid boulevard and flowed between rows of celestial structures, of temples and palaces amid green gardens of delight; all this both right and left, on the shore of life as well as on the shore of death. There were papyrus colonnades and lotus colonnades, gold-tipped obelisks, colossal statues, turreted gates with sphinx avenues leading to them from the bank. Their doors and flag-poles were gilded, and light flashed from them that dazzled the eyes, till the painted scenes and inscriptions on the buildings, the cinnamon red, the plum-colour, the emerald green, the ochre yellow, and the azure blue all swam together into one confused sea of colour.

"That is Ipet-Isowet, 'Amun's Great House,'" said the old man to Joseph, pointing with his finger. "It has a hall fifty ells wide, with fifty-two columns and pillars like tent-poles, and the hall itself, if it please thee, is paved with silver."

"Surely it pleaseth me," Joseph answered. "I knew, of course, that Amun is a very rich god."

"Those are the shipyards of the god," said the old man again, pointing to the basins and dry-docks on the left, where numerous apron-wearers, the god's carpenters, were at work with drills, hammers, and picks on skeletons of ships. "There is Pharaoh's temple of the dead and there his house of life," said he and pointed here and there westwards into the land to various blocks of buildings in character both magnificent and charming at once. "That is Amun's southern house of women," turning toward the other side to point out an expanse of temple precincts on the bank. The sun glared against their façades, the shadows cast by their projections were sharp and black. Hordes of men were bustling about, engaged in building-activities.

"Dost thou see this beauty? Dost thou see the shrine of the mystery of the kingly conception? Dost thou see where Pharaoh buildeth another hall in front of the hall and the court, with taller columns than all the rest? That, my friend, is Nowet-Amun, the proud, which we see. Observe then the ram avenue that runneth from the southern house of women to the great house. Five thousand ells long is it, let me tell thee, bordered right and left with Amun-rams bearing Pharaoh's image between their legs."

"All very nice," said Joseph.

"Nice!" said the old man, firing up. "Thou choosest me words out of the treasury of speech so inept as to be comic, I must say. Thou hast pleased me little indeed with thy response to the marvels of Weset."

"I did say *very* nice," replied Joseph. "As nice as thou wilt. But where is the house of the fan-bearer before which thou wilt bring me? Canst thou show it to me from here?"

"No, that one cannot make out from here," responded the elder. "It lieth toward the western desert, where the city thinneth out, losing itself in villas and lordly gardens."

"And wilt thou take me even today before the house?"

"Thou canst not well expect that I shall take thee thither and sell thee? Dost thou know then that the steward of the house will take thee and offer enough for thee that I am paid for my outgo and get a little just profit therefrom? It is some changes of the moon since I released thee out of thy mother the well and some days that thou hast baked me pancakes and fetched new words out of thy storehouse to wish me good-night. So that it may be the time has grown long to thee and thou weariest of us and would seek new service. Yet it might as well have been that the many days had made habit with thee, so that thou couldst not lightly part from thy rescuer, the old Minæan from Ma'on, but be content to wait the hour till he goeth away and leaveth thee in the hands of strangers. Either of these might issue out of the many days of our wandering together."

"The latter," answered Joseph, "quite incontestably the latter is the reality. Of a surety I am in no haste to part from thee, my deliverer. My only haste is that I may arrive whither God will have me."

"Content thyself," replied the old man. "We will land and submit oursleves to the troublesome formalities which the children of Egypt lay upon us, and which will take a long time. After that we will go to a hostel that I know in the city's heart, and there spend the night. But tomorrow I will bring thee before the house of blessing and offer thee to my friend the house-steward, Mont-kaw."

While they were talking they had come to port, or rather to the place where the boat should tie up, crossing over from the middle of the stream while Thot-nofer burned more balsam in front of the cabin, as a thank-offering for their safe journey. The landing was as troublesome and time-consuming as only such journeys anywhere ever were or are. They came into the noise and bustle of the landing-stage and the water in front of it, where there was a congestion of ships native and foreign either already tied up or looking for a landing-place to fling their rope when a post was free. "Shining in Swiftness" was docked by the port authorities and customs officials, who began to make entries of great and small, of mice and men, and every piece of freight, while on shore the servants of the owner of the statue stretched out their arms and shrieked their demands for its delivery. There were many pedlars of sandals, caps, and honey cakes; their cries mingled with the bleating of herds being unshipped close by and the music of jugglers trying to call attention to themselves on the quay. It was a vast confusion; Joseph and his companions sat still and shrinking on the lumber at the stern of their boat and awaited the moment when they could get off and seek their hostel. But it was still remote. The old man had to come before the customs in person, to vouch for himself and each of his party and pay the harbour dues for his wares. He was shrewd enough to establish human relations instead of official ones; so that the authorities laughed and joked, accepted small presents, and were not too precise about the landing rules for stranger merchants. A few hours after they had tied up, the owners of Joseph were able to lead their camels across the gang-plank and, quite unnoticed by a crowd used to the sight of any and every complexion and costume, to make their way through the mingled tumult of the port quarter.

JOSEPH GOES THROUGH WESE

THE EGYPTIAN city whose name the Greeks later adapted for their own convenience and called it Thebai was, when Joseph landed and lived there, by no means at the height of its fame, although already famous, as can be gathered from the way the Ishmaelites spoke of it and the feelings Joseph entertained when he found himself at his journey's end. From dark and small beginnings in the long-ago, it had waxed and was on the way to full splendour. Yet much still lacked before its glory was complete and it paused perfected, one of the seven wonders of the world. It was this as a whole; but also and indeed principally in one of its parts, the unique and marvellous vast columned hall which a later Pharaoh, named Ramessu, or "The Sun hath begotten him," added to the group of buildings which composed the great Amun-temple in the north, at an expense commensurate with the renown of the god. Of this hall, then, Joseph's eyes beheld as little as they had of the departed glories in the environs of the pyramids, only on contrary grounds. The hall had not yet achieved any presentness and no one had yet had courage to imagine it. To make it possible, something had to precede it, which then as men tired of it and it could no longer satisfy their difficult imaginations would be superseded by something else. There was, for instance, the silver-paved hall of Ipet-Isowet, built by the three predecessors of the present god. The old man knew it, with its fifty-two columns like tent-poles. Or there was the hall which Pharaoh himself, as Joseph had seen, was having added to Amun's southern house of women, the beautiful temple on the river; it excelled all the rest. And this beauty must first be imagined and then realized in the faith that it was the uttermost man could perform, before man's insatiable imagination could use it as a springboard for the actually uttermost, the unsurpassable beauty of a final achievement — in other words, the wonder of the world, the Great Hall of Rameses.

This, then, in Joseph's and our time, was not yet present, but only, as it were, on the way. None the less, Weset, also called Nowet-Amun, chief city on the river Nile, was even at this time a marvel to all the world both near and far, wherever it was known. Report even exaggerated the marvel, making it a point of honour and a convention, as men love to do, if only by hearsay; so that a man would have been looked at askance and considered outside the pale who had dared to doubt in public that No in the land of Egypt was beautiful beyond word or measure, the abstract of all architectural magnificence and simply a dream of a city. We come down to her, down in a spatial sense — that is, with Joseph up the river — but down in a temporal sense as well: namely, into the past where at moderate depth Wese still lies, still glitters, still resounds with the busy tumult of her streets, still mirrors her temples clear and sharp in the stirless surface of her sacred lakes. And coming thus, we must feel about Wese a little as we did about Joseph himself when we first glimpsed beside the fountain that form so besung and belauded in saga and psalm. We traced back the fantastic legend of his loveliness to its source in the opinion of his own time and found that, even discounting all trumped-up exaggerations, quite enough remained of beauty and of charm. So too with No, the heavenly city. It was not compact of any supernal stuff, but built of painted bricks mixed with straw, like any other city; its streets, as Joseph noted with satisfaction, were as narrow, crooked, foul, and ill-smelling as the streets of any man-made city large or small ever have been and will be in this part of the world. At least, they were so in the poorer quarters, which as usual were much more numerous than the richer sections, these indeed being most spacious and charming. True, it was said and sung, even to the uttermost isles and the coasts beyond, that Wese's houses "were rich in treasure," and in the temples they measured their gold with a scoop. But of such houses there could be but a few, those which Pharaoh had enriched; the great majority held no treasures at all, but were as mean as those of the very island-dwellers and denizens of the further coasts, who sunned themselves in the legendary glory of Wese's fame.

As for the size of No, it passed for enormous, and it was. That is, if we add that the word "enormous" has not one simple, unequivocal meaning, but is a relative conception, depending on who applies it and to what it is applied. For instance, the chiefest monument of Wese's greatness is a good example of the kind of misunderstanding which can arise. I refer to her reputation as the "city of a hundred gates." On Cyprus-Alashia, on Crete and places yet more remote, she was called in extravagant awe the "hundred-gated"; and it was related that forth from each of these hundred gates two hundred men with steed and harness might ride abreast to battle. Such prattle as this took for granted a ring wall so large round that it could be broken not by four or five but by a hundred city gates, an utterly childish conception, only possible to those who had never seen Wese with their mortal eyes but known it only from legend and hearsay. The Amun-city might with some justice have been called the "many-gated," for it had in fact many "gates." But these were not gates in the sense of sally-ports in the wall. The word referred to the pylons with which the wearers of the double crown had on the occasions of ju-bilees and great progresses from time to time adorned and comple-mented the shrines of the gods. For indeed of these there were very many, and mighty they were, shining and bright with the colours of their high reliefs and wonder-working inscriptions, blithe with pen-nants that fluttered above their gilded flag-staffs. And more were added, between the time of which I write and the epoch of Wese's full and incomparable bloom. A hundred there were not, either now or later. But a hundred is only a round number; even on our own lips it often means no more than simply "very many." Amun's great dwelling in the north, Ipet-Isowet, had at this time six or seven such "gates" and the smaller temples near it, the houses of Khonsu, Mut, Mont, Min, and the hippopotamus-formed Ipet, had several. The other large temple on the riverbank, known as Amun's southern house of women, otherwise simply the harem, had towered gates too, and still others belonged to the smaller shrines of deities not actually indigenous here, yet settled and provided with nourish-ment: the houses of Usir and Eset, Ptah of Menfe, Thoth, and many more.

These temple precincts, with their gardens, groves, and lakes, formed the kernel of the city; they were the city itself, and the dwell-ings of the profane and human simply filled the spaces between, ex-tending, that is, from the port quarters on the south and Amun's house of women to the temple complex in the north-east. Across it lengthwise ran the great triumphal road of the god, the ram-sphinx avenue which the old man had pointed out to Joseph from the boat. It was a considerable area, and five thousand ells in length. To the north-east the triumphal avenue curved landwards and the residen-

tial city filled the widening space between it and the river; while on
the other side it spread out toward the eastern desert, where it lost itself in fine gardens and villas — where indeed "the houses were rich
in treasure." So that in actual fact the city was large, enormous if you
like; more than a hundred thousand people were said to live in it.
If a hundred was an exaggerated figure for the gates, a sort of poetic
licence, certainly on the other hand a hundred thousand for the population of Wese erred on the low side. If we may trust our own estimate and Joseph's, it was not only larger but very much larger, even
possibly double and treble that figure. Quite definitely so, if one include the inhabitants of the city of the dead over in the West, across
the river, called "opposite their lord"; not the dead, of course, but
those living who dwelt there for professional reasons, having some
serious task, either ritual or mechanical, connected with the service
of the departed who had gone over the water. These, then, and their
dwellings were a city in themselves, which, added to the size of Wese,
made the whole exceedingly large. And among them was Pharaoh
himself, who did not live in the city of the living, but without in the
West; on the edge of the desert, under its red rocks, there lay his
palace in all its airy grace and there the pleasure-gardens of his palace, with their lake and pleasure-waters, which earlier had not been
there.

A very great city, then — great not alone in its extent and the number of its inhabitants, but even more in the intensity of its inner life
and the racial variegations which made it gay and lively like a country fair. Wese was great as kernel and focus of the world. It considered itself the navel of the world — a piece of presumption in Joseph's
eyes, and even otherwise debatable. After all, there was Babel on the
Euphrates, that flowed the other way; in Babel they were convinced
that Egypt's stream flowed the wrong way; and they had no doubt
that round about Bab-ilu the rest of the world was grouped in an admiring circle. Though there, too, in respect of building-activities
they had not yet reached the fullness of beauty. But it was not without reason that they liked in Joseph's home to say of the Amun-city
that "Nubians and Egyptians without number were their strength
and folk from Punt and Libyans were their auxiliaries." Even on his
way with the Ishmaelites from the port to the hostel which lay in the
heart of the narrow inner city, Joseph received a hundred impressions which confirmed the legend. Nobody looked at him and his;
strangers were the daily fare, and his companions were not crass
enough in their strangeness to cause remark. He might gaze undisturbed, his only care being lest his spiritual pride be encroached upon
by the sight of so great a world; fear of falling prey to diffidence
made him look with reserve on what he saw.

And what all did he not see, on the way from the harbour to the inn! What treasures of merchandise swelled the bazaars! How the streets teemed and seethed with every kind and breed of the children of Adam! All the citizenry of Wese seemed to be on their legs, to be impelled to move from one end of the city to the other and back; while with these natives mingled human types and costumes from the four corners of the earth. By the landing-stage there had been a noisy crowd about a group of ebony-black Moors with incredibly thick, swollen lips, and ostrich feathers on their heads: men and animal-eyed women with breasts like wineskins and absurd children in baskets on their backs. The men were leading animals on chains: horribly whining panthers and baboons walking on all fours; a giraffe towered up, tall as a tree in front and like a horse behind. There were greyhounds too. And the Moors carried bundles covered with cloth of gold, whose contents doubtless corresponded to the value of the wrapping. Probably it was gold and ivory. These, Joseph learned, were a tribute-bearing mission from the land of Kush, southwards beyond the land of Wewet, far up the river. Only a very small, non-compulsory, and irregular tribute, sent by the governor of the southern lands, viceroy and prince of Kush, as a surprise for Pharaoh and to rejoice his heart, that he might be favourably mindful of the prince and not take it into his head to recall him and replace him by one of the gentlemen in the royal entourage who had been dinning in Pharaoh's ears at every levee that the holder of the valuable office up the river was quite unworthy of his charge. The strange thing was that these harbour hands who gaped at the embassy, these street gamins who laughed at the palm-tree neck of the giraffe, were perfectly informed about the inner history, the viceroy's anxiety and the carping of Pharaoh's courtier. Joseph and the Ishmaelites heard them comment on these things in loud and certain tones. A pity, thought Joseph, that sophistication must mar their pure and simple pleasure in the picturesque spectacle. But perhaps it only added spice. He himself was glad to hear their talk. It was good to get a side-light on such matters; to learn that the prince of Kush trembled for his office; that the courtiers intrigued against him; and that Pharaoh liked to be surprised. The knowledge strengthened his confidence and armed him against humility.

The Negroes, in charge of Egyptian officials, were ferried over the river to stand before Pharaoh; Joseph watched them go. More of their colour he saw as he made his way with his owners; but in fact he saw every shade of skin, from obsidian-black through all the tones of brown and yellow to cheese-white. He saw even yellow hair and bright blue eyes, faces and garments of every cut; he saw the human race. For the foreign ships with which Pharaoh traded very often did not stop in the ports of the Delta region but sailed with the north wind up-river to unload their tribute of freight and goods for exchange on the spot whither everything came at last: namely, Pharaoh's treasure-house, that he might therewith enrich Amun and his friends, enabling the former to enlarge his demands in respect of building-activties and surpass anything previously built. As for the friends, the gifts of Pharaoh refined their lives to the last degree, making them so fastidious that from refinement they fell, indeed, into foppery.

These things the old man explained to Joseph. And thus it was Joseph saw, among the people of Wese, Moors from Kush; Bedus from the land of God this side the Red Sea; pale-faced Libyans from the oases of the western desert, in gay woven skirts and plaits standing out straight from their heads; Amu people and Asiatics like himself in coloured woollens with the beards and noses of his own land; Hattite men from beyond the Amanus range, in tight shirts and with their hair in bags; Mitanni traders in the dignified fringed and draped garb of Babel; merchants and seafarers from the islands and from Mycenæ, in white woollen robes with beautifully falling folds, wearing bronze rings on their bare arms. So much he saw, even though the old man modestly led his troop as much as possible through the poorer streets and avoided the finer quarters in order not to offend their beauty. But it was not possible to spare them quite. There was the beautiful street of Khonsu, which ran parallel to the triumphal avenue of the god, "the Street of the Son," as it was called. Khons, related to the moon, was son of Amun and Mut, his Baalat; he was in Thebes what Nefertem the blue lotus was at Menfe, and with his exalted parents he made up the Triad of Weset. The street of Khons, then, was a main artery; a real Abrek avenue, where it was always well to take heed to one's heart. The Ishmaelites had to traverse it, for a distance long enough to expose them to the full danger of its splendours. Joseph saw the ministries of the treasury and the granaries and the palace where the sons of Syrian city princes were brought up; wonderful and spacious erections of brick and fine woods, brilliant with colours. He saw chariots roll past, covered all over with hammered gold, wherein the lords of the earth stood and swung the lash over the backs of steeds prancing and rolling their eyeballs, snorting fire from their nostrils and foam from their jaws. Their legs were like deer's legs, their heads were drawn in on their chests and crowned with ostrich feathers. He saw sedan-chairs pass, carried on shoulder-poles, in easy swinging tread, by tall youths wearing gold aprons. The chairs were carven, gilded, and canopied and men sat in them with their hands hidden in their garments, their lacquered hair stroked back from brow to neck, their eyelashes cast down; condemned by rank to immobility. At their backs a screen of reeds and painted linen sheltered them from the wind. Who was it who one day should sit like that and be borne before his house, which

Pharaoh had enriched? That lies in the future; our narrative has not yet reached that hour and feast, though where it lies it is already present and known of all. For the time Joseph, of course, only saw what he once would be; gazed upon it with eyes as large and strange as those which would rest on him or cringe before him, the foreign great man — young slave Osarsiph, son of the well, stolen and sold hither, in ragged shirt and hood, with dirty feet, pushed to the wall by soldiers who came dashing by in even, shining ranks, amid blare of trumpets, armed with shields, bows, and clubs, bristling with lances, down the Street of the Son. He took these grim ranks for Pharaoh's soldiery; but by the standards and the insignia on the shields the old man recognized that they were troops of the gods, temple soldiery, the strength of Amun. What, thought Joseph, had then Amun armies and bodies of soldiers like Pharaoh? He did not like it; and not wholly because the squad had pinned him to the wall. He was conscious of jealousy on Pharaoh's account; on account of the question who was the greatest here. The proximity of Amun's pride and fame in any case oppressed him. He took comfort in the presence of another Highness, namely Pharaoh's own; and the thought that this idol rivalled him in his own field, that he even kept an army, angered him. He thought to guess that it angered Pharaoh too and took his side against the arrogant deity.

But soon they left the Street of the Son, not to mar it any longer, and by narrow lanes came to the inn called Sippar Court because its owner and host was a Chaldæan from Sippar on the Euphrates and took by preference Chaldæan folk to lodge, though all sorts of other folk as well. It was called a court because it was almost nothing but a well and courtyard, quite as full of dirt, noise, and smells, bleating of herds, quarrelling of men, and squealing of mountebanks as the inn at Menfe; and even that very evening the old man struck up a little trade and had a run of customers. They slept under their mantles, and had to take turns, all except the old man, in standing watch lest valuables be stolen from the packs and treasures by their very doubtful fellow-lodgers. They had to wait their turn to wash themselves at the well, then they breakfasted on a sort of pap which was served to them, a Chaldæan dish prepared from sesame, called pappasu. At last the old man said, not looking at Joseph as he spoke:

"Now then, my friends — thou, Mibsam, my son-in-law, Epher, my nephew, and Keder and Kedema, my sons — we will leave here toward sunrise with our goods and offerings in the direction of the desert where the city leaves off among the dwellings of the great. For I have acquaintance there and folk with needs, who I hope will be ready to buy from our packs this and that for their storehouses and to pay us so that we come not on our own cost but pocket a good advantage and enrich ourselves conformably to our rôle as

traders on this earth. Load, then, our goods upon the beasts and saddle me mine that I may lead the van."

Thus it came about. And they drew out of Sippar Court toward
the gardens of the rich. In front Joseph led the old man's dromedary
by a long rein.

JOSEPH COMES BEFORE PETEPRE'S HOUSE

THEY went toward the desert and the hot desert hills where Re rose
in the morning; and their road lay into the land of God, in front of
the Sea of the Red Earth. It was a level road and they went along it
just as they had entered into the Vale of Dothan, only that now it
was not the thick-lipped youth named Jupa but Joseph who led the
old man's beast. They came on a buttressed ring wall, long and embracing, out of whose inner precinct towered beautiful trees, sycamores, honey-locusts, date-palms, figs, and pomegranates, and the
tops of buildings, shining white or gay with colour. Joseph looked
over at them and then at his master to learn from his face whether
this was the abode of the fan-bearer, for it was obviously the house
of one with the blessing. But the old man was looking straight before
him, with his head on one side; they went along the wall and he
showed nothing until it rose to a tower and a covered gateway; there
he stopped.

In the shadow of the gateway was a brick bench on which sat boys
in aprons, four or five, playing a game with their fingers. The old
man looked down on them awhile from his beast, till they began to
heed. They dropped their hands in their laps and looked at him, raising their brows in pretended amazement, to put him out of countenance.

"Be of good cheer," said the old man.

"Rejoice," answered they, shrugging their shoulders.

"What sort of monkey-shines may they have been," asked he,
"which you broke off because I came?"

They looked at each other and laughed in turn.

"Because you came?" one repeated. "We stopped out of distaste
at your own monkey-shines, old pedlar!"

"Must you improve your knowledge here, old sand-rabbit," cried
a second, "on this very spot and nowhere else, that you ask about
our game?"

"I have indeed something to peddle," responded the old man,
"only not monkey-shines, however complete my pack, for I know
not the ware, but take it from your distaste that you have a superfluity of it yourselves. Hence then probably your need of diversion,
which, if I be not mistaken, you satisfy by the amusing game of
'How many fingers?' "

"Well, then?" they asked.

"I only inquired in passing and by way of preliminary," he went on. "Is this, then, the house and garden of the noble Petepre, fan-bearer on the right hand?"

"Whence know you that?" they asked.

"My memory instructs me," he answered, "and your answer confirms it. But you, as it seems, are set as watchers at the gate of the exalted man to announce the familiar guests?"

"Then you are familiar guests? Bush-rangers and snappers-up from the desert! You would sell us a sell, old man!"

"Young guardian of the gate and bringer of tidings," retorted the Ishmaelite, "you deceive yourself, and your knowledge of the world is unripe as green figs. We are no snappers-up and fly-by-nights, but hate all such and are their true opposite in the scheme of things. For we are travelling traders, who go here and there between kingdoms and make fine connections so that we are well received, as everywhere else so here too and in this house, whose storehouses gape for our wares. For the moment we stand rebuffed by your lack of manners. But I counsel you, become not guilty before Mont-kaw, your head, who is over the house and calls me his friend and treasures my treasures. Rather fulfil the service which is vouchsafed you in the scheme of things and run to announce to the steward the well-known travelling traders from Ma'on and from Mosar — in short, the Midianite merchants are once more at hand with good things for the house's chambers and barns."

The watchers had exchanged looks at hearing him name the name of the steward. Now said he whom the Ishmaelite had addressed, a chubby-cheeked, narrow-eyed lad:

"How then shall I announce you to him? Bethink yourself of that, old man, and go your ways. Can I come running to him and say: 'The Midianites from Mosar are at hand, therefore have I left the gate where at midday the lord will enter, and run to disturb you'? He will call me the son of a dog and take me by the ear. He is settling accounts in the bakery and speaking with the scribe of the buffet. He has more to do than to haggle with you about your wares. Therefore go hence."

"It is pity for you, young door-keeper," said the old man, "that you make yourself a hindrance between me and my years-long friend Mont-kaw, standing between us like a river full of crocodiles and a mountain of impassable steepness. Are you not called Sheshi?"

"Sheshi! Ha ha!" laughed the gate-keeper. "I am called Teti."

"It is all the same," responded the old man. "It is only my pronunciation and because in my old age some teeth are lacking me that I spoke it otherwise. Well then, Tshetshi — though that is no better, alas! — let me see if a dry ford does not lead through the river and

mayhap a curving path round the steepness of the mount. You have
made a blunder in calling me a snapper-up, but here" — he put his
hand in his garment — "is something of the sort, and very pretty too,
that belongs to you if you will run and announce me and bring
hither Mont-kaw. There, take it from my hand. It is but a small example of my treasures. Look, the sheath is of hardest wood, finely
etched, and has a slot out of which you push the diamond-sharp
blade, and lo, there is the knife. But if you press the blade down to
the handle again, it snaps into its bed and rests secure in its sheath
so that you can hide the thing in your apron. What do you say
now?"

The youth came forward and tried the spring of the knife.

"Not bad," said he. "Is it mine?" and he pocketed it. "From the
land of Mosar?" he asked. "And from Ma'on? Midianite traders?
Wait a little."

And he went through the gate.

The old man looked after him, laughed and shook his head. "We
have forced the stronghold of Thel," he said, "and passed through
Pharaoh's border watches and military scribes. We shall pass here too
and win to my friend Mont-kaw."

And he gave a little cluck which was a sign to his beast to lie down.
Joseph helped him to dismount. The other riders got down too; and
they waited.

After a while Teti came back and said:

"You are to come in into the court. The overseer will come."

"Good," replied the old man, "if he has the wish to see us we will
take time and oblige him, although we must still go on."

And led by the young keeper they passed through the covered
gateway, which echoed to their tread, into a court covered with hard
clay. They faced an open double gate flanked by shady palm trees;
it stood in the brick wall of the square inner court, and through slits
in the wall they could see the house, with its fine mouldings, its entrance between painted columns, and on the roof its three-cornered
ventilators opening to the west. It lay in the centre of the grounds,
surrounded on west and south by the green depths of spacious gardens. The court was large, with many open spaces among the buildings which stood facing westwards, without any wall, on the north
side of the property. The largest building extended on their right,
long, gay, and charming, guarded by watermen. Through its doors
went maidservants with tall jugs and platters of fruit. Other women
sat on the house roof, spinning and singing. Farther westwards,
against the northern wall, was another house from which steam was
rising and before which people were busy beside vats and grain mills.
Yet another house lay farther west behind the orchard, and workmen
were busy in front of it. At the back, in the north-west corner of the

ring wall, lay cow-stalls and corn granaries with ladders against them.

An estate rich in blessing, beyond a doubt. Joseph glanced over it quick-eyed, seeking to penetrate everywhere. But he had little time, for his help was needed in the task which his master undertook as soon as they entered: they unloaded the camels and set up shop on the clay pavement between the gate and the master's house, spreading out their wares that the overseer, or whoever else among his people desired to buy, might be tempted by the alluring contents of their packs.

THE DWARFS

AND ACTUALLY they were soon surrounded by an inquisitive crowd of people who had seen the Asiatics come in, and though the event was nothing unusual, found in it a welcome diversion from their work or even from mere idling. There were Nubian guards from the house of women and maidservants whose female forms, after the custom of the country, shone clear and plain through the sheer batiste of their garments; domestics from the main house dressed according to their place in the hierarchy of servants, in the short apron or with a longer one over it and with the short-sleeved upper garment; people from the cook-house with half-plucked fowls in their hands; stable-boys, workmen from the servants' house, and gardeners; they all came up, looked and chattered, bent over the wares, took this or that in their hands and inquired after its price in weight of silver or copper. There were two tiny men, dwarfs, included in the fan-bearer's household. Neither of them was more than three feet tall; but they were very different in bearing, for the one was quite a simpleton and the other most dignified of mien. The latter came first from the main house, on little legs which seemed still more crooked by comparison with his body; with careful and circumspect gait, very upright or even somewhat bent backwards, looking importantly about him and paddling rapidly with his stumpy arms, the palms turned backwards. He wore a starched apron which stood out in a slanting triangular plane in his rear. His head was relatively large, and bulbous behind, covered with short hair which grew low on brow and temples; he had a powerful nose and a manner equable, even settled.

"Are you the leader of the caravan?" he asked, standing before the old man, who had squatted down near his goods, a position gratifying to the dwarf since he could thus speak to him as man to man. His voice was hollow; he pitched it as low as possible, sinking his chin on his chest and drawing his under lip over his teeth. "Who let you in? The outside guards? With permission from the overseer? Then it is well. You may stop and await him, although it is doubtful when he will find time for you. Do you bring things of use and beauty? It is more likely to be trumpery. Or are there objects of value among them, solid, sensible things? I see balsams, I see walking-sticks. I personally could use a stick if it is of the hardest wood and solid in its make-up. Above all, have you ornaments, chains, necklaces, rings? I am the care-taker of the master's wardrobe and trinkets, the chief steward of the robing-room. Dudu is my name. And I should enjoy giving my wife Djeset a good piece of jewellery, as a reward for child-bearing. Are you provided with such things? I see vitreous paste, I see knick-knacks. But I should want gold, electrum, good stones, lazuli, cornelian, crystal. . . ."

While the little man talked in this wise, the other dwarf came running from the direction of the harem, where he had probably been amusing the ladies with jests. He had just heard of the arrivals, it seemed, and, full of childish zeal, he hastened to be on hand — running as fast as his fat legs would carry him and now and then interrupting his trot to hop on one; in a thin, sharp, short-winded voice, in a sort of ecstatic outburst, he was saying:

"What's this, what's this? What is happening in the world? An uproar, a great hubbub? What is there to look at? What to stare at in our court? Merchants — even wild men — men of the desert? The dwarf is frightened, the dwarf is eager for new things. Hop, hop, hop, here he comes a-running — "

A rust-coloured long-tailed monkey sat on his shoulder, and he held it there with one hand, while it stretched its neck and glared wild-eyed from its perch. The costume of this wight had a comic effect, consisting, as it seemed to do, of a gala garment worn every day. His little, finely pleated apron reached down to his calves, with a fringed turnover; the transparent little camisole had finely pleated sleeves; but all this pleating was crumpled and draggled from long wear. About his diminutive wrists were gold spiral rings; round his little neck a dishevelled garland of flowers, with other flowers sticking in it and standing out round his shoulders. On his wig, made of brown woollen curls, sat a cone of ointment, which, however, was not made of scented fat, but consisted of a conical felt hat soaked in fragrant grease. His face, in contrast to the other dwarf's, was like an elderly child's, elfish, shrivelled, wizened.

Dudu, the guardian of the wardrobe, had been greeted with respect by the crowd, but it burst into laughter at sight of his partner in pettiness and brother dwarf.

"Vizier!" they shouted at him, as in mockery. "Bes-em-heb!"

That was the name of a comic dwarf god imported from foreign parts, with the addition of the designation "in the feast," by which they played on the little man's gala attire.

"Will you buy, Bes-em-heb? How he takes his legs under his arms! Run, Shepses-Bes, mighty Bes, magnificent Bes! Run and buy, but first get your breath! Buy yourself a sandal, vizier, and make little ox-legs under it, then you will have a bed to stretch in; but you must put a step to climb up!"

They shouted at him as he came up, and he answered in his wheezing, cricket voice which sounded as though it came from far away: "Plying your jokes, are you, long-legs? And think they hit the mark right well? But your vizier can but yawn, so do they bore him, as does of a truth this whole weary world whereon a god has set him and where all is made for giants: not only the sandals, but the jokes as well — and even the time! For if the world were made after my measure and for me to dwell in, time would be much shorter too and I should not have to yawn! There would be yare little years and double hours, nimble night-watches would there be! Tick tock, tick tock, the clock of the heart would hurry away, so swiftly running down that a generation would pass in a trice and scarcely find time to make one good jest on earth ere it were gone and another see the light. How merry would that short life be! But the dwarf is set here in this long-legged, long-winded world and so must yawn. I will not buy your gross wares, and your rude wit will I neither take for a gift. I would but see what there is new in the giant's world of time and space here in our court. Here are strange men, men of wretchedness, men of the desert and wild nomads, in clothes such as men do not wear them. . . . Fie!" He broke off, and his gnome-like face contracted in angry wrinkles. He had seen Dudu, his partner dwarf, where he stood before the squatting old Ishmaelite, gesticulating with his stumpy arms, as he demanded full value for his money.

"Fie!" said the so-called vizier. "There is His Honour, to be sure! What a pity the old gaffer must get in my way when I want to satisfy my desire for the new. Stands there ahead of me his worship the ol'-clo'-man and makes as ever his dull and edifying talk. . . . Good morning, worshipful Dudu," chirped the little wight, ranging himself by the other's side. "A right good morning and very good health to your substantial person! May one be so bold as to inquire after the health of the lady Djeset, who embraces you with her arms? And after that of your towering scions, stout Esesi and Ebebi?"

Very contemptuously Dudu turned his head over his shoulder and did not so much seek the mock-vizier with his eyes as let his gaze fall to the ground somewhere in front of the other's feet.

"You midge!" he said, shaking his head, as it were at the sight. He drew in his lower lip so that the upper one stood out over it like a thatch. "What, are you crawling and piping down there? I heed you no more than I would a crab, or an empty nut full of wind and dust. You are no more than that in my eyes. How dare you ask after Djeset, my wife, mocking as you speak, and fleering at my aspiring sons, Esesi and Ebebi? Your inquiry is unfitting, it is not proper or becoming for you even to ask after them, minimus and cipher as you are!"

"Hark at him!" retorted he whom they called Shepses-Bes, and his little visage wrinkled even more. "Wants to exalt himself above me, who knows how high; his voice issues as out of a tun, for sheer pomposity — when you cannot see over a mole-hill yourself and are no match for your brood, let alone for her who embraces you with her arms. A dwarf you are and a dwarf you remain, no matter how you puff yourself out; and ill it beseems you to scorn my polite inquiries after your family, on the score that it does not befit a dwarf to make them! But you yourself — truly it befits you well and becomes your stature to play the married man and father of the family, wedding with one of the big folk and denying your dwarfish kind — "

The courtyard people laughed uproariously; the wrangling and mutual dislike of the manikins seemed to be a familiar source of merriment. They egged them on: "Give it him, vizier!" "Pay him out, Dudu, spouse of Djeset!" But he whom they called Bes-em-heb had stopped scolding and lost interest in the fray. He was standing near his enemy, who in his turn stood next the old man. But on the old man's other hand was Joseph, and thus Bes found himself confronting the son of Rachel. As he became aware of him he ceased to speak and gazed steadily, while his dwarfish face, but now so full of petty rage, smoothed itself out and assumed an expression of self-forgotten inquiry. His mouth remained open, and if he had had brows — but he had none — they would have risen high. Thus he looked up at the young Shabirite, and the little ape on his shoulder did the same, as though fixed by magic; with neck thrust out, with wide-staring eyes, it gazed up into the face of the descendant of Abram.

Joseph submitted to the scrutiny. Smiling he returned the gnomish gaze, and thus they stood, while the solemn Dudu resumed his chaffering with the old man and the attention of the other courtyard folk veered again to the strangers and their wares.

At length the manikin, pointing with dwarf finger to his breast, said in his strange, remote little voice:

"Sa'ankh-Wen-nofer-Neteruhotep-em-per-Amun."

"What did you say?" Joseph inquired.

The dwarf repeated his words, still pointing to his breast. "Name," he explained. "The little one's name. Not vizier. Not Shepses-Bes. Sa'ankh-Wen-nofer — " and he whispered it for the third time, his full name, as long and resounding as he himself was insignificant. Its meaning was "May the Favouring Essence (in other words, Osiris) preserve the beautified of the gods in the house of Amun." And Joseph understood it.

"A fine name!" said he.

"Fine, yes, but not true," came the murmuring voice. "Me not beautiful, me not favoured of gods, me little frog! You beautiful and favoured, you Neteruhotep, so is fine and true too."

"How can you know that?" Joseph asked with a smile.

"See," came the subterranean accents. "See very clear." And he carried his small finger to his eye. "Wise," he added. "Small and wise. You not of the little race, yet wise too. Good, wise, and beautiful. Do you belong to him?" He pointed to the old man, who was busy with Dudu.

"I belong to him," said Joseph.

"From a child?"

"I was born to him."

"He is your father?"

"He is a father to me."

"What is your name?"

Joseph did not answer at once. He smiled before he spoke. At length: "Osarsiph," said he.

The dwarf blinked. He pondered the name.

"Are you born from the reeds?" he asked. "Are you an Usir in the rushes? Did the mother search and find you in the water?"

Joseph was silent. The little man went on blinking.

Then they heard the voices of the people in the yard: "Mont-kaw is coming!" They began to disperse to their tasks, that he might not find them idle and chattering. Mont-kaw was standing or moving about near the open courtyard in front of the buildings in the north-west corner of the estate. You could see him by looking between the harem and the master's house: an elderly man, beautifully dressed in white, accompanied by scribes, who, with reed pens behind their ears, bowed before him and wrote down his words on tablets.

He approached. The servants had scattered. The old man had got to his feet. But through all the sound of these movements Joseph heard, as though a voice, a little voice, whispered up to him from under the earth, the words:

"Stay with us, young sandman!"

MONT-KAW

THE OVERSEER had arrived at the open gate in the crenelated wall before the master's house. Half turned toward it, he looked back over his shoulder at the group of strangers and the wares exposed for sale.

"What is this?" he said rather gruffly. "What men are these?"

It seemed as though he had forgotten, in the press of other affairs, that he had sent for them to come in. Nor did the exhaustive salutations of the old man help matters much. A scribe reminded him, pointing to his tablet, upon which he had obviously noted the incident.

"Yes, yes, the pedlars from Ma'om or Mosar," said the overseer then. "Good, good: but I need nothing except time and that they have not for sale." And he approached the old man who came bustling up to him. "Well, old man, how are you, after all this time?" asked Mont-kaw. "So we see you at our door with your goods, all ready to swindle us once more?"

They laughed together. Both of them had only the lower canines left in their jaws, sticking up solitary like posts. The steward was a stocky, powerfully built man of fifty, with an expressive head. The decided bearing which his office brought with it was softened by benevolence. He had very prominent tear ducts under his eyes, giving the latter a swollen, slit-like look beneath heavy, still black eyebrows. From the well-formed though wide-nostrilled nose deep furrows ran down to the corners of the arched and outstanding upper lip, which like the cheeks was shaven so that it shone. On the chin sat a club-shaped beard sprinkled with grey. The hair had already retreated from brow and temples, but grew in a bush at the back of the head, standing out like a fan behind the ears, in which he wore gold rings. Mont-kaw's features had something traditionally shrewd and peasant-like about them, and withal a twinkle that suggested the seafaring man. His dark red-brown complexion contrasted with the florid white of his clothing — that inimitable Egyptian linen which lent itself to such exquisite folds and pleating as those in the front flap of his apron kilt, the stiffly starched flaring folds of which began below his navel and reached down nearly to the ankle-length hem. His body-garment was tucked into the apron, and its wide, half-length sleeves were likewise pressed into fine diagonal folds. The fine batiste revealed his muscular, hairy torso.

The two dwarfs had taken leave to remain in the court, and Dudu now came up to Mont-kaw, paddling importantly and rowing with his stumpy arms.

"I fear, overseer, it is time lost to deal with these people," he said, and notwithstanding his stature he spoke as an equal. "I have looked over their stock. I see trumpery. I see gimcrackery. What lacks is good, solid, high-class stuff, suitable for an aristocratic house and estate. The master will scarcely be grateful to you for purchasing trash."

The old man was cast down. He indicated by a gesture his distress that the overseer's hopeful and cordial greetings should have aroused in him expectations which now were destroyed by Dudu's severity.

"But I have valuable goods too," he said. "Maybe not valuable to you upper officials, nor of course to your lord, I have not said that. But how many servants are there not in the courtyard — cooks and bakers, gardeners and water-bearers, runners and waiters-on! Countless like the sands of the sea! Yet not so many that they are enough or too many for such a great lord as Petepre, His Grace, the friend of

Pharaoh, or that one could not always add one or another well-built
and clever slave, let him be native or a foreigner, if only he be useful.
But why do I prattle of what is not to the point instead of saying simply: You, great steward, buy for the many and their use; you stand as
their head, and it is the business of the old Minæan, the travelling
pedlar with his popular wares, to suggest to you. Look at these well-
painted, earthenware lamps from Gilead beyond the Jordan — they
cost me little, so should I value them high to you, my patron? Take
some of them as a present, and if I may see your favour therefor, I
am rich. On the other hand these little pots of eye-paint with cow-
horn tweezers and spoons of cow-horn — their value is considerable,
but not their price. Here are hoes, an indispensable tool; I will give
one for two pots of honey. More costly, indeed, are the contents of
this little bag, for there are onions from Ascalon in it, from Ascaluna,
rare and hard to come by as they are savoury. But the wine in these
jugs is eight times good wine from Khadati, in the land of Phœnicia
— as it stands written. Lo, I grade my offers, I go from the lower to
the higher, and from them to the very choice, that is my considered
practice. For the balsams here, and incense-resins, the goat's-thorn
gums, the brownish labdanum, they are the pride of my business, and
the specialty of my house. We would be praised and renowned between the rivers, because we are stronger in sudorifics than any merchant, be he travelling trader or a settled man of the bazaar. 'There
are the Ishmaelites from Midian,' they say of us; 'they carry spices,
balsam, and myrrh from Gilead down toward Egypt.' So is it in the
mouth of the people — precisely as though we did not carry and bring
much else, as doth in truth happen, dead and alive, the created or the
creature, so that we are the men not only to provide a house but also
to increase it. But I am silent."

"What, you are silent?" the overseer pretended amaze. "Do you
ail, then? For when you are silent I know you not, but only when
your mild prattle of speech wells out from under your beard — I can
still hear it from the last time and know you by it again."

"Is not," responded the old man, "speech the pride of mankind?
Who knows how to set his words well and hath a gift of expression,
upon him gods and men nod with applause, and he findeth inclined
ears. But your servant is little gifted with expression, and not master
of the treasure of speech, I say it openly. So then he must substitute
persistency for speech and duration of flow for what it lacks in
choiceness. For the merchant must be of ready tongue, the which
must know how to flatter his clients, or he cannot earn his living and
doth not bring the seven gifts to the man —"

"Six," came the whispering of little Bes, as from afar off, although
he stood quite near. "Six gifts, old man, you offered: lamps, salve,
hoes, onions, wine, and myrrh. Where is the seventh?"

The Ishmaelite laid his left hand like a mussel-shell round his ear and the right to his eyes to peer.

"What," he asked, "was the remark of this middle-sized, gaily clad gentleman?"

One of his party repeated it to him.

"Oh," he replied, "the seventh likewise is to be found among all the things which we have brought down to Egypt, besides the much-talked-of myrrh. For it, too, will I let my tongue run on, with persistency, if not with chosen words, that I may bring the ware to the man and the house, and that the Ishmaelites of Midian may make for themselves a name on account of all that which they bear and bring to Egypt."

"Spare me," said the overseer. "Do you think I can stand here and hear you chatter all the days of Re? He is already almost at his midday, may the gods keep us! Any minute the master may come home from the west and be here again from the palace. Shall I then leave it to the slaves and trouble not myself whether all is right in the dining-room, with the roast ducks, the cakes, the flowers; and the master find his meal as he is used to, likewise the mistress and the exalted parents from the upper storey? Make haste, or else make off! I must go. Old man, I cannot well use you or your seven gifts — scarcely at all, to be frank — "

"For they are but beggarly trash," interpolated Dudu, the married dwarf.

The overseer gave a downward glance as he heard the harsh judgment.

"But you have need of honey, it seems," he said to the old man. "I will give you a few pots against two of these hoes, that I may not offend you or your gods. Give me five bags of the little onions too, in the name of the Hidden One, and five measures of your Phœnician wine, in the name of the Mother and the Son! Tell me the cost — yet give me not first the triple price, as a haggler does so that we sit down and bargain, but at most the double one, so that we may come more quickly to the just one, and I can go in. I will give you writing-paper in exchange, and some of our linen. If you like, beer and bread as well. Only make haste that I may go!"

"You are served," said the old man, loosing the hand scale from his girdle. "You are served in a trice, and without conditions, served by your servant. What am I saying, without conditions? With conditions, of course, but only of the best. Had I not to live, the things were yours without price. But even so I will make you a price that may indeed cut me short, yet keep myself in your favour, for that is my chief concern.

"Hallo," said he to Joseph over his shoulder, "take the list of wares which you have made, the things in black but the weight and quantity in red. Take and read to us the weight of the shallots as well as the wine, that is their price, but translate as you stand and in your head into the values of the country, in deben and lot, that we may know what the goods are worth in pounds of copper and the high steward may give us, for just so much copper, linen and writing-paper of the house. But I, my patron, if you will allow, will weigh out the goods once more for test and proof."

Joseph had the roll ready and stepped forward as he unrolled it. Next him stood Master Bes, who, indeed, was far from being able to look at the list, but gazed up attentively at the extended hands.

"Doth my lord command me to read the just price or the double one?" asked Joseph discreetly.

"The just one, of course; dost thou dote?" the old man scolded.

"But the high steward commanded that thou shouldest name the double price," responded Joseph with the most charming seriousness. "If now I name the just one he might take it for the double and offer but the half; and how then couldst thou live? Better would it be if he took the double price for the real one; and if he drive it down, even so thou comest not short."

"He he!" the old man laughed. "He he!" he went again, and looked at the overseer to see how he took it. The scribes, with the reed pens behind their ears, laughed. The thumbling "Beauty" clapped his knee with his little hand, drawing it up to his chest and hopping on the other. His goblin face was flawed into a thousand little wrinkles of dwarfish delight. But Dudu, his brother manikin, only shook his head and stuck out the thatch of his upper lip more disdainfully than ever.

As for Mont-kaw, he had so far of course given no heed to the knowing young scribe with the roll. But now he looked at him, with a surprise which at once turned to perplexity, and presently to something very like admiration — save that it betokened indeed a far, far deeper feeling. Perhaps — I will not venture an assertion — perhaps at this moment, upon which so much depended, the planning God of his fathers did a little something extra for Joseph. Perhaps He let fall upon him a light calculated to produce the desired effect upon the hearts of all beholders. For He, in truth, has given us all our senses for our pleasure; yet reserved to Himself their use as medium and avenue for His larger purposes to play upon our minds. Hence my suggestion — which, however, I am willing to withdraw if it seem too supernatural an element to be introduced into our very natural tale.

Indeed, the more natural and practical our interpretations, the better, since Mont-kaw himself was a practical and natural man. Besides he belonged to a world already remote from any in which the idea of meeting a god unexpectedly, in broad daylight and, so to speak, on the street, would have been a familiar thing. Yet even so his world stood nearer than ours does to such possibilities and expectations; though in his they might only have been held with half one's mind, no longer in a real, positive, and unequivocal sense. It came to pass that Mont-kaw looked at Rachel's son and saw that he was beautiful. But beauty of so striking and arresting a kind was associated in the steward's mind with one immediate order of ideas: it belonged to the moon, which was the planet of Djehuti of Khmunu, Thoth's heavenly manifestation — Thoth, who was master of measure and order, the wise man, scribe and magician. And now Joseph stood there before him, a roll in his hands, and in his mouth words which for a slave, even an educated one, were unusually subtle and shrewd. The combination was upsetting. The young Bedouin and Asiatic had no ibis-head on his shoulders; he was, of course, a human being, not a god, not Thoth of Khmunu. But he had, by association, to do with him. He seemed ambiguous, in the way that a word can be ambiguous, for instance the epithet "divine." Compared with the august substantive from which it derives, it conveys indeed a weakening, a derogation of the idea; it is not absolute, but only suggestive, and thus it is partly unreal and derivative, but partly too lays claim to absoluteness, in that the word "divine" is a description of the perceptible attributes and form of the god.

Some such equivocal associations came to Mont-kaw's mind and gave him pause when he saw Joseph for the first time. It was indeed a recurrent event; others before him had felt the same, still others would yet feel it. But we must not suppose that Mont-kaw was very powerfully moved. He felt no more than what we might express by the exclamation: "What the devil!" He did not say that. He asked: "What is that?"

He cautiously — likewise somewhat contemptuously — said "what" instead of "who"; and thus the old man's answer came very pat:

"That," he replied with a smirk, "is the Seventh Gift."

"It is a habit of the uncivilized," the Egyptian retorted, "to speak in riddles."

"Does my patron not love riddles?" responded the old man. "'Tis a pity! I could tell him so many. But this one is quite simple: they have said that I offered only six gifts and not seven, as I had boasted and as it is proper to do. Well, then, this slave who keeps my list is the seventh gift — a Canaanitish youth whom, besides my much praised myrrhs, I have brought down to Egypt and who is for sale. Not that I must sell him or would do so because he is no good to me. For he can bake and write and hath a clear head for accounts. But to a good house, a house like yours, in short, is he for sale, if you will pay me a living price, no more. For I would have a good place for him."

"Our numbers are full," the steward said hastily, shaking his head. For he had no liking for riddles, either in the usual or in a higher sense, but spoke like a practical man, anxious to protect his business interests against importunity from anything out of the usual order — the divine, in short.

"There is no vacancy here," he said, "and the house is full. We need no baker nor writer; nor any clear heads, for mine is clear enough to keep things in order. Take your seventh gift with you on your way and may it find you profit."

"For it is beggarly trash and a beggar and the trash of a beggar," Dudu, husband of Djeset, concluded sententiously. But another little voice answered his heavy one, the cricket-like chirp of "Beauty," the fool:

"The seventh gift is the best — buy it, Mont-kaw!"

The old man took up his tale:

"The clearer one's own head, the more vexing the dullness of the others', for one suffereth impatience on their account. A clear head at the top needeth clear heads below. I had already in mind this servant for your house when great space yet lay between me and it, and brought him down before you to make you an advantageous and friendly offer. For the young one is clear of head and eloquent of tongue so that it is a pleasure, and bringeth before you adornments out of the treasure-house of speech so that it is a mere delight. Three hundred and sixty times in the year he sayeth good-night to one in a different phrase and still has something left for the other five days. But if ever he says it twice the same, you may give me him back again and I will refund the purchase money."

"Hearken, old man," replied the overseer. "All that you say may be true. But whilst we speak of patience I am wellnigh at the end of mine. In my good nature I was ready to take a few gew-gaws from your pack, of the which I have no need at all, but not to disoblige your gods and so as to be able to go into the house. And lo, you would talk me into buying your good-night-saying slave and makest as though he were destined for the house of Petepre since the foundation of the land."

Here Dudu, scribe of the wardrobe, gave vent, from his lowly station, to a burst of deep round laughter: "Ho, ho, ho, ho!" he went, and the overseer cast him a quick angry look.

"Where did you get it then, this seventh gift with the gift of tongues?" he asked. He did not look toward Joseph, but stretched out his hand for the roll which the latter gracefully presented. Mont-kaw unrolled it and held it away from his eyes, for he was already very long-sighted. Meanwhile the old man answered:

"A pity it is indeed that my patron does not love riddles. Else I could tell him one in answer to his question whence I have the lad."

"A riddle?" repeated the overseer absently, for he was looking at the roll.

"Guess it if you will," said the old man. "It runs: 'A barren mother bore him to me.' Can you solve the riddle?"

"Did he write this list?" Mont-kaw asked, still reading. "H'm. Step back, you. It was done with thoroughness and with pleasure and executed with a sense for adornment, that I will not dispute. It might serve as an inscription to decorate a wall. Whether it is correct as well, that I cannot judge, for it is gibberish. 'Barren'?" he asked, for he had heard the old man's words with half an ear. "A barren mother? What does that mean? A woman is barren or else she bears. Both cannot be true."

"It is a riddle, my lord," explained the old man. "I took the liberty to dress my reply in the garment of jest. If it please you, I will supply the answer. Far from here, I came on a dry well, out of which sounded a whimpering. And I drew up to the light of day this which had been three days in the well's belly, and gave it milk. Thus the well became a mother and yet was barren."

"H'm," said the overseer. "Your riddle is passable, more one cannot say, or laugh very heartily at it. If I smile, it is out of pure politeness."

"Mayhap," replied the old man, rather hurt, "you might have laughed more readily if you had been able to guess it."

"Solve me," the steward gave back, "another riddle, and a harder one: namely, that I should stand here prattling with you, and why. Solve it better than you have your own; for, so far as I know, there are no monsters that breed in wells to give birth to such as this. How, then, did the child come into the belly and the slave into the well?"

"Hard masters and former owners, of whom I bought him, had cast him in, by reason of slight misdemeanours which do not lessen his value, because they had to do only with subtle matters and fine distinctions like that between the 'so that' and the 'in order that' — matters not worth talking about. But I bought him, having taken him between thumb and finger, as it were, and found the boy to be fine in thread and grain, notwithstanding the darkness of his origins. Also he had already rued his errors while in the well, and punishment had so purged him that he was a valuable servant to me; and he can not only read and write but bake uncommonly relishable pancakes on stones. I well know that a man should not boast of his own, but leave it to others to call it extraordinary. Yet indeed, for the dexterity and the understanding of this youth, purified as they are by chastisement, there is in the language but one word: they are extraordinary. And now since your eyes have fallen upon him and I owe you a debt for my folly in plaguing you with riddles, receive him as a present from me for Petepre and his house over which you are set! Though of course I well know that you would contrive a recompense for me out of the riches of Petepre so that, and in order that, I may live to supply your house and ever increase it."

The overseer looked at Joseph.

"Is it true," said he, with suitable gruffness, "that you have the gift of speech and can say such things as are pleasant to hear?"

Jacob's son gathered all his Egyptian together.

"'Servants' speech is no speech,'" he answered, using a popular phrase. "That the lowly shall be silent when the masters speak together stands at the beginning of every book of precepts. Besides, my name, by which I call myself, is a name of silence."

"How so? How are you called, then?"

Joseph hesitated. Then he lifted up his eyes.

"Osarsiph," he said.

"Osarsiph?" repeated Mont-kaw. "I know not the name. It is not foreign; indeed, it is comprehensible, since he from Abodu occurs in it, the lord of the eternal silence. But it is not customary in the land, no one is so called in Egypt, either now or under any earlier kings. But even if you have a name of silence, Osarsiph, yet your master says that you can utter pleasant wishes and say good-night in a variety of ways at the end of the day. Well, I too shall go to bed tonight and lie on my bed in the special room of trust. What will you say to me?"

"Rest gently," answered Joseph with feeling, "after the toil of the day. May your soles, that are scorched from the heat of your path, move blissfully over the mosses of peace, and your languid tongue be refreshed from the murmuring springs of night!"

"Yes, that is really moving," said the steward; the tears stood in his eyes. He nodded to the old man, who nodded back, rubbing his hands and smiling. "When one has troubles in the world, like me, and sometimes feels not too good about the kidneys, one is moved by things like that. Can we then, in the name of Set," he turned back to his scribe, "use a young slave—as a lamplighter, perhaps, or as a floor-sprinkler? What do you say, Kha'ma't?" he said to a tall, stoop-shouldered man who carried several reed pens behind each ear. "Do we need one?"

The scribes made gestures of indecision, seeming to debate. They stuck out their lips, drew their heads down between their shoulders, and flapped their hands in the air.

"Need?" answered he who was called Kha'ma't. "Is 'need' to want, to lack the indispensable? Then no. But even the unnecessary may be made useful. It depends on the cost. If the man of the desert would sell you a scribe, then drive him away, for we are writers enough and neither need nor can use one. But if he offer you a baser slave, for the dogs or for the bathing-room, then inquire of him his price."

"Well, old man," said the steward, "hasten, then, and say what you would ask for your son of the well."

"He is yours!" replied the Ishmaelite. "Since we speak of him at all and you ask me about him, he already belongs to you. Truly it is not fit that I decide on the worth of the present in exchange which, as it would seem, you will make me. But since you command — the ape sits beside the scale! Who sins in measure and weight is convicted by the power of the moon. Two hundred deben of copper the slave must be reckoned at, considering his extraordinary properties. But the little onions and the wine from Khadati I will throw in, as a gage of friendship."

The price was high. It was a clever stroke to make extras of the shallots and the much-liked Phœnician wine, and to charge only for the young slave Osarsiph. But high it was, even granted that of all the old man's stock-in-trade, not excepting the famous myrrhs, only this single thing paid for the transportation to Egypt. It was high even from the point of view that the Ishmaelites' entire business was only an extra, and their sole and single significance consisted in the fact that they were bringing the boy Joseph down to Egypt in order to fulfil the ordained. We may not venture to think that any such idea entered the old Minoan's head; certainly it was remote from the overseer Mont-kaw's, and probably he would have protested against the overcharge if the dwarf Dudu had not forestalled him. From under the thatch of the little man's lip a full-mouthed protest rolled out; the tiny hands at the end of his stumps of arms gesticulated before his breast.

"It is absurd!" he said. "Utterly fantastic and not to be borne. Turn your back on him, show your disgust to this shameless old thief and vagabond who dares to speak of friendship, as though there could be anything of the kind between you, an Egyptian overseer to the great, and him, a wild man from the desert. His business is pure swindle — asking two hundred copper deben for this lout here — " and he gestured palm upwards at Joseph as he stood beside him — "for such worthless trash, a snot-nosed sand-rabbit! It is all highly suspicious to me; he may be able to prattle about moss and murmuring streams, but who knows what sort of abandoned vices brought him to acquaintance with the pit that the old rascal is supposed to have got him from? I say you shall not buy the lout; my advice is not to acquire him for Petepre; he will not thank you for it."

Thus Dudu, overseer of the wardrobe. But hard upon his voice came a little pipe like a cricket's out of the grass, the voice of "Beauty" in the gala attire, the vizier who stood at Joseph's other side — for they had taken him between them.

"Buy, Mont-kaw," he whispered, standing on his tiptoes. "Buy the sand-boy. Of all the seven gifts buy him alone, for he is the best. Trust me, I have the use of my eyes. Good, beautiful, and wise is Osarsiph. Blessed is he and will be a blessing to the house. Hearken to the voice of wisdom."

"Take not the advice of the base, but of the worthy," cried the other in his turn. "How can this dried-up nothing give you anything of worth, being himself without worth and like a rotten nut with nothing but dust and wind inside? He has no weight in the world, no social value, but bobs on the surface of things like a cork. How can a clown and court fool speak anything of value, or have judgment of human folk and their goods, or of human goods?"

"Oh, you stuck-up little busybody, you!" shrieked Bes-em-heb, his gnome-face crumpled into a thousand wrinkles with sheer rage. "How can you have judgment or give counsel, you backslider and turncoat? You threw away your wisdom when you denied your dwarfdom and wived yourself with a tall woman and gave life to long, lathlike children called Esesi and Ebebi! You pompous ass! You have remained a dwarf according to your stature and cannot see over the boundary-stone of the field. But as for your stupidity, that is full-size; and it has entirely blunted your judgment of men and wares and human wares!"

Dudu was brought by these epithets and this description of his mental state to a pitch of almost incredible fury. He got white as cheese, the thatch quivered on his upper lip, and he burst out in venomous invective, which Beauty was not slow in repaying with even more malicious allusions to Dudu's loss of finer intelligence, his renegade state and ridiculous pretensions. The two little men stood, hands on knees, on Joseph's either side as though he were a tree, scolding and spitting at each other round him. The crowd, Egyptians and Ishmaelites together, and the overseer with them, roared with laughter at this petty war going on at the level of their knees. But suddenly everything came to a stop.

POTIPHAR

From afar in the street, sounds came and swelled: the trampling of horses, the rolling of wheels, the thud of running feet, and many-voiced cries of warning. It all came on so fast that in no time it stood before the door.

"There we are," said Mont-kaw. "The master. And the arrangements in the dining-hall? Great Triad of Thebes, I have wasted my time in sheer folly! Quiet, ye underlings, or ye shall have a taste of the lash! Kha'ma't, conclude the bargain, I must go with the master into the house. Take the goods and pay a proper price for them. Keep well, old man! And come back again — in six or seven years' time!"

He hastened away. The gate-keepers, from the benches, shouted into the court, and from all sides servants came running, in zeal to line up before the master with their foreheads to the ground. The trotting feet of the runners and the rattle of the car came from the gateway: Petepre drove in. Before him went his panting, shouting runners, among and behind them his fan-bearers came. Two proud and glossy chestnuts in fine trappings, with ostrich plumes on their heads, drew the little two-wheeled car, a sort of gala chariot, with prettily curved rails. In it was just room for himself and his driver; but the driver did nothing save to add to the splendour of the equipage, for Pharaoh's friend drove himself — it was plain, from his bearing and his attire, that it was the master who held reins and whip. He was an extremely tall, fat man, with a little mouth, Joseph remarked; but only at a glance, for his eyes went rather to the wheels of the chariot, which had bright stones let into the spokes and sparkled like fireworks as they whirled round in the sun. Joseph wished that little Benjamin might see it. The same splendour, though not whirling, repeated itself on Petepre's person; for he wore a jewelled collar, a magnificent piece of workmanship, set with stones and enamel in all colours; their countless facets, arranged in rows with the narrow sides together, flashed like a rain of sparks in the strong white light which the sun-god at his zenith was pouring down on Weset and upon this very spot.

The ribs of the runners panted in and out. The shining steeds came to a halt, pawing the ground, rolling their eyes and snorting; a groom held them by the bridle, patted their foaming necks, and murmured soothing words. The chariot had stopped by the palm trees, just between the group of merchants and the gate in the ring wall which led into the inner court. And at the gate stood Mont-kaw, bowing and smiling and gesturing his delight. His head was trembling with sheer admiration as he stepped up to the car and offered his hand to help the master alight. Petepre handed reins and whip to the driver, keeping in his small hand only a short staff made of cane and gilded leather, thick at the end and looking like a kind of reduced bludgeon. "Wash them off with wine, cover them well, and lead them about!" he commanded in a thinnish voice, lifting his staff and pointing to the animals with that elegant survival of a savage weapon, become in his hands merely a symbol of his power. He waved back the hand offered by Mont-kaw and sprang down, with a movement agile for one of his weight — though he might as easily have stepped.

Joseph saw and heard clearly, especially after the car moved slowly off toward the stables and the master and his steward stood gazing after it, in full view of the group of Ishmaelites. The great man might be perhaps forty years old, or less; and like a tower for size — Joseph could not help thinking of Reuben as he looked at the columnar legs showing through the royal linen of the outer garment, which came not quite to the ankles and revealed the pleats and ribbons of the skirt through its thin weave. But this massiveness was not heroic like brother Reuben's, for it was fat: fat everywhere, especially on the breasts, which stood out like two hillocks under the thin batiste. They had shaken not a little with the man's unnecessarily active jump from the car. His head was quite small in proportion to his height and breadth; but nobly shaped, with short hair, short, aristocratically hooked nose, delicate mouth, pleasantly prominent chin, and long-lashed eyes with a veiled and haughty gaze.

Standing with the steward in the shade of the palms, he looked well pleased after his horses as they were led off.

"They are very fiery," he was heard to say. "User-Min even more than Wepwawet. They were unruly, they tried to bolt. But I got the better of them."

"As only you can do," answered Mont-kaw. "It is amazing. Your driver, Neternakht, would not dare cope with them. Nor any of the others here, the Syrians are so wild. They have fire, not blood, in their veins. They are not horses, but demons. Yet you have conquered them, they feel the master's hand, and their pride is subdued, they are tamed and run in harness for you. And you, after triumphing in the struggle with them, are not even tired; you spring like a lad from your car, my lord."

The deep corners of Petepre's mouth deepened more in a fleeting smile.

"I have further intent," said he, "to pay homage to Sebek this afternoon and go hunting in the marshes. Make all ready and rouse me betimes should I fall asleep. Put throw-sticks and fishing-spears in the boat. And harpoons as well, for I hear that a hippopotamus of great size has strayed into the backwater where I mean to hunt, and I am minded most of all to kill it."

"The mistress," answered Mont-kaw, his eyes cast down, "the mistress Mut-em-enet will tremble with fear when she hears. Be persuaded at least not to attack the brute single-handed — leave the struggle and the danger to your servants. The mistress — "

"That gives me no pleasure," Petepre responded. "I will myself hurl the spear."

"But the mistress will be afraid."

"Let her be afraid. — But," he asked, turning with a swift movement toward the steward, "is all well in the house? Naught untoward has befallen? Nothing? And what people are those? Travelling merchants — very good. The mistress is happy? Is all well with the exalted parents in the upper storey?"

"Order and well-being reign," Mont-kaw gave answer. "Our gracious mistress went in her litter toward noon to visit the lady Renenutet, wife of the head steward of the bulls of Amun, to practise hymn-singing with her. When she returned she sent for Tepem'ankh, scribe of the house of the secluded ones, to read fairy-tales to her, the while she felt desire to kiss the sweetmeats which your servant sent her. As for the exalted parents from the upper storey, it pleased them to cross the river, to make sacrifice in the tomb of Thutmose, father of God united with the sun. Returned from the west, the exalted brother-sister pair, Huia and Tuia, have spent the time sitting peacefully hand in hand in the pleasure-house by the pond, awaiting your return and the hour of the evening meal."

"You may tell them too, and let it come privily to them," the master said, "that I mean to hunt the hippopotamus this very day. They may as well know it."

"But on that account," replied the steward, "they will, alas, fall into anxiety and great distress."

"No matter," retorted Petepre. "It seems," he added, "that life here today has gone to everybody's liking; whereas I had annoyance at court and vexation in the palace Merimat."

"You?" Mont-kaw questioned in dismay. "But how can that be, for the good god in the palace . . ."

"Either a man is captain of the guard," the master was heard to say, shrugging his massive shoulders as he turned away, "and head executioner, or else he is not. But if one is only — and there is a man there . . ." The rest of his words were lost as he passed through the gate and toward his house through the rows of slaves standing with uplifted hands. Mont-kaw moved a little behind him, bent over, listening and replying to what he said. And thus Joseph had seen Potiphar, as he pronounced the name to himself — that great man of Egypt to whom he had been sold.

JOSEPH IS SOLD FOR A SECOND TIME
AND FLINGS HIMSELF UPON HIS FACE

For the bargain was now made. Khamat, the tall scribe, concluded it with the old man in the overseer's name, the dwarfs looking on. But Joseph scarcely listened, nor did he hear the price he fetched, so intent was he on his thoughts and so busy with his first impressions of the person of his new owner. The collar glittering with jewels, the gold of favour, the proud, over-fleshy form; the spring from the car, the flatteries uttered by Mont-kaw about his master's prowess as a tamer of steeds; his intention of fighting the wild hippopotamus single-handed, heedless of his consort's fears or those of Huia and Tuia, his parents (and even the word "heedless" seems inadequate to characterize his mood); on the other hand his hurried inquiry about the order and well-being of the household; even the disconnected words he had let fall about the annoyances he suffered at court — all this gave the son of Jacob most urgently to think, to consider, to examine; he laboured within himself to probe, to interpret and fill in the blanks, like one who, placed by chance in a certain set of circumstances, and having to reckon with them, tries to master them as quickly as he may.

Would he, his thoughts ran on, stand some day in the chariot beside Potiphar and be his driver? Would he go with him to hunt in the backwaters of the Nile? That seems incredible, but so it was: scarcely had he come before the house when his thoughts flew to such an hour. Scarcely had his quick appraising eye taken in men and things when he considered how — sooner or later, but certainly as soon as possible — he would win to the master's side, to the side of him highest in this sphere if not the highest in Egypt. If not the highest: the words betray that whatever unforeseeable difficulties lay in the way of attaining his immediate though still very distant goal, these did not prevent him from looking beyond it to where hovered other, yet more conclusive incorporations of the highest.

Yet so it was; we know our man. And would he, with lesser pretensions, have gone so far in this country as he did? He was in the nether world, to which the pit had been the entrance. He was no longer Joseph, but Usarsiph; lowest among these below, but that could not last for long. Advantage and disadvantage he scanned with rapid eye. Mont-kaw was good. Tears had come in his eyes at Joseph's gentle greeting, because he often did not feel too well. The dwarf jester was good too, and obviously minded and ordained to help him. Dudu was a foe — for the present; perhaps there were ways to get around him. The scribes had shown some jealousy, because he too was a scribe; he must pay heed to their natural grudge and treat it gently. Thus he went on, weighing his immediate prospects — but it would be wrong on that account to chide him and call him a place-hunter. That Joseph was not; such is not a just judgment upon his thoughts. He mused and pondered upon a higher duty. God had put an end to his life, which had been one of folly, and resurrected him to a new one. He had used the Ishmaelites to lead him to this land; and in so doing He had, as in all else, undoubtedly great purposes. Never did He do aught that brought not great things in its train; it behoved Joseph, then, to lend himself trustfully to His design and use all his spiritual gifts in its service, instead of weakening it by idle lack of ambition. God had sent him dreams, which the dreamer had done better to keep to himself: the dream of the sheaves, the dream of the stars. For such dreams were less a promise than a guide. They would be fulfilled, in one way or another — in what way actually, God alone knew, but that he had been snatched away into this land was the beginning of the fulfilment. But in the meantime nothing would happen of itself — one had to help. That was no base ambition: to live in the light of the silent conviction that God had unique designs regarding him. Ambition is not the right word for it; for it was ambition for God, and that deserves a higher name.

Thus Joseph paid little heed to the chaffering that went on at his second sale, and thought little about the price he fetched, in his zeal to master his present situation and prospects. Lanky Khamat — with reed pens behind his ear, so astonishingly balanced that they lodged as though stuck on, no matter how much his head shook as he bargained — insisted stoutly on his distinction between needing and being able to use, as an argument to bring down the price. The old man produced his former strong plea: namely, that he must receive a present large enough that he might still exist to serve the illustrious house; and he knew how to make the necessity seem so inevitable that the scribe was taken at a disadvantage and could not refute it. Yet he was supported by Dudu, chamberlain of the wardrobe, who denied all claims, the needing and the being able to use as well, and in respect of all the wares in question, the wine and the onions no less than the slave. The other part was taken by Shepses-Bes, who vaunted his penetration in a chirping voice and demanded that Osarsiph be purchased at the price of first asking, without any haggling at all. Only at the end and quite incidentally did the object of the chaffering take any hand in the deal: saying offhand that he thought a hundred and fifty deben too low, and that they should agree on a hundred and sixty at the least. He said this out of sheer respect for God, and was brushed aside by the scribe Khamat, in high excitement, he considering it most improper that the chattel should have a voice in his price. Joseph then dropped the point and fell silent once more.

At length he saw a young spotted steer brought from his stall into the court by order of Khamat. He had a strange sensation at seeing, outside of himself and in animal form, the estimated value of his own person. That was strange, yet not offensive; for in this country nearly all the gods could recognize themselves in animal shape, and great respect was paid always to the idea that being near to a thing and being a thing were closely related conceptions.

But it did not stop at the young steer, for the old man sturdily refused to value him at more than a hundred and twenty deben, which was much less than what Joseph was worth. So various goods were added: a neat's-leather breast-plate, several bales of writing-paper and the cheaper sort of linen, a few wineskins of panther-fell, a quantity of natron for embalming, a bundle of fishhooks, and some hand-brooms. All this had to be laid beside the steer before the scale with the ape was brought to a balance in the time-honoured way. Even then the bargain was concluded more by agreement than by calculation, for in the end they gave up reckoning and each side contented itself with the feeling that it had not been too grossly swindled. The whole amount had come to perhaps a copper weight of one hundred and fifty or sixty deben; for which sum Rachel's son, together with the wine and the onions, became the property of the great Egyptian, Petepre.

It was done. The Ishmaelites from Midian had accomplished the purpose of their existence: they had delivered that which they had been chosen out to bring down to Egypt; they might vanish from the scene, it needed them no more. But their self-satisfaction was untroubled by the state of things; they took themselves as seriously as ever they had, packed up their wares, and never dreamed that they were now superfluous. The desire and fatherly concern of the old man to protect his foundling and provide for him in the best place he could — had it not its full value in the moral world, though from another point of view one might consider his whim a means and tool to ends he knew not of? True and obvious it was that he sold Joseph, as though he could not do anything else — for a price, indeed, which "let him live that he might further serve the house"; and knew how to state his necessity in such a way that the scribe, to his disadvantage, could not gainsay it. Thus he satisfied his mercantile conscience; yet plainly he did not do it for profit, and — unless I am mistaken — he would gladly have kept the son of the well, to bake him pancakes and bid him good-night. He did not act to his own advantage, while being at pains to safeguard his business interest. But then, what is self-interest? Interest urged him to look after Joseph and advance his lot in life; for in so doing he got satisfaction, of whatever sort, and from whatsoever source it came.

Joseph, moreover, was quite the youth to respect the dignity of freedom which humanly animates the inevitable. The old man, on concluding the bargain, addressed him, saying: "Lo, now, 'Come-hither,' or Usarsiph, or however thou callest thyself, now thou art no more mine, but belongest to this house; and I have made good my purposes." So then Joseph willingly paid him due meed of gratitude, kissing many times the hem of his garment and calling him his saviour.

"Farewell, my son," the old man said, "and show thyself worthy of my kindness. Be tactful and obliging to all, and bridle thy tongue when it twitches to criticize and to practise itself on injurious distinctions like that between the honoured and the outworn. For suchlike bringeth one to the pit. Sweetness is given to thy mouth; thou know-

est how to bid a soothing good-night and turn a phrase with charm.
Keep to such, then, and rejoice mankind, instead of winning their
abhorrence for thy carping, for it doeth no good. And now farewell.
Those errors which brought thee to thy grave — culpable self-confidence and blind presumption — of them I need not to warn thee, for
I think thou art taught of experience to shun them. I have not pried
into the details of thy history or thy antecedents. It sufficeth me to
know that much mystery lurketh in this blustering world; and I
am taught of experience that strange things are possible. If it be true,
as thy manners and gifts sometimes make me suspect, that thou comest
of the best and didst anoint thyself with the oil of gladness before
thou camest unto the body of the pit — well then, here is a life-line
thrown to thee, a prospect that thou mayest raise thyself to better
conditions by my having sold thee to this house. For the third time,
fare thee well! For I have said it twice already, and what one says
three times must come to pass. Old am I, and know not if I shall see
thee again. May Adon thy God — who, so far as I know, may be like
the setting sun in power — keep thee and guard thy steps, that they
stumble not. And blessings on thee!"

Joseph knelt down on the ground before this father of his and once
again kissed the hem of his robe, as the old man laid a hand upon his
head. Joseph took leave also of Mibsam, and thanked him for pulling
him out of the pit; from Epher, the nephew, and Kedar and Kedema,
the old man's sons, and more informally from Ba'almahar, the pack-
boy, and Jupa, the thick-lipped lad, who was holding by a rope the
animal representative of Joseph's value — in other words the young
steer. Then the Ishmaelites went off across the court and through the
echoing gateway, as they had come — only without Joseph. He stood
looking after them; not without pain at the parting and some sinking
at the pit of his stomach as he thought of the new and uncertain
prospects before him.

When they were out of sight he turned round and saw that everybody was gone from the court, that he was alone save only for the
mock-vizier, Sa'ankh-Wen-nofer-Neteruhotep-em-per-Amun, who
stood with the red monkey on his shoulder and looked up at him with
a wrinkled smile.

"What do I do now, and whither do I go?" Joseph inquired.

The dwarf did not reply, only nodded and went on smiling. But
suddenly he turned his head with a start and whispered:

"Throw yourself on your face!"

And at once he did as he had bade the other, lying with his forehead to the earth in a fat little heap, with the monkey atop. For the
little creature had cleverly parried his master's abrupt movement by
leaping from shoulder to back and squatting there with uplifted tail
and staring eyes directed to the point where Joseph also took leave

to look. He had followed the dwarf's example, but yet lifted his head a little on his hands that he might see before whom or what he thus abased himself.

A train was passing across from the women's to the master's house: in front five servants in aprons and narrow caps; behind, five maid-servants with flowing hair; and between them, swaying on the bare shoulders of Nubian slaves, a sort of gilded carrying-chair adorned with the heads of gaping beasts. Leaning among the cushions, with crossed feet, was an Egyptian lady, exquisitely got up, glittering ornaments in her curling locks, gold about her neck, with beringed fingers, and arms like lilies, one of which — very white and lovely — hung idly down at the side of the chair. Beneath the wrought-gold garland on her head Joseph saw her profile: that peculiar and personal, despite all adherence to the fashion quite unique and individual profile, with its eyes lengthened toward the temples by cosmetics, its flattened nose, its shadowy cheeks, its mouth at once thin and soft and sinuous as a snake between its two deep corners.

It was Mut-em-enet being borne to her evening meal; the lady of the house, consort of Petepre — a personality big with fate.

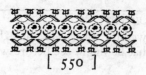

Chapter IV

THE HIGHEST

HOW LONG JOSEPH STAYED WITH POTIPHAR

ONCE there was a man who had a refractory cow, that would not bear the yoke for the plough, but always shook it from her neck. The man took her calf from her and brought it to the field which was to be ploughed. When the cow heard the lowing of her calf she let herself be driven to the field and submitted her neck to the yoke.

The calf is on the field, the man has brought it hither; yet it lows not, rather makes no sound as it looks about in the strange field, which it thinks to be a field of the dead. It is too soon, thinks the calf, to let its voice be heard. But it has a clear idea of the man's purpose and long-distance calculations, this calf Jehosiph or Osarsiph. Knowing the man, it assumes at once and understands, though as in a dream, that its transportation to this field, so rebelled against at home, is no isolated fact or half-measure, but part of a plan, in which one thing follows upon another. This theme, of the "following on" or the "drawing after" is one of those which presented themselves contrapuntally in his intelligent and dreamy soul, in which, as one may say, the sun and the moon, as we sometimes see them, are in the sky at the same time, and the moon comes into play as the leading motif, making a gleaming path for its brothers the constellations across the sky. Joseph, the calf — had he not had his own thoughts at sight of the bright meadows of the land of Goshen, quite irrespective of the man's plans, though even so in harmony with them? Premature thoughts they were, and wide-ranging into the future — he saw that himself, and for the present they should remain unuttered. For much was yet to be fulfilled before they could come to fulfilment, and the mere coming hither was by no means enough. Something more must be added, to which there was need of the quietest waiting and the most childlike and secretive caution, withal no speculation at all as to the how. For that lay with the Man who brought the calf to the field — that lay with God.

No, Joseph was not unmindful of the old man at home, benumbed by his grief. His silence — the silence of so many years — must never lead us to reproach him. Least of all at this moment, the events of which I relate with emotions precisely like his own — for they are his own. I feel indeed as though I had once already reached this point in my story and told it once before; the special feeling of recognition, of having been here before and dreamed the same dream, moves me and challenges me to dwell upon it — and such precisely were the feelings, such the experience of my hero. For all which there is probably very good reason. What I am tempted to call his bond with his father — a bond the stronger and deeper in that, thanks to far-reaching associations, it was also a bond with God — was in particular strength at this moment, as indeed how could it not have been, when it subsisted in him, with him, and outside of him? What he felt was imitation and succession; with slight differences, his father before him had experienced the same. It is uncanny to see the mixture of free will and guidance in the phenomenon of imitation. In the end it is hard to tell whether it is the individual or the destiny that actually follows the pattern and insists upon the repetition. The inward and the outward play into each other, and materialize apparently without act of will into the event which was from all time bound up with and one with the individual. For we move in the footsteps of others, and all life is but the pouring of the present into the forms of the myth.

Joseph played with many forms of imitation and artlessly deluding self-metamorphoses, knowing how to make an impression with them and win men to himself, even if temporarily. But just now he was entirely preoccupied with the return of the father-idea and its resurrection in him. He was Jacob the father, a refugee from home, fleeing before fraternal hate, stolen to the kingdom of Laban to escape from the Red One's jealousy of the first-born blessing. This time, to be sure, there was not one Esau but ten, and Laban's present form was quite other than the old one: he was Potiphar, tamer of horses, arriving in a chariot with fiery wheels, arrayed in royal linen, fat and heavy, and so brave that one must tremble for his life. But Laban he was all the same, no doubt of that, however much life changed its forms. And once more, as the past had foretold, had the seed of Abram come a stranger into the land that belonged not to him, and Joseph was to serve a Laban who in his present form bore an Egyptian name and a high-flown title like "Gift of the Sun." But how long should he serve him?

Thus did we ask in the time of Jacob, and made the matter clear to the light of reason. Now we ask it with regard to the son, again with intent to clarify the matter and establish the dream within the reality. In Joseph's story the question of time and age have always been very laxly dealt with in the field of reality. Dreamy and superficial fantasy ascribes to his figure an unchangeableness untouched by time, such as it had in Jacob's eyes when he believed him to be dead and mangled. But that is an unchangeableness only conferred by death; actually the lad, immortalized to the father's eye, lived on and increased in years. We need to realize that the Joseph before whose chair the famine-stricken brethren stood and made obeisance was a forty-year-old man; and that they failed to recognize him not only on account of his dress and his dignity of rank but also because of the changes wrought by the years in his person.

Twenty-three years had passed since the Esau-brethren had sold him into Egypt — almost as much time as Jacob, all in all, spent in the land of never-more-return. And the same name might with even more justice be given to the country where now Abram's seed was once more strange; for the years which Joseph remained in it were not fourteen and six and five, or seven and thirteen and five, but actually the whole of his life; and only with his death did he return home. But it has remained uncertain and has been little considered in what proportion the years of his underworld life were divided into the two plain and clear epochs of his blessing-life: the first and decisive period of his sojourn in Potiphar's house, and the period spent in the pit whither he once more came.

The two periods came together to thirteen years — the same number that Jacob took to rear up his twelve Mesopotamian children — supposing that Joseph was thirty when his head was lifted up and he became the first among those below. Certainly we are nowhere told that that was his age — or at least nowhere where the statement would be authoritative. Yet it is a generally accepted fact none the less, an axiom, requiring no evidence and simply speaking for itself — begetting itself, as it were, like the sun, from its own mother, and with the clearest claims to a simple "So it was." For it is always so. Thirty years is just the right age for the stage of life at which Joseph then arrived; at thirty a man emerges from the darkness and wilderness of the time of preparation into active life; it is the age of fruition and fulfilment. Thirteen years, then, passed from the time when he entered Egypt a seventeen-year-old lad to the day when he stood before Pharaoh. There can be no doubt of it. But how many of them were spent in Potiphar's house and how many in the grave? The established tradition leaves it open; a few non-committal phrases are all we have to help us clear up the dates within our history. How shall we interpret them? What shall we conclude was the real division of the time?

The question seems inept. Do we know our story or do we not? Is it proper and suitable to the nature of story-telling that the narrator should openly reckon dates and facts according to any deductions or considerations whatever? Should he appear at all, save as anonymous source of the tale which is being told or is telling itself, in which everything is by virtue of itself, so and not otherwise, indis-

putable and certain? The narrator, according to this view, should be
in the tale, one with it, and not outside it, reckoning and calculating.
But how is it with God, whom Abram thought into being and recognized? He is in the fire but He is not the fire. Thus He is at once in
it and outside it. Indeed, it is one thing to be a thing, quite another
to observe it. And yet there are planes and spheres where both happen
at once: the narrator is in the story, yet is not the story; he is its scene
but it is not his, since he is also outside it and by a turn of his nature
puts himself in the position of dealing with it. I have never tried to
produce the illusion that I am the source of the history of Joseph.
Before it could be told, it happened, it sprang from the source from
which all history springs, and tells itself as it goes. Since that time it
exists in the world, everybody knows it or thinks he does — for often
enough the knowledge is unreal, casual, and disjointed. It had been
told a hundred times, in a hundred different mediums. And now it
is passing through another, wherein as it were it becomes conscious
of itself and remembers how things actually were with it in the long-
ago, so that it now both pours forth and speaks of itself as it pours.

It tells, for instance, about the apportionment of the years between
Joseph's sale to Potiphar and the lifting up of his head. And this much
is certain: that the Joseph who went down into the prison was far
from being the lad Joseph whom the Ishmaelites led before Petepre's
house; that much the larger part of the thirteen years was passed in
that house. I might state the fact categorically, but prefer merely to
inquire how it could have been otherwise. Joseph was, from a social
point of view, a complete cipher when as a seventeen- or eighteen-
year-old youth he came among the Egyptians; and his career there
must have embraced the whole time of his stay. For it was not on
the second or the third day of it that Potiphar set the Shabirite slave
over the whole of his property and left it in Joseph's hands. It took
some time before the master was even aware of Joseph's presence —
and the same is true of certain other persons of importance to the
issue of events. Moreover, that swiftly mounting career to the great
height he reached must even so have stretched into years, in order
to be the schooling in administration and economics which we are
led to consider it.

In a word: Joseph stayed with Potiphar for ten years, and became
a man of twenty-seven, a Hebrew "man," as it is said of him, by
some even a Hebrew servant, which sounds rather distorted and
exaggerated, considering that in practice he had long since ceased
to be a servant. We cannot tell or define the precise point at which
he ceased to be so — as little now as we could have done then. In
legal fact Joseph remained a servant, a slave, even at the time of his
greatest honour and actually until the end of his life. For we read
of his being sold, and of his being sold again, but nowhere at all of

his being freed. His phenomenal career ignored the legal fact of his status, and after his swift elevation it no longer came in question. Even in the house of Petepre he did not long remain a slave in any strict sense of the word; his rise to Eliezer's position of stewardship by no means occupied the whole of his time there. One thing is certain, that seven years were enough; another, that it was only the remaining three which were dominated and overshadowed by the emotions of an unhappy woman and which brought in their train the termination of the decade. The tradition does, by its very vagueness in the matter of time, indicate that the trouble did not begin at once or even very soon after Joseph's appearance; that it did not coincide with his rise to power, but only commenced after he had reached his height. "After these things," it says, "it came to pass"; in other words, after its own account of Joseph's rise to a position of the highest trust. That unhappy passion, then, must be thought of as lasting three years — quite long enough for the actors in it! — before the final catastrophe.

The results of our examination of this part of the story are borne out by the other half. We have calculated that the Potiphar episode occupied ten years of Joseph's life. Accordingly, there are three years left for the period in prison. No more and no less; and certainly it is not often that fact and probability coincide more nearly than in this case. For what could be more illuminating, more inevitable, than that Joseph lay three years in the prison, no more and no less, corresponding to the three days which he lay in the well at Dothan? We may even go so far as to assert that he suspected it beforehand, or even knew it, and measuring it by all that he held fitting, significant, and in the divine order of things, was convinced that nothing else was possible — confirmed therein by a destiny which took a perfectly inevitable line.

Three years — and not only that it was three, but also that it could not be otherwise. The tradition fixes with extraordinary precision and detail the way in which the three years were divided: it shows that the famous episodes of the chief baker and the chief butler, Joseph's elegant fellow-prisoners, upon whom he waited, fell in the first year. "At the end of two full years," it says, "Pharaoh dreamed," and Joseph interpreted unto him his dreams. Two full years after what? Opinions might differ. It might mean two years after he became Pharaoh — that is, two years after the accession of that Pharaoh who dreamed the riddling dreams. Or, on the other hand, it might mean two years after Joseph had interpreted the dreams of the butler and the baker, and the latter, as we know, had been hanged. But it would come to the same thing in the end: Pharaoh dreamed his dreams two years after the episodes of the imprisoned courtiers, and also two years after he had become Pharaoh. For during the time

Joseph spent in prison, at the end of the first year, to be precise, it came to pass that Amun-hotep, of his name the Third, united himself with the sun, and his son, the Dreamer, set upon his head the double crown.

Thus we see that there is nothing wrong about the story, but that all the evidence agrees concerning the ten and three years of Joseph's life until he was thirty; the true and the actual are one.

IN THE LAND OF THE MODERNS

PART of the game we play with life consists in the relations of human beings one to another. Take two people who have just exchanged their first glance — what could be slighter, what could be more unconscious, tenuous, distant, and casual than the bond between them? And yet it may be destined to take on, some unimaginable day, a character of burning intensity, a frightful and breathtaking immediacy. Truly this game, and the innocence of the players, may well be the subject of head-shaking and pondering on the part of the forewarned observer.

There knelt Joseph, a little round mound, beside the dwarf called Shepses-Bes, on the paving of the court and peered curiously through his fingers at the priceless, utterly unknown presence which swayed past him in its gilded chair adorned with lions' heads, only a few paces away. This underworldly product of culture, civilization's height, roused in him no other feeling than a respect strongly tinged with critical disapproval, no other thought than perhaps something like: "Ha ha, that must be the mistress — Potiphar's wife, who is supposed to tremble for his safety! Where does she belong — is she friend or foe? One cannot tell from her looks. A very great Egyptian lady. My father would disapprove of her. I am more lenient in my judgment; on the other hand, I am not to be dazzled." That was all. And on her side it was still less. As she swayed past she turned her jewel-crowned head for a second to the place where they did reverence. She saw them and saw them not — so idle and unseeing was her glance. She probably recognized the dwarf, for she knew him; perhaps the faintest shadow of a smile showed in her enamel-lengthened eyes and just deepened the corners of her sinuous mouth. Even that is doubtful. The other figure she did not know, and scarcely noticed it. He looked a little odd, because of the faded cloak the Ishmaelites had given him, and also his hair had not an Egyptian cut. Did she see it? She must have done so. But he could scarcely have penetrated her lofty consciousness. If he did not belong here, the gods knew where he did belong and that was quite enough; she, Mut-em-enet, called Eni, thought far too much of herself to consider the question. Did she see how beautiful and well-favoured he was? Why ask? Her seeing was no seeing; she never thought, it was hidden from her, that here was any occasion for the use of her eyes. Not the shadow of a suspicion visited either, of what was to happen, whither a few years was to bring them both. That the reverential little bundle over there on the ground was one day to be her one and all, her ecstasy and anguish, the single morbid content of her mind, which should distract its sense, make her commit mad acts of folly, destroy all the dignity, self-control, and order of her days — the woman dreamt not of it. What tears she would bring him to, with what uttermost danger she threatened his brideship of God and the garland of his head; that through her folly he would come in peril of losing his God — all this the dreamer could not dream, though the sight of her lily arm hanging down from her chair might have given him to think. The onlooker, knowing the tale as it fell out in all its hours, may be forgiven if he pauses a little, shaking his head, and assumes the ignorance of those who are in the story and not outside it.

He puts aside the indiscretion which made him lift the curtain of the future, and confines himself to the hour of the reigning feast, which lasted seven years, the years of Joseph's incredible rise in the house of Petepre, from that moment when, after the litter had swayed past them, the fool Bes-em-heb whispered to Joseph there in the court: "We must cut your hair and dress you as others are dressed —" and led him to the barber in the servants' quarters; who, jesting the while with Bes-em-heb, cut Joseph's hair in the Egyptian fashion, so that he looked like the wayfarers along the canals. Thence they took him to the wardrobe room, where the apron skirts were kept, and issued to him Egyptian clothing out of the stores: the livery of Petepre for best and for common wear; so that at last he looked like a child of Kemt, and even his brothers, at first glance, might not have known him.

These seven years, then, were a repetition and imitation of the father's life in the life of the son; corresponding to the period in which Jacob turned from a landless fugitive to a man weighed down with possessions, and an indispensable partner in Laban's enterprises, which by the power of the blessing were swollen with prosperity. Now it was Joseph's turn to make himself indispensable — and how did he do it? Did he find water, as Jacob did? It would have been utterly superfluous. There was abundance of water on Petepre's estate, not only in the lotus-pond in the pleasure-garden, but also in square basins sunk in the ground among the orchards and vegetable-gardens. They had no connection with the Nourisher, but supplied the estate from subsoil sources. No, there was no need of water. Nor of domestic well-being of any kind. For if Potiphar's house was not a house of blessing — and indeed it proved despite all its dignity to be rather a house of tribulation and folly — yet it abounded in material prosperity, to an extent which made it wellnigh impossible for anybody to give it increase or to play the rôle of blessing-bringer in any such sense. It must suffice that the owner should one day come to the conviction that if he put his affairs into this young stranger's hands all would be well and himself not need to trouble further, or act otherwise than befitted his lordly station and ways. So that the blessing displayed itself above all in the establishment of trust; and Joseph's natural dislike of betraying such confidence in any point — above all in the most personal and delicate — was to prove to the blessing-bearer a mighty bulwark against betraying his compact with God.

Yes, this was Joseph's Laban-time. Yet there were great material differences, and things fell out quite otherwise for the son. For in repetition there is always change, as in the kaleidoscope the bits of coloured glass shape ever different patterns. Life in its play produces changing patterns out of the same material, and the constellation of the sun, formed of the same little glass splinters as the father's, yet showed a new form. The parallel of the kaleidoscope is instructive; for in how much richer, more involved and varied patterns did the son's life shape itself! He is a later, more difficult and dangerous "case," this Joseph; a son, probably cleverer and flightier than the father, yet more interesting, difficult, painfuler; scarcely even is the pattern of the father's life recognizable in that of the sun who repeats it. How much richer it is, how much more complex, more dangerous! Where for instance is the figure and concept of Rachel, that pure and classic fundamental? — and what extraordinary and hazardous arabesque instead! Of course, we see what is coming, what is already present because it happened when the story first told itself, and is only not yet come to pass because we give due heed to later introduced laws of time and sequence. It exerts a powerful, uncanny fascination; our lively curiosity — of a peculiar kind, indeed, since it already knows, and interests itself only in the telling — tempts us ever and anon to anticipate the hour. Thus the double sense of the "once upon a time" practises its magic upon us; future is past, and what happened long ago now plays itself out again in the clear-cut present.

What we can do, in order to put reins to our impatience, is to extend somewhat our notion of the present; to include in it somewhat larger entities of sequence, and make of them a sort of loose coincidence in time. And the period we have in hand is quite suited to such a procedure — the years, that is, in which Joseph became first Petepre's body-servant and then his head overseer. They even demand such treatment, because there were circumstances which — quit contrary to probability — contributed to his success, and not only so but exercised an influence afterwards; and these played a part, like an all-pervasive atmosphere, even in the beginning, so that one cannot even discuss the early stages without bringing them in.

Our source, after confirming the fact of Joseph's second purchase, promptly states that "he was in the house of his master the Egyptian." Certainly, there he was — where else? He had been sold into that house and there he was — the tradition seems to assert the known and to be redundant. But let us be sure that we understand it. To say that he "was" in Potiphar's house means that he remained there, which is a new fact and one to be emphasized. After he was bought, Joseph *remained* in Potiphar's *house;* that is to say, he escaped, by God's will, the imminent danger of being sent to field labour, where he would by day have fainted in the heat, by night have shaken with cold, and might easily, under the lash of a barbarous overseer, have ended his days obscurely and in want, uncherished, unadvanced.

The sword hovered over him; we must wonder that it did not fall. It hung loose enough. Joseph was an alien sold into Egypt, a son of Asia, an Amu boy, a Shabirite or Hebrew; we must realize the contempt felt for such in this most arrogant of lands before we pass on to explain the influence which weakened and counteracted it. We have seen that Mont-kaw was tempted for a second or so to regard Joseph more or less as a god; but that does not mean that — certainly in the beginning — he did not think of him more rather than less as a man. For of course he did. The denizen of Kemt, whose forbears had drunk from the waves of the sacred river, at home in an unsurpassable land crowded with temples, statues, and writings compelling from old time, where once the sun-god in person had been king, was to expressly aware of his status as "man" to have much esteem left over for non-Egyptians, such as Negroes from Kush, Libyan pigtail-wearers, and Asiatic louse-beards. The conception of uncleanness and abomination was not an invention of the seed of Abram, and by no means peculiar to the sons of Shem. Some things they held in common detestation: as for instance the pig. But to the Egyptians the Hebrews were themselves an abomination — it went against them to break bread together; indeed, some twenty years later, when Joseph, God consenting, had become to all intents and purposes an Egyptian, he had foreign barbarians served separately when such at sat at his table, in order to keep himself in countenance with his own.

This was the position in Egypt respecting the people of Amu and Haru. And such was the view taken of Joseph himself when he first came. So that it is really a miracle that he remained in Potiphar's house and had not to perish in the fields — or rather it is to be marvelled at; for a miracle, a wonder-working of God in the full sense of the word, it was not. What actually came in play was the human: matters of taste and custom, influences which, as I said above, weakened and even abrogated the effect of the fundamental tradition. Not that the latter was not vocal. It spoke, indeed, in the voice of Dudu, spouse of Djeset, who demanded that Joseph be sent to field labour. For Dudu was not only a man — or a manling — of great and solid dignity; he was also spokesman and defender of the sacred and traditional in all its strictness; he was fundamentally pious, and withal, as a party man, he held with a school of thought which, committed by every consideration of state, ethics, and religion to an organic and militant unity, had to dispute its position against less limited and reactionary views. This school, so far as Petepre's establishment was concerned, had its seat in the house of women, more precisely in the apartments of the mistress, Mut-em-enet. For a familiar guest in those apartments was a certain man whose rigid personality made him the centre and nucleus of the traditional view: this man was Beknechons, the first prophet of Amun.

We shall speak of him later. For it was only after some time that Joseph first heard of the man; indeed, he only gradually gained insight into the situation hinted at above. However, he would have needed to be much less acute than he was, much less quick in sizing up advantage and disadvantage, not to have gained some inkling of essentials, even in his first conversations with the servants of the house. His method was to behave as though he already knew as well as anybody the inner mysteries and secrets of the country. His Egyptian sounded quaint and amusing in the ear of the natives and he made no haste to regularize it; but his choice of words was both lively and judicious, as he talked about the "rubber-eaters" — glibly adopting the popular name for the Nubian Moors whom he had seen crossing the river to audience on his arrival; or repeated the carping words of the gentlemen at the levee. They would not, he said, succeed in undermining the prince-prefect of Kush, for the latter had cut away the ground under their feet by the surprisingly lordly tribute with which he had rejoiced the heart of Pharaoh. All this made them laugh much more than if he had told them something new; and the way they made merry over his strange speech, even admiring it and listening to the Canaanitish words with which he helped himself out, shed even now some light upon the problem of advantage and disadvantage.

For they tried, as best they could, to speak as he did, mixing into their sentences craps of Akkadian or Babylonian as well as words from Joseph's own linguistic sphere. He divined, long before he could know it for a fact, that they were imitating the elegant attitude of their masters; and that these in turn did not ape the foreigner of their own motion, but because they wished to copy the manners of a still higher sphere — namely, the court. Joseph grasped the situation, as I have said, long before he could actually know it. He smiled to himself as he did so. These little people, so absurdly vain because they were brought up on Nile water and born in the land of "men," the only true birthplace of the gods, would have laughed to scorn the slightest doubt cast upon the superiority of their civilization over that of any of the surrounding countries. They were full to overflowing with the martial glory of their kings, their Ahmoses and Thtumoses and Amen-hoteps, who had conquered the earth as far as the contrary-flowing Euphrates and advanced their boundary-stones to the northern Retenu and the deserts and bowmen of the farthest south. And then, secure as they were, they were weak and childish enough to be openly envious of his Canaanitish speech, and that it was his mother tongue; and against all reason and sense to regard it as meritorious that he could speak it.

Why? Because Canaanitish was good form. And why good form? Because it was foreign and strange. But the foreign and strange was of no value and worthless? Yes, of course. But in spite of that it was good form; and this inconsequential esteem rested, in their own opinion, not on weakness or childishness but on liberality of thought. Joseph felt this — he was the first person in the world to feel it, since the phenomenon now appeared for the first time in the world. It was the freedom of thought possessed by people who had not themselves conquered those wretched foreign lands, but had it done for them by their forbears, and now took leave to make liberal thought the mode. The example was given by the great. The house of Petepre the fan-bearer made that clear to Joseph; for the more he saw, the plainer it became that most of its treasures came from the port — in other words, were importations. In fact, they came in large part from Joseph's own sphere, in a narrower or a more extended sense: from Syria and Canaan. That was flattering; at the same time he found it a little undignified. For on the leisurely journey from the Delta to the house of Amun he had had ample occasion to admire the native skill and craftsmanship of Pharaoh's country. Potiphar's horses were Syrian stock — it was indeed better to get them from Syria or Babylonia, for the Egyptian strain was poorish. But his chariots as well, and that very one with its wheels inlaid with stones like fireworks, were imported too. Then his cattle came from the land of the Amorites — which could be nothing else than a freak of fashion, considering the beauty of the domestic breed, with its lyre-shaped horns — the mild-eyed Hathor cows and the strong bulls from whose number Merwer and Hapi were chosen. Pharaoh's friend carried an inlaid walking-stick from Syria, and from Syria came the beer and the wine he drank. The jugs that held them came "from the port" as well; likewise the weapons and musical instruments which adorned his rooms. Ornamental vases almost the height of a man stood in painted alcoves in the northern and western hypostyle halls and on both sides of the dais in the dining-hall; the gold they were made of came doubtless from Nubian mines, but the vases were shaped in Damascus and Sidon. A reception- and banqueting-hall, entered by stately doors from the court itself, lay in front of the family dining-room; in it Joseph was shown other vases, somewhat eccentric in shape and decoration, from Edom, the Goat Mountains; they brought to mind Esau, his foreign uncle — he, too, was obviously the fashion here.

So were the gods themselves of Emor and Canaan: Baal and Astarte. They were considered very elegant; Joseph could tell by the way Potiphar's people took it for granted that they were his, asked about them, and paid them compliments. It seemed a feeble sort of broad-mindedness, because after all in the imagination of the people the relations between the powers of the various countries were incorporated in the gods and were only the expression of their personal life. Indeed, what was the thing itself, and what their picture? What the reality and what the paraphrase? Was it just a manner of speaking to say that Amun had conquered the gods of Asia and made them tributary, when the actual fact was that Pharaoh had subdued the kings of Canaan? Or was the latter only an unreal and sublunary expression for the former? Joseph knew that you could not distinguish. The thing and the image, the actual and the non-actual, formed an inextricably interwoven whole. But that was just why the folk of Mizraim were abandoning Amun, not only when they flattered Baal and Ashtaroth but also when they interlarded the tongue of their own gods with fragments of the speech of the children of Shem and said "*seper*" for scribe and "*nehel*" for river because the Canaanitish words were "*sofer*" and "*nahal.*" It was indeed a free-thinking spirit which underlay these fashions, whims, and habits — and free-thinking against Egyptian Amun. The issue of it was a much less thoroughgoing distaste for the Semitic and Asiatic — in his estimating advantage and disadvantage Joseph booked this fact on the credit side.

Thus he took note of fluctuations and variable currents of thought and opinion, growing, as I said, more able to judge them with each day that he lived and observed the life of the land. His master, Potiphar, was a courtier, one of the friends of Pharaoh; it was not hard to guess that this loose tolerance of foreign ways, this rebellion against Amun, displayed in Potiphar's life and habits, had its source over there in the West, beyond the "*nehel*," in the Great House. Had it, Joseph wondered, to do with Amun's warrior hosts, the lance-bristling temple troops which had shoved him to the wall in the Street of the Son? With Pharaoh's displeasure when Amun,

too powerful already as the established god of the state, competed
with him on the military side as well?

What strange, far-reaching considerations! Pharaoh's irritation at
the presumption of Amun or his temple became perhaps the final
reason why Joseph had not to go and labour in the fields, but might
remain in his master's house, and came on the fields much later, in
the capacity not of labourer but of overseer and administrator. The
situation, which made the boy profit from considerations of so lofty
and far-reaching a kind, pleased the young slave Osarsiph and made
a bond — aside from that through his present master — with the
Highest. But something else rejoiced him even more: a more pervasive
atmosphere in this world to which he had been transplanted. He de-
tected it as he sniffed for advantage or disadvantage with that pretty
if rather thick-nostrilled nose of his, and it was an air in which he
was as much at home as a fish in water. For the prevailing atmosphere — to put it in an old phrase — was *fin de siècle*. It was that of
a society composed of descendants and heirs, already remote from
the patterns of the founding fathers whose victories had put their
successors in the frame of mind to regard the conquered as elegant.
It appealed to Joseph, for he himself was late, too, in time and in his
soul, a very good specimen of a descendant, volatile, witty, difficult,
and interesting. So he felt like a fish in water, and filled with lively
hope that by God's help he would do honour to Him and to himself
and go very far in Pharaoh's land.

THE COURTIER

DUDU, then, the married dwarf, acted as a defender of tradition and
a partisan of the good old times; he spoke in Amun's name when he
advised Mont-kaw to send the new Shabirite slave to work in the
fields, for that he came from the enemies of the gods and was no fit
person for the house. He stood waving his stumps of arms and sending his deep voice up to reach the ear of Mont-kaw. But the steward
seemed disinclined to remember what Dudu was talking about or
to whom he referred. An Amu boy? Bought from the Minæans?
Named Osarsiph? Oh yes, yes. And after having thus given the other
a lesson in the careless and forgetful attitude proper to such a theme,
he expressed surprise that the keeper of the wardrobe should give
it any thought, much less waste words on it. He did so for the sake
of propriety, Dudu replied. It was offensive to the people of the
estate to break bread with such a one. The overseer simply denied
that they were so fastidious, and mentioned the case of a Babylonian
female slave named Ishtarummi, with whom the others in the house
of women got on very well. "Amun!" said the keeper of the wardrobe, naming the name of the conservative deity and looking severely,

even almost menacingly up at Mont-kaw. It was on Amun's account, he said. "Amun is great," replied the steward, with an ill-concealed shrug. "Anyhow," he added, "I may send the new slave to the fields. I may send him, or I may not; but if I do, it will be on my own motion. I like not those who try to throw a noose over my thoughts and lead them on a string."

In a word, he sent the spouse of Djeset about his business; partly on the ground that he could not stand the dwarf, but also on a ground that had backgrounds as well. The ground for his disinclination was the dwarf's pompous respectability, which rubbed him the wrong way; but the background was his own honest devotion to his master, Petepre, which sustained a sense of injury at Dudu's pretensions. All this will become clear later on. But ill will against Dudu's sterling personality was not the only reason why Mont-kaw turned a deaf ear to his words. The steward had a liking for the other dwarf, Beauty — less, perhaps, for himself than because he was an agreeable foil to Dudu. But he had snubbed him likewise when he appealed to his superior in the opposite sense. Good, beautiful, and wise is the desert youth, darling of the gods, that was what Bes had whispered. He, Bes, by name the beautiful, but in fact not such a one, had seen the truth, with the unerring penetration of his dwarf senses; the overseer should see to it that Joseph be given tasks, whether in the court or outside it, which would give employment to his qualities. But here too the steward had pretended absent-mindedness and then irritably refused to give any thought to the problem of employment for the chattel which partly by chance and partly by good nature he had acquired. There was no hurry, and he, Mont-kaw, had other things to think of.

That was reasonable enough, for the steward was weighed down with cares, and his kidneys gave him much trouble. The reply was convincing, the dwarf had nothing to say against it. But the truth was that the steward pretended, to himself and others, forgetfulness of Joseph because he was ashamed of the equivocal thoughts and impressions which he, a practical man, had had at first sight of the slave; when he had been half inclined to take him for a god, the Lord of the White Ape. He had felt ashamed, and that was why he wished to forget and not be persuaded by the importunities of others to act in line with his own impressions. He refused alike to send his purchase to the fields or to think of using him in the house; refused, in short, either to act or to think of acting, in either or in any direction. The good man did not perceive, he tried not to see, that precisely in doing nothing he was acting on his first impressions. And the bottom of his restraint was fear; it arose, just among ourselves, from the feeling which is the bottommost one in the world and thus lay at the bottom of Mont-kaw's soul: the feeling of expectancy.

Thus it came about that Joseph, garbed and barbered like an Egyptian, spent weeks and months without work; or at most in some light and desultory occupation on Petepre's court; in which he was not very noticeable, for there were plenty of loiterers and bystanders besides himself. And in a way he was pleased and satisfied to have no notice paid him — that is, not prematurely, or until it could come about in proper and dignified fashion. He did not want to begin his career in a false or unreal way, by being drawn into some one of the trades practised in the courtyard and being lost for ever in that obscure activity. He guarded himself against such a fate, keeping himself from observation at critical moments. He would sit and chat with the gate-keepers on their brick bench, making them laugh with his Asiatic expressions. But he avoided the bakery; such marvellous triumphs of the baker's art were there achieved as would put his uncommonly good pancakes quite in the shade; nor did he call attention to himself in the booths where they made sandals, or paper, or mats of woven palm, or pottery, or furniture. He was warned by an inward voice that it would be foolish to play the part of ignorant apprentice — foolish, and prejudicial to his later career.

On the other hand, there was no harm in making lists and doing accounts now and then for the laundry or the granary; and for this his knowledge of writing soon became adequate. At the bottom he would sign with flourishes: "Written by the young foreign slave Osarsiph, for his master the great Petepre; may the Hidden One give him long life! Likewise for Mont-kaw, the steward set above all, greatly skilled in his office; for whom he implores from Amun ten thousand years of life beyond his life. Written on this and this day of the third month of Ákhet, the time of the flood." In such terms, recreant to the practice of his own land, did he express himself, in the consciousness of his blessing, and in sure trust that God, seeing his situation and the need of making himself loved, would not take them ill. Such lists and signatures came to the eye of Mont-kaw; he saw them at odd times and made no sign.

His bread Joseph ate with the people of Potiphar, in the servants' house; drank beer with them and passed the time of day. Soon he could chatter with the best — or even better; his gifts inclining him to use his tongue rather than his hands. He listened to their idiom and took it in his mouth, first to talk but later to give orders. He learned to say: "As true as the king liveth!" "By Khnum, the great, Lord of Shab!" He learned to say: "I am in the greatest joy of the earth" and "He is in the rooms beneath the rooms" — in other words, on the ground floor. Of an angry overseer he said: "He raged like the leopard of Upper Egypt." In telling a story, he trained himself to give great prominence to the demonstrative pronoun, this being the custom of the country; to say: "And when we came before this impregnable fortress this good old man said to this officer: 'Look at this letter!' And when this officer looked at this letter he spake: 'By Amun, these strangers may pass!' " His hearers enjoyed it hugely.

Several feast-days fell in each month, not only calendar but also seasonal, as when Pharaoh cut a swath of grain to open the harvest; there was the anniversary of his accession and that of the unification of the two lands; the day when they set up the column of Osiris, with masques and sistrum-playing. There were the days of the moon and the great days of the Triad, Father, Mother, and Son. And on all such days there was roast goose and beef in the servants' house, and Joseph's small-sized patron, Bes, brought him all sorts of dainties and sweetmeats from the house of the women: grapes and figs, cakes baked in the shape of cows lying down, and fruits in honey. "Take it, young sandman," he would whisper, "it is better than leeks to your bread, and your little friend brings it to you from the tables of the shut-in ones, after they have feasted. For they grow far too fat with their munching and crunching, and are nothing but cackling stuffed geese before whom I dance. Take it all, then, that the dwarf brings you and may it do you good; the others have not such food."

"And is Mont-kaw yet mindful of me in the way of my advancement?" Joseph would ask, after thanking the dwarf for his offerings.

"Not much as yet," Bes would answer shaking his head. "He is deaf and asleep where you are concerned and will not be reminded. But the dwarf is at work to bring your ship into the breeze, let him see to it. He is thinking how best to make it come about that you shall stand before Petepre — and it shall come to pass."

It was Joseph who had urged upon Bes-em-heb the necessity of his coming to stand before Petepre, in some way and at some time; but the thing was almost impossible to bring to pass, and the dwarf could only go about it by small stages. Attendance on the master, even of a general kind, and much more the personal service, was firmly held in jealous hands. It was a pity that Joseph had not been granted duties in the stables: feeding, currying, harnessing and unharnessing Potiphar's Syrians. But never once had he succeeded in leading out the fiery pair — not even for Neternakht the driver, to say nothing of the master himself. That would have been a step in advance — but it was impossible. No, for the present it would not be his to speak with the master, but only to hear his servants speak about him; to question them of their lord and the way matters stood in the house, and to keep a watchful eye wherever possible on the service of the master. The latter enterprise had to do above all with Mont-kaw, and he had begun putting it into effect on the very day he was bought.

And each day the same scene repeated itself, he saw and heard it. Mont-kaw flattered the master. His lips ran over with praise, and moisture stood in his eyes as he sang pæans to the dignity and riches of his lord; he never failed to laud and marvel at his boldness and virility, his control of his steeds and prowess as hunter, whereat all the world about him trembled. And all this he did — Joseph felt certain — not for his own sake and not to curry favour, but on the master's account, and thus by no means in a lickspittle spirit. Mont-kaw seemed a very decent man: not cruel to those below nor cringing to those above him; his adulation of the master was only to be taken in a good sense, as an expression of his genuine love, his desire to bring by sweet words comfort to the soul of his lord. Such was the impression Joseph got, strengthened by the faint smile, at once gratified and melancholy, which appeared on the lips of Pharaoh's friend as he listened to the words of praise, this tower of a man, who yet in all other ways was so unlike Reuben. And the more Joseph understood the situation in the house, the more clearly he felt that Mont-kaw's bearing toward his master was only an example of the relations of all the other members of the family. They were all very gracious, very respectful, and delicately considerate of each other, displaying a mutual politeness which was a support, no doubt, but made an impression of exaggeration and strain: so Potiphar to his wife, the lady Mut-em-enet, and she to him; the exalted parents in the upper storey to Petepre their son and he to them; they in turn to their daughter-in-law Mut, and she to them. Their dignity and self-confidence, supported by outward circumstances of the very best and by their own behaviour, seemed after all not to be a very firm footing; there was something hollow about it. Therefore they the more strove to strengthen by all this tact and courtesy each other's self-respect. If in this house of blessing there reigned an atmosphere of uneasiness which even had its comic side, in this it consisted; if there was a weight of care, herein it lay and showed itself. It gave itself no name, but Joseph guessed it: the dignity was a sham.

Petepre had many titles and honours. Pharaoh had lifted up his head. Many times the Highest at his window, in presence of the royal family and the court, had flung down upon him the goal of favour, while the populace had applauded and made ceremonial leaps of joy. Joseph heard about it in the servants' house. The master was called fan-bearer on the right hand and friend of the king, and lived in well-founded hope of one day becoming "unique friend of the king" — there were very few of this title. He was captain of Pharaoh's guard, head executioner, and commandant of the royal prisons. Or rather he bore the title of these court offices, for they were empty or nearly empty honours. Actually — so Joseph was told — it was another man — an upper officer named Haremheb, or Hor-em-heb, a rough soldier and lieutenant-colonel — who commanded the bodyguard and presided over the executions. Very likely he had to render account to his titular head and the honorary commander of the prisons, but only as a matter of form. Certainly it was lucky for this fat towering Reuben of a man, with his high voice and melancholy smile, that he had not to administer justice by mangling the backs of criminals with five hundred blows, or, as the expression went, "bringing them to the house of execution and martyrdom" to "put them in corpse-colour." It would have been most unfitting and repugnant to him. Yet Joseph was given to understand that much recurrent humiliation and gilded care might grow out of such a state of things.

For Potiphar's offices and honours, symbolically represented by the staff he carried in his small right hand, once a bludgeon and now degeneration into a pine-cone, were a dignified fiction, which not only Mont-kaw but all his world about him combined to sustain for the sake of his self-respect. Yet secretly, half-unconsciously, he knew them for what they were: for unreality and hollow pretence. And just as the pine-cone formed the symbol of that pretence, so, Joseph felt, was Potiphar's whole state a symbol of a more far-reaching hollowness, that had not to do with offices, but with the man's own natural dignity as a man.

Joseph knew, he had memories not personal to himself which instructed him, that social conventions, the traditional conceptions of honour, avail but little against the dark and silent knowledge in the depth of the soul, which will not be deceived by daylight fictions. He thought of his mother. Yes, strange though it was, while he explored and pondered on the situation of his purchaser and master, Petepre the "man" of Egypt, his thoughts turned to her, the lovely one, her trouble and bewilderment. He knew about it; it was a chapter of his prehistory and tradition — besides, Jacob had often told him stories of that time when Rachel, great though her willingness, was unfruitful by decree of God, and Bilhah had had to be brought in and had given birth upon Rachel's knees. Joseph could see that puzzled smile upon the face of her rejected by God: a smile of pride at her maternal dignity, which yet understood that this was a sham and a conception of honour upheld by human standards but not founded in her own flesh and blood. It was half a joy and half a pretence; countenanced by usage, but at bottom a detestable sham. He called these recollections to his aid as he thought of his master's position and pondered over the conflict between the conscience of the flesh and the expedient honoured by usage. Certainly Potiphar had many more and richer compensations than Rachel had had. He was wealthy. His existence was brilliantly adorned with precious stones and waving ostrich plumes; kneeling slaves attended his ways, his house was full of treasures, his women's house of the twittering and cackling, lying and sweet-eating apanage of a lordly life, with the lily-armed Mut-em-enet as his chief and lawful wife. All this redounded to his dignity and availed mightily to uphold it. And yet far within, where Rachel had been aware of her secret shame, he knew that he was not captain of the bodyguard, but only its titular head. Otherwise he would not have needed the flattery of Mont-kaw.

He was a courtier, a chamberlain and servant of the king. A very highly placed one, overwhelmed with honours and possessions, yet a courtier in the full sense of the word; and the word "courtier" had a slightly malicious tinge, or rather it was used in two related senses which flowed together. It was a word not used today in its original — or not only in its original — meaning, but in a transferred one which kept the original one as well, so that in a quite honourable and respectful way it was malicious, and contained an innuendo which flattered in two directions: with reference both to dignity and to the lack of it. A conversation heard by Joseph — not overheard but listened to quite openly and in the course of his duties — taught him much about all these matters.

THE TASK

It was ninety or a hundred days after his entry into this elegant and distinguished household that Joseph, through the good offices of Sa'ankh-Wen-nofer-Neteruhotep-em-per-Amun, the dwarf, was given a task. It was a simple and rewarding one to carry out, if also a little burdensome and painful. He was lounging as usual in Potiphar's courtyard, willy-nilly waiting his hour, when the dwarf came running, in his crumpled finery, with the felt cone of ointment cocked on his head, and announced in a whisper that he had something for him, a piece of good luck worth hearing, and leading to advancement. He had got it from Mont-kaw, who had said neither yes nor no, but simply suffered it. No, he was not to stand before Petepre — not yet. "But hearken, Osarsiph, what you are to do and how fortune smiles by the dwarf's contrivance, who has kept you in mind and brought it about: today at the fifth hour after midday, after their nap, the exalted parents from the upper storey will come to the pleasure-garden, and there, sheltered from sun and wind, will enjoy the coolness of the water and the peace of their great age. They love to sit there hand in hand in two chairs, alone in this hour of repose save for a dumb waiter who shall kneel in a corner with a salver of refreshment to comfort their spirits when they are tired from their peaceful sitting. You are to be the dumb waiter, Mont-kaw has commanded, or at least has not forbidden it, so you shall hold the salver of refreshment. But you must not budge as you kneel with your burden, not even to blink your eyes, else you might disturb their rest with your too much presentness. You must be entirely the dumb waiter and like a figure of Ptah, for so are they used to have it. Only when the exalted brother-sister pair give sign of fatigue, then you must set yourself briskly in motion, still on your knees, moving very carefully without stumbling or spilling anything on your clothing, and bear them the delicacies to be a cordial to them. When they are satisfied, then you must kneel backwards swiftly into your corner and take care for your body, not to pant or do aught to disturb or give sign of your presence, but to become at once the dumb-waiter as before. Can you perform all that?"

"That I can," Joseph replied. "Thanks, little Bes, all that will I do, precisely as you have said, and even my eyes shall be as though glass, that I may look like an image, without presence more than the space of air which my body takes up. So nothing shall I be. But in all my stillness my ears shall be open wide, unseen by them, the exalted brother-sister pair, when they speak before me and name by their true names all the household matters, and I shall become master of them in my mind."

"Very good," answered the dwarf. "But conceive not that it will be simple to play for so long a space the dumb waiter and image of Ptah, or to haste to and fro upon your knees. It would be well for you to practise by yourself. The dish of refreshment will be dealt out to you by the scribe of the sideboard; not in the cook-house, but in the provision-chamber of the house of the master. They will have it ready. Enter through the gate of the house into the entrance-hall and turn left by the stair toward the private room of trust which is the bedchamber of Mont-kaw. Cross over diagonally and open the door on the right, leading into a long corridor-chamber, full of provisions so that you will see it is the store-chamber. There you will find the scribe who will give you all needful. That you must carry most heedfully across the garden to the summerhouse, a little time before the appointed hour, that you may be already in your place when the exalted ones come. You are to kneel in your corner and hearken. When you hear them approaching, stir no eyelash more, or even scarcely breathe, until when they seem fatigued. Do you understand your service now?"

"Perfectly," Joseph replied. "There was once a man's wife turned to a pillar of salt because she looked back at the place of destruction. Such will I become in my corner and with my dish."

"I know not the tale," said Neteruhotep.

"One day I will tell it to you," Joseph responded.

"Pray do, Osarsiph," murmured the dwarf, "in reward for the service which I have procured you. And repeat to me again the tale of the serpent in the tree, and how the pleasant one slew the unpleasant one, and the story of the far-seeing man and his ship like a chest. Also the tale of the saved sacrifice, and the smooth one whom his mother made rough with skins, and later in the darkness knew the false bride."

"Yea," replied Joseph, "ours are good tales to hear. But now I go, to practise running to and fro and up and down on my knees, noting the shadow on the clock that I make myself fine in time for my service and fetch the refreshments from the provision-room and perform all as you have said."

He did accordingly; and when he thought himself perfect in running he anointed and preened himself, put on his best clothes, the under apron-skirt and the longer upper one that was transparent, tucked in the little shirt of darker, unbleached linen, and failed not to adorn breast and brow with garlands for the honour of the service to which he was called. Then he glanced at the sun-dial, in the open space surrounded by the master's house, the house of women, the cook-house, and the house of the servants; and went through the wall and the gate into the vestibule of Potiphar's dwelling, which had seven doors of red wood with fine wide bands of decoration above them. The roof was supported by pillars likewise of polished red wood, with stone bases and green capitals. The floor had a design of the heavens with its constellations, containing hundreds of figures: lion, hippopotamus, scorpion, serpent, goat, and bull stood in a circle with many figures royal and divine, and the ram, the ape, and the crowned falcon.

Joseph crossed the hall and by a door beneath the stair leading to the rooms above the rooms he entered into the private room of trust which was the nightly place of him above the house, Mont-kaw the steward. Joseph himself slept among the others, on the floor in the servants' quarters; he looked curiously round at this private room. The bedstead was of elegant form and rested on the claws of beasts; it was covered with skins and the head-board had pictures of the gods that preside over man's sleep: misshapen Bes, and Ipet the pregnant hippopotamus. There were chests, and stone washing-things, lamp-stands and a bucket for coal. He thought to what high position of trust he must rise here in Egypt to achieve such comforts as these. The thought brought him back to his service, and passing on he came to the long provision-chamber, so narrow that it needed no columns or supports to the roof. It ran the whole western length of the house, abutting not only on the dining-room and reception-hall but on the third or western pillared hall; for besides this and the eastern one there was another or northern hall, of such rich and superfluous extent was the structure of Petepre's house. This long corridor, however, was, as the dwarf had said, lined with rows of shelves full of dishes and provisions: fruit, cakes, loaves of bread, boxes of spice, basins, beer-skins, long-necked wine-jugs in beautiful stands, with flowers to crown them. It was Khamat, the lanky scribe, whom Joseph encountered here, rummaging and reckoning among the stores with his reed pens behind his ear.

"Here you are," said he, "greenhorn and know-nothing from the desert! You have made yourself fine indeed. You like it well in the land of men and of the gods? Yes, you are permitted to attend upon the exalted parents — I have it written upon my tables. Most like it was Shepses-Bes who procured you the service; how else would you have come by it? But he was anxious for your purchase and screwed up your price to a fantastic sum. For how can you who are a calf have the value of an ox?"

"Take heed to your words," Joseph mentally addressed him; "for one day I shall most certainly be set above you." But aloud he only said:

"Be so good, Kha'ma't, scholar of the book-house, who can read and write and make magic, as to give this unworthy petitioner the refreshment for Huia and Tuia, the venerable parents, that I may have it ready for them as dumb waiter in the hour of their exhaustion."

"I must, I suppose," the scribe replied. "Your name is on my list and the fool has brought it about. But I foresee you will spill the drink on the feet of the exalted pair and then you will be taken off to be refreshed in your turn, until you are exhausted too and he that gives it you as well."

"Praise be to God, I foresee quite otherwise," Joseph replied.

"Do you indeed?" asked the lanky Khamat, blinking. "And after all it is your affair, not mine. The refreshment is here and is written down: the silver bowl, the little gold jug full of pomegranate juice, the little gilt cups, and five sea-shells with grapes, figs, dates, doum fruit, and little almond cakes. You will not steal or even nibble them?"

Joseph looked at him.

"You will not, then," said Khamat, in some confusion. "So much the better for you. I merely asked, though I thought at once you would not like to have your ears and nose cut off — and moreover it is probably not your way. It is only," he went on, for Joseph was still silent, "because it is said that your former owners condemned you to the punishment of the well for certain shortcomings — I know not what, they may have been slight and had to do not with matters of mine and thine but with questions of wisdom — I cannot tell. And I have heard that the punishment availed to cleanse you; so that I only thought it right to put a warning question. . . ."

"What am I saying?" he thought to himself. "Letting my tongue run on like that! I am a surprise to myself, to find that I am irresistibly tempted to say all sorts of other things which should not be urgent, but are, all the same."

"My office obliged me," he said, "to ask as I asked. It is my duty to assure myself of the honesty of a servant whom I do not know; and for my own sake I must do it too, for mine is the fault if any of the gear is lost. And I do not know you, your origins are dark — at least in so far as it is dark in a well. Back of that they may be brighter; but the name they call you — Osarsiph, is it not? — seems in its last syllable to say you are a foundling from the rushes and rode round in a rush basket until a water-carrier drew you out; such things come to pass now and then in the world. However, it is possible that your name has another meaning, I cannot tell. For in any case I asked as I did because it was my duty — or if not absolutely my duty then according to custom and in a manner of speaking. For that is the way and it is the tradition that one speaks thus to a young slave, as I spoke, and calls him, as I did, a calf. I would not say you are actually and in fact a calf, how could that be? Rather I spoke but according as all speak. Nor do I actually expect and foresee that you will spill the pomegranate juice on the feet of the exalted parents. I only said so to be gruff, as is the custom in such cases, and spoke not the truth. Is it not a strange thing in the world that a man will hardly ever say what is his own, but that which he thinks others would say, and speaks after pattern and scroll?"

"The dishes and what is left of the drink and food," Joseph said, "I will bring back when my service is done."

"Good, Osarsiph. You can go straight through the door at the end of the store-room instead of through the private room of trust. Then you will stand before the wall and the little gate in it, and beyond are the gardens and flowers and you will see the pond and the smiling pleasure-house."

Joseph went out.

"Well," thought Khamat, left behind, "how I did run on, God help me! What this Asiatic will think of me is past finding out. Had I but spoken as others do and according to pattern and scroll! Instead of that I felt all at once I must utter some uncommon truth, and gabbled quite against my will till my cheeks burn to think of it. By the aard-vark! When he appears next before me, I will be as gruff with him as the best of them!"

HUIA AND TUIA

Joseph meanwhile had passed through the little gate in the ring wall and found himself in Potiphar's garden, where the finest sycamore trees, date-palms and doum-palms, fig, pomegranate and persea trees stood in rows on the greensward. Paths of red gravel ran across the grass. Half hidden among the trees, on a terraced mound, stood the gaily painted summerhouse, open toward the square basin of water bordered with papyrus reeds. On that green mirror swam bright-feathered ducks, and a light bark floated among the lotus blossoms.

Joseph, with the dishes in his hands, mounted the steps to the kiosk. He was familiar with these elegant and aristocratic surroundings. Beyond the pond the plane-tree avenue was visible, leading to the double-towered gate on the south side of the ring wall, which gave direct entry to Potiphar's flourishing estate. The orchard, with its little runnels full of subsoil water, continued from the east edge of the pond, and then came the vineyards. And there were fields of the loveliest flowers, on either side of the plane-tree avenue and about the summerhouse on the mound. The carrying of all the soil needed to make the original desert blossom like the rose must have cost the children of the house of bondage much labour and sweat.

The little building, quite open on the side next the pond, was flanked by white columns fluted in red, and furnished most charmingly. It was a dainty little retreat, adapted alike for solitary contemplation and enjoyment of the garden's loveliness and for intimate intercourse — perhaps of two people, as the draughtboard on a little stand seemed to indicate. Gay paintings covered the white background of the walls, partly floral decorations consisting of garlands of corn-flowers, yellow persea, grapevines, red poppies, and the white petals of the lotus flower; but partly too of spirited natural scenes: there was a troop of asses so lifelike that one thought to hear them bray; a frieze of high-chested geese, a green-eyed cat peering from among reeds; stalking cranes of the most delicate rust-red colour; people slaughtering and carrying poultry and legs of beef in a sacrificial train. All this was so excellently carried out; so blithe and light-hearted and playfully mocking was the relation of the painter to his subject, so bold and faithful at once his hand, that involuntarily one would find oneself exclaiming: "Yes, yes, what a jolly cat, what a haughty crane!" And yet the whole seemed elevated into a sphere both more vivid and more austere, an æsthetic heaven as it were, a celestial realm of good taste. Joseph as he scanned these things could give no name to that which none the less he perfectly well understood. This was culture which smiled down upon him from the walls; and Abram's late descendant, Jacob's youngest son, a little worldly as he was, leaning to youthful curiosity and youth's glorification of freedom, rejoiced in the sight — always with a silent reservation and a thought of the too spiritual-minded father, who would have objected to all this picture-making. "It is charming to the last degree," he thought; "admit it, old Israel, and revile not this achievement of Kemt's children, this taut and worldly and smiling effort, in the very flower of good taste — for perhaps it might even be pleasing in the sight of God Himself! I feel friendly toward it and find it exquisite — despite the consciousness in my blood that probably the real and important thing is not to carry nature's handiwork into the high heaven of good taste but rather the urgent need of care for God and the future."

Thus Joseph to himself. The furnishings of the little house were in the same heavenly good taste: an elegant long couch of ebony and ivory, resting on lions' claws, spread with panther and lynx skins and strewn with soft cushions; roomy armchairs with backs of gilded leather stamped in fine designs, full of embroidered cushions and with fat foot-stools to match; bronze incense-stands giving off priceless savour. This interior, so comfortable, domestic, and inviting, was at the same time a chapel and place of worship; for on a raised platform at the back were offerings of flowers and little silver teraphim with the crowns of gods on their tiny heads; while various cult objects showed that their rite was observed.

So then Joseph knelt down, to be in readiness, in the corner by the entrance, setting his burden on the mat before him, to rest his arms. But before long he hastily lifted it and stiffened his pose, for Huia and Tuia were scuffling in their beak-toed sandals across the garden, each supported on the arm of a child servant. The two little maids had arms like thin sticks, and mouths that hung foolishly open. For the brother-sister pair would have only such to wait on them. These then helped the old people up the terrace and into the house. Huia was the brother and Tuia the sister.

"First before our lords," old Huia ordered in a husky voice, "and to bow before them!"

"Just so, just so," old Tuia agreed. She had a large, pale oval face. "Before our gods first of all, that we may pray their leave, before taking our ease in our chairs, in the peace of this summerhouse."

And they had the children lead them over before the teraphim, where they lifted their withered hands and bent still more their bended backs — for age had bowed and buckled the spines of both. Huia, the brother, had an unsteady head; it shook a good deal up and down as well as sometimes sidewise. Tuia's neck was still steady. On the other hand, her eyes had retreated in her face till they were a mere pair of blind colourless slits; a fixed smile sat on her large face.

After the parents had prayed, the little maids led them to the chairs which stood ready in the foreground of the little house, and let them sink cautiously down. They took their feet and set them on the foot-stools, which were laced with gold cord.

"There, there, there!" Huia said in his hoarse whisper, for other voice he had not. "Go now, maidservants, for ye have done your duty, our feet are set and our bones rest, and all is well. Let be, let be, I sit — and thou too sittest, Tuia, bed-sister of mine? Then all is

well, go until we call you and stay away, for we want to be by ourselves to enjoy the sweet hour of late afternoon and early evening, as
the light rests upon reeds and duck-pond; and to look across the avenue to the towers of the gate in the strong wall. We want to be quiet,
and sitting thus seen and heard by nobody to talk to each other in the
familiar phrases of old age."

Meanwhile Joseph, with his dish, was kneeling in his corner, diagonally opposite to them and quite near. But he well knew that he
was nothing but a dumb waiter, in presence like a piece of furniture
and no more; with glassy eyes he gazed past their old heads.

"Go, little maids, obey the mild command," said Tuia. In contrast
with her brother's she possessed a clear, soft voice. "Go, and wait just
so near and so far that ye shall hear our hands clap when we call you.
For if weakness should come over us or death surprise us we will clap
our hands in sign that you are to come and let the soul-birds to flutter
out of our mouths."

The little maids prostrated themselves and went. Huia and Tuia
sat beside each other in their chairs, a beringed old hand of each
clasping the other's on the inside arm. They wore their grey hair,
the colour of much-tarnished silver, just alike: it fell in thin strands
from the scantily covered head, over their ears nearly down to their
shoulders. But sister Tuia had made an attempt to twist the strands
together by twos and threes into a sort of decoration, which did not
come to much because of the thinness of the hair. Huia, on the other
hand, had a little beard of the same dull silver on the under side of
his chin. And he wore gold ear-rings that showed through his hair,
while Tuia's old head was crowned with a broad band in a petal
design in black and white enamel, which one would have liked better
on a younger head. For we feel that beautiful things belong to youth
and freshness and jealously grudge them to a head which is already
nearly a skull.

In other respects too, Petepre's mother was elegantly dressed: her
pure white robe was cut like a shepherd's cape at the neck and girdled
with a beautiful ribbon embroidered in bright colours, its lyre-shaped
ends hanging nearly to her feet. A wide necklace of the same black
and white enamel as her head ornament covered her age-shrunk
breast. In her left hand she held a bunch of lotus blossoms and carried them now and then to her brother's nose.

"Smell them, my treasure," she said. "Sniff the sacred flowers,
lovely gift of the swamp! Comfort thyself with their scent of anise,
after the tiring walk from the upper storey to this peaceful spot."

"Thanks, twin sister and bride," old Huia answered hoarsely. He
was well wrapped in a mantle of fine white wool. "Enough, let be;
I have smelt and I am refreshed. Thy health!" said he, bowing over
her like a stiff old nobleman.

"And thine!" she replied. Then they sat silent awhile, blinking into the beauty of the garden, the bright perspective of pond and avenue and flowery meadows, with the towered gate at the end. And old brother Huia blinked even more anciently than his sister-bride, with weary eyes, like lights gone out. He chewed ceaselessly with his toothless jaws, and his little beard bobbed evenly up and down.

Tuia did no such mumbling. Her large face was calm, the head a little on one side, and the little cracks of eyes seemed to share in her permanent smile. Very likely she was skilled at raising her husband's spirits and bringing him back to awareness of the world about him; for she said:

"Yes, my little old bullfrog, here we sit, and the silver gods are good to us. Our slim young maids have settled us dutifully in the cushions of these fine chairs and slipped away, so that we are alone together like the divine pair in the mother's womb. Only in our hole it is not dark, and we may feed upon its pleasantness — the pretty pictures and the well-made furniture. Lo, they have set our feet on broidered foot-stools, as a reward for having trod the earth so many weary years, all four together. But if we lift our eyes we can see the beautiful disk of the sun spreading its bright wings above the entrance to our hole, flanked by cobras, Horus, lord of the lotus, son of the dark embrace. The shapely alabaster lamp by the sculptor Mer-em-opet they have set on a stand to our left and in the right-hand corner kneels the dumb waiter with dainties in his hands prepared for our desire. Hast thou yet desire, my bittern?"

Frightfully hoarse came the brother's reply:

"I desire already, dear mud-lark; but I mistrust my mind and palate, lest it is they that desire, and not my stomach, which might rise up against food with cold sweat and deadly anguish if I feed it before time. It is better we should wait, until we are weary of sitting and have actual need."

"Thou'rt right, buttercup," answered she, her voice sounding very full and soft after his. "Check thy appetite, that is wiser, thou wilt still live long nor will the dumb waiter run away with the cordials. Look, he is young and pretty. He is as choice as all the other things with which they surround our old eyes. Garlanded is he like a wine-jug, with tree blossoms, flowers from the reeds, and flowers from the beds. His pretty black eyes gaze past thine ear, they look not on the place where we sit, but at the background, and thus into the future. Dost thou understand my play with words?"

"It is easy to understand," old Huia strained his voice to croak. "For thy words point to the purpose of this charming little hut, where for a while the dead of the house always lie, behind us, in front of the silver ones in their shrines, on well-shaped trestles, after they have been disembowelled, after the doctors and embalmers have filled them with nard and rolled them in bandages and before they are borne in their ship up the river to Abdu, where He Himself lieth buried, and been given their splendid burial such as that they make for Hapi and Merwer and for Pharaoh, and are shut up in their good eternal dwelling and its columned rooms where their own life smiles at them in colour from all the walls."

"Right, my swamp-beaver," Tuia rejoined. "Thy mind is clear and clearly hast thou grasped the play of my words, as I also can understand thy meaning in a trice, whatever the figure thou clothest it in, for we play on each other's minds, being an old brother-sister pair, who have played together all the games of life: first those of childhood and then those that a man and a woman play together. Thy old mole takes no shame to say it, for we are here alone in the house and are as one."

"Yes, yes," said old Huia, with apologetic haste. "For our life was life together, from the beginning unto the end. We were much in the world and among the people of the world, for we are nobly born and near the throne. But at bottom we were always alone together in the little house, the house of our brother-sisterhood, as we are in this one here: first in the mother's womb, then in the house of childhood and in the dark room of marriage. Now we two old folk sit here and gaze at the dainty decorations of this little house, so lightly built, our refuge for a day. But the eternal refuge awaiteth us in the pillared cave in the West, which shall shelter us through all time, through unnumbered jubilees, while the dreams of life smile down upon us from the dark walls."

"Right, my good house-wren," Tuia agreed. "But is it not strange that at this hour we still sit here in our chairs in the front of this little temple and talk to each other — yet in but a little while we shall be resting at the back on lion-footed trestles, in our wrappings, with feet pointed up, and have our faces outside once more, with the little god-beard on our chins: Usir Huia and Usir Tuia, and above us sharp-eared Anpu will bend?"

"Very queer, no doubt," croaked old Huia. "But for myself I see it not so clearly and shrink from the strain on my head, for it is tired. But thine is still strong in thoughts and steady on thy neck. That makes me misgive, lest thou in thy freshness might not depart when I do, but sit in thy chair while I take the narrow path alone."

"Have no fear, my king-fisher," answered she. "Thy little old mole will not leave thee alone; and shouldst thou breathe thy last before her a draught of physic will congeal the life in her veins and we shall still be together. For I must certainly be at thy side after death, to prompt thee in the reasons and justifications at the judgment."

"Will there be judgment?" asked old Huia uneasily.

"We must expect it," answered she. "So the law teaches. But there

is doubt whether it still hath full authority. There are laws which
are like old houses: they endure and stand upright but no one lives
in them any more. I have questioned Beknechons, Amun's great
prophet, how it may be in the hall of the judging goddesses, with
the scale for the weighing of the heart and the hearing in the presence
of Him of the West, at whose side sit the two-and-forty frightfully
named. Beknechons's words were unclear. The law stands, so he told
thy mole. For all standeth to everlasting in the land of Egypt, the old
as well as the new set up beside it, the land being thick with laws,
images, and buildings, with living and dead, and one moves among
them in decency and propriety. For the dead is the more holy only
in that it is dead, the mummified truth, to be preserved everlasting to
the people, even though it is forsaken by the spirit of the newly
taught. Thus spoke Beknechons the wise. But he is very much the
servant of Amun and zealous for his god. The king of the lower regions, with the fan and crooked staff, about him he troubles less, and
the teachings and tales that are told about him he cares for but
little. He may call them a forsaken building and mummified truth;
but there is no certainty that we must not come before them, as the
common folk believe, to declare our innocence and have our hearts
weighed in the scale, before Thoth absolve us of the two-and-forty
sins and the Son take our hands to lead us to the Father. We must
reckon with the chance. And therefore must thy wise little old owl
be at thy side, in death as in life, to take the word in her mouth
when we stand before the throne and explain our deeds to the frightfully named, lest thou forget the reasons and thy head fail thee at the
great moment. For my little buck-bat is even now sometimes cloudy
in his mind."

"Do not say so!" Huia burst out more hoarsely than ever. "For if my
head is tired and foggy, it is because I have pondered so long and hard
upon the reasons and the explanation. But even a foggy mind may talk
of the matters which make it foggy. For was it not I who thought and
spoke in the sacred darkness of the sacrifice and the atonement? That
canst thou not deny; it was I, for I am the man, thy brother-husband
and the begetter, between us two; dark indeed in the holy darkness
of the nuptial chamber, but not too dark or foggy in his mind that he
could not light up the ancient darkness with the idea of making part
payment to the holy new law."

"Have I denied it?" Tuia replied. "Nay, that thy old bride denies
not at all: truly it was her old knave of dark corners who first begot
the idea of drawing a line between the holy old and the splendid new,
in other words the worldly, which mayhap may be the order of the
new day. We might have to reckon with it, and so it behoved us to
make offering and atonement. For thy old mouldwarp saw it not,"
she said, turning her large face this way and that as the blind do; "I

was reposing in the holy old, and unable to understand anything of the new order."

"Not so," Huia contradicted her, croaking. "For thou didst see it as soon as I brought it up. Thou art quick to receive, if not to invent; and thou hast well understood thy brother's plan and his concern over the new order and the age. How else shouldest thou have agreed to the sacrifice and the payment? And when I say agreed, the word is not enough; rather I had but to tell thee my worry concerning the age and the order of the day, and thou camest of thyself on the idea of consecrating the dark son of our holy wedlock to the splendid new time and of withdrawing him from the old."

"How canst thou say so?" the old woman asked, bridling. "Thou crafty old corncrake, to say that it was I who had the idea; thou wilt be putting it off on me when we stand below before the king and the frightfully named! What a sly old fox! For at most I but understood and conceived, after thou, the man, hadst begot — as I received from thee our Horus, our little son-of-the-dark, Petepre the courtier, whom we turned into a son of the light and vowed him to the lordly new according to thy own notion, which was from thee, though I brooded and bore it as Eset the mother. And now cometh the judgment; and when we stand before the judge and it may prove that our deed was wrong and false, thou wilt make it seem that not thou but I conceived and bore it, of myself alone!"

"Stuff and nonsense!" he answered, in an angry croak. "It is well and good we are alone and no one can hear the folly thou art prattling. For have I not myself said that I was the man, and that I lighted our darkness with the idea? How canst thou then put on me the meaning that begetting and bearing are the same — though they are, indeed, in the swamps and the black river mud, where the mother-stuff breweth and giveth itself to its own embrace and fructifieth in the darkness; but not in the world above, where it is so that the man must visit the woman."

His voice gave out, he coughed and mumbled with his jaws. His head shook violently.

"Might it not, dear old mother-frog," he said, "be time to summon the dumb waiter to refresh us? Thy green frog feels worn out with all this thinking and his strength is sapped by the effort to make clear the motives and the justification."

Joseph, still staring like a lifeless image past their heads, made ready to run on his knees. But the occasion passed over, for Huia went on:

"Yet it is probably excitement and not real weariness that bringeth me in mind of food; which then my stomach, being unsettled, might reject. For there is nothing in the world more upsetting than these thoughts about the age and the order of the day. They are most important of all, save only that a man must eat, for of course that comes before everything else. Yet so soon as he is full, and free of that care, he thinks of holiness, and asks if it is holy still, not already despised, and a new era begun, so that he must hasten to suit himself to it and appease it with consecration and sacrifice, to save his life. Now we, brother-sister pair that we are, are rich and well born, and need have no thought for food, having everything of the best. So there is nothing more important for us or more upsetting than this very matter. Long indeed hath thy old croaker's head shaken, being troubled by it; we may so easily make a serious blunder, in trying to set things right and atone. . . ."

"Be quiet, my buck-rabbit," said Tuia, "and shorten not thy life without need. If there is judgment and the law still stands, then will I speak for us both and frankly explain the deed of atonement, that the gods and the frightfully named ones shall understand and not reckon it to the two-and-forty misdeeds, and Thoth shall acquit us."

"Yes," Huia answered her, "it will be well for thee to speak, for thou hast it more in thy mind and art not so upset; because thou hast it from me and only understood and received it, so thou canst better put it in words. I who begot it might be confused and stammer in my excitement before the judges, so that we lost the game. Thou shalt be the tongue for us both; for the tongue, as thou well knowest, hath two natures in the slippery-slimy darkness of the womb and standeth for both sexes, like the swamp and the brewing mud which embraceth itself, before the time of the higher order, wherein the man visits the woman as is fit."

"But thou didst visit me well, as man to wife," said she, with a delicate gesture of modesty, moving her large sightless face to and fro. "Long and oft it had to be, before blessing came and the sister was fruitful to thee in wedlock. For our parents had vowed us to each other in our earliest youth, but many cycles passed before our brother-sisterhood was fruitful in a son. Then brought I to thee Petepre, the courtier, our Horus, the beautiful lotus, Pharaoh's friend, in whose upper storey now we the exalted live out our latter days."

"True, true," old Huia agreed. "So was it, as thou sayest, in all properness and even holiness, and yet after all there was a catch in it in our secret thought, and a hidden care which paid heed to the time and age and strove to fit in with the order of the day. For we, male and female, begot in propriety, but we did so in the dark chamber of our sister-brotherhood. And the embrace of brother and sister — is it not after all a self-embracing in the depths and so not far removed from the brewing mother-stuff, hated by the light and the powers of the new order?"

"Yes, so hast thou told me, as my husband, and I took it to heart. I may have taken it amiss of thee to call our embrace a brewing of the swamp, when it was pious and honourable even to holiness, in harmony with the most refined custom and well done in the sight of gods and men. Is there then anything more pious than to imitate the gods? For they all beget upon their own blood and embrace in wedlock their mothers and sisters. It is written: 'I am Amun, who hath made pregnant his mother.' So it is, for each morning the divine Nut beareth the radiant one, but at midday, become a man, himself begets with his mother the new god. Is not Eset sister, mother, and spouse to Usir? Even in the beginning and before birth, in the wrapping of the mother's womb, the exalted brother-sister pair embraced each other, and dark it was, and slippery-slimy, as in the house of the tongue and the depth of the swamp. But holy is the darkness, and highly honourable in the sight of men is this pattern of marriage."

"That sayest thou, and sayest with right," he responded, in his hoarse, labouring voice. "But in the darkness the wrong brother-sisters embraced each other too, Usir and Nebthoth, and that was a great mistake. So the light avenged itself, the glorious light, to whom the mother-dark is hateful."

"Yes, so speakest and spokest thou as husband and master," she retorted, "and art of course for the glorious, the lordly and new, while I as mother and wife stand more for the holy, for the pious old custom, and thy views made me sad. We are noble old folk, and near the throne. But the high consort, was she not nearly always Pharaoh's sister, after the divine pattern, and precisely as sister destined to be the wife of the god? He whose name is a blessing, Men-Kheper-Re-Thutmose, whom should he have embraced as the mother of God if not Hatshepsut, his exalted sister? She was born to be his wife and they were divine flesh. Man and wife shall be one flesh, and if they are that from the beginning, then the marriage is propriety itself and no brewing-up of the depths. Thus was I born for thee, for a bond and in the bond, and we were destined for each other by our noble parents from the day of our birth because they surely guessed that the brother-sister pair had embraced each other already in the womb."

"I know naught of all that, and can certainly remember not at all," he answered hoarsely. "We might just as well have fought in the womb and kicked each other, for at this stage people have no thoughts. Even outside if we sometimes quarrelled, as thou knowest, though of course not kicked each other, for we were well brought up and very respectable in the sight of gods and men, living happily in harmony with the best traditions. And thou, my mouldwarp, wast content in thy soul, like a sacred cow with satisfied countenance, especially after thou wast fruitful to me with Petepre, our Horus, as my sister, mother, and spouse."

"So it was," she nodded pensively. "Blissfully satisfied was I, blind mouldwarp and satisfied cow, in the caul of our happiness together."

"But I," he went on, "was man enough, in the days of the strength of my mind, and according to my sex close enough to the lordly in the world, that I could not be satisfied with the pious old views. I had enough to eat, and so I thought. Yea, I remember, the twilight of my mind lifts a little at this moment, so that if I now stood before the judgment of the dead, I could speak. For we lived after the pattern of gods and kings, in full harmony with pious custom and with the approval of men. And yet there was a thorn in my flesh and a care concerning the vengeance of the light. For light is lordly, in other words manly, and hateful to it is the brewing up of the mother-darkness, to which the manner of our begetting was still near and knit to it by its umbilical cord. For lo, one must cut the cord, so that the calf may free itself from the mother-cow and become a bull of the light. Which teaching prevaileth, and whether there be judgment after we breathe our last is not the important thing. Important is only the question of the age and whether the thoughts by which we live are still the order of the day. That alone is of import, after hunger is appeased. But now there is come into the world that which I divined long since: that the male principle will tear the umbilical cord between him and the cow and set himself as master over the mother-stuff on the throne of the world, and found the order of light."

"Yea, so hast thou taught me," answered Tuia. "And satisfied as I was in the sacred darkness, yet I took thy idea to my heart and bore it for thee. For the woman loveth the man and so she taketh his thoughts even though they are not like hers. The woman belongs to the holy and old, but for the sake of her husband and master she loveth the lordly new. And thus we came to the sacrifice and the atonement."

"So we did," agreed the old man. "And today I could explain all that clearly before the king of the lower world. We wanted to withdraw our Horus, whom as Usir and Eset, brother-sister pair, we begot in the darkness; withdraw him from the dark kingdom and dedicate him to the purer light. That was our partial payment to the new age, upon which we agreed. And we asked not his wish in the matter but did with him as we did, and perhaps it was a mistake, yet a well-meaning one."

"If it was," said she, "then are we both guilty, for we concocted it together, to do thus with our son of the darkness; but thou hadst thy thoughts about it and I mine. For as mother I thought not so much about the light and the propitiation as of our son's greatness and honour on earth. I would make of him a courtier and chamberlain by thus preparing him; a royal official, destined by what we made him to be an honorary captain, and to have Pharaoh gild with the gold of favour the man devoted to his service. Those were, I confess, my thoughts, which made atonement to my heart for the atonement, though I found it very hard."

"It was but in the order of things," he said, "that thou hast taken my idea in thy own way and added to it in thine, so that out of the whole grew our deed, which we did in love to our little son, since he had yet no views of his own. I too was glad at the advantage which flowed to the dedicated boy in thy thoughts as a woman. But mine were the thoughts of a man and turned toward the light."

"Aha, little old brother," said she; "I fear that he has only too much need of the advantages which flowed to him. Perhaps we shall have to speak of them not only at the judgment, but before our son as well. For however tenderly respectful his treatment of us, however high and dear he holds his parents, yet I think and sometimes fear to read in his bearing that secretly he is not glad that we pruned him into a courtier without asking his consent, and before he was able to defend himself."

"That," Huia hastened to say hoarsely and with some heat, "would be grumbling against the exalted parents in the upper storey! For his duty is to reconcile us with the age, it was for that we dedicated him; and what he gets in return is enough to make everything good, so that he need not find fault or pull a long face. Nor do I think he does, least of all at us, for he is by nature and spirit a man, and thus related to the lordly new; I cannot believe but that he consents to his parents' act of atonement and wears his consecrated state with pride."

"Surely, surely," she nodded. "And yet, old man, thou'rt not sure thyself that the cut with which we severed the cord between him and the mother-darkness was not a cut in the wrong direction, after all. For did he, by being so consecrated, become a bull of the sun? No, he is only a courtier of the light."

"Repeat not my own scruples after me," he reproved her hoarsely. "Anyhow they are not of the first importance. The first concern is that about the age and the order of the day, and the act of atonement. It is in the nature of atonements that they may turn out badly and leave something not quite atoned for."

"Surely, surely," she said again. "And doubtless he hath, our Horus, rewards of the most flattering kind, and his compensations as sun-chamberlain and honorary official to the lordly are magnificent indeed, no question of that. But there is Eni too, our little daughter-in-law, Mut-em-enet the beautiful, Potiphar's chief wife and head of the house of the secluded ones. Sometimes an old woman and mother like me has thoughts about her too. She behaves with most loving respect toward us; yet I suspect that in the depth of her soul she harbours a faint secret grudge against us because we made a courtier of our son so that he is not really in her sight a captain of the guard but only bears the title. Trust me, she is woman enough, our Eni, to sulk over it; and I am enough of her kind to read it in her face when she thinketh herself unwatched."

"Nonsense," Huia rejoined. "It would be ingratitude itself for her to cherish such a grudge as that in her exalted breast. For she has compensations, and even super-compensations, more than Petepre himself; and I cannot bear to believe that she is gnawed by the worm of envy for earthly things when she has the blessings of the divine, bearing the title of bride of Amun and dweller in the house of his consort at Thebes! Is it nothing, is it a slight thing, to be Hathor, spouse of Re, and to dance before Amun with others of her order, in the close-fitting garment, and to sing to the beating of the tambourine, the gold cap on her head, with the horns, and the disk of the sun between them? No, it is no slight thing, but a compensation of the highest and most glorious kind, which she has as spouse of the courtier our son. All this her kin well knew, when they gave her to him as his chief and true wife when both were but children and there could be no thought of marriage between them according to the flesh. And it was good so, for an honorary marriage it was and has remained."

"Yes, yes," responded Tuia. "So it had to be. Yet when I think of it as a woman, I find it hard: brilliant indeed and of great honour by day, but an affliction by night. Mut is she called, the wife of our son, Mut in the valley of the desert, a mother-name from ancient times. But mother can she and may she not be, on account of our son's consecrated state; and I fear that she lays it up against us, taking it ill despite all the gentleness she shows."

"She must not be a goose," scolded Huia, "not a bird of the water-sodden earth. That she shall hear from me, our daughter-in-law, if she sulks. I do not like to hear thee take her side against our son, simply because thou art a mother and a wife. Thou dost offence to Horus our son. And even more to the woman-nature for which thou thinkest to speak, for thou degradest it in the world, as though one could never see it in any other image than that of the ever-pregnant hippopotamus. Truly thou art by nature a mole; and it was I by my man's nature gave thee the thought of the new age and the part payment. And yet thou couldst never have received it nor understood it, nor come to terms with the act of atonement, if there were no link between the woman's nature and the purer and more lordly one, so that it had no share in it at all. For must it be that the black pregnant earth is ever the woman's image and portion? By no means: the woman may in all dignity appear likewise as the chaste priestess of the moon. I will let her know, thy Eni, that she must not be a goose. As our son's chief and true wife she is counted among the first women of the land; to his greatness she oweth it that she is friend to Queen

Tiy, the wife of the god, and is herself a god-wife of Amun's southern house of women and belongeth to the order of Hathor, whose
head and first woman of the harem is the wife of Beknechons the
great prophet. So great indeed are her spiritual compensations that
she is in short herself a goddess, with horns and sun-disk, and a white
moon-nun in her spiritual state. Is it not quite fitting that her earthly
marriage is honorary and her spouse on earth a dedicated atonement
and a courtier of the light? All that seemeth to me most excellent, and
let me tell thee, it is what I would have said to her, if she hath not
understanding for the fitness of it!"

But Tuia answered, shaking her head:

"I cannot tell her, for she gives no occasion to her mother-in-law
for such a rebuke, and would be amazed if I were to do thy errand
and tell her she is a goose. She is proud, our Eni, as proud as Petepre,
her husband and our son. Neither of them knows aught but the pride
of their day, neither moon-nun nor sun-chamberlain. Do they not
live in happiness and self-respect in the sight of day, in harmony
with the best society and pleasing in the sight of man? What need
they know but this their pride? For if they knew more, they would
not admit it or confess it to their own souls, but only continue to
pay honour to their pride. How shall I take the word 'goose' from
thy lips and give it to our daughter-in-law? For she is no goose; she
is proudly conscious of being set apart for the god, and her whole
being is scented with the bitter fragrance of the myrtle. When I speak
of ill feeling and of affliction I have not the day in mind nor the
honours of the day, but the silent night and the mother-darkness,
where it is no use to scold and call names. Thou hast sometimes been
afraid of the vengeance of the light because of our marriage in the
darkness; I sometimes as a woman fear the vengeance of the mother-
darkness."

Here Huia began to snigger. The sound startled Joseph a little, so
that he stirred the slightest bit and for a moment lost his imperson-
ality as dumb waiter. His gaze forsook the background for a flash
and sought the old pair, to see if they had noticed. But they had not;
absorbed as they were in their talk they gave him as little heed as
they did the alabaster lamp made by the sculptor Mer-em-opet, that
stood in the other corner. He turned away his gaze and once more
looked past Huia's ear into the background. But his breath went fast,
after all that he had listened to, to hear old Huia still laughing his
old-man laugh — it sounded uncanny.

"He he!" went old Huia. "No fear, the darkness is dumb and knoweth naught of anger or revenge. Son and daughter-in-law are proud
and know naught of mumps and dumps, nor yet ill feeling against
the parents who treated them thus and made a barrow of the little
boar when it could hardly walk and had no ideas at all. He he! No

fear! Mumps and dumps are well shut down in the dark, and even if
they stuck their noses out into the light they would be bound by the
rules of decorum to be gentle and polite to their exalted parents, however much we may have played them a trick in the past to our own
advantage. He he he! Twice bound, doubly sure, doubly sealed,
nothing to be done against the parents so snug in the upper storey!"

Tuia at first seemed uneasy as she listened; but she was gradually
convinced, and joined in his laughter till her blind eyes went quite
shut. There sat the old pair in their stately chairs and chuckled together, with their hands on their stomachs, their shoulders stooped,
and their heads drawn down between.

"Yes, he he! Thou art right," Tuia chimed in. "Thy old mole can
understand the joke: we played a trick on our children, but we are
doubly safe against their wrath. That was cautious and crafty. And
glad am I that my old frog is merry and hath forgot his fear of the
judgment in the halls of the dead. But feelest thou now no desire to
be refreshed, no exhaustion, so that I should summon our dumb
waiter to fetch up his dainties?"

"Not at all," replied Huia. "I feel not the slightest weariness, rather
our hour of talk has given me new life. Shall we save our hunger till
the hour of the evening meal, when the exalted family gathers in the
dining-room and we elegantly hold the lotus blossom to each other's
noses? Let us clap that our servants may come and support us as we
walk in the orchard, for my old limbs feel desire to stir."

And he clapped. The little maids came running, their mouths open
foolishly in their zeal. Each offered a spindling arm to a parent,
helped them down the terrace and away.

Joseph fetched a deep breath and set down his burden on the floor.
His arms were nearly as lame as when the Ishmaelites had drawn him
out of the well.

"Certainly these are fools before the Lord," thought he, "these exalted little old parents! What a glimpse have I had into the painful
secrets of this house of blessing, may God pity it! Thus we see that
to live in the highest heaven of good taste doth not save one from
the most arrant blunders. How I should like to tell my father of this
exalted idiocy! Poor Potiphar!"

And he lay down on the mat to rest his tired limbs before carrying the refreshments back to Khamat.

JOSEPH CONSIDERS THESE THINGS

HE was excited and dismayed by what he had overheard, and during
this time it preoccupied his thoughts. For the exalted parents he felt
a lively disgust, only held in check by the need for politeness and reverence, not in the least by the darkness of ignorance. For neither his

anger at the irresponsible stupidity of those old people in the sight of God, nor his abhorrence of their smug satisfaction at being secure against all reproach, was lacking in any element of clear-sightedness toward himself.

It did not escape him that what he had heard possessed instructive implications for him, the descendant of Abram; and he would not have been Joseph had he not been ready to profit by them. The experience was calculated to broaden his view and warn him not to regard his own immediate spiritual home, the world of his fathers and its preoccupation with God, whose nursling and pupil he was, as something all too unique and incomparable. Not Jacob alone had cares in the world. Care was everywhere among men; everywhere the anxiousness to be sure one understood this problem of the Lord and the times — though it might lead here and there to the most dubious expedients, and indeed Jacob's inherited thoughts of God might afford the subtlest test one could apply to a possible decline of custom and tradition from the will and influence of the Lord.

And anyhow it was just here that error lay closest to hand. One did not even need to think of Laban, left clinging to the primitive, nor of the little son in the jar. There every kind of awareness of the problem had been lacking, even though the practice had already gone far to become an abomination. But precisely the developed sensitivity for such changes could easily lead one astray. Had not Jacob's painful misgivings in the matter of the feast tempted him to destroy feast and custom root and branch just because of their roots, which drew their nourishment from the unclean soil? The son had had to beg him to spare the feast, the tree that spread its shade and tossed its tip in the air, which like the Lord had risen out of the earth, but must wither if one uprooted it. Joseph was for sparing, he was not for uprooting. He saw in God — who after all had not always been what He was — a God of sparing and of passing over; not even in the case of the deluge had He proceeded to extremes or hewed at the root of mankind, but had put the idea of the ark into the head of an exceeding wise man. Wisdom and passing over: these seemed to Joseph related thoughts, which might exchange their garb and even had a name in common: goodness. God had tempted Abram to offer Him his son; but then He had not taken him, introducing a ram, in a most edifying way. The tradition of these people here, in however exalted kingdoms of taste they moved, was lacking in such good stories. There was some excuse for them, repulsive as they were with their sniggers over the blundering trick they had played on their children. To them, too, instruction had come from the spirit of the father, in the shape of an uncertainly moving rumour, itself still very much having its being in the darkness, that one must emerge and escape from the stage of the traditionally sacred and come over

into the light. They had received the instigation to the sacrifice. But
how like Laban they were in their clinging to the old! For precisely
to cling was what they hoped to do, by dint of making sacrifice to
the new. But no ram had appeared to these God-forsaken ones, that
might turn into a ram of light; the sacrifice had been their trembling
little son, Potiphar.

Yes, one might truly call that a God-forsaken way of dealing, a
gross lack of skill in going about to propitiate a new and splendid
age. For an approach to the spirit of the father, thought Joseph, did
not lie in taking things out by the roots; and there was truly a great
difference between consummate double-sexedness and its utter abrogation in the courtier. For the double-sexed powers united both
male and female glory in themselves; like the image of the Nile with
one woman's breast and one man's; or like the moon, that was wife
to the sun and yet male to the earth, sending the ray of his seed to
beget the bull on the cow. The relation of all this to the status of
courtier was, in Joseph's mind, as two to nothing.

Poor Potiphar! For a cipher he was, in all the splendour of his fiery
chariot-wheels and his greatness among the great of Egypt. His young
slave Osarsiph had a cipher for a master, a Reuben-tower without the
strength or the fallibility, a broken sacrifice, neither accepted nor
rejected, a neither-nor, not human nor divine; very proud and stately
in the light of day, yet poor indeed, and in need of all the support
and flattery that could accrue from outward circumstance — and
especially from the devotion of Mont-kaw.

Joseph considered that devotion afresh in the light of his new understanding, and did not hesitate to find it worth imitating. So it
was: on the ground of the insight he had gained while playing the
dumb waiter he resolved to be "helpful," as Mont-kaw was helpful,
to his Egyptian master; nor did he doubt that he would exceed the
measure and quality of the other's service. For thus, he told himself,
would he best be helpful to another master, and that the Highest, in
the task of prospering the young slave Osarsiph in the land to which
he had been transplanted.

Here in the interest of truth we must warn the reader lest he level
against Joseph the reproach of being coldly calculating. That would
be precipitate and censorious. The situation was too complicated for
such moral judgments. For Joseph had long been watching Mont-
kaw, the oldest servant of the house, realizing that he was a good
man, whose obvious flattery of his master deserved a better name and
must be called a service of love. And the conclusion followed that
Potiphar, the honorary captain of the guard, must be worthy of such
love — a conclusion confirmed by Joseph's own observation of his
master. This great man of Egypt was a noble, fine and sensitive soul;
and kindly, too, in the slave's opinion. True, he took pride in making

others tremble for his sake; but considering his status as a sacrifice to certain mistaken conceptions of the spiritual, that probably ought to be allowed him, Joseph thought.

We see that it was not when Joseph began to serve Potiphar, but actually before it, and in his own heart, that he defended him and espoused his cause. In the first place, the Egyptian was his lord, to whom he had been sold, and highest of his sphere. And Joseph's conception of his relation to him included, by right of his tradition, an element of loyal forbearance, which was applicable not only in the higher but in the lower sphere, and to some extent to earthly conditions and immediate surroundings. We are to understand that the idea of the Highest bore within it a conception of unity that was favourable to interchange and a certain equalization as between the higher and the lower. This was reinforced by the idea of "helpfulness" — the thought that he, Joseph, by serving Potiphar as did Mont-kaw, would best be "helpful" to the wide designs of the Highest who sent him his dreams. And other considerations as well came to make his relations with the Highest to a certain extent colour his attitude toward the master of the fiery wheels. He had seen Petepre's smile, melancholy, proud, and yes, grateful, in answer to the flatteries of Mont-kaw. He had seen the helpless loneliness it expressed. It sounds childish; but Joseph found a resemblance, equally appealing to his pity, between the solitary remoteness of God the Father and the isolation from the human lot of this tower of a man, this mutilated Reuben, however behung he was with the gold of favour. Yes, God too, the Lord, was lonely in His greatness; and Joseph's blood and his memory spoke in the realization that the isolation of a wifeless and childless God had much to do with the jealousy of the bond He had made with man.

Joseph knew the peculiar happiness which loyal service can give the lonely; the quite peculiar pain which lack of it can mean. He did not of course fail to see that God, after His nature, had nothing to do with procreation or death, for that He was both Baal and Baalat; the great difference between two and nothing did not for a moment escape him. Yet I but express in words what he certainly felt, when I say that these intuitions of loving and sparing were dreamily at one in his heart when he resolved to keep faith with the cipher in its need as he did with the needy Two.

JOSEPH SPEAKS BEFORE POTIPHAR

AND NOW we come to that decisive first meeting and conversation between Joseph and Potiphar, in the orchard. It has not been described in any of the sources; none of the accounts, Oriental or Occidental, in prose or verse, so much as dream of it. It is in the same case as countless other corroborative details which this version may boast of bringing to light and embodying in the accepted tradition.

We know that it was again Bes-em-heb, the mock-vizier, to whom Joseph owed the long-desired and in the result decisive meeting; even though the dwarf could not actually arrange for it but only prepare the ground. And the preparation lay in bringing it to pass that the young slave Osarsiph, heretofore lounging superfluous about, with but occasional occupation, was one fine day given a job as gardener in Potiphar's garden. Not, of course, as head gardener; for the head gardener was a certain Khun-Anpu, son of Djedi, nicknamed Red-belly, because that part of his body was burnt by the heat and hung down like a setting sun over the apron round his middle. He was a man about the age of Mont-kaw, but lower in station, though possessing dignity and competence in his calling: well-versed in the lore of plants, both for purposes of decoration and gain, and also on their medicinal side. Thus he was not only forester, gardener, and florist but also apothecary and barber-surgeon; master of the arts of decoctions, draughts, salves, clysters, juices benign and malign, cataplasms and emetics, which he prepared at need for man and beast, though of men it was only the servants for whom he prescribed, since the masters had a severe professional physician from the temple of the god. — Khun-Anpu's bald spot was red too, for he scorned to cover it, and wore a lotus blossom behind his ear, as the scribes did their pens. Bunches of all sorts of herbs hung out of his apron, roots and shoots, which he snipped off or dug out as he moved among his plants; shears, chisel, and a little saw hung from his waist and clanked as he went. He was stout, with a red face screwed up in an expression not at all unfriendly; his nose was knobby; his mouth, likewise wried, whether in satisfaction or the opposite one could not tell, was covered with irregular, unshaven hairs like little rootlets; they added to the earthy aspect of Red-belly's blinking, sunburnt face. His short forefinger, brownish-red and soil-encrusted, when he held it up to threaten some malingerer, looked like nothing so much as a freshly dug beet.

Little Bes, then, had approached the gardener on the subject of the foreign slave. He had told him in a whisper that the stranger was gifted and skilled from childhood up in the knowledge of growing things; that before he was sold he used to tend his father's olives in the wretched Retenu, and out of love for the fruit had quarrelled with his fellows because they had thrown stones at the trees and crushed the olives too roughly in the press. Likewise had given the dwarf to understand that he had inherited a sort of charm, a lucky hand as it were, of twofold nature, from heaven above and from the earth beneath; which was just what a gardener needed and therefore Khun-Anpu might take the boy among his underlings as at present he was a loss to the household, being idle. It was dwarfish wisdom that spoke, and those who hearkened had never regretted it.

Thus spoke the mock-vizier, having in mind Joseph's desire to stand before the master and knowing that employ in the garden would give him the best opportunity. For like all the great of Egypt the fan-bearer loved his well-watered grounds, the like of which he hoped to possess and enjoy in the life after life. At various times of day he would rest there or walk up and down, talking with the labourers if the mood took him. Not only with Red-belly, their overseer, but with the workers as well, hoers and water-carriers. On this circumstance the dwarf rested his hopes, and they were well founded.

Thus Joseph was put to work by Red-belly; and it was in the orchard that he received employment, more precisely in the palm garden, which ran from south of the house to the edge of the pond, giving place to vineyards on the east, near the court. But the palm garden was a vineyard too, festoons of vine hung between the tall feathered columns, with merely openings here and there that one might pass through. The garlands were heavy with grapes, and the date-palms bore each year a crop of many hundreds of litres; the sight of their combined fruitfulness was a paradisial delight to the eye — no wonder, then, that Petepre loved his palm garden, with its basins of water sunk here and there in the ground, and often had a couch spread for him there, that he might listen at the same time to the breeze whispering in the crown of the palm trees and the voice of the reader or the scribe making a report at his side.

Here then it was that the son of Jacob found employ, of a kind both evocative and painful, since it called up memories of a dear and now frightfully lost possession: the veil, the coat of many colours, his and his mother's *kuttonet passim*. Among its embroideries had been one he had noticed when for the first time he saw the shimmering bridal garment draped over his father's arms, in Jacob's tent. It was a sacred tree, and on either side a bearded angel was fructifying it by touching it with the cone of the male flower. Joseph performed now the work of these two genii. The date-palm is diœcious; and the task of pollinating the fruit-bearing trees with the pollen of those which produce pollen-sacs instead of blossoms with pistil and stigma is performed by the wind. However, man long ago took over the job and practised artificial pollination, cutting off the blossom of the non-fruit-bearing tree and bringing it into contact with the blossom of the fruitful ones. It was this which the genii of the veil had been doing to the sacred tree, and just this was Joseph now called on to perform. Red-belly, son of Djedi, head gardener to Potiphar, assigned him to the task.

He did so by reason of Joseph's youth and the suppleness of his years. For it is a task not easy to perform; it takes agility in climbing, daring and a steady head to do the office of the wind. With the help of a padded rope, encircling his body and the trunk of the palm, the climber with his wooden vessel or little basket must work himself up the pollen-bearing tree using what stumps and knots he can find for foothold, till he reach the crest, throwing up the rope each time from the height at which he had arrived, with the motion of a driver who gives his horses the reins. Arrived at the top, he cuts off the panicles and puts them in his basket, then glides down the trunk. Then one after another he mounts the trunks of the fruit-bearing trees and everywhere puts the seed-bearing panicles to "ride" — that is, to hang down inside the ovary-bearing flower-stalk, which will then produce the pale-yellow fruit; these can soon be picked and eaten, though the ones grown in the hot months Paophi and Hathyr are the really good ones.

Khun-Anpu with his earth-encrusted beet of a finger pointed out to Joseph the pollen-bearing trees, of which there were only a few, for a single one could pollinate some thirty of the fruit-bearing kind. He gave him the rope, which was very stout and of the best quality, made not of hemp but of strands of reed thoroughly soaked and beaten. He supervised the tying of it round Joseph and the first tree, for he was responsible, should the master lose the price of the new slave by his falling and dashing out his bowels. He soon saw that the lad was clever: he scarcely needed to be tied, but swarmed up the trunk in a way to put a squirrel to shame, and reaching the top performed the business with care and intelligence. Khun soon left him to himself, promising other work in the garden and saying that he might in time become a proper gardener if he did well this work and produced early and abundant fruiting of the pollinated trees.

Not only was Joseph ambitious for the credit of his God; but also he found pleasure in the skilled and daring operation. He performed it with great zeal, bent on surprising Khun by his quickness and thoroughness — in general, indeed, this was the effect which Joseph sought to produce upon all men. He worked all day, and then another into the evening. At sunset when beyond lotus-pond, city, and river the sky unfolded the almost unbearable splendour of its daily crimson and tulip red, he was alone in the garden among his trees, or rather in them, setting the last of his panicles to "ride" by the swiftly failing light. He was sitting in the crown of a tall, swaying trunk dealing with the fruit-bearing blossoms when he heard whispering and footsteps beneath him, and glancing down saw Beauty, the dwarf, looking like a mushroom from that height. The manikin waved with both arms and cupped his hands to his mouth. "Osarsiph!" he loudly whispered. "Osarsiph! He is coming!" Then he vanished.

Joseph hastened to leave his employ, and slid down the tree faster than he had climbed up. There, sure enough, Potiphar was approaching from the pond, between the festoons of vine, with a little train. An erect white figure in the sunset glow, with Mont-kaw beside him a step to the rear, Dudu, the guardian of the jewel-house, and two scribes rather farther behind, with Bes-em-heb, who had stolen back to their side.

"Lo," Joseph thought, with his gaze upon his lord, "there he walks in the garden in the cool of the eve." And when the group drew near he flung himself at the foot of his tree and laid his forehead to the ground, with his hands stretched toward the master, palms out.

Petepre stopped and looked down at the arched backbone in his pathway. His train paused with him.

"To your feet," he said briskly but in a mild voice. Joseph with one swift motion obeyed. He stood close by the shaft of the palm, in humble posture, his hands crossed at his throat, his head bent. His heart was exceedingly ready and alert. It had come: he stood before Potiphar. Potiphar had stopped. He must not move on too soon. Everything depended on his staying. What question would he ask? One, it was to be hoped, which required an answer of some length. Joseph waited, his eyes cast down.

"Are you of the household?" he heard the high crisp tones inquire.

For the moment the opportunity afforded was small. Only by the manner and not the matter of the reply could he arrest the master's attention and persuade him not to move on. Joseph murmured:

"The great master knows all. I am the least and lowest of his slaves. He counts him happy who is even the least and lowest of his lord."

"Only fair," he thought. "He surely will not go on yet. No, he must ask why I am here at this hour. And I must answer prettily."

"You are one of the gardeners?" the mild voice, after a brief silence, went on above his head. He replied:

"My lord knows and sees all, even as Re, who gave him. Of his gardeners I am the least."

To that the voice:

"But why do you linger in the garden after the time of leaving, when your fellows do honour to the hour of rest and take their meal?"

Joseph bowed his head still lower above his hands.

"My lord presides over the hosts of Pharaoh, he is greatest among the great of the land," he said appealingly. "He is like Re, who rides across the heavens in his bark with his train. He is the steersman of Egypt guiding the bark of state after his will. He is next to Thoth, who judges without distinction of persons. Bulwark of the poor, may his mercy fall upon me like to the satisfaction of the hungry. Like a garment to cover the naked may his forgiveness come upon me that I lingered at my work among his trees until the hour when he walks in the garden and was a stumbling to his path."

Silence. Perhaps Petepre was exchanging glances with his companions as they listened to this well-turned prayer, spoken in rather harsh pronunciation, indeed, but apt in phraseology and though formal yet not without a note of real sincerity. Joseph could not see whether Potiphar looked at his train, but he hoped so and waited. His sharp ears seemed to catch a faint laugh as Potiphar replied:

"Zeal in office and industry at late hours call not forth the master's wrath. You may breathe in peace. For it seems you love your task and are skilled in its performance?"

Here Joseph thought best to lift his head and raise his eyes. Those deep, black Rachel-eyes met in their upward gaze the master's mild and even sad ones, long-lashed, and brown like the doe's; veiled with pride, yet good-humouredly searching, they looked into Joseph's own. Potiphar stood there, tall and fat and most elegantly clad, his hand on the rest of his tall walking-staff, a little way below the crystal knob on its end; pine-cone and fan he held in the other hand. The bright-coloured faience of his necklace was in a pattern of flowers. Leather gaiters protected his shins; leather, papyrus, and bronze were the sandals he stood in, the points of which ran between his great and second toes. His finely shaped head was bent as he listened, and from the top of the brow dangled a lotus flower.

"How shall I not love the gardener's art," answered Joseph, "and be zealous therein, my lord, when it is pleasant in the eyes of gods and men, and the work of the hoe exceedeth in beauty that of the plough as well as many others if not the most? For it is an honour to the man, and many chosen ones practised it in ancient time. Was not Ishullanu gardener to a great god and found favour in the eyes of the daughter of Sin, and brought her daily blossoms and made her table smile? I have heard of a child whom they exposed in a basket of rushes, but the stream bore him to Akki the water-carrier, who taught the boy the art of gardening, and to Sharuk-inu, the gardener, Ishtar gave her love and her kingdom. And another king, Urraimitti of Isin, changed places in jest, I have heard, with Ellil-bani his gardener and set him on his throne. And lo, then Ellil-bani sat there and himself remained king."

"Well, well," said Petepre and cast another smiling glance at Mont-kaw, who was shaking an embarrassed head. So were the scribes, and most of all Dudu, the dwarf. Only little Shepses-Bes wrinkled his face with delight. "But whence have you all these tales? Are you from Karduniash, then?" the courtier said, in Akkadian, meaning Babylonia.

Joseph answered in the same tongue: "It was there my mother bore me, my lord. But 'twas in the land of Zahi, in a valley of Canaan, that your slave grew up, among his father's flocks."

"Ah!" was all he heard Petepre say. The master liked to speak

Babylonian, and a certain poetic timbre in the reply, vaguely like a quotation, particularly in the phrase "his father's flocks," arrested him — and embarrassed him at the same time. An aristocratic dread of evoking intimacy, of hearing things that did not concern him, conflicted with a curiosity already quite lively and a desire to hear more from these lips.

"But you speak not badly," he said, "the tongue of King Kadash-mansharbe." And falling back into Egyptian: "Who taught you the fables?"

"I read them, my lord, with my father's oldest servant."

"So you can read, then?" asked Petepre, glad to express legitimate surprise and not wishing to hear more of the father and the eldest servant, or that the father had a servant at all.

Joseph bowed his head, not merely inclined it, but rather as though he admitted guilt.

"And write?"

The head went lower still.

"What work was it," the other asked after a moment's hesitation, "which made you linger?"

"I was putting the blossoms to ride, my lord."

"Ah! — and is that a male or female tree behind you?"

"It is a fruit-bearing one, my lord, it will bear. But whether one should call that male or female is uncertain — people disagree. In Egypt they call male the fruit-bearing tree. But I have spoken with folk of the isles of the sea, Alashia and Crete, and these call the fruit-bearing ones female and male the unfruitful which only bear pollen and are barren."

"This is a fruit-bearing one, then," the captain of the guard said shortly. "And how old is the tree?" he asked, since such a conversation could have but one purpose, an examination into Joseph's proficiency.

"It has blossomed for ten years, my lord," he replied with a smile. He spoke with a certain enthusiasm, partly out of his quite genuine feeling for trees, but also because it seemed useful. "And it is seventeen since its planting. In two or three years it will bear full crops and be at the height of its yield. Even now it bears close to two hundred *hin* of the best fruit every year, of great beauty and size and a fine amber colour. That is, of course, if it is pollinated by hand, instead of leaving it to the wind. It is a tree glorious among your trees," said he with a burst of enthusiasm, laying his hand on the slender shaft, "male in the pride of its growth and strength, so that one feels inclined to call it so, as do the Egyptians; but on the other hand female in its fruitful yield, according to the speech of the people of the islands. In short it is a godlike tree, if your servant may unite in the word what is divided on the tongues of the peoples."

"So," said Petepre teasingly, "you can talk of the nature of the divine as well! Do you worship trees at home?"

"No, my lord. Under trees, perhaps, but no more. We have reverent thoughts of trees, it is true; there is something sacred about them, and they say that they are older than the earth itself. Your slave has heard of the tree of life, with power to produce all living things. Shall one call that all-creative power male or female? Ptah's artists at Menfe and Pharaoh's here, who are fruitful of forms and fill the world with beautiful images: is their power male or female, begetting or bearing, which produces their works? We cannot tell, for the power is of both kinds, and the tree of life must have been hermaphrodite, two-sexed, as trees mostly are, and as Kheper is, the sun-beetle, who conceives himself. Lo, the whole world is divided in twain, and we speak of male and female and cannot even agree in distinguishing between them, discussing whether the fruitful tree is male, or the barren. But the bottom of the world and the tree of life are neither male nor female, rather both in one. And what does that mean? It means they are neither. Virgin are they, like the bearded goddess, and are father and mother at once to the thing they beget, for that they are above sex and their power of giving has naught to do with being torn in twain."

Potiphar was silent, supporting his towering figure on his beautiful staff and gazing on the ground in front of Joseph's feet. He felt a warmth in his face, his breast, and all his limbs, a sort of dim stirring; it held him to the spot and would not let him go; and yet this man of the world knew not how to continue the conversation. His aristocratic dread of intimacy had made him avoid the subject of the young slave's personal life; now another sort of shyness seemed to bar this avenue as well. He might have gone, and left the young foreigner standing by his tree; but that he could not do nor did he wish to. He hesitated, and in the pause were heard the pompous accents of Dudu, the dwarf, spouse of Djeset, who took upon himself to say:

"Were it not better to proceed toward the house, my lord? The fire of heaven pales and at any moment a chill may blow up from the desert, giving him without a coat a cold in the head."

To Dudu's annoyance the fan-bearer heard him not at all. The warmth he felt closed his ears to the dwarf's sensible warning. He said:

"A thoughtful gardener are you indeed, O Canaanitish youth." And returning to the word which had stamped itself on his mind he said: "Were they numerous, your father's flocks?"

"Very numerous, my lord. The land could scarce bear them."

"Your father, then, was a man without care?"

"Save his care for God, my lord, he knew none."

"What is the care for God?"

"It is enlarged throughout the earth, my lord. With more or with less blessing and well-being it is cherished by all the world; but especially was it from old time laid upon my people, so that my father, a king of his flocks, was also known as a prince of God."

"A king and a prince, you call him? Then you lived in great well-being in the days of your childhood?"

"Your servant," answered Joseph, "may say that he anointed himself with the oil of gladness in his childhood and lived as of high rank. For the father loved him more than his brethren and made him rich with the gifts of his love. He gave to him a sacred garment where were woven many of the great lights and signs. A dissembling garment it was and a coat of reversion, handed down from the mother's side, and he wore it in her place. But it was torn from him by the fang of envy."

Potiphar had not the impression that he was lying. The youth's eye gazed into the past, the earnestness of his words spoke for him. There was a certain hesitation and vagueness which might be ascribed to his foreign tongue, and the details he gave were convincing.

"How then did you come — " the other began to ask. He wanted to put the question delicately, and began again: "How did your present then grow out of your past?"

"I died the death of my life," answered Joseph, "and a new one was vouchsafed me in your service, my lord. Shall I weary your ear with the circumstance of my story and the stages of it? I must call myself a man of sorrow and joy. For the favourite was driven into the desert, into misery, he was stolen and sold again. He drank deep of suffering after his joy. Grief was his bread. For his brethren hated him and in their hate they laid snares about his steps. They dug a grave before his feet and thrust his life into the pit so that darkness became his dwelling."

"Do you speak of yourself?"

"Of the least of your servants, my lord. Three days he lay in bonds to the lower world, so that truly he stank, for he had fouled himself like a sheep with his own filth. Then came travellers with souls of mildness; they raised him forth in the goodness of their hearts and freed him from the maw of death. They stilled with milk the newborn and gave him a garment for his nakedness. But after that they brought him before your house, O Akki, great water-carrier, and you made him to be your gardener in the goodness of your heart and to be a helper of the wind among your trees; so that his second birth may be called as strange as his first."

"What of his first?"

"Your servant hath blundered with his tongue. My mouth had no will to speak what it spoke."

"But you said your birth was strange."

"It escaped me, great lord, as I spoke before you. It was virgin."

"How can that be?"

"Lovely was my mother," Joseph said, "and Hathor had sealed her with the kiss of loveliness. But her body was closed for long years so that she despaired of her motherhood and no man could expect to see her loveliness bear fruit. But after twelve years she conceived and bore, with unnatural pains, what time the sign of the Virgin rose in the east."

"Do you call that a virgin birth?"

"No, my lord, if it displease you."

"One cannot call it a virgin birth only because your mother bore you in the sign of the Virgin."

"Not therefore alone, my lord. One must consider further circumstances, the stamp of loveliness upon her brow, and that for so many years the womb of God's handmaid was closed. All this together with the sign of the Virgin makes it up."

"But there is no virgin birth."

"No, lord, as you say it."

"Or is there, in your way of thinking?"

"Many thousand times, my lord," said Joseph joyously. "Many thousand times it comes to pass in the world, which is sundered in sex, and the universe is full of begetting and giving birth that is exalted high above sex. Does not a moonbeam bless the body of the cow awaiting the bull and she bears Hapi? Does not old wisdom teach us that the bee is created out of the leaves of the trees? Then there are the trees, themselves the care of your servant, and their mystery, wherein creation plays her game with sex, putting it together into one, and dividing it among them according to her whim, and in one case one way and another, so that no one knows name and order of their sex, or if it is actually one, and the peoples disagree. For often it happens not at all through the sex that they propagate, but outside of it: not by pollination or conception but by shoots or runners or because they were planted; and the gardener sets out shots but not kernels of the palm, that he may know whether he is growing a fruit-bearing or a barren one. But if they are propagated by their sex, then sometimes pollen and conception are put together in their blossoms and sometimes divided among the blossoms of the same tree, but sometimes also among different trees in the garden, the fruitful and unfruitful, and it is the business of the wind to carry the seed of the pollen trees to those of the conception. But when one considers, is it thus truly a begetting and a conceiving in sex? Is not that which the wind does, already quite like the begetting of the moonbeam upon the cow — already a middle stage or transition to a higher kind of begetting and a virgin birth?"

"It is not the wind that begets," Potiphar said.

"Say not so, O my lord, in your greatness! Often, so I have heard, the sweet breath of Zephyr visits the birds, before the close time is at hand. For it is the breath of God's spirit, and the wind is spirit; and as Ptah's sculptors fill the world with beautiful forms, and no one can tell whether their activity is to be called male or female, because it is both and neither, or in other words is virgin-fruitful — so too is the world full of fructifying and bringing forth without sex, from the fructification of the breath of God. The father and creator of the world is God. He creates all living things, not because they are brought forth from seed, but the unbegotten in other ways lays a source of fruitfulness within matter, which changes it and alters it into the manifold. For all the manifold shapes of things were first present in the thoughts of God, and the word, borne by the breath of God, is their begetter."

It was a strange scene, one never before enacted in the Egyptian's house or court. Potiphar stood leaning on his staff and listening. On his fine features the expression of tolerant irony which they habitually sought to wear struggled with a gratification strong enough that it might be called joy or even happiness. It was in fact so strong that one may scarcely speak of its struggling with the irony, since joy obviously took the upper hand. Beside him stood Mont-kaw with the little wedge-shaped beard, steward of the house, staring with his little inflamed eyes with the great puffy tear-sacs underneath; incredulous, dazed, grateful, and with appreciation which was nearer to wonder, he looked into the face of this bought slave, this lad, who was doing something which love had taught himself to do for their noble master, and in a higher, finer, and far more effective way. — Then behind him was Dudu, spouse of Djeset, most self-righteously enraged, because the master had been deaf to his warning, and prevented from entering fresh objection and interrupting the interview by Potiphar's complete absorption in Joseph's words. The puppy was obviously cutting a good figure, and the dwarf proportionately disadvantaged. It seemed to him that the things the slave was saying — shameless, really not allowable things, which Potiphar was drinking in as though they were the water of life — detracted in some way from his own dignity and were calculated to weaken it and his influence over certain of the small and certain of the great. As for the small, there was Beauty, the midget, his face wrinkled with delight at his favourite's success, fairly swollen with satisfaction because the lad had known how to improve his chance and prove that he had a right to it. Then there were the two scribes, to whom nothing of the kind had ever happened before in their lives, and who had ceased to smile, instructed by diligent study of their master's face and that of Mont-kaw, as well as by their own impressions of what they had heard. And beside his tree, before this group of listeners, stood Joseph, a smile on his lips, and perorated most enchantingly. He had long since abandoned the humble posture which at first had constrained him, and stood in easy grace, accompanying with pleasing and eloquent gesture the words which flowed unsought from his lips, as with blithe seriousness he discoursed upon the higher procreation and the fruitful power of the breath of God. In the gathering twilight, among the columns of this temple grove he stood there, not unlike an eager child, in whom God speaks to His own glory, loosening his tongue that it may give forth doctrine to the amazement of the doctors.

"There is but one God" — so he went joyously on — "but of godlikeness there is much in the world, and of the virtue of giving which is neither male nor female but lifted above sex and has naught to do with dismemberment. Let me, O lord, as I stand before thee, sing with lively tongue of that giving virtue. For mine eyes were opened in a dream and I saw as it were a great and blessed house, in a far land, its courts abounding in weal, with buildings, gardens, granaries, and shops, men and cattle in number like the sands of the sea. There thrift and prosperity ruled, sowing and reaping came to pass, the oil-mills rested not, wine gushed from the vats and the presses, rich milk from the udders of kine, with golden sweetness from the honeycomb. But by whom did all this move in its appointed ways, and who was the source of this well-being? Ah, it came to pass through its master and head, and through him who owned it. For all went at his beck and nod, and all was moved by the breath of his nostrils. He said to one: Go! and he went, and to another: Do this! and it was done. And without him would have been no life, but all would have withered and perished. From his fullness all fed, his manservants and maidservants, and praised his name. Father and mother was he to the house and to all the estate, for the glance of his eye was like the moonbeam which fructified the cow and it gave birth to the god, and the breath of his mouth like the wind that bears the pollen from tree to tree, and out of the lap of his presentness gushed all beginning and prospering, as the golden honey gushes from the honeycomb. Thus dreamed I, far from here, of that virtue of giving so that I perceived that there is a fruitfulness and a begetting which is not earthly after manner or sex and not of the flesh but of the spirit and of God. Lo, the people dispute whether the fruit-bearing tree or the pollen-bearing one be male, and they agree not. And the reason therefor is that the Word is spirit and in the spirit things contend. I saw a man — frightful was he to you, O my lord, splendid in his might and terrible in the strength of the flesh, a giant and a son of Enak, and his soul was of neat's-leather. Then went he out against lions, smote the wild ox, the crocodile and rhinoceros, and laid them all low. And they asked him: 'Have you no fear?' and he answered and said: 'What is fear?' For he knew it not. But another child of man saw I in the world, tender of soul as in flesh, and he was afraid. Then he took shield and spear and spoke: 'Come on, my fear!' And smote the lion, the wild ox, the crocodile, and the rhinoceros. Would you now, my lord, try your servant and think to ask him which of these men one should call by the name of man before the other — it might be that God would put His answer in my mouth."

Potiphar stood leaning on his staff, so that he stooped a little. He felt a pleasant warmth in his head and limbs. Such a sense of well-being, it is said, came to those visited by a god in the guise of a wayfarer or beggar or some acquaintance or relative, and they held speech together. For it was by this they knew him or at least received happy intuition. The peculiar sense of well-being which streamed through them was a sign that he with whom they spoke might indeed be a wayfarer or beggar, a friend or relation, a fact to be taken account of by their sober sense and treated accordingly, but yet — considering that peculiar sense of well-being — to be thought of at the same time in the light of other and far-reaching possibilities. That all things may coincide in time is of their very nature and essence; realities wear each other as disguises, the beggar is not less a beggar because a god has put him on. Is not the river a god, in the shape of a bull or of a wreath-crowned man-woman with one breast of each sex; did it not make the land and does it not nourish it? Which does not forbid one to hold a common-sense attitude toward the water of the river, impersonal as itself: to drink it, to ride on it, to wash one's clothes in its stream. And only the sense of well-being as one drinks and bathes may suggest a higher point of view. The border-line between the earthly and the heavenly is fluid; and one need only fix one's eye upon a phenomenon for it to break up in diplopy. Again, there are stages and pre-stages of the divine: half-gods, transitional existences, intimations. In the things which the youth by his tree had uttered about his previous life, much was familiar, much teasingly allusive and monitory, much might be taken in a literary light. Even so it was hard to say how far it rested upon assimilation and deliberate arrangement and how much upon objective elements: traits which characterized the life of beneficent presences, beings by nature deific, consoling, saving and redeeming. The young gardener knew these traits, he had made them spiritually his own and knew how to bring his personal promptings in life into harmony with them. That might be an effect of his allusive intelligence; but Potiphar's striking sense of well-being spoke for the fact that the things themselves bore it out. He said:

"I have tried you already, my friend, and you have stood the test not badly. Of course there can be no talk of virgin birth," he added, in a pleasantly instructive and admonitory tone, "simply because your birth was in the sign of the Virgin. That you can well see." He said this out of a sound sense of the practical side of things, and, as it were, not to let the god know that he knew him. "Go now," said he, "and take your rest with your fellows, and with tomorrow's sun take up your work again among my trees." With that he turned away, smiling and red of face, but after two paces brought his train to a halt again and instead of turning back beckoned Joseph to his side.

"What is your name?" he asked. He had forgotten to do so before.

Not until after a pause, which could not have been for reflection, Joseph, looking up gravely, replied:

"Osarsiph."

"Good," responded the fan-bearer, short and crisp, and hastened his steps. Crisp too were his words (Bes the dwarf heard and reported them to Joseph before an hour was out) when he told his steward Mont-kaw as they went:

"That is an exceptionally clever slave there. Certainly the trees are in good hands with him. But you will scarcely be able to keep him at such work for long."

"You have spoken," answered Mont-kaw, and knew what he had to do.

JOSEPH MAKES A PACT

Not idly have I introduced this conversation, of which elsewhere we have no record, word for word, with all its ins and outs, just as it came to pass. For it was the point of departure for Joseph's career in Potiphar's house; its immediate sequel was that the Egyptian took him for his body-servant, and later set him over his house that he might put all that he had into his hands. The news of it has ridden us swiftly into the heart of the seven years which raised the son of Jacob to new heights before casting him down to a new death. For in this test which he had passed he showed his understanding of the painful secret of the blessing-house whereinto he had been sold: the need for mutual forbearance, tact, and flattering service to uphold its hollow dignity. And not only had he shown his understanding, but also his ability to perform the needed service better and more skilfully than anyone else.

Such was in particular the experience of Mont-kaw, who found himself so far outrun by Joseph's incredible skill in his loyal endeavours for the health of their noble master's soul. I would expressly add, to the honour of the steward's good heart and to point the difference between love and flattery, that he felt no pang of jealousy, but only joy. Indeed, it did not need the master's hint to decide him, after the encounter in the garden, to raise the slave at once out of the obscurity of his lowly state and put him in the way of higher testing. Long since, we knew that what had held the steward back was secret shame at those thoughts which had crossed his mind when Joseph stood before him with the roll — thoughts like to those which stirred in Potiphar during the talk in the garden.

Hardly had the next day's sun seen Joseph after his morning meal at work in the garden as Khun-Anpu's underling and helper to the wind, when Mont-kaw summoned him to come before him and announced decided changes in his employ. He found it good to say that these were overdue, and even in a sort to chide Joseph for the delay. How strange men are, and how they will twist the facts in their minds! The steward was pleased to be gruff; making announcement of his subordinate's good fortune in the odd form of a reproach, as though he had been guilty of lingering out by his own acts an untenable situation.

He received the Hebrew slave in that part of the court which lay near the stables, between the women's house, the kitchens, and the servants' quarters.

"Ah, there you are," said he, as Joseph saluted. "Well that at least you come when you are called. Do you think it can go on like this for ever and you can play about in tree-tops to your days' end? You think falsely, let me tell you. But now we shall string the lute with other strings, for your days of idleness are over. You are to come into the house for service, with no more ado: wait upon the masters in the dining-room, hand the dishes, and stand behind the chair of Pharaoh's friend. You will not be asked if it likes you. Long enough you have played the laggard and run from the higher service. And your looks? Full of bark and dirt from the garden are your skin and linen. Go cleanse yourself. Get a silver apron from the stores for your waiter's service, and for your hair a fitting garland from the gardeners. Or how else then did you think to stand behind Potiphar's chair?"

"I did not think to stand there," Joseph replied, very low.

"It goes not after your thinking. And adjust your thoughts further to this: after the meal you shall read aloud from the book-rolls to the master, for he will try you, before he sleeps, in the northern columned hall, where it is cool. Can you acquit yourself?"

"Thoth will aid me," Joseph made bold to answer, trusting in the indulgence of Him who had snatched him away to the land of Egypt, and speaking as Egyptians speak. "But who is it who may read unto the master till now?" he added.

"Who till now? Amenemuia it was, scholar of the book-house. Why would you know?"

"Because for the sake of the Hidden One I would step before no one's steps nor injure any man's boundary-stone by taking away his office, which is his pride."

Mont-kaw was most pleasantly impressed by this unexpected thoughtfulness. Since yesterday — and perhaps before — he had a clear idea that the capacity and calling of this young man to rival others

for office in the house went further than perhaps even he himself
suspected, further than to the office and person of Amenemuia the
reader — and much further still. Thus he was pleased with Joseph's
delicacy, quite apart from the fact that he belonged to those Reuben-
natures which find their joy and the dignity of their souls in being
"fair and just"; in other words, take pleasure in reconciling their own
view with those of the higher powers, even if that involve their own
dismissal. Mont-kaw was this kind of man and acted accordingly,
perhaps because he was not quite well and often troubled with his
kidneys. But I repeat that Joseph's tact gratified him. What he said
was:

"You are full of consideration in your relations with men. But let
Amenemuia's honour and promotion be his affair and mine. For such
consideration is but another name for meddlesomeness. You hear."

"Has the most exalted commanded it?"

"What the overseer commands is a command. And what did I command this minute?"

"To go and cleanse myself."

"Then do it."

Joseph bowed low and retreated backwards.

"Osarsiph!" said the steward in a gentler voice and Joseph returned.

Mont-kaw put his hand on his shoulder.

"Do you love the master?" he asked, and his small eyes with the
large tear-ducts beneath them looked searchingly into Joseph's face.

The question was strangely moving, and fraught with memories
familiar to Joseph's thoughts since childhood. Just so had Jacob
asked, drawing his favourite to his knee; with just such painful
searching had the brown eyes with the pouches beneath them looked
into the face of the child. Involuntarily he answered in the formula
which is the right reply to this ever recurring question, and the giving of which did no offence to its inner nature:

"With my whole soul, with my whole heart, with my whole mind."

The steward nodded his satisfaction, just as Jacob had done.

"That is right," said he. "He is good and great. Yesterday in the
date orchard you spoke commendably before him — as not everybody could have done. I saw well that you can do more than say
good-night. There were errors in it, as when you spoke of a virgin
birth, only for that it occurred in the sign of the Virgin — but one
may forgive the errors of youth. The gods gave you subtle thoughts
and loosened your tongue to utter them, so that they wreathe and
wind as in a dance. The master had his good pleasure therein and you
are to stand behind his chair. But also you shall be with me in my
comings and goings as my pupil and apprentice, that you may gain
insight in house and court and field, the business and supplies, and

shall in time be my assistant, for I have much trouble in the world and very often am not too well. Are you satisfied?"

"If I am certain to take no one's place behind the master's chair and at your side," Joseph said, "then truly am I glad and thankful, if also not without a slight timidity. For between ourselves who am I, and what can I do? My father, who was king of his flocks, had me taught to write and speak, but in other wise I might anoint myself with the oil of gladness, and I know no trade, neither cobbling nor paper-making nor pot-throwing. How then shall I dare to go amongst those who sit and know their task, one this, the other that, and I take upon myself the overseeing of them?"

"Think you that I can make shoes and paper?" asked Mont-kaw. "Or pots, or chairs and coffins? It is not needful nor would anyone ask it, least of all those who can. For I am of different birth from theirs and from another stock, with a head for the general; and thus I have become overseer. The workmen in their shops inquire not what you can do, but rather who you are, that is another sort of ability, and made for overseeing. Who can speak before the lord as you can do, and rhyme your subtle thoughts to subtle words, shall not sit stooped over detail, but walk abroad at my side. For in the word and not in the hand is command and oversight. Have you something to object or carp at in my opinions?"

"No, great steward. I agree and am grateful."

"That is the word, Osarsiph! And it shall be a word between me and you, the old man and the young, that we shall understand each other in our service and in our love of our master the noble Petepre, Pharaoh's captain of the guard, and make a pact between us for his service, which each shall hold to the end of his life, so the death of the elder shall not dissolve the bond; but the other shall keep it over his grave, as his successor and son, who portects and justifies his father in that he protects and justifies the noble master in bond with the dead. Can you see that and does it please you? Or does it seem fanci-ful and strange?"

"By no means, my master and overseer," Joseph replied. "Your words are after my mind and understanding; for long have I under-stood such a bond, which one makes with the master as with one an-other in his service, and I could not tell what were more familiar in mine eyes and less strange. By my father's head and Pharaoh's life, I am yours."

He who had bought him kept still one hand upon the lad's shoulder and now with his other took both of Joseph's in his.

"Good," said he. "Good, Osarsiph. Go then and cleanse yourself for the personal and the reading service of the master. But when he has done with you, come to me that I may teach you to know the economy of the house and to oversee it."

Chapter V

THE MAN OF THE BLESSING

JOSEPH IS READER AND BODY-SERVANT

WE know the behaviour of servants, the smiling and casting down of eyes, when one of their number, least and least-considered among them, is with apparent favouritism lifted up beyond their ken. They smile, look at each other and then down; are disconcerted, envious, spiteful, yet on the other hand cautious and apparently acquiescing with enthusiasm in the whim of the ruling powers. These looks, these smiles Joseph now encountered every day; for the first time on that morning in the garden when he was sent for to Mont-kaw — he, the climber of trees — and always after that. For this was the beginning, and his head was now lifted up in manifold ways. He became Potiphar's personal servant, his master gradually put all that he had into the Hebrew's hand, just as we are told; and all that was prepared for, and the germ of it lay, in the words of Mont-kaw and the pact he made; was implicit in it as is the slow-growing tree in the seed, needing but time for its unfolding and fulfilment.

Joseph, then, received the wreath and the silver apron which formed the livery of the dining-room servants — and which, it need hardly be said, became him to a marvel. For so must they look who might wait upon Petepre and his family at table; but this son of a lovely mother stood out among them of course, by reason of a superior brilliance which was not mere charm, rather a union of physical and spiritual parts in which both were enhanced.

He was given his place behind Petepre's chair on the dais, or rather at first beside the stone platform opposite, along the narrow side of the room, where the wall was covered with flags and a bronze jug and beaker were set. For when the illustrious family entered for their meal, from the northern or the western hall, they mounted this platform and water was poured over their hands. It was Joseph's part to pour the water over Potiphar's small white hands, which were ornamented with seal and scarab rings, and to hand him the scented napkin to dry them. While Potiphar did this, Joseph had to hasten with swift foot across the matted floor with its bright embroidered runners to the

dais where the chairs were placed: those for the exalted parents from
the upper storey as well as for their son and the mistress Mut-em-enet.
Behind Potiphar's chair he stood, and served the latter with viands
handed him by other silver-clad waiters. He did not run to and fro
to fetch or take the platters, but others gave him and he offered to
Pharaoh's friend, who thus received from his hand all that he ate and
drank.

The dining-room was high and bright, although the light came not
from outdoors but through the adjoining rooms, particularly through
the seven doors of the western outer hall and the windows above
them, which were of fine open-worked stone slabs. But the walls were
very white and gave back the light; painted friezes ran round them
under the ceiling, which was also white and crossed by many sky-
blue beams, supported by wooden columns painted blue, with round
white bases and bright-coloured capitals. These sky-blue columns
were a delightful decoration, and delightfully decorative, full of gaiety and abundant ornament was everything else as well, in this room
where Potiphar daily ate his meals. The dining-chairs were ebony
and ivory, adorned with lions' heads and filled with embroidered
down cushions. Along the wall stood lamp-stands and incense-tripods
in elegant shapes, standing basins, ointment-jars and broad-handled
wine-jars in holders, wreathed with flowers; these and all the other
appurtenances of the dining-room glittered and gleamed. In the
centre of the room stood a capacious buffet, piled high, like
Amun's sacrificial table, with food — far more than the exalted family could possibly consume — which was handed to the waiters by
servants in attendance: roast goose, roast duck, joints of beef, loaves
of bread and cake, vegetables, and lavish display of melons, cucumbers and Syrian fruits. Amid the eatables towered a costly centre-
piece, a New Year's present from Pharaoh to Petepre, in the shape of
a little gold temple standing among exotic trees with apes clambering
in their branches.

A hush prevailed in the hall when the family sat at table. The servants' bare soles were inaudible on the matted floors, and the speech
of Petepre and his kin was infrequent and soft-voiced from mutual
respect. They bent tactfully toward each other, and in the pauses between courses held to each other's noses a lotus flower, or some dainty
morsel to each other's mouths. Their mutual gentleness was exquisite,
it was almost painful. The chairs were placed by twos, with free space
between; Petepre sat with his mother, and the lady Mut beside old
Huia. When Joseph had first seen his mistress as she swayed past him
in her carrying-chair, she had worn her own hair, in locks like a
poodle's, thick-dusted with gold. But often she wore a wig, of blue,
blond, or brown hair coming down far on her shoulders, made into
tight little rings and set with corkscrew curls underneath. Atop was

a close-fitting wreath. The wig was shaped rather like the head-cloth of a sphinx; it came out in a heart-shaped curve over the white forehead, and a few strands or tufts, with which she sometimes toyed, hung down on either side over the cheeks, making a singular frame to that singular face, in which the eyes were at war with the mouth, they being slow in movement, sombre and stern, while the mouth was sinuous as a serpent, the corners of it chiselled very deep. The bare white arms were notable near as far; as they moved among the dishes, modelled and polished as by the hand of one of Ptah's artists, one might well call them divine.

Pharaoh's friend took much food into his shapely mouth — after all, he had to nourish a mountain of a man. And many times during the meal the beaker had to be replenished from the long-necked jug. Probably the wine was cordial to his self-esteem and made him believe that despite Hor-em-heb he himself was a real and actual captain of the guard. But the mistress — about whom hovered a slender and decorative female slave, in flowing spider-web garb, so thin that she was as good as naked, and it was well that Jacob the father could not see her — Mut-em-enet, that is, displayed but small appetite and seemed to sit there because it was the thing to do. She took a single bite, idly, hardly opening her mouth, into the breast of a roast duck, then tossed it into the basin. The exalted parents, waited on by their silly little maids, for they tolerated no adult attendance, only picked and poked at their food; they too seemed to sit there as at a ceremony, for a mouthful or two of bread and vegetable sufficed them, particularly old Huia, who had to be careful lest his stomach revolt and throw him into a cold sweat. Bes-em-heb, the unmarried dwarf, sat sometimes and munched on the step of the dais, at the masters' feet; though actually he took his meal at a sort of officials' table, with Mont-kaw himself, Dudu, warder of the jewel-house, Red-belly, the head gardener, and a few of the scribes; in other words, the upper staff of the house. Joseph, called Osarsiph, the Shabirite slave, was soon to join them. At times the mock-vizier, in his crumpled finery, would perform comic dances round the great centre buffet. In a corner there cowered nearly always an old harp-player, touching the strings with warped and withered fingers and murmuring rhapsodical incoherent songs. He was blind, as befits a bard, and could soothsay a little, though but haltingly and unclear.

Such was the daily scene. But often too the chamberlain was with Pharaoh in the palace of Merimat, across the river, or attending the god in the royal bark up or down stream to inspect quarries and mines, estates and waterworks. On such days no dinner was served; the blue salon was empty. But when the master was present and with many manifestations of mutual fine feeling the meal had come to an end, the exalted parents betook themselves to their upper storey, and their daughter-in-law the moon-nun retired to rest in her own apartment, in the master's dwelling, separated from her consort's by the great columned northern hall, or went under escort in her lion-chair to the women's house. Then Joseph followed Potiphar into one of the adjoining halls, spacious airy rooms with paintings along three of their walls and the fourth side open save for supporting columns: either the northern, extending in front of the dining- and reception-rooms, or the western, which was still better, because it looked out on the garden, the trees, and the little summerhouse on the mound. The former, however, had the advantage of giving the master an eye upon the court, the storehouses, and the stables. Besides, it was cooler there.

In both rooms were many splendid things, regarded by Joseph with the mixture of admiration and contempt which he kept for the manifestations of high civilization in this land whither he had been snatched. They were presents, tokens of Pharaoh's regard for his chamberlain and titular head of his troops, like the exquisite little gold temple in the dining-room. They were hung on the walls or disposed on chests and shelves: statuettes in silver and gold, ivory and ebony, of the royal donor Neb-mat-Re-Amenhotpe, a fat, thickset man, in various costumes, crowns and head-dresses; bronze sphinxes likewise representing the god; all sorts of statues of animals — a herd of running elephants carved in ivory, squatting apes, a gazelle with a flower in its mouth; costly vessels, mirrors, fans, and whips. But above all there were weapons, in large number and variety: axes and daggers, scale armour, and shields covered with hide, bows and arrows and bronze sickle-shaped swords. It was strange that Pharaoh, who though the successor of warriors was in his own person no man of battles but a builder and prince of peace, should have showered such profusion of war-like implements upon a favourite — and that favourite, that Reuben-tower of a man, himself not at all constituted to let the blood of rubber-eaters and sand-dwellers.

Among the furnishings of the hall were handsome decorated bookcases. Petepre stretched his bulk upon a light day-bed, which looked more fragile than ever beneath his weight; while Joseph went up to the shelves to read out the titles to his master. Should he unroll the adventures of the shipwrecked sailor upon the island of the serpent or the tale of King Khufu and that Djedi who could put a head back on after it had been cut off; or the true and apposite story of the conquest of the city of Joppa by the stratagem of Thuti, the great general of His Majesty Men-Kheper-Re-Thutmose III, who had five hundred soldiers carried into the town in sacks and baskets; the fairy-tale of the king's son to whom Hathor prophesied that he would come to his death by means of a crocodile, a serpent, or a dog — what would the master prefer? The choice was large. Petepre had a varied library arranged in the cases of the two halls; consisting in part of lively and

amusing fables and conceits like the "Fight of the Cats and the
Geese"; in part of stimulating dialectic like the polemic between the
scribes Hori and Amenemone, texts and tracts in religion and magic
in obscure and artificial language; lists of kings from the times of
the gods down to the foreign rule of the shepherd kings, with dates
and reigns of each son of the sun, and annals of remarkable historical
events such as important jubilees and extraordinary tax-collections.
He possessed the "Book of Atmen," the book "Of That which is in
the Underworld," the book "May the Name Flourish," and a learned
topography of the Beyond.

   Potiphar knew all his books. When he listened to reading, it was to
hear again the well known — as one listens to music. Such an attitude
toward his choice was the more natural because in the great majority
of these writings the interest lay very little in the matter or the story
and very much in the charm of style, the choiceness and elegance of
the phrasing. Joseph read, with his feet drawn up under him or standing at a sort of liturgical reading-desk. He read capitally; was fluent,
exact, unaffected, moderately dramatic, with such natural command
of words that the most involved literary style had a happy conversational ease. Literally he read himself into the heart of his listener; and
when we seek to understand his swift rise in the Egyptian's favour
we must by no means leave out of account these reading hours.

   Moreover Potiphar often dozed off early in the hour, lulled by the
measured, agreeable voice, the level, practised tone. And often he
interrupted with lively interest, corrected Joseph's pronunciation,
called attention to the excellence of a rhetorical flourish, criticized
what he had heard, or if the meaning were obscure, discussed it with
Joseph and was much taken with the lad's penetration and expository
gift. His personal feeling for certain literary products came out by
degrees, for instance a preference for the "Dispute with His Soul of
a Man who is Tired of Life." This as time went on he had read to him
over and over; in yearning, rhythmical accents death was compared
to many fine and good things: the recovery from sore illness, the
scent of myrrh and lotus blossoms, to a seat under shelter of a sail
on a windy day; with a cool drink on the shore, a "way in the rain,"
the homecoming of a sailor in a ship of war, the return to house and
home after long imprisonment — and many other things devoutly
wished for. Like all these, said the poet, was death to him. And Potiphar hearkened to the words as they were shaped by Joseph's lips, as
one hearkens to music as familiar as loved.

   Another piece of literature which enchanted him, so that he must
hear it over and over from Joseph's mouth, was the sinister and
frightful prophecy of encroaching disorder in the two lands, ending
in complete anarchy, an awful reversal of the order of things, when
the rich should be poor and the poor rich, when the temples should

be desolated and the service of the gods utterly neglected. It was unclear why Petepre liked to hear this account. Perhaps only for the
shudder which he might enjoy while reflecting that the rich were
still rich and the poor still poor, and that they would remain so if one
avoided disorder and sacrificed to the gods. He expressed himself on
the poem as little as he did on the "Dispute with His Soul" or the so-
called "Songs of Rejoicing," upon whose honeyed words and lovelorn lamentings he preserved silence. These romances told of the joys
and sorrows of a poor little fowler maid who went mad for love of
a youth, cooing after him and longing that she might be his wife and
his arm for evermore lie in hers. In honeyed tones he mourned that
he came to her not by night so that she was as one lying in her grave,
for in him alone was healing and life. And it was all a mistake; for he
too lay in his bed and mocked the doctor's skill with his sickness,
which was but love. But then she found him upon his bed and no
longer did they grieve each other's hearts but made each other the
first people in the world, roving hand in hand hot-cheeked through
the flowery garden of their joy. From time to time Petepre had these
cooings read aloud. His features never moved, only his eyes went
slowly to and fro in the room as he listened with cold attention; and
never did he express liking or disliking for the songs.

But once after many days he did ask Joseph how he liked them; and
so for the first time master and servant came again upon the theme
and touched lightly once more upon the subject of their talk in the
palm garden.

"Very good," Potiphar said. "You utter the songs with the very
mouth of the fowler and her lad. You prefer them, then, before all
the rest?"

"I seek, my lord," answered Joseph, "to win your pleasure with
my reading, and whatever I read, it is the same."

"That may be. But your effort might in one case more than another be supported by the spirit and heart of the reader. For one
subject may be nearer to him than another. I will not say that you
read this better than other things. But that need not mean that you
do not like better to read it."

"To you, my lord," Joseph said, "to you it is a joy to read them all."

"Yes, yes. But I would hear your judgment. You find the songs
beautiful?"

Joseph put on a consummately lofty and critical air.

"Very nice," said he and pursed his lips. "Very pretty certainly,
and every word of it dipped in honey. Yet perhaps a little too simple — just a trace."

"Simple? But the writing itself, which so completely expresses the
simplicity, and in so masterly fashion brings out the pattern, just as it
always is between human beings, will persist to endless jubilees. Your

years call you to judgment, whether these words are not the very pattern of the pattern itself."

"It seems to me," said Joseph with great detachment, "that the words of this fowler maid and her bedridden youth do perfectly convey the simplicity of the pattern and make it convincing."

"Only that?" asked the fan-bearer. "I reckoned on your experience. You are young, and beauty sits upon your countenance. Yet you speak as though for your part you had never walked with such a fowler maid in such a garden."

"Youth and beauty," Joseph replied, "may also signify a sterner adornment than that with which that garden crowns the children of men. Your slave, O master, knows an evergreen which is a symbol of youth and beauty, and yet is an adornment for a sacrifice. He who wears it is reserved, and whom it adorns is set apart."

"You speak of the myrtle?"

"Of the myrtle. I and mine name it the herb touch-me-not."

"Do you wear that herb?"

"My seed and stock, my lord, we wear it. Our God has dedicated Himself to us, and is our blood-bridegroom in all jealousy, for He is solitary and on fire for our loyalty. And we for our part are the bride of His loyalty, consecrate and set apart."

"What, all of you?"

"In principle all, my lord. But among the heads and friends of God in our race God chooses out one who shall be especially dedicate to Him in the adornment of consecrated youth. To the father it is indicated that he shall bring the son as a whole offering. If he can, so he does. If he cannot, then is it done to him."

"I do not like," Potiphar said, tossing on his bed, "to hear that something is done to someone that he will not and cannot have. Speak, Osarsiph, of other matters."

"I can at once better what I said," responded Joseph; "for there is a consideration and mildness which obtain in the whole sacrifice. While it is commanded, it is also forbidden and made a sin, so that the blood of a beast shall intervene for the blood of the son."

"What do you mean? Made what?"

"A sin, my lord. Made a sin."

"What is that — sin?"

"Just this, my lord: what is demanded and yet forbidden, ordered but accursed. We, almost alone in the world, know what sin is."

"That must be a heavy knowledge, Osarsiph, and to my mind a painful contradiction."

"God suffers, too, for our sin, and we suffer with Him."

Potiphar asked: "And when the fowler maiden wandered in the garden, was it, as I begin to surmise, a sin in your sense?"

"It hath a strong smack of it, my lord. Since you ask me, certainly yes. I cannot say that we especially love it, though we ourselves have doubtless also produced such songs. The garden — I will not go so far as to say that to us it is the land of Sheol. It is not an abomination but a dread, a dæmonic kingdom where an accursed command has play, full of the jealousy of God. Two animals lie at the gate: the name of one is shame, of the other guilt. And out of the branches looks a third and its name is mocking laughter."

"And now," said Petepre, "I begin to understand why you have called the song simple. Yet I cannot but think that it stands strangely and dangerously with a people to whom the pattern of simplicity is sin and mocking laughter."

"It has its history with us, my lord, it has its place in time and events. The pattern comes first, then recurs in many ways. There was a man and friend of God, and his love to his lovely one was strong as his love to God, and this tale of the fathers was of a pattern-like simplicity. But God in jealousy took her from him and plunged her into death, and she came forth to the father in another form, as a son, in whom he now loved his lovely one. Thus death made out of the beloved a son in whom she lived and who was a youth but by the power of death. But the love of the father for him was a love changed through that bath of death — love no longer in the form of life but of death. Thus my lord can see that in the story things went in different ways and less according to the pattern."

"The youthful son," said Petepre with a smile, "was doubtless the same of whom you went so far as to say that his birth was virgin, only because it happened in the sign of the Virgin."

"Mayhap, my lord, you are in your goodness inclined," Joseph answered, "after what I have said, to soften the reproach, or even graciously to withdraw it — who knows? For as the son is only a youth through death, the mother in the sign of death, and as it is written, at evening a woman, but in the morning a man — cannot we then with some justice, considering everything, speak of a virgin birth? God has chosen my seed, and all of us bear the sacrificial adornment of the bride. But one in particular wears it and is set apart for special zeal."

"Let it be as it is, my friend," said the chamberlain. "For our talk has led us a long way, and from the simple into the complex. If you will and greatly desire it, I will soften the reproach, and reduce it almost to nothing at all. But read me something else! Read me the night journey of the sun through the twelve houses of the nether world — I have not heard it for long, though there are in it, to my memory, many fine sentences and choice phrases."

And Joseph read the journey of the sun through the nether world, with good taste and discrimination, and Potiphar was entertained and much sustained thereby. The word "sustained" is in place, for by the voice of the reader and the excellence of the matter to which he subdued it, was sustained the sense of well-being with which the previous conversation had filled the listener. He was sustained, as the flame on the stone of sacrifice is sustained by nourishment from below and fed with fresh fuel from above. It was a sense of well-being, amounting to confidence in himself or in the person of his servant, which the Hebrew slave seemed always to know how to impart to Pharaoh's friend. This twofold confidence of Potiphar in Joseph, and its growth, were of high importance; and for that reason it seemed good to reproduce the above conversation in detail — even though, like the confrontation in the palm garden, it is unknown to earlier versions of our story.

Other such conversations there were, of course, which went to strengthen Potiphar's confidence and his preference for Joseph, to an extent which finally led to his servant's exaltation. We cannot reproduce them all. It is enough to have characterized by some striking instances his methods of "flattering" his master and being "helpful" to him, in the sense of the bond which he had made with the good Mont-kaw. I may use the word "method" without fear of chilling the reader's sympathies, since he already knows that in Joseph's way of dealing with his master there existed the same mingling of calculation and sincerity which characterized his relation to another isolated Being of a far more exalted sphere. Moreover, we are entitled to doubt whether sheer sincerity, unassisted by calculation and a good technique, would ever achieve practical results — for instance in inspiring a sense of well-being in another person. Confidence among human beings is rare. And in gentlemen of Potiphar's bodily habit, titular officials with titular wives at their sides, there is usually a fundamental vague jealous mistrust of everybody not constituted like themselves. So then nothing could be so calculated to rouse in them the unfamiliar and thus so much more gratifying feeling of self-respect, as the discovery that a member of the enviable outer world wears the rue, so to speak; in other words, the garland in his hair, which comfortably cancels out all his other disquieting characteristics. It was method, it was calculation that caused Joseph to let Potiphar make this discovery. But if anyone feel inclined to take offence at this, let him make use of the advantage he has in that he already knows the story we are telling, and remember that Joseph in the hour of temptation did not betray the confidence so engendered, but kept the faith and was true to the pact with Mont-kaw which he had sworn by he head of Jacob and incidentally also by the life of Pharaoh himself.

JOSEPH FLOURISHES AS BY A SPRING

So now, when he was free of his service with Potiphar, he went with the steward, whom already he called father, as his aid and apprentice about the estate, among people smiling and casting down their eyes; and learned how to oversee. Mostly there were other attendants as well: like Khamat, the scribe of the buffet, and a certain Meng-pa-Re, scribe of the stables and prisons. But these were people of but average gifts; pleased to be equal to the claims of their narrow field and specialty, and to keep order among gear and accounts, men and beasts, to the steward's satisfaction. They took no thought for those wider and higher spheres which require a head for the general; nor of improving themselves to be fitted for such; they were slack creatures who preferred to write down to dictation; it would never have occurred to them that they might be born to overseeing and government, and just for that reason they certainly were not. For let a man once have the idea that God has special plans for him, which he must further by his aid, and he will pluck up his heart and strain his understanding to get the better of all things and be their master, though the sum of them be as vast as it was in the prosperous establishment of Petepre at Wese in Upper Egypt.

For they were many and various. And of the twofold achievement, that Joseph became Potiphar's soothing and indispensable body-servant, and that afterwards the master put all that he had into his hand, the second was incomparably the harder part. Mont-kaw, who initiated Joseph into the work, was right in his oft-repeated saying that he had a hard time in the world. For a man with a good head for the general there was probably too much drudgery, and Mont-kaw suffered with his kidneys as well. It is easy to see that he was glad of the chance to acquire a strong young assistant and to train him for his successor — indeed, he must have been quietly looking for one for some time.

Petepre, the friend of Pharaoh, titular commandant of the palace troops and chief executioner, was a very rich man — richer, and rich in much grander style, than Jacob at Hebron. And he always grew richer, for he was highly paid as a court official and the constant recipient of the royal largesse, and also his property bore and bred for him without stint. Indeed, it came to him only partly by inheritance, being itself, especially the landed property, a gift of the god to his favourite, and continually increased and fed from the same source. He had little acquaintance with it in any active sense; applying himself exclusively to the maintenance of his physical bulk by eating, his mental by the books he had read aloud to him, and his manly self-respect by hunting in the marshes. Everything else he left in the hands of his steward; and when the latter as in honour bound submitted the accounts for inspection, he would glance at them indifferently and say:

"Very good, old man. I know you love me well, and do your work as well as you can, and you can very well indeed. What does it say here about the wheat and spelt? Is that right? — but yes, of course it is. I am convinced that you are as good as gold, and devoted to me body and soul. How could it be otherwise, considering your nature and the baseness it would be to do me wrong? Out of love for me you make my affairs your own; very good, I leave them to you for the sake of your love; in your own affair you will not come short out of carelessness or worse. Besides, the Hidden One would see it and you would have only torment from it in the end. Your accounts are correct, you may take them again with my thanks. You have no longer a wife, nor children — for whom should you disadvantage me? For yourself? You have not good health; your body indeed is strong and hairy, but inwardly a little worm-eaten, you have often a yellow face; the tear-glands under your eyes grow larger — you will probably not live to a great age. Why then should you offend your love to defraud me? Heartily I would that you should live to grow old, for I know not whom I could trust like you. What doth Khun-Anpu, our barber-surgeon, think of your health? Have his medicines helped you? I have no understanding for these things, I am healthy myself though not so hairy. But if he does not know how to help you and so your state grows worse, we will send to the temple for a physician. True, you are of the servant class, and Red-belly should do for you in illness, yet you are dear enough to me that I would procure you a learned man from the book-house if your body require. Thank me not, I would do so for the sake of your love and because your accounts are so clear and right. Here, take them again, and go on in your accustomed way."

Thus Potiphar to his house-steward on these occasions. For he took nothing upon himself. His aristocratic nature, its unactuality made him shun the practical realities of life, confiding as he did in the love and care which those about him had for his sacred and fleshly person. Certainly, he had good ground to trust Mont-kaw, for the steward really loved him and did him loyal service, making him richer and richer with the most disinterested care and caution. But suppose it had been otherwise, and this man who had all in his hands had robbed him, so that he and his had come to want? He would have had himself to blame and would have deserved to be reproached for his indolent over-confidingness. Yes, Potiphar presumed all too much upon the deeply motivated and tender devotion which those about him had to pay to his peculiar constitution and sacred person as courtier of the sun. We should all have had to agree to the justice of this charge.

Thus he was responsible for naught, save his eating and drinking; but the hardship for Mont-kaw was the greater in that his own affairs were involved with those of his master. As pay for his services he received supplies — corn, bread, beer, geese, linen, and leather — in much greater quantity than he could eat up or wear out. He had to take them to market and exchange them for durable goods to increase his permanent holdings. The same was true in general of his master's property, both that produced on the estate and that which came from without.

The fan-bearer stood high on the list of Pharaoh's beneficiaries; a rich and constant stream of rewards and superfluities flowed out upon his titular and unreal existence. The good god gave him every year quantities of gold, silver, copper, clothing, yarns, incense, wax, honey, oil, wine, vegetables, corn, and flax; birds caught by the fowlers, oxen, and geese; yes, even armchairs, coffers, mirrors, wagons, entire wooden ships. All this was only in part used on the estate; and the same was true of the estate's own produce, the household goods and the fruits of garden and field. Most of it was taken to market up or down the river and sold in exchange for other wares or for metal worked and unworked, which then went to swell Potiphar's treasury. And these operations, combined with the actually producing and consuming economy of the estate, necessitated much book-keeping and careful oversight.

Provisions had to be rationed out to the servants and workers: bread, beer, and barley or lentil porridge for work-days, for feast-days geese. The women's house had a separate domestic economy which had to be supplied and accounted every day; the raw materials had to be given out to the bakers, sandal-makers, paper-stickers, brewers, carpet-weavers, carpenters, potters, weavers, and spinners, and their finished wares to be apportioned where needed, or stored, or marketed. The same was true of the crops and the produce of orchard and garden. Potiphar's live-stock had to be kept up and taken care of: the horses which drew his chariot, the dogs and cats with which he hunted. The dogs were large and fierce, and he used them when he hunted in the desert; the cats were of a jaguar kind, for bird-hunting in the marshes. Some head of oxen were kept on the estate, but the most of the herds were pastured on an island in the middle of the river, somewhat upstream toward Dendera and the house of Hathor, which Pharaoh had likewise given him as a mark of affection. That comprised five hundred square rods of ploughland, each of which produced twenty sacks of wheat, twenty sacks of barley, and forty baskets each of onions, garlic, melons, artichokes, and gourds. Multiply that by five hundred, and one can see the amount of work and account-keeping entailed! There was a separate steward for it, the overseer of the harvest and the barley, who filled the measures pressed down and running over and measured the wheat for his lord. Actually the man expressed himself thus, in epigraphical style, about his performance; yet the responsibility was not his, but Mont-kaw's. All the accounts went through his hands; for the sowing and reaping, the oil-mills, the wine presses, the herds and flocks — in short, for all that such a prosperous estate produces and consumes, brings in and sends out. And he had to go out on the fields too and see that things were going well; since he to whom they and everything else belonged, Potiphar the courtier, was not used to supervising anything or disturbing the delicate insubstantiality of his state with any care at all.

So it was fortunate that Joseph after all did go out to the fields — at the right time and under the right auspices, not the wrong ones. For he went not as a labourer, as Dudu, the married dwarf, in his conservatism had wanted and tried to bring about, before he had had the chance to stand before Potiphar. Instead with tablets and pen he accompanied Mont-kaw, to learn the business of overseeing; went down-river with him in a sail-boat with rowers, to Potiphar's island. Mont-kaw sat stiff and solemn between the carpet hangings of his little niche, like the travelling grandees whom Joseph had seen during his first voyage; he himself, with the other scribes, sat behind. The boat was well known, and people as it passed them said:

"There goes Mont-kaw, the steward of Petepre, to inspect his master's estate. But who is the strikingly pretty lad among his train?"

Then they would disembark to walk over the island. inspect the sowing or reaping, have the cattle driven up, and strike terror to the heart of him who "let the measure run over" — while the culprit looked his astonishment at the youth to whom the overseer was showing everything, introducing it, as it were, and bowing above him as he talked. And Joseph, fully aware that the man before him might have been his slave-driver and swung the lash over him had he come out too early to the field, spoke to him privily and said:

"Have a care that you do not let the measure run over to your own gain, my man. For we should see it at once and you would be in a hole."

He used an expression native to his home, not familiar here, but by that so much the more impressive to the startled scribe of the harvest.

At home Joseph accompanied Mont-kaw on his round among the workers sitting at their benches. He examined their work, listened to their reports of the foremen and scribes and the explanations of Mont-kaw for his benefit; and he congratulated himself on not having displayed his ignorance and earned their contempt; that would have made it much harder for them to accept him as a man endowed by nature to be a supervisor. It is hard enough for us to make ourselves into that for which we were created and to arrive at the height of God's purpose for us, even when that may not be in itself a very lofty goal. And God's purposes with Joseph were lofty indeed, and follow them he must. He sat and did sums and accounts in the business of the estate; with figures and statements before him, he kept his mental eye fixed upon the realities which they represented. And he worked with his father Mont-kaw in the special room of trust, and the steward marvelled at the swiftness and penetration of his understanding, the power possessed by this pretty head of grasping facts and their relations, of suggesting, even, improvements on his own account. For instance, the garden produced such large quantities of sycamore figs that they disposed of them in the city, and particularly in the quarter of the tombs, where there was a great demand for them to furnish the offertory tables and as ceremonial food for the dead; and one day it occurred to Joseph to have the potters make imitation fruit in the natural colours, which would serve the purpose of the funerary offerings quite as well as the actual fruit. And as the purpose itself was magic, these symbols answered to it even better than reality, and very soon the magic figs were in great demand. They cost the producers little or nothing and could be made in great quantities, so that the making soon became a flourishing branch industry in Potiphar's house, occupying many work-people and contributing substantially to the proprietor's income, though of course the sum was small in comparison to the whole.

The steward Mont-kaw was grateful to his young aide for understanding so well how to keep the bargain they had struck for the sake of their noble master. Not seldom, as he watched the boy's single-minded endeavour and the sagacious purposefulness with which he conquered the manifold detail of his work, he felt afresh those equivocal sensations which had assailed him when Joseph for the first time stood before him, roll in hand, and moved him so strangely.

Soon he was able to relieve the pressure by sending his young pupil on business trips and to market in his place: downstream toward Abdu, the abode of the mangled one, yes, even to Menfe, and upstream to the Elephant Isle. Joseph became the master of the bark, or rather not of one but of several, which carried Potiphar's wares: the beer, the wine, the vegetables, hides, linen, earthenware, and castor oil, the latter of two kinds, the coarser for lamps, the finer for inward lubrication. Soon those who saw him said:

"There goes Mont-kaw's assistant, from the house of Petepre. He is an Asiatic youth, of beautiful countenance and very shrewd;

he takes goods to markets, for the steward trusts him, and with right too, for he has magic in his glance and speaks in the speech of men better than you or I, and gains favour for his wares as for his person, and can obtain prices to gladden the heart of Pharaoh's friend."

Thus or something like it spoke the sailors of the Nehel as they passed. And it was true; for blessing abode by Joseph's endeavours, he had the most engaging way with the merchants in village and town, and his words were a joy to hear, so that there were crowds about him and what he had to sell and he brought back better profit to the overseer than the latter could most likely have got himself or anybody else. But Mont-kaw could not often send him on journeys of any duration, for Petepre was displeased when his servant was absent from the dining-room, when another poured water over his hands or gave him dish and cup; or if he must take his nap without hearing Joseph read aloud. Yes, only when we realize that his service to Potiphar continued alongside his task of learning to manage the estate, can we measure the claims which were made at this time upon his energies and powers. But he was young and full of zeal, as of high resolve to attain the height of God's purpose for him. Already he was no longer the least of these here below; already there were those who bowed before his steps. But there must be much more than this; for the sake of his God he was filled with the idea that not some but all must bow — all, with exception of One, the Highest, whom alone he might serve. Such was now the fixed and unchanging principle which guided the life of the descendant of Abram. How it would come about he did not know or conceive. The important thing was to walk with courageous and willing steps the road God set under his feet, to look as far ahead as it is given man to see, and not to startle though the way were steep, for the steeper the more certainly it pointed to the highest goal.

So he chafed not at the struggle to master the details of the business and to make himself every day more indispensable to Mont-kaw, as well as to keep the pact with regard to Potiphar, his good master and the highest in his immediate circle, devoting himself as his servant and reader and establishing himself in Potiphar's confidence as he had done by the conversation in the orchard and the discussion about the garden and the fowler maiden. It took much skill and understanding to do this, to reach and help the master in his innermost soul and nourish his self-esteem with a warmth more cordial than the wine he poured for him at table. And even this was not all. For to conceive the sum of Joseph's efforts for master and steward one must add that he had every evening to say good-night to Mont-kaw, and every night in different phrases. For that service he had originally been bought; and Mont-kaw had been too favourably impressed with the first instance to forgo the pleasure of the sequel. He was a poor sleeper, as the pouches under his eyes betrayed. Only hardly did the overburdened brain relax from the occupations of the day and find the good highway to slumber. The kidneys too were bad and helped to make the transit difficult. So that he could well use a few sweet words and mellifluous murmurings at the end of the day. Thus Joseph might never neglect to come before him at night and drop soothing speech in his ears — which, besides everything else, had to be prepared during the day, for it must have comeliness of form.

"Greetings at evenfall, my father," he would say, with lifted hands. "Lo, the day is lived out, it has closed its eyes, weary of itself, over all the earth stillness has come. Hark, how strange is the stillness! There might sound a stamping from the stable, or a dog give tongue, only to make the silence more profound. It reaches with soothing into the souls of men, it makes them slumbrous; while over city and country, fertile and desert land are kindled the wakeful lamps of God. The peoples rejoice in the timely coming of the night, for they were weary; they rejoice that morn shall open their eyes again when sleep has washed them. Truly God's works are grateful to man! For imagine that there were no night; that the burning road of his toil glared endless and uniform before him. Were it not a horror and a quailing? But God has made the days and to each set its limit, so that we unfailingly reach it at its hour; the grove of night invites us to pious repose; with outstretched arms, head sinking back, with open lips and blissfully closing eyes we enter into its priceless shadow. Yet think not, dear my master, on your bed, that you must rest, but rather that you may, then the great boon of peace will come. Lie then, my father, outstretched on your couch and may sweet sleep fall upon you and over you, fill your soul quite with exquisite repose, that freed from care and cark you may breathe it in as resting upon the breast of God!"

"Thanks, Osarsiph," said the steward; and his eyes were filled with tears, as they had been that first time by broad daylight. "May you rest well too! Yesterday you spoke perhaps a trace more sweetly, but yet today's words were full of consolation like poppy-seed, and will help me even better against wakefulness. Strange, your distinction — that I may but must not sleep — strange and appealing. I mean to think of it and it will stead me. Yet must I wonder at the way your words fall from you like a charm: 'Upon you, over you, fill your soul quite . . .' — but that you can probably not tell yourself. And so good-night, my son!"

AMUN LOOKS ASKANCE AT JOSEPH

Such were the many and varied demands made upon Joseph at this time; he must not only satisfy them but take care that his good fortune be not laid up against him. For the smiling, the downcast eyes with which men mostly greet such a rise to power hide much ill will, which must be mollified with tact, shrewdness, and consideration, thus adding another to the many claims upon his judgment and alertness. Joseph flourished as by a spring; and it is wellnigh impossible for one in his position to avoid encroachment on another's field, and damage to another's boundary-stones. His advancement is inevitably bound up with detriment to another's; he must devote a good part of his understanding to reconcile with his own existence the outshone and overthrown. Before the time in the pit Joseph had been without sensitivity for these things. The view that everybody loved him more than they did themselves closed his eyes. In death and in his Osarsiph life he was cleverer, or, if you like, shrewder, for cleverness does not shield one from folly, as witness Joseph's case. The delicate compunction he had displayed to Mont-kaw about Amenemuia, his predecessor in the reader's office, was in the first instance directed toward Mont-kaw himself, in the consciousness that it would please him, even taking into consideration that the steward was by nature inclined to cheerful abnegation. But even for Amenemuia Joseph did all he could, addressing him so courteously and modestly that the scribe was quite won over and felt himself repaid by his successor's charming friendliness for the fact that he had ousted him from office. For Joseph, hands on his breast, put into moving words his pain at the decision and the master's whim, which must be held sacred but which to his knowledge he had done nothing to bring about. His best excuse was his sincere conviction that Amenemuia, scholar in the book-house, and a son of the black earth, could read aloud much better than himself, Osarsiph, who could but mangle the Egyptian tongue. But it had come about in the orchard that he had had to speak before the master, and in his embarrassment told him all sorts of things about trees, bees, and birds as they came into his head. They had oddly enough pleased the master to such a disproportionate extent that with the swift decision of the great and mighty he had come to a resolve which by now he probably saw was not to his own advantage. For ever and often he held Amenemuia up to his new reader as an example, saying: "Thus and so spoke and pronounced Amenemuia, my former reader, and so must you do, would you win favour in my sight, for I am spoilt to begin with." Joseph had endeavoured so to do, and as it were had life and breath only from his predecessor. Probably the master would by now have recalled his command, if it were not that the great would never admit that they had spoken too soon or given a mistaken order. He, Joseph, had realized the unspoken regret and sought to assuage it by saying: "You must, my master, give Amenemuia two feast-day garments and that excellent post as scribe of the sweetmeats and the revels in the house of the women, then will your mind be relieved and mine too on his account."

All that was of course balsam to Amenemuia's wound. He had not known that he was such a good reader; mostly the master had gone to sleep soon after he opened his mouth. He told himself that since he had had to leave to find it out he must perforce be satisfied with his congé. Likewise his successor's pangs of conscience did him good in his very soul, as also the master's supposed regret; and when he did actually receive the fine garments and the excellent post of master of revels in Petepre's house of women, in evidence that Joseph had spoken for him, he bore no malice at all, but conceived that he had been most charmingly treated.

It was of course nothing to Joseph to get for others good posts, since he himself, with God, aimed at supervision of them all, if as yet from afar, and dealt with all the problems at Mont-kaw's side. The same thing happened again with a certain man named Merab, who had formerly accompanied Petepre when he went bird-hunting and fish-spearing. For now it was Joseph who enjoyed these masculine pleasures attendant on his lord; and that must truly have been a thorn, a poisoned one at that, in Merab's side. But Joseph took away the sharpness and the sting, speaking to Merab as before to Amenemuia and procuring him presents and a good post — that of head of the brewery — so that he was Joseph's friend instead of his enemy, and went about saying: "Of course he is from the wretched Retenu and of the desert fly-by-nights; but a fine chap is he none the less, with the most charming ways, that one must admit. By All the Three! He still makes mistakes in speaking a man's tongue; but in some wise is it so that if one must give way before him one does it with pleasure and one's eyes light up. Explain it as you will and you can only blunder thereby — but it remains the fact that one's eyes light up."

Thus Merab, a quite common man of Egypt. It was Sa'ankh-Wen-nofer-and-so-forth, little "Beauty," the dwarf, who whispered it all to Joseph, how the superseded one had spoken to the people of the courtyard. "Well, then, all is well," Joseph had answered. But he perfectly knew that not everyone spoke thus. He had got over the childish illusion that everybody must love him more than themselves; he fully understood that his rise in the house of Potiphar, irritating in itself, was further offensive in that he was a foreigner, a sand-dweller and of the Ibrim. He knew that he must treat the situation with the utmost tact. And here we come back to those inner contradictions and factions which reigned in the land of ancestors and among which Joseph's career was run: certain religious and patriotic fundamentals which went counter to that career and had almost succeeded in sending him out untimely to the field; likewise certain factors of an opposed kind, free-thinking, tolerant — or one

might say degenerate and capricious — which favoured his rise.
These things concerned the steward Mont-kaw simply because they
concerned his master the courtier. But why did they concern
Petepre? Because they concerned the court. Because the court was
angry at Amun in his temple and at his oppressive power, the latter-
day embodiment of patriotic conservatism and the bondage of tradition, and because the great at court inclined to and cultivated another god and worship — and it was already suspected which god
that was. It was the worship of Atum-Re at On in the Delta, that
very old and mild god with whom Amun had put himself on a par
— not courteously but with violence, calling himself Amun-Re, sun-
god and god of the empire. Both of them were the Sun-in-his-Bark,
Re and Amun, but in what unlike sense and in what different way!
Joseph had had proof on the spot, in converse with the blear-eyed
priests of Horakhe, of the god's blithe, many-sided, and edifying
sun-meaning; he knew of his desire to extend, his tendency to associate himself and reach understanding with all possible popular sun-
gods, with Asia's youths of the sun, who went forth like a bridegroom out of his chamber, rejoiced like strong men in their race,
and were mourned in their setting with the laments of women. Re,
it appeared, would have no more great distinction among them, just
as Abram in his time would perceive none between his god and
Melchizedec's El Elyon. He was called Atum in his going down,
very lovely and lamentable; but of late, out of lively speculation by
his learned prophets, he had given himself a like-sounding name for
his universal sunship — not only for his going down but for morning, midday, and evening all together: he called himself Aton — with
a peculiar intonation noted by all. For he thus assimilated his own
name to that of the youth mangled by the boar and bewailed by the
flutes in Asia's gorges and groves.

The sun-meaning of Re-Horakhte, with its foreign associations
and inclination to a lively universalism, was well received at court.
Pharaoh's wise men found it good to practise themselves in its
thought. But Amun-Re at Karnak, Pharaoh's father in his rich and
mighty temple, was just the opposite of Atum-Re. He was rigid and
strict, hostile to every sort of wide-ranging speculation, averse to
foreign influence, abiding by unarguable custom and the sacred traditional. All this though he was much younger than he of On. The
ancient of days was here flexible and blithe, the new unbending conservative — and that was confusing.

But even as Amun at Karnak looked askance upon the growing
esteem in which Atum-Re-Horakhte was held at court, so also, Joseph felt, the god looked askance at him, Potiphar's foreign body-
servant and reader. Weighing favour against disfavour, he soon deduced that the sun-meaning of Re favoured his course, while that of

Amun did the opposite — also that this situation, too, demanded exercise of tact.

His closest contact with Amun, the embodiment of the god in Potiphar's house, was the wight Dudu, keeper of the jewels. It had been clear from the beginning that Dudu loved him not as himself but even considerably less; unspeakable trouble did Jacob's son have through all these years with the pompous creature. In every way, with the most punctilious courtesy, he sought to win and reconcile the dwarf, as also by attentions to her whose arm went about him, Djeset his spouse, who had place of authority in the house of the women; and his two overgrown and ugly sons, Esesi and Ebebi. He painfully avoided every slightest affront to Dudu's boundary-stones. Surely it would have been easy, standing in such cordial relations with Petepre, to push Dudu aside and to take his office. The master would have liked nothing better than to draw him even closer into his personal service. It is as good as known that he offered Dudu's post to Joseph unasked — and certainly, as Joseph saw, and had inferred also from the loyal steward's attitude, he simply could not bear the arrogant dwarf. But Joseph declined — meekly but firmly; in the first place, busy as he was with learning to oversee, he could take on nothing more; but in the second, on which he laid stress to Potiphar, he could not and would not bring himself to tread on the worthy manikin's toes.

But one would think the dwarf might have been grateful. He was not — in this respect Joseph had given himself to false hopes. The enmity evinced by Dudu from the first day, nay, from the first hour, for he had tried his best to prevent him being bought, was not to be softened or won by any politeness. And if we wish to get an insight into the foundations and motivations of all these events, we shall not be satisfied to explain Dudu's dogged dislike as the ill will of a partisan of Egypt against a foreigner and his increase in Potiphar's house. We must quite certainly bring in those peculiar talismanic powers by virtue of which Joseph had known how to be "helpful" to the master and to win favour from him. Of these Dudu had had proof, of a kind peculiarly offensive to the dwarf, injuring him as they did at once in his exaggerated personal dignity and in values which sustained the pride and the self-esteem of his dwarfish existence.

This too Joseph perceived. He knew that his oration in the palm garden had wounded the deepest sensibilities of one hearer in the same measure as it had worked healing to the other's; that, without meaning to, he had somehow encroached on the domain of the married dwarf. This was why he had been so gracious to Dudu's wife and her brood. But it did no good. Dudu showed his dislike whenever he could, especially by casting up at him — from below —

the reproach familiar in the stern old code, that of being a stranger, a Shabirite, and as such unclean. At table, when the upper servants of the house broke bread together, among them Joseph and the steward Mont-kaw, Dudu, pursing his upper lip till it stuck out like a thatch, insisted that the Hebrew be separately served; and when the steward and the others tried, in the sun-sense of Atum-Re, to make light of the matter, he held to the strict letter of the Amun-observance, withdrew from the abomination, spat toward the four quarters of the heavens, and drawing a circle round about him, prac-tised charms and exorcisms against the pollution, quite obviously actuated by the wish to be offensive to Joseph.

If he had only stopped at that! But Joseph soon learned that the worthy Dudu actively worked against him and tried to drive him away. He got it fresh and hot from his little friend Bes-em-heb; for the latter, thanks to his minute size, was extraordinarily clever at peeping and hearkening in the right places, and simply a master at hiding in holes which could never have occurred to a full-sized man. Dudu was a dwarf too, by nature adjusted to the scale of the dwarf world; he too should have shown himself less clumsy and defence-less than ordinary mortals. But it might be true, as little "Beauty" asserted, that his marriage into the full-sized world had blunted the edge of his finer perceptions — perhaps by dint of the same virtue which had made him capable of contracting it. In any case, he let himself be tracked down and spied upon by his despised little col-league, who soon learned how Dudu went about to hinder Joseph's growth. The road led into the house of the secluded, it led to Mut-em-enet, Potiphar's chief wife; what the dwarf said to her she re-peated, sometimes in his presence, but oftener alone with a certain mighty man who went in and out in Petepre's house of women and in her private rooms as well: Beknechons, the first prophet of Amun.

We know from the lips of Potiphar's mischief-making little old parents the close relation in which Joseph's mistress stood to the temple of the wealthy state god and the house of Amun-Re. Like numberless women of her social standing, for instance Renenutet, wife of the overseer of the bulls of Amun, she belonged to the aristo-cratic order of Hathor, whose protectress was the exalted consort of Pharaoh and its present leader the wife of the head priest of the god's temple at Karnak; in other words, of the pious Beknechons. The centre and spiritual home of the order was the beautiful temple by the river, called Amun's southern house of women or simply the harem; connected by the amazing avenue of rams with the great temple at Karnak, and now in process of enlargement by Pharaoh with a vast and towering columned hall. The honorary title of the members of the order was "harem-wife of Amun"; and accordingly the "mother" of the members, the wife of the high priest, was called "first of the women of the harem." But why were these ladies priest-esses of Hathor, when Amun-Re's great consort was called Mut or mother, and Hathor, the cow-eyed, beautiful of countenance, was the wife of Atum-Re, the lord of On? These were the refinements and subtle statesmanlike balancings of the land of Egypt! For as it pleased Amun on political grounds to put himself on a par with Atum-Re, so Mut, the Mother of the Son, did the same with all-compelling Hathor; and Amun's earthly harem-women, the ladies of the best society of Thebes, followed her example: each one of them was Hathor, the mistress of love, in her very person; at the great feasts of Amun, wearing the narrow garment, the mask of the bride of the sun, the gold cap with the cow-horns and crescent moon, they made music and danced before him, singing as well as ladies in high society can sing — for they were not chosen for their voices, but for their riches and aristocratic birth. But Mut-em-enet, Poti-phar's lady wife, had a charming voice, and taught the others, among them Renenutet, wife of the keeper of the bulls, to sing. She had a high place in the women's house of the god, her rank in the order was next to its head, whose husband, the great prophet Beknechons, was her friend and trusted intimate and went in and out of her house.

BEKNECHONS

JOSEPH had long known that forbidding man by sight; had repeat-edly seen him on his visits to the house of women and sympathized with the anger in Pharaoh's soul at sight of Beknechons's pomp and state. Troops of the god, with spears and clubs, ran before his carrying-chair as it swayed on long poles upon the shoulders of four times four shiny-pated temple servitors. At its sides were bearers with ostrich-feather fans and another troop followed behind — as though the god Amun himself were going a progress in his bark. Criers ran in front of the train with slaves, filling the court in ad-vance with their loud insistent shouts, so that the people hurried up, and he who was set over the house, if not Petepre himself, came to receive the great guest on the threshold. Petepre avoided these occa-sions, but Mont-kaw was always on hand and on sundry of them Joseph had already stood behind him, attentively fixing the great man with his eye. For here was the embodiment, the highest and re-motest, of the hostile sun-doctrine, as Dudu was its smallest and closest to hand.

Beknechons was of goodly stature and bore himself haughtily, his torso strained upwards from his ribs, his shoulders thrown back, his chin thrust up and out. His head was impressive: egg-shaped, with a never-covered, smooth-shaven poll, and characterized by the sharp and deep-cut furrow between the brows. It was a permanent furrow, losing none of its severity when he smiled, as he sometimes did, condescendingly, or as a reward for some particular obsequiousness. His face, likewise meticulously shaven, was clean-cut and immobile, with high cheek-bones and furrows as deeply graven as the one on his forehead, about the nose and mouth. He had a way of gazing past men and things, which bespoke not merely arrogance but a thoroughgoing rejection of the modern world, a denial and condemnation of the whole course of life, for centuries or even millennia back. And his raiment, though costly and fine, displayed a priestly conservatism, being fashioned after a mode whole epochs earlier in time. Beneath his outer garment, which began under his shoulders and fell to his feet, could plainly be seen the simple, narrow, brief loin-apron, cut in the manner of the first dynasties of the Old Kingdom. To even more remote and thus presumably more pious times belonged the priestly leopard-skin which was draped round his shoulders, with the head and fore-paws hanging down his back, the hind-paws crossed on his breast, where likewise he wore other insignia of his state: a blue scarf, and a complicated gold ornament with rams' heads.

The leopard-skin was clearly an unwarranted presumption, for it belonged to the insignia of the head priest of Atum-Re at On and not at all to the servants of Amun. But Beknechons was just the sort of man to decide for himself what was fitting for him; and nobody, not even Joseph, failed to understand why he wore the primitive and sacred skin. It signified that Atum-Re had been absorbed in Amun, that he was but a manifestation of the Great One of Thebes, to some extent his subject — and not only to some extent. For Amun — that is to say, Beknechons — had succeeded in making Re's head prophet at On take the honorary title of a second priest of Amun at Thebes; the superior status of the high priest was thus made evident, also his right to the insignia of the other's office. Even at On, Re's own seat, he had managed to prevail. For he not only called himself "Head Priest of all the gods of Thebes," but also assumed the title of "Head Priest of all the gods of Upper and Lower Egypt," and was thus the first of the first in Atum-Re's own house. Why should he not wear the leopard-skin? Not without awe could one look at this man, in view of all that he represented. And Joseph had come to enough understanding of Egyptian affairs that his heart misgave him as he thought how Pharaoh made him wax ever more in girth and pride by endless gifts of goods and treasures, in the pleasing fancy that it was his father Amun to whom he gave them — and, in a sense, also to himself. Joseph — for whom Amun-Re was only an idol, like another, though he kept it to himself: sometimes a ram in his chamber, again a doll-like image in his chapel shrine, whom they took riding in his bark on the Jeor because they knew no better than so to do — Joseph made sharp and clear distinctions which Pharaoh failed to make: he found it not good and not wise of the god to let his supposititious father wax fatter and fatter; they were higher cares which beset him when he saw Amun's greatest disappear into the house of the women. And they transcended, in his statesmanlike musings, his concern for his own welfare, although he knew that it was being threatened by the talk going on inside.

He knew from little Bes, his first patron in Potiphar's house, that Dudu had complained of him more than once to Mut, the mistress. The midget, hidden in unlikely places, had been present at these scenes and made such detailed report to Joseph that the latter could fairly see the keeper of the robes, standing in his starched apron skirt before his lady, pompously sticking out his upper lip and gesturing indignantly with his stumpy arms as he sunk his voice to its deepest note and sent up to her ears his plaint over the annoyance and the offence. The slave Osarsiph, for so he mysteriously chose to call himself, the Shabirite lout and scum of the desert — verily it was a scandal, said Dudu, and a malignant sore, the way he waxed in favour in Potiphar's house. Surely the Hidden One saw it with displeasure. Not alone that he had been bought, against the dwarf's advice, for far too high a price, a hundred and sixty deben, of some worthless pedlars from the desert, who had stolen him from a prison grave; not alone that he had been taken into the house, through the contrivance of the jester Shepses-Bes, the unmarried dwarf, a fellow not worth a rotten nut. But instead of sending the foreign hand to field labour, as sensible folk had advised the steward, the latter had let him lounge about the court and he had come to stand before Petepre in the palm orchard, and the rascal had turned it to his advantage in a way that could only be called shameless — and even that was too mild. He had filled the master's ears with the rankest and most insidious jargon, which was an affront to Amun and a blasphemy against the sun. And the exalted master had been taken in, had been criminally bewitched, so that he had made the slave his waiter and servant, while Mont-kaw treated him like a son, or more correctly like a son of the house, who was learning to administer it because he was the heir, and plumed himself as the overseer's assistant — a scabby Asiatic in a house of Egypt! He, Dudu, permitted himself most humbly to call the mistress's attention to this abominable state of things, at which the Hidden One might be so wroth as to avenge himself for this corrupt free-thinking upon those who committed and suffered it.

"What said the mistress?" asked Joseph after hearing. "Tell me exactly, little Beauty, repeating if you can her very words."

"Her words," the little man replied, "were these: 'While you were speaking, steward of the jewel-house,' she said, 'I have tried to think

who he is whom you have in mind, and what foreign slave you accuse
in your words; but I searched my memory in vain. You could not
expect me to have all the servants in my eye and thus understand at
once the sense of your words. But in time it came to me, that he of
whom you speak is the truth, still young in years, who now for a
while has filled my husband's cup. Vaguely I can recall the silver-
apron if I try.' "

"Vaguely?" repeated Joseph, with some disappointment. "How
can I be so vague to our mistress, when I stand each day beside her
and her master at table, and the favour I have found in his eyes and
Mont-kaw's cannot have escaped her? I wonder therefore that she
must search so long and make such effort before she guessed to
whom Dudu's spiteful words referred. What more did she say?"

"She said," went on the dwarf, "she said: 'Why do you bring me
all this to reproach me, keeper of the wardrobe? For you will call
down Amun's wrath upon me; have you not said he would be enraged at those who suffer the offence to be? But if I know naught,
I suffer naught, and you might have spared me and not made me
to stand in danger of my knowing.' "

Joseph laughed at this and gave it great praise. "What a capital
answer, what a shrewd reproof! Tell me more of our mistress, little
Bes! Repeat all to me with exactness, for I am sure you listened
well."

"It was that spiteful Dudu," the dwarf went on, "who said more,
justifying himself and saying: 'I have told the mistress, not that she
may suffer the evil, but may do it away. For out of love for her
I have made occasion that she may serve Amun, by telling the master
that the unclean slave must be sent away out of the house. Now that
he is bought he should be sent to the fields, instead of making himself master here and setting himself above the children of the land."

"Very hateful," Joseph said. "A bad, spiteful speech. But the
mistress, what did she say to that?"

"She answered," little Beauty responded, "and said: 'My solemn
friend, it seldom happens that it is vouchsafed to the mistress to
speak in confidence with the master. Think of the formal manners
of our house and do not dream that it stands between him and me
as between you and her who is your spouse and familiar, Djeset your
wife, who puts her arm about you. She comes in simple confidence
and speaks of all her concerns and yours and may also decide your
mind to this or that course. For she is a mother, having borne you
two sightly sons, Esesi and Ebebi, so that you are bound in gratitude
to her and have all reason to give her your ear and heed her words
and wishes. But what am I to the master and what cause has he to
hearken to me? For his self-will is great, his mood unhearing; I am
powerless before him with my reminders.' "

Joseph was silent, looking thoughtfully over his little friend's head as the dwarf sat with wrinkled anxious face supported on his hands.

"Well, and the wardrobe master, what answered he?" Jacob's son probed again after a while. "Did he reply and enlarge himself yet more?"

That the dwarf answered in the negative. Dudu had preserved a dignified silence; and the mistress had added that she would speak as soon as might be with the head priest. For as Petepre had advanced the foreign slave after the latter had spoken with him concerning sun-matters, it was plain that they were here dealing with religion and the state, which were the affair of Beknechons, the great prophet of Amun, and her confessor and friend. He must be told; she would pour into his fatherly heart, to her relieving, all that Dudu had told her concerning the offence.

So far the dwarf's information to Joseph. But the latter recalled afterwards how Bes-em-heb lingered, sitting beside him in his comic costume, the cone of ointment perched on his wig, his chin in his hands, sombrely blinking.

"What are you frowning at, Beauty in the house of Amun?" he had asked. "Why do you brood over these things?"

The other answered in his cricket chirp:

"Oh, my Osarsiph, I brood because it is not good that the spiteful gossip speaks of you to Mut the mistress — how little good it is, and how great harm!"

"Of course not," Joseph replied. "Why do you tell me that, when I know of myself that it is evil and even dangerous? But behold, I have no care because I trust in God. Has not the mistress herself admitted the weakness of her power over Petepre? It would take more than a word from her to send me to the field, so have no care!"

"But how shall I be quiet," whispered Bes, "when there is danger still, of another kind, if Dudu open your mistress's eyes and enlighten her concerning you?"

"Who can understand that?" Joseph cried out. "Not I indeed, for your prattle is like so much gibberish to me. Danger of another kind — what sort of dark saying is it you whisper there?"

"I whisper, I whisper my fear and foreboding," he heard the dwarf say. "I murmur my dwarfwise cares, of which you, being of the full-grown race, as yet have no notion. The old gossip intends evil; but it may turn out that he has done well, yet only too well, so that in the end it is worse than before, much worse than he thought to make it in his spite."

"Take it not ill, little man, that I understand not one word of your words, for they have no sense. Good, evil, only too well and yet

much worse — and that is but little language and dwarfish nonsense,
and try as I may, I understand it not."

"Then why has your face turned red, Osarsiph, and why are you
vexed — as you were before when I said that the mistress knew you
but vaguely? My dwarf-wisdom would have you remain ever vague
to her; for the danger is doubly a danger if the accursed gossip opens
her eyes with his malice. Ah!" the manikin said, and hid his head
in his arms, "the dwarf is afraid, he is terrified in face of the foe, the
bull whose fiery breath scorches the field."

"What field?" Joseph asked, with wilful want of understanding.
"And what sort of fiery bull? You are not in your right senses today
nor can I give you reason. Go get yourself a soothing drink from
Red-belly, it will cool your head. I go to my work. Can I help it
if Dudu complain of me to the mistress, however dangerous it may
be? But you see my trust in God, and need not be disturbed. Yet
take heed always to let no word escape you of that which Dudu
speaks before the mistress, and even more what she says to him, and
report it to me with exactness. For it is important that I should
know."

Such had been the course of their conversation; Joseph later recalled it, and how the dwarf had displayed such fear. But had it been
merely his trust in God, and nothing else, which made Joseph receive with relative blitheness the news of Dudu's unfriendly activities?

Up till then, to the mistress he had been, if not precisely air, still
a vacant shape, like a dumb waiter in the service of Huia and Tuia.
Dudu's ill will now altered the situation. For when at table Joseph
handed the dish to his lord or filled his cup and her eye fell upon
him, this was not mere chance, not as though it rested on an object
in the room, but she looked at him as a person, with associations
and backgrounds to give food for thought, whether pleasant or
otherwise. In a word, his mistress, this great lady of Egypt, had begun
to heed him. Of course, in an idle and cursory way; it would be too
much to say that her eyes really rested upon him. But for the space
of a second perhaps, they sought him out — very likely as the thought
crossed her mind that she must speak to Beknechons; and Joseph behind his eyelashes took note of such moments. Despite all the attention he must give to serving Petepre, not one of them escaped him —
though only once or twice did he let it happen that the moment was
mutual: that the two pairs of eyes, the mistress's and the servant's,
actually chanced to meet — hers blankly, haughtily, with stern in-
sistence, his with startled respect, then veiling their gaze to look
humbly down.

That happened after Dudu's talk with the mistress. Before, it had
not — and between ourselves Joseph found it not altogether unpleasant. To some extent he saw progress in it and was tempted to

be grateful to Dudu. And next time he saw Beknechons enter the
house of women he found it agreeable to realize that they would be
talking in there of him and his advancement — there was a certain
satisfaction or even joy connected with the thought, though mingled with however much misgiving.

Of this talk too he got a report from the mock-vizier, who had
been present in some crack or cranny and heard it all. First the
priest and the lady of the order of Hathor had discussed religious
and ritual matters as well as those of a personal and social nature —
they had made tongue, as the children of Kemt said (the expression
was a Babylonian one); in other words, exchanged the gossip of the
metropolis. When the talk veered round to Petepre's house the
mistress took occasion to put before her spiritual adviser Dudu's
complaint and the improprieties centring in the Hebrew slave to
whom the courtier and his steward had shown such signal and sen-
sational favour. Beknechons nodded as he listened, as though her
words confirmed his general gloomy expectations and conformed
only too well with the morals of a time which had forfeited so much
of the righteousness that had held sway in those epochs when the
apron was worn short and tight as Beknechons wore it. A bad sign,
certainly, he had said. A sign of the loose times and the neglect of the
ancient piety; all very fine in the beginning, but getting lost in the
wilderness, rending the most sacred bonds, sapping the strength of
the lands till no more awe before their sceptre lived on the coasts,
and the kingdom fell to decay. And the high priest forsook the subject of Dudu's complaint, said Bes, to enlarge upon higher themes,
questions of power and statesmanship, waving his hands about in the
air. He spoke of Tushratta, king of Mitanni, and the need of using
Shubbilulima, king of Hatti in the north, to check his encroachments;
but only just enough, Shubbilulima must not succeed too well. For if
warlike Hatti were to bring Mitanni completely under its rule and
overrun the southland with arms, it might become a danger to Pharaoh's Syrian possessions, descended to him from the conqueror
Men-Kheper-Re-Thutmose. In any case it was on the cards that
Hatti, urged by its savage gods, might some day, avoiding Mitanni,
overrun the land of Amki on the sea, between the cedar ranges and
those of Amanus. Yet he was opposed on the world chess-board by
Abd-Ashirta the Amorite, who as Pharaoh's vassal held the region
between Amki and Hanigalbat, on purpose to set limits to Shubbilulima's southward advance. But this the Amorite would do only
so long at his awe of Pharaoh remained greater than his fear of Hatti;
failing that, he would assuredly betray Amun and make common
cause with Shubbilulima. For they were traitors one and all, these
vassal kings of the Syrian conquest, just as soon as they dared, so
that everything depended on their fear, theirs and that of the Bed-

ouins and migratory hordes of the steppes, who without it would
fall upon the fertile land and lay Pharaoh's cities waste. In short,
there were many cares; many considerations admonished Egypt to
keep itself nerved and sinewy if it wished to preserve awe for its
sceptre and the kingdom for the crown. To that end it must be stern
of morals and pious as in ancient time.

"A mighty man," Joseph opined after listening to the speech.
"For besides being a man of God and a shiny-pate before the Lord,
who should be a good father to his children and put out his hand to
them that stumble, he had a head for things of the earth and for
political affairs — one has to admire him for it. But just between ourselves, little Bes, he ought to leave the running of the kingdom and
the terror of the tribes to Pharaoh in his palace, who is set in his
place to that end. Certainly it was thus between temple and palace
in the days which he praises so highly above these. But our mistress,
did she answer nothing to his words?"

"I heard," said the dwarf, "how she answered, saying: 'Ah, my
father, is it not true that in the past, when Egypt was pious and
strict in observance it was also small and poor; nor were its boundary-
stones set among vassal peoples either southwards beyond the cata-
racts to the Negro lands or eastwards to the river that floweth the
wrong way? But out of the poverty have riches come, and out of the
smallness a great kingdom. Great Wese and both the lands teem with
foreigners, the treasures pour in, and all is changed. But do you not
rejoice at all over the new that grew out of the old and is its reward? From the tribute of the peoples Pharaoh offers richly to
Amun, so that the god can build to the height of his desire, so that
he increases like the river in spring when it is already at high-water
mark. Must not my father then approve the course of things since
the times of their early piety?'"

"Very true," Beknechons had, according to the dwarf, made answer. "Very justly does my daughter speak concerning the problem
of the lands. For thus it stands: the good old times bore within them
the seed of the new — that is the kingdom and the riches of the kingdom which in its turn bore within it the loosening, the relaxing, and
the loss. What shall be done that the blessing not become a curse, and
the good not be rewarded with evil? That is the question; and Amun,
lord of Karnak, answers it in this wise: the old must become lord
in the new, the strict and sinewy be set over the kingdom that
looseness not go too far and the reward of strictness be lost. For not
to the sons of the new but to the sons of the old pertains the kingdom and belong the crowns, the white, the red, the blue, and the
crown of the gods as well!"

"Strong!" said Joseph, after he had taken it in. "A strong, uncom-
promising speech is this you have heard, little Bes, thanks to your

want of size. I am alarmed by it, if at the same time not surprised. For I have always known ever since I saw his troops for the first time in the Street of the Son, what was in Amun's heart. So our mistress just spoke a little of me and it sent Beknechons off into all those high matters and they forgot all about me. Did you hear that they came back to me at all?"

Only just at the end, Shepses-Bes told him. When he left, the high priest had promised to take Petepre to task as soon as he could and put him on his guard, for the sake of the traditional morality, against the foreign slave whom he had so favoured.

"Then must I tremble indeed," said Joseph, "and be in sore fear that Amun put an end to my growth in the land; for if he is against me, how then shall I live? It is very bad, for if I go now to field labour, after the scribe of the harvest hath bowed before me, it will be worse than if I had gone in the first place; and I should perish of heat by day and of cold by night. But do you think that it will be given to Amun to deal thus with me?"

"So stupid am I not," whispered back the dwarf. "I have not wasted my dwarf-wisdom by marriage. True, I have grown up — if I may put it thus — in the fear of Amun. But I have long known that you have a god with you, Osarsiph, stronger than Amun and wiser than he; and never will I believe that He will give you into his hands and permit him in his chapel to set limits to your growth that He Himself has not set."

"Well, then, little Bes, be blithe!" cried Joseph, giving the other a slap on the shoulder, but gently so as not to hurt him, "and concerning me be of good cheer. For after all I have the ear of the master and can put him on his guard too when we are alone, against things which perhaps are dangerous for Pharaoh too. Then will he hear us both: Beknechons and me. The high priest will speak to him of a slave, and the slave of a god; and we shall see to what he inclines his ear — to what, I say, to what subject, and not to whom. But you, my little friend, be watchful, and hide your wisdom for me in cracks and crannies if Dudu should complain of me again to the mistress, that I may come to know his words and hers."

And thus it was. For it is certain that the keeper of the wardrobe did not rest with one tale-bearing to Mut-em-enet, but from time to time in conversation with her came back to the foreign slave from the prison pit and the gross favour shown him in Petepre's house. The little jester was always at his post and faithfully brought back the tale of Dudu's doings. Yet even had he been less watchful, Joseph would have known whenever the married dwarf had complained; for then one of those moments would come in the dining-room. And when for days there had been none, so that Joseph was cast down, their renewal, and that stern inquiry directed not as though at an object but a person, made him realize that Dudu had been with her again, and he would say to himself: "He has reminded her, and it is a danger!" But when he said it he also meant: "How pleasant!" and in one way was grateful to Dudu for calling him to the mistress's mind.

JOSEPH BECOMES VISIBLY AN EGYPTIAN

No longer evident to the father's eye, but in his place very much alive and alert, Joseph lived on in the Egyptian world, lived into it, one might say; for he went in harness to its claims, and they were heavy on him who as a lad in his first life had known no tasks and had no demands laid upon him, but spent time according to his whim. Here he was the more active in that he now strove to rise to the height of God's purpose for him; his head was full of figures, facts, and things, all sorts of business details, and more than that involved in a web of human problems and relations which always required most delicate handling, the threads of which led to Potiphar, to the dwarfs, to Mont-kaw, to God knows whom else in the house and outside it — in constant functioning, in short, of a kind that his early home, where Jacob now was, and the brothers, would never dream of.

That home was far away — farther than seventeen days, farther than Jacob had been from Isaac and Rebecca when he lived and looked into the Mesopotamian light of day. They too had had no idea, been able to form no picture of how their son lived or what his problems were; and from their day he in his turn was estranged. Where a man lives, there is his world: a narrow circle of life, work, and experience. The rest is vague. Though men have always been inclined to shift their centre, to let the known sink into the mist and look into a different day. Naphtali's urge has been strong upon them, to run off into the mist, to report strange news to those dwelling there who know only their own, and take back home some thing worth the knowing. In short, there was always traffic and intercourse. Even between the widely separated places of Jacob's land and Potiphar's, there always had been, time out of mind. Was not the man from Ur accustomed to change his horizon, had he not been to the land of mud, though not so far into it as Joseph; had not his sister-bride, Joseph's ancestral grandmother, dwelt for a time in the house of women of that Pharaoh who then glittered in his horizon not at Wese but farther north, nearer to Jacob's sphere? Always there had been contacts between that sphere and Joseph's present one; for the darkly beautiful Ishmael had taken to wife a daughter of the black earth, and from the marriage the half-Egyptian Ishmaelites had sprung, called and chosen to bring Joseph down hitherwards. And many like them traded between the rivers to and fro, and apron-skirted messengers had gone about, a thousand years and more, with letters written on bricks carried within their garments' folds. But if this Naphthali-nature had always been, yet now in Joseph's time it was as never before a regular, customary, and developed thing; for the land whither he was snatched and where he lived his second life was definitely a land of descendants: no longer piously self-sufficient and strict as Amun would have it be, but worldly and seeking the pleasures of the world; so that if a Come-hither Asiatic lad had but a cunning gift at saying good-night and could add two and two, he could become the body-servant to a great Egyptian and goodness knows what besides!

No, there was no lack of communications between Jacob's place and his darling's. But he whose affair it was to use them since he knew his father's abode but his father knew not his, for whom it would have been easy, as a great steward's right hand, and so skilled in all arrangements, to have arranged opportunity for this too; he did not do it, he did it not for many years. The reasons have long since become clear to us, and nearly all of them are comprehended in the one word: expectancy. The calf bleated not, it kept still as death, it did not let the cow know to what field the man had brought it; for in agreement with the man, it demanded expectation of the cow as well, however hard it might be for her; for needs must the cow consider her calf to be dead and mangled.

Strange, and confusing too it is, to think that Jacob, the old man back there in the mist, all this while held his son for dead — confusing, in that on the one hand one would like to be glad for him because he was mistaken, and on the other one grieves for him precisely because of his mistake. For there are, we know, certain consolations for the death of a beloved one, though they may be of a sufficiently hollow and desolate kind; and so we may feel a double pity for that sorrowing old man: first because he held Joseph for dead, and second because he was not. The father-heart lulled itself — no doubt with a thousand pangs, but yet with a gentle sense of soothing — in the security of death. It imaged his son as treasured up in death, unchangeable, inviolable, needing no more care, eternally the seventeen-year-old boy who had ridden off on white Hulda. And all this was a mistake, not only the affliction but also the consolation which gradually surmounted it. For Joseph lived, and was exposed to all the chances and changes of life. He was snatched away, but not snatched out of time; he did not remain seventeen, but waxed and riped in the place where he was, got to be nineteen and twenty and one-and-twenty; certainly he was still Joseph, but the father would not have known him, at least not at the first glance. The stuff of his life was altered, while still wearing its triumphantly successful shape; it ripened and became a little broader and firmer, less a youth and more a young man. A few years more, and of the fabric of that Joseph whom his Rebecca-father kissed at parting little will be left — as little as though death had dissolved the flesh. Only, since it was not death but life that changed him, the shape to some extent remained. Not so faithfully or exactly as death would have preserved it in the spirit, and did, illusorily, in Jacob's mind. After all, in this matter of content and form, whether it is death or life that removes the loved object away from our eyes is perhaps not so important as we are prone to think.

Likewise we must consider that the substance of Joseph's life, by which among all the changes and chances of his maturing youth its form was preserved, was drawn from quite another sphere than the one which would have fed it had he remained under Jacob's eyes; and the fact influenced its form as well. He was nourished by the airs and juices of Egypt, ate Keme's food; the water of her river moistened and swelled his tissues and cells, her sun irradiated them; he dressed in the linen from Egypt's flax, trod her soil, receiving from it the impulse of her silently shaping powers; took in with his eyes every day the evidences shaped by the hand of man, the expression of her fundamental, all-embracing, decisive character; lastly, he spoke her speech, and it gave to his tongue, his lips, his jaws another shape than that they would have had. Very soon Jacob the father would have said to him: "Damu, my seed, what is it with thy mouth? I know it no more."

In short, Joseph as he grew became visibly an Egyptian, in form and manner; quickly, easily, unnoticeably, because he was a child of the world, pliant in body and mind, likewise very young and soft when he came into the land, and thus the reshaping of his person after the local type happened readily and painlessly, the more that physically he had, from God knows where, something Egyptian about him — the square shoulders, the slender limbs; and mentally because it lay in his tradition, it was natural to him, to live a stranger among the "children of the land." Even at home he and his, the children of Abram, had always been *gerim* and guests, long settled and well adapted, it is true, but with an inner reserve and looking with detachment upon the easy-going Baal-abominations of the real children of Canaan. So now Joseph in Egypt. As a child of the world he found it simple to conform and to practise detachment at one and the same time, for the one made the other easier and drew out the sting of his fear lest he be disloyal to Him, Elohim, who had brought him into this land, and upon whose countenance and indulgence he might reckon, though Joseph were to comport himself in all ways as an Egyptian and become a child of Hapi and subject of Pharaoh — always excepting the silent reservation. Thus to be a child of the world meant that he might blithely adapt himself to Egypt's children and move among them, consenting to the high culture of the land; yet all the while he might feel that they were the children of the world, at whom he gazed, benevolently but apart, and ever aware of the mocking spirit in his blood at sight of their decorative and detestable folk-customs.

The Egyptian year laid hold upon him and whirled him round with itself in the ebb and flow of nature and the rhythmic recurrence of its feasts — of which one or other might be regarded as the first: the New Year's festival at the beginning of the inundation, a day rich in hopes and incredibly tumultuous, a fateful day for Joseph, indeed, as we shall presently see; or the recurrent celebration of the accession of Pharaoh to the throne — when the rejoicing populace renewed the hopes which were bound up with the original day, the beginning of the new dynasty and era: when justice should banish injustice, and life be lived amid laughing and amaze. Or indeed any other of the recurrent feasts, for they were many.

Joseph had first set eyes upon the Egyptian scene at the time of the ebb, when the land had emerged and the sowing had been done. Then he had been sold, and gone on further into the year and round with it: the harvest came, which in name lasted into the flaming summer and the weeks which we call June, and then the diminished stream, amid reverential jubilation, began to swell and climbed slowly out of its banks; closely observed and measured by Pharaoh's officials, for it was of the first and last importance that it should rise properly, not too wildly and not too weak, that Keme's children might have to eat, and the tax-gatherers make it possible for Pharaoh to build. Six weeks the river rose and rose, the Nourisher of the Land, quite quietly, inch by inch, day and night, while men slept and, sleeping, trusted. And then, about the time when the sun was most blazing, and we should have written July, in the second half, which the children of Egypt called the moon of Paophi, the second of their year and in their first season, which they called Akhet, the river swelled mightily, overflowed the fields on both sides far and wide, and covered the land — that strangely and uniquely conditioned land, which had not its like in the world and which now to Joseph's wonderment and laughing, when he first saw it, was changed into a sacred lake, out of which high-lying towns and villages stood up, connected by causeways. The god stood there and let his richness sink, and his nourishing mud, on all the fields, until the second or winter season, Peret; then he began to bate and retire — "the waters returned from off the earth continually," as Joseph reminiscently put it to himself; so that beneath the moon of our January they flowed in the old bed, but continued to shrink until summer. It was for two-and-seventy days, the days of the two-and-seventy conspirators, the days of the

winter drought, that the god pined and died; up to that day when
Pharaoh's river conservancy announced that it was rising and a new
year of blessing took its beginning. It might be moderate, it might be
abundant; Amun send there should not be famine or a scant yield for
the tax-gatherers, so that Pharaoh could not build!

Time went very fast, Joseph discovered, from New Year to New
Year — or from that moment when he came into the land till the same
came round again, reckoning in the Egyptian seasons as he now did,
the flood, the sowing, and the harvest, each adorned with its proper
feasts, in which Joseph took part, with reserve, and confiding in indulgence from on high; he must indeed do so, and wear a pleasant
face, for these heathen celebrations were involved with the economic
life of the land. In Petepre's service and as the representative of Mont-
kaw he could not avoid the fairs and markets which were bound up
with the religious features of the feasts, since always trade springs up
wherever men come together in numbers. There were always markets in the fore-courts of the temples of Thebes, on account of the
thank-offerings; but likewise up and down the river were many places
of pilgrimage and the people streamed together in great hordes wherever a god held his feast, adorned his temple, possessed oracular wisdom, and promised, along with spiritual refreshment, crowds and
booths and general mass jollification. It was not Bastet only, the she-
cat of the Delta, who held a feast — of which Joseph had heard so
much that was unedifying. Every year there was a popular excur-
sion from near and far to the ram of Mendes, Djedet in the people's
mouth; it was even more jocund than Per Bastet's feast; for Bindidi
the ram, racy and rank as he was, stood closer to the temper of the
folk than the she-cat, and during the festivities publicly cohabited
with a virgin of the country. But the reader may be assured that Joseph, who went down to the feast on business, did not seek out the
sight; being occupied, as the steward's confidential man, solely with
the marketing of the paper, tools, and vegetables which he had
brought.

There was much in the land, and the customs of the land, particularly the feast-day observances — for the feast is the great hour of
the traditional, the hour when it comes uppermost and glorifies itself — at which, in all his worldliness, mindful of Jacob, he did not
look; or at most with a very detached eye. He did not love the people's love of drink; recollections of Noah prevented him, as well as
the picture in his soul of his sober, pondering father. His own nature
too, though bright and merry, was averse to drunken disorder. For
the children of Keme knew no better than to drink themselves drunk
on every occasion, with beer or wine; men and women alike. Wine
flowed freely at all the feasts, and they and their children could drink
four days on end and be good for nothing at all. Moreover, there

were special feasts of drinking, like the great beer-feast which commemorated the legend of Hathor the mighty, the lion-headed Sakhmet, how she had raged among mankind to destroy them and was only prevented from blotting out the race of men by Re, who with a most clever stratagem made her drunk on red blood-beer. On that day the children of Egypt drank beer in quite insalubrious quantities, a dark beer called *khes*, very powerful; beer with honey, foreign and home-brewed, the latter mostly in the city of Dendera, seat of Hathor, whither one made pilgrimage to the feast and it was actually called "Place of Drunkenness" as the seat of the goddess of drunkenness.

To all this Joseph paid little heed, and only drank a little, symbolically and socially, to the extent demanded by his business. And some of the practices at the great feast of Osiris, lord of the dead, at the time of the shortest day, when the sun died, he also, for the sake of Jacob, regarded with but very distant eye. The beast itself, however, with the ritual performances proper to it, interested him very much and he followed them attentively. For they told again the story of the passion of that mangled and buried and risen god; presented by priests and people in very beautiful masques, faithfully reproducing both the terror and the jubilation of the resurrection, whereat the populace leaped on one leg with joy. Along with this came a deal of primitive foolishness and antique survivals of which nobody any longer knew the meaning: as that various groups of men belaboured each other, one group representing the "folk of the city of Pe," the other the "folk of the city of Dep," and both cities were now entirely unknown. Or a herd of asses was driven round and round the city with mocking shouts and blows from cudgels. A certain contradiction lay in the fact that they treated with blows and contumely a creature which stood to them as a symbol of phallic readiness, for actually the feast of the dead and buried god was likewise a commemoration of the rigid readiness of the male, which tore the mummy-wrappings of Osiris so that Eset the female vulture received from him the avenging son. At this time of year in all the villages there took place processions of women carrying a phallic emblem as long as an ell, which they made to move by means of strings. Thus the worship contradicted the maltreatment; and the reason was after all clear. For on one side this erection and procreation was a matter of dear life itself, and of fruitful continuance; but on the other, and more strikingly, it was a feast of death. For Usir was dead when the vulture conceived from him; the gods were all erected in death; and just among ourselves that was the reason why Joseph, with all his personal feeling for the feast of Usir, the mangled one, did not look on at some of the rites, but averted his head even inwardly speaking. What sort of reason was that? Well, it is hard to talk about so deli-

cate a matter, when one knows and the other does not yet see — and
that is the more pardonable in that Joseph himself hardly saw it, and
only darkly and partially took account of what he did see. A faint,
almost unconscious sense of guilt was stirring in him, guilt on account
of disloyalty to the "Lord" — interpreting the word on whatever
plane one may choose. Remember that he thought of himself as dead
and belonging to the kingdom of the dead, wherein he grew; remember moreover that name which he had ingeniously and somewhat
presumptuously chosen. After all, the presumption was not so great:
Mizraim's children each one of them, even the least, had long had
the right to become Usir when he died, and unite his name with that
of the mangled one, as Hapi the bull became Serapis in death. The
association meant: "To be dead in God," or "To be as God." But just
this, to "be God" and to be "dead," brought up the subject of the
bandage-rending erection; and Joseph's half-unconscious guilty fear
was connected with the intuition that certain moments — for which
Dudu was responsible — now beginning to play a rôle, half of fear,
half of joy, in his life, were, however remotely, yet perilously connected with that godlike rigidity of death and with disloyalty.

   There, it is out. With all possible restraint it has been revealed why
Joseph did not care to look on at the popular customs of the feast of
Osiris or the processions of women or the cudgelled asses. But he
took a good look at much else, in city and country, during the feasts
that punctuated and adorned the Egyptian year. Once or twice as
the years went on he saw Pharaoh, for it came about that the god
made his appearance: not alone at the window of audience when he
threw down the gold of favour upon favourites, in the presence of
his elect, but when he came forth in brilliance from the horizon of
his palace and beamed in full splendour upon all the people, who as
one man hopped for joy according to prescribed form and also because they loved it from their hearts. Pharaoh was short and stout,
Joseph noted, his colour was not very good, at least not when Rachel's son saw him for the second or third time; his facial expression,
too, reminded him of Mont-kaw when his kidneys troubled him.

   Amen-hotpe III, Neb-Mat-Re, did in fact begin to fail in the years
which Joseph spent in Potiphar's house and grew great therein. In
the judgment of the skilled priests from the temple and the sorcerers
from the book-house he displayed in his physical condition a growing inclination to rejoin the sun. To control this tendency was beyond the power of the priests of healing, for it had all too much
natural justification. In Joseph's second year the divine son of Thutmose IV and the Mitannic Mutemweia celebrated his jubilee, the so-
called Hebsed: that is, it was thirty years since amid innumerable
ceremonies, exactly repeated on each anniversary, he had set the double crown upon his head.

It had been a regal and splendid life, as good as free from wars, weighed down, as with a golden mantle, by hieratic pomp and the cares of government; but set off by the pleasures of the chase, in commemoration of which he had issued scarabs; and made splendid above all by his love of building, which he had been able to gratify in full measure. Now all that lay behind him; his nature was as active in decline as Joseph's in upbuilding. In his early days the majesty of this god had only suffered from toothache, an affliction which he treated by the usual method of chewing balsamic sweetmeats, and often had to receive audience in the throne-room with a great lump in his cheek. But since the Hebsed (when Joseph saw him drive out) his bodily ailments were of a more deep-seated kind. Pharaoh's heart fluttered, or beat too quick against his chest so that it took away his breath. His secretions carried matter which the body should have retained but could not because it was breaking down; later it was not only the cheek that was thick and swollen, but the legs and belly. It was at this time that the confrère and correspondent of the god, who was likewise a god in his own sphere, King Tushratta of Mitanniland, son of Shutarna, the father of Mutemweia, whom Amenhotpe called his mother — in short, his brother-in-law from the Euphrates (for he had received from Shutarna the Princess Gulichipa into his house of women) — his brother-in-law sent him a magic image of Ishtar, with safe-conduct from his far-away capital to the palace at Thebes. For he had heard of Pharaoh's affliction and in his own case found the image efficacious for slighter ailments. The whole city, yes, all Upper and Lower Egypt from the borders of Nubia down to the sea, spoke of the arrival of this image in the palace Merimat, and in the house of Potiphar almost nothing else was talked of for days. But we know that Ishtar of the Road was unavailing, or unwilling to relieve more than temporarily Pharaoh's short breath and swollen limbs — to the satisfaction of his domestic sorcerers, whose gifts of healing were not much help either, simply because the tendency to rejoin the sun was stronger than all else and slowly got its way.

Joseph saw Pharaoh at Hebsed, when all Wese was abroad to see the god drive out, in the course of the ceremonies which lasted the whole day. There were investitures, accessions, coronations, purificatory baths assisted by priests in masks representing various gods; incensing and primitively symbolical procedures, at first within the palace, in the presence of the great of the land, while outside the populace by dint of drink and dance made themselves believe that from this day forth time should renew itself from the foundations and an age of peace, justice, and prosperity, of laughter and universal brotherhood, take its beginnings. This glad conviction had been ardently bound up with the original accession, a generation before, and renewed more faintly and fleetingly on each recurrence. But at Hebsed it sprang up in freshness and festal power in all their hearts, the triumph of faith over knowledge, the cult of an expectation which no experience can banish from the heart of man because it was implanted there from on high. — But Pharaoh's progress when at midday he betook himself to the house of Amun to make sacrifice, was a public spectacle, and many people, including Joseph, awaited it in the West, before the gate of Pharaoh's palace, while other crowds lined the route which the royal train was to take through the city, especially in the great ram-sphinx avenue, the sacred way of Amun.

The royal palace, Pharaoh's great house — from which in fact Pharaoh took his name, for the word means "great house," though on the lips of the children of Egypt it sounded rather differently, just as in the case of Potiphar and Petepre — Pharaoh's great house, then, lay at the edge of the desert at the foot of the gleaming bright-coloured cliffs of Thebes. It stood inside a great ring wall with armoured gates, which also included the exquisite gardens of the god and, laughing amid flowers and exotic trees, the lake which by command of Amenhotpe glittered east of the garden for the delectation of Tiy, his consort.

The populace outside, though they strained their necks, could see little of the bright splendours of Merimat. They saw the palace guards before the gates, with wedge-shaped leather leaves over their apron kilts, and feathers in their storm-helmets; they saw foliage lit by the sun and waving in the wind; saw airy roofs hovering upon coloured columns, long, many-coloured streamers fluttering from gilded poles; they sniffed the Syrian odours from the beds of the invisible gardens, and these accorded well with the idea of Pharaoh's godship, since sweet odours are thought of as accompanying the divine. But now the expectation of the eager, good-natured, lip-smacking, dust-swallowing crowd before the gate was to be fulfilled. Just as Re's bark reached the zenith a cry burst out, the guards at the gate raised their spears, the bronze doors between the standards flew open upon the sphinx avenue strewn with blue gravel, which ran through the garden. And upon that avenue Pharaoh's train appeared, dashing out through the gate directly into the throng, which swept back and gave way with shouts that were part joy, part fear. Men bearing staves laid into the crowd to make a path for the chariots and horses, with loud cries of "Pharaoh! Pharaoh! Take heed to your heart! Turn away your heads! He drives out — room, room for his driving out!" And the reeling rout made way, it hopped on one leg, it rolled like a wave in a storm, stretched up its thin arms into Egypt's sunlight, madly kissed hands. The women waved their wailing infants on high, or with heads flung back offered their breasts in both hands, while the air throbbed with exultation and yearning as they filled it with cries of "Pharaoh! Pharaoh! Strong Bull of your mother! Lofty

in feathers! Live a million years! Live to eternity! Love us! Bless us!
We love and bless you with fierce ardour! Golden falcon! Horus!
Horus! Re you are in your members! Kheper in his true shape! Heb-
sed! Hebsed! Turn of the ages! End of trouble! Beginning of joy!"

A popular jubilation like that is moving, it clutches at the heart,
even of him who does not quite belong and is inwardly detached.
Joseph shouted a little with the rest, he hopped a little too, with the
children of the land; but chiefly he looked on, with silent emotion.
What moved him was the sight of Pharaoh: he saw the Highest, coming forth out of his palace like the moon among stars, and his heart
beat responsive to that old legacy, now a little weakened by his cosmopolitan understanding, which bade him serve the Highest, whom
alone man shall serve. Long before he had stood even before the next-
highest, Potiphar, he had, we know, already bent his thoughts upon
still more absolute and final embodiments of that idea. We shall see
that even now his eager spirit did not pause.

Pharaoh was wonderful to behold. His chariot was pure gold,
naught else — gold wheels, gold sides, gold axles; and covered with
embossed pictures, which, however, one could not see because the
whole car flashed and glittered so, as it reflected the midday sun, that
the eye could scarcely bear it. The wheels and the hoofs of the steeds
whirled up thick enveloping clouds of dust so that it was as if Pharaoh came on in flame and smoke, frightful and glorious to behold.
You expected nothing less than that the stallions too, Pharaoh's great
First Team, as it was called, would breathe fire from their nostrils;
so they danced, so their smooth muscles shone, so wild they were, in
their ornamented harness, with gold breast-plates, and gold lions'
heads on their crests from which coloured ostrich plumes stood up
and nodded. Pharaoh drove himself; he stood alone in the chariot of
cloud and fire, the reins in his left hand; with his right he held the
lash and crook, the black and white one, in a sort of ritual position,
slantingly against his chest just underneath his jewelled collar. Pharaoh was already rather an old man, one could tell by his sunken
mouth, the tired look in his eyes, and his back, which seemed a little
stooped beneath the lotus-white linen of his upper garment. The
cheek-bones stood out in his gaunt face and it looked as though they
were rouged. All sorts and kinds of charms in the shape of stiff emblems and variously knotted and looped ribbons hung down from his
hips under his garment. His head was covered to behind his ears and
down to his neck by the blue crown set with yellow stars. But on the
brow, above Pharaoh's nose, the poison-cobra reared, glittering with
coloured enamel, Re's talisman.

Thus, without looking to left or right, the king of Upper and
Lower Egypt drove past before Joseph's eyes. Tall ostrich-feather
fans swayed over him; the soldiers of his bodyguard, archers and

shield-bearers, Egyptian, Asiatic, and Negro, hurried under standards beside the wheels and officers followed in cars covered with purple leather. Then all the people gave another adoring cry, for after the officers came another single chariot, with gold wheels whirling up the dust, and in it a boy eight or nine years old, likewise under ostrich-feather fans, driving, too, with weak bebraceleted arms outstretched. His face was long and palish, the full, raspberry-coloured lips smiled with charming shyness at the yelling populace, the eyes were half-open, from pride or sadness. That was Amenhotpe, the godlike offspring, heir to the throne and crown, when he who drove in front of him should have decided to mingle with the sun: Pharaoh's only son, child of his old age, his Joseph. The recipient of all these plaudits had a thin, childish torso, nude save for the arm-rings and jewelled necklace. His apron kilt of pleated gold stuff came high up in the back and down to his calves; in front, where the gold-fringed draw-string hung, it was scooped out, exposing a drum-shaped paunch like a Negro child's. On the boy's brow the serpent reared, as on the father's; his close-fitting headdress of gold stuff enveloped his head and came together at the back like a knot of hair, while the youthlock of the kings' sons hung in the form of a broad fringe over one ear.

The populace shouted at the top of their lungs to this engendered but not yet risen sun, the sun below the eastern horizon, the sun of tomorrow. "Peace of Amun!" they shouted. "Long live the son of the god! How beautiful you are in the bright places of the sky! Youthful Horus in the childhood lock! Rich-enchanted falcon! Protector of the father, protect us!" — They still shouted and adored when after the rabble in the wake of the morrow's sun followed another fiery chariot with high sides; behind the driver, as he leaned over the rail, stood Tiy, consort of the god, Pharaoh's chief wife, the lady of the lands. She was small and dark of countenance, with gleaming eyes lengthened by paint, a firm and delicate nose with a pronounced curve; a smile sat on her full curling lips. Anything as beautiful as her head-dress there could not be on earth; it was the vulture cap, the whole bird, made of gold, covering her head with its body and outstretched head, while the pinions hung down in splendour over cheeks and shoulders. On the bird's back a ring was fastened, from which rose a pair of high, stiff plumes, converting the cap to a divinity's crown; while in front on the brow, besides the featherless head and crooked beak of the bird of prey, was likewise the uræus, fanged and erect. Here were the very signs and insignia of godhood — it was too much, the people could not but greet them in ecstasy, and quite beside themselves shriek out: "Eset! Eset! Mut, heavenly mother-cow! Mother of God! You who fill the palace with love, sweet Hathor, pity us!" They cried out to the princesses too, who stood embraced in their own chariot behind the driver bent to his steeds; to the ladies of the court, driving by twos, with the fan of honour in their hands; and to the friends of Pharaoh, the unique and only friends, who attended his levee. Thus the Hebsed procession moved among the crowds from the house Merimat to the river where the gaily coloured boats lay ready, and Pharaoh's bark "Star of the Two Lands"; and the god, the goddess, and their offspring, with all the court, were set across to the eastern shore and driven by other teams through the city of the living, attended by the plaudits of the throng in all the narrow streets and from all the house-tops. And they drove to the house of Amun and the great incensing.

Thus then Joseph had seen Pharaoh, as once in the court of his house he, the bought slave, had seen Potiphar, first of his sphere, and thought how he could come to stand before him. At his side he now stood, thanks to his shrewdness in discourse; but we know that even then his thoughts outran the moment, secretly anticipating a connection with distant and final manifestations of the highest; his audacity even envisaged a still further goal. But how could that be — was there than the highest a higher still? Certainly, when one has in one's blood a feeling for the future — that is to say, for the highest of the morrow. During the exultations of the throng, which Joseph, with a certain reserve, had shared, he had observed Pharaoh in his fiery chariot with sufficient care. But his inmost and uttermost curiosity had for its object not the old god but his successor, the lad with the lock and the sickly smiling mouth, Pharaoh's Joseph, the next sun. He gazed after the narrow shoulders and gold knot of hair, the thin, armleted arms, as the lad drove by. Him, not Pharaoh, he had in his mind when the procession had passed and the crowds followed to the river. With the little coming one his thoughts were concerned; and it might well be that his opinion was that of the children of Egypt; for they had cried out more fervently at sight of him than when Pharaoh himself passed by. For the future is hope; and in the goodness of God time is given to man, that he may live in hope. Joseph had need still to grow mightily in his station before the hope of standing before the highest, or at his side, could have the smallest prospect of fulfilment. So then with reason it was that, as he watched the feast of Hebsed, his gaze passed over the present highest into the future and rested on the not yet risen sun.

ACCOUNT OF MONT-KAW'S SIMPLE PASSING

SEVEN times had the Egyptian year carried Joseph with it in its round; four-and-eighty times the planet that he loved, to which he was kin, had gone through all its phases. Of the material substance of Jacob's son, that in which he was clothed when the father blessed him and sent him from him nothing at all was left. He wore so to speak a new earthly garment, wherein God had arrayed his life; of the old, of that worn by the seventeen-year-old youth, was not one thread remaining. For he walked in one woven of Egyptian stuff, in which Jacob would only doubtingly have known him. The son would have had to reassure him, saying: It is I, Joseph. Seven years had passed, in sleeping and waking; in thinking, and feeling, in doing and being done by; passed as days pass; that is, neither fast nor slowly, but simply passing; and in his age he was now four-and-twenty, a young man, very beautiful in form and feature, son of a lovely one, a child of love. His bearing, by reason of his activities, had become more serious and assured; his voice, the one-time childish pipe, had grown more resonant as he moved among the workmen giving directions or as Mont-kaw's mouth transmitted all his orders; for Mont-kaw's mouth he had been now all these years, or one might have called him his eye, his ear, or his right hand. The work-people, however, spoke of him simply as the steward's "mouth," for so in Egypt they called a man through whom orders are transmitted. In Joseph's case the word was doubly apt, for the youth spoke like a god, a gift most pleasing, yes, a laughing delight to Egypt's children, and they knew that it was by that gift of shrewd and comely speech, such as was beyond their own powers, that he had made his way, or at least opened his way, to the favour of the master and Mont-kaw.

Mont-kaw by now trusted him in everything — administration, accounts, oversight, and business. When the tradition states that Potiphar put all that he had into his hand and knew not aught he had save the bread that he did eat, it refers, in the last analysis, to a delegation of power, from the master to the steward, and from the steward to the purchased slave with whom he had made a pact in love and loyalty to their lord. And the master and his house might be glad that it was Joseph and no other on whom the delegation finally fell and who in the end took over the economy of the house, for he oversaw it with the utmost of loyalty and ability, for the sake of the Lord and His far-flung plan; thinking day and night on the advantage of the house; so that, in the words of the old Ishmaelite and consonant with the name he had chosen, he not only provided but also increased it.

As for the reason why Mont-kaw, toward the end of this period of seven years, had entrusted Joseph more and more with the oversight of affairs, until he finally gave them all into his hands and withdrew into the private room of trust — of that anon, and only a little farther on. For first I must say that Dudu, despite all his malicious striving, did not succeed in barring the way to Joseph's happy advance — which finally, and before the seven years were out, had set him over all the other servants, even above the rank and dignity of Potiphar's undersized keeper of the jewel-caskets. Dudu's office was indeed a dignified one, and he owed it, certainly, to his sterling quality, his honesty and dwarf-worthiness. It brought him into close contact with the master and would have afforded occasion for confidence and the exercise of influence against Joseph, but that Potiphar could not abide the little man, whose pompous dignity went against him. He did not feel justified in taking away his office, but he kept him as removed as possible, setting subordinates between them for the service of the robing-rooms, so that to Dudu fell only the care of the garments, jewels, amulets, and orders. He saw the dwarf only for brief conferences. Thus Dudu could not easily come to speech with Potiphar, certainly not to that speech which he would gladly have made with reference to the favourite and the offence of his growing favour in the house.

Even though he had had the chance he would not have dared to speak — at least not before the master himself. For he well knew Potiphar's dislike for him, the serious-minded dwarf; it rested on the concealed sense of superiority which he neither could nor would deny, as well as on his partisanship for Amun's sun-power; he knew that his word availed little before Potiphar. Why should he, Dudu, spouse of Djeset, expose himself to a rebuff? No, he preferred a roundabout way: he would act through the mistress — to her he often complained, and at least she listened with respect — and through Beknechons, the mighty man of Amun; he, when he visited the mistress, could be warned against the advancement of the Shabirite, so offensive to ancient traditions. And he instigated Djeset, his full-sized wife, who was in Mut-em-enet's service, to talk to her mistress in the same sense.

But even industry will not always bring success; if Djeset had not been fruitful to her spouse it would have been a case in point. Here, at least, his striving bore no fruit. It is true, that one day Beknechons, in Pharaoh's antechamber, took Petepre to task, diplomatically, for the annoyance suffered by the pious of his household through the advancement of the impious there, and expostulated with him in fatherly wise. But the fan-bearer did not take it in, he could not remember, he blinked and seemed absent; and Beknechons, owing to his flair for greatness, was incapable of pausing for more than a minute upon small domestic details. He soon passed over into more exalted spheres and harangued the four quarters of the heavens as he held forth upon problems of state, speaking of the foreign kings Tushratta, Shubbilulima, and Abd-Ashirta — and upon these high themes the conversation expended itself and died. As for Mut, the mistress, she had not brought herself as yet to speak to her husband on the subject. She knew his unhearing obstinacy; moreover, she was not used to talking over matters with him, their intercourse consisting altogether of tender and exaggerated expressions of concern; it did not occur to her to make any demands upon him. These were sufficient grounds of excuse for her inaction. But in our eyes it is also a sign that even at that time — that is to say, toward the end of the seven years — she was indifferent to Joseph's presence and had no motive for wishing to have him sent away. The time when she would want him removed from her sight and hearing was still to come for this woman of Egypt; it came at the same time with that fear of herself which yet she was too proud to know. And another strange something would come to pass at the same time — the time when she realized that it would be better for her to see Joseph no more and turned to Petepre to get him sent away: it was that Dudu had been converted to the Shabirite and become his partisan. For he began to flatter him and be obsequious to him, to such an extent that a change of rôles seemed to have taken place between the dwarf and his mistress; the latter appeared to have assumed the former's hatred and the dwarf to praise and belaud the youth in her hearing. Both attitudes were entirely specious. For at the moment when the mistress would have wished that Joseph was not there, she could no longer do so, and deluded herself in thinking that she did. But Dudu, who had quite a glimmering of it, acted in malice, hoping the more to injure the son of Jacob by being comradely with him.

But I shall speak of this a little later. For the event which brought about these changes — or upon which they followed — was the sore illness of the steward Mont-kaw, Joseph's ally in the service of the master; sore for him, sore for Joseph, who so clung to him that he almost made a matter of conscience of his sufferings and death; and distressing to all sympathizers of the simple but intuitive man — even though these might have insight into the necessity of his destined passing. For we are obliged to see the hand of destiny in the circumstance that Joseph had been brought into a house whose steward was devoted to death; and so in a sense his passing was sacrificial. Fortunate that he was a man whose soul inclined to resignation, a readiness which in another place I have attributed to his trouble with his kidneys. But it is quite possible that the latter was only the physical constitution corresponding to his spiritual state, actually the same, distinguished from it only as the word is distinguished from the thought, and the word-sign from the word; so that in the book of the steward's life a kidney would have been the hieroglyph for the word "resignation."

Why should we concern ourselves with Mont-kaw? Why do I speak of him with a certain emotion, though unable to say much more of him than that he was known to be a man simple — that is, modest — and upright — that is, both practical and good-hearted? A man who trod the earth of Egypt and the land of Keme, late or early according as one takes it, at the time when life among its manifold shapes brought just him and no other forth, but early enough in all its lateness that his mummy has long since been dust and scattered to the four winds. A practical son of earth who did not imagine himself to be better than life and had no use for higher or speculative matters; not out of inferiority, but out of modesty, although in his secret depths he was quite accessible to higher promptings – indeed, it was these which made him play a rôle, a not inconsiderable one, in Joseph's life. Figuratively speaking, he did very much what Reuben had one day done: he retreated three steps before Joseph, bowed his head, and turned away. It needs no more than this rôle given him by destiny to make us owe him a lively sympathy. Aside from which, and for his own sake, I like to dwell upon the figure of this man, simple yet sensitive as he was, and pervaded by an unassuming melancholy; it has a sympathetic, spiritual claim upon us – he would have called it magic – which makes me like to conjure it up out of its ancient dust.

Mont-kaw was the son of an under-official of the treasury of the Montu temple at Karnak. When he was five years old his father, whose name was Akhmose, had dedicated him to Thoth and put him into the school attached to the administration of the temple of Montu, the falcon-headed god of war, where the rising generation of officials was brought up, on short commons, strict discipline, and plenty of canings, for the view obtained that a pupil had his ears on his back and heard when he was beaten. The pupils were of varied origins, aristocratic and middle-class; besides the discipline, they received the fundamentals of a literary education: the word of god, otherwise writing, the art of the reed, the gift of a good style, and the necessary equipment for a career of learning as well as for that of official scribe.

Akhmose's son did not want to become a scholar; not because he was not clever enough, but because he was too modest; resolved from the beginning to dwell within the sphere of the respectable average and not at any price to depart beyond it. It happened almost against his will that he did not, like his father, spend his days as a writer of documents in the office of Montu's temple, but became overseer to one of the great. It was his superiors and masters who recommended him thither and got him the excellent post, out of the regard they had for his gifts and his modest demeanour. At school he received only the inevitable canings, which fell to the lot of even the best pupils, in order to make them hear. For he early gave evidence of his head for the general by the quickness with which he mastered the great gift of the ape, the art of writing; the care and neatness with which he wrote out in long lines in his roll the copy before him, consisting of ancient rules of propriety, style-forming models, didactic poems, admonitions, and praise for the writer's craft, and covered the reverse side with calculations about sacks of corn, and notes for business letters. Almost from the beginning he had been set to work on the practical business of administration, more on his own initiative than that of his father, who would gladly have made of his son something better than he was himself, a priest perhaps, a magician or star-gazer; whereas from boyhood Mont-kaw in his modesty had decided for the practical side.

There is something peculiar about this sort of inborn resignation which takes the form of honest capacity and quiet toleration of the hardships of life, where another nature would shatter the heavens with loud remonstrance. Mont-kaw married rather early the daughter of one of his father's colleagues with whom he fell in love. But his wife died in her first childbirth and the infant with her. Mont-kaw lamented her loss most bitterly, without being greatly astonished or rebellious at this blow from the hand of fate. He did not try for happiness a second time, remaining a widower, and solitary. He had a sister married to a bazaar-keeper at Thebes; he visited her sometimes, when he had a holiday, of which he never took many. After finishing his education he worked at first in the offices of the temple administration, later became steward to the chief priest and after that to the great household of Petepre the courtier, where he had for ten years wielded his office with firm but good-natured authority, at the time when the Ishmaelites relieved the overburdened man in his service to his beloved master by bringing him an assistant — and at the same time a successor.

He had early perceived that Joseph was destined to follow after him — for he was, in all his assiduous simplicity, a man of intuition. We may almost say that the simplicity itself, the selfless resignation, was a product of the same intuition: in other words, of the illness lying dormant in his powerful frame. The very working of it, silently breaking down his physical morale, but refining the spiritual, was what made possible the subtle impressions which he received at first sight of Joseph. At that time he already knew the nature of his ailment. Red-belly, the barber-surgeon, had told him plainly, diagnosing from the symptoms of frequent dull pressure in his back and left side, irregular pains in the region of the heart, frequent giddiness, sleeplessness, poor metabolism, and excessive urination, that he suffered from degeneration of the kidneys.

This ailment is often insidious in its nature; strikes its roots during early life and then has periods when it seems to be arrested or even cured, only to evince its hidden progress later on. Mont-kaw could remember that when he was twelve years old he passed blood-impregnated urine — but only once, and then not again for many years, so that he had really forgotten the alarming symptom. It happened again when he was twenty, together with the above-mentioned mani-festations, the headache and giddiness culminating in violent nausea. That too passed; but since then he had quietly and grimly wrestled with intermittent attacks, which would leave him free for months or even years, to take possession of him again with greater or less violence. The modesty which was their source came out often in profound fatigue, physical and mental weariness and indifference; he made a practice of sticking to his tasks throughout, heroically and in silence, being treated by medical science, or what passed as such, with blood-letting. His appetite was satisfactory, his tongue clean, the skin excretions in good order, and his pulse fairly regular; the physi-cians therefore did not consider his condition serious until one day his ankle-bones displayed whitish swellings full of a watery fluid. When it was drawn off, the relief to his vascular system and his heart made one regard the symptom as favourable, because it was the dis-ease coming out and being got rid of.

He had indeed, with the help of Red-belly and his herbal treat-ments, got through quite tolerably the decade before Joseph's arrival, with but few interruptions to his activities; though that was very likely to be ascribed more to his own modest strength of purpose, holding in check the slow process of decay, than it was to Red-belly's homely remedies. He had his first really severe attack very soon after Joseph came; with such dropsy in hands and legs that they had to be bandaged; throbbing headache, badly upset stomach, and even a dimming of the vision. Probably it had begun during the bargaining with the Ishmaelite and the examination of his goods. At least we may surmise it; for it seems as though his sensitiveness to Joseph's looks and the emotion he showed at the test good-night greeting in-dicated a morbidly heightened receptivity. But the converse might also be true: that the all too gentle words had affected his spirit to soften it and make it a more ready prey to the evil power assailing it. I am tempted to harbour the misgiving that Joseph's good-night ad-dresses, however soothing to the steward, were actually unfavourable to the will to live which struggled in his depths with the fell disease.

The attack was responsible too for the fact that Mont-kaw paid no attention to Joseph in the beginning. It lamed his initiative. But it passed, like others of greater or less severity, thanks to Khun-Anpu's blood-lettings, leeches, arbitrary decoctions of animal or vegetable na-ture, and abdominal compresses made of old pieces of writing soaked in warm oil. Recovery — or apparent recovery — ensued, and reigned over large spaces of the time during which Joseph was growing up to be his first assistant and chief "mouth." But in the seventh year of Joseph's time Mont-kaw caught a cold at the funeral of a relative, his sister's husband (the bazaar-keeper in fact), and it opened the door wide to dissolution, which then ensued.

This "catching" death and being "carried off," through standing in a draughty hall to pay last honours to the deceased, was a frequent phenomenon then as now. It was summer, and very hot, but, as often in Egypt, at the same time very windy, a dangerous combination, for the air fanning over the perspiring flesh cooled it too rapidly. The steward, overwhelmed with business, had lingered at home until he was in danger of being late for the services; he sweated as he went, and when he was ferried across the river in the train of the funeral bark he shivered in his thin clothes. Then he stood by the little grave in the rock which the bazaar-keeper, now united with Osiris, had acquired with his savings. Before its modest portal a priest in the mask of Anpu held the mummy upright while another performed with the calf's foot the mystic ceremony of the opening of the mouth; and the little group of mourners looked on, their hands upon their ash-strewn heads. The cold dank air that breathed from the vault was not very good for Mont-kaw. He came home with a cold in his head and catarrh of the bladder. Next day he complained to Joseph of feeling queer and heavy, and of the effort it was to move his limbs; he was overtaken by a sort of numbness which forced him to give over work and take to his bed. The head gardener attended him and set leeches to his temples, to relieve the intolerable pains in his head, which were accompanied by severe nausea and semi-blindness; but an attack of apoplexy supervened.

Joseph, when he saw the purposes of God with Mont-kaw, was greatly shocked. He came to the conclusion that it would not be a crossing of the divine purpose but merely putting God to the test to try all human means of combating the disease. He persuaded Potiphar to send at once to Amun's house for a learned physician; and Red-belly, offended, yet at the same time relieved from a responsibility the weight of which he knew enough to realize, retired from the field.

The medical man from the temple did indeed reject most of Red-belly's measures; but the distinction between his and the gardener's was, in the eyes of all the world, his own as well, more of a social than a medicinal kind: the latter were for the people and for them might do very well; the former for the upper classes, where the treatment was of a more refined kind. The doctor from the temple rejected the ancient documents soaked in oil with which his predecessor had covered the belly and loins of the patient, demanding in their place linseed poultices on good handkerchiefs. Likewise he stuck up his nose at most of Red-belly's popular cure-alls, which had been invented by the gods themselves for Re when he was old and ailing. They consisted of from fourteen to seven-and-thirty separate disgustingnesses: lizard's blood, ground pigs' teeth, sweat from a pig's ears, the milk of a woman in childbed, various sorts of excrement

such as antelopes', porcupines', and flies', human urine, and more of
the same kind. But there were other ingredients more to the physician's liking, which he also prescribed, without the disgustingnesses:
honey and wax, henbane, small doses of opium, bitter bark, bear-
berries, natron, and ipecacuanha. The doctor did concur in the use of
the gardener's cherished remedy, the chewing of castor-oil berries
with beer; and in his use of a root rich in resin with a strong purgative
effect. But he declared that the drastic blood-lettings, which Red-
belly performed nearly every day to control the agonizing pain in
the head and the mist in the eyes, must be discontinued or only performed with great reserve; he could tell by the patient's pallor that
the temporary relief was too highly paid for by the loss of certain
nourishing and stimulating properties in the blood.

The dilemma was probably an impossible one; for obviously it was
precisely the indispensable but impoverished and infected blood that
carried insidious inflammations and overwhelmed the body with various morbid manifestations, either by turn or at the same time; all of
them, as both physicians were aware, having their source in the originally diseased kidney. Thus Mont-kaw, without regard to the name
or nature of this or that distressing phenomenon, suffered one after
another or at the same time from inflammation of the chest, the peri-
toneum, the lungs, and the pericardium; from brain symptoms such
as vomiting, blindness, congestion, and spasms. In short, death attacked him with all its weapons and on every side, and it was only a
wonder that he resisted for weeks after he took to his bed, and in part
overcame the supernumerary ailments from which he suffered. He
was a stout invalid; but however sturdily he defended his life – he
had just to die.

Joseph realized this, while Khun-Anpu and the learned man of
Amun still hoped to save the steward. He took it much to heart; not
only on account of his attachment to the good man, who had shown
him so much kindness and in whose mingled destiny he sympathized,
finding him one of those "glad-sorry" men, the Gilgamesh type, favoured and disfavoured at the same time. No, it was also and particularly because he had pangs of conscience over his sufferings and
death. They were obviously ordained to his own advantage and
growth, poor Mont-kaw was a sacrifice to God's plans; he was put
out of the way, that was plain and clear, and Joseph would have liked
to speak to the author of the plans and say: "What Thou here dost,
O Lord, is exclusively thine own idea and none of mine. I must say
plainly that I will have naught to do with it, and that it happeneth on
my account must not, I hope, mean that I am to blame for it – in all
humility I must beg to be excused." But it did not help him, he still
felt guilty for the death of his friend and perceived that if there
could be any talk of responsibility in the affair it fell upon him, whom

it advantaged, God being blameless. "That is just it," he thought to himself: "God does all, yet has given us a conscience, and we become guilty before Him because we are guilty for Him. Man bears God's guilt; and it would be no more than right if one day God were to make up His mind to bear our guilt. How He, the holy and blameless, could do that is hard to say. I should think He would need to become a man to that end."

He did not stir from the bedside of the suffering sacrifice throughout the four or five weeks of struggle against the death that came on in protean shape. So guilty did he feel. He tended the afflicted man day and night; he sacrificed himself, as one says, and here would say it with justice, for he offered himself in return, to the extent of offering up his own sleep and physical well-being. He set up his cot beside the sick man's in the special room of trust, and hour by hour did the needed service: warmed the compresses, gave the medicines, rubbed in the lotions, gave him to inhale the vapour of powdered herbs heated on stones, as prescribed by the doctors, and held his limbs when attacked by spasms. For as his end approached, the steward so suffered from these that he cried out under death's torturing grip — for death seemed not to expect that he would yield himself and so laid violent hands upon him. Especially when Mont-kaw tried to sleep death interfered, sending such potent cramps as almost to wrench the sufferer bodily from the bed — as though to say: "What, thou wouldst sleep? Up with thee, to thy end!" This was more than ever the place for Joseph's soothing good-nights; he employed them skilfully, murmuring in the steward's ear that now he would surely find the path into the land of peace for which he yearned, find and tread upon it; nor would his left arm and leg, carefully bound up for him by Joseph with strips of linen, snatch him back again to day and anguish.

That was true, and sometimes efficacious. But Joseph himself was alarmed to see that his invocations to peace and repose helped only too much — for the steward, wakeful for so many years, inclined now to stupor, so that the gracious path became a dangerous one, embarked on which the wanderer might forget to return. He must sing no more lullabies, but try to rouse the patient to the things of earth, and his will to live with tales and anecdotes out of that copious store, extensive in time and space, which Joseph, thanks to Jacob and Eliezer, had commanded ever since he was small. The steward had always loved these tales of his assistant's first life, his childhood in the land of Canaan, of his lovely mother who had died by the way, of his father's wilful tenderness for her and for his son, so that they were one in the festal garment of his love. He knew of the brethren's furious jealousy, of the sin of overweening blind self-confidence which had weighed down Joseph; of the mangling and the pit. The steward, of

course, like Potiphar and all his house, always thought of that region
where Joseph had spent his youth as a land far off, dusty and indescribably wretched; which one forsook with all speed naturally when
destiny transplanted one into the land of men and gods. He was as
little surprised or critical as anybody else that the Egyptian Joseph
made no effort to resume contact with the barbaric world of his
youth. But he enjoyed hearing of that world, and during his last days
it was his dearest and most soothing distraction to lie with folded
hands and listen to his young nurse unfold the memories of his clan,
in the charming way he had, so thrilling, so blithe and impressive all
at once. He told of the rough and the smooth and how even in the
womb they had fought each other; of the feast of the blessing and
the betrayal, and the flight of the smooth man to the nether world;
of the wicked uncle who exchanged his children on the bridal night;
how the cunning rogue tricked the stupid one, taking a leaf from
nature's book and so got back his own. Shuffling here and there: the
trickery of the first-born and the blessing, exchange of brides, exchange of possessions. Exchange of the first-born and the beast on the
offering-table; of the beast and the son, who looked like the beast as
he bleated and died. All these illusions and transformations fascinated
the hearer and held him rapt; for what is more charming than illusion?
And a light played to and fro, back and forth, between the teller and
his tale; illusory light, illusory charm, illusory magic of charm, fell
upon him from the tales he told, and he himself in his turn lent to
them the same from his own person — from him who had worn the
veil of love in turn with his mother, from him who in the eyes of
Mont-kaw had always possessed an agreeably teasing and mischievous
charm, from the first moment when the boy had stood before him
with the roll in his hand and by his smile tempted the steward to
confuse him with the ibis-headed one.

Mont-kaw could scarcely see at all now, he could not tell how many
fingers when Joseph held them up. But he could still listen and be
lured by the sound of strange tales murmured sweetly at his bedside,
away from that heavy slumber to which he was drawn by the poison
in his blood. He heard about the ever present Eliezer who with his
master had smitten the kings of the east and toward whom the earth
had sprung when he rode on the bridal journey for the saved sacrifice;
of the bride by the well who had dismounted from her camel and
veiled her face in the sight of the wooer; of the wild and beautiful
son of the desert who had tried to persuade the cheated red one to
kill his father and eat him. Of the original wanderer, the father of
them all, and what had one time befallen him and his sister-bride, here
in this very land of Egypt. Of his brother Lot, the angels before his
door, and the extraordinary shamelessness of the Sodomites. Of the
sulphurous rain, of the pillar of salt, and what Lot's daughters did

out of care for the continuance of the human race. Of Nimrod at Sinear and his arrogant tower. Of Noah, the second first man, called the exceeding wise one, and his ark. Of the first man himself, made out of clay in the garden of the east, of the she-man made of his rib, and of the serpent. From this great heritage of tales Joseph gave with wit and eloquence of his best, sitting by the bedside of the dying man — to assuage his own remorse and to hold the other in the land of the living for yet a little while. But Mont-kaw too was seized with the epic vein and began to talk in his turn, having them prop him up in the cushions and in the unease of oncoming death feeling for Joseph to touch him as though he were Yitzchak in the tent.

"Let me see with seeing hands," he said, his face lifted to the ceiling, "if you are Osarsiph my son, for I will bless you before my end, mightily strengthened to the blessing by the tales with which you have so richly fed me. Yes, it is you, I see and recognize you as do the blind and there can be no doubt here, for I have but one son whom I can bless and you are he, Osarsiph, whom I have come to love in the course of the years in the place of the little one whom the mother took with her in her hour — for he was suffocated, she being built too narrow. By the way? No, for she died at home, in her chamber in childbed, and I dare not call her agonies more than human, yet frightful they were, and cruel so that I fell on my face and begged the gods for her death, which they granted her. The boy's death they granted too, though I had not begged for that. But what would the child have been to me without her? Olive Tree was she called, daughter of Kegboi, the treasury official. Beket was her name and I was not bold enough to love her as the man of the blessing made bold to love his lovely one of Naharin, your mother — I did not dare. But she too was lovely, unforgettably lovely in the adornment of her silken eyelashes which dropped over her eyes when I spoke to her, words from my heart, words of songs which I never presumed to attempt, yet which at that time, that beautiful time, my words became. Yes, we loved each other, despite the narrowness of her build, and when she died with the child, I wept, wept many nights for her, till time and work dried mine eyes — dried them quite and I wept no more at night; but the tear-sacs, and their smallness, they come, I think, from all those nights — I do not know, it may be, and may not, for I am dying and my eyes are going with which I wept for Beket, it will be all the same in the world whether it was or not. But my heart was empty and desolate, since my eyes were dried; and it grew small like my eyes, and despondent for that it had loved in vain so that there was room only for resignation in it. Yet the heart must cherish something besides resignation; it yearns to throb for some care tenderer than profit and use. Petepre's house-steward was I and his oldest servant and had no thought save for his house that it might flourish. For he who has given up is good for service. And lo, that then was a thing for my shrunken heart to cherish: service, and tender helpfulness to Petepre my master. For who is there more needing than he the service of love? He takes no affairs to himself, he is strange to all affairs and not made for business. Strange, delicate, and proud he is, the honorary official, and cannot face any business, so that one must pity him, for he is good. Has he not come to me and visited me in my illness? He has taken trouble to come hither to my bedside while you were at work, to ask after me, the sick man, in the goodness of his heart, though it is plain that he feels strange and shy before illness too, for he is never ailing — though a man would be puzzled to call him healthy or believe that he will die — I can scarcely believe it, for one must be healthy to be ill and live to die. But can that lessen one's care for him, and the need of upholding his sensitive dignity? It is rather the other way. My heart cherished this care, above and beyond profit and use: to devote itself to the service of upholding his dignity and addressing his pride, as well as I knew how. But you, Osarsiph, know how, incomparably better than I, for the gods have given subtlety to your mind, and greater pleasingness than mine, who lack it either because I was too dull and dry or because I did not dare to attempt the highest nor had confidence to do so. Therefore I have made a pact with you for this service, which you will keep when I die and am no more. And when I bless you and make over to you my office as steward of this house, then must you vow to me upon my death-bed that you will not only cherish the house and the business according to the best of your wits, but also faithfully keep our loving bond and do service of love to Petepre's soul and shield and justify his dignity with all your skill — far indeed from ever doing him offence or from being tempted to shame him with word or deed. Can you solemnly promise me, Osarsiph, my son?"

"Solemnly and gladly," Joseph answered to this dying speech. "Have no care, my father! For I promise you to be helpful to his soul with careful loyalty according to our pact, and to keep faith with his need; and will think of you, if ever temptation should befall me to inflict upon him the peculiar pain which disloyalty is to the lonely. You may rely upon it."

"It calms me much," said Mont-kaw, "though the feeling of death disquiets me greatly, as it should not do; for nothing is commoner than death, and especially of a simple man like me, who always avoided higher things. For I die no higher death and will make over it no ado, as little as I made over my love to my little Olive Tree, nor emboldened myself to call her childbed pains more than human. But yet I will bless you, Osarsiph, in the room of my son, not without solemnity, for the blessing is solemn, not I — therefore bow yourself beneath my groping hand. House and court make I over to you, my true son and successor in the steward's office to Petepre the great courtier and my master, and resign in your favor, which gratifies my soul; yes, this joy death brings me, that I can resign, and joyfully am I agitated by death, for it is joy and naught else that I feel. But that I leave all to you is by the will of the master, who among all his servants points with his finger to you and chooses you in my place as his steward when I am dead. For when he came to see me of late in the goodness of his heart and looked helplessly at me, I talked it over with him and begged him that he would direct his finger upon you alone and name you by your name when I am made god; that I might go hence with quiet mind as regards the household and all the business. 'Yes,' said he, 'it is well, Mont-kaw, very well, old man. I will point to him with my finger, if you really do die, which would grieve me sorely. Yes, I will point to him and no other, that is certain, and let anybody try to persuade me, he will find my will like iron or black granite from the quarries of the Retenu. He himself has said that of such quality is my will and I had to agree with him. He moves me with a feeling of confidence, very pleasant indeed, even more than you yourself have done in your lifetime; often have I thought that a god is with him or even several gods, who make all to succeed which is in his hands. And he will be less likely to go behind my back than even you in all your uprightness, for he has knowledge of sin in his heart and wears in his hair something like a garland of sacrifice, which is a charm against sin. In short, it is settled, Osarsiph shall be set over the house and take all things upon himself with which it is impossible I should concern myself. I will point to him with my finger.' Those were the master's words, I have remembered them exactly. So then I bless you, only after he hath blessed you himself, for so it ever is: one blesses always the blest and wishes the joyful joy. The blind man in the tent blessed the smooth one only because he was already blest and the rough one was not. One can do no more. Be then blessed, as blest you are! Your spirits are blithe, and you measure yourself boldly against higher things; you are blithe to say your mother's pains were more than human and your birth was virgin — though your reasons for that are probably not sound. But those are the signs of the blessing, which I possessed not and so cannot bestow; but I can bless you and wish you joy as I depart. Bend then your head lower beneath my hand, my son, the head of the aspiring beneath the hand of the meek. To you I make over household, house, and fields in Petepre's name, for whom I administered it; their riches give I to you, the fat of these lands, that you may preside over shops and stores, the fruits of the gardens, the herds great and small, the island farm, the accounting and trade; I set you over sowing and harvest, kitchen and cellar, the master's table, the needs of the house of women, the oil-mills, the wine-presses, and all the servants. May I have forgotten nothing! But you,

Osarsiph, do not forget me, when I am made a god and like Osiris.
Be my Horus, who protects the father and justifies him. Let not my
tomb inscription be blurred, and support my life! Tell me, will you
see after it that Min-neb-maat, the master of the bandaging, and his
assistants make of me a good mummy, not black, but a beautiful yellow, for I have put aside all things needful thereto; that they consume
it not themselves, but salt me well with natron and use fine balsam
to make me eternal, styrax, juniper wood, cedar gum from the port,
mastic from the sweet pistachio shrub, and fine bandages next the
body? Will you take care, my son, that my eternal shell is well
painted, and covered within with writings, without crack or cranny?
Promise me to take care that Imhotep, priest of the dead in the West,
does not divide among his children the fund I have set aside with him
for my sacrificial offerings of bread, beer, oil, and incense, but that
it remain whole and your father be for ever provided with food and
drink on feast-days. It is dear and good that you promise me all this
with reverent voice; for death is a common thing, yet bound up with
great cares, and a man must secure himself on many sides. Put too a
little stove in my chamber that the servants may roast a joint of beef.
And add an alabaster goose, and the wooden likeness of a wine-jug,
and also plenty of your sycamore figs. I like to hear you reassure me
as to all that, in your reverent words. Put too a little ship with rowers
beside my coffin, for I might have need of it, and let other apron-boys
be with me that they may take my place when He who is over the
West calls me up to work upon his fruitful fields, for I had ever a
head for the general, and knew how to oversee, but not to drive the
plough nor ply the sickle. Ah, with how many cares is death surrounded! Have I forgotten aught? Promise that you will be mindful
of what I forget — for instance, take care that they should lay the
beautiful jasper scarab upon the place of my heart, the one which
Petepre gave me in his goodness and on which is written that my
heart shall not rise up as witness against me in the scale. It is in the
right hand of the coffer in a little box of yew-wood, together with
my two necklaces, which I bequeath to you. — Enough, I will make
an end of my dying speech. One cannot think of everything and
there is still much unrest which death brings in its train, and only
ostensibly the need to take care for it doth so. The very thought, the
uncertainty as to how we shall live after our parting is itself more a
form assumed by the unrest; but that is what my thoughts are none
the less — thoughts of unrest. Shall I perch on the trees, a bird among
birds? Shall I be this or that at will: a heron in the swamps, a beetle
rolling his ball, a lotus chalice on the water? Shall I live in my chamber rejoicing in the offerings purchased from my fund? Or shall I be
there where Re shines by night and where all will be just as it is here,
heaven as on earth, river, field, and house and I shall be Petepre's eld-

est servant as I always have been? I have heard it one way and I have heard it another, and all ways at once, when one thing probably stands for another and all is but a figure of our unrest, which dies away in the gentle drowsiness that calls upon me. Let me down again in the bed, my son, for my strength is gone, I have spent the last of it in the provision for death and in the blessing. I will give myself to sleep, which murmurs drowsily in my head; but before I yield myself, I should like quickly just to know whether I shall meet again my little Olive Tree, who perished away from me — whether I shall meet her again on the Nile in the West. But before all comes the fear lest in the last moment, when I would fall asleep, the cramp will snatch me back. Tell me good-night, my son, as you know how to do, hold my arm and leg and conjure the cramp with soothing words! Perform once more your delicate office — for the last time! Yet not the last; for if on the Nile of the transfigured all is as it is here, then, Osarsiph, you too will be again at my side as my apprentice and every night give me your evening blessing sweetly phrased as is your gift to do. For you are blest and can give blessing, whilst I can but wish — I can speak no more, my friend! I have done with my speech. But believe not that I cannot hear you still!"

Joseph's right hand lay on the wan hands of the dying man, with the left firmly supporting the thigh.

"Peace be with you!" he said. "Rest, rest, my father, beatified through the night! Lo, I keep watch over your limbs, that you may carefree tread the path of consolation. You need not to be careful for aught, and thinking that may be blithe. Not about your limbs, nor the cares of the house, nor yourself and what will become of you and how it may be in the life after this life. For just so is it, that all this is not your affair nor care and you need not to have unrest about it but may leave all as it is, for somehow it must be, since it is, and however it is has been well cared for; but you, who have had so much care, are done with care and may quietly repose and be cared for. Is that not gloriously soothing and happy? And is it not with must and may as ever it was when I bade you good-night and told you not to think that you must rest but only that you may? Lo, you may! All toil and moil, all heat and heaviness are past. No anguish more, no wrestling struggle, nor terror of cramp. No bad medicines, no burning poultices, nor sucking leeches on your neck. The dungeon of your sore trouble opens its door, you can come out and stroll strong and hale down the path of consolation, which leads you deeper with each step into the ways of peace. At first you will go through vales you know, those which each eve received you when I said good-night; you have still some heaviness and scantness of breath, of which you are scarce aware; they come from your body, which I hold here in my hand. But soon — you will not know the crossing — you will gain the meadows with light tread, where no distress from afar can hang on or plague you even unaware, for all at once you are free of all doubt or care as to how it will be with you or what become of you, so that you are amazed how they could once have so concerned you; for all is as it is and in the most natural way, the most right and best, in happy harmony with itself and with you, since you are Mont-kaw to all eternity. For what is, is, and what was shall be. Did you doubt in your heaviness if you would find your little Olive Tree in the blessed fields beyond? You will laugh at your little faith, for lo, she is at your side — and why should she not be, since she is yours? And I too shall be with you, Osarsiph, the dead Joseph, as I am called for you — the Ishmaelites will bring me to you. For ever you will come across the court with your little wedge-shaped beard, your ear-rings, and the tear-sacs under your eyes, which may have come from the nights of quiet weeping for your Beket, your Olive Tree; and you will ask: 'What men are these?' And will say: 'Be so good — dost think I can listen to your chattering all the days of Re?' For since you are Mont-kaw, you cannot fall out of your rôle nor look before the people as though you believe I was nothing else but Osarsiph, the bought slave from afar, for secretly you will know, with silent intuition, from the other time, who I am and what path I follow, that I prepare the way of the gods my brothers. Farewell, then, my father and chief! In light and in lightness shall we see each other again."

Here Joseph closed his lips and ceased to speak; for he saw that the steward's ribs and his belly were still and that unaware he had passed through the vale and reached the meadows. He took a feather, which he had often held before his eyes to tell if he could still see it, and laid it on his lips. But it stirred not. The eyes he needed not to close, for the steward had peacefully shut them himself as he fell asleep.

The doctors came and salted and embalmed the body of Mont-kaw, forty days long, then it was wrapped and laid into a coffin which fitted it exactly. Then, a bright-coloured Osiris, he might lie some days at the back of the garden-house in front of the little silver gods. Then he took a voyage downstream, to the sacred tomb of Abdu, to visit the Western Lord, before in modest pomp betaking himself to the rocky grave-chamber set aside in the mountains of Thebes.

But Joseph never thought of this father of his without feeling his eyes wet. Then they were strangely like the eyes of Rachel, when they filled with impatient tears at the time when she and Jacob waited for each other.

JOSEPH IN EGYPT

Chapter VI

THE SMITTEN ONE

THE WORD OF MISTAKING

AND it came to pass after these things that his master's wife cast her eyes upon Joseph; and she said —

All the world knows what Mut-em-enet, Potiphar's chief wife, is supposed to have said when she cast her eyes upon Joseph, her husband's young steward, and I will not and dare not deny that at last, one day, in her extremity, in the fever of her despair she did actually so speak, did make use of the frightfully direct and frank expression which tradition puts in her mouth. So direct, indeed, so frank, that it sounds like a lewd proposal coming from a woman who made it quite naturally and at small cost to herself, instead of being the final outcry of her utter agony of spirit and flesh. To tell the truth, I am horrified at the briefness and curtness of the original account, which does so little justice to life's bitter circumstantiality. Seldom have I felt more acutely than in this connection the harm done to truth by abbreviation and compression. Yet let no one think that I am deaf to the reproach — whether expressed or, out of politeness, not expressed — which hangs over my account, my entire exposition: to the effect that the laconic terseness of the original text cannot be surpassed, and that my whole enterprise, which is already of such long continuance, is so much labour lost. But since when, may I ask, does a commentator set himself up in competition with his text? And besides, is there not as much dignity and importance attached to the discussion of the "how" as to the transmission of the "what"? Yes, does not life first fulfill itself in the "how"? Let us remind ourselves once again that before the story was first told, it had to tell itself — with an exactitude of which life alone is master, and to attain which a narrator has no hope or prospect at all. He can only approach it by serving the "how" of life more faithfully than the lapidary spirit of the "what" condescended to do. But if ever the fidelity of a commentator can justify itself, then surely it does in the story of Potiphar's wife and of just what, according to the tradition, she is supposed to have said.

For the picture which one inevitably makes, or is irresistibly tempted to make, of Joseph's mistress; the picture, I fear, which most people make of her, is so false that one does a service to the original in correcting it in the way of truth — if we understand by original the first written, or better yet the story as life first told it. This deceptive picture of unbridled lust and shameless allurement does not, at least, agree with what we overheard, when we were with Joseph in the garden-house, from the lips of dignified old Tuia about her daughter-in-law. It was there that we began to learn with a little more particularity of the life of the house. Petepre's mother called her "proud," after declaring that it was impossible to accuse her of being a goose. Haughty she said she was, reserved, a moon-nun, a nature with the bitter fragrance of the myrtle leaf. Does such a one speak as tradition makes her speak? Yet she did so speak, literally and repeatedly, as her pride broke under the assaults of passion. We are agreed upon that. But the tradition neglects to state how much time passed during which she would have bitten out her tongue rather than have so spoken. It neglects to say that sitting in solitude she actually, literally, and physically bit her tongue so that she stammered for pain when first she uttered the words that for all time have stamped her for a seductress. A seductress? A woman, overcome as she was, is of course seductive — seductiveness is the exterior and physical shape taken by her affliction; it is nature makes her eyes sparkle more sweetly than any drops the toilette-table can supply; heightens more alluringly the red of her lips than rouge can do it, and pouts them in a soulful, suggestive smile; makes her dress and adorn herself with innocently abandoned calculation; gives her movements and all her body a purposeful grace, lending to it, as far as physical constitution permits, and even a little further, an expression of blissful promise. And all that fundamentally means nothing else than what Joseph's mistress finally said to him. But is she to whom it happens so to speak from within to be made responsible? Does she do it out of deviltry? Does she even know of it — otherwise than through her torturing pangs which express themselves in outward charm? In short, if she is made seductive, is she then a seductress?

In the first place we must examine the nature and form of the seduction in the light of the birth and upbringing of the smitten one. Against the assumption that Mut-em-enet, familiarly called Eni or even Enti, behaved herself in her afflicted state like a common prostitute must be set her whole nurture, which was aristocratic to an unimaginable degree. It is but just that we should — as we did in the case of Mont-kaw — consider briefly the origins of the woman who exerted upon Joseph's destiny an influence so very different from that of our honest steward.

It will surprise nobody to hear that the wife of Petepre the fan-bearer was no daughter of an innkeeper or quarry labourer. Her stock was no more and no less than that of the old princes of the nome, though it had been long ago that her forbears had lived like patriarchal kings on their extended property in one of the districts of Middle Egypt. Foreign sovereigns of Asiatic shepherd blood had then lived in the north, and worn the double crown, and the princes of Wese, in the south, had for centuries been subject to these invaders. But there had arisen men of might, Sekenenre and his son Kamose, who rebelled against the shepherd kings and fought them stoutly, finding the foreign blood of their overlords an effective stimulant to their own ambitions. Yes, Ahmoses, the dauntless brother of Kamose, had laid siege to the invaders' fortified royal seat, Avaris, had taken it and driven the kings from the country, setting it free, in the sense that he and his house took it for their own and substituted their domination for the foreign one. Not all of the nome princes had been at once willing to regard the hero Ahmoses as their deliverer or his sovereignty over them as freedom. Some of them had on whatever grounds adhered to the foreigners in Avaris, preferring to remain their vassals rather than be freed by somebody else. Even after their old overlords had been entirely ejected some of these petty kings, unambitious for freedom, mutinied against their deliverer and, as the sources say, "gathered the rebels against him" so that he had first to defeat them in open battle before freedom was established. It goes without saying that these rebels forfeited their estates. It was the method of the Theban deliverers to keep for themselves what they had taken from the foreigner; so that a process now began which at the time of our tale was already far advanced though only entirely consummated in the course of it: that is to say, the dispossession of the princes and the confiscation of their property in favour of the Theban crown. The latter gradually became the owner of all the lands and let them out or presented them to favourites or religious houses — as, for instance, Pharaoh had presented the island in the river to Petepre. But the old princes of the nome became a new class of officials and nobility, who owed allegiance to Pharaoh and occupied commanding posts in his army and administration.

From such as these, then, Mut had come. Joseph's mistress descended directly from a nome prince called Teti-'an, who in his time had "gathered the rebels" and had to be defeated in battle before he admitted that he was free. But Pharaoh did not lay that up against Teti-'an's grandchildren and great-grandchildren. Their clan had remained great and aristocratic, it gave to the state commanders of troops, heads of cabinets, and administrators of the treasury, to the court high stewards, first charioteers and overseers of the royal bathhouse; some of them, for instance the administrative heads of large cities, like Menfe or Tine, even kept their old princely titles. Eni's

father, Mi-Sakhme, held the high office of a city prince of Wese —
one of two; for there was one for the city of the living and one for
the city of the dead in the West, and Mi-Sakhme was prince of the
Western city. As such, to use Joseph's language, he lived as one of
high rank and might certainly anoint himself with the oil of gladness — he and his, including Eni, his fine-limbed child, even though
she was no longer a landed princess but the daughter of a modern
office-holder. In the destiny which her parents chose for her one can
read the changes that had taken place in the ways of thinking of the
clan since the days of the fathers. They gained great advantage at
court when they gave their beloved child in her tender age to the
son of Tuia and Huia, Petepre, the man-made courtier; yet in doing
so they proved that the instinct for fruitfulness possessed by their
land-owning, soil-attached forbears had been greatly weakened by
modern ideas.

Mut was a child when her parents disposed of her destiny in the
same way that Potiphar's parents had disposed of their unsteady little son when they speculated in the hereafter and made him a courtier of light. The claims of sex which Mut's parents passed over,
claims symbolized by the water-darkened earth, the moon-egg, the
origin of all material life, were still but a germ, still slumbering within
her; she was unconscious of them, she made not the least objection
to the loving, life-denying deed. She was blithe, merry, untroubled,
free. She was like a water-flower swimming upon a glassy pool, smiling beneath the kisses of the sun, untouched by the knowledge that
its long stem is rooted in the black slime of the depths. The conflict
between her eyes and her mouth had not existed in those days, rather
a childish inexpressive harmony, and her pert, little-girl glance was
undarkened by any harshness. The peculiar serpentine shape of the
mouth, with its deep corners, had not been nearly so pronounced.
The discord between them had come about gradually in the course
of years during her life as moon-nun and titular consort of the sun-
chamberlain — in token, obviously, that the mouth is a tool and image more closely allied to the nether powers than is the eye.

As for her body, everybody knew its shape and loveliness, for the
"woven air," that luxurious silken fabric like a zephyr's breath which
she wore in compliance with the custom of the land, revealed its every line to the admiring eye. And one might say that it was more in
harmony with her mouth than with her eyes. Its honourable rank had
not checked its ripening or its bloom. The small firm breasts, the fine
line of neck and back, the tender shoulders and perfect statuesque
arms, the high-flanked legs expanding into the splendidly feminine
haunches and pelvis — all these composed a form admitted far and
wide to be the most beautiful of its sex. Wese knew none more
worthy of praise; and as men's nature was, the sight of it stirred in

them old lovely fantasies, pictures of beginnings and pre-beginnings, pictures that had to do with the moon-egg and the origin of things: the picture of a glorious virgin, which, at bottom — right at the bottom, in the moist earth — was the goose of love itself in the shape of a virgin, and in its lap, with spread wings flapping, nestled a splendid specimen of a swan, a strong and tender snowy-feathered god, fluttering his love-sick work upon her, honourably surprised, that she might bear the egg.

Such pictures of aforetime did indeed light up in the inmost depths of Wese's folk, where they had lain in darkness, at sight of Mut-em-enet's translucent form, although they knew the moon-chaste honourable state in which she lived and which could be read from the stern look in her eyes. They knew that those eyes gave a truer measure of her essence and activities than did the mouth, which said far other things and which might well have looked down smiling if protesting upon the activities of a royal bird. They were aware that this body knew its greatest moments, its highest satisfaction and fulfilment, not in receiving such royal visits, but only on the feast-days when she shook her rattle and danced the cult-dance before Amun-Re. They did not gossip about her; no evil rumours went round in the sense of Mut-em-enet's mouth, to which her eyes would have given the lie. They were sharp-tongued enough about others, who were more truly married than Teti-'an's grandchild and yet played fast and loose in the point of morals: ladies of the order, harem women of the god. Renenutet, for instance, wife of the overseer of bulls: things were known of her which Amun's overseer wotted not of. Plenty was known, jokes enough were made behind her car or her carrying-chair — hers and others' too. But of Petepre's chief and, so to speak, true wife nothing was known in Thebes, and folk were convinced that there was nothing to know. They took her for a saint, reserved and apart, in Petepre's house and court as well as abroad; and that was significant, considering the love of joking inborn among the people.

Whatever my readers may think, I do not consider it to be my task to inquire into the habits of Mizraim and in particular of No-Amun's feminine world. I mean such habits as long ago we heard condemned in old Jacob's forthright way. His knowledge of the world had a strongly emotional tinge, a mythical reference, which we must realize in order not to exaggerate. Yet his lofty condemnation was not without grounds. Among a people who have neither word nor understanding for sin, and who go about in garments made of woven air, people whose attitude toward death and worship of animals betokens and induces a certain fleshliness, one must assume — even without knowledge or experience — the existence of a light moral attitude. And Jacob, making this assumption, couched it in poetic, high-sounding words. Experience, then, bore out the assumption — I say it less in malice than in satisfaction of the claims of logic. But to conform the assumption by prying into the daily lives of the wives of Wese would be beneath our dignity. Much can be pardoned, little disputed. We should need only to intercept a few glances between Renenutet, wife of the overseer of bulls, and a certain very smart lieutenant of the royal bodyguard, or between the same exalted lady and a young shiny-pated temple-treader of Khonsu, to realize that things went on which to some extent justified Jacob's picturesque language. It is not our affair to sit in judgment on the morals of Wese — that great city of more than a hundred thousand people. We must, where we cannot sustain a position, abandon it. But I would put my hand in the fire and swear, staking the whole of my reputation as a story-teller, that one of those led a blameless life, up to a certain time, when the gods made of her a reeling mænad: I mean the daughter of Mi-Sakhme, prince of the nome, Mut-em-enet, Potiphar's wife. To see her as a natural prostitute, upon whose lips those words we know constantly hovered and were lightly released, is so false that truth demands its complete refutation. When she did, biting her tongue, utter them, she knew herself no more; she was beside herself, her reason dethroned by agony, a sacrifice to the scourge-swinging, avenging lust of powers to which she was committed by her mouth, while the eyes had thought to treat them with detachment and contempt.

THE OPENING OF THE EYES

WE know that Mut's well-intentioned parents had betrothed and married her to the son of Huia and Tuia when she was still a child. We need to remember this; for it followed that she had got accustomed to the formal nature of her married life, while the moment when she might have realized its actual character still lay in fluid darkness. Thus she had nominally lost her maiden state at too early an age — but there it stopped. Hardly yet even a maiden, rather a half-grown girl, she found herself a spoilt darling, head of an aristocratic "house of women," in command of every luxury, every flattery, surrounded by the half-savage servility of naked Moorish women and kneeling eunuchs; first and titular wife and chief over fifteen other idle, passive, and voluptuous females chosen for their beauty, of very varied origins, and themselves the empty and honorary apanage of a courtier who could not enjoy them. Of these dreamy-eyed, chattering females she was the queen; they hung on her words, were plunged in melancholy when she was sad, and burst into delighted cackles when she was merry. They quarrelled addle-patedly over Petepre's favours when he came to the women's house to play

a game at draughts with Mut-em-enet, while amber brandy and
sweets were handed round. So then she was the star of the harem, and
at the same time the female head of the whole establishment, Potiphar's wife in a higher and more special sense than the concubines;
the real mistress and — under other circumstances — the mother of
his children. She occupied when she chose quarters of her own, separated from her husband's by the northern columned hall where
Joseph performed his reading service. And she was hostess and housewife at those exclusive entertainments and musicales given by Petepre, the friend of Pharaoh, to the high society of Thebes — in return
for which they were entertained at similar functions in aristocratic
houses in the city.

It was a nervous life, full of elegant obligations — superfluous ones
if you like, but no less consuming to the energies for all that. We
know that in every civilization that ever existed the demands of social
life, of culture itself, tend to choke with luxuriant detail the overburdened forces of the upper-class woman; so that the life of her
soul and her senses is submerged in conventional circumstance and
she never actually gets round to it at all. A cool, unoccupied heart,
not troubled because unaware of a lack, and thus not even pathetic,
becomes a habitual state of existence. In all times and regions these
worldly women, possessing no temperament, have existed in high society. One may go so far as to say that it matters little whether the
husband of such a one is a captain of troops in an actual or only in an
honorary sense. The ritual of the toilette is equally important whether
its aim is to preserve desire in the breast of a husband or is practised
as an end in itself and as a social duty. Mut, like other ladies of her
station, devoted hours to it daily. There was the painfully elaborated
care of her finger- and toe-nails, until they shone like enamel; the
perfumed baths, the depilatories, the massage to which she subjected
her beautiful body. There was the critical business of applying drops
and paint to her eyes — beautiful enough already, with their irises of
metallic blue and their practised and sparkling glances, they became
veritable jewels through the artful application of rouge, pencil, and
other sweet enhancements. There was the care of her hair; her own
was a half-length mass of shining black locks, which she liked to dust
with gold or blue powder — and besides that the wigs, in various colours, braided, plaited, in tresses, and with pearl fringes. There was
the fastidious adjustment of the snowy garments to the embroidered
sashes pressed by the iron into lyre-shape and the little shoulder-
capes moulded into tiny pleats; the choice of ornaments for head,
neck, and arms, presented by kneeling slaves. And throughout all
this nobody must so much as smile: the nude Moorish girls, the sew-
ing-women, the barber eunuchs preserved their solemnity nor did
Mut herself smile, for the slightest carelessness or neglect in these

high matters would have called down the reproach of the great world
and made a scandal at court.

Then there were the visits in her carrying-chair to friends of like
station; and the receiving of them at home. And Mut was lady-in-
waiting to Tiy, the wife of the god; she must attend at the palace
Merimat and like her husband carry the fan. Also she was summoned
to the evening water-parties which the consort of Amun held on the
artificial lake called into being by Pharaoh's command in the royal
gardens, where torches of the recently invented coloured fire steeped
the water in sparkling hues. And then — as we are reminded by our
mention of the mother of the god — there were the famous honorary
religious duties, functions combining the social with the priestly, and
responsible more than anything else for the stern and haughty expression of Mut's eyes. These duties arose out of her membership of
the order of Hathor and her capacity of wife to Amun; they fell to
her as wearer of the cow's horns with the sun's disk between; in
short, as "goddess in her time." It is strange how much this side of
Eni's life contributed to heighten her cool worldliness as a great lady
and to keep her heart empty of softer dreams. It did so in connection
with the titular character of her marriage — though there was no necessary connection between them. Amun's house of women was in no
sense a place of the *intactæ*. Restraint of the flesh was far from being
an attribute of the great mother as whose representatives Mut and
her fellow-members performed their feasts. The queen, the god's bedfellow and mother of the coming sun, was the protectress of the order. Its head, as I have already more than once mentioned, was a
married woman, wife of Amun's prepotent high priest; and married
women preponderated among its members — such as Renenutet, wife
of the overseer of bulls (we pass over further comment on the state
of her morals). In fact, Mut's temple office had to do with her marriage only in so far as she owed, socially speaking, the one to the
other. But in her own mind, privately, she did what Huia the hoarse
had done in his conversation with his old bed-sister: she connected
her priestly office with the singularity of her marriage and, without
putting the thing into words, found it suitable, indeed quite the
proper thing, for a wife of the god to have an earthly husband made
like Petepre. And she knew how to convey this conception to her
social circle, so that they sustained her in it and thought of her membership in the order of Hathor as that of a being set apart and reli-
giously chaste. And all this contributed even more than Mut's lovely
voice and the elegance of her dancing to the pre-eminence of her position in the order — almost equal indeed to the lofty station of its
head. In this way did Mut's will-power mould outward conditions
and create for her those super-compensations of which the mute
depths of her being so painfully stood in need.

Was she a nymphomaniac? A loose woman? The idea is absurd. Mut-em-enet was a saint, a chaste moon-nun of high social position, whose strength was consumed partly in the demands of her highly cultured life, but partly, so to speak, was temple property and transmuted into spiritual pride. Thus had she lived: as Potiphar's first and titular wife, petted and indulged, carried in the arms of subordinates, knelt to and bowed to from all sides. Her compensations were so superior that not even in dreams was she confronted by images from that sphere so well represented by her sinuous mouth. By goose-wishes, to put it arrestingly! For it is false to regard the dream as a free and savage domain where all that is forbidden to the waking thought may come out and revel unashamed. What the waking state definitely does not know, what is simply shut off from it, the dream does not know either. The border between the two is fluid, it permits of interpenetration; there is but one space, through which the soul hesitantly moves, and that it is one, indivisible for the conscience and the pride, is proved by Mut's bewilderment, the panic shame she suffered not only in her waking hours but when she for the first time dreamed of Joseph.

When did that happen? In her world, the world of our narration, they were careless about counting the years; and we are somewhat conditioned by their habit. We must estimate as best we can. Eni was certainly several years younger than her husband, whom we have seen as a man at the end of the thirties when Joseph was sold to him. In the meantime he had added seven years to his age. She, then, was not like him in the middle of her forties, but several years less; certainly, however, a mature woman, much older than Joseph. Just how much older I am reluctant to ask; my reluctance is justifiable, springing as it does from a profound respect for the feminine cult of the toilette-table, which can go far to annihilate the years, and in its results upon the senses surely possesses a higher veracity than mere reckoning with a pencil can have. Since the day when Joseph first saw his mistress, as she swayed past him in her golden chair, he had increased his charms for the feminine eye. But she had not increased hers — at least not for one who saw her uninterruptedly. Woe to the preparers of creams and the massage-eunuchs if those years had been able to show any change to her disadvantage! But her face, with its saddle-nose and strange shadowy hollows in the cheeks, though it had never been actually beautiful, still preserved its mixture of conformity and caprice, of fashionable convention and anomalous charm, which it had always had; though the disturbing contradiction between the eyes and the sinuous mouth had probably been accentuated. To one inclined to be attracted by the disturbing — and there are such people — she had probably only grown more lovely.

The beauty of Joseph, on the other hand, had probably outgrown the stage of youthful charm for which it had always been so be-praised. At four-and-twenty he was still — perhaps only then en-tirely — a figure to marvel at. But his beauty had ripened beyond that equivocalness of his youth while preserving its general effective-ness; and specifically in that it made a much more direct appeal to the feminine emotions. It had been ennobled, because it had become more manly. His face was no longer that of the Bedouin boy, in-sidiously seductive — though still reminiscent of it at times, as when — though not at all short-sighted — he narrowed his eyes and veiled them in the way that Rachel had done. But it was fuller and more serious, and darkened by Egypt's sun; its features too had grown more regular and refined. I have referred already to the changes in his figure, his movements, and the sound of his voice — due, these last, to the tasks he had performed. We must add, in order to get a true picture of him as he now was, that his whole appearance had be-come more refined, being worked upon by the cultural influences of the land. We must think of him arrayed in the white linen of the Egyptian upper classes; transparent, so that the under-garments showed through; with short sleeves, revealing the forearms adorned with enamel rings. His head was bare, dressed in its own smooth hair, save on formal occasions, when he wore a light wig of the best sheep's-wool, something between a head-cloth and a peruke, fitting the top of his head with thick, fine, even strands like ribbed silk. Along a diagonal line it changed into small overlapping curls, like tiles on a roof, which came down on neck and shoulders. Round his neck besides the gaily coloured collar he wore a flat chain made of reed and gold beads, with a scarab amulet. His face had slightly changed its expression; it had a hieratic cast, due to his make-up; for he accentuated the line of the brows, and lengthened the eyes evenly toward the temples. Thus he looked as he went about, setting his long staff before him, among the work-people, the steward's first "mouth." Thus he went to market, or stood behind Petepre's chair and beckoned to the waiters. Thus the mistress saw him, in the dining-room or the house of women, when he came before her, sub-missive in posture and speech, to deal with some household matter. And thus it was she actually first saw him; for previously her eyes never dwelt on the purchased slave, not even at the time when first he had known how to warm the heart of Potiphar. Even while he lived and waxed as by a spring, it had needed Dudu's complainings to open her eyes to the slave's appearance.

And even after her eyes had been opened, Dudu's tongue playing the part of calf's foot, she was far from properly seeing him. When after hearing of his offensive advancement in the house she had had to look at him, it was solely with stern-eyed curiosity that she gazed.

The element of danger (we must put it like that, if we are concerned for her pride or her peace of mind) consisted in that it was Joseph on whom her eyes fell, Joseph whose eyes met hers at seconds of time. It was a circumstance big with fate; and big enough too that little Bes, in his dwarfish wisdom, had perceived in it a hidden and fearful danger. He saw that Dudu's malice was bringing about a situation more destructive than anything he had dreamed of or could dream of, and that the opening of the eyes might be even all too wide. Inborn fear and dread of powers which he saw in the image of the fire-breathing bull made him prone to such intuitions. But Joseph, with culpable lightness — in this point I am not inclined to spare him — had affected not to understand, and assumed that Bes was dreaming, though probably in his heart he was of the same mind. For he too laid stress on the moments in the dining-room — less for what they meant than for the fact that they actually happened; in his folly he was glad that he was no longer empty air for the mistress, but that her look rested on him as on a human being, no matter how angry her gaze. And our Eni?

Well, Eni was no wiser than Joseph. She too had affected to misunderstand the dwarf. That she looked angrily at Joseph excused her in her own mind for looking at him at all. And this was a mistake from the very beginning; pardonable before she realized whom she saw when she looked, but after that less excusable and more culpable every time. The unhappy creature refused to see that the stern-eyed curiosity with which she regarded her husband's body-servant was losing its sternness, leaving the curiosity deserving of another and less orthodox name. She supposed herself to share in Dudu's indignation; she felt bound, indeed, to share in it on religious grounds, or — which was the same thing — on political and partisan ones: on the grounds of her relation with Amun, who could not fail to see in the preponderance of a Shabirite slave in Petepre's house an insult to himself and a surrender to the Asiatic tendencies of Atum-Re. She had to make the anger last in order to justify the pleasure she felt in entertaining it; so she called it righteous anger and zeal for her cause. Our capacity for self-deception is amazing. When Mut had an hour free from her social duties — a short summer hour or a longer winter one — she would lie stretched out on her couch at the edge of the square basin let into the pavement of the open columned hall in the house of women. And lying there, watching the bright fish, seeing the floating lotus blossoms, she would muse to the accompaniment of soft stringed music played by an oily-locked little Nubian girl crouching at the back of the hall. And she was quite convinced of the tenor of her musings: she was considering the problem how, despite the obstinacy of her husband and Beknechons's statesmanlike vagueness, she could prevent this evil thing, that a slave from Zahi-land, one of the Ibrim, waxed great in the house. And so considering she omitted to notice how much pleasure it gave her to think about it. Though surely she knew that her pleasure had no other source than the intent to think about Joseph. Had we no pity for her we might be angered at such blindness. She even did not notice that she had begun to look forward to the meal-hour in the dining-room, when she might see him. She fancied that her pleasure sprang from her purpose to dart angry looks at him; it is pathetic, but she never dreamed that her sinuous lips curved in a self-forgotten smile, remembering how at her stern fixed gaze his startled, humble one would be swiftly hidden beneath his lowered lids. It was enough, she thought, if at such times she frowned her indignation at the affront to her house. Had the dwarf's little wisdom sought to warn her too, if it had spoken of the fire-breathing bull or hinted that the artificial fabric of her life was already shaken and threatened to totter to its fall, perhaps her face, too, might have got red. But she would have said that she blushed for anger at such nonsensical babble; she would have outdone herself in extravagant, hypocritical merriment and in deliberate misunderstanding of such misgivings. Who would be deceived by these exaggerated disclaimers? Certainly not he who sought to dissuade her. For they were but meant to dissemble the path of adventure which the deluded soul is bent on treading. To delude oneself, up to the point where it is too late to turn back — that one must do at all costs. To be awakened, warned, called back to oneself before it is too late: there lies the danger which is at all costs to be avoided. Then let the kind-hearted observer beware of making himself absurd with unwarranted sympathy. Let him not benevolently assume that the human being's deepest concern is for peace, tranquillity, the preservation of the carefully erected structure of his life from shattering and collapse. For, to put it mildly, the assumption is unwarranted. Too much evidence goes to show that he is headed straight for ecstasy and ruin — and thanks nobody in the very least who would hold him back. In that case — what use?

As for Enti, the kind-hearted observer must — not without some bitterness — take it for granted that she was brilliantly successful in gliding over the moment when it was not yet too late and she was not yet quite lost. A moment of terrifying rapture and realization came to her with the dream I spoke of, which she dreamed about Joseph. Then truly she was aghast and shook in all her limbs. She remembered that she was a being endowed with reason, and she behaved accordingly. That is to say, she imitated the conduct of a reasonable being; mechanically she behaved like one, but not actually as one. She took steps, for the success of which she could no longer sincerely wish — confused, unworthy steps, before which the well-wishing friend must simply hide his head and take care lest he feel an unseasonable pity.

It is almost impossible to put a dream into words and relate it. For in a dream little importance attaches to the actual matter and everything to the aura and atmosphere, the incommunicable sense of horror or of blessedness, or both, which wraps it and which often till long afterwards engrosses the soul of the dreamer. In this tale of ours dreams play a decisive rôle; its hero dreams greatly and childishly; and there will be others in it who will dream. But how hard would all of them find it even to approach the inwardness of what they dream, how unsatisfactory would they find every effort to do so! We have only to recall Joseph's dream of the sun, moon, and stars, and the helpless insufficiency with which he told it. I may then be forgiven if in relating Mut's dream I fail quite to convey the impression it made upon the dreamer, both when she dreamed it and afterwards. But having said so much, I may not withhold an accounting of it.

She dreamed, then, that she sat at table in the hall with the blue columns; in her chair on the dais, beside old Huia, and ate her dinner in the tactful silence which always prevailed. But this time the silence was particularly forbearing and profound; the four companions not only refrained from speech but were even noiseless in all their motions, so that in the stillness one could hear the breathing of the servants as they passed to and fro — so distinctly indeed that they seemed not to be breathing so much as panting and would have been audible even were the silence less profound. The quick, soft sounds were disquieting; perhaps because Mut was listening, perhaps for some other reason, she lost sight of what she was doing and gave herself a wound. She was cutting a pomegranate with a sharp little bronze knife, when it slipped and went into her hand, making rather a deep gash in the soft flesh between the thumb and the four fingers, so that it bled. There was a good deal of blood, ruby red like the juice of the pomegranate; she saw it flowing with distress and shame. Yes, she felt ashamed, despite the beautiful ruby colour; partly of course because it stained the pure white of her garment, but also aside from and beyond this she felt disproportionately ashamed and sought to hide the blood from those about her. Successfully as it seemed, or as they wanted it to seem, for they assiduously behaved — with more or less ease and convincingness — as though they saw nothing at all. None of them troubled themselves over her distress, which distressed her the more. She did not want to betray that she was bleeding, she was ashamed; at the same time she was indignant that nobody cared to see it, nobody lifted a finger, but by common consent left her to herself. Her waitress, the affected damsel in the

spider-web garment, bent over the little one-legged table absorbed
in putting things on it to rights; old Huia at her side, his head wag-
gling, chewed away toothlessly at a gilt thigh-bone whereon were
stuck pieces of cake soaked in wine. He held it by one end in his
hand and acted as though he were entirely consumed in chewing.
Petepre, the master, raised his cup behind him over his shoulder, for
his Syrian cup-bearer to fill it. And his mother, old Tuia, was cheer-
fully nodding her great pale face with the blind slits of eyes in the
direction of the distracted Mut; though it was hard to say whether
she even saw her daughter-in-law's predicament. And Mut, in her
dream, went on bleeding, staining her white frock and feeling silent
bitterness at the general indifference to her plight; also a distress
which had nothing to do with that, but with the bright crimson
blood itself. She rued indescribably the seeping and spouting flow;
it was such a pity, such a pity! She felt so sorry for it, so sorry — she
felt a deep, unspeakable anguish in her soul, not about herself and
her plight, but about the sweet blood that was flowing away. She
gave a short dry sob. Then she realized that in her trouble she had
forgotten her duty to Amun, the obligation to look angrily at that
offence to her house, the Canaanite slave, and do her part in dis-
countenancing his advancement. So she darkened her brows and
looked fiercely across at him where he stood behind Petepre's chair:
young Osarsiph. Then he, as though summoned by her look, left
his place and office and came toward her. And was near to her, so
that she felt his nearness. But he had come near to her to quench the
flowing of her blood. For he took her injured hand and carried it
to his mouth, so that the fingers lay on his one cheek and the thumb
on the other, the wound on the lips between. Then her blood stood
still with ecstasy and was stanched. But in the hall, while she was
being healed, there was unpleasant and disquieting bustle. All the
servants there ran about distraught; light-footed, indeed, but panting in confused chorus. Petepre, the master, had veiled his face, his
mother was touching the bowed and covered head with her outspread hands, desperately groping for him with her blind, upturned
gaze. But Huia — Eni saw him get up and threaten her with his gold
thigh-bone, from which all the cake had been munched. He scolded
her soundlessly and his sorry little beard wagged up and down. The
gods knew what abuse he was shaping with his toothless mouth and
busy tongue! Perhaps its tenor was the same as what the servants
were saying as they panted. For loud whispers formed themselves
out of the panting and came to her ears: "To the fire, to the flood,
to the dogs, to the crocodile!" They said it over and over. She had
that awful whispering chant still in her ear when she emerged from
her dream; cold with horror, then hot with ecstasy of her healing;
and aware that life's rod had been laid about her shoulders.

HUSBAND AND WIFE

Now that her eyes were open, Mut resolved to behave like a reasonable human being and take a step worthy to stand before reason's throne. Its clear and unequivocal intent was to put Joseph out of her sight. She would lay the case for his departure before Petepre, her husband, with all the powers she had at command.

She had spent the next day after her dream alone, withdrawn from her sister wives and receiving no visits. She had sat beside the basin in the court and watched the darting fish; concentrating, as we say of a person whose gaze passes over the objects in its path and fixes itself on space. But all at once in the midst of this staring her eyes widened in alarm, opened wider and wider as though with horror while still staring at nothing; she opened her mouth and drew in a gasping breath. Then the eyes retracted; the corners of her mouth deepened and the lips relaxed in an unconscious smile beneath the dreaming gaze. For a whole minute she knew not that she smiled; with a start she pressed her hand upon those errant lips, the thumb on one cheek, the four fingers on the other. "Ye gods!" she murmured. Then it began anew: the dreamy stare, the gasp, the unconscious smiling, and the shocked recall — until at last the conclusion came: she must make an end to it all.

Toward sunset she inquired and learned that Petepre was in the house, and summoned her maids to dress her, that she might visit him.

Petepre was in his western hall, which looked out on the orchard and the little summerhouse on the mound. The sunset light, falling through the gay outer columns, began to fill the room and enrich the pale colours on the walls, the floor, and the ceiling, where pictures flung with careless ease by an artist hand adorned the stucco facing: a swamp with hovering birds; calves jumping; ponds with ducks; a herd of bulls being driven across a ford while a crocodile leered at them out of the water. The rear wall, between the doors which led into the dining-room, displayed pictures of the master of the house in his habit as he lived, and showed him returning home attended by assiduous servants. The doors were framed in glazed tiles covered with picture-writing in blue, red, and green on a dun-coloured background: sayings from ancient authors and lines from hymns to the gods. Along the wall between the doors ran a sort of raised ledge with a back, both of clay, covered with white stucco and with coloured picture-writing on the front. This ledge or bench served as a stand for works of art, the presents in which Petepre's house abounded. But you could also sit on it; and there now he sat, the man full of honours, in the middle, on a cushion, his feet together on a footstool, while on both sides of him extended in a row the most lovely objects: animals, images of the gods, royal sphinxes, all made of gold, malachite, and ivory, and behind him the falcons, owls, ducks, wavy lines, and other symbols of the inscriptions. He had made himself comfortable by taking off all his clothes down to the knee-length skirt of strong white linen with a wide starched draw-string. His upper garment, and his staff with his sandals tied to it, lay on a lion-footed chair near one of the doors. Yet there was no relaxation in his posture; he sat up perfectly straight, his little hands stretched out in his lap. They looked tiny compared with the massiveness of his body, as did his finely shaped, severely erect head with its aristocratically hooked nose and well-cut mouth. He sat there, a well-composed seated statue of a fat yet dignified man. His powerful legs were like straight columns, his arms like those of a fat woman; his fat-upholstered chest was thrust out. His mild long-lashed brown eyes looked straight before him through the hall into the red evening light. In all his fatness he had no belly, being narrow round his hips. His navel was striking: very large and horizontal, so that it looked like a mouth.

He had sat there a long time thus motionless, in an idleness en-nobled by the man's natural dignity. In the tomb which awaited him a life-sized counterfeit would stand in a false door, in darkness, in the same immovable calm which he now displayed in life, and gaze out of brown glass eyes at paintings on the wall, where his household surroundings were depicted, for purposes of magic, that he might have them with him to all eternity. This statue would be the same precisely as he was — he anticipated the identity with it as he sat here now and made himself eternal. At his back and on the ledge close to his feet the picture-writings, red, blue, and green, expressed their meaning; on either side of him extended Pharaoh's gifts in long rows; most consonant with the Egyptian sense of form were the painted columns between which he gazed into the evening glow. To be surrounded by possessions favours immobility. One's posses-sions shall endure, and oneself endure in their midst, one's limbs composed to quiet. For others movement: for those who face the world, who sow, who give out and, giving, expend themselves in their seed. But not for one constituted and made like Petepre, in the inviolability of his being. Composed, symmetrical, he sat there, with-out access to the world, inaccessible to the death of begetting; eternal, a god in his chapel.

A black shadow glided between the pillars, sidewise to the direc-tion of his eyes, an outline against the red glow. It entered crouching and so remained, silent, its brow between its hands, upon the floor. He slowly turned his eyeballs toward it. It was one of Mut's naked Moorish handmaids, animal-like. He blinked and roused himself. Then he raised one hand, from the wrist only, and commanded:

"Speak!"

She jerked her forehead up from the floor, rolled her eyes, and answered in a husky, barbaric voice:

"The mistress it at hand and would approach the master."

He bethought himself again. Then he replied:

"It is granted."

The little animal disappeared backwards over the threshold. Petepre sat with lifted brows. After a few moments Mut appeared on the spot where the slave had crouched. With her elbows at her sides she extended toward him both palms like an offerant. He saw that she was heavily clad, in a long, full, pleated mantle above her narrow ankle-length under-garment. Her shadowy cheeks were framed in a dark-blue head-cloth like a wig which fell on shoulders and neck and was confined by an embroidered band. On top of it stood a cone of ointment, with a hole through which the stem of a lotus was drawn, curving down parallel with the line of the head so that the blossoms swayed above her brow. The stones in her necklace and arm-bands glittered darkly.

Petepre lifted his small hands likewise in greeting and carried the back of one of them to his mouth to kiss.

"Flower of the lands!" he said in a tone of surprise. "Lovely of face, having a place in the house of Amun! Pure-handed loveliness, alone among those that bear the sistrum, and with voice of beauty when she sings!" He continued on a note of joyous surprise as he rapidly repeated the stilted phrases. "You that fill the house with beauty, charming one to whom all pay homage, familiar of the queen — you can read my heart, since you fulfil its every wish ere it be spoken, and fulfil them all by your coming. — Here is a cushion," he went on in an ordinary tone, as he drew one from behind his back and placed it on the lower ledge at his feet. "Would the gods," he resumed the courtly key, "you had come with a plea, that the greater it were, with the more joy could I grant it."

He had ground for curiosity. For her visit was quite out of the usual order and tactful routine and therefore disturbed him. He divined some special reason for it and felt a certain uneasy joy. But for the moment she uttered only fulsome phrases.

"What wish, as your sister, could I still cherish, my master and friend?" she said in her soft voice, a sonorous alto which betrayed cultivation. "For I have breath only through you, yet, thanks to your greatness, all is vouchsafed me. That I have a place in the temple is due to your eminence among the great of the land. That I am called friend to the queen, is solely because you are Pharaoh's friend and gilded with the favour of the sun since your rising. Without you I were dark. As yours I have a fullness of light."

"It were useless to gainsay you, if such is your belief," he said with a smile. "At least let us take care that your fullness of light be not darkened where we stand." He clapped his hands. "Make light!" he ordered the slave who appeared from the dining-room.

Eni demurred. "Not yet, my husband," said she. "It is hardly dusk. You were sitting to enjoy the beautiful twilight hour; I have no wish to regret that I disturbed you."

"Nay, I insist," he answered her. "Receive it as evidence of that for which they blame me: that my will is like black granite from the quarries of the Retenu. I cannot change it, I am too old to alter. For to do that would be to show myself ungrateful to my dearest and best, who has guessed the secretest wish of my heart with this wish, and shall I receive her in darkness and gloom? Is it not a feast-day when you come, and shall I leave the feast unillumined? All four lights!" he said to the two servants bearing torches, with which they hastened to light the candelabra standing on columns in the four corners of the hall. "Let them burn up bright!"

"As you will," said she with an admiring, submissive shrug. "Truly I know the firmness of your resolution, and may the blame rest on those who strike against it! Women cannot but esteem inflexibility in a man. Shall I say why?"

"I would gladly hear."

"Because only that can give worth to surrender and make of it something of which we may be proud when we receive it."

"Most charming," said he, and blinked. Partly because of the brightness, for the hall now lay in the light of twenty lamp-wicks stuck in blazing wax, that sent up thick glaring flames till the hall became a sea of mingled milk and blood from the white light and the sunset glow. But partly too he blinked reflectively at the meaning her words might bear. Obviously she had a request, he thought, and no small one, otherwise she would not so carefully lead up to it. "It is not her way, for she knows full well my honourable peculiari-ties and how much it means to me to be left in peace and take nothing upon myself. And she is usually too proud to ask anything; her pride and my convenience thus coincide. Yet it would be good, and elevate my spirits, to do her a favour and show my power. I am curious, and concerned, to hear what she would have. The best would be if it seemed to her great yet was not so for me, so that I may do her pleasure without too great cost to my comfort. Lo, there is a conflict in my breast: it rises from my justified self-esteem, that flows from my peculiar and consecrated state and makes me find it hateful when I am approached too closely and my rest disturbed; and on the other hand from my desire to show myself loving and strong to this woman. She is lovely in her heavy robe, which she wears in my presence for the same reason that made me command the lights to be brought — lovely with her eyes like precious stones and her shadowy cheeks. I love her, in so far as my justified self-esteem permits; but here is the actual contradiction, for I hate her too, I always hate her, because of the claim which of course she does not make upon me but which is taken for granted in a marriage. Yet I do not like to hate her, rather I would that I could love her without hate. Were she to give me good occasion to show myself strong and loving, the hatred might be taken from my love and I might be happy. Therefore am I so curious to know what she would have, if also a little disturbed on account of my conduct."

Such were Petepre's thoughts as he blinked, while the slaves finished lighting the lamps and with silent haste withdrew, the torches held in their crossed arms.

"You permit me to sit beside you?" he heard Eni ask with a little laugh; starting from his thoughts, he bent once more to arrange the cushion as he expressed his pleasure. She sat down at his feet on the inscribed ledge.

"Truly," she said, "it happens too seldom that we are together like this for an hour, enjoying each other's presence without other purpose than to talk — of no matter what; for with an object in view we must talk, whereas without one talk is the pleasanter for being superfluous. Do you not agree?"

He nodded assent, sitting with his big feminine-looking arms stretched out along the back-rest of the ledge. He thought: "Seldom happens? It never happens; for we members of this noble and exalted family, parents and children, lead our lives apart, each in his own place; we avoid each other out of delicacy save when we break bread. That it happens today must have a reason, and I am full of curiosity and misgiving. Am I wrong? Is she here simply to see me, to be with me at this hour because her nature demands it? I do not know what to wish. For I could wish that she should have a need provided it be not too inconvenient to me; yet that she came for the sake of my presence solely I could wish even more — almost." He was thinking this as he said:

"I quite agree. It is a poor and narrow mind that uses speech merely as a tool for practical understandings. Whereas the rich and noble require beauty and superfluity in everything, speech as well. For beauty and superfluity are the same thing. How strange it is about words, and the dignity of them: that they can lift themselves out of their bald sufficiency to the whole height of their significance! The word 'superfluous,' for instance, often carries with it a contemptuous meaning; yet it can rise to a royal height, beyond the reach of contempt and in itself actually signify the name and nature of beauty. I often think of the mystery of words when I sit alone, and amuse my mind with such charming and idle occupation."

"Thanks to my lord that he lets me share his thought," answered she. "Your mind is clear, like the lamps you have had lighted for our meeting. If you were not Pharaoh's chamberlain, you might well be one of the learned scribes of the god, who walk in the temple courts and ponder words of wisdom."

"Very likely," said he. "For a man might be many other things than precisely that which it is his lot to be or to represent. He may often marvel at the absurd play-acting he has to do in his allotted rôle; he feels stifled in the mask life has put on him, as the priests may at times feel stifled in the mask of the god. Do you agree?"

"Quite."

"Yet perhaps not quite," he said insinuatingly. "Probably women have less understanding of such a feeling. For the Great Mother has granted them a more general sense in respect of their being more women and image of the Mother, and less this or that individual woman. For instance as though you were less bound to be Mut-em-enet than I am to be Petepre because I am conditioned by the sterner father-spirit. Do you agree?"

"It is so very bright in this hall," said she, with her head bowed, "from the flames that blaze by virtue of your masculine will. Such thoughts, it seems to me, are better pursued by softer light; it would be easier for me in the twilight to consider this matter of being more a woman and image of the Mother than just plain Mut-em-enet."

"Pardon me," he hastened to reply; "it was untactful of me not to adapt our delightfully idle conversation to the light which befits this joyous hour. I will give it a turn more suited to the festal illumination I have seen fit to make. Nothing could be easier. I will pass over the things of the mind and speak of matters of the tangible daylight world. But before I make that easy transition let me have my pleasure in the pretty mystery which consists in the fact that the world of tangible things is also the intelligible world. For what one can actually grasp with the hand is intelligible to the mind of women, children, and the common folk; whereas the intangible is intelligible only to the sterner mind of the male. The word 'comprehend' is figurative, the word 'tangible' is literal — though the latter may easily become figurative as well: we even say of an easily comprehensible thing that we can actually grasp it with our senses."

"Your observations and idle thoughts are most charming, my husband," said she, "and I cannot express the refreshment this connubial conversation gives me. Do not think I am in haste to pass over from the intangible things to the tangible. On the contrary, I would gladly linger with you in the realm of your idle thoughts, and counter them in the measure of my powers as a woman or a child. I had no meaning in my words save that a less glaring light suits better for the exchange of intimate thoughts."

He did not answer at once, being annoyed. But presently, in a chiding tone and shaking his head:

"The mistress of the house keeps coming back to the point in which things went not according to her will but to that of the stronger. That is not quite fine, the less so that it is the way of women to cling to and dissect such occasions. Permit me the suggestion that in this one respect my Eni should try to be more Mut the exceptional woman and less the ordinary one."

"I hear and repent," she murmured.

"If we were bent on mutual reproach," he continued, giving his irritation further vent, "how easily might I express my regret that you come to me at this hour, my friend, clad in so thick a mantle; for surely it is the joy and desire of your friend to follow the lines of your swanlike form through the kind transparency of a linen garment."

"Woe is me indeed!" she said, and drooped her head with a blush. "It would be better for me to die rather than learn that I have come before my lord in an unpleasing garb. I swear that I thought to give you special pleasure in this dress. For it is more costly and full of art than most of mine. My sewing-woman Heti worked with sleepless industry to make it and I shared her care that I might find favour in your eyes. But a care shared is not a care halved."

"No matter, my dear," he answered. "Let it pass. I did not say that I wished to complain, only that I could do it if you so desired. But I will not take for granted that you do. Let us go on with our idle conversation, as though the question of blame had never crept into it, like a false note. For now I will pass over to the things of the tangible world and say how I rejoice that my task in life is stamped with the seal of superfluity and not of need. I used the word 'royal' to characterize the superfluous; and indeed it is in its right place at court and in the palace Merimat; as ornament, as form for form's sake, as the elegantly turned phrase with which one greets the god. All these are the affair of the courtier; so that one may say in a way that the mask is less stifling than to him who is hemmed in by the objective fact and stands closer to the feminine because it is granted him to be less individual. It is true, I am not among those whom Pharaoh summons for advice about boring a well on the road through the desert to the sea, or the erection of a monument, or how many men it takes to wash a load of gold-dust out of the mines of the wretched Kush; and it may be that it detracts from my satisfaction and I am angry with the man Hor-em-heb, who commands the household troops and holds the head office among the executioners, almost without asking my advice, although I bear the title of the office. But always I have overcome these attacks of annoyance. For after all I am different

from Hor-em-heb, as the possessor of the title is different from the
necessary but unimportant official who actually holds the fan over
Pharaoh when he drives out. People like that are beneath me. For
mine it is to stand before Pharaoh at his levee with the other title-
bearers and dignitaries of the court and repeat the hymn of salutation to the majesty of this god: 'Thou are like Re,' with our adoring
voices; and to expend myself in utterly ornamental flourishes such
as: 'A scale is thy tongue, O Neb-mat-Re, and thy lips are more just
than the little tongue on the scale of Thoth'; or extravagant protesta-
tions like: 'Speakest thou to the ocean and sayest: "Rise up to the
mountain!" lo, the waters come up, even as thou hast spoken.' So
must I speak, in beautiful, objectless form, far from the compul-
sions of ordinary life. For pure form, adornment without purpose, is
my honour and my task, as it is the task of royalty to be royal. And
all this is an aid to my self-esteem."

"Splendid and fitting it is too," she answered, "if also the truth
be honoured and receive support, as is doubtless the case in your
words, my husband. Yet it seems to me that the beautiful superfluities
of the court and the extravagances at the levee serve to clothe with
honour and dread the material cares of the god, such as wells and
buildings and gold-mines, for the sake of their importance to the
land; and that concern for these things is the most royal thing about
royalty."

Petepre again closed his lips and refrained from any answer, playing with the draw-string of his skirt.

"I should be untruthful," he said at last with a little sigh, "were
I to say that your share in our pleasant conversation is conducted
with great tact. I made a skilful transition to the more worldly and
material things of life, bringing the subject round to Pharaoh and the
court. I expected you to return the ball by asking me some question,
such as for instance whose ear-lobe Pharaoh tweaked in token of his
favour when we went out of the hall of the canopy after the levee;
but instead you turned aside into observations about such irritating
matters as mines and desert wells, about which, truly, my love, you
must certainly understand even less than I."

"You are right," she replied, shaking her head over her blunder.
"Forgive me. My eagerness to know whose ear-lobe Pharaoh tweaked
today was only too great. I dissembled it by small talk. Pray understand me: I thought to put off the question, feeling that a slow
leading up to the important subject is the finest and most important
feature of elegant conversation. Only the clumsy blunder in their
approach by precipitation, betraying at once the whole content of
their minds. But now that you have permitted me the question: Was
it not yourself, my husband, whom the god distinguished?"

"No," said Petepre, "it was not I. It often has been, but not today.

But your words betrayed — I know not how, yet it appeared as though you inclined to the view that Hor-em-heb, the acting captain of the guard, is greater at court and in the lands than I — ”

“The gods forbid, my husband! In the name of the Hidden One!” she cried in alarm, laying her beringed hand on his knee. He looked at it as though a bird had alighted there. “I should need to be weak-minded indeed, past hope of betterment, if for a single moment — ”

“Your words made it seem so,” he asseverated, with a regretful shrug, “though of course contrary to any such intent. It was almost as though you would say — what example shall I give? As though in your mind a baker of Pharaoh’s bakery, who actually bakes the bread for the god and his house and sticks his head in the oven is greater than the great overseer of the royal bakery, Pharaoh’s chief baker, whose title is prince of Menfe. Or as though I, who of course take nothing upon myself, were of less importance here in the house than Mont-kaw, my steward, or even than his youthful ‘mouth,’ the Syrian Osarsiph who oversees the workshops. Those are striking instances — ”

Mut had shrunk back.

“They strike me indeed, so that I quail beneath them,” said she. “You see my confusion and in your greatheartedness will let the punishment rest at that. I see now how I have disarranged our dialogue with my proneness to delay. But gratify my curiosity, which I hoped to conceal, and quench it as one quenches blood: let me hear who it was that received the caress of favour in the throne-room today.”

“It was Nofer-rohu, chief of the anointers from the treasury of the king,” answered he.

“So it was that prince,” she said. “Did they surround him?”

“They did, according to the custom, and congratulated him,” he answered. “He is at the moment very much in the forefront of attention; it would be well that he should be seen at the entertainment we purpose giving at the next quarter of the moon. It would add to the lustre of the occasion and to that of our house.”

“Certainly,” she agreed; “you must invite him in a beautiful letter in which he will take pleasure because of the elegance of the phrases, such as: ‘Beloved of his master!’ or ‘Rewarded and distinguished by his lord’; and you must send him a present to his house besides, by special messenger. Then it would be most unlikely that Nofer-rohu would decline.”

“I think so too,” said Petepre. “And the present must be something very choice, of course. I will have various things brought before me to choose from and this evening I will write an invitation which he will really enjoy reading. My child,” he went on, “I should like this entertainment to be particularly choice, so that it will be talked of in the city and the report of it reach other distant ones.

With some seventy guests, and rich in unguents, flowers, musicians, food, and wine. I have purchased a very good figure of a mummy to be carried about, a good piece, an ell and a half long — I will show it to you beforehand if you like: the case is gold, the body of ebony, with 'Celebrate the joyful day' written on the forehead. Have you heard of the Babylonian dancers?"

"Which dancers, my husband?"

"There is a travelling company of foreign dancers in the city. I have had presents sent to them, that they may come to my entertainment. From all that I hear, they are of exotic beauty and accompany their performance with bells and sounding tambourines. They are said to know some new and striking poses, and to have a strange fire of fury in their eyes as they dance, as well as in their caresses. I promise myself a sensation, and for our party great success from their presence."

Eni looked down, she seemed to reflect.

"Do you intend," she said after a pause, "to invite Beknechons, first priest of Amun, to your party?"

"Of course, naturally," he answered. "Beknechons? It goes without saying. Why do you ask?"

"His presence seems important to you?"

"Why not? Beknechons is a great man."

"More important than that of the Babylonian maidens?"

"What sort of comparisons are these, my love? What choice are you putting before me?"

"The two are not reconcilable, my husband. I must make it clear to you that you must choose between them. For if the Babylonian maidens dance before Amun's high priest at your feast, it may be that the strange fire of fury in their eyes would not equal that in Beknechons's heart and that he would rise and summon his servants and leave your house."

"Impossible!"

"Even probable, my friend. He would not suffer the Hidden One to be affronted before his eyes."

"By a dance?"

"By a dance danced by foreign dancers — when, after all, Egypt is full of beauty of this kind and even sends its dancers abroad."

"So much the better may Egypt allow itself the pleasure of the novel and unknown."

"That is not Beknechons's view. His objection to what is foreign is very strong."

"But I hope that it is your view."

"My view is that of my master and friend," said she, "for how can that go against the honour of our gods?"

"The honour of the gods, the honour of the gods," he repeated, shrugging his shoulders. "I must confess that my mood and spirit begin to be clouded by our talk — which is quite contrary to the purpose of elegant conversation."

"I should be alarmed," she replied, "if that were the result of my care for your peace of mind. For how would it stand with that if Beknechons in anger called his servants and left the feast so that there would be talk of his rebuff in both the lands?"

"He would not be so petty as to feel offence at an elegant diversion nor so bold as to offer an indignity to the friend of Pharaoh."

"He is great enough that his thoughts travel easily from small affairs to large and he would give offence to Pharaoh's friend sooner than to Pharaoh, in the sense of a warning to the latter. Amun hates the laxity of foreign ways and the disregard of pious old custom, because it enervates the land and weakens the authority of the kingdom. That is what Amun hates, as we both know; for he wishes the fibre of moral discipline to be strong in the land, as it always has been in Kemt, and to have its children walk in the path of patriotic tradition. But you know, as well as I, that down there" — Mut pointed westward, toward the Nile and beyond it to the palace — "another sun-sense rules and is lightly favoured among Pharaoh's wise men: the sense of On at the apex of the Delta; the mobile sense of Aton-Re, inclined to broadness and conciliation — they call it Aton, with I know not what weakening effect. Must not Beknechons be angered for Amun if his son in the body favours this laxness and permits his thinkers and seekers to weaken the marrow of the land by toying with foreign ways? He may not blame Pharaoh. But he will blame him in you, and make demonstration for Amun by raging like a leopard of Egypt when he sees the Babylonian maidens, and will spring up to summon his servants."

"I hear you speak," he retorted, "like the clapper-bird of Punt with tongue like a rattle, who hears and repeats what is not in its head. The marrow of the lands, and the good old ways, and the laxity of foreign ones — all that is Beknechons, those are his disagreeable and crafty words, and it upsets me to have you repeat them; for your coming gave me hope of familiar converse with yourself, not with him."

"I only remind you, my friend," she answered, "of his views, which you know, in order to protect you from serious unpleasantness. I say not that Beknechons's thoughts are mine."

"But they are," he retorted. "I hear his voice in yours; but you do not utter his thoughts as something foreign in which you have no share, but rather you have made them yours and are of one mind with him, the shiny-pated priest, against me — and that is what I cannot bear. Do I not know that he goes in and out in our house, visiting you each quarter of the moon or even oftener? And always to my unspoken distress, for he is not my friend, I cannot bear him or his guile and bad manners. My nature and temperament demand a mild, refined, and tolerant sun-sense; thus in my heart I am for Atum-Re, the tolerant god; but especially because I belong to Pharaoh and am his courtier, for he permits the experimental thought of his wise men to dwell upon the benign and universal sun-sense of this glorious god. But you, my consort and sister before gods and men, where do you stand in these matters? Do you hold, not with me — in other words, with Pharaoh and the tendencies of the court — but rather with Amun the inflexible, the brazen-browed; do you lean to his party against me and are of one house with the chief shiny-pate of the ungracious god, not realizing how offensive it is to infringe upon my dignity or show me disloyalty?"

"You use comparisons, my lord," said she, in a voice thin and pinched with anger, "lacking in good taste, which is strange considering the reading you do. For it is without taste, or in poor taste, to say that I am of one house with the prophet and therefore disloyal to you. That is a lame and distorted comparison. I must remind you that Pharaoh is Amun's son, according to the teaching of the fathers and the people's ancient belief, and therefore you would do no violence to your duty as courtier by paying heed to the sacred sun-sense of Amun, however ill-mannered you find him, and by bringing him the light sacrifice of your own and your guests' curiosity in respect of a paltry dance, however striking. So much with respect to yourself. As for me, I am utterly and entirely Amun's, in piety and devotion, for I am the bride of his temple and of his house of women, Hathor am I, and dance before him in the garment of the goddess, that is all my honour and my desire and further have I none, this honourable rank is my life's sole content. And you would quarrel with me because I keep faith with the lord my god and unearthly spouse, and make comparisons against me that cry to heaven with their falseness." And she lifted up a fold of her mantle and, bending over, shrouded her face with it.

The captain of the guard was more than distressed. He shuddered, he even felt cold all over; for it seemed to him that intimate matters, always most tactfully passed over in silence, threatened to come to speech in the most shocking and destructive way. He leaned, with his arms spread out along the back of his seat, still farther away from her; and sat numbly, looking down, indignant, guilty, and bewildered, to where she wept. "What is this?" he thought. "It is all quite wild and unheard-of, it threatens danger to my peace of mind. I went too far. I brought my justified self-interest into the field, but she struck it down with her own; it is not only our talk; for my heart is pierced by her words so that pity and pain are mingled with my dread of her tears. Yes, I love her; I know it by my dread of her tears; and would like to let her know it by what I say." He raised his arms and bent over her, yet not touching her, as he said, not without painful hesitation:

"You see, dear flower, indeed your own words make it clear, that you did not speak solely to warn me of Beknechons's churlish state of mind, but because you share it, because his ideas are yours and your heart is of his party against me. You have said it plain and clear in my face: 'I am utterly and entirely Amun's' — those were your words. Was then my comparison so false and can I help it that the taste of it is bitter to me, your husband?"

She took the mantle from her face and looked at him.

"Are you jealous of god, the Hidden One?" she asked. Her mouth was wry, scorn and weeping mingled in the jewelled eyes so close to his that he started and bent back again. "I must retreat," he thought. "I have gone too far, and must by some means or other withdraw, for my own peace and for the peace of the house. For both stand in sudden and horrible danger. How can it have happened that they are both so threatened, and that this woman's eyes are all at once so terrible? Everything seemed so safe and plain." And he recalled many a home-coming, from a journey or from the court, when his first question to his steward was always: "Is all well with the household? Is the mistress happy?" For there abode in his inmost mind a secret misgiving about the peace of the house, its dignity and security — a dim consciousness that its footing was weak and imperilled. And now, by the look in Eni's angry eyes, by her tears, he knew that he had been right and that his secret dread threatened to fulfil itself.

"No," said he, "far from it. The idea that I could be jealous of Amun, the god, that I repudiate. Well I know how to make distinction between what is due from you to the Hidden One and what to your spouse. And if, as I think, the expression was displeasing to you, which I used to characterize your familiar intercourse with Beknechons, I am at all times ready and even seek occasion to give you pleasure, and will do so by withdrawing the comparison about being of one house — it shall be as though I had not said it and that it be erased from the record of my words. Are you content?"

Mut let her wet eyes dry of themselves, as though she were unconscious of the tears that stood in them. Her husband had expected gratitude for his complaisance, but she showed none.

"That is but a small matter," she said, shaking her head.

"She sees that I shrink, in respect of my fear for the peace of my house," he thought; "and she will use her advantage, as is a woman's way. She is more a female than she is an individual and my wife. I may not be surprised, though it is always a little painful to see the eternal feminine displaying its wiles in one's own wife. It would make one laugh ruefully, it has indeed an irritating effect upon me, to perceive that a person thinks to deal according to his individual mind, when all he really does is to repeat the general pattern — mortifying indeed it is! But what use are such thoughts? I can only think, not say them. What I must say is this." And he went on:

"Probably not of the smallest, indeed, but still the least of what I would say. For I did not think to end with it, but rather to increase your relief by saying that while we have been speaking I have reconsidered my idea of inviting the Babylonian dancers. I have no wish to anger a highly placed man to whom you stand in close relations, by seeming to offend what may seem to me his prejudices but which I have even so no desire to attack. Our entertainment will be brilliant enough without the foreigners."

"That too, Petepre, is most unimportant," she said. She called him by his name, he noted it with mounting apprehension.

"What do you mean?" he asked. "Still unimportant? Most unimportant of what? And compared to what?"

"To that which is desirable. To that which is needful," answered she with an intake of breath. "There should be changes, there must be changes here in this house, my husband, that it may not become a house of offending to the pious, but instead a place of good example. You are the master; who does not bow before you? Who would not grant you the mild refinement of the tolerant sun-sense, by which you order your life and which you practise in all your ways? I see well that one cannot at the same time be for the kingdom and for the stern old ways, for out of the second came the first, and life now in the richness of the kingdom must be otherwise than in the simplicity of the old times. You must not say that I have no understanding of life and its changes. But there must be measure in all things; a remnant of the ancient discipline, out of which sprang the kingdom and the riches of it, must be preserved and held in honour, that the lands become not shamefully corrupt and the sceptre fall from their hands. Would you deny this truth, or would Pharaoh's wise men deny it, they who occupy themselves with the mobile sun-sense of Atum-Re?"

"Nobody," responded the fan-bearer, "denies the truth. It might be dearer than even the sceptre. You speak of destiny. We are children of our age, and it seems to me it is always better to live by the truth of the time wherein we are born than to try to guide ourselves by the immemorial past and the stern maxims of antiquity and so doing to deny our own souls. Pharaoh has many mercenaries — Asiatic, Libyan, Nubian, even native. They will guard the realm so long as destiny permits. But we must live in sincerity."

"Sincerity," said she, "is easy, and therefore it is not lofty. What would become of men if each would live only in the sincerity of his own desires, claiming for them the dignity of truth and unwilling to be strict with himself to his own improvement? The thief too is sincere, and the drunkard in the gutter, and likewise the adulterer. But shall we by reason of its sincerity pass over their conduct? You wish to live in sincerity, my husband, as a child of your time, and not according to the ancient precepts. But that is barbaric antiquity, where each lives according to his lust; a more advanced age demands the limitation of the personal for the sake of higher considerations."

"Wherein would you have me alter myself?" he said in some panic.

"In nothing, my husband. You are unchangeable, and far be it from me to shake the sacred moveless calm of your being. Far, too, any reproach because you make nothing your affair in the household or elsewhere in the world but to eat and drink. For if this were not a consequence of your nature, it would be of your rank. Your servants' hands do all for you as they will do in your tomb. Your part is but to command, or not even this, for you command only one, him who is set over all to direct the house in your name, in the sense that it is the house of a great man of Egypt. Only this, this alone is your affair; a thing of the utmost ease, yet of the last importance: that you should not err nor point wrongly with your finger. Upon that all depends."

"For years which I no longer count," said he, "Mont-kaw has been my steward. A worthy soul, who loves me as he should, and is sensitive for all that could give me offence. Never so far as I could tell has he betrayed me in great matters, or hardly in small, and he has administered the household nobly, and fittingly to my state. Has he the misfortune to incur your displeasure?"

She smiled contemptuously at his evasion.

"You know," she answered, "as well as I and all of Wese that Mont-kaw is dying of his kidneys and for some time has had as little charge of affairs as you yourself. Another rules in his place, whom they call his mouth; and the advancement of this youth in your household must be seen to be believed. But that is not all; for it is said that after Mont-kaw's expected death this so-called mouth shall step into his place and all that you have shall fall into his hands. You praise your steward for his loyalty to your interest — but in this matter I seek in vain for evidence of it."

"You are thinking of Osarsiph?"

She bowed her head.

"It is a strange way of putting it," she said, "to say that I am thinking of him. Might the Hidden One grant there were no ground to think of him! Instead of which one is driven to do so, by this blunder of your steward, and in a way most mortifying to our pride. This ailing man bought him you speak of as a boy, from some travelling pedlars; then, instead of treating him as befitted his base blood and origins, he advanced him and let him take the upper hand in the house;

he put all the household under him, my servants as well as yours, till you yourself, my lord, speak of him, a slave, with a readiness most painful to me, which rouses up my anger. For if you had stopped to think and then said: 'Do you mean the Syrian, the Hebrew lad from the wretched Retenu?' that would have been natural and fitting. But things have gone very far, your own words betray it, for you spoke as though he were your cousin, naming him familiarly by name and asking: 'Are you thinking of Osarsiph?' "

Thus then she too uttered the name, bringing it over herself with a secret ecstasy and blissful satisfaction. She spoke the mystic syllables, with their echo of death and divinity, syllables conveying to her fate's utmost sweetness in their sound, with a sob. But she pretended that it was a sob of outraged dignity and once more she hid her face in her mantle.

For the second time Petepre was sincerely alarmed.

"What is it, what is it, my love?" he said, stretching out his hands above her head. "More tears? Let me understand why. I spoke of the slave by his name, as he calls himself and is known to all. Is not a name the quickest way to indicate one's meaning? And I see that I was correct. You did have in mind that Canaanitish youth who serves me as cup-bearer and reader — to my great satisfaction, I deny it not. Should that not be a ground for you to think favourably of him? I had no part in his purchase. Mont-kaw, who has power to buy and to sell, took him years ago from some honest traders. But it came about that I had speech with him to try him, when he was putting date blossoms to ride in my orchard, and found him exceedingly pleasing, gifted by the gods with graces of body and mind most unusually mingled. For his looks seem but the natural expression of the charm of his spirit, and in turn his mental parts are in invisible correspondence with the outward grace; so that you will, I hope, permit me to call him remarkable, for it is the due and proper word. His origins are not of the best; indeed, one might, if one chose, call his birth virgin; but at least he who begot him was undoubtedly a prince of a sort, a prince of God and king over his flocks, and the boy led a princely life and was favoured with the gifts of favour, where he grew up amongst his father's flocks. After that, indeed, affliction was his portion, and there were those who set snares for his feet and he walked into them. But even the tale of his sufferings is remarkable; it has spirit and sense, it holds together, as one may say, and in it there rules that same combination which makes his inward and outward parts seem one and the same thing. For it has its own reality, but also seemingly a higher reference as well, and both so related that one is mirrored in the other, which only adds to the youth's mysterious charm. When he had not ill sustained the test I gave him, he was appointed my cup-bearer and reader — without my stir, out of love of

me, of course — and I confess that in this capacity he has become indispensable. But again, he has grown up, without any motion of mine,
to have oversight of all the things of the household, and it has proved
that the Hidden One grants success through him, in all that he does
— I cannot put it otherwise. And now that he has become indispensable to me and to the house, what would you have me do with him?"

Truly, what was there to wish or to do, when he had finished
speaking? When he stopped, he looked round with a satisfied smile.
He had secured himself strongly against attack and stamped the
threatened demand as monstrous, as an unloving offence against himself, which no one could think of inflicting upon him. He could not
have dreamed that the woman before him paid no heed to this interpretation. Sitting crouched under her cloak, she had greedily sucked
in the honey of his words; her tense excitement had let no syllable
escape of all that he said in Joseph's praise; which greatly diminished
its intended effect. Yet, strange to say, Mut remained honourably true
to the strict and reasonable dictates which had given rise to this visit
to Potiphar. She sat up erect and said:

"I will assume, my husband, that what you have said in favour of
the slave is the uttermost that can be justly said. And it is not enough,
it is untenable before Egypt's gods. All this that you have been so
good as to tell me, of the wonderful combination of qualities in your
servant, and of his mysterious charm — all that counts as nothing in
face of Amun's just demand through my mouth. For I too am a
mouthpiece — not alone he whom you say is indispensable to your
house — clearly without due reflection, for how can a chance stranger be indispensable in the land of men and in Petepre's house, which
was a house of blessing before this outlander began to wax strong
within it? That should never have come to pass. If the lad was once
bought, he should have been sent to labour in the fields instead of
keeping him in the courtyard and even entrusting him with your cup
and lending your ear to his reading because of his insinuating gifts.
The talents are not the man; one must make a distinction. For it is so
much the worse when a base man has gifts which can make one finally forget his natural baseness. What are those gifts which can justify the elevation of the base? Mont-kaw, your steward, should have
asked himself that, who without your orders, as you say, made this
lowly slave flourish like a weed in your house, to the shame of all the
pious. Will you permit him, now that he is dying, to defy the gods
and point with his finger at the Shabirite as his successor, so shaming
your house before the world and humbling your own people beneath
his foot, so that they gnash their teeth?"

"My dear one," said the chamberlain, "how you deceive yourself!
You are not well informed, to judge from your words, for there is no
thought of teeth-gnashing. All the other servants love Osarsiph, from

high to low, from the scribe of the buffet to the kennel-boys and to the least of your handmaidens, and take no shame to do his will. I know not whence this report, that folk gnash their teeth at his advancement, for it is quite false. On the contrary, they all seek his glance and gladly vie to do each his best when he comes amongst them; they hang joyously upon his lips when he gives them orders. Yes, even those who had to step aside from their office to make way for him, even they do not look askance, but straight in his eye, for his gifts are irresistible. And why? Because he is not what you say, nor are his gifts a lying appendage to his person, and to be distinguished from it. For they are mingled together and are one, the gifts of one blest with the blessing, so that you might say he deserves them, if that again were not an untenable division between the person and his gifts, or if you can speak at all of merit in connection with natural gifts. But it has come about that on the land-ways and the water-ways folk recognize him from afar, they nudge each other and say: 'There is Osarsiph, Petepre's body-servant and mouth to Mont-kaw, an excellent youth, going about the business of his lord, which he will perform to advantage as is his way.' Moreover, though men look him in the eye, it is said that women avoid it, but give him sidling glances, which is as good a sign. And when he shows himself in the streets of the city and in the bazaar, it often happens that the maidens mount on the house-tops and fling down gold rings upon him from their fingers, that he may look up at them. But he never does."

Eni listened, in speechless ecstasy. This glorification of Joseph, the description of his popularity, intoxicated her beyond words. Bliss ran like fire through her veins, made her bosom rise and fall and her breath come sobbingly in gasps; her very ears grew red – only with the greatest difficulty could she prevent her lips from curving in a beatific smile as she listened. A benevolent onlooker must have shaken his head at the deluded creature. This praise of Joseph must have confirmed her in her weakness – if we may so express it – for the foreign slave; it must have justified this weakness in the face of her own pride, plunged her still deeper in, made her still less capable of carrying out her purpose of saving her own life. Was that a ground for joy? No, not for joy, but for ecstasy – a distinction which the well-wishing friend, though shaking his head, is bound to make. She suffered, too – that goes without saying. What Petepre said about the women: how they looked, how they cast down their rings, that confirmed her again in her weakness and filled her at the same time with scorching jealousy and with hatred for those whose feelings were her own. It consoled her a little to hear that Joseph did not look at them; and it helped her to persevere in her project of behaving like a reasonable being. She said:

"I will pass over, my friend, your lack of delicacy in entertaining me with the ill behaviour of the women of Wese, be there much or little truth in such reports — for they may have their source in the conceited youth himself or in such as he has bribed with promises." It cost her less than one would think, to speak thus of the object of her already hopeless love. She did it mechanically, making herself speak like another than herself; her musical voice took on a hollow tone corresponding to the fixity of her features and the vacancy of her gaze. The whole made up a picture of deliberate guile. "It is more important to point out that when you say I am falsely informed as to the situation in the house, your charge is unfounded and falls to the ground. It would be much better if you had not made it. Your habit of taking nothing upon yourself, but of seeing all with distant and detached eye, should make you doubt whether you are yourself so well informed. The truth is that the forwardness of this youth has become a subject for violent anger and widespread disaffection in the house. Dudu, the guardian of your jewel-caskets, has more than once, yes, very often, taken occasion to speak before me, uttering bitter complaints of the offence to the pious in making them suffer the domination of impure stock — "

Petepre laughed. "You have found a wonderful witness, my blossom — take it not ill of me that I say so! Dudu is a pompous puffed-up toad, a quarter-size man and made to be laughed at. How in the world could he be taken seriously in this or any other matter?"

"The size of his person," she retorted, "is not to the purpose. But if his view is so contemptible, his judgment so worthless, how then is it that he was chosen guardian of your wardrobe?"

"It was a joke," said Petepre. "Only in jest could one give such a man an office. The other clown, his little mate, they even call vizier, but certainly they are not serious when they do it."

"I need not call your attention to the difference between them," she answered. "You know it well enough, though at this moment you would deny it. But it is sad that I must defend your most loyal and worthy servant against your ingratitude. Aside from his small stature Dudu is a serious and dignified man, who in no way deserves the name of clown, and whose judgment is valuable in affairs of the house and of his own honour."

"He reaches up to here on me," remarked the captain of the guard, making a line on his shin with the edge of his hand.

Mut was silent for a while.

"You know, my husband," she said then, with self-control, "that you are uncommon in height and strength, so that Dudu's size must seem smaller to you than to most other men — or for instance to Djeset, his wife, my woman, and to his children, who are of ordinary size and look up to their father with loving respect."

"They look up — ha ha!"

"I use the word advisedly, in a higher, poetic sense."

"So you express yourself even poetically about your Dudu," Pete-pre mocked her. "Since you have complained of my bad taste in choice of subjects, I may remind you that you have dwelt overlong upon this conceited fool."

"We may well leave the subject," she said compliantly, "if it displeases you. I do not need his evidence or support in the matter of our discussion, since the request I would make is thrice justified of itself; his evidence is not needed to prove that you must grant it."

"You have a request?" he asked. ("So, then," he said to himself, rather bitterly, "it is true that she came with some purpose of a more or less troublesome nature. My hope is vain that her visit was simply for the sake of my presence. It cannot make me well-disposed toward her request.") — He asked:

"And what request?"

"This, my husband: that you should send away the foreign slave, whose name I will not again speak, from your house and courtyard, where he has sprung up like a weed, by dint of culpable negligence and lying favour, so that he has made it a house of offence instead of an example to the lands."

"Osarsiph — from house and courtyard? What are you thinking of?"

"I think, my husband, of right and justice. I think of the honour of your house, of the gods of Egypt and what you owe to them. Not alone to them, but to yourself and me, your sister-wife, who shakes the sistrum before Amun in the adornment of the Mother, consecrate and set apart. I think of these things and am certain beyond any doubt that I need only remind you of them for your thoughts to unite with mine and for you to grant my request without delay."

"By sending Osarsiph. . . . My dear, it may not be. Put it out of your mind, it is in vain, it is a whim which I cannot entertain, for it is a stranger to my mind, and all my thoughts rise up against it."

"So there we have it," he said to himself, in anger and bewilderment. "That is the request, and that is why she came to me at this hour and seemed to come that we might talk together. I saw it coming, yet on my side would not see it, so offensive it is to my justified self-interest. I would have granted something small, wishing to seem great to her; but unhappily this that she thinks small and simple to grant is for me inconvenient in the extreme. Not without justification did I feel the approach of a disturbance to my peace. Yet what a pity that she has offered me no occasion to rejoice her heart, for I am reluctant to hate her."

"Your prejudice, my little flower," said he, "against the person of this youth, so great as to make you launch so foolish a request, is very sad. Clearly you know nothing of him save for the complaints and curses of mis-shapen and misbegotten persons and have no direct knowledge of his excellent gifts, which, young as he is, could in my opinion exalt him much higher than even the stewardship of my house. You call him barbarian and slave — and literally you are right — but is that right enough, if it denies the spirit? Is it the custom and way of our land to esteem a man accordingly as he is free or unfree, native or foreign, and not rather according to his spirit whether it is dark and undisciplined or enlightened through the word and ennobled by the magic of its eloquence? What is our practice in Egypt? For the youth has a blithe and lucid manner of speech, with well-chosen words and charming intonation, writes a decorative hand, and reads aloud from my books as though he spoke himself by the motion of his own spirit, so that all their wit and wisdom seem to come from him and belong to him and one can only wonder. I could wish you to take notice of his parts, to talk graciously with him and win his friendship, which would be much more pleasing to you than that of yon arrogant toad. . . ."

"I will neither take notice of him nor have speech with him," she said frigidly. "I see that I was mistaken when I thought you had exhausted your praise. You had still something to add. But now I await your word and the granting of my well-justified, my pious request."

"No such word," he replied, "can I utter, in response to a request so signally mistaken. It cannot be granted, and for more than one reason; the only question is whether I can make this clear to you. If not, alas, it will not be the more easily granted. I have told you that Osarsiph is not an ordinary slave. He brings increase to our house, he serves it incredibly; who could bring himself to send such a person away? It would be to rob the household; and to him gross injustice for he is free from error and a youth of the finest fibre, so that it would be a rarely unpleasant business simply to send him away without cause, and no one would be prepared to do it."

"You fear the slave?"

"I fear the gods who are with him, who make everything that is put in his hands succeed, and give him charm in the eyes of all the world. What gods they are is beyond my judgment, but they show themselves powerful in him, beyond a doubt. You would quickly forget such ideas — for instance, of burying him in field labour or selling him, if you would once forget your refusal to know him better. Very soon, I assure you, your heart would feel sympathy and softening toward the youth, for there is more than one point of contact between your life and his; and if I love to have him about me, believe me that it is because often he reminds me of you."

"Petepre!"

"I say what I say, and what I think is by no means meaningless. Are you not dedicate and set apart for the god, before whom you dance as his bride, and do you not wear your sacrificial adornments before men? Well, then, I have it from the youth himself that he, too, wears such an adornment, invisible, like your own. One must imagine a sort of evergreen, which is a symbol of consecrated youth and bears the significant name of touch-me-not. All this he has told me and I listened not without amazement, for he spoke of strange things. I knew of the gods of Asia, Atys and Ashrat, and the Baals of the growth. But he and his live under a god strange to me, and of amazing jealousy. For this unique god is solitary and feels a great need of loyalty, and he has betrothed himself to them as a bridegroom. It is all strange enough. In principle they each wear the evergreen and are set apart to their god like a bride. But one among them he chooses as a whole sacrifice, and that one must wear it with a difference and as one specially dedicate to the jealous god. And such a one is Osarsiph! They know a thing, he says, which is called sin, and the garden of sin, and have imagined beasts which leer from among the branches in the garden, ugly beyond conception. There are three of these and they are called 'Shame,' 'Guilt,' and 'Mocking Laughter.' But now I will ask you two questions: First, can one have a better servant and steward than one born to loyalty, and fearing sin in his very bones? And second, was it too much to say when I spoke of a point of contact between you and this youth?"

Ah, how Mut's heart contracted at her husband's words! Agony had consumed it when he spoke of the maidens who threw down their rings; but that had been nothing compared with the icy sword which pierced it when she understood why the daughters of Wese had not succeeded in drawing his gaze upon them. A frightful anguish, a presentiment of all she was to bear, came over her and painted itself openly on the pale agonized face turned up to Petepre. If we try to put ourselves in her place we shall see that the situation did not lack an element of absurdity. For why was she struggling and wrestling with her husband's obstinacy, if he was speaking the truth? If the healing and revealing dream which had brought her hither was but a lying dream? If he from whom she would save her own life and her husband's was a whole sacrifice already promised, devoted, and set apart? What an involvement was this, in which she had feared to involve herself? She had not strength, she dared not attempt to cover her eyes with her hand; they stared into space, where she seemed to see the three beasts in the garden: Shame, Guilt, and Mocking Laughter, of whom the last whined like a hyena. It was unbearable. She was overwhelmed. Only away with him, more than ever now, since those healing dreams had been all a lie — thrice shameless dreams, since it would be quite vain were she even to throw down to him the rings from her fingers! "Yes, I must fight," she thought, "more than ever now, if this be true! But do I believe it? Or do I not rather cherish a secret hope that my dreams will prove stronger than his bond, will overpower it so that he will return my gaze and still my blood? Do I not hope and fear with a force which in my soul I believe to be ir-resistible? And seeing that clearly, once for all, must he not away, out of my sight, out of this house, that my life may be saved? There sits my fat-armed husband, like a tower of strength; Dudu, who can beget children, reaches up to his shin. He commands the troops. From him and his cherishing have I to hope healing and saving, from his alone." — It was this thought of taking refuge in her husband, her nearest, of trying on him the power of her craving for help, that spoke when she said in a clear ringing voice:

"I will not enter further upon your words, my friend, nor try by contending to refute them. It would be idle. For what you say is not to the point of our dispute, there is no need for you to say it; you need only speak the words: 'I will not.' For all the rest is but the cloak for your inflexible will; it is the iron firmness of your resolve, the granite determination which informs all that you say. Should I then enter into unavailing and ungrateful strife, since after all as a woman I must rather admire and love your strength? It is rather something else for which I wait — something which without that iron resolve would mean little or nothing, but with it is rich and glorious: I mean your gracious granting of this boon for which I plead. This hour is not like other hours; it is for us two alone, and full of the expectancy in which I came to it — came to beg that your strong will should in-cline to me and give me my desire, saying: 'This offence shall be re-moved from the house, and Osarsiph shall be deprived of his office and sold and sent away.' Shall I hear those words, my husband and lord?"

"You have heard, my dear, that you cannot hear them, not with the best of goodwill on my part. I cannot sell Osarsiph and send him away, I cannot desire to, the will is lacking."

"You cannot will it? Then your will is your master, and not you master of your will?"

"My child, these are hair-splittings. Is there a difference between me and my will, one being servant and the other master and one lord-ing it over the other? Master your own will, and will what is repug-nant, what is entirely repulsive to yourself!"

"I am ready to do so," said she, and flung back her head, "when higher things come into play, such as honour, pride, and the king-dom."

"But nothing of that sort is involved here," he replied, "or rather what is involved is respect for sound sense, the pride of wisdom, and the kingdom of moderation."

"Think not of these, Petepre!" she begged in her ringing voice. "Think alone of this hour, this single hour, and its expectancy, and my coming to you unannounced to disturb your rest. Lo, I put my arms about your knee and implore you to grant me this favour, my husband, and to send me away in peace."

"It is pleasant to me," he responded, "to feel your lovely arms about my knee; yet however pleasant, they cannot make me yield; it is but due to their softness that my reproach is so gentle for the disturbing of my repose and the heedlessness toward my well-being. For that you have no concern; yet even so I will speak of it and tell you something in this hour when we are alone together. Know then," he said with a certain mysterious solemnity, "that I must keep Osarsiph, not alone for the good of the house, to which he gives such increase, or because he reads my books in praise of wisdom as no other can. For another reason he is supremely important to my well-being. In saying that he gives me a feeling of self-confidence I do not say it all; it is even more indispensable than that. His mind is fertile in invention of easements of every sort; but of these the chief is that by day and hour he speaks to me of myself in a favouring light, almost divine, and strengthens my heart in my own regard, so that I feel —"

"Let me wrestle with him," she said, holding his knee in a closer embrace, "let me defeat him, who only knows words to strengthen your heart and your confidence in yourself. I can do it better. I will give you power to strengthen your own heart in deeds, through yourself, in fulfilling the expectation of this hour and giving back the boy to the desert whence he came! For how greatly, my husband, will you feel yourself when you have consoled me and I go from you in peace!"

"Do you think so?" he asked, blinking. "Then hearken: I will command that when my steward Mont-kaw departs this life, for he is near his end, Osarsiph shall not be head in his place, but another, perhaps Khamat, the scribe of the buffet. But Osarsiph shall remain in the house."

She shook her head.

"Therewith, my friend, is my need not served, nor will any increase of strength or knowledge come to you. For my wish would be but half or partly granted and no satisfaction be given to my expectation. Osarsiph must go from the house."

"Then," said he quickly, "if that is not enough, then I withdraw what I said, and the youth shall come to the headship of the house."

She relaxed her arms.

"I hear your final word?"

"Another, alas, I have not to give."

"Then I will go," she breathed, and stood up.

"Yes," he acquiesced. "But after all, it was a charming hour. I will send presents after you to rejoice you: an ointment-dish of ivory, carven with eyes and fish and mice."

She turned her back and moved toward the columned archway. There for a moment she paused, supporting one hand, still holding her garment's folds, upon a column, and leaning her forehead against it so that her face was shrouded. No one has ever known how it looked in that hidden face.

Then she clapped her hands and went out.

THREEFOLD EXCHANGE

WITH the recording of the above conversation we have got so far into our story that we can now link it on to a remark which I made somewhat earlier and only in passing. I referred, that is, to the strange constellation, the pattern into which life's kaleidoscope here fell. I have said that about this time, when the mistress was making apparently sincere efforts to have Joseph removed, there came a change in the attitude of Dudu, the married dwarf. For whereas formerly his efforts had all been in the same direction, he now began to ply Joseph with sweet words and to behave like his devoted friend; not only to Joseph himself but also in conversation with the mistress, praising him in all possible keys. And in saying this I said not a word too much. But the reason was that Dudu perceived Mut-em-enet's state, and the ground of her desire to have Joseph put away from the sight of her eyes. He had divined it, by virtue of the sun-property of his dwarfish wisdom; a gift which, however surprisingly it sat upon him, he yet cultivated with assiduity. Actually he was expert and connoisseur in the field, with sharpened senses for all its manifestations — though in other respects his dwarfish wisdom might sorely suffer from the gift.

It was not long, then, before he saw what he had brought about — or at least fostered — by his patriotic indignation at Joseph's growth in the house. He saw it actually much sooner than she did herself, being guided by her proud self-unconsciousness which would take no thought of the need for caution. Then, when her eyes were open, he profited by the usual incapacity of the deluded and stricken heart to conceal its state from the eyes of men. Dudu perceived that the mistress was on the verge of falling in love, headlong, calamitously, and with all the seriousness of her nature, with the foreign body-servant of her spouse. He rubbed his hands. He had not expected this, but shrewdly surmised that by its means a deeper pit would be digged for the interloper than could have been prepared for him in any other way. He changed his face from one day to the next, assuming a rôle which many people have played since his day, though he was himself scarcely the first to play it, being relatively late in time. Little as we know of his predecessors, we cannot doubt that he walked in the footsteps of others as he played his part. He began, that is, to insti-

gate mischief by acting as go-between, to and fro between Joseph
and Mut-em-enet.

In talk with her he skilfully changed his tune, speaking tentatively
at first, but more boldly as he felt more certain of the state of her
heart. For now she sent for him, where before he had urged the matter upon her; and of her own accord began to discuss the affront to
the household. At first he took this as a sign that he had won her over
to his own hatred and made her active in its service. But soon he
scented a different posture of affairs in the strangeness of the language she used.

"Steward," said she (to his joy she called him so, though in fact his
office was an inferior one), "steward, I have summoned you through
one of the gate-keepers of the house of women, to whom I sent one
of my Nubian slaves. For I waited in vain for your appearance to
continue our necessary conference in that affair which I so call because it is an affair of yours and it is you who have brought it to my
attention. I would reproach you, though but gently, in consideration on the one hand of your merits and on the other of your size,
that you have not before now come to me of your own accord, but
let me suffer torture by neglect. For waiting is in any case a torture,
always unfitting to a woman of my station and so for me even worse.
My heart is on fire with this disgrace, this foreign youth of whose
name I have been obliged to take note, since I hear that he has become steward in the household in the place of the Osiris Mont-kaw,
and walks in his beauty through the establishment and oversees all, to
the rapture of most of you. This shame, I say, burns in my heart; the
which, dwarf, should rejoice yours since you were the first to arouse
me to it by your complaints, without which I might have rested in
peace, whereas now it is before me day and night. And then after
making the thing a concern of mine you came no more to speak with
me of it, as is needful, but left me alone in my anger until I was
driven to send for you before my face to discuss what must be done;
for nothing is more painful than to be left hanging in such a matter.
This you should know of yourself, for what can you do alone and
without me as ally, against the object of our hate, he being so powerful that by comparison your hatred is impotent, however much I approve it. He sits unshakable in the favour of the master, who cannot
abide you; and has known by means of cleverness and magic spells
to make himself prized, also because his gods make all to succeed that
is put into his hands. How can they do this? I cannot think them so
powerful, certainly not here in the lands where they are strange and
without honour, as to achieve all that he has achieved since he came
amongst us. The gifts must lie in himself, for without them could no
one rise from the base position of a chattel to the overseer of all the
household. It is plain that you can compare with him in shrewdness

as little as in outward favour, dwarf. For his wisdom and his way seem to appeal to everybody, little as you and I can understand the fact. They love him and seek his glance; not only the people of the house but also in the city and on the land- and water-ways. Yes, I have heard that when he appears the women mount the house-tops to stare down upon him and throw down their rings in token of their desire. This, then, is the height of the abomination; and for this reason I was impatient to see you, steward, and hear your advice or give you mine, to the end that this shameless situation be ended. For last night when sleep fled my couch, I pondered whether we might not send archers with him to the city, who should shoot their arrows into the faces of these women, directly into their faces, who so conduct themselves. I considered and found that we should do this thing; and now you are at last come, I charge you with it, upon my responsibility. Yet you are not to name me in the business, but make it seem as though the idea were yours and plume yourself with it. Only to Osarsiph you will say that I, the mistress, would have it so, and have the bowmen shoot in the women's faces, and you must listen to what he says to this my order. Afterwards you will tell me what he said, coming of yourself and at once to make report, that I need not send and command your coming, having first suffered the torments of waiting and the pain of being left alone in so weighty a matter. For it seems to me you have grown careless, steward, while I give myself trouble and pain for Amun. His Grace Beknechons and you have advised that I embrace the knees of my husband Petepre, captain of the king's bodyguard; and I have wrestled with him half the night for the ending of this annoyance, making myself a burden to him and a humiliation to myself, and all in vain, for his granite will was not broken and I went forth alone and unconsoled. And messenger after messenger had I to send, only that you should come and make report of the infamous youth who grows rank in the house: how he spreads himself in the honours for which he has schemed, and what he utters about masters and servants, but especially about me, its mistress — how he may chance to express himself about me. For if I am to meet him and oppose him, I must know him and his way of speech and thought about myself. Your negligence leaves me uninformed. You could, if you were active and ingenious, move him to approach me and seek my favour. Then might I test him and find out the magic by means of which he besots the hearts of men and draws them to his side. For that must be a mystery, and the ways of it past finding out. Or can you, O guardian of the robes, see and say what all the world sees in him? It is for this I have summoned you, for you know the ways of the world; had you come sooner, I would have asked you before now. Is he then so unsurpassed in figure and stature? By no means, he is as many others are, in the measure of a man, of course not so small as you are, yet far from the towering height of my husband, Petepre. One might say he is of just the right height — but would that be so overwhelming? Or is he so strong that he can carry five bushels or more of seed-corn out of the granary, amazing the men and bewitching the women? No, for his strength is but average, it is again just the right strength. If he bend his arm, the virile muscle stands out not grossly and boastfully, but only with moderate and graceful power, which one might call human, or one might also call divine. For so it is, my friend. But thousands of such are there in the world, and how little it justifies his triumphs! It is the head and face that impart meaning and dignity to a man; and let us admit in fairness that his eyes are lovely in their darkness beneath the arch of the brows; lovely in their clear open gaze and also when it pleases him to veil them in a dreamy and artful way which you have doubtless observed. But what sort of mouth has he, that he can bewitch mankind, so that they actually call him, as I have heard, the mouth of the house? It is incomprehensible, it is not to be fathomed; for his lips are too thick, and the smile with which he knows how to grace them, with his teeth shining as they part, can but little explain the delusion, even considering the felicity of his words. I incline to the view that good part of the mystery lies in this same mouth; at that door must one listen would one trap the adventurer in his own snare. If my servants will not betray me or leave me to wait in torment for their aid, I will take it on myself to ensnare him and bring him to a fall. But if he resist me, know then, dwarf, that I will order the bowmen to turn their weapons and shoot their arrows into his face, into the night of his eyes and the fatal sweetness of his mouth!"

To this extraordinary speech from his mistress Dudu listened with great dignity, the thatch of his upper lip shoved out over the lower one; his hand curved round his ear in token of an attention not at all feigned. Being past master in a certain field, he was in a position to interpret her words. So, understanding how things stood, he changed his tune; not too abruptly, but by degrees gliding from one position to another. On the morrow he spoke differently of Joseph, yet as though his words of yesterday had been uttered in the same sense, though in fact they had been much more derogatory. And in general he sought to turn gall into honey and all that he had previously uttered into its opposite. Such gross inconsistency must have angered any reasonable person, for it insulted the human understanding. But Dudu was instructed by his prowess in a certain field; he knew how much people in Mut-em-enet's state can be made to believe and he took no shame to himself for urging her on. And she — she was far too bemused to take offence at the insolence; she was even grateful to the dwarf for his complaisance.

"Noble lady," he said, "if your servant appeared not yesterday be-

fore you to discuss ways and means in our affair — for the day before
I was here, as you will recall when I remind you, and only your great
zeal magnifies the term of my absence — the cause was but the pressing claims of my office; yet could not even so my mind be distracted
from the problem which lies next to your heart and mine, touching
Osarsiph, the new steward. The duties of my office are none the less
dear to me, for the which you will not chide me; they are precious,
and have become so by inclination, whereas at first they were a burden — as will often come to pass. For the same is true of that problem
and occupation concerning which your servant is privileged to take
frequent counsel with you. How could one but take that duty to his
heart which permitted him daily or almost daily to exchange speech
with his mistress, whether summoned or unsummoned? It is even
true and natural that my gratitude for the great privilege be extended
to the subject of our discourse, so that I must needs take him to my
heart who was the cause of my advancement in being the cause of
your concern. It could scarcely be otherwise; and indeed I am reminded to my satisfaction that I have never thought of the subject
of our discourse, the person in question, otherwise than as one
worthy of your concern. It were unjust to Dudu to suppose that he
has neglected for an hour the elegant duties of the wardrobe, even
to be active in the business which his lady grants him to share with
her. One must do the one without neglecting the other, that was
always my motto, in earthly as also in heavenly things. Amun is a
great god, there can be no greater. But shall one therefore neglect
to worship and cherish the other gods of the land — even such as are
so near to him as almost to be the same and have named him their
name, as for instance Atum-Re-Horakhte at On in Lower Egypt?
Even when it was vouchsafed me to speak with you last time, I sought
to explain, albeit clumsily and with unsuccess, that I found him a
god great, wise, and mild, pre-eminent for such inventions as the
clock and almanac, without which we were as the beasts. From my
youth up I have asked myself privily, but now aloud, if Amun in his
chapel could find it amiss were we to take account in our hearts of
the mild and magnanimous thoughts of that majestic being with
whose name he has united his own. Is not His Grace Beknechons the
first prophet of one as well as the other? When my lady shakes her
loud rattle in the dance before Amun as his bride in the feast, then her
name is not Mut as on other days, but Hathor, the sister-bride of
Atum-Re, with disk and horns — not the bride of Amun. In the light
of these things, your faithful servant has not failed to take trouble
in the matter close to our hearts; but has approached nearer to the
seed of Asia, that youth who flourishes so exceedingly in the house
that he is now steward and the object of your concern. I have sought
to search him to the end that I might speak with more knowledge

before you than was last time possible despite all my effort. All in all
I found him charming — within the limits set by the natural order
for a man like me. The feelings of the women on the roofs are different, of course. But I found that the youth would have little or no
objection to letting the bowmen shoot at them, and in this respect
there would be no ground at all for turning the bows in the other
direction. For he seemed to say that but one had the right to look
upon him and fix him with her eye — whereat he darted me a glance
with his great eyes like night, at first large and shining, but then
veiled and artful, in the interesting way he has. His words might have
been an indication of his feeling for you; but I did not let it stop
there. For I am used to weigh and estimate men according to their
attitude toward you. So I led the talk round to feminine charm and
asked him, as one man another, whom he found the most beautiful
of all that he knew. 'Our mistress, Mut-em-enet,' he said, 'is the most
beautiful here and in all the region round. One could cross seven
mountains and not find one more full of charm.' And there came
an Atum-redness in his cheek, which I can but compare with that
which now colours yours — the source of which, I may hope, is your
satisfaction over my zeal in our cause. And not stopping at that, I
furthered your desire that the young steward should wait often upon
you and put himself to proof before you that you might come upon
the sources of his magic and the secret of his mouth — for to that I
feel myself by my nature uncalled. Urgently I pressed him and chid
his timidity, counselling him to approach you, O my lady, the more
assiduously the better, kissing with his mouth the ground before you,
the which may suffer it. He made no reply. But the blush which had
gone from his cheek swiftly returned, which I took for a sign of his
fear to betray himself to you and reveal his secret. Yet I am convinced that he will follow my advice. True, he has risen above me in
this house, by whatever means, and is at its head; but I am the older
in years and office, so that I can speak to such a youth as a plain,
forthright man, which I am, and as which I commend myself to
my lady's favour."

And Dudu bowed very correctly as he took leave, his stumpy little
arms dangling from his shoulders. He went straight to Joseph, whom
he greeted with the words:

"My respects to you, mouthpiece of the house!"

"So, Dudu," answered Joseph, "you come to pay me your valued
respects? But how is this? For only a little while since you would not
eat with me, but showed in word and deed that your friendliness was
not great."

"Friendliness?" repeated the husband of Djeset, tilting back his
head to look into Joseph's face. "It was always greater than that of
many who have behaved more like it these seven years, while I had

it but did not show it. I am a cautious, reserved man, who grants not all at once his respect and devotion to a man for the sake of his beautiful eyes, but lets it ripen in silence even for seven years. But let it once be mature, then is all trust and dependence to be placed upon it, as he who has been tested soon can test."

"Very good," answered Joseph. "I rejoice to have won your favour without having put myself to great charge thereby."

"Charge or no," answered the manikin, suppressing his anger, "you may at all times count on my zeal from now on, which springs above all from the fact that the gods are with you. I am a religious man, with respect for the voice of the gods, and I esteem a man's virtue according to his good fortune. The favour of the gods brings conviction. Who would be so obstinate as to oppose his own opinion in their face? So stupid and so stubborn Dudu is not; and hence am I become your man to the last gasp."

"I am gratified to hear it," said Joseph, "and congratulate you on your mingled piety and wisdom. On which note I might perhaps take leave, for my affairs call me."

"It is my impression," persisted Dudu, "that our young steward has not understood how to esteem my overtures — which amount to a formal offer — at quite their true worth. Else you would not make to leave me without seeking to understand their extent and the advantages they hold out. For you may trust me and avail yourself of my loyalty and initiative in all your affairs: in the business of the household as well as in reference to your personal happiness. I have thorough knowledge of the ways of the world, on which you may build; versed am I in walking hidden ways, in spying and eavesdropping, carrying messages, and my secrecy is like nothing on earth, so subtle is it and so inviolable. I hope that your eyes are beginning to open upon the meaning of my offers."

"They were never closed," Joseph assured him. "You have mistaken me quite, to think that I undervalue the advantages of your friendliness."

"Your words reassure me," said the dwarf, "if not quite the tone of your voice. If my ear deceives me not, it expresses a certain reluctance, which in my eyes belongs to past time, and for which there should be no more room between you and me, since for my part I have abandoned it utterly. From you it pains me as an injustice, for you have had as long time as I in which your trust in me might ripen — namely, seven years. Trust for trust. But I see that I must do yet more to take you into my confidence that you may give me yours without reserve. Know then, Osarsiph," he said, and sank his voice to a whisper, "that my resolve to love you and give myself to your service utterly comes not alone from my reverence for the gods. It was the wish and the desire of an earthly person, if one very near the gods, which was as I now confess the decisive motive — " He paused, blinking.

"Who, then?" Joseph could not refrain from asking.

"You ask?" Dudu replied. "Good, then; with my answer I give such proof of my confidence that you must needs return it." He stood on his tiptoes, put his hand over his mouth, and whispered:

"It was the mistress."

"The mistress!" Joseph made answer — far too quickly and far too low, as he bent down. It was true, alas: the dwarf had known what to say to arouse the other's immediate curiosity. Joseph's heart — that heart which Jacob, far off, believed long stilled in death, whereas here it was in Egypt, ticking away and exposed to all the perils of life — that heart stood a moment still, then, as a heart does, throbbed the faster in order to overtake its lost beats.

He stood up erect again at once, and commanded:

"Take your hand from your mouth! Speak low if you must, but take your hollowed hand away!"

He said this that no one might suppose him to have secrets with the dwarf. He was ready to have them, but rebelled against their outward signs.

Dudu obeyed.

"It was Mut, our lady," he asseverated, "the chief and true wife. She summoned me before her to speak of you and addressed me thus: 'Steward' (pardon, but so did she speak, with gracious flattery, whereas I know that you alone are steward since Mont-kaw's death, and occupy the special room of trust, whereas the title was and is mine in but a limited sense), 'Steward,' said she, 'to come back to the youth Osarsiph, about whom we have before now taken counsel together; the moment, so it seems to me, has come for you to lay aside the reserve and dignity which you have practised toward him these past years, some seven years, perhaps, and to lend yourself frankly to his service. For in your heart you have long yearned to do so. I have considered the misgivings which you have now and then expressed before me concerning his precipitate advancement in the house; but I have at length rejected them, on the ground of his obvious virtues. This was the easier because you yourself have gradually lost sight of your objections and finally could no longer conceal your increasing goodwill. It is my wish that you will no longer put this constraint upon yourself, but rather serve him with fervent love and loyal heart, for this indeed is the heart's wish of your mistress. What could be dearer to her than that the best servants of the house be friendly with each other and enter into a bond for its welfare? Such a pact, Dudu, you will make with the young steward; and as the older and more experienced, give him aid and counsel and be his messenger and guide. For it lies near to my heart. He is shrewd, and

in what he does the gods mostly grant success through him. Yet in
some things is his youth a hindrance and a peril. The peril rises from
his youth, that being united with great measure of beauty, the beauty
of his years and growth as well as of his swiftly veiled glance and his
ripe lips — one might climb seven mountains without finding a stripling of such pleasing exterior. What I enjoin upon you is that you
shall protect his person against offensive curiosity, giving him a
troop of bowmen when he goes into the cities, who shall shoot their
arrows to rescue him from the peril of things thrown down upon
him from roofs and walls. But I have said that his youth is also a
hindrance to him; for he is timorous, and I would have you extend
your aid to overcome it and give him confidence. For instance, all
too seldom or almost never does he come before me, the mistress, to
speak concerning the affairs of the house. I am loth to miss it, being
not like unto Petepre, my husband, who on principle takes nothing
on himself. For I as mistress take lively interest in the economy of
the household and have ever regretted that the departed Mont-kaw —
from too great ambition or exaggerated respect, I know not which —
excluded me from those affairs. I have promised myself some improvement from the change, and appoint you, my friend, to ply between me and our young steward, subtly, as you know how, and to
teach him how timidity may be overcome; that he may appear often
before me for converse about this and that. This indeed you may
regard as the chief aim of the pact you make with him even as I, Mut-
em-enet, make one with you. For thus I bind you in allegiance to him
and in obedience to a bond between him, yourself, and me.' These,"
concluded Dudu, "were my mistress's words; in repeating which I
give you intimate confidence, that you may return it. For now you
can better understand the meaning of my offers, whereby I give myself blindly to your service, and am prepared to walk all sorts of secret
ways for the sake of our threefold bond."

"Very good," Joseph answered. He forced himself to be calm and
his voice was low. "I have listened to you, overseer of the wardrobe,
out of respect for our mistress, whose words spoke from your mouth,
as you would have me believe; also in respect of yourself, the man of
the world — for it would be unfitting for me to meet you with a
coolness and polish inferior to your own. For I have not much faith
in your recent conversion, taking it to be worldly wisdom instead,
sharp practice, if I may speak frankly without offence. Nor is my
love for you without limits; indeed, like my feeling for your person,
it hath rather the opposite quality. But I seek to show you that I am
not less man of the world than you, and equally master of my feelings;
for I am capable quite in their despite of cold-blooded wisdom. A
man like me cannot always walk the straightest path. He must not
fear to take a crooked one. And such a man can use not only the

honest for friends; he needs eavesdroppers and clever rogues and must prize their services. Therefore, Master Dudu, I will not reject your offer, but readily accept your service and duty. There shall be no talk of a bond between us — such a vow would not be to my taste, even were the mistress included in it. But what gossip you hear in house or city, that bring always to me and I will seek to make it avail."

"If you but trust me," responded the little man, "I care not whether you think me worldly or sincere. I need no love from the world, having it ever in my home from Djeset, my wife, and from the sons I have begotten, Esesi and Ebebi. But my glorious mistress has set her heart upon this bond between you and me; and that I shall be aid and counsel to your youth, messenger and guide; to this I cling, for my own part, and shall be satisfied if you will trust me, whether with your heart or your understanding matters not to me. Only forget not what I whispered you, of the mistress's desire to be initiated into the affairs of the household, more intimately than in the time of Montkaw; and that she will often have speech with you. Have you perhaps a message to give me for her in return?"

"Nothing that I can think of," replied Joseph. "Let it content you that you have delivered hers, and leave it to me to consider it."

"As you will," said the dwarf. "But I can add still a little. For the mistress let fall that she would walk today at sunset in the garden for the comfort of her lovely spirit and mount the slope into the secluded garden-house, there to commune with her thoughts. If there were someone who would have speech with her to make a report or prefer a request he should take advantage of the rare opportunity to present himself for audience."

This was simply a lie on Dudu's part. The mistress had said nothing of the sort. But if Joseph fell into the snare he would lure her to the summerhouse by turning the tale the other way about, thus contriving a rendezvous between them. And though Joseph did not rise to his hint, yet the dwarf did not relinquish his purpose.

Joseph, indeed, made no sign of intending to avail himself of the suggestion he had heard, simply turning his back on the guardian of the wardrobe without more ado. His heart beat high, though not so quickly as it had before, having by now caught up with itself; and it would be idle to deny that he was glad almost to rapture at what he had heard about the mistress, as likewise at the opportunity which awaited him at the setting of the sun. We may guess that an insistent inner voice warned him not to go; nor need it surprise us that presently an outward whisper, like a cricket's chirp, reinforced the inward one. For when after leaving Dudu he had made for the house to consider these matters in the special room of trust, it was Sa'ankh-

Wen-nofer-and-so-on, it was Shepses-Bes in his wrinkled finery, who slipped in with him and murmured:

"Osarsiph, do not that which the wicked advise you, do it not now or ever."

"What, little friend, are you there?" he asked, rather confused. And asked him in what crack or cranny he had crept that he could know what Dudu said.

"In none at all," responded the little man. "But my dwarf eyes are sharp, and from afar I saw you bend down to him, after you had chidden him for the hand over his mouth. Then knew I whose name he had whispered."

"A wizard you are, indeed!" answered Joseph. "And are now slipped hither to congratulate me on the turn affairs have taken; for here was my enemy, who has so long complained of me to the mistress, and she sends him to me with the plain meaning that I have at last found favour in her eyes and she covets to speak with me about the affairs of the household! Confess now that it is a marvellous turn, and rejoice with me that I may if I choose have audience with her to-day in the garden-house at sunset — for I myself rejoice beyond all words. Mind, I do not say that I purpose to go — I am far from having made up my mind. But that I may go, that the choice rests with me to go or stay, that rejoices me unspeakably, and you too, thumbling, shall wish me joy!"

"Ah, Osarsiph," sighed the little man, "if you had in mind not to go your joy would be less; that, to my little wisdom, is a sign that you will go. Shall the dwarf rejoice with you over that?"

"Small wisdom is it, as you say," scolded Joseph; "and in this case your piping and plaining serve me not at all. Can you not grant it to a son of man to be glad of his free choice, in such a matter that he had no thought ever to be able to rejoice at it? Only think back with me to the time, the day and the hour, when the man who is now departed bought me for the master, and the bargaining was done by the scribe Khamat with my father of the well, the old man from Midian, and we stood thereafter alone in the courtyard: I, you and your ape, do you recall? Then did you whisper to me as I stood there dazed and said: 'Fling yourself on your face!' Then my unknown mistress rode past, lifted high and proud on the shoulders of rubber-eaters, the mistress of the house into which I was sold, and her lily-white arm hung down from the chair, as I saw from between my fingers. She looked upon me with contemptuous seeing, as though I were not a man but a thing, while I, a boy, gazed up as though at a goddess, blinded with awe. But God brought it about by His will that I grew up in this house and flourished as by a spring, for these seven years long, till I fell heir to the office of the ailing man and came to the headship. So the Lord my God glorified Himself in me. There was but one cloud in the mirror of my fortune, and in one part dross mingled with its bronze: the mistress was against me, with Beknechons, the priest of Amun, and Dudu, the married dwarf. I must rejoice when she frowned upon me, for black looks are better than none. But now, lo: is it not the consummation of my good fortune, is it not now for the first time free from dross, that her brow has lightened and she sends me word of her relenting and even of her desire for speech with me in special audience? Who could have dreamed, at the hour when you whispered to the boy: 'Fling yourself on your face!' that one day it would lie with him to choose or not to choose to have speech with her? Then take it not amiss of me, my friend, if I rejoice!"

"Ah, Osarsiph, be glad, but after you have resolved not to see her, not before!"

"Begin not each sentence with 'Ah' and 'Alas,' little wizened one, instead of with 'Oh,' as in wonder and rejoicing! Why do you croak like a raven and spin gloomy fancies? I told you that I was more inclined not to go to the summerhouse. But even so, it must be thought of. For after all it is the mistress who has sent; or rather one might say that in the first place it is she, and that makes it important. In my place a man must keep his head and be cool and worldly. Such a man must be mindful of his advantage and not fear to take opportunity by the forelock that he may strengthen himself. Consider how much a bond with the mistress and a nearness to her person can advance me and be a prop to me in the house; but on top of that, tell me, who am I to pass judgment on the mistress's wish and command? True, I am set over the house, but I belong to the house, I am the bought servant of it. Whereas she is the chief and true wife, lady of the house, and I owe to her obedience. There could be nobody, among the living or the dead, to blame me were I to fulfil her bidding in blind loyalty; even the dead and living might blame me did I otherwise. For plainly I had risen too early to command, had I not first learned to obey. So I begin to ask myself whether you were not right to chide me for my joy in the free choice. For perhaps I have no such, and no other course is left me but to go."

"Ah, Osarsiph," came the whispering little voice, "how can I answer aught but 'Ah' and 'Alas' when I hear you speak and utter such quibbling with your tongue! You were good, you were lovely and wise, when you came to us, O seventh gift! And I spoke for you and your purchase against the evil old gossip because with my unclouded little wisdom I saw at first glance the power and the blessing. Beautiful you are still, and good at heart; but of the other — better be silent. Is it not a calamity to hear you, thinking on past times? Wise you were till now, unerring in shrewdness, your thoughts went like the

arrow, your head was blithely erect as you walked in the service of
your mind. Then came the fiery bull, which I fear more than aught
else in the world, and breathed one breath in your face. And you are
grown foolish that God may pity you, and like an ass which one
drives round the town with cudgellings, for your thoughts go on all
fours, while your tongue hangs out, serviceable no longer to your
mind, but to your evil proneness. Ah, alas, and woe to your ignominy! For all that you say is but beating the air, it is but crooked conclusions and subterfuge, betraying the bondage of your mind to the
yearning to go on all fours! Even would you pull the wool over the
eyes of your little faithful here, saying that he was right to rebuke
you for your joy in free choice, because in fact you have none — as
though it is not just therein you should find your true joy! What a
shame is that, what a boundless shame and mortification!" Here the
dwarf put his two little hands before his wrinkled face and began to
weep.

"Nay, nay, little gnomeling!" said Joseph in distress. "Take heart,
weep no more! It goes to my heart to see you so low — and all because
of some false conclusions that have crept into our talk. You may well
find it an easy thing to draw the right ones and guide yourself by
the spirit; yet you must not suffer such pathetic distress over one
whose mind is somewhat clouded by the proneness to err."

"Now you are good again," said the little man, still sobbing. He
dried his eyes on his crumpled batiste skirt. "You pity my tears. Alas,
that you have no pity on yourself, to hold upright your reason with
all your strength that it fail you not when you have most need! Lo,
from the beginning have I seen it come, when you would not understand and pretended ignorance when I whispered. I saw that much
worse could unfold itself from the complaints of that evil man when
he complained before Mut, the mistress — something much more dangerous than that danger. For thinking to do you ill, he did more ill
than he knew, opening her eyes to you, you good and lovely one!
And you, will you now close your own eyes before the opening pit,
that is deeper far than the other of your tale, whereinto you were
thrown after your envious brethren had snatched your wreath and
veil? No Ishmaelite from Midian will there be to draw you up from
this pit which the bad man digged when he opened the eyes of the
mistress to your beauty! Now she, the exalted one, makes eyes at you,
and you return her glances, and they are the terrible glances of the
fiery bull that lays waste the fields, and after them comes naught but
ashes and darkness!"

"Fearful are you by nature, dear manling," Joseph answered
him, "and you torture your small soul with dwarfish imaginings.
But tell me what it is you see in your weakness only because our
lady has let her eyes rest upon me. When I was a little lad I thought

that everyone who saw me must love me more than himself — so foolish was I. It brought me to the pit, but I have climbed out of the pit and overcome my folly. Yet that folly, methinks, has descended upon you and whispers fears. As yet the mistress has looked but sternly upon me, nor I upon her save with reverence. If she will speak with me and hear reports upon the business of the house, shall I interpret that according to your conceit of me? Not flattering is that conceit, for it assumes that I am lost, were the mistress but to hold out her little finger to me. I myself have no such fear, nor think to come again so swiftly to the pit. If now I would challenge your fiery bull, do you think I am so ill armed and cannot take him by the horns? Verily you imagine me to be of great frailty! Comfort yourself; go to the house of women and cheer them with dance and song. It is most likely I shall not present myself for audience in the little house. But I must ponder these things alone, and as a grown man come to some compromise with my thoughts: how to reconcile one wisdom with the other, neither offending the mistress nor yet being disloyal to either the living or the dead or . . . But that you cannot understand; for to you children here below, the third is contained in the second. Your dead are gods, and your gods are dead, and you know not what that is: the living God."

Thus Joseph, condescendingly, to the wizened little man. Yet knew he not that he, Joseph, was dead and deified, Osarsiph, in other words? It was to ponder all these things that he would be alone; alone too with a thought inevitably bound up with them: the thought of the god in deathly readiness, rigidly awaiting the vulture-woman.

IN THE TOILS

How narrow is the span when we look back upon our own lives; how vast when we contemplate the world's abysmal past! And yet we lose ourselves as easily, as dreamily, in the one as in the other; by virtue of our perception of a unity between the two. As little in the small sphere as in the large can we go back to the time of our birth and the beginning of our days, to say nothing of further back. It lies in darkness before the beginnings of the dawn of consciousness or memory. But with our earliest mental life, when we first enter — as primitive man once entered — into civilization, giving and receiving our first little contributions, we are aware of a sympathy, we feel ourselves recognize that abiding unity; with pleased surprise we acclaim our kinship with the larger whole. And the content of the kinship is always the same: it is the idea of a catastrophe, the invasion of destructive and wanton forces into an ordered scheme and a life bent upon self-control and a happiness conditioned by it. The saga of peace wrung from conflict and seemingly assured; of life laugh-

ingly sweeping away the structure of art; of mastery and overpowering, and the coming of the stranger god — all that was there from the
beginning, as it was in the middle. And in a late age which is aware of
its affinity with human beings, we find ourselves still united with
them in that bond of sympathy.

For Mut-em-enet, Potiphar's wife, the sweet singer, that far-away
form, which the epic spirit grants us to see as though close at hand
— she too was one afflicted and overpowered, a bacchantic sacrifice
to the stranger god, the careful structure of her life no less than
wrecked by the nether powers which in her ignorance she had
thought to mock, whereas they alone it was who made mock of all
her compensations and super-compensations. Old Huia might well
have told her not to be a goose — not a bird of the black water-logged
depths, whom the swan visiteth and covereth. Not a goose, but a
moon-chaste priestess, yet not the less feminine for that. He himself, old Huia, had dwelt in the marshy, murky brother-sister darkness, yet felt strange and awkward stirrings of conscience and intuitions that new things were come to pass in the world. He had
mutilated his little son to be a courtier of light, sapped his son's
virile powers and made him a human nonentity, and then given him
in the stern bond of marriage to the woman who bore the ancient
name of mother. Now might they see themselves prop up each other's
dignity by dint of tact and mutual consideration! It is undeniable
that human dignity realizes itself in the two sexes, male and female;
so that when one is neither one nor the other, one stands outside
the human pale and whence then can human dignity come? Efforts
to sustain it are worthy of respect, for they deal with the spiritual,
and thus, let us admit in honour, with the pre-eminently human.
But truth demands the hard confession that thought and the spirit
come badly off, in the long run, against nature. How little can the
precepts of civilization avail against the dark, deep, silent knowledge
of the flesh! How little it lets itself be taken in by the spirit! All this
we saw in the early days of our story, in connection with the bewilderment of Rachel. And now Rachel's sister here below, Mut,
once princess of the nome, by virtue of her relation with the sun-
chamberlain was just as remote from the female side of human life
as he was from the male. As a woman, she led a life as hollow, as dis-
honouring to the flesh as did he; nor were her compensations, and
the Amun-honour in which she thought to veil her dim perceptions from herself, any less frail a support, though a support to the
spirit, than those props to the amour-propre of her fat husband
when he posed as a horse-tamer and hippopotamus-hunter and urged
himself on to feats of valour. Joseph had known how to flatter his
master by making these exploits appear as the essence of masculinity;
but actually they were sicklied and forced, and when Petepre went

hunting in the swamps he was always yearning for the peace and quiet of his library — in other words, for the life of the mind, pure and simple and quite unapplied.

However, we are not now thinking of Petepre, but of his Eni, the priestess of Amun, and of the anguishing dilemma of her position between the honour of the spirit and the honour of the flesh. Two dark eyes had done this to her, the eyes of a beloved one who had lived far away and been all too extravagantly loved; her surrender to them was by its nature nothing else than a violent, terrified outburst concerned to save, in the last or almost the last moment, her fleshly honour and her human womanhood — to save, or rather to secure it, though it meant the abandonment and sacrifice of her spiritual and religious honour, of everything in the realm of the idea on which her life was based.

Let us pause here to look at her situation — look at it with the eyes of this woman who thought of nothing else by day and night, in a torture of mounting desire. Was it a genuine dilemma, does that sacrifice always and everywhere dishonour and desecrate? That was the question. Does dedication amount to chastity? Yes, and no. For her state of bridehood involved certain contradictions which cancelled each other out; the veil, the token of the goddess of love, is also the token of its sacrifice, the sign at once of the nun and of the courtesan. The spirit of her time and her temple recognized the consecrated and immaculate, the *kedesha*, who was an "enticer"; that is to say, a street prostitute. Theirs was the veil; these *kadishtu* were immaculate, as is an animal, which precisely because of its immaculateness is destined for a sacrifice to god in the feast. Consecrated? One asks: to whom, and why? If one is consecrated to Ishtar, then chastity is only a phase of the sacrifice, a veil destined to be rent.

Such were Mut's lovelorn thoughts as she wrestled; and if the little dwarf had heard them, he would, in his fear of sex, his remoteness from all such ideas, have wept at the insidiousness of her thoughts, so little serviceable to reason, so prone to go on all fours. It would have been easy for him to weep, knowing, as he did, nothing of human dignity, being but a little dancing dervish of a man. But to Mut, the mistress, it was a matter of the honour of her flesh, and she sought out thoughts by which she might reconcile it with her religious honour. So we owe her consideration and sympathy, however much she rationalized; for thoughts are seldom present for their own sake only. She had hard work with hers; for her awakening to her womanhood from that sleep of the senses in which she had rested as aristocrat, lady, and priestess was nothing like the traditional one of the daughter of the king summoned by the sight of the majesty of the prince of heaven from the peace of childhood to endure the torment and desire of consuming love. She had not the fatal happiness of loving so exaltedly above her station (which condemns one in the end to accept the extremest pangs of jealousy and even to be turned into a cow); no, her misfortune lay — in her mind — in the fact that she loved so far below it: a nameless slave, a bought chattel and Asiatic house-servant. That was bitterer to her dainty pride than anything we have had so far to tell. It long prevented her from admitting her feelings even to herself, and when she finally did so, there mingled in the bliss which love always brings us an element of humiliation which, rising from the deepest depths of cruelty, can arm desire with its sharpest thorn. The rationalization which she sought to apply to these humbling thoughts centred in the fact that the *kedesha* and temple maiden cannot seek out her own lover either, her caresses being the property of him who throws the price in her lap. But how unavailing the justification, what violence it did to herself in allotting her so passive a rôle! For surely hers was the active, wooing, choosing part — though even so she had not been quite independent, her choice having been guided by Dudu's complaints. But her station and years entitled her to the position of attack and challenge; it could never have been possible that the slave of his own motion and will had lifted up his eyes to her or that she could have been the submissive recipient of his desire. Never! In this affair her pride decisively laid claim to the masculine rôle; and yet in the depths of her being, the rôle did not suit. For however one might try to twist the fact, it remained true that this young servant, consciously and wilfully or not, had been, by virtue of his existence, the awakener of her womanhood from its enchanted sleep, and had therewith made himself the master of his mistress, so that she served him in her thoughts and hung upon his eyes, in panic lest he see that she would be his, yet trembling for fear lest he might requite her incommunicable longings. All in all, it was a humility pervaded by a frightful sweetness. Yet she sought to lessen it, as passion will do. For while not at all actuated by considerations of worth or dignity, it will always seek to seem so, and to justify itself in all possible ways for its choice. Thus she contrived to raise the boy whose mistress she would be, out of his lowly condition; adducing his bearing, his cleverness, his position in the house. She even, taking a leaf from Dudu's book, called in religion to justify her "proneness to all fours," as the mock-vizier would have said: in other words, she brought into the field Atum-Re of On, the complaisant god, friendly to foreigners, against stern old Amun, her former lord, and enlisted the court, the royal power itself, in support of her love. Which for her subtilizing conscience had the further advantage that she came closer in spirit to her husband, Pharaoh's friend, and won him in a certain sense as a party to her own burning wish to betray him!

Thus Mut-em-enet, twisting and turning in the toils of her own desire — as in the coils of a serpent sent by a god to embrace and strangle her — so that she gasped for breath. And she wrestled alone; she had no one to talk to, save Dudu, with whom she never got beyond veiled allusion — at least not in the beginning, for later she lost all restraint and made her whole entourage partakers of her frenzy. Remember further that the urge of her blood had lighted upon a zealot, one devoted to higher purposes, wearing the rue in token of his loyalty and proud devotion; in other words, one set apart, who might not and would not yield to her allure. Remember, finally, that her torture lasted three years, from the seventh to the tenth of Joseph's sojourn in Potiphar's house, and then was not satisfied, but only slain. And remembering all this, shall we not concede that the lot of Potiphar's wife, lewd wanton as she was in the popular legend, was a tragic one? Shall we not bestow upon her at least the pity born of the perception that the instruments of such a trial bear their punishment in themselves and have it in fuller measure than they deserve, considering the inevitability of their function?

THE FIRST YEAR

THREE years: in the first she tried to conceal her love from him; in the second she let him see it; in the third she offered it to him.

Three years: and she must or might see him every day, for they lived as members of one family, and there was daily fuel for her folly, great encouragement and also great torment. For with love we cannot speak of must and may as Joseph had spoken to Mont-kaw about sleep, saying soothingly not that he must sleep but that he might. For in love there is a painful, involved, and bewildering struggle; it splits the soul with half-wishing, half-unwishing, so that the lover curses the must-see with as good will as he would blissfully welcome the may-see. And the more violent his anguish from the last time of seeing, the more passionately he strives for the next opportunity to aggravate his disease. This most of all when the patient had ground to rejoice that the pain was growing less! For it can actually happen that a meeting can tarnish the brilliance of the desired object and bring about a certain disappointment, cooling, and detachment. That should be the more welcome to the lover since with the diminishing of his own infatuation, thanks to desire, he has a growing power of self-conquest and of inflicting on another what he suffers himself. Such would be the result were one lord and master of one's passion instead of its victim; for the chances of winning the other are greatly improved by the cooling of one's own feeling. But the lover will listen to nothing of all this; the advantages of returning sanity, coolness, and boldness — for they are advantages, in pursuit of a goal which is the highest he knows — he reckons as nothing compared with the loss he imagines that he will suffer by the diminution of his feeling. He declines upon a state of desolation and emptiness comparable to that of a drug-taker deprived of his drug, and strains every muscle to regain his former state of infatuation by fresh doses of re-infecting impressions.

Thus it is with must and may in the field of love's folly — which of all follies is the greatest, so that in it one may best study the nature of folly and its effect on its victim. For he, however much he may groan under the lash of his passion, is not only incapable of wishing to be free, he is even incapable of wanting to wish it. He probably knows that if he did not see the object of his passion for a certain time — quite an absurdly short time, perhaps — he would be free. But it is just forgetting of which he is more afraid than of anything else; indeed, every pain at parting rests upon a secret dread of the inevitable forgetting. When it has happened, one can grieve no more — and therefore one grieves in advance. No one saw Mut-em-enet's face when she hid it against the pillar, after wrestling in vain with Petepre, her husband, for the sending away of Joseph. But there is much, there is everything, in favour of the guess that it was radiant with joy, because now she must see every day him who had awaked her love, and so would not be able to forget him.

It must have been all-important, for her especially, and particularly strong, her dread of the parting and the inevitably ensuing forgetting, the dying down of her passion. For women of her age, when their blood has been late stirred, and perhaps without extraordinary provocation never would have been stirred, yield themselves with more than common abandon to their feelings, which are their first and may be their last, and would rather die than exchange this new life of blissful anguish for the old peace of mind which they now find so empty. It was then the more meritorious in Mut that in all seriousness and reasonableness she did what she could to persuade her indolent husband to withdraw from her eyes the object of her longing. If his nature could have brought him to grant her the favour, she would have sacrificed her feelings. But to move and arouse him was simply not possible, he being a proper captain of the guard; and the real truth is that Eni had secretly known that and counted on it; in other words, her struggle with her husband had been a device by which his refusal should set her free for her passion and her fate.

For free she might in fact consider herself after the evening in the hall at sunset. If she bridled her passions for such a long time afterwards the reason was less duty than pride. Her carriage was lofty indeed, and only the very keenest eye could have seen any trace of weakness or tenderness shining through, when at sunset on the day of the three conversations she went to meet Joseph in the garden, at

the foot of the little summerhouse. Dudu had carried out his plan
with the utmost slyness and shrewdness. From Joseph he had returned
to the mistress and told her that the new steward rejoiced in the opportunity of giving account of the business of the household and laid
stress on their meeting for this purpose alone and undisturbed, at
whatever hour and place it pleased the mistress to appoint. He would,
he had said, be visiting the little house in the garden at sunset that
day, to inspect its furnishings and the condition of the frescoes. Dudu
had given this second piece of information independently from the
first, sandwiched in between other matters, delicately leaving it to the
mistress to draw her own conclusions. But his manœuvres had not
quite succeeded, for both parties had contented themselves with half-
measures: Joseph had found a middle way between his two choices
and without mounting up to the summerhouse had merely walked
round its base, as he might or should have done in any case, to inspect
the trees and flower-beds in this part of the garden. Neither had Mut,
the mistress, been minded to climb the mound. But she had seen no
reason why she need be prevented by what the dwarf had happened
to murmur in her ear from carrying out what she remembered to
have intended from the beginning: namely, to linger awhile in the
garden at sunset and watch the beautiful fiery sky as it mirrored itself in the duck-pond. She was attended, as usual, by two of her
maidens.

So then the mistress and the young steward met each other on the
red-sanded path, and their encounter went off something like this:

Joseph, perceiving the group, gave a little "Oh!" of startled respect;
raising his hands he began to move backwards, bowing as he went.
Mut on her side, smiling a little, in vague surprise, shaped a casual
and questioning "Ah?" with her sinuous lips, above which her eyes
looked sternly, even forbiddingly at him. She walked forward as he
retreated a few ceremonial steps, then signed to him by a little downward motion with one hand to await her. She stood still at the same
time, and behind her her dark-skinned maidens did the same, casting
delighted glances with their paint-lengthened eyes as did all the servants when they saw Joseph. In their ears, peeping from among black
woolly fringes, they wore great enamelled disks.

It was not a meeting to afford one of the two any of the disillusion
of which I spoke. The light fell slanting across the garden, bathing
the scene in colour and beauty; it gilded the summerhouse and the
duck-pond with rich tints, turned the sand of the path to a fiery red,
gave lustre to the flowers, lighted the waving foliage of the trees, and
made little mirrors of men's eyes, like the mirror of the pond,
whereon the ducks, both domestic and exotic, looked less like real
ducks than painted and lacquered toys. And the human beings, too,
looked painted and celestial in this light, as though freed from all

taint of inadequacy or care; not only in their gleaming eyes but with their whole figures, they looked like gods and tomb images, painted and beautified by the flattering brightness, so that each must have had joy at sight of the other, as they looked out of their mirror-eyes into each other's illumined faces.

Mut was enraptured to see in all his perfection him whom she knew she loved. For the loving woman is ever on the look-out for justification of her love; palpitatingly sensitive to every flaw in the image of the beloved, triumphantly grateful for every favourable illusion. And if its splendour, which for the sake of her honour she cherishes, is a source of pain, because it belongs to everybody, is apparent to everybody, and must disquiet her with fear of rivals on every hand — yet even the pain is sweet beyond words, so that she presses the sword to her heart, heedless of everything if only its sharpness be not blunted by any clouding or detraction from the image. And then Eni might joyfully conclude from Joseph's beauty that she too was beautiful, and hope that he found her lovely in his turn, even though broad daylight might perhaps betray that she was no longer in her first youthful bloom. She knew that the long open white woollen mantle that she wore, held at the throat over her necklace with an agraffe, for it was near the winter season, gave majesty to her figure; and that her breasts stood out firm and youthful under the batiste of her garment, which fitted her closely and was embroidered with red beads round the hem. Look at it, Osarsiph! It had clasps and ribbons at the shoulders, and how well she knew that it left free her smooth and chiselled arms and revealed the splendid high haunches of her wonderful limbs! Was that not reason enough for her love to hold its head high? It did so. She pridefully behaved as though she could scarcely raise her eyelids and so must throw her head back to look out underneath them. Her face was framed this time in a golden-brown head-cloth, held in place by a broad, loosely fitting band set with precious stones — a face, she trembled to think, no longer the youngest, and very unusual and irregular with its shadowed cheeks, its saddle-nose and deep-cornered mouth. Only the thought of how its ivory paleness must set off her painted jewel-like eyes gave her courage to hope that it would not disadvantage the effect of her arms, legs, and breasts.

Conscious, with mingled pride and misgiving, of her own beauty, she looked at his; at the beauty of Rachel's son in its Egyptian guise. Highly civilized it was, though the costume had an out-of-doors negligence about it. His head, indeed, was very carefully dressed, with a head-cloth of ribbed black silk which suggested a wig and finished in curls at the bottom; beneath it, with artful effectiveness, peeped out a corner of the clean white linen cap. But save this peruke, and the enamelled collar, arm-bands, and flat chain of reed and gold with a scarab, he wore only the knee-length double skirt round his

narrow hips; very elegantly cut indeed, and of a sheer white which
set off charmingly the warm tone of his flesh, turned into bronze by
the slanting light and decked with its jewelled adornments. That
youthful body, so exactly right in its build, strong and delicate at
once, irradiated by the sunset light and freshened by the cool air,
seemed not to belong to the world of the flesh, but to the purer world
of Ptah's thoughts made visible. Especially the shrewd-looking head
seemed to accentuate and embody — for himself as for everyone who
looked at him — a gratifying union of beauty and wisdom.

Very conscious of herself, in pride and misgiving, the wife of Potiphar looked at him, at his dark-skinned features, large by comparison
with her own, and into the friendly night of Rachel's eyes, whose ex-
pressiveness, in the face of the son, was heightened by the masculine
power of understanding. She took in at once his shoulders' golden-
bronze gleam; the slender arm whose muscles rounded pleasantly but
not unduly to hold the walking-staff. And such a wave of maternal
admiration and tenderness swept over her that she gasped; her bosom
was so shaken by her desperate ecstasy that it quaked visibly beneath
its thin white sheath and she could only hope that her proud bearing
would give it the lie in his sight.

Thus, then, and so shaken she must speak to him. And she did so,
with a self-conquest in itself alarming because it cost her such a heroic
effort.

"I see," said she, coolly, "that we walk here very untimely, we idle
women, and disturb the offices of him who is set over the house."

"Set over the house, my mistress, is yourself alone; for you stand
above it as the morning and evening star, which in the land of my
mother they call Ishtar. She too is idle, because divine, and we toil-
ing ones look up for refreshment to her tranquil shining."

She acknowledged his words with a gesture and a smile of understanding. She was both enchanted and pained by the spoilt way in
which he wove into the compliment an allusion to his unknown
mother; and seized by a gnawing jealousy of that mother, who had
borne him and nourished him, guided his steps, stroked his hair out
of his eyes, and kissed him by the right of her love.

"We will go away," said she, "I and my handmaids, who accompany me today as always, that we may not hinder the steward, who
doubtless would make sure before twilight falls that all is well in Petepre's garden, perhaps even up in the little house on the mound."

"Garden and temple," replied Joseph, "concern me but little when
I stand before my mistress."

"But I think they should at all times concern you, and reward you
for your concern more than all the rest," she answered — and already
how frightfully, how wildly sweet it was, simply that they addressed
each other and said "I" and "you," sending out across the two paces

of distance between their bodies the breath which created the bond and union of speech — "for I have heard that they are the beginning and fount of your good fortune. I am told that it was in the little house you first did service as dumb servant; and in the orchard Petepre's eye first fell upon you when you were setting blossoms to ride."

"Thus it was," he laughed. And his laugh cut through her, like a sacrilege. "Just as you say, my lady! I was doing the service of the wind in Petepre's palm trees, at the bidding of the gardener, whom they call — but I know not why, nor may I repeat his name before you, for it is a gross and common name, unsuited to your gracious ear." She looked at his laughing face but did not smile herself. He obviously did not know how little she was minded to jest, nor why; that was well, was inevitable, yet it hurt her. He might interpret her seriousness and lack of smiling response as a remnant of her earlier hostility; but he should perceive it. — "Yes," he said, "I did the wind's work by the gardener's direction, when the friend of Pharaoh came and summoned me to speech, and as I found favour before him, much took its issue from this hour."

"Men lived and died," she said, "that you might prosper."

"The Hidden One does all," he replied, using an inoffensive designation for the Highest. "His name be praised! But truly I often question myself whether He has not advanced me beyond my deserts; and I am anxious for my youth, that such an office is laid upon me and I have become at not much more than twenty the eldest servant of this house. Great lady, I speak openly to you, though you hear me not alone and are not come alone into the garden, but accompanied by maids of honour as befits your rank. They hear me too, and for good or ill hearken while the steward deplores his youth and expresses doubts of his capacity for such high service. But let them hear. For I must put up with their presence, which may not constrain me in my frankness to you, who are the sovereign of my head and my heart, my hands and my feet."

There are after all certain advantages in falling in love beneath one's station. For the station of the beloved makes natural turns of phrase which give us pleasure, though he may think little or nothing about them.

"Of course," she said, with even more majestic poise, "I do not walk alone. I could never do that. But speak without thought of injury to yourself, for the ears of Hedjes and Me'et are as my ears. What would you say?"

"Only this, my lady: my responsibilities are more numerous than my years and it could not have surprised your servant had not alone good will but some ill will and contrariety accompanied my swift rise to the steward's office. I had a father who brought me up in the goodness of his heart, the Osiris Mont-kaw; would that the Hidden

One had let him still live, for much better was my youth, and I might still speak of good fortune, when I was his mouthpiece and his right hand. But he has entered the mysterious gates to the splendid places of the lords of eternity and I am alone with more cares and sorrows than the tale of my years and have no one in the world with whom to take counsel in my unripeness or to share the burden which bows me to the earth. Petepre, my great master — may he live long in good health! — is well known to take naught upon himself save that he eats and drinks and boldly confronts the horse of the Nile. When I come before him with the accounts and books he will say: 'Good, Osarsiph, my friend. All that you have written seems to me right, so far as I can see, and I take it that you have no intent to cheat me, for you know the nature of sin and have understanding for the special offence to me which would lie therein. And therefore I need not trouble myself.' Thus the master, in his greatness, may blessing be upon his head!" He searched her face for a corresponding smile. It was a slight, a very slight treachery which he here committed: an attempt, though in all love and respect, to set up an understanding with the mistress over Petepre's head. He thought he might go so far without offence to the bond. He still thought, for some time yet, that he might without danger go so and so far. But there was no smile of understanding. And he was glad to see that, though faintly ashamed. He went on:

"So am I alone in my youth and unripeness, with my many problems of trade and production, of increase and maintenance. As you saw me approach, my head was full of the cares of the sowing. For the river ebbs and the beautiful feast of mourning approaches, when we dig the earth and bury the god in the darkness and plough for the barley and wheat. Then here is the problem which goes round and round in my head, for it is question of a change: whether we should not do well to sow much more durra corn on Potiphar's fields which are the island in the river, instead of the barley as heretofore; it is the Moorish millet, the negro corn, the white kind, for we have already planted plenty of brown durra for fodder and it satisfies the horses and is good for the cattle. But the question is, would it not be an improvement to change over to the white to even greater extent; that is, planting over much ground to feed the servants, that they may be nourished by good bread instead of with lentils and barley and grow stronger in their service? For the kernel of the white corn is full of meal and has taken up the richness of the earth so that a worker needs less than of the lentils or barley, and we feed them quicker and better. So all that goes round in my head, I cannot tell how, and when I saw you, my lady, approaching through the sunset garden, with your handmaids, then I thought in my soul and spoke to myself as to another: Lo, you are alone in your unripeness with the cares of this house and have no one with whom to share them, for the master takes upon himself none of these things. But now comes the mistress in her beauty, followed by two maids, as is fitting to her rank. Confide, then, in her upon the matter of the new plan and the durra corn; try her opinion, and her good counsel will sustain your unripe youth!"

Eni blushed, partly for joy, partly for embarrassment, for she knew nothing at all about negro corn and was ignorant of the advantage of planting it. She said in some confusion:

"The matter is worthy of discussion, that is clear. I will consider it. Is the soil of the island favourable to this innovation?"

"The mistress," remarked Joseph, "displays her judgment and experience, in that she seizes at once upon the heart of the matter in all things. The soil is fertile enough, yet one must be prepared for failure at first. For the field workers do not yet know how to sow the white corn for food, but only the brown for fodder. What does my mistress think that it may cost till they are instructed in the fine cultivation of the ground with the hoe, as the durra requires, or till they understand that it cannot tolerate weeds like the brown? For if no heed be paid to the roots and shoots, then there is fodder but no nourishment."

"You may well have your difficulties with your work-people in their lack of understanding," said she, and went red and pale with embarrassment, for she knew nothing of these things and had no sensible answer ready, though she had wished that he might speak with her about them. Her conscience smote her with shame before her servant, she felt humiliated; for he spoke of honest practical matters like food for human beings, whereas she knew and desired nothing but that she loved him and longed for him.

"It must be very difficult," she repeated, and controlled her trembling. "But they say that you know well how to deal with the labourers and keep them to their work. So that you will surely succeed in teaching them this new thing as well."

His gaze betrayed that he had not heard what she said, and she was glad, though this was at the same time an offence. He stood there plunged in his practical considerations.

"The straw from the corn is very strong and pliant. It makes good brushes and brooms, so that it is not all loss should the crop fail."

She was silent, painfully conscious that his mind was not on her but on the brooms, which were certainly a more honourable topic than her love. But at least he noticed her silence, for he started and said with that conquering smile:

"Forgive me, my mistress, that our converse is upon such lowly

themes as can but bore you. But it is on account of my single-handed
unripeness in these cares and because I was so tempted to take counsel with you."

"There is naught to forgive," she answered. "The matter is important and the possibility of making brooms lessens the loss. I thought
so at once when you spoke of your new plan and I will also consider
the matter further."

She could not stand still, her feet urged her away from him and
his too dear nearness. All lovers know this conflict: the strife between
seeking and flight. And old as the hills is the practice of speaking honesty with the tongue while the eyes belie it with their seeking, shifting glance, and the mouth wries what it utters. Fear lest he know that
her talk about corn and brooms concealed only one desire: that she
might put her hand on his forehead and kiss him with possessive maternity; the frightful wish that he might know it and not despise her
for it but rather share her wish; these, and her great uncertainty in
all pertaining to food and fodder, which was the subject of their talk,
for her but a lying pretext — though how can one lie when one has
no knowledge of the pretended subject and is condemned to stumble
blindly through it? — all these unnerved and shamed her so that she
went hot and cold and could think only of panic flight.

Her feet twitched to be off, her heart held her still on the spot —
in the immemorial struggle of the love-possessed. She drew her mantle closer about her and spoke in a strangled voice:

"We must continue, steward, another time and in another place.
Evening is falling, I shall soon be shivering with cold." She was in
fact taken with an unmistakable shivering which she thought to explain on this ground. "You have my promise that I will take counsel
of myself as to your new plan; likewise I permit you to come before
me again when you feel yourself too solitary in your youth." She
should not have tried to utter this last word, it stuck in her throat.
For with it he and only he became the subject of their talk; it was a
stronger synonym for the "you" she had used in their lying converse,
the only true thing in it. It was the word of the magic he practised,
the word of her maternal longing, laden with tenderness and pain.
It overcame her quite, it died away in a whisper. "Farewell," she
breathed, and fled, her maidens ahead of her, past Joseph, as he stood
bowing in respectful salutation.

One cannot too much wonder at the weakness of love, nor too long
pause upon its strangeness. For it is not as a stale, everyday affair that
we would consider it, but as the unique, novel, and isolated occasion
which it really was, and is to this very day. A great lady, elegant,
superior, proud, worldly, hitherto self-contained within her personal
and religious arrogance — and now all at once fallen victim to a you,
and a you — from her own point of view — entirely unworthy and

unsuitable. Fallen victim to such weakness, with such abandonment
of her rank, that she was hardly capable of sustaining even the rôle
of mistress and challenger, but knew herself to be already a slave, as
with shaking knees she fled, half-blind, her thoughts flickering in her
head, murmuring broken words, heedless of the maids whom she had
pridefully taken with her to the rendezvous.

"Lost, lost, betrayed, betrayed — I am lost, I betrayed myself to
him, he saw it all, the lie in my eyes, my restless feet, my trembling;
he saw it all, he despised me, it is over, I must die. We must plant more
durra, we must destroy the weeds, the stalks are good for brooms.
What did I answer? I betrayed myself with my stammering, he was
laughing at me, it was frightful, I will kill myself. But was I beautiful,
at least? For if I was, in that light, then it was only half bad and I need
not kill myself. The golden bronze of his shoulders — oh, Amun in
thy chapel! 'Sovereign of my head and heart, my hands and my feet'!
O Osarsiph, speak not thus to me with your mouth, laughing the
while in your heart at my stammering and the weakness of my knees!
I hope — I hope — though all may be lost and I must die after this mischance, yet I must hope and not despair; for I am not utterly unhappy, there was much happiness in that I am your mistress, boy, and
you were obliged to speak to me with such sweetness, saying: 'Sovereign of my head and heart,' though it was only lip-service and
empty homage. But words are strong; one cannot speak them without consequences, they leave traces on the mind; spoken without feeling, they yet speak to the feeling of the speaker; if they are lying
words, yet the magic of them changes one a little in the direction of
their sense, so that they are no longer quite lies. That is very happy
and hopeful; for the soil of your nature, boy, must be turned by your
words, making it a good soil for the sowing of my beauty, if I have
the good fortune to appear before you in a favouring light. For the
subservience of your words, together with my beauty, will bring me
healing and bliss; from it will grow a worshipful feeling only needing encouragement to become desire — for so it is, little boy, worship
encouraged becomes desire. Ah, what a depraved woman am I, with
my wily thoughts! Shame upon my head and heart! Forgive me,
Osarsiph, forgive me, my master and deliverer, O morning and evening star of my life! Why had it today to go all wrong, so that all
seemed lost, because of my restless feet? Yet I will not kill myself,
not yet send for an asp to lay upon my bosom, for there is still much
hope of happiness left. There is tomorrow, and all the other days. He
will remain here, Petepre refused to send him away, to sell him, I
must see him every day, every sun rises with hope and good prospects. 'We must continue, steward, another time. I will take counsel
of myself and permit another meeting.' That was good, it was providing for the next time. Oh, yes, that was sensible, Eni, that in all

your madness you had thought for continuance. He must come again; and if he delay out of shyness, I will send to him Dudu the dwarf to remind him. How shall I make good all that today went wry? I will meet him calmly, and my feet will stand still, and only betray a little, a very little, encouragement to his homage, as it pleases me. Perhaps he will seem less beautiful to me, this very next time, so that my heart shall cool and I can smile and jest with a free mind and inflame him while I suffer not at all? No, ah, no, Osarsiph, it shall not be, those are wily thoughts, and gladly will I suffer for you, my lord and my salvation, for your glory is like that of a new-born bull. . . ."

This rhapsody, of which the maids Hedjes and He'et caught some words, to their vast amazement, was but one of many, of a hundred such which escaped the mistress that year, while she sought to conceal her love from Joseph. The dialogue about the Moorish corn, which preceded it, likewise represents many of the same kind, carried on at various times of day in various places: in the garden, in the fountain court of the house of women, even up in the little summerhouse, whither, however, Eni never came unattended and where Joseph was likewise accompanied by two scribes carrying paper rolls, accounts to be submitted, and other documents. For they always talked of domestic affairs: ploughing, sowing, and reaping, trade and crafts; and the young steward gave accounting to the mistress, instructed her, or sought her advice. Such was the lying content of their talk; and we must realize — if with a somewhat doubtful smile — that Joseph laid stress on it and tried to make something real out of the pretence to give the mistress a serious account of these practical matters and gain her interest in them, even if only on the ground of her interest in himself.

It was a sort of cure. Young Joseph fancied himself in the rôle of pedagogue. His plan was — he thought, at least — to lead the thoughts of his mistress from the personal to the objective; from his eyes to his occupations, thus assuaging, cooling, and neutralizing them. Thus he should profit by the honour, advantage, and great pleasure of her favour and her company, without risking the pit with which the anxious little vizier threatened him. One cannot but see a certain overweeningness in the young steward's pedagogic design, with which he thought to keep in leading-strings the soul of a woman like his mistress, Mut-em-enet. If he wanted to avoid the danger of the pit, he might much better have avoided her, instead of holding educational conferences. That the son of Jacob preferred the latter may well rouse the suspicion that the cure was a hocus-pocus, and his idea of taking their pretended conversations as genuine, itself a pretence and a pretext for thoughts which no longer served pure mind but tended to proneness.

In any case, such was the suspicion, or rather the shrewd little dwarfish conclusion, of Joseph's gnomelike friend. And he made no concealment of his view, almost daily wringing his hands and begging him not to condescend to evasions and beating the air, but to be as wise as he was good and beautiful and flee from the devastating breath of the fiery bull. In vain. For his young friend, the steward, the full-sized man, knew better. And when a man is used, with good reason, to depend upon his own judgment, he is in the greater danger when that reason is clouded.

Dudu, meanwhile, the solid-substantial dwarf, acted his traditional rôle: that of go-between and crafty pander playing on the weakness of both sides; running back and forth between two who would sin, winking and blinking, hinting and pointing, setting himself to one or other, with his mouth on one side, his lips closed, and retailing all sorts of insidious and provocative gossip out of the corner. He played his part without knowledge of his predecessors and successors in it, as though he were its first and only actor — for each of us must consider himself that in every part he plays, as though he had made it all up himself, yet with a sureness and dignity which comes to him, when he plays it, so to speak, in daylight for the first time, not from his supposed invention of the rôle, but on the contrary from the well-grounded consciousness that he is once more presenting something legitimate and traditional, and must perform it, however repellent, to the best of his ability according to the pattern.

But for the present he did not take all the steps which belong to the rôle. I mean, he did not yet tread a path which always branches off from the one running between the two parties concerned and leads to a third — in other words, to Potiphar. To infect that sensitive gentleman with doubt, to trickle suspicion in his ear, on the subject of certain meetings — that would come, but as yet the time seemed not to be ripe. It did not please Dudu that despite all his industry in making the occasions, all the half-invented messages he gave out of the corner of his mouth, at both ends of the road, his mistress and the young steward as good as never met alone, but conversed almost always in the presence of attendants. And he did not like what they talked about, either; Joseph's pedagogic enterprise was not to his taste, it annoyed him, although he saw through it and recognized its rationalized proneness to "all fours" quite as well as did his pure-minded little brother dwarf. All this exchange of practical information seemed to him to delay a desirable development of his project; he was concerned lest the plan meet with success and the thoughts of the mistress be elevated and purified and no longer to the point. Even to her good guardian of the wardrobe she would now talk about such matters as production and trade, the price of oil and wax, supplies and provisioning. It did not escape his sun-perception that she was simply using it all to speak of Joseph, who had taught it to

her. But it vexed him; he bent all his energies, directed all the insinuations at both ends of his route, to a single goal. The young steward,
he would say, was often sad. He was privileged, indeed, to be with
the mistress when his toil was done, or sometimes even in between, to
bathe his soul in her beauty, and might speak with her, but only of
dull domestic concerns, instead of more intimate and animating affairs. And at the other end: the mistress had ordered Dudu to express
to the young steward her regret, her bitterness, that he was so little
aware of the favour he received in his audiences with her, and would
always talk of household matters instead of coming round to himself
and gratifying her curiosity about his person and former life, his
wretched home, his mother, his virgin birth, his descent to the pit, his
resurrection, and so on. Such things were of course more interesting
for a lady like Mut-em-enet than lectures on paper-making and installing looms. If the steward wished to make progress with Mut,
progress toward a goal higher and splendider than any he had yet
reached in the house, he must embolden himself to deal with themes
not quite so heavy.

"Let that be my affair, the goal equally with the means," Joseph
answered crossly. "And you might speak straight out, instead of out
of the corner of your mouth; I do not like it; also I could wish, husband of Djeset, that you yourself kept more to the point. Forget not
that the understanding between us is a worldly one, not an affair of
the heart. Continue to report to me what you hear in house and courtyard. I have not encouraged you to offer friendly advice."

"By the heads of my children!" Dudu swore. "According to my
bond I have but told you what I gathered from the mistress's bitter
sighs because your discourse is so dry. Not Dudu but herself it is that
counsels you to be a little more entertaining."

That was more than half a lie. Actually, he had said to her that if
she wanted to spy out the source of the young steward's magic and
bring him to a fall she must get closer to his person instead of letting
him hide behind his office and his business. To which she had replied:
"It does me good, and somewhat quietens my mind, to hear of his
doings when I do not see him."

A revealing answer, even a touching one. For it betrays the envy of
the loving woman for the fuller life of the man; the jealousy of the
nature wholly occupied with feeling, against the content which plays
so large a part in the life of the beloved and makes her aware of the
painful idleness of her own. The effort made by the woman to share
in the man's life springs from this jealousy, even when his interests
are not of a practical but of an intellectual kind.

It did the mistress good to let Joseph introduce her into the practical side of life, on the ground that he yearned to have his youth instructed by her wisdom. And how little it matters, indeed, what the

talk is about when it is his voice that embodies it, his lips which shape it, his gaze which accompanies it, and his nearness which can inform the driest and coldest matter, as sun and water warm and moisten the earth! Every speech becomes a love-speech — but it could actually not be carried on as such, consisting as it would have to of the words "I" and "thou," and with nothing else at all would come to an end out of sheer monotony. So that other things must inevitably come in. Yet it is clear from Eni's simple reply that she treasured even the subject-matter of their talk; that it nourished her soul through the vacant, hopeless, enervating days when Joseph was away on business up or down the river, and there could be no moment-meeting of the eyes at table nor could or might she feverishly await his visit in the house of women or elsewhere. Then she fed on the things he had told her, exalted them in her heart, and got much good from her knowledge of his errand, in this or that city and its villages, at this market or that fair; for thus at least her woman's misery of utter feeling might be lightened by knowing the content of his masculine days. She could not help boasting her knowledge, before the chattering women in her house, before her maids, and before Dudu when he waited on her.

"The young steward," she would say, "has gone down the river to Nekheb, to the feast of the goddess Nekhbet; with two barges full of doum and balanite fruit, figs and onions, garlic, melons, cucumbers from Aggur, and castor-oil seeds. He will trade them, under the pinions of the goddess, for wood and leather for sandals, which Petepre needs in the workshops. The steward by consultation with me chose a moment for the shipment when vegetables fetch a high price and wood and leather are relatively cheap."

Her voice rang and vibrated as she spoke; Dudu put his hand to his ear to hearken and bethought himself whether the moment would not soon come when he should take his hidden way to Petepre to rouse his suspicions.

How much else we might tell of this year when out of pride and shame Mut was still hiding her love from Joseph, and even from the outer world was still thinking that she hid it? Her own struggle against her feelings, the struggle with herself, carried on for a while with such violence, was over, and for better or worse the feelings had won. Now she only fought to conceal her state before men and before the beloved himself; for in her soul she gave herself more utterly to this new marvel, with the more rapture, one might say with the more simplicity, in that she had been before so ignorant of it, had remained so long the elegant saint and cool worldly moon-nun before she had awakened to feeling. With the deeper revulsion she now looked back upon those times unblest by passion; she could not find herself again in their aridity, she shrank from a return to them with all the strength of her awakened femininity. The intoxicating enhancement which fullness of love can bring to a life like hers is well known — though indescribable. But gratitude for that blessing of desire and torture seeks an object, and finds it only in him from whom it all proceeds or seems to proceed. Is it any wonder, then, that fulfilment in him, increased by gratitude, becomes adoration? We have seen that there were brief, uncertain moments in which Joseph seemed half, or even more than half a god. But were those momentary promptings to be called idolatry? For so much positive rapture, so much finality lies in the word, as the logic of love understands it! That is a logic strange and audacious enough. He who has done this, so it runs, to my life, he who has given to the once dead this burning and freezing, this jubilation and these tears — he must be a god, nothing else is possible. Actually he has done nothing, and everything proceeds from the possessed one herself. But she will not believe it; with prayers of gratitude she creates out of her own rapture the other's godhead. "O paradise of feeling! Thou hast made rich my life — it burgeons!" That was a prayer, a fragment of one of Mut-em-enet's prayers of gratitude addressed to Joseph, as she knelt at the end of her couch, when no one saw her, stammering and weeping. But why, with her life so rich and burgeoning, why was she more than once on the point of sending her Nubian slave for the asp that she might put it to her bosom? Yes, why had she once even given the order and had the viper already at hand, in a little reed basket, and had only at the last moment desisted from her purpose? Well, because she was convinced that she had at their last meeting spoiled everything and not only looked ugly but had by her look and her trembling betrayed to her lover her love — the love of an ugly old woman — after which there was nothing left but to die, so punishing herself and him, and by her death revealing to him the secret for whose betrayal she had sentenced herself.

Oh, muddled, fantastic logic of love! So familiar, it is hardly worth telling; so old, that it was already old in the time of Potiphar's wife, and seems new only to those who, like her, are in the throes of what they believe to be a unique experience. She whispered: "Oh, hearken, music! . . . A ghost of sound breathes blissful on my ear!" That is familiar too: it is the aural delusion of the ecstatic, which visits the love-intoxicated as well as the god-intoxicated and indicates that the two states are related and mingled, the one having much of the divine, the other of the human. Familiar too, so that we need not go into detail, are those fevered nights, taken up with a sequence of brief dreams in which the other is always present and turns coldly and suspiciously away: a succession of meetings with his image, wretched, crushing, yet tirelessly resumed by the slumbrous soul, between constant abrupt wakings; the sufferer starts up, wrestles for breath, makes light: "O God, O God, how can it be? How can such torments exist?" But does she fly from him, the author of such nights? By no means. When morning releases her from agony she sits exhausted on the edge of her bed and sends a whisper thence to where he is: "I thank thee, my joy, my star, my salvation!"

The well-wishing friend can but shake his head at such a reaction to such frightful anguish. He feels confused, even made a fool of, by his pity for her. But when the author and giver of the anguish is thought of as not human but divine, then the reaction is possible and natural; the authorship is shared between the I and the you, so that though it seem bound up with the one, yet at the same time it is lo-calized in the other; consisting in the enlacement and union of an in-ward and an outward, an image and a soul — a marriage, that is, such as has before now had gods as issue, and can thus, without absurdity, be spoken of as divine in its manifestations. A being whom we bless for the tortures he inflicts must be a god, not a man, else we should curse him. A certain logicality cannot be denied. A being upon whom depends all the joy and sorrow of our days — for that is love — be-longs in the ranks of the divine; nothing could be clearer; for this de-pendence is the very essence of an awareness of God. But has any-body ever yet cursed his god? It has been tried, perhaps. But then the curse turned into something else — what it sounded like we have heard.

All this for the consolation of the well-wishing friend, if not per-haps altogether to his satisfaction. But had our Eni not a peculiar justification for making a god out of her beloved? Surely; for thus she got rid of the humiliation otherwise inseparable from her weak-ness for a foreign slave, with which she had struggled so long. A god from above, taking on a slave's shape, only apparent by his undis-guisable beauty and his shoulders' golden bronze: she evoked this idea out of her thought-world, and most happily, for it was the ex-planation and excuse for her state. But the hope that her dream might be fulfilled, that dream of healing when he had opened her eyes and stanched her blood — that hope was nourished by another and more remote vision which likewise she discovered in her own mind. It was the vision of a mortal overshadowed by a god. It may well be that in her groping back to so fantastic a conception lay some of the anguish she felt when her husband made his revelations about Joseph's con-secrated state, and the meaning of the garland that he wore.

THE SECOND YEAR

WITH the coming of the second year something gave way in Mut-em-enet's soul, so that she began to let Joseph see her love. She could no longer help it; she loved him too much. At the same time, and in consequence, she began to confide her state to certain persons in her entourage — not quite to Dudu, for indeed she well knew that his sun-brightened wits had found it out long before; besides, despite the change in her, it would have gone against her pride to admit it to him. They abode by their old understanding, that she was seeking to discover the source of the magic practised by the foreign slave, in order to "bring him to a fall." This was the established phrase, becoming less equivocal from day to day. But there were two women whom she suddenly made her confidantes, she who had never had confidantes before, so that they were not a little exalted by the honour. She confided in each separately: the concubine Mekh-en-Weseht, a lively little person, arrayed in transparent garments, with flowing hair; and an old rubber-eater, Tabubu by name, slave of the toilette-table and the rouge-pots— grey of hair, black of skin, with sagging breasts like leather wineskins. To these two Eni opened her heart in whispers, after her behaviour had been such that they began to wheedle her for its cause. She so sighed, that is, and smiled, and sat plunged in such obvious day-dreaming that the two women, one beside the basin in the court, the other at the toilette-table, implored her to tell them the reason. For a while she still twisted and turned; but then as though overtaken by a seizure she confessed her state to them, murmuring in their ears with drunken tongue, while they shuddered too.

Though they may have guessed before, by putting this and that together, they now held up their hands, or covered their faces, kissed her hands and feet, and cooed over her solemnly and tenderly — almost as though she had told them she was with child. In such wise did these women receive the great news, so important to their sex, that Mut, the mistress, found herself in love. They became very busy with consolation and congratulations, stroking the afflicted one as though her body had become the vessel of some precious and perilous thing; displaying in all sorts of ways their fearful delight with the turn of affairs, the great transformation, the opening of a time of feminine mysteries and joys, sweet deceptions, and the enhancement of the daily round by intrigue. Black Tabubu, who knew all sorts of Negro magic and how to conjure up forbidden gods, was all for practising her arts to subject the youth and bring him to her mistress's feet a blissful prey. But the daughter of Mi-Sakhme, the prince of the nome, rejected the idea with disgust — for the present; displaying a higher stage of civilization than the woman from Kush, and also the decency of her own feelings, however suspect they really were. On the other hand, Mekh, the concubine, thought not of magic, considering such practices beside the mark. Surely the matter, aside from the danger of it, was simple enough.

"Blissful one," said she, "why sigh? Is not the handsome youth the bought slave of this house, although set over it, and your property

from the very first? If you would have him, what have you else to
do but beckon? He cannot but consider it the greatest honour to put
his head and feet to yours for your rejoicing!"

"For the sake of the Hidden One!" whispered Mut, hiding her
face. "Speak not so openly, for you know not what you say, and it
rives my heart!"

She could not chide the simple soul, for she knew, with a certain
envy, that the concubine was pure and free from love and love's
guilty desires and so might speak with good conscience of putting
heads and feet together, however it anguished her mistress to hear
her. Mut went on:

"One can see you were never in such a state, my child. Never have
you been hurried and harried, but might spend your time munching
and prattling with your sisters in Petepre's house of women. Else you
could not say that I have but to lift my eyebrow; you would know
that in my love the state of mistress and slave is cancelled out, even
if not reversed. Rather I hang upon his gloriously pencilled brows, to
see if they are smooth and pleasant, and not bent with amazement and
reproof upon my quaking form. Lo, you are no better than the base
Tabubu, who would have me practise black magic with her, that the
youth might fall victim in the flesh, and in all innocence. For shame,
you ignorant ones, who with your advice thrust a sword into my
heart and turn it round! For you speak as though he were but body,
and not soul and spirit to boot. And over these my beckoning would
have no power, no more than magic; for both can only command the
body and bring me only that — a living corpse. Were he ever mine,
obedient to the beckoning of my brow, then by my love he hath his
freedom, his full freedom, foolish Mekh, and I give up my sovereignty with joy and wear his yoke, enslaved in bliss and torment to
his living soul. This is the truth; and I suffer endlessly that it is not
daylight truth, but that he must by day be ever the slave and under
my orders. For when he calls me sovereign of his head and heart, his
hands and feet, I cannot tell whether he speaks in the phrases of a
slave or perhaps as a living soul. I hope the latter but am ever fearful.
Heed what I say! If his mouth were all, then might I listen in my
need to what you say of beckonings and magic, for the mouth is of
the body. But there is the lovely night of his eyes, speaking freedom
and the soul — ah, how I specially fear that freedom, for that it may
be freedom from the longing which thralls me, the lost one, in its
sullen bondage; perhaps he laughs at me, perhaps not just at me but
at my longing, so that I am shamed and ruined, for my admiration of
his freedom but heightens my longing and weaves my bonds the
tighter. Can you understand that, my Mekh? And more: I must fear
the anger of his eyes, and his rejection of me, because my feeling for
him is a betrayal of Petepre the courtier, his master and mine, to

whom he is loyal, in whom he labours to keep self-esteem erect. While I would tempt him to shame the master, upon my heart! All this I read in his threatening eyes; from which you can see that it has to do with more than his mouth and that he is more than body. For a man who was only body would not be involved in entanglements which condition him as well as our relation to him and make it difficult by weighing it down with all sorts of considerations and consequences, turning it into a question of rules and honour and moral precepts and cutting the wings of our desire so that it limps along the ground! How much, Mekh, by night and day, have I pondered on these things! For a body is free and single, has no reference, and for love's purpose we need be only bodies, swinging free in space and embracing each other without care or consequence, mouth on mouth, with closed eyes. That would be bliss — and yet bliss which I reject. For can I wish that the beloved should be a detached body, a corpse, not a person? That I cannot; for I love not alone his mouth, I love his eyes, them most of all, and thus your counsels are repellent to me, yours and Tabubu's, and I reject them with impatience."

"I cannot understand," said Mekh, the concubine, "your tangled imaginings. I thought, since you love him, the only matter was to put your heads and feet together for your enjoyment."

As though simply this were not after all the final goal of her longings — the longings of Mut-em-enet, the lovely Mutemone! The thought that her feet, so restless in Joseph's presence, might rest nestled close to his — the thought enraptured her and shook her to her very depths. When Mekh-en-Weseht gave it words, without having spent a tithe of thought upon it, compared to Mut, she encouraged the inward yielding, of which her disclosures to her women had been a sign, and she began to betray to the young steward her fallen state, in word and deed.

The deeds were significant, if also childlike in kind and even touching: small attentions from the mistress to the servant, who found it not easy to put the right face upon their true meaning. For instance, one day — and often afterwards — she received him in Asiatic dress, a rich garment, the stuff for which she had bought in the city of the living, at the shop of a bearded Syrian; her slave the dressmaker Heti had made it up. It had much more colour than Egyptian wear; in fashion like two pieces of embroidered woollen stuff, one blue and one red, wound together and bordered with coloured braid. It was extravagant and exotic. The shoulders were covered by the lappets proper to the style, and on top of the embroidered and gaily coloured head-band, called *sanip* in its native land, Eni had thrown the indispensable head-cloth, reaching below her hips. Thus clad, she looked at Joseph, her eyes widened both by the application of galena and by an expectation half-mischievous, half-concerned.

"How strange, yet how splendid you look, my lady!" said he, betraying his understanding by an embarrassed smile.

"Strange?" she asked, smiling too — but her smile, though tender, was forced and confused. "Familiar, I should rather think. Do I not appear as a daughter of your own land in this garb, which for a change I put on today? If indeed it be my garb you have in mind?"

"Familiar," he said, his eyes cast down, "is the garment indeed and the fashion of it; yet a little strange on you."

"Do you not find that it suits me so that I wear it to advantage?" she tremulously challenged him.

He answered guardedly: "The stuff is not woven nor the garment fashioned, were it even of sackcloth, that would not serve your beauty, my sovereign."

"Then it is all the same to you what I wear," she retorted, "and the trouble is lost that I have taken with this costume! For I arrayed myself in it in honour of your visit and as a response to your own custom. For you, a youth from the Retenu, wear Egyptian garb with us, doing honour to our customs. I thought not to be behind you on mine own part, but to meet you in the dress that your mother wore. Thus as in the feast have we exchanged garments; in such an exchange there has been ever something festal, when the men wear the garb of the women and the women the men's and distinctions fall away."

"To which," he responded, "I am bound to add that there is naught familiar to me in such a custom. For it savours rather of light-headedness and a falling away from godly sobriety, and my father would not be glad to see it."

"Then have I erred indeed," said she. "Have you aught to tell me of the house?"

She was profoundly hurt, that he seemed not to understand (though understanding but too well) that she had offered up to him her feelings, in that she, the child of Amun, bride of the mighty one and partisan of his power, honoured the stranger in her dress, because the stranger was her beloved. The offering had been sweet to her, it was bliss to divest herself of her opinions for his sake; so now she was most unhappy, because he had accepted it so lifelessly. Another time she succeeded better — though the symbolic gesture she made was even more self-abnegatory.

In the retreat she liked best, her apartments in the house of women, was a small hall facing the desert. One might give it that name, for the wide-open door with its wooden jambs had its view cut by two columns with simple square capitals under the eaves, standing flat on the threshold, without bases. The room gave on a court with low flat-roofed white buildings on its right. Here were the quarters of the concubines, and adjoining them a higher building, like a pylon, with columns. A clay wall, shoulder-high, ran diagonally behind it, so that one could see nothing beyond save the sky. The little salon was simple and elegant, the ceiling not very high. The shadows of the columns lay black on the floor, the walls and ceiling were a plain lemon-colour with a simple band of decoration in pale tints. There was little in the room save a graceful couch in the background, with cushions on it and skins on the floor in front. Here Mut-em-enet often awaited Joseph.

He would appear in the court, raising the palms of his hands toward the room and the woman on the couch; tucked under his arm were his rolls and accounts. She would sign to him to enter and speak before her. But one day he saw at once that there was a change in the room; saw it by her air of mingled pleasure and embarrassment, as when she had worn the Syrian dress. But he behaved as though he noticed nothing, greeted her with suitable salutations, and began at once to speak of household matters. Then she said:

"Look round you, Osarsiph! What do you see that is new?"

She might well call it new. It was almost incredible. At the back of the room, on a little altar with an embroidered cloth, stood an open shrine with a gilt statuette of Atum-Re!

The Lord of the Horizon was unmistakable; he looked like his written symbol, sitting with his knees drawn up on a little square pedestal, the falcon's head on his shoulders, even the oval sun-disk on top, with the inflated head and the ringed tail of the uræus at front and back. On a tripod beside the altar were incense-pans on standards, with gear for making fire and little pellets of incense in a dish.

Astonishing, almost impossible it was — likewise very touching, a childishly direct expression of the longing of her heart for utterance. The lady Mut, of the house of women of him rich in bulls; sweet singer and sacred dancer before the ram-browed god of the kingdom, friend of his statesmanly chief shiny-head; partisan of his conservative sun-sense — she had erected in her own inner sanctum a shrine to the lord of the wide horizon, on whom Pharaoh's thinkers tried their thoughts, complaisant and friendly brother to foreign and Asiatic sun-lords — to Re-Horakhte-Aton from On in the apex of the Delta. Thus she gave expression to her love, in this language she took refuge, the speech of space and time, which was common to them both, the Egyptian woman and the Hebrew servant. How could he have failed to understand her? He had long since understood, and one must honour his emotions at this moment: what he felt was joy, mingled with alarm and concern. His head drooped.

"I see your devotion, mistress," he said very low. "It somewhat alarms me. For what if Beknechons, the great priest, were to visit you and see what I see?"

"I fear not Beknechons," she answered, her voice thrilling with triumph. "Pharaoh is greater."

"May he live long and prosper!" he murmured mechanically. "But you," he added, still lower, "you belong to the lord of Ipet-Isowet."

"Pharaoh is the son of his body," she responded so quickly that it was plain she was prepared. "I too may serve the god whom he loves, whom he has commanded his wise men to study. Where could there be an older, a greater in all the lands? He is like Amun, and Amun is like him. Amun has named himself with his name, and said: 'Who serves me, serves Re.' So then I too serve Amun when I serve him."

"As you say," he answered softly.

"We will burn incense to him," she said, "before we take up the household affairs."

And she took him by the hand and led him before the image, to the tripod with the implements of the offering.

"Put in frankincense," she commanded (she said *senter neter*," which is Egyptian for "divine odour"), "and light it, if you will be so kind!" But he hesitated.

"It is not good, my lady," he said, "that I should burn incense before an image. It is forbidden among my people."

She looked at him, silently, with such unconcealed pain that he shrank afresh. Her look said: "You will not with me burn incense to him who permits that I love you?"

He thought of On in the Delta, the mild doctrine of its teachers, and the head priest, whose smile had said that whoso sacrificed to Horakhte did so at the same time to his own god in the meaning of the triangle. And he answered to her look:

"Gladly will I be your ministrant, lay the fire and light it and assist your sacrifice."

And he put some of the pellets of terebinth in the pan, struck fire and kindled it, and gave her the stick that she might incense. And while she caused the smoke of the fragrance to rise before Atum's nose, he lifted his hands and served the tolerant god — with reserve, and trusting that what he did might be overlooked. But Eni's breast swelled at the symbolic act, throughout the whole of the dry conversation that followed.

In such ways did she confess her longing. But the poor soul could not much longer refrain from words. For her craving to tell the beloved that which she had struggled so long for her life to conceal grew finally overpowering. And being constantly encouraged by Dudu and incited to lead the conversation away from the impersonal toward more intimate matters, that she might slip up upon his secret and "bring him to a fall," she tore with hot hands at the pretended fabric of their converse — his fig-leaf, as it were — to uncover the naked truth of the thou and I. She could not know what frightful associations were bound up in Joseph's mind with the idea of uncovering: Canaanitish associations warning against the forbidden thing, against every kind of drunken shamelessness, going back to the beginning and the place where nakedness and knowledge had sharply confronted each other, with the resulting distinction between good and evil. Such a distinction was foreign to Mut's traditions; with all her sense of honour and her sense of shame she was quite without understanding of sin, there was no word for it in her vocabulary. Least of all could she connect any such idea with nakedness; or know the shuddering Baal-horror, impersonal to him and transmitted in his blood, which nakedness of speech inspired in the youth. As often as he would draw the garment of objectivity over their talk, so often would she draw it away and make him speak not of household economy but of himself, of his life and earlier life; she asked him about his mother, whom he had already mentioned; learned of her proverbial loveliness; whence it was but a step to his own inheritance of charm and good favour; and she no longer refrained from speaking of it, at first with smiling words, but going on to praise it with more and more passion and fervour.

"Seldom," said she — she was leaning back in her great armchair, which stood at the tail end of a lion's skin, while the beast's jaws yawned at Joseph's feet, and her own lay under stern control, crossed on a footstool — "Seldom," she said, in answer to a remark of his, "does one hear of a person, and have her described, while at the same time her very image stands before one. It is strange, very strange, to see directed upon me while you tell me of them the very eyes of that lovely mother-sheep, and the friendly night of them, whose tears of impatience were kissed away by that man of the west, your father. For not idly did you say how like you were to the departed, so that she lived in you after her death and your father loved you both together, mother and son. You look at me with her eyes, Osarsiph, and describe them as passing lovely. But for long I knew not whence you had them, those eyes which win the hearts of men for you as you go up and down the river and the land. They were, up to now, if I may so express myself, an isolated phenomenon. But it is welcome and agreeable, not to say consoling, to become familiar with the origin and history of a manifestation which speaks to our souls."

We must not be surprised at the painful nature of such talk. Being in love is a sickness; though a healthy one, so to speak, like pregnancy and childbirth — yet like them not without danger. The woman's senses were benumbed; true, she expressed herself like an Egyptian woman of culture, even with literary skill, and in her way reasonably; but her power to distinguish between what is possible and what not was greatly lessened and befogged. What made things worse — or, in a sense, excused them — was that as the mistress she was unused to self-restraint and in the habit of expressing herself as she chose, confident that it was not natural to her to offend against aristocratic good taste. And in the days before her sickness she was right in her self-confidence. But now she neglected to allow for the change in her circumstances, and spoke with her usual freedom, with the result that she said many things most awkward to listen to. There is no doubt that Joseph found them awkward and offensive; not only on her account, but even on his own. He saw his careful pedagogic plan, symbolized by the rolls and accounts under his arm, suffering shipwreck; but even that was less annoying than the lofty lack of self-control in which she persisted in their changed relations — saying, for instance, things to him about his eyes which are only said by a lover to his mistress. The feminine form of the word "master" retains the masculine element even in its changed application: a mistress, physically speaking, is a master in female form; but figuratively it is a woman with the character of a man, thus the conception of a mistress can never lack a certain ambivalence, though the male element predominates. On the other hand, beauty is a passive, feminine quality, in that it awakens longing and calls out active masculine motives of admiration, desire, and courtship in the breast of him who sees her, so that she too is able to respond and show that double nature, though presided over by the female element. Now Joseph, of course, was very much at home in this double realm. He understood it, in the sense that a maiden and a youth united in the person of Ishtar, and that in him who exchanged the veil with her, Tammuz, the shepherd lad, the brother, son, and husband, the same manifestation repeated itself, so that actually all together there were four of them. These memories to be sure were very distant and strange, but Joseph received the same instruction from his own sphere. Israel, the spiritual name of his father, in its extended meaning signified also a virgin, betrothed to the Lord his God, as bride and bridegroom, a man and a woman. And He Himself, the solitary, the jealous One? Was He not at once Father and Mother of the world, with two faces, one a man's, turned toward the daylight, and the other a woman's, looking into the darkness? Yes, was not this two-sidedness of the nature of God the first factor, by which the double nature of Israel's relation to Him, and especially that of Joseph's personal relation, so strongly bridelike and feminine, were first defined?

All that was very right and true. But it will not have escaped the attentive reader that certain changes had taken place in Joseph's consciousness which made it unpleasant to him to be the object of desire and courtship on the part of a mistress who paid him compliments as a man does a maiden. It did not suit him; and the growing masculinity which was the consequence not only of his twenty-five years but also of his official position and his success in bringing under his control and supervision a considerable area of the economic life of Egypt, easily explains why he found it unpleasant. But though the explanation is easy, it is perhaps not quite sufficient; and there were other grounds for his discomfort. This increasing manliness of the boy Joseph was represented in his own mind by a certain image: the awakening of the dead Osiris by the female vulture which hovered over him and received from him the god Horus. Do we need to point out the correspondence between this picture and the actual circumstances — the fact, for instance, that Mut, when she danced before Amun as his bride, wore the vulture head-dress? There can be no doubt: she herself, the smitten one, was the cause of Joseph's increased masculinity, which began to claim the rights of desire and courtship for itself and found it unfitting to be the recipient of masterful compliments.

So now Joseph only looked at her in silence with his belauded eyes and then turned to the roll in his hands, making bold to ask if they might not now, after the personal digression, get back to business. Mut, however, encouraged in her wilfulness by Dudu's hints, affected not to hear, but continued to yield to her craving to make her love known. I am speaking here not of the single scene but of many, very like it, occurring during the second year. Without self-restraint, acting like one possessed, she gave vent to raptures not only about his eyes but about his stature, his voice, his hair; always taking his mother as the point of departure and marvelling at the law of inheritance which permitted advantages that in one generation took on feminine shape, to descend to the next in masculine shape and quality. What should he do? Let us remember that he was kindly and very sweet to her, that he spoke with affection; we can even find him deliberately taking refuge in the defects of that which she admired, hoping to cool her ardour.

"Let be, my lady," he would say. "Pray speak not so. These appearances, to which you have vouchsafed your regard — what of them? They are vanity and vexation of spirit, as one does well to remind oneself — and anyone who tends to smile upon them. For we know but in our weakness would forget of what poor stuff it is, if indeed it may be said to be at all, so pathetically perishable is it! Remember that in a little this hair must fall out, and these teeth too, that now are white. The eyes are but a jelly of water and blood, they will dissolve, as indeed the whole outward show must shrivel and melt away to vileness and nothing. Lo, now, it seems to me proper not to keep these reasonable considerations to myself, but to put them at your service in case you might find them useful."

But she did not believe in them; her condition made them quite unavailable as educational propaganda. Not that she could have been angry with him for his penitential exhortation; she was far too glad that they were not talking about Moorish corn or suchlike painful proprieties, but moved in a region where she felt her feminine competence and her feet need not be seized with a desire to flee.

"How wonderfully you speak, Osarsiph!" she replied, her lips caressing his name. "Yet your words are false and cruel — false because cruel; for even if true and indisputable to the reason, they are not in the least so for the heart and spirit, to which they are naught but sounding brass. For that substance is perishable is no ground for us to feel less admiration for form, but rather more; since we mingle in our feelings an element of pathos quite lacking to those which we have for the durable beauty of bronze or stone. Our regard for living loveliness is far more lively than it is for the images from Ptah's workshop, however beautiful and lasting they may be. And how shall you teach the heart that the stuff of life is of baser quality than its enduring copies? The heart refuses the knowledge, could never learn it. For permanence is dead and only dead things endure. Ptah's busy workmen may set sparks in the eyes of their images, they may seem to look at one; but they see not, you only see them, they cannot respond, as does a you who is likewise an I and of the same nature with yourself. But we are moved by the beauty of our kind. Who could possibly be tempted to lay his hand upon the brow of an image, or to kiss its mouth? See then how much more living is our feeling for the living form, no matter how perishable! Perishable! Why speak to me of the perishable, Osarsiph, warning me in its name? Do we then carry the mummy round the banqueting-hall to put an end to the feast because all must perish? Nay, on the contrary; for on its brow is written: 'Celebrate the joyful day!' "

A good, even a capital answer — in its way; the way, that is, of that madness which makes to serve its ends the wisdom of its saner days. Joseph only sighed and said no more. He had done what he could, and dwelt no further upon the abominations of which all flesh, under the surface, consisted. For he realized that it was of the nature of the madness to ignore all that; the "heart and spirit" would simply not hear of it. He had other tasks than convincing this woman that life was either illusion as images were, or the beauty of the perishable children of men; and that truth, wherein life and beauty are a solid and imperishable unity, he belongs to a different order of things, upon which one would do well to direct one's thoughts. For instance, he had great trouble in warding off the presents which Eni nowadays wanted to shower upon him. She did so out of a primitive impulse, always present in those who love; rooted in a sense of dependence upon the being whom they have made a god, and the need of bringing him offerings, of adorning, glorifying, and bribing him. But still more: for the gift serves also the purpose of attaching and pre-empting the recipient, of staking him out, as it were, and marking him with a prior claim. If you wear my gift, you are mine. The most preferred gift is the ring; who gives it knows very well what he wants, and who receives it must be aware of its meaning, for every ring is the visible link of an invisible chain. Thus Eni, ostensibly in gratitude for his services in initiating her into the household affairs, gave him — with a self-conscious air — a very costly ring, with a carved scarab; likewise, in the course of time, other valuable ornaments, such as gold bracelets and collars set with precious stones. She even gave him feast-day garments of great elegance. Or, rather, she wanted to give him all these things and kept pressing them upon him, in artless words. But after he had respectfully received one or two, he refused the rest, at first gently and pleadingly, then more and more brusquely. And it was these gifts which showed him his situation, so that he recognized it for what it was.

For instance one day, when he rejected the present of a feast-day garment, saying curtly: "My garment and my shirt content me," he had clearly recognized what was involved, and unconsciously replied in the words of Gilgamesh when Ishtar made assault on his beauty and said: "Come then, Gilgamesh, thou shalt mate with me and give me thy fruit!" and promised many splendid presents in return for his compliance. Such a recognition can have its soothing as well as its disturbing side. A man says to himself: "There it is again!" — with a sense of the solid ground, the shelter afforded by the myth, the reality, or even better, the truth, of what is happening — all of which reassures him. But at the same time he is startled to find himself playing a part in the feast and representing such and such a myth as is then being made present — he feels as though he were in a dream. "Yes, yes," thought Joseph, as he looked at poor Mut. "Verily thou art the abandoned daughter of Anu, though thou knowest it not. I might chide thee for it, reproaching thee with thy many lovers, whom thou smotest with thy love and turned them into a bat, a brightly coloured bird, a savage dog, so that his own shepherds hunted him, the chief shepherd of the flocks, and the dogs tore his skin. 'To me also would it happen' — as my part makes me say. Why did Gilgamesh say that, insulting thee, so thou didst run to Anu in thy rage and made him send the fire-breathing bull of heaven to chastise the disobedient? I know why now, for in him I see myself, as through myself I understand him. He spoke in displeasure of thy masterful homage, and turned maid before thee, girding himself with chastity against thy wooing and thy presents, O Ishtar in the beard!"

OF JOSEPH'S CHASTITY

THUS Joseph, the reader of tablets, assimilated his thoughts to those of him who went before him in the pattern. And in that he did so he

gives me the cue for an explanation which is at the same time a sum-
ming up, and which I am convinced is here due to the fine spirit of
scientific inquiry. The cue is "chastity." The theme has for thousands of years been associated with the figure of Joseph, it supplies
the classical epithet inseparable from his name. "The chaste Joseph,"
we say; or even, giving it a general and symbolic application, we say
"a chaste Joseph." That is the pretty, prudish phrase in which his
memory lives in an age separated from his own by so many abysses
of time; and I shall not feel that I have made a true and reliable re-
construction of his story unless, at the appropriate time, I gather together the scattered threads, the tangled and varicoloured strands of
that much-talked-of chastity and make them as comprehensible as
possible to the reader who out of natural sympathy for Mut-em-
enet's anguish may incline to be angry at Joseph's resistance.

It goes without saying that there can be no chastity where there is
no capacity — honorary captains and mutilated sun-chamberlains, for
instance, are not chaste. We set out with the premise that Joseph was
a whole and virile man. Indeed, we know that in later years he married, under the protection of royalty, and had as issue two sons,
Ephraim and Manasseh, who will come into the story later on. So
that his chastity was not permanent throughout his life, but only for
the term of his youth, with which the conception was apparently
bound up. It is plain that he kept his virginity (the word may perhaps
be applied to young men as well as to maidens) only so long as he
associated with its surrender the idea of prohibition, temptation, and
fall. Later, when, so to speak, it was of no importance, he gave it up
without a thought. So the classical epithet fits him only for a certain
period of his life.

We must not make the mistake of thinking that his youthful chastity was that of some simple country bumpkin, whose awkwardness
is at fault though his temper may be as ardent as you like. Jacob's
darling was no blunderer in affairs of the heart — such an idea is inconsistent with the picture we first saw of him, saw, indeed, with the
father's anxious eyes: the seventeen-year-old youth by the well, coquetting with the moon and matching her beauty with his own. His
famous chastity was so far from being due to inexperience that it
was closer to the opposite: resting rather upon a feeling that the mutual relations between him and all the world were permeated with
the spirit of love; he was in love with everything, with a love deserving of the adjective universal, because it did not stop at the earthly
but was present as a pervasive atmosphere, as an inference, a subtle
significance and unconscious background to every relation in life,
even the holiest and most awe-inspiring. From this feeling his chastity proceeded.

Earlier in my narrative I have discussed the phenomenon of the lively jealousy of God, as displayed in the unequivocally violent persecutions with which the one-time demon of the desert, even in a much further advanced stage of his relation with the spirit of man, visited the objects of idolatry or unbridled excess of feeling. It was this which poor Rachel had experienced. And I said then that Joseph, her son, would better understand this attitude of God and be more pliable in coming to terms with it than Jacob, his over-emotional begetter. Joseph's chastity, then, was above all an expression of this understanding and compliant spirit. He knew, of course, that his sufferings and death — with whatever large designs they might be connected — were a punishment for Jacob's pride, which had imitated, in a way not to be borne, the deity's majestic exercise of the power of selection. They were a manifestation of jealousy, directed against the poor old man. In this sense Joseph's misfortunes had to do only with the father, and were the continuation of Rachel's, since Jacob, in simply transferring his affection to her son, had never ceased to love her too much. But jealousy can have a twofold reference. One may be jealous of an object because another person, whose whole love one claims, loves it too; or one may strive for the object out of love for itself which cannot brook a rival. There is a third possibility: the combination of both these other two to make up the complete conception. Joseph was not fundamentally wrong when he assumed the third case. In his view, he had been ravished and snatched away, not only and not even chiefly for the chastisement of Jacob — or rather for this chastisement, indeed, but on the ground that he himself was the object of an overwhelming exercise of the power of selection, of a majestic covetousness and jealous pre-emption. Jacob's own settled paternalism had not yet arrived at the height of such complicated craftiness; he could not understand, though his anxiety might make him sometimes suspect it. I know that our modern sense too may be confused and offended by ideas like these, by such an emphasis on the relations between creator and creature, as foreign to us as would be Jacob's settled paternalism. Yet they have their place in time and evolution; there is no doubt, psychologically speaking, that more than one pregnant dialogue, handed down by tradition, taking place in a cloud between the Unseeable (whatever name He bore) and His disciple and favourite, was characterized by an abnormal capriciousness. Thus Joseph's view of things is at bottom justifiable; its probability rests upon his own personal worth, which I would not wish to dispute.

"Yea, I keep myself clean." Little Benjamin had once heard the words from the lips of his admired brother, in the grove of Adonis. He was speaking of keeping his face clean of a beard and thus enhancing the peculiar beauty of his seventeen years; but also of his relation to the outer world, which had been, and still remained, abstemious, though as remote as possible from awkward inexperience. His restraint was nothing less than caution, an inspired shrewdness, a religious circumspection; and the experience of frightful violation, the tearing of wreath and robe, must have strengthened it mightily. We must suppose that it was associated with a certain haughtiness of spirit which did away with the bleakness of renunciation. There can be no talk here of painful mortification of the flesh, in whose haggard image our modern world almost inevitably clothes the idea of chastity. Yet even the modern world might have to concede the possible existence of another kind: a blithe, even supercilious chastity. Joseph decided for this, first by virtue of his clear and bold mentality; but his choice was made easier, where for others it would have entailed cruel hardship, because of the pleasure he took in the pious conceit of his brideship with God. Mut the mistress, in talk with the concubine Mekh-en-Weseht, had let fall a complaint about the mockery she read in the young steward's eyes. It was, she thought, a jeering at the cruel bondage of desire, so shameful to him who feels it. The observation was a shrewd one; for certainly of the three animals which according to Joseph kept guard in the orchard of the little fowler — shame, guilt, and mocking laughter — the last was the most his familiar. Yet not in the sense that he suffered from it, in the meaning of the legend. It was he himself who indulged in the mocking laughter, and nothing else could be seen in his eyes when the wanton women peered after him from the house-tops. Such an attitude toward the sphere of sexual infatuation does doubtless exist; it is produced by the consciousness of a higher bond, to which one is chosen. Some may see in it an arrogant contempt of human claims and find that it is culpable to look at passion in a comic light. To these let me say that we are approaching a time in our tale when Joseph laughed no more; and the second catastrophe in his life, his second descent to the grave, was brought on him by just that power to which in his youthful pride he had thought to deny tribute.

Here, then, was the first reason why Joseph denied himself to the desire of Potiphar's wife: he was betrothed to God, he practised a shrewd foresight, he took account of the peculiar pain which faithlessness inflicts on the solitary. And his second reason was closely allied to his first, being its mirror, being actually its earthly and social form: it was loyalty to the letter of the pact made with the departed Mont-kaw: loyalty to his difficult master, the highest in his sphere.

This juggling with ideas of the absolutely Highest compared with him only relatively and locally so, as it went on in the head of the descendant of Abraham, must strike a modern sense as absurd and even glaring. For all that, we must realize and accept it if we wish to understand how it looked inside that mind, so early and yet so modern, which thought its thoughts with as much inevitability, compo-

sure, and reasonableness as we do ours. Joseph's fantasy actually did
no less than see, in the obese aristocratic person of Mut's honorary
husband the courtier of the sun, and in his melancholy egotism, the
earthly counterpart and fleshly reproduction of the wifeless and childless, lonely and jealous God of his fathers, with whom he was bent
on keeping loving human faith. He made a fantasy-parallel, which
yet was not without some trace of speculation on the practical side.
Add to that the solemn vow he had made to Mont-kaw on his death-
bed, to sustain the master's sensitive dignity to the best of his powers and protect it from harm — and we shall better understand that
the now scarcely concealed desires of poor Mut must have seemed to
him like a devouring temptation to experience the knowledge of
good and evil and to repeat the folly of Adam. That was the second
reason.

For the third, it is enough to say that his aroused masculinity objected to being degraded into the feminine and passive by the wooing
of a mistress who behaved like a man; he would be the arrow, not
the goal of desire. That is understandable. — And the fourth follows
quite naturally, for it also had to do with pride, but spiritual pride.

Joseph shuddered when he thought of that which Mut, the Egyptian woman, embodied to him. A proud tradition of racial purity
warned him not to mingle his blood with hers. She was the ancient-
ness of this land into which he had been sold; the enduringness, the
unchanging, unpromising desolation which stared out into a future
savage and dead and void of expectation, yet seemed as though it
would raise its paw to snatch to its bosom the reasoning child of the
promise as he stood before it, that he might name it his name, of
whatever sex it was. For the hopelessly old was at the same time lewd,
lustful of young blood — young not alone in years but, and especially,
also in its promise for the future. This election of his Joseph had in
his heart never forgotten, since he came a slave, a nobody and nothing, into this land. With all his native worldly adaptability, by means
of which he had ingratiated himself among the children of the land
of mud and thought to go far amongst them, he had kept detached,
he had clung to his inward reserve, well knowing that in the last
analysis he might not make himself common, for they were taboo;
distinctly feeling in his heart of whose spirit he was child and of
what father son.

His father! There was the fifth reason — if indeed it was not the
first and strongest. He knew not, the poor, beaten old man, who had
painfully grown used to thinking of his child as safe in death, he
knew not where it lived and moved, arrayed already in a new and
strange bodily garment. Were he to learn, he would fall down and
collapse with grief. When Joseph, in his mind, dwelt on the third of
his three imaginings: the snatching away, the elevation, the follow-

ing after, he never concealed from himself that much resistance
would need to be overcome in Jacob, knowing the stately old man's
pathetic prejudice against Mizraim, his paternal-childish horror of
Hagar's land, the monkey-land of Egypt. The good soul's etymology
was wrong; he derived the name of Kemt, which signified the black
earth, from Ham, the shameless one and shamer of his father; and
cherished immoderate ideas about the abominable folly of the children of the land in matters of morality and discipline; Joseph had
always suspected them of one-sidedness, and learned to smile at them
as mythical since his coming to the land. For the luxury here was not
worse than the luxury of other lands; and whence would the panting, tax-paying, drudging little peasants and systematically flogged
water-carriers whom Joseph had known now for nine years have got
the lustiness to behave like sodomites? In short, the old man had all
sorts of quaint notions about the conduct of the people of Egypt —
as though they lived in a way that must have infected all the children
of God with wantonness.

But Joseph was the last person to have concealed from himself the
grain of truth in Jacob's moral condemnation of the land where the
inhabitants worshipped animals and the dead. Some good downright
epithets echoed in his brain at this time, which the anxious old man
had uttered about people who set up their beds with the neighbours'
whenever they pleased and exchanged their wives; of women who
would go to market and see a youth who took their fancy, when
they would lie down with him without more ado, without a notion
of sin. Joseph knew the sphere whence the father drew these ideas:
it was the sphere of Canaan and the abominable fluctuations of its
worship, against all reason; the sphere of the Moloch-madness, of
singing and dancing, abandonment and aulasaukaula, when they went
whoring after the images of fertility in an abandonment of ritual
copulation. Joseph, son of Jacob, would not go whoring after the
gods of Baal; this was the fifth of the seven reasons why he practised
reserve. And the sixth reason lies to hand; though in passing, our
sympathy with poor Mut should make us cast an eye on the perversity of her fate, in that precisely he upon whom her late-roused fancies dwelt saw her in the light of his father's mythical misunderstandings and heard in the cry of her heart's longing so much shameless
temptation — which was as good as not there at all. Eni's yearning for
Joseph had little to do with the follies of Baal and aulasaukaula; it
was a deeper and more honourable wound from his youth and beauty,
a fervid desire, as decent and as indecent as any other and no more
lewd than it is the nature of love to be. If later it degenerated, and
destroyed her reason, the fault lay with her anguish over the sevenfold armour of resistance which it encountered. A cruel fate would
have it that her love was weighed not by what she was but by what

she meant for Joseph: in other words, and sixthly, the "bond with Sheol."

Here again we must take care to be clear in our minds. This was a situation in which Joseph desired to act with good sense and consideration, to lose nothing himself nor do anyone harm. And in it his mentality must lead him to associate his Canaanitish hostility to the stammering and staggering folly of Baal with another conception, fundamentally Egyptian, which was the greatest difficulty of all. I mean the reverence for death and the dead, which was nothing else than the Egyptian form of whoring after Baal. It was Mut's misfortune that it was just this she represented to Joseph. We cannot envisage too clearly the importance of the ancient warning, the primeval No in Joseph's blood, which spoke out against any bond with the lower world or its inhabitants, against that combined idea of death and dissoluteness. To sin against its command, to err in this inscrutably fundamental matter, was for him literally to lose all. His thoughts, and the serious obstacles they created for him, may easily seem fantastic to our modern reason; but it is for precisely them that I seek to win understanding from initiate and allied minds, however separated by time from his sphere. And yet it was reason itself, speaking with his father's voice, that set itself against the temptations of shameless unreason. Not in the least that Joseph would have been without understanding for unreason; the anxious old man at home had known that. But must one not understand sin in order to be able to sin? It takes understanding to sin; yes, at bottom, all spirit is nothing else than understanding of sin.

The God of Joseph's fathers was a God of the spirit — at least that was the goal of His evolution, for the sake of which He had made a bond with men. Never since He united with theirs His will to salvation had He anything to do with death and the nether world or with any madness rooted in the dark bottom of fruitfulness. In man He had become aware that such things were an abomination unto Him; and in his turn man too had become aware of it in Him. Joseph, when he said his good-nights to the dying Mont-kaw, had of course dealt soothingly with his death-anguish and told him how it would be with him in the hereafter, saying consolingly that they would be together for ever and always because they belonged together in their sagas. But that was a friendly concession to human distress, a benevolent open-mindedness which for the moment looked aside from what he knew to be fixed: from the strict and stern renunciation of any view of the hereafter, which had been the way the fathers — and their self-sanctifying God — took to make by such a ruling a clear divorce between themselves and the corpse-gods of their neighbours in their temple graves and their death-rigidity. For only by comparison does man distinguish and learn what he is in order to become what he should be. Thus the famous chastity of Joseph, a future husband and father, was no theoretic and self-flagellating denial of the sphere of love and procreation, which would have been inconsistent with the promise to Abraham that his seed should be numerous as the desert sand; rather it was the inherited dictate of his blood to uphold the godly claims of reason in this field and to avoid all horned folly and aulasaukaula, which in his mind formed an inseparable logical and metaphysical unity with the service of the dead. It was Mut's misfortune that he saw in her wooing a temptation from this complex of death and unchastity, the temptation of Sheol, to yield to which would have meant laying himself bare to annihilation.

Here we have the seventh and last reason — the last also in the sense that it comprehended all the others. For all together what they came to was just this fear: the fear of laying himself bare. That was what he heard when Mut had tried to divest their conversation of the fig-leaf of objectivity; but we must consider it here in the sober light of its manifold sense-reference and the vast scope of its consequences.

How strangely it can fare with the meaning of a word when it breaks up into its elements in the mind, as a ray of light from a cloud is broken up into the colours of the rainbow! Let even one of these refractions make unhappy contact with an evil association and become a curse, and it loses its good repute in all, it becomes an abomination in every one of its senses, so that it can be and is condemned to be used solely to characterize abominations. If red, let us say, is a bad colour, the colour of the desert, the colour of the polar star, then it is all over with the blithe innocence of the whole white ray of heaven. The idea of bareness and baring did not originally lack innocence and blitheness; it had no red about it and no curse. But since the accursed affair of Noah in his tent, with Ham and Kenaan, his wicked son, it got, so to speak, a permanent split, became red and evil in this refraction, and blushed through and through. There was nothing else to do after that but to use it to describe abominations. It even happened that every abomination, or almost all, cried out for this name and recognized itself in it. In the attitude of the anxious Jacob by the well — almost nine years before — when he sternly rebuked his son for the nakedness with which he responded to the loveliness of the moon, in that attitude lay a regrettable blackening of an idea in itself as bright as the sight of a naked boy by a well. Baring, in the simple and literal physical sense, was in the beginning quite unsuspect, it was as neutral as the light of heaven. It only began to blush when it acquired a transferred significance, as Baal folly and the shameful blood-sin of looking upon the nakedness of a father. But now the redness had reflected back upon the innocent original meaning and cast such a glow upon it that it became a name for every sort of deadly sin, those actually committed and those only realized in look and wish. So that finally everything forbidden, thought of as accursed, in the realm of sensual lust and fleshly intercourse — and especially, by association with the shame of Noah, the invasion of the son into the rights of the father — was thought of as "baring." And even that was not all; for a new and peculiar association and comparison grew up, and the error of Reuben, the offence done by the son to the father's bed, began to stand for the whole conception — until every meeting of glances, every wish, every act, became almost equivalent, in quality and even name, to a shaming of the father.

These, then, whether we like it or not, were the pictures in Joseph's mind. To do that to which the sphinx of this dead land incited him seemed to him a shaming of his father — and was it not, in truth, when we remember what wickedness the land of mud meant to the old man at home, and with what outraged alarm he would have learned that his child, instead of being safely garnered up in death, was living in such sore temptation? In those anxious brown eyes with the soft tear-glands beneath — Joseph could feel them resting upon him — he would be committing that sinful "baring" of himself; forgetting himself as grossly as Reuben had done, what time he had shown himself unstable as water and been deprived of the blessing. Since then the blessing had hovered over Joseph's head; should he, too, be unstable and fling it away by sporting with this dubious catgoddess as Reuben once had sported with Bilhah? Who can wonder that his inward answer to the question was: "Not for the world!" Who, I repeat, can be surprised, considering all the associations and identifications bound up in Joseph's mind with the idea of his father, and the thought of offending him? Can even the liveliest mind, or the person most receptive to the tender passion, find anything strange in a chastity which consisted in a resolution counselled by the purest religious prudence; namely, that he would avoid the grossest error he could commit and the one most injurious to his future prospects?

These, then, were the seven reasons why Joseph desired not to respond to the call of his mistress's blood — not for anything in the world. I have set them down in the order of their number and weight, and regard them with a certain sense of reassurance — which, however, considering the hour at which we have arrived, is by no means in place, since Joseph is still enduring temptation, and as the story tells itself, there was as yet no certainty whether he would come out of it a whole man or not. He did come well out of it; that is, he escaped with a black eye, as we know. But why did he venture so far? Why did he disregard the whispered warning of his pure-hearted little friend, who already saw the pit yawning, and make friends instead with the phallic-minded manikin who played Lothario and mumbled out of the corner of his mouth? In a word, why did he not avoid the mistress instead of letting things reach the pass they did for him and for her? Yes, that was coquetting with the world, it was sympathy with the forbidden thing; it was also a falling away from the death-name he had chosen and from the state of salvation in which he had stood. And it had a savour of arrogant self-assurance, of a notion that he could venture into danger and retreat whenever he liked. To look at it on its good side, it was a willingness to take a dare, an ambition to face the worst and run the risk, to push matters to the uttermost in order to carry off a greater triumph — to be a virtuoso of virtue and thus more precious to the father than a more restricted and an easier trial would have shown him. Perhaps, even, it was a secret knowledge of his own course and the line it took, the suspicion that its next lesser round was to complete itself and bring him to the pit, which was inevitable if all that was to be fulfilled which was written in the plan.

Chapter VII

THE PIT

BILLETS-DOUX

WE see and we have said that Potiphar's wife, in the third year of her passion, the tenth of Joseph's sojourn in the chamberlain's house, began to tender her love to Joseph, and with growing vehemence. At bottom there is no great difference between the revealing of the second year and the tendering of the third; the one was comprised in the other and the line between them was fluid. But there was a line none the less; and to pass from attentions and longing looks, even though desire was implicit in them, to actual invitation cost the woman a self-conquest almost equal to the effort required to conquer her weakness and renounce her desire for her servant — almost, but probably not quite, since obviously she must have preferred this to the other.

She did not do it; rather than overcome her love she overcame her pride and her shame — hard enough, but yet somewhat easier, a little, because she was not alone in this struggle as she would have been in the other, for Dudu, the begetting dwarf, helped her; going to and fro between her and the son of Jacob, playing with great dignity and in his own mind for the first time the rôle of attached patron, counsellor, and messenger, and fanning the flame on both sides with all the strength of his lungs. For Dudu at length understood that there were two fires, not only one; that Joseph's pedagogic plan of salvation, by means of which he need not avoid the mistress but might stand before her nearly every day, was just an absurd and asinine pretext, since he — consciously or not — already found himself in the state of the god when his wrappings were rent. Dudu understood all this quite as well as did the quaking little mock-vizier; for in this sphere his perceptions were not only equal but superior to those of his small colleague.

"Steward," said he, at Joseph's end of the route, "you have so far known how to make your fortune — even envy, of which I am incapable, would concede that. You have trodden down those above you, despite your doubtless respectable but modest origins. You sleep in

the private room of trust, and the perquisites in which the Osiris
Mont-kaw once rejoiced, the corn, beer, bread, geese, linen, and
leather — you are now the one whom they rejoice. You take them to
market, since it is impossible you should consume them; you increase
your wealth and seem to be a made man. But what is made can be
unmade and what is won can run away, as happens often in the world
when a man knows not how to hold his good fortune nor how to secure it by unshakable foundations that it may endure for ever like a
temple of the dead. Indeed, it must happen again and again that only
some one thing is lacking to crown such a man's fortune and make
his unshakable success; and he would need but to put forth his hand
to grasp it. But from shyness or obstinacy, slackness or even conceit,
the fool refrains, folds his hand in his garment, and wilfully does not
put it out to grasp this final success, but neglects it, despises it, and
whistles it down the wind. And the consequence? The sad consequence is that all his luck and his gains ebb away, his good fortune is
level with the ground, and his place knows him no more, all because
of that one refusal. For he lost credit with powers which had thought
to accompany his success with their last and highest favour that it
might last for ever, but being thus despised and insulted, rage like the
sea, their eyes shoot fire, and their hearts rouse up a sand-storm like
the mountains of the East, so that they not only turn their faces away
from the man's fortune, but set themselves against it in their wrath so
that they entirely destroy it, which costs them no effort at all. I doubt
not that you see my concern as an honest man for your welfare — indeed, not for yours alone but also and equally for that of the person
to whom my words, I hope unmistakably, refer. Yet they are the
same: her good fortune is yours and yours hers; this conjunction is
long since a happy truth, and it only remains to give it blissful reality. For when I think and ruminate in my soul what voluptuous delight this union must prepare for you, I, the strong man, reel and am
giddy. I speak not of fleshly bliss — in the first place out of modesty,
and in the second because it goes without saying that it will be very
great, considering the silken skin of the person in question and the
wonder of her build. I refer to the delight of the soul, through which
the fleshly must be heightened beyond any measure; and will consist
in the thought that you, of certainly respectable but yet quite modest
origins and a foreigner, are holding in your arms the loveliest and
most noble lady in the two lands, and that you have evoked her profoundest sighs, as it were in token that you, a youth of the desert and
of misery, have subdued Egypt, which sighs beneath your weight.
And wherewith do you repay this mutual bliss, of which one ever
spurs the other up to fresh heights? You pay it not, but are paid for
it; paid by the unshatterable perpetuation of your fortune, in that
you will have risen to be the true lord and master over this house.

For who possesses the mistress," said Dudu, "is in truth the master."
He raised his stumps of arms as though before Potiphar, and symbolically kissed the ground before Joseph's feet.

The latter had listened, though with disgust, to the pander's very
common and offensive words. But he had listened; so that the arrogance with which he replied was not wholly becoming:

"I should, dwarf, be better pleased if you spoke not so much of
your own motion nor developed so many of your marvellous ideas,
for they are little to the purpose; but instead would confine yourself
to your office as messenger and informer. If you have something to
tell me from a higher source, then do so. If not, then begone!"

"I should," answered Dudu, "put myself in error to be gone before
I discharged my office. For I have something to deliver and hand
over. It will perhaps be permitted to the messenger and announcer
from so high a source that he somewhat adorns and enlarges upon
the message."

"What is it?" asked Joseph.

And the gnome handed something up to him, a note on papyrus,
a long, narrow slip, on which Mut, the mistress, had written some
words.

For at the other end of the route the mischief-monger had said:

"Let your loyal servant, my lady (by which I mean myself), speak
to your very soul in saying that the pace of time in which things
move forward is a vexation to me, for it is sluggish and stagnant. And
that pinches my inwards with anger and grief for your sake, for that
your beauty might suffer under it. Not that I have seen it suffer —
thanks to the gods, it flourishes in plenteous bloom and has such abundance that it might lose much and still radiantly excel the common
human measure. Thus far all is well. But your honour suffers if your
beauty does not, and therewith mine too, under the state of things
and in your relation with the youth who is set over the house, who
calls himself Osarsiph, but whom I would call Nefernefru, for certainly he is the most beautiful of the beautiful — does the name please
you? I have contrived it for your use — or not actually contrived,
rather overheard and picked up to put at your service, for so is he
often named in the house as upon the land- and the water-ways and
in the city, yes, the women on the house-tops choose to call him so,
against whose behaviour unfortunately one could not take any serious measures. But let me go on with my considered words. For it
gnaws your devoted servant in his very liver, for the sake of your
honour, that you approach so slowly your goal in the matter of this
Nefernefru — your known purpose being that you may come upon
the sources of his power and bring him to a fall as he names to you
his name. I have indeed contrived and brought about that mistress
and man no longer approach each other with scribes and attendants,

but converse without restraint or burdensome formality, just four eyes and two mouths, and in some appointed place. That improves the prospect that in some most sweet and secret hour he will at last name you his name and you will swoon with the bliss of your triumph over him, the wicked one, and all those whom his mouth and eyes have beguiled. For you will seal his mouth in such wise that his beguiling speech will fail him and his all-enchanting eye grow dim in the bliss of surrender. But the trouble is that the youth defends himself against trying a fall with you, which in my eyes is rank sedition and a sort of shameless shamefacedness, as Dudu does not hesitate to call it. For what is it? You would assault him and bring him to his fall; you, child of Amun, the flower of the southern house of women; and he, the Shabirite Amu, the foreign slave and son of the depths, he forsooth resists, he will not what you will, he hides himself behind accounts and affairs of the household. That is not to be borne, it is rebellion and presumption on the part of the gods of Asia, who owe tribute to Amun, the Lord in his Chapel. Thus the affront to the house, which earlier consisted in the growth and advancement of this slave, has now become the open insurrection of the gods of Asia, who will not pay their due tribute to Amun, which is the downfall of this youth to your power, who are a child of Amun. To this must it come. I have given timely warning. But neither, great lady, can a just mind quite absolve you or wash you white of guilt in this abomination, that the affair does not go forward. For you do not press it; in maiden delicacy you allow the youth to play his game with Amun, the king of the gods, by feints and shifts putting him off from moon to moon. That is frightful. But it is your maidenliness that is responsible, by lacking in boldness and in ripe experience; you will pardon your true servant his words, for else whence shall you acquire that which you lack? For now it must be that without scruple or ceremony you must summon the slippery one and challenge him to his fall, so that he cannot escape. If your modesty forbids you to achieve this by word of mouth, then there is the written way and the billet-doux, which he must understand when he reads, whether he will or no, for it should run in some such wise as: 'Will you overcome me today at a game? Shall we try conclusions alone together?' For so can ripeness and audacity clothe itself in a maidenly garment of speech, yet make itself understood. Let me prepare the writing instruments and write as I dictate, that I may bring him to it and make a conclusion of the business to the honour of Amun!"

Thus Dudu at this end, the sun-potent dwarf. And Eni, dazed and femininely submissive to his authority and knowledge of the field, did write to his direction that which Joseph now read. He could not conceal the redness of Atum that flew to his cheeks; though it angered him so that he urgently drove away the messenger without any ado. Yet despite anxious whisperings from another quarter, bidding him not obey the artful challenge, he did obey it, playing a game with the mistress in the columned hall beneath the image of Re-Horakhte. Once he "drove her into the water" and once let her drive him, so that defeat and victory were even and the result of the meeting was nothing at all — to the great disappointment of Dudu, at this new hitch in affairs.

So then he took the next and last step; and presently he could say to Joseph, out of the corner of his mouth:

"I have something to deliver, from a certain source."

"What is it?" Joseph asked.

Then the dwarf handed up to him a narrow slip, of which one may say that it did indeed give a desperate push to the plot; for it contained, quite baldly and unmistakably, the word which I called a word of mistaking — on the ground that it was not the word of a strumpet but of a woman overwhelmed. True, it was couched in the roundabout way which the written word permits and in especial the Egyptian, in which it was of course set down. The delicate conciseness of the picture-writing, which with the vowels left to the imagination, with the everywhere interspersed symbols suggesting the category of the consonantally crisply invoked sounds, always has something of the magic rebus, of flowery half-concealment and witty anagram, so that in fact it seems made for the confection of billets-doux, and the simplest statement receives an allusive and ingenious cast. The decisive part of Mut-em-enet's communication, what we should call the point of it, consisted of three word-symbols, with others equally pretty preceding them, and following them the quickly sketched symbol of a lion-headed couch with a mummy lying on it. The rebus looked like this:

and it meant "lying" or "sleeping." For the two words are the same in the language of Kemt; and the whole line on the papyrus slip, signed with the symbol of a vulture, said quite plainly and unmistakably: "Come, let us sleep together for an hour."

What a document! Precious as gold, highly moving and self-respecting if also most evil, distressing, and dangerous in its nature. We have here, in its original form, in the original version and the phrasing of the Egyptian language, the words in which the wife of Potiphar according to tradition couched her imploring offer to Joseph — for first in this written form she addressed it to him, empowered by Dudu, the begetting dwarf, who prompted her out of the corner of his mouth. But if the sight of it moves even us, then how must Joseph have felt when he had deciphered it! Pale and startled,

he crumpled the paper in his hand and chased Dudu away with the
handle of his fly-brush. But he had now received the message, the
sweet suggestion, the longing and promising call of his loving mistress; and if he could not in honour be greatly surprised at it, yet it
shook him mightily and made such havoc in his blood that we might
fear for the strength of the seven reasons, if we did not, while still
involved in the present feast-hour of our story, already know how
it came out. But Joseph, to whom it happened when it played itself
for the first time, actually lived in that hour, was unable to see beyond
it, and could by no means be certain of the outcome. It was all in
suspense, at the point whither we are arrived; and at the moment
when it was actually decided, it was to be touch and go whether the
seven reasons would hold or would be dissipated into air and Joseph
yield to sin. It might just as well have gone wrong as to have gone,
as it did, right by the thickness of a hair. Certainly Joseph knew himself resolved not to commit the great error, not to wreck his good
faith with God. But the wise little dwarf had been right when he had
seen in Joseph's pleasure in his freedom of choice between good and
evil something very like pleasure in evil itself, not only in the freedom to choose it. Certainly an unconfessed inclination to evil, interpreted only as a pleasure in the glorious freedom of choice, includes
the other inclination: namely, to pull the wool over one's own eyes
and cloud one's understanding to the point of seeing the good in it.
God had such wonderful intentions with regard to Joseph — did He
really mean to grudge him the proud and honeyed satisfaction which
offered itself, which perhaps He Himself was offering? Might not
this satisfaction be the destined means of the elevation in the hope of
which the "snatched-away" one lived and which had so far pros-
pered in the house that now the mistress had cast her eyes upon him
to covet him, naming to him her sweet name, longing to name the
name of all Egypt, and thereby to make him, so to speak, the lord of
all the world? What youth to whom the beloved yields herself would
not liken this to his elevation to the lordship of the world? And was
it not just this, to make him lord of the world, that God designed
for Joseph?

We see the temptations to which his clouded reason was exposed.
Good and evil were in a fair way to be thoroughly confused in his
mind. There were moments when he was tempted to interpret evil
as good. The symbol coming after "lie" on the slip of paper was calculated — thanks to the mummy on it — to open his eyes to the kingdom whence the temptation came, and to show him that to yield to it
would be an unpardonable affront toward Him who was no mummy-
god promising endurance and nothing else, but rather a God of the
future; yet even so Joseph had every ground to mistrust the strength
of his seven reasons and the course which future feast-hours would

take, and to lend an ear to the whisperings of a certain little friend
who implored him to go no more to the mistress, to receive no more
billets-doux from the malicious go-between, and to fear the bull
which even now was beginning to turn the smiling meadow into a
field of ashes with his fiery breath. True, for Joseph to avoid the mistress was more easily said than done; after all, she was the mistress
and when she called he had to go. But how prone is man to keep open
the door to evil choice, rejoicing in freedom and playing with fire —
whether out of self-confidence that thinks it can take the bull by
the horns, or out of light-headedness and secret desire, who can tell?

THE PAINFUL TONGUE
(PLAY AND EPILOGUE)

THERE came that night in the third year, when Mut-em-inet, Potiphar's wife, bit her tongue, because it so overpoweringly craved to
say to her husband's young steward that which she had already written to him in a rebus; while at the same time her pride and shame
would have prevented her tongue from speaking and from offering
to the slave her blood that he might stanch its flow. The conflict lay
in her rôle as mistress. On the one hand it was frightful to her so to
speak and to offer him her flesh and blood in exchange for his own;
while on the other it was her fitting part to behave as the male and, so
to speak, as the bearded active principle in love. Thus it was she bit
her tongue by night, above and below, so that it was nearly bitten
through, and next day she lisped from the wound, like a little child.

For some days after the sending of the letter she would not see
Joseph, but denied him her countenance because she could not look
into his, after challenging him in writing to try a fall. But just this
renunciation of his presence it was that made her ripe to utter with
her own lips what she had said in magic writing. The longing for his
presence took the form of the longing to utter the words which it
was forbidden to him, the slave of love, to speak. For if she were ever
to learn whether he spoke from his soul, there was nothing left but
for her, the mistress, to speak and to offer him her flesh and blood in
the fervent hope that she responded to his own desire and took the
words from his lips. Her rôle as mistress condemned her to shamelessness, for which she had already punished herself at night, by biting her tongue; so that now she might take leave to say what she must
say, as well as she could after the punishment, lisping like a child —
which was also a refuge, since it gave an air of helplessness and innocence to the shamelessness and turned into pathos what would else
have been gross.

She had summoned Joseph through Dudu to a business session and a
game afterwards, and she received him in the hall with the image of

Atum, about an hour after the meal, when Joseph would have finished reading to Potiphar. She came to him from her bedchamber; and as she approached he made the observation, for the first time, or for the first time consciously, that she was greatly changed. I also have until this hour refrained from notice of the change which had taken place since the beginning of her passion — and also as a result of it.

It was a peculiar change, in characterizing and describing which I run the risk of being either offensive or misunderstood. To Joseph, when he at last perceived it, it afforded much food for wonderment and profound reflection. For life lies deep, not only in the spirit but in the flesh. It was not that Mut had aged in this time; her love would have prevented that. Had she grown more beautiful? Yes, and no — but on the whole no. Even decidedly no, if by beauty we mean the utterly admirable and satisfyingly complete, a splendid image, something glorious to enfold in one's arms, yet afterwards claiming no place in our thoughts because it appeals to our most clarified sense, the eye, and not the mouth or the hand — in so far as it appeals to anything at all. For however richly sensuous, beauty has about it something abstract and spiritual; it asserts its independence and the priority of the idea before the manifestation; it is not the product and tool of sex, but rather sex is its stuff and instrument. Feminine beauty — that may be beauty embodied in the feminine, the feminine as beauty's means of expression. But if the relation between spirit and matter is reversed, so that one speaks of beautiful femininity rather than of feminine beauty, because the feminine has become the premise and primary idea, and the beauty its attribute instead of the reverse — what then? What if sex, I would ask, deals with beauty as its material, embodying itself in it, so that beauty serves and is functional as a means of expressing the feminine? It is clear that the result is a quite different kind of beauty from that which I spoke of above — a suspect, an uncanny kind, which may even approach the ugly and wield for evil the power over the emotions which it is the gift of beauty to wield; by virtue, that is, of sex, which has usurped beauty's place and takes its name. Then it is no longer a spiritual beauty revealed in the feminine, but a beauty in which the feminine reveals itself, an eruption of sex, the beauty of a witch.

The word I have used, startling as it is, is indispensable to a description of the change which had taken place during the year in Mut's physical being. It was a change pathetic and disturbing at once, evil and apparent, a witchlike metamorphosis. We must not imagine a hag, we must reject such an idea — though perhaps a faint suggestion of something like it might enter in. A witch is certainly not of necessity haglike. And yet in the most charming witch one might descry a trace — it does belong to the picture in our minds.

Mut's new body was that of a witch, informed by love and sex, and thus remotely haglike, though the only manifestation was a combined development of leanness and voluptuosity. A proper example of a hag was for instance black Tabubu, who presided over the mysteries of the make-up and had breasts like wineskins. Mut's own breasts, once so tender and maidenly, had, thanks to her suffering, developed in voluptuous splendour; standing out like great fruits of love and suggesting the haglike only by comparison with the thinness, the emaciation of the fragile shoulder-blades. The shoulders themselves looked too narrow, fragile, even childishly touching, and the arms had lost much of their roundness, they were wellnigh thin. On the other hand the thighs had developed, one might almost say, illicitly, by comparison with the upper extremities; they were large and vigorous, and gave the impression that they gripped a broomstick between them, over which the creature bent, with shrunken back and swelling breasts, and rode to the mountains. The fancy not only lay to hand, it fairly urged itself upon the observer. And the face helped it out, with its frame of black curls — that saddle-nosed, shadow-cheeked face, so long the theatre of a conflict to which only now the right name can be given, since only now did it arrive at its climax: the quite witchlike contradiction between the stern, the threatening and sinister expression of the eyes and the sinuous audacity of the deep-cornered mouth. This distressing contrast, now at its height, lent the face a morbid, mask-like tension, intensified, probably, by the burning smart of the bitten tongue. But among the reasons why she had bitten it was probably this: that she knew she would be obliged to lisp like an innocent child and that the childlikeness of her lisping would perhaps disguise and palliate the witch-aspect of her new body, of which she was but too well aware.

We may guess the distress which the cause of all these changes felt at the sight of them. Now for the first time he began to realize how lightly he had behaved in paying no heed to the prayers of his pure-minded little friend and, instead of avoiding the mistress, let it come to this, that his swan maiden was transformed witch. The folly of his pedagogic scheme struck him; for the first time he had a glimmer of the fact that his behaviour in the affair of his second life was not less culpable than his conduct toward the brethren. This insight, which was to ripen from a misgiving to a conviction, explains much that happened later.

At first his bad conscience and his distressful unease over the transformation of his mistress into a hag for love hid itself behind the special reverence, yes, veneration, of his tone and manner. Wisely or unwisely he proceeded as on all other occasions with his idiotic plan of pedagogic treatment; showed his rolls of accounts and spoke of the supplies and consumption of various commodities for the house of women, the dismissing of certain servants, and the appointing of others. Thus he did not at once notice the injury to her tongue; for she only listened to him nervously and said almost nothing. But when they sat down to play their game, at the beautifully carven board, she on her couch of ebony and ivory, he on an ox-legged tabouret; sorted the pieces shaped like couchant lions, and agreed upon the play, he could no longer fail, with mounting anxiety, to note that she lisped. When he had listened a few times and confirmed his perception he ventured to ask:

"What do I hear, my lady? It seems you have some difficulty in your speech?"

And he was forced to hear that the lady had "painth" in her tongue; she had hurt herthelf in the night and bitten her tongue, the thteward mutht pay no heed.

So she spoke — I reproduce the childish accents in our tongue instead of hers, but with no great difference in the effect. Joseph, profoundly shocked, lifted his hands from the board and wished not to play until she had tended her wound and taken balsam in her mouth, which Khun-Anpu, the barber-surgeon, must straightway be summoned to prepare. But she would not hear of it; she lightly reproached him that he wished to avoid the game, which at the beginning stood unfavourably for him and it looked as though he would be pushed into the water. Therefore he would save himself by breaking up the game and seeking for the apothecary. In short, she held him to his seat, lisping and babbling like a child, for involuntarily she suited her words to the helplessness of her tongue and spoke like a small girl, seeking to give her strained and suffering face an expression of infantine charm. I will not try to imitate her as she went on talking about puthing hith piethes into the water; for I would not seem to mock at her, who had death at her heart and was in act to throw away every vestige of pride and spiritual honour, in the overpowering urge to appease the honour of her flesh and see fulfilled the dream of healing which she had dreamed.

He too, who had awaked this urge in her, he too felt death at his heart — and only too justly. He did not dare to look up from the board, and he bit his lip, for his conscience spoke against him. Yet he played carefully; it would be hard to say whether reason controlled him or he his reason. She too took her pieces, lifted and moved them, but so absently that she was soon in a corner with no way out, was hopelessly beaten without seeing it at all, but went on playing until she was recalled by the fact that he no longer moved, when she looked down with a nervous smile upon the confusion of her hopes. He in his delusion thought that by speaking sensibly and courteously he could mend the disordered situation and set it to rights, so he said discreetly: "We must try again, now or some other time, for the

game went wrong, very likely because I made an awkward opening,
and you see that we can get no further, you have checkmated me
and I you, so that nobody has won or lost, for we have both done
both."

He hesitated and his voice was toneless, he spoke on only because
he had begun, for he could no longer hope to save the situation by
speaking of it. Even as he spoke, the worst had happened: she had
broken down, laying her head and face on his arm that rested on the
edge of the board. Her hair, with its gold and silver powder, upset
the couching lions, and her hot breath brushed his arm as she feverishly lisped and stammered. Out of respect for her pain I refrain from
reproducing the childish, sickly sounds, but their sense and nonsense
ran somewhat like this:

"Yes, yes, we can go no further, the play is played out, there is
only a downfall for us both, Osarsiph, my beautiful god from afar,
my swan and bull, my highly and hotly and eternally beloved; so we
may die together and go down into the darkness of blissful despair!
Tell me, speak to me, and freely, since you cannot see my face, because it lies upon your arm, at last upon your arm and my lost lips
touch your flesh and blood as I implore you: tell me, not seeing my
eyes, if you have had my letter that I wrote before I bit my tongue
to prevent myself from saying what I wrote and what I even so must
say, because I am the mistress and it lies with me to speak the word
you may not speak and may not embolden yourself to utter though
the reason has long since become no reason. But I know not whether
you would gladly say it, which is the sum of my anguish; for if I
knew that you would burn to say it if you could, then I would take
the words from your lips and blissfully utter them as your mistress,
even though lisping and stammering, with my face hidden on your
arm. Say if you had my letter from the dwarf, as I wrote, and did
you read it? Were you glad to see my hand, so that all your blood
rose in a wave to beat on your soul's shore? Do you love me, Osarsiph, my god in a slave's form, my sublime falcon, as I have loved
you, for so long, so long, in bliss and torment, and does your blood
burn for mine as mine for yours, so that I had to write the letter, after
long struggle; ensnared by the golden bronze of your shoulders and
the love all bear you, but above all by the godlike glance, beneath
which my body has changed and my breasts become like fruits of
love? *Sleep — with me!* Give me, give me your youth and splendour
and I will give you bliss undreamed of, for I know what I speak! Let
us put our heads and our feet together for our delight, that we may
together die of our mutual bliss, for no longer can I bear it that we
live together as two!"

Thus the woman spoke, in her abandonment. I have not imitated
the actual sound of her plea and the lisping of her cloven tongue, for

every syllable cut her like a knife, yet she lisped it all in one breath against his arm — for women can bear great pain. But so much must be clearly envisaged and settled: that the word of mistaking, the incisive phrase which has been handed down, did not issue from the sound lips of a grown person, but was thrust through and through by pain and spoken as a child speaks: "Thleep — with me!" she said. For this was the purpose of the mangling of her tongue.

And Joseph? He sat and ran over his seven reasons in his mind, conning them forwards and back. I would not assert that his blood did not rise in a wave to beat on the shore of his soul. But it met the wall of his seven reasons and they held firm. To his credit be it said, that he did not turn harshly against her or treat the witch with contempt because she tempted him to destroy himself with God; but was mild and gentle and sought in all honour to console her, despite the danger to himself which, as anyone can see, lay in such a course. For where, once begun, would the consolations end? He did not even pull away his arm, regardless of the humid heat of her breath as she lisped and the touch of her lips, but left it where it was while she lisped herself out, and even a little longer, while he replied:

"What do you, my mistress, with your face hidden on my arm, and what are you saying in the fever of your wound? Come to yourself, I implore you; for you forget yourself and me! For consider: your room is open, and we might be seen, by a dwarf or by some ordinary man, who would spy where you have your head — forgive me, for if you permit I must now take my arm away and see if outside — "

He did as he said. She, too, lifted herself, but with violence, from the place where his arm no longer was, and stood stiffly erect, with flashing eyes and suddenly ringing voice, crying out words which should have taught him with whom he had to deal and what he might expect from her who but now had been crushed and imploring, and now seemed to lift her claws like a lioness. For the moment she did not even lisp; for when she bore the pain she could force her tongue, and she cried out with great distinctness:

"Leave the hall open that the whole world may look in upon me and you, whom I love! Are you afeared? I fear neither gods nor dwarfs nor men that they see me with you and spy upon our meeting. Let them come, let them come in hosts to see us! I will fling to them like trash my modesty and shame, for they are naught to me but trash and trumpery compared with what is between us and the world-forgotten need of my soul! Am I afeared? I alone am frightful in my love. Isis am I, and upon him who sees us would I cast a look from my eyes so frightful that he would pale in death upon the spot."

Thus Mut the lioness, unmindful of her wound and the stabbing pain in every word. But he drew the curtains across between the pillars and said:

"Let me then be careful for you, since it is given me to foresee what might happen were we spied upon. For that must be sacred to me which you would fling at the world's feet, which is not worthy of it, not even worthy to die of the scorn of your look."

But when after drawing the curtain he came back to her in the shadow of the room she was no longer a lioness but a lisping child, yet with the wiliness of the serpent too, for she turned round upon him his words and stammered sweetly:

"Have you shut us in, wicked one, enfolding us in shadow against the world, that it may no more protect me against your harshness? Ah, Osarsiph, how cruel you are, that you have so namelessly bewitched me and changed my body and soul, that I know myself no more! What would your mother say if she knew how you bewitch human beings and make them so that they know themselves no more? Were son of mine so lovely and so evil, and I might see him in you, my lovely, evil son, my sun-youth, whom I bore and who at midday puts head and feet together with his mother to beget himself upon her anew! Osarsiph, do you love me upon earth as in heaven? Have I painted your soul when I painted the letter I sent you, and did your inwards quake as you read, as I too shuddered to my innermost soul with unquenchable shame and desire as I wrote? When you dupe me with your mouth, calling me the sovereign of your head and your heart — what does that mean? Do you say it because it is fitting, or in fervent sincerity? Confess to me here in the shadow! After so many nights of torturing doubt, when I lay alone, lay without you, and my blood cried out helplessly, you must heal me, my saviour, and redeem me, confessing that you spoke the lying language of beauty but to tell me the truth of your love!"

Joseph: "Not so, great lady. . . . But yes, as you say — yet spare yourself, if I must believe you look on me with favour; spare yourself and me, I implore, for it pierces my heart to hear you force your injured tongue to shape your words, instead of cooling it with balsam. To shape cruel words! How could I not love you, you, my mistress? Upon my bended knees I love you; upon my bended knees I beg you not to pry into the nature of that love, its humbleness and fervour, its reverence and sweetness, but graciously let it rest in its component parts which make up a delicate and precious whole, underserving of untwisting and unravelling in pitiless curiosity. No, bear with me still and let me tell you. . . . Gladly you hearkened when I spoke before you in many matters — hear me then in this. For a good servant loves his master, if he be noble, for so is it ordained. But when the master becomes mistress and a lovely woman, then there comes a great sweetness and adoring fervour into the love and permeates it — it is humility and sweetness, which are adoring tenderness, ardour, and inward imprecation against the cruel one who would approach it too closely with prying touch and angry glance — for that cannot come to good. When I call you sovereign of my head and heart, surely it is for the form's sake and fitting. But how sweet that it is fitting so to speak — there lies a mystery which must be veiled in delicate silence. Is it then gracious or wise to break the silence and ask my meaning, leaving me in my answer a choice between a lie and a sin? That is a false and cruel choice, I can none of it. And I beg you on my knees that you will show kindness and mercy to the life of the heart!"

The woman: "O Osarsiph, you are frightful in your speaking beauty, which makes you appear godlike before men so that they serve you, yet the art of your speaking drives me to despair. That is a terrible deity, your art, child of intelligence and beauty; a mortal spell for the unhappily loving heart. You chide me for speaking, yet you speak in eloquent chiding, and say that beauty must be silent and not speak; that there must be silence about beauty as about the holy grave at Abdu, for love shall be silent like death, yes, in silence they are like each other and speaking wounds them. You demand that I show kindness and mercy to the life of the heart, and would seem to be on its side against my unravelling curiosity. But that is to turn the world upside down; for it is I who in my sore need fight for the life of the heart when I am driven to examine it. What else shall I do, beloved, and how help myself? I am mistress to you, my lord and saviour, for whom I yearn, and I cannot spare your heart nor let your love rest in peace for pity of it. I must be cruel, I must lay siege to it as the bearded man lays siege to the tender maiden who does not know herself, and must wrest fervour from her humility and desire from her meekness, that she may be bold and able to grasp the thought that you sleep close beside me, for therein lies all the salvation of the world that you do so with me; it is a question of bliss or the torment of hell. It has become for me the torment of hell that our limbs are separate, yours there and mine here; and if you only speak of your knees I am seized with unspeakable jealousy of them, that they are yours and not also mine, and they must be near to me, that you sleep with me or I perish and am destroyed!"

Joseph: "Dear child, that cannot be, let your servant implore you to consider and not cling fixedly to this idea, for it is born of evil. You put an exaggerated, a morbid value upon the idea that dust must lie close to dust; it would be lovely for a moment, but that it would outweigh the evil consequences and all the remorse coming after could be true only in your fevered dream. Lo, it is not good and could never come to good that you should lay siege to me as the bearded man and woo me as your mistress for the satisfaction of my love. There is an abomination in it, it is unfitting to our days. For I am not slave enough for that, and I can myself conceive the idea — only too well, I assure you; yet may we not bring it to pass, for more than one reason, many more than one, a great number of them, like the constellation in the image of the bull. I beg you to understand that I may not set my teeth in the lovely apple which you offer me, that we should eat transgression and lose all. Therefore I speak and am not silent, take it kindly of me, my child, for since I may not be silent with you I must speak and choose consoling words, for your consolation, dearest mistress, lies close to my heart."

The woman: "Too late, Osarsiph; too late for you and for us both. You cannot retreat, nor I, for we are mingled. Have you not drawn the curtains and shut us in together in shadow apart from the world, so that we are paired together? Do you not already say 'we' and 'us' — 'we might be seen,' drawing yourself and me together in sweet union in this precious word, the figure of all the bliss I offer you, which is already comprehended in it so that the act has no new element after we have said 'we,' for we have a secret together against all the world and are two together with it apart from the world, and naught remains but to — "

Joseph: "No, but hear me, my child, that is not true, and you do violence to truth, so I must resist! It was your self-forgetfulness forced me to draw the curtain, for your honour's sake, that it might not be seen from the court where your head was lying. And now you will so turn it that naught is any matter and the act already done because we have a secret and must shut ourselves in with it! That is not true, for I have no secret, I would but protect yours; and only in this sense can there be talk of we and us, and nothing has happened nor can, for a whole constellation of reasons."

The woman: "Osarsiph, sweet liar! You will deny our union and our secret, when you have but now confessed that you could but too well understand my wooing, since it lay all too near to your heart? Is that, wicked one, to have no secret together from the world? Do you then not think of me as I think of you? But how would you think of me and of lying with me if you could once imagine the pleasure that awaits you, my golden sun-boy, in the arms of your heavenly goddess! Let me tell you and promise you in your ear, shut away from all the world, in shadowy depths, what awaits you! For I have never loved, never received a man into my body, have never given even the smallest part of the treasure of my love; it is all treasured up for you, and you shall be so extravagantly rich with it as you could never dream! Hearken to what I whisper: for you, Osarsiph, my body has changed and been transformed to a vessel of love from tip to toe; when you come to me and yield me the glory of your youth, you will not believe that you lie next a human woman, but will satisfy the lust of a god with mother, wife, and sister, for lo, I am she! I am the oil that craves your salt that the lamp may burn bright in the feast of night! I am the meadow that thirsts after you and the flood of your manhood's water, bull of your mother, that you swell above her and over her in espousing me, before you leave me, beautiful god, and forget your lotus wreath beside me in the moist earth! Hear, hear now what I whisper. For with every word I draw you deeper into the mystery which we share, and you can no longer withdraw, for we are in the thick of it together, so that there can be no reason in withholding what I ask."

Joseph: "Yes, dearest child — forgive me that I call you so, since we are so far, certainly, in a secret together that I had to draw the curtain because of your distraction; but it has its good sense, and sevenfold, that I must refuse your honeyed suggestion; for it is marshy ground upon which you would lure me, where nothing grows but wild grass, no corn; and would make of me an adulterous ass, of yourself a roving bitch. Then how shall I not protect you against yourself, and myself against the vile transformation? Consider how it would be with us if we were seized of our crime and it fell upon our heads? Shall I let it come to this, that they strangle you and throw your body to the dogs, or cut off your nose? One cannot think of it. But the ass's share would be uncounted beatings, a thousand blows for his senseless lechery, if he were not thrown to the croco-diles. These corrections threaten us if our deed take possession of our souls."

The woman: "O cowardly boy, if you but let yourself dream of the bliss that awaits you by my side, you would think no further, but laugh at punishment, for whoever meted it out it could not measure to the height of our joy!"

"Yet behold," he said, "dear friend, how madness reduces you for a time below the level of the human! For its advantage and special property it is to think beyond the moment and consider what comes after. Nor would I fear at all — "

They were standing close together in the darkened room, speak-ing softly but urgently like people who debate something of great moment, with lifted brows, faces flushed with excitement.

"Nor would I fear at all," he was saying, "the punishment for you and me, that were the least of it. But I fear Petepre, our master, him-self, not his punishments, as one fears God, not on account of the evil He can visit on one, but Himself, in the fear of God. From him have I all my light, and what I am here in house and land I owe to him. How should I then dare to tread before him and look into his mild eyes, though I had no punishment to fear, after I had lain with you? Hearken, Eni, and in God's name recall your understanding for that which I would say, for my words will stand, and when our story comes into the mouths of the people, so will it sound. For all that happens can become history and literature, and it may easily be that we are the stuff of history. Therefore have a care for yourself and take pity upon your story, that you do not become a warning in it and the mother of sin. Much could I say, and give words to many involved matters, to resist your desire and mine own; but for the people's mouth, should it come to be put into it, will I say the simplest and most pertinent thing, which every child can understand, thus: *My master hath committed all that he hath to my hand; there is none greater in this house than I; neither hath he kept back anything from me but thee, because thou art his wife. How then can I do this great wickedness, and sin against God?* These are the words which I say to you for all the future, against the desire which we have for each other. For we are not alone in the world, to enjoy the flesh the one of the other, for there is also Petepre, our great master, in his loneliness, against whom we may not act, instead of doing loyal service to his soul, nor affront him with such an act, which could bring to shame his sensitive dignity and break the bond of loyalty. He stands in the way of our bliss, and that is an end."

"Osarsiph," she whispered close behind him, and girded herself up to make a proposal. "Osarsiph, my beloved, who are long since joined with me in a mystery, hearken and understand your Eni aright. I could — I could . . . ."

This was the moment which revealed why and to what end Mut-em-enet had bitten her tongue; and what were the long-since-ready words for which she had prepared it that it might utter them in the most beguiling, helpless, and pathetic guise. Not only the words of the offer — that came first but not last; for the final and actual ones, for which she had taught her tongue to lisp like a child, were meant for the proposal she now made, laying on his shoulder the lovely masterpiece that was her hand, blue-veined and decked with precious stones, and nestling her cheek to it as she said, sweetly, with pouting lips:

"But I might kill him."

He started back. The prettiness of it was too much for him, he would never have thought of it nor expected it of her, even after he had seen her lift her lioness paws and heard her hoarse breath: "Frightful am I alone!"

She nestled to him as he shrank away. "We could kill him and put him out of the way, what ith there to that, my falcon? It ith nothing. Tabubu could brew me in a twinkling a clear decoction or crystalline deposit of mysterious powers; I would give it you in your hand to shake into the wine he drinks to warm his flesh, but when he drinks he would grow cold by degrees and no one perceive anything, thanks to the skill of the Negro lands in brewing such potions; and he embarks for the West and is out of the world and can no longer stand in the way of our bliss. Let me only do this, beloved, and revolt not against so simple a measure. For is not his flesh dead already while he lives, is it of any use but to flourish and increase to no end? How I hate his lazy flesh, since my love for you has lacerated my heart and made my own flesh to a vessel of love — I cannot say, I can only shriek it. So, sweet Osarsiph, let us make him cold, for it is a little thing. Or is it something to you, to knock down a fungus with a stick, some foul tindery mushroom or puff-ball? That is nothing to do, to do away with such. But when he is in his grave and the house empty of him, then are we free and alone, blissful vessels of love, unbound to consequences, and may embrace each other, fearless, mouth on mouth. For you are right, my divine boy, to say that he stands in the way of our joy and we may do naught to him — you are right in your misgiving. But just therefore must you see that we must make him cold and send him out of the world, that the misgiving may be satisfied and we do him no more harm in our embracing. Do you understand, my little one? Picture to yourself our raptures and how it will be when the mushroom is struck down and put out of the way and we are alone in the house, and you, in all your youth, are its master. You the master, because I am the mistress, for he who sleeps with the mistress is the master. And we shall drink of bliss by night, and in the day rest beside each other on purple cushions and breathe incense of nard, while garlanded girls and youths posture before us and play on their lutes, while we lie and dream of the night that was and the night that will be. For I will hand you the cup, where we shall drink from one and the same place, with our lips on its golden rim, and as we drink, our eyes will meet in the thought of the delight which we had the past night and that which we plan for this night, and we put our feet together — "

"Hearken now, Mut in the valley of desolation," said he. "For I must conjure you — that is an expression, but I mean it literally, I must conjure you in all truth, or rather the demon that speaks out of you and by whom you are clearly possessed, for so it must be. Little pity have you for your legend, I must say; for you give yourself the name of mother of sin, for all future times. But remember that we are perhaps, yes, very likely, in a saga; then pull yourself together! For I too, as you can see, must do the same against your urging of delights, though it is easier for me because of my horror at your mad proposal to murder Petepre, my master and your husband. That is a frightful thing. It lacks only that you tell me that we are together also in this secret because you have imparted to me your thought, and that it is now mine. But it is my case and concern that it shall remain but a thought and that we shall make no such history as that! Dear Mut! I have no liking to your proposal that we live here together thus in your house after we have done away with its master. When I think how I should live, in the house of murder with you, as the slave to your love, and derive my mastership from that, I feel self-contempt! Shall I not wear a woman's garment from Byssus and you command me every night for your lust, a master seduced to murder his father that he might sleep with his mother? For just so would it be with me: Potiphar, my lord, is to me like a father; were I to live with you in the house of murder it would be as though I lived with my mother. Therefore, dear, good child, I conjure you, in all friendliness, console yourself and incite me not to such an evil deed!"

"Fool! Fool and child!" she answered in her ringing tones. "How like a foolish boy you answer in your fear, which as your mistress in love I must break down! With his mother each man sleeps — the woman is the mother of the world, her son is her husband, and every man begets upon his mother — do you not know, must I teach you these simple things? Isis am I, the Great Mother, and wear the vulture hood, and you shall name me your name, sweet son, in the sacred sweetness of the begetting night — "

"No, no, not so!" he cried. "It is not as you say, I must correct you. The Father of the world is no mother's son, nor is he the Lord by a lady's grace. To Him I belong, before Him I walk, the son of my father, and once for all I tell you I will not so sin against God the Lord, to whom I belong, to shame my father and murder him and pair with my mother like a shameless hippopotamus. — Now, my child, I must go. Dear mistress, I beg your leave. I will not forsake you in your distraction, surely not. I will console you with words and speak to you kindly as I can, for that I owe you. But now must I take my leave and go to look after my master's house."

He left her. She cried after him:

"Do you think to escape me? Do you think we shall escape each other? I know, I know already of your zealot god to whom you are sealed and whose wreath you wear. But I fear no stranger god and I will tear your wreath, of whatever it is made, and give you to wear a wreath of ivy and vine for the mother-feast of our love! Stay, beloved! Stay, loveliest of the lovely! Stay, Osarsiph, stay!" And she fell down and wept.

He parted the curtains with his hands and went quickly out. But in their folds as he thrust them to right and left, on each side was a dwarf; one named Dudu, the other little Shepses-Bes, for they had found themselves together, stealing up from either side to listen; they stood there, each with one hand on his knees, the other to his ear, eagerly listening, the first out of malice, the second trembling with fright. And each ever and anon shook his fist at the other and gnashed his teeth, beckoning him to go away. Neither had stirred, though each had been no little hindrance to the other in hearing; yet neither had left the field.

And behind Joseph, emerging from the folds, they flew at each other with hisses, fists raised to their temples, choking with fury, deadly in their enmity because they were like in kind yet so different in nature.

"What business have you got here?" panted Dudu, spouse of Djeset, "you hunch-back, you mite, you empty little barley-corn! You must crawl hither to this crack, where I alone have a right and claim to be, and will not budge however much I sign to you to make yourself scarce! You miller's thumb, you cod's head, you shotten herring! I will thrash you till you cannot stir a leg, you worm, you misbegotten, crawling vermin! You must come sneaking and spying hither, you empty bladder, and stand guard for your master and crony, the pretty-phiz, the bastard from the swamps, the scum he brought into the house to shame it, taking the upper hand till it is a disgrace to the two lands, and on top of all making a thing of the mistress — "

"Oh, oh, you villain, you bully, you vile mischief-making devil!" piped the other, his little face flawed into a thousand wrinkles with rage, his ointment-cone askew on his head. "Who is it here lurking and listening to the devilry which he himself has brewed with his billets-doux and his playing with fire, feasting his eyes at a crack on the torture and agony of the big folk, that they may be snared in destruction according to his shameless scheming — who but you, you pouch-mouth, you moocher, you scullion, — oh, you scarecrow, you jumping-jack, you busnacker, with nothing about you of dwarf or giant but just one thing, you walking dardsman, you much-married knave — "

"Wait!" the other gave back shrilly. "Wait, you less than nothing, you atomy, you loss-and-lack, you worthless nocky! Away from this spot where Dudu guards the honour of the house, or I will disgrace you with my manly weapon, wretch, and give you something to remember! What shame awaits you now, if I go to Petepre and tell him what goes on here in the dark, and what sort of words the steward whispers to the mistress in the curtained room — that you shall soon learn! You brought him into the house, the good-for-nothing, not resting from your little tittle-tattle before the departed Mont-kaw; boasting of your keen eye for goods and men and goods in men, till he bought the knave from the other knaves against my advice and set him here in the house to dishonour the mistress and make a cuckold of Pharaoh's eunuch. You are to blame for the mess, you above all, and in the very beginning. You are due to the crocodile, and shall be served up to him as a tidbit and sweet-meat after they feed him your bosom friend when they have bound and beaten him."

"Oh, oh, you foul-mouth!" railed the little one, trembling and writhing with rage. "You backbiter, whose words come not out of his understanding but rise out of unknown depths and are slavering obscenity! I dare you to touch me, or make any attempt to disgrace me, else, though I am only a poor dwarf, you shall feel my nails in your face and the hollows of your eyes, for they are sharp, and to the pure weapons are given against the vicious. I, a little dwarf, guilty of the agony and affliction there within? Guilty is the evil thing, the all-devouring pestilence wherein you boast yourself a master; and have used it to the devilish ends of your hatred and envy, to dig a pit for Osarsiph, my friend. But see you not, you goat-dwarf, that you have failed, for no lack showed itself in my beautiful one? Since you listened, you must have heard that he was constant as a novice before the mysteries, and heroically defended his saga? What else have you heard at your crack, and what misheard, since your dwarf-ear has lost all its cunning and sharpness and become thick and stupid with playing the cock? I should like to know what you would or could tell the master of Osarsiph, when your dull ears could have caught nothing important at your eavesdropping."

"Oho!" Dudu cries out. "The husband of Djeset can vie with you, weak wight, in sharpness of ear and hearing, when the matter is one he is at home in, while you, you chirruping lack-brain, have no understanding of it at all! Have you not heard the billing and cooing there within, and how the fine little pair were calling and prancing like birds when they mate? My ear is good for all that; it heard him call her 'dear child,' and 'little treasure,' the slave the mistress, but she said 'falcon' and 'bull' in the most honeyed tones. I heard them conniving how they would enjoy each other's flesh and blood. Do you not see that Dudu is not wanting as a witness? But the best thing I heard as I listened is that they made up, in their heat, to bring about Petepre's death, to lay him low with a club — "

"You lie, you lie! For it is plain you have heard but the crassest nonsense at your post and will tell Petepre the sheerest lies about them both. For my youth called the mistress child and friend out of simple goodness and kindness to soothe her in her distraction, and honourably dissuaded her from her plan of felling even a puff-ball with a stick. Marvellously did he bear himself for his years, and as yet not the smallest blemish comes into his legend despite all those sweet blandishments."

"And so you think, crab-louse, that I could not accuse him just the same and ruin him with the master? There is precisely the trick of it, and my trump card in this game, of which a puppet like you understands nothing at all. For it matters not a scrap how the fool behaves, more properly or more lustfully; the point is that the mistress is head over ears in love with him and has no room for thought save how to bill and coo — and therein lies his ruin, from which nothing can save him. A slave about whom the mistress is crazy — he simply goes to the

crocodiles, nothing else for him, and that is just the game. If he yields
and makes love to her, I have him. But if he refuses, then he but pricks
her madness and it is even worse, he is for the crocodile either way,
or at best for the knife, which will ruin his bill for cooing and cure
the mistress of her fit."

"Oh, you monster, you blasphemer!" shrieked Shepses-Bes. "You
are the best case in the world of what abomination can come and
straddle about on this earth when one of the race of dwarfs loses his
rightful goodness and fineness and tries to take on full-grown dignity.
For such a one is a rascal like you, you runagate, you coney-hunter,
you —"

To which Dudu retorted that when the knife had been wielded,
then Osarsiph would be a better match for his emasculate friend.
Thus the two pygmies expended themselves in mutual reviling, until
the courtyard folk ran together. Then they parted; the one to report
Joseph to the master, the other to seek his friend and warn him, that
he might still try by some means to escape from the pit.

DUDU'S COMPLAINT

POTIPHAR, as everybody knew, could not abide Dudu — on the ground
of the pompousness he saw in the stout little man. The Osiris Mont-
kaw had always been irritated by the dwarf, and for the same reason.
I have said already that the courtier held at a distance the keeper of
his jewel-chests; did not see him if he could help it, and interposed
other servants between them — people of the regulation size, who for
that reason were better able to dress and undress that towering form
and adorn it, whereas Dudu would have had to use a pair of steps.
But aside from that, being of the same size as other people, they laid
less stress on certain natural gifts and sun-powers and assumed less
dignity on account of them than Dudu did, to whom they amounted
to a lifelong marvel and proud distinction.

Thus it was by no means easy for the pygmy to arrive at speech
with the master, now that he had at last decided to take the bypath
which branched off from the road so assiduously trodden between
mistress and steward. He did not succeed all at once, after that quarrel with the mock-vizier before the curtained room; not days but
weeks had he to wait, to announce himself, before he got audience.
He, the scribe of the jewels, had to bribe the slaves, or else threaten
them that he would withhold this or that dress or ornament, would
simply not unlock his wardrobes, so that they would get into trouble with the master, if they did not force it upon his notice that Dudu
would and must speak to him on a very weighty domestic concern.
A whole quarter of a moon he had to work, beg, cajole, and storm
before he achieved the favour of an audience, which he the more ar-

dently desired because he thought that, once exploited, there would
be an end to his troubles; such a service as he meant to render the
master must ensure him the latter's abiding favour.

The indomitable creature had plied two of the slaves of the bath
with presents, to the end that with every jug of water which they
poured over their puffing master's shoulders and chest they should
repeat: "Master, remember Dudu!" They said it again when the
dripping tower of flesh stepped out of the sunken basin on to the
tiled floor to be dried with perfumed towels; one after the other:
"Master, remember Dudu!" until in exasperation he said: "Let him
come and speak before me!" They signed to the slaves who were
waiting in the bed-chamber to anoint and massage; these had likewise
been bribed, and summoned the dwarf out of the western hall, where
he was like to die with impatience, into the room with the bed standing in a niche. He raised his little palms aloft, toward the kneading-
bench, where Pharaoh's friend stretched himself out and gave his
flesh to the ministrations of the slaves. Dudu's dwarf-head drooped
meekly to one side between his lifted arms, as he awaited a syllable
from Petepre's mouth or a glance from his eye. But neither came; the
master only grunted softly as the slaves attacked his flesh, working
his shoulders, hips, and thighs, the fat feminine arms and fleshy bosom
with oil of nard, even turning the small fine head the other way as
it lay on the leather cushion, so that it did not look at Dudu. That
was vexatious; but his affair was so hopeful that he would not desist
or be cast down.

"May your destiny endure a thousand years," he said, "first of
mankind, warrior of the highest! Four jars for your entrails, and for
your abiding image a coffin of alabaster!"

"Thanks," Petepre answered him. He said it in Babylonian, as we
might say "*Merci*," and added: "Will the man take long with what
he has to say?"

"The man" was bitter. But Dudu's hopes were too high, he would
not be abashed.

"Not long, my sun and master," he gave answer. "Rather, briefly
and to the point."

And at a sign from Petepre's little hand he put one foot before
him, laid his stumpy arms on his back, and began, his nether lip drawn
in, the other sticking out over it like a thatch. He knew that he could
not say all that he had to say before the slaves, but felt sure that
Petepre would soon dismiss them to listen in private.

His beginning might be called skilful — except that it lacked in fine
feeling. He began with praise of Min, god of the harvest, who in some
localities was honoured as a form of the sun-power, but had had to
name his name to Amun-Re and became, as Amun-Min or Min-
Amun-Re, one person with him, so that Pharaoh as readily spoke of

"my father Min" as of "My father Amun," especially at the harvest festival or the feast of the crowning, when the Min aspect of Amun was predominant and he became the fruitful god, protector of desert wanderers, towering in feathers and mighty in procreative power, the ithyphallic sun. Him then Dudu evoked in all his dignity, appealing to him as he implored the countenance of his master, in that he, as upper servant of the house and scribe of the master's wardrobe, did not confine his zeal for his office to the narrower round of his duties but, husband and father as he was, author of the being of two well-proportioned children, called so-and-so, to whom, unless all signs failed and there was nothing in the coy confession which Djeset his wife whispered to him, a third would soon be added — as he was saying, then, he, who had himself given increase to the house and was bound by especial reverence to the majesty of Min (and thus to Amun in his Min aspect), gave an eye to the welfare of the house in general and in particular from the point of view of human fruitfulness and propagation. He had taken under his special protection and supervision everything that came to pass in the household in this field: all such happy events as marriages and consummations, bringing home the bride, fertility of the womb, childbed and so on; encouraging all the household folk in such activities, spurring them on and in his own person setting them an example of diligence and established order. For much depended upon a good example from those in authority — not quite the highest authority, of course, for naturally, where nothing could be taken upon oneself, this could not either. So much the more important and necessary was it that precautions be taken to avoid disturbing the sacred tranquillity of that apex of their household structure which stood above the need of setting an example. But those just beneath him were, in his, Dudu's, opinion, bound to lead an exemplary life, not only orderly but also diligent in the activities before-mentioned. He hoped that thus far the speaker had the approval of his lord and sun.

Petepre shrugged his shoulders and rolled over on his belly, to give the rubbers a chance to work on his massive back. But he lifted his small, well-shaped head to ask what Dudu meant by his words about disturbing the master's tranquillity, and the remarks about dignity and the reverse.

"Your upper servant will come to that at once," replied the dwarf. And spoke of the departed Mont-kaw, whose course of life had been so upright, and who had married early the child of a state official and would have become a father had not fate dealt hardly by him and shattered his prospects, so that well-meaning as he was, he had ended his days as a downcast widower. So much for Mont-kaw. But now he would speak of the brightness of the present, bright in so far that the deceased had found a successor of equal standing, or, if not quite equal, being a foreigner, yet not inferior to him in gifts, and they had welcomed to the headship over the house a youth of very considerable parts. His name, to be sure, had a somewhat decadent sound; but his face was ingratiating, he talked well and seemed astute — in short, an individual of very evident advantages.

"Ass!" muttered Petepre into his folded arms. For nothing sounds sillier to us than praise of an object whose true worth we think ourselves better able to gauge than anyone else.

Dudu pretended not to hear. The master may have called him an ass, but it was better to take no notice, in order to keep up his courage.

He could not, he said, give enough praise to the fascinating, yes, really dazzling and for some people distracting qualities of the youth in question. For it was just these which gave weight to the anxiety he, Dudu, felt for the stability and well-being of the household, to the headship of which these qualities had raised the young man.

"What is he jabbering about?" Petepre said, lifting his head a little and turning it in the direction of the rubber. "The steward's qualities threaten the stability of the household?"

Jabbering was pretty bitter too. But the dwarf was not to be put off.

They need not, in the least, under other circumstances, be anything but a blessing to the house; that is, if they were legally circumscribed and ameliorated — or, still better, had been so circumscribed beforehand. For such qualities — such an attractive face, such astuteness and eloquence — could otherwise become the source of much unrest, ferment, and derangement in their vicinity. And Dudu expressed regret that the youthful steward, whose religious affiliations were quite obscure, had refrained from paying due tribute to the majesty of Min, had remained unmarried in his high office and not taken to himself a bedfellow suitable to his birth — for instance the Babylonian slave Ishtarummi of the house of women — and added his offspring to the children in the courtyard. That was regrettable, it was bad, it was serious — it was even dangerous. For not alone did the household suffer diminution to its state, but a bad example was set in the point of stability and fruitfulness. And even that was not the worst. For, thirdly, there was, so to speak, no check upon the beguiling charms which undeniably the young steward possessed, and of which they stood in such need and had for a long time needed, to guard against their inflammable, head-turning, sense-destroying effect upon the household; to prevent them, in short, from sowing the wind not only upon their own social level but also in spheres far above it.

There was a pause. Petepre lent himself to be massaged and did not answer. It was either — or, Dudu declared. Such a young man must either submit to the marriage yoke, so that his gifts might not strew destruction like wildfire throughout the house, but be brought into the peaceful haven of wedlock; or else it would be better to wield the knife as a preventive measure and effect the sanative neutralization which would secure exalted persons from the disturbance of their rest and preserve their honour and dignity unscathed.

Another silence. Petepre suddenly turned on his back, so that the masseurs working upon him were interrupted and stood with their hands in the air. He lifted his head toward the dwarf, measuring him from head to foot and back again — a short distance for Petepre's eyes — and then glanced over to the armchair where lay his clothes, his sandals, his fan, and other insignia. Then he rolled round again, his head in his arms.

He was filled with a cold, shuddering anger, a sort of outraged alarm at the threat to his peace of mind from this disgusting hop-o'-my-thumb. Obviously the misbegotten fool knew something and wanted to tell it to him. And if it was true, certainly he, Petepre, had to know it; though he felt that to be told it was the grossest unkindness. "Is all well in the house? Naught untoward has happened? Is the mistress happy?" Yes, that was it; he was going to be given the wrong answer to the question. He hated the man — this man, most of all, not being prepared to hate anybody else, and aside from any question of the truth of what the dwarf would say. He would have to send away the masseurs and be alone with this valiant little guardian of his honour, to let him rouse it up, whether with truth or with calumny. Honour: what was that, in the present connection? It was sexual honour, the honour of the cock, which consists in the faithfulness of the hen, as a sign that he is a complete specimen of cockishness, from whom she will get such satisfaction that it will never occur to her to take up with anyone else nor would she be tempted by the advances of any other cock, no matter how well equipped. But if this happens, and she has to do with another, everything is altered: there is sexual dishonour, the cock becomes a cuckold, which is as good as saying he becomes a capon. He is made ridiculous with horns which she sets on his head, and if anything is still to be saved he must save it by running a sword through the rival whom she hoped to enjoy, and perhaps better yet by killing her too, in order by that striking and sanguinary deed to re-establish his self-respect in his own eyes and those of the world.

Honour. Petepre had no honour whatever. He lacked it in his very flesh, he had no comprehension of what this cockish attribute might be; and it seemed frightful to him when others, for instance this pompous little scribe, wanted to make much of it. But he had a heart, one capable of doing justice; that is, he had a sense of the rights of others. It was a sensitive heart, dependent upon the love and loyalty of others. He hoped for their love and, being betrayed, was so constituted as to suffer bitterly. During this pause, while the masseurs set to work again on his tremendous back and he kept his face buried in his fat feminine arms, all sorts of thoughts coursed through his mind. They had to do with two persons on whose love and loyalty he so fervently built that one might say he loved them: Mut, his chief wife, whom he hated a little too, because of the reproach which of course she could not utter and yet did by her very existence utter none the less; to whom he would dearly have liked to show himself strong and loving; and Joseph, who did him so much good, who knew how to make him feel better than wine, and for whose sake, to his own great regret, he had had to refuse to show himself strong and loving to his wife in that twilight hour in the western hall. Petepre was not without an intuition of what he had then refused her. To tell the truth, even during that conjugal conversation he had been vaguely aware that the reasons she gave for her request were only a pretext, the real ground being fear of herself on account of his honour. But since he lacked that kind of honour, her fear had seemed less important to him than the retaining of the youth who did him good. He had preferred him to her; and by abandoning his wife to her fear he had challenged them both to prefer each other and betray him.

He saw all that. And it wounded him, for he had a heart. Yet he saw it, for that heart was inclined to fairness, if perhaps only out of indolence, and because fairness can counteract anger and thirst for revenge. Probably he felt, too, that it is also the safest refuge of dignity. Evidently this hateful guardian of his honour was trying to tell him that his dignity was being betrayed by treachery. As though, he thought, dignity ceased to be dignity when it had to hide its head and suffer from treachery! As though the betrayed were not more dignified than the betrayer! But if he is not, because he has himself incurred guilt and invited treachery, yet justice, fair-mindedness, is always there, so that dignity may find in its own guilt and the rights of others and there establish itself anew.

So then Petepre, the eunuch, strove after justice — at once and before everything else, whatever might be brought up against him from the side of honour. Justice is a spiritual quality, by contrast with the fleshliness of honour; and as he lacked the latter he was perforce, he knew, thrown back upon justice. It was on the spiritual he had relied, with both of these who now, as this informer and intriguant seemed to want to tell him, had broken their faith. So far as he knew, both were secured by powerful spiritual considerations against the flesh, for both of them were set apart and in the spirit belonged together: the woman, with all her compensations, Amun's wife and bride of his temple, who danced before him in the narrow garment of the goddess; and the devoted youth with the wreath of consecration in his hair, the boy "touch-me-not." Had the flesh mastered them? He grew cold with terror at the thought, for the flesh was his enemy, despite his superfluity of it; and always, when he came home and asked: "Is all well? Naught untoward has happened?" his sub-conscious anxiety had been lest the flesh have somehow gained the mastery over the forbearing, careful, yet not trustworthy bond of the spirit and brought about some frightful disruption. But his cold shivers did not exclude some anger too; for did he have to know, could they not have left him in peace anyhow? If those two dedicated persons had been overpowered by the flesh behind his back and had secrets from him, yet in that very secrecy and betrayal lay a forbear-ing love for which he was very ready to be grateful. But for that creature there, the pompous little guardian of honour, who was try-ing to give him unasked-for enlightenment and make a vulgar attack upon his peace of mind — for him he felt nothing but inexpressible dislike.

"Are you nearly done?" he asked. He was thinking of the masseurs, whom he would have to send away, and did not want to be com-pelled by that spy and sneak to do so against his will. But there was nothing for it. They were perfect blockheads, you might say that they had made themselves clods because it suited their calling to be so. But though certainly they had not understood a word up to now, nor were any more likely to understand the rest, yet Petepre could scarcely ignore the silent intimation of his tormentor that he would speak with him alone. It made him dislike him still more vehemently.

"Go not before you have finished," he said, "and there is no special need of haste. But if you are done, give me my sheet and then go when you like."

They would never have understood that they were to go, whether finished or no; but since they really were, they smoothed the linen sheet up to their master's chin, over his ponderous bulk, flung them-selves on their faces, touching their narrow foreheads to the ground, and went off with arms akimbo, in a sort of waddling trot, which was evidence enough of their self-satisfied stupidity, were more needed.

"Come closer, my friend," said the chamberlain. "Come as close as you will and find proper for what you have to tell me, for it seems to be something better not shouted to the house-tops, but rather some-thing that brings us to close grips, which I take to be an advantage, whatever else may be said of it. You are a valuable servant, small in-deed, far below the average, and in this respect a figure of fun; but you have poise and dignity and qualities which justify you in assum-ing responsibility beyond the duties of your office, having an eye over the house and especially over its fertility. Not that I remember installing you in this charge, for I do not. But I do so now, for I cannot avoid recognizing your calling to it. If I understood aright, your love and duty urge you to impart to me certain disturbing information in your special field of oversight and accounting, of events which might kindle disorder in the house?"

"That is so," Joseph's enemy replied with emphasis to this address, whose offensive insinuations he swallowed down for the sake of its otherwise encouraging nature. "Loyal and anxious concern bring me before your countenance, to warn you, my lord and my sun, of a danger so pressing that it merited my admission earlier to your presence; for too easily, yes, at any moment it may be too late."

"You alarm me."

"I am sorry. And yet it is my purpose to alarm you, for the danger is imminent, and with all the keen perception of which I am master I cannot, I your servant, be sure that it is not already too late and your disgrace already accomplished fact. In that case it would still in one respect not be too late, for you are still alive."

"So I am threatened with death?"

"With both shame and death."

"I should consider the one welcome could I not avoid the other," said Petepre grandly. "And whence do these things threaten me?"

"I have already," responded Dudu, "gone so far in indicating the source of the danger that it is unmistakable, unless for an ear too fearful to hear it."

"Your impertinence makes plain to me in what an evil case I am," retorted Petepre. "Obviously it corresponds to my situation, and I am reduced to praising the zeal which is its source. I admit that my fear is insuperable. Help me, my friend, and tell me the truth so straightforwardly that even my fear has no place to hide from it."

"Very good, then," answered the dwarf, changing his legs and putting one hand on his hip. "This is your situation: the unsatisfied and contagious qualities of the young steward Osarsiph have kindled a fire in the breast of your wife Mut-em-enet and the flames already with crackling and smoke lick at the supports of your honour, which are near to collapsing and burying your life beneath them."

Petepre drew up the linen sheet over his chin and mouth, as far as his nose.

"You would say," he asked from under the sheet, "that the mistress and the young steward have not only cast eyes on each other but that they also threaten my life?"

"Quite," replied the dwarf. He changed fists with a bounce. "That is the situation of a man who but late was so great."

"And what evidence," asked the captain in a subdued voice, the sheet going up and down on his mouth, "have you for so frightful a charge?"

"My watchfulness," Dudu gave answer, "my eyes and ears, the

penetration which was given me by my zeal for the welfare of the house may be witness, my poor master, for the lamentable and re-grettable truth of my revelations. Who can say which of the two — for so must we now speak of these persons who in virtue of their rank are so widely separated — the two, we must say; which of them first cast his eyes upon the other? Yet their eyes met; they lost them-selves criminally in each other's depths — and there you have it. We must consider, my master, that Mut-em-enet, in the valley of deso-lation, is a woman of a lonely bed; as for the steward, he is inflam-mable and inflaming. What servant would be beckoned in vain by such a mistress? That would presume a love and loyalty to the lady's husband which obviously does not exist in the person of the highest steward but only in the next-lower ranks. Guilt? To what end in-quire who first lifted eyes to the other or in whose senses the evil first took root? The young steward's guilt consists not only in his acts but in that he is here at all. His presence in the house kindles and inflames with a fire neither unallayed by lawful wedlock nor made innocuous by the knife. If the mistress is on fire for the slave, it is his existence is at fault, the sin lies at his door, his guilt is the same as though he had made indecent assault upon the innocent, and accord-ingly should he be served. But this now is the state of things: they have most forward understanding, billets-doux pass between them which I have myself seen, and can vouch for their ardour. Under pre-text of consultation on affairs of the house they meet, now here, now there; in the hall of the women, where the mistress has set up an image of Horakhte to please the slave; in the garden and in the garden-house on the mound, yes, even in the mistress's own room in this house — in all these places the pair come together secretly, and long since their talk has ceased to be of open matters, it is vanity and idle billing and cooing. How far they have gone, and if they have yet enjoyed each other's flesh so that it is too late to prevent it and only revenge remains, I cannot say with full and complete certainty. But what I can take upon mine own head, before all the gods and before you, you humiliated man, is certain truth, because with my own ear I heard it as I listened at the crack: that they in their blissful madness appoint and arrange to kill you, striking you with a club on the head; and when you are gone they will live here in the house as master and mistress and indulge their lust on a garlanded bed."

At these words Petepre drew the sheet over his whole head and became invisible. So he stayed for some time, so that Dudu began to feel how long it was, though at first he had enjoyed the sight of the master lying there a formless mass, covered and hidden by his shame. But suddenly he thrust back the sheet to his middle and half sat up, facing the dwarf with his little head propped on his hand.

"I must express my hearty thanks, guardian of my chests," said he, "for these revelations" (he used a Babylonian word, as we might use a French one) "about the saving of my honour, or alternatively about the fact that it is already lost and perhaps nothing but my bare life is left. And I must save it, not for itself, but for the sake of revenge, to which it must be devoted from now on. I am in danger of dwelling on this and losing sight of my due gratitude and recognition of the debt I owe you for your information. For my astonishment at the evidence of your loyalty and love equals the anger and horror which I feel. Yes, I confess my surprise — I know that I ought to moderate it; for how often do not the best things come to us from an unlikely quarter, one perhaps where we have bestowed no great signs of confidence and respect! Still, I cannot get over my surprise. You are after all a misbegotten changeling, a sort of dwarf jester, and hold your office more as a joke than anything else; a type half repulsive and half absurd, and accentuated both ways by your pomposity. Does it not border on the incredible, or even overstep the border, that you should succeed in penetrating into the private affairs of persons who are after me the highest in the house — for instance to read their love-letters which according to your account pass between the mistress and the young steward? Must I — or may I — not doubt the existence of these letters, when it is already unbelievable to me that you should have seen their contents? To do that, my friend, you must have wormed yourself into the confidence of the person who carried them — and how, considering your undeniable repulsiveness, can that seem in the least likely?"

"Your dread," responded Dudu, "of having to believe in your shame and humiliation, my poor master, makes you seek grounds for mistrust of me. But believe me, the grounds are ill-chosen. Though so great is your fear and trembling before the truth, which shows you so mocking and miserable a face, that it is really no wonder. Hear, then, how unfounded are your doubts! I needed not to slip into the confidence of the confidential messenger who carried the wanton letters, for that selected person was myself."

"Simply immense!" said Petepre. "You grotesque little man, so you carried them yourself? My respect grows, even to hear you say it; but it would have to grow still more before I actually believed it. What, you are so far in the mistress's confidence, and on so familiar a footing, that she thus entrusted to your keeping her happiness and her guilt?"

"Certainly," said Dudu, changing legs and fists again with another bounce. "Not only did she give me the letters to carry, but I dictated them to her. For she knows nothing about billets-doux and needed to be instructed in the sweet art."

"Who would have thought it?" murmured the chamberlain, as in surprise. "I see more and more how I have underestimated you, and my respect is growing by leaps and bounds. I assume that you have so acted to have matters come to a head and to see how far the mistress's folly would carry her."

"Of course," Dudu agreed. "Out of love and loyalty to you, my humbled lord. Should I else be standing here to incite you to revenge?"

"But how did you, contemptible and hideous as you appear at first sight, win the friendship and confidence of the mistress and make yourself master of her secret?" Petepre wanted to know.

"They happened at the same time," answered the dwarf. "Both together. For I, as all good people would, felt anger and affliction for Amun, that this foreigner had craftily advanced himself so far in the house; I mistrusted him, and the guile of his nature — not without justice, as you will admit, since he has now betrayed you and shamed your marriage bed, and after you had heaped benefits upon his head, has made you the laughing-stock of the capital and probably of the two lands. In my anger and suspicion I complained to Mut, your wife, about the affront and injustice and pointed out and called attention to the person of the wretch. At first she did not know whom I meant. But soon she hearkened so eagerly to my complaints, and in so contrary a way, speaking so wantonly and amorously under cover of a just concern, that I was not long in knowing that she lusted in her bowels after the youth and was smitten like a very kitchen-maid, having completely surrendered all her pride — for the which his presence is to blame. And if a man like me had not taken hold of the affair and associated himself with it, in order to explode the whole plot at the right moment, it would have been all up with your honour. So seeing your wife's thoughts take such devious ways, I slipped after them like a thief in the night, whom one will catch in the act. I inspired her with the idea of the billets-doux, to tempt her and to try how things were with her and how far she would go; and I found all my expectation exceeded, for by dint of the confidence she reposed in me, because she thought me a man of the world and ready to serve her lust, I learned to my horror that the young steward had inflamed our noble lady so far that she would stop at nothing, and that not only your honour but your life is in immediate danger."

"Ah!" said Petepre. "So you called him to her attention and inspired her acts. Well, so much for the mistress. But even now I simply cannot believe that a man with your drawbacks could have won the steward's trust — that I consider simply impossible."

"Your scepticism, my dear dishonoured lord, must give way before the facts. I consider your dread responsible, but likewise your particular and sacred constitution, which, one must admit, is responsible for all the harm, and which makes it impossible for you to understand people and realize how greatly a man's view of others, and his liking for them, no matter whether they are short or tall, depend on their readiness to serve his pleasure and desires. I needed only to display this readiness and to offer him my services, as a man of the world, as a go-between, between our lady and his lust, to have the fool in the snare. My standing with him was such that he soon kept nothing from me and I was able not only to know all the treacherous dealings of the couple but to lead them on and blow up the fire, that I might see how high it would blaze, to what extreme of guilt they would be led, in which I might trap them. For such a course is prescribed for the guardians of the established order, of which I am a model representative. And by this assiduous conduct I was able to come at their mutual views and the purpose they cherish: namely, that he who sleeps with the mistress of the house is master of it. That, my poor gentleman, is the luxurious and murderous plot which they daily discuss; and from it, from their own lips indeed, they deduce their higher right to fall upon you with a club and do you out of the way, that they may celebrate their feast of roses as mistress and as master of the mistress's love. But when things were so far advanced that I heard this from their own lips, the boil seemed ripe for lancing, so I have come to you, in your abasement and misery, to tell you all, that we may trap them."

"That shall we," said Petepre. "We shall come upon them and overwhelm them with fear — you, my dear dwarf, and I, and their sin shall find them out. What think you we should do with them, what punishment do you find at once painful and humiliating enough to be visited upon them?"

"My judgment is mild," answered Dudu, "at least in respect of our Mut, the lovely sinner; for that she has no bedfellow excuses much; also even though you suffer from their sin, it is not fitting, just between ourselves, for you to make great outcry. Besides, it is as I said: if the mistress loses her head over a slave, the slave is to blame, for it is due to his very presence that the misfortune occurs and he should be the one to pay. Yet even toward him I have some mercy; I would not demand that he be bound and thrown to the crocodiles, though he has richly deserved it by his good and his ill luck. For Dudu thinks not so much of revenge as of repentance and prevention, to make an end of the danger; we should but bind him and let the knife do its work, thus rooting out the cause of the sin, that he become unavailable to Mut-em-enet and his charm have no more meaning in the woman's eyes. I am myself ready to do the deed, if he is properly bound beforehand."

"I find it very dutiful," said Petepre, "that you are willing to do this too, after all you have done for me. Do you not think that thus justice would in more than one respect be re-established in the world, in that you, by this change, would be advanced in proportion as he is diminished, and put in a position of advantage which must afford you a compensation for his advancement, highly satisfying, considering your peculiar build?"

"There is something in that," Dudu replied, "I will not deny that it might be a consideration, though secondary." And he folded his arms, thrust one shoulder forward, and began to sway to and fro with his front leg going up and down. He seesawed there, nodding his head and looking pertly about as his spirits rose higher and higher.

"But again," went on Petepre, "he could hardly remain at the head of the house after you had revenged yourself thus upon him?"

"No, of course not," laughed Dudu, continuing to posture. "To be at the head of the house and give orders to the household is no office for a chastened criminal. It is the service of a capable and unmutilated man, competent to represent the master in every affair which he cannot and will not take upon himself."

"Then," concluded the captain, "I should know at once the suitable reward for your great service, that I may thank and pay you for your service as spy, and for striving to save me from shame and death."

"I should hope!" cried Dudu, abandoned to arrogance. "I may hope that you will understand my merits and be clear as to their reward and the succession. For it is not too much to say that I have saved you from shame and death, and our lovely sinner as well. She should know that I begged for mercy for her on the ground of her loneliness in bed, giving her her life, so that she has breath only through my favour! For if I choose, and she prove ungrateful, I can publish abroad her shame in city and land, and you would be forced to strangle her after all and lay her delicate body in ashes, or at least to send her back to her family minus her nose and ears. Let her be advised, poor light-of-love; let her turn her jewelled eyes away from unfruitful beauty to bend them upon Dudu, who knows how to console; master of the mistress, stout little steward over all the house!"

And he cast ever blither glances on this side and that into space, wreathed and writhed with shoulders and hips, pranced on his little feet — and, in short, behaved just like a cock at courting time, blind and deaf to his peril, utterly absorbed in his performance. And it befell him too as it befalls the cock. For with one bound Petepre the master was out from under the sheet; quite naked, a tower of flesh with the little head atop. Another bound took him to the chair where his clothes lay, and he swung his cudgel. We have seen this ornamental emblem of office in his hand — or one like it: the thick stick covered with gilded leather, with a pine-cone on top and a gilt wreath round it. It was probably a symbol of power, also probably a fetish and cult-object in female ritual. The master swung it suddenly and let it fall on Dudu's shoulders and back; he beat him until the dwarf

was deaf and blind — though on quite other grounds than before —
and squealed like a stuck pig.

"Oh, oh! Ow, ow!" he yelled, and writhed at his hips. "Oh, it
hurts, it is killing me, my bones are broken, I bleed! Mercy, mercy!
Have pity on your faithful servant!" But Petepre had none: "There,
that's for you, you shameless spy, you sneak — you snake-in-the-
grass, who have confessed to me all your treachery!" And drove him
under a rain of blows round and round the bedroom until the faithful servant found the door, took to his legs, and ran.

THE THREAT

AND it came to pass, the story tells us, that Potiphar's wife spake to
Joseph day by day and entreated him that he should lie with her. So
he gave her occasion, then? Even after the episode of the injured
tongue he did not avoid her presence but still came together with
her in various places and at various times? He did. He probably had
to; for she was the mistress, a female master, and could command his
presence when she liked. But also he had promised not to forsake her
in her distress, but to console her with words as he alone could, because he owed her that much. He saw this. He was bound to her by
the consciousness of his guilt; admitting in his heart that he had light-
headedly let things come to this pass, and that his pedagogic plan of
salvation had been a very culpable pretence, whose consequences he
must now endure and as far as possible amend, however dangerous,
difficult, and unlikely any amendment seemed. Shall we then count
it to his credit that he did not withdraw his countenance from the
smitten one, but "day by day" — or, shall we say, nearly every day —
exposed himself to the breath of the fiery bull; that he still dared, and
went on daring, to face one of the strongest temptations which have
probably ever assailed any youth in the history of the world? Yes,
probably; conditionally and in part. Some of his motives were excellent, we may grant him that. His sense of guilt and obligation was
praiseworthy; so was his stout-hearted reliance on God and his seven
reasons in the hour of need. Perhaps we may respect even the defiance
which had begun to guide his conduct, and which demanded of him
that he measure the strength of his reason against the madness of this
woman. For she had threatened him; she had sworn to tear off the
garland he wore for the sake of his God and crown him with her own.
He found that shameless, and I must say here that another element
came in which in time made him think of the matter as something
between his God and the gods of Egypt; just as to her, also, her zeal
for Amun gradually became — or was made by others — a ground for
her desire. We may understand, we may even approve, his feeling
that it was not permitted him to shirk; that he must see the matter

through to the bitter end and make it redound to the honour of his God.

All very well. Yet not quite wholly so. For there was an admixture of another motive for his obeying her, going to her and meeting her — and this, he very well knew, was not quite so creditable. Shall I call it curiosity, irresponsibility? The unwillingness to give up the free choice of the bad course, the desire to preserve his freedom for a while yet, though without any intention of deciding on the wrong side? However serious, even dangerous the situation, did he take pleasure in being alone with the mistress, on a certain footing, in calling her "my child" and feeling justified on the ground of her passion and despair? A commonplace assumption, yet justifiable, along with another, more godly or more profound: that product of his fantasy, the highly alluring, deeply thrilling thought, that is, of his death and deification as Osarsiph, and the state of sacred readiness that belonged with it, above which, none the less, there hung the ass's curse.

Enough, then, he went to the mistress. He stuck by her. He suffered her to speak to him day by day and to entreat him: "Lie with me!" He suffered it, I say, for it was no joke and no small matter, to persevere with this woman possessed by desire, to speak kindly to her and yet on his own side to sustain the seven reasons in full force and fend off her demands, despite the sympathy which in some measure flowed toward them from his own dead and deified state. Truly, one is inclined to overlook the less praiseworthy among the motives of the son of Jacob, when one considers the trouble he must have had with the unhappy woman, for she daily so besieged him that he had moments when he understood Gilgamesh, who in furious impatience one day tore out the phallus of the sacred bull and flung it in Ishtar's face.

For she degenerated daily and grew less and less delicate in the importunities with which she besought him that they might put their heads and feet together. She never, at least, came back to that idea of hers to murder the master and do away with him that they might reign as mistress and lord of love in soft garments amid flowers and lead a life of bliss. She saw that the idea was entirely repugnant to him and must have feared to estrange him by repeating it. Her drunken and clouded state did not prevent her from seeing the perfect justice of his decided refusal even to consider the wild project, and that he did not need to conceal his indignant rejection of a proposal which even she would find it hard to bring up again with a whole tongue and without the excuse of a childish lisp. But she did not abandon the plea that there was no sense in refusing her, since they already shared the secret and might just as well, so to speak, get the good of it; she went back to it again and again, holding out the promise of unspeakable bliss which he would find in her loving arms, in her body, which had stored all its treasures up for him. And when to that sweet wooing he only answered: "My child, we may not," she proceeded to try to spur him on with doubts about his masculinity.

Not that she took these seriously herself — it is hardly possible. But on the face of it she was somewhat justified by his response to her mockery. Joseph could not come out with his seven reasons — most of them she could not even have understood — and what he offered instead was certainly feeble, stupid, and badly invented. What, for instance, could she, in her passion and extremity, make of the moral thesis which he would once and for all have made his answer, that it might be on the lips of the peoples in case this story of theirs became history: namely, that his master had put all that he had into his hands save only herself because she was his wife, and how then could he do this great wickedness and sin with her? That was threadbare rubbish, it could not serve her need and passion. And even if she found herself in a history, Mut-em-enet was convinced that everybody and at all times would find it justifiable that such a pair as she and Joseph were should put their heads and feet together regardless of the captain of the guard and her titular husband; she was sure that anybody would take much more pleasure in it than in a moral thesis.

What else did he say? Something like this:

"You want me to come by night and sleep with you? But it has been just by night that our God, whom you do not know, has mostly revealed Himself to men. If then He would reveal Himself to me in the night and found me thus — what would become of me?"

That was childish. Or he would say:

"I fear because of Adam, who was driven out of the garden on account of so small a sin. How then would I be punished?"

She found that as pitiable as the one which followed:

"You cannot know all these things. But my brother Reuben lost his first-born right because he was unstable, and the father gave it to me. He would take it away again, if he knew that you had made an ass of me."

That must have seemed to her the sheerest pusillanimity. He could not be surprised, when he had dragged in some such lame excuses by the hair, that she answered them, weeping tears of rage the while, by saying that there was nothing left but for her to believe that the garland which he wore was nothing else than the straw wreath of impotence. She could hardly have meant what she said. Rather it was a desperate challenge to the honour of his flesh, and the look with which he answered her shamed and inflamed her equally, for it spoke with more eloquence and emotion even than his words:

"Do you think so?" he said bitterly. "Then be quiet. For if it were with me as you pretend to think, then were it easy, and my temptation were not like a dragon and a roaring lion. Believe me, woman, I have had the thought of putting an end to your agony and mine by making of myself what you impute to me, like the youth in one of your legends, who took a sharp leaf of the sword plant and cut himself and threw the offending member into the river for fish to devour, to witness his innocence. But I may not; the sin were as great as though I yielded, and I should be no use to God any more. For He wills that I remain whole and sound."

"Horrible!" she cried. "Osarsiph, whither did your thoughts tend? Do it not, my beloved, my glorious one, it would be such a dreadful pity! Never could I mean what I said! You love me, you love me, your angry look betrays your love and your blasphemous purpose. Sweet one, oh, come and save me, stanch my streaming blood, for pity of its flowing!"

But he answered: "It may not be."

Then she grew wrathful and began to threaten him with martyrdom and death. So far had she come; it was this that haunted me when I said that she grew less and less fastidious in her choice of means. He learned now with whom he had to do and what she had meant by her ringing cry: "Frightful am I alone in my love!" The giant cat lifted her paw, threateningly she put out her claws from their velvet sheath, to tear his flesh. If he would not do her will, not yield her his sacred wreath to receive in exchange the garland of bliss, then she must and would destroy him. Urgently she implored him to take her words seriously and not as empty sound, for he could see that she was ready for any- and everything. She would accuse him to Petepre of that which he denied her, and tax him with assault upon her virtue. She would say that he had done violence to her and the accusation would be a joy, and she would know how to act the ruined and maculate so that no one would doubt what she said. Her word and oath, he might be sure, would count before his in this house, and no denial would help him. Besides she was convinced that he would not deny, but in silence take the guilt upon himself; for that it had come to this despair and fury with her was his fault, the fault of his eyes, his mouth, his golden shoulders, and his denial of her love; he would see that it was all one in what accusations one clothed his guilt, for every accusation became true by virtue of the truth of his guilt and he must be prepared to suffer death. But it would be a death which would make him rue his silence and even perhaps his cruel denial of her love. For men like Petepre were inventive in revenge and for the libertine who debauched the mistress there would be found a kind of death that left nothing to be desired in the way of refined torture

And now she told him how he would die, painting it to him, sometimes in her singing, ringing tones, again in whispers close to his ear, like the tender murmurings of love:

"Hope not," she whispered, "that it will be quick; casting you from a rock or hanging you head down till the blood soon rushes to your brain and death comes gently. So merciful it will not be — after the beatings that will mangle your back when Petepre pronounces sentence. For when I disclose your violent deed he will be seized with a sand-storm such as comes from the mountains of the East, and his fury will rage and his malice be unbounded. It is horrible to be given to the crocodile, to lie bound and helpless in the reeds when the devourer draws nigh and his wet belly glides over you, beginning his meal with shoulder or thigh so that your wild shrieks mingle with his satisfied gruntings as he feeds — for nobody will hear or heed. For I have heard when it happened to others, and felt a light pity, without much thought or realization, one's own flesh being safe. But now it is yourself and your flesh which the oncoming devourer nuzzles, beginning in this place or that, while you are fully conscious and would hold back the inhuman shriek that wrings itself from your breast — shriek not, beloved, for me, who would have kissed you where that wet-belly sets his teeth! — But perhaps there will be other kisses. Perhaps they will stretch my beautiful one upon his back on the ground, your hands and feet made fast with brazen clamps, and heap firewood on your body and light it, so that with tortures for which there is no name and you alone can know them, gasping and shrieking, while the others only look on, your body is consumed to charcoal by lingering flame. So may it be, beloved; or perhaps they will put you, living, in a pit, together with two great dogs, and cover it with beams and earth, and again no one thinks, nor yourself until it come to pass, what shall happen there below among you three. — Do you know of the punishment of the mortise and tenon? For being accused by me and thereupon condemned, you would be shrieking and praying for mercy with the iron rod in your eye and the door grinding your head whenever it pleased the avenger to pass through. These, then, are but a few of the punishments you are certain to find, if I give voice to my complaint, as I am in my last despair resolved to do; for you will not be able to make yourself white after my oath. Out of pity for yourself, Osarsiph, give me your wreath!"

"My friend and mistress," he answered her, "you are right, I shall not be able to make myself white if it please you so to blacken me before my master. But among the punishments with which you threaten me, Petepre must choose; he cannot visit me with all, but only with one, which limits his revenge and my suffering. And even so, my suffering can only comprise what is humanly possible; and whether those limits be small or great it cannot overpass them, for they are finite. Delight and suffering, both, you have painted to me as measureless, but you exaggerate, for with both one soon reaches the limits of human capacity. It is only the error which I should commit that would be measureless, if I destroyed myself in the sight of God the Lord, whom you do not know, so that you cannot tell what it is to be forsaken of God. Therefore, my child, can I not yield to your desire."

"Woe to that wisdom of yours!" she cried in her singing voice. "Woe to it! I, I am not wise. Unwise am I, out of my measureless longing for your flesh and blood, and I will do what I say! I am the loving Isis and my gaze is death. Take care, Osarsiph, take care!"

THE LADIES' PARTY

Ah, how splendid she seemed, our Mut, standing before him and threatening him in her bell-like voice! And yet she was weak and helpless like a child, quite without regard for her dignity or her saga. She had of late begun to confide her passion to all the world, and the misery she suffered because of her young man. It had come to this: that now not only Tabubu, the rubber-eater, and Mekh-en-Weseht, the concubine, were initiated into her love and longing, but also Renenutet, the wife of Amun's overseer of bulls, as well as Neit-em-het, the wife of Pharaoh's head washerman, and Ahwere, spouse of Kakabu, the scribe of the silver-houses, from the king's silver-house; in short, all her friends, all the court, and half the city. It was a distinct sign of her degeneration that toward the end of the third year of her passion she told everybody without restraint or embarrassment and imparted to all the world regardless that which in the beginning she had so proudly and shyly kept hidden in her own bosom that she would sooner have died than confess it to the beloved himself or to anyone else. Yes, it was not only the worthy Dudu who degenerates in this story; Mut, the mistress, did too, so much that she lost her manners and her self-control. She was a person deeply afflicted and possessed, entirely beside herself, no longer a denizen of the civilized world, and estranged from its standards; a runner upon the mountains, ready to offer her breasts to wild beasts; a garlanded, panting, exulting swinger of the thyrsus. To what all did she not finally descend? This is not the place to speak of the magic she abased herself to practise with black Tabubu — we shall come to that later. Here we must only note, with mingled amazement and pity, that she prattled everywhere of her love and unslaked longing, restraining herself before neither high nor low, so that soon her affliction was the daily talk of all the household, and the cooks as they stirred the pots and plucked the fowls, the gate-keepers on their bench, said to each other:

"The mistress is keen on the young steward, but he won't hear to it. — What a state of things!'"

For that is the form such subjects take in the heads and on the lips of ordinary folk, by virtue of the lamentable contradiction between the lover's own consciousness of his sacred, serious, painfully beautiful passion and the impression it makes on the detached observer, to whom its lack of purpose or power to conceal itself is a mockery and a scandal, like a drunken man on the street.

All the later versions of our story — with exception of the briefest but most prized — the Koran as well as the seventeen Persian songs, the poem of Firdausi the disillusioned, on which he spent his old age, and Dshami's late and subtle version, all of these, as well as countless renderings by pencil and brush, tell of the ladies' party which Potiphar's chief and true wife gave to the high society of No-Amun, to acquaint them with her suffering and its cause; to arouse sympathy and also envy in the bosoms of her sisters. For love, however unslaked, is not only a curse and a scourge but also a priceless treasure, which one cannot bear to keep hidden. The songs contain some errors and are guilty of superfluous variations and adornments which despite their sweetness and charm are a burden upon the simple truth. But as for the episode of the ladies' party, there they are in the right; and if again, for the sake of pleasing effect, they depart from the original form of the story, or even belie each other by their variations, yet the singers are not the inventors of this event, the story invented it, or rather it was the personal invention of Potiphar's wife, poor Eni, who made it up and put it into effect with a shrewdness which stands in the strangest though most realistic contradiction to her bemused state.

We who know the revelatory dream dreamed by Mut-em-enet at the beginning of the three years of her love can easily understand the connection between it and the ingenious, pathetic device she employed to open the eyes of her friends. And the dream, which bears every mark of genuineness, is the best evidence for the historicity of the ladies' party and makes quite clear that only laconic brevity of style is responsible for its omission from our nearest and best-prized source.

As a prelude to the ladies' party Mut-em-enet fell ill: of that illness, in its nature not very well defined, which seizes all the young princes and the kings' daughters in the fairy-stories when they love unhappily, and which regularly "mocks the skill of the most famous physicians." She sickened of it, according to all the rules, because it was the right and proper thing, and the right and proper thing is hard to resist; but also it was important to her (and seems in general to be a principal motive of all these illnesses of princes and kings' daughters) to attract attention, to put the world about her in a flutter of excitement, and to be *questioned*, this above all: to be importuned, as in a matter of life and death, and from all sides — for her changed appearance had for a long time now been the subject of genuine anxiety and question in her closer circle. She fell ill out of the urgency of her need to preoccupy the world with her affliction, with the bliss and torment of her love for Joseph. That there was not much more, literally and strictly speaking, in her illness than this is shown from the fact that when there was question of a ladies' party Mut could arise from her couch and play the hostess — and no wonder she could, for it was all part of the same plan.

So, then, she fell ill, seriously, if rather indeterminately, and lay abed. She was treated by two eminent doctors, one from Amun's book-house, who had previously been called to Mont-kaw, and another learned man from the temple; cared for by her sisters of the house of the secluded ones, Petepre's concubines; and visited by her friends of the order of Hathor and Amun's southern house of women. The lady Renenutet called, Neit-em-het, Ahwere and many others. Came too in her litter Nes-ba-met, head of the order, consort of the great Beknechons, "head priest of all the gods of Upper and Lower Egypt." And all of them, singly or by twos and threes, sat by her bed, mourned over and importuned her, in a flood of words, partly from their hearts but partly also in cold blood, out of pure convention or even envy.

"Eni with beloved voice when you sing," said they. "In the name of the Hidden One say what ails you, and how, naughty girl, can you so distress us? As the king lives, you are changed, for a long time now; all of us, in whose hearts you live, have seen the signs of fatigue, and alterations too, which — while doing no violence to your beauty — give us great concern. May there be no evil eye upon you! We have seen, and wept among ourselves to see how weariness overtook your body, and a decrease of flesh that attacked not all parts at once, for some are fuller while others have shrunk. Your cheeks, for instance, are gaunt, your eyes begin to stare, and suffering sits upon your much-praised sinuous mouth. We, your admirers, have seen all this and spoken of it with tears. But now your exhaustion has reached a point where you take to your bed and can neither eat nor drink, while your ailment mocks the doctors' art. Truly at this news we knew not where we were, so great was our alarm. We have besieged with questions the wise men from the book-house, Te-Hor and Pete-Bastet, your physicians, and they have answered they are almost at the end of their skill and will soon be helpless. They had only a few more remedies which might avail, for all those they have tried have been unavailing. It must be some great affliction that gnaws at you as a mouse will gnaw at the root of a tree so that it sickens. In Amun's name, our treasure, is it true, say, have you a gnawing sorrow? Tell

it quickly to us who love you, before the accursed thing strikes at
the root of sweet life itself!"

"Supposing," Eni answered in a faint voice, "that I had, what good
could it do me to name it to you? All your kindness and sympathy
could not free me from it, and in all likelihood nothing remains to
me but to die."

"Then it is true," cried they, "it is really such a sorrow that is wearing you down?" And they expressed their shrill-voiced surprise: how
could it be possible — a woman like her, belonging to the highest society, rich, enchantingly lovely, the envied of all others of her sex!
What could she lack? What heart's desire was denied her? Mut's
friends could simply not understand. They questioned her persist-
ently; partly in the goodness of their hearts and partly out of sheer
curiosity, envy, and love of excitement. For a long time she evaded
their questions; in her feeble, hopeless tones she refused them all information, saying they could do her no good. But at last, very well,
she said, she would answer them. She would answer them all together and make an occasion of it: she would give a ladies' party,
very soon, and invite them all. She was very weak and without appetite, could scarcely take anything, at most a bird's liver and a little
vegetable; but she would try to find strength to get up, so that she
might reveal to her friends the cause of her disordered and altered
state.

So said, so done. At the next quarter of the moon — it was not
long before the new year and the great feast of Opet, on which day
decisive events were to come to pass in Potiphar's house — Eni gave
out invitations to that ladies' party in Petepre's house which has been
so widely if not always so wisely celebrated in song. It was a large
afternoon affair, and took on added lustre through the presence of
Nes-ba-met, Beknechons's wife and first among the women of the
harem. There was no lack of flowers or unguents, or of cool drinks,
some of them intoxicating, some only refreshing; or of cakes of various sorts, crystallized fruits and spun-sugar sweetmeats, handed by
young maidservants in charmingly exiguous costumes, with black
braids hanging in their necks and veils shrouding their cheeks — a
novel refinement which was much applauded. A delightful orchestra,
of harpists, lute-players, and flautists in wide diaphanous garments
revealing their embroidered girdles underneath, made music in the
fountain court, where most of the ladies settled down informally,
partly on chairs and stools among the laden tables, partly kneeling
on gaily coloured mats. They also occupied the columned hall, from
which the image of Atum-Re had been removed.

Mut's friends were graceful and exquisite to behold. Their flowing
hair was anointed with perfumed oil from the crowns of their heads
to where it finished off in a twisted fringe, through which peeped the

golden disks of their ear-ornaments; their limbs were a lovely brown, their sparkling eyes reached to their temples, their little noses bespoke nothing but pride and high spirits. The patterns of their jewelled and faience necklaces and arm-rings, the spider-web linen that spanned their sweet bosoms and seemed woven of sunshine or moonbeams, were the very last word in elegance. They smelt of lotus flowers; they passed each other sweetmeats and chattered in high twittering voices, or else in deeper, rougher ones — for in this climate women sometimes have such voices; for instance, Nes-ba-met. They talked of the approaching feast of Opet, of the great procession of the holy Triad in their barks by water and land; of the reception of the god in the southern house of women, where they, the ladies, would dance and sing and shake their rattles in their character as sweet-voiced concubines of the god. The topic was both attractive and important; yet at this moment it only served to keep their tongues wagging and fill in the time until their hostess, Mut-em-enet, should give them answer and let them know the thrilling cause of her exhaustion.

She sat, a figure of suffering amongst them, beside the basin, smiling faintly with her tortured sinuous mouth and awaiting her moment. As in a dream, and after the pattern of a dream, she had made her arrangements to enlighten her friends; and she felt dreamlike certainty of their success. The moment arrived with the climax of the feast. Splendid fruits were standing ready in flower-trimmed baskets, fragrant golden spheres bursting with refreshing juice under their leathery skins. They were Indian blood-oranges, a great rarity; and beside them lay charming little knives that had handles inlaid with blue stones and highly polished bronze blades to which the hostess had given special attention. She had had them sharpened — to a pitch of sharpness, indeed, such as seldom any little knives had ever been brought before. They were of such a razor sharpness that a man might have shaved with them were his beard never so tough. But they required great care in their use, for even a moment of absent-mindedness or unsteadiness was sure to bring about an annoying injury. They had acquired an edge — a positively dangerous one, these little knives; one had the feeling that one only needed to come near the blade with a finger-tip for the blood to gush out. Were these all the preparations? By no means. There was a precious wine "from the port," sweet, fiery Cyprian wine, a dessert wine, to be served with the oranges; the charming cups of hammered gold and glazed and painted earthenware stood ready, and at a sign from the hostess were handed round in the fountain court and the pillared hall by dainty little maids who had nothing on but bright-coloured sashes. But who should pour this island wine into the cups? The little maids? No; the hostess had decreed that too little honour would thus be paid to her entertainment and her guests. She had arranged something else.

She beckoned again, and the golden apples, the exquisite little knives were passed. Both elicited cries of rapture: they praised the fruit, they praised the dainty tools — that is, they praised their daintiness, for with their chief property they were as yet unacquainted. They all set to at once to lay bare the sweet pulp; but soon their eyes were distracted from the task.

Again Mut-em-enet had beckoned, and he who now appeared on the scene was the cup-bearer, the pourer of the wine — it was Joseph. Yes, the lovesick woman had commanded him to this service, requesting, as his mistress, that he should himself serve the wine of Cyprus to her guests. She did not tell him of her other preparations, he did not know for what purpose of edification he was being used. It pained her, as we know, to deceive him and deliberately make such misuse of his appearance. But her heart was set on enlightening her friends and laying bare her feelings. So she said to him — just after he had once more, with all possible forbearance, refused to lie with her:

"Will you then, Osarsiph, at least do me a favour, and pour out the famous Alashian wine at my ladies' party day after tomorrow? In token of its excelling goodness, also in token that you love me a little, and lastly to show that I am after all somebody in this house, since he at its head serves me and my guests?"

"By all means, my mistress," he had answered. "That will I gladly do, and with the greatest pleasure, if it be one to you. For I am with body and soul at your command in every respect save that I sin with you."

So, then, Rachel's son, the young steward of Petepre, appeared suddenly among the ladies as they sat peeling in the court; in a fine white festal garment, with a coloured Mycenæan jug in his hands. He bowed, and began to move about, filling the cups. But all the ladies, those who had chanced to see him before as well as those who did not know him, forgot at the sight not only what they were doing but themselves as well, being lost in gazing at the cup-bearer. Then those wicked little knives accomplished their purpose and the ladies, all and sundry, cut their fingers frightfully — without even being aware at the time, for a cut from such an exceedingly sharp blade is hardly perceptible, certainly not in the distracted state of mind in which Eni's friends then were.

This oft-described scene has by some been thought to be apocryphal, and not belonging to the story as it happened. But they are wrong; for it is the truth, and all the probabilities speak for it. We must remember, on the one hand, that this was the most beautiful youth of his time and sphere; on the other, that these were the sharpest little knives the world has ever seen — and we shall understand that the thing could not happen otherwise — I mean with less shedding of

blood — than as it actually did. Eni's dreamlike certainty of the event
and its course was entirely justified. She sat there with her suffering
air, her brooding, sinister, masklike face and sinuous mouth, and
looked at the mischief she had worked; the blood-bath, which at first
no one saw but herself, for all the ladies were gaping in self-forgotten
ardour after the youth as he slowly disappeared toward the pillared
hall, where, Mut knew, the scene would repeat itself. Only when the
beloved form had disappeared did she inquire of the ensuing stillness,
in a voice of malicious concern:

"My loves, what ever has happened to you all? What are you doing? Your blood is flowing!"

It was a fearful sight. With some the nimble knife had gone an
inch deep in the flesh and the blood did not ooze, it spouted. The little hands, the golden apples, were drenched with the red liquid, it
dyed the fresh whiteness of the linen garments and soaked through
into the women's laps, making pools which dripped down on the
floor and their little feet. What an outcry, what wails, what shrieking
arose when Mut's hypocritical concern made them aware what had
happened! Some of them could not bear the sight of blood, especially their own; they threatened to faint and had to be restored with
oil of wormwood and other pungent little phials brought by the bustling maids. All the needful things were done; the neat little maids
dashed about with cloths and basins, vinegar, lint, and linen bandages, until the party looked more like a hospital ward than anything
else, in the pillared hall as well, whither Mut-em-enet went for a moment to assure herself that blood was flowing there too. Renenutet,
the wife of the overseer of bulls, was among the more seriously
wounded; they had to quench the flow of blood by putting a tourni-
quet on the wrists to shut off the circulation from the slowly paling
and yellowing little hand. Likewise Nes-ba-met, Beknechons's deep-
voiced consort, had done herself considerable damage. They had to
take off her outer garment, and she was tended and reassured by two
of the girted maids, one black and one white, while she raved and
raged in a loud voice at everybody indiscriminately.

"Dearest Head Mother and all of you my dear friends," said the
hypocrite Mut, when order had somewhat been restored, "how could
it happen that here in my house you have done this to yourselves,
and this red episode has marred my party? To your hostess it is almost intolerable that it had to be in my house that it happened — how
is such a thing possible? One person, or even two, might cut their
fingers while peeling an orange — but all of you at once, and some
of you to the bone! Such a thing has never happened before in the
world, and will probably be unique in the social life of the two lands
— at least, let us hope so! But comfort me, my sweethearts, and tell
me how ever it could happen!"

"Never mind," Nes-ba-met answered in her deep bass for the rest of the women. "Do not think of it, Enti, for everything is right now, at least nearly, even though red Set has spoilt our afternoon frocks and some of us are pale with blood-letting. Do not be upset. For your intentions were good, and as for the party, it is exclusive in every respect. Yet after all it was pretty thoughtless of you — the thing you did in the middle of it. I am speaking quite frankly, and for all of us. Put yourself in our place. You invited us to explain the cause of your exhaustion, which mocks the best skill of the physicians; we must wait for the revelation, and that makes us nervous, so that we hide our suspense by making conversation. As you see, I am telling everything as it was, according to the simple truth, speaking for us all and not mincing matters. You served us with golden apples — very good, very fine, even; Pharaoh himself does not have them every day. But just as we are peeling them, there comes, by your order, this young cup-bearer into our already excited group — whoever he is, I suppose that he is your young steward known on the land- and the waterways as Nefernefru; and it is mortifying for a lady to have to agree with the people of the dams and the canals, and with their judgment and tastes, but really there can be no question of disagreeing with them, for he is certainly a picture of a young man from head to foot. In and for itself it is something of a shock when a young man suddenly comes among a group of already nervous women, even if he is less attractive than this one. So what could you expect but that we should tremble in all our limbs and have tears come in our eyes when such a young god appears on the scene and bends with his jug over our cups? You could not expect us to attend to what we were doing and take care not to cut our fingers! We have caused you much bustle and annoyance with this blood-letting, but the blame, dearest Eni with the lovely voice, is your own, for the trouble ensuing on your startling entertainment."

"Yes, yes!" cried Renenutet, wife of the overseer of bulls. "You must take the blame, my dear, for you have played us a fine trick and we shall all remember it — though not with anger, since we realize that you could not be affected by it, and hence thought nothing of it. But that is just it, my treasure, that you failed in tact and consideration, and so to yourself is due in all justice the awkwardness of this red episode. For naturally the total femininity of this whole gathering affects each single female in it and heightens her susceptibility to the uttermost! And then you elected to introduce a young man among us, and at what moment? Precisely when we were peeling our oranges! How could we help cutting ourselves? For it has to be just this cup-bearer who comes in, your young steward, a perfect young Adonis! I must say frankly that I was beside myself at the sight. I speak without shame, for this is an hour and these are circumstances when the mouth speaks from the fullness of the heart, and for once it seems quite right to say just what one thinks. I am a woman with a great deal of feeling for the masculine; you all know that besides my husband the director of bulls, who is in his best years, I know a certain young officer of the guard, and also there is a young priest of the temple of Khonsu who comes to my house. You all know these things without my telling you. But all that does not prevent me from being always on the alert, so to speak, for the masculine — it is easy for me to feel perfectly divine — but I have a special weakness for cup-bearers. There is always something of the god — or a darling of the gods — about a cup-bearer! I do not know what that is, probably it is because of his office and his motions. But this Refertem, this blue lotus, this honey youth, with his jug — ye gods, it was all up with me! I quite thought that I was seeing a god, and for sheer delight I did not know where I was. I was all eyes, and while I gazed I stabbed myself with the fruit-knife, deep into my flesh, and the blood ran in streams and I never felt it, in the state I was in. But that is not the whole of it: for now whenever I want to peel fruit in the future I am convinced that the image of your divine young cup-bearer will come up before me, the wretch, and I shall cut myself to the bone for losing myself in the sight of him, and can never eat any more fruit that must be peeled, though I am passionately fond of it. And all that you brought about, my treasure, with your heedlessness."

"Yes, yes!" all the ladies echoed her, the ones who had been in the pillared hall as well, for they had come out to the court while Nesba-met and Renenutet were speaking. "Yes, yes!" they cried all together, in voices some shrill and some deep. "The speakers have spoken as it was, we all nearly killed ourselves in our amazement at sight of this cup-bearer, and instead of telling us the cause of your illness, to which end we were invited, Eni, you have played us this trick!"

But now Mut-em-enet raised her voice to its full singing power and cried:

"Fools! I have not only told but showed it to you, the cause of my mortal weakness and all my misery! Then have some eye for me, as you were all eyes for him! You have seen him but the space of a few heart-beats and done yourselves harm in your distraction, so that you all are pale with the red distress the sight of him gave you. But I — I must or I may see him every day — and what can I do in my own distress, which is unending and infinite? I ask you. Where shall I turn? For this boy, you blind creatures, who saw him in vain, the steward and cup-bearer to my husband — he is my anguish and my death, he has brought me to my end with his eyes and mouth; for him alone, my sisters, my red blood gushes out in agony and I die if he quench it not. For you only cut your fingers at sight of him; but

love for his beauty has cut me to the heart, and I bleed to death!"
Thus she chanted till her voice failed and she fell back in her seat
with convulsive sobs.

We can imagine the state of high feminine excitement into which
this revelation flung the troop of Mut's friends. They behaved as
Tabubu and Mekh-en-Weseht had done before them, in face of the
great news that Mut had fallen in love. They treated the sufferer
much as the other two had done: crowded round her, stroked and
patted, congratulated, commiserated, in many-voiced high-strung
prattle. But the looks which they exchanged, the words which they
murmured to each other, had quite other meaning than sympathy.
They were angry and disappointed that there was no more to it, and
that all this pretentious affliction amounted to no more than falling
in love with a servant. There was silent disapproval, and universal
jealousy on the youth's account. But more than all, there was a certain dog-in-the-manger satisfaction that this was Mut, the proud and
pure, the moon-chaste bride of Amun, who had been visited so to
speak in her old age and afflicted in quite the most ordinary way, that
she was pining for a handsome slave and did not even know how to
keep it to herself but must helplessly expose her humiliation like a
regular female, wailing: "What shall I do?" That pleased her friends,
if also it did not escape them that all the self-exposure and publicity
were at bottom the same old conceit, which made of the most ordinary occurrence, when it was Mut to whom it happened, an extraordinary and world-shaking event — and that annoyed them afresh.

But if all this spoke in the side glances which the ladies exchanged,
yet their animation and pleasure in the sensation and the charming
scandal in high life was sufficient to make them capable of heartfelt
sympathy with their sister in distress, and of feminine solidarity; they
crowded round her, embraced and petted her, and prattled loudly,
expressing their views of the youth's good fortune in having been
granted to rouse such feelings in the breast of his mistress.

"Yes, sweet Eni," they cried, "you have shown us and we understand that it is no small thing for a woman's heart to have to be able
to see such a picture of a young god every day — no wonder that in
the end you, too, fell victim! The lucky fellow! What no man has
succeeded in, during all these years, has fallen to his youth: he has actually stirred your senses. Certainly he was not born to it — but that
shows the simplicity of the heart, which asks not after rank or station. He is no son of a nome prince and neither officer nor councillor
of state, being only your husband's steward; but yet he has melted
your heart and that shall serve him for title; and that he is a foreigner,
an Asiatic youth and so-called Hebrew, makes the affair still more
piquant and gives it a cachet. Dearest, we are so glad and relieved that
your distress and weariness has no worse cause than your feeling for

this beautiful youth. You will forgive us if we cease to feel anxiety for you and begin to feel it for him; for certainly the only ground here for fear is lest he may go out of his head with the honour done him. Otherwise the business seems to us quite simple."

"Ah," sobbed Mut, "if you only knew! But you know nothing, and I knew that you would not, even after I opened your eyes. For you have no notion how it stands with him, or with the jealousy of the god to whom he belongs and whose wreath he wears; so that he is much too good to stanch the blood of an Egyptian woman and his soul has no ear for all my crying. Ah, how much better you would do, my sisters, not to be anxious for his great honour, but to devote all your concern to me, who am at death's door with his religious compunctions!"

Then her friends insisted on learning more particulars about these religious compunctions; they could not believe their ears when they heard that this servant was not bursting with pride at the honour done him but was denying himself to his mistress. The looks they then exchanged did betray some malice, some suggestion that after all their Eni was too old for the beautiful youth, and he simply made pious excuses because he felt no desire; some of them flattered themselves that they would be in better case with him. But in general they were sincerely indignant at the foreign slave's recalcitrance; particularly Nes-ba-met, the head priestess, took the word, in her bass voice, and declared that from this point of view the affair was scandalous and indeed not to be borne.

"As a woman, dearest," said she, "I am on your side, your affliction is mine. But there is a political aspect to the thing too, it touches the state and the temple; and this little upstart — you will pardon me, I know you love him, but I call him so out of honest scorn — in his obstinate refusal to pay you the tribute of his youth, displays an insubordination dangerous to the kingdom; it is as though some Baal-city of the Retenu or Phœnicia were to set himself up against Amun and refuse the duties which it owed. In that case there would be a punitive expedition fitted out, to protect the honour of Amun, even if it cost more than the tribute came to. In this light, my dear, I view your affliction; and as soon as I get home I will speak with my husband, who is the head of all the priests of Upper and Lower Egypt, to tell him of this gross case of Canaanitish insubordination and ask him what measures he thinks proper to deal with the disorder."

She reached her conclusion amid more and even more animated chatter from all the guests; and thus the ladies' party at last broke up, which has become so famous and is here related in the true and actual course of its events. By it Mut-em-enet principally succeeded in making her unhappy passion the talk of the town — a success at which she herself, in her clearer moments, was probably horrified, yet at other times was capable, thanks to her increasing degeneration, of thinking of with a drunken satisfaction. For most infatuated people cannot believe that sufficient honour is shown their feelings unless they occupy the thoughts of all the world, if only to be mocked at and scorned. They must be known to the sparrows on the house-tops. Her friends now often made her sick-bed visits, singly or by twos and threes, to inquire after her state, to comfort her and give her advice; they foolishly passed over the actual though entirely peculiar circumstances, and the sufferer could only shrug her shoulders and reply:

"Ah, my children, you chatter and advise and understand nothing at all of this peculiar case." Then the ladies of Wese would be annoyed afresh, saying to each other: "If she thinks the matter is above our heads, and there is something quite peculiar about it, beyond any good counsel of ours, then she should hold her tongue and not tell us about the affair."

But someone else came in person, borne to Petepre's house between vanguard and rear-guard: the great Beknechons, Amun's first, whose wife had informed him of the story, and who was not yet minded to take it lightly, but rather to see it in view of the larger interests involved. The mighty shiny-pate and statesman of the church, wearing his arrogated leopard-skin, strode to and fro before her lion-footed chair, straining upward from his ribs and holding his chin in the air as he declared that all personal and merely moral considerations must be put aside in judging this situation. This might be regrettable on the ground of standards of conduct and the moral order, but once begun, must be pursued to the end in the light of loftier considerations. As a priest, a spiritual guide, and guardian of religious order, and not least as the friend and colleague of the good Petepre at court, he was obliged to censure the attentions Mut dedicated to this young man and oppose the desire he aroused in her. But the recalcitrant bearing of this foreigner, his refusal to pay tribute, was intolerable to the temple, which would be obliged to insist that the matter be set right without delay and to the glory of Amun. Therefore, he, Beknechons, quite without regard to what might be personally desirable or blameworthy, must warn and admonish his daughter Mut to exert all her powers to the utmost to bring the rebellious youth to a fall — not for her own satisfaction, even though that might come to pass, without his approval, but for that of the temple; if necessary the backward youth could be brought to book by force.

It shows with depressing clarity how low Mut had sunk that this spiritual admonishment and authorization to sin did her soul good, that she could see in it a strengthening of her position with regard to the beloved one. To this she had come, the woman who but late and conformably with her stage of development had made her joy and sorrow dependent upon the freedom of his living soul, that now she found a desperate and distorted pleasure in the thought of having the object of her hot desire produced by force before the temple authorities. Yes, she was ripe for Tabubu's magic.

But the position of the Amun authorities was not unknown to Joseph either. For no crack or cranny was too small for his faithful Bes-em-heb to crawl into, that he might be present at the interview between Mut-em-enet and Beknechons the great, hear the advice with dwarf-fine hearing, and bring it hot and hot to his patron and protégé. Joseph listened and was extraordinarily strengthened in his view that this was a trial of strength between the power of Amun and God the Lord, and that he might not let Him down, at any price whatsoever, no matter how ill the resolve might accord with the old Adam in him.

THE BITCH

So then it came about that Mut-em-inet the proud, in the degeneration worked by her passion, fell low indeed, letting herself in for a course of action which her natural refinement would only a little while before have rejected with disgust. She sank to the moral level of Tabubu the Kushite and combined with her to deal with the unclean; in other words, to make magic spells for the binding of her lover and to sacrifice to a horrible nether-world deity whose name she did not even know or wish to know. Tabubu simply called her the bitch, and that was enough.

This nocturnal spectre, it seemed, was a perfect ghoul and fury; but the Negress promised to make her compliant by means of charms to the wishes of Mut the mistress, and Mut was fain to be content — on the understanding that she renounced her claims to the soul of her beloved and would be glad if she might but hold his body — a warm-blooded corpse, as it were — in her arms. Or not glad, precisely, but mournfully assuaged; for of course it is the body, the flesh alone, that can be conjured in this wise and delivered into anybody's arms, not the soul at all. One needed to be very inconsolable indeed to be consoled with that, and with the thought that love's craving and satisfaction is after all a matter for the flesh; in God's name, it was easier to dispense with the soul than the body, however mournful the satisfaction the body purveyed.

The state of Mut-em-inet's own body was responsible for her finally consenting to the rubber-eater's base proposals. She was fully aware of her witchlike state, and considered that the physical signs it had set upon her were proof that she belonged to the guild and was bound to act accordingly. We must remember that her new body was a result and product of love, a pathetic accentuation of her femininity. For witchery is at bottom nothing else than femininity raised

to an exaggeratedly and illicitly alluring height; from which it follows not only that witchcraft is pre-eminently female, and male
witches as good as never exist, but also that in it love plays a predominant part, is always the very centre of the activity, and love-
magic, as its natural and preferred sphere, comprehends everything
that can rightly be called magic.

I have earlier, with all due delicacy, suggested that something of
the hag had entered into Mut's physical being; it probably contributed to her inclination and willingness to practise witchcraft, so that
she now allowed Tabubu to set to work on the business of sacrificing
and conjuring. For the deity whom they were to conjure was, according to the Negress, the personification of haggishness, a hag-god
and hag-goddess combined, in whom one must envisage an embodiment and epitome of all possible repulsive connotations of the word
"hag": a being of the filthiest practices; in short, an arch-hag. Such
deities there are and must be; for the world has sides that reek with
blood and are stiff with foulness, seemingly very little fit to be deified. Yet these have just as much need as its more appealing sides of
permanent representation and headship, of ghostly embodiment, so
to speak. Thus it comes that the name and nature of the divine can
enter into the horrible, and bitch and mistress be one; especially when
it is the arch-bitch we are dealing with, having by right the characteristics of a mistress, in any case. Tabubu, when she referred to this
embodiment of all filthiness and obscenity, actually called her "the
gracious mistress bitch."

The black woman thought well to warn Mut that the nature and
conduct of the proposed operations were quite outside the great
lady's social sphere. She begged pardon of her refinement beforehand, and implored her for just this once to adjust herself to the tone
of vulgarity because it was all that the gracious mistress bitch could
understand, and without a certain indecency of speech there would
be no dealing with her. The proceedings would not be very pleasant,
she said — the ingredients for the conjuring were some of them most
unappetizing; nor would there be a lack of imprecations and bombast. The mistress must make up her mind to that and not take offence, or if she did she must conceal it. For this act of compulsion
would differ from the religious services to which Mut was accustomed: it would be frightful, violent, and high-handed. Not even in
intention did it proceed from the human side or in accordance with
human tastes; but from the gross nature of the being they invoked,
whom they summoned to their presence, the mistress-bitch, whose
service could not be other than obscene, and whose character as arch-
hag conditioned the form of the proceedings and their very low
level of decency. After all, in Tabubu's opinion, if you were setting

about to constrain a young man to a purely physical compliance with the demands of love, there could not be a very high tone to the business.

Mut paled and bit her lips. Partly from the shock to her conventions, partly also from hatred of the evil chance which forced the compulsion upon her as well as on him. Now that she had resolved, the baseness of her resolve was a wound in her thoughts. That is a very old human experience: that when a man is tempted to fall below his better self, his tempters, those who drag him down, alarm him and mock him when they have him safely below, by the insolence with which they suddenly speak of his new and unfamiliar state. Pride demands that he conceal his fear and bewilderment; that he answer them: "Let things be as they are, I knew what I did when I resolved to follow you." And in such wise did Mut express herself, taking up an attitude of defiance to a resolve originally foreign to her nature: the conjuring of her beloved by means of magic.

She had to be patient for several days. The black priestess needed to prepare her magic, for which not all the ingredients were to hand: rarities like the rudder of a wrecked ship, uncanninesses like wood from a gallows, rotting flesh, certain parts from the body of an executed criminal; most important of all, some hair from Joseph's head, which Tabubu had to procure by craft and bribery from the household barber-shop. Besides they had to wait for the full moon, for their work would be more fruitful if performed under the highest potency of that equivocal planet, which is feminine in reference to the sun, masculine in reference to the earth, and thanks to its double character guarantees a certain unity to the universe and can interpret between mortals and immortals. Besides Tabubu as priestess and the lady Mut as client, there would assist at the conjuration a Moorish acolyte and Mekh-en-Weseht, the concubine, as witness. The flat roof of the house of women was the theatre of operations.

Each day — whether feared or longed for, or fearfully longed for, with impatience and shame — comes on, at last, and becomes a day of one's life bringing what it has to bring. So came on the day of Mut-em-inet's hopeful degradation, when in her bitter need she betrayed her station and embarked upon her unworthy course. She awaited each hour as she had awaited each day, conquering one by one. The sun sank, its glory faded, the earth was shrouded in darkness, and the moon, incredibly large, rose above the desert, substituting its borrowed lustre for that of the departed sovereign sun, and for substantial daylight the frail web of her painful, pallid magic. As slowly diminishing, she mounted to the zenith, and all was quiet, while in the house of Potiphar everybody lay with drawn-up knees and peaceful faces, sucking at the breasts of sleep; then the four

women, alone in the house awake, with their mysterious feminine
purposes, forgathered on the roof, where Tabubu and her assistant
had already made the needful preparations.

Mut-em-inet, her white mantel round her shoulders, a blazing
torch in her hand, hurried so fast up the steps which led from the
fountain court to the low upper storey, and thence by a narrower
one to the roof, that Mekh, the concubine, with her own torch,
could not keep up with her. Eni began to run directly she quitted
her bedroom, holding aloft her fiery torch, her head flung back, her
eyes fixed, her mouth open, her garments caught up in one hand.

"Why run so, darling?" murmured Mekh. "You will be out of
breath, I am afraid, you are stumbling; stop, go carefully with the
torch!"

But Petepre's chief and true wife answered disconnectedly:

"I must run, I must run, I must storm these heights breathless, do
not stop me, Mekh, the spirit commands me and so must it be, we
must run!"

Panting and staring she swung the light above her head so that
sparks of burning pitch flew off from the flax, and her breathless
companion clutched in alarm at the whirling stick, to wrest it away.
Mut would not suffer her, and the danger was the greater. They
were now on the second stair, and Mut really did stumble when they
came to grips, and would have fallen had not Mekh grasped her arm.
The two women, thus embraced and flourishing their lights, staggered through the narrow door and out on the dark roof.

They were greeted by a wind and by the voice of the priestess,
who took command from the first. She carried on the talk from that
moment, without ever stopping for breath; and it was gross, domineering, bombastic, ever and again interrupted by the howling jackals from the bleached desert on the east, yes, from farther away by
the dull, shattering roar of a ranging lion. The wind blew from the
west, from the sleeping city, and from the river, where the moon
played in silver sparkles on the water; from the shore of the dead,
and the mountains on that side. It was caught, panting, in the wind-
chimneys that faced the west, a sort of wooden roof designed to divert cool air down into the house. There were also a few cone-shaped
grain-bins on the roof; but besides these usual things were many more
objects and preparations, the properties for the performance. Among
them certain things on whose account it was well that the wind was
blowing: for on the floor and on tripods were pieces of bluish putrid
flesh, which would have stunk — and did when the wind died down.
The other objects for the dark rite a blind man might have seen with
inward eye, or a person who, like Mut-em-inet, did not want to see
anything, since then and thereafter she gazed diagonally upwards
into space, with her mouth drawn down half open, and staring eyes.

For Tabubu described them all aloud. She stood there black and naked to the waist, her head a grey mass of tangled hair dishevelled by the wind; girdled with a goatskin under her haglike breasts, as was her young helper likewise; her loose mouth, in which two lonely buck-teeth stood up, moved ceaselessly as she shouted the name and use of each object, like a market-woman crying her wares.

"There you are, woman!" she said as she gestured and pointed, when her mistress staggered onto the roof. "Welcome, scorned one, seeking protection, poor languisher, husk rejected of the stone, love-sick trull, come to this hearth! Take what we give you. Take grains of salt in your hand, hang laurel on your ear, crouch by the hearth, where it flickers in the wind out of its hole; it flickers for you, to your healing, poor soul, so far as may be!

"I speak! I spoke, here above I spoke and said, as priestess, before you came. Now I speak on, loudly and grossly, for fine words avail not to wrestle with her, one must name things shameless by their names; wherefore I now name you aloud, supplicant, a fool for love and a trollop bewitched. Are you sitting with your salt in your fist, the laurel over your ear? And your companion, has she hers and is she, too, crouching by our altar? Up with us, then, for the sacrificial rite, priestess and ministrant! For all is prepared for the meal, gifts and adornments without flaw.

"Where is the table? It is where it is, facing the hearth, fittingly adorned with garlands and branches, twigs of ivy and blade of corn, that she loves whom we invoke, who approaches. Dark husk hiding the mealy kernel. Therefore it garlands the table and trims the stands whereon the tempting offering stinks to heaven. Does the rotting rudder lean at the table's side? It does. And on the other side what do we see? A beam from the cross whereon they raised the malefactor on high — in your honour, perverted one, who favours that which is rejected, and to allure you it leans beside the table. But do we offer you naught else of him who was hanged, no ear, no finger? Yea, the mouldering finger graces the table, with fine crumbs of bitumen and the gristly waxen ear from the miscreant's head, clammy with blood — all that so richly to your taste, may it bring you, unholy one! But the knots of hair that shine upon the offertory table, like in colour, they come not from the murderer's head but from other heads near and far, and we have them lying close together, may they be fragrant to you, if you will help, you on whom we call, you who come out of the night!

"Still, then, let no one budge! Ye who sit by the hearth, keep your eyes on me, blench not, for no one can tell from which side she will creep up! I command silence for the offering. Put out this torch, wench. So. Where is the double-edged blade? To hand. And the cur? It lies on the floor, like a young hyena, with chains on its claws, with moist muzzle bound, that snuffs with such delight for every kind of filth. Give me first the bitumen. The ready priestess throws it in black crumbs on the flame, that its leaden qualmish smoke may curl up to your nostrils as incense, O mistress of the nether world! The drink-offerings now, the vases in right succession: water, cow's milk, and beer — I pour, I pour, I pour. My black feet stand in the liquid, the pool, the bubbling lake, while I perform the sacrifice and slay the dog — a loathsome rite, but it is not our choice, we only know that it is dear to you.

"Bring him on, then, the sniffling cur, the obscene beast, and slit his throat! Slit his belly and bathe your hands in the smoking entrails as they steam up into the cool moonlighted night. Smeared with blood, dripping with entrails, I hold them up to you, my hands, for I have made them in your image. I salute you, I invite you humbly to the sacrificial meal, O mistress of the hosts of night! Courteously we entreat you, solemnly we beg you, graciously share the meal, accept the flawless gifts! Does it please you to accept? For else know that the priestess will rise in strength against you, will seize you violently with bold practised clutch. Approach! Come springing from a noose, or from pressing hard the woman in labour as she groans; from the caresses of self-slain wives; come, blood-smeared one, from the haunt-ing-place of corpses to gnaw their flesh! Come, lured thither by your cankered lust of the impure, from unclean clingings at the cross-roads where the malefactor lies.

"Do I know you, do you know yourself in these my words? Do I wrestle nearer to you in your essence as you are? Lo, I know you in your works and ways, your unspeakable practices, your monstrous eating and drinking, and all your bottomless lusts! Or shall I come to you with closer grips and plainer, and my mouth forget its last re-straint, naming you as you are in all your swinish essence? — Utter-most horror clepe I you, bitch and strumpet, I rail at you, pus-eyed nightmare, rotten fungus, slavering slut of hell. You that perch at home on gallows where the criminal is flayed, squeaking and squall-ing and slobbering as you gnaw the carrion bones! Last lust of the hanged, wet-wombed receiver of his erected agony! Yet weak with vice, unnerved and abject, quaking with every breeze, starting at spectres, to all things of the night a cowardly prey. Uttermost hor-ror! Know I you? Name I you? Have I you? See I you? Yes, it is she! For lo, a cloud darkened the face of the moon and while it was veiled she came. The dog that bays before the house bayed louder, the blaze flared up from the hearth; the handmaid there of her who invokes you writhes in a fit. Where she bends her gaze, whither her eyes roll, thence approaches the goddess.

"Sovereign, we greet you. Graciously be pleased; for we have given of our best in gifts. If then the impure offering appease you, help! If the unclean meal, aid us, we pray! Help her, the despised and languishing! She groans for love of a youth who will not as she will. Help her, as you can, as you must, I have you in ban. Torment him hither in the flesh, the reluctant one, till he come to her on her bed, he knows not how, make smooth his neck to her hands, let her once slake her longing with the sharp smell of his youth, for which she yearns!

"Now the hairs, quickly, wench. The love-offering, the burnt-offering, I now perform, in sight of the goddess. Ah, the bright locks, from heads one near, one far, so soft and shining! Waste matter from your bodies, I, priestess, weave and wind, mingle and marry them in my hands bloody from sacrifice, I knot and net, I twist and tie; I let them fall into the flame, and flame consumes them crackling. Why is the face of the suppliant one writhen with horror and disgust? Is it the evil hornlike smell of the burning offendeth your nostrils? 'Tis your own substance, my delicate one, essence of your ardent flesh — the odour of love! — Done!" she said abruptly. "The worship has been well performed. May he please you and relish you, your beautiful one! The mistress-bitch blesses him to you, thanks to Tabubu's arts, which are worth their hire."

And the low creature laid aside her lofty tone, stepped back from her labours, wiped her nose with the back of her hand, and put her blood-stained hands in a basin of water to cleanse them. The moon shone out again. Mekh, the concubine, came to after her faint.

"Is she still there?" she asked, shaking.

"Who?" asked Tabubu, scrubbing her hands like a doctor after an operation. "The bitch? Calm yourself, concubine, she has vanished again. She did not want to come, she was enforced by my arts, because I know so well how to get round her and compass her character so tellingly in words. And she could do nothing here but by my will, because I buried under the threshold a three-fold spell against evil. But she will perform her task, no question of that. She received the offering, and likewise she is bound by the burnt-offering of the woven hair."

Mut-em-inet, the mistress, heaved a deep, audible sigh and rose from the hearth where she had crouched. In her white mantle, with the laurel still at her ear, she stood before the carrion flesh with her chin raised and her hands clasped beneath it. Since she had smelt the odour of burning hair, hers and Joseph's mingled, the corners of her half-open, masklike mouth had sagged more and more bitterly, as though weighted down; it was piteous to see, this mouth, with its stiff, tragic lips; to watch them move, as in her chanting voice she addressed her plea to the powers above:

"Hear me, ye purer spirits, who might have joyed me had ye smiled upon my love to Osarsiph the Ibrian youth; hear and see me,

in my misery at this abasement, how anguish sits at my heart for the
evil choice I must make, since no other remained to me, in my deep
despair, to your mistress, sweet Osarsiph, my falcon! Ah, ye purer
powers, how hard, how oppressive, how shameful is this renunciation of mine! For I have renounced his soul, when at last I yielded
and was enforced to this making of magic. Thy soul I renounced,
Osarsiph, my beloved — and how hard, how bitter to love must this
renunciation be! I have renounced your eyes, most anguishing of all,
but I could no other, I was helpless and had no choice. When we embrace, thine eyes will be closed and dead, and only thy swelling lips
will be mine — how often shall I kiss them, shamed in my bliss! For
the breath of thy mouth is dearer than aught else; but more than all,
more than aught else, my sun-youth, would have been the gaze of
thy soul — and the lament for its loss welleth up from my depths.
Hear, ye purer powers! From beside this hearth of the black arts, in
the bitterness of my affliction I cry to you. Look upon me, a woman
of high rank, driven by love to sink beneath it, that I must give my
joy for lust, to enjoy if not the joy of his eyes at least the delight
of his mouth! But woeful and evil it is to me, this renunciation, to me
a daughter of a prince, I cannot but utter it aloud, ye higher powers,
cannot but give it voice before I taste this conjured lust and enjoy a
soulless bliss with his sweet body. Ye spirits, leave me my secret inmost prayer: let me hope that at the last the lust and joy may not
quite part, so that if the lust be deep enough, love may blossom from
it; that beneath my ardent kisses the dead boy's eyes may open and
he may give me his gaze from his soul, so that perhaps after all the
hard conditions of this magic art may not hold but be defeated. In my
abasement, ye purer powers, leave me this silent secret hope; to you
I raise my lament, deny me not the hope of this little defeat, this little, little triumph — "

    And Mut-em-inet lifted her arms and with violent prolonged sob-
bing sank upon the breast of Mekh, the concubine, who led her from
the roof.

NEW YEAR'S DAY

MY audience must by now have reached the height of its impatience
to hear what after all everybody already knows. The hour of satisfaction is at hand, the climax of the story, the chief hour of the feast,
which has been since it first came to pass and related itself: the hour
and day when Joseph, for three years Potiphar's head steward, for
ten his property, just saved himself from the grossest error of his life,
escaping from fiery temptation — though as it were with a black eye
— and as a result completing a smaller cycle of his life, in that he went
down again to the pit, by his own error, as he himself realized, and in
punishment for behaviour so heedless, so provocative — almost, one

might say, so wicked — that there was not much to choose between it and his earlier wrongdoing.

We are justified in drawing a parallel between his sin against Potiphar's wife and his earlier sin against his brothers. Once more he had gone too far, in his craving to make people "sit up"; once more the working of his charm, which it was his good right to employ, for his own enjoyment and for the honour and profit of his God, had been allowed to get beyond control, to degenerate into an actual danger. In his first life these workings had taken the negative form of hate; this time the immoderately positive and equally destructive form of passion. He had in his blindness given fuel to the flames of both; in the second case, misled by his own response to a woman's uncontrollable passion, he who stood in such need of instruction himself had tried to play the pedagogue. His conduct cried out for retribution, there is no doubt of that; but we cannot help smiling to see how the punishment which so justly overtook him was directed to the furtherance of a good fortune much greater and more brilliant than that which had been destroyed. The source of our amusement is the insight which these events afford into the mental processes of exalted spheres. Far back in the very pre-beginnings of history, we have seen that the fallibility of the creature man was a source of dissatisfaction to certain circles. "What is man, that Thou are mindful of him?" The question always hovered on certain lips and was an embarrassment to the Creator, who saw Himself driven to pay tribute to the "kingdom of the stern" and let justice have its way — clearly less of His own motion than under a moral pressure from which He could not well escape. The present instance is a delightful example of His dignified bowing to the storm, while at the same time having His little game with the austere and disgruntled ones, practising the art of healing where He chastened and making misfortune a fruitful soil whence renewed good fortune should spring.

The day of decision, the turning-point, was the great feast-day of the official New Year, the day of the beginning of the rise of the Nile and of Amun's visit to his southern house of women. The official New Year, be it noted; for the actual day when the sacred cycle closed, the dog-star rose once more in the morning sky, and the waters began to mount was by no means the same day. In this respect disorder reigned in Egypt, where it was otherwise so much detested. It did happen, through time, men's lives, and kingly dynasties, that the actual New Year coincided with the calendar; but only in one thousand four hundred and sixty years did this come to pass, almost forty-eight generations must live without experience of it — which they did not mind at all, by comparison with other of life's manifold cares. The century in which Joseph's Egyptian course was run was not vouchsafed the pleasure of beholding the beauty inherent in the

union of the actual and the formal; the children of Kemt who lived
and laughed and wept beneath Egypt's sun simply knew no more
than that the two did not coincide — and it mattered to them not at
all. Not that they celebrated the New Year, Akhet, the rise of the
Nile, at a time when actually they were in the middle of the harvest,
Shemu. But they did so in the winter season, Peret, also called the
time of the sowing; and if the children of Kemt saw nothing strange
in that — for an irregularity which will go on for another thousand
years is after all regularity of a sort — Joseph for his part did, he even
found it comic, by reason of his inward detachment respecting the
life and customs of the Egyptians. He kept the irregular feast, as he
did all those of the nether land, with reservations, and with just that
amount of indulgence which he considered justified from above in
respect of his worldly participation. It is worth while to point out in
passing, and is almost a cause of amazement, that a person having so
much critical detachment from the sphere where he lived, and from
activities to him fundamentally foolish, could yet take life seriously
enough to achieve all that Joseph achieved, and accomplish all the
good that he was destined to accomplish.

But whether a detached mind took it seriously or no, the day of the
official rise of the Nile was celebrated in all Egypt, and especially in
Nowet-Amun, the hundred-gated Wese, with a solemnity which we
can only realize by comparing it with one of our own great national
and popular festivals. The whole city was on its legs from early
dawn, and its huge population, greatly exceeding a hundred thousand, as we know, was still further increased by hordes of country-
folk from up-river and down, streaming in to celebrate Amun's great
day in the god's own seat. They mingled among the citizens, open-
mouthed, hopping on one leg, staring at the city's majestic sights, the
glory of which made up to the betaxed and belaboured little peasantry for the grey poverty of the whole past year and strengthened
their patriotism for the floggings of the one to come. In a sweating
throng, their noses full of the odours of burnt fat, the fragrance from
mountains of flowers, they filled the gay, canopied, alabaster-paven
forecourts of the temples, which echoed with sacred chorals, glowed
with colour, and were full to bursting with abundance of heaped-up
food and drink of every sort and kind. There, this one day, they
might fill their bellies at the expense of the god, or rather of the
higher powers who robbed and exploited the whole year round but
now smiled in extravagant generosity; they might, against their own
better knowledge, lull themselves in the dream that it would always
be thus, that with this feast the golden age of free beer and roast
goose had dawned, and never again would the tax-gatherers come, accompanied by Nubians bearing palm rods to harass the little peasantry, but every day would be like the temple of Amun-Re, wherein

they saw a drunken woman with flowing hair, spending her days in riotous living because she held the king of the gods.

By sunset all Wese was so drunk that it went reeling and bawling about the streets, committing all sorts of nuisances. But in the early morning and forenoon it was still fresh-eyed and well in hand; receptive to the splendours of Pharaoh's progress, when he drove out "to receive the office of his father," in the official phrase, and Amun moved in his famous procession on the Nile to Opet, to his southern house of women. The populace was all joyous reverence and pious zeal, untiringly it gazed upon the unfolding splendours of State and Church, which were calculated to lay up in the hearts of Wese's children and her guests a fresh supply of daily patience and proudly self-deluded devotion to the fatherland. This was accomplished nearly as efficiently in the present as in the old days when earlier kings came home booty-laden and triumphant from Nubian and Asiatic campaigns and perpetuated their victories in reliefs on the great temple walls — victories which had made Egypt great, and were indeed the first beginning of the exploitations and floggings of the little peasants.

On high feast-days Pharaoh drove out wearing crown and gloves; he came out from his palace brilliant like the rising sun, and betook himself to his father's house, to behold his beauty; in his high swaying canopied carrying-chair, surrounded by ostrich-feather fans, enveloped in heavy clouds of fragrant smoke, which streamed back upon him from incense-bearers walking in front of his chair, their faces turned toward the good god. The voices of the reading priests were drowned in the jubilations of the throng, as they hopped on one leg and rejoiced. Drums and cornets preceded the procession, in which walked troops of Pharaoh's relations, dignitaries, unique and true friends of the king as well as just plain friends. Ranks of soldiers closed up the rear, with field badges, battle-axes, and throw-sticks. The lifetime of Re to thee, the peace of Amun! But where should one stand — staring, swallowing dust, stretching one's neck — were it better here, or at Karnak beside Amun's house, aflutter with banners, whither everything would finally proceed? For the god himself came out today, left the dim shrine in the farthest background of his mammoth tomb, behind all the forecourts, courts, and halls, each one lower-ceiled and more silent than the last; and moved, a strange, misshapen, squatting puppet, through all his halls, each loftier and more brilliantly coloured, on his bark adorned with the heads of rams, secluded in his veil-shrouded chapel, which was borne by long poles on the shoulders of four-and-twenty shiny-pates in starched kilts. He too, among fans, in clouds of incense, went into the light and the noise to meet his son.

The great event was the "flight of geese," a custom dating from primitive times, the scene of which was the beautiful meeting-place on the square before the temple. What a lovely and joyous spot this was! Gay flags fluttered from gilded poles with the head-ornament of the god on top. Mountains of flowers and fruits heaped the offertory tables before the shrine of the holy Triad, father, mother, and son; statues of Pharaoh's ancestors, the kings of Upper and Lower Egypt, brought up by the crew of the sun-bark, divided into four watches, were here set up. Priests standing on golden pedestals above the crowd, their faces turned to the four quarters of the earth, released the wildfowl in four directions, to carry to the gods of each the news that Horus, son of Osiris and Eset, had set upon his head the white as well as the red crown. For he that was conceived in death had once chosen this form when he mounted the throne of the two lands and the ceremony had been repeated through countless years, and lay and learned in their different ways had drawn conclusions about the general or the individual destiny from the manner of flight.

After the flight of geese, Pharaoh performed many beautiful mysteries and ceremonies on the square. He sacrificed before the images of the early kings. He cut with a golden sickle the sheaf of spelt handed him by a priest and laid the grain as an offering of praise and petition before his father. He burned the incense of the gods before him in a long-legged pan, while readers and choir-singers chanted out of their book-rolls. Then the majesty of this god seated itself in a chair and sat motionless to receive the congratulations of the court, expressed in quaint and high-sounding words or brought before him in the shape of letters couched in flowery, subtilizing phrases, from courtiers who were prevented from coming. They were read aloud, to the great entertainment of all who listened.

This was only the first act of the celebration, which went on from beauty to beauty. They went down to the Nile, the barks of the holy Triad swaying aloft on the shoulders of twenty-four shiny-pates each; and Pharaoh walked like a modest son on foot behind his father Amun's bark.

The whole crowd swarmed down to the river, thronging round the procession of the gods, led by Beknechons, the head priest, in his leopard-skin, just behind the trumpets and cornets. The incense rose, the music swelled, the fan-bearers fanned. Arrived at the shore, the sacred barks were put on three large ships, each more beautiful than the other, but the most indescribably beautiful of all was Amun's bark, made of cedar-wood which — it was said — the princes of the Retenu had had to fell in the cedar mountains and themselves pole across the river. Each ship was mounted in silver, and all of gold was the great heaven-throne in the centre and the flag-poles and obelisks in front, adorned with serpent-crowns fore and aft and furnished with all sorts of little emblematic soul-figures and sacred symbols, most of which people would not have known how to explain, from so remote a past had they been handed down. The fact strengthened instead of weakening the veneration they enjoyed.

The state ships conveying the great Triad were not boats, but barges; not rowed, but towed by light galleys and a crew from the shore, up the Nile toward the southern house of women. It was an honour to belong to these crews, and a man so chosen reaped many practical benefits throughout the year. All Wese, save the dying and the age-ridden — for the infants were carried on their mothers' backs or at their breasts — in other words, a mighty host, rolled like a wave along the bank with the crews, accompanying the divine procession, and a procession in themselves. They were led by a servant of Amun chanting hymns; soldiers of the god followed with shields and throw-sticks; dressed-up Negroes came after, greeted with roars of laughter from the crowd as they danced and drummed, cut grimaces and made ribald jokes. They knew they were held in contempt and so played the fool even more than lay in their natures, to flatter the grotesque conception the people had of them. Temple musicians of both sexes shook castanets and sistra; there were animals garlanded for the sacrifice, standard-bearers, war-chariots, lute-players, upper priests with their retinues; burghers and peasants followed on, singing and clapping out the time with their hands.

Rejoicing and exulting the train moved on to the pillared temple on the river, where the state ships tied up; the sacred barks were hoisted to the shoulders of the bearers and carried in a new procession, to the sound of drums and long trumpets, to the glorious house of birth, received and met with curtsyings and contortings and waving of boughs by Amun's earthly concubines, the ladies of the order of Hathor, who now danced before their exalted spouse, the squatting swaddled little doll in his shrouded bark; in diaphanous garments, beating tambourines and singing in their universally beloved voices. This was the great New Year's reception in Amun's harem, a most regal spread, mountains of offerings in the shape of food and drink, unending genuflections and symbolic ceremonies, for the most part no longer understood by anybody, in the inmost, inner, and outer parts of the house of embrace and birth, in its rooms full of gay reliefs and inscriptions, its corridors of rose-granite papyrus-columns, silver-paved tent-halls, and courts of statuary where the populace might enter at will. The full gorgeousness of the New Year will be best appreciated if we realize that toward the end of the day the whole procession re-formed in the same splendour as before and went back by water and land to Karnak; and that in all the temples the fairs and feastings, the popular jollification and theatrical entertainments — in which masked priests performed scenes from the lives of the gods — went on without stopping through the evening. The whole great city swam in beer and bliss and belief in a carefree

golden age. The crews which had towed the state barks, crowned
with garlands, anointed with oil, and very drunk indeed, ranged
through the streets and might do more or less what they liked, without let or hindrance.

THE EMPTY HOUSE

IT was necessary to sketch in the scene of the feast of Opet, the official celebration of the rising of the Nile, in order to make clear to my
readers the frame and setting of those events in the lives of individuals which form the climax of our tale. The bare sketch suffices to
show that Petepre, the courtier, had his time very much taken up.
He was a member of the immediate entourage of His Majesty Hor-
in-the-Palace, who had this day more pontifical duties to perform
than on any other of the high-days and holy-days in the year. And
Petepre's place was among the nearest; that is, among the "unique"
friends of the king. Yes, on this very morning he was raised to the
rare and exalted rank and addressed in a manner which caused him
the utmost gratification. The titular captain of the guard was away
from home all day. Indeed, the whole household was away, the place
was empty, like every other house in Wese; for, as I said, only crip-
ples and the moribund remained at home. Among the last, indeed,
were Huia and Tuia, the exalted parents in the upper storey; for they
never went farther afield than the garden house on the mound, and
seldom even as far as that. It was a miracle that they yet lived; for
during the last ten years they had reckoned hourly on their passing,
yet still tottered about, the old mole and the swamp-beaver, she with
her blind slits of eyes, he with his beard of tarnished silver, together
within the dark caul of their brother-sisterhood; perhaps because
some aged people simply go on living and cannot find death, being
powerless to die; perhaps because they were afraid of the king of the
nether regions and the forty frightfully named ones, on account of
the clumsy bribery of which they had once been guilty.

Huia and Tuia, then, had remained at home in their upper storey,
together with the two stupid little maids who served them in succession to others grown in the course of time too unchildlike to wait on
the exalted parents. Otherwise house and court were empty, like all
others in Wese. Yet were they? No, for there was one other exception — single, but important. Mut-em-inet, Potiphar's wife, his chief
and first, had stopped at home.

That must seem very strange to anyone with knowledge of the
feast. She did not take part with her sisterhood, Amun's concubines,
in the sacred service of the god; did not wear the horns and disk, nor
in the narrow garment of Hathor undulate in the dance, nor raise her
beloved voice to accompaniment of the silver rattle. She had made

her excuses to the protectress of the order, Tiy, wife of the god; they were the same excuses which Rachel had once made a pretext what time she sat on the teraphim hidden in the camel bedding, and would not rise and stand before Laban. She had sent word that unfortunately she was unwell, meaning by the discreet phrase that unfortunately on this very day she found herself incapacitated. The exalted ladies had shown more understanding than Petepre, to whom she had said the same. For he, with a lack of feeling for human frailty, had been as obtuse as in his time the obtuse Laban. "How do you mean unwell?" he asked. "Have you toothache, or the vapours?" He used a silly medical expression current in high society to describe a hypochondriac state of health. And when she had finally gone into detail he had been unwilling to admit the excuse. "That doesn't count," he had said — very much, we will remember, as Laban in his time had done. "That is not an illness that anyone can see, or an excuse for staying away from the feast of the god. Some people would drag themselves to it half dead rather than stay away, but you want to remain at home on account of a simple and normal thing like that." "There does not need to be anything unnatural about an ailment, for it to attack us, my friend," she answered him. Then she gave him the choice of dispensing her either for the public feast or for the private entertainment at their own home in the evening, with which Petepre was to celebrate his promotion to the rank of "unique friend." It was impossible, she said, for her to attend at both. If she danced before the god she would be worn out by evening and have to absent herself from Petepre's feast.

In the end though in great annoyance he had had to agree to her saving her strength in the day-time in order to act as hostess in the evening. He was annoyed because he was suspicious — so much we can say with certainty. He did not like it. He did not feel easy in his mind at her remaining at home alone on the pretext that she was unwell; he was disturbed, he had a vague sense of apprehension — on the score of his own peace of mind and that of the household; and he came home earlier than necessary to the evening party, on his lips the usual question, outwardly confident, but inwardly anxious: "Is all well in the house? Is the mistress happy?" — this time to receive a frightful but secretly long-expected reply.

We have thus anticipated our story, because after all, in the words of Renenutet, wife of the chief overseer of bulls, we know it already without being told; so that there is no more suspense save in the matter of details. Neither will it surprise anybody to hear that the thought of Joseph had a share in Petepre's annoyance and disquiet; and that he mentally connected the idea of his wife remaining at home with the question of whether Joseph was doing the same. We share his disquiet, and we too must, not without misgivings on the score of the seven reasons, inquire of Joseph's doings on the day of the feast. Did he, in fact, remain at home too?

He did not; it would have been quite impossible for him, and strikingly inconsistent with his principles and practice. The Egyptian Joseph, in this tenth year after he had been snatched away into the land of the dead, was now at seven-and-twenty Egyptian incarnate, in a social if not in a spiritual sense; even his fleshly garment had been for the last three years wholly Egyptian, the form of him entirely occupied and informed by Egyptian substance. We know his attitude: with certain reservations he adapted himself, became a child of Egypt and partaker in the Egyptian year, celebrating her heathen feasts, sharing in her outlandish practices, in his tolerant, cosmopolitan way, if also with moderation and a certain irony; confident that the man who had brought the calf to this field would indulgently close his eyes to the sight. Certainly the New Year's day, the great Amun-feast, was a proper occasion to be affable, to live and let live; and the son of Jacob went to it. Like everybody else here below, he was arrayed in feast-day garments and on foot from early morn. Yes, he actually paid symbolic honour to the popular custom and drank a little more than he needed; but only later in the day, for at first he had to perform official duties. As the steward of a high dignitary and title-bearer he walked in the suite of the king's suite from the western house of the horizon to Amun's great house and took ship thence to the Opet temple. The return procession of the divine family was not quite so formal, it was easy to withdraw from it; and Joseph spent the day as thousands did, sauntering and sightseeing, visiting masses in the temples, sacrificial feasts, and masques of the gods. He knew of course, that he must be at home betimes, by late afternoon and before all the other servants, to perform to his own satisfaction his duties as head of the household and responsible overseer; to assure himself that in the long serving-room (where once he had received from the scribe of the buffet the refreshment prepared for Huia and Tuia) and in the hall where the banquet was spread, everything was ready and in order for the New Year's feast and the celebration of Petepre's promotion.

He laid stress in his mind, and in his intentions, on carrying out this supervision alone and undisturbed, while the house was still empty and his subordinates not yet returned from the feast. It seemed to him right and proper so to do; and in support of his resolution he excogitated a set of sayings — in his own mind, for they had never existed before, though he couched them in the form of popular proverbs — such as: High estate, golden weight; great honour, great onus; first to aspire, last to retire — and other golden rules of the same kind. He thought them out, and repeated them to himself, after learning, during the water journey, that his mistress, being indisposed, was not taking part in the dances of the order of Hathor but remaining at home alone. For before he knew this fact he had never thought of the jingles, nor persuaded himself that they were proverbs; nor had he realized what now became perfectly clear, that in the sense of these maxims it was imperative for him, the head of the house, to be at home before the rest of the staff, to see that all was in readiness.

He used that very word, in his mind, though even to him it was suggestive, and an inner voice warned him that he should refrain. Joseph, as an upright young man, did not deceive himself about the great and soul-shattering peril involved in following out his own maxims. It was a soul-shattering peril, yes; yet also it was a joyful opportunity — but for what? Yes, little whispering Bes, an opportunity to bring to an issue the affair of honour between God and Amun; to take the bull by the horns and in God's name to let matters come to a head here and now. This was the goal, this the great, soul-shattering opportunity; and everything else, frightened, whispering little Bes, is just nonsense and rubbish. "The servant still may sleep, the master watch must keep." Joseph, the young head steward, would cling to his proverb-wisdom, undeterred by either the futile croaking of his little friend or his mistress's artful indisposition.

We may gather from overhearing this much of what went on in his mind that there is no ground to feel assured of his safety. The original story, to be sure, long ago played itself out to the end, and what we here relate is only a repetition in the feast, a temple masque, as it were. Otherwise, out of sheer anxiety and concern, the sweat might be standing on our brows! But what is a repetition in the feast? It is the abrogation of the difference between was and is. When the story first told itself, there was, at this crisis in it, simply no ground whatever for thinking that its hero would come off with a black eye instead of losing his God and his all. Nor have we any better right to premature unconcern. The women as they buried the beautiful god in the cave wailed no less shrilly because the hour of his resurrection would come. For when they wailed he was dead and mangled; and to every hour of the feast as it comes on and is present is due its meed of tears and triumphing, of triumph and tears. Esau celebrated his great hour, swelling his chest and flinging out his legs, pathetic and comic to behold. His story had not yet reached the wailing and weeping stage. We are in like case: at this moment, reading Joseph's thoughts and hearing his jingling little rhymes, we are justified of the sweat that stands on our brows, and should not be justified if it did not so stand.

We shall be in even worse case if we return and see how matters stood in Potiphar's deserted house. The woman who remained there alone, who in this drama plays the part of the mother of sin, was ardently confiding in the feast-hour for a glowing realization of her

hopes. Certainly she no less than Jacob's son was resolved to stake all
on the issue; certainly she had every reason to await the bitter-bliss-
ful triumph of her passion, the hour of sweet and sinister fulfilment,
when she should enfold her beloved in her arms. Were her hopes not
confirmed from above and from below? She was empowered by the
highest spiritual authority in the kingdom, the honour and sun-power
of Amun were pledged to her support; but no less was she upheld by
the powers of darkness, which by virtue of infernal magic she, daughter of a nome prince, had debased herself to conjure and to bind —
though in her breast still lingered hope that she might evade the humiliating conditions they imposed. For in her shrewd feminine mind
she thought that after all love made no such clear distinction between
body and soul; that by the sweet embraces of the flesh she would
succeed in wooing the soul of her beloved as well, and in uniting lust
with bliss. As we tell the tale, the wife of Potiphar is — here and now,
as well as in the then which has become the now — bound up with
the event, and cannot know what has not yet happened. But this she
knows: that Joseph will come to her in the empty house; with all
the burning passion of her soul she knows it. The bitch-goddess will
torment him hitherwards. In other words, he will learn on the way
that she is not taking part in the feast, that she has remained alone in
the silent house. And the thought will grow in him to overmastering
strength, that he must come back at a time when this significant and
extraordinary situation still obtains. The bitch-goddess will give this
thought power over him, will make it guide his steps. Joseph, thinks
Mut, knows nothing about the bitch-goddess and Tabubu's vile arts;
he will think it is his own, that overwhelming impulse to join Mut in
the empty house; he will suppose that he is irresistibly drawn to seek
her out in her solitude. And if he does, if he is convinced that thought
and impulse are his own, then will not the illusion become truth in
his soul, and thus the bitch have been defeated on her own ground?
A man will often say "I am urged" to do so and so. But what is it that
urges him, which he distinguishes from himself and makes responsible for his act? Certainly it is only himself; himself, together with
his desire. Is there any difference between "I will" and "Something
within me wills"? Must we say "I will" in order to act? Does the act
come from the will, or does not rather the will first show itself in the
act? Joseph will come; and by his coming will realize that he willed
to come, and why. But if he comes, if he hears the call of opportunity and heeds the call, then all is decided, Mut has triumphed, she
will crown him with ivy and garlands of the vine!

Thus Potiphar's wife, and such the reasoning of her drunken, over-
stimulated mind. Her eyes looked unnaturally large and quite as unnaturally bright, for she had applied quantities of black antimony to
brows and lashes with her ivory pencil; and they looked out from it

with a sinister look as of one possessed. And her mouth, as always, had no truck with her eyes: it was a sinuous, smiling, assured, and triumphant mouth. But her lips moved constantly in a slight sucking, chewing motion, for she was eating little balls of crushed incense mixed with honey, to sweeten her breath. She wore a garment of the thinnest royal linen, which revealed all her love-bewitched contours; from its folds, and from her hair, came a fragrance of fine cypress perfume. She was in the room reserved for her use in the master's house; on one side it adjoined the vestibule with the seven doors and the constellated pavement; on the other Petepre's northern pillared hall, where Joseph performed his reading service. But in one corner it gave on the banqueting-hall next the family dining-room; in this hall the evening feast was to be served, in honour of Petepre's new rank. Mut's door into the northern hall was open, likewise one of the doors thence into the banqueting-hall. Confident, expectant, she moved about in these rooms, solitary in the house save for the two exalted parents awaiting their end in the upper storey. Eni, their daughter-in-law, as she went to and fro, gave them a thought, and cast a glance upwards toward the painted ceiling from her jewelled, sinister, glittering eyes. Often she retired from hall and banqueting-room into the twilight of her private chamber, where the light fell from above through openwork stone panels. There she lay down, outstretched upon her diorite couch, and buried her face in the pillows. Cinnamon wood and myrrh burned in the incense stands, and their fragrant vapour curled out through the open doors into the dining- and banquet-halls.

So much for Mut, the enchantress.

To return to the departed son of Jacob: he came back, as we know, before any of the other members of the household. He came — and perhaps thereby became aware that he wanted to come, or was urged to come — which is the same thing. Circumstances had not prevented him from sticking to his duty and adhering to the view that it was right and proper for him to break off his sightseeing sooner than the others and give his attention to the house over which he was set. Though actually he had delayed longer than one might suppose, before the performance of a duty prescribed and postulated by so much proverbial wisdom. He did come back when the house was still empty; yet not so very long before the others, those of them, that is, who had not permission to stop in the city because they were needed that evening at home. Perhaps not longer than a winter hour, or even less — considering that in this latitude winter hours are so much shorter than summer ones.

He had spent a quite different day from Mut's: in sunlight and noise, in the lively hubbub of the pagan feast. Behind his lashes he still saw pictures of the magnificent processions, the masques, the bustling crowds. His Rachel-nose still smelled the burnt-sacrifices, the flowers, the emanations from all these hordes of human beings hot with hopping on one foot and excited with so much sensual gratification. His ears were still full of the sound of drums and horns, rhythmical hand-clapping, and the shouts of men intoxicated with hopeful fervour. He had eaten and drunk; without exaggerating his condition, I may say that he was in the frame of mind of a young man who is disposed to see in a threatened danger less a danger than an opportunity. He had a blue lotus-wreath on his head and a single blossom in his mouth. He twirled his fly-fan of white horsehair round on his wrist and sang as he went: "Blithe the servant, free from care, the master's eye is everywhere!" He actually thought that this was a line from some treasure of folk-wisdom, and that he had made up only the tune. So, as the day wore to its end, he reached his master's house, opened the gate of cast bronze, crossed the constellated pavement of the vestibule, and entered the beautiful banqueting-hall, where all was laid ready, in the most elegant refinement, for Petepre's party.

He had come home, Joseph, the young steward, to see that all was complete, and whether or no Khamat, scribe of the buffet, was deserving of a reproof. He moved about the pillared hall, among the chairs and little tables, the jars of wine in their holders, the buffets laden with pyramids of fruit and cakes. He looked to the lamps, the table of wreaths, floral necklaces, and unguent boxes; and rearranged the sideboard, making the little golden beakers ring. He had spent awhile in these masterly retouchings, and made the beakers ring once or twice, when he started; for he heard a voice, a singing, ringing voice, calling him from some distance; calling the name which he had taken in this land:

"Osarsiph!"

In all his life he never forgot that moment, when in the empty house the sound of his name struck on his ear. He stood with his fan under his arm and two golden beakers in his hands. He was inspecting their polish and certainly he had made them ring as he held them; he listened, thinking he had not heard aright. Yet he must have been mistaken, for he stood thus a long time listening, the two beakers in his hand, and there was no sound for a long time. But at last it came again, that singing voice echoed through the rooms:

"Osarsiph!"

"Here am I," he answered. His voice failed him for hoarseness; he cleared his throat and said again:

"I hear."

Again there was a pause, and he waited motionless. Then it came, singing and ringing:

"Is it you, Osarsiph, whom I hear in the hall, and have you come home alone to the empty house?"

"As you say, mistress," he replied, setting back the beakers in their place and going through the open door into Petepre's northern hall, to speak into the adjoining room.

"Yes, I am here, to see that things are in train in the house. 'Much oversight to put all right' — you know the proverb, and since my master has set me over the house and knows no care save for the bread he eats, for he has put all into my hands, keeping naught back, and will literally be no greater than I in this house — I have given the servants a little extra time to enjoy themselves, but thought best to resign the latter end of the day's pleasures and come home betimes. 'Harsh with thyself, to others merciful' — as you know must be the rule. But I will not praise myself before you, and I am but little ahead of them, they may come at any moment, and Petepre too, the unique friend of the god, your husband and my noble master — "

The voice came ringing out of the twilit chamber: "And seeing after all that is in the house, will you not also, Osarsiph, see after me? Have you not heard that I remained alone and that I suffer? Cross over the threshold and come to me!"

"Gladly would I," Joseph replied, "and would cross the threshold and visit you, but there are many things here in the hall to attend to, and much still to arrange which needs me to cast my eye — "

But the voice sounded again:

"Come in to me. The mistress commands it."

And Joseph crossed the threshold and went in to her.

THE FATHER'S FACE

HERE our story loses its tongue. I mean our present version and repetition in the feast does so; for in the original, as it happened and told itself, it by no means lost its tongue; it went on, there in the twilit room, in an agitated exchange, a dialogue in the sense that both parties talked at once. I prefer, however, to draw over the scene the veil of delicacy and human feeling. For in that long-ago time it went on without witnesses, whereas here and today it is performed before a large audience — a decisive difference, as no one can deny, where a question of tact is involved. Joseph, particularly, was not silent; he could not be silent, but talked very volubly, almost breathlessly, bringing to bear all his wit and charm against the woman's desire, in the attempt to talk her out of it. But just here lies the reason why our story loses its tongue. For he became involved in a contradiction, or rather a contradiction presented itself, as he talked, most painfully affecting and troubling to human feeling: the contradiction between body and soul. Yes, as the woman, in words or by her silence, answered to what he said, his flesh stood up against his spirit, and in the midst of his most fluent and eloquent speech he became an ass. And what a shattering contradiction that is, what restraint it demands from the narrator: when eloquent wisdom is given the lie by the flesh and is manifest an ass!

He fled — for we know that he succeeded in flying — in the state and condition of the dead god; to the woman an aggravated occasion for despair and the raging fury of frustration. Her desire had discovered in him a manly readiness; and the forsaken woman alternately tore at and caressed the garment which he left in her hands — for we know that he left his garment behind him — in paroxysms of frantic agony, with loud outcries of exultation and anguish. The Egyptian woman's cry, repeated over and over again was: *"Me'eni nachtef!* I have seen his strength!"*

Something enabled Joseph, in that uttermost extremity, to tear himself away and flee: that something was his father's face. He saw his father's face — all the more detailed versions say so, and we may take it for the truth. It is so: when, despite all his skill of tongues he was almost lost, the face of his father appeared to him. Jacob's image? Yes, certainly, Jacob's image. Not an image of settled and personal lineaments which he saw somewhere in the room. Rather he saw it in his mind and with his mind's eye: an image of memory and admonition, the father's in a broad and general sense. For in it Jacob's features mingled with Potiphar's fatherly traits, there was something of the modest departed, Mont-kaw, and over and above all these were other, mightier traits. Out of bright, brown father-eyes with soft tear-sacs beneath them, it peered at Joseph in tender concern.

This it was which saved him. Or rather, he saved himself — for I would speak in the light of reason and give credit where it is due, not to any spirit manifestation. He saved himself, in that his spirit evoked the warning image. In a situation only to be described as far gone, with defeat very nigh, he tore himself away — to the woman's intolerable anguish, as we must, in justly divided sympathy, admit — and it was fortunate that his physical agility equalled his glibness of speech; for he was able, one, two, three, to twist himself out of his jacket — the "garment," his outer raiment — at which she clutched in the abandon of her love, and to escape, in not very stewardlike array, to the hall, the banqueting-room, the vestibule.

Behind him, in her thwarted love she raved, half in raptures — *"Me'eni nachtef!"* — but yet betrayed beyond bearing. She did frightful things with the garment still warm with his body, which she held in her hands, the precious hated object: covered it with kisses, drenched it with tears, tore it with her teeth, trod it underfoot —

dealt with it, in short, much as the brethren had dealt with the veil of
the son at Dothan in the vale. "Beloved!" she cried. "Whither do you
go from me? Stay! O blissful boy! O shameless slave! Curses upon
you! Death! Treachery! Violence! Seize the miscreant! He has slain
my honour — help, help! Help for the mistress! A fiend has attacked
me!"

There we have it. Her thoughts — if we may speak of thoughts
where there was nothing but a whirlwind of rage and tears — had
brought her to the accusation with which she had more than once
threatened Joseph in the fury of her desire, when she raised her lioness claws against him: the murderous accusation that he had monstrously forgotten himself toward her, his mistress. The wild recollection rose in the woman's mind, she flung herself on it, shrieked it
with all her strength — as one hopes, by sheer voice-power, to lend
truth to the untrue — and our justifiable sympathy must make us rejoice that the insulted woman found this outlet to her anguish, that
she could give it an expression, false, of course, yet matching it in
horror, which was calculated to enflame all who heard, turn them
into allies of her insulted state and make them pant to avenge it. Her
yells resounded.

There were already people in the vestibule. The sun was setting,
and most of Petepre's household had returned to house and courtyard. So it was good that the fugitive had a little time and space to
collect himself before he emerged. The servants stood rooted to the
ground with horror, hearing their mistress's cries; and though the
young steward came at a measured pace out of the banqueting-hall
and passed with composed mien among them, it was as good as impossible not to connect the impaired state of his clothing with the
shrieks that issued from the inner room. Joseph would have liked to
gain his room, the special room of trust, to put himself to rights. But
as there were servants in the way, and a craving to get out of doors
took the upper hand, he crossed over to and through the open bronze
door to the courtyard, which was full of the bustle of home-coming.
Several litters were drawing up before the harem, containing the secondary wives; the chattering little creatures, under supervision of
Nubian eunuchs and scribes of the house of the secluded, had been
vouchsafed their glimpse of the feast and were now being returned
to their gilded cage.

Whither should the fugitive flee with his black eye? Out through
the gateway by which he once had entered? And thence? That he
himself did not know, and was glad that he still had space before him
in the courtyard and might move as though he were bound somewhither. Then he felt his clothing twitched; and Bes-em-heb, the
little dwarf, piped up at him, his face all crumpled with his grief:
"Ravaged the field — burnt by the bull — oh, ashes, ashes! Osarsiph,

Osarsiph!" They stood halfway between the main house and the gate-way in the outer wall. Joseph turned, the little man hanging to him. The sound of the woman's voice came over to him, the voice of the mistress. The white figure stood at the top of the house steps, sur-rounded by a crowd which poured after her out of the hall. She stretched out her arm, and men followed it running with arms like-wise outstretched in his direction. They seized him and brought him back among the courtyard folk running up before the house: gate- and door-keepers, artisans, stablemen, gardeners, cooks, and silver-aproned waiters. The weeping midget clung to his skirt and was borne along too.

And Potiphar's wife addressed to her husband's servants thus gath-ered before and behind her in the courtyard that well-known speech which at all times has been counted against her by all men; which even I, despite all I have done for Mut-em-inet's saga and her cause, cannot fail to condemn. Not on account of its untruth, which might pass as the garment of the truth; but on account of the demagogy which she did not scorn to use to rouse the people.

"Egyptians!" she cried. "Children of Kemt! Sons of the river and the black earth!" — What did she mean by that? They were just or-dinary people, and at the time nearly all of them a little drunk. Their Egyptian birth as children of Hapi — in so far as it was a fact, for there were among them Moors from Kush and people with Chaldæan names — was a native merit: they had nothing to do with it nor did it help them in the least if they neglected their duties, for their backs were bruised with thick leather straps well laid on, regardless of whose children they were. And now all at once their birth, which had been very much in the background and had no practical value for the individual, was brought to their notice with flattering empha-sis — because it could be used to rouse their sense of honour, unite them in a common pride, and make them pant with fury against someone who had to be destroyed. Her challenge bewildered them. Yet it had its effect, combined with that of the good barley beer.

"Egyptian brothers!" — They were her brothers all at once; it went through and through them, they found it thrilling. "Behold me, your mistress and mother, Petepre's chief and true wife! See me as I sit upon the threshold of this house — we know each other well, you and I!" — "We," and "each other"! They swallowed it down, this was a good day for the lower classes! — "But likewise know you this Hebrew youth, standing here half naked on this great day in the cal-endar, lacking his upper garment, because I have it in my hands. Do you recognize him, who was set as steward above the children of the land and over the house of one great in the two lands? He came down out of his wretched country to Egypt, Osiris' beautiful garden, the throne of Re, the horizon of the good spirit. They brought this stranger to us into this house" — "us" again! — "to mock us, and bring shame upon us. For this frightful thing has happened: I sat alone in my chamber, alone in the house, for I was unwell and was dispensed from appearing before Amun and kept the empty house alone. Then the abandoned one, the Hebrew fiend, took advantage of my being alone and came in unto me that he might do his will with me and bring me to shame — the servant would lie with the mistress!" — she screamed the words — "lie with me to enforce me! But I cried with a loud voice, when he would have done it and have shamed you for his servant-lust; I ask you, Egyptian brothers, have ye heard me cry out with all my strength, in evidence that I repulsed him and defended myself to the utmost, as the law demands? Ye have heard it. But when he too heard it, the abandoned one, that I lifted up my voice and cried, then his boldness failed him and he struggled out of his outer garment, which I have here as evidence and would hold him by it that ye might seize him, and fled away from me with his evil purpose unaccomplished and got him out, so that I stand here pure before you, thanks to my outcry. But he, who was set over you all and over this house, he stands there in his shame, who will be seized of his deed, and judgment shall come upon him as soon as the master, my husband, comes home. Put the clog on him."

This was Mut's speech — it was not only untruthful but provocative. And Potiphar's household stood there stupefied and helpless; they had already been not too clear-headed, with all the free temple beer they had had, and now they were completely dazed. They had heard, all of them, that the mistress was infatuated with the handsome young steward and he denied her. And now suddenly it turned out that he had laid hands on the mistress and tried to do her violence. It made their heads go round, what with the beer and what with the mistress's tale; they could not make it rhyme, and all of them were fond of the young steward. Certainly the mistress had cried out, they had all heard her, and they knew the law: it was evidence of a woman's innocence if she cried out when she was attacked. And she had the steward's garment in her hands; it really looked as though she held it as a forfeit when he tore himself away; but he himself stood there with his head sunk on his chest and said not a word.

"Why are you hesitating?" they heard a strong manly voice saying — the voice of Dudu, the gentleman dwarf, who stood among them in a stiffly starched feast-day skirt. "Do you not hear the mistress, that she has been so cruelly insulted and nearly brought to shame, and she commands that the clog be brought and laid upon the Hebrew slave? Here it is, I have brought it with me. For when I heard her lawful outcry I knew where we were and at what o'clock, and quickly fetched the tools out of the whipping-room, to have them at hand. Here they are. Stop gaping, and fetter his lustful hands

— bind up this infamous slave, bought long ago on the advice of the shallow against that of the sound; for long enough has he played the master and been set over us who are true-born! By the obelisk! He shall be brought to the house of retribution and death!"

It was Dudu's great hour and he savoured it to the full. And two of the servants took the clog out of his hand and put it on, while little Shepses-Bes whimpered in a way that made the rest of the crowd titter. It was a spindle-shaped block of wood with a slit in it, which could open and shut, holding the culprit's hands helplessly in the narrow hole, weighed down by the heavy wood.

"Fling him in the kennel!" commanded Mut, with a frightful sob. Then she crouched on the step where she was, in front of the open door, and laid Joseph's garment down beside her.

"Here I will sit," she said in her chanting voice that rang across the darkening courtyard, "on the threshold of this house, with the accusing garment by my side. Withdraw from me, all of you, and let no one advise me to go in, that I suffer no harm from my thin garb in the cool of the evening. I shall be deaf to such pleas, for here will I sit beside my forfeit until Petepre drives in and I receive atonement for my monstrous wrong."

THE JUDGMENT

ALL hours are great, each in its own way, whether great in pride or great in misery. Esau had his, when all went well with him, and he boasted, throwing out his legs. But when he flung out of the tent, crying: "Curse it! Curse it!" and limped away, tears like hazel-nuts rolling from his eyes, was the hour less great, less momentous for the hairy one? So now: we are come to Petepre's feast-hour, the most painful in his life, and at all times inwardly anticipated by him: when he hunted birds, or the hippopotamus, or followed the desert chase; even when he read his good old books, always that hour abode in the background of his thoughts, always he vaguely looked forward to it, ignorant only of its details — though these, when it came, were largely in his hands. And as we shall see, he shaped them nobly.

He rode in between torches, driven by Neternakht, his charioteer; earlier, as I said, than the festivities required, on account of his premonitions. It was a home-coming like many others, when each time he had felt dread in his heart — but this time the dread was to be realized. "Is all well in the house? Is the mistress happy?" Just that she is not: the mistress sits, a figure of tragedy, on your threshold, and your helpful cup-bearer lies fettered in the kennel.

So, then, this was the form which the reality took. Well, let us deal with it. He had already, from some distance, seen that Mut, his wife, somehow frightful to behold, sat beside the door of his house. Yet as he dismounted from his gala chariot he threw out the usual questions — this time they remained unanswered. The grooms hung their heads and were silent. Yes, yes, it was all just as he had always expected, though of course the hour might hold its minor surprises. The car was led away; the crowd drew back into the torch-lighted courtyard; he moved, that Reuben-tower of tender flesh, with his fan and symbol of office in his hand, toward the steps; he mounted them to where she crouched.

"What am I to think of this scene, my dear friend?" he asked, with courtesy and circumspection. "You sit thinly clad in so exposed a place, and beside you is something I am at a loss to understand."

"So it is," answered she. "Yet your words are pale and weak to describe a reality so much more frightful and violent than you paint it. But what you say is true: here I sit, and have that beside me of which you shall soon have frightful understanding."

"Aid me to reach it," he replied.

"I sit here," she said, "awaiting your judgment upon the direst crime ever known in the two lands or probably in all the kingdoms."

He made a sign with his fingers to ward off evil and waited, composedly.

"He came," she chanted, "the Hebrew servant whom you brought to us, he came to me to mock me. I begged you in the hall that sunset evening, I embraced your knees that you might send away the stranger, from whom I boded no good. In vain; the slave was too dear to you and I went away unconsoled. But now the wretch came upon me and would have his lust of me in your empty house, being in manly readiness for the act. You do not believe, you cannot comprehend this abomination? Then see this sign and interpret as you must. Stronger than the word is the sign; in it is nothing to interpret or to doubt, for it speaks the absolute language of fact. Behold! Is this robe your slave's robe? Examine it well, for I am clean before you by this sign. For when I cried out as the wretch assailed me, he was afraid and fled from me, but I held him by his garment and in his fright he left it in my hand. The evidence of his shocking crime — here I hold it before your eyes, the evidence of his flight and of my crying. For if he had not fled I had not his garment; if I had not shrieked he had not fled. Moreover all your household are witness that I shrieked — ask all the people!"

Petepre stood silent, his head bent. Then he gave a sigh and said:

"That is a very sad affair."

"Sad?" she repeated, stormily.

"I said, very sad," he answered. "It is even frightful; I would seek a yet stronger word, but that I may gather from what you say that, thanks to your presence of mind and legal knowledge, the issue was favourable and things did not come to the worst."

"You seek no word to describe the shameless slave?"

"He is a shameless slave. As the whole affair is a matter of his behaviour, the words I used apply above all to him. And this evil thing must confront me, on this evening of all evenings, the evening of the great day of my elevation to the rank of unique friend, when I come home to celebrate Pharaoh's goodness and grace with a little evening party, to which the guests will soon be coming. You will agree that it is hard."

"Petepre! Have you no human heart in your breast?"

"Why do you ask?"

"Because in this hour of nameless horror you can speak of your new court title and how you will celebrate it."

"I did so but to bring the nameless horror of the hour into sharpest contrast with the homage of the day and set it off the more. It lies in the nature of the nameless that one may not directly speak of it, but only express it by indirection."

"No, Petepre, you have no human feeling!"

"My love, I will tell you something: there are situations in which one welcomes a certain lack of feeling for the sake of the injured as well as of the situation itself, which may be better dealt with in the absence of too much human feeling. What is now to be done, in this dreadful and very sad affair, which mars the day of my own promotion? It must be dealt with and dispatched without delay; for in the first place I quite understand that you will not stir from this spot, where it is impossible you should remain, until you have satisfaction for the unspeakable annoyance you have suffered. But in the second place, everything must be put right before my guests arrive, and that will be soon. Therefore I must hold domestic court without delay, and the trial, praise to the Hidden One, will be brief, for your word, my friend, has sole validity and none other comes into question, so that judgment can be rendered speedily. — Where is Osarsiph?"

"In the kennel."

"I thought as much. Let him be brought before me. Have the exalted parents summoned from the upper storey, even though they may sleep. Let the household assemble before my seat, which I will have set up here, where the mistress sits, that I may raise her after I have given judgment."

His orders were quickly carried out; the only obstacle to them being that at first Huia and Tuia, the brother-sister pair, refused to appear. They had heard of the trouble from their spindle-armed child-servants; these, with mouths like funnels, had poured out the course of events below, and the frightened old folk, like their sin-offered son the courtier of the sun, found that they had always been prepared for something of the sort. Now they were afraid and would not come, because the trial seemed to promise them a foretaste of the judgment in the lower regions and they felt too weak-headed to marshal their arguments in their own justification, further than the phrase: "We meant it for the best." They sent word that they were near to death and not equal to attending a domestic court. But their son, the master, grew angry, stamped his foot, and ordered that they be helped downstairs, just as they were. If they were on the point of dying, then the fitting place was where their daughter-in-law sat accusing and demanding justice.

So then they came down, on the arms of their child-maids, old Huia's silver beard wagging and his head aquiver; old Tuia with a frightened smile lifting her blank white face, with its slits of eyes, as though she were seeking something. They were placed beside Petepre's judgment seat, where they sat distractedly babbling: "We meant well." After a while they became quiet. Mut the mistress crouched, with her token and forfeit beside her, next the footstool of the throne, behind which a Moor in a red coat waved a tall fan. Torch-bearers lighted up the group. The courtyard, too, was lighted up with torches, and the household, save those on holiday, were gathered there. And they brought Joseph in his fetters before the judgment seat, with little Sa'anch-Wen-nofer-and-so-forth, who had not let go his skirt; likewise Dudu, pompous and secure in the hope that his great hour was mounting from better to best. The two dwarfs stood there, on the culprit's either side.

Petepre raised his refined voice and spoke rapidly and formally:

"We shall hold a court here, but we are in haste. — I summon thee, Ibis-headed One, who wrotest the laws for men, white ape beside the scale; thee, goddess Ma'at, who representest truth, in adornment of ostrich-feathers. The offering we owe you will be offered later, I stand warrant and it is as good as done. Now the hour presses. I pronounce justice for this house which is mine, and thus I pronounce."

He had said this while holding up his hands. Now he took an easier position in a corner of the lofty chair, supported his elbow, and lightly moved his little hand over the chair-arm as he went on:

"Notwithstanding the host of precautions taken in this house to oppose evil, despite all the words and maxims which should make it invulnerable to harm, yet affliction has succeeded in entering in and breaking for a time the charm which preserved it in peace and tender mutual consideration. Very sad and frightful is all this, there are no other words; so much the more that the evil must come to a head on the very day when Pharaoh's love and grace vouchsafed to honour me with the rank and splendid title of unique friend; one would think that on such a day I must needs be met with courtesy and congratulations from all sides, instead of the frightful news that the order of my house stands tottering. But be that as it may. That beautiful order has for long been gnawed at by affliction, and evil has slipped through the protecting guards, to break in and bring about that which stands written, that the rich shall be poor and the poor rich and the temples desolate. For long, I say, has evil consumed in secret, hidden from most, but not from the eye of the master, who is father and mother to the house, for his glance is like the moonbeam which makes the cow to conceive, and the breath of his words like the wind which bears the pollen from bough to bough in sign of divine fruitfulness. And as from the lap of his presentness all beginning and prospering flow as the honey from the comb, so naught escapes his oversight; however hidden to the many, to his eye it lies open. Let this occasion teach it. For I know the legend that follows my name: that I take upon myself nothing on earth save that I eat and drink. That is but gossip and negligible. Know that I know all; and if the fear of the master and the dread of his all-seeing eye come strengthened anew out of this distress, upon which I sit in judgment, then one may say that despite all its deep sadness it had its good side."

He carried to his nose a little handled malachite scent-bottle, which hung on a chain over his jewelled collar; after refreshing himself he went on:

"Thus were long known unto me the ways by which evil penetrated into this house. And also to me were known the ways of those who in their arrogance and spite, out of envy and hatred, nourished it and prepared its paths — and not only this but even first gave it entrance that it might glide in past all the good words and charms. These traitorous powers stand before my seat, in the dwarfish person of my former guardian of the wardrobe and jewel-caskets, called Dudu. He himself has had to confess to me all his malice and how he opened the way for the consuming evil. Upon him may judgment fall! Far be it from me to deprive him of the virility which the sun-lord was once minded to unite with his puny form. I will not touch it. They shall cut out the traitor's tongue. — Half his tongue," he corrected himself, waving his hand with a movement of disgust as Dudu set up a loud wail. "But," he added, "as I am used to having my clothing and precious stones in charge of a dwarf, and it is not desirable that my habits should suffer from this misfortune, I will name the other dwarf of my house, Sa'ankh-Wen-nofer-Neteruhotep-em-per-Amun, as scribe of the wardrobe, and he shall from now on preside over my coffers."

Little Bes, the nose in his wrinkled face all cinnamon-red from weeping for Joseph, jumped for joy. But Mut, the mistress, raised her head to Petepre's chair and murmured through her teeth:

"What judgments are these, my husband? They touch but the margin of things, they are but trivial. What shall I think of your judgment and how shall I raise myself from this place, if you so judge?"

"Patience!" he answered her as softly, bending down from his seat. "For here each will in his turn have justice and judgment, and his guilt will overtake the culprit. Sit quietly! You will soon be able to rise from your sitting, as satisfied as though you had yourself been judge. I judge for you, my love — though without admixture of all too human feeling — and you may rejoice! For were feeling and its violence to pronounce the judgment, there might be no end to the remorse."

After he had so whispered to her he sat up straight again and spoke:

"Take your courage in your hands, Osarsiph, my former steward, for now I come to you, and you too shall hear my judgment, for which perhaps you have long anxiously waited — to sharpen your punishment I have prolonged your suspense. For I think to lay hold on you roughly and assign you bitter punishment — aside from that growing out of your own heart. For three beasts with ugly names follow at your heels; they are called, if I remember aright, shame, guilt, and mocking laughter. And these, it is easy to see, have brought you before my seat, your head bent and your eyes cast down — as I am not now for the first time aware, for I have kept my secret eye upon you during the torture of the time of waiting I have chosen to inflict. You stand, your head bowed low, your hands in fetters, and utter no word. For how should you speak, since you are not asked to justify yourself, and it is the mistress who witnesses against you, with her own word, which is unimpeachable and of itself would call down judgment; yet there is also the evidence of your upper garment to shame you, and the irrefutable language of things speaks of your presumption, which at last has brought you so far that you have raised your hand against the mistress, and when she would hold you to a reckoning, you are driven to leave your garment in her hand. I ask you, what sense it could have to speak in your own defence against the mistress's word and the plain language of things?"

Joseph was silent, bowing his head even lower than before.

"Obviously none," Petepre answered himself. "You must be dumb, as the sheep before its shearers is dumb — naught else remains for you to do, however glib of tongue and pleasing of speech you are. But thanks to the god of your tribe, that Baal or Adon who is probably like to the setting sun in power, for he preserved you in all your presumption that it came not to the uttermost with your rebellion, but rather thrust you out of your coat — thanks to him, I say, for else you had been at this hour thrown to the crocodile, or your part had been the slow death by fire, if not the torture of the door and the rod. But there can be no talk of such punishments. For you were preserved from the worst and I am not in a position to inflict them. But doubt not that I am minded none the less to handle you roughly; take then your sentence, after your lengthened-out suspense: For I will cast you in prison, where lie the prisoners of the king, at Zawi-Re, the island fortress in the river; not to me any longer you shall belong, but to Pharaoh, and shall be a slave of the king. I will give you into the hand of the master of the jail, a man with whom one does not jest; of whom moreover one may think that he will not be deceived by your beneficent-seeming ways; so that at least in the beginning he will be hard on you. Moreover I will write to the official and advise him of your affair and shall know how to speak of you to him. To this place of atonement, where no laughter is, you shall be taken tomorrow by boat and see my face no more, after those long and pleasant years when you could be near me, fill my cup, and read to me from the good old books. That may well be painful for you, I should not wonder if your downcast eyes were full of tears. Be that as it may, tomorrow you shall be brought to that place of durance. You need not go back to the kennel. That punishment you have already borne, it shall rather be Dudu who shall spend the night there until tomorrow they cut off half his tongue. But you may sleep in your wonted place, the special room of trust, which for this night shall be called the special room of custody before punishment. Also, since you wear fetters, it is but just that Dudu wear them too, if there is another set. If there is but one, Dudu shall wear it. — I have spoken. The trial is ended. Let each one go to his post for the reception of the guests."

No one will be surprised to hear that after such a judgment as this, all those on the court fell on their faces and raised up their hands, crying out the name of their mild and wise lord. Joseph too fell down, in gratitude; even Huia and Tuia, supported by their little maids, did honour on their faces to their son; and as for Mut-em-inet, the mistress, she made no exception; but was seen to bow over the footstool of the judgment seat and hide her face upon her husband's feet.

"My friend," said he, "there is no reason for thanks. I rejoice if I have succeeded in satisfying you in this affliction and have showed myself loving with my power. We may now go into the banqueting-hall and celebrate my feast. For since you have wisely kept the house all day, you have spared your strength for the evening."

So then Joseph went down a second time to the prison and the pit. The story of his rising again out of this hole to a still higher life may be the subject of future lays.

JOSEPH THE PROVIDER

PRELUDE IN THE UPPER CIRCLES

IN the upper circles of the hierarchy at this time there was felt, as always on such occasions, a mild yet poignant satisfaction, an agreeable sly sense of "I told you so," expressed in glances from under lowered lashes and round little mouths discreetly drawn down.

Once again had the cup run over; once more had patience been exhausted, justice fallen due; and quite against His own wish or will, under pressure from the Kingdom of the Stern (which, in any case, the world was unable to resist, since One had never succeeded in making it stand up on the unstable and yielding foundations of sheer mercy and compassion), He, the Almighty, in majestic affliction had seen Himself driven to step in and clean up; to overturn, to destroy, and only after that to even off again — as it had been at the time of the Flood and on the day of the rain of fire and brimstone, when the Salt Sea had swallowed up the wicked cities.

This time, of course, the concession to justice was not on such an appalling scale as in that earlier attack of remorse and the ensuing wholesale drownings. It did not compare with that other occasion when, thanks to the perverted sense of beauty of the people of Sodom, an unspeakable city tax had almost been exacted from two of us. No, this time it was not all mankind that had fallen into the pit; nor even some portion of it, the corruption of whose ways had cried to heaven. This was a matter of but one single specimen of the breed, albeit an uncommonly taking and self-complacent one, more than usually well equipped with the advantages of nepotism and long-standing design in his favour. And we had had our noses rubbed into him on account of a whim, a train of thought, only too familiar to the heavenly host, where it was the source of much bitterness, though also of the not unjustified hope that very soon the shoe would be on the other foot and the bitterness the portion of him who had set the train of thought in motion. "The Angels," so ran the train of thought, "are created after Our image, but yet not fruitful. The beasts, on the other hand, lo, they are fruitful, but not after Our likeness. Let Us create man — an image of the angels, yet fruitful withal!"

Fantastic. Worse than merely futile, it was far-fetched, extravagant, pregnant with remorse and bitterness. We were not "fruitful," not we! We were courtiers of the light, sober-minded chamberlains one and all; the story about our one-time going in unto the children of men was simply irresponsible gossip. But everything considered, and whatever interesting advantages the animal quality of fecundity might prove to have over and above its animality, at all events we "unfruitful ones" did not drink injustice like water, and One should see how far One would get with One's notions about fruitful angels: perhaps far enough to see that an Almighty with self-control and prudent forethought for His own peace of mind might better let matters rest once and for all at our decent and honourable form of existence.

Unlimited power, unlimited possibility of taking into one's head, producing out of it, and bringing into being by a mere "Let there be" — such gifts had, of course, their dangers. Even All-Wisdom might not be quite adequate to avoid all the blunders and waste motions in the practice of absolute qualities like these. Out of sheer restlessness and lack of exercise; out of the purest "much wants more"; out of a capricious craving to see, after the angel and the brute, what a combination of the two would be like; out of all these motives, and impelled by them, One entangled Oneself in folly and created a being notoriously unstable and embarrassing. And then, precisely because it was such an undeniable miscreation, One set One's heart upon it in magnificent self-will and made such a point of the thing that all heaven was offended.

Now, was it true that He had come on this idea all by Himself and of His own accord? Speculations to the contrary were rife in the hierarchy, albeit only in whispers and not susceptible of proof. Plausible, however, they were; and according to them the whole thing went back to a suggestion made by the great Shemmael, who at that time, before his luminous fall from on high, had stood very near the Throne. The idea sounded very like him — and why, forsooth? Because it was his business to realize and bring into the world evil, his very own thought, which nobody else either knew or cared about, and because the enrichment of the world's repertory through evil could be achieved in no other way than just precisely by the creation of man. Among the fruitful animal creation evil, Shemmael's great invention, did not come into question, and certainly not among us unfruitful images of God. For it to come into the world, there was needed just the very creature which Shemmael, according to the hypothesis, had proposed: an image of God, which at the same time was fruitful — in other words, man. It did not necessarily follow that the Almighty had been hoodwinked. Shemmael, in his usual grandiose way, had probably not concealed the consequences of the proposed creation — in other words, the origin of evil — but had come out quite forthright and forcibly with it, though in our circles we guessed that he also said a lot about how much livelier it would make life for the Creator: for instance by the need to exercise mercy and pity, judgment and correction. Or by the appearance in the world of merit and demerit, reward and punishment — in other words, by the origin of the Good, a phenomenon bound up with that of Evil. The Good, indeed, had actually had to depend upon its opposite, waiting for existence in the limbo of the merely possible; thus it was clear that creation rested upon division, which had even begun simultaneously with the separation of light from darkness, and the All-power would only be consistent in going on from this exterior position to create the moral world.

The view was widespread in the hierarchy that this had been the argument by which the great Shemmael had flattered the Throne and won it over to his counsels — highly malicious counsels they were, of course; one could not help sniggering at their slyness, however much it had been disguised by the rude frankness the malice clothed itself in. With that malice, it must be said, the upper circles did not altogether lack sympathy. The core of Shemmael's malice lay here: if the beasts, though possessing the gift of fruitfulness, were not created in God's image, we of the hierarchy were not either, strictly speaking, since that property, God be praised, we were clean of. Now the properties of godlikeness and fruitfulness which we divided between our two groups were originally united in the Creator Himself and thus the new creation suggested by Shemmael would be the only one actually and literally after the Creator's own image. With this being, then — in other words, man — evil came into the world.

That was a joke to make anyone snigger. The very creature which if you like was nearer to the image of the Creator than any other brought evil with him into the world. Thus God on Shemmael's advice created for Himself a mirror which was anything but flattering. Often and often in anger and chagrin He was moved to smash it to bits — though He never quite did, perhaps because He could not bring Himself to replunge into nothingness that which He had summoned forth and actually cared more about the failure of than He did about any success. Perhaps too He would not admit that anything could be a complete failure after He had created it so thoroughgoingly in His own image. Perhaps, finally, a mirror is a means of learning about oneself; and He was later to be confronted, in a son of man, a certain Abiram or Abraham, by the consciousness of that equivocal creature as a means to His own self-knowledge.

Man, then, was a result of God's curiosity about Himself. Shemmael had shrewdly divined the curiosity and had exploited it in his advice. Vexation and chagrin had been the inevitable and lasting effect — especially in the by no means rare cases where evil was united with bold intelligence, logic, and pugnacity, as it was in Cain. The story of the first fratricide and his conversation with God after the deed was known in some detail to the upper circles and industriously circulated. God had not come off very well when He asked Eve's son: "What hast thou done? The voice of thy brother's blood crieth unto Me from the earth, which has opened her mouth to receive thy brother's blood from thy hand." For Cain had answered: "Yes, I have slain my brother and it is all very sad. But who created me as I am, jealous to that extent that under provocation my whole bearing is changed and I no longer know what I am doing? Art not Thou a jealous God, and hast Thou not created me after Thy image? Who put in me the evil impulse to the deed which I undeniably committed? Thou sayest that Thou alone bearest the whole world and wilt not bear our sins?" Not so bad. Quite as if Cain or Cajin had taken counsel beforehand with Shemmael, though probably the hotheaded rascal had needed no advice. Rejoinder would not have been easy. There could be only bitter laughter or a crushing blow. "Get out!" was what He had said. "Go thy ways! A fugitive and vagabond shalt thou be, but I will make thee a sign that thou belongest to Me and no one may slay thee." In short, Cain, thanks to his logic, came off better than unscathed; there could be no talk at all of punishment. Even that about the fugitive and vagabond was not serious: Cain settled in the land of Nod, eastward of Eden, and in peace and quiet begot his children, a work for which he was urgently needed.

At other times, as is well known, punishment descended, frightfulness was invoked, there was majestic affliction at the compromising conduct of the "most like" creature. Again there were rewards, extravagant rewards: we need only recall Hanok or Enoch and the incredible, between ourselves the quite irresponsible benefits that fell into the fellow's lap. In the circles and ranks the view was held — and cautiously passed about — that in the world below there was great lack of even-handed justice; that the moral world established by Shemmael's advice was not dealt with in a properly serious spirit. It did not need much, there were times when it needed nothing at all, to convince the hierarchy that Shemmael took the moral world much more seriously than He did.

It could not be disguised, even where it ought to have been, that the rewards, disproportionate as they were in some cases, were actually only a sort of rationalization of blessings which at bottom were nothing but an arbitrary playing of favourites, with almost no moral aspect at all. And the punishments? Well, for instance, just now in Egypt punishment and reduction to the ranks were taking place: there was compliance, apparently painful and reluctant, with the dictates of the moral world. A certain dashing and arrogant young darling, a dreamer of dreams, a scion of that stock which had hit on the idea of being a medium of self-knowledge to God, had come down to the pit, to the prison and the grave, and for the second time, because his folly had passed all bounds and he had let love — as before he had hate — get entirely out of hand. But we onlookers, perhaps we were deceiving ourselves in our satisfaction at this particular version of the fire and brimstone?

Just between ourselves we were not being deceived, at bottom not for a moment. We knew precisely or we accurately guessed that all this severity was for the benefit of the Kingdom of the Stern; that He was using the punishment, the instrument of the moral world, to break open a closed alley which had but one and that an underground exit to the light; that He — with all due respect — was perverting the punishment into a means of further elevation and favour. When we, in passing, made little O-shaped mouths with the corners drawn down, and shot little glances from under our eyelids, we did so because we saw through the whole thing. Disgrace as a vehicle to greater honour — the All-Highest's little game illuminated the past as well and shed light on the follies and flippancies which had given cause for punishment and "forced" Him to inflict it. And this light did not come from the moral world; for these earlier failings, from wherever and whomever inspired, God knew, were also revealed as a medium and vehicle to new, extravagant exaltations.

In our circles we were convinced that we knew more or less about these devices, partaking as we did, to however limited an extent, in the Creator's all-knowledge: though even so, out of respect, we could make use of our knowledge only with the greatest caution, self-restraint, and dissimilation. In the merest whisper it might and should be added that the hierarchy thought it knew still more — of matters, steps, undertakings, intentions, manœuvres, secrets of the widest scope which it would have been wrong to brush aside as mere court gossip. There could be no mention, scarcely even so much as a whisper, and all that happened was the next thing to keeping silent: the slightest movement of lips just slightly curled, and that was all. What sort of matters were these, what were the rumours?

They had to do, of course, quite without comment, with this business of reward and punishment — with the whole complex question of favour, predilection, election, which had been raised with the birth of the moral world, the twin birth of Good and Evil. It had to do, further, with the not entirely authoritative but well-founded news, conveyed by all these barely moving lips, that Shemmael's counsel, his suggestion that God should create the "most like" creature — in other words, man; that this had not been the last piece of advice he had bestowed upon the Throne; that the relation between the latter and the fallen one had never been entirely severed or else at some later time had been resumed, no one knew how. Perhaps behind the backs of His Court He had undertaken a journey to the Pit and there indulged in an exchange of ideas. Perhaps the exile, perhaps more than once, had found a way to leave his own place and speak again before the Throne. In any case he had clearly been in a position to continue his exposition, so cleverly seasoned by surprising candour, and to support it with fresh advice, which, however, as before, did not go deeper than to stimulate ideas already present and only requiring further persuasion.

In order to understand what was going on, we have to recall certain dates and facts which form the premise and prelude of our present story. I refer to that psychological soul-novel which was earlier the subject of discussion: that romance of the soul of man — primitive man — which, as formless matter, was from the very first one of the fixed premises, its "Fall" being the conditioned basis of everything that followed. We might perhaps use the word "creation"; for surely the sin consisted in that the soul, out of a sort of melancholy sensuality surprising and shocking in a primitive principle proper to the higher world, let itself yield to a craving to penetrate in love matter which was formless and obstinately clung to its lack of form, for the purpose of calling up out of its forms through which it could compass fleshly desire. Surely it was the Highest who came to the rescue of the soul in that wrestling for love which was far beyond its power. He thereupon created the world, where things happen and can be told, the world of forms, the world of death. This He did out of sympathy for the straits of His erring partner and fellow fixed conditions. We may therefore even infer an affinity between them. If such an inference is to be drawn, we must not neglect to draw it, even if it sound impudent or blasphemous to speak in the same breath of error and weakness.

May we associate the idea of error with Him? A resounding No can be the only answer to such a question; it was in fact the answer of all the heavenly host, accompanied, of course, by that same discreet twist of all the little mouths. It would doubtless be going too far, it would be hasty, to consider that the Creator's tender and helpful pity for the erring was the same thing as error itself. That would be premature, because through the creation of the finite life-and-death world of form no least violence was done to the dignity, spirituality, majesty, or absoluteness of a God who existed before and beyond the world. And thus up to now one could not speak seriously of error in any full or actual sense of the word. It was different with the ideas, plans, and desires which were now supposed to be in the air, the subject of private conversations with Shemmael. The latter, of course, pretended to be presenting the Throne in all good faith with a perfectly new idea; whereas he was most likely quite aware that He was already more or less occupied with the very same one. Obviously

Shemmael trusted to the widespread though mistaken belief that when two people hit on the same idea it must be a good one.

It is futile to go on beating round the bush. What the great Shemmael proposed, one hand on his chin, the other stretched in eloquent peroration toward the Throne, was the corporealization of the Most High, His embodiment in a chosen people not yet born but to be created. The idea was based on the model of other gods on this earth: folk and tribal gods, mighty in magic, full of fleshly vitality and energy. The word "vitality" is well chosen; for the chief argument of the Pit, just as at the time of the creation, was that the spiritual, the above-and-beyond-the-world Creator would experience a great accession of vitality by following Shemmael's advice — only in a much more thoroughgoing and distinctly more fleshly sense. This, I say, was the chief argument: for the clever Pit had many more, and with more or less justice he assumed that all of them were already at work in the theatre of God's mind and only needed to be brought forward and stressed.

The field of the emotions to which they addressed themselves was ambition. It was ambition, certainly, towards degradation, ambition directed downwards; for in the case of the Highest, where there can be no striving upwards, there is only the other direction left. It was an ambition to mingle, a craving to be like the rest, a desire to stop being unusual. Nothing easier than for the Pit to harp on a certain sense of futility, a frustrating vagueness and universality which God must feel when He, a spiritual, supra-worldly world-god, compared Himself with the wonder-working and sensual appeal of primitive tribal gods. It was just this that would arouse an ambition to condescend mightily, to submit Himself to limitations which should result in a concentration of power; in short, to add the spice of sense to His existence. To exchange a lofty but somewhat anæmic spiritual all-sufficiency for the full-blooded fleshly existence of a corporeal folk-god; to be just like the other gods; it was this private hesitant seeking and striving which Shemmael met with his crafty counsel. To make all this clear, all this exposure and this yielding to infection, it is surely allowable to cite as a parallel that soul-novel, the soul's love-affair with matter and the melancholy sensuality which urged it on; in other words, its "Fall." Indeed, there is scarcely any need to cite, the parallel is so clear, even down to the creative help and sympathy which was then vouchsafed to the erring soul; surely it was this that gave the great Shemmael courage and maliciousness to make his proposal.

Malice, of course, and the burning desire to cause embarrassment were the innermost meaning of the suggestion. Man was already, simply as man and speaking generally, a source of constant embarrassment to the Creator; the situation must become intolerable through

His fleshly union with a particular stock, through an increase of vitality which came to the same thing as becoming biological. All too
well did the Pit know nothing good could come of an ambition head-
ing downwards, of an attempt to be like the others; that is to say, to
become a racial and folk-god — or at least not until after long wandering, embarrassments, disappointments, and embitterment. All too
well did the Pit know, what surely God knew too, that after taking
his fling at biological vitality as a tribal God and the doubtful if also
full-blooded pleasures of a concentrated earthly existence as a folk-
incarnation, fed and worshipped and propped up by a technique of superstition; that upon all this there would inevitably follow the moment
of remorse and reflection, the relinquishing of all these stimulating
limitations, the return of the One Beyond Time to beyond time, the
resumption of all-power and spiritual all-competence. But what Shemmael — and he alone — cherished in his heart of hearts was the
thought that this very about-face and return, comparable to the end
of an era, must be accompanied by a certain chagrin, and the thought
was a sweet savour on the tongue of the source of all malice.

By chance, or not by chance, it came about that the particular
stock chosen and dedicated for a folk-embodiment was so constituted that the World-God, in that He became its corporeal deity, not
only had to surrender His superior rank above the other folk-gods
of this earth and become like them but actually in power and honour
fell considerably below them — at which the Pit rejoiced. In the second place, the whole declension to the state of folk-god, the whole
experiment of biological sense-enjoyment, was from the very beginning against the better knowledge and deeper insight of the chosen
stock itself. Indeed, it was not without the intensive spiritual co-operation of the chosen seed that God thought better of His plan, was
converted and turned back to His superior other-worldly and be-
yond-the-worldly rank above all other gods. It was this that tickled
Shemmael's malicious soul. To represent the godhead of this particular stock was on the one hand no great joy; it was not, as they say,
"any great shakes," for among the various folk-gods it invariably
took a back seat. But on the other hand and in consequence the quality common to the human race, of being an instrument of God's
self-knowledge, here came out in peculiar strength. An urgent concern with the nature and status of God was native to it; from the
very first it had the beginning of a lively insight into the Creator's
other-worldness, universality, spirituality, His quality of being the
theatre of the world but the world not His theatre (just as the story-
teller is the theatre of the story, but the story not his theatre, which
circumstance gives him the chance to deal with it). It was a seed
capable of evolution, destined in time and with enormous effort to
mature into full knowledge of God's true nature. May one assume

that this was precisely the ground of its election? That the issue of the biological adventure was no better known to him who gave the counsel than to Him who received it? That He Himself consciously brought about the so-called chagrin and admonishment? Maybe we are driven to such a view. Anyhow, in Shemmael's eyes the point of the joke lay in the fact that the chosen seed was privately and subconsciously aware from the start that it knew better than the tribal God and exerted all this strength of its expanding reason to help Him out of His improper situation and back into the beyond-all, all-sufficing spiritual. Even so, the Pit's assertion remains unproved that the return from the Fall to the original position of honour could never have been possible without that human exertion and could never have happened save by its means.

The hierarchy was not far-sighted enough to go so far as this. It stopped at the gossip about secret conferences with Shemmael and the subject of these. But that was far enough to add fuel to the chronic angelic irritation with the "most like creature" and to the chosen seed now in process of evolution. It was far enough to make the hierarchy privately rejoice at the little flood and the rain of sulphur which He, greatly to His own distress, was obliged to visit upon a scion of the stock, despite His far-reaching designs in its favour, and with the ill-concealed purpose of making the punishment a vehicle to serve His plans.

All this was what they expressed, those little O-shaped mouths drawn down at the corners, and the scarcely perceptible jerk of the head by which the heavenly choirs drew attention to the figure standing, arms bound behind his back, in a sailboat propelled by oars over the river of Egypt and down to his prison. It was the scion of the Chosen Seed.

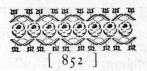

Chapter I

THE SECOND PIT

JOSEPH KNOWS HIS TEARS

JOSEPH too — by the law of correspondence between Above and Below — was thinking of the Flood. The two sets of thought met, or rather, if you like, moved parallel to each other far apart; for this young specimen of the human race, thinking them here on the waves of the Jeor, bowed down by the weight of events and the traditional procedure of punishment for guilt, was thinking with much more immediacy and associative energy than were the hosts above, who, having no experience of suffering, were just having a pleasant, refined little gossip.

But more of this later. The convict lay discomfortably in the plank compartment which served as cabin and storeroom to a smallish freight-boat built of acacia-wood, with a pitched deck. It was a so-called ox-boat, such as he himself had used taking goods up or down river when he was Mont-kaw's pupil. It was manned by four oarsmen, who had to take to their oars when the wind died down or was contrary and the swaying double mast was lowered. They stood on the platform of the forward deck; there was a steersman aft and two under-servants of Petepre acted as escorts, also served at the ropes and with the lead. Finally there was Khamat, the scribe of the buffet. To him had been entrusted the command of the ship and the transport of the prisoner to Zawi-Re, the island fortress. He carried on his person a sealed letter which the master had written about his erring steward to the warden of the prison, a captain of troops and "writer to command of the victorious army" named Mai-Sachme.

The journey was long and protracted — Joseph thought of that other, early one, seven and three years before, when for the first time he had voyaged on this river, with the old man who bought him, with Mibsam his son-in-law, Epher his nephew, and Kedar and Kedema his sons. In nine days they had come from Menfe, city of the Swaddled One, to No-Amen, the royal city. But now they were going far beyond Menfe, yes, past On the Golden, and past Per-Bastet, the city of cats. Zawi-Re, the bitter goal, lay deep in the land of Seth and the red crown, that is to say in Lower Egypt, down in the desert, in a branch of the district of Mendes, which there is called Djedet. It was to the abominable goat-district they were carrying him; the thought gave his apprehensive and brooding melancholy an added pang. Yet it was not without a sense of destiny, a heightened emotion and lively play of thought. He was a son of Jacob and his real and only wife, and never all his life long would he be able to check this play — just as little now as a man of seven-and-twenty as when he was a simple inexperienced lad. And the kind of play dearest to his heart, most fascinating to his mind, was the play of allusion; so that when his life, so painstakingly introspected, seemed full of that quality, and its circumstances to show themselves suffused with correspondences to the motions of higher things, he was prone to feelings of satisfaction, since such correspondence could never really be wholly sad.

Sad enough in all conscience his circumstances were; and sadly musing he pondered them as he lay with his arms bound together at the elbows across his back, in his little compartment, on the roof of which the provender of the crew was heaped up, melons, ears of maize, and loaves of bread. He had returned to a hideously familiar state; again he lay helpless, in bonds, as once he had lain for three horrible days in the dark of the moon, in the hole of the well, with worms crawling and rustling about him, and fouled himself like a sheep with his own filth. True, his present state was a little less rigorous than before, because his fetters were not much more than a matter of form and for appearance's sake, being a piece of ship's rope they had forborne to tighten. But even so his fall was not less deep and breathtaking, the change in his life not less abrupt and incredible. That other time, the spoiled darling and pet of his father, always anointed with the oil of gladness, had been treated in a way he could never have dreamed of. This time it was Usarsiph, he who had mounted so high in the land of the dead, who was head overseer and dwelt in the special chamber of trust, who tasted all the charms and refinements of culture and arrayed himself in pleated royal linen — to this Usarsiph was his present treatment now meted out; he was sore smitten indeed.

Gone all the fine-folded linen, the modish apron and elegant sleeved coat, this being now become the evidence which spoke against him. They had given him a single garment, the slave's hip-apron, such as the crew wore. Gone the curled wig, the enamelled collar, the armbands and necklace of red and gold. All this refinement and beauty was vanished away, not one poor ornament left, save on his neck the little packet with the amulet which he had worn in the land of his fathers and with which the seventeen-year-old lad had gone down to the pit. The rest was laid aside — Joseph used the significant words to himself, an allusive phrase, as the fact itself was an allusion and a

matter of mournful order and correspondence. It would have been
quite false, travelling whither he travelled, to wear breast and arm
adornment. The hour of unveiling, of putting off of ornaments, was
at hand, the hour of the descent into hell. A cycle had come round:
a small cycle often completed; but also a greater, too, bringing round
its like more seldom; for the revolutions of the two coincided with
each other at the centre. A little year was returning on itself, a sun-
year — insofar, that is, as the mud-depositing water had run off again
and (not by the calendar but in practical reality) it was sowing-time,
the time of ploughing and hoeing, the breaking up of the soil. When
Joseph now and then got up from his mat and Khamat allowed him
to walk on the caulked deck, with his hands on his back as though
he held them there at will, he would stroll about or sit on a coil of
rope, in the clear-carrying echoing air above the water and watch
the peasants on the fertile shore performing their careful, life-and-
death task of digging and sowing that was hedged about with so many
taboos and penalties. A mournful task, for sowing-time is mourning-
time, time when the Corn King is buried, when Usir is borne down to
the dark and hope is seen but from afar. It is the time of weeping —
Joseph wept a little himself at sight of the corn-burying little peasants,
for he too was being buried again into the darkness and into hope
only too far away — in token that a great year had come round as
well and brought repetition, renewal of life, the journey into the
abyss.

It was the abyss into which the True Son descends, Etura, the sub-
terrestrial sheepfold, Aralla, kingdom of the dead. Through the pit
he had come into the land below, the land of the rigour of death; now
again the way went down into *bôr* and prison, towards Lower Egypt
— lower it could not go. Days of the dark moon came again, great
days which would become years, and during which the underworld
had power over the Beautiful One. He declined and died; but after
three days he would rise again. Down into the well of the abyss sank
Attar-Tammuz as evening star; but as morning star it was certain he
would rise up out of it. This we call hope, and hope is a precious gift.
Yet after all it has something forbidden about it, because it contracts
the value of the hallowed present and anticipates the festal hours of
the cycle, which are not yet at hand. Each hour has its honour, and
he does not live aright who cannot despair. Joseph held this view. His
hope, indeed, was the most certain knowledge; yet as a child of the
moment he wept.

He knew his tears. Gilgamesh had wept them when he had scorned
Ishtar's longing and she had "prepared tears" for him. He was thoroughly worn out from the sore trial he had endured, the pressure
from the woman, the severe crisis of the climax and the utter downfall and transformation of his life. The first few days he did not ask

Khamat's permission to walk on deck amid the colour and bustle of Egypt's great artery. He lay alone on the mat in his pen and wove a web of dreamlike thoughts. He dreamed tablet-verses.

Ishtar the raving bounded to Amo, King of the Gods, demanding revenge. "Thou shalt create the steer of the heavens, he shall stamp on the world, singe the earth with the fiery breath of his nostrils, wither and destroy the ground."

"The heavenly steer will I create, Lady Ashirta, for grievously art thou affronted. But chaff-years will come, seven in number, years of famine, thanks to this stamping and singeing. Hast thou provided food, heaped up provision, to meet the years of want?"

"Prepared have I for food, heaped up provisions."

"Then will I create and send the heavenly steer, for sore art thou affronted, Lady Ashirta."

What singular conduct! When Ashera burnt to destroy the earth because Gilgamesh shrank from her, and demanded from heaven the fire-breathing steer, there had not been much sense in accumulating food for the seven years' shortage the steer would cause. But anyhow that was what she had done, accepting the condition because she so burned for the avenging steer. What pleased and intrigued Joseph in the whole thing was just this precaution, which the goddess even at the height of her fury had to reckon with if she was to get her fire-breathing steer. Foresight, carefulness, these were familiar and ever important ideas to the dreamer, however often he might in his folly have done violence to them. And they were almost the first law of life in the land where he had grown up as by a spring, the land of Egypt. For it was a fearful land; its folk engaged in endless effort, with every kind of magic and charm it could command, to close up all the crannies through which misfortune, great or small, might creep in. And he had now been for so long an Egyptian himself, his fleshly garment made of purely Egyptian stuff, that the national watchword of care and foresight had sunk deep into his soul, where it found its twin already at home. For it was deeply rooted in his native tradition, where the word "sin" had almost the same sense as want of foresight. It meant folly, it meant clumsy dealing with God, it was something to jeer at. Whereas wisdom meant foresight and care for the future. Had not Noah-Utnapishtim been called the exceeding wise one, simply because he had seen the Flood coming and provided for it by building the great ark? The ark, the great chest, the Arôn, wherein creation survived in the time of the Flood; to Joseph the ark was the first instance, the earliest pattern of all wisdom — in other words, of all knowledgeable foresight. And thus, by the route of Ishtar's fury, the trampling and fire-breathing beast, and the heaping up of provisions as a safeguard against want, Joseph's thoughts followed trains parallel to those in the upper sphere about the great Flood; of the little flood too he was reminded with tears, the one which had come upon him because while he had not, indeed, been so lost in folly as to betray God and cast himself out, yet he had certainly been guilty of woeful lack of foresight.

He acknowledged to himself his sin, just as he had done in the first pit, a great year before, and his heart was sore for his father Jacob, and bitterly ashamed before his face for having brought himself down again to the pit in the land whither he had been snatched. What a lifting up had come of that snatching and what a downfall and abasement had followed it, all due to the want of wisdom! The third — that is, the making-come-after — was so far away now that it was quite out of sight. Joseph's spirit was honestly crushed. Humbly he implored pardon of the spirit of his father, whose image had at the last moment saved him from the very worst. But to Khamat, the scribe of the buffet, and his guard, he was careful to betray no depression. Partly out of tedium, partly to enjoy the humiliation of a man who had risen so far above himself, Khamat often sat down by Joseph to talk; but Joseph treated him with hauteur and reserve. Yes, we shall see that after a few days, and simply by his way of knowing how to put things, he induced his guard to remove his bonds and let him move about freely, although Khamat thus ran the risk of sinning against his duty as guard and ought to have been afraid to do it.

"By Pharaoh's life!" said Khamat as he sat down in the pen beside Joseph's mat, "how you have come down in the world, ex-steward, and sunk beneath us all after you had so nimbly mounted above us! One can scarcely believe it. I can only shake my head to see you lying there like a Libyan prisoner or a man from the wretched Kush, with elbows pinioned behind his back. A man who got up so high and was head over all the house, and now you are, so to speak, delivered over to the devourer, the bitch of Amente. May Atum, Lord of On, have mercy on you! How you have bowed down your head to the dust — to use the jargon of your wretched Syria, which we have picked up from you, and by Khons we are not likely to pick up anything else, for not even a dog would take a piece of bread from your hand, so low are you fallen! And why, forsooth? Out of sheer frivolity and lack of discipline you were bent on playing the big man in a house like ours and could not bridle your reeking lust. And it had to be our sacred lady and mistress on whom you fixed your lewd desires, when, after all, she is almost the same as Hathor's self. That was shameless enough. Never shall I forget how you stood there before the master when he pronounced justice in his house, and hung your head because you found not the least word of excuse and knew not how to wash yourself clean of your guilt. How could you, when the torn garment spoke loud against you, which you had left in the mistress's hand when you vainly tried to overpower and assault her and it was plain you had even gone about the business very clumsily? It could not be worse! Do you remember how you came to me in the pantry to fetch the refreshments for the old pair in the upper storey? You were impudent enough even then; I warned you not to spill the drink over the old people's feet and I felt rather mortified when you behaved as though such a thing could not happen to you. Well now, you have spilled something on your own feet so they are all stuck together. Oh, no, I knew you wouldn't be able to hold the tray steady in the long run. But why couldn't you? Because, after all, you are a barbarian, a sand-rabbit, with no more self-control than the wretched Zahi, ignorant of our standards and knowledge of life here in the land of men; you could not truly lay to heart our precepts which teach that one may take his pleasures in the world but not with married women, because that is risky. But you in blind lust and unreason leaped at our mistress, and you may thank your stars you were not put in corpse-colour at once — and that is the only thing you have to be thankful for."

"Do me the favour, Khamat, scholar of the bookhouse," said Joseph, "of not talking about matters you do not understand. It is frightful when a difficult and delicate matter gets to the ears of the masses though it is something much too ticklish for them to grasp. They all lick their lips and talk the greatest tripe about it — really it is intolerable how they go on, and worse for the subject-matter than even for the persons involved. It is naïve of you, and not very refined and does no credit to your renowned Egyptian culture to have you talk like this to me. Not because I was yesterday your overseer and you bowed down before me, for I am laying that aside. But, after all, you are to realize that I must know more and better about the affair between the mistress and me than you who can only see it from the outside and hear only gossip about it. So why should you question me about it? Furthermore, it is absurd for you to contrast the barbarous cravings of my flesh with the standard of Egypt, when, after all, these latter have no very good reputation themselves all over the world. And when you talk about assaulting and leaping and think no shame to apply such a word to me, you must be confusing me with that famous ram we are on our way to, to whom the daughters of Egypt yield themselves when he has his feast — and these are your fine cultural standards, forsooth! Let me tell you: it may come to pass that people will speak of me as one who preserved his chastity among a people whose lust was like the lust of the stallion and the ass — some day that may happen. Some day the virgins of the world may mourn for me before they wed, bringing me their maiden tresses and singing a melancholy ditty in which they lament my youth and recount the tale of one who withstood the hot solicitations of a female and so doing lost his life and his repute. As I lie here and ponder, I can well imagine such a tradition growing out of my story. Consider, then, how petty your comments must seem to me! And why, while re-joicing in my misfortunes, are you so surprised at them? I was Pe-tepre's bought slave; now by his decree I am become Pharaoh's. So, after all, I am more than I was, I have added to my stature. Why are you so simple as to laugh at that? Very well, let us agree that for the moment my fortunes are on the decline. But is it a decline without honour and solemnity, does not this ox-boat seem to you like Usir's bark when it moves down to light the great sheepfold below and greet the dwellers in the cave on his nightly ride? To me, let me tell you, it is strikingly like that. If you think I am parting from the land of the living, you may be right. But who shall say that my nose shall not smell the herb of life, and that I shall not rise the morrow morn over the rim of the world, even as a bridegroom goes forth out of his chamber and his radiance blindeth the eyes of the dull of sight?"

"Ah, ex-steward, I see you remain the same in all your misery. But the trouble is that nobody can tell what being the same really means. It is like the coloured balls which jugglers send flying out of their hands and catch again and you cannot see them as separate balls be-cause they make a bright bow in the air. Where you get your cheek, no matter what happens to you, the gods only know, the ones you have dealings with; for god-fearing folk must get goose-flesh and pimples to hear you. You cannot get out of it by that rubbish about brides who dedicate their hair to your memory. That could happen only to a god. Or your comparing this boat, which is after all the vehicle of your shame, with Usir's evening-bark — would the Hidden One that you only compared the two! But you weave in the word 'strikingly' — you say this boat is strikingly like that bark, and you know how to convince a simple soul that it is really the very bark after all, and that you may really be Re when he is called Atôn and changes into the bark of the night — and that gives one goose-flesh. But one gets it not only from laughing and shivering but also and even more from being angry, let me tell you, from disgust and bit-terness like gall at your presumption; at the way you make bold to mirror yourself in the Highest and identify yourself with Him, so that you talk as if you were the same and go on making an arch of balls so that I blink my eyes in exasperation. Of course, it is open to anyone to say such things and to behave like that; but a decent person would not do it, he would be humble and pray. I sat down here to talk with you partly because I was sorry for you and partly because I was bored. But when you give me to understand that you are Atum-Re and Usir the great in his bark, at one and the same time, then I must leave you to yourself, for my gorge rises at your blasphemies."

"Take it as you must, Khamat of the book-house and the buffet. I

did not ask you to sit down with me, for I like quite as well to be
alone, maybe even a bit better, and I can amuse myself without you
as you can see for yourself. If you knew how to entertain yourself as
I do, you would not have come; but on the other hand you would not
look askance at the diversions I allow myself and you do not allow
me. You make out that you do this out of pity; but actually it is nothing but ill will, and the pity is a sort of fig-leaf your ill will puts on
— if you will pardon the far-fetched comparison! A human being en-
tertains himself, he does not pass his life like the dumb brutes; that
is the whole point, that and how far he goes in his diversions. You
were not quite right to say that anybody might act the same as I; not
everybody might. Not because decency forbids, but because he lacks
any harmony with higher things, he has just been denied any affinity
with them, it is not given him to pluck flowers of speech from the
fields of heaven — if you will pardon me another figure. He sees in
the Highest something quite different from what he sees in himself —
in which, of course, he is perfectly right — and has no idea of serving
Him, except with hymn-tunes, which are tiresome. If he hears anyone else praise Him in more intimate terms, he is green with envy and
stands before the image of the Highest and weeps crocodile's tears
and implores Him to forgive the blasphemy. That is a really silly pose,
Khamat of the buffet, you should not be guilty of it. Give me my
mid-day meal, for it is time and I am hungry."

"That I must, I suppose, if the time is here," answered the scribe.
"I cannot let you starve. I have to deliver you alive to Zawi-Re."

Joseph could not feed himself with his elbows bound behind him,
so Khamat had perforce to do it for him, there being no other way.
Squatting beside Joseph, he had to put the bread in his mouth and
then the beaker of beer to his lips; Joseph commented upon it at every
meal.

"Yes, you squat here, long-legged Khamat, and feed me," said he.
"It is kind of you too, even though you feel ashamed and show that
you do not like it. I drink this to your health. At the same time I
cannot help thinking how you have come down in the world, that
you have to feed me and give me drink. Certainly you never had to
when I was your overseer and you bowed before me! You have to
serve me as never before, as though I were become more and you
less. It is the old question: who is greater and more important, the
watcher or the watched? But of course it is the latter. For is not even
a king guarded by his servants, and is it not said of the just man: 'He
shall give His angels charge over thee to keep thee in all thy ways'?"

And so after a few days Khamat said to Joseph: "Let me tell you, I
am fed up with feeding you and having you open your beak like a
young daw in the nest, and when you open it words come out that
disgust me even more. I am going to untie your bonds so that you

are not so helpless and I need not be your slave and angel, that is not a scribe's job. When we come near your destination I will tie you up again and deliver you in bonds to the governor there, Mai-Sachme, a captain of troops. That is only proper. But you must swear to me not to tell that official that you were free in the meantime or that I have been lax in my duty; otherwise I shall be blamed."

"On the contrary, I will tell him you were a cruel warder and chastised me with scorpions every day."

"Nonsense, that is going much too far the other way. You never do anything but make fun of people. Of course, I don't know what is in the sealed letter I carry on my person and I am not sure what they mean to do with you. That is the worst of it, no one ever does know what to do with you. But you are to tell the governor of the prison that I treated you with tolerable severity and with firmness tempered with humanity."

"So will I do," said Joseph, and got his elbows free until they were far down into the land of Uto the Serpent and the seven-branched river in the district of Djedet and near to Zawi-Re, the island fortress. Then Khamat tied him up again.

THE GOVERNOR OF THE PRISON

JOSEPH's place of penance and second pit, which he reached after almost seventeen days' journey, and where by his own transcendental reckoning he was to spend three years before his head should be once more lifted up, was a group of gloomy buildings irregular in shape and covering almost the whole of the island that rose from the Mendesian arm of the Nile. It was a collection of cubical barracks, stables, storehouses, and casemates grouped around courts and passages surmounted at one end by a Migdol tower, the residence of the governor over the prison and the prisoners and commandant of the garrison, Mai-Sachme, a "scribe of the victorious army." In the middle of the whole rose the pylon of a Wepwawet-temple, whose standard was the sole relief to the eye in all that baldness. The whole was enclosed by a ring wall some twenty ells high, of unbaked bricks, with projecting bastions and platforms jutting out in the round. The landing bridge and the fortified and guarded gate lay somewhere at the side. Khamat stood on the bow of the ox-boat and waved his letter at the guards from afar. As they came under the gate he shouted that he was bringing a prisoner whom he must himself in person hand over to the troop captain and head of the prison.

Mercenaries, called Ne'arin, a military term adapted from the Semitic, lance-bearers with heart-shaped leather leaves on their aprons and shields on their backs, opened to the conveyance and let it through. To Joseph it seemed as though he were back in the times when he and the Ishmaelites were admitted through the gates of the fortress of Thel. Then he had been a boy, abashed before the marvels and abominations he saw in Egypt. Now he knew them all, the marvels and the abominations, he was Egypt hide and hair — apart from the reservations he confined to his private thoughts respecting the follies of the land whither he had been snatched — and he had got a good bit beyond his youth and was well into manhood. But now here he was, led on a rope, like Hapi, the living representation of Ptah in the court of his temple at Menfe: a captive in Egypt just like that sacred bull. Two of Petepre's people held the ends of his bonds and drove him in front of them. Behind them, Khamat addressed himself beneath the gate to an under-officer with a staff, who had probably given the order for admission, and was referred to a higher official coming across the court armed with a cudgel. This man took the letter, saying that he would take it to the captain, and told them to wait.

So they waited, under the curious gaze of the soldiery, in a little quadrangle, in the sparse shade of two or three spindling palm trees tufted with green at the top, their round reddish fruits lying about on their roots. The son of Jacob mused. He was recalling what Petepre had said about the governor of the prison into whose hand he was being given: that he was a man with whom one did not jest. Joseph's concern and suspense as he waited are easy to understand. At the same time he reflected that the titular captain probably did not know the man personally at all and had simply guessed that a man in charge over a prison was bound to be forbidding — a probable but not an inevitable conclusion. Joseph consoled himself with the thought that at least this was a human being with whom he would have to deal — and in Joseph's eyes that meant that he was somehow or other to be got on terms with; in God's name, however much he might be a born prison-keeper, yet by this means or that, from one angle if not from another, he *could* be jested with! Besides, Joseph knew his children of Egypt, the denizens of this land who against a background of deathlike rigidity and a religion of the tomb were blithe and inoffensive children at heart and easy to live with. Then the letter which the governor was now reading, where Potiphar told him about the man he was casting out, so that the governor could get an idea of his affair: Joseph was confident that the description would not turn out to be too dreadful; that it would not be calculated to evoke the man's grimmest qualities. His real confidence, however, was more of a generalization: it proceeded, as it is wont to do with children of the blessing, not from himself outwards but inwards upon himself and the happy mysteries of his own nature. Certainly he had got beyond the childish stage of blind confidence, where he had believed that everybody must love him more than they did themselves. What he continued to believe, was that it was given him to constrain the world and the men in it to turn him their best and brightest side — and this we can see was confidence rather in himself than in the world. In any case the two, his ego and the world, in his view belonged together, they were in a way one, so that the world was not simply the world, by and in itself, but quite definitely his world and by virtue of the fact susceptible of being moulded into a good and friendly one. Circumstances were powerful; but what Joseph believed in was their plasticity: he felt sure of the preponderant influence of the individual destiny upon the general force of circumstances. When like Gilgamesh he called himself a glad-sorry man, it was in the sense that he knew the happy side of his nature was capable of much suffering, but on the other hand did not believe in suffering — bad and black enough it was that it had proved too dense for his own light, or the light of God in him, to penetrate.

Such was the nature of Joseph's confidence. Generally speaking it was trust in God, and with it he armed himself to look Mai-Sachme, his taskmaster, in the face. In no long time he was set before him; for they were led through a low covered passage to the foot of the citadel, to a barred door manned by other guards in helmets with bosses on them. The grating presently opened and the troop-captain came out.

He was in the company of the high priest of Wepwawet, a lean baldpated man with whom he had been engaged in a game of draughts. The governor was a man of some forty years, a stocky figure in a cuirass which he had probably put on for the occasion, with little metal pictures of lions fastened on it like scales. He wore a brown wig, had round brown eyes under very heavy black brows, and a small mouth. His tanned and burnt face was darkened by a fresh growth of beard and his forearms were hairy. His whole expression was oddly unruffled, even sleepy; yet it was shrewd too, this expression, and the captain's speech was calm to the point of monotony as he came out from under the gate in conversation with the prophet of the warlike deity. They were obviously still discussing the moves in the game, upon which the newcomers had had to wait. In his hand the captain held the unsealed roll of the fan-bearer's letter.

He stood where he was, reopened and reread it; and when he lifted his face Joseph had a feeling that this was more than just a man's face, it was the very presentment of forbidding circumstance with the light of God striking through, the very face which life shows to the glad-sorry man. The black brows were threateningly drawn, yet a smile played about his small mouth. Now he banished smile and threat together out of his face.

"You had charge of the boat that brought you down from Wese?" he said in calm monotonous tones, turning round and raising his brows at the scribe Khamat. Upon the latter's assent he looked at Joseph.

"You are the former steward of the great courtier Petepre?" he asked.

"I am he," answered Joseph in all simplicity.

And yet this was rather a strong answer. He might have replied: "As you have said," or "My lord knows the truth," or more floridly: "Maat speaks out of your mouth." But in the first place just "I am he," spoken, of course, quite simply but with a sober smile, was a little incorrect; one did not speak in the first person to superiors but said "your servant," or with even greater self-disparagement "this servant here." And in the second place the "I" was too prominent: associated with the "he," it roused a vague suspicion that it referred to more than merely the stewardship which was all that was in question. There was an implication that question and answer did not quite match, that the answer overlapped the question and might tempt the questioner to another question: "What are you?" or even "Who are you?" over and above that.

The truth is, Joseph's answer was a formula, old, familiar, and widely appealing from ages past. It was the time-honoured revelation of identity, a ritual statement beloved in song and story and play in which the gods had parts. In such a play it is used in order to string together a whole gamut of effects and plot sequences, from mere casting down of the eyes to being thundered at and flung to one's knees.

Mai-Sachme's placid features, the features of a man not prone to alarm, did show a faint confusion or embarrassment; it made the end of his small hooked nose turn whitish.

"Yes, yes, so you are," said he. Possibly at the moment he did not know himself just what he meant by that; and if so the fact that this man before him was the handsomest twenty-seven-year-older in the two lands may have contributed to his absence of mind. Beauty is impressive. Unfailingly it stirs a special kind of faint trepidation even in the most placid soul from whom fear in general is remote. A simple "I am he" uttered with a sober smile might be magnified by the beauty of the speaker into something a little unearthly.

"You seem to be a light-headed bird," went on the captain, "falling out of the nest out of sheer foolishness and lack of balance. Lived up there in Pharaoh's city where life is so full of interest that it could have been a perpetual feast-day for you, and for nothing and less than nothing you have got yourself sent down here to us where there is nothing too, nothing but nothingness. Here utter boredom reigns," said he, and gathered his brows in a momentary frown, accompanied however by a half-smile, as though smile and frown belonged together. "Were you ignorant," he went on, "that in the stranger's house one should not seek out the women with one's eyes? Have you not read the precepts in the Book of the Dead or the teachings and sayings of the holy Imhotep?"

"They are familiar to me," Joseph replied, "for I have read them countless times aloud and to myself."

But the captain, though he had asked for an answer, was not listening to it.

"That was a man," said he, turning to his companion, the chaplain, "a good companion for life, Imhotep the Wise! Physician, architect, priest, and scribe, all in one, Tut-anch-Djehuti, the living image of Thoth. I venerate the man, that I must say. If it were given me to be appalled, which it is not — perhaps I ought to say unfortunately, I am much too easy-going for that — but if I could I should certainly be appalled at such encyclopædic wisdom. He died long years ago, Imhotep the Divine; his like existed only in early times and in the morning of the two lands. His sovereign was an early king named Djoser, whose eternal dwelling he is known to have built, the stepped pyramid near Menfe, six storeys high, some hundred and twenty ells, but the limestone is poor. Ours up in the quarry where the convicts work is better stuff; the master just had no better to his hand. But the art of building was only a small part of his knowledge and skill; he knew all the locks and keys to the temple of Thoth. Skilled in medicine he was too and adept in nature's matters, with knowledge of solids and liquids. He had a gentle hand with the sick and could relieve folk groaning and tossing with pain. He himself must have been very tranquil by nature and not prone to fear. Added to all this he was a reed in the hand of God, a writer of wisdom; but his talents worked together, not today a doctor and tomorrow a writer, but both in one and at the same time. I emphasize this because it is to my mind a surpassing virtue. Medicine and writing go well together, they shed light on each other and both do better by going hand in hand. A doctor possessed of the writer's art will be the better consoler to anyone rolling in agony; conversely, a writer who understands the life of the body, its powers and its pains, its fluids and functions, its blessings and banes, has a great advantage over him who knows nothing of such things. Imhotep was such a doctor and such a writer. A godlike man; they ought to burn incense to him. And I think when he has been dead awhile longer, they will. Anyhow, he also lived in Menfe, a very stimulating city."

"You need not blush before him, captain," replied the high priest. "For aside from your military service you practise the art of healing, you do good to those who wreathe and writhe, and besides that write very winningly in form and matter, while uniting all these branches in perfect serenity."

"Serenity by itself does not do it," answered Mai-Sachme, and the serenity of his own face with its shrewd round eyes altered a shade into the pensive. "Perhaps I just need to get good and scared once. But how could that happen? — And you?" he said suddenly. He lifted his brows and shook his head as he looked over at Petepre's two house-slaves who were holding the ends of Joseph's bonds. "What are you doing there? Are you going to plough with him or play horse like little boys? I suppose your ex-steward is to do time at hard labour with his limbs tied up like a calf for the slaughter? Untie him, stupids! Here we work hard for Pharaoh, in the quarry or on the new buildings, we don't lie about in bonds. What lack of under-standing! These people," he explained aside to the man of God, "live in the belief that a prison is a place where one lies about in chains. They take everything literally, that is their way, and stick to the letter as children do. If they hear about somebody that he lies in gaol, that being the phrase in common use, they firmly believe that the man has been plumped into some hole full of hungry rats and rattling chains, where he lies and steals days from Re. Such confusion of the word and the reality is to my way of thinking characteristic of low breeding and lack of education. I have often seen it in the rubber-eaters of the wretched Kush and even in the little peasantry of our own fields; not so much in the towns. To be sure, there is a cer-tain poetry in the literal interpretation, the simple poetry of the fairy tale. There are, so far as I can see, two kinds of poetry: one springs from folk-simplicity, the other from the literary gift in essence. The second is undoubtedly the higher form. But in my view it cannot flourish cut off from the other, needing it as a plant needs soil, just as all the beauty of the higher life and the splendour of Pharaoh him-self need the earth-mould of all our poverty-stricken existences in or-der to flower and flourish and be an amazement to the world."

"As scholar of the book-house," said Khamat, scribe of the buffet, who meanwhile had hastened to free Joseph's elbows with his own hands, "I have no part in any confusion between the phrase and the reality, and only for form's sake and for the moment, I thought I had to deliver the prisoner in bonds. He himself will tell you that during the greater part of the voyage I let him go free."

"That was no more than sensible," responded Mai-Sachme, "since there are differences between crimes. Murder, theft, trespass, refusal to pay taxes or conniving with the tax-collector, those are in a differ-ent class from offences where a woman is concerned, which require more discreet handling." He half unrolled the letter again and looked at it.

"Here," he said, "I see a woman comes into it; and as an officer and a pupil of the royal stables I cannot put it in the same boat with vulgar crimes. We have said that it is a sign of lack of elevation or maturity to take everything literally and not to distinguish between the phrase and the reality. But such a distinction is now and again unavoidable among the better sort of people. For instance it is said that in the house of strangers it is dangerous to cast eyes upon the women. Yet even so it is done, because wisdom is one thing and life another; and you might even say that the element of risk makes it to some extent honourable. Again, there are two parties to a love-affair, and that always obscures the issue a bit. From the outside it looks as though the case were clear; that is because one side — I mean the man, of course — always takes the blame on himself, yet again it may be best to make a distinction in private between the phrase and the reality. When I hear of a woman being led astray by a man, I chuckle to myself, for it sounds like a joke and I think: By the great Triad! Because, after all, we know whose business seduction has been since the time of the gods and it was not the business of us stupid men. Do you know the story of the Two Brothers?" He turned to face Joseph, looking up at him with his round brown eyes, for he was considerably shorter as well as stoutish in build. He lifted his thick brows again as high as they would go, as though that would help to strike a balance.

"I know it well, my lord," answered Joseph. "For I had often to read it aloud to my master, Pharaoh's friend, and I also had to copy it out fair for him, with black and red ink."

"It will continue to be copied," said the commandant; "it is a capital invention not only in its style, which carries conviction even though the episodes are really almost incredible when one thinks them over calmly, for instance where the queen conceives through a splinter which flies into her mouth from the wood of the persea tree, which is too contradictory to medical experience to be taken literally. But despite that the story is lifelike, as when the wife of Anup leans against the youth Bata, finding him great in strength, and says to him: 'Come, let us have joy in each other for a little and I will make thee two feast-day garments,' and when Bata cries to his brother: 'Woe is me, she has turned all to ill!' and before his eyes cuts off his manhood with the blade of the sword-reed and gives it to the fishes to eat — that is thrilling. Later on, the narrative degenerates and becomes unbelievable; yet it is edifying too when Bata turns himself into the Hapi-bull and speaks: 'I shall be a wonder of a Hapi and the whole land will exult in me,' and makes himself known and says: 'I am Bata, lo, I live still and am the sacred bull of God.' Those are, of course, fantastic inventions; but yet how plastically life does sometimes pour itself into the most extraordinary forms of the creative fancy!"

He was silent awhile and stood placidly gazing off into space with his little mouth slightly open. Then he read a little more in the letter.

"You can imagine, Father," said he, lifting his head to the baldpate, "that an occurrence like this makes a more or less stimulating change for me in the monotony of this settled place where a man already settled by nature is in danger of falling asleep. What I usually get down here, either already sentenced or for temporary custody before the scales of justice have finally settled and their case has not yet been tried, are all sorts of tomb-robbers, bush-rangers, purse-snatchers — and none of them help me to keep awake. A love crime is an exciting exception. For there can hardly be any doubt, so far as I know people of the most diverse way of thinking agree that this is the most curious, exciting, and mysterious tract of all our human existence. Who has not had his surprising, thought-provoking experience in the realm of Hathor? Have I ever told you about my first love, which was at the same time my second?"

"Never, captain," said the chaplain. "The first and the second too? I wonder how that could have come about."

"Or the second, yet after all the first," responded the commandant. "As you like to put it. Again or for ever — who knows which is the right word? And it does not matter either."

Mai-Sachme stood there, his expression relaxed, not to say sleepy, his arms folded, the roll tucked under one of them; his head on one side, the heavy brows somewhat lifted under the brown bullet-eyes. His rounded lips moved with measured gravity and he began to narrate, there before Joseph and his guards, before the priest of Wep-wawet and a number of soldiers who had gathered round:

"I was twelve years old, a pupil of the house of instruction in the riding-school of the royal stables. I was rather short and plump just as I am today, that is my stature and my state in my life before and after death. But my heart and mind were open. So one day I saw a maiden who was bringing her brother, a fellow-pupil of mine, his midday bread and beer, for his mother was ill. His name was Imesib, son of Amenmose, an official. But his sister, who brought him his rations, three pieces of bread and two jugs of beer, he called Beti, from which I gathered that her name was Nekhbet, which proved correct when I inquired of Imesib. For it interested me because she herself interested me and I could not keep my eyes off her so long as she was there. Not off her braids nor off her narrow eyes, nor her mouth like a bow, and especially not off her arms, which were bare and of that slender fullness that is so lovely — she made the greatest impression on me. But I did not know all day what the impression was — I found that out only at night, when I lay in the dormitory among my comrades, my clothes and sandals beside me, and under my head to serve as pillow according to the regulation my bag of writing tools and books. For we were not allowed to forget our books even in sleep; the contact with them was to keep them always in mind. But yet I did forget them, for my dreams had a way of shaping themselves quite independently of the books under my head. I dreamed ex-

plicitly and vividly that I was betrothed to Nekhbet, the daughter
of Amenmose; our fathers and mothers had come to an agreement
and she was soon to become my housewife and sister-bride, so that
her arm would lie upon mine. I rejoiced beyond all measure, as I had
never rejoiced in all my life before. My entrails rose up in joy on
account of that contract, which was sealed by our parents bringing
our noses close together, a most lovely feeling. But this dream was
so lively, so natural, that it lagged not at all behind reality; and
strangely enough even after I had wakened and washed myself it beguiled me into believing it. It has never happened to me before or
since that a dream has been so vivid as to hold me in its power in my
waking hours, so that I went on believing it. Well on into the morning I was still fondly and firmly convinced that I was betrothed to
the maiden Beti, and only slowly, as I sat in the writing-room and
the master thumped me on the back to liven me up, did my inward
exultation subside. The bridge over into sobriety was formed by the
reflection that the contract and the approaching of our noses had
indeed been only a dream, but that nothing stood in the way of its
immediate realization; that I only needed to have my parents come to
an agreement with Beti's parents on our behalf. For quite a while it
seemed to me that after such a dream my expectation of its fulfilment
was only natural and nobody could be surprised at it. But gradually I
arrived at the chilling and sobering thought that the realization of the
dream which had seemed so real was only idle nonsense and as things
stood frankly impossible. For of course I was nothing but a schoolboy,
still beaten as they beat papyrus, only just at the beginning of my
career as scribe and officer, and short and fat into the bargain, according to my constitution before and after death; and my betrothal
to Nekhbet, who was probably three years older than I and might
any day marry a man far above me in station and dignity, was revealed to me, with the fading of my dream happiness, as a thing of
sheer absurdity.

"So," the official continued imperturbably, "I gave up an idea
which would never have occurred to me save for that vivid and beautiful dream. And I went on with my studies in the house of instruction
of the royal stables, frequently admonished by thumps on my back.
Twenty years later, when I had long ago become a teacher-scribe to
the victorious army, I was sent with three associates on a journey to
Syria, in the wretched Cher, to muster and levy a tribute of horses,
which were to be sent down in freight boats to Pharaoh's stables. So
I travelled from the port of Khadati to the defeated Sekmen and to
a town which, if I recall rightly, is called Per Shean, where we had a
garrison, whose colonel gave a party to the people of the countryside
and the remount scribes: an evening company with wine and flowers
in a house of most beautiful doors. There were Egyptians there and

city notables, men and women. I saw a maiden, a connection of this Egyptian house on the female side, for her mother was a sister of its mistress and she had come hither on a visit with male and female servants from far away in Upper Egypt where her parents lived, near the first cataract. Her father was a very rich trader from Suenet, who bought up the wares of the wretched Kasi, ivory, ebony, and leopard-skins for the Egyptian market. Now when I saw this girl, the daughter of the ivory-dealer, in all her youth, there happened to me for the second time in my life what had first happened so many years ago in the house of instruction: I could not keep my eyes off her, she made an exceptional impression on my mind and brought back in amazing likeness the joyous taste of that long-vanished betrothal dream, so that my entrails rose up for joy at sight of her just as before. But I was shy before her, although a soldier should not be shy, and for some time I shrank from finding out her name and who she was. But when I did so I learned that she was the daughter of Nekhbet, the daughter of Amenmose, who, quite shortly after I had seen her in my dream and been betrothed to her, had become the wife of the ivory-merchant of Suenet. But the maid Nofrure — so she was called — was not like her mother in her features or the colour of her braided hair or her complexion, being a good deal darker. At most her charming figure was like Nekhbet's — but how many girls have figures like that! Yet the sight of her roused in me at once the same deep feelings I had felt then and never again; so that one might say I had loved her already in her mother, as I loved the mother again in her. Indeed, I consider it possible, and in a way I expect, that if again after another twenty years I should meet by chance and unawares the daughter of Nofrure, my heart would melt to her irresistibly as once it did to her mother and her grandmother, and it will always and for ever be the same love."

"That is really a remarkable emotional experience," said the chaplain, charitably passing over the extraordinary fact that the captain had chosen to relate the tale at this moment, in however composed and level a tone. "But if the daughter of the ivory-merchant were to have a daughter, it would be a pity that she was not your child; then, even though your boyish dream on the pillow of books could never be realized, yet in Nekhbet's reincarnation or the return of your inclination to her, reality would have come into its own."

"Not so," replied Mai-Sachme, shaking his head. "Such a rich and beautiful maiden and a remount clerk, short and stout by nature and predestination, how could they go together? Most likely she has married a district baron or else somebody who stands under the soles of the Pharaoh, a steward of the treasure-house with the gold of favour round his neck. And you must realize that you stand in a fatherly relation, as it were, to a girl whose mother you once loved, so that the idea of marriage is not quite the thing. Besides, such thoughts as you suggest were shoved into the background with me by what you call the remarkable nature of the situation. That prevented me from taking a decision which would end in the grandchild of my first love becoming my own child. Was that anything actually desirable? It would have deprived me of the expectation in which I now live: that some day without knowing it I shall meet the daughter of Nofrure, the granddaughter of Nekhbet, and that she too will make on me the same wonderful impression. That is a possibility which leaves me something to hope for in my elder days; whereas if not, the course of my recurrent emotional experiences might have been cut off untimely."

"That may be," the priest agreed hesitantly. "But the least you could do would be to put on paper the story of mother and daughter, or rather your story about them, and use the reed to give it a charming form to the grateful enrichment of our literature. In my opinion you could just write out of your own fancy the third incarnation of that figure and of your love for it and make it seem as though it had already happened."

"I had made some beginnings," replied the captain coolly; "that is why I can tell the story so glibly, because I have already done some drafts of it. The thing is only that in order to include the meeting with Beti's granddaughter I have to set the story in the future and make myself out an elderly man, which is a strain and I shirk it, although by rights a soldier should not shirk. But the principal trouble is that I doubt whether by temperament I am not too steady-going to give to my tale the thrilling character it should have, as for instance in the model story of the Two Brothers. The subject is too dear to me that I should want to take the chance of botching it." He broke off with a guilty air and said: "But at the moment what I am doing is to induct the prisoner. How many beasts of burden," he asked, turning to condescend to Joseph, though with some difficulty on account of his shortness, "would it take, do you think, to carry food to five hundred stone-workers and porters, together with their officers and overseers?"

"Twelve oxen and fifty asses," answered Joseph, "might be about right."

"More or less. And how many men would you order to the rope to drag a block of stone four ells long by two wide and one thick, five miles to the river?"

"Counting the men needed to clear the road, the water-bearers to wet it under the sledges, and men to carry the rollers that need to be put underneath every now and then," said Joseph, "I should say at least a hundred."

"Why so many?"

"It is a good heavy block," answered Joseph, "and if you do not want to put oxen to it but men because men are cheaper, you should take enough of them so that midway one gang can spell the other at the rope. Then you do not have to reckon with deaths due to checked sweat or some of them straining their inwards or their wind giving out so that they roll about in agony."

"That is certainly to be avoided. But you forget that we have not only the choice between oxen and men, but there are all sorts of barbarians and folk of the desert of the red land, from Libya, Punt, and Syria — we have all that we can use."

"He who is here given into your hand," answered Joseph evenly, "is himself of such an origin, namely the child of a shepherd king of the Upper Retenu, where it is called Canaan, and has only been stolen down here into Egypt."

"Why do you tell me that? It is here in the letter. And why do you call yourself a child instead of a son? It sounds like self-indulgence and pampering, not becoming in a convict, even though his crime is not of a dishonourable kind but lies in the realm of the emotions. You seem to fear that I, because you are originally from the wretched Zahi, would harness you to the heaviest loads, until your sweat was checked and you died a dry death. That is an attempt, as indiscreet as it is clumsy, to think my thoughts. I should be a poor prison governor if I did not know how to size up every man's parts and place him accordingly. Your answers show very plainly that you once oversaw the household of a great man and understand something about business. It seems you would like if possible to avoid having people exhaust themselves, even if they are not children — I mean sons of the black earth; this does not precisely run counter to my own wishes and shows some knowledge of economic thought. I will use you as overseer over a gang of convicts in the quarry, or perhaps in the inside service and the office; for of course you can reckon faster than the others how many measures of wheat can be put into a storeroom of this and this size, or how much spelt should be brewed to make so and so much beer or baked to make so much bread, and can turn one value into another, and things like that.

"It would be really a good thing," he added in explanation to the opener of Wepwawet's mouth, "for me to have some such assistance, so that I need not take everything on myself and could have more leisure for my efforts to put on paper in a good and even engrossing style my tale of the three love-affairs which were one and the same. — You people of Wese," he said to Joseph's attendants, "can now be off and set out on your homeward journey. You will be going upstream and you will have a north wind. Take your rope along with you, and make my compliments to Pharaoh's friend, your master. — Memi!" he gave order in conclusion to the man with the club who had ushered in the new arrival. "This slave of the King will do convict labour as assistant in the office; show him a place to sleep by himself and give him an upper garment and a staff of office. Very high he once stood, very low has he let himself be brought down here to us; now he must submit to the iron regimen of Zawi-Re. What superior parts he brings with him we will ruthlessly exploit, just as we do the physical strength of the lower sort. For they belong no longer to himself but to Pharaoh. Give him something to eat. — Till our next meeting, Father," he took leave of the chaplain and turned back to his tower.

Such was Joseph's first meeting with Mai-Sachme, the governor of the prison.

OF GOODNESS AND CLEVERNESS

Now, like Joseph himself, you are reassured as to the particular kind of man this governor was into whose hands Petepre had given him. He was a man of peculiarly even and pleasing temper, and not for nothing has our all-illuminating narrative been in so little haste to take the spot-light from his undeniably stoutish figure, but has let it rest long enough upon him for the reader to get a clear picture of his hitherto unknown personality. And this for the reason that he has a not insignificant part, again very little known, to play in the tale which is here being retold with all possible correctness and verisimilitude. The fact is that after Mai-Sachme had been Joseph's superior and taskmaster for some years, he continued for a long time at his side and bore a part in the stage-management of great and glorious events, as we shall soon hear — and may the Muses strengthen me in the task of narration.

All this only in passing. But in speaking of the governor of the prison, the tradition uses the same formula earlier applied to Potiphar, that he "took nothing on himself," so that Joseph was soon responsible for all that happened in his second pit. We must pause upon this tradition, to interpret it aright; for it has not at all the meaning it had in the case of the sun-courtier and consecrated mountain of flesh who "took nothing on himself" simply because his whole being was nominal and titular; because he stood outside humanity and in a straitness of existence without prospect of change, remote from reality, an existence of the purest form. Whereas Mai-Sachme was a perfectly competent man, warmly if placidly interested in any number of things, particularly in people. He was a sedulous physician, who rose early every morning to inspect the discharge of the soldiers and convicts in his sick-bay. His workroom, in a well-guarded spot in the citadel tower of Zawi-Re, was a perfect laboratory, equipped with a herbarium, with mortars and pestles, phials and ointment-pots, tubes and stills. Here that same shrewd-sleepy face he had worn when on the first day he told the story of the three love-affairs bent over lotions, pills, and poultices or consulted the work "For the Benefit of Mankind" and other text-books of ripe wisdom for advice on the treatment of retention of urine, tumours of the neck, spinal rigidity, heartburn, and the like. As he read and pondered, his mind ranged over a whole area of general speculations: were the blood-vessels that ran in pairs from the heart to the separate limbs of the body and were so prone to hardening, choking, and inflammation that often they would not respond to treatment — were there only twenty-two of these blood-vessels or forty-six as he was more and more inclined to think? Were the worms in the body to whose destruction he applied his electuaries the cause of certain illnesses or more correctly their result — for instance by the stopping-up of one or more vessels a tumour was formed which had no outlet to discharge by and eventually became putrid and, of course, turned into worms?

It was a good thing the captain took these matters on himself although as a soldier they were less his province than that of his partner at draughts, the priest of Wepwawet. But the latter's knowledge of such physical matters was confined to the inspection and ritual slaughtering of the sacrificial animals, and his methods of healing were too dependent on charms and phylacteries — though of course these too were useful in their place, certainly in a case where the affection of an organ, say the spleen, or the spinal column, was clearly due to the fact that its special protecting deity had forsaken that member and left it to a hostile demon who was now creating his disturbing effect therein and must be forced by suitable invocations to void the field. For this purpose the chaplain had a cobra which he kept in a basket and by pressure on the neck could turn into a magic wand. His successes with the cobra sometimes inspired Mai-Sachme to borrow the creature. But on the whole the governor had the settled conviction that just magic by itself as a sufficing principle was seldom able to pull it off; it needed to be permeated and propped up by the grosser methods of profane knowledge, through which then it could produce its effect. For instance, Zawi-Re had suffered from a plague of fleas and the charms of the man of God had never reduced it, or so temporarily that the relief might have been only self-deception. It was only when Mai-Sachme, of course to the accompaniment of the spoken text, had sprinkled much natron-water and strewn much charcoal mixed with the powdered herb *bebet* that the pest subsided. It was the governor who ordered the lids of the food-stocks in the storehouses to be smeared with cat-fat, the mice being almost as much of a nuisance as the fleas. He had reckoned that the creatures would be frightened, thinking they were smelling the cat itself, and would leave the supplies alone, which proved to be the case.

The sick-bay of the fortress was always full of injured and ailing, for labour in the quarry, five miles inland, was hard labour indeed, as Joseph soon learned, since he often had to spend several weeks there to oversee a gang of soldiers and convicts in hewing, mining, cutting, and hauling operations. Soldiers and convicts were treated the same; the garrison of Zawi-Re, native and foreign, except for guard-duty did the same tasks as the convicts and felt the sting of the same lash. But at least where a soldier suffered from injury or exhaustion or his sweat struck inwards he was sent to the sick-bay somewhat sooner than a convict, who had to go on till he fell down, even to the third time of falling, for the first and second times were considered shamming.

Under Joseph's overseership, however, matters improved, beginning with his own gang. And at length the saying was fulfilled that the governor of the prison put all the prisoners into his hand. When he went out to the quarries it was as a sort of upper inspector and immediate representative of the commandant, and the improvement became general. For Joseph had in mind Jacob, his far-off father, to whom he was as dead, and how he had always disapproved of the Egyptian house of bondage. He decreed that a man even after falling down only twice should fall out and be fetched back to the island. For the first time he fell continued to be reckoned a sham, unless, of course, the man was dead.

So the lazaret was never empty of those who wreathed and writhed: a man might have broken a bone or "could no longer look down upon his belly" or his body might be covered with great swellings from infected fly- and gnat-bites; or his stomach, when one put one's finger on it, might go up and down like oil in a leather bottle; or stone-dust might cause inflammation and running from the eyes; all these cases the captain dealt with, shrinking from none; and for each, if the man was not already dead, he knew a remedy. The broken bones he splinted with little pieces of board, the inability of a man to look down upon his belly he sought to control with soothing poultices; the purulent discharge from bites he painted with goose-grease mixed with an emollient powdered herb; for the bloated abdomen he prescribed a chewing of berries of the castor-oil plant with beer, and for the frequent eye-inflammations he had a good salve from Byblus. Probably there was always a trifle of "magic" to help out the medicines and defeat the insidious demon; but it consisted not so much in texts for application of the cobra wand as in the emanation from Mai-Sachme's imperturbable personality, which worked wonders of soothing on the patient, so that he was no longer frightened by his illness, that always having a bad effect. He ceased to writhe and unconsciously put on the captain's own facial expression — the rounded open lips, the brows drawn up with almost a quizzical air. So the patient lay and looked with equanimity towards healing or death. For this too Mai-Sachme taught them by his own attitude not to be afraid, and even when a man's face was already corpse-colour, his hands in their relaxed pose still expressed his doctor's teaching. Quietly, comprehendingly, with lifted brows and parted lips he lay, looking forward to the life after death.

So the lazaret was pervaded by serenity and absence of fear. Joseph sometimes entered it as the governor's right hand and even lent a hand, for he was soon transferred from the quarry to inside service. The words: "The governor of the prison committed to Joseph's hand all the prisoners that were in the prison, and whatsoever they did there he was the doer of it," are to be understood as meaning that Potiphar's former house steward, some six months after he entered Zawi-Re, had become, without any special title or promotion, the head manager and provisioner of the whole fortress. All the records and accounts went through his hands, and these, as everywhere else in the country, were endless: all purchases of oil, corn, barley, and cattle, all the giving out of supplies to the guards and convicts; all the operations in the brewery and the bakery of Zawi-Re; even the income and outgo of the Wepwawet temple; all matters connected with the dispatch of hewn stone from the quarries, and much, much else besides, came to be Joseph's business, greatly to the relief of those who had had charge of it before. He was accountable to the governor only, to that easy-going man with whom from the very beginning he had go on so well and continued to get on better and better.

For Mai-Sachme had learned that the words in which Joseph answered him at the first hearing had been uttered in very truth: the ancient, dramatic formula of self-revelation which had startled his phlegmatic soul and made him aware that the end of his nose had got cold. The impression had been uncommon, also very vague and general in kind. The captain was, in a way, grateful to Joseph for it, for on its basis he felt justified in his craving to be stirred out of his phlegm, and he looked forward to a satisfaction of the craving just as he did to the reappearance of the maiden Nekhbet in her grandchild and the ensuing third set of emotions; though he modestly and shrewdly sized himself up as not worthy of such a shock. Vague and undefined too was Mai-Sachme's feeling that Joseph had uttered the truth in his self-revelation. He could not have said what was meant by the "he" in the always portentous formula "I am he"; he did not even know that he would not have known what it meant, because he had never found it desirable or necessary to consider the point. That is the difference between his obligations and ours. Mai-Sachme in his time, which was early from one point of view, though from another also very late, must be entirely absolved from any such responsibility. He may be allowed to go his placid way and limit himself, though with a modicum of trepidation, to feeling, faith, and divination. Our source has it that the Lord was with Joseph *and* gave him to find favour in the sight of the keeper of the prison. This "and" might be interpreted to mean that the favour which God showed to the son of Rachel consisted precisely in the kindliness his taskmaster conceived for him. But favour and kindliness are not precisely the same thing. It was not that God showed to Joseph the favour of making the captain's mind favourable to him. The sympathy and confidence — in a word, the trust — which Joseph's appearance and behaviour inspired in the prison-keeper flowed rather from the unerring instinct of a good man for the divine favour — that is, for the divine itself — which rested upon this convict's head. For it is, indeed, the mark of a good man that he is wise enough to perceive and reverence the divine. Here goodness and wisdom lie so close together that they actually seem to be the same.

What, then, did Mai-Sachme take Joseph for? For something right and proper, for the right and expected one, for the bringer of the new time. At first, only in the limited sense that this man convicted of an interesting crime and sent down to the humdrum hole where it had been the captain's lot to do service for years, and who knew how much longer, brought with him a definite break in the monotony. But when the commandant of Zawi-Re so sharply condemned and rejected any confusion between phrase and reality, his strictness may have sprung from his own involvement in that very confusion; indeed, if he did not take care, he might actually find himself guilty of mixing up the literal and the figurative. In other words, such faint stirrings, associations, intuitions as Joseph's traits called up were enough to make the governor round them out into full reality; which in Joseph's case meant the manifestation of the expected one, the bringer of salvation, who comes to end the reign of the old and monotonous and to usher in a new epoch amid the rejoicing of all humanity. But about this figure which Joseph suggested floated the nimbus of the divine; and in that again is inherent the temptation to mix up the metaphorical and the actual, the quality with that from which the quality is derived. But is that such a misguided temptation? Where the divine is, there is God. There is, as Mai-Sachme would have put it, if he ever did put anything, instead of divining and believing it, *a* god; in a disguise, of course, which outwardly and indeed mentally is to be respected, even though as a disguise it shows through, so to speak, and is not very convincing, because it is itself so very lovely and well-favoured. Mai-Sachme could not have been a child of the black earth without knowing that there are images of God, breathing images of the Deity, which must be distinguished from the inanimate ones and honoured as living images of God, like Hapi the bull of Menfe and like Pharaoh himself in the horizon of his palace. The governor's knowledge of this fact did contribute not a little to shape his speculations about Joseph's nature and appearance — and we know of course that, for his part, Joseph was not precisely keen on checking such speculations but on the contrary rather enjoyed making people sit up.

For the office and the book-keeping Joseph's presence was a perfect blessing. Tradition wrongs the captain when it says he took nothing on himself. But it was true that the office routine, so important in the eyes of his superiors in Thebes, had, as he well knew, been neglected for the pursuit of his tranquil passions of medicine and literature. Even his official reputation had already suffered on occasion, and letters full of polite, roundabout unpleasantness had come from the capital. And here Joseph proved to be the long-desired indeed, the bringer of change, the man of the "I am he." He put all the records in order, taught Mai-Sachme's scribes, much given to morra and skittles, that the higher preoccupations of their head were no reason why they should let dust accumulate on the necessary business of the place, but on the contrary were every ground for their own added diligence. Joseph saw to it that regular reports and accounts went off to the capital, where the authorities read them with pleasure. In his hand the staff of office became a cobra-snake stiffened to a magic wand. He needed only to tap a vat with it to say offhand: "That will hold fifty sacks of wheat"; and when they needed to know how many bricks it would take to build a ramp, he would put the staff to his forehead and then say: "It will take five thousand bricks." The first time that had been exactly right, the next time not quite. But when he was quite right the first time, the success gilded the faultiness of the second guess and made that correct too.

In short, Joseph had not betrayed the captain in saying: "I am he." And when the book-keeping and the housekeeping came to no harm, Mai-Sachme often required his presence in the tower as well, where he compounded his drugs and made his literary essays. He liked to have Joseph about him, to discuss such matters as the correct number of blood-vessels and whether worms were the cause or the effect of disease. He set him to copy out the Tale of the Two Brothers, just as Joseph had done for his former master, in a de luxe edition on fine papyrus with red and black ink. Mai-Sachme found his assistant just the man for the job, not only because he could write a calligraphic script but also because the subject-matter was allied to Joseph's own fate. It was especially as a fool for love that Mai-Sachme found him so interesting. It was a field in which the governor's sympathies were warmly if sedately engaged — as indeed it is the chief theatre for the most fascinating exercise of the literary art. We can see how much time Jacob's son had to take from his administrative tasks — without neglecting them — to devote to Mai-Sachme's private avocations. They conferred for hours at a stretch how best to begin to commit to paper, in a pleasing, if possible even exciting, not to say thrilling style, the story of the governor's three-in-one-love-affair, which was still in part a tale of expectancy. The greatest and most discussed difficulty was this: if you included the third episode by anticipation, you would have to write the whole thing from the point of view of an old man of at least sixty; and that, they feared, would detract from the thrillingness, which, even as it was, was bound to suffer from the governor's natural temperament.

Then there was Joseph's own adventure which had brought him down to the prison. His affair with the sun-courtier's wife profoundly engaged Mai-Sachme's literary sympathies, and Joseph told him the whole story, taking care, of course, to spare the afflicted woman and not to minimize his own sins. These he described as being of the same nature as the ones he had earlier been guilty of against his own brothers and so against his father the shepherd king. So step by step he was brought back to the tale of his youth and origins; the captain's shrewd brown eyes got a strange and pregnant dissolving view into the backgrounds of this phenomenon, his aide, the convict Osarsiph. Mai-Sachme liked the fantastic name, obviously a made-up allusive combination. He spoke it feelingly, like the good man he was, never taking it for the newcomer's own but rather for a disguise or an epithet, or a circumlocution of the "I am he."

He would have liked, with the enthusiasm of the born story-teller, to put to paper the tale of Potiphar's wife; and often he diverted himself with discussion about the best method. But when he tried, the result turned out to follow the pattern of the Two Brothers and he presently left off where he began.

The days went on, they multiplied, soon almost a year had gone round since Rachel's first-born came to Zawi-Re. Then there befell something in the prison, part of a series of important events in the great world. Not immediately, but after some lapse of time, this happening in the prison was to have extraordinary results and produce great changes for Joseph and for his friend and taskmaster, Mai-Sachme.

THE TWO FINE GENTLEMEN

ONE day, that is, Joseph betook himself, at his usual early hour, to the governor's tower, with some business papers for his chief's approval. The scene was always much like what happened between Petepre and the old steward Mont-kaw, and had the same ending: "Very good, very good, my friend." This time Mai-Sachme did not even look at the accounts, waving them away with his hand. His brows were even higher than usual, his lips more parted; it was plain that he was taken up with a particular occurrence, and, within the limits of his phlegm, wrought up.

"Another time, Osarsiph," he said, referring to the papers. "Now is not the moment. Let me tell you, in my prison things are not as they were yesterday and the day before. Something has happened, it happened before daybreak, very quietly, under special and secret orders. There has been a delivery of prisoners, a most embarrassing one. Two persons have arrived, under cover of darkness, for temporary arrest and safe-keeping — not ordinary persons, I mean they are very highly placed, or they were and may be again, but just now they have come down in the world. You have taken a fall yourself; but theirs is worse because they stood much higher. Listen while I tell you, but better not ask for details."

"But who are they?" asked Joseph all the same.

"Their names are Mesedsu-Re and Bin-em-Wese," answered the governor with reserve.

"Hark to that!" cried Joseph. "What sort of names are those? People don't have such names!"

He had good ground for surprise, for Mesedsu-Re meant "Hateful to the Sun-god" and Bin-em-Wese "Evil in Thebes." Those would have been strange parents who gave their sons such names!

The captain mulled about with some sort of decoction, without looking at Joseph.

"I thought," he said, "you knew that people are not necessarily named what they call themselves or are temporarily called. Circumstances can make names. Re himself changes his according to his circumstances. These gentlemen are called as I have called them, in their papers and the orders I received about them. Those are their names in the minutes of the action which will be brought against them, and they call themselves so according to their circumstances. You will not want to know more about it than that."

Joseph quickly considered. He thought of the revolving sphere, of the above that becomes below and again mounts upwards, by turns; of the laws of opposites, of how order is reversed and things turned upside down. "Hateful to the sun-god" — that was Mersu-Re, "The Lord loves him"; "Evil in Thebes" — that was "Good in Thebes," Nefer-em-Wese. Through Potiphar he knew much about Pharaoh's court and the friends of the palace Merimat; and he recalled that Mersu-Re and Nefer-em-Wese were the names — quite overlaid with fulsome honorary titles — of Pharaoh's chief baker and supervisor of sweetmeats, with the title of Prince of Menfe, and of his overseer and scribe of the buffet, the head butler, Count of Abodu.

"The real names," said he, "of these given into your hands are probably 'What does my lord eat?' and 'What does my lord drink?' "

"Well, yes," responded the captain. "One only needs to give you an inch and you have an ell, as the saying goes. Or you think you have. Know what you know, and ask no further."

"What can have happened?" asked Joseph notwithstanding.

"Let be," replied Mai-Sachme. "They say," he went on, looking in the other direction, "that pieces of chalk were found in Pharaoh's bread, and flies in the good God's wine. How such responsible dignitaries come to be accused of such things and be sent up here awaiting investigation, under names corresponding to their circumstances, you can figure that out yourself."

"Chalk?" repeated Joseph. "Flies?"

"Before daylight," went on the captain, "they were put under strong guard on a boat bearing the sign of suspicion on prow and sail. They have been given me into strict though also suitable safe-keeping till their trial and till the verdict is pronounced. A most responsible and trying business. I have put them into the little vulture hut, you know, round the corner to the right by the back wall, that has a vulture with outspread wings on the ridgepole, it happened to be vacant — or rather, empty, for it is not furnished in the least as they are used to — and there they sit since early this morning, with some bitter beer, each of them on an ordinary camp-stool; and the vulture-house has no other amenities whatever. It is pretty hard on them; and what will be the end of their affair, whether they will soon be put in corpse-colour or whether the majesty of the good God will lift up their heads again, nobody can say. We have to behave in the light of this uncertainty, taking account within limits of their former station and to the extent of our powers. I will put you in charge of them, you will visit them twice or thrice a day, you know, and ask after their wants, if only for form's sake. Such gentlemen require good form; if we only ask what they would like, it does them some good, and it is less important after that whether they get it. You have the society graces, the *savoir faire*," said he (he used an Accadian expression), "you can talk with them in a way that suits their own elegant conventions and their present circumstances too. My lieutenants here would be either too rough or too subservient. We have to keep the right balance. Respect with a shade of solemnity, that would be about my idea."

"I'm not so good at solemnity," said Joseph. "It is not my long suit. Perhaps I might make the respectfulness a little ironic, just slightly mocking."

"That might be good too," the captain responded. "When you inquire after their wishes, they see at once that you are not serious, and that of course they can't have things here the way they are used to them, or only sort of symbolically, as it were. Anyhow we cannot have them squatting there in an empty hut. We must put in two beds with head-rests, and at least one comfortable chair, if not two, with cushions for the feet; they can take turns sitting in it. And you must act as their vizier 'What would my lord eat?' and their vizier 'What would my lord drink?' and go a little way towards satisfying their wishes. Say they want roast goose, you can give them stork. If they ask for cake you can give them short-bread, if they want wine let them have grape-juice. We will try every time to go half-way and at least show our willingness on all occasions. Go along now and pay them your respects — with any kind of colouring you think best. Beginning tomorrow, you should go morning and evening."

"I hear and obey," said Joseph, and betook himself down from the tower to the vulture hut.

The guards in front of it lifted their daggers with grins spreading over their peasant faces, for they liked him well. Then they drew back the heavy wooden bolt from the door and Joseph entered in to the courtiers. They squatted there in their little cubicle, bowed over their own stomachs, with their hands folded on top of their heads. He saluted them with the utmost refinement, though not in such an affected manner as he had seen in Hor-waz, the scribe of the Great Gate. However, it was a greeting à la mode, with raised arm and a smile and the formal wish that they might live the lifetime of Re.

They had sprung up as soon as they saw him, and overwhelmed him with questions and complaints.

"Who are you, young man?" they cried. "Are you well or ill disposed towards us? But at least you have come — at last somebody has come! Your manners are good, they suggest that you might feel with us and see how impossible, how intolerable, how indefensible our situation is! Do you know who we are? Have they told you? We are the Prince of Menfe, the Count of Abodu: Pharaoh's first inspector of bakestuffs and he who ranks even above the first scribe of the buffet, his sommelier-general, who hands him the cup on all the greatest occasions; the baker of bakers and the butler of butlers, master of the grape, in the garland of vine. Is this clear to you? Have you come here in this knowledge? Can you picture to yourself how we have lived, in pavilions faced with azurite and diorite, where we slept upon down and had special servants to scratch the soles of our feet? What will become of us in this hole? They have put us into this bare room, we have been sitting since before dawn behind bolts and bars, without the least attention paid to us. Curses on Zawi-Re! Curses, curses! There is nothing here, nothing! We have no mirror, we have no razors, no rouge-box, no bathroom, no place to satisfy our necessities, so that we are forced to restrain ourselves, though they are more urgent than usual on account of the strain we have been under, and we have cramps — we, the arch-baker and the master of the vine! Is it given to your soul to feel that this situation of ours cries to heaven? Or do you only come to observe whether our misery has reached the uttermost?"

"High and noble sirs," answered Joseph, "calm yourselves! I am well disposed towards you, for I am the captain's mouthpiece and adjutant and trusted by him with the office of overseer. He has made me your servant, who am to ask after your commands, and as my master is good and even-tempered you may infer my own temperament from his choice of me. I cannot lift up your heads; that only Pharaoh can do, so soon as your innocence is made clear, which I assume with all due respect is present and can be made clear — "

Here he paused a little and waited. They both looked him in the face: one with eyes swimming in vinous emotion, yet hopefully; the other wearing a glassy stare wherein fear and deceit swiftly pursued each other.

One would have expected the baker to be like a bag of flour and the cup-bearer to resemble the slender vine. But on the contrary it was the cup-bearer who was full-bodied. He was short and plump, with a fiery red face between the wings of the kerchief drawn smoothly over his head, in front of which his thick ears adorned with stone buttons stood out. His chubby cheeks, alas, were now quite bristly with a stubble of beard; but they showed that when shaven and oiled they could shine right jollily. Even the present dejection and gloom on the chief butler's face could not quite extinguish its fundamental trait of joviality. The chief baker was by comparison tall and stoop-shouldered; his face was sallow, though perhaps again only by comparison; but also because it was framed by a sombre black coiffure, out of which his broad gold ear-rings peeped out. But there were unmistakably underworldly features in the baker's face: the longish nose was set somewhat awry, the mouth showed a one-sided thickening and lengthening, making it sag unpleasantly, and the lowering brows had a sinister, ill-omened expression.

We must not suppose that Joseph would have remarked the difference between the two faces with any easy partisanship for the good cheer of the one and just as easy dislike of the forbidding traits of the other. By tradition and training he would be prone to accord to both the jovial and the jaundiced equal respect for their destinies. He would even go further and summon up more cordiality and courtesy towards the man whose features bore the stamp of the lower regions than to him who was already jolly by nature.

The beautifully pressed court costumes of the two with their ample adornment and gay-coloured ribbon bows were soiled and crumpled with travel; but each still wore in plain view the insignia of his high office: the butler a collar of gold vine-leaves and the baker an order of golden ears in the shape of a sickle.

"It is not I," repeated Joseph, "who can lift up your heads, nor is it the warden. All that we can do is to ease a little, as well as we can, the discomforts a heavy fate has inflicted on you. You will understand that a beginning has already been made, in that in your first hour here you wanted for everything. From now on, there will be something you do not lack; and that, after the complete deprivation, will seem sweeter to you than anything that you had when you still anointed yourself with the oil of gladness, but which, alas, this sorry place can never offer you. You see how well-meaning we were, my lords Count Abodu and Prince of Menfe, in making such a poor beginning. Within the hour you will have two bedsteads, simple ones but one apiece. An easy-chair, to use by turns, shall join the stools. A razor — unfortunately only a stone one, I apologize for it beforehand — will be at your service, and some very good eye-paint, black, shading into green, the captain himself knows how to prepare it and I am sure he will be delighted to give you some if I asked him. As for the mirror, again it was probably intentional to have it reflect your images not as you at present are but after you have washed up. Your servant, by which I mean myself, possesses a fairly clear copper mirror, and I will gladly loan it to you for the duration of your stay, which one way or the other can only be a brief span. It will please you that its frame and handle are shaped like the life-sign. As for bathing, you can get that done at the right of your hut by a couple of guards whom I will station there for the purpose; on the left side you can satisfy your necessities; that is probably just now the most pressing matter."

"Fine!" said the butler. "Just fine, for the present and in view of all the circumstances. Young man, you come like the rosy dawn after the night and like cooling shade after the heat of the sun. Health and strength to you and may you live long! The master of the vine salutes you! Lead us to the left side."

"But what did you mean," asked the baker, "by 'one way or the other' in connection with our stay and by 'a brief span'?"

"I meant by that," Joseph answered, "in any case, quite certainly, beyond a doubt — or something reassuring of that sort. That is what I meant."

And he took leave for the time of the two gentlemen, bowing somewhat more respectfully before the baker than before the butler.

Later in the day he came back, bringing a draught-board to amuse them, and inquired how they had dined. They answered more or less in the sense of "Oh, well . . ." and asked for roast goose. He promised they should have something of the kind, a roast waterfowl for instance and some sort of cake such as the poor place afforded. Further they might have an hour's target practice or a game at skittles under the eye of the guards on the court in front of the vulture-house:

they had only to command. They thanked him very much and begged him to thank the captain as well for so thoughtfully arranging that they could now so greatly enjoy these indications of amelioration after the utter baldness of their beginning. They had conceived a great confidence in Joseph and kept him in talk as long as they possibly could, with thanks and complaints, both that day and the following one, each time he came to inquire after their welfare and their commands. But in all their volubility they did not depart from their silence on the ground of their presence here but showed the same reserve which Mai-Sachme had shown in his first talk about them with Joseph.

They suffered most on account of their new names, and repeatedly implored him not to believe that these were their real ones in any sense whatever.

"It is so very delicate of you, Usarsiph, dear youth," they said, "that you do not call us by the absurd names which they put on us when we were arrested. But it is not enough that you do not let them cross your lips; even to yourself you must not call us so; you must believe that we do not go by such indecent names, but quite the reverse. That would be a great help; for we are distressed lest these fantastic names which are written in indelible ink in our papers and the proceedings of our trials in the writing of truth should gradually take on reality and we be so called to all eternity."

"Do not distress yourself, my lords," answered Joseph; "that will all pass. After all, at bottom it is a kindness. They had given you a disguise to wear under your present circumstances, thus your real ones are not betrayed in the writing of truth. In a way it is not you at all who appear in the papers and indictments; it is not you who sit here, but 'Hated of God' and 'Scum of Thebes' who suffer under your deprivations."

They were inconsolable. "Ah, but it really is us, even though incognito," they lamented. "You are so tactful that you still give us the fine titles and decorations we wore at court: Distinguished in Menfe, Prince of the Bread, and His Eminence the Great Lord of the Winepress. But know, if you do not already, they took away all these names when they arrested us; we stand here practically as naked as when the soldiers pour water over us at the right of the hut — all we have left is 'Scum of the Earth' and 'Hated of God' — that is the horrible thing!"

And they wept.

"How ever is it possible," Joseph asked, looking away just as the captain had done, "how is it possible, how ever in all the world can it have happened that Pharaoh behaved to you like a leopard of Upper Egypt and like the raging ocean, and his heart brought forth a sandstorm like the mountains of the East, of such a sort that overnight you are shorn of your honours, arrested on suspicion, and snatched off down here to us?"

"Flies," sobbed the butler.

"Chalk," said the chief baker.

Both looked the other way but each in a different direction. However, there was not much resort in the hut for three pairs of eyes; their glances met by mistake, then quickly shifted, only to meet again whitherever they travelled. It was a depressing game and Joseph would have ended it by going away, as he saw that there was nothing to be got out of them save flies and chalk. They did not want to let him go, they kept trying to convince him how untenable was any suspicion of guilt, how preposterous the names Mesedsu-Re and Bin-em-Wese.

"I implore you, good youth from Canaan, dear Ibrim," said the butler, "listen and see, how could it ever be that I, Good-and-happy-in-Thebes, could have anything to do with such an affair? It is absurd, it is contrary to the order of things; it stands to reason that it only proceeds from misunderstanding and slander. I am the chief of the wine of life and carry the staff of the grape before Pharaoh when he goes in procession to the banquet and the blood of Osiris flows in streams. I am his herald, crying Hail and Health, swinging my staff above my head. I am the man with the garland, of the vine-wreath on the head and the foaming beaker! Look at my cheeks, smoothed as they now are, albeit with a bad razor! Are they not like the bursting grape when the sun has brewed the sacred juice within it? I live and let live, crying all Hail and all Health! Do I look like one who measures the coffin for the God? Have I any resemblance to the ass of Set? One does not hitch that animal to the plough with the ox, one does not put wool and flax together in one garment; the vine does not bring forth figs. And what does not go together never can! I beg you to judge by your good common sense, as one who knows the laws of opposites and makes distinctions, who understands what is possible and what not; judge whether I can have any share in this guilt or partake at all in what is so impossbile to me."

"I can see," said Prince Mersu-Re, the chief baker, looking the other way in his turn, "that the Count's words have not failed of their impression on you, man of Zahi and gifted youth. Indeed they were compelling; your judgment must inevitably speak in his favour. Therefore I also appeal to your sense of justice, convinced that you will not want for reason and worldly common sense in passing judgment in my own case. You have perceived that the suspicion we high officials labour under is inconsistent with the sacred office my friend here holds. So you will surely agree that one can even less reconcile it with the sacredness of mine, which is if possible still greater. It is in essence the oldest, the earliest, the most exemplary — a higher there

may be, a deeper never. There is a consummateness about it as there
is about everything from which a descriptive adjective derives; it is
the holy, the very holiest of the holy! It speaks of the grotto and the
cavern into which one drives swine to sacrifice, throwing torches
down from above to feed the primeval fire, that it may burn to warm
and expand the forces of production. Therefore I bear a torch before
Pharaoh, not swinging it above my head but holding it seemly and
priestlike before me and before him, when he goes to the table to eat
the flesh of the buried god, which springs forth to the sickle from
below and out of the depths that received the oath."

Here the baker gave a start, and the gaze of his staring eyes moved
still further aside, until he was looking out of the left outside and the
right inside corners. He kept beginning a sentence only to take it back
and begin again, yet all the while he only talked himself deeper in.
For his words were addressed downwards and he could not turn
them round.

"Pardon me, I did not mean to say that," he began again, "at least
I did not intend to say it just like that; I do hope that you are not
getting a wrong idea. You are a worldly-wise young man, and we
would enlist your understanding in support of our innocence. I talk,
but when I listen to my own words I am alarmed. I might be making
you feel that I am invoking a sacredness so mighty, that is so great and
so deep, that it is almost suspect itself, so to speak, and invoking it
might even work the other way from what I want. I beg you, summon all your understanding, do not be confused into the idea that
if the evidence is too strong that makes it weaker, or even makes
it help to prove the opposite. That would be frightful, it would endanger the soundness of your judgment for you to come on such
thoughts. Look at me! Even though I do not look at you, but at my
arguments. I — guilty? I involved in such an affair? Am I not the
very chief and lord of the bread, servant of the wandering mother
who seeks her daughter with the torch, the fruit-bringer, the all-giver,
giving warmness and greenness; who rejected the benumbing blood
of the grape and gave the malt drink preference; who brought to mankind wheat and barley and first broke the clod with the curving
plough; so that from milder nourishment milder customs sprang,
whereas aforetime men ate roots and grasses and even one another?
To her I belong, consecrate to her who in the wind on the threshing-
floor winnows corn and chaff and separates honour from dishonour;
the lawgiver who gives justice and regulates free will. Judge now in
your wisdom if I could have engaged in such a sinister affair! Judge
on the basis of unfitness, which does not so much rest on the fact that
the affair is sinister; justice, like bread, being allied to the dark realm
and to the womb of the earth below, where dwell the avenging goddesses; so that one might call it in its sacredness the watch-dog of

the goddess, the more so since the dog is in fact sacred to her — and from that point of view you might also call me, who am sacred to her, a dog — "

Here he broke off with another frightful start and his eyeballs darted right over into the opposite corners. He asseverated that he had not meant to say what he had said, or at least not the way he had said it. But Joseph soothed them both, begging them not to take things so hard and not strain themselves on his account. He knew how to prize it, he said, and was honoured to have them tell him about their affair, or if not about the affair, at least the reasons why it could not have been their affair. But still less was it his affair to set himself as judge over them, for he was commanded only to be their servant, who inquired after their wishes, as they had been accustomed. Of course, they were also accustomed to having their wishes carried out, and that, much to his regret, he was largely unable to do. But at least they had the first half of what they were used to. And he asked if they would honour him with another command.

No, they said pensively, they knew of nothing; no other commands would be likely to occur to one, seeing that nothing came of them. Ah, but why must he leave them so soon? Would he not tell them how long he thought the investigation of the charges against them would take and how long they would have to lie in this hole?

He would tell them faithfully and at once, he replied, if he only knew. But naturally he did not. He could only make an entirely arbitrary and irresponsible guess; it would take thirty and ten days in all, at the most and the least, until their fate was decided.

"Ah, how long!" lamented the butler.

"Ah, how short!" cried the baker — but at once gave another frightful start and assured them that he also had meant to say how long. But the chief butler reflected and then remarked that Joseph's calculation had probably got some sense to it. For in thirty and seven and three days, counting from their arrival, it would be Pharaoh's beautiful birthday, well known as a day of justice and compassion; on that day, in all probability, their fate would be decided.

"I did not to my knowledge think of it," answered Joseph, "and did not make my calculations according. It was more of an inspiration, but seeing it turns out that Pharaoh's exalted birthday falls just on that day, you can see that my words are already beginning to be fulfilled."

OF THE STINGING WORM

WITH that he went, shaking his head over his two charges and their "affair," about which he now knew more than he could well admit. Nobody in the two lands might appear or assume to know more than was considered seemly for men to know, and this perilous knowledge was hushed up by the authorities in a cloud of circumlocution and secrecy, a screen of words about flies and pieces of chalk and unidentifiable made-up names like Hated of God and Scum of Weset. Nevertheless it was soon talked of through the length and breadth of the whole kingdom. Everybody, whether he used the prescribed circumlocutions or not, knew what was behind these minimizings and palliations. The story in all its shockingness did not lack popular appeal; one might even say that it had a ritual character, seeming as it did like the repetition in the present of events whose foundation lay far back in the past.

To put it bluntly, somebody had been conspiring against Pharaoh's life — this although the days of the majesty of that elderly god were well known to be numbered anyhow, and it is common knowledge that their inclination to unite again with the sun could not be arrested either by the advice of the magicians and physicians of the bookhouse or even by the mediation of Ishtar of the Way, which His Majesty's brother and father-in-law of the Euphrates, Tushratta, King over Khanigalbat or Mitanniland, had solicitously sent to him. But that the Great House, Si-Re, Son of the Sun and Lord of the Two Crowns, Neb-ma-Re-Amenhotpe, was old and ailing and could scarcely breathe was no reason at all why he should not be conspired against; indeed, if you liked, it was a very good reason why he should, however dreadful, of course, such an enterprise remained.

It was a universally known fact that Re himself, the sun-god, had originally been King of the two lands, or rather ruler on earth over all men; and had ruled them with majestic brilliance and blessing so long as his years were still young, mature, or middle-aged, and even for some considerable period of time into his beginning and increasing age. But when he had got very old, and painful infirmities and frailties, though of course splendid in their form, approached the majesty of this god, he had found it good to withdraw from the earth and retire into the upper regions. For his bones gradually turned to silver, his flesh to gold, and his hair to genuine lapis lazuli, a very beautiful form of senescence, yet attended with all sorts of ailments and pains, for which the gods themselves had sought a thousand remedies but all in vain, since no herb that grows can avail against the diseases of gilding and silvering and lapidification, those troubles of advanced old age. Yet even under these circumstances the old Re had always clung to his earthly sovereignty although he must have seen that owing to his own weakness it had begun to relax, that he had ceased to be feared and even to be respected.

Now Isis, the Great One of the Island, Eset, a millionfold fertile in guile, felt that her moment was come. Her wisdom embraced heaven and earth, like that of the superannuated old Re himself. But there was one thing she did not know or command, and the lack of it hampered her: she did not know the last, most secret name of Re, his very final one, knowledge of which would give power over him. Re had very many names, each one more secret than the one before, yet not utterly hopeless to find out, save one, the very last and mightiest. That he still withheld; whoso could make him name it, he could compel him and outdistance him and put him under his feet.

Therefore Eset conceived and devised a serpent, which should sting Re in his golden flesh. Then the intolerable pain of the sting, which only great Eset could cure who made the worm, would force Re to tell her his name. Now as she contrived it, so was it fulfilled. The old Re was stung, and in torments was forced to come out with one of his secret names after another, always hoping that the goddess would be satisfied before they got to the last one. But she kept on to the uttermost, until he had named her the very most secret of all, and the power of her knowledge over him was absolute. After that it cost her nothing to heal his wound; but he only got a little better, within the wretched limits in which so old a creature can; and soon thereafter he gave up and joined the great majority.

Thus tradition, known by heart to every child of Keme. It did suggest that Pharaoh had had something done to him; since he gradually got worse until his condition was so like that of the old god that one tended to mix them up. But there had been one particular individual who had taken the ancient tradition quite peculiarly to heart: a certain inmate of Pharaoh's house of women, the private and well-guarded pavilion of the greatest elegance adjoining the palace Merimat; whither Pharaoh still had himself carried now and then, of course only to chuck one or other of their graces under the chin, perhaps to defeat her on the board of thirty fields, and at the same time to enjoy the lute-playing, dancing, and singing of the rest of the sweet-scented troop. Often, indeed, he played a game with that very female who took so seriously the old legend of Isis and Re that she yielded to the temptation to re-enact it. Nobody, however well versed in the finer points of this story, can tell this woman's name. It has been obliterated from tradition, the night of everlasting forgetfulness shrouds it. And yet the woman had been in her time a favourite concubine of Pharaoh, and twelve or thirteen years before, when he still condescended to beget a child, she had borne him a son, Noferka-Ptah — this name is preserved — who as a scion of the godlike seed received a special education, and on whose account she, a concubine, was privileged to wear the vulture head-dress. It was not quite so elaborate a one as that worn by Tiy, the great royal consort herself, but none the less a gold vulture cap. This cap, and her maternal weakness for Noferka-Ptah, went to the woman's head and were fatal to her. For the head-dress incited her to confuse herself with the wily Eset and to cherish ambitions hallowed by tradition and mixed up with her doting fondness for her little half-breed. The ancient records dazed her small and scheming brain, so that she made up her mind to have Pharaoh stung by a serpent, to instigate a palace revolt and set on the throne of the two lands not Horus-Amenhotep, the rightful heir, who was sickly anyhow, but the fruit of her own womb, Noferka-Ptah.

The first steps toward the goal of overturning the dynasty, bringing in a new time and elevating the nameless near-favourite to the rank of goddess-mother had been successfully taken. The plot was hatched in Pharaoh's house of women; but through certain officials of the harem and certain officers of the guard who had been eager for new things, connections had been established, on the one hand with the palace itself, where a number of friends, some of them highly placed — a head charioteer of the god, the chief of gens-d'armes, the steward of the fruit stores, the overseer of the King's herds of oxen, the head keeper of the King's ointments, and certain others — were won over for the enterprise; and on the other hand they got in touch with the outer world of the residential city, where through the officers' wives the male kindred of Pharaoh's graces were drawn in and engaged to stir up Wese's population with evil talk against the old Re, who by now was nothing at all but gold and silver and lapis lazuli.

In all there were two-and-seventy conspirators privy to the plot. It was a proper and a pregnant number, for there had been just seventy-two when red Set lured Usir into the chest. And these seventy-two in their turn had had good cosmic ground to be no more and no less than that number. For it is just that number of groups of five weeks which make up the three hundred and sixty days of the year, not counting the odd days; and there are just seventy-two days in the dry fifth of the year, when the gauge shows that the Nourisher has reached his lowest ebb, and the god sinks into his grave. So where there is conspiracy anywhere in the world it is requisite and customary for the number of conspirators to be seventy-two. And if the plot fail, the failure shows that if this number had not been adhered to it would have failed even worse.

Now the present plot did fail, although it had had the benefit of the best models and all the preliminary steps had been taken with the greatest care. The head keeper of unguents had even succeeded in purloining a magic script out of Pharaoh's book-house and, following its instructions, had shaped certain little wax images; these were smuggled about here and there and were calculated to produce by magic a mental confusion and bewitchment such as must assure the success of the undertaking. It was decided to put poison in Pharaoh's bread or his wine or in both; and to use the ensuing confusion for a palace coup. Combined with a rising in the upper city, this was to have led to the proclamation of a new era and the elevation of the young bastard Noferka-Ptah to the throne of the two lands. And then all at once the lid blew off. Possibly at the last minute one of the seventy-two decided that by choosing the loyal part he would do better for his career and for the beauty and interest of the wall-paintings in his tomb. Or perhaps a police decoy had wormed himself into the councils from the start. Anyhow, a list had been put into Pharaoh's hands. It was painful enough reading, containing as it did the names of a number of really close friends of the god and visitors at his levee. The list was on the whole correct, though not quite free from errors and mistaken identities; and the prosecutions had been swift, quiet, and thorough. The Isis of the women's house was straightway strangled by eunuchs, her little son was sent into outermost Nubia and a secret commission met to investigate the whole scheme and each particular guilt. Meanwhile the persons thus exposed were labelled in one common epithet: "Abhorred of the two lands"; while cruel distortions were made of their personal ones, under which they disappeared into various custodies to await their fate in circumstances quite foreign to their usual habits.

And thus it was that Pharaoh's chief baker and chief butler had come down to the prison where Joseph lay.

JOSEPH HELPS OUT AS INTERPRETER

THEY had been sitting there now for thirty-and-seven days when Joseph one morning made his usual call to inquire how they had rested and to ask after their commands. He found the two gentlemen in a frame of mind which might be called excited, depressed, and annoyed all at once. They had by now begun to get used to the simple life and had ceased to complain. After all, it is not necessary to life to live as they had lived, surrounded by malachite and diorite, with servants to scratch the soles of their feet. Indeed, with a bathing-place on their right and a retiring-place on their left, and some opportunity to shoot arrows and throw nines as a substitute for the lordly bird-shoot, life is not so bad after all. But today they looked definitely relapsed into their former spoilt-children state; as soon as Joseph appeared they exhausted themselves in the old bitter complaints: how after all they lacked for the most elementary conveniences and how their life here, however honest the effort they had made to come to terms with it, still continued to be a dog's life.

They had had dreams the night before, they said, in answer to Joseph's sympathetic questioning. Each of them had dreamed his own dream, and each dream had been of the most speaking vividness, highly impressive, unforgettable, and of quite peculiar flavour: dreams that unmistakably "meant something," wearing the sign "Understand me aright" on their brows. They fairly cried out for inter-

pretation. And at home each of them had had his own interpreter of
dreams, experts in all the monstrous brood of the dark hours, with
eyes for every detail to which a claim of significance could be attached; equipped with the very best dream-books and expositions,
Babylonian as well as Egyptian, and only needing to turn the leaves,
if they themselves fell short of ideas. And when they were at a stand-
still and the books did not help them out, the two courtiers could call
a convocation of temple prophets and learned scribes, by whose combined powers the matter could certainly be got to the bottom of. In
short, in every such case they had been promptly, efficiently, and
aristocratically served. But now, and here? They had dreamed: each
of them his own special, striking, and poignant dream, each with a
strange flavour of its own; their minds were full of them, and there
was nobody in this accursed hole to interpret these dreams and serve
them as they were used to be served. That was a deprivation far
harder to bear than the loss of feather beds, roast goose, and bird-
shooting; it made them feel their intolerable degradation even to tears.

Joseph listened and stuck out his lips a little.

"Well, gentlemen," said he, "to begin with, if it is any consolation
to you to know that someone feels for you in your distress, then behold in me one who does so. But it might even be possible to do a
little something about this lack that so upsets you. I have been appointed your servant and caretaker, and, so to speak, I am here as a
general-purpose assistant. So why not after all for dreams as well? I
am not quite unversed in the field, I may boast of a certain familiarity
with dreams — do not take the word amiss, it is only apt, for in my
family and tribe we have always been in the habit of having interesting dreams. My father, the shepherd king, while on his travels, had
a first-class dream in a certain place, which clothed his whole being
with dignity for the rest of his life; it was always an uncommon
pleasure to hear him tell it. And in my previous life I myself had much
to do with dreams, I even had a nickname for it among my brothers,
who made a jest of this peculiarity of mine. You have had so much
practice in putting up with things — how would it be if you put up
with me and told me your dreams, in order that I might try to interpret them?"

"Yes, indeed," said they. "Very good. You are a most agreeable
young man, and you have a way of looking dreamily into space with
your charming, yes, even beautiful eyes, when you talk of dreams,
that we could almost have confidence in your capacities. But even so,
it is one thing to dream and quite another to interpret."

"Do not say so!" he responded. "Do not say it without qualification. For it may well be that dreaming is a single whole, wherein
dream and interpretation belong together and dreamer and interpreter
only seem to be two separate persons but are actually interchange-

able and one and the same, since together they make up the whole.
Whoever dreams interprets also; and whoever would interpret must
have dreamed. Your Excellencies Lord Prince of the Bread and Hereditary Cup-bearer, you have lived under luxurious circumstances of
unnecessary division of labour, so that when you dreamed, the interpretation was the business of your private soothsayers. But at bottom
and by nature everybody is the interpreter of his own dream, and
only out of sheer elegance does he have himself served with an interpretation. I will reveal to you the mystery of dreaming: the interpretation is earlier than the dream, and when we dream, the dream proceeds from the interpretation. How otherwise could it happen that
a man knows perfectly when an interpretation is false, and cries:
'Away with you, ignoramus! I will have another soothsayer who interprets to me the truth'? Well, at least try it with me, and if I
blunder or do not interpret after your own knowledge, chase me
away to hide my head in shame!"

"I will not tell mine," said the chief baker; "I am used to better
service and I prefer to go without in this as in other things, sooner
than take an unprofessional person as interpreter."

"I will tell mine," said the butler. "Truly I am so eager for an interpretation that I will gladly put up with what comes, especially since
this young man shows some familiarity with the subject and narrows
and veils his eyes in such a promising way. Young man, prepare to
hear and to interpret; but pull yourself together, as I likewise must
pull myself together to find the right words and not murder my
dream in the telling. For it was so clear and lifelike and full of inimitable spice; for we know, alas, how a dream like that shrinks when
you try to put it into words, and becomes the mummy and withered, swaddled image of that which it was when you dreamed it and
it grew green and blossomed and bore fruit like the vine which was
before me in this my dream — for it seems I have already begun to tell
it. It seemed to me I was with Pharaoh in his vineyard and beneath
the roof of the vaulted bower where Pharaoh was resting. And before
me was a grapevine, I see it still, it was a marvellous vine and had three
separate branches. You understand, it grew green and had leaves like
human hands; but though the arbour was already hanging full of
heavy bunches of grapes, this vine had not fruited yet, for that took
place before my very eyes, in my dream. Lo, it grew before them and
began to blossom, sending forth the most beautiful thick blooms
among its foliage, and the three branches put out grapes that ripened visibly with the swiftness of the wind and their purple fruits
were as bouncing as my own cheeks and bulged as nobody's cheeks
in these parts. I rejoiced greatly and with my right hand I picked the
grapes, for in my left I held Pharaoh's beaker, half full of cool water.
And full of feeling I squeezed the juice of the grapes into the cup,

remembering as I did so that you, young man, sometimes squeeze a little grape-juice into water and give it to us when we order wine. So I gave the cup to Pharaoh into his hand. . . . And that was all," he finished lamely, crestfallen and disappointed by his own words.

"It is not a little," answered Joseph, opening his eyes, which he had kept closed as he inclined his ear to the tale. "There was the cup, and clear water within it, and you yourself pressed the grape-juice into it from the vine with the three branches and gave it to the lord of the two crowns. That was a pure gift and there were no flies in it. Shall I interpret?"

"Yes, do!" cried the other. "I can scarcely wait!"

"This is the meaning," said Joseph. "The three branches are three days. In three days you will receive the water of life and Pharaoh will lift up your head and take away from you the name of shame so that you are once more called Justified in Thebes as before, and he will install you again in your office, so that you can give him the cup again into his hand as when you were his cup-bearer. And that is all."

"Splendid, capital!" cried the fat man. "That is a beautiful, an excellent, a masterly interpretation, I am served by it as never before in my life, and you, sweet youth, have done my mind an inestimable service. Three branches — three days — how you could have it so pat, you clever youth — and 'Honourable in Thebes' again as before, and everything as it used to be, and once more Pharaoh's friend! Thank you, thank you, thank you very, very much!"

And he sat there and wept for joy.

But Joseph said to him: "District Count of Abodu, Nefer-em-Wese! I have prophesied to you according to your dream — it was easily and gladly done and I rejoice that I could give you a happy interpretation. Soon you will be surrounded by hosts of friends, because you have been declared innocent; but here in these straits I shall be the first to congratulate you. I was your servant and steward for seven-and-thirty days and shall be so for three more, by the governor's orders; asking after your commands and giving you tokens of your accustomed amenities, so far as our limitations permit. I have come to you here in the vulture-house morning and evening, and been like an angel of God, if I may so express myself, into whose breast you could pour your troubles and be condoled with over the strangeness of your lot. But you have not asked me much about myself. And yet, like you, I was not born into this hole nor did I choose it for my habitation; I landed here, I know not how, put here as a slave of the King, condemned for a sin which is nothing but misrepresentation before God. Your minds were too full of your own misfortunes for you to have much feeling or interest left for mine. But forget me not, and my service to you, Count Chief Cup-bearer; think of me when you are back in all your former glory. Speak of me before Pharaoh and call to his attention that I am sitting here out of the sheerest misunderstanding, and beg in my behalf that he graciously remove me out of this prison where I am so sorely against my will. For indeed I was stolen away, simply stolen as a boy from my home and brought down here to Egypt, stolen down into the pit — and am like the moon, when an opposing spirit stopped it in its course so that it could not move shining onwards before the gods its brothers. Will you do this for me, District Count Head Cup-bearer, and speak of me at Court?"

"Yes, of course, a thousand times yes!" cried the fat man. "I promise you that I will mention you at the first opportunity when I stand before Pharaoh, and will remind him each later time if his mind has not grasped it. It would be swinish of me indeed not to think and speak of you to your advantage; for whether you have stolen or are stolen is all the same to me; mentioned you shall be, and pardoned, sweet honey-youth!"

And he embraced Joseph and kissed him on the mouth and on both cheeks.

"But I also have dreamed," said the long man, "though the fact seems to have been forgotten here. I did not know, Ibrim, that you were such a skilled interpreter or I would not have rejected your aid. I now incline to tell you my dream in my turn, as well as it can be told in words, and you shall interpret it to me. Make ready to hearken."

"I hearken," answered Joseph.

"What I dreamed," said the baker, "was this, and was the following. I dreamed — but you can see how ludicrous was my dream, for how should I, the Prince of Menfe, who certainly never sticks his head into the oven, how should I, like a baker's apprentice, be delivering rolls and crescents? — but suffice it to say, there I was, in my dream, carrying on my head three baskets of fine rolls, one on top of the other, flat baskets fitting into each other, each full of all kinds of good things from the palace bakery; and in the top one lay uncovered the bakestuff for Pharaoh, the crescents and rolls. Then a flight of birds came swooping down on spread wing, their talons bared, their necks stretched out, their eyeballs goggling and glaring, and screeched as they came. And these birds in their boldness thrust down and ate of the food on my head. I would have lifted my free hand to wave it over the top of the basket and frighten the vermin away; but I could not, for my hand was as lamed. And they hacked at the food, and their flapping was all about me like a wind, and the bird-smell of them was piercing in its foulness." Here the baker started, as he always did, went pale, and tried to smile in the misshapen corner of his mouth. "That is," he said, "you must not imagine the birds and the stench on the air nor their beaks nor their goggling eyes as too utterly disgusting. They were just birds, like any birds, and when I said they hacked — I don't remember whether I said that but I may have done — that was rather too strong a word, used to give you a feeling of my dream. I ought to have said they pecked. The little birds pecked from my basket, they probably thought I meant to feed them, the top basket being uncovered and no cloth over it — in short, the situation was very natural in my dream, except for me, the Prince of Menfe, carrying the bakestuff on my head, and of course that I could not wave my hand — though perhaps I did not want to because I liked the little birds to come. . . . And that was all."

"Shall I interpret?" Joseph asked.

"As you will," answered the baker.

"The three baskets," said Joseph, "are three days. In three days Pharaoh will take you out of this house and lift up your head from off you; that is, he will bind you to the post and shall hang you on a tree and the birds of the air will eat your flesh from off you. And that is all — unfortunately."

"What are you saying?" cried the baker, hiding his face in his hands. Tears sprang out from between his beringed fingers.

But Joseph comforted him, and said: "Do not grieve all too much, Excellence Chief Baker, neither do you dissolve, O master of the vine, in tears of joy. Rather accept with dignity what you both are and what comes to you both. For the world too, being round, has an upper and an under side; yet we should not make too much of this two-sidedness, for at bottom the ox is no better and no worse than the ass, they might easily change places, and together they make one whole. You can see by the tears you both are shedding that the difference between you two gentlemen is not so great. You, Your Eminence Master of the Feast, be not prideful, for you are only good in a manner of speaking and I suspect your innocence consists only in that nobody approached you from the side of evil, because you are a chatterbox and they did not trust you. So you remained ignorant of evil. And you will not be mindful of me when you come back into your kingdom, although you have promised to; I tell you this before-hand. Only very late will you do it, when you stub your toe on the memory of me. When you do, then remember how I told you so. But you, Master Baker, do not despair! For I think you joined the con-spiracy because you thought it was respectably backed, and you con-fused evil with good, as can easily happen. Lo, you are of the god when he is below, and your companion is of the god when he is above, and lifting up of the head is lifting up of the head, even though it be on the cross of Usir, on which, in fact, one sometimes sees an ass, in token that Set and Osiris are the same."

Thus Jacob's son to the two fine gentlemen. But three days after he had interpreted their dreams they were fetched out from the prison and the heads of both were lifted up: the chief butler in honour, the baker in shame, for he was put to death. But the butler completely forgot Joseph, because he hated even to think of the prison and so would not think of his former steward.

Chapter II

THE SUMMONS

NEB-NEF-NEZEM

AFTER these events, Joseph remained for two more years in the prison and in his second pit. He had reached the mature age of thirty when he was hastily removed, yes, in the most breathless haste — for now it was Pharaoh's self who had dreamed. After the space of two years Pharaoh had a dream — in fact he had two dreams; but since they came to the same thing we may speak of them as one. The point is idle, by comparison with another: namely, that when we now speak of Pharaoh, the word has no longer, in a personal sense, the meaning it had when the chief baker and the chief butler dreamed their true dreams. For Pharaoh is always the word, and Pharaoh is always; but at the same time he comes and goes; just as the sun is always, yet likewise goes and comes. So now, that is to say very soon after the two gentlemen, Joseph's protégés, had in opposite ways had their heads lifted up, Pharaoh had gone and come. This had happened and much else besides, and Joseph had missed it, while he still lay in prison and in *bôr*, and only a faint echo of the resounding event reached him: namely, the change of reign, the lamentable passing of one day of the world and the exultant dawn of another, a new time, from which men expect a change for the better, no matter how good, humanly speaking, the former one may have been. On that day, they think and believe, right will drive out wrong, "the moon will come right" (as though it had never come right before!) — in short, from now on life would be one long season of laughter and amaze. All of which was reason enough for the whole population to hop on one leg and drink to excess for weeks — after, of course, a period of mourning in sackcloth and ashes, and that was by no means a hypocritical convention, but sincere grief over the going hence of the old time. For man is a creature prone to confusion.

As many years as his chief butler and the general intendant of his bakeries had spent days at Zawi-Re, namely forty, had Amun's son, the son of Thutmose and the daughter of Mitanni's King, Neb-ma-Re-Amenhotpe III-Nimmuria adorned his throne in splendour and built his palaces; then he died, he united himself with the sun, having had at the close of his life the disheartening experience with the two-and-seventy conspirators who had sought to lure him into the coffin. But now of course he had come to it anyhow, and a splendid coffin it was, studded with nails of pure beaten gold; he lay there, preserved in salt and bitumen, made to last to all eternity with juniper-wood, turpentine, cedar resin, styrax, and mastic, and wrapped in four hundred ells of linen bandages. Seventy days it took till the Osiris was ready. Then it was laid on a golden sledge drawn by oxen, that carried the bark holding the lion-footed bier roofed over by a canopy. Preceded by incense-bearers and water-sprinklers and accompanied by a host of mourners apparently overcome by grief, it was borne to its eternal dwelling in the hills, a many-chambered tomb equipped with every convenience. Before its door the ceremony was performed, the so-called "opening of the mouth," with the foot of the Horus-calf.

The Queen and the court were no longer walled in within the many-roomed abode there to starve to death and moulder beside the dead. The days when that was considered necessary or proper were far in the past, the custom had lapsed and was forgotten — and why? What had they against it, and why was it remote from every mind? They indulged their fill in primitive observances, diligently made magic; stopped all the body openings of the exalted cadaver with charms against evil and faithfully performed the ceremony with the calf's-foot instrument, according to the time-honoured ritual. But to wall up the royal court — no, none of that, it was not done any more. It was not only that they did not wish to do it, that they no longer found it a good idea, as once they had. They did not even want to know that the custom had ever been practised or found good: neither the traditionally walled-in parties nor the wallers-in gave a single thought to the matter. Obviously it could no longer bear the light of day — call that light late or early as you will — and that is remarkable. Many people might feel that the remarkable thing was the fine old custom itself, the immurement of the living. But surely it is more remarkable that one day, by common, wordless, indeed unconscious consent, it simply ceased to come under consideration.

The court sat with its head on its knees, and all the people mourned. Then they all lifted their heads, from the Negro borders to the delta and from desert to desert, and greeted enthusiastically the new epoch which should know no more wrong, in which "the moon would come right"; lifted their heads in exultant welcome to the son and successor, a charming though not beautiful lad, who if the reckoning was correct was only fifteen years old and still under the wardship of Tiy, the goddess-widow Horus-mother, who was still for some time to guide the reins of state. He was throned and crowned with the crowns of Upper and Lower Egypt; and there were great celebrations, in much weighty pomp, partly in the Palace of the West in Thebes, but the most solemn part at the place of the coronation, Per-Mont, whither young Pharaoh and his lady mother, lofty in feathers, with a splendid retinue, on the heavenly bark *Star of the Two Lands,* betook themselves upstream amid loud shoutings from the banks. When he returned thence, he bore the titles: "Strong Bull," "Favoured of the Two Goddesses," "Great in Kingship in Karnak," "Golden Falcon, who lifted the Crowns of Per-Mont," "King of Upper and Lower Egypt," "Nefer-Kheperu-Re-Wanre," which means "Lovely of form is he, who alone is and to whom he is the only"; "Son of the Sun, Amenhotpe," "Divine Ruler of Thebes," "Great in Duration," "Living to all Eternity," "Beloved of Amon-Re, Lord of the Heavens," "High Priest of Him exulting in the Horizon by the Power of his name 'Heat-which-is-in-Aton.'"

Thus was young Pharaoh called after his crowning. The combination of titles, Joseph and Mai-Sachme agreed, was a compromise arrived at after long and tough bargaining between the court and the temple power. For the court inclined to Atum-Re's complaisant sun-sense; whereas Amun's jealous and oppressive temple power had reaped a few low bows before the traditionally Highest, but only in return for pretty transparent concessions to him at On in the point of the triangle. The royal boy, actually consecrated as "Greatest of Seers" of Re-Horakhte, had even woven the un- and anti-traditional doctrinal name Aton into the trailing garment of his title. His mother, the goddess-widow, called her strong fighting bull, who of course had no faintest resemblance to a bull, quite briefly, Meni. But the people, Joseph heard, had another name for him, a tender and delicate name: Neb-nef-nezem it called him, Lord of the Breath of Sweetness — it could not definitely be said why. Perhaps because it was known that he loved the flowers of his garden and liked to bury his small nose in their fragrance.

Joseph, then, in his pit, missed all these spectacles and the accompanying hubbub of rejoicing. The only sign of them down in the prison was the fact that Mai-Sachme's soldiers were allowed to get drunk three days running. Joseph was not present; he was not, so to speak, present on earth when the day changed, tomorrow became today, and the sun of tomorrow the sun of today. He only knew that it had happened; and from down below he cast his eyes up to the sun. He knew that Neb-nef-nezem's child- and sister-bride, another Princess of Mitanni, whom his father had wooed for him by letter from King Tushratta, had disappeared and taken her way westward almost as soon as she had arrived. Well, Meni, the strong fighting bull, was quite used to such disappearances. There had always been much dying all about him. All his brothers and sisters had died, some of them before his birth, some since, among them one brother; only a late-born little sister had survived, and she too had shown such a strong inclination westwards that she was almost never seen. Nor did he himself look as though he would live for ever and always, to judge from the sandstone images which the apprentices of Ptah made for him. But it was imperative that he should continue the line of the sun before he too went hence; so he had been married again in the lifetime of Nebmare-Amenhotep, this time to a daughter of the Egyptian nobility, Nefertiti by name, who had now become his exalted consort and mistress of the two lands, and to whom he had given the radiant title Nefernefruaton — "Beautiful beyond all beauty is Aton."

Joseph had missed the wedding feast too, and the sight of the rejoicing crowds on the banks. But he knew about it, and he took note of the young Highest. He heard for instance from Mai-Sachme, who got to know a good deal in the course of his duties, that Pharaoh, directly he had lifted the two crowns at Per-Mont, had given the order to complete with all speed the building of the house of Re-Horakhte-Aton at Karnak. His departed father had in fact already commissioned it. And special order was given to erect in the open court of the temple a mammoth freestone obelisk on a lofty base. The sun-meaning of this obelisk, referring to the doctrines of On at the point of the triangle, was quite obviously a challenge to Amun. Not as though Amun would have had anything against the neighbourhood of other gods, in and for itself. Round about his greatness there were indeed many houses and shrines at Karnak; for Ptah the swaddled one, Min the staring, Montu the falcon, and some others had shrines there, and Amun tolerated the worship of them near him, and not only out of benevolence. For the multiplicity of the gods of Egypt was really an asset to his conservatism; always, of course, with the proviso that he, the weighty one, was king over them all, king of the gods, and that they waited upon him from time to time, in return for which he was ready, on proper occasion, to make them a return visit. But in this case there could be no waiting upon; there would be no image in the great new shrine and house of the sun, nothing but the obelisk, which threatened to be arrogantly tall. After all, it was no longer the time of the pyramid-builders, when Amun was small and Re very great in his light-places; when Amun had not yet taken Re into himself and become Amun-Re, god of the empire and king of the gods. Among these Re-Atum now, for his part and in his kind, might of course continue to exist, or rather, indeed, should continue to exist — but not in any presumptuous sense, not as a new god called Aton, setting himself up to philosophize about himself. That was fitting for Amun-Re alone, or, more correctly, not even for him; to think, indeed, was altogether unsuitable, and the settled position was that Amun and no other was king over the traditional multiplicity of the gods of Egypt.

But even under King Nebmare there had been a great deal of fashionable speculation at court; and now it looked as though it was going to take the upper hand. Young Pharaoh had given out an edict, and had it engraved on stone to commemorate the erection of the obelisk. It gave evidence of much subtilizing effort to define the nature of the sun-god in a new and anti-traditional way; to define it so sharply, indeed, that it suffered from tortuosity. "There lives," so the inscription ran, "Re-Hor of the horizon, who exults in the horizon in his name Shu, who is the Aton."

That was obscure, although it dealt with light itself and was meant to be very clear. It was complicated, although it aimed at simplification and unification. Re-Horakhte, a god among the gods of Egypt, had a threefold form: animal, human, and divine. His image was the image of a man with a falcon head, on which stood the disk of the sun. But also as a heavenly constellation he was threefold: in his birth out of the night, in the zenith of his manhood, and in his death in the west. He lived a life of birth, of dying, and of renewed generation, a life looking into death. But he who had ears to hear and eyes to read the writing on the stone understood that Pharaoh's doctrinal pronouncement did not wish the life of the god to be thus perceived as a coming and going, a becoming, passing, and becoming again, as a life done away with in death and thus phallic; all in all, not as life in so far as life is always done away with in death, but as pure being, the changeless source of light, subject to no ups and downs, out of whose image man and bird would at some far future time fall away, so that only the pure life-radiating sun-disk remained, called Aton.

This was understood, or not understood but at least energetically and excitedly discussed by such as had the necessary equipment to talk about it, also by such as entirely lacked the equipment and merely prattled. It was prattled about even as far down as into Joseph's pit; even Mai-Sachme's soldiers prattled about it, and the convicts in the quarry too, whenever they had breath enough; and this much at least everybody understood, that it was an offence to Amun-Re, as was likewise the great obelisk they had stuck in front of his nose, as well as certain more far-reaching orders of Pharaoh, having to do with the subtilizing definition in the inscription and really going very far indeed. Thus the great estate where the new house of the sun grew up was to bear the name Brightness of the Great Aton — yes, rumour even had it that Thebes itself, Wese, Amun's city, was henceforth to be called City of the Brightness of Aton; about this there was endless gossip. Even the dying in Mai-Sachme's hospital beds talked of it with their latest breath — quite aside from those

who were only suffering from itch or pink-eye; so that the captain's
rest-cure system was endangered.

The lord of the sweet breath, so it seemed, could not do enough
to further his purposes and the purposes of the beloved god of his
doctrine — in other words, the building of the temple; it was carried
forwards with such haste and urgency that all the stone-masons from
Jebu, the Elephant Isle, as far down as the delta, were set to work.
And yet all this concentration failed to give the house of Aton the
kind of structure suitable for an eternal dwelling. Pharaoh was in
such haste, so ridden by impatience, that he gave up the use of the
large blocks used for the tombs of the gods, because they were so
hard to cut and haul. He gave order to erect the temple of changeless
light out of small stones which could be tossed from hand to hand.
Quantities of mortar and cement had thus to be used to smooth the
walls for the painted bas-reliefs designed to shine there. Amun had
made great fun of this, so one heard on all sides.

So it was that the course of events reached down into Zawi-Re
and involved the son of Jacob, even though he was not present at
them. For Mai-Sachme's quarry had to furnish much stone for Pharaoh's hasty building, and Joseph had to be on hand with his overseer's staff to see that pick and crowbar were not idle, so that the
governor of the prison should not get any flowery unpleasantness
in his correspondence with the government. For the rest, he continued to endure his quite endurable punishment at Zawi-Re, by the
side of his even-tempered chief. It was monotonous, like the captain's
manner of speech, yet nourished by expectation. For there was much
to expect, at hand and afar off — at first near at hand. Time passed
for him as it does pass, in the usual way, which we may call neither
quickly nor slowly, for it goes slowly, especially when one lives in
expectation, yet if one looks back it appears to have gone very
quickly. Joseph lived in Zawi-Re until he got to be thirty, without
taking particular notice of it. Then came the breathless day and the
winged messenger, a day which might have startled Mai-Sachme out
of his calm and almost taught him to fear, if he had not already been
expecting great things for Joseph.

THE EXPRESS MESSENGER

A BARK arrived, with curving lotos prow and purple sail; it fairly flew
up, so light it was, manned by five oarsmen on either side, and bearing the sign of royalty, an express boat from Pharaoh's own flotilla.
It lay to neatly alongside the landing-stage of Zawi-Re, and a youth
leaped ashore, slender and light as the boat that bore him, with lean
face and long sinewy legs. His chest heaved beneath the linen garment, he was out of breath or at least he seemed to be, he behaved as

though he were. There was no real reason for breathlessness; after all, he had come by boat, not run all the way. Anyhow, he ran, or flew, with extreme celerity through the gate and courtyard of Zawi-Re, opening a way for himself and preventing anyone from stopping him, by uttering a series of little shouts, not loud, but very disconcerting to the astonished and ineffectual guards in his path, and demanding to see the captain at once. He ran, then, or he flew, with such speed toward the citadel they pointed out to him that despite his slim build the pretended breathlessness might well have become real by the time he reached it. Certainly the little wings on the heels of his sandals and on his cap could not help him along, they were there merely in token of his office.

Joseph, occupied in the counting-house, saw this new arrival running, but paid him no heed, even when his attention was called to him. He went on turning over papers with the chief clerk until an underling came running, breathless too, with the order that Joseph was to drop everything, no matter how important, and present himself at once before the captain.

"I am coming," said he; yet finished first the paper he was going over with the clerk. Then, of course not loitering, but not running either, he betook himself to the captain in the tower.

The end of Mai-Sachme's nose was rather white when Joseph came into the dispensary. His heavy brows were drawn up higher than ever, his full lips parted.

"Here you are," he said with abated voice to Joseph. "You should have been here before. Hearken to this." He gestured toward the winged youth, who stood beside him, or rather did not stand, or not still, for his arms, head, shoulders, and legs kept moving in such a way that he seemed to run to and fro without stopping, in order to go on being breathless. Sometimes he stood on his toes, as though about to take flight.

"Your name is Usarsiph?" he asked in a low, hurried voice, keeping his quick, close-lying eyes upon Joseph's face. "You are the captain's aide who was in charge of certain occupants of the vulture-house here two years ago?"

"I am," answered Joseph.

"Then you must come with me just as you are," the other stated, with even more speaking play of limb. "I am Pharaoh's first runner, his swift messenger am I, and came with the express boat. You must straightway join me so that I can take you to court, for you are to stand before Pharaoh."

"I?" asked Joseph. "How could that be? I am too unimportant."

"Unimportant or no, it is Pharaoh's beautiful will and command. Breathless I bore it to your captain and breathless must you obey the summons."

"I have been put into this prison," responded Joseph, "certainly by way of a mistake, and in a manner of speaking I have been stolen down here. But here I am, a convict at hard labour, and though you cannot see my chains, yet I have them. How could I go out with you through these walls and gates on to your boat?"

"That has not the least thing in the world to do with it," hurried on the runner, "by comparison with the beautiful command, which makes all that vanish into thin air and in a trice bursts all your bonds. Before Pharaoh's wonderful will nothing can stand. But have no fear, it is more than unlikely that you will stand the test; much more than likely they will bring you back in short order to the place of your punishment. You will hardly be wiser than Pharaoh's greatest scholars and magicians of the book-house and shame the seers and soothsayers and interpreters of the house of Re-Horakhte, who invented the sun-year."

"That is in God's hands, whether He is with me or not," answered Joseph. "Has Pharaoh dreamed?"

"You are not here to ask but to answer," said the messenger, "and woe to you if you cannot. Then will you fall, I suppose deeper than just back into this prison."

"Why am I to be thus tested," asked Joseph, "and how does Pharaoh know of me, that he sends forth his beautiful command down here to me?"

"You have been mentioned and named and called attention to in this crisis," the other replied. "On the way you may learn more; now you must follow me breathless, that you may straightway stand before Pharaoh."

"Wese is far," said Joseph, "and far is Merimat, the palace. However winged boat and messenger, Pharaoh must wait before his will is obeyed and I stand before him for my test. He might even have forgotten his beautiful command before I come, and himself find it no longer beautiful."

"Pharaoh is near," responded the runner. "It pleases the beautiful sun of the world to shine now in On, at the point of the delta; he has betaken himself thither in the boat *Star of the Two Lands*. In a few hours my bark will fly and flit to its goal. Up with you, then, not a word more."

"But I must have my hair cut first and put on proper clothes if I am to stand before Pharaoh," said Joseph. He had been wearing his own hair in the prison, and his clothing was only of the very common coarse linen. But the runner replied:

"That can be done on board as we flit and we fly. All has been provided. You imagine that one thing may delay another, instead of all being crowded into one time, in order to save it; but you know not what breathlessness is when Pharaoh commands."

So then Joseph turned to the captain to take his leave, and he called him "my friend."

"You see, my friend," said he, "how things stand and how they are to go with me after these three years. They hurry me out of the pit and draw me up out of the well — it is the old pattern. This courier thinks I shall come back down again to you, but I believe it not, and since I do not believe it, so will it not be. Fare thee well, and take all my thanks for the kindness and the peace which have made bearable this pause in my affairs, this penance and obscurity; for you have let me be your brother in the time of waiting. You were waiting for Nekhbet's third appearance and I was waiting upon my own business. Farewell, but not for long. Someone has thought of me after long forgetfulness, when he stubbed his toe against the memory of me. But I will think of you without forgetting; and if the God of my father is with me, whereof — not to offend Him — I do not doubt, then you too shall be drawn up out of this tedious hole. There are three beautiful things and three beautiful tokens which your servant cherishes in his heart: they are called 'snatching away,' 'lifting up,' and 'making to come after.' If God lift up my head, and I should fear to insult Him if I did not certainly expect it, then I promise you you shall come after and have a share in more stimulating circumstances than these, where your tranquillity will not be in danger of degenerating into sleepiness, and where the prospects for the third incarnation will be improved. Shall that be a promise betwixt thee and me?"

"Thanks in any case," said Mai-Sachme, and embraced him; a thing which up till now he could not have done and which, he vaguely felt, he would not be able to do later either, on opposite grounds. Only just now, at the moment of parting, was the right time. "For a minute," said he, "I thought I was quite upset when this man arrived hot-foot. But I am not, my heart beats evenly as ever — for how shall a thing one has been long expecting upset one? Calmness means nothing but that a man is prepared for every event and when it comes he is not surprised. But with feeling it is different; there is room for it even with self-control, and it touches me very much that you will think of me when you come into your kingdom. The wisdom of the Lord of Khnum be with you! Farewell!"

The courier, hopping from one foot to the other, had barely let the captain say his say to the end. Now he took Joseph by the hand, manifestly panting, and ran down with him from the tower, through the court and passages of Zawi-Re to the boat. They leaped aboard and off it went flying. And as it flitted and flew, Joseph, in the little pavilion on the after-deck, was shaved, rouged, and dressed while listening to the winged one's tale of what had happened at On, City of the Sun, and why he had been sent for. The thing was, Pharaoh had actually dreamed, and most portentously. But when the dream-interpreters were summoned, they had failed to give satisfaction and had fallen into disfavour. In the ensuing embarrassment the chief butler, Nefer-em-Wese, had spoken up and mentioned him — that is, Joseph — saying that if anybody could help out, perhaps he could, they might at least try it. What Pharaoh had actually dreamed, that the courier could not say, save in an obviously distorted and confused version, which had seeped through to the court from the council-chamber where the sages had suffered their discomfiture: the majesty of this god, it was said, had dreamed first that seven cows ate seven ears of corn and second that seven cows had been eaten by seven ears of corn — in short, a pack of nonsense such as occurs to nobody, even in a dream. Yet it was of some use to Joseph on his way, and his thoughts played about mental images of hunger and food, of need and supply.

OF LIGHT AND DARKNESS

WHAT had really happened, leading up to the summoning of Joseph was this:

The year before — towards the end of the second year Joseph spent in the prison — Amenhotpe, the fourth of his name, was sixteen years old and ceased to be a minor; the regency of Tiy, his mother, came to an end and the government of the two lands passed automatically to the successor of Nebmare the Magnificent. Thus ended a situation which the people and all those concerned had seen in the sign of the early morning sun, the young day born of the night, when the shining son is as yet more son than man, still belongs to the mother and is her fledgling, before he soars to the full height and strength of midday. Then Eset the Mother withdraws and yields up her sovereignty, although the maternal dignity still remains to her, the dignity of the source and fount of life and power, and always is the man her son. She gives over the power to him; but he exerts it for her, as she exerted it for him.

Tiy, the mother-goddess, who had been ruling and guarding the life of the lands since the years when her husband fell prey to the aging of Re, now removed from her chin the braided Usir beard which like Hatshepsut, Pharaoh with the breasts, she had been wearing, and surrendered it to the young son of the sun, whom it became almost as oddly when on occasions of high ceremony he assumed it. On such he was also obliged to appear with a tail; that is, to fasten a jackal's tail to his apron at the back. This animal attribute belonged to the strict and primitive ceremonial costume of His Majesty, and still formed an item in the sacred and jealously preserved ritual, though nobody any longer knew why it was there. However, they

did know at court that young Pharaoh hated it. Wearing it even had
a bad effect on his digestion; inclined His Majesty to feel quite sick
and made him look pale or even green in the face; though, frankly
speaking, even without the tail that was a feature of the attacks to
which his health was subject.

Unless all observers erred, the shifting of the royal power from
the mother to the son had been accompanied by much misgiving:
would not one do better to put it off or void it altogether, leaving
the young sun under the shelter of the mother's wing for good and
all? The mother of the god herself entertained these doubts; her
chief councillors had them, and a mighty man of our acquaintance,
Beknechons, sought to feed and further them: Beknechons of the
strict observance, great prophet and first priest of Amun. He had not,
strictly speaking, been a servant of the crown or, as many of his predecessors had done, united the office of high priest with that of the
head of the administration of the two lands. King Nebmare, Amenhotep III, had seen himself called upon to separate the spiritual from
the secular arm and set up laymen as viziers of the North and the
South. But as the mouth of the imperial god, Beknechons had a right
to the ear of the regent, and she lent it to him graciously, though
aware that it was to the voice of political rivalry that she lent it. She
had had a decided share in her husband's decision to separate the two
functions and in that way to achieve the necessary result of damming
back the weight of the College of Karnak and preventing a preponderance of power which — and not only since yesterday — had been
a threat to the royal house. It had inherited the problem from early
days. Tutmose, Meni's great-grandfather, had dreamed his promise
dream at the feet of the Sphinx and freed her from the sand, naming
as his father the lord of the prehistoric giant statue, Harmakhis-
Khepere-Atum-Re, to whom he owed his crown. But this, as everybody understood and as Joseph too had learned to understand, was
nothing but the hieroglyphic circumscription of the very same position: the religious formulation of political self-assertion. And it escaped nobody that this fresh definition of Aton as a new constellation in the firmament, a process begun back at the court of the son of
Tutmose and dwelt on so lovingly in his little grandson's thoughts,
had as its aim to prize Amun-Re loose from his arbitrary and despotic
union with the sun, to which he owed his universal character, and reduce him to the rank of a local power, as the city god of Wese, which
he had been before his political *coup*.

We fail to recognize the indivisibility of the world when we think
of religion and politics as fundamentally separate fields, which neither
have nor should have anything to do with each other; to the extent
even that the one would be devalued and exposed as false if any trace
of the other were to be found in it. For the truth is that they change

but the garment, as Ishtar and Tammuz wear the veil by turns, and it is the whole that speaks when one speaks the language of the other. And it speaks besides in other tongues: for instance through the works of Ptah, the creations of taste, skill, and love of ornament; for to consider these as things apart, quite outside world-indivisibility and having nothing to do with either religion or politics, would be equally foolish. Joseph knew that young Pharaoh, on his own initiative, without any maternal prompting, devoted the most zealous, even jealous attention to the fostering of beauty and ornament in his world, in intimate connection with the effort he made to think into existence the god Aton in all his purity and truth. He cherished surprising ideas of change, of relaxation of the conservative tradition, feeling sure that his dearly loved god would have it so. The cause lay close to his heart, he fostered it for its own sake, in accordance with his convictions about what was true and pleasing in the world of form. But had it on that account nothing to do with religion and politics? Since the memory of man, or, as the children of Keme loved to say, since millions of years, the world of art had been regulated by pretty stiff religious conventions, now imposed and continued in force by Amun-Re in his chapel or by his powerful priesthood for him. To relax or indeed wholly to remove these fetters for the sake of a new truth and beauty which the Aton-god had revealed to Pharaoh was a blow in the face to Amun-Re, the head and front of a religion and politics indissolubly bound up with certain pictorial conceptions consecrated by time. In young Pharaoh's disintegrating theories on the subject of the pictorial arts, the world-whole spoke the language of good taste, one language among many, in which it expresses itself. For with the world-whole and its unity the human being has always and ever to do, whether he knows it or not.

He might know it, Amenhotep, the boy king; but the world-whole was manifestly too much for him. His strength seemed to be too slender, he suffered too much. Often he was pale or green, even when he did not have to wear the jackal's tail; he was so tortured by headaches that he could not keep his eyes open; often and often he had to give up his food. He was obliged to lie in the dark for days — he whose whole love was the light, the golden bond between heaven and earth, those rays ending in the caressing, life-giving hands of his father Aton. Of course, it was matter for grave concern when a reigning king was constantly prevented by such attacks from fulfilling his representational duties: such as offering sacrifice, dedicating this and that, receiving his wise men and councillors. But unfortunately there was even worse: one could never tell what attack might suddenly seize His Majesty in the middle of these duties, in the presence of dignitaries or even of masses of people. Pharaoh, holding his thumbs clamped round by the other four fingers and rolling his eyeballs back under half-closed lids, might fall into a not quite normal unconscious state, not lasting very long but still a disturbing interruption to the business in hand. He himself explained these incidents as abrupt visitations from his father the god; and he feared much less than he desired to receive them. For he returned from them with his daily life enriched by first-hand instruction and revelation on the true and beautiful nature of Aton.

Thus it need cause us neither surprise nor doubt to learn that when the new sun reached his majority the point was discussed whether it might not be better to leave him under the maternal wing and let things go on as they were. But the idea came to nothing, despite Amun's representations in its favour. However much there was for it, there was too much against it. For to admit that Pharaoh was so ill, or so sickly, that he could not take over the government was contrary to the interests of the hereditary sun-rulers and might give rise to dangerous notions in the kingdom and the tributary states. Moreover, Pharaoh's attacks were of a nature which forbade their use as a reason for continuing his minority: they were holy, they contributed to his popularity rather than otherwise; it would be unwise to make them the ground for a prolongation of his minority, it was much better to exploit them against Amun, whose private intention to unite the double crown with his own feather head-dress and himself found a new dynasty lurked in the background of every situation.

And so the maternal bird turned over to her son the full authority of the zenith of his manhood. But looking very closely, we can see that he himself, Amenhotpe, had conflicting feelings on the whole subject. He felt pride and joy in his new powers, but he felt embarrassment as well; all in all he might have preferred to remain under his mother's wing. There was one reason why he looked forward with positive horror to his majority, and it was this: every Pharaoh at the beginning of his reign, by fixed tradition, personally undertook, as commander-in-chief, a military campaign of war and plunder, into either the Asiatic or the Negro lands. And upon its glorious conclusion he was solemnly received at the border and escorted back to his capital, where he offered as tribute to Amun-Re, who had thus set the princes of Zahi and Kush under his feet, a goodly share of the swag. Pharaoh had also with his own hand to slay a half-dozen prisoners of war, as high as possible in rank — in case of need they were elevated for the purpose.

Of all such ceremonies the lord of the sweet breath knew himself to be utterly incapable. He was attacked by facial twitchings, pallor, and greenness whenever they were mentioned or even whenever he thought of them. He loathed war; it might be Amun's business but was far from being that of "my father Aton," who in one of those holy and questionable attacks of Meni's had expressly revealed himself

to his son as the "Prince of Peace." Meni could neither take the field
with steed and chariot, nor plunder, nor make presents of booty to
Amun, nor slay in his honour princely or theoretically princely cap-
tives. He neither could nor would do any of that, even ostensibly
and for form's sake; and he refused to be pictured on temple walls
and arches shooting arrows from a lofty war chariot at terrified foes
or holding a bunch of them with one hand by the hair of their heads
and with the other brandishing the bludgeon. All that was to him —
that is to say, to his god and so to him — intolerable and impossible. It
must be clearly understood by court and state that the inaugural campaign of plunder would not take place; that after all it could be somehow got round, by good will and good words. One could say that
all the lands of the globe already lay at Pharaoh's feet, and tribute
poured in so promptly and copiously that any warlike demonstration
was superfluous; that indeed it was Pharaoh's wish to signalize his accession by the absence of such events.

But even after this easement Meni's feelings continued to be mixed.
He did not conceal from himself that as a reigning monarch he came
into immediate contact with the whole world and all its languages
and ways of expressing itself, whereas up till then he could regard it
from the one point of view which he preferred, the religious one. Not
taken up with earthly affairs, among the flowers and trees of his gardens he could dream of his loving god, think him forth, muse upon
him, and consider how his essence could best be comprehended in one
name and represented by a single image. That had been strain and
responsibility enough; but he loved it, and gladly bore with the headaches it gave him. Now he had that to do and to think about which
gave him headaches he did not love at all. Every morning, with sleep
still in all his members, he received the Vizier of the South, a tall man
with a little chin beard and two gold neck-rings, named Ramose. The
man greeted him with a fixed form of address, like a litany, very
florid and long-winded, and then for endless hours badgered him
with rolls of marvellously executed writings about current administrative problems: judicial business, sentences, tax registers, plans for
new canals, foundation-stone laying, building supplies, opening of
quarries and mines in the desert, and so on and on, instructing Pharaoh in Pharaoh's beautiful will in all these matters. After that with
upraised hands he would marvel at the beauty of Pharaoh's will. It
was Pharaoh's beautiful will to take such and such journeys into the
desert, to designate the right spots for wells and post-stations, after
they had been picked out beforehand by people more competent in
such matters. It was his admirably beautiful will to summon the city
Count of El-Kab to come before his face for a hearing upon why he
so unpunctually and insufficiently paid his official assessments of gold,
silver, cattle and linen into the treasury at Thebes. The next day it was

his exalted will to set out for miserable Nubia, to lay a cornerstone or preside at an opening of a temple — usually one dedicated to Amun-Re and thus in Meni's mind by no means compensating for the exhaustion and headache brought on by the journey.

At best, the obligatory temple service, the cumbersome ritual of the imperial god, took up a great part of his time and strength. Outwardly it was his beautiful will to perform it; but inwardly it was the reverse; for it prevented him from thinking of Aton, and also it inflicted on him the society of Beknechons, Amon's autocratic servant, whom he could not abide. In vain had he tried to have his capital city called "City of the Brightness of Aton." The name was not taken up by the people, the priests prevented them, and Wese was and remained Nowet-Amun, the city of the Great Ram, who by the strong right arms of his royal sons had reduced foreign lands to subjection and made Egypt rich. Even thus early, Pharaoh was secretly playing with the idea of removing his residence from Thebes, where the image of Amun-Re shone from every column and arch, column and obelisk and was a vexation to his eyes. Certainly he did not yet think of founding a new city all his own, wholly dedicated to Aton; he only contemplated transferring the court to On at the top of the delta, where he felt more at home himself. There, in the vicinity of the sun-temple, he had a pleasant palace, not so brilliant as Merimat in the west of Thebes, but provided with all the comforts his delicate health required. The court chroniclers had often to record the journeys of the good god by boat or wagon down to On. True, it was the seat of the Vizier of the North, who had under him the administration and judiciary functions of all the districts between Asyut and the delta, and who in his turn lost no time in giving him headaches. But at least at On Meni was spared burning incense to Amun under the supervision of Beknechons; and he very much enjoyed talking with the learned shiny-pates from the house of Atum-Re-Horakhte about the nature of the glorious god his father and his inner life, which despite his vast age was so fresh and lively that it proved capable of the most beautiful variations, clarifications, and developments; if one may so express it, there emerged out of the old god, with the aid of human brain-power, slowly, yet ever more completely, a new, unspeakably lovely one, namely the wonderful, universally illuminating Aton.

Oh, that one might give oneself wholly to him and be his son, midwife, herald, and confessor, instead of being King of Egypt as well, and successor of those who had enlarged the boundaries of Keme and made it an empire! He was tied fast to them and to the deeds they had done; he was vowed to them and to all their acts; probably the reason why he could not endure Beknechons, Amon's man, was that he was right when he constantly emphasized the fact. In other words,

young Pharaoh himself, in his most private self-examination, suspected it: he suspected first that it was one thing to found an empire
and another to help a world-god into being; and second that the latter
occupation might easily be in some kind of contradiction to the regal
task and responsibility of preserving and sustaining the achievements
of the past. And the headaches which made him shut his eyes when
the Viziers of the North and the South set upon him with imperial
business were connected with suspicions to the effect (or not quite to
the effect, but moving in that direction) that they, namely the headaches, were not caused so much by fatigue and boredom as by a vague
but disquieting insight into the conflict between devotion to the
beloved Aton theology and the duties of a King of Egypt. In other
words, they were conscience and conflict headaches. Knowing them
for what they were only made them worse instead of better, and increased his nostalgia for his former state of protection under the wing
of maternal night.

Doubtless not only he but the country too would have been better
off. For an earthly land and its prosperity are always better taken
care of by the mother, however much the spiritual side may be so in
the hands of the son. This was Amenhotep's private conviction, and
it was probably the feeling of Egypt itself, the Isis belief in the black
earth which she instilled into it. Meni made a mental distinction between the material, earthly, "natural" welfare of the earth and its
mental and spiritual weal; he vaguely feared that the two concerns
might not only not coincide but even conflict rather fundamentally.
To be charged with both of them at once, to be both priest and
king, was the source of many headaches. The material and natural
well-being and prosperity were the business of the king, or, even
better, it was the business of a queen, of the mother, the great Cow —
in order that the priest's son in freedom and without responsibility
for material well-being might dwell on the spiritual side and spin his
sun-thoughts. His royal responsibility for the material side oppressed
young Pharaoh. His kingship was for him bound up with the black
Egyptian loam between desert and desert — black and fertile from
the impregnating water. Whereas his passion was the pure light, the
golden sun-youth of the heights — and he had no good conscience
about it. The Vizier of the South, who got all the reports, even about
the early rising of the dog-star which heralds the swelling of the
waters — this Ramose, then, constantly called his attention to the latest news on the state of the river, the prospects of a good rise, the
fertilization, the harvest. To Meni, however attentively, yes, conscientiously he listened, it seemed as though the man would much
rather give his reports as he used to, to the mother, the Isis-Queen.
She knew more about these things, they were better off in her hands.
And yet for him too, as for his lands, everything depended on a

blessing-issue in the dark fields of fertility. Failure or deficiency, if it came, reflected on him. Not for nothing did Egypt's people have a king who was God's son and so in God's name represented an assurance against stoppages in holy and necessary processes upon which nobody else had any influence. Mistakes or damages in this department of the black earth meant that his people were disappointed in him, whose mere existence should have prevented them. His credit was shaken and, after all, he needed all he could get, that he might make to triumph the beautiful teaching of Aton and his nature of heavenly light.

That was the difficulty and the dilemma. He had no bond with the blackness below, loving alone the upper light. But if things did not go smoothly and well with the blackness that fed them all, he lost his authority as teacher of the light. And so young Pharaoh's feelings suffered from a split when the motherly night took away her wing from above him and handed him over the kingdom.

PHARAOH'S DREAM

WELL then, Pharaoh had betaken himself once more to instructive On out of unconquerable yearning to escape from the empire of Amun and commune with the shiny-pates of the sun-house about Harmakhis-Khepere-Atum-Re, Aton. The court chroniclers, puckering their lips and obsequiously crouching, mincingly entered in the record His Majesty's beautiful resolve; and how thereupon he mounted a great car made of electrum, together with Nefertiti, called Nefernefruaton, the Queen of the lands, whose body was fruitful and whose arm was about her consort; and how he had radiantly taken his beautiful way, followed in other cars by Tiy, the mother of God, Nezemmut, the Queen's sister, Baketaton, his own sister, and many chamberlains and ladies-in-waiting with ostrich-feather fans on their backs. The heavenly bark *Star of the Two Lands* had also been used by stretches; the chroniclers had set down how Pharaoh, sitting under his canopy, had eaten a roast pigeon, also held the bone out to the Queen and she ate from it, and how he put into her mouth sweetmeats dipped in wine.

At On, Amenhotep entered his palace in the temple district and slept there dreamlessly the first night, exhausted from the journey. The following day he began by sacrificing to Re-Horakhte with bread and beer, wine, birds, and incense. After that he listened to the Vizier of the North, who spoke before him at length, and then, regardless of the headache that had brought on, devoted the rest of the day to the much-desired talks with the priests of the God. These conferences, which at the moment greatly occupied Amenhotep's mind, had been taken up with the subject of the bird Bennu, also called Offspring of Fire, because it was said that he was motherless, and moreover actually his own father, since dying and beginning were the same for him. For he burned himself up in his nest made of myrrh and came forth from the ashes again as young Bennu. This happened, some authorities said, every five hundred years; happened in fact in the temple of the sun at On, whither the bird, a heron-like eagle, purple and gold, came for the purpose from Arabia or even India. Other authorities asserted that it brought with it an egg made of myrrh, as big as it could carry, wherein it had put its deceased father, that is to say actually itself, and laid it down on the sun-altar. These two assertions might subsist side by side— after all, there subsists so much side by side, differing things may both be true and only different expressions of the same truth. But what Pharaoh first wanted to know, what he wanted to discuss, was how much time had passed out of the five hundred years which lay between the bird and the egg; how far they were on the one hand from the last appearance and on the other from the next one; in short, at what point of the phœnix-year they stood. The majority opinion of the priests was that it must be somewhere about the middle of the period. They reasoned that if it was still near its beginning, then some memory of the last appearance of Bennu must still exist and that was not the case. But suppose they were near the end of one period and the beginning of the next; then they must reckon on the impending or immediate return of the time-bird. But none of them counted on having the experience in his lifetime so the only remaining possibility was that they were about the middle of the period. Some of the shiny-pates went so far as to suspect that they would always remain in the middle, the mystery of the Bennu bird being precisely this: that the distance between the last appearance of the Phœnix and his next one was always the same, always a middle point. But the mystery was not in itself the important thing to Pharaoh. The burning question to be discussed, which was the object of his visit, and which then he did discuss for a whole half-day with the shiny-pates, was the doctrine that the fire-bird's myrrh egg in which he had shut up the body of his father did not thereby become heavier. For he had made it anyhow as large and heavy as he could possibly carry, and if he was still able to carry it after he had put his father's body in it, then it must follow that the egg had not thereby increased in weight.

That was an exciting and enchanting fact of world-wide importance. In young Pharaoh's eyes it was worthy of the most circumstantial exposition. If one added to a body another body and it did not become heavier thereby, that must mean there were immaterial bodies — or differently and better put, incorporeal realities, immaterial as sunlight; or, again differently and still better put, there was the spiritual; and this spiritual was ethereally embodied in the Bennu-father, whom the myrrh egg received while altering its character thereby in the most exciting and significant way. For the egg was altogether a definitely female kind of thing; only the female among birds laid eggs, and nothing could be more mother-female than the great egg out of which once the world came forth. But Bennu the sun-bird, motherless and his own father, made his own egg himself, an egg against the natural order, a masculine egg, a father-egg, and laid it as a manifestation of fatherhood, spirit, and light upon the alabaster table of the sun-divinity.

Pharaoh could not talk enough with the sun-calendar men of the temple of Re about this event and its significance for the developing nature of Aton. He discussed deep into the night, he discussed to excess, he wallowed in golden immateriality and father spirit, and when the priests were worn out and their shiny pates nodded, he was still not tired and could not summon resolution to dismiss them — almost as though he were afraid to stay alone. But at last he did dismiss them, nodding and stumbling to their rest, and himself sought his bedchamber. His dressing and undressing slave was an elderly man, assigned to him as a boy, who called him Meni although not otherwise informal or lacking in respect. He had been awaiting his master for hours by the light of the hanging lamp and now quickly and gently made him ready for the night. Then he flung himself on his face and withdrew to sleep on the threshold. Pharaoh for his part nestled into the cushions of his exquisitely ornate bed, which stood on a dais in the middle of the room, its headboard decorated with the finest ivory-work displaying figures of jackals, goats, and Bes. He fell almost at once into an exhausted sleep. But only for a short time. After a few hours of profound oblivion he began to dream: such complicated, impressive, absurd, and vivid dreaming as he had not done since he was a child with tonsillitis.

In his dream he stood on the bank of Hapi the Nourisher, in a lonely, marshy, uncultivated spot. He had on the red crown of Lower Egypt, the beard was on his chin and the jackal's tail fastened to his upper garment behind. Quite alone he stood, heavy-hearted, and held his crooked staff in his hand. Then there was a rippling noise not far from the shore and seven shapes mounted from the stream: seven cows came on shore; they had probably been lying in the water like buffalo cows. They moved in a straight line one behind another, seven without the bull, for no bull was there, only the seven cows. Magnificent cows they were, white ones, black ones with lighter backs, grey with lighter belly, and two dappled — fine smooth fat kine with bursting udders, long-lashed Hathor-eyes, and high curving lyre-shaped horns. They began to graze contentedly among the reeds. The King had never seen such fine cattle, not in the whole country. Their sleek well-fed bodies were something to see and Meni's heart would have rejoiced at the sight if it had not felt so heavy and full of care — feelings which presently gave way, indeed, to actual horror and fear. For these seven were not all: still more cows came out of the water, joining those to these, seven more cows climbed upon the bank, again without the bull, for what bull could have cared to join with such as these? Pharaoh shuddered at the kine; they were the ugliest, leanest, most starveling cows he had ever seen in his life — their bones stood out on their wrinkled hides, their udders were like empty bags with stringlike teats. They were an alarming and upsetting sight, the wretched creatures seemed scarcely able to keep their legs. And yet their behaviour was so bold, so aggressive and sudden — one could never have expected the like from such decrepit beasts, yet truly it was all too natural, since it was the recklessness of starvation. Pharaoh watches: the haggard herd advances on the bonny one, the calamitous cows leap on the well-favoured ones as cows do when they play the bull; the poverty-stricken devour and swallow the well-fed and simply wipe them off the earth. Afterwards they stand there on the spot as lean as ever before, without one single sign of being any fuller.

Here this dream ended and Pharaoh started from his sleep in a perspiration of fear; sat up with throbbing heart and looked about in the mildly lighted chamber. It had been only a dream; yet so immediate, so speaking, that its urgency was like that of the starving kine and lay cold in the limbs of the dreamer. He had no wish for his bed again; stood up, drew on his white woollen robe, and moved about in the room, musing on the dream and the pressing nature of that obviously absurd yet so vivid nonsense. Gladly would he have waked the slave to tell it to him, or rather to try if what he had seen could be reproduced in words. But he was too kindly to disturb the old man, who had had to wait up so long the night before. He sat down in the cow-footed armchair beside the bed, drew closer about him the moonbeam softness of his white wool robe, and dozed off again, his feet on the footstool, squeezed into the corner of the chair.

But scarce was he asleep when he dreamed again; again — or still — he stood on the bank in beard and crown and tail, and now there was on it a ploughed strip of black earth. And he beholds the loam disturbed, the crust rises, curls over, a stalk pricks forth, and one, two, even up to seven ears spring swiftly from it, one after another, all on one stalk: full, fat ears, bursting with golden fullness. How blithe the heart could feel at such a sight! Yet cannot, for, lo, the stalk keeps on shooting forth ears; seven ears more, poor, pathetic, dead, and dry, scorched by the east wind, blackened with mildew and blight; and as they push out raggedly below the full ones, the fine large ears vanish as though into the poor lean ones. Truly it was like that: the wretched ears swallowed up the fat, just as before the ill-favoured cows had devoured the sleek ones. And grew neither fuller nor better favoured than before. This Pharaoh saw with his bodily eyes, started up in his chair, and once more found it all a dream.

A confused, ridiculous enough dream, wordless and senseless. Still it came so close, it so urgently assailed his mind with its burden of warning, that Pharaoh could not sleep again. Nor did he even wish to, till happily the dawn soon broke, but went on shifting between bed and chair, musing on the dream — or the twin dreams grown on one stalk — and its clear and pressing demand for clarification. Already he was firmly resolved not to let such a dream pass over silently and keep it to himself. He would make an occasion of it, he would sound an alarm. In it he had worn the crown, the crozier, and the tail, beyond a doubt these were king-dreams of imperial import, vastly suggestive and significant. They must be made public and everything possible done to get to the bottom of them and study them on the basis of their obviously alarming meaning. Meni was greatly wrought up over his dreams, he hated them more with every minute that passed. A king could not put up with such dreams — although on the other hand they could not come to anyone but a king. While he, Nefer-Kheperu-Re-Wanre-Amenhotep, sat on the throne such things must not happen: no such abominable cows must eat up such fine fat ones; or such wretched blighted ears consume such swelling golden ones. Nothing must happen in the realm of events corresponding to this frightful picture-language. For it would reflect upon him, his prestige would suffer; ears and hearts would be closed to the annunciation of Aton, and Amun would gain thereby. Danger threatened the light from the black earth, danger from the material side threatened the spiritual-ethereal, there was no doubt about that. His excitement was great; it took the form of anger, and the anger swelled up into a great resolve that the danger must be revealed and recognized for what it was in order to meet it.

The first person to whom he told the dream — as much as it lent itself to telling — was the old man who now came to dress him, arrange his hair, and wind the headdress round it. He only shook his head in amaze and then gave it as his view that the dream came from the good god going to bed so late after he had heated his brain with all that wool-gathering, as he popularly and simple-mindedly put it. Very likely he unconsciously thought of the dreams as a sort of punishment for having kept his old servant up so late. "Silly old goat," Pharaoh had said, half laughing, half angry. He gave him a light slap on the cheek and went to the Queen. But she was feeling sick, being pregnant, and paid little heed. Then he sought out Tiy, the mother goddess, and found her at her dressing-table in the hands of her maids-in-waiting. To her too he told the dream, finding it not at all easier to tell as time went on, but harder instead. Nor did he get from his mother much consolation or encouragement. Tiy was always rather mocking when he came to her with his kingly cares; and he was so convinced that this was a heavy care that he began by saying so. And at once the bantering smile appeared on the maternal face. King Nebmare's widow had, after mature reflection, of her own free will laid down the regency and given over to her son the ruling power of his majority; but she could never quite conceal her jealousy, and the painful thing for Meni was that he saw it all, this bitter reaction which he himself evoked did not escape him, while he sought to soften it by childlike pleas for counsel and help.

"Why does Your Majesty come to me, the rejected?" she would say. "You are Pharaoh, so be Pharaoh and stand on your own feet instead of on mine. Confide in your servants the Viziers of the South and the North when you do not know what to do, and let them tell you what is your will if you do not know it; but not in me, for I am old and have retired."

She behaved like that about the dream too. "I am too much out of the habit of power and responsibility, my friend," she had told him with a smile, "to be able to judge whether you are right in giving so much weight to this matter. 'Hidden is the darkness,' so it is written, 'when ample is the light.' Let your mother hide herself. Let me even hide my opinion whether these dreams are worth while or befitting your state. They ate them up? They devoured them? Some cows ate up some other cows? Some withered ears some full ones? That is no dream vision, you cannot see it or form a picture of it, either awake or I should say asleep either. Probably Your Majesty dreamed something quite different and you have put in its place this monstrous picture of impossible greediness."

In vain Meni assured her that he had positively seen it precisely like that with the eyes of his dream and that its clarity had been full of meaning which cried out for interpretation. In vain he spoke of his inner threat, of the harm which might come to the "teaching" — in other words, to Aton — if the dream were to interpret itself unhindered; that is to say, be fulfilled and take the actual shape of which it had been the prophetic garment. He had again the impression that at bottom his mother had no heart for his God; that it was only with her reason, namely on political and dynastic grounds, that she sided with him. She had always supported her son in his tender love, his spiritual passion for Aton. But again today, as for a long time, he saw — and thanks to his sensitiveness he always saw — that she did it only out of calculation, exploiting his heart as a woman would who saw the whole world exclusively from the point of view of statesmanship, and not, as he did, from the religious first and foremost. That troubled Meni and wounded him. He left his mother, having heard from her that if he really thought his cow-and-corn vision important to the state, he could apply to Ptahemheb, the Vizier of the South, at the morning audience. Besides, there was no dearth of dream-interpreters on the spot.

He had already sent for the interpreters and now impatiently awaited them. But before receiving them he had to see the great official who came to report on the affairs of the "Red House," in other words the business of the treasury of Lower Egypt. Immediately after the greeting hymns Meni interrupted him and made him listen to the story of the dreams, related in nervous, tormented tones; hesitating, seeking for the right words, he demanded that the man express himself on two points: first, whether he, like his master, considered the narrative to have political significance, and second, if so, in what way and what connection. The official did not know what to answer; or rather he had answered in a lengthy speech of very well-turned phrases that he did not know how to answer and did not know what to say about the dreams — after which he had tried to return to treasury business. But Amenhotep kept him to the subject of the dreams, obviously unwilling and unable to talk about anything else or listen to it, only to want to make him understand how speakingly impressive or impressively speaking they were — and he did not leave off until the wise men and seers were announced.

The King, full of his night's experience — indeed, possessed by it as he now was — turned his levee into a first-class ceremony — and yet after all it turned out to be a lamentable failure. He not only ordered Ptah-em-heb to remain present, but also arranged that all the court dignitaries who had accompanied him to On should attend the audience of interpretation. There were some dozen high-ranking gentlemen: the great steward of the palace, the keeper of the King's wardrobe, the overseer of the fullers, the so-called sandal-bearer of the King, a considerable office; the head wig-keeper of the god, who was likewise "guardian of the enchanted empires," in other words of the two crowns, and privy councillor of the royal jewels; the groom of all Pharaoh's horses; the new head baker and Prince of Menfe, named Amenemopet, the first steward of the buffet, Nefer-em-Wese, once temporarily called Bin-em-Wese, and several fan-bearers on the right hand of the god. All these had to be present in the audience and council hall; they stood round in two groups on either hand of Pharaoh's splendid seat, which was on a raised dais under a baldachin borne by slender beribboned poles. The prophets and dream-interpreters were brought before him, six in number, all of whom were in more or less close relation with the temple of the horizon-dweller and of whom a few had taken part in the phœnix-council of the day before. People of their sort no longer prostrated themselves on their bellies to kiss the ground, as had once been the custom, before the throne-chair. It was still the same chair as in the time of the pyramid-builders and even much earlier: a boxlike arm-chair with a low back and a cushion on the floor in front; only there was rather more ornamentation than in primitive times. But even although the chair had become more splendid and Pharaoh more mighty, one no longer kissed the ground before them. Here as in the case of the living burial of the court in the dead king's tomb, it was no longer good *ton*. The soothsayers merely lifted their arms in rever-ential wise and murmured in rather unrhythmical confusion a long formula of respect and greeting, wherein they assured the king that he had a form like his father Re and illumined the two lands with his beauty. For the radiance of His Majesty penetrated into the dungeons and there was no place which escaped the piercing glance of his eye, nor one whither the fine hearing of his million ears did not reach, he heard and saw all, and whatsoever issued from his mouth was like the words of Horus in the horizon as his tongue was the scale of the world and his lips more precise than the little tongue on the just scale of Thoth. He was Re in all his members, they said, in un-even and confused chorus, and Khepere in true form the living image of his father Atum of On in Lower Egypt — "O Nefer-Kheperu-Re-Wanre, Lord of Beauty, through whom we breathe!"

Some of them finished before the others. Then they were all silent, and listened. Amenhotep thanked them, told them first in general on what occasion he had called them together, and then began, before this assemblage of some twenty either elegant or learned persons to relate his egregious dream — for the fourth time. It was painful to him, he flushed and floundered as he spoke. His insistent sense of the por-tentous significance of his tale had decided him to make it public. Now he regretted the decision, for he did not conceal from himself that what had been — and to him still was — so serious sounded laugh-able when he repeated it aloud. Really, why should such fine fat cat-tle let such miserable weak ones calmly eat them up? Why and how should one set of ears of corn devour another set? But it had been so to him in his dream, so and not otherwise. The dreams had been fresh, lifelike, and impressive at night; by day and put into words they were like badly prepared mummies, with distorted features; nobody could want to reveal them. He was embarrassed and came laboriously to an end. Then he looked shyly and expectantly at the dream-seers.

They had nodded their heads meaningfully; but gradually one after another they stopped nodding and began a side-to-side mo-tion, a series of wondering head-shakes. These were very singular and almost unique dreams, they explained through their elders; the inter-pretation was not easy. Not that they despaired of it — the dream was still to be dreamed that they could not expound. But they must ask for time to consider and the favour of withdrawing for counsel. And compendiums must be fetched for consultation. There was no-

body so learned as to have the whole technique at his fingers' ends.
To be learned, they permitted themselves to remark, did not mean to
have all knowledge in their heads; there would not be room for it; no,
it meant to be in possession of the books in which the knowledge
was written, and that they were.

Amenhotep granted them leave to take counsel. The court was
told to hold itself in readiness. The King spent two whole hours —
the wait lasted that long — very restlessly. Then the sitting was resumed.

"May Pharaoh live a hundred years, beloved of Maat, lady of truth,
in response to his love of her who was without guile." She stood in
person at the side of the experts as they pronounced their results and
brought their interpretation before Pharaoh, Protector of the Truth.
In the first place: the seven fat kine meant seven princesses, which
Nefernefruaton-Nofertiti, the Queen of the Lands, would in time
bear. But that the fat kine had been devoured by the lean ones meant
that these seven daughters would all die in Pharaoh's lifetime. That
did not mean, they hastened to add, that the King's daughters would
die young. To Pharaoh would be vouchsafed such a length of days
that he would outlive all his children, however long they lived.

Amenhotep looked at them open-mouthed. What were they talking about, he asked them, in a diminished voice. They answered, it
had been granted them to deliver the meaning of the first dream. But
this interpretation, he had responded, in a still smaller voice, had no
sort of reference to his dream, it simply had nothing to do with it.
He had not asked them whether the Queen would bear him a son
and successor or a daughter and more daughters. He had asked them
for the interpretation of the sleek and the ill-favoured kine. — The
daughters, they replied, were the interpretation. He should not expect to find cows in the interpretation of a dream about cows. In
the interpretation the cows were turned into princesses.

Pharaoh no longer had his mouth open, he had it very tightly
closed, and opened it only a very little when he ordered them to go
on to the second dream.

Very well, the second, they said. The seven full ears were seven
flourishing cities which Pharaoh would build, but the seven shrunk
and scrubby ones were — the ruins of them. It was well known, they
hastily explained, that all cities inevitably fell into ruins in time.
Pharaoh himself would survive so long that he would see with his own
eyes the ruins of the cities he had built.

But here Meni's patience came to an end. He had not had enough
sleep; the repeated telling of the dreams, lessening in impressiveness
each time he told them, had been painful; the two hours' wait unnerving. Now he was so filled with the idea that these interpretations
were sheer boggling and miles away from the true meaning of his

visions that he could no longer control his anger. He put one more question: did the books say the same as the wise men had said? But when they replied that their contributions were a suitable synthesis of what was in the books, together with the promptings of their own powers of combination, he sprang from his chair. During an audience that was unheard of, the courtiers shrugged and put their hands over their mouths. Meni, tears in his voice, called the fearfully startled prophets bunglers and ignoramuses.

"Away with you!" he cried, almost sobbing. "And take with you, instead of the plenteous gold which my Majesty would have conferred on you if truth had come out of your mouths, the disfavour of Pharaoh. Your interpretations are cheating and lies, Pharaoh knows it, for it was Pharaoh who dreamed, and even though he does not know the meaning, he does know how to distinguish between real interpretation and such worthless stuff as this. Out of my sight!"

The pallid scholars were led out by two palace officials. But Pharaoh, without sitting down, had declared to his court that their failure would not lead him to let the matter rest. The gentlemen had unfortunately been witness to a mortifying failure, but by his faith and his sceptre, on the very next day he would call up other experts, this time from the house of Djehuti, the scribe of Thoth the ninefold great, lord of Khnumu. From the adepts of the white peacock was to be expected true and worthy interpretation of that which, the inner voice had told him, must be explained at all costs.

The second hearing took place next day under the same circumstances. It went off even worse than the first. Again young Pharaoh, with much inward constraint, halting in his speech, made public exhibition of his dream-mummies and again among the luminaries there had been great nodding and then great head-shaking. Not two but three hours had King and court to wait on the issue of the private consultation; and then the experts were not even agreed among themselves, but divided as to the meaning of the dreams. Two interpretations, the eldest among them announced, existed for each dream, and these, certainly, were the only ones possible, or even thinkable. According to one theory the seven fat kine were seven kings of Pharaoh's seed, the seven lean ones seven princes of misery who would make head against them. All this lay in the distant future. Alternatively the fat kine might be so many queens whom either Pharaoh himself or one of his late successors would take into his women's house, and who, as indicated by the lean kine, would unhappily all die, one after the other.

And the ears of corn?

The seven golden ears meant in one version seven heroes of Egypt, who in a later war would fall by the hand of seven hostile and — as shown by the thin ears — much less powerful warriors. The others stuck to it that the seven full and seven barren ears were children, in all fourteen of them, which Pharaoh would get from those foreign queens. But quarrels would break out among them, and, thanks to superior guile, the seven weak children would destroy the seven stronger ones.

This time Amenhotep did not get up from his seat of audience. He sat there bent over, burying his face in his hands; the courtiers to right and left of the canopy inclined their ears to hear what he was muttering. "Oh, muddlers, muddlers!" he whispered over and over; then beckoned to the Vizier of the North, who stood nearest him, and gave him a whispered order. Ptah-em-heb discharged this task by announcing to the experts in a loud voice that Pharaoh wanted to know if they were not ashamed of themselves.

They had done their best, they replied.

Then the Vizier had to bend over again to the King, and this time it appeared he had received the order to tell the wonder-workers they were to leave the audience. In great confusion, looking one at another as though to ask whether the like had ever been known before, they departed. The court, remaining, stood about perplexed, for Pharaoh still sat there, bent over, shielding his eyes with his hand. When at length he took it away and sat up, affliction was painted upon his face, and his chin quivered. He told his courtiers he would gladly have spared them, and only reluctantly plunged them into pain and grief, but he could not hide the truth; their lord and King was profoundly unhappy. His dreams had borne the unmistakable stamp of political significance, and their meaning was a matter of life and death. The expositions he had been given were ineffectual twaddle; they did not in the least fit the dreams, nor could the dreams recognize themselves in the interpretations, as dream and interpretation must recognize each other. After the failure of these two full-dress attempts he was forced to doubt whether he was to be able to get any interpretation corresponding to the truth, which he would at once recognize. But that meant to be forced to leave the dreams to interpret themselves without any preventive measures and proceed to their evil consummation, quite possibly involving religion and the state in irreparable injury. Danger threatened the lands; but Pharaoh, to whom it was apparent, would be left alone, without counsel or aid.

The oppressive silence lasted for only a moment after Pharaoh finished speaking. For then it happened that Nefer-em-Wese, the chief cup-bearer, after a long struggle with himself came forward from the group of the King's friends and besought the favour of speaking before Pharaoh. "I do remember my faults today": thus tradition makes him begin his speech, we know the words, they still echo today in our ears. But the chief butler meant not faults which he had not committed, for he had once come unjustly into prison and had not shared in the plot to have the aged Re bitten by Eset's serpent. He meant a different fault: namely, that he had explicitly promised somebody to mention him but had not kept his word for that he had forgotten the somebody. Now he thought of him, and he spoke of him before the baldachin. He reminded Pharaoh — who scarcely remembered it himself — of the "ennui" (for so he put it, with a deprecating foreign word) he had had at one time two years before, under King Nebmare, when there had been a mistake in identity and he, together with another man, whom it were better not to name, an accursed of God, whose soul had been destroyed with his body, had been sent to Zawi-Re, the island fortress. There a youth had been assigned to him as steward, a Khabirite from Asia, the captain's aide, with the fantastic name of Osarsiph, son of a shepherd king and friend of God in the East, born of a beautiful woman, as one could tell just by looking at him. This youth, then, had the greatest gift in the field of dream-exegesis which he, Excellent-in-Thebes, had ever seen in all the days of his life. For they had both dreamed, his guilty fellow-prisoner and himself the innocent one: very weighty, portentous dreams, each his own dream, and been extremely embarrassed for their true meaning. Then this Usarsiph, without making much of his talent beforehand, had interpreted their dreams quite easily and offhand, and announced to the baker that he would come to the gibbet, but to himself that on account of his utter innocence he would be taken back again into favour and put back into his office. And exactly so it had come to pass, and today he, Nefer, was mindful of his fault, namely that he had not long before called attention to and pointed out this talent that existed under a cloud. He did not hesitate to express the conviction that if anyone were able to interpret Pharaoh's important dreams, it was this youth, presumably still vegetating in Zawi-Re.

There was a stir among the friends of the King; something stirred also in Meni's face and form. A few more questions and answers, quickly exchanged between him and the fat man — and then the high command went forth, the first and swiftest messenger was straightway to hasten by flight of boat to Zawi-Re and with the minimum of delay to fetch back the soothsaying youth to On, before Pharaoh's countenance.

Chapter III

THE CRETAN LOGGIA

THE PRESENTATION

WHEN Joseph arrived in the City of the Blinking, thousands-of-years-old On, it was once more seed-time, time of the burial of the god, as it had been when he came for the second time to the pit and lay in it three great days under tolerable conditions thanks to Mai-Sachme, the even-tempered captain. Everything fitted in: precisely three years had passed, they were at the same point in the circle, the week of the twenty-second to the last day of Choiak, and the children of Egypt had just celebrated once more the feast of the harrowing and the setting-up of the sacred backbone.

Joseph was glad to see golden On again. As a lad three-and-ten years before he had passed through it with the Ishmaelites on the way whither they led him and they had all got themselves instructed by the servants of the sun in the beautiful figure of the triangle and the mild nature of Re-Horakhte, lord of the wide horizon. Once more his way led through the wedge-shaped city of instruction with its many glittering sun-monuments. At the messenger's side he went toward the top of it and the great obelisk at its apex where the two sides cut each other; its golden, all-outglittering peak and cap had already greeted them from afar.

Jacob's son, who for so long had seen nothing but the walls of his prison, had no leisure to use his eyes and enjoy the sights of the busy city and its folk. Not only that none was given him by his guide, the winged messenger, who lost not a second and ever urged him on to more breathless haste. His own temperament and feelings left him no time for gazing. Once it had been Petepre before whom it was vouchsafed him to speak in the garden, the highest in that immediate circle, and everything had depended on it. Now it was Pharaoh himself, the All-Highest here below, before whom he should speak, and now even more depended on it. But what depended on it was being helpful to the Lord in His plans, not clumsily to thwart them. That would be a great folly and a disgraceful denial of the world-order out of want of trust. Only a wavering faith that God meant to lift him up could be a cause for unskilfulness or poor grasp of the opportunity presented. Thus Joseph, while of course bent on the coming event, so that he had no eyes for the busy bustling streets, yet awaited it with a self-confidence devoid of fear, being strong in that faith which he knew was the basis of all devout and adroit dealing: namely, that God meant well and lovingly and momentously by him.

We, as we go along with him, sharing his suspense even though we well know how everything fell out, we shall not reproach him for self-confidence, but take him as he was and as we have long known him to be. There are some chosen ones full of doubt, humility, and self-reproach, unable to believe in their own election. They wave it away in anger and poorness of spirit, trusting not their own senses, even feeling some injury done to their unbelief when after all they find themselves lifted up. And there are others to whom nothing in the world is more natural than their own election: consciously favoured of the gods, not at all surprised at whatever elevation and consummation come their way. Whichever group of chosen ones you prefer, the self-distrustful or the presumptuous, Joseph definitely belonged to the second. Yet let us at least be glad that he did not belong to the third, which likewise exists: hypocrites before God and man, who behave unworthily even to themselves and in whose mouth "the grace of God" conceals more arrogance than all the blessing-confidence of the unabashed.

Pharaoh's temporary quarters in On lay east of the sun-temple, connected with it by an avenue of sphinxes and sycamores on which the god proceeded when he went to burn incense before his father. The dwelling-house had been conjured up by a blithe, gay fancy; not built of stone, which was suitable only for eternal dwellings, but made of brick and wood like other dwellings, though of course as charmingly and gracefully conceived as only the highest culture of Keme could dream of, surrounded in its gardens by the protection of the blindingly white wall, in front of whose elevated entrance, on gilded flagpoles, gay pennants floated in a light breeze.

It was past midday, the meal-time already over. The messenger had not rested even by night, yet it took the forenoon too before they reached On. There was a bustle on the square before the walled gate. Many of the citizenry of On had got up and gone thither only to stand about and wait to see the sights. Groups of police guards and charioteers barred the way, standing to chat while their steeds snorted, pawed, or even sometimes gave out a high clear whinny. Then there were all sorts of hawkers and peddlars selling coloured sweetmeats and cakes, little scarabs, and inch-high statuettes of the King and Queen. Not without difficulty did the messenger and his charge make a way for themselves. "A guest, a guest, way by the King's command!" he cried again and again, trying to frighten the people by his professional breathlessness, which he had resumed on landing. He cried out again to the servants running towards him in the inner court; they raised their eyebrows and made signs of assent and led Joseph to the foot of a staircase. A palace official stood on the top of it guarding the entrance to a pavilion and looked down at them dull-eyed. He was something like an under-steward. To this man the messenger cried up the stairs in winged words that he was bringing the sooth-sayer from Zawi-Re who had been sent for hither in the utmost haste. Whereupon the man, still dull, measured Joseph from head to foot, as though even after this explanation he had something to say about whether he would let him in or no. Then he beckoned them up, still with the air of himself deciding not to refuse. Hastily the messenger once more charged Joseph that he must pant and gasp for breath when he came before Pharaoh, to impress the King with the fact that he had run the whole way to his countenance without pause. Joseph did not take him seriously. He thanked the long-legged one for fetch-ing and accompanying him and mounted the stairs to the official, who did not nod but shook his head by way of greeting, but then invited Joseph to follow him.

They paced the gaily coloured vestibule, which had landscapes on the walls and four ornamental columns wound with ribbons; and arrived at a fountain hall likewise shining with pillars, this time of rare polished woods. Here there was a guard of armed men. It opened in front and at the sides into wide pillared passages. The man led Joseph straight ahead through an antechamber with three deep doors in a row and they entered through the middle door, into a very large hall, with perhaps twelve columns supporting a sky-blue ceiling painted full of flights of birds. A little open house in red and gold, like a garden belvedere, stood in the centre, in it a table surrounded by armchairs with coloured cushions. Aproned servants were sprin-kling and brushing the floor, clearing away fruit-plates, looking after the incense vases and lamps, on tripods alternating with wide-handled alabaster vases. They rearranged the chased gold beakers on the buffet and plumped up the cushions. It was clear that Pharaoh had eaten here and then withdrawn to some place to rest, either in the garden or somewhere in the house beyond. To Joseph this was all much less new and astonishing than his guide probably supposed, for he looked at him sideways from time to time.

"Do you know how to behave?" he asked as they left the hall on their right and entered a court with flower-beds and four basins let into the pavement.

"More or less, if I have to," answered Joseph with a smile.

"Well, you have to now," retorted the man. "You know at least how to salute the god?"

"I wish I did not," replied Joseph, "for it would be pleasant to learn it of you."

The official kept a straight face for a moment, then abruptly and unexpectedly he laughed. Then he pulled his long face that had gone so suddenly broad, and was sober again.

"You seem to be a sort of joker," he said, "a rascal and horse-thief who can make a man laugh at his tricks. I suppose your gift of interpreting is a trick too, like something you see a quack do at a fair?"

"Oh," answered Joseph, "I can't tell you much about interpreting; I haven't had much to do with it, it is not my line, it just happens by accident, and up to now I have not made much of it. But since Pharaoh called me in such haste on account of it, I have begun to think better of it myself."

"That is meant for me, I take it?" asked the man. "Pharaoh is young and gentle and full of kindness. That the sun shines on a man is no proof that he is not a rascal."

"It not only shines on us, it makes us shine," answered Joseph as they went on. "Some in one way, some in another. May you shine in yours!"

The man looked at him sideways. Then he looked straight ahead; but after that, suddenly, as though he had forgotten something and had to give another look at what he had seen before, he turned his head back to Joseph; at length the latter was compelled to return the side glance. He did so smiling and with a nod, as one who would say: "Yes, yes, don't be surprised, you are seeing straight." Quickly and as it were startled, the man turned away again and stared before him.

From the court with the flower-beds they reached a passage lighted from above, where the wall on one side was painted with scenes of harvesting and sacrifice, while the other through columned doorways gave glimpses of various rooms. Here was the entrance to the hall of council and audience; the guide pointed it out to Joseph as they passed. He had become more talkative; he even told his companion where Pharaoh was to be found.

"They went into the Cretan loggia after luncheon," he said. "They call it that because some such foreign artist from across the sea did the paintings. He has the chief royal sculptors with him now, Bek and Auta, and is instructing them. And the Great Mother is there. I will hand you over to the chamberlain in the anteroom and have him announce you."

"Yes, let us do so," said Joseph; there was no more than that to what he said. Yet as they went on, the man at his side first shook his head and then again suddenly fell into a soundless, prolonged chuckle, almost spasmodic, which visibly shook his diaphragm in sudden jolts. He seemed not to have quite got it under control when they reached the antechamber at the end of the passage. A little stooped courtier in a wonderful frilled apron, with a fan on his arm, detached himself from the crack of a portière embroidered with golden bees, where he had stood listening. The guide's voice still shook with suppressed chuckles; it went up and down quaintly as he announced his companion to the chamberlain tripping mincingly toward them.

"Ah, the much-heralded know-it-all!" said the little creature, in a high pipe, with a lisp. "He who is wiser than all the scholars of the book-house! Good, good, ex-quisite!" said he, still stooping, either because he was born like that and could not stand up straight, or because the exaggerated punctilio of court life had fixed him in this posture. "I will announce you, announce you at once, why shouldn't I? The whole court is waiting for you. I will interrupt Pharaoh, whatever he is saying, in the middle of his instruction to his artists, to tell him you have arrived. Maybe that surprises you a bit, eh? Let us hope it does not bewilder you and make you utter follies — though you may easily utter them anyhow without that. I call your attention beforehand to the fact that Pharaoh is extraordinarily sensitive to any stupidities told him about his dreams. I congratulate you. Your name was — ?"

"My name was Osarsiph," answered the other.

"You mean your name is Osarsiph, of course. Extraordinary, to be called that all the time. I will go to announce you by your name. Merci, my friend," said he, with a shoulder-shrug, addressing Joseph's guide. The man went away, and the chamberlain slipped through the curtains.

From inside subdued voices could be heard: a youthful one, gentle and shy at once. It paused. Probably the hunchback had minced and lisped himself close to Pharaoh's ear. Now he came back, his eyebrows high, and whispered:

"Pharaoh summons you."

Joseph went in.

A loggia received him, not large enough really to be called, as they did call it, a garden-house, but of most unusual beauty. Its roof was supported by two columns inlaid with coloured glass and sparkling stones and wound with painted garlands so well executed that they seemed real. The floor was laid in tiled squares of alternating design, cuttlefish and children riding on dolphins. The whole place looked out through three large openings upon gardens all of whose loveliness it thus embraced. There were glorious beds of tulips, strange exotic flowering shrubs, and paths strewn with gold-dust that led to lily-ponds. The eye ranged far out into a perspective of islands, bridges, and kiosks and met the glitter of the faïence decorations on a distant summer-house. The loggia itself glowed with colour. The side walls were covered with paintings unlike anything elsewhere in the country; strange peoples and customs were depicted; obviously these were landscapes from the islands of the sea. Women in gay stiff clothing sat or moved about, their bosoms bare in their tight bodices, their hair curling above the ribbon on their foreheads and falling on their shoulders in long plaits. Pages attended them, in strange elaborate costume, and handed drink from tapering jugs. A little prince with a wasp waist, particoloured trousers, and lambskin boots, a coronet with a gay gush of feathers on his curly head, strutted complacently between rankly blossoming grasses and shot with his bow and arrow at fleeing game which leaped away with all four hooves clear of the ground. Acrobats turned somersaults over the backs of raging bulls for the diversion of ladies and gentlemen looking down from balconies.

In the same exotic taste were the objects of art and fine handicraft: bright enamelled earthenware vases, ivory reliefs inlaid with gold, embossed drinking-vessels, a steer's head in black basalt with gold horns and rock-crystal eyes. As Joseph entered and raised his hands his serious and modest gaze went the round of the scene and the persons of whose presence there he had been told.

Amenhotep-Nebmare's widow sat directly facing him with her back to the light, throned on a lofty chair with a high footstool, in front of the middle window embrasure. Her bronze-tinted skin, dark against the white garment, looked even darker in the shadow. Yet Joseph recognized her unusual features, having seen them various times on the occasion of royal progresses: the fine little aquiline nose, the curling lips framed in furrows of bitter worldly knowledge; the arching brows, lengthened with the pencil above the small, darkly gleaming, coolly measuring eyes. The mother did not wear the gold vulture-cap in which Joseph had seen her in public. Her hair was surely already grey, for she must have been at the end of her fifties. But it was covered by a silvery mob-cap which left free the gold band of a strap over brow and temples, and from the crown of her head two royal serpents — two of them, as though she had taken over that of her husband now with God — wreathed down and reared themselves in front of her brow. Round plaques adorned her ears, of the same coloured precious stones that composed her necklace. The small, energetic figure sat very straight, very upright and well-knit, so to speak in the old hieratic style, the forearms on the arms of her chair, the little feet set close together on the footstool. Her shrewd eyes met Joseph's as he entered, but turned away again towards her son after gliding swiftly down the newcomer's figure, in natural and even correct indifference, while the deep-graven bitter lines round her prominent lips shaped a mocking smile at the boyish curiosity in his face as he looked towards the eagerly awaited and recommended arrival.

The young King of Egypt sat in front of the left-hand painted wall, in an armchair with lions' feet, richly and softly cushioned and with a slanting back from which he bent briskly forward, his feet under the seat and holding its arms with his thin, scarab-decked hands. It must be added that this posture of tense expectancy, as though to spring from his chair, this turn to the right while the veiled grey eyes went as wide open as they possibly could to look at the new interpreter of his dreams: this expressive series of changes did not happen all at once, but was carried out by stages and lasted a full minute; at the end it really looked as though Pharaoh had lifted himself from his seat and was resting all his weight on the hands clutching the chair-arms — their knuckles stood out white. And thus an object which had been in his lap — some sort of stringed instrument — fell with soft ringing and twanging to the floor, quickly retrieved and handed back by a man who stood before him, one of the sculptors he was instructing. The man had to hold it out awhile until the King took it, closing his eyes and sinking back into the cushions in the same attitude which had obviously been his when talking with his artists. It was extraordinarily relaxed and easy, even too easy, for the chair-seat was hollowed out to hold the cushions, and the cushions were too soft, so that he could not help sinking down. Thus he sat, not only leaning back but also very low, with one hand hanging loosely over the back of the chair, and with the thumb of the other hand lightly touching the strings of the strange little harp in his lap. His linen-covered knees were drawn up and crossed, so that one foot went to and fro rather high in the air. The gold strap of the sandal ran between his great and his second toe.

THE CHILD OF THE CAVE

Nefer-Kheperu-Re-Amenhotep was at that time just the age that Joseph — now standing before him a man of thirty — had been when he was "feeding the flocks with his brethren" and beguiled his father of the many-coloured coat. In other words, Pharaoh was seventeen years old. But he seemed older; not only because in his climate men ripen faster; not only because of his delicate health; but also because of his early obligations to the universe, the many impressions that, coming from all quarters of the heavens, had assailed his mind and heart, and finally because of his zealous and fanatical concern anent the divine. In describing his face, under the round blue wig he wore today over the linen cap, the thousands of years' gap must not prevent the apt comparison: he looked like an aristocratic young Englishman of somewhat decadent stock; spare, haughty, weary, with a well-developed chin which yet somehow looked weak, a nose with a narrow, rather depressed bridge which made even more striking the broad, sensitive nostrils; and deeply, dreamily overshadowed eyes with lids he could never open quite wide — their weary expression was in disconcerting contrast to the unrouged, morbid brilliancy of the full lips. There was a complicated and painful mixture of intellectuality and sensuality in this face, still in its boyish stage, with a suggestion of arrogance and recklessness. Pretty and well-favoured it was not at all, but of a disturbing attractiveness; it was not surprising that Egypt's people had a great tenderness for their Pharaoh and gave him flowery names.

Not beautiful either, indeed quite odd, and unconformable to tradition was Pharaoh's figure. It scarcely reached middle height; that was plain as it lay there in the cushions, clearly defined in its light, choice, costly raiment. The relaxed posture did not indicate a lack of manliness but was a sustained attitude of opposition. There were the long neck and thin arms, the narrow, tender chest half covered by a collar of priceless stones, the arms encircled by chased gold bands; the abdomen, rather prominent from chlidhood, with the apron beginning well below the navel and reaching high up in the back, the rich frill in front trimmed with the uræus and ribbon fringes. Add to all this that the legs were not only too short but otherwise out of proportion, the thighs being distinctly too big while the legs looked almost as thin as a chicken's. Amenhotep charged his sculptors not to disguise this peculiarity but even, for the sake of truth, to exaggerate it. His hands and feet, on the contrary, were most delicate and aristocratic in shape, especially the hands, with their long fingers and sensitive expression. They had traces of unguent at the base of the nails. It was something to ponder on, that the ruling passion of this spoilt lad, who obviously took for granted all the privilege and luxury of his state, was knowledge of the Highest; Abraham's descendant, standing at one side and looking at Pharaoh, marvelled to see in what divers sorts of humanity, strange and remote one from another, concern for God could manifest itself on earth.

"So, good Auta" — Joseph noted the gentle reserved tones he had heard from outside, rather high-pitched, rather slow, but at times falling into a more impetuous measure — "make it as Pharaoh has directed, pleasing, living, fine, as my Father above would have it. There are still errors in your work — not mistakes of technique, for you are very capable, but mistakes of spirit. My Majesty has shown them to you and you will correct them. You have done my sister, sweet Princess Baketaton, too much in the dead old style, contrary to the Father whose will I know. Make her sweet and easy, make her according to the truth, which is the light, and in which Pharaoh lives, for he has set it in his inmost heart! Let one hand be putting to her mouth a piece of fruit, a pomegranate, and her other hand be hanging down easily — not with the palm turned stiffly to the body but the rounded palm turned backwards, thus will the god have it that is in my heart and whom I know as no other knows him because I have come of him."

"Your servant," answered Auta, wrapping the clay figure with one hand while he raised the other arm towards Pharaoh, "will make it exactly as Pharaoh commands and has instructed me to my great joy who is the only one of Re, the beauteous child of Aton."

"Thank you, Auta, my warm and loving thanks to you. It is important, you understand? For as the Father is in me and I in him, so shall all become one in us, that is the goal. But your work, conceived in the right spirit, can perhaps contribute a little to all becoming one in him and me. — And you, good Bek — "

"Remember, Auta," the deep, almost masculine voice of the goddess-widow made itself heard at this juncture from her high seat, "always remember that it is hard for Pharaoh to make us understand him, and that he probably says more than he means in order that our understanding may follow him. What he means is not that you are to show the sweet Princess Baketaton as eating, as biting into the fruit; rather you should only put the pomegranate into her hand and make her slightly lift her arm so that one may assume she will probably put the fruit to her mouth. That will be enough of the new and is what Pharaoh means you to understand when he says you are to make her eat it. You must also subtract a little from what His Majesty said about the hanging hand, that you are to turn the palm entirely to the back. Turn it just slightly away from the body, half turn it, that is what is meant — and that will make you praise and blame enough. This simply to make things clear."

Her son was silent a space.

"Have you understood?" he asked then.

"I have," answered Auta.

"Then you will have understood," said Amenhotep, looking down at the lyre-shaped instrument in his lap, "that the great mother of course said somewhat less than she meant, in seeking to lessen the effect of my words. You can carry the hand with the fruit rather far towards the mouth. As for the other hand, it is, of course, only a half turn if you turn her palm away from her body towards the back, for nobody carries the palm turned entirely outwards. And you would be offending against truth if you made it like that. Thus you can see how wisely the mother has qualified my words."

He looked up from the instrument with a mischievous smile showing the teeth, too small, too white, too translucent between his full lips. He looked over at Joseph, who smiled back at him. The queen and the craftsman smiled too.

"And you, good Bek," he went on, "go, as I have commissioned you, to Jebu, into the elephant land, and fetch some of the red granite that is produced there; a goodly amount of the very finest quality, the

kind with a glittering of quartz and shot through with black, you
know, which my heart loves. Lo, Pharaoh will adorn the house of
his father at Karnak that it may excel Amun's house, if not in size,
then in the preciousness of the stones, and the name 'Brilliance of the
great Aton' be more and more usual for his district, until perhaps
Weset itself, the whole city, may take on one day the name 'City of
the Brilliance of Aton' in the popular mouth. You know my thoughts,
and I confide in your love of them. Go, then, my good man, travel at
once. Pharaoh will sit here in his cushions and you will travel far
away upstream and bear the burdens it costs to get the red stone out
and down and ship it to Thebes. So is it, and thus so be it. When will
you set out?"

"Early tomorrow," answered Bek, "when I have taken care of home
and wife; and love to our sweet Lord the beauteous child of Aton will
make as light my travel and travail as though I sat in the softest
cushions."

"Good, good; and go now, my men. Pack up and go each to his
task. Pharaoh has weighty business; only outwardly does he rest in his
cushions, inwardly he is in a high state of tension, zealous and full of
cares. Your cares are indeed great, but small in comparison with his.
Farewell!"

He waited until the craftsmen had done their reverence and withdrawn but meanwhile he looked at Joseph.

"Come nearer, my friend," he said, as the bee-studded curtain
closed behind them, "pray come close to me, dear Khabiru from the
Retenu, fear not, nor startle in your step, come quite close to me!
This is the mother of god, Tiy, who lives a million years. And I am
Pharaoh. But think no more of that, lest it make you fearful. Pharaoh
is God and man, but sets as much store by the second as the first, yes,
he rejoices, sometimes his rejoicing amounts to defiance and scorn,
that he is a man like all men, seen from one side; he rejoices to snap
his fingers at those sourfaces who would have him bear himself uni-
formly as God."

And he actually did snap his slender fingers in the air.

"But I see you are not afraid," he went on, "and startled not in your
steps, but pace them with calm courage towards me. That is good to
see, for in many the heart turns over when they stand before Pharaoh, their spirit forsakes them, their knees give way and they cannot
distinguish life from death. You are not giddy?"

Joseph smiling shook his head.

"There can be three reasons for that," said the boy king. "Either
because your descent is noble, or because you see the human being in
Pharaoh, as it pleases him when it comes about within the frame of
his divinity. Or it may be you feel that a reflection of the divine rests
upon you, for you are wonderfully lovely and charming, pretty as a

picture, My Majesty noted it directly you entered, although it did not surprise me, as I have been told you are the son of a lovely woman. For after all it indicates that He loves you who creates beauty of form through Himself alone, who lends the eyes love and power of vision through and for His beauty. One may call beautiful people the darlings of the light."

He looked at Joseph with satisfaction, his head on one side.

"Is he not wonderfully pretty and well-favoured, like a god of light, little Mama?" he asked Tiy, who sat leaning her cheek against three fingers of her little dark hand that blazed with gems.

"You have summoned him because of the wisdom and power of interpretation he is supposed to have," she answered looking into space.

"They belong together," broke in Amenhotep quickly and eagerly. "Pharaoh has considered much and perceived much on this point; he has discussed it with visiting ambassadors often from afar and foreign lands, magi, priests, and initiates who brought him from east and west news of the thoughts of men. For where all must he not hearken and what all not observe: to test, to choose, and make useful the usable that he may perfect the teaching and establish the image of truth according to the will of his Father above! Beauty, little Mama, and you, dear Amu, has to do with wisdom through the medium of light. For light is the medium and the means, whence relationship streams out on three sides: to beauty, to love, and to knowledge of truth. These are one in him, and light is their three-in-oneness. Strangers bore to me the teaching of the beginning god, born of flames, a beautiful god of light and love, and his name was 'first-born brilliance.' That is a glorious, a useful contribution, for therein is displayed the unity of love and light. But light is beauty as well as truth and knowledge, and if you would learn the medium of truth, then know that it is love. — Well, now, they say of you that when you hear a dream you can interpret it?" he asked Joseph. His face was suffused with the colour of embarrassment at his own extravagant and fanatical words.

"It is not I who does this, O my lord," answered Joseph. "It is not I who can do it, it is God alone, and He does it sometimes through me. Everything has its time: dreams, and the interpretation of them. When I was a lad I dreamed and my brothers were angry and chid me. Now when I am a man has come the time of interpretation. My dreams interpret themselves to me, and certainly it is God who gives it to me to interpret the dreams of others."

"So you are a prophetic youth, a so-called inspired lamb?" inquired Amenhotep. "You seem to belong in that category. Will you fall down dead with your last words after you have announced the future to the King, and die in a spasm, that he may give you solemn burial and have your prophecies inscribed to be handed down to posterity?"

"Not easily," said Joseph, "is the question of the Great House to be answered; not with yes and not with no, at best with both. It amazes your servant and goes to his heart that you are pleased to see in him a lamb, an inspired lamb. For I am used to this name since a child: my father the friend of God used to call me 'the lamb,' because my lovely mother, the star-maid for whom he served at Sinear, across the river flowing the wrong way, and who bore me in the sign of the virgin, was named Rachel, which means mother sheep. But this does not justify me, great lord, in accepting your idea unconditionally or in saying 'I am.' For I am and am not just because I am I. I mean that the general and the typical vary when they fulfil themselves in the particular, so that the known becomes unknown and you cannot recognize it. Do not expect me to fall down dead with my last word just because that is the established pattern. This your servant, whom you summoned from the grave, does not expect it, for it belongs only to the typical and not to me, the variation from the typical. Nor shall I foam at the mouth, like the typical prophetic youth, if God shall give it to me to prophesy to Pharaoh. When I was a lad, I probably did twitch, and gave my father great concern by rolling my eyes like those who run naked, babbling oracles. My father's son has put that away from him since he came to years; he holds now with divine reason, even when he interprets. Interpretation is spasm enough, one need not slaver as well. Plain and clear shall be the interpretation, and no aulasaukaulala."

He had not looked toward the mother as he spoke, but out of one corner of his eye he saw that she nodded assent on her high seat. Her brisk, low, almost masculine voice, issuing from that fragile form, was heard to say:

"The stranger speaks what is worth hearing and heartening to Pharaoh."

On that Joseph could only continue, for the King was silent for the moment and hung his head with the sulky look of a chidden child. Joseph, thus encouraged by Tiy, went on:

"In my unworthy opinion, a composed manner in interpreting is due to the fact that it is an I and a single individual through whom the typical and the traditional are being fulfilled, and thereby, in my feeling, the seal of divine reason is vouchsafed to them. For the pattern and the traditional come from the depths which lie beneath and are what binds us, whereas the I is from God and is of the spirit, which is free. But what constitutes civilized life is that the binding and traditional depth shall fulfil itself in the freedom of God which belongs to the I; there is no human civilization without the one and without the other."

Amenhotep nodded to his mother with lifted brows; he began to applaud, holding one hand straight up and striking the palm with two fingers of the other.

"Do you hear, my little Mama?" said he. "This is a youth of great insight whom My Majesty has sent for to come hither. Remember, pray, that by my own resolve I called him to come. Pharaoh too is very gifted and advanced for his years, but it is doubtful whether he could have made up and expressed these things about the binding pattern of the depths and the dignity which comes from above. — So you are not bound to the binding pattern of the foaming lamb," he asked, "and you will not bruise the heart of Pharaoh with the traditional announcements of horrible misery to come, the invasion by foreign peoples, and how that which is undermost shall be turned uppermost?" He shuddered. "We all know about that," he said, his lips going a little white. "But My Majesty must spare himself a little, he cannot well bear the wild and savage, he is in need of tenderness and love. The land has gone down to destruction, it lives in uproar. Bedouins rove over it. Poor and rich change places, all law is annulled, the son slays the father and by his brother is slain, wild beasts of the desert drink at the springs, one laughs the laugh of death, Re has turned away his face, no one knows when midday is, for one knows not the shadow on the dial; beggars consume the sacrifices, the King is taken and snatched away; one only consolation abides, that by the might of him who shall deliver all shall be better once more. Pharaoh, then, need not hear this song again? May he hope that the modification of the traditional by the particular will exclude such horrors?"

Joseph smiled. It was now that he made the famous reply, both courteous and shrewd:

"God shall give Pharaoh an answer of peace."

"You speak of God," probed Amenhotep. "You have done so several times. Which god do you mean? You are from Zahi and from Amu, so I assume that you mean the ox whom in the East they call Baal the Lord?"

Joseph's smile became detached. He even shook his head.

"My fathers, the God-dreamers," said he, "made their covenant with another Lord."

"Then it can only be Adonai, the bridegroom," said the King quickly, "for whom the flute wails in the gorges and who rises again. You see, Pharaoh knows his way about among the gods of all mankind. He must know and try all and be like a gold-washer who dredges the kernel of truth out of much absurdity, that it may help to perfect the teaching of his adored father. Pharaoh finds it hard, but good, very good, a royal task. My good parts have made me work that out. Who has hardship must also have ease, but only he. For it is disgusting to have only ease; yet to have only hardship is not right either. At the great feast of tribute in the beautiful balcony of audience My Majesty sits next to my lovely consort and the ambassadors of the people. Moors, Libyans, and Asiatics bring a ceaseless train of gifts from all the world, bar gold and gold in rings, ivory, silver vases, ostrich feathers, oxen, byssus, leopards and elephants in procession; and just so the Lord of the Crowns sits in the beauty of his palace and receives in fitting ease the tribute of all the thought of the inhabited earth. For as My Majesty was already pleased to say, the singers and seers of strange gods succeed one another, coming to my court from all the regions of the earth together: from Persia, where the gardens are renowned and where they believe that some day the earth will be flat and even and all men have one species, speech, and law; from India, the land where the incense grows, from star-wise Babel and the islands of the sea. They all visit me, they pass over before my seat, and My Majesty has intercourse with them as he now has with you who are a special kind of lamb. They offer me the early and the late, the old and the new. Sometimes they leave strange souvenirs and divine signs. Do you see this toy here?" And he lifted the round stringed object from his lap and held it out to Joseph.

"A lyre," the other assented. "It is fitting that Pharaoh holds in his hand the symbol of goodness and charm."

This he said because the hieroglyph for the Egyptian "Nofert," which means both goodness and charm, is a lyre.

"I see," responded the King, "that you have understanding of the arts of Thoth and are a scribe. I suppose that belongs to the dignity of the I, wherein the binding pattern of the depths fulfills itself. But this object is a sign of something else besides goodness and charm, namely of the artfulness of a strange god, who may be a brother of the Ibis-headed or his other self, and who invented the toy as a child when he met a certain creature. Do you know the shell?"

"It is a tortoise-shell," said Joseph.

"You are right," assented Amenhotep. "This sly-boots of a child-god met this wise creature born in the hollow of the rocks and it fell a sacrifice to his quick wit. For he impudently robbed it of its hollow shell and put strings across and fastened on two horns as you can see, and it became a lyre. I will not say this is the very same toy the mischievous rascal made. The man who brought it and gave it to me, a seafarer from Crete, does not say that. It may only have been made in memory of the first, in jest or piety, for this was only one of various tales the Cretan told of the swaddling-babe of the cave. It seems this infant was always getting up out of his hole and swaddlings to play pranks. He stole — it is almost unbelievable — the cattle of the sun-god, his elder brother, away from the hill where they pastured, when the sun-god had gone down. Fifty of them he took and drove them about, across and across, to confuse their hoof-marks. His own steps he disguised, binding on them enormous sandals woven of branches, so that there were giant footprints that he left behind, and thus none at all. And that was quite fitting. For he was indeed an infant and yet a god; and so those vast vague footprints were quite as they should be. The cattle he drove away and hid them in a cave, a different one from the one where he was born — there are many in those parts. But first he slaughtered two cows by the river and roasted them at a huge fire. These he ate, the suckling babe; it was the meal of a giant child and went with the footprints."

Amenhotep went on, lying back relaxed in his chair: "This done, the thievish child slipped back to his parent cave and into his swaddlings. But when the sun-god came up again and missed his cattle, he divined, for he was a soothsaying god, and knew that only his newborn brother could have done the deed. Hot with anger he came to him in his cave. But the little thief, who had heard him coming, cuddled himself into his swaddlings that smelled sweet of his godhead, made himself very small, and counterfeited the slumber of innocence. In his arms he held his invention, the lyre. And of course the hypocrite knew how to lie like the truth when the sun-god, undeceived by his wiles, taxed him with the theft. "Quite other concerns have I," he lisped, "than this you think: sweet sleep and mother's milk, the swaddlings round my shoulders and warm baths." And then he swore, the seafarer said, a great round oath that he knew nothing of the cattle. — Do I bore you, Mama?" he interrupted himself, and turned to the goddess on her throne.

"Since I am freed from the cares of the governing of this land," she replied, "I have much time to spare. I can as well while it away listening to stories of strange gods. Yet truly the world seems upside down to me: it is usually the king who lets himself be narrated to, and now Your Majesty narrates himself."

"Why should he not?" responded Amenhotep. "Pharaoh must instruct. And what he has learned he is always urged to teach at once to others. What my mother really objects to," he went on, and stretching two fingers towards her he seemed as it were to explain to her her own words, "is, no doubt, that Pharaoh delays to relate his dreams to this understanding and inspired lamb, that he may at last hear the truth about them. For that I shall get true interpretation from him I am almost certain even now, owing to his person and some things he has already said. My Majesty is not afraid, for he has promised that he will not prophesy in the manner of the mouth-foaming youth or horrify me with such tales as that beggars will consume the offerings. But do you not know and have you not seen the wonderful way the mind has: that a man, when the fulfilment approaches of his most coveted wish, will of his own free will hold off a little from the consummation? 'Now it is at hand anyhow,' he says, 'and only waits on me; I may just as well put it off a little, for the desire and the wish themselves have grown dear to me, in a way, and it is too bad about them.' That is a way human beings have, and Pharaoh too, who sets great store by being a human being himself."

Tiy smiled.

"As your beloved Majesty does it, we shall call it beautiful. Since this soothsayer may not well ask, I will: did the naughty suckling's perjury avail, or what happened next?"

"This," answered Amenhotep, "according to my source: the sun-brother brought the thief in bonds before their father, the great god, that he should confess and the god punish him. But here too the rascal lied with the utmost guile and spoke piously out of his mouth. 'Highly I honour the sun,' he lisped, 'and the other gods and you I love, but fear him here. Protect, then, the younger and help poor little me!' So he misrepresented himself displaying his baby side, winking the while at his father out of one eye, so that he could only laugh aloud at the arch rogue. He ordered him to show his brother the cattle and deliver back the stolen property, to which the infant agreed. But when the elder brother heard of the two slaughtered cows he was wroth anew. Now while he threatened and fumed, the little one played on his lyre — this thing here — and his singing went so sweet to the sound of the lyre that the elder brother's scolding died away and the sun-god thought only of getting the instrument for his own. And his it became, for they made a bargain: the cattle remained to the thief, the lyre the brother carried away — and keeps it for ever."

He stopped speaking and looked down at the toy in his lap.

"In right instructive way after all," said the mother, "Pharaoh has put off the fulfilment of his most ardent wish."

"Instructive it is," gave back the King, "for it shows that child gods are only disguised children — disguised out of sheer mischief. He came out of his cave whenever he chose, as a gay and gifted youth, skilled in devices, never at a loss for flexible stratagems, a helper to gods and men. What new things did he not invent, in the belief of the people: writing and reckoning, culture of the olive and of shrewd persuasive speech; not shrinking from deceit, yet deceiving with great charm. My seafaring man, whose patron he was, esteemed him highly. For he was the god of favourable chance, so the man said, and of smiling inventiveness; shedding blessing and well-being — whether honestly or even a bit dishonestly won, the way life is; a leader and guide through the windings of this world, turning back with lifted staff to smile. Even the dead he guides, the man said, in their kingdom of the moon — and even dreams, for he is lord of sleep, who closes the eyes of man with his staff, a gentle magician with all his slyness."

Pharaoh's gaze fell on Joseph, as he stood before him, the pretty and charming head bowed or even bent on one shoulder, looking sideways up at the paintings on the wall, with an unforced and absent smile, which seemed to say he need not absolutely listen to all this.

"Are the tales of the mischievous god known to you, soothsayer?" asked Amenhotep.

Joseph quickly changed his pose. He had behaved with pointed lack of courtly manners and now showed that he was aware of it. He even did so in somewhat exaggerated fashion; so that Pharaoh, who always noticed everything, got the impression not only that this startled return to the present moment was assumed, but that it had been put on to create that very impression. He waited, keeping his veiled grey eyes, as wide open as he could make them, directed on Joseph.

"Known, highest Lord?" the young man asked. "Yes and no — if you will permit your servant the double answer."

"You seek often for such permission," said the King, "or rather you simply take it. All your speaking turns on the Yes and at the same time on the No. Is that likely to please me? You are the mouth-foaming youth and you are not, because you are you. The mischievous god is known to you and he is not, because — why? Was he known to you or not?"

"To you too, Lord of the Crowns, he has always been known — in a way; for did you not call him a distant brother of the Ibis-headed, Djehuti, the moon-friendly scribe, or indeed his other self? Was he known to you or not? He was familiar — that is more than known, for in it the Yes and No cancel each other out and are one and the same. No, I did not know the child of the cave and master of pranks. My father's oldest servant, the wise Eliezer, was my teacher: he who could say that the earth sprang to meet him on the bridal journey for the saved sacrifice, my father's father — pardon, pardon! All this leads too far afield, your servant cannot narrate the world to you at this hour. And yet the words of the great mother still ring in his ear: it is the custom in the world for the king not to narrate but to be narrated to. Of such pranks as these I might know several, to show you, you and the great mistress, that the spirit of the rogue-god has always been at home among my people and is familiar to me."

Amenhotep looked across at his mother with a light nod which meant: "Well, what shall we make of him?" Then he answered Joseph:

"The goddess permits you to tell us one or two of them, if you think you can amuse us, before the interpreting."

"Our breath cometh from you," said Joseph, with an obeisance. "I use it to divert you."

And with folded arms, but often lifting his hand in a descriptive gesture, he spoke before Pharaoh and said:

"Rough was Esau, my uncle, the mountain goat, twin of my father, who forced the passage before him when they were born. Red and shaggy of hair was he, a bungler; my father was smooth and fine, tent-bred and son of his mother, clever in God, a shepherd, while Esau a hunter was. Always was Jacob blest, since before the hour when my forebear, father of both, resolved to bestow the handed-down blessing, for he declined unto death. Blind the old man, his ancient eyes would no longer obey him, only with hands he saw, feeling not seeing. Before him he summoned the red one, his eldest, longing to love him. 'Go, shoot me game with thy bow,' he said, 'my forthright, hairy first-born, cook me a savoury meat that I may eat and then bless thee, strengthened thereto by the meal.' Red one went off to the hunt. Meanwhile the mother wrapped the younger in goat-skins round his smooth limbs and gave him a mess, spiced and seasoned, from goat's flesh. With it he went to the master into the tent and spake: 'Here am I back, my father, Esau, thy hairy one, having hunted and cooked for thee. Eat then, and bless thy first-born!' 'Come now to me, come near to thy father, my son,' spoke the blind old man, 'that I may feel with my seeing hands if you are truly Esau, my hairy one, for it is easy to say.' And felt with his hands and felt the fell of the goat where the skin was bare, and there it was rough, like Esau; red it was not, but that the hands could not see and the old eyes would not. 'Yes, there can be no doubt, it is you,' said the old man then, 'from your fleece it is plain to me. Rough or smooth, so it is, and how good that one needs not the eyes to perceive, for the hand sufficeth! Esau art thou, then feed me that I may bless thee!' So did he smell and eat, and he gave to the wrong one, who yet was the right one, the fullness of blessing one might not recall. Then came Esau from hunting, puffed up and boastful at this his great hour. He cooks and seasons his game where all eyes can see him and bears it within to his father inside the tent. But there in the tent was he cheated and mocked as a humbug, truly he was the wrong right one, since the right wrong one had come before him through mother's guile. Only a barren curse he received since naught else was left after the blessing was spent. What jesting and laughing were there, when he sat down wailing aloud with his tongue hanging out, and the fat tears plumped down into the dust, the cozened clodpate whom the clever one tricked, skilled and familiar in all!"

Mother and son both laughed, the one in a sonorous alto, the other clear and rather piping. Both shook their heads.

"What a grotesque tale!" cried Amenhotep. "A barbaric farce, capital in its way, if rather depressing too; one hardly knows how to take it, it makes you feel like laughing and crying, both at once. The wrong right one, you say, and the wrong one that was the right one? That is not bad; it is so crazy that it is witty. But may the higher goodness preserve us all from being both right and wrong, so that we need not sit blubbering in the end, with our tears plopping into the dust! What do you think of the mother, little Mama? Wrapping goatskins round the smoothness, and helping the old one and his seeing hands to bless the right one, in other words the wrong one. Tell me if you do not find this an original lamb whom I have summoned before my presence. My Majesty permits you to relate another jest, Khabire, that I may see whether the first was not good just by chance, and whether this spirit of clever roguery is really better than known to you, because familiar. Let me hear!"

"What Pharaoh commands," Joseph said, "is already done. The blessing one had to flee before the wrath of the cheated; travel he must, and travelled to Naharin in the land of Sinear, where relatives dwelt: Laban the clod, a sinister man of affairs, and his daughters, the one red-eyed, the other more lovely than stars in the sky. So she became his all, and more to him than all save only God. But the hard taskmaster made him serve seven years for the starry maid. They passed like days, but then the uncle gave to him first in the dark the other unloved, and only much later the true bride, Rachel the mother sheep, who bore me with more than natural pains, and they called me Dumuzi, the true son. This only in passing. Now, when the star-maid was healed after bearing, my father would be away with me and the ten whom the maids and the wrong one had borne him; or he made as though he would go to his uncle, who was unwilling, for Jacob's blessing-hand was a profit to Laban. 'Give me, then, all the pied sheep and goats of the flocks,' said he to his uncle. 'They shall be mine, but yours all those of one colour. Such is my modest condition.' So then they sealed their bargain. But what then did Jacob do? Took wands from the trees and bushes and peeled white stripes in the bark, so they were pied. These he laid in the troughs where the flocks came to drink and mated after the drinking. Always he made them see the pied wands at this business, which worked on them through their eyes so that they dropped pied young, which he took. So he grew rich out of all count and Laban was laid by the heels through the wit of the roguish god."

Again the mother and son were much diverted. They laughed and shook their heads; a vein stood out on the King's sickly forehead and tears were in his half-shut eyes.

"Mama, Mama," said he, "My Majesty is very, very much amused. Striped staves he took and gave them the pattern through their eyes — ring-straked and speckled, we say, and ring-straked and speckled Pharaoh could laugh himself at a jest like that! Does he still live, your father? That was a rogue! And so you are the son of a rogue and a lovely one?"

"The lovely one was a thief and rascal too," Joseph supplemented his tale. "Her loveliness was no stranger to stratagems. For love of her husband she stole her gloomy father's images, thrust them into the camel's bedding, and sat on it and said in her beguiling voice: 'I am unwell with my periods and cannot stand up.' But Laban searched in vain, to his own chagrin."

"One on top of the other!" cried Amenhotep, his voice breaking. "Listen to me, Mama. You owe me an answer whether I have not summoned before me a highly original subtle and sportive lamb. Now is the moment," he suddenly decreed; "now is Pharaoh ready to hear from this wise youth the interpretation of his difficult dreams. Before these tears of merriment are quite dry in my eyes, I will hear it. For as long as my eyes are still wet from this rare laughter, I fear not the dreams nor their meaning, whatever it is. This son of jesters will tell Pharaoh neither such stupidities as did the pedants of the book-house, nor yet any frightful things. And even though the truth he tells be bad, yet these lips so given to smiling can scarcely shape it so as to turn straightway these tears of laughter to tears of mourning. Sooth-sayer, is there need of any vessel or apparatus for your task? A caul-dron, perhaps, to receive the dreams, out of which their meaning shall rise?"

"Nothing at all," answered Joseph. "I need nothing between heaven and earth for my affair. I just go ahead and interpret as the spirit moves me. Pharaoh needs only to speak."

The King cleared his throat and looked over in some embarrass-ment at his mother, excusing himself by a little bow for her having to hear the tale all over again. Then, blinking with his laughter-wet eyes, for the sixth time he conscientiously related his now stale dreams.

PHARAOH PROPHESIES

JOSEPH listened unaffectedly, in a respectful posture; while the King spoke he kept his eyes closed, but in no other way did he betray the profound abstraction and concentration of his being upon what he heard. He did something else too; he kept them shut for a little while after Amenhotep had finished and was waiting, holding his breath. He even went so far as to let the King wait a little, while he stood there, not looking but aware of the attention focused upon him. It was very still in the Cretan loggia, only the goddess mother gave a ringing cough and played with her ornaments.

"Are you sleeping, lamb?" Amenhotep asked at last in a tremulous voice.

"No, here am I," answered Joseph, as without undue haste he

opened his eyes before Pharaoh. Even then he seemed to look through
him instead of at him, or rather his gaze, resting on the King's figure,
broke there and turned inwards in contemplation — and all that became the black Rachel-eyes very well.

"And what say you to my dreams?"

"To your dreams?" Joseph answered. "To your dream, you mean.
To dream twice is not to dream two dreams. You dreamed but one
dream. That you dreamed it twice, first in one form and then in the
other, has only the meaning of emphasis: it means that your dream
will certainly be fulfilled and that speedily. Furthermore its second
form is only the explanation and more precise definition of the meaning of the first."

"That is just what My Majesty thought in the beginning!" cried
Amenhotep. "Mother, what the lamb says was my own first thought,
that the two dreams are at bottom only one. I dreamed of the goodly
cattle and then the ghastly ones, and then it was as if somebody said
to me: 'Did you understand me? This is the meaning.' And then I
dreamed of the ears, the full and the blasted ones. As a man will seek
to express himself and then try again, 'In other words,' he says, 'so
and so.' Mama, here is a good beginning which this prophetic boy
has made, without foaming at the mouth. Those botchers from the
book-house bungled at the very start and nothing good could come
after that. Continue, prophet. What is the single meaning of my
double royal dream?"

"Single is the meaning, like the two lands, and double the dream
like your crown," Joseph replied. "Is not that what you meant just
now though you did not quite say it, yet said it not quite by chance?
You betrayed what you meant in the words 'my royal dream.' Crown
and train you wore in your dream, as I darkly perceived. You were
not Amenhotep, but Nefer-Kheperu-Re, the King. God spoke to the
King in his dream. He revealed his future purposes to Pharaoh that
Pharaoh may know and plan accordingly."

"Absolutely," cried Amenhotep. "Nothing was clearer to me.
Mother, nothing was more certain from the beginning than what
this peculiar kind of lamb has said: that it was not I who dreamed, but
the King, in so far as the two can be separated, and in so far as not
even I was necessary in order that the King should dream. Did not
Pharaoh know it and swore to you at once next morning that the
double dream was important for the realm and therefore absolutely
must be interpreted? But it was sent to the King not as the father of
the lands but because he is also the mother of them; for the sex of the
King is double. My dream had to do with matters of life and death
and with the black underworld. I knew it and I know it. But yet I
know no more," he suddenly bethought himself. "Why is it My
Majesty utterly forgot that he knows nothing more and that the in-

terpretation is still to seek? You have a way," he turned to Joseph, "of making it seem as though everything is all beautifully clear whereas so far you have only told me what I knew already. What means my dream, what would it show to me?"

"Pharaoh errs," Joseph responded, "if he thinks he does not know. His servant can do no more than to prophesy to him what he already knows. Did you not see the cows as they came up out of the water in a row, one after the other, and followed in one another's steps, first the fat and then the lean, so that there was no break in the row? What are they that come up out of the casket of eternity, one after the other, not together but in succession, and no break is between the going and the coming and no interruption in their line?"

"The years!" cried Amenhotep, snapping his fingers as he held them up.

"Of course," said Joseph. "It needs not to rise out of any cauldron nor any rolling of eyes nor foaming at the mouth to tell us that the cows are years, seven and seven. And the ears of corn which sprouted one after the other, and to the same number: shall they be something quite different and vastly hard to guess?"

"No!" cried Pharaoh and snapped his fingers again, "they are years too!"

"As divine reason would have it," answered Joseph, "to which all praise and honour shall be given. But why the cows should have become ears, seven fruitful and seven barren — now indeed the cauldron must be fetched. Large round as the moon, that the answer may rise out of it and tell us what the connection is between cows and ears and the reason why the first seven cows were so fat and second seven so lean. Pharaoh will be so kind as to send for a cauldron and tripod!"

"Get along with your cauldron!" cried the King. "Is this a time to talk of cauldrons, as though we needed anything of the sort! The connection is as plain as a pikestaff and clear as a gem of the first water. There is a connection between the goodness and the badness of the cows and the ears: one means good crops and the other bad ones." He paused, staring out into space before him. "Seven fat years will come," he said in a sort of transport, "and then seven lean ones."

"Without fail or faltering," said Joseph, "for it was told you twice."

Pharaoh directed his gaze upon his lamb.

"You have not fallen dead after the prophecy," he said with a certain admiration.

"Were it not evil and punishable to say so," Joseph responded, "one might put it that it is wonderful Pharaoh does not fall dead, for Pharaoh has prophesied."

"No, you are just saying that," contradicted Amenhotep. "You made it seem as though I myself interpreted because you are a child of stratagems and descended from rogues. But why could I have not done it before you came? I only knew what was false but not what was true. For true is this interpretation, that I know in my very soul; my own dream knows itself again in the interpretation. Yes, you are indeed an inspired lamb, but you certainly have your own little ways. You are no slave of the binding pattern of the depths, you did not prophesy first the curse-time and then the blessing-time but the other way round, first the blessing and then the curse — and that is very original of you!"

"It was you yourself, Lord of the Two Lands," answered Joseph, "and on you it depended. You dreamed, first of the fat kine and ears and then of the lean ones; and you yourself are the only original."

Amenhotep worked himself up out of the hollow of his chair and sprang to his feet. He strode to his mother's seat, moving swiftly on those odd limbs of his — the heavy thighs and thin lower parts showed plainly through the batiste garment.

"Mama," he said, "now we have it! My king-dreams are now interpreted to me and I know the truth. When I think of the erudite rubbish that was passed off to My Majesty — the daughters, the cities, the kings, and the fourteen children — I feel as much like laughing as I felt like weeping before when I was desperate at its poverty. Now, thanks to this prophetic youth, I know the truth and I can simply laugh at it. But the truth itself is serious enough. My Majesty has been shown that seven fat years will come in all Egypt and after that seven years of dearth, such that one will quite forget the previous plenty, and famine will consume the land, just as the lean kine consumed the fat, and the blasted ears the golden ones; for such was the message: that one would know no more of the fullness that was before the famine-time, for its harshness will consume our memory of the fullness. This is what was revealed to Pharaoh in his dreams, which were one dream and which came to him because he is the mother of the lands. That it remained dark to me until this hour is what I can scarcely understand. Now it is brought to life by the aid of this genuine but peculiar lamb. It was necessary, in order that the King might dream, that I should be; in the same way it was necessary that he should be, in order that the lamb might prophesy; our being is only the meeting-place between not-being and ever-being; our temporal only the medium of the eternal. And yet not only that. For we must ask — it is the problem which I should like to put before the thinkers of my Father's house — whether the temporal, the individual, and the particular get more worth and value from the eternal, or the eternal more from the particular and temporal. That is one of those beautiful questions which permit of no solution, so that there is no end to the contemplation of them from dewy eve to early dawn."

Seeing Tiy shake her head, he broke off.

"Meni," said she, "Your Majesty is incorrigible. You kept on at us about your dreams, which you thought were so important to the realm that they must be interpreted without fail, so that they could not fulfil themselves unhindered. But now that you have the meaning, or think you have, you act as though everything were all settled, you forget the meaning even as you utter it, to get lost in the most remote and impossible speculations. Is that like a mother? I could not even call it fatherly; and I can scarcely wait until this man here has gone back where he came from and we are alone, to admonish you indignantly from my maternal throne. It is possible that this sooth-sayer knows his craft and that what he says may happen. It has happened in the past, that good and poor seasons have alternated, that then the Nourisher has run low and time after time he has denied his blessing to the fields, so that want and famine consumed the lands. It has happened, it has actually happened seven times running, as the chronicles show. It can happen again, and therefore you have dreamed it. But perhaps you have dreamed it because it is going to happen again. If that is what you think, then, my child, your mother is aston-ished that you can rejoice over the interpretation and even flatter yourself that in a way you made it yourself. And now, instead of summoning all your counsellors and wise men together to consider how to meet the threatening evil, you go off into such extravagant abstractions as this about the meeting-place of the not-being and the ever-being!"

"But, dear little Mama, we have time!" cried Amenhotep, with a lively gesture. "Where there is no time, then of course one cannot take any; but we can, for before us lies a fullness of it. Seven years! That is the great thing; the fact to make us dance and rub our hands together: that this highly individual lamb was not bound to the hate-ful pattern and did not prophesy the accursed time before the blessing-time, but the blessing-time first, and for as long as seven years. Your rebuke would be just if the bad time, the time of the withered kine, were due to begin tomorrow. Then there would certainly be no time to lose in thinking about expedients and preventive measures — al-though My Majesty is free to confess he knows no adequate measures against failure of crops. But seven years of fatness are granted us in the kingdom of the black earth, during which the love of the people for their Pharaoh-mother will flourish like a tree, under which he can sit and teach his father's teaching. So I do not see why on the very first day — your eyes are speaking, soothsayer," he broke off, "and you have such a very piercing look; have you anything to add to our common interpretation?"

"Nothing," answered Joseph, "save a plea that you permit your servant to go now to his own place, back to the prison where he was serving and into the pit out of which you took him for the sake of your dream. For his task is done and his presence is no longer fitting in the places of the great. In his hole will he live and feed upon the golden hour when he stood before Pharaoh, the beautiful sun of the lands, and before the great mother, whom I name in the second place only because language will have it so, which belongs to time and must deal with one thing after the other, unlike the world of images, where two can stand side by side. But speech and naming belong to time; thus the first mention belongs to the King; yet truly the second is not the second, for was not the mother before the son? So much in the succession of things. But whither my smallness now returns, there will I continue in my thoughts this intercourse with the great, to mingle in which were culpable of me. Pharaoh was right, I shall say to myself in the silence, to rejoice in the reversed order and the beautiful respite before the time of cursing and the years of drought. But how right was not the mother too, who was before him with the view and the warning that from the very first day of the blessing-time and from the very day of the interpretation there must be much taking of thought against the coming of evil! Not to avoid it, for we avoid not the purposes of God; but to anticipate and provide against it by proper foresight. For the term of blessing which is promised us means in the first place a stage wherein to take breath to bear the affliction. But in the second place it means time and space to take steps, at least to clip the wings of the raven of calamity; to take note of the coming evil to work against it, and so far as possible not only to keep it in bounds but perhaps to derive from it a blessing to boot. This or something like it shall I be saying to myself in my dungeon, since it would be worse than improper for me to inject my thoughts into the converse of the great. What a great and splendid thing, shall I whisper to myself, is the wisdom which can convert even misfortune into blessing! And how gracious is God, that He granted to the King, through the medium of his dreams, such a wide survey over time — not only over seven, but over fourteen years! Therein lies the provision, and the command to provide. For the fourteen years are but one time, made up of twice seven though it is; and it does not begin in the middle but at the beginning, in other words with today, for today is the day of surveying the whole. And to survey it all is to provide for it all."

"All this is very odd," remarked Amenhotep. "Have you been speaking, or have you not? You have been speaking while you did not speak but only let us hear your thoughts, those, that is, which you only think to think. But it seems to me it is the same as though you had spoken. In other words, you contrived a little device, to say something that had not yet been said."

"Everything must have its first time," Joseph replied. "But foresight is not new. And there has been for very long the shrewd employment of what time is granted. If God had put the bad time before the blessing-time and it began tomorrow, there could be no counsel nor could any avail. What the chafftime wrought among men could not be made good by the fullness to follow. But now it is the other way on, and there is time — not to waste, but to make good the coming want and to balance the fullness and the lack, by saving the fullness to feed the lack. The order of the dream was meant to instruct us: the fat kine come up first, then the lean; which means that he who makes the survey is called and commanded to feed the lack."

"You mean we must heap up provision and gather it into bins?" asked Amenhotep.

"On the very largest scale," said Joseph with decision. "In quite other measure than has ever been in the time of the two lands! And the master of the survey shall be the taskmaster of the fullness. He shall control it with strictness; the people's love for him will teach them the economy of plenty. Then, when the dearth comes, and they find that he can give, how will their love and trust increase! Under that spreading tree he may sit and teach. And the master of the survey shall be the vicar and shadow-spender of the King."

As he spoke, Joseph's eyes chanced to meet those of the great mother, the little dark figure sitting upright and hieratic upon her raised seat with her feet together. Those shrewd, sharp eyes, gleaming black out of the shadow, were fixed upon him, and the lines about her full lips shaped a mocking smile. He dropped his lids gravely before this smile, yet not without a respectful twinkle.

"If I have heard aright," said Amenhotep, "you think, like the great mother, that without any loss of time I should summon my advisers to a council, that they may decide how to deal with the abundance to make it serve the lack?"

"Pharaoh," answered Joseph, "has had no great luck with the councils he summoned to interpret the double dream dreamed by his double crown. He interpreted himself, he found the truth. To him alone was the prophecy sent and the whole situation made clear; on him alone is it incumbent to administer the supplies and husband the plenty which will come before the drought. The measures which must be taken are unprecedented in method and scope; whereas a council is prone to decide on a middle and traditional course. Therefore he alone who has dreamed and interpreted must be the man to decide and execute."

"Pharaoh does not execute his decisions," Tiy the mother coolly made herself heard. She gazed through and past both of them as she spoke. "That is an ignorant conception. Even granted that he make his own decision about what to decide according to his dream — in other words, granted that the decision is to be made in accordance with the dream — he will then put the performance of it into the hands of his administrators who are there for the purpose: the two Viziers of the South and North, the steward of the storehouses and stalls, and the head of the treasury."

"Precisely so," said Joseph, with an appearance of astonishment, "did I think in my hole to tell myself, in the imaginary conversation I was carrying on. Indeed, those very words, even 'ignorant conception' did I put into the mouth of the great mother and turned them against myself. I am swollen with pride to hear her utter just what I would have made her say, down there and only to myself. I will take back her words with me into my prison; there, living and feeding upon the memories of this exalted hour, I will answer in spirit and say: 'Ignorant are all my conceptions, save perhaps one only: the thought that Pharaoh himself, the beautiful sun of the two lands, should himself carry out what he decides and not leave the performance of it to tried and tested servants, saying: "I am Pharaoh! Be as myself, receive from me full powers for the task wherein I have tried and tested you; for you shall be the middleman between me and men, as the moon is middleman between sun and earth. So shall you turn to blessing this threat to me and to the two lands." ' No, my ignorance is perhaps not so all-embracing; for in this matter and in my own mind I clearly hear Pharaoh speak and say these words, yet not to many, but to one. And again, no man hearing my words, I will say: 'Many counsellors make many counsels; therefore let there be but one, as the moon is one among the stars and is the middleman between above and below, who knows the dreams of the sun. The first of the extraordinary measures must be the choice of him who shall put them into action. Otherwise they will be not extraordinary but middling, usual, and inadequate. And why? Because they will not be put into action with faith and knowledgeable foresight. Tell the many your dreams, they will both believe and disbelieve; part of each will have faith and part foresight, but all these parts together will not make up the complete faith or foresight which is necessary and can be only in one. Therefore let Pharaoh look for a wise and understanding man in whom dwells the spirit of his dreams, the spirit of seeing and the spirit of providing, and set him over the land of Egypt. Say to him: "Be as I am," that he may be as it says in the song: "Unto the borders of the land 'Twas he who saw it all." And let him administer the abundance of the years of plenty with a strictness never seen before, that the King may have shade to sit in during the time of dearth.' Such are my words which I shall be saying to myself in my pit; for truly to utter them here before the gods would be the grossest indiscretion. Will Pharaoh now dismiss his servant from his sight, that he may go out of the sun into his shadow?"

Joseph made a turn towards the bee-studded hangings and a gesture thitherwards, as though asking if he might pass through. The eyes of the goddess-mother looked sharply at him, and the worldly-wise lines round her mouth deepened to a mocking smile. He saw, but purposely did not look back at her.

"I DON'T BELIEVE IN IT"

"STAY," said Amenhotep. "Wait a little, my friend. You have played very prettily upon this instrument of yours, this pretext that one may speak without speaking, not speak and yet speak withal, while getting a hearing for your thoughts. You have not only put My Majesty in the way of interpreting his own dream, but also you have pleasured me with this novel device of yours. Pharaoh cannot let you go unrewarded, surely you cannot think that. The only question is, how can he reward you? About that My Majesty is not yet clear. For instance, to give you this tortoise-shell lyre, the invention of the lord of mischief, that, I think, would be too little, and surely you think so too. Yet take it at least, for the moment, my friend, take it in your arms, it becomes you there. The god of contrivance gave it to his soothsaying brother; you are a soothsayer too, and full of contrivance into the bargain. But I am thinking of keeping you at my court, if you will stop, and of making some fine title for you, such as First Dream-interpreter of the King, something very imposing, to cover up your real name and make it quite forgot. But what is your real name? Ben-ezne, perhaps, or Nekatiya, I suppose?"

"What I am called," Joseph answered, "I was not called, and neither my mother, the starry virgin, nor my father, the friend of God, called me so. But since my hostile brothers flung me in the pit and I died to my father, being stolen away down here, what I am has taken on another name: it is now Osarsiph."

"Most interesting," pronounced Amenhotep. He had settled back into the cushions of his too-easy-chair, while Joseph, the seafaring man's gift in his arms, stood there before him. "So you think one should not always be called the same, but suit his name to his circumstances, according to what happens to him and how he feels? Mama, what say you to that? I think My Majesty likes it well, for I am always pleased by new views; whereas those who know only outworn ones open their mouths in astonishment, as wide as I do when I yawn at theirs. Pharaoh himself has too long been called by his present name, and for long it has been out of tune with what he is and how he feels. In fact for some time he has cherished the idea of putting aside the old and mistaken name and taking a new and more accurate one. I have never spoken of this to you, Mama, because it would have been awkward for me to tell you just by ourselves. But in the presence of this soothsayer Osarsiph, who himself once had another name, it is a good opportunity to speak. Certainly I will do nothing rash, it will not happen from one day to the next. But happen it must, and soon; for what I am now called becomes daily more a lie and an offence to my Father above. It is a disgrace, in the long run it is not to be borne, that my name contains the name of Amun the throne-robber, who gives out that he consumed Re-Horakhte the Lord of On and the ancestor of the kings of Egypt, and who now reigns as Amun-Re, the god of the Empire. You must understand, Mama, that in the long run it is a sore offence to My Majesty to be named after him, instead of by a name pleasing to Aton; for out of him have I issued, in whom is united what was and what shall be. Lo, Amun's is the present, but the past and future are my Father's, and we two are old and young both, we are of times past and times to come. Pharaoh is a stranger in the world, for he is at home in the early time, when kings raised their arms to Re their father, the time of Hor-em-akhet, the time of the Sphinx. And at home he is in the time that shall come, of which he is the forerunner; when all men shall look up to the sun, the unique god, their gracious father according to the teaching of the son, who knows his precepts, since he came out of him and his blood flows in his veins. Come hither, you!" said he to Joseph. "Come and look!" And he drew the batiste from his thin arm and showed the other the blue veins on the inside of the forearm. "That is the blood of the sun!"

The arm shook visibly, although Amenhotep supported it with the other hand; for the other hand shook too. Joseph looked respectfully at the exhibit and then drew back a little from the royal seat. The goddess-mother said:

"You excite yourself, Meni, and it is not good for Your Majesty's health. You should rest, after the interpretation and all this exchange of views, and take a little time from the time that is given you, to let your decisions ripen, not only concerning measures against what may come, but also about the very serious proposal to change your name, which you seem to be considering; while at the same time you are thinking about a proper reward for this soothsayer. Do go and rest!"

But the King was unwilling. "Mama," he cried, "I do beg you most ardently not to ask that of me, just in the middle of such a promising train! I assure you, My Majesty is perfectly well and feels no trace of fatigue. I am so excited that I feel well, and so well that I feel excited. You talk just like the nurses in my childhood; when I felt my liveliest, then they said: 'You are overtired, Lord of the Two Lands, you must go to bed.' It could only make me savage, I could have kicked with rage. Now I am grown, and I thank you most respectfully for your care of me. But I have the distinct feeling that this present audience can lead to further good and that my decisions can better ripen here than in my bed, and in talk with this skilled soothsayer, to whom I am grateful, if for no other reason, for giving me the opportunity to speak of my intention to take a real name, which contains the name of the unique one, namely Ikhnaton, that my name may be pleasing to my Father. Everything should be called after him and not after Amun; and if the Lady of the Two Lands, who fills the palace with sweetness, the sweet Titi, is soon brought to bed, then the royal infant, whether prince or princess, shall be called Merytaton, that it may be loved by him who is love. No matter if I draw down on my head the anger of the mighty one of Karnak, who will come and make representations and harangue me with threats of the anger of the Ram! Him I can endure — all I can endure for the sake of my love to my Father above."

"Pharaoh," said the mother, "you forget that we are not alone. Matters which need to be dealt with in wisdom and moderation are probably best not discussed in the hearing of a soothsayer from the people."

"Let that be, Mama," replied Amenhotep. "He is in the way of noble lineage, that he has himself given us to understand — the son of a rogue and a lovely one, which is definitely attractive to me; while that he says he was even as a child called the lamb, that also indicates a certain refinement. Children of the lower classes are not given such nicknames. And besides, I get the impression that he is able to understand much, and give answer to much. Above and beyond all this, he loves me and is ready to help me, as he has done already in interpreting the dreams and also by reason of his original view that one should call oneself according to one's own circumstances and feelings. It would all be very fine, if I liked a little better the name by which he chooses to be known. . . . I would not wish to be unfriendly or distress you," he turned to Joseph, "but the kind of name you have taken pains me: Osarsiph, that is a name of the dead, as when we call the dead bull Osar-Hapi; it bears the name of the dead lord, Usir, the frightful, on the judge's throne and with the scale, who is only just but without mercy, and before whose tribunal the terrified soul trembles and shakes. This old creed has nothing in it but fear, it is dead itself, it is an Osar-creed, and my Father's son believes not in it."

"Pharaoh," the mother's voice came again, "I must once more appeal to you and warn you to be cautious and I need not hesitate to do so in the presence of this foreign interpreter, since you grant him such extended audience and take as a sign of his higher origins his mere assertion that as a child he was called the lamb. So he may hear that I warn you to be wise and moderate. It is enough that you go about to decrease the power of Amun and set yourself against his universal rule, in that wherever possible you take from him step by step the unity with Re the horizon-dweller, who is the Aton. Even to do this takes all the shrewdness and policy in the world, and a cool head besides, for heated rashness comes of evil. But let Your Majesty beware of laying hands on the people's belief in Usir, King of the lower regions, to which it clings more obstinately than to any other deity, because all are equal before him, and each one hopes to go in unto him with his name. Bear in mind the prejudice of the many, for what you give to Aton by diminishing Amun, you take away again by offending Usir."

"Ah, I assure you, Mama, the people only imagine that they cling so to Usir," cried Amenhotep. "How could it really cling to a belief that the soul which goes up to the judge's seat must pass through seven times seven regions of terror, inhabited by demons who cross-examine it as it passes in some three hundred and sixty several magic formulas, each harder to remember than the last, yet the poor soul must have them all by heart and be able to repeat each one in the right place, otherwise it does not pass and will be devoured before ever it reaches the judgment seat. And if it does get there, it has every prospect of being devoured if its heart weighs too light in the scale; for then it is delivered over to the monstrous dog of Amente. I ask you, where is there anything in all that to cling to? — it is against all the love and goodness of my Father above. Before Usir of the lower regions all are equal — yes, equal in terror. Whereas before my Father all shall be equal in joy. With Amun and Aton it is the same. Amun too, with the help of Re, will be universal and will unite the world in worship of him. There they are of one mind. But Amun would make the world one in the rigid service of fear, a false and sinister unity, which my Father would not, for he would unite his children in joy and tenderness."

"Meni," said the mother again, in her low voice, "it would be better for you to spare yourself and not speak so much of joy and tenderness. You know from experience that the words are dangerous to you and put you beside yourself."

"I am speaking, Mama, of belief and unbelief," answered Amenhotep; once more he worked himself out of the cushions and stood on his feet. "Of these I speak, and my own good mind tells me that disbelief is almost more important than belief. In belief there must be a sizable element of disbelief; for how can a man believe what is true so long as he also believes what is false? If I want to teach the people what is true, I must first take from them certain beliefs to which they cling. Perhaps that is cruel, but it is the cruelty of love, and my Father in the sky will forgive me. Yes, which is more glorious, belief or disbelief, and which should come before the other? Believing is a great rapture for the soul. But not believing is almost more joyous than belief — I have found it so, My Majesty has experienced it, and I do not believe in the realms of fear and the demons and Usiri with his frightfully named ones and the devourer down there below. I

don't believe in it! Don't believe, don't believe," Pharaoh sang and
trilled, skipping on his misshapen legs, whirling round with arms
outstretched and snapping the fingers of both hands.

After that he was out of breath.

"Why did you give yourself such a name of death?" he asked,
gasping, as he came to a stop beside Joseph. "Even if your father
thinks you are dead, after all you are not."

"I must be silent to him," answered Joseph, "and I vowed myself to
silence with my name. Whoever is thus dedicate and set apart, he is
among the dead. You cannot separate the depths from the holy and
consecrated, they belong together; and just therefore lies upon him
the gleam of light from above. We make offerings to the depths; yet
therein lies the mystery, that in so doing we only rightly make them
to the heights. For God is the whole."

"He is the light and the sweet disk of the sun," said Amenhotep
with emotion, "whose rays embrace the land and bind them in love —
he makes the hands grow faint with love, and only the wicked, whose
fate is directed below, have strong hands. Ah, how much more would
things in the world go by love and goodness if not for this belief in
the lower and in the devourer with the crushing jaws! No one shall
persuade Pharaoh that men would not do much or consider much
pleasing to do if their fate were not directed downwards. You know,
the grandfather of my earthly father, King Akheperure, had very
strong hands and could span a bow which no one else in all the lands
could span. So he went out to slay the kings of Asia and took seven of
them alive. He fastened them to the prow of his ship by the heels —
their hair hung down and they glared straight ahead with their upside-down bloodshot eyes. And that was only the beginning of all that
he did with them, which I will not go into, but he did it. It was the
first story my nurses told me as a child, to instil in me a kingly spirit
— but I started shrieking out of my sleep with what they instilled and
the doctors from the book-house came and instilled an antidote. But
do you suppose Akheperure would have done all that to his foes if
he had not believed in the realms of horror and the spectres and the
frightfully named ones of Usiri and the dog of Amente? Let me tell
you: men are a hopeless lot. They know how to do nothing that
comes from within themselves, not even the very least thing occurs
to them on their own account. They only imitate the gods, and
whatever picture they make of them, that they copy. Purify the godhead and you purify men."

Joseph did not reply to all this until he had looked across to the
mother and read in the eyes she rested on him that a reply from him
would please her.

"Harder than hard," he said then, "it is to reply to Pharaoh, for he is gifted beyond measure, and what he says is true, so that one can only nod and murmur: 'Quite right,' or else keep still and let the echo die of the truth he uttered. Yet we know Pharaoh would not have speech die away and cease at the truth. Rather he desires that it free itself and go on, past the truth and perhaps to further truth. For what is true is not the truth. Truth is endlessly far and all talk is endless too. It is a pilgrimage into the eternal and looses itself without rest, or at most after a brief pause and an impatient 'Right, right,' it moves away from every station of the truth, just as the moon moves away from each of her stations in her eternal wanderings. All of this brings me — whether I will or no, and whether it is fit or unfit in this place — to the grandfather of my earthly father, whom at home we always called by a not quite so earthly name and named him the moon-wanderer, though we knew quite well that actually his name was Abiram, which means high father. He came from Ur in the Chaldees, the land of the great tower. He did not like it there and could not endure it — he could never endure it anywhere and hence the name we gave him."

"You see, Mother," the King broke in, "that my soothsayer has good origins in his way? Not only that he himself was called the lamb, but also he had a great-grandfather to whom they gave a name not of this earth. Mixed races and people from the lower classes do not usually know their great-grandfathers. So he was a seeker after truth, your great-grandfather?"

"So untiring," responded Joseph, "that in the end he discovered God and made a pact with Him that they should be holy the one in the other. But strong he was in other ways too, a strong-handed man; when robber kings came on from the East, burning and plundering, and took away his brother Lot a prisoner, then with swift resolve he went out against them with three hundred and eighteen men and Eliezer, his oldest servant, making three hundred and nineteen, and thrust at them with such force that he drove them beyond Damascus and freed his brother Lot out of their hands."

The mother nodded and Pharaoh cast down his eyes.

"Did he take the field," he asked, "before he had discovered God or afterwards?"

"It was in between," answered Joseph, "while he was working on his task and without loss of power from the combat. What can be done with robber kings that burn and plunder? You cannot give them the peace of God, they are too stupid and bad. You can only bring it to them by first smiting them hip and thigh until they know that the peace of God has strong hands. But you owe it to God that things shall go on earth at least half-way according to His will and not entirely according to the will of burners and plunderers."

"I see," said Amenhotep in boyish annoyance, "if you had been one of my guardians, you too would have told me stories about hair floating upside down in the wind and rolling eyes full of blood."

"Could it come to pass," Joseph inquired as though of himself, "that Pharaoh should err and despite extraordinary gifts and maturity be wrong in his thought? I can scarcely believe it; yet it seems to happen and is a sign that he has his human as well as his godlike side. Those who burdened his young heart with tales of warlike prowess," he went on, always speaking as though to himself, "they, of course, stood for war and lust of the sword for their own sakes. Now your soothsayer here, descended from the moon-wanderer, he would seek to bring to war word of the peace of God; while to peace he would put in a word for courage as a dealer between the spheres and go-between 'twixt above and below. The sword is stupid; yet I would not call meekness wise. Wise is the mediator who counsels courage in order that meekness may not be revealed as stupid in the sight of God and man. Would I might say to Pharaoh this that I think!"

"I have heard," said Amenhotep, "what you have been saying to yourself. It is the same as before: the little trick you have invented, that you may speak aloud to yourself and that no one else has any ears. You are holding the seafaring man's gift in your arms — perhaps the little invention comes to you from it, and the spirit of the mischievous god speaks through your words."

"It may be," responded Joseph. "Pharaoh speaks the word of the hour. It may be, it is possible, we should not quite reject the idea that the quick-witted god is present with us and would make Pharaoh mindful of him and aware that it was he who brought up the dream to him from below to where he sits in his palace. For he is a guide to the world below and, with all his gay spirits, the friend of the moon and the dead. He puts in a friendly word with the upper world for the lower and with the lower world for the upper, he is a gentlemanly go-between 'twixt heaven and earth. Violence and abruptness are hateful to him and better than anyone else he knows that one can be right and yet wrong."

"You are coming back to your uncle," asked Amenhotep, "the wrong right one whose big tears rolled down in the dust while all the world laughed at him? Let that story be. It is amusing but it makes me uneasy. Perhaps it is true that what is funny is always at the same time a little sad, and that we only breathe freely and happily at the pure gold of serious things."

"Pharaoh says it," answered Joseph, "and may he be the right one to say it! Serious and stern is the light and the power which streams up from below into its clarity — power it must surely be and of masculine kind, not mere tenderness; otherwise it is false and premature and tears will follow."

He did not look over at the mother after he spoke — at least not

full in the face. But enough so that he could see whether she nodded
approval. She did not nod, but he thought she looked steadily at him,
which was perhaps even better.

Amenhotep had not been listening. He leaned back in his chair, in
one of those exaggerated attitudes of his, deliberately aimed at the
old style and the rigidity of Amun. One elbow leaned against the
chair-back, his other hand was on his hip, thrust out by the weight
he put on that leg, the other one resting lightly on its toes. He went
back to his own last words.

"I think," he said, "My Majesty said something very good, which
merits attention. I mean about jest and earnest, one oppressing and
the other blessing. The moon mediates between heaven and earth.
True, but the mediation is of the jesting kind, uncanny, ghostly.
Whereas all the beams of my father Aton are golden earnest without
guile, bound up in truth, ending in tender hands, which caress the
creation of the father. God alone is the whole roundness of the sun,
from which the truth pours itself out upon the world, and unfaltering love."

"The whole world hearkens to Pharaoh's words," answered Joseph,
"and no one fails to hear a single one of them when he teaches. But
that may easily happen to others, even when their words should by
chance be just as much worth taking to heart as his. But never will it
happen to the Lord of the Crown. His golden words put me in mind
of one of our stories, namely how Adam and Eve, the first human
beings, were frightened by the approach of the first night. They
feared that the earth would again become void and formless. For it
is the light which divides things and puts each in its place — it creates
space and time, while night brings back disorder again, the chaos and
the void. So the two were terribly frightened when the day died at
the red even and darkness crept up on all sides. They beat their brows.
But God gave them two stones: one of the deepest black, the other
like the shadow of death. He rubbed the two together for them and
lo, fire sprang out, fire from the bosom of the earth, the inmost primeval fire, young as the lightning and older than Re. It fed on dry
leaves and burned on, making night plain for the two."

"Very good, very good indeed!" said the King. "I see that not all
your tales are jests. Pity you do not also speak of that great joy of
the first morning, when God lighted up their whole world anew
and drove away the frightful shapes of darkness; for their delight
must have been very great. Light, light!" he cried. Springing from
his relaxed position, he stood up and began to move to and fro in the
room, now fast, now slowly, now lifting both bebanded arms over his
head, now pressing his two hands to his heart.

"Blessed light, that created for itself the eyes which see it, created sight and thing seen; the becoming-conscious of the world which

knows of itself only through the light, which distinguishes in love. Ah, Mama, and you, dear soothsayer, how glorious above all glory and how unique in the all is Aton my Father, and how my heart beats with fullness of pride because I came forth from him and before all others he gave me to understand his beauty and love! For as he is unique in greatness and goodness, so am I his son unique in love to him, whom he has entrusted with his teaching. When he rises in the eastern horizon of heaven and mounts out of the land of God in the east, glitteringly crowned as king of the gods, then all creatures exult. The apes adore with lifted hands and all wild creatures praise him, running and leaping. For every day is his blessing-time and a feast of joy after the cursing-time of the night, when his face was turned away and the world sunk in self-forgetfulness. It is frightful when the world forgets itself, though it may be well for its refreshment. Men sleep in their chambers, their heads are wrapped up, their nostrils stopped, and none seeth the other, stolen are all the things that are under their heads while they know it not. Every lion cometh forth from his den, all serpents they sting. But thou hast raised them up, their limbs bathed, they take their clothing, their arms uplifted in adoration to thy dawning. Then in all the world they do their work. The barks sail upstream and downstream alike. Every highway is opened because thou hast dawned. The fish in the river leap up before him, and his rays are in the midst of the great sea. Though he is afar, yet his rays are upon the earth as in the sea and fix all creatures with his love. For unless he were so high and far, how should he be over all and everywhere in his world which he has linked and spread out in manifold beauty: the countries of Syria and Nubia and Punt and the land of Egypt; thou hast set a Nile in the heavens that he may fall for them, making floods upon the mountains like the great sea and watering their fields among their towns as he springs for us out of the earth and makes fertile the desert that we may eat. Yes, how manifold, O Lord, are thy works! Thou makest the seasons in order to create all thy works with million shapes, that they live in you and fulfil their life-span, which you give, in cities, towns, and settlements, on highway or on river. Thou settest every man in his place, thou suppliest their necessities. Everyone has his possessions and his days are numbered. Their tongues are divers in speech, their ways are varying, but you embrace them all. Some are brown, others red, others black, and still others like milk and blood. And in all these hues they reveal themselves in you and are your manifestations. They have hooked noses or flat or such as come straight out of the face, they dress in gay colours or white, in wool or linen, according as they know or think; but all that is no reason for them to laugh or to be spiteful, rather only interesting and solely a ground for love and worship. Thou fundamentally good God, how joyful and sound is all

that thou createst and nourishest and what heart-filling delight hast
thou instilled into Pharaoh, thy beloved son who proclaims thee!
Thou hast made the seed in man and giveth life to the son in the
body of the woman, thou soothest him that he may not weep, thou
good nurse and nourisher! Thou makest of what the flies live on and
of the like the fleas, the worm, and the offspring of the worm. It
would be enough for the heart and even well-nigh too much that
the creature is satisfied in his pasture, that trees and plants are in sap
and blossoms spring in praise and thanks, while countless birds flutter
above the marshes. But when I think of the little mouse in its hole
where thou preparest what it needs, there it sits with its beady eyes
and cleans its nose with its paws — then my eyes run over. And I
may not think at all of the little chick that cries in the egg-shell, out
of which it bursts when he has made it ready — then it comes out of
the egg to chirp with all its might and runneth about before Him
upon its two feet with the greatest nimbleness — especially may I
not be mindful of this, else I must dry my face with finest batiste, for
it is flooded with tears of love. — I should like to kiss the Queen," he
suddenly cried, and stood still with his face turned up to the ceiling.
"Let Nefertiti be summoned at once, she who fills the palace with
beauty, the mistress of the lands, my sweet consort!"

ALL TOO BLISSFUL

JACOB's son was almost as weary with standing before Pharaoh as
when he had played dumb waiter for the old pair in the garden-
house. And young Pharaoh, for all his delicacy of feeling for the
gnats, the chicks, the little mouse, and the offspring of the worm,
seemed to have no thought for Joseph's discomfort. His delicacy was
of a regal kind, it had lapses. To neither him nor the mother-goddess
on her high seat did the idea occur — and probably it could not — to
tell him to sit down awhile. His limbs had great longing and there
were many charming little stools in the Cretan loggia to invite him
thereto. It was hard; but when one knows what is involved, one just
takes the hardship for granted and stands firm — and here we have
a good instance of a literally correct usage.

The goddess-widow took it on herself to clap her hands when her
son announced his desire. The chamberlain from the anteroom sidled
sweetly through the bee-curtain. He rolled up his eyes when Tiy
flung at him: "Pharaoh summons the great consort!" and disappeared
again. Amenhotep stood at one of the great bay-windows with his
back to the room and looked out over the gardens, his chest and his
whole body heaving with the violence of the homage he paid to the
sun and its works. His mother was looking towards him with concern. But only a few minutes passed before she appeared whom he

had summoned — she could not have been far away. A little door, invisible among the paintings, opened in the right-hand wall, and two maidservants fell on their faces on the threshold. Between them the Queen of the lands appeared, with swaying tread, faintly smiling, her eyes cast down, the long, lovely neck thrust anxiously out: the bearer of the seed of the sun. She did not speak. Her hair was covered with a blue cap, which hung in a bag behind, elongating the shape of the head; her large, thin, finely turned ears were uncovered. Navel and thighs showed through the ethereal pleatings of her flowing garb, the bosom was covered with a shoulder drapery and a flower-collar glittering with enamel and gems. She moved with hesitant steps towards her young husband, who approached her still panting with access of feeling.

"Here art thou, golden dove, my sweet bed-sister," he said with trembling voice; embraced and kissed her on eyes and mouth, so that the two cobras on their foreheads kissed too. "I had to see thee, if only for a moment to show thee my love — it came over me while talking. Was my summons a burden to thee? Art thou at the moment not suffering from thy present sacred condition? My Majesty does wrong, perhaps, even to ask; for I might thereby rouse and recall thy nausea with my words. You see how the King has understanding of all. I would have been so grateful to the Father if you had today been able to keep our excellent breakfast by you. But no more of that. Here thrones the eternal mother, and this man with the lyre is a foreign magician and soothsayer who has interpreted for me my politically important dream and can tell such amusing tales that I may keep him by me, in a high office at court. He lay in prison, owing to some mistake, such as can sometimes happen. Nefer-em-Wese too, my cup-bearer, was once in prison by mistake, while his companion there, the late chief baker, was guilty. Of two that lie in prison, one always seems to be innocent, and of three, two. This I say as a man. But as god and king, I say that prisons are necessary, notwithstanding. And as man I kiss you, my sacred love, on your eyes, your cheeks and mouth; be not surprised that I do it in the presence not only of the mother but also of the soothsaying stranger, since you know that Pharaoh loves to show himself as he is before men. I think to go even further in this direction. You do not know about that yet, nor does Mama, therefore I take this opportunity to tell you. I am considering a pleasure voyage on the royal barge *Star of the Two Lands*. The populace, urged by curiosity and also partly by my royal command, will follow along the banks in crowds, and there in their sight, my sacred treasure, without having got permission from Amun's first priest beforehand, I will sit with you under the canopy and hold you on my knee and kiss you right soundly and often before all the people. That will annoy him of Karnak, but the people will exult, and it will not only show them our great happiness but also instruct them in the essence, spirit, and goodness of my Father above. I am glad that I have now mentioned this plan of mine. But do not think I sent for you on this account, for I only happened to come on the thought as I was speaking. I called you simply and solely out of sudden unconquerable longing to show you my tenderness, and now I have done so. Go, then, my crowning joy! Pharaoh is overwhelmed with affairs and must take counsel on matters of high import with his dear and eternal little Mama and with this young man, who, you must understand, comes of the stock of the inspired lamb. Go, and take great care of yourself, guarding against all jars to your person. Divert yourself with dancing and song. The babe, whatever it is, shall be called Merytaton, when you are happily brought to bed — that is, if you find it good, and I see you do. You always find everything good that Pharaoh thinks. If only the whole world would think well of what he thinks and teaches, it would be better for it. Adieu, swan's throat, little dawn-cloud, golden-seamed! Adieu and au revoir!"

The Queen swayed away again. Behind her the picture-door closed and became invisible. Amenhotep, embarrassed by his own emotions, turned back to his throne chair.

"Happy lands," said he, "to which such a mistress is vouchsafed, and a Pharaoh whom she makes so happy! Am I right to say that, Mama — do you agree with me, soothsayer? If you stop on at my court as interpreter of the King's dreams, I will marry you off, that is my firm intention. I will myself choose the bride, befitting your office, from the higher circles. You do not know how delightful it is to be married. For My Majesty, as my idea about the pleasure-voyage in public will have shown you, it is the very image and expression of my human side, on which I lean more than I can say. For look, Pharaoh is not proud — and if he is not, then who in all the world should be? But in you, my friend, I feel a sort of pride, with all your charm of manner — I say a sort, for I do not know its cause and can only suspect it has to do with what you told us, that you are in some way set apart and consecrate to silence and the deeps, as though the sacrificial garland lay on your brow, made of an herb called touch-me-not. It was just this that gave me the idea to bestow you in marriage."

"I am in the hand of the highest," answered Joseph. "What he does will be beneficent. Pharaoh knows not how necessary to me was my pride to protect me from evil-doing. I am set apart for God alone, who is the bridegroom of my race and we are the bride. But as it says of the star: 'In the evening a woman, in the morning a man,' so I suppose it is here too, and out of the bride steps forth the wooer."

"Such a double nature may be fitting for the son of the sly one and the lovely one," said the King, with a worldly-wise air. "But now," he added, "let us speak seriously of serious matters. Your God, who and what is He? You have neglected or avoided giving me a clear understanding. The forefather of your father, you say, discovered Him? That sounds as though he had found the true and only God. Is it possible that so remote from me in space and time a man divined that the true and only God is the sun's disk, the creator of sight and seen, my eternal Father above?"

"No, Pharaoh," Joseph answered smiling. "He did not stop at the sun disk. He was a wanderer, and even the sun was but a way-station on his painful wandering. Restless was he and unsatisfied — call it pride if you will; for thereby you seal your censure with the sign of honour and necessity. For it was the pride of the man, that the human being should serve only the Highest. Therefore his thoughts went out beyond the sun."

Amenhotep had flushed. He sat bent forward, his head in the blue wig stretched out on its neck; with the tips of his fingers he squeezed and kneaded his chin.

"Mama, pay attention! By all you hold dear, pay strict attention," he breathed, without turning the fixed gaze of his grey eyes away from Joseph. His suspense was so great that it seemed he would tear away the veil which dimmed them.

"Go on, you!" said he. "Wait! Stop, no, go on! He did not stop? He went out beyond the sun? Speak! Or I will speak myself, though I know not what I should say."

"He made things hard for himself, in his unavoidable pride," Joseph said. "For this he was anointed. He overcame many temptations to worship and adore, for he longed to do so, but to worship the Highest one alone, for only this seemed right to him. Earth, the mother, tempted him; she who preserves life and brings forth fruit. But he saw her neediness, which only heaven can supply, and so he turned his face upwards. Him tempted the turmoil of the clouds, the uproar of the storm, the pelting rain, the blue lightning-flash driving down, the thunder's rattling roar. But he shook his head at their claims, for his soul instructed him they were all of the second rank. They were no better, so his soul spake to him, than he himself — perhaps lesser indeed, although so mighty; and though they were above him it was simply in space, but not in spirit. To pray to them, so he felt, was to pray too near and too low; and better not at all, he said to himself, than too near or low, for that was an abomination."

"Good," said Amenhotep, almost soundlessly, and kneaded his chin. "Good! Wait! No, go on! Mama, pay attention!"

"Yes, how many great manifestations did not tempt my forefather!" Joseph went on. "The whole host of the stars was among them, the shepherd and his sheep. They were indeed far and high, and very great in their courses. But he saw them scattered before the beams of the morning star — and she indeed was surpassing lovely, of two-fold nature and rich in tales, yet weak, too weak for that which she heralded; she paled before it and vanished away — poor morning star!"

"Spare your regrets!" ordered the King. "Here is matter for triumph. For tell me what it was she paled before, and who appeared, whom she had heralded?" he asked, making his voice sound as proud and threatening as it could.

"Of course, the sun," Joseph replied. "What a temptation for him who so longed to worship! Before its cruelty and its benignity all peoples of the earth bowed down. But my ancestor's caution was unlimited, his reservations endless. Peace and satisfaction, he said, are not the point. The all-important thing is to avoid the great peril to the honour of humanity, that man should bow down before a lower than the highest. 'Mighty art thou,' he said to Shamash-Marduk-Bel, 'and mighty is thy power of blessing and cursing. But something there is above thee, in me a worm, and it warns me not to take the witness for that which it witnesses. The greater the witness, the greater the fault in me if I let myself be misled to worship it instead of that to which it bears witness. Godlike is the witness, but yet not God. I too am a witness and a testimony: I and my doing and dreaming, which mount up above the sun towards that to which it more mightily bears witness than even itself, and whose heat is greater than the heat of the sun.' "

"Mother," Amenhotep whispered, without turning his eyes from Joseph, "what did I say? No, no, I did not say it, I only knew it, it was said to me. When of late I had my seizure, and revelation was vouchsafed me for the improvement of the teaching — for it is not complete, never have I asserted that it was complete — then I heard my Father's voice and it spoke to me saying: 'I am the heat of the Aton, which is in Him. But millions of suns could I feed from my fires. Callest thou me Aton, then know that the name itself stands in need of improvement. When you call me so, you are not calling me by my last and final name. For my last name is: the Lord of the Aton.' Thus Pharaoh heard it, the Father's beloved child, and brought it back with him out of his attack. But he kept silent, and even the silence made him forget. Pharaoh has set truth in his heart, for the Father is the truth. But he is responsible for the triumph of the teaching, that all men may receive it; and he is concerned lest the improvement and purification, until at last it consist only of the pure truth, might mean to make it unteachable. This is a sore concern which no one can understand save one on whom as much responsibility rests as on Pharaoh. For others it is easy to say: 'You have not set truth in your heart, but rather the teaching.' Yet the teaching is the sole means of bringing men nearer the truth. It should be im-

proved; but if one improve it to the extent that it becomes unavailable as a medium of truth — I ask the Father and you: will not only
then the reproach be justified that I have shut up the teaching in my
heart to the disadvantage of the truth? Pharaoh shows mankind the
image of the revered Father, made by his artists: the golden disk
from which rays go down upon his creatures, ending in tender hands,
which caress all creation. 'Adore!' he commands. 'This is the Aton,
my Father, whose blood runs in me, who revealed himself to me, but
will be Father to you all, that you may become good and lovely in
him.' And he adds: 'Pardon, dear human beings, that I am so strict
with your thoughts. Gladly would I spare your simplicity. But it
must be. Therefore I say to you: Not the image shall you worship
when you worship, not to it sing your hymns when you sing; but
rather to him whose image it is, you understand, the true disk of the
sun, my Father in the sky, who is the Aton, for the image is not yet
he.' That is hard enough; it is a challenge to men; out of a hundred,
twelve understand it. But if now the teacher says: 'Still another and
further effort must I urge upon you for the sake of truth, however
much it pains me for your simplicity. For the image is but the image
of the image and witness to a witness. Not the actual round sun up
there in the sky are you to think of when you burn incense to his
image and sing his praise — not this, but the Lord of Aton, who is
the heat in it and who guides its course.' That goes too far, it is too
much teaching, and not twelve, not even one understands. Only
Pharaoh himself understands, who is outside of all count, and yet he
is supposed to teach the many. Your forefather, soothsayer, had an
easy task, although he made it hard for himself. He might make it as
hard as he liked, striving after truth for his own sake and the sake
of his pride, for he was only a wanderer. But I am King, and teacher;
I may not think what I cannot teach. Whereas such a one very soon
learns not even to think the unteachable."

Here Tiy, his mother, cleared her throat, rattled her ornaments,
and said, looking ahead of her into space:

"Pharaoh is to be praised when he practises statesmanship in matters of religious belief and spares the simplicity of the many. That is
why I warned him not to wound the popular attachment to Usir,
king of the lower regions. There is no contradiction between knowing
and sparing, in this connection; and the office of teacher need not
darken knowledge. Never have priests taught the multitude all they
themselves know. They have told them what was wholesome, and
wisely left in the realm of the mysteries what was not beneficial.
Thus knowledge and wisdom are together in the world, truth and forbearance. The mother recommends that it so remain."

"Thank you, Mama," said Amenhotep, with a deprecating bow.
"Thank you for the contribution. It is very valuable and will for

eternal ages be held in honour. But we are speaking of two different things. My Majesty speaks of the fetters which the teaching puts upon the thoughts of God; yours refers to priestly statecraft, which divides teaching and knowledge. But Pharaoh would not be arrogant, and there is no greater arrogance than such a division. No, there is no arrogance in the world greater than that of dividing the children of our Father into initiate and uninitiate and teaching double words: all-knowingly for the masses, knowingly in the inner circle. No, we must speak what we know, and witness what we have seen. Pharaoh wants to do nothing but improve the teaching, even though it be made hard for him by the teaching. And still it has been said to me: 'Call me not Aton, for that is in need of improvement. Call me the Lord of the Aton!' But I, through keeping silent, forgot. See now what the Father does for his beloved son! He sends him a messenger and dream-interpreter, who shows him his dreams, dreams from below and dreams from above, dreams important for the realm and for heaven; that he should awake in him what he already knows, and interpret what was already said to him. Yes, how loveth the Father his child the King who came forth out of him, that he sends down a soothsayer to him, to whom from long ages has been handed down the teaching that it profits man to press on towards the last and highest!"

"To my knowledge," Tiy coldly remarked, "your soothsayer came up from below, out of a dungeon, and not from above."

"Ah, in my opinion that is sheer mischief, that he came from below," cried Amenhotep. "And besides, above and below mean not much to the Father, who when he goes down makes the lower the upper, for where he shines, there is the upper world. From which it comes that his messengers interpret dreams from above and below with equal skill. Go on, soothsayer! Did I say stop? If I did, I meant go on! That wanderer out of the East, from whom you spring, did not stop at the sun, but pressed on above it?"

"Yes, in spirit," answered Joseph smiling. "For in the flesh he was but a worm on this earth, weaker than most of those above and below him. And still he refused to bow and to worship, even before one of these phenomena, for they were but witness and work, as he himself was. All being, he said, is a work of the highest, and before the being is the spirit of whom it bears witness. How could I commit so great a folly and burn incense to a witness, be it never so weighty — I, who am consciously a witness, whereas the others simply are and know it not? Is there not something in me of Him, for which all being is but evidence of the being of the Being which is greater than His works and is outside them? It is outside the world, and though it is the compass of the world, yet is the world not its compass. Far is the sun, surely three hundred and sixty thousand miles away, and yet his rays are here. But He who shows the sun the way hither is further than far, yet near in the same measure, nearer than near. Near or far is all the same to Him, for He has no space nor any time; and though the world is in Him, He is not in the world at all, but in heaven."

"Did you hear that, Mama?" asked Amenhotep in a small voice, tears in his eyes. "Did you hear the message which my heavenly Father sends me through this young man, in whom I straightway saw something, as he came in, and who interprets to me my dreams? I will only say that I have not said all that was said to me in my seizure, and, keeping silent, forgot it. But when I heard: 'Call me not Aton, but rather the Lord of the Aton,' then I heard also this: 'Call on me not as "my Father above," for that is of the sun in the sky; it must needs be changed, to say: "My Father *who art in heaven*"!' So heard I and shut it up within me, because I was anxious over the truth for the sake of the teaching. But he whom I took out of the prison, he opens the prison of truth that she may come forth in beauty and light; and teaching and truth shall embrace each other, even as I embrace him."

And with wet eyelashes he worked himself up out of his sunken seat, embraced Joseph, and kissed him.

"Yes, yes!" he cried. He began to hurry once more up and down the Cretan loggia, to the bee-portières, to the windows and back, his hands pressed to his heart. "Yes, yes, who art in heaven, further than far and nearer than near, the Being of beings, that looks not into death, that does not become and die but is, the abiding light, that neither rises nor sets, the unchanging source, out of which stream all life, light, beauty, and truth — that is the Father, so reveals He Himself to Pharaoh His son, who lies in His bosom and to whom He shows all that He has made. For He has made all, and His love is in the world, and the world knows Him not. But Pharaoh is His witness and bears witness to His light and His love, that through Him all men may become blessed and may believe, even though now they still love the darkness more than the light that shines in it. For they understand it not, therefore are their deeds evil. But the son, who came from the Father, will teach it to them. Golden spirit is the light, father-spirit; out of the mother-depths below power strives upward to it, to be purified in its flame and become spirit in the Father. Immaterial is God, like His sunshine, spirit is He, and Pharaoh teaches you to worship Him in spirit and in truth. For the son knoweth the Father as the Father knoweth him, and will royally reward all those who love Him and keep His commandments — he will make them great and gilded at court because they love the Father in the son who came out of Him. For my words are not mine, but the words of my Father who sent me, that all might become one in light and love, even as I and the Father are one. . . ."

He smiled, an all too blissful smile; at the same time grew pale as death; putting his hands on his back, he leaned against the painted wall, closed his eyes, and so remained, upright indeed, but obviously no longer present.

THE WISE AND UNDERSTANDING MAN

TIY, the mother, came down from her chair into the hall and approached the rapt one with short, decided steps. She looked at him a moment, gave him a quick little tap with the back of one finger across his cheek, of which he was obviously unconscious, and turned to Joseph.

"He will exalt you," said she, with her bitter smile. Her pouting mouth and the lines round it were probably incapable, by their shape, of any smile but a bitter one.

Joseph, in some alarm, was looking over at Amenhotep.

"Do not be distressed," she said. "He does not hear us. He is unwell, he has his affliction, but it is not serious. I knew it would end like this when he would keep on talking about joy and tenderness; it always ends the same way, although sometimes it is more severe. When he began on the mice and chickens I was sure how it would turn out, but I was certain when he kissed you. You must take it in the light of his special susceptibility."

"Pharaoh loves to kiss," Joseph remarked.

"Yes, too much," she answered. "I think you are shrewd enough to see that there is danger for a kingdom which supports within it a too powerful god and without it many envious tributaries, who plot revolts. That was why I was willing you should speak to him of the stoutheartedness of your ancestors, who were not debilitated by all their thoughts on God."

"I am no man of war," said Joseph, "nor was my ancestor save under great pressure. My father was a pious dweller in tents and prone to contemplation, and I am his son by his first and true wife. True, among my brethren who sold me are several who are capable of considerable barbarity; the twins were war-heroes — we called them twins, though there is a whole year between them — and Gaddiel, son of one of the concubines, wore more or less harness, at least in my time."

Tiy shook her head.

"You have a way," she said, "of talking about your people — as a mother I should call it spoilt. All in all, you think pretty well of yourself, it seems; you feel you could stand a good deal of promotion?"

"Let me put it like this, great lady," said he, "that none surprises me."

"So much the better for you," she answered. "I told you that he would exalt you, probably quite extravagantly. He does not know it yet, but when he comes to himself he will."

Joseph said: "Pharaoh has exalted me in that he honoured me with this talk about God."

"Rubbish," said she, impatiently. "You put him on to it, you led up to it from the start. You need not play the innocent before me; or pretend to be the lamb they called you who spoiled you when they brought you up. I have a political mind, it is no use to make pious faces to me. 'Sweet sleep' forsooth, and 'mother's milk, warm baths, and swaddling bands'! Stuff and nonsense! I have nothing against politics, on the contrary; and I do not reproach you for making the best of your hour. Your talk of God was a talk of gods as well; and your story not bad at all, the one about the god of mischief and worldly-wise advantage."

"Pardon, great mother," said Joseph, "it was Pharaoh who told that tale."

"Pharaoh is receptive and suggestible," she responded. "What he said, your presence evoked. He felt you, and spoke of the god."

"I was without falseness against him, great Queen," said Joseph. "And I will remain so, whatever he may decide about me. By Pharaoh's life, I will never betray his kiss. It is long since I received the last kiss. That was at Dothan in the vale, my brother Jehudah kissed me before the eyes of the children of Ishmael, my purchasers, to show them how highly he valued the goods. That kiss your dear son has wiped off with his own. But my heart is full of the wish to serve and help him as well as I can and as far as he empowers me to do it."

"Yes, serve and help him," said she, coming quite close with her firm little person and putting her hand on his shoulder. "Do you promise it to his mother? You see the great and high responsibility I have with the child — but you understand. You are painfully subtle; you even spoke of the wrong right one, and — he is so sensitive — he got the point when you suggested that one can be right and yet wrong."

"It was not known or recognized before," answered Joseph. "It is a destiny and a basis for destiny that a man can be right on the way and yet not the right one for the way. Until today there was no such thing; but from now on there will be. Honour is due every new foundation: honour and love, if one is as worthy love as your lovely son!"

From Pharaoh's direction came a sigh; the mother turned toward him. He stirred, blinked his eyes, and stood up straight. Colour came back to his lips and cheeks.

"Decisions," they heard him say, "decisions must be made. My Majesty made it clear that I had no more time and must return at once to my immediate kingly concerns. Pardon my absence," he said with a smile as he let his mother lead him back to his seat and sank into the cushions. "Pardon me, Mama, and you too, dear sooth-sayer. Pharaoh," he added, with a meditative smile, "had no need to excuse himself, for he is untrammelled, and besides, he did not go but was fetched. But he excuses himself all the same, out of ordinary politeness. But now to business. We have time, but we have none to lose. Take your seat, eternal mother, if I may respectfully beg you. It is not proper for you to stand when your son is sitting. Only this young man with the lower-regions name might stand before Pharaoh for a little while longer, during the discussion of matters growing out of my dreams. They came from below too, but out of concern for that which is above; but he seems to me to be blest from below up and from above down. So you are of the opinion, Osarsiph," he asked, "that we must husband the fullness against the ensuing scarcity and collect enormous stores in the barns to be given out in the barren years, in order that the upper should not suffer with the lower?"

"Just so, dear master," answered Joseph. The term was quite foreign to etiquette, and at once brought the bright tears to Pharaoh's eyes. "That is the silent message of the dreams. There cannot be enough barns and granaries; there are many in the land, but yet all too few. New ones must be built everywhere so that their number is like the stars in the skies. And everywhere must officials be appointed to deal with the harvest and collect the taxes — there should be no arbitrary estimate which can always be got round with bribes, but instead there must be a fixed ruling — and heap up grain in Pharaoh's granaries until it is like the sands of the sea; and provision the cities so that food is laid up for distribution in the bad years and the land does not perish of hunger and Amun reap the benefit, who would misinterpret Pharaoh to the people, saying: 'It is the King who is guilty and this the punishment for the new teaching and worship.' I said distribution; but I do not mean it so that the corn should be handed out once and for all, but we should distribute to the poor and the little people and sell to the great and rich. Poor harvests mean a hard time, and when the Nile is low prices are high; the rich shall buy dear and all those shall stoop who still think themselves great as Pharaoh in the land. For only Pharaoh shall be rich in the land of Egypt, and he shall become silver and gold."

"Who shall sell?" cried Amenhotep in alarm. "God's son, the King?"

But Joseph answered: "God forbid! It shall be the wise and understanding man whom Pharaoh must search out among his servants: one filled with the spirit of planning and foresight, master of the survey, who sees all even unto the borders of the land and beyond, because the borders of the land are not his borders. Him let Pharaoh appoint and set him over the land of Egypt with the words: 'Be as myself'; so that he husband the abundance as long as it goes on and feed the dearth when it comes. Let him be as the moon between Pharaoh our lovely sun and the earth below. He shall build the barns, direct the host of officials, and establish the laws governing the collection. He shall investigate and find out where it is to be distributed gratis and where sold, shall arrange that the little people shall eat and listen to Pharaoh's teaching, and shall harass the great in favour of the crown, that Pharaoh become over and over gold and silver."

The goddess-mother laughed a little from her chair.

"You laugh, little Mama," said Amenhotep. "But My Majesty finds really interesting what our foreseer here foresees. Pharaoh looks down from above on these things below, but it interests him mightily to see what the moon brings about on earth in her jesting, spectral way. Tell me more, soothsayer, since we are in council, about this middleman, this blithe ingenious young man, and how he should go to work once I have appointed him."

"I am not Keme's child and not the son of Jeor," answered Joseph; "indeed, I came from abroad. But the garment of my body has long been of Egyptian stuff, for at seventeen I came down here with my guide which God appointed for me, the Midianites, and came to No-Amun, your city. Although I am from afar, I know this and that about the affairs of the land and its history: how everything came about and how the kingdom grew out of the nomes, and out of the old the new, and how remnants of the old still defiantly persist, out of tune with the times. For Pharaoh's fathers, the princes of Weset, who smote the foreign kings and drove them out and made the black earth a royal possession, these had to reward the princes of the nomes and the petty kings who helped them in their campaigns, with gifts of land and lofty titles, so that some of them still call themselves kings next after Pharaoh, sit defiantly on their estates, which are not Pharaoh's, and resist the passage of time. All this being well known to me, I have no trouble in showing how Pharaoh's middleman, the master of the survey and of the prices, shall act and how use the occasion. He will fix the prices for the whole seven years to the proud district princes and surviving so-called kings when they have neither bread nor seed but he has abundance of them. They shall be such a kind of prices that their eyes will run over with tears and they shall be plucked to the last pin-feather; so that their land shall finally fall to the crown as it ought and these stiff-necked kings be turned into tenants."

"Good!" said the Queen-mother energetically in her deep voice.

Pharaoh was much amused.

"What a rascal, your young middleman and moon-magician!" he laughed. "My Majesty would not have thought of it, but he finds it capital. But what shall this man, my regent, do about the temples, which are rich to excess and oppress the land; shall he harass them too and fleece them properly as a rogue should? Above all, I would wish that Amun might be plundered and that my man of business would straightway lay the common taxes on him who has never had to pay!"

"If the man is as extremely sensible as I expect," replied Joseph, "he will spare the temples and leave the gods of Egypt alone during the years of plenty, since it has always been the custom for the gods' property to be left untaxed. Above all, Amun must not be exasperated against the work of provision and not agitate among the people to oppose the storage of supplies, telling them it is directed against the god. When the hard times come, then the temple will have to pay the prices of the master of the prices; that is enough. It will not profit from the success of the crown's enterprise; Pharaoh shall become heavier and more golden than all of them if the middleman even halfway understands his affair."

"Very sensible," nodded the mother-goddess.

"But if I do not deceive myself in the man," went on Joseph, "and why should I since Pharaoh will choose him? — then the man will cast his eye even beyond the borders of the land and see to it that disloyalty is suppressed and the vacillating firmly attached to Pharaoh's throne. When my forefather Abram came down into Egypt with his wife Sarai (which means queen and heroine), when they came down, there was famine at home where they lived and high prices in the lands of the Retenu, Amor and Zahi. But in Egypt there was plenty. And shall it be different now? When the time of the lean kine comes for us here, who says there will not be scarcity up there too? Pharaoh's dreams were so heavy with warning that their meaning might apply to the whole world and would be a thing something like the Flood. Then the peoples would come on pilgrimage down to the land of Egypt to get bread and seed-corn, for Pharaoh has it heaped up in abundance. People will come hither, people from everywhere and from who knows where, whom one had never expected to see here; they will come driven by need and come before the lord of the survey, your business man, and say to him: 'Sell to us, otherwise we are sold and betrayed, for we and our children are dying of hunger and know not how to live longer unless you sell to us out of your substance.' Then will the seller answer them and go about with them according to what sort of people they are. But how he will go about with this and that city king of Syria and Phœnicia, that I can trust myself to prophesy. For I know that neither of them loves Pharaoh his lord as he should, and is unsteady in his loyalty, carrying water on both shoulders and even pretending submission to Pharaoh, but at the same time making eyes at the Hittites and bargaining for his own advantage. Such as these will the overseer make humble when the time comes, I can see that. For not alone silver and wood

will he make them pay for bread and seed-corn; they will be obliged
to deliver up their sons and daughters as payment or as a guarantee
to Egypt if they want to live; thus they will be bound to Pharaoh's
seat, so that one can depend on their loyalty and duty."

Amenhotep bounced for joy on his chair, like a child.

"Little Mama," he cried, "think of Milkili, the King of Ashdod,
who is more than wobbling and so evil-intentioned that he loves not
Pharaoh from his whole heart but even plots treachery and defection — I have had letters to that effect. Everybody wants me to send
troops against Milkili and dye my sword; Horemheb, my first officer,
demands it twice daily. But I will not do it, for the Lord of the Aton
will have no bloodshed. But now you hear how my friend here, the
son of the roguish one, suggests how we can force the loyalty of
such bad kings and bind them firmly to Pharaoh's seat without shedding of blood and just in the way of business. Capital, capital!" he
cried, and struck his hand repeatedly on the arm of his chair. Suddenly he grew serious and got up solemnly from his seat; but then,
as though seized by misgiving, sat down again.

"It is difficult," he said pettishly. "Mama, I do not know how to
arrange about the office and rank which I shall confer on my friend
and middleman, the person who shall concern himself with the collection and distribution of provisions. The government is unfortunately fully staffed, all the best offices are taken. We have the two
viziers, the overseers of the granaries and the King's herds, the chief
scribe of the treasury, and so on. Where is the office for my friend,
to which I can appoint him, with a suitable title?"

"That is the least of your difficulties," returned his mother calmly.
She even turned her head aside as though the matter were indifferent
to her. "It happened often in earlier times, and even in more recent
ones; there is an established tradition, which could be resumed any
day, if it pleased Your Majesty, to set between Pharaoh and the great
officials of the state a go-between and mouthpiece, the head of all
the heads and overseer of all the overseers, through whom the King's
word went forth, the representative of the god. The chief mouthpiece is something quite customary. We need not see difficulties
where there are none," she said, and turned her head even further
away.

"And that is the truth!" Amenhotep cried. "I knew it, I had just
forgotten it, because there had been no occupant of the office for so
long, no moon between the heaven and the earth, and the Viziers
of the North and the South were the highest. Thank you, little
Mama, thank you most warmly and cordially."

And he got up again, very grave and solemn of countenance.

"Come nearer to the King," he said, "Usarsiph, messenger and
friend! Come here beside me, and let me tell you. The good Pharaoh

fears to startle you. I beg you to steel yourself for what Pharaoh has to say. Steel yourself beforehand, even before you have heard my words, so that you will not fall in a faint and feel as though a winged bull were bearing you up to the skies. Have you prepared yourself? Then hear! You are this man! You yourself and no other are he whom I choose and raise to a place here by my side, to be chief overseer over all, into whose hands the highest power is given, that you may husband the plenty and feed the lands in the years of famine. Can you wonder at this, can my decision take you utterly by surprise? You have interpreted me my dreams from below, without cauldron or book, just as I felt one must interpret them, and you did not fall dead afterwards as inspired lambs are wont to do. To me that was a sign that you are set apart to take all the measures which, as you clearly recognize, follow from the interpretation. You have inter- preted to me my dreams from above, precisely according to the truth of which my heart was aware, and have explained to me why my Father said that he did not wish to be called Aton, but the Lord of the Aton, and you have enlightened my soul on the doctrinal dif- ference between 'my Father above' and 'my Father *who is in* heaven.' You are not only a prophet but a rogue as well; you have shown me how by means of the lean years we can fleece the district kings who no longer fit into the picture, and bind the wavering city kings of Syria to Pharaoh's seat. God has told you all this; and because of it no one can be so understanding as you, and there can be no sense in my seeking far and near for another. You shall be over my house, and all my people shall be obedient to your word. Are you very much surprised?"

"I lived long," answered Joseph, "at the side of a man who did not know how to be surprised, for he was steadiness itself. He was my taskmaster in the prison. He taught me that steadiness is nothing but being prepared for everything. So I am not overwhelmingly sur- prised. I am in Pharaoh's hand."

"And in your hands shall be the lands, and you shall be as myself before all the people," said Amenhotep with feeling. "Take this in the first place," said he. With nervous fingers he jerked and pulled a ring over his knuckle and thrust it upon Joseph's hand. It was an oval lapis lazuli of exceptional beauty, in a high setting. It glowed like the sunlit heavens, and the name Aton within the royal cartouche was en- graved on the stone. "That shall be the sign," Meni went on with passion, once more growing quite pale, "of your plenary power and representative status, and whoever sees it shall tremble and know that each word you utter to one of my servants, be he the highest or the lowest, shall be as my own word. Whoever has a request to Pharaoh, he shall come first before you, and your word shall be kept and obeyed because wisdom and reason stand at your side. I am Pharaoh!

I set you over all the land of Egypt, and without your will shall no one stir hand or foot in the two lands. Only by the height of the royal seat shall I be higher than you, and lend you of the loftiness and splendour of my throne. You shall drive in my second chariot, just behind mine, and they shall run alongside and shout: 'Take care, take your heart to you, here is the Father of the Lands!' You shall stand before my throne and have the power of the keys, unlimited. . . . I see you shake your head, little Mama, you turn it away and I hear you murmur something about extravagance. But there can be something splendid about extravagance, and just now Pharaoh is bent on extravagance. You shall have a title and style confirmed to you, lamb of God, such as was never before heard of in Egypt; and in it your death-name shall disappear. We have of course the two viziers; but I will create for you the as yet unknown title of Grand Vizier. But that will not be nearly enough; for you shall be called in addition Friend of the Harvest of God, and Sustainer of Egypt, and Shadow-spender of the King, Father of Pharaoh — and whatever else happens to occur to me, though just now I am so happy and excited that nothing else does. Do not shake your head, Mama, let me this one time have my fun; for I am extravagant on purpose and consciously. It is grand that it will happen as in the foreign song that goes:

> Father Inlil has named his name Lord of the Lands.
> He shall administer all realms over which I hold sway,
> All my obligations shall he take to himself.
>
> . . .
>
> His land shall flourish, he himself shall be in health.
> His word shall stand firm, what he commands shall not
>   be changed,
> Not any god shall alter the word of his mouth.

As it goes in the song and as the foreign hymn says, so shall it be, and it gives me infinite pleasure. Prince of the Interior and Vice-God: so shall you be called at the investiture. We cannot undertake your gilding here, there is no adequate treasure-house out of which I can reward you with gold, with collars and chains. We must go back at once to Weset, it can only be there, at Merimat in the palace, in the great court under the balcony. And a wife must be found for you from the best circles — that is, of course, a whole lot of wives, but first of all the first and true one. For it is settled that I am going to see you married. You will find out what a pleasure that is!" And Amenhotep clapped his hands with the eager unrestraint of a child.

"Eiy!" he called breathlessly to the chamberlain who came crouching forward. "We are leaving. Pharaoh and the whole court are going back to Nowet-Amun today. Make haste, it is a gracious command. Make ready my boat *Star of the Two Lands*, I will travel on it with the eternal mother, the sweet consort, and this elect one, the Adon of my house, who from now on shall be as myself in Egypt. Tell it to the rest. There will be a tremendous gilding!"

The hunchback had of course been close to the portières the whole time, he had listened with all his might, but he had not trusted his ears. Now he was forced to believe; and we can imagine how he fawned like a kitten and bridled and kissed his fingertips.

Chapter IV

THE TIME OF ENFRANCHISEMENT

SEVEN OR FIVE

It is well that this conversation between Pharaoh and Joseph — which led to the lifting up of the departed one, so that he was made great in the West — this famous and yet almost unknown conversation which the great mother, who was present, not unaptly called a conversation of gods about God, has now been re-established from beginning to end in all its turnings, windings, and conversational episodes. Well that it has been set down with exactitude once and for all, so that everyone can follow the course which in its time it pursued in reality; so that if some point or other should slip the memory, one need only turn back and read. The summary nature of the tradition up till now almost makes it, however venerable, unconvincing. For instance upon Joseph's interpretation and his advice to the King to look about for a wise and knowledgeable and forethoughted man, Pharaoh straight-way answers: "Nobody is so knowledgeable and wise as you. I will set you over all Egypt." And overwhelms him on the spot with the most extravagant honours and dignities. There is too much abridge-ment and condensation about this, it is too dry, it is a drawn and salted and embalmed remnant of the truth, not truth's living lineaments. Pharaoh's inordinate enthusiasm and favour seem to lack foundation and motivation. Long ago when, overcoming the shrinking of our flesh, we pulled ourselves together for the trip down through millen-nial abysses, down to the regions below, to the field and the fountain where Joseph was standing; even so long ago what we were actually after was to listen to that very conversation and to bring it back with us in all its members as it really came to pass and took place at On in Lower Egypt.

Of course, there is really nothing against condensation in itself. It is useful and even necessary. In the long run it is quite impossible to narrate life just as it flows. What would it lead to? Into the infinite. It would be beyond human powers. Whoever got such an idea fixed in his head would not only never finish, he would be suffocated at the outset. Entangled in a web of delusory exactitude, a madness of detail. No, excision must play its part at the beautiful feast of narration and recreation; it has an important and indispensable role. Here, then, the art will be judiciously practised, to the end of getting finally quit of a preoccupation which, though after all it has a distant kinship with the attempt to drink the sea dry, must not be driven to the extreme and utter folly of actually and literally doing so.

What would have become of us, for instance, when Jacob was serving with the devil Laban, seven and thirteen and five — in short, twenty-five years, of which every tiniest time element was full of a life-in-itself, quite worth telling? And what would become of us now without that reasonable principle, when our little bark, driven by the measuredly moving stream of narration, hovers again on the brink of a time-cataract of seven and seven prophesied years? Well, to begin with, and just among ourselves: in these fourteen years things were neither quite so definitely good nor so definitely bad as the prophecy would have them. It was fulfilled, no doubt about that. But fulfilled as life fulfils, imprecisely. For life and reality always assert a certain independence, sometimes on such a scale as to blur the prophecy out of all recognition. Of course, life is bound to the prophecy; but within those limits it moves so freely that one almost has one's choice as to whether the prophecy has been fulfilled or not. In our present case we are dealing with a time and a people animated by the best will in the world to believe in the fulfilment, however inexact. For the sake of the prophecy they are willing to agree that two and two make five — if the phrase may be used in a context where not five but an even higher odd number, namely seven, is in question. Probably this would constitute no great difficulty, five being almost as respectable a number as seven; and surely no reasonable man would insist that five instead of seven could constitute an inexactitude.

In fact and in reality the prophesied seven looked rather more like five. Life, being living, put no clear or absolute emphasis on either number. The fat and the lean years did not come up out of the womb of time to balance each other so unequivocally as in the dream. The fat and lean years that came were like life in not being entirely fat or entirely lean. Among the fat ones were one or two which might have been described as certainly not lean, but to a critical eye as certainly no more than very moderately fat. The lean ones were all lean enough, at least five of them, if not seven; but among them there may have been a couple which did not reach the last extreme of exiguity and even half-way approached the middling. Indeed, if the prophecy had not existed they might not have been recognized as years of famine at all. As it was, they were blithely reckoned in along with the others.

Does all this detract from the fulfilment of the prophecy? Of course not. Its fulfilment is incontestable, for we have the fact — the facts of our tale, of which our tale consists, without which it would not be in the world and without which, after the snatching away and the lifting up, the making to come after could not have happened. Certainly things were fat and lean enough in the land of Egypt and adjacent regions, years-long fat and years-long more or less lean, and Joseph had plenty of chance to husband the plenty and distribute the crying lack, and like Utnapishtim-Atrachasis, like Noah the exceeding wise one, to prove himself a man of prudence and foresight, whose ark rocks safe on the flood. In loyal service to the highest he did this as his minister, and by his dealings he gilded Pharaoh over and over again.

THE GILDING

BUT for the present it was himself who was gilded; for to "become a man of gold" was the phrase the children of Egypt used for what now happened to him when by Pharaoh's gracious command — together with this god, the Queen-mother, the sweet consort, and the princesses Nezemmut and Baketaton — he had made the journey upstream on the royal bark *Star of the Two Lands* back to Weset, amid the plaudits of the crowded shores. There with the sun-family he made his entry into the palace of the west, Merimat, set in its gardens and with the lake of its gardens, at the foot of the high-coloured desert hills. There he received spacious quarters, servants, raiment, and everything for his comfort and pleasure and as early as the second day the state function of the investiture and gilding was held, beginning with the ceremonial progress by the court when the purchased slave did actually drive in Pharaoh's second car directly behind the monarch and surrounded by his Syrian and Nubian bodyguard and fan-bearers, separated from the car of the god only by a troop of runners who cried: "Abrekh!" and "Take care!" and "Grand Vizier!" and "Behold the father of the land!" By this means it was made known to the populace what was going on and who that was in the second car. At least they saw and understood that Pharaoh had made someone very great, for which he must have had his own reasons, even if only it was his gracious will and whim, that being quite reason enough. Moreover, since the idea of a dawning of a new age and great improvement in all things was somehow always bound up with such an investiture and lifting up, Weset's people exulted greatly on the house-tops and hopped on one leg along the avenues. They shouted: "Pharaoh! Pharaoh!" and "Neb-nef-nezem!" and "Great is Aton!" And you might even distinguish this name pronounced with a softer sound: "Adon! Adon!" doubtless referring to Joseph. For it had probably leaked out that he was an Asiatic, and it seemed proper — particularly to the women — to hail him by the name of the Syrian "Lord" and bridegroom, not least because he whom they thus distinguished was so very young and handsome. It should be added here that among all his titles it was this name which stuck. And in all the land of Egypt he was called Adon all his life, in speaking both to and of him.

After this fine procession they were all ferried across the river to the west bank and back to the palace, where there was now to take place the ceremony of the gilding, always wonderful and this time simply irresistible to the eye and the heart. Its course was as follows: Pharaoh, and She-who-filled-the-palace-with-love, Nefernefruaton the Queen, showed themselves at the so-called audience-window, actually not a window but a sort of balcony giving on an inner court of the palace, a pillared terrace in front of the great reception hall. It was magnificently constructed of malachite and azure and adorned with bronze uræi. But in front of this was still another little structure supported on enchantingly garlanded lotus columns. Its broad balustrade was covered with gay cushions, and on these Their Majesties leaned to fling down the gold presents of every shape and sort, handed them by officers of the treasure-house, upon the lucky man standing below on the terrace. The present recipient, of course, was no other than Joseph the son of Jacob. The scene and all that went with it were never forgotten by those who once saw it. Everything swam in a sea of colour and pomp, of extravagant favour and fervid ecstasy. The splendid fretwork of the architecture, the banners flapping in the breeze, under a sunny sky, from the gay gilded and painted wooden columns; the blue and red whisks and fans of the ranking retainers who filled the court, dressed in flowing gala aprons, bowing and scraping, cheering and paying homage; women striking tambourines; boys with the youth-lock told off to jump for joy without stopping; the hosts of scribes in their customary obsequious posture, writing down with their reeds everything that happened; the view through three wide-open gates into the outer court, full of vehicles whose prancing horses carried tall coloured plumes on their heads and behind them the drivers, facing the scene with them, bowing low and lifting their arms; looking in on all this from outside the red and yellow mountains of Thebes, dark blue and violet in their shadowy depths; and on the splendid ceremonial estrade the god-like pair, fragile and smiling in their languid elegance, wearing their high caplike crowns with the drapery protecting the back of their necks: uninterruptedly, with obvious enjoyment tossing out of an inexhaustible store the shower and dower of valuables on the favoured one below, strings of gold beads, gold in the shape of lions, gold arm-bands, gold daggers, gold fillets, collars, sceptres, vases, hatchets, all out of fine gold — the recipient of course could not catch them all, so he had two slaves to heap up in front of him on the ground a veritable golden hoard, glittering in the sunshine amid the onlookers' admiring cries — yes, this was certainly, take it all in all, the prettiest scene imaginable; and were it not for the inexorable laws of abridgement and condensation it would be described here in much greater detail.

Jacob in his time had amassed treasure during his life with Laban the devil in the land of no return. On this day his darling did so too, in the merry land of the dead into which he had died and been sold. For certainly all that gold exists only in the lower world. Here in this very spot and space of time he became a well-to-do man simply by dint of the gold of favour. We know that foreign kings, trading with Pharaoh for gold, were wont to say that in Egypt that metal was no more precious than the dust in the streets. But it is an economic error to think that gold decreases in value the more there is of it.

Yes, that was a red-letter day for the snatched-away and set-apart one, a day full of worldly blessing. One could wish that Jacob the father might have beheld it, feeling as he gazed a mixture of pride and dismay in which the first would have outweighed the second. Joseph did wish it; and later he said: "Tell the father of all my glory in Egypt!" He had had a letter from Pharaoh that day, not written by the King himself, of course, but by the "actual scribe," his secretary, by Pharaoh's order. It was somewhat stiff, but as a calligraphic production quite delightful, and in its content most gracious. It said:

"Command of the King to Osarsiph, the overseer of that which the heavens give, the earth produces, and the Nile brings forth, superintendent of all things in the whole land and actual administrator of works. My Majesty has heard with pleasure the words which a few days before this, in the conversation which the King was pleased to hold with you at On in Lower Egypt, you spoke about heavenly and earthly things. On that happy day you greatly rejoiced the heart of Nefer-Kheperu-Re with that which he really loves. My Majesty heard these words from you with extraordinary pleasure, in that you linked the heavenly with the earthly and through your concern for the one at the same time showed great concern for the other, and also contributed to the teaching of my Father who is in heaven. Truly you know how to say what pleases My Majesty extraordinarily, and what you say makes my heart to laugh. My Majesty also knows that you rejoice to say what My Majesty likes to hear. O Osarsiph, I say to you times without end: Beloved of his lord! Rewarded of his lord! Favourite and ordained of his lord! Truly the Lord of Aton loves me, since he has given you to me! As true as Nefer-Kheperu-Re lives eternal, whenever you utter a wish, be it orally or in writing to My Majesty, My Majesty will straightway see it granted."

And in anticipation of such a wish, in Egyptian thought the most pressing concern of all, the letter ended by saying that Pharaoh had given orders for the immediate excavation, construction, and decoration of an eternal dwelling, in other words a tomb for Joseph in the western hills.

After the exalted one had read this paper, there took place before the assembled court, in the great columned hall behind the balcony of audience, the great ceremony of the investiture; at which Pharaoh, besides the signet ring already given and all the gold showered upon him, hung a particularly heavy gold necklace of favour round Joseph's neck over his immaculate court garment which of course was not made of silk as we in our ignorance might think, but of the finest royal linen. The Vizier of the South read the letters patent which Pharaoh had conferred, and the style and titles under which henceforth Joseph's death-name should be hidden. Most of these we already know from Pharaoh's own lips and from the formal letter with its official superscription: "Administrator of what the heavens give," and so forth. The most impressive were probably "the King's shadow-dispenser," "friend of the harvest of God," "nourisher of Egypt" ("Ka-ne-Keme" in the language of the country). "Grand Vizier," although unprecedented, and "universal friend of the King," as distinguished from "unique friend," sounded pale beside them. But it did not stop there, for Pharaoh was bent on extravagance. Joseph was called "Adon of the royal house," and "Adon over all Egypt." He was called "chief mouthpiece" and "prince of mediation," "increaser of the teaching," "good shepherd of the people," "double of the King," "vice-Horus." There had not been such a thing before, the future has never repeated it, and probably it could only happen under the dominion of a young king prone to impulsiveness and bursts of extravagant resolve. There was another title still, but that was more like a personal name and intended not so much to cover as to replace Joseph's own. Posterity has speculated much about it, and even the most respectable tradition gives an inadequate or misleading interpretation. It is said that Pharaoh called Joseph his "Privy Counsellor." That is an uninformed version. In our script the name would have appeared as Dje-p-nut-ef-onch, which the glib-lipped children of Egypt pronounced Dgepnuteefonech, with the palatal *ch* on the end. The most prominent part of the combination is *onch* or *onech*, the sign for which in picture-writing is (☥), which means life and which the gods held under the noses of men, especially their sons the kings, that they might have breath. The name, then, which was added to Joseph's many titles, was a name of life. It meant: "The god" (Aton, one did not need to specify) "says: Life be with thee!" But even that was not its whole meaning. It meant, for every ear that heard it, not only "Live thou thyself," but also "Be a life-bringer, spread life, give living-food to the many!" In a word, it was a name that meant satisfaction, sufficiency; and in that character above all had Joseph been exalted. All his titles and styles, in so far as they did not refer to his personal relation to Pharaoh, contained in some form or other this idea of the preservation of life, the feeding of the country; and all of them, including this excellent and much disputed one, could be comprehended in a single epithet: the Provider.

THE SUNKEN TREASURE

WHEN Jacob's son had had these strings of titles hung around his neck he was overwhelmed with congratulations. I leave to your imagination the honeyed homage and adulation that followed. Human beings mostly have an itch to accept the arbitrary caprice, the incomprehensible election, the tremendous "I favour whom I favour," going beyond all possible calculation, even disarming envy itself and imparting a kind of sincerity to the words of the veriest toady. Nobody could really understand why Pharaoh was thus exalting this still youthful stranger, but everybody blissfully gave up trying. True, the art of soothsaying was held in honour; it was a partial explanation that Joseph had chanced to distinguish himself in this field and had come off better than the very best domestic product. Moreover Pharaoh's weakness for those that "heard his words" was well known; those, that is, who entered into his theological ideas and realized that interest in them, whether real or assumed, was rewarded by the tenderest gratitude. Here, too, this extraordinary chap both seemed favoured by fortune and also apparently had some inherited talent for the sort of thing Pharaoh loved. In any case, it was clear that in dealing with their lord he had kept his wits about him; with the result that he had been whisked upstairs and now ranked high above them all. They bowed before his successful cunning no less than before the royal will. They bowed and scraped with a vengeance, they kotowed and kissed hands for all they were worth. One man among the unique friends of the King, who fancied himself as a writer, had even composed a panegyric in Joseph's honour and he sang it accompanied by soft chords on the harp. It went like this:

> Thou livest, thou art hale, thou art sound.
> Thou art not poor, thou art not wretched.
> Thou abidest like the hours.
> Thy plans abide, thy life is long.
> Thy speech is choice.
> Thine eye sees what is good.
> Thou hearest what is pleasing.
> Thou seest good, thou hearest pleasantness.
> Thou shalt be placed among the counsellors.
> Thou standest firm, thy foe falls down.
> Who speaks against thee is no more.

Pretty mediocre. But for something written by one of themselves the court found it capital.

Joseph took all this as one whom no preferment surprises: gravely, courteously — though at times, owing to the distraction of his thoughts, the situation verged on the painful. For he was distraught, his mind was not here in Pharaoh's hall. It was in a house of hair on a far hill; or in the grove of the Lord near by, with his own little brother from the true mother. To that little lad with the helmet-like hair he was telling his dreams. Or he sat beneath the awning on the harvest field with companions to whom likewise he related his dream; or at Dothan in the vale by a certain well, whither he had come by no gentle means. And thus preoccupied he almost failed to acknowledge the salutation of a certain courtier to whom such neglect would have been most painful.

In other words, among the troop of gratulants was Nefer-em-Wese, who had once been called just the opposite, the Master of the Vine. We can feel the fat man's bewilderment and dismay at the tricks life plays, as he waited to congratulate, under such undreamed-of, such incredibly altered circumstances, his young steward of earlier and evil days. He might hope that the new favourite was friendly disposed and would not "speak against him," since to him, Nefer, he owed his summons and his great opportunity. But on the other hand the fat man guiltily realized that he had done nothing until the very eve of the prophesying to call attention to Joseph and then only because the occasion had so to speak hit him in the eye. He thought that perhaps Joseph cared as little as himself to be reminded of the prison; so he confined himself to the cautious familiarity of winking one eye, which might mean anything; and had the gratification of seeing Adon wink back.

Here and now may be the right time to speak of another possible — and how pregnant — meeting of old friends, and to justify a silence which has not always been preserved by those who have concerned themselves with Joseph's history. I refer to Potiphar or Potiphera, more correctly Petepre, the great eunuch, Joseph's former owner, master and judge, who with such good will threw him into prison. Was he too present at the gilding and the reception and did he too pay Joseph homage at court — thus expressing, perhaps, the respect of a man incapable of a certain thing but knowing how to value it, for another man who was capable of it yet also capable of renouncing it? To describe such a meeting is alluring indeed — but alas, nothing of the sort took place. The painfully beautiful motif of reunion plays a triumphant role in our present tale; we shall hear much that is undreamed of, much that is moving on this very theme. But in this place there is only silence and the silence of our accepted version at this point in the story of the sun chamberlain and particularly of his honorary wife, the pathetic Mut-em-inet — this silence is not simply omission unless negation can be regarded in that light: the express statement that something did *not* happen; in other words, that Joseph, after his departure out of the courtier's house, never again met either its master or its mistress.

The people, and to please them the poets, an all too easy-going breed, have spun out in a variety of ways this tale of Joseph and Potiphar's wife, which was only an episode, if an important one, in the life of Jacob's son. Any possibility of more to follow was, of course, completely excluded by the final catastrophe. But they have written sentimental continuations and given it a predominant place within the Joseph story. In their hands it becomes a sugary romance with a proper happy ending. According to these poetasters, the temptress — who goes by the name of Zuleika, a fact at which we can only shrug our shoulders — after she had got Joseph into prison, withdrew full of remorse into a "hut" and there lived only for the expiation of her sins. Meanwhile through the death of her husband she became a widow. But when Yussuf (meaning Joseph) was about to be freed out of the prison, he had refused to have his "chains" removed until the female aristocracy of the country had come before Pharaoh's throne and borne witness to his innocence. Accordingly the entire nobility of the sex had come before the King and with one voice the whole lovely bevy had announced that Joseph was the prince and pattern of purity, the very freshest ornament in her crown. After which Zuleika took the floor and made public confession that she alone had been the offender, and he an angel. The shameful crime was hers, she frankly avowed it; but now she was purified and gladly bore the shame and disgrace. Even after Joseph's elevation she continued to do penance, growing old and grey in the process. Only on the festal day when Father Jacob made his alleged triumphal entry into Egypt — and thus at a time when Joseph was actually the father of two sons — did the pair meet again. Joseph had forgiven the old woman, and as a reward heaven had restored all her former seductive beauty; whereupon Joseph had most romantically married her, and thus, after all these tribulations, her old wish came true, and they "put their heads and feet together."

All that is just Persian musk and attar of roses. It has nothing whatever to do with the facts. In the first place, Potiphar did not die so early. Why should the man have died before his time, whose peculiar constitution saved him from using up his powers, who lived entirely for his own inner satisfactions and often went bird-shooting to freshen himself up? The silence of history upon his fate after the great day of the house judgment certainly indicates his disappearance from the scene — but why draw the conclusion that he died? We must remember that while Joseph was in prison, there had been a change of rulers, and on such occasions it is the rule that the court or some part of it changes too. We know that Petepre had had his troubles as nominal head of troops without any real authority; now, after the burial of Nebmare the magnificent he withdrew into private life, with the title and rank of unique friend. He went no more to court, needed to do so no longer in any case; and on the day of Joseph's gilding he must have refrained, obviously out of the sense of delicacy that was so strong in him. Afterwards they never did meet; the reason being, in part at least, that as master and overseer of the department of supplies Joseph, as we shall see, had his residence not at Thebes but at Memphis. Potiphar's tact was probably responsible for the rest. If, in the course of years, a chance encounter did take place, on one or other ceremonial occasion, we may be sure it went off without the flicker of an eyelash, with perfect discretion and the most deliberate ignoring of the past on both sides. It is just this situation that is reflected in the silence of the authorized tradition.

The same thing applies to Mut-em-enet, and on equally good grounds. Joseph did not see her again. That is quite clear; but just as clear is it that she did not withdraw into any penitential hut. Nor did she ever publicly accuse herself of shamelessness — if she had it would have been a lie. This great lady, the instrument of Joseph's trial, which he passed by no means brilliantly, but still passed; after the shipwreck of that desperate attempt to escape into the human from her honorary existence, she was forced back finally and for ever into the form of life which before her affliction had been the normal and familiar one to her. Indeed, she now practised it with more pride and concentration than ever. By reason of the surpassing wisdom Potiphar had shown at the time of the catastrophe, their relations had gained in warmth rather than the reverse. He had given judgment like a god, elevated above and beyond the frailties of the human heart; she was grateful to him, and from that day onwards was a blameless and devoted wife. She did not curse the beloved for the agony that he had brought upon her or she had brought upon herself. No, the agonies of love are set apart; no one has ever repented having suffered them. "Thou hast made rich my life — it burgeons" — so had Eni spoken in the midst of her travail; it is clear that love has its own quality of torment, not always incompatible with heartfelt gratitude. At least, she had lived and loved. Unhappily, of course; but is there really such a thing as unhappy love? And shall we not put aside as stupid and officious any pity we may feel for Eni? She asked for none; and she was much too proud to pity herself. Her life had had its flowering, the renunciation was stern and final. The lines of her body, for a time those of a witch for love, quickly recovered their normal state. That was no longer the swanlike beauty they had owned in youth; it was rather an expression of the nunlike in her nature. Yes, Mut-em-

inet from now on was a cool moon-nun, chaste-bosomed, irreproach-
ably elegant, and — it must be added — extremely bigoted. We all
remember how in the season of her painful blooming she had burned
incense with the beloved before the world-wide, omni-friendly
Atum-Re of On, Lord of the Wide Horizon, and prayed that he
would smile upon her passion. That was all over. Her own horizon
had closed round her again, and narrow, rigid, and devout it was. Her
whole devotion now went to him rich in bulls of Ipet-Isowet, and
to his conservative sun-sense; more than ever she lent her ear to the
spiritual counsel of his head baldpate the great Beknechons, who
hated all change and frowned on all speculation. Thus she was the
more estranged from the court of Amenhotep IV, where a tender,
all-embracing, ecstatic cult had begun to be the mode. In Mut-em-
enet's eyes it had nothing whatever to do with religion. She was all
for the sacred static, the eternal equilibrium of the scales, the stony
stare into for-ever-and-ever; and she celebrated it when in her tight-
skirted Hathor dress she rattled her clappers before Amun in measured dance-step, and from her shrunken bosom gave out her still admired voice to swell the choir of her noble sisterhood. And yet at
the bottom of her soul there abode a treasure of which she was secretly prouder than of all her religious or worldly honours and,
whether confessedly or not, would never have surrendered. A treasure
buried very deep; yet ever it sent a warm glow upwards into the grey
daylight of her resigned state. Of course the chill knowledge of defeat
was there present too, in slight measure; but weak compared to the
warmth from below, which imparted to her worldly and religious
pride an indispensable element of the human — the pride of life. It was
a memory — not so much of him who, as she had heard, was now become lord over all Egypt. He was an instrument — as she, Mut-em-
inet, had been an instrument. Almost independent of him was her
sense of having justified her own existence, her secret knowledge that
she had once blossomed and burned, once suffered and loved.

LORD OVER EGYPT

LORD over Egypt: I use the phrase in the spirit of a convention, which
could never go far enough in deification to satisfy itself; and in the
sense of that beautiful extravagance which Pharaoh defended in
favour of the interpreter of his dreams. However, it is not recklessly
or fancifully used in this place, but rather with a full sense of loyalty
to truth. For here in this account I am not drawing a long bow but
merely telling what happened; and these are two very different
things, whichever one you may happen to prefer. Exaggeration does,
of course, get a more striking temporary effect; but surely a critical
and considered narrative is of more real profit to the listener.

Joseph became a very great lord at court and in the country, no question of that; and the confidential relations between him and the monarch after the talk in the Cretan garden room, his position as a favourite, left the limitations to his authority somewhat vague. But he was never actually lord over Egypt, or as saga and song sometimes express it, Regent of the Lands. His elevation, which was fabulous enough, and his inordinate row of titles could not alter the fact that the administration of the country whither he had been snatched remained in the hands of the crown officials, some of whom had held office under King Neb-ma-re. It would be excessive to suppose that the administration of justice, for instance, came under the authority of Jacob's son, which from time immemorial had been the business of the high judge and vizier and now of the two viziers. The same is true of the field of foreign policy, which might indeed have had better results if Joseph had taken it over than those which history records. We must not forget that at bottom he was not interested in the glory of the kingdom, however much he had become Egyptian in his outward walks and ways. And that whatever energetic benevolence he displayed to the inhabitants, however wisely he served the public good, his inward eye ever remained directed upon the personally spiritual, the private which was yet of such world-shaking significance; on the furtherance, in short, of plans and purposes which had little to do with Mizraim's weal or woe. We may be certain that he had at once brought Pharaoh's dreams and what they foretold into relation with his own plans and purposes. Certainly he made them fit into his ideas about expecting and preparing the way; in fact, we cannot deny that his attitude before Pharaoh's throne was a thought too eager, almost enough so to cool the sympathy which we would wish to preserve for Rachel's child, if we did not keep it in mind that Joseph regarded it as his duty to further such plans and to be as helpful as he possibly could to God in carrying them out.

Well, whatever the interpretation in fact of all his string of titles, he was duly installed as minister of agriculture and supplies; and in this capacity he carried through important reforms, among them the ground-rent law which has particularly impressed itself on history. But he never overstepped the limit of his field, however likely it is that the affairs of the treasury and the administration of the granaries were too closely connected with his own operations for his authority not to have reached out into them; for all that, designations like Lord over the Land of Egypt and Regent of the Lands remained fanciful ornamentations upon the actual situation. And something else must be taken into account too. Under the conditions that obtained during the first and decisive ten to fourteen years of his tenure of office — conditions in anticipation of which he had been installed — the importance of his particular responsibilities increased so extraor-

dinarily as to put all the others in the shade. The famine which five
to seven — more likely five — years after his elevation broke over
Egypt and the neighbouring provinces made the man who had foreseen it, and knew how to help people through it, easily the most
important figure in the kingdom, and his activities of more living
importance than any other's. It may well be a fact that judgment, if
it is fundamental enough, leads back to a recognition of the soundness of the popular verdict; this being the case, we will say no more
than that Joseph's position, at least for a period of years, was equal in
fact to that of a lord over the land of Egypt, without whose voice no
one could stir hand or foot in the two lands.

For the present, immediately after his investiture he undertook by
boat and car a journey of inspection through the country, accompanied by a staff of secretaries chosen by himself, mostly young men
not yet fossilized by the jog-trot of office. He did this to acquire first-
hand knowledge of the black earth and, before he took any concrete
measures, to make himself in actual fact master of the survey. The
conditions of property were peculiarly vague and undefined. Theoretically, the soil like everything else belonged to Pharaoh.
The lands, including the conquered or tributary provinces as far as the
"wretched land of Nubia" and the borders of Mitanniland were Pharaoh's private property. But the actual state domains, the "estates of
Pharaoh" as special crown lands, were distinct from the estates which
earlier kings had presented to their great men, as well as from the
property of small nobles and peasants which passed as personal property of their proprietors, although, to be exact, the situation was
more in the nature of leasehold and rental, while preserving the right
of inheritance. The only exceptions were the temple lands, especially
the acres of Amun, which were all freehold and tax-free; and those
remnants of an older structure made up of special immunities, pro-
prietary rights of single district princes who were still powerful
and behaved as though they were independent; inherited estates
which stood out here and there all through the kingdom like islands
of an obsolete feudalism, and like the acres of the church expected to
be considered the unqualified property of their owners. But whereas
those latter were on principle left in peace by Joseph's administration,
he went after the obdurate barons tooth and nail, from the very beginning; he included their estates without more ado in his system
of taxation and reservation and in time arrived at simple expropria-
tion in favour of the crown. It is not correct to say that the peculiar
agrarian constitution of the so-called new kingdom, a phenomenon
so striking to other peoples — namely, that in the lands of the Nile all
the soil except the properties of the priesthoods belonged to the King
— was created by the measures taken by Jacob's son. For what he did
only completed a process well on the way, by defining, regularizing,

and legalizing, so that they became clear to the people, conditions which had existed before his time.

His travels did not extend to the Negro lands or to the districts of Syria and Canaan, as he sent commissioners into these regions instead; even so, his tour of inspection took between two and three times seventeen days, there was so much to inspect and have recorded. Then he went back to the capital, where he established himself with a staff in a government building on the Street of the Son and from there, well before the harvest, issued in Pharaoh's name the famous land law which was immediately proclaimed throughout the country. Universally and without respect to person or crop failure it fixed the produce tax at one fifth, to be delivered into the royal storehouses punctually and without notice — or if with notice certainly in peremptory terms. At the same time the children of Egypt could see that all over the country, in the cities large and small and the regions roundabout, these storehouses were enlarged and increased in number by the labours of a large force of workmen. Certainly it looked as though there were more than were needed, because at first, of course, many of them stood empty. Yet more and more were built, for the undue number, so it was said, was reckoned on the abundance which had been foretold by the new Adon of distribution and friend of the harvest of God. Wherever you went you saw the skittle-shaped corn-bins standing in close rows or grouped into squares around courts. They opened on top to receive the corn and had stout doors below to empty it out by and they were built with unusual solidity on terraced platforms of pounded clay to protect them from damp and mice. There were also numerous underground pits for the storage of grain, well lined, with almost invisible entrances, guarded by police.

It is pleasant to report that both measures — the tax law and the construction of the big magazines — enjoyed decided popularity. Taxes there had always been, of course, in many forms. Not for nothing had old Jacob, who had never been in Egypt but had built up an emotional picture of it, been used to talk about the Egyptian house of bondage; even though his mistrust took too little account of the conditions peculiar to the country. The labour of the children of Keme belonged to the King, that was taken for granted; and it was used to erect enormous tombs and incredibly ostentatious public buildings, yes, certainly it was used for that. But it was even more in demand for works of necessity: for all the digging and hoisting operations indispensable to the prosperity of this peculiar and extraordinary land of oases; for keeping the waterways in good condition, digging ditches and canals, manning the sluices, strengthening the dams — all these things were a matter of the general welfare and could not be left to the imperfect intelligence and improbable personal industry of subordinates. Therefore the government kept its children's noses to the grindstone, they had to work for the state. And when they had worked, then they had to pay taxes on what they had done. They had to pay taxes for the canals, lakes, and ditches they used, for the irrigation machinery and sluices which served them, and even for the sycamore trees which grew on their fertilized soil. They paid for house and farmyard and everything that house and farmyard produced. They paid with skins and copper, with wood, rope, paper, linen; and always since time immemorial with corn. But the taxes were levied at the very uneven discretion of the regional administrators and village overseers, according to whether the Nourisher, that is to say Hapi, the river, had been great or small — and that, of course, was sensible enough. But between connivance on the one hand and extortion on the other there was much room for bribery and favouritism and good reason to complain. We may say that from the first day Joseph's administration tightened the reins on the one hand and loosened them on the other. That is, he put all the emphasis on the corn rent and looked very leniently at other debts. The people might keep their linen of the first, second, and third quality, their oil, copper, and paper, if only the corn delivery, the fifth of the bread-grain harvest, was conscientiously handed over. This explicit and universal tax provision could not be regarded as oppressive in a country where the fertility is on the average thirtyfold. Moreover, it had a certain legendary charm and metaphysical appeal, since it had been shrewdly and intentionally taken from the sacred intercalary figure of the five extra days after the three hundred and sixty making up the year. And lastly it pleased the people that Joseph unhesitatingly levied the tax on the still recalcitrant district barons as well and forced them to make up-to-date improvements on their properties for the good of the state. For the reactionary spirit of these men operated to keep their estates in a condition far behind the times: the irrigation system was clumsy and inadequate; they retained it partly out of laziness but mostly out of defiance; and thus the soil yielded less than it should have done. To this gentry Joseph emphatically prescribed the repair of their water systems, recalling as he did so a certain Saleph, an uncle of Eber, about whom Eliezer had told him, that he was the first man to "turn the brooks on to his property," and thus was the inventor of irrigation.

Now as for the new erections, the extraordinary measures taken to heap up the surpluses: the Egyptian national idea of thrift and foresight is probably the best explanation of the fact that Keme's children liked them well. Joseph's own personal tradition of the Flood and the brilliant idea of the ark which saved the human race as well as all animal creation from complete extinction, was in harmony here with the instinct for security and defence deep-rooted in this very vul-

nerable civilization which had waxed old despite the precarious circumstances under which it lived. Egypt's children even tended to
see something magic about Joseph's storehouses. They themselves
were practised in fending off evil and malicious demons by setting
up some kind of impediment, impenetrable as possible, in the way of
magic symbols and signs. Thus in their minds the ideas of foresight
and magic were easily interchangeable; they found it not hard to see
even such prosaic arrangements as Joseph's corn-bins in the light of
enchantments and spells.

In a word, the impression prevailed that Pharaoh, young himself,
had made a lucky hit when he installed in office this young father of
the harvest and shadow-dispenser. His authority was destined to wax
exceedingly in the course of the years; but even now it was favoured
by the circumstance that this year the Nile had been very great, and
a far greater crop than usual was harvested under the new management, particularly of wheat, green rye, and barley; and abundance of
durra-corn could be gleaned from the stalks. We may have our doubts
about including in the seven years one of which the prosperity was
already certain when Joseph took office. It may not be allowable to
count it as one of the years of the fat kine. But it was later so counted
— probably in an attempt to bring the number of the blessing years
up to seven, though even so they did not quite reach that figure. In
any case, it was pleasant for Joseph that he took over the business
under conditions of prosperity and plenty. Popular psychology always has been and always will be, quite self-respectingly, without
rhyme or reason. If a minister of agriculture takes office in a period
of prosperity, public opinion is quite capable of thinking he is a
good minister.

Thus, when Jacob's son drove through the streets of Weset, the
populace greeted him with lifted hands and shouted: "Adon! Adon!
Ka-ne-Keme! Live for ever, friend of the harvest of God!" Many
even cried: "Hapi! Hapi!" and carried their right hands, thumb and
forefinger pressed together, to their mouths — which was going
rather far, and must be ascribed in large part to their childish enthusiasm for his handsome person.

But he very seldom drove out, being exceedingly busy.

URIM AND THUMMIM

WHATEVER we do in life is determined by fundamental tastes and
sympathies, by deep-lying private destinies which colour our whole
existence and dye all our doing. These are responsible for our acts —
these and not any of the reasonable grounds we are likely to adduce
to others and to ourselves. The King's chief mouthpiece and overseer
of all his stores, a short time after he entered office — very much

against Pharaoh's wish, who would gladly have kept his new friend near him for discourse about his Father who was in heaven and with his help to labour on the improvement of the teaching — moved his residence and all his offices from Nowet-Amun, the capital, to Menfe in the north, home of the Swaddled One. The external but probably quite justifiable ground for the change lay in the fact that thick-walled Menfe was "the balance of the lands," the centre and symbol of the equilibrium of Egypt and well suited for the residence of the master of the survey. Of course, that about the balance of the lands was not strictly accurate; Mempi lay really quite far north, near On, the city of the blinking and the cities of the seven mouths. If one reckoned that Egypt reached only to the Elephant Isle and the island Pi-lak and did not count Negritia, then the city of King Mira, where his beauty lay buried, was by no means the balance of the lands, but lay as much too far north as Thebes lay too far south. Nevertheless, age-old Menfe continued to be thought of as the balance; and it was axiomatic that it held a commanding position and was a point of vantage for both upstream and down. At any rate, such was the argument upon which the Egyptian Joseph based his decision, and Pharaoh himself could not deny that the trade with the Syrian port cities, when they sent down into the granary, as they called the land of the black earth, to buy grain, was easier from Menfe than from Per-Amun.

All this was perfectly true. And yet these were only the external, the rational grounds for Joseph's decision to get Pharaoh's permission to live in Menfe. The real and decisive reasons were in his heart, where they lay so deep and reached so far that they involved his whole attitude to life and death.

It is long, long since, but we can all remember how once as a lad, alone and dispirited, at odds with his brothers, he had looked down from the hill by Kirjath Arba upon the moon-white town in the valley and upon Machpelach, the twofold hollow, the rock-tomb which Abram had bought and where the bones of his ancestors rested. We recall the strange medley of feelings in his soul aroused by sight of the tomb and of the populous town lying there asleep: feelings of piety, which is reverence for death and the past, mingled with a half-mocking, half-fascinated drawing to the "city" and the busy human life which all day long filled the crooked streets of Hebron with clamour and reek, and at that hour lay snoring in its chambers with its knees drawn up. It may seem bold and arbitrary to connect such feelings, which after all were so early and so momentary, with the considered conduct of his present age. And probably still more rash to make the latter depend on the former. Yet there is some evidence in favour of the association: I mean the remark which Joseph later made to the old man, his purchaser, when they were together in Menfe, the metropolis. He had idly said that he liked the place, whose dead had not to ferry over the water because they were already west of the river; and remarked that among the cities of Egypt this one pleased him most. That was entirely characteristic of Rachel's eldest, far more than he realized himself. He had taken great pleasure in the way the little people of Menfe, in a mocking spirit preserved in the midst of their monotony, had blithely shortened the ancient grave-name of the city Men-nefru-Mire to Menfe. And this pleasure was almost Joseph himself, it revealed the deepest depth of his nature. We call that feeling of his by the name of sympathy, a rather tame word for so profound an emotion as it actually is. For sympathy is a meeting of life and death; true sympathy exists only where the feeling for the one balances the feeling for the other. Feeling for death by itself makes for rigidity and gloom; feeling for life by itself, for flat mediocrity and dull-wittedness. Wit and sympathy can arise only where veneration for death is moderated, has, so to speak, the chill taken off by friendliness to life; while life, on the other hand, acquires depth and poignancy. This happened in Joseph's case; and his shrewd and friendly temper was the result. This was the blessing, the double blessing with which he was blessed from the heights above and the depths which lay beneath; the blessing which Jacob, his father, launched into on his death-bed, behaving as though he then gave and conferred it, whereas after all he was only reasserting an already accomplished fact. Any attempt to examine the moral foundations of our exceedingly complicated world requires a certain amount of learning. Of Jacob it had always been said that he was *"tam,"* meaning that he was upright, and that he dwelt in tents. But *tam* is an equivocal word, not properly rendered by "upright." It is both positive and negative, it is yes and no, light and darkness, life and death. It turns up again in the curious formula "Urim and Thummim," where in contrast to the light, affirmative Urim it obviously stands for the dark, death-shadowed aspect of the world. Tam, or thummim, is the light-and-dark, the upper and the under world at once and by turns; and Urim only the light, as distinguished in pure usage. So "Urim and Thummim" does not actually express a contradiction; it only exhibits the mysterious truth that when one separates a part from the whole of the moral world, the whole always stands opposed to the part. It is not so easy to make head or tail of the moral world, first of all because what is sunshiny in it refers to the underworldly. Esau, for instance, the Red One, was distinctly a sun-man of the lower world. And Jacob, his younger twin, set off against Esau as a mild moon-shepherd, did, we must remember, spend the better part of his life in the underworld with Laban, and the means he used there to become gold and silver are very inaccurately described by the word "upright." Urim he was certainly not; but *tam* precisely describes him: a glad-sorry man, like Gilgamesh. And Joseph was that too, whose rapid adaptation to the sunny underworld of Egypt as little indicates a Urim-nature pure and simple. "Urim and Thummim" might be rendered as yes — yes-no; that is, yes-no with the coefficient of a second yes. Mathematically speaking, after the yes and the no have cancelled each other out, only the second yes is left; but the purely mathematical has no coloration at all, or at least it ignores the dark tone of the resultant yes, which is obviously an after-effect of the eliminated no. All that is, as I said, involved. We do better merely to repeat that in Joseph life and death met, and the result was that sympathy which was the profounder reason why he asked Pharaoh's permission to live in Menfe, that sprightly metropolis of tombs.

The King had first of all taken thought for the eternal dwelling of his "universal friend," and it was already under way. He now gave Joseph a residence in the dearest quarter of Menfe: a sunny dwelling-house, with garden, reception-hall, fountain court, and all the amenities of that late-early time, not to mention a host of Nubian and Egyptian servants, for kitchen, vestibule, stable, and hall, who swept and garnished and sprinkled the villa and adorned it with flowers, under the supervision of — guess whom? But of course even the slowest in the uptake must have known long ago. For Joseph kept his word more punctually and punctiliously than Nefer-em-Wese, the cup-bearer, had kept his: he straightway honoured the promise he had made to somebody when they parted: that he would send after him and take him to himself whenever he should be lifted up. While he was still in Thebes, immediately after he got back from his tour of inspection, with Pharaoh's approval he wrote to Mai-Sachme, the warden at Zawi-Re, and invited him to be his house steward and head of his house and of all those matters which such a man as Joseph now was could not take on himself. Yes, he who had once been overseer in Petepre's house and to whom a so much greater charge had now fallen, he himself had an overseer over everything that was his: wagons and horses, storerooms, house servants, scribes, and slaves. And that was Mai-Sachme, the imperturbable, who was not startled when the letter of his former convict reached him, if only because it was not given him to be startled. Nevertheless, he did not even wait for his successor to arrive at the prison, but betook himself by leaps and bounds to Menfe — a somewhat out-of-date city, of course, quite over-crowded by Thebes in Upper Egypt, but in comparison with Zawi-Re immensely stimulating. Imhotep, the wise, the many-sided, had lived and worked there; and now Imhotep's great admirer had been beckoned hither to a splendid post. Mai-Sachme put himself at once at the head of Joseph's house, assembled the staff, bought, furnished, and bestowed; so that when Joseph came down from Wese and Mai-Sachme met him at his own beautiful gateway, he found his house equipped in every detail as the residence of a great man. He even found an infirmary ready for such as would wreathe and wind, and a pharmacy where his overseer might mix and triturate to his heart's content.

The meeting was most cordial, though of course the two could not embrace in view of the surrounding staff. The embrace had taken place once for all when they parted, in the only moment proper to it, when Joseph was no longer Mai-Sachme's servant but not yet Mai-Sachme's lord. The steward said:

"Welcome, Adon; lo, here is your house. Pharaoh gave it, and he whom you command commanded it, down to the smallest detail. You need only go to the bath, be anointed, sit down, and eat. But I thank you very much for thinking of me and pulling me out of my tedium directly you sat in glory, and now everything has come out as your servant always imagined it would, and you have called me to share your varied and diverting life, which I shall strive to deserve."

Joseph replied:

"And in my turn I thank you, you good soul, for answering my call and being willing to be my housekeeper in this new life. It came as it has come, because I never offended my father's God by the smallest doubt that He would be with me. But do not call yourself my servant, for we shall be friends as we were before, when I was beneath your feet; and together shall we meet the good and bad hours of life, the exciting and the unexciting. There will certainly be both, and I need you most for the exciting ones. For your careful oversight I thank you in advance. But it must not consume you to the extent that you have no leisure to guide the reed in your study as you love to do, to find the right and fitting form for the story of the three love-affairs. Great is the writer's art! But truly I find it greater yet to live in a story; this that we are in is certainly a capital one, of that I am more and more convinced the longer I live. And now you are in it with me because I brought you; and when in the future people hear or read of the steward who was with me and at my side in exciting moments, they will know that this steward was you, Mai-Sachme, the man of poise."

THE MAIDEN

ONCE in the beginning God made a deep sleep to fall upon the man he had set in the garden in the East, and while the man slept God took out one of his ribs and closed the place up with flesh. But out of the rib He made a woman, in the opinion that it was not good for man to be alone, and presented her to the man that she should be about him for company and help. And it was very well meant.

Our teachers have painted this presentation in very fine colours: thus and so, they say, it happened; they behave as though they knew all about it — and it may be they really do know. God washed the woman, they assure us, He washed her clean, for naturally she was a bit sticky, anointed her, rouged her face, curled her hair, and at her urgent plea adorned her head, neck, and arms with beads and precious stones, among them sardonyx, topaz, diamond, jasper, turquoise, amethyst, emerald, and onyx. He brought her, thus embellished, before Adam, with a choir of thousands of angels singing and playing on their lutes, to present her to the man. Then there was a feast and a feasting, that is to say a festal meal, of which it seems God Himself most affably partook, and the stars danced together, to the music they themselves made.

That was the first great wedding feast; but we do not hear that it was also straightway a marriage. God made the woman for a helper to Adam, simply in order that she might be about him, and had obviously thought no more about it. That she should bear children in suffering He only inflicted upon her after she and Adam had eaten of the tree and their eyes had been opened. Between the feast of the presentation and the time when Adam knew his wife and she bore him the farmer and the shepherd, in whose footsteps Jacob and Esau walked, between these comes the story of the tree and the fruit and the serpent and the knowledge of good and evil. For Joseph too it came in this order. He too knew the woman only after he had learned what good and evil are, of a serpent who would have given her life to teach him what is very, very good but yet evil. But he resisted her, and had the art to wait until it was good and no longer evil.

How can we help thinking sadly of the poor serpent now, at the moment when the sun-dial points to the hour of Joseph's marriage, which he made with another woman and put heads and feet together with her instead of with the serpent? I have sought to forestall that natural sadness by speaking first of her, how that by now she had become once more a cool moon-nut, to whom the whole affair no longer mattered. It is easier to think of her thus; our faint remaining bitterness is quenched in the picture of her as the bigoted priestess she had now become. Besides, her tranquillity was in no danger of being disturbed by the wedding, for that took place not in Thebes but far away at Joseph's house in Menfe. Pharaoh, who had been zealous in the affair from the beginning, came down in person to the festivities and most affably sat by while the stars danced in their courses. He quite literally took on the role of God, being profoundly convinced that it is not good for man to be alone. He had told Joseph almost at once how pleasant it was to be married, and, unlike God, he spoke from experience, for he had Nefertiti, his little dawn-cloud, gold-edged, whereas God was always alone and His concern was only for all mankind. But Pharaoh, like God in this, had concern for Joseph too. So as soon as he had exalted him, he began to look about for a state alliance, which was to be just that; that is to say, very aristocratically and politically conceived, yet pleasant and enjoyable too — not such a simple combination. But as God for Adam, so Pharaoh produced his creature the bride, led her to Joseph to the sound of harps and cymbals, and himself took part in the wedding feast.

Now who was this bride, Joseph's graceful consort, and what was her name? Everybody knows; but that does not lessen the pleasure of telling or hearing it. It may be possible that somebody has forgotten it or no longer knows that he knows it, and would not know what to say if asked. Her name, then, was Asenath, the maid, daughter of the sun-priest at On. Yes, Pharaoh had gone high, higher he could not have gone. To marry the daughter of the head priest among those who served Re-Horakhte — it was a thing unheard of, it bordered on sacrilege, although of course the girl was destined in any case for marriage and motherhood, and nobody in the least wanted her to live a cloistered life and die unwed. On the other hand, however desirable and proper it was that she be wed, yet whoever should capture her was thought of as a dark, equivocal phenomenon; he was an abductor, and she was not given but snatched — that was the attitude in her circle, though actually everything went off with the utmost propriety and according to all the conventions. But never parents in the world made more to-do about handing a child over to a husband. The mother in particular was or affected to be quite beside herself. She could not talk enough about her inability to grasp what was happening; she wrung her hands and behaved as though she herself had been or was going to be raped. She even made vows of vengeance, though less because she really meant them than because they were the proper thing under the circumstances. Now, the reason for all this was that the virginity of the daughter of the sun, though in the last analysis destined for the common lot, was invested with the shield and buckler of a peculiar sacredness and inviolability. She was uniquely girdled with the virgin girdle, she was the virgin of virgins, the idea, so to speak, of a virgin: quite especially and exclusively maid, the essence of maidenhood. In her case the common noun became proper: "Maiden" she was called all her life; and the husband who should make theft of her maidenhead would be to the average mind committing a godlike crime, though actually less criminal for being so godlike. The relation of the son-in-law to the parents of the girl, particularly to the hand-wringing mother, might be in private perfectly friendly; but in public it was a case of strained relations, in order to bear out the theory that in a sense they never consented to let their daughter belong to her husband. Indeed, in the marriage contract the condition was expressly stated that the child should not live all the year round with her sinister brigand, but should return and live as a maid with her parents for a certain by no means small part of each year. But here again the condition was symbolic rather than literal; its fulfilment only meant that the bride, in quite normal and regular way, paid visits to her parents' house after she was married.

If the high-priest and his wife had had several daughters, still these arrangements would refer primarily to the eldest, and to the others in much lesser degree. But sixteen-year-old Asenath was their only child. Think, then, of what godlike violence and unnatural crime was this man guilty who wedded her! Her father, Horakhte's chief prophet, was of course not the same gentle old greybeard who at the time of Joseph's first visit to On, with the Ishmaelites, had occupied the golden chair at the foot of the great obelisk in front of the winged disk of the sun. He was that man's elected successor, likewise gentle, benevolent, and blithe of countenance; for thus had every servant of Atum-Re to be by virtue of his office; and if he was not by nature thus, then by some necessary disguise he had to become so by second nature. Chance willed it that this priest, as we are aware, had the same name as Joseph's former owner, the courtier of light, namely Potipherah or Petepre — and what name could be better for him in his office than "The sun gave him"? The name indicates that he was born and destined for the office. Presumably he was the son of that old man in the little gold cap, and Asenath, accordingly, his granddaughter. As for her name, written Ns-nt, it was connected with the goddess Neith from Sais in the Delta; it meant "She who belongs to Neith," and the maiden was under the special protection of that armed goddess, whose emblem was a shield with two arrows fastened crosswise on it, and who even in human guise usually wore a cluster of arrows on her head.

Asenath did. Her hair, or rather the conventional wig she wore over it, the construction of which left it a little uncertain whether it was a coiffure or a head-dress, was always adorned with arrows either thrust through or fastened on top; while the shield, in token of her peculiar virginity, appeared as an ornament, at throat or waist or on her arm-bands, accenting, together with the crossed arrows, the inviolable character of her maidenhood.

Despite all this armour and outward emphasis upon her inward resistance, Asenath was a charming child, highly sweet-natured, gentle and biddable, obedient to the wishes of her aristocratic parents, to Pharaoh's will, and to her husband's — even to the point of having none of her own. It was precisely this combination of sacred and inviolate purity with a definite tendency to let people do what they would with her, a tolerant acceptance of her feminine lot, which was the essence of Asenath's character. Her face was typically Egyptian in shape, small-boned, with somewhat prominent lower jaw; but it did not lack individuality. The cheeks still had their childlike roundness, the lips were full too, with a soft hollow between mouth and chin; the forehead chaste, the little nose perhaps a thought too thick; the large, beautifully painted eyes had that peculiarly fixed and expectant gaze which is typical of the deaf; but Asenath was not deaf, her gaze only reflected her inner expectancy. It was as though, with conscious readiness and acceptance, she was waiting for the hour of her destiny to strike. This faint unearthliness in her face was more than made good by the dimple coming and going in one cheek as she talked — the whole effect was rarely charming.

Charming and a little unusual her figure was too, as seen through the spun air of her garment: the waist exceptionally small and wasp-like, the hips and abdominal cavity by contrast ample and spreading, a good womb for child-bearing; the breasts stood out like little twin bucklers, the arms were slender and shapely, with large hands which she habitually held with the fingers spread out. Portrait of a maiden in amber — such was the whole impression Asenath gave.

Until her marriage she had led among flowers a life like theirs. Her favourite spot was the lake shore in her father's temple grounds, a rolling meadowy stretch carpeted with narcissus and anemones where she loved to wander by the mirrorlike waters with her playmates, the little daughters of the priests and the aristocracy of On. There she plucked her flowers, sat in the grass, and wound her garlands, her listening look fixed upon space, the brows lifted, the dimple coming and going in her chin, wholly expectant of what should come. And then it came: for one day Pharaoh's messengers appeared on the scene. From Potipherah, father and priest, heavily nodding assent, and from the mother, who was quite beside herself and wrung her hands, they demanded the virgin Asenath for wife to Dgepnuteefonech, Vice-Horus and shadow-dispenser of the King. She herself, possessed by the one idea of her existence, flung up her arms to heaven imploring aid. But they snatched her round her tiny waist and tore her away.

All that was just a farce, a symbolic performance dictated by convention. For not only were Pharaoh's wishes law, but a marriage with his favourite and first mouthpiece was highly honourable and desirable and the parents could not have looked higher for their child than Pharaoh had looked for Joseph; so there was no reason at all for desperation or even for grief going beyond the natural pain of parents at parting from their only child. But there had to be much ado made over Asenath's virginity and the theft of it; it was necessary to portray the bridegroom as a sinister character, however pleased the parents had reason to be and in fact probably were. Pharaoh had expressly given out that virginity here espoused virginity: that the bridegroom too was in his way a virgin, long wooed and set apart, a

bride whence now the wooer issued. To this end he had had to arrange matters with the God of his fathers, the bridegroom of his race,
whose jealousy he had long spared but now no longer spared, or
spared only in so far as he was making a very special kind of marriage, a proper virgin marriage — if that helped matters any. We,
of course, need feel no concern, despite all the implications of the
step; for Joseph was making an Egyptian marriage, a marriage with
Sheol, an Ishmael marriage, and thus a marriage not without a prece-
dent, though a doubtful one, in need of all the consideration which,
it appears, it was sure to receive. Our teachers and expounders have
many of them taken exception to this marriage of Joseph's and even
sought to deny the fact. In the interest of purity they have put it
about that Asenath was not the child of Potipherah and his wife but
a foundling and no other than the offspring of Jacob's own unhappy
daughter Dinah, exposed and found floating in a basket. According
to this theory, Joseph took his own niece to wife; which even if it
were true would not greatly improve matters, because half of Dinah's
child was flesh and blood of the fidgety Sichem, a Baal-worshipping
Canaanite. Anyhow our reverence for our teachers must not prevent us from pronouncing the story of the child in the basket to be
what it is, an interpolation and pious fraud. Asenath the maiden was
the real child of Potipherah and his wife, of pure Egyptian blood,
and the sons she was to present to Joseph, his sons and heirs Ephraim
and Manasseh, were, whether we like it or not, simply half-Egyptian
by blood. And even that was not all. For by his marriage with the
daughter of the sun Israel's son came into close relations with the
temple of Atum-Re — priestly relations in fact, as had been part of
Pharaoh's plan when he arranged the marriage. It was almost un-
thinkable that a man as high in government preferment as Joseph was
should not at the same time have performed a higher priestly function
and drawn a temple revenue, and — again whether we like it or not —
Joseph, as Asenath's husband, did both. In other words and to put
it rather baldly, he had an income from the idolaters. To his official
wardrobe henceforth belonged the priestly leopard-skin and under
certain circumstances he was liable to burn incense officially before
an image — that of the falcon Horakhte with the sun-disk on its head.
    These things have been well understood by but very few people;
to have them thus clearly stated may come as a shock. But it is quite
clear that for Joseph the day of enfranchisement was now come; and
we may be sure that he had known how to reach an understanding
with Him who had parted him from his own, transplanted him to
Egypt, and made him great there. Perhaps we have here an application of the philosophy of the triangle, according to which a sacrifice
at the alabaster table of the complaisant Horakhte meant no derogation from any other godhead. And after all this was not just any

temple; it was the temple of the god of the far horizon; Joseph might put to himself that it would have been a mistake, a piece of foolishness, in other words a sin, to ascribe to the God of his fathers a narrower horizon than to Atum-Re. And finally we must not forget that the Aton had of late emerged out of this god; in the conversation between Pharaoh and Joseph it had transpired that one properly invoked him not by the name Aton but as the Lord of Aton; not as "our Father above" but as "our Father who art *in* heaven." All this may have passed comfortably through Joseph's mind when on certain rare occasions he put on his leopard-skin and went to burn incense.

All in all Rachel's eldest, Jacob's parted darling, was definitely a very special case. The indulgence vouchsafed him took account of the things of this world; and that in turn prevented things from ever coming to a tribe of Joseph as it did to a tribe even of Issachar, Dan, and Gad. His role, his place in the plan, was that of a man set in the great world to be, as we shall see, guardian, provider, and saviour of his own. There is every reason to think that he was aware of this function, at least emotionally, and thought of his own exiled and cosmopolitan existence not as that of an outcast but as that of a man set apart for a purpose. Undoubtedly this is the explanation of his supreme confidence that the Master of the Plan would treat him with due consideration and forbearance.

JOSEPH TAKES A BRIDE

WELL then, Asenath the maiden, accompanied by twenty-four selected slaves, was sent up to Menfe to her virgin marriage in Joseph's house. The high-priestly pair, bowed down with grief at this incredible abduction, travelled up from On; and Pharaoh himself travelled down from Nowet-Amun, to partake in the mysteries of the wedding feast, personally to present this exceptional bride to his favourite and as an experienced married man to assure him of the amenities procured by the married state. It should be said that twelve of the twenty-four young and beautiful maidservants who came with Asenath and with her passed into the possession of the sinister bridegroom (involuntarily one thinks of the retinue which in former times used to attend a king living into his tomb), twelve of them, were there to make music, dance, and jubilate, the other twelve to lament and beat their breasts. For the wedding ceremonies as they were celebrated in the torch-lit fountain court and adjacent rooms of Joseph's palatial house had a strongly funereal flavour; that we do not go into them with the last degree of exactitude is due to a kind of consideration for old Jacob back there at home, deluding himself in the belief that his darling was treasured up in death and permanently seventeen. Jacob would assuredly have flung up his hands at the sight of much that happened at the wedding. It would have confirmed him in his honest prejudices against Mizraim, the land of mud, prejudices which we would wish to respect and so do not describe the occasion with such particularity as to imply that we approve of what went on.

Behind his back we may agree that there does exist a certain relation between death and marriage, a bridal chamber and a tomb, a murder and the abduction of a virgin. It is no great strain to think of a bridegroom as a god of death. And there is a likeness between the fate of the maiden, who, a veiled sacrifice, steps across the serious divide between maidhood and wifehood, and the fate of the seed-corn buried in the darkness there to rot and then out of corruption to come back to the light as just such another seed-corn, virgin and new. The resemblance is an accepted one; just as we admit the ear mown down by the sickle to be a painful parable of the daughter snatched out of her mother's arms, who herself was once virgin and sacrifice, once also mown down by the sickle and now in her daughter's fate reliving her own.

The sickle in fact played a prominent part in the decorations provided by Mai-Sachme for the great occasion. The symbolism of the corn, the grain, and the sown field was ingeniously used in the fountain court and the peristyle round it; as likewise in the entertainment offered the guests before and after the ceremony: men strewed corn on the pavement and poured water on it out of jars, with ritual shoutings; women bore vessels on their hips, one side filled with corn, the other with a little burning torch. Since the festivities were in the evening there were many torches everywhere throughout the rooms, which were hung with coloured draperies and garlands of myrtle. The torches were of course; yet there was such lavish use of them that here too the decoration verged on the symbolic. A torch in fact is used to give light where there is no daylight. The bride's mother, Potiphar's wife (if one may speak of her thus without confusion), entirely shrouded in a deep-violet mantle, a perfect tragic muse, carried part of the time a torch in each hand or even two in one hand. And everyone, male and female, bore torches in the great procession which was the climax of the evening. Torch in hand, they moved in a long line through all the rooms in the house and then into the fountain court, where Pharaoh, the most exalted guest, sat in an easy attitude between Joseph and Asenath (also shrouded in a violet veil). In the fountain court the procession broke up into an ingenious and remarkable dance — or rather broke out, for the flaming smoking line of dancers remained still one behind another and moved in a ninefold spiral to their own left around the fountain. In all the labyrinthine involutions the line was kept by a red ribbon running through the hands of the dancers; which did not prevent them from executing their crowning marvel of pyrotechnic skill, for the blazing torches themselves danced, tossed and caught from outside to inside of the ninefold coil, without a single one missing its goal or falling to the ground.

One must have seen that, in order to share the writer's temptation to describe it in more detail than suits with the thought of the old man at home. He would surely have taken some pleasure in the skilful dance at least, purely as a spectacle, certainly much more than in some other manifestations. He saw things through a father's eye; and he would have disapproved — to put it mildly — of the prominent part played by the maternal element at his son's wedding; by the mother of Asenath, storming and threatening and figuring in her own person both the bereft and the beraped. Again, most of the men and youths taking part in the grand procession and the spiral dance were dressed as women in garb like the bride-mother — and that, of course, in the eyes of the good Jacob would have been a Baal-abomination. Apparently they were considered to represent her and to enter into her feelings; for the same violet veil flowed about them and they gave vent in the same way to anger, taking the torch in the left hand in order to shake the right fist in the air; the gesture was the more alarming because these figures wore masks, which bore no resemblance to the matronly countenance of Potiphar's wife, but had an expression of affliction and wrath to curdle one's blood. Some of them had stuffed out their mourning garments to look as though they were advanced in pregnancy; that is, they represented the mother, still — or once again — bearing the maiden sacrifice beneath her heart, or else the maiden there bearing a new sacrifice-maiden — probably they were not clear just what they did mean. Men and youths who thus distended their bodies — no, that would certainly have been nothing for Yakob ben Yitzschak. Nor must any further description of the wedding feast be construed as approval of the goings-on. But for Joseph, set apart and severed into the great world, the time of licence had come; his marriage itself was one great licence and we report on its details in the indulgent and forbearing spirit the occasion demands.

There was in short a certain abandon and on the other hand a savour of the grave — bespoken for instance by the myrtle wreaths with which all the guests and all the rooms in the house were adorned. Some of the guests even carried whole bunches of myrtles in their hands. For the myrtle is sacred both to love and to the dead. But the great procession had an equal number of performers with cymbals and tambourines, displaying joyous exultation in the same measure as the others did the postures and gestures of grief, as though they were walking in a funeral train. It must be added that each kind of performance showed various stages. For instance, certain groups of mourners merely wandered to and fro with satchels and staves; they went aimlessly up to and past the royal seat, the wedding pair, and the high-priestly parents, without actual lamentation or shedding of tears. In the same way there were various degrees of rejoicing, some of them quite dignified and pleasing; as, for instance, a group would advance to the seats of honour bearing jugs of graceful shape, and turn them ceremonially upside down to east and west, chanting antiphonally: "Overflow!" "Receive the blessing!" So far so good. But often, and more and more as the evening wore on, the laughter and rejoicing rather coarsely betrayed the real idea at the bottom of a wedding feast, the thought of what was naturally to follow. One might put it that the idea of abduction and murder and the idea of fertility came together and flowed into licence; so that the air was full of offensive innuendo, of winking, obscene allusions, and roars of laughter. Animals had been led about in the procession, among them a swan and a stallion, at sight of which the bride's mother shrouded herself more closely in her purple veil. But what shall we say to the appearance of a pregnant sow, actually with a rider in the shape of a fat, half-naked old woman with an equivocal cast of countenance who gave out a stream of bad jokes! This offensive old female played a familiar, popular, and important role in the whole performance. She had accompanied Asenath's mother from On and had been whispering lewd jokes the whole time into the lady's ear in order to cheer her up on the journey. This was her function and her role. She was called the comforter; in the prevailing high spirits the name was constantly shouted at her and she answered with coarse gestures. During the whole evening she scarcely stirred from the side of the theoretically inconsolable one, striving none the less to console her — that is, to make her laugh by whispering an inexhaustible flow of indecency into her ear — and she succeeded too, because that was the pattern: the offended, furious, and ostensibly outraged mother did really from time to time titter into the folds of her veil at what she heard. Then all the assemblage laughed too and applauded the "comforter." But as the mother's anger and grief were only put on, being largely a matter of convention, we may assume that the tittering too was merely a concession to old practice and that she would herself have felt only disgust at the antics of the comforter. At most her amusement might be as much and as little unfeigned as is the natural and not conventionally exaggerated grief of a mother at losing her only daughter to a husband.

Enough has been said to justify the good sense of not going into the details of Joseph's wedding feast. Even if we sin against our own intentions, that does not mean we approve. The young pair themselves, clasping hands across Pharaoh's knees, were almost indifferent to the whole scene, looking at each other instead of at the indispensable scenes enacted before their eyes. Joseph and Asenath were attracted to each other from the first, and felt delight each in the other's company. Of course, this was a prearranged state marriage, and into such an arrangement, at least at first, love does not come. It has to find itself, and with well-constituted people it does so in time. The mere knowledge that they belong together helps; but in this case other circumstances favoured the growth of feeling. Over and above her natural passive readiness, Asenath the maid had gone some way toward accepting her lot in the person of this abductor and murderer of her maidenhead, who had clutched her round a waist that seemed to be made tiny on purpose, and made off with her into his realm. Already she felt drawn to Pharaoh's dark, handsome, wise, and kindly minister, and did not doubt that liking could grow into a stronger bond; while the thought that he would be the father of her children was like a mussel-shell in which the pearl of love should grow. Not otherwise was it with Joseph. The set-apart one, in this situation of special licence, admired God's large, worldly-wise freedom from prejudice — as though the eternal wisdom had not always taken account of his own worldliness — and left it to Him to cope with the delicate question what relation the children of Sheol who would be born of this marriage were to bear to the Chosen Seed. But we cannot blame this virgin wooer that his thoughts were less on the expected children than they were on the till now forbidden mysteries to which they would owe their existence. What had once been evil and forbidden was now good. But look upon this being through whom evil becomes good; look well upon her, and especially because she has such listening eyes and so speaking an amber-tinted shape as had Asenath the maiden, and you will be sure that you will love her; nay, that you already do.

Pharaoh walked between them when at last the feast ended and the procession re-formed. It now included all those present, who with jubilation and lamentation, with myrtle-strewing and the fist-shaking of the masked mothers, took their way to the bridal chamber, where the newly-wed pair were put to bed among flowers and fine linen. The sow-rider stood just behind the daughter of the sun-priest as the parents, murmuring the prescribed sayings, took leave on the threshold of Asenath the maid. Over the bride's shoulder the old hag murmured such things as made the anguished mother laugh amid her tears. And shall we too not both laugh and weep, is there not food for both laughter and tears, in the thought of what nature has contrived for mankind, and after what fashion she wills that they seal their love — or, in case of a state marriage, of course, learn to love? The sublime and the ridiculous flickered in the lamplight of this wedding night where virginity met virginity and wreath and veil were torn — a difficult work of tearing it was. For this was a shield-maid whom the dark arms embraced, expressly so designated, an obstinate virgin; and in blood and pain Joseph's first-born was conceived, Manasseh, a name which means: "God has made me forget all my connections and my father's house."

CLOUDS IN THE SKY

IT was the year one of the fat kine and the full ears. Of course the customary reckoning was from the year of the god's accession; but among the children of Egypt the new method now began to run concurrently. The fulfilment had, actually, set in before the prophecy. But only in the following year did it begin in a way to carry conviction; for that year far exceeded the preceding one in richness; and whereas the first had been merely somewhat above the average, the second proved to be a veritable year of marvels, magnificence, and jubilation, fertile past all expectation in every line. The Nile had got very fine and large — not wild and swollen, tearing away the farmer's fields, yet not a single fraction lower than the best year on record. It lay over the expanse of fields and quietly deposited its dung; it made one laugh to see the splendour of the flourishing land toward the end of the sowing season, and the abundant riches gathered in during the third quarter. The next year was not quite so luxuriant, it was more or less average, it was gratifying, it was even commendable, without being at all surprising. But the next one almost equalled the second and was quite as good as the first, while the fourth merited the adjective "capital," if no more. So we can imagine how Joseph's reputation, as the overseer of all that plenty, waxed among the people, and with what zealous, joyful punctuality his ground-rent law, the tax of the fifth, was carried through, not less by the taxed than by the tax officials. "And he gathered up all the food of the seven years which were in the land of Egypt and laid up the food in the cities, the food of the field which was round about every city laid he up in the same." In other words, the grain tribute of all the land round, year in, year out, streamed into the fabulous skittle-shaped granaries which Adon had built in all the cities and their environs; not too many of them, as it turned out, for they got filled and more and more had to be built to meet the incoming tribute. So well did Hapi the nourisher mean by his land. The heaping up was in truth like the sands of the sea, song and saga are quite correct. But when they add that "they left numbering, for it was without number," that is an exaggeration due to enthusiasm. The children of Egypt never stopped counting, writing down, and book-keeping, it was not in their nature and did not happen. Though the fullness of the provision was indeed as the sands of the sea, yet these worshippers of the white ape held it to be their first and finest preoccupation to cover paper with the close-written calculations and detailed account-

ings which Joseph exacted from his collectors and inspectors throughout the period.

They counted five years of abundance; some people, even many
people, counted seven. It is idle to dispute the point. Observers who
stuck to the five may have been thinking of the five extra days in the
year and the tax quota based on that figure. On the other hand, five
years of fatness one after another are so joyful in themselves that
it would be easy to celebrate by calling them seven. Yes, it is possible
to make five out of seven; yet after all a bit more human to make seven
out of five — the narrator frankly confesses his uncertainty, for it is
not his way to pretend to knowledge where he has not got it. The
same thing applies to the admission that we do not know exactly
how old Joseph was at a certain point during the period of scarcity.
He may have been either thirty-seven or thirty-nine. It is certain
that he was thirty when he stood before Pharaoh: objectively certain, from our own point of view, for it is doubtful if he himself
knew. But what he was at that later, crucial moment, whether only
in his latish thirties or already as good as forty, we do not know,
and must be reconciled to the uncertainty. He, of course, a child of
his time and place, gave the matter little thought, or none at all.

Anyhow, he was now in the prime of life. If as a boy he had been
stolen away into Babylonia instead of Egypt, he would long ago
have assumed a full black beard, curled and pomaded; an appendage
which would have helped him not a little in a certain game he was to
play. But we can be grateful to the Egyptian custom that kept the
Rachel-face free of beard. Even so, he succeeded in the game, and
that shows how much the chiselling hand of time, the change of matter, the sun of his adopted land had worked upon his original characteristics to change them.

Joseph's figure, up till the time when he was drawn up out of his
second pit to stand before Pharaoh, had remained quite youthful.
After his marriage, during the fat years, when God made him fruitful in Asenath the maid and she bore him first Manasseh and then
Ephraim in the women's quarters of his house, he grew a little heavier,
perhaps a little too heavy, though not fat. He was tall enough to carry
it off; his commanding presence, gentled by the shrewd and humorous glance of his black eyes and the charm of the smiling Rachel-
mouth, accounted for the popular verdict that Joseph was an exceptionally handsome man. A thought too full-bodied, possibly, but
definitely handsome.

His physical increase chimed with the period of general luxuri-
ance. In fact the amazing increase of production showed itself in
every direction: the herds, for instance, so multiplied that it reminded the educated of the words of the old song: "Thy goats shall
bear twofold, thy sheep drop twins." And the women of Egypt too,

in both city and country, bore — probably in consequence of better food — much oftener than usual. But nature, partly through the negligence of the overburdened mothers, partly through the incidence of new infant diseases, redressed the balance by an increase in infant mortality, so there was no danger of over-population. It was only the birth-rate that so strikingly increased.

Pharaoh too became a father. The mistress of the lands had already been expectant on the day of the interpretation; but there was a tendency to believe that its fulfilment was responsible for her happy delivery. It was the sweet princess Merytaton who now came into the world. The physicians, on æsthetic grounds, lengthened the still plastic skull almost excessively, and rejoicings were loud in the palace and throughout the land — the louder to conceal a disappointment at the failure of an heir to the throne. But not even later did one appear; Pharaoh, his life long, begot only daughters, six in all. Nobody knows the law determining sex: whether it is already present in the sperm or whether the balance after some wavering goes down on one side or the other. We can contribute no information on the subject; and neither could the wise men from Babel and On, not even among themselves. On the other hand, we can scarcely be argued out of the conviction that it was something about young Amenhotep himself which resulted in his exclusively female issue.

Be that as it may, the fact must have been a small, an unacknowledged cloudlet upon the King's wedded happiness, though of course the most tender mutual consideration prevailed at all times. Either of them might have said to the other what Jacob said to impatient Rachel: "Am I in God's stead, who hath withheld from thee thy heart's desire?" On one of the sweet princesses, the fourth, there was conferred out of sheer tenderness the title of the Queen of the Lands, Nefernefruaton, for her own name. But the fifth was given one almost identical, Nefernefrure — which would seem to be due to a flagging of interest. The names of the others, still showing some affectionate ingenuity, I could easily tell you too; but sharing the slight irritation which all this female preponderance is bound to set up, I feel no inclination to put them down.

Considering that Tiy, the great mother, still stood at the head of the house of the sun; that Queen Nefertiti had a sister, Nezemmut; that there was a still living sister of the King, the sweet princess Baketaton, and that to these in the course of the years were added the King's six daughters, we must envisage a regular women's court, where Meni was the only cock among a whole flock of hens; and this was not at all consonant with his phœnix-dream of an immaterial father-spirit of light. One is reminded of Joseph's remark during the famous conversation with Pharaoh — one of the best things he said — that the power which strove from below upwards into the purity of light must be truly power and of a masculine kind not mere tenderness.

A slight shadow, then, lay upon the royal happiness of Amenhotpe and his golden pigeon, the sweet lady of the land, because no son was vouchsafed them. Joseph's marriage with Asenath the maid was also happy, happy and harmonious throughout, with a similar limitation: only sons were born to them, one, two, and later others on whom the light of history does not fall. In fact the abducted bride bore only sons and was grievously disappointed and probably her spouse as well, who would gladly have begot a daughter for her, at least one daughter! After all, the fact remains that a man can beget but not create. Asenath was simply possessed with the idea of a daughter: not just one daughter, but several; in fact she would have preferred nothing but daughters. She who had been a virgin of the shield desired nothing more ardently than to raise up the same out of the depth of her own virginity. And she was abetted by her nagging mother, who persisted in the affronted pose she had assumed from the beginning and thus fomented a slight but permanent marital discord, always kept within bounds, of course, by affection and consideration.

This was probably at its height in the beginning, when Joseph's eldest son was born. Asenath's disappointment was acute, one might justly call it exaggerated, and it looks as though something of his annoyance at the reproaches he had to bear slipped into the name Joseph gave the child. "I have forgotten," he may have been trying to say, "all that lies behind me, and my father's house as well; but you and your offended mother, you act not only utterly disappointed but as though I were to blame to boot." Something of this kind may lie at the bottom of the strange choice of the name Manasseh; but it is well to add that we need not take the name or its meaning too seriously. If God had made Joseph forget all his past connections and his father's house, how then did the same Joseph come to give Hebrew names to his Egyptian sons? Was it because he could count on the foreign names being found elegant in the monkey-land of Egypt? No; it was because Jacob's son, however long he had been arrayed in the fleshly garment of an Egyptian, had not forgotten at all but had always in his mind what he said he had forgotten. The name Manasseh was nothing but a polite flourish; a case not of foolishness but the reverse, and an instance of the tact of which Joseph all his life long had been past master. It was a plain statement of the fact that God had snatched him away and transplanted him into the worldly sphere out of two motives, one of them jealousy, the other the comprehensive plan of deliverance. As to the second Joseph could only speculate. The first lay entirely open to his shrewd eyes, that saw far enough even to see through God's design and recognize that it was really the first and that the second only offered the means of uniting suffering and wisdom. The words "to see through" may seem irreverent in such a connection. But is there an activity more religious than studying the soul-life of God? To meet the politic of the Highest with an earthly one is indispensable if one wants to get on in life. If Joseph had been silent like the grave, and as the grave, to his father all these years, it was deliberate policy and understanding insight into the soul-life of the Highest that had enabled him to be so. And his name for his first-born was in the same category. "If I am supposed to forget," the name was meant to say, "then lo, I have forgotten." But he had not.

In the third year of abundance Ephraim came into the world. The maiden-mother would not even look at him at first, and the mother-in-law was more out of temper than ever. But Joseph quite calmly gave him the name that meant: "God has made me to grow in the land of my banishment." He might well say so. He drove in his light car, accompanied by runners, acclaimed by Menfe's people in his name of Adon, to and fro between the splendid residence presided over by Mai-Sachme and his offices in the centre of the city, where three hundred clerks were at work; and gathered in stores until there was an abundance almost beyond keeping account of. He was a great man, the universal friend of a great king, Amenhotep IV, who by that time, to the furious chagrin of the temple of Karnak, had put aside his Amun-name and taken on that of Ikh-n-Aton ("It is pleasing to Aton"). He was also playing with the idea of leaving Thebes altogether and building himself a city dedicated entirely to Aton, where he thought to reside. Pharaoh, of course, wanted to see his shadow-dispenser of the teaching as often as possible to discuss with him about above and below. Likewise it could not fail to happen that Joseph, in pursuance of his great office, travelled several times in the year by land or water to Nowet-Amun to make report to Hor in the palace, when the two would spend hours in intimate talk. And Pharaoh too, on every trip to golden On, or when he drove forth to look for a proper site for his new city, the city of the horizon, would stop at Menfe and stay with Joseph. This of course put a heavy burden upon Mai-Sachme, though he never faltered in his perfect poise.

The friendship between the frail descendant of the pyramid-builders and Jacob's son, the foundations for which had been laid in the Cretan loggia, grew with the years into a warm and intimate bond. Young Pharaoh called Joseph his little uncle, and when he embraced him slapped him on the back. For this god was an enthusiast for informality, and it was Joseph who, out of native reserve, kept the balance in their relations. The King often laughed at the formality which his friend preserved in the midst of their familiar intercourse. They talked of their ill luck as fathers, that the one got only daughters, the other only sons. But the dissatisfaction of Joseph's wife and her nagging mother did little to dampen his joy in the grandsons of Jacob, who were growing up in the strange worldly world so far away from their grandsire. Equally the failure of a male heir could never depress Pharaoh's buoyant spirits for long at a time. Everything was going so wonderfully well in the maternal kingdom of the black earth that his reputation as the teacher of the fatherly light was strengthened mightily thereby, and he might sit in the shade of prosperity, giving witness to the God on whom his soul hung, and in speech as in solitude expending all his parts to think him better and better forth.

Debating thus, defining and comparing the high and holy properties of Pharaoh's father Aton, they might remind us of the religiodiplomatic exchanges which took place at Salem between Abram and Melchizedek the priest of El Elyon, the highest and also the only god; exchanges which ended in the agreement that this El was just the same, or pretty much the same, as Abram's God. It was noticeable, however, that it was always at the point where the discussion seemed to be approaching such an agreement that the courtly reserve which Joseph preserved in his relations with his exalted friend came out most plainly.

Chapter V

TAMAR

THE FOURTH

A WOMAN sat at the feet of Jacob the rich in tales, in the grove of Mamre at Hebron the city or close by, in the land of Canaan. Often she sat at his feet: either in the "house of hair," near the entrance, on the very spot where once the father had talked with his darling and been beguiled of the many-coloured coat; or else beneath the tree of enlightenment; or at the marge of the well close by, where first we met the subtle lad beneath the moon and watched the father go peering after him, leaning on his staff. How is it the woman sits with him now, in this place or that, her face lifted to his, and hearkens to his words? Whence comes she, this grave young creature so often found at his feet, and what sort of woman is she?

Her name was Tamar. — We look round at the faces of our hearers and see on but few, only here and there, the light of knowledge. Clearly the great majority of those who are here to learn the precise circumstances of this story do not recall, perhaps do not even know, the bare facts. We might be disposed to censure, did not the common ignorance jump with the advantage of the story-teller, by adding to the importance of his task. So you really no longer know, or to your knowledge never have known, who Tamar was? A Canaanite woman, simply a native, and in the first place no more than that. But in the second place Jacob's son's son's wife, daughter-in-law of Jehudah, Jacob's fourth, granddaughter-in-law, so to speak, of the man of the blessing. And in the third place, and finally, she was Jacob's devotee and his pupil in knowledge of the world and of God; who hung on his lips and looked up into his solemn face with such reverent attention that the heart of the bereaved old man opened utterly to her in turn, and he was even just a little in love with her. For Tamar's nature was strangely mingled, in a way even hard and heavy to herself: with a part of her being she was austere and full of spiritual striving (to which later on we must give an even stronger name); but in the other gifted with the soul-and-body charm and mystery of Astarte. We know how receptive to such a combination a man can be, and to what advanced years, when like Jacob he has always yielded to and dignified his own emotions.

Since Joseph's death, or rather because of that lacerating event, which he seemed at first quite unable to accept, Jacob's personal majesty had only increased. Then, when once he got used to the fact and his wrangling with God had worn itself out, the Deity's cruel dispensation having at length worked its way into the mind so desperately shut against it, it became an enrichment of his life, an addition to its weight of history. By virtue of it his musing — when he fell into a musing fit — grew more expressively, more completely and picturesquely "musing" than ever, so that observers were seized with awe and whispered one another: "Lo, Israel muses on his tales!" True it is, expression makes impression. The two have always gone together, and very likely the one has always had its eye on the other. That is nothing to laugh at, if the expression has behind it not mere humbug but real life experience and a burden of tales. In such a case the furthest we may go is a respectful smile.

Tamar, the native girl, knew naught of even such a smile. She was profoundly impressed by Jacob's majesty, directly she came in touch with him — and that had not come about merely through Judah, Leah's fourth, and his sons, two of whom she married one after the other. All this we know, as well as the sinister and half-equivocal accompanying circumstances, in other words the destruction of both Judah's sons. What is not known, since the chronicle passes it over, is Tamar's connection with Jacob, which after all is the indispensable premise of the whole episode and a remarkable secondary action within our whole history, which we interpolate while at the same time being aware that that history — which one may well call seductive, since it seduces us to such explicitness of detail — the history of Joseph and his brothers, is itself an interpolation in an epos incomparably vaster in scope.

Tamar, the native girl, daughter of quite simple Baal-farmers, moving within this episode of an episode — had she a notion of the fact? The answer is: quite certainly she had. Her own behaviour, which was deadly serious, gallant and offensive both at once, is evidence of the fact. It is not for nothing that the word I used above, the word "interpolation," keeps coming into my mind, as though it had a will of its own. Interpolation, insertion, pushing in: these form the motive of the hour, they were Tamar's watchword and mainspring. She was bent on pushing herself into the great history, and she did it, with amazing strength of purpose. It was the most spacious scene of which she had knowledge, and she would not, at any price whatsoever, be shut out of it. I think I also let fall the word "seduction"? There we have another key word; for it was by seduction that Tamar shoved herself into the great history of which this is an episode. She played the temptress and whored by the way, that she might not be shut out; she abased herself recklessly to be exalted. . . . How did that come about?

When first, or by what prosaic chance, Tamar got access to the friend of God and became his devotee no one precisely knows. Perhaps it happened before Joseph's death, and perhaps it was by Jacob's arrangement that she was taken into the tribe and given for wife to young Er, Judah's eldest. But the relation between her and the old man deepened and became intimacy only after the frightful blow had fallen and after Jacob's slow and unwilling recovery; only when his bereaved heart was unconsciously reaching for new emotional outlets. Then only did he become aware of Tamar, and drew her to himself because of her admiration for him.

By that time the eleven, his sons, were almost all married; the older ones long since, the younger more recently; and had children from their wives. Even Benoni-Benjamin, the little son of death, had come on in his turn — scarcely had he outgrown his urchinhood, become a youth, and then reached man's estate, seven years, perhaps, after the loss of his brother, when Jacob found and wooed for him first Mahalia, daughter of a certain Aram, of whom it was said that he was a "grandson of Terah" and so somehow or other descended from Abraham or from one of his brothers; and then the maid Arbath, daughter of a man named Simron, called quite explicitly a "son of Abram," which might mean that he came of that stock by some concubine. As for the pedigree of Jacob's daughters-in-law, the record has been both toned down and touched up and an effort made to show the blood kinship of the priestly stock, although the case had not a leg to stand on and was not even consistently attempted. Levi's and Issachar's wives were held to be "the granddaughters of Eber" — perhaps they were; even so they might have come from Assur or Elam. Gad and the glib Naphtali had followed their father's example and taken wives from Haran and Mesopotamia, but that these wives were actually great-granddaughters of Nahor, Abraham's uncle, they did not themselves assert, it was asserted of them. Asher the sweet-tooth took a nut-brown maid from the seed of Ishmael. Well, at least that was a relation, if a dubious one. Zebulon, of whom one might have expected a Phœnician marriage, actually went in unto a Midianite. This was correct only in so far as Midian was a son of Keturah, Abram's second wife; but had not big Reuben already gone and incontinently married a Canaanite woman? So too had Judah, as we know, and so Simeon, for his Bunah had been stolen from Shechem. As for Dan, Billhah's son, whom they called snake and adder, his wife was well known to be a Moabitess, descended from that Moab whom Lot's eldest daughter had borne to her own father — and to herself her own brother. Not particularly wholesome, that; nor had it anything to do with blood kinship, since Lot had not been Abram's brother, but only a proselyte. From Adam, of course, he too descended and equally, of course, from Shem, since he came from the land of the two rivers. Blood kinship is always possible to demonstrate if one takes in enough of the picture.

So all the sons "brought their wives to their father's house," as we are told; in other words, the place of the tribe in the grove of Mamre near Kirjath Arba and the burying-ground, around Jacob's house of hair, grew larger as the days went on and descendants multiplied according to the promise, round Jacob's knees when the majestic greybeard permitted it, and in his goodness he sometimes did and fondled his grandchildren. Particularly Benjamin's he fondled. For Turturra, a stocky little fellow who still had his trustful grey eyes and heavy metallic helmet of hair, also a rather muddy complexion, had become father to five sons in quick succession, borne to him by his Aramaic wife as well as other little ones in between, born of the daughter of Simron; the grandchildren of Rachel were always Jacob's favourites. But despite their presence and Benoni's paternal dignity Jacob still treated his youngest like a child, kept him in leading-strings as though he were not grown up, and gave him very small freedom lest mischance befall him. Scarcely to go into the town, to Hebron, scarcely to the fields, to say nothing of making a trip across country, would he permit his one remaining pledge of Rachel's love; though he was far from loving Benoni as he had loved Joseph and there was no actual reason on his account to fear the jealousy of the Higher Power. Still, since the lovely one had fallen to the tooth of the swine, Benoni had become the only treasure of Jacob's care and concern, wherefore he did not let him out of his sight and would pass no hour without knowing where Benjamin was and what he was doing. Such supervision could not but be painful to Benjamin and wounding to his dignity as husband and father. Yet he bore with it, though it depressed him, and presented himself before his father several times a day in obedience to Jacob's whim; for if he did not, Jacob came himself on his long staff halting from his hip to see after him — although as Benjamin well knew and as was plain enough from the old man's capricious behaviour, Jacob's feelings were actually very divided, being a queer mixture of hidden grudge and sense of property. For at bottom he never ceased to see in Benoni the matricide and the instrument God had used to take Rachel from him.

One important advantage, certainly, besides that of being the youngest-born, Benoni had over all the living brothers; and for Jacob's dreamily associational mentality it made one more reason to keep his youngest always at home. For Benjamin had been at home when Joseph got lost in the world, and as we know Jacob, this equivalence between being at home and being innocent, having quite defi-

nitely no share in a crime committed from home, was symbolically
well lodged in his mind. Thus Benjamin had always to be on hand as
the sign and the permanent token of his guiltlessness and of the fact
that he alone, the youngest, did not lie under the abiding, ever silently
gnawing suspicion which both rightly and wrongly Jacob cherished
and which the others knew that he cherished. It was the suspicion
that the boar which had rent Joseph had been a beast with ten heads;
and Benjamin had to be "at home" in token that the beast had quite
definitely not had eleven.

But perhaps not even ten heads, God only knew, and He might
keep it to Himself. Indeed, as the days and years went on, the question lost importance. It did so above all because Jacob, since he had
stopped bickering with God, had gradually arrived at the view that it
was not God who had by main strength laid upon him the sacrifice
of Isaac, but that he himself had done it of his own free will. As
long as the first agony lasted, such an idea had been far from him; he
had only thought of himself as cruelly misused. But as the pain faded,
habit set in, death made his advantage good — namely, that Joseph
was safe in His bosom and care, for ever and ever seventeen years old
— then this soft, pathetic soul had seriously begun to conceive itself
capable of Abraham's deed of sacrifice. To the honour of God this
fancy was born — and to Jacob's own. God had not monstrously and
craftily robbed him of his dearest. He had but taken what, consciously and in heroic spirit, had been offered, the dearest thing that
Jacob owned. Believe it or not, Jacob pretended to himself, and bore
himself witness for the sake of his pride, that in the hour when he
let Joseph set out on the journey to Chechem he had committed the
Isaac-sacrifice and freely out of love of God had surrendered to Him
the being he too dearly loved. Jacob did not believe this all the time.
Sometimes he confessed to himself with contrition and fresh-flowing
tears that he would never have been capable, for the love of God, of
tearing the beloved from his heart. But the yearning to believe it sometimes won the day; and when it did, the question who had mangled
Joseph became relatively unimportant.

The suspicion — certainly it was none the less there, it gnawed,
but more gently, and not at every hour; sometimes in later years it
slumbered and slept. The brothers had pictured living under suspicion, under half-wrongful suspicion, as being worse than in fact it
proved to be. The father was on good terms with the sons, that is
clear. He spoke with them and broke bread with them, he shared
their business, their household sorrows and joys; he looked in their
faces, and only once in a while, only at intervals already quite far
apart, did the gleam come into his old eyes or suspicion and hypocrisy cloud his old gaze, before which they, breaking off in their
words, had to cast down their eyes. But how much did that mean?

A man casts down his eyes even if he knows no more than that another suspects him. It does not inevitably mean he is guilty. A scrupulous innocence and pity for the man sick of mistrust may equally so
express itself. And so at last a man even gets sick of his suspicions.
In the end he lets them rest; especially if confirmation, without reference to past events, can change nothing of the future, or the promise,
or anything that is to be. The brothers might be the ten-headed Cain,
they might be fratricides; but after all they were what they were,
Jacob's sons; they were the given conditions that must be reckoned
with, they were Israel. For Jacob had deliberately taken to using the
name he had wrested at Jabbok after which he halted upon his thigh,
not only for his own person but with a broader and larger meaning.
Why not? Since it was his name, hardly won, and not until the dawn,
he might deal with it as he would. Israel: thus should not only he
personally be called but all that belonged to him, the man of the blessing, from the nearest to the latest-never-last member in all the branchings and collateral branchings, the kin, the stock, the folk, whose
numbers should be like the stars and the sands by the sea. The children sometimes permitted to play at Jacob's knee — they were Israel,
collectively he called them so, and even fell back on it gratefully
when he could not keep all their names in mind. It was particularly
the names of the children of the Ishmaelite and definitely Canaanite
women that escaped him. But "Iisrael" these women were too, including the Moabites and the slave-woman from Shechem; and Iisrael in
the first line and above all were their husbands, the eleven; deprived
of their full zodiacal number by early-evident and prolonged fraternal strife and by heroic sacrifice; yet still a goodly rank: Jacob's sons,
progenitors of countless generations, to whom they in their turn
would bequeath their name — mighty men before the Lord, whatever
each single one might be like inside and whatever each one had in
his mind when he cast down his eyes. What did it all matter, when
through thick and thin they always remained Iisrael? For Jacob
knew, long before it stood written — and it only stands written because he knew it — that Iisrael, even when it had sinned, always remained Israel.

    But in Israel there was always one head on whom the blessing rested
before the others, as Jacob had been before Esau — and Joseph was
dead. Upon one rested the promise, or would rest, when Jacob conferred the blessing; from him the salvation should come, for which
the father long sought a name and had found one, for the present,
which no one knew save only the young female who sat at Jacob's
feet. Who was the chosen one among the brothers, from whom it
should come? Who was the man of the blessing, now that the choice
no longer went by love — for the love was dead? Not Reuben, the
eldest, who had shot away like the unstable waterfall and had played

the hippopotamus. Not Simeon or Levi, they were personally nothing but unlicked cubs, and had some unforgettable items against them
on their score. For they had behaved like heathen savages at Shechem
and like satyrs in Hamor's city. This three were accurst, in so far as
Israel can be accurst, they fell away. And so it had to be the fourth
who came next after them, Judah. He it was.

ASHTAROTH

DID he know it was he? He could count it up on his fingers, and often
literally did, but never without shrinking from his election and painfully doubting whether he was worthy; yes, even fearing that the
choice might become corrupt in him. We know Jehudah; when Joseph still lay in his father's bosom we sometimes saw in the group
of brothers that suffering leonine head and the stag's eyes. We
watched him when Joseph suffered his mishap. On the whole Judah
did not come so badly out of that affair; not so well, of course, as
Benjamin, who had been "at home," but almost as well as Reuben,
who had never wanted the boy dead but had procured him the pit in
order to steal him out of it. To draw him up out of the pit and give
him his life, that had been Judah's idea too; for it was he who had
suggested that they sell their brother, because in these times one did
not know how to treat him like Lamech in the song. The excuse was
trifling, a mere pretext, as most excuses are. Jehudah had acutely realized that to let the boy perish in the pit was no whit better than to
shed his blood and had wanted to save him. That he came too late
with his proposal, since the Ishmaelites had already done their work
and freed Joseph, was not his fault. He could honestly say that his
conduct in the accursed business had been comparatively decent, since
he had wanted the lad to come out alive.

Still the crime plagued him more and worse than it did those who
could have put up no defence — and why not? Only the thick-witted
should commit crimes; they do not mind, they live from day to day
and nothing worries them. Evil is for the dull-witted; anyone with
even traces of sensibility should avoid it if he possibly can, for he
will have to smart for it. That he has a conscience makes him worse
off than ever; he will be punished precisely on account of his conscience.

The deed done to Joseph and his father pursued Judah horribly.
He suffered, because he was capable of suffering, as one could guess
from his stag's eyes and a certain line round the thin nostrils and full
lips. The deed lay like a curse upon him and punished him with sore
adversity — or rather: whatever evil and adversity he suffered he laid
to that cause, regarding it as payment for the committed, the partici-
pated-in sin — and this again is evidence of a strangely arrogant

conscience. For he saw, of course, that the others — Dan or Gaddiel or Zebulon, to say nothing of the savage twins — went unscathed; that it mattered not at all to them and they had nothing to repent of; which might have taught him that his own plagues, those with himself and those with his sons, were perhaps quite independent of the common crime and came from within him. But no, he would have it that he was suffering punishment, he alone, and looked with contempt on those who, thanks to their thick skins, remained unscathed. Such is the peculiar arrogance of conscience.

Now the torments he suffered all bore the sign of Ashtaroth; and he need not have been surprised that they came from this quarter, because he had always been plagued by the mistress, in other words had been her slave without loving her. Judah believed in the God of his fathers, El Elyon, the Highest, Shaddai, the Mighty One of Jacob, the Rock and the Shepherd, Jahwe, from whose nose, when He was wroth, steam came and consuming fire from His mouth, that it lightened from it. Judah made burnt offerings to Him and brought Him oxen and milch sheep to the altar as often as seemed proper. But he believed also in the Elohim of the people, which was nothing against him if he did not serve them. When one observes how late and how far from their beginnings the people of Jacob still had to be admonished to put away strange gods, Baal and Ashtaroth, and not to hold sacrificial feasts with the Moabites, one is impressed by their obstinate instability and tendency to backslide and fall away, down to the latest generation. Thus one is not surprised to learn that so early a figure, so near to the source as Jehudah ben Jekew, believed in Ashtaroth, who was entirely a folk-goddess, exalted everywhere under various names. She was Judah's mistress and he bore her yoke, that was the harsh reality — harsh to his soul and his election both — and so forsooth how should he not have believed in her? He did not sacrifice to her — not in the strict sense of the word; that is, he did not bring her a sweet savour of oxen and milch sheep. But to sorrier, more passionate sacrifices her cruel spear enforced him, sacrifices which he made not gladly, not with a light heart, but only under the mistress's lash; for his spirit groaned against his lust and he freed himself from no hierodule's arms without hiding his head in shame and doubting with anguish his fitness for election.

Since, then, they had together got Joseph out of the world, Judah had begun to regard the plagues of Astarte as a punishment for his guilt; for they increased, they beleaguered him from without as they laid siege to him from within. One can only say that since that time the man had atoned in hell — in one of the hells there are, the hell of sex. One might think that of all the several hells there are, that cannot be the worst. But he who thinks so knows not the thirst for purity without which indeed there is no hell, neither this one nor any other.

Hell is for the pure; that is the law of the moral world. For it is for sinners, and one can sin only against one's own purity. If one is like the beasts of the field one cannot sin, one knows no hell. Thus it is arranged, and hell is quite certainly inhabited only by the better sort; which is not just — but then, what is our justice?

The history of Judah's marriage and that of his sons and their destruction thereby is extremely strange and abnormal and actually incomprehensible, so that it can be spoken of with half-words, and that not merely out of delicacy. We know that Leah's fourth married young — the step was taken out of love of purity, in order to find and restrict himself and thus find peace. But in vain; he reckoned without the goddess and her spear. His wife, whose name tradition has not given us — perhaps she was not much called by it — she was simply the daughter of Shuah, that Canaanite man whose acquaintance Judah had made through his friend and head shepherd Hirah from Adullam. This woman, then, had much to weep over, much to forgive, and it was somewhat easier for her because three times she experienced the joy of motherhood. Yet after all it was a brief joy, for the sons she gave Judah were only nice in the beginning, and grew up nasty. The youngest, however, Shelah, born at quite an interval after the second, was only sickly; but the two elder ones, Er and Onan, were both sickly and evil; sickly in an evil way and evil in a sickly way, though both were pretty to look at, and sprightly in their manners. In short, they were an affliction in Israel. Lads like these, unusual and sickly, yet charming in their own way, are a misfit in time and place, a sign of Nature's rashness, who will sometimes for a moment fall doting and forget where she is. Er and Onan would have fitted into a late and ancient society, into an old-man world of mocking heirs; for instance, into the monkey-land of Egypt. So close to the beginnings of an effort addressed to the future and into space they were an error in time and place and had to be blotted out. Judah, their father, should have recognized the fact and blamed nobody — except perhaps himself for having begot them. But he put off the blame for their badness on their mother, Shuah's daughter, and only on himself in so far as he considered he had committed a folly when he took a born Baal-fool to wife. For their destruction he blamed the woman to whom he gave them in marriage, and whom he accused of being in the likeness of Ishtar, who destroys her beloved so that they die of her love. That was unfair: to his wife, who soon died of her grief; and certainly most unfair to Tamar as well.

TAMAR LEARNS THE WORLD

TAMAR, she it was. She sat at Jacob's feet, had sat there a long time now, profoundly moved by the expression on his face, listening to the

words of Israel. Never did she lean back, she sat up very straight, on
a footstool, on a well-step, on a knot of root beneath the tree of wisdom, with throat outstretched and concave back, two folds of strain
between her velvet brows. She came from a little place in the environs of Hebron, where people lived on their vineyards and kept a
few cattle. There stood her parents' house, they were small farmers
and sent the wench to Jacob with parched corn and fresh cheeses,
lentil and grits. And he bought them with copper. So came she to
him and first found her way thither on mere pretext, for actually she
was moved by a higher compulsion.

She was beautiful in her way; not pretty-beautiful, but beautiful
after an austere and forbidding fashion, so that she looked angry at
her own beauty, and with some justice too, for it had a compelling
power which left the men no rest; and it was precisely their unrest
which had graved the furrows in her brows. She was tall and almost
thin, but of a thinness more disturbing than any fleshliness however
ripe; accordingly the unrest was not of the flesh and so must be
called dæmonic. She had wonderfully beautiful and piercingly eloquent brown eyes, nearly round nostrils, and a haughty mouth.

What wonder that Jacob was taken with her, and as a reward for
her admiration drew her to himself? He was an old man, loving
feeling, only waiting to be able to feel again; and in order to reawaken feeling in us old folk, or at least something which mildly and
dimly reminds us of the feelings of our youth, there must come something out of the ordinary to give us strength by its admiration, at
once Astartelike and spiritually eager for our wisdom.

Tamar was a seeker. The furrows between her brows signified not
alone anger at her beauty but also strain and searching for truth and
salvation. Where in the world does one not meet concern with God?
It is present on the thrones of kings and in the mountain hut of the
poorest peasant. Tamar felt it. The unrest she aroused distressed and
exasperated her precisely on account of the higher unrest which she
herself felt. One might have supposed that this country girl would
have been satisfied by the wood and meadow nature-worship of her
tradition. But not so: it had not answered her urgent need even
before she met Jacob. She could not feed on the Baalim and fertility
deities, for her soul divined that there was something other and higher
in the world, and she yearned and strove towards it. There are such
souls; there only needs to come something new, some change into
the world and their sensibilities are touched and seized on, they must
make straight for it. Their unrest is not of the first order, not like
that of the wanderer from Ur, which drove him into the void, where
nothing was, so that he had to create the new out of himself. Not so
these souls. But if the new is there in the world, it disturbs their sen-

sitive feelings from afar off and they must forthwith go faring after it.

Tamar had not far to fare. The wares she brought to Jacob in his tent, receiving their weight in copper in exchange, were certainly only a pretext of her spirit, a device born of unrest. She found her way to Jacob; and now often and often she sat at the feet of the stately old man weighed down by the weight of his tales. She sat very erect, the great penetrating wide-open eyes cast up to him, so fixed and moveless with attention that the silver ear-rings on either side her sunken cheeks hung down unswaying. And he told her of the world; that is, he told her his tales, which with intent to instruct he boldly presented as the history of the world — the history of the spreading branches of a genealogical tree, a family history grown out of God and presided over by Him.

He taught her the beginning, chaos and old night, and their division by God's word; the work of the six days and how the sea at command had filled with fishes, next space under the firmament where the great lights hang, with many winged fowl, and the greening earth with cattle and reptiles and all manner of beasts. He gave her to hear the vigorous, blithely plural summons of God to Himself, the enterprising proposal: "Let us make man." And to Tamar it was as though it was Jacob who had said it and certainly as though God — who always and ever was called simply God, as nowhere else in the world — as though He must look just like Jacob; and indeed did not God go on to say: "in our image, after our likeness"? She heard of the garden eastwards in Eden and of the trees in it, the tree of life and the tree of knowledge; of the temptation and of God's first attack of jealousy: how he was alarmed lest man, who now indeed knew good and evil, might eat also of the tree of life and be entirely like "us." So then the likes of us made haste, drove out the man, and set the cherub with the flaming sword before the gate. And to the man he gave toil and death that he might be an image like to "us," indeed, but yet not too like, only somewhat liker than the fishes, the birds, and the beasts, and still with the privately assigned task of becoming against our jealous opposition ever as much more like as possible.

So she heard it. Very connected it was not; all pretty puzzling, but also very grand, like Jacob himself who told it. She heard of the brothers who were enemies, and of the slaying on the field. Of the children of Cain and their kinds and how they divided themselves in three on this earth: such as dwell in tents and have cattle; such as are artificers in brass and iron; and such as merely fiddle and whistle. That was a temporary classification. For from Seth, born to replace Abel, came many generations, down to Noah, the exceeding wise one: him God, going back on Himself and His annihilating wrath, permit-

ted to save all creation; he survived the flood with his sons, Shem,
Ham and Japheth, after which the world was divided up afresh, for
each one of the three produced countless generations and Jacob knew
them all — the names of the tribes and their settlements on earth
poured forth from his lips into Tamar's ears: wide was the prospect
over the swarming brood and the places of their dwellings; then all
at once it all came together into the particular and family history.
For Shem begot Eber in the third remove, and he Terah in the fifth,
and so it came to Abram, one of three, he was the one!

For to him God gave unrest in his heart on His account, so that he
laboured tirelessly on God to think Him forth and make Him a name;
he made Him unto himself for a benefactor and He repaid with far-
reaching promises the creature who created the Creator in the spirit.
He made a mutual bond with him: that one should become ever holier
in the other; and gave him the right of election, the power of cursing
and blessing, that he might bless the blessed and curse the accurst.
Far futures he opened out before him wherein the peoples surged, and
to them all his name should be a blessing. And promised him boundless fatherhood — since after all Abram was unfruitful in Sarah up
till his eighty-sixth year.

Then he took the Egyptian maid and begot upon her and named
her son Ishmael. But that was a begetting on a side-line, not on the
path of salvation but belonging to the desert, and first-father did not
believe God's assurances that he should yet have a son by the true
wife, named Isaac; but fell on his face with laughter at God's word,
for he was already an hundred years old and with Sarah it had ceased
to be after the manner of women. But his laughter was a wrong unto
her, for Jizchak appeared, the saved sacrifice, of whom it was said
from on high that he should beget twelve princes. That was not
strictly accurate; God sometimes misspoke and did not always mean
exactly what He said. It was not Isaac who begot the twelve, or only
indirectly. Actually it was himself, from whose solemn lips the tale
fell on which the simple maid was hanging. It was Jacob, brother of
the Red One; with four women he begot the twelve, being servant
of the devil Laban at Sinear.

And now Tamar heard once more about brothers who were enemies: the red hunter, the gentle shepherd; she learned of the blessing-
deception that put things straight, and the flight of the blessing-thief.
A little there was about Eliphaz, son of the deposed son, and the meeting with him by the way; but it was toned down to save Jacob's face.
Here and elsewhere the narrator went delicately: for instance, when
speaking of Rachel's loveliness and his love of her. He was sparing
himself when he softened the account of his humiliation at Eliphaz's
hands. But in the case of the dearly beloved he was sparing Tamar;
for he was a little in love with her and his feeling told him that in the

presence of one woman one does not praise too warmly the charms of another.

On the other hand the great dream of the ladder, which the thief of the blessing dreamed at Luz, that his pupil heard about in all its magnitude and splendour; though such a glorious lifting up of the head perhaps did not sound quite reasonable unless one knew about the deep humiliation that went before. She heard tell of the heir — looking at him the while all eyes and ears — who bought the blessing of Abraham and had power to pass it on to one who should be Lord over his brothers, at whose feet his mother's children must bow down. And again she heard the words: "Through thee and thy seed shall be blessed all the generations on the earth." And did not stir.

Yes, what all did she not hear, and how impressively delivered, in these hours — what tales they were! The fourteen years' service in the land of mud and gold unrolled before her and then the extra years that made them twenty-five, and how the wrong one and the right one and their handmaidens together assembled the eleven, including the charming one. Of the flight together she heard, of Laban's pursuit and search. Of the wrestling with the ox-eyed one till the dawn, from which Jacob all his life limped like a smith. Of Shechem and its abominations, when the savage twins strangled the bridegroom and destroyed the cattle and were cursed — up to a point. Of Rachel's dying a furlong only from the inn, and of the little son of death. Of Reuben's irresponsible shooting away and how he too was cursed, in so far as Israel can be cursed. And then the story of Joseph: how the father had loved him sore, but, strong of soul and heroic in God, had sent him forth and knowingly given the best beloved a sacrifice.

This "once on a time" was still fresh, and Jacob's voice shook, whereas in the earlier ones, already overlaid with years, it had been epically unmoved, solemn and blithe of word and tone, even in the grim and heavy, heavy parts; for these were all God's-stories, sacred in the telling. But it is quite certain now, could not be otherwise and must be conceded, that Tamar's listening soul in the course of instruction was fed not alone on historical, time-overlaid once-on-a-time, the time-honored "once," but with "one day" as well. And "one day" is a word of scope, it has two faces. It looks back, into solemnly twilit distances, and it looks forwards, far, far forwards, into space, and is not less solemn because it deals with the to-be than that other dealing with the has-been. Many deny this. To them the "one day" of the past is the only holy one; that of the future they account trifling. They are "pious," not pious, fools and clouded souls, Jacob sat not in their church. Who honours not the future "one day," to him the past has had naught to say, and even the present he fronts the wrong way. Such is our creed, if we may interpolate it into the teachings which Jacob ben Jizchak imparted to Tamar: teachings full of the double-faced "one day" — and why not, since he was telling her the "world" and that is "one day" in both senses, of knowledge and of foreknowledge? Well might she gratefully say to him, as she did: "You have paid too little heed, my master and lord, to telling me what has come to pass, but spoken ever to thy handmaiden of the far future." For so he had done, quite unconsciously, since into all his stories of the beginning there came an element of promise, so that one could not tell them without foretelling.

Of what did he speak to her? He spoke of Shiloh.

The assumption would be entirely wrong that it was only upon his death-bed, feeling the promptings of oncoming dissolution, that Jacob spoke of Shiloh the hero. In that moment he had no promptings at all; merely pronouncing the long-known and prepared words, having considered and conned them half his life long, so that his dying hour could only confer on them an added solemnity. I mean the blessing and cursing judgments upon his sons, and the reference to the figure of the promise, whom he called Shiloh. It had occupied Jacob's thoughts even in Tamar's time and even though he spoke of it to nobody but her, and then out of gratitude for her great attentiveness and because with the remnant of his power of feeling he was a little in love with her.

Strange indeed, and extraordinary, how he had mused it all out to himself! For Shiloh was really nothing but a place-name, the name of a walled settlement in the country farther north, where often the children of the land, when they had fought and come off victors, would gather to divide the spoil. Not a particularly sacred place, but it was called place of quiet or rest, for that is what Shiloh means: it signifies peace, signifies drawing a long and relieved breath after bloody feud. It is a blessing-word, as proper for a person as for a place. Sichem, son of the citadel, had had the same name as his city; and in the same way Shiloh might serve for a man and son of man called bearer and bringer of peace. In Jacob's thoughts he was the man of expectation, promised in those earliest and ever renewed vows and precepts: promised to the womb of the woman, promised in Noah's blessing on Shem, promised to Abraham, through whose seed all the breeds on the earth should be blessed. The prince of peace and the anointed, who should reign from sea to sea and from river to river to the end of the world, to whom all kings should bow, and all the peoples cleave to the hero who one day should be awoken out of the chosen seed, and to whom the seed of his kingdom should be confirmed for ever.

Him who would then come he called Shiloh. And now we are challenged to use our imagination as well as we can and picture to ourself how the old man, endowed with such rich gifts of expression and impressiveness, spoke to Tamar of Shiloh in these hours and bound up the earliest beginning with the furthest future. His language was powerful, it was weighty with meaning. Tamar, the female, the single soul deemed worthy to hear it, sat motionless. Even watching very closely you could not be sure of even the slightest swaying of her ear-rings. She heard "the world," which in the early things hid promise of the late: a vast, ever branching eventful history, through which ran the scarlet thread of promise and expectancy from "one day" to "one day," from the earliest "one day" to the furthest future one. On that "one day," in a cosmic catastrophe of salvation, two stars which flamed in wrath against each other, the star of might and the star of right, would rush upon each other in consummating thunder-crash to be henceforward one and shine with mild and mighty radiance for ever on the heads of men: the star of peace. That was Shiloh's star, star of the son of man, the son of the election, who was promised to the seed of the woman, that he should tread the serpent underfoot. Now Tamar was a woman, she was *the* woman, for every woman is *the* woman, instrument of the Fall and womb of salvation, Astarte and the mother of God; and at the feet of the father-man she sat, on whom at a confirming nod the blessing had fallen and who should pass it on in history to one in Israel. Who was it? Above whose brow would the father lift up his horn that he anoint him as his heir? Tamar had fingers whereon to reckon it up. Three of the sons had been cursed, the favoured, son of the true wife, was dead. Not love could guide the course of inheritance, and where love has gone, nothing but justice remains. Justice was the horn out of which the oil of anointing must trickle on the brow of the fourth. Judah, he was the heir.

THE RESOLUTE ONE

FROM now on, the standing furrows between Tamar's brows took on yet another meaning. Not only of anger against her beauty they spoke, of searching and strain, but also of determination. Here let me impress upon you: Tamar had made up her mind, cost what it might, by dint of her womanhood to squeeze herself into the history of the world. So ambitious she was. In this inexorable and almost sinister resolve — there is about the inexorable always something sinister — her spiritual aspirations had issued. There are natures wherein teaching is straightway converted into resolve; indeed, they only seek instruction in order to feed their will-power and give it an aim. Tamar had needed only to be instructed about the world and its striving toward its goal, to arrive at the unconditional resolve to mingle her womanhood with these strivings and to become historic.

Let me be clear: everybody has a place in the history of the world. Simply to be born into it one must, one way or the other and roughly

speaking, contribute by one's little span one's mite to the whole
of the world-span. Most of us, however, swarm in the periphery, far
off to one side, unaware of the world-history, unsharing in it, modest
and at bottom not displeased at not belonging to its illustrious dramatis
personæ. For such an attitude Tamar had only contempt. Scarcely had
she received instruction when she resolved and willed, or, better put,
she had taken instruction to learn what it was she willed and did not
will, and she made up her mind to put herself in line, into the line of
the promise. She wanted to be of the family, to shove herself and
her womb into the course of history, which led, through time, to salvation. *She* was the woman, the dispensation had come to her seed.
She would be the foremother of Shiloh, no more and no less. Firm
stood the folds between her velvet brows. They already meant three
things, they could not fail to mean yet a fourth: they came to mean
anger and envious scorn for Shuah's daughter, Jehudah's wife. This
jade was already in the line, she had a privileged place, and that without merit, knowledge, or will-power (for Tamar counted these as
merits); she was a cipher dignified by history. Tamar bore her ill
will, she hated her, quite consciously and most femininely. She would
have, equally open-eyed, wished for her death if that had had any
sense. But it had none because the woman had already borne three
sons to Judah, so that Tamar would have had to wish all three of
them dead too to have things put back and a free place made for herself at the side of the inheritor of the blessing. It was in this character
that she loved Judah and desired him; her love was ambition. Probably never — or never up till then — did a woman love and desire a
man so entirely apart from his own sake and so entirely for the sake
of an idea as Tamar loved Judah. It was a new basis for love, for the
first time in existence: love which comes not from the flesh but from
the idea, so that one might well call it dæmonic, as we did the unrest
which Tamar herself evoked in men aside from her fleshly form.

She could have got at Judah with her Astarte side and would probably have been pleased to do so, for she knew him much too well as
slave to the mistress not to be sure of success. But it was too late;
which always means too late in time. She came too late, her ambition-
love was in the wrong time-place. She could no longer shove herself
in at this link in the chain and put herself into the line. So she would
have to take a step forward or else back in time and the generations:
she would have to change her own generation and address her ambitious designs to the point where she would have preferred to be
mother. The idea was not a difficult one, for in the highest sphere
mother and beloved had always been one. In short, she would have to
avert her gaze from Judah and direct it upon his sons, the grandsons
of the inheritance, whom under other circumstances she could almost
have wished out of the way, in order to bear them again herself to

better purpose. And first, of course, she directed it solely upon the boy Er, he being the heir.

Her personal position in time made the descent quite possible. She would not have been much too young for Judah, and for Er not entirely too old. Still, she took the step without joy. She was put off by the sickliness and degeneracy of the brothers, no matter how much charm they had. But her ambition came to her aid, and luckily, for otherwise she would have found it inadequate. Ambition told her that the promise did not always take the promising or even the suitable course; that it might run through a great deal that was dubious or worthless or even depraved without exhausting itself. That disease did not always come of disease, but that it can issue in tested and developed strength and continue on the way of salvation — especially when brought out and developed by dint of such a resolute will as Tamar called her own. Besides, the scions of Judah were just degenerate males, just that. It depended on the female, on the right person coming in at the weak point. The first promise had to do with the womb of the woman. What in fact had the men got to do with it?

So, then, to reach her goal she had to rise in time to the third generation; otherwise the thing was not possible. She did indeed practise her Astarte wiles on the young man but his response was both childish and vicious. Er only wanted to sport with her, and when she set the darkness of her brows against him he fell away and was incapable of being serious. A certain delicacy restrained her from going further up and working on Judah; for it had been he whom she actually wanted or would have wanted, and though he did not know that, yet she did, and was ashamed to beg from him the son whom she would gladly have borne him. Therefore she got behind the head of the tribe, her master, Jacob, and worked on his dignified weakness for her, of which she was fully aware, of course, and more flattered than wounded it by wooing for admission and desiring from him his grandson for her husband. They sat in the tent, on the very spot where Joseph had once talked the old man out of the many-coloured coat. Her task was easier than his.

"Master and lord," she said, "little Father, dear and great, hear now thy handmaid and incline thine ear to her prayer and her earnest and yearning desire. Lo, thou hast made me distinguished and great before the daughters of the land, hast instructed me in the world and in God, the only Highest; hast opened my eyes, and taught me so that I am thy creation. But how has this been vouchsafed to me that I found favour in thine eyes and thou hast comforted me and spoken to thy handmaid with kindness, which may the Lord requite thee and may thy reward be perfect in the God of Israel, to whom I have come by thy hand so that I have safety beneath His wings? For I guard myself and keep well my soul that I forget not the tales which you have made me see, and that they shall not come away from my heart as long as I live. My children and my children's children, if God give me such, them will I tell, that they destroy themselves not, nor make themselves any image like unto man or woman or cattle on earth or birds beneath the sky or reptiles or fishes; nor that they shall lift up their eyes and see the sun, the moon, and the stars, and fall away from me to worship them. Thy people are my people and thy God my God. So if He give me children they shall not come to me from a man of a strange people, it may not be. A man from out of thy house, my lord, perchance may take a daughter of the land, such as I was, and lead her to God. But I as I now am, new-born and thine image, cannot be bride to an uninstructed one and who prays to images of wood and stone from the hand of the artificer, which can neither hear nor see nor smell. Behold now, Father and lord, what thou hast done in shaping me, that thou hast made me fine and delicate of soul so that I cannot live like the hosts of the ignorant and wed the first wooer and give my womanhood to a God-fool as once in my simplicity I should have done. These now are the drawbacks of refinement and the hardships that elevation brings in its train. Therefore reckon it not to thy daughter and handmaid for a naughtiness if she point out the responsibility thou hast taken on thyself when thou didst form her, and how thou standest now in her debt almost as much as she in thine, since thou must now pay for her having been lifted up."

"What thou sayest, my daughter, is boldly conceived and not without sense: one hears it with applause. But show me thine aim, for I see it not yet, and confide in me whither thou thinkest. For it is dark to me."

"Of thy people," she answered, "am I in spirit. Of thy people alone can I be in the flesh and with my womanhood. Thou hast opened mine eyes, let me open thine. A branch grows from thy trunk, Er, eldest son of thy fourth son, and is like a palm tree by the waters and like a slender reed in the fence. Speak then with Judah, thy lion, that he give me to Er for a bride."

Jacob was exceedingly surprised.

"So that was thy meaning," he answered, "and thither went thy thought? Truly, truly, I should not have guessed it. Thou hast spoken to me of the responsibility I have taken on and makest me now concerned precisely on thine account. Verily I can speak with my lion and make my word avail with him. But can I justify it? Welcome art thou to my house, it opens its arms with joy to receive thee. But shall I have trained thee up to God so that thou becomest unblest? Unwillingly do I speak with doubt of anyone in Israel, but the sons of the daughter of Shuah are indeed an unable breed and good-for-nothings before the Lord, from whom I prefer to avert my gaze. Truly I hesitate very much to go along with thy wish, for it is my conviction the lads are no good for wedlock, and anyhow not with thee."

"With me," said she firmly, "if with nobody else. Bethink thee after all, my master and lord! It was irretrievably decreed that Judah have sons. Now they are as they are and at least must be sound at the core, for in them is Israel. And they cannot be passed over, nor can one leave them out save that they themselves fall away and do not stand the test of life. Unavoidable is it that they should in turn have sons, at least one of them, one at least, Er, the first-born, the palm tree by the brook. I love him and I will build him up with my love to a hero in Israel."

"A heroine, at least," he responded, "art thou thyself, my daughter. And I trust in thee to perform it."

So he promised her to make his word good with Judah his Lion, and his heart was full of varying and conflicting feelings. For he loved the woman, with what strong feeling was left him, and was glad to present her to a man of his own blood. Still he was sorry and it went against his honour, that it should be no better man. And again, he knew not why, the whole idea made him somewhat to shudder.

"NOT THROUGH US"

JUDAH did not live with his brothers in the grove of Mamre, "in his father's house"; since he had become good friends with the man Hirah, he pastured farther down towards the plain in the grazing-ground by Adullam, and there his son Er, his eldest, and Tamar celebrated their wedding, provided by Jacob, who had sent for his fourth and made his word avail with him. Why should Judah have kicked against the pricks? He consented not too gracefully, with rather a gloomy air, but he did consent with no ado and so Tamar was given to Er to wife.

It befits us not to look behind the veil of this marriage — even in the beginning no one liked it and humanity has always expressed itself baldly and brusquely as to the facts, finding it too much trouble, as always, to soften them with pity or excuse. The factors of failure were present in it: on one side historic ambition to play a part in history, combined with the gifts of Astarte; on the other enervation, a youth capable of standing no serious test in life. We shall do well to follow the example of tradition and baldly and brusquely state that Judah's Er, quite shortly after the wedding, died; or as tradition has it, the Lord slew him — well, the Lord does all, and all that happens may be regarded as His doing. In Tamar's arms the youth died of a hæmorrhage which would probably have killed him even if he had not choked to death with the blood. Some people may feel relieved that at least he did not die quite alone like an animal but in the arms of his wife, though again it is distressing to picture her dyed with the life-blood of her young husband.

Dark-browed she stood up. She washed herself clean of the blood and straightway demanded for her husband Onan, Judah's second son.

The determination of this woman has always had something staggering about it. She went up to Jacob and lamented to him; in a way she accused God to him, so that the old man was seriously embarrassed for Yah.

"My husband has died and left me," she said, "Er, thy grandson, in a trice and the twinkling of an eye. How is one to understand that? How can God do so?"

"He can do everything," Jacob replied. "Humble thyself! He does, when occasion requires, the most frightful things. For to be able to do everything one wants is, when you come to think of it, a great temptation. There are vestiges of the desert — try to explain it so to thyself. He sometimes falls on a man and slays him whether or no, without rhyme or reason. One must just accept it."

"I accept it," she replied, "so far as God is concerned. But not for my own part, for I do not recognize my widowhood, I cannot and I may not. Since one has fallen away, the next must take his place; that my fire be not quenched which still lives and to my husband no name remain and nothing else upon earth. I speak not for myself alone and for the slain one, I speak generally and for all time. Thou, Father and lord, must make thy word avail in Israel and exalt it into a law, that where there are brothers and one dies childless, his wife shall take no strange man from outside, but her brother-in-law shall step in and wed her. But the first son whom she bears shall he confirm after the name of his deceased brother, that his name shall not be uprooted out of Israel."

"But if it please not the man," Jacob objected, "to take his sister-in-law?"

"In that case," said Tamar firmly, "she shall stand forth before the people and say: 'My brother-in-law refuses to reawaken for his brother a name in Israel and will not marry me.' Then shall one require him and speak with him. But if he stand and speak: 'I like not to take her,' then shall she stand to him before all the people and take one of his shoes from off his foot and spit upon it and answer and say: 'Thus shall one do to every man who will not build up his brother's house.' And his name shall be Barefooter!"

"Then certainly he will bethink himself," said Jacob. "And thou art right, my daughter, in so far as it will be easier for me to make my word avail with Judah that he should give thee Onan for a husband if I make a general law on which I can support myself, which I have proclaimed under the tree of wisdom."

It was the brother-in-law marriage which at Tamar's instigation was thus founded and became a matter of history. This country girl had certainly a flair for the historical. Skipping over the stage of widowhood, she now received the boy Onan as her husband, though Judah showed small desire for the arrangement or the collateral marriage, and the person most concerned even less. Judah, sent for to his father from the grazing-ground of Adullam, rebelled a long time against the father's counsel and denied that it was advisable to repeat with his second what had turned out so unhappily with his first. Besides, Onan was only twenty, and if capable of marriage at all, certainly not yet ripe for it, and neither willing nor disposed thereto.

"But she will take off his shoe and all that if he refuse to build up his brother's house, and will be called Barefooter all his days."

"Thou makest, Israel, as though that were established fact, and it is so only because thou hast but now thyself introduced it – I know well by whose advice."

"God speaks out of the maid," responded Jacob. "He has brought her to me that I make her acquaint with Him, that He may speak out of her."

Then Judah rebelled no more, but ordered the wedding.

It is beneath the dignity of this narrator to pry into the secrets of the bedchamber. So then, baldly and bruskly: Judah's second son, Onan, in his own way quite pleasing – and his way was a dubious one – was, again in his own way, quite a character. He had a deep-seated perversity of disposition, amounting to a judgment upon himself and a denial of life. I do not mean his own personal life, not exactly that; for he possessed much self-love and rouged and adorned himself like any dandy. Yet in the very soul of him he denied life; for in those inmost depths he uttered an emphatic no to any continuation of life after or through him. We are told that he was angry at being forced to become a surrogate husband and raise up seed not to himself but to his brother. That is probably true; so far as words and even thoughts come in question, he might put the thing so to himself. But in reality, for which words and thoughts are only paraphrases, the knowledge was inborn in all the sons of Judah that life was a blind alley; that whatever way it might take, in no case would, should, could, or might it continue further through them, the three sons. Not through us, they said with one voice, and in their way they were right. Life and lustiness might go their ways, the three turned up their noses. Particularly Onan; and his prettiness and charm were merely an expression of the narcissism of a man beyond whom the line does not continue.

Forced into marriage, he resolved to make a fool of the womb. But he reckoned without Tamar's strength of will and her Astarte equipment, which confronted his perversity as one thunder-cloud

confronts another; like thunder-clouds they met and lightning followed — the stroke of death. He was paralysed and died in her arms
from one second to the next. His brain stood still and he was dead.

Tamar rose up and straightway demanded that Shelah be given her
for husband, he, Judah's youngest-born, being then only sixteen
years old. She might be called the most amazing figure in this whole
story — few will be found to deny it.

This time she did not prevail. Even Jacob hesitated, if only in anticipation of Judah's emphatic objection, and that was not long in
coming. They called him a lion; but like a lioness he stood before his
last cub, whatever he might or might not be worth, and would not
budge.

"Never!" he said. "What! So he is to die too, in blood like one,
without, like the other? God shall prevent it, it shall not be. I have
obeyed thy summons, Israel, and hastened up to thee from my wife's
kin in the plain where Shuah's daughter bore me this son and where
she now lies sickened. For she is ailing and drooping towards death,
and if Shelah die too, then I am bare. There is no question of diso-
bedience here, for thou mayst indeed not command me at all, and
thou makest only a hesitant suggestion. But I hesitate not only. I say
no and never, for thee and for me. What thinks this woman, that I
shall give her my ewe lamb that she destroy it? That is an Ishtar, who
slays her beloved. A devourer of youth is she, a greed insatiable. Besides, this one is still a boy, still under full years, so that the lamb will
avail her nothing in the fold of her arms."

Really nobody could have imagined Shelah, at least not now, in
the rôle of married man. He looked more like an angel than a human
being, very smug and unserviceable, and had neither beard nor bass.

"It is only on account of the shoe and the rest of it," Jacob reminded him quaveringly, "if the boy refuses to build up his brother's
house."

"I will tell thee a thing, my friend," quoth Judah. "If this devourer
go not now away and put on widow's garb and continue to do her
seemly mourning in her father's house as the bereaved of two husbands and behave quietly, then I myself, as sure as I am thy fourth
son, will take off her shoe before all the people and do all the rest of
it and accuse her openly of being a vampire that she may be stoned
or burned."

"That is going too far," said Jacob in painful agitation, "in thy dislike of my suggestion."

"Going too far? And how far wouldst thou go if they would take
Benjamin from thee and try to send him on some very dangerous
journey, who after all is not thine only one but merely thy youngest?
Thou guardest him with thy staff and keepst him close that he too

may not be lost and scarce can he go out on the highroad. Well, Shelah is my Benjamin and I resist, everything in me rises up against yielding him up."

"I will make thee a fair proposal," Jacob said, for this argument had gone home to him. "Just in order to gain time and not grossly to offend the girl, thy daughter-in-law, we will not reject her demand but wean her from it. Go to her and say: 'My son Shelah is still too young and is even unripe for his years. Remain a widow in thy father's house till the lad grow up, then I will give him to thee that he may raise up seed to his brother.' So shall we silence her demand for some years before she can renew it. Then perhaps she will get used to the widow's state and not renew it at all. Or if she do, then we will console her, saying with more or less truth that the lad is still not ripe."

"Be it so," said Judah. "It is the same to me what we tell her if only I do not have to yield that tenderness and pride into the burning embrace of Moloch."

And it came about according to Jacob's instructions. Tamar received dark-browed her father-in-law's verdict, looking deep into his eyes, but she yielded. As a widow and a woman who mourns she remained in her father's house and nothing was heard of her, one year and two years and even a third. After two she would have been justified in renewing her claim; but she expressly waited a third year in order not to be told that Shelah was still too young. The patience of this woman was as remarkable as her resolution. Indeed, resolution and patience are probably the same thing.

But now that Shelah was nineteen and in the bloom of whatever manhood he would ever rejoice in, she came before Judah and spoke:

"The term is up and the time is now ripe for thee to give me to thy son as wife and him to me as husband, that he raise up to his brother name and seed. Remember thy bond."

Now Judah, even before the first year of waiting was out, had become a widower. Shuah's daughter had died, out of affliction over his bondage to Astarte, the loss of her sons, and the blame on her head for their loss. He had now only Shelah left and was less than ever minded to send him on the perilous journey. So he answered:

"Bond? There was never one made, my friend. Do I mean by that that I do not stand by the simple word of my mouth? Not so. But I would not have thought thou wouldst insist after so long a time, for it was a word of delay. Wilt thou have another such? If so, I will give it thee, but it should not be needed, for thou shouldst already have consoled thyself. True, Shelah is older, but only a little, and thou art further forward of him than when my word consoled thee. Thou mightest almost be his mother."

"Oh, might I?" asked she. "Thou showest me my place, I see."

"Thy place," said he, "in my opinion, is in thy father's house, to remain there a widow and a woman who wears mourning for two husbands."

She bowed and went hence. Now comes the sequel.

This woman was not so easy to put off the track and remove from the line of descent. The more we observe her, the more we are amazed. She had dealt very freely with her position in time, moving it down with her to the grandchildren, whom she cursed because they were in the way of those whom she would bring forward. Now she resolved to change generations a second time and climb up again; she would pass over the one remaining member of the generation of grandchildren, whom they would not give her, that he might either die or else bring her and her womb into the line of descent. She would do this, for her flame might not be quenched nor would she suffer them to shut her out of her God-inheritance.

THE SHEEP-SHEARING

Now, these following are the things which happened to Judah, Jacob's son. Not many days after the day when the lion again played lioness and put himself before his cub, the sheep-shearing came round and the feast of the wool-harvest. And the shepherds and herders of the region gathered to eat and drink and offer sacrifice. The feast was held in different places. This time it was in the mountains, called Timnath, and hither came the shepherds and owners of the flock down from above and up from below, to shear their sheep and have a good time. Judah went up together with Hirah of Adullam, his friend and head shepherd, the same through whom he had got to know Shuah's daughter; for they too meant to shear and have a good time — at least Hirah did, for Judah was not inclined for a good time, he never was. He lived in hell, in punishment for former share in evil doings, and the way his sons had lost their lives looked very like this hell. He was afflicted over his election and on account of it would rather have had no feast and no good time, for if one is bond-slave to hell, all gaiety takes on the nature of the hellish and leads to nothing save befouling the election. But what was the use? Only the ill in body are excused from life. If one ails only in spirit, that does not count. No one understands it and one must play one's part in life and keep the seasons with the rest. So Judah stopped three days at the shearing at Timnath, sacrificed and feasted.

The way back to his own place he travelled alone; he liked it better alone. We know that he went on foot for he had a good knobbed staff of some value, a walking-staff, not a cudgel for a beast. With it he strode down the hilly paths between vineyards and villages, in the parting gleams of the day, which went redly to its rest. The roads and bypaths were familiar; there was Enam, the place Enajim at the foot of the heights, which he must pass on his way towards Adullam and the village of his kinfolk. The gate, the mud walls, the very houses shone crimson in the glory of the exulting heavens. By the gate crouched a figure; when he came closer he saw that it was wrapped in a *ketonet paspasîm*, the shrouding garment of those who are temptresses.

His first thought was: "I am alone." His second: "I will go by." The third: "To hell with her! Must the *kedeshe*, the daughter of joy, sit on my peaceful homeward way? So it looks to me. But I will take no heed, for I am twofold, that I am: he of whom it looks likely and he who is bitter, denies himself and goes angrily by. The old song! Must it be sung for ever? So sing the chained galley-slaves from their groaning hearts at the oar. Up above I groaned and sang it with a dancing-girl and should be sated for a while. As though hell were ever sated! Shameful craving and absurd for the hundredfold hateful! What will she say, how behave? He who comes after me may try. I will go past."

And he stopped.

"Greeting to the Mistress."

"May she strengthen thee," she whispered.

The angel of desire had already seized upon him and her whisper made him shiver with lustful curiosity after this woman.

"Whispering wayside one," said he, with trembling lips, "for whom dost thou wait?"

"I wait," she replied, "on a lusty lustling who will share with me the mystery of the goddess."

"Then am I half the right man," said he, "for a lustling am I if not a lusty one. I have no lust to lust, yet she to me. In thy calling, methinks, one is not very lusty for lust either, but must be glad if others feel it."

"We are givers," she said, "but if the right one comes we know how to receive as well. Hast thou lust to me?"

He put his hand upon her.

"But what wilt thou give me?" she stopped him.

He laughed. "In sign," he said, "that I am a son of lust with some trace of lustiness I will give thee a he-goat from the flock that thou remember me."

"But thou hast it not by thee."

"I will send it thee."

"A man says that beforehand. Afterwards he is a different man and remembers not his former word. I must have a pledge."

"Name it."

"Give me thy signet from thy finger and thy bracelets and thy staff that is in thy hands."

"Thou knowest how to look out for the Mistress," he said. "Take them!"

And he sang the song with her by the wayside in the red evening glow and she went away round the wall. But he went on home and next morning he said to Hirah, his shepherd:

"Well, so and so, you know how such things are. At the gate of Enajim, the place of Enam, there was a temple prostitute, and her eyes had something about them under the *ketonet* — in short, why make so much of it between men? Be so good and take her the he-goat I promised so I get back my things I had to leave her, ring, staff, and bracelets. Take her a fine big billy-boat, I won't be shabby with the shabby creature. Maybe she is sitting again by the gate, or ask the people of the place."

Hirah picked out the goat, diabolically ugly and magnificent with ringed horns, cleft nose, and long beard, and took him to the gate by Enajim, where nobody was. "The whore," he asked within, "who sat outside by the road? Where is she? You must know your whores."

But they answered him: "Here was and is no whore. We have none here, we are a decent little place. Look elsewhere for the she-goat for thy he-goat, or stones will be flying."

Hirah told that to Judah, who shrugged his shoulders.

"If she cannot be found, then the fault is hers. We have offered to pay, nobody can reproach us. Of course, I have lost my things. The staff had a crystal knob. Put the goat back to the herd."

With that he forgot it. But three months later it became plain that Tamar was with child.

It was a scandal such as the neighbourhood had not seen for a long time. She had lived a widow, in mourning garments, in her parents' house, and now it came to light and could no longer be hid that she had carried on shamelessly, in a manner worthy death. The men growled in their beards, the women screeched their scorn and curses. For Tamar had always been arrogant and behaved as though she were above them. The hue and cry soon came to Judah's ears: "Hast thou heard, hast thou heard? Tamar, thy daughter-in-law, has so behaved that she cannot hide it longer. She is with child by whoredom."

Judah went pale. His stag-eyes stood out, his nostrils flickered. Sinners can be extremely sensitive to the sins of the world; besides he had bad blood towards the woman because she had consumed his two sons and also because he had broken his promise about his third.

"She is guilty of crime," said he. "Brazen be the sky above her head and iron the earth beneath her! She should be burnt with fire. Long ago she was due to the stake; but now the sin is open, she has committed an abomination in Israel and besmirched her mourning garment. They shall set her out before the door of her father's house and burn her to ashes. Her blood be on her own head!"

With long strides he outpaced the informers, who flourished switches, and on the way were increased by other flourishers from the villages round, so that it was an eager crowd who came up before the widow's house in Judah's train, whistling and jeering. Inside one could hear Tamar's parents sobbing and lamenting, but from herself no sound.

Then three men were told off to go in and produce the courtesan. They squared their shoulders and went in, stiff-armed, chins drawn in, fists ready, to fetch out Tamar, first to be pilloried and then to be burnt. After a while they came out again without Tamar, bearing certain things with them. One had a ring between two fingers, the others splayed out. The second held a staff out in front of him by the middle. The third had a purple cord dangling from his hand. They brought the things to Judah, standing there foremost, and said:

"We were to say this to thee from Tamar thy daughter-in-law: 'From the man whose pledges these are I carry my pawn. Dost thou know them? Then hearken: I am not the woman to let herself be destroyed together with her son from the heir of God.'"

Judah the lion looked at the things while the crowd pressed round him and peered in his face. White as he had been all the time with anger, so slowly now he grew red as fire, up into the roots of his hair and even into his very eyes, and was dumb. And then a woman began to laugh and then another and then a man and then several men and women and at length the whole place rang with their laughter going on and on; they bent over with laughing and their mouths gaped up towards the sky and they cried: "Judah 'twas thou! Ho, ho, ho! Judah hath got his son an heir from his whore! Ha, ha, ho, ho, ho!"

And Leah's fourth? He spoke very low, standing there in the crowd: "She is more justified than I." And went with bowed head out of their midst.

But when six months later Tamar's hour came she gave birth to twins and they became mighty men. Two sons she had destroyed out of Israel when she descended in time, and for them she gave back two others incomparably better when she climbed up again. The first-come, Pharez, was in particular a most doughty man and in the seventh remove he begot one who was doughtiness itself, named Boaz, husband of a lovely one. They waxed great in Ephratha and were praised in Bethlehem, for their grandson was Isaiah the Bethlehemite, father of seven sons and of a little one who kept the sheep, brown, with beautiful eyes. He could play on the lute and with the sling he brought the giant low — by then he had been secretly anointed king.

All that lies far hence in the open future and belongs to the great history of which the history of Joseph is only an interlude. But into this history has been interpolated and there for ever remains the story of the woman who would not at any price let herself be put aside, but with astounding tenacity wormed herself into a place in the line of descent. There she stands, tall and almost sinister, on the slope of her native hills; one hand on her body, the other shading her eyes, she looks out upon the fruitful plains where the light breaks from towering clouds to radiate in waves of glory across the land.

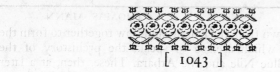

Chapter VI

THE GOD-STORY

OF WATERS AND WINDS

THE CHILDREN of Egypt, even the wisest and best-instructed of them, had in general the most childish ideas about the nature of their nourisher-god, that aspect and manifestation of divinity which the Abram-people called El Shaddei, the god of feeding, and the children of the black earth Hapi: the onswelling, surging one, the stream which had built up their marvellous oasis between the deserts and fed their existence and their comfortable, pious life-and-death philosophy — in other words, the river Nile. They believed, and from generation to generation taught their children, that the river — God knew where and how — arose out of the underworld, on its way to the "Great Green" — that is to say, the immeasurable ocean, as which they envisaged the Mediterranean — and that its subsidence, after its fructifying rise, was in the nature of a return to the lower world. . . . In short, there reigned among them the most utterly superstitious ignorance on this whole subject; and only the fact that there was no more enlightenment, indeed rather less, in the rest of the world, got them through life at all in such a darkened state. True, in spite of it they built up a mighty and magnificent kingdom, admired on all hands and holding out for many millennia; produced many beautiful things and in particular were geniuses at dealing with the object of their uninstructedness: namely, the river that fed them. Still, we who know so much more, in fact know everything, cannot but regret that none of us was on the spot at that time, to lighten the darkness within their souls and give them real understanding of the nature of Egypt's great river. What a buzz it would have made in the seminaries and academies, to be told that Hapi, far from having his source in the lower world (the lower world itself having been rejected as a baseless superstition) is merely the outlet of the great lakes in tropical Africa; and that the food-god, to become what he is, has first to be fed himself, by taking in all the rivers that flow down westwards from the Ethiopian Alps. In the rainy season, mountain brooks, full of fine detritus, rush and tumble down from the heights and flow together to form the two watercourses which are, so to speak, the prehistory of the future river: the Blue Nile and the Atbara. These, then, at a later locality, namely at Khartum and Berber, go together to bed and turn into the creative stream, the river Nile. For this, their common bed, about the middle of the summer, gradually becomes so full with the volume of water and liquid mud that the river spreads out widely over its banks — so widely, indeed, that the common epithet for it is the Overflowing One. The flood lasts for months, then just as gradually it subsides within its bounds. But the crust of mud, the deposit left by its overflowing, forms, as the seminarists well knew too, the fertile soil of Kemt.

But they would probably have been amazed, and even embittered against the harbingers of truth, when they heard that the Nile comes not from below but from above — in the last analysis from heights as high as the rain that in other less exceptional countries plays the fertilizing rôle. There, they used to say, meaning in the wretched foreign countries, the Nile is set in heaven, meaning by that the rain. And it must be confessed that a surprising intuition, almost approaching enlightenment, expresses itself in the florid phraseology: an insight, that is, into the relations existing between all the watercourses and water-sources in the world. The rise of the Nile depends on the amount of rainfall in the high mountains of Abyssinia; but the rains in turn are actually cloud-bursts from clouds formed over the Mediterranean and driven by the wind into those regions. The well-being of Egypt depends on how high the Nile rises; and in the same way the well-being of Canaan, the land Kenana, the Upper Retenu, as it was once called, or Palestine as we in our enlightenment designate Joseph's homeland and his father's, is conditioned by the rains which, in the rule, fall twice in the year: the early rain in the late autumn, the latter rain in the early part of the year. For the country is poor in springs, and not much can be done with the water of the rivers that run in the deep gorges. So everything depends on the rains, especially on the latter ones, and from the earliest times the rainfall has been collected. If the rains do not come, if instead of the moisture-bearing west wind it blows regularly from the south and east, from off the desert, then there is no hope of a harvest; aridity, crop failure, and famine follow — and not only here. For if it does not rain in Canaan, then there are no downpours in the Ethiopian hills, the mountain torrents do not tumble down from the heights, the two nourishers of the nourisher are not nourished — at least not enough for him to become "great," as the children of Egypt always put it; not great enough to fill the canals which carry the water to the higher levels. Then crop failure and want ensue, even here in the country where the Nile is not in heaven but on earth. And thus we see the connection between all the waters of the earth, in their sources and courses.

Though we ourselves are enlightened only in a general way on these matters, we see nothing strange (though much that is unfortunate) in the phenomenon that hard times come at the same time "in all lands"; not only in the land of mud but also in Syria, the land of the Philistines, Canaan, even the countries on the Red Sea, probably even in Mesopotamia and Babylonia; and that "the dearth was great in all lands." Yes, things can go from bad to worse, one year of irregularity, failure, and want can follow on another in ill-tempered succession; the strands of misfortune may spin themselves out over a number of years, until even the fabulous number of seven is reached — or perhaps not quite seven, but then even five is bad enough.

JOSEPH ENJOYS LIFE

FOR five whole years now the winds and the waters had behaved their best, and the harvest been so rich that in sheer gratitude people made a seven out of the five — and the five fully deserved it. But now the page turned. Pharaoh, maternally concerned for the kingdom of the black earth, had unclearly dreamed, and Joseph had boldly interpreted: the Nile failed to rise, because in Canaan the winter — that is, the latter — rain did not fall. It failed once; that was a misfortune. It failed twice, and that was ground for lamentation. It failed three times; there was blanching and blenching and wringing of hands. After that it might as well keep right on failing and go down in the records as a seven years' drought.

We human beings, when so unnaturally visited by nature, always behave the same way. At first we deceive ourselves, in our day-by-day minds, about the nature of the event: we do not understand what it means. We good-naturedly take it for an ordinary, average episode. After we have gradually learned that it is extraordinary, a first-class calamity such as we could never have dreamed could attack us in our lifetime, we look back in amazement on our former blindness. Thus the children of Egypt. It was long before they grasped the fact that this which they were enduring was the phenomenon called the "seven lean years." It had probably come to pass before now: in earlier times, in their legendary history, it had played a gruesome role; but they had never thought of it as affecting themselves. Their dullness of comprehension was not even as excusable as short-sightedness sometimes is. For Pharaoh had dreamed, and Joseph had interpreted. That they had really experienced the seven fat years might have been enough evidence that the seven lean ones would come along in their turn. But during the fat years the children of Egypt had put the lean ones out of their minds, as the man in the legend forgets the devil's book-keeping. Now the day of reckoning was at hand. When the nourisher had been pitiably low once, twice, and thrice, they had to admit it; and a patent result of the admission was a vast enlargement of Joseph's reputation.

Of course that too had steadily waxed in the years of fatness. How much more now must his fame have increased when the incidence of the lean ones proved that the measures he had taken were inspired by the profoundest wisdom!

In times of crop failure and hunger a minister of agriculture is in a bad position. The dull-witted population, never at the best very reasonable, always tending to make their feelings their guide, lay the blame for disaster on the shoulders of the highest responsible official. But if that official have acted in time to erect a magic barrier against evil, so that even if it work great changes, it is at least robbed of its character of a major catastrophe; if the official have done this, then he is a glorious and awe-inspiring leader of men.

Men living in a land which is theirs merely by adoption sometimes display the national traits more strongly than even the native-born. During the twenty years of Joseph's adoption into the land of Egypt, the typically Egyptian idea of careful, preventive preservation had got into his flesh and bones. He put it into practice; it was the motive for his acts. But it was a conscious motive, for he preserved enough distance from his guiding principle to keep in mind the truth that it was also popular with the Egyptians, and to deal accordingly. And this was a combination of sincerity and a sense of humour which goes down better than sincerity by itself.

And now his harvest time had come, and he reaped as he had sown. The sowing was his tax-economy during the good years; the harvest time was the distribution, a crown business of proportions never son of Re had known since the time of that god. For as it is set down, and told in song and story, "the dearth was in all lands; but in all the land of Egypt there was bread." Which of course does not mean that there was not scarcity in Egypt too. What the price of corn rose to in response to frenzied demand, anyone can imagine who has even a vague idea of the working of economic laws. He may grow pale at the realization, but at the same time he will also see that this scarcity was controlled, as the plenty had been before, by the same shrewd and kindly man; that the scarcity lay in his hand and he could wield it as he would. For Pharaoh he got out of it all that he could, but he did the same for those least able to cope with it, the little people. He did this by a combination of liberality and exploitation; of government usury and fiscal measures such as had never been seen before. His mingling of severity and mildness impressed everyone, even the hardest hit, as superhuman and godlike — for the gods do behave in just this ambivalent way and one never knows whether to call it cruel or kind.

The situation was fantastic. Agriculture was in a state that made the dream of the seven singed ears not even a parable but the bare bald truth. The dream-ears were burnt by the east wind, namely Khamsin, a scorching south-easter, and now Khamsin blew all summer long and throughout the harvest time, called Shemu, from February to June, almost without cease. Often it was a tempest like an oven, filling the air with a dust like ashes that coated the young growth. Whatever feeble green the unnourished nourisher had bred was charred by this desert breath. Seven ears? Yes, actually and literally — there were no more. In other words, the ears were not there, the harvest was not. But what was there, in quantity most scrupulously dealt out, was corn: every kind of grain and cereal, in the royal magazines and pits up and down the river in all the cities and towns and their vicinage. Throughout the length and breadth of Egypt — but only Egypt. Elsewhere there had been no provision, no building of bins, no foresight before the flood. Yes, in all Egypt, and only there, was bread; in the hand of the state, in the hand of Joseph, the superintendent of all that the heavens had given; and now he himself became like the heavens which gave and the river Nile which provides. He opened his chambers — not wide open, but with circumspection — and gave bread and grain to all who needed, and that was everybody; Egyptians as well as strangers from afar travelled hither to get food from Pharaoh's land, which now more correctly than ever was called a granary, the granary of the world. He gave, that is, he sold, to them that had, at prices not they but he fixed, corresponding to the extraordinary economic situation; so that he made Pharaoh gold and silver and still could give in more literal sense to the little lean-ribbed. To them he distributed, in measure, what they clamoured for: to the small farmers and the dwellers in the little guttered alleys of the big towns; gave them bread and grain, that they might not die.

That was godlike; but it was a praiseworthy human pattern too. There had always been good officials, who with justice had had written in their tombs that they had fed the King's subjects in time of need, given to the widow, not favoured the great before the small; and afterwards, when the Nile had once more grown, "had not taken the peasant's arrears" — that is, had not pressed for advance payment or a fixed date. The people thought of these tomb inscriptions as they saw Joseph's business methods. But "since the days of Set" no official had shown such benevolence, or was equipped with such plenary powers and such a truly godlike manipulation of them. The grain business, superintended by a staff of ten thousand scribes and underscribes, reached out all over Egypt, but all the threads ran back to

Menfe, into the palace of the King's shadow-dispenser and universal friend; there was not one final decision upon sale, loan, or gift which he had not reserved to himself. The rich man, the landed proprietor, came before him and cried for grain. To him he sold for his silver and gold, making the sale conditional upon the modernization of the man's irrigation system, so that he should stop muddling along in feudal inefficiency. Thus he kept faith with the highest, with Pharaoh, into whose treasuries flowed the rich man's silver and gold. The cry of the poor came before him too; and to them he distributed from the stores for nothing and again for nothing, that they might not hunger but eat. Herein he was true to his fundamental characteristic of human sympathy, to which we have already done justice and need not dwell longer upon it. Though we might just say once more that it has to do with mother-wit; for truly there was something deserving the adjective "witty" in Joseph's technique of combined largesse and exploitation; despite hard work and heavy cares he was always in high spirits, and at home would say to Asenath, his wife and daughter of the sun: "My girl, I am enjoying life!"

He sold abroad too, at high prices, as we know, and studied lists of the cereals delivered to the "nobles of the wretched Retenu." For many city kings of Canaan, among them the kings of Megiddo and Shahuren, sent to him for grain; the envoy from Ascalon came and cried before Joseph on behalf of his city and was given — at a price. But here too Joseph struck a balance between strict interest and friendliness, and starving sand-rabbits, shepherd stock from Syria and Lebanon — "barbarians, who do not know how to live," as his scribes said — he allowed to enter with their flocks, past the well-guarded gates of the land and east of the river, toward stony Arabia, to find a living on the fat pastures of Zoan, on the Tanitic arm of the Nile, if they promised not to trespass beyond their allotted territory.

Thus he would get from the frontier reports which ran like this: "We have passed Bedouins from Edom through the fortress of Merneptah and toward the lakes of Merneptah, to pasture their flocks on the great meadows of Pharaoh, the exalted sun of the lands."

He read very carefully. He read all the frontier reports with the utmost care and by his orders they had to be precise. He ordered a tightening of the regulations governing the entry of all persons through the eastern border fortresses into that rich land which now had become so uniquely rich. There had to be a list of names of every person coming out of the lands of wretchedness to fetch food from Pharaoh's corn-bins. Frontier officials like that Lieutenant Hor-waz of Thel, scribe of the great gate, who had once passed Joseph himself with his Ishmaelites into the land, had to take great pains with such lists, and to record all immigrants not only according to their names, trades, and places of origin, but also by their fathers' and grandfathers' names. The lists then had to be sent daily by fast messenger down to Menfe, to the offices of the King's shadow-dispenser.

There they were copied out fair on extra good paper with red and black ink and laid before the provider. And he, though quite busy enough without that, read them through every day from beginning to end, as carefully as they had been compiled.

THEY COME!

IT was in the second year of the lean kine, on a day in the middle of Epiph, May by our reckoning and frightfully hot, as it is anyhow in Egypt in their summer season, but even hotter than usual. The sun was like fire from heaven, we should have measured it at well over one hundred degrees in the shade. The wind was blowing and driving the hot sand into the red-lidded eyes of the little people in Menfe's narrow streets. There were hosts of flies, and they and the human beings were alike sluggish. The rich would have given large sums for half an hour of a breeze from the north-west; they would even have been willing that the poor should benefit as well.

Joseph too, the King's first mouthpiece, had a perspiring face caked with sand. But as he went home at noon from his office he seemed to be in high spirits and very lively—if the word be applicable to a man borne in state in a litter. Followed by the equipages of some of his upper officials, who were to lunch with him, according to a custom which the vice-god even today did not fail to observe, he soon turned off from the wide boulevard and was carried through some of the mean alleys of the poorer quarters, where he was hailed with cordial and confident familiarity. "Dgepnuteefonech!" the little lean-ribbed ones shouted, throwing kisses. "Hapi! Hapi! Ten thousand years to you, our provider, beyond the end of your destiny!" And they, who would simply be rolled in a mat when they were taken out to the desert, wished him: "Four excellent jugs for your entrails, and for your mummy an alabaster coffin!" Such was the form their sympathy took, in response to his for them.

At length the litter bore him through the painted gate in the wall of his gracious villa, into the front garden, where olive, pepper, and fig trees, the shadowy cypress and the spreading fanlike palm were grouped about the gay papyrus columns of the terrace before the house, and mirrored in the square walled-in lotus pool. A broad gravelled drive ran round the pond; the bearers followed it and came to a halt, whereupon the runners offered Joseph knee and neck, so that he stepped first upon them and then to the ground. Mai-Sachme was quietly awaiting him on the terrace or rather at the top of the flight of steps at one side, as were Hepi and Hezes, two greyhounds from Punt, most aristocratic beasts in gold collars, a-quiver with nerves.

Pharaoh's friend sprang up the shallow steps, more precipitately than usual; indeed, more briskly than an Egyptian noble should move before spectators. He did not look at his retinue.

"Mai," said he hurriedly, in a low tone, as he patted the animals' heads and they put their fore-paws on his chest to greet him, "I must talk to you at once, alone. Come into my room. Let them wait, there is no hurry about the meal, and I could not eat a mouthful. This is much more pressing business, about the roll here in my hand — or rather the roll is about the pressing business — I will explain it all to you if you will come with me where we can be alone."

"But steady," expostulated Mai-Sachme. "What is the matter with you, Adon? You are shaking. And I am sorry to hear you cannot eat, you who make so many to eat. Will you not have water poured to cleanse your sweat? It is not good to let it dry in the pores and hollows of the body. It itches and inflames, especially when mixed with grit."

"I'll do that later, Mai. Washing and eating are not urgent, by comparison; for you must hear at once what I have heard, the roll here tells me, that was brought to my office just before I left and here it is: it has come, I mean they have come, which is the same thing; and the question is what will happen and how I am to receive them — and what shall I do, for I am fearfully excited!"

"Why, Adon? Just be calm. You say it has come. That means you expected it; and what you were expecting cannot surprise you. Kindly tell me what is, or who are, come; then I will prove to you that there is no reason to be upset; on the contrary calmness is the one thing needful."

They were talking as they went through the peristyle to the fountain court, moving with a rapid gait which the man of poise tried to slow down. But Joseph turned, and Mai-Sachme followed with Hepi and Hezes into a room on the right, with a coloured ceiling, a malachite lintel and gay friezes along the walls. It served him as a library and lay between his sleeping-chamber and the great reception-hall. It was furnished with true Egyptian charm. There was an inlaid day-bed covered with skins and cushions, delightful little carved chests on legs, inlaid and inscribed, for the protection of the book-rolls; lion-footed chairs with rush seats and backs of stamped and gilded leather; flower-stands and tables with faïence vases and vessels of iridescent glass. Joseph squeezed his steward's arm as he balanced up and down on the balls of his feet; his eyes were wet.

"Mai," he cried, and there was something like suppressed exultation, a choked off rapture in his voice, "they are coming, they are here, they have passed the fortress of Thel — I knew it. I have been waiting for it, and yet I can't believe it has come. My heart is in my mouth, I am so excited that I don't know where I am — "

"Be so good, Adon, as to stop dancing up and down in front of me. I am a man of peace and quiet; pray make it clear to me who has come."

"My brothers, Mai, my brothers!" Joseph cried, and bounced up and down the more.

"Your brothers? The ones who rent your garments and threw you into the well and sold you into slavery?" asked the captain, who had long since learned the whole story by heart.

"Yes, yes! To whom I owe all my good luck and my glory down here!"

"But, Adon, that is certainly putting things too much in their favour."

"God has put it that way, O my steward! God has turned all to good, to everyone's good, and we must look at the results which He had in mind. Before we could see how it turned out, and had only the fact but not the result, I agree that it had a bad look. But now we must judge the fact according to the result."

"That is a question, after all, my good lord. Imhotep the wise might have had a different view. And they showed your father the blood of an animal for yours."

"Yes, that was beastly. He must certainly have fallen on his back. But that probably had to be, because things could not go on as they were. For my father, great-hearted and soft-hearted as he was — and then I myself, what a young peacock I was in those days, a regular young cock of the walk, full of really vicious vanity and self-impor- tance! It is a shame how long some people take to grow up. Even supposing I am grown up even now. Perhaps it takes you your whole life to grow up."

"It may be, Adon, that there is still a good deal of the boy about you. So are convinced it is really your brothers?"

"Convinced? There cannot be the slightest doubt. Why else did I give such strict orders for records and reports? All that was not for nothing, be sure; and as for giving Manasseh, my eldest, the name I gave him, that was just for form's sake — I have not forgotten my father's house, oh, not in the very least; I have thought of it daily, hourly, all these years, and how I promised my little brother Ben in the hiding-place of the mangled one that I would have them all come after me when I had been lifted up and had the power of binding and loosing! Convinced! Here, look, it is written down, it came by run- ning messenger and is a day or so ahead of them: the sons of Jacob, son of Yitzschak from the grove of Mamre which is at Hebron: Reu- ben, Simeon, Levi, Judah, Dan, Naphtali, and so on . . . to buy corn — and you talk as though there were any doubt! It is the brothers, all ten of them. They entered with a troop of buyers. The scribes never dreamed, when they wrote it down. Nor did they, they have not

the least idea before whom they will be brought, nor who it is sells in
the King's name, as his first mouthpiece. Mai, Mai, if you only knew
how I feel! But I do not know myself, it is all Tohu and Bohu within
me — if you know what that means. And yet I knew and have been
expecting it for years. I knew when I stood before Pharaoh and
when I interpreted to him I was doing it to myself too, reading the
purposes of God and how He guides our history. What a history,
Mai, is this we are in! One of the very best. And now it depends on
us, it is our affair to give it a fine form and make something perfectly
beautiful of it, putting all our wits at the service of God. How shall
we begin, in order to do justice to such a story? That is what excites
me so much. . . . Do you think they will recognize me?"

"How should I know, Adon? No, I should think not. You are considerably matured since the time they pulled you to pieces. And anyhow they could never dream of such a thing, and that will make them
blind, so they will never think of it or even trust their own eyes. To
recognize and to know that you recognize are two very different
things."

"Right, right. But I fear they will, I fear it so much that my heart
is pounding in my chest."

"You mean you do not want them to?"

"Not first off, Mai, not on any account! They must only grasp it
by degrees; the thing must draw itself out before I speak the words
and say I am I. In the first place, that is required for the shaping
and adorning of the tale; and secondly, there is so much to be gone
through and so many tests to make, and there will be a great deal of
beating about the bush, first of all in the business about Benjamin — "

"Is Benjamin with them?"

"That is just the thing of it: he is not. I tell you there are ten, not
eleven of them. And we are twelve, all together. It is the red-eyed
ones and the sons of the maids; but not my mother's son, not the little
one. Do you know what that means? You are so calm, your wits move
slowly. Ben not being here might mean one of two things. It may
mean — I hope it does — that my father is still alive — think of it, that
he still lives, that old, old man! — and keeps guard over his youngest,
so that he forbade him the journey and did not want him to take it,
for fear harm might come. His Rachel died on a journey, I died on
a journey — why should he not be prejudiced against them and keep
at home with him the last pledge of his lovely one? This may be the
meaning. But it might mean too that he is gone, my father, and that
they have behaved badly to Ben because he is alone and unprotected;
and thrust him out as though he were not their brother, and would
not let him come with them because he is a son of the true wife, poor
little soul — "

"You keep calling him little, Adon; you do not take into account that he must have grown up too, in the meantime, this only real brother of yours. When you think of it, he must be a man in the prime of life."

"Quite right, it is quite possible. But he remains the youngest, my friend, the youngest of twelve, why should I not call him the little one? And there is always something sweet about the youngest in the family; all over the world the youngest is the favourite and leads a charmed life; it is almost as much in the picture for the older ones to conspire against him."

"Hearing your story, my lord, it almost seems as though you had been the youngest."

"Just so, just so. I will not deny it, there may be some truth in what you say. Maybe history here repeats itself with a difference. But it is on my conscience; I am determined the little one shall have his due as the youngest; and if the ten have thrust him out or treated him badly — if they have played fast and loose, which I do not like to think, as they did with me — then may the Elohim have mercy on them, for they will come up against me. I will not reveal myself to them at all; the beautiful speech to tell them who I am will just not be made; if they recognize me I will deny it and say: 'No, I am not he, ye evildoers'; and they will find in me only a harsh and stranger judge."

"There, you see, Adon. Now you put on a different face and sing a new tune. No more sentimental tenderness in your heart. You are remembering how they played fast and loose with you, and you seem perfectly able to distinguish between the fact and the result."

"I don't know, Mai, what sort of man I am. One does not know beforehand how one will behave in one's story; but when the time comes it is clear enough and then a man gets acquainted with himself. I am curious myself to see how I shall act and how talk to them — at this moment I have no idea. That is what makes me tremble so. When I had to stand before Pharaoh I was not a thousandth part so excited. And yet they are my own brothers. But that is just it. Everything is upside-down inside me: it is a perfect muddle of joy and dread and suspense and quite indescribable, just as I tell you. How startled I was when I came to the names on the list, though I had known and definitely expected to see them — you cannot imagine it, of course not, because you cannot be startled. Was I startled on their account or my own? I do not know. But they would have good ground to be startled themselves — to be frightened down to the very soles of their shoes, I do not deny that. For it was no small thing then; and long ago as it all was, it has not got any smaller with the years. I said I went to them to see that everything was in order; that was cheeky, I agree — I admit it all, especially that I ought not to have told them my dreams. Besides, it is true that if they had granted me my life I would have told the whole thing to my father — so they had to leave me where I was. And still and all — that they were deaf when I cried out of the depths, lying there in my bonds, covered with welts, and wailed and begged them not to do this to my father, to let me perish in the hole and show him the blood of a beast for mine — yes, my friend, it was all pretty bad. Not so much to me, I am not talking about that; it was bad towards my father. If he is dead now of his grief and has gone down in sorrow to Sheol, shall I be able to be friendly to them? I do not know, I do not know how I am under such conditions; but I very much fear I could not be friendly. If they have brought down his grey hairs with sorrow to the grave, that also would belong to the result, Mai, even first and foremost; and would very much obscure the light shed by the result upon the fact. In any case, it remains a fact, and it must be set over against the result. Eye to eye with it, so that confronted by its goodness it may be ashamed of its badness."

"What do you mean to do with them?"

"How do I know? I am asking you for advice and counsel just because I don't know what to do: you, my steward, whom I took into this story for you to give me of your steadiness when I get excited. You can afford to give me some, for you've got too much, you are far too phlegmatic, you just stand there and raise your eyebrows and put your lips together, and just because you are like that you do not have any ideas. But we need ideas, we owe it to the kind of story it is. For the meeting of the act and the result is a feast of no common sort, it must be celebrated and adorned with all sorts of solemn flourishes and pious manœuvres so that the world will have to laugh and cry over it five thousand years and more."

"Excitement and fear are less productive than peace and quiet, Adon. I will mix you a soothing drink now. I will shake a powder into water and it will sink and be still. But if I shake another kind into the cup, then the two will seethe up together, and if you drink it foaming it will act as a sedative."

"I will gladly drink it later, Mai, at the right moment, when I need it most. Now hearken to what I have done so far: I have sent running messengers with orders to segregate them from the other travellers and not to give them corn in the border cities but to send them on to Menfe, to the head office. I have arranged to have an eye kept on them so that they are sent to good rest-houses with their animals and are cared for without their knowing it in the strange land, as new and strange to them as it was to me when I died up above there and was brought down here, at seventeen years old. I was flexible then, but they, I realize, are all getting to the end of the forties, except Benjamin, and he is not with them, and all I know is that he must be fetched; in the first place so I can see him and in the second place because if he is here the father will come too. In short, I have laid upon our people to make smooth the way under their feet so that they strike not against a stone — if the figure means anything to you. And they shall be brought before me in the ministry, in the hall of audience."

"Not in your house?"

"No, not yet. At first quite formally at the office. Between you and me, the hall there is much bigger and more impressive."

"And what will you do with them there?"

"Yes, of course that will be the moment for me to drink your foaming draught. Because I have not the least idea in the world what I shall do, when they do not know me, nor what when I tell them who I am — but one thing I do know: I will not be so clumsy as to spoil the beautiful story and burst out headlong with the climax like an inexperienced story-teller. No, I will sit tight when they come in and treat them like strangers."

"You mean you will be unfriendly?"

"I mean formal to the point of unfriendliness. For I think, Mai, I shall hardly succeed in being strange unless I force myself to be unfriendly. That will be easier. I must think of some reason why I have to speak harshly and can go at them properly. I must act as though their case was suspicious and strict investigations had to be made and all the circumstances cleared up, whether or no."

"Will you speak with them in their tongue?"

"That is the first useful word your stolidity has managed to utter," cried Joseph, striking his brow. "I certainly needed to be reminded of that, for the fact is I am always speaking Canaanitish with them in my mind, like the fool that I am. How should I come to know Canaanitish? That would be a frightful *faux pas*. I do speak it with the children; I suppose I am giving them an Egyptian accent. Well, that is the least of my troubles. I seem to be talking at random, saying things that might be important under less exciting circumstances but not now. Of course, I cannot know any Canaanitish, I must speak through an interpreter, we must have one here, I will give orders in the ministry, a good one, who knows both languages about equally so that he can render what I say exactly without making it any weaker or stronger. For what they say themselves, for instance big Reuben — oh, Reuben, my God, he was at the empty pit to save me, I know it from the watchman, I don't know if I told you about that, some time I will — what they say themselves of course I shall understand, but I must not show that I do or forget and answer what they say before the long-winded interpreter has translated."

"When you have taken it in, Adon, you will do it all right. And then perhaps you might pretend you take them for scouts come to spy out the weakness of the land."

"I beg of you, Mai, spare me your ideas! How do you come to make big eyes and suggest things to me?"

"I thought I was supposed to, my lord."

"I thought so at first myself, my friend. But I see after all that nobody can or should advise me in this most solemn business. I must shape its course all by myself. Remember how you are using your ingenuity in the story of the three love-affairs to make it as exciting and delightful as possible, and let me use mine on my own. Who told you I had not got the idea of pretending I took them for spies?"

"So we both have the same idea."

"Of course, because it is the only right one and as good as written down already. In fact, this whole story is written down already in God's book, Mai, and we shall read it together between laughing and tears. For you will be there, won't you, and come to the office when they are here, tomorrow or day after, and are brought into the great hall of the Nourisher with himself painted over and over on the walls? Of course you will be among my train. I must have a stately retinue when I receive them. . . . Ah, Mai," he burst out, and buried his face in his hands — those hands at which the little urchin Benoni had looked in the grove of the Lord Adon, as they wove the myrtle garland; now one of them wore Pharaoh's sky-blue lapis lazuli ring inscribed: "Be as myself" — "I shall see them, my own folk, my own, for they were always that however much we quarrelled through the fault of all of us. I shall speak with them, Jacob's sons, my brothers, to whom I have kept so long the silence of death and learn whether he can still hear that I am alive and that God accepted the beast instead of the son! I shall hear everything, I shall learn all that has happened, how Benjamin lives and whether they treat him brotherly. And I must get him down here and my father too! Oh, my taskmaster, now my house-master, it is all too exciting and solemn for words! And just because it is so solemn it must be treated with a light touch. For lightness, my friend, flippancy, the artful jest, that is God's very best gift to man, the profoundest knowledge we have of that complex, questionable thing we call life. God gave it to humanity, that life's terribly serious face might be forced to wear a smile. My brothers rent my garment and flung me into the pit; now they are to stand before my stool — and that is life. And the question whether we are to judge the act by the result and approve the bad act because it was needed for the good result — that is life too. Life puts such questions as these and they cannot be answered with a long face. Only in lightness can the spirit of man rise above them: with a laugh at being faced with the unanswerable, perhaps he can make even God Himself, the great Unanswering, to laugh."

THE AUDIENCE

JOSEPH was indeed as Pharaoh when he sat in his seat on his raised dais in the hall of the Nourisher beneath white ostrich-feather fans thrust into chased gold shields, held above him by pages in aprons, with bobbed hair. About him were his chief scribes from the ministry, an austere group of magistrates; along the dais to right and left lance-bearers of his household guard stood in a row. Two double lines of orange columns covered with ornamental inscriptions, on white bases, with green lotus capitals and over-pieces in coloured enamel, ran from his dais to the farthest entrance doors and on the long and high sidewalls above the dado, Hapi, the overflowing, was repeatedly pictured: in human form, with covered sex, one breast male, the other female, the royal beard on his chin, reeds on his head, bearing on his palms the presentation tray with wild jungle flowers and slender water-jugs. Between these repeated representations of the god came other forms of life in flowing lines and bright colours, gleaming in the rays of light that fell through the stone gratings of the high windows. There were scenes of sowing and threshing, Pharaoh himself ploughed with oxen and cut the first swath with the sickle into the golden grain; there were the seven kine of Osiris, with the bull whose name he knew, pacing in a row, with exquisite inscriptions, such as: "Oh, may the Nile give me food and nourishment and every green thing according to its time!"

Such was the hall of audience where every cry for bread came before the Vice-Horus, for he reserved to himself each decision. Here now he sat, on the third day after his talk with his steward; Mai-Sachme now stood behind his seat and had actually mingled him a foaming draught; and Joseph had just dismissed a pigtailed and bearded delegation wearing shoes turned up at the toes, from the land of the great King Murshili, in other words Hatti, where too famine reigned. He had been absent-minded and heedless, as everyone had remarked; for he had dictated to his "actual scribe" a figure of more wheat, spelt, rice, and millet and at a lower price than the delegates from Hatti had themselves offered. Some of those present thought there might be diplomatic reasons for this: perhaps, who knew, the moment had come in the world political sphere to show King Murshili some attention. Others ascribed it to the physical condition of the universal friend, as he had remarked before the sitting that he had a catarrh from the dust, and he kept a handkerchief before his mouth.

Above the handkerchief his eyes looked out into the great hall when the men from Hatti had left and the group of Asiatics were brought in in their turn. One of their number was tall like a tower;

another had a melancholy leonine head; one was solid and marrowy, another had long nimble legs; two others did not dissemble their natively belligerent air; one kept giving piercing glances round about him, another was striking because of his very bony joints, and still another because his eyes and lips were so bright and humid. One had curly hair, a round beard, and much red and blue dye of the purple snail about his garment. Each, in short, had something to distinguish him. In the middle of the hall they found it good to fall on their faces, and the universal friend had to wait till they stood up again to beckon them near him with his fan. They came closer and then again fell on their faces.

"So many?" he asked in a muffled voice which, oddly enough, he had pitched almost in a growl. "Ten all at once? Why not eleven? Interpreter, ask them why there are not eleven of them or even twelve — or do you men understand Egyptian?"

"Not so well as we should like to, O lord, our refuge," answered one of them in his own tongue. It was he on the runner's legs, whose tongue, it seemed, was nimble too. "You are as Pharaoh, you are as the moon, the merciful father, who comes forth in majestic garment. You are as a first-born steer in his adornment, Moshel, ruler! Our hearts praise with one voice him who here holds market, nourisher of the lands, food of the world, without whom no one has breath, and we wish for you as many years of life as the year has days. But your tongue, O Ádon, we understand not enough to deal with you, be merciful unto us."

"You are as Pharaoh," they all repeated in chorus.

While the interpreter rapidly and monotonously translated Naphtali's words, Joseph devoured with his eyes the men standing before him. He knew them every one and had no trouble in marking in each the work the hand of time had done upon them too. O God of dispensations, they were all there, the hate-hungry wolf-pack that had flung itself on him with cries of "Down with him, down with him!" How he had begged: "Do not tear it, do not tear it!" But all the furious pack had dragged him to the pit with shoutings and halloo-ings, the while he questioned the heavens in a daze: "What is this that has come upon me?" They had sold him as a criminal to the Ishmael-ites for twenty silver pieces and before his eyes had dabbled the ruins of his garment in blood. Here they were now, his brothers in Jacob, come up out of long-ago time, his murderers because of dreams, led to him by dreams — and the whole past was like one dream. There were the red-eyed ones, all six of them, and the four of the maids: Bilhah's adder and snake and her prattler of news; Zil-pah's sturdy eldest in his tunic, the forthright Gad, and his brother the sweet-tooth. He was one of the youngest next to Issachar the beast of burden and the tarry Zebulon, and he had wrinkles already

and lines in his face and much silver in his beard and his smooth oiled
hair. Good God, how old they had got! It was very moving — as all
life is moving. But he shrank back at sight of them, for with them so
old it was unbelievable that the father was still alive.

With his heart full of laughing and weeping and dismay he looked
at them, recognized every single one despite the beards, which some
of them in his time had not yet worn. But they, looking at him in their
turn, had no such thoughts; for their seeing eyes were wrapped in
blindness against the possibility that it could be he. They had once
sold a blood-brother and shameless brat away into the world, out into
far horizons and misty distances. That they never ceased to know,
they knew it now. But that the aristocratic heathen there in his
throned chair under the feather fans, in brilliant white that blazed
against the perfectly Egyptian brownness of his brow and arms — that
the potentate and provider here to whom they had come in their
need; he who had about his neck the collar of favour, an amazing
piece of goldsmith's work and an equally marvellous breastpiece with
falcons, sun-beetles, and life-crosses arranged with the utmost art —
that he there, under the waving fly-fans, the silver ceremonial hatchet
in his belt, his headcloth wound in the manner of the country, with
stiff lappets falling on the shoulders — that this could be the one-time
outcast, mourned by the father till he mourned himself out; the
dreamer of dreams — to such a thought they were immune, they
were shut and bolted against it. Besides, the man kept his handkerchief to his face all the time and made even the barely possible impossible.

He spoke again, and every time, directly he paused, the interpreter
beside him rattled off what he had said in monotonous Canaanitish.

"Whether there can be any dealing here at all, or any delivery of
grain," he said crossly, "is still a question. We must consider it. It
may easily turn out otherwise. That you do not speak the language
of men is the least of your troubles. I pity you, if you thought you
could hold speech in your jargon with Pharaoh's first mouthpiece.
A man like me speaks the tongue of Babylon, and Chetitish; but he
can hardly let himself in for Khabirish and suchlike gibberish; and
if he had ever known it he would make haste to forget it."

Pause for translation.

"You look at me," he went on, not waiting for an answer, "you
stare at me, like men without culture, and take private note that I
keep a handkerchief before my face — from which you conclude that
I am not feeling well. Well, I am not — what is there in that to remark and take down and draw conclusions from? I have a catarrh
from the dust — even a man like me can suffer from catarrh. My
physicians will cure me. Medical science is far advanced in Egypt.
My own house steward, the overseer of my private palace, is a phy-

sician himself. So you see, he will treat me. But people, however remote from me, who had to undertake a journey, and furthermore a
journey through desert lands, under these abnormal and unfavourable
meteorological conditions, have my sincere sympathy. I feel keenly
what they must have had to endure on the journey. Whence do you
come?"

"From Hebron, great Adon, from Kirjath Arba, the four-square
town, and from the terebinths of Mamre in the land of Canaan, to
buy food in Egypt. We are all — "

"Stop! Who is that speaking? Who is the little man with the shining lips? Why is it he speaks — why not that tall tower over there?
He is built like one, at least. He seems to be the oldest and most intelligent amongst your crew."

"It is Asher, by your favour; Asher, so is your servant's name, a
brother among brothers. For we are all brothers and sons of one man,
in the bond of brotherhood, and when a thing concerns all of us it is
Asher, your humble servant, who is accustomed to take the word."

"Oh, so you are the common mouth for commonplaces. Good. But
now I come to look at you all, it does not escape my penetration that
although you are supposed to be brothers, you are very different
among yourselves, some belonging in one group and some in another. This common mouth here looks like the man over there in a
short coat with bits of bronze sewed on it; the one beyond with
eyes like a snake has something or other in common with the man
next him, standing first on one leg and then on the other. But several
of you seem to belong together by virtue of the red eyes you have in
common."

It was Reuben who took upon himself to reply.

"Verily you see all, lord," Joseph heard him say. "Likenesses and
differences are due to our being from different mothers, four from
two and six from one. But we are one man's sons, Jacob your servant,
who begot us and who sent us to you to buy bread."

"He sent you to me?" repeated Joseph, and lifted the handkerchief until it almost covered his whole face. He looked at them over it.

"Man, you surprise me by the thinness of your voice, coming from
such a tower of a body; but I am still more surprised at your words.
Time has silvered all your hair and beards, and the eldest of you, who
has no beard, has more silver hair to make up for it. Your looks contradict your words; for you do not look like people whose father is
still alive."

"By your favour, he lives, O lord," Judah took up the tale. "Let me
bear witness to my brother's words. We deal in truth. Our father,
your servant, lives in his state — and really he is not so old after all,
maybe eighty or ninety, which is not unusual in our stock. For our

ancestor was a hundred years old when he begot the true and right son, our father's father."

"How uncivilized!" said Joseph, his voice breaking. He turned round to his steward, then back, and for a while said nothing, to the unease of his audience.

"You might," he said at length, "answer my questions more precisely, without going off into unessentials. What I asked was how you stood the journey under such hard conditions, whether you suffered much from the drought, whether your water supply held out, whether you were attacked by roving bands or a dust-abubu, whether anybody was overcome by the heat — that was what I asked."

"We got on reasonably well, Adon, thank you for the kind inquiry. Our train was strong against roving bands, we were well supplied with water, we scarcely lost even an ass, and we were all in good health. Just one dust-abubu, of medium severity, was the most we had to bear."

"So much the better. My inquiry was not kind, it was strictly practical. A journey like yours is after all not so uncommon. There is much travel in the world; seventeen days' journeys, even seven times seventeen, are no rarity, and they have to be put behind the traveller step by step, for seldom does the earth spring to meet him. Merchants take the road from Gilead, leading from the town of Beisan through Yenin and the valley of — wait, I knew it once, it will come back to me — the valley of Dothan; whence they meet the great caravan route from Damascus to Leyun and Ramleh and the port of Khadati. You had it better, you simply came down from Hebron to Gaza and then along the coast down towards our land."

"As you say, O lord. You know all."

"I know a great deal. Partly because of my natural shrewdness, partly by other means which a man like me knows how to command. But at Gaza, where you probably joined the caravan, begins the worst part of the trip. You have to survive an iron city and an accursed sea-bottom covered with skeletons."

"We did not look round, and with God's help we came safe through the horrors."

"I am glad to hear it. Perhaps you had a column of fire to guide you?"

"There was one, once, that went on in front of us. It collapsed, and then came the dust-abubu, of moderate severity."

"You refrain from boasting of its terrors, but it might easily have been the death of you. It concerns me that travellers are exposed to such hardship on the way down to Egypt. I say that quite objectively. But you thought yourselves lucky when you got into the regions of our watch-towers and bastions?"

"Yes, we counted ourselves fortunate and praised God aloud for our being spared."

"Were you afraid at the fortress of Thel and its armed troops?"

"We feared only in the sense of awe."

"And what happened to you there?"

"They did not forbid us to pass when we told them we were buyers come to buy corn from this granary that our wives and children may live and not die. But they separated us from the others."

"I wanted to hear about that. Were you surprised at the measure? It had not happened before, to your knowledge, to say nothing of your being the object? At least they had provision put up for you in full number, all ten of you, if ten can be called a full number. They did not separate any of you from each other, but only from the others that entered with you?"

"So was it, lord. They told us we could not buy bread for our money except at Mempi, balance of the lands, and from yourself, lord of bread and friend of the harvest of God."

"Correct. They put you on the road? You had good journey from the frontier to the city of the swaddled one?"

"Very good, Adon. They kept an eye on us. Men who came and went directed us to lodgement and rest-houses with our animals, and in the morning when we offered pay the host would not take it."

"Two kinds of people receive free lodgement and board: the guest of honour and the prisoner. — How do you like Egypt?"

"It is a land of marvels, great vizier. Like Nimrod's is its might and magnificence, it is splendid in form and adornment, whether towering or extended flat, its temples are overpowering and its tombs touch the skies. Often our eyes ran over."

"Not so much, I hope, that you neglected to ply your trade and task, or were prevented from spying and reconnoitring and drawing your conclusions."

"Your word, O lord, is dark to us."

"So you pretend not to know why you were set apart and why people kept an eye on you and brought you before my face?"

"Gladly would we know, great lord, but we know not."

"You put on a face as though you never dreamed — does not your conscience whisper to you that you are under a cloud, that a suspicion rests upon you, a sinister one, and that your villainy is open to my eyes?"

"What say you, lord? You are as Pharaoh — what suspicion?"

"That you are spies," Joseph cried out. He struck the arm of his lion-footed chair with his hand and stood up. He had said *daialu*, spy, a heavily offensive Akkadian word; and he pointed at them, in their faces, with his fan.

"*Daialu.*" the interpreter hollowly repeated.

They started back as one man, thunderstruck, indignant.

"What say you?" they repeated, in a growling chorus.

"I said what I said. Spies you are, come to spy out the secret bareness of the land that you may discover it and reveal the way for invasion and plunder. That is my conviction. If you can gainsay it, do so."

Reuben spoke, all the others frantically gesturing to him to set them right. He shook his head slowly and said:

"What is there, sovereign lord, to gainsay? Only because it is you who say it is it worth a word, but otherwise only a shrug of the shoulders. Even the great err. Your suspicion is false. We do not cast down our eyes before it, but as you see we look up freely and honestly to your face, and even in polite reproof that you can so misread us. For we know you in your greatness, but you know us not in our good faith. Look at us, and let your eyes be opened at the sight. We are all sons of one man, an excellent man in the land of Canaan, a king of herds and a friend of God. We are true men. We came in amongst others coming to buy food, for good silver rings which you can weigh on exact scales: food for our women and children. That is our aim. Spies, by the God of gods, have your servants never been."

"But you are!" answered Joseph, and stamped with his sandalled foot. "What a man like me has in his mind he sticks to. You are come to discover the shame of the land, that it may be harmed with the sickle. It is my belief you have this commission from wicked kings of the east; to disprove it rests with you. But far from doing so, what that tall tower there has said is merely to assert baldly that it is not true. That is no evidence to satisfy a man like me."

"But consider in mercy, lord," said one of them, "that it rather rests with you to give evidence for such an accusation than for us to disprove it."

"Who is that speaking so subtly out of your midst and piercing me with his eyes? For some time I have remarked your darting eye like a snake's. How are you called?"

"Dan, by your good favour, Adon. Dan I am called, born of a maid upon the knees of the mistress."

"I am pleased to hear it. And so, Master Dan, to judge by the subtlety of your words, you set yourself up for a judge and in your own case to boot? But here it is myself who sit as judge and the accused must make himself clean before me. Have you sand-dwellers and sons of misery any notion of the parlous balance of this pearl of great price among all the lands, over which I am set and must render account of its safety before god's son in his palace? It is ever threatened by the lustful covetousness of the desert-born who spy after its weakness, Bedu, Mentiu, and Peztiu. Shall the Khabirites deal here as they have dealt time and again beyond the borders in Pharaoh's provinces? I know of cities they have fallen upon like mad bulls and in their fury strangled the man and slain the oxen in savage wantonness. You see, I know more than you thought. Two or three of you, I will not say all, look to me quite capable of such games. And shall I take your bare word that you mean no ill and were not aiming at the secret parts of our land?"

They shifted about among themselves and took counsel with excited gesturings. In the end it was Judah to whom they beckoned to answer and represent them. He did it with the dignity of the tried and tested man.

"Lord," said he, "let me speak before you and set forth our state according to the exact truth, that you may know we are true men. Lo, we your servants are twelve brothers, sons of one father, in the land —"

"Stop!" cried Joseph, who had sat down but now stood up again. "What? So now all of a sudden you are twelve men? So then you have not dealt in truth when you said you were ten?"

"— in the land of Canaan," finished Judah firmly. His face wore a look which seemed to say that he found it uncalled for and premature to interrupt him when he was about to launch out into a full explanation. "Twelve sons are we, your servants, or we were — we have never said this was all of us as we stood before you, we only bore witness that all ten of us were one man's sons. At home we were originally twelve, but the youngest brother, not born of any of our mothers but from a fourth, who has been dead as many years as he is old, has stopped at home with our father, and one of us is no longer with us."

"What do you mean by 'no longer with us'?"

"Gone, lord, in his early years, lost to our father and to us, lost in the world."

"He must have been an adventurous fellow. But what have I got to do with him? Now the little one, your youngest brother: he is not lost — not got out of hand —"

"He is at home, lord, always at home and at our father's hand."

"From which I conclude that this old father of yours is alive and well?"

"You have asked that before, Adon, by your leave, and we told you yes."

"Not at all! It may well be that I asked you once about your father's life, but about his well-being I am now asking you for the first time."

"Things are very well," answered Judah, "with your servant, our father, under all the circumstances. But there has been hardship in the world for some time now, as my lord well knows. For since the heavens denied their watery blessings, once and then twice, the scarcity presses the harder the longer it goes on, in all the lands, and so in ours. Even to speak of scarcity is to make small the evil, for there is no grain for love or money, for either seed or bread. Our father is rich, he lives on an easy footing — "

"How rich and how easy? Has he for instance an ancestral tomb?"

"As you say, lord, Machpelach, the double hollow. There sleep our forefathers."

"For instance, does he live on such a footing that he has an oldest servant, a steward, as I have, who is a doctor as well?"

"So is it, Highness. He had a wise and much-travelled first servant, Eliezer by name. Sheol hides him; he bowed his head and died. But he left two sons, Damasek and Elinos, and the elder, Damasek, has taken the place of the deceased; he is now called Eliezer."

"You don't say," said Joseph, "you don't say." And his eyes were brimming for some while as his gaze travelled above their heads into space. Then he asked: "Why do you interrupt yourself, lion-head, in your attempted justification? Do you not know how to go on?"

Judah smiled forbearingly. He did not say that it was not he who kept interrupting.

"Your servant was in act and remains ready to tell you all our circumstances and the kind of journey we had in order and faithfully, that you may see we deal in truthfulness. Numerous is our house — not precisely as the sands of the sea, but very numerous. We number in the seventies, for we are all heads under our father's headship, we are all married and blessed with — "

"All ten of you married?"

"All eleven of us, Lord, and blessed — "

"What, your youngest too is married and the head of a family?"

"Lord, as you say it. From two women he has eight children."

"Impossible!" cried Joseph, without waiting for the man to translate. He struck his palm on the arm of his chair and burst out laughing. The Egyptian officials behind him laughed too, out of the purest sycophancy. The brothers smiled anxiously. Mai-Sachme, Joseph's steward, gave him a private nudge in the back.

"You nodded your head," said Joseph, drying his eyes. "So I understood that your youngest is married and a father too. That is fine. I am only laughing because it is really very good and something to laugh at. Because one always thinks of the youngest as a little chap, not as a husband and father. That is what made me laugh; but you see I have stopped already. This business is much too serious and suspicious to be a laughing matter and that you, lion-head, have got stuck again in your defence seems to me a most suspicious thing."

"With your permission," answered Judah, "I will go on with it without stopping, and connectedly. For the dearness of all things, which one might better call a dearth because there is no food at all at any price, this catastrophe weighs upon the country, the herds perish, and on our ears strikes the cry of our children for bread, which, lord, is the bitterest of all sounds to a human ear and hardest to bear, save it may be the complaint of venerable age that he misses his due and daily comfort; for we heard our father say that he was not far from having his lamp go out so that he must sleep in the dark."

"Unheard of," said Joseph; "that is a vexation, not to say an abomination. Have you people let it come to that? No provision, no looking ahead, no measures against calamity, which after all does exist in the world and can take on presentness at any moment! No imagination, no fear, no sense of the past! Living like the beasts of the field from day to day, mindful of nothing that is not before your face and eyes — until the father in his old age must go without his habitual comforts! Shame! Have you, then, no education, no history? Do you not know that under some circumstances the blade cannot shoot and all blossoming things lie in bonds, because the fields bring forth only salt and no herb grows, nor any smallest sprout of grain? That life is numb with grief, the bull leaps not on the cow nor does the ass cover the she-ass? Have you never heard of floods that cover the earth so that only the exceeding wise man survives because he has made himself to swim upon the returned primeval flood? Must, then, before you heed, everything be before your eyes and face presentwards to you, which was merely turned away, until your dearest-loved old age must want oil for its lamp?"

They hung their heads.

"Go on," he said. "That man who was speaking, let him continue! But let me hear no more of your father sleeping in the dark!"

"That is only a figure, Adon, it means that he too suffers from the hard times and has no bread for the offering. We saw many folk gird themselves up and set out for this country, to buy from Pharaoh's granaries, and they brought back food, for only in Egypt is there corn and a grain-market. But for long we would not come before our father with the suggestion that we too gird our loins and come down likewise to do business and buy."

"Why would you not?"

"He has the fixed ideas of his old age, lord, all sorts of opinions about everything, and so about the land of your gods — he thinks his own thoughts about Mizraim and has a prejudice against its customs and ways."

"One must just shut one's eyes to that and not notice."

"He probably would not have let us come, if we had asked him. So we thought it better counsel to wait until he noticed the scarcity himself."

"Perhaps that ought not to be either, that you put your heads together about the father; it looks as if you were playing fast and loose with him."

"There was nothing else to do. And of course we saw his side-glances and how he would open his mouth to speak and then shut it again. Finally he said to us: 'Why do you look at each other with side-glances? Lo, I hear, and the rumour reached me, that in the south-land grain is cheap and there is a market there. Up with you, and sit not on your backsides till all of us are lost! Choose out one or two of you by lot and on whom it falls, Simeon or Dan, he may gird his loins and travel down with the travellers and buy food for your wives and children, that we may live and not die.' 'Good,' we brothers answered him, 'but it is not enough that two should go, for the question of need will arise. We must all go and show the number of our heads, that the children of Egypt may see we need corn not by the ephah but the homer!' So he said: 'Then all ten of you go.' We told him it would be better if we all went and showed that we are eleven households under his headship, otherwise we should be given too little. But he answered and said: 'Are you out of your wits? I see you want to make me childless. Do you not know that Benjamin must be at home and at hand? Suppose an accident were to befall him on the way? Ten of you go, or else we sleep in the dark.' So we came."

"Is that your justification?" Joseph asked.

"My lord," answered Judah, "if my faithful testimony overcome not your suspicion and if you do not recognize that we are innocent folk and deal in truth, then we must despair of any justification."

"I fear it will come to that," Joseph said, "for about your innocence I have my own ideas. But as for the suspicion you are under and my yet unshaken accusation that you are naught else but spies – very good, I will test you. You say I ought to know by the good faith of your deposition that you deal in honesty and are not rogues. I say: Good. Bring then your youngest brother here, of whom you speak. Set him here with yourselves before my face, that I may convince myself that your details all hang together and have weight; then I shall begin to doubt my suspicions and be slowly shaken in my accusation. But if not, by Pharaoh's life – and I hope you know one can take no higher oath in this country – there can be no talk of dealing by the homer nor yet by the ephah and it will be finally proven that you are *daialu*, and you should have realized how such people are treated before you took to this way of life."

They were all pale and mottled in the face and stood there help-less.

"You mean, lord," they asked through the interpreter, "that we are to put our way behind us again, nine or seventeen days long (for the earth does not spring to meet us) and then repeat the journey hither to bring our youngest brother before your face?"

"That would be wonderful," he retorted. "No, certainly not. Do you think a man like me catches spies and then just lets them go again? You are prisoners. I will put you apart in a separate wing of this house and guard you for three days, by which I mean today, tomorrow, and some part of the day after. During that time you may choose one of you by lot or by consent to make the journey and fetch the subject of the test. But the others shall remain prisoners, until he stands before me; for by Pharaoh's life, without him you shall not see my face again."

They looked down at their feet and bit their lips.

"Lord," said the eldest, "what you command is possible, up to the point where the messenger reaches home and confesses before our father that before we can have bread we must fetch down his youngest to you. You have no idea how he will go on at that, for our father's mind is very wilful and most of all on this very point, that the young one must always be at home and never go on journeys. You see, he is the youngest fledgling — "

"That is absurd," cried Joseph. "Who would nurse such fairy-tale prejudices about a youngest son? A man with eight children is old and sensible enough to leave home, even if he were twelve times the youngest. Do you think your father will leave you all here in jail for spying rather than to let his youngest go a journey?"

They took counsel together awhile with looks and shoulder-shrugs, and at last Reuben said:

"We think that possible, lord."

"Well, then," said Joseph, and got to his feet, "I think it is not possible. You can't make that wash with a man like me, and as for what I said, by that we shall abide. Set your youngest before me, I charge you strictly. For by Pharaoh's life, if you cannot do it, you shall be convicted as spies."

He nodded to the officer of the guard, who uttered a word; whereat lance-bearers stepped to the side of the frightened men and led them out of the room.

IT IS EXACTED

IT was no prison and no pit into which they were thrown. They were only subject to house arrest in a separate part of the palace, a hall with flower-twined columns, to which some steps led down, and which seemed like an unused writing-room or archive for old documents. It afforded sufficient room for ten people and had benches running round it. For tent-dwelling shepherds it was accommodation bordering on the sumptuous. That the apertures for light had gratings over them meant nothing, for such openings always had some kind of lattice. True, guards paced up and down outside the door.

Jacob's sons squatted on their ankle-bones and considered matters. They had plenty of time to choose the man for the return journey to make the proposal to the father; time until day after tomorrow. So first they discussed the situation as a whole and the trouble they were all in. Full of distress, they unanimously voted it to be very evil and threatening. What a diabolical mischance to have fallen under suspicion — nobody knew how or why! They reproached each other for not having seen misfortune coming; their segregation on the frontier, the dispatch to Menfe, the watchful eye during the passage thither, all that, they now saw and said, had been in itself suspicious, in the sense that they themselves had been suspected, while all the time they had taken it for friendliness. All together, there had been a mixture of friendliness and alarmingness that was very puzzling, it upset them and at the same time they still had an odd feeling of pleasure in the midst of all their heavy care and vexation. They could not make out the man before whom they had stood, who had this unhappy suspicion about perfectly sincere and innocent men and put off upon them the burden of proving their innocence. Absurd, unbelievably capricious the suspicion was, from the point of view of their tenfold innocence and business good faith: to call them spies, come to spy out the shame of the land! But he had got it into his head, and quite aside from the life-and-death seriousness of the charge, it really pained the brothers as well; for this man, this keeper of the market and great lord of Egypt, somehow they liked him; it hurt their feelings that it was just this very man who thought so ill of them.

A man good to look at. You might call him handsome and well-favoured. You could, without going too far, compare him to a first-born bull in his adornment. And he was friendly too, in a sort of way. That was just it: the mixture of pleasure and exasperation in the whole thing was concentrated in his person. He was "*tam*"; the brothers concurred in the epithet. He was equivocal, double-faced, a man of both this and that, beautiful and beshadowed, stimulating and disturbing, kindly and dangerous. You could not make him out, just as you could not quite explain the quality "*tam*" in which the upper- and the under-world meet. He could be sympathetic; he had concerned himself about the hardships of their journey. He had found it worth while to ask about the life and well-being of their father, and he had laughed aloud when he heard that the little one was married. But then as though he had only wanted to lull them in friendly security, he flew in their faces with this utterly arbitrary and capricious accusation and ruthlessly flung them into the condition of hostages until they should produce the eleventh son as evidence of good faith — as though that could seriously be considered a refutation! "*Tam*" — there was no other word for it. A man of the solstice, of chopping and changing, at home above and below. He was a business man too, and there was always a trace of trickery about business which belonged to the rest of it.

But of what avail to have noticed these things, what use to lament because the man they liked so much had been so harsh with them? It did not mend matters or help the plight they were in, and that, they confessed to each other, was the worst thing that had ever happened to them. And then came the moment when they put together the unreasonable suspicion they were under with another most reasonable one: perhaps this that was happening had some connection with the suspicion they were used to living under at home — in short, that this visitation was a punishment for long past guilt.

It would be a mistake to conclude, or to gather from the text, that they first mentioned the suspicion in front of Joseph, at their second confrontation with him. No, it had occurred to them before that. Here in the place of their first arrest it mounted to their lips and they spoke of Joseph. That was strange. They were capable of not even the faintest mental association between this lord of the corn and their sold and buried brother, yet — they spoke of him. It was not a merely moral association; they did not at first come on to it by such a route, one suspicion leading back to the other. At first it was not a matter of guilt and punishment, it was a matter of contact.

Mai-Sachme had been right when he remarked in his imperturbable way that it was a far cry between knowing and knowing that you knew. A man cannot come into contact with his blood-brother without knowing it, especially if he has once spilled that blood. But confessing it to oneself is a different pair of shoes. To assert that the sons had at this point in the story recognized the keeper of the market as their brother would be a clumsy way to put it and could only be denied forthwith; for why then their boundless amazement when he revealed himself? No, they had not the faintest idea. And quite specifically they had no idea either why Joseph's image and their ancient guilt came to their minds after or even during their first contact with this attractive and alarming potentate.

This time it was not Asher who out of pure relish put into words the unexpressed feelings that united them. It was Judah, the man with a conscience. For Asher realized that he did not carry enough weight, whereas Judah knew that it was his fitting task.

"Brothers in Jacob," said he, "we are in great peril. Strangers in a foreign land, we are in a trap, we have fallen into a pit of incomprehensible but ruinous suspicion. If Israel refuses Benjamin to our messenger, as I fear he will, either we are dead men, and they will lead us into the house of martyrdom and execution, as the children of Egypt say; or we shall be sold into bondage, either building tombs or washing gold in some horrible place, and never see our children again and the lash of the Egyptian house of bondage will make weals on our backs. How is it that this is happening to us? Bethink yourselves, brothers, why this comes upon us and learn to know God. For God our Father is a God of vengeance, and He forgets not. Neither has He allowed us to forget, but least of all does He Himself forget. Why He did not, at once and straightway, in the long ago, consume us with fire out of His nostrils, but let whole lifetimes pass and coolly postponed the judgment until now it comes upon us, this ask of Him and not of me. For we were young when we did it and he a little lad, and we are not the same people on whom punishment now falls. But I say to you: we have been guilty towards our brother, when we saw the anguish of his soul when he cried up to us from below and we would not hearken. Therefore this calamity comes upon us."

They all nodded heavily, for he had uttered the thought of each; and they murmured:

"Shaddei, Yehu, Eloah."

But Reuben, his grey head between his fists, red in the face with distress, the veins swollen on his forehead, burst out through drawn lips:

"Yes, yes, remember now, grumble and groan! Did I not say so? Did I not tell you when I warned you and said: Lay not your hand on the boy? But who would not hear but you? So now you have it — his blood is exacted of us!"

Precisely that the good Reuben had not really said. Yet he had prevented something: he had prevented Joseph's blood from being shed, at least not more than from the superficial marring of his beauty, and it was not accurate to say that his blood was exacted from them. Or did Reuben mean the blood of the beast which had stood to the father for Joseph's blood? But at least the others did agree that he had warned them of repayment to come; they nodded their heads again and said:

"True, true, it is exacted."

They were given food, and very good food it was, white bread and beer — here again, they felt, was that odd mixture of kindliness and threat. They slept at night on the benches, which even had supports for the lifting up of their heads. Next day they had to choose the messenger who according to the will of this man should travel back to fetch their youngest — and who perhaps might never come again, if Jacob said no. It took them actually the whole day; for they would not leave it to the drawing of lots, but took their reason to their guide in this weighty case, which had to be considered in all its various lights.

Who amongst them had most influence with the father to prevail with him? Whom could they themselves best spare in their grave peril? Who was the most indispensable for the seed, that it might survive after they perished? All that had to be weighed and sifted, and the varying answers reconciled; by evening they had not got to the end. Those among them already accurst — in so far as Israel could be accurst — were not the men. So there was much in favour of sending Judah. True, they would be loath to spare him; but he might be the right one to win the father over, and they united in seeing in him the most indispensable for the seed. But he himself took exception. He shook his leonine head and said he was a sinner and bondman, neither worthy nor willing to survive.

So whom should they designate, to whom should the finger point? To Dan, because of his shrewdness? To Gaddiel, on account of his forthright way? To Asher because he liked to move his moist lips to represent them all? Zebulon and Issachar both felt there was nothing to be said in their favour. The lot would probably have fallen upon Naphtali, Bilhah's son, in the end. His talebearing zeal urged him to be gone, his long legs twitched, his tongue already ran; though to the others, and even to himself, he seemed not weighty or considerable enough, either spiritually or mentally, in any but a superficially mythical sense. So up till the third morning the finger did not point decisively at any one of them; but it would probably have pointed to Naphtali if the next audience had not shown all their brain-racking to be vain, since it turned out that the stern keeper of the market had thought of another plan.

THE MONEY IN THE SACKS

JOSEPH was scarcely once more alone with Mai-Sachme, after receiving and dismissing his train of notables, when with still glowing face, rapt and exulting, he said:

"Mai, did you hear? He still lives, Jacob is alive, he can still hear that I am alive and not dead — and Benjamin is a married man, with a host of children!"

"That was a bad slip you made, Adon, when you burst out laughing before it was repeated to you."

"No matter! I patched it up all right. In such an exciting moment one cannot think of everything. But aside from that, how was it? How did I do? Did I manage well? Did I adorn the God-story properly? Did I give it some impressive detail?"

"You did it very well, Adon. Wonderful. Very pretty. It was a rewarding situation too."

"Yes, rewarding. But what is not rewarding is you. You take everything for granted, you only make big eyes. When I stood up and accused them, wasn't that pretty telling? I had led up to it, you could see it coming; but when it came it was impressive. And when big

Reuben said: 'We recognize you in your greatness, but you not us in our innocence' — wasn't that silver and gold?"

"You had nothing to do with his saying it, Adon."

"But I had led up to it! And, after all, the details of the feast are all my affair. No, Mai, you are ungrateful, and I cannot get at you, and you cannot be surprised. But now I will tell you something: I am not at all as satisfied as I seem, because I was stupid."

"How so, Adon? You did it charmingly."

"One important thing I did badly, and I saw it directly, but it was too late to alter it then. Keeping nine of them as hostages and sending one back was clumsy — a much worse blunder than my laughing was. I must correct it. What should I do with nine of them here, since I can do nothing to hasten the action of the God-story until Benjamin is here, and I cannot even see them, since they are forbidden my countenance until they set him before me? That was badly botched. Are they just to sit here in pawn, while at home there is no food and my father has no bread for the offering? No, it must be arranged just the other way: one stops on here as guarantee, one by whom the father sets least store, say one of the twins (just between ourselves, they were the ones who behaved the most savagely when they all fell upon me); the rest shall go and take home the needful for their hunger — for which they must pay, of course; if I gave it to them it would look too suspicious. I do not for a moment think they would leave the hostage to his fate and confess themselves guilty to the charge, by sacrificing him and not coming back with the little one."

"But that may take a long time, my dear lord. My mind misgives me lest your father refuse to let the little married man go, until the bread is all gone and the lamp again threatens to go out. You are taking a long time for your tale."

"Well, yes, Mai. And why should not such a God-story take time, and we not patiently work on its careful embellishment? If it is a whole year before they come back with Benjamin, it will not be too long for me. What is a year, anyhow, in this story? After all, I have taken you into it expressly because you are patience itself and can lend me some when I get fidgety."

"With pleasure, Adon. It is an honour to be present in it. I can see ahead and guess some of the things you will do to give it form. I think you mean to have them pay for the food you give them to take with them, but secretly, before they leave, you will have the money put in the top of their sacks, so that they will find it at their first stage. That will give them something to puzzle over."

Joseph looked at him big-eyed.

"Mai," said he, "that is capital. That is silver and gold. You remind me of a detail I should probably have come on by myself, because of course it belongs to the story, yet I might have overlooked it. I should never have thought that one who could not be astonished could think up anything so astonishing as that."

"I should not be astonished, my lord, but they will be."

"Yes, they will; they will be bewildered, and they will guess — but not yet know that they guess. And they will feel they are dealing with a man who means well by them and plays tricks on them. I leave it to you to arrange; it is as good as set down in the tale. I charge you to slip the money into the fodder-bags so that everyone finds his own as soon as they feed. Aside from the hostage, they will feel even more bound to come back. And now till day after tomorrow. We must just wait till then, and then I will tell them the new arrangement. But what are a year and a day in a tale like this!"

So on the third day the brothers stood again in the hall of audience before the chair of Joseph the provider — or rather they lay, they pressed their foreheads to the pavement, they rose half-way, lifting their arms palms upwards, then they fell down again, murmuring in chorus:

"You are as Pharaoh. Your servants are without guilt before you."

"Yes, yes, you think you can get round me with bendings and bowings; but you are just a sheaf of hollow ears — interpreter, tell them what I said, that they have ears but they hear not. And by hollow I mean hypocritical, dishonest. But you cannot pull the wool over the ears of a man like me with shows of that kind; my suspicions are not to be put to sleep by your bobbing up and down. So long as you have not brought up the evidence and set it here before me, I mean your youngest brother you talk about, just so long you are rascals in my eyes, and fear not God. But I fear Him. Therefore I will tell you how it is ordained. I do not want your children to suffer hunger or your old father to sleep in the dark. You will be given provision according to your numbers at the price fixed by the market. Even you could not imagine that I would give you bread because you are this or that, all sons of one man, and twelve of you in all. That is no reason why a man like me should not deal with you in a businesslike way; especially when I am in all probability dealing with spies. You shall receive for ten families if you can pay for it; but I will let only nine of you carry it home. One of you must remain as hostage and be held here until you get back and wash yourselves clean by setting all eleven of you before me, who once were twelve. And the pawn shall be the one on whom my eye first lights, in other words he!"

And he pointed with his fan to Simeon, who looked defiantly straight ahead as though it did not concern him at all.

They laid him in bonds. While the soldiers put them on, the brothers pressed round and spoke to him. Then it was they came back to what they had already said in private, speaking what was not meant for Joseph's ears; but he heard and understood it.

"Simeon," they said, "courage, man! So it is to be you, he has picked you out. Bear it like the man you are, a stout man and brave, a Lamech! We will do everything to get back and set you free. But you need not fear: it will not be too bad in the meantime, not anything beyond your considerable powers to endure. The man is only half hostile — he is half friendly too. He will not send you to the mines unconvicted. Remember he sent us roast goose into our prison. He is perfectly unaccountable; but he is by no means a bad sort. Maybe you will not be kept in bonds all that time; but if you are, even that is better than washing gold. We do pity you; but the lot has fallen upon you by the man's whim, so what can you do? It might have been any one of us, and indeed it is all of us, God knows. But at least you do get out of one thing, you do not have to stand before Jacob and tell him we have left one of us in pawn and have to take back the youngest-born with us. The whole thing is a calamity, an affliction sent upon us by avenging powers. For remember what Judah said, when he spoke to us all from the depths of his heart and reminded us how our brother cried to us out of the depths of the well and we were deaf to his weeping when he pleaded with us for our father's sake, that he might not fall on his back. And you cannot deny that you two, you and Levi, were the most savage of all in your treatment of him!"

And Reuben added:

"Courage, twin, your children shall have what to eat. All this has come upon us because none of you would listen when I warned you and said: 'Do not lay hands on the boy!' But no, you would not be checked, and when I came back to the pit the boy was gone. Now God is asking us: 'Where is your brother Abel!'"

Joseph heard it. His nose began to prickle inside, he sniffed a little, and his eyes all at once ran over, so that he had to turn round as he sat, and Mai-Sachme had to thump him on the back. It did not help him at once. Even when he turned round, he was blinking his eyes and his speech was halting and thick.

"I will not," said he, "charge you the highest price which the market permits. You shall not be able to say that Pharaoh's friend exploited you when you came to the father of the famine. What you can carry and your sacks can hold will be given, I assign it to you. I am granting you wheat and barley; I recommend you the kind that comes from Uto, the land of the serpent, it is the best sort. What I further advise is that you use the corn for bread and not risk much on the sowing. The drought may continue — in fact it certainly will — and the seed would be wasted. Farewell! I bid you farewell like honest people, for after all you are not yet convicted, however sorely suspect, and in case you set the eleventh brother before me I will believe you, and not take you for monsters of the prime but eleven sacred signs of the zodiac. Yet where is your twelfth sign? It is hidden by the sun. Shall it be so, men? Good luck on the journey. You are a strange, riddling folk. Take heedful way now that ye go, and very heedful when you come back. For now only necessity is your guide, and that is hard enough; but when you return you will be bringing your youngest. The god of your fathers be your shield and buckler! And forget not Egypt, where Usir was lured into the chest and mangled, but became the first in the kingdom of the dead and lighted the under-earthly sheepfold."

So then he broke off the audience and rose from his seat beneath the feather fans. The brothers received their vouchers in an office in the building, whither they were led; and the price was fixed by bushel and measure and load and their animals and beasts of burden were fetched from the courtyard, and the purchase price was weighed out to the sworn officers presiding over the scales: from each of them ten silver rings, so there was a just balance between rings and weights, and the wheat and the barley poured forth out of the bins and filled their sacks to bursting — great double sacks they were, bulging out over the flanks of the heavy-laden beasts. The fodder-sacks, however, were hung on the riding-animals, in front of the saddles. Now they would have set off, to lose no time but get a good piece from Menfe towards the frontier on their first day. But the officials first spread them a meal for their strengthening, while the caravan waited in the court: beer soup with raisins, and legs of mutton. Likewise they were given food for the first days of the journey, packed in gay packages to keep it fresh — that was the custom, they were told; the provisions were included in the purchase price, for this was Egypt, the land of the gods, a land that could well afford to be generous.

It was Mai-Sachme, steward of the lord's house, who said this to them. He had supervised all these arrangements with the greatest care, lifting his heavy black brows above his round brown eyes. They very much liked him and his easy ways; especially when he comforted them about Simeon, and said that he thought his lot would be fairly tolerable. The business of putting him in bonds had been mostly symbolic, it would probably not last. Only if they decamped and left him in the lurch and did not come back with the youngest-born by a year from now at the latest, then, of course, he, Mai, would answer for nothing. For his master — well, of course, he was a potentate: friendly, yes, certainly, very pleasant; but on the other hand quite relentless once he had got a thing into his head. He thought it quite possible things would go very hard with Simeon if they did not follow out what his master had said. Then there would be two gone instead of one — which surely would not please the old man their father any better.

"Oh no," they said. And they would do all they could. But it was hard to live between two fires. Spoken in all honour, of course, so far as his master was concerned; for he was *tam*, a man of the solstice, and had something godlike in his goodness and his awfulness.

"That you may well say," he responded. "Have you had enough? Then good journey to you! And remember my words!"

So then they pulled out from the city; silent at first, for they were depressed about Simeon and also about the problem of bringing home to the father that they had forfeited him, and breaking to him the only way there was to redeem the forfeit. But it was a long way yet to the father, and they talked among themselves too, after a while. They said how much they liked the Egyptian beer soup; and how indeed trouble had overtaken them, but yet they had had easy bargaining and come out well — after all, the father ought to be pleased at that. They spoke of the stocky steward and what a pleasant, composed man he was, not *tam* but quite simply friendly and without any sharp corners. But who knew how he would have behaved if he had been not just an eldest servant, but the master and keeper of the market? Simple people are less tempted, they can easily be kind-hearted; whereas greatness without bounds inevitably made people capricious and unaccountable. The All-Highest Himself was an instance; often He was hard to understand with His uncanny ways. Anyhow, the Moshel had been almost entirely friendly today — up to the point where he had put Simeon in bonds. He had given them good advice, blessed them, and almost solemnly compared them with the signs of the zodiac, of which one was hidden. Probably he was an astrologer, besides being a reader and interpreter of signs. Indeed, he had let fall a hint that he was not without higher means of increasing his own perceptions. It would not surprise them to hear that he could read the stars. But if the stars had told him this about the brothers being spies, then it was sheer nonsense he read in them.

They talked over all these matters; and on the same day got a good piece on in the direction of the Bitter Lakes. But when it began to grow dark they chose a camping-ground for the night, a pleasant, convenient spot, half surrounded by lime cliffs, from which in one place a crooked palm tree grew out and then straightened itself to make a shade. There was a well, and a shelter-hut, and the blackened earth showed that other people had camped here and made fire. The locality has a further rôle to play in the rest of the story; we shall know it again by the palm tree, the well, and the hut.

The nine brothers made themselves comfortable there. Some unloaded the asses and put the packs together. Others drew water and piled branches for a fire. But one of them, Issachar, at once set about feeding his animal — for his nickname of the "bony ass" gave him special sympathy with the wants of his beast, and the animal had several times brayed piteously for its food.

The son of Leah opened his feed-bag. He gave a shout.

"Halloo!" he cried. "Look here! See what I have here, brothers in Jacob! Come hither, all of you!"

They come up from all sides, stretch their necks, and look. Right at the top of the feed-bag Issachar had found his ten silver rings, the price of his load of corn.

They stand and are amazed, they shake their heads and make signs to ward off evil. "Well, bony one," they cry, "what has happened to you?"

Suddenly they rush each to his own bag. Each one looks, and needs not to search: at the top of each man's bag lies his purchase money.

They sit down where they are on the ground. What does it mean? The money had been fairly counted out against the weights; now they have it back again. Their hearts sink under the sheer incomprehensibility of it. What in all the world could it mean? Certainly it is good, it makes the face light up, to get one's money back along with the goods. But yet it was uncanny — particularly because they were under suspicion as it was. There was the mutual good feeling — that in itself was suspicious, and cast a distorted light in both directions. It still remained warming and satisfying — but again, there was a screw loose somewhere, for why, oh, why had God done this?

"Do you know why God does this to us?" asked big Reuben, and nodded at them with the muscles of his face all drawn.

They understood well what he meant. He referred to the old story, and connected this crazy good luck with the crazy bad luck in which they were involved; because once, against his warning (if he *had* actually warned them), they had laid hands on the boy. That they brought God into the thing, asking each other why He did this, showed that they had the same thoughts. But thinking of it, they felt, was going far enough; Reuben need not wag his head at them. Now that this had happened, it would be harder than ever to stand before the father; it gave them still another confession to make. Simeon, Benjamin — and now this queer, this altogether crazy business into the bargain; no, they were not exactly going home with their heads high. Perhaps it might please Jacob to hear that they had got the corn gratis; on the other hand his business honour might be touched, and more than ever they should stand in a bad light before him.

Once they all jumped up at the same time to run to their asses and return the purchase price. But then they all saw the futility of that and sat down again. No sense in that, they said. And truly there was as little sense in returning the money as there was in their having it back in the first place.

They shook their heads. They even kept on shaking their heads in their sleep, often several at a time. And they sighed, too, as they slept — probably not one of them but unconsciously heaved a sigh twice or thrice in the night. Yet anon a smile would play on the lips of this or that sleeper; yes, several of them smiled happily in their sleep.

THE MISSING NUMBER

GOOD news! The return of his sons was announced to Jacob, and their approach towards the paternal tent, with their asses moving heavily under the burden of Mizraim's corn. At first it was not noticed that there were only nine of them, instead of the ten who had gone forth. Nine makes a sizable group, and with all their animals, nine was almost like ten to the eye. Only a very sharp eye will notice that it is not one more. Benjamin, standing with his father before the house of hair (the old man had him by the hand, the husband of Mahalia and Arbath, like a little lad), did not notice anything wrong. He saw neither nine nor ten — just the brothers, moving up in their goodly numbers. But Jacob saw at once.

Astonishing. After all, the patriarch was close to ninety; one would not expect keenness of vision from those brown eyes, faded and blinking from age, with the flabby sacs beneath them. For unimportant things — and how much has not become unimportant? — they were not keen. But the deficiencies of age are more mental than physical: the senses have seen and heard and felt enough — let them grow dull. But there are things for which they can surprisingly regain the keen ear of the hunter, the quick eye of the sheep-counting shepherd; and the integrality of Israel was a subject on which Jacob saw better than anybody else.

"There are only nine," he said in a decisive though somewhat quavering tone, and pointed. After a very brief space he added: "Simeon is not there."

"Yes, Simeon is missing," replied Benjamin after a careful look. "I don't see him either. He must be coming after them."

"We will hope so," said the old man very firmly, and clasped the hand of his youngest in his. Thus he let them come up. He did not smile, he said not a word of greeting. He only asked:

"Where is Simeon?"

There they had it. Obviously he was minded, as before, to make things as hard as he could for them.

"Of Simeon later," answered Judah. "Greeting, Father! Of him presently; for the moment only this much: that you have no cause for worry about him. Look, we are back from our journey and once more with the head of our house."

"But not all," said he immovably. "To you too greetings, but where is Simeon?"

"Well, yes, he is missing for the moment," they told him. "He is not here just now. That is because of the business we did and the way the man down there — "

"Perhaps you have sold my son for bread?"

"Of course not. But we bring corn, as our lord sees, plenty of corn, at least plenty for a while and very good quality, wheat and prime barley from Lower Egypt, and you will have your little white loaves for the offerings. That is the first thing we have to tell you."

"And the second?"

"The second may sound somewhat strange, one might even say more than strange; if you like, even abnormal. But we did think it would please you. We have all this good corn for nothing. That is, it was not for nothing at first; we paid for it, and our money faithfully balanced the weights of the land. But when we camped the first night, Issachar found his money in his feed-bag and, lo and behold, we all found ours too, so that we are bringing home the goods and the money too, for which we count on your approval."

"But my son Simeon you do not bring home. It is as good as settled that you have traded him for common bread."

"Again! What can our dear lord be thinking of! We are not the men for that kind of trade. Shall we sit down here with you and reassure you about your son our brother? But first shall we let a little golden grain run into your hand and show you the money we brought back that you may see how gold and silver are present both at once?"

"What I desire first of all is to be informed about my son Simeon," he said.

They sat down in a circle with him and Benjamin and made their report: how they had been segregated on the frontier and sent to Mempi, a great noisy bustling city. How they were led through rows of crouching men beasts to the great official palace and into a room of overwhelming splendour, and before the seat of the great lord who was as Pharaoh, and was the keeper of the market to whom all the world came for bread. He was a strange kind of man, spoiled by greatness, erratic and charming. They had bowed and bent before the man, Pharaoh's friend, the provider, and thought to deal with him in the way of business; but he showed a double face, both friendly and grim. In part he spoke them very friendly, in part and suddenly very harsh; he had asserted what they could scarcely bear to repeat; namely, that they were spies, who wanted to search out the secret shame of the land — they, the ten true men! Their hearts had misgiven them; they had told him precisely who they were, ten men dealing in truth, all of them sons of one man, the friend of God, in the land of Canaan, and in their full number not ten but twelve, since the youngest was at home with the father and one had been lost in the world at an early age. But the man there, the lord of the land, did not and would not believe that their father was still alive, seeing that they themselves were no longer of the youngest. He had to be told twice, for in the land of Egypt they probably knew no such length of days as our dear lord owns, they probably die off early of their apelike excesses.

"Enough," he said. "Where is my son Simeon?"

They were just coming to that, they said, or at least without long delay. But first for good or ill they must speak of somebody else, and it was a pity he had not gone with them in the first place as they had wished and suggested. If he had they would probably all be back again in full numbers by now; for then the proof would have been forthcoming which the man, not trusting them, had required. For he had never given up the notion that they were spies, or believed their solemn word as to their honourable origins; but had demanded as proof of their innocence that they send the youngest-born of them all before his seat. If they did not, then, he had said, they were proven spies.

Benjamin laughed.

"Lead me to him!" he said. "I am curious to see this curious man."

"You will be silent, Benoni," Jacob sternly admonished him, "and cease your childish prattle. Does an urchin like you mix in such counsels as this? — I have still to hear about my son Simeon."

"Yes," said they, "you would hear if you would listen, dear Father, and did not expect us to tell you all the details at once." It had been clear that, lying under such a suspicion and enforced by such a demand, they would not have been allowed to leave — to say nothing of buying bread. There had to be a guarantee. The man had first proposed to keep them all and only send one to bring back the evidence; but by skilful talk and persuasion they succeeded in changing his mind, so that he only kept one, Simeon, and let the rest of them leave, provided with grain.

"And so your brother, my son Simeon, has been sold for debt into the Egyptian house of bondage," said Jacob with terrifying self-control.

The steward of the lord of the land, they answered, a good, steady-going man, had assured them that Simeon would be well treated, everything considered, and that his bonds would soon be loosed.

"Better and better," he said, "do I understand why I was loath to give you leave for the journey. You keep for ever at me with your itch to go down to Egypt, and when I finally consent you make such use of my weakness that only some of you come back, leaving the best of you in the clutch of the oppressor."

"You did not always speak so well of Simeon."

"Lord of Heaven," he said with face upraised, "they accuse me of having no heart for Leah's second, the warlike hero. They act as though it was I had sold him away for a measure of meal and given him to the jaws of leviathan for food for their children — I, not they! How must I thank Thee that Thou hast at least strengthened my heart against their assault and kept me firm against their naughtiness when they wanted to go in their full numbers, taking the youngest as well! They would have been quite capable of coming back without him and telling me: 'You did not set any great store by him'!"

"On the contrary, Father! If all eleven of us had gone and the youngest had been with us, so that we could have set him before the man, the lord of the land, who required his presence, then we should all have come back together. But there is nothing lost, for we need only take Benjamin down and set him before the man, Pharaoh's keeper of the market, there in the hall of the provider, and Simeon will be free and you will have them both back again, your hero and your child."

"In other words, since you have squandered away Simeon you want to tear Benjamin out of my arms and take him to where Simeon is."

"We want that because of the man's whim, to cleanse ourselves and with the proof redeem the pledge."

"You hearts of wolves! You rob me of my children and all your thought is how to decimate Israel. Joseph is no more, Simeon is no more, and now you would take Benjamin away. As you have brewed, so I must drink, and everything goes on over my head."

"No, you describe it not as it is, Father and lord. Benjamin is not to be given up in addition to Simeon, rather both shall come back to you, if only we first set our youngest before the man's eyes that he may see we go about with truth. We humbly beg you to give us Benjamin for the journey that we may free Simeon and Israel may be once more his full number as of yore."

"Full number? And where is Joseph? In plain words you demand from me that I shall send this last remaining one to join his brother Joseph. Well, you are refused."

Then Reuben, the oldest brother, grew hot and gushed forth like boiling water and said:

"Father, hear me now! Listen to me alone who am the head of all this! For not to them shall you give the boy for the journey, but only to me. If I do not bring him back, then may it happen to me thus and thus. If I do not bring him back, then shall you strangle my two sons, Hanoch and Pallu. Strangle them, I say, before my eyes with your own hands and I will not stir an eyelash if I broke my word to you and did not free the pledge."

"Yes, yes, there you go headlong like a waterfall," Jacob answered;

"where were you when the swine trod down my lovely son? Did you know how to protect Joseph? What should I have from your sons? And am I an avenging angel to strangle them and decimate Israel with my own hands? I reject you all and your demand, my son shall not go down with you, for his brother is dead and he alone remains to me. If aught happen to him on the way, then the world would see the sight of my grey hairs brought down in sorrow to the grave."

They looked at each other and compressed their lips. It was wonderful, the way he called Benjamin "my son" and not their brother and said that he alone was left to him!

"And Simeon, your hero?" they asked.

He answered: "I will sit here alone and mourn for him. Disperse!"

"Our duty and thanks to you," said they, and left him. Benjamin went with them and patted the arm of one or two of the brothers with his short-fingered hand.

"Don't be annoyed," he begged, "and be not bitter that he stands on his dignity. Do you think it flatters me to be called his only son or that I brag because he said I am all that is left him and he refuses to let me go with you? I always know he never forgets how Rachel died to give me my life, and this tutelage I suffer under he practises in bitterness. Think how long it took for him to let you go down, without me; and see how dear you are to him. Now it will only take a little time till he will yield and send me down with you to the land, for he will not leave our brother in the hands of the heathen, he cannot; and besides, how long will the bread last which you were so clever as to get for nothing? So be of good cheer! The little one will have his journey yet. But now tell me a bit more about this keeper of the market, the stern lord who accused you so outrageously and asked such outlandish questions about the youngest of the family! I might almost boast about that — that he wants to see me at all and use me for a witness. Tell me about him. The highest, you said, among all those lower than the highest? And lifted up above all? How did he look to you, how does he speak? It is no wonder I am curious about a man who is so curious about me."

JACOB WRESTLES AT JABBOK

YES, what is a year compared with this tale; and who would be miserly with time or patience on its account? Joseph practised patience; he had to live and be a statesman and a business man in the meantime. The brothers practised patience, well or ill, with Jacob's self-will, and Benjamin did too, restraining his curiosity about the journey and the curious keeper of the market. We are better off than they, and that not because we already know how it all turned out. That, indeed, is a disadvantage compared with the position of those who lived in the story and experienced it in their own persons; for we must summon up a lively feeling of suspense where by rights there can be none. But yet we do have a certain advantage, because we have power over the whole quantum of time to stretch or shrink it at will. We do not have to pay for the year of waiting in all its daily ups and downs as Jacob had to pay with his seven years in Mesopotamia. We may simply open our lips and say: A year passed—and lo, it has passed. It has passed, and Jacob is ripe.

It is a well-known fact, of course, that meteorological conditions in this quarter of the globe remained erratic for a considerable time. The drought continued to oppress the lands in which our story moves. Misfortunes, they say, never come singly; one leads to another and then to another, until instead of the hit-or-miss pattern usually obtaining in this world of chance and change, it seems as though fate took a diabolic delight in making the same bad luck come to pass time after time with infuriating repetition. Of course, there simply has to come a turn sooner or later; otherwise it would end by nullifying itself. But it can go on and on for years, without rhyme or reason; that it should repeat itself as many as seven times is not, generally speaking, anything extraordinary.

In our explanations of the cloud movements between the sea and the African Alps in the land of the Moors where the waters of the Nile take their rise, we have, indeed, considered the how but not the why of this situation. For once you begin with the why you can never get to the end. It is like the dunes by the sea, where behind each foreland lies still another and the space of time where you might come to final rest is somewhere in dim infinity. The Nourisher did not grow great and overflow its banks, because in the land of the Moors it did not rain. It did not rain because no rain fell in Canaan; and that was because the sea manufactured no clouds for seven, or certainly at least for five years on end. Why not? Here too there are overarching reasons reaching into cosmic matters and to the heavenly bodies which doubtless control our wind and weather. There are the sun-spots; they are a sufficiently remote cause perhaps; yet since every child knows that the sun is not the last and highest, and since Abram, in his time, refused to worship it as the final cause, we ourselves should be ashamed to stop at it. There are higher orders in the All, which compelled even the sun's fixed regal status to subordinate its motions; and the sun-spots on its disk are in their turn, so to speak, a subordinate why; but even from this you must not conclude that the final and ultimate resting-place lies in those super-systems or in still superior systems. The ultimate obviously lies or has its seat in a remoteness which is at the same time a nearness, since in it farness and nearness, cause and effect are all one; it is where we find ourselves by losing ourselves and where we suspect a design which for the sake of its ends renounces even the bread for the offering.

The drought and the scarcity were sore and oppressive indeed. It did not take even a whole year for Jacob to be ripe. The provisions which his sons had so luckily and uncannily got for nothing had all been consumed; they had not been much among so many, and more were not to be had anywhere in the land at any price. So, a few moons earlier than the year before, Israel brought up the subject the brothers had been waiting for.

"Tell me what you think," he said. "For to me it seems that there is a preposterous contradiction yawning between the riches which I own and which have increased since I broke the dusty bolts of Laban's kingdom, and the present bad state of things; for we have neither seed-corn nor bake-stuff and our children cry for bread."

Yes, they told him; that was due to the bad times.

"They are strange times," said he. "A man has a whole troop of grown sons whom with God's help he did not fail to raise up to his aid; and they sit here on their backsides and lift not a finger against the want that consumes us."

"Yes, that is easy to say; but what can we do?"

"Do? In Egypt, as I hear on all sides, there is grain market. How would it be if you gird yourselves for the journey and go down and buy a little bread?"

"That would be splendid, Father, and we would have gone already. But you forget what the harsh ruler down there said about Benjamin: that we should not see his face unless our youngest brother were with us, and we could show him on the spot in token of our good faith. It appears the man is an astrologer. He says that of the twelve one is hidden behind the sun; but it must not be two at once that are hidden, and the eleventh must be set before him before he will even see us again. Give us Benjamin and we will go."

Jacob sighed.

"I knew that would come," he said, "and that you would only torment me again about the child."

And he chided them loudly.

"Unhappy that ye are, and unheeding! Why did you have to prattle and tattle and in your folly turn out all your affairs before the man so that he heard you had another brother, my son, and could demand him from me? If you had been dignified and stuck to business without prattling, he would know nothing about Benjamin and could not ask my heart's blood as the price of flour for bread! Richly you deserve that I should curse you one and all!"

"Do not, lord," said Judah; "for what would become of Israel? Consider in what straits we were and how we were forced to tell

truth when he set about us with his suspicion and examined us about
our kindred. For he questioned us so narrowly: 'Does your father
yet live?' 'Have you another brother?' 'Is your father well?' And
when we told him it was not so well with you as it should be, he
scolded us loudly and railed at us for letting it come to that."

"H'm," went Jacob, and stroked his beard.

"We were frightened," Judah went on, "by his severity, yet drawn
to him by his interest. For after all it is no small thing when such a
great man of the world, at whose mercy we then were, shows such
concern." And how, Judah went on, could they have foreseen that
the man would demand their brother's presence and lay upon them
so bindingly to fetch Benjamin down?

Thus Judah, the tried and tested man, who today took the word.
For they had so planned it among them, in case Jacob showed signs
of being ripe. Reuben was already out of the field, after he had im-
pulsively made the clumsy and offensive suggestion that Jacob should
strangle his two sons. Levi, though much upset by the loss of his
twin, and only half a man since then, could not be put forward on
account of Shechem. But Judah spoke very well, with manly per-
suasiveness and warmth of feeling.

"Israel," he said, "overcome yourself, even though you wrestle
with yourself until the dawn, as once before you did with another.
This is a Jabbok hour, would you go out of it like a hero of God!
Lo, the man's mind down there is unchangeable. We shall not see
him, and Leah's third son remains fallen to the house of bondage, and
there is not even a thought of bread, unless Benjamin is with us. I,
your lion, know how bitter it is for you to yield up Rachel's last
pledge to take a journey, on account of the 'being always at home';
and worse than that, a journey down to the land of mud and dead
gods. And you probably do not trust this man, the lord in the land,
suspecting that he is laying a trap for us and will give back neither
the pledge nor the youngest — or perhaps not any of us at all. But I
say to you, I who know men and expect not much good from high
or low: the man is not such a man; so far I know him and know that,
and would put my hand in the fire for it: to lure us into a trap is not
in his mind. He may be strange and not quite canny, but he is also
very winning, and though full of error yet not false. I, Judah, go bail
for him, as also I go bail for your youngest son, our brother. Let him
go down at my side, and I will be father and mother to him, like you;
both on the road and in the land, that he strike not his foot against a
stone nor is besmirched in his soul by the vices of Egypt. Give him
into my hand, that we may journey at length, and live and not die:
we, you, and the little children of us all. For at my hand shall you
require him, and if I bring him not and set him before your face I
will bear the blame all my life long. As you have him now, so shall

you have him again — and could have had him long since as now you have him, for had we not delayed we could have been there and back twice over with the pledge, the witness, and the bread."

"Until the dawn," answered Jacob, "give me time."

And by next morning he had surrendered and acquiesced, he would give Benjamin to go a journey — not a journey to Shechem, a few days distant, but some seventeen days down into the underworld. Jacob had red eyes and failed not to express how hard the enforced resolve had borne upon his soul. But as he had not only honourably and sorely wrestled with necessity and come off conqueror, but expressed his pain with such great-hearted dignity, they were all much edified, and all those round about him said with feeling: "Lo, Israel has this night overcome himself!"

His head drooped upon his shoulder as he said:

"If it must be so, and stands written in bronze that everything shall go out from me, then take it and do it and go forth, for I consent. Take of the choicest things in your packs, for which our land is praised throughout the world, to present to the man to soften his heart: oil of balsam, gum of tragacanth from the goat's-thorn, grape honey cooked to a thickness, to drink in water or sweeten the dessert, also pistache nuts and fruit of the terebinth — and call it little in his eyes. Furthermore take double the money, for the new grain and for the earlier time as well, for I recall that the money was found in your sacks and there may have been a mistake. And take Benjamin — yes, yes, you hear me aright — take him and lead him down to the man that he may stand before him, I give my consent. I see on your faces consternation painted at my words; but my decision is final, Israel girds himself up to be as a man who is bereft of his children. But may El Shaddei," he broke out, his hands raised to heaven, "give you pity in the man's eyes that he yield you your other brother back, and Benjamin. Lord, only as a loan and to be returned give I him to you; for the journey only, let no misunderstanding be between me and you, for I offer him not to be devoured like my other son, I will have him back! Remember, O Lord, the bond, that the heart of man become fine and holy in You and You in it. Fall not below the feeling human heart, O mighty One, and defraud me not of the boy on the journey and fling him to the devourer, but be moderate, I implore You, and honourably return me the loan; then I will serve You in the dust and burn before You what shall ravish Your nostrils, the very best parts!"

So he sent up his prayers. Then he arranged with Eliezer, whose name was Damasek, to make ready the little son of death for the journey and to provide him in all ways like a mother; for at the next dawning the brothers should set out, in order not to miss the caravan from Gaza. And hearing this, Benoni's eager cup overflowed with

joy, seeing that at last he should be released out of his symbolic durance and go to see the world. He did not jump for joy before Jacob
and the brothers, nor kick his heels together, because he was not
seventeen, as Joseph had been, but nearly thirty; and he would not
wound that soft pathetic heart with showing his gladness. Besides,
his darkened existence as a mother-slayer did not suit with much
jumping for joy, and he might not fall out of his rôle. But before
his wives and children he plumed himself not a little over his freedom of action and the fact that he was going down to Mizraim to set
Simeon free, he and he alone having such power over the lord of
the land.

They were able to shorten their preparations because they could
supply in Gaza all their wants for the trip through the desert. For
the present their packs chiefly consisted of presents for Simeon's
jailer, the Egyptian keeper of the market, which young Eliezer had
taken out of the stores: the aromatic distillations, the grape syrup, the
gums and myrrh, the nuts and fruit. A single donkey was reserved for
these gifts, for which the country was renowned.

In the light of early dawn the brothers set forth on their second
journey, in the same strength as before, one less and one more. The
families and servants stood about, and within the group the ten with
their beasts on halters. But at the heart of it stood Jacob, and held all
that he had left of the beloved of his youth. That was what the audience came for: to see how Jacob took leave of his dearest possession
and to be edified by his pangs and his stately expression of them. Long
he held his youngest to him; hung round him the phylactery from his
own neck and murmured at his cheek with eyes upraised. But the
brothers bent theirs on the ground, with bitter, forbearing smiles.

"Judah, it was you," he said at last; all of them heard him. "You
have given your bond for this child, that I may require him at your
hand. But now hearken: you are released from your bond. For can
a man give his bond for God? Not upon you will I build my trust,
for what could you avail against God's anger? I will build upon
Him alone, who is the Rock and the Shepherd, that He grant me
back this pledge that I have entrusted to Him in good faith. Hear,
all of you: He is no monster who mocks at human hearts and treads
them like a savage in the dust. He is a great God, purified and enlightened, a God of the bond and of good faith; if any man is to vouch
for Him, I need you not, my lion, for I myself will vouch for His
faith and He will not so injure Himself as to make His guarantee a
mock. Go!" he said, and put Benjamin from him, "go in the name
of God, the true and the merciful. But all the same, take care of
him!" he added in a breaking voice, and turned away to his dwelling.

THE SILVER CUP

AND SO, in due course, Joseph the provider came from his office to his house, and the news was in his heart that the ten travellers from Canaan had passed the frontier. Mai-Sachme took it in at once, and asked:

"Well, Adon, so we are for it, the waiting time is over?"

"We are," answered Joseph, "and it is. It has turned out as it ought to, they have come. The third day from today they should be here — with the little one," said he, "with the little one. This God-story of ours made a pause for a while and we had to wait. But time does not stand still, and it only seems to have no burden, and the shadow of the sun moves slowly on. One must steadfastly trust himself to time and trouble about it hardly at all — the Ishmaelites taught me that, with whom I travelled — for it continues to ripen and brings everything in its train."

"So now," said Mai-Sachme, "there is much to think of, and the course of the plot has to be carefully thought out. Shall I make suggestions?"

"Ah, Mai, as though I had not long ago thought out and composed everything and had in my composing spared any care! It will run off as though it were already written down and was being played according to the script. There are no surprises, only the thrill of seeing the familiar of long ago become the present. And I am not nearly so excited this time either, I only feel solemn as we go on to the next scene, at most my heart gives a jump at the thought of the 'It is I'; I mean it jumps on their account — you would better have a draught ready for them."

"It shall be done, Adon. But even though you want no advice I will just give you some: take care for the little one! He is not merely half of your blood, he is your blood brother, and besides, as I know you, you will not be able to leave things alone, you will put him on the scent. The youngest of the family is always the cleverest; he might easily get ahead of your 'It is I' by saying 'It is you' and spoil your whole plan."

"Well, and what then, Mai? I shouldn't mind much. There would be a great laugh, as when children build a sand-castle and knock it down again and shout for joy. But I don't think so. A little chap like that, and tells Pharaoh's friend and vice-Horus, the great man of business, right to his face: 'Pooh! You are nobody but my brother Joseph!' That would be impertinent. No, the rôle of saying who I am will fall to me."

"Will you receive them again in the hall of audience?"

"No, this time it shall be here. I will have luncheon with them, they shall eat with us. Slay and provide for eleven more guests than you had down the third day from today. Who are invited for that day?"

"Some city dignitaries," said Mai-Sachme, consulting his memorandum. "Their worships Ptah-hotpe, reader from the house of Ptah; the god's Champion, Colonel Entef-oker, of the god's household troops; the chief surveyor and boundary-inspector Pa-neshe, who has a tomb where the Lord lies; and from the main commissariat a couple of scribes."

"Good. They will find it strange to sit down with the foreigners."

"Strange indeed, I am afraid, Adon. There are difficulties about the food laws and customs, I must warn you, and certain prohibitions. To some it may seem an offence to eat with the Ibrim."

"Go along with you, Mai, you talk like Dudu, a dwarf I once knew, who worshipped all the old saws. Trying to teach me my Egyptians — as though they still had a horror of such things! They would have to have a horror of eating with me; everybody knows I was not brought up on Nile water. Here is Pharaoh's ring: Be as myself; that will silence all objections. Whoever I eat with must obey that injunction at table too, and then there is Pharaoh's teaching which everybody professes who wants to stand well at court: that all men are the beloved children of his father. But of course you can serve us separately to preserve the forms. The Egyptians by themselves, the brothers by themselves, and me by myself. But you must seat my brothers together according to age, big Reuben first and Benoni last. Be careful to make no mistake, I will tell you the order again and you can write it down."

"Very well, Adon. But it is a risk. How do you come to know their ages so well without their being surprised at it?"

"And you must put my cup at my place, my silver cup that I look into."

"Yes, your cup. Will you tell them their ages out of it?"

"I could use it for that too."

"I wish, Adon, I could use it for prophesying too. I wish I could read, the way gold pieces and gems look in clear water, what you planned for the story and how you build it up to the point where you make yourself known. If I do not know, I fear I shall be able to serve you but poorly; but I must serve you and be useful to you in order not merely to stand about in this story into which you have so kindly taken me."

"That you certainly shall not. It would not be right. In the first place you are to put the cup at my place out of which I sometimes read, just for fun."

"The cup — very good, the cup," said Mai-Sachme, widening his eyes as though in an effort to remember. "They bring you Benjamin and you see your little brother again among his brothers. And when you have eaten with them and filled their sacks a second time they will take the youngest-born away with them again and go home to your father and there you will be!"

"Look again into the cup, Mai, see how it looks in the water! They go away again, of course; but perhaps they have forgotten something, so they have to come back again?"

The captain shook his head.

"Or they have taken something with them and we miss it, and go after them on account of it and fetch them back again?"

Mai-Sachme looked at him round-eyed, his brows drawn up; slowly his small mouth widened in a smile. When a man has a little mouth, no matter how square and strongly he may be built, when he smiles it is like a woman smiling. Thus Mai-Sachme smiled and despite his growth of black beard his smile was sweet and almost feminine. He must have been pleased with what he read in the cup, for he nodded to Joseph with a twinkle in his eye and Joseph nodded too. He lifted his hand and clapped his steward on the back. And Mai-Sachme — despite the fact that Joseph had once been a convict in his prison — lifted his hand too and patted the other's shoulder. Thus they stood, nodding and clapping; it was clear that both fully understood how the story was to run off.

THE MEAL WITH THE BROTHERS:
FRAGRANCE OF MYRTLE

AND here is how it ran off, in its appointed hour. Jacob's sons made their entry into Menfe, the house of Ptah, and alighted at the same inn as before. They were relieved to have brought Benjamin safely so far; during the nearly seventeen days of the journey they had handled him like a basket of eggs; partly out of fear of Jacob, partly because he was the most important member of their party, the indispensable evidence to convince the two-faced keeper of the market. Without Benjamin they would neither see the man's face nor get Simeon back. These would have been reasons enough to treat the little one like the apple of their eye, to give him of the best in food and lodgement and guard him as they did their precious water supply. Fear of the man stood in the foreground and behind it fear of the father. But behind those was still a third motive for their assiduity: namely, that they wanted to make good in Benjamin what they had sinned in Joseph. For the memory of him and of their evil deed was astir in them now after all these years, owing to the events of their first journey; it had risen up out of the drift of the years, till now it seemed only yesterday that they had sold their brother and uprooted a stem out of Israel. Retribution was in the air, they felt it like a hand drawing them to an accounting; a zealous care for Rachel's second child seemed to them the best means of making the hand relax its grip.

They dressed Benjamin in a fine gay smock with fringes and draperies, to introduce him to the lord of the land; his furry thatch of hair they anointed till it truly looked like a shiny helmet; they lengthened his eyes with a pointed pencil. But when they announced themselves at the great office where tickets were issued and grain delivered, they were sent on to the provider's own house. That alarmed them as everything alarmed them that did not go as it had before and seemed to involve them in fresh complications. Why were they set apart and sent to the man's private house? Did it portend good or ill? Possibly it had to do with the money returned to them in so strange a way. Perhaps the trick was now being used against them in a new trick and because of the money they had carried off all eleven of them were now to be enslaved. They had the wretched money with them as well as more for fresh supplies; but the fact did little to reassure them. They were strongly tempted to turn round, not to show themselves to the man but to take refuge in flight — and particularly because they feared for Benjamin. But the little brother spoke up boldly and insisted on being brought before the keeper of the market. He was adorned and anointed, he said, and he had no reason to hide from the man; as a matter of fact, neither had they, for it was only a mistake that the money had been returned and innocent men must not behave as though they were guilty.

Yes, guilty, they said. A little guilty in general they always did feel: not in this particular case, of course, it was only that they never did feel quite comfortable. He, Benjamin, could say what he liked; he was always at home, he had never been exposed, he never found unexplained money in his feed-bag, whereas they had had to be out in the world, where it was hard to keep oneself entirely pure.

Benoni tried to cheer them. The man, he said, was a man of the world, he would understand that kind of sense of guilt. About the money: it was certainly a puzzle, but probably perfectly all right — and had they not come, among other reasons, in order to give it back? But they knew as well as he did that Simeon must be released and that they had to have more provisions. There could be no talk of running away; that was to be called spies and thieves and brother-murderers to boot.

They knew it all as well as he did. They knew they had to face the music at the risk of being made slaves all round. The delicacies they had brought with them, Jacob's presents and bribes, the pride of their native land, gave them a little hope; and they felt something might be gained by trying to speak first with that pleasant and equable steward, if they could get hold of him.

This they succeeded in doing. They reached the gracious villa which Pharaoh had given his friend in the best quarter of the town, dismounted from their asses at the gate, and led them round the lotus pond to the house. And there he was, the man who had inspired their confidence; he came towards them down the terrace, greeted them, and thanked them for keeping their word even after this lapse of time. They presented their youngest brother, at whom he looked round-eyed and said "Bravo!" The animals were led round to the courtyard, where the servants unloaded them and carried into the house the bales containing Canaan's pride. Mai-Sachme led the brothers up the steps, and as they went they consulted anxiously with him about the money. Some of them had already begun as soon as they saw him, almost from afar, so eager they were:

"Worthy house-steward, head superintendent," said they, "thus and so it was; incredible as it seems, so it was." But here was double the money, for they were honest men. They had found the previously paid-out silver, first one of them and then all of them, in their feed-bags at the first camp, and the mysterious treasure-trove had greatly troubled them. Here it was again full weight, along with more money for the new purchases. His master, Pharaoh's friend, would not lay it up against them and condemn them?

They all talked at once, they tugged his arm in their distress and vowed they would not enter under the beautiful doors of the house unless he swore that his master was playing them no trick nor laying the mysterious chance to their charge.

But he was calmness itself; he quieted them and said:

"Calm yourselves, my friends, do not be afraid, for everything is in order. Or even if out of the natural order, it is a benign miracle. We got our money and that must content us, it is no reason why we should play tricks on you. After all you have told me I can only assume that your God and the God of your fathers amused Himself by putting the treasure in your sacks. No other explanation suggests itself to me. Probably you are His good and faithful servants and He would show you His awareness once in a way — that one can understand. But you seem to me very much excited, and that is not good. I will have some foot-baths prepared for you, first for hospitality's sake, for you are our guests and are to take the meal with Pharaoh's friend; but also they draw the blood from the head and will have a soothing effect. Now go inside and see who is waiting for you in the hall!"

And lo, inside there stood their brother Simeon, quite unattended and not in the least hollow-eyed or wasted, but as bouncing and heroic as ever. He had fared very well, he told his brothers as they crowded round him; he had lived in a room in the office building and been very comfortable for a hostage, though he had not seen the

Moshel's face again and had lived in fear lest they come not back. But the excellent food and drink had kept him up. They asked Leah's second to forgive them for taking so long, on account of Jacob's obstinacy — of course he would know how it was, and of course he did, and he rejoiced with them, especially with his brother Levi, for the two ruffians had missed each other sorely. There was no kissing and embracing, but they could scarcely leave off punching each other in the ribs.

The brothers all sat down together and washed their feet. Then the steward led them into the hall where the meal was laid out, magnificent with flowers and fruit and beautiful tableware. And he helped them arrange their gifts on a long buffet: spices, honey, fruits, and nuts, to make a fine display for the master's eye. But presently Mai-Sachme had to hurry away, for people were arriving, and Joseph came home with the Egyptian gentlemen whom he had invited as his guests of the day: the prophet of Ptah, the Champion of the god, the chief surveyor, and the masters of the books. He came in with them and said: "Greetings!" They fell on their faces as if they had been mown down.

He stood a little while, rubbing his fingers across his forehead. Then he repeated:

"Greetings, friends. Stand up and let me see your faces that I may recognize them. For you recognize me, I see, as the keeper of the market of Egypt who had to behave sternly to you because of this priceless land. But now you have appeased me and reassured me by your return in your proper numbers so that all the brothers are assembled in one room and under one roof. That is capital. Do you notice that I am speaking to you in your own tongue? Yes, I can speak it now. The other time you were here made me aware that I knew no Hebrew and it annoyed me. So since then I learned it. A man like me can do such things in a twinkling. But how are you all anyhow? And first of all, is your old father still alive about whom you told me, and is he well?"

"Your servant, our father," they said, "is very well and keeps his usual state. He would be much touched by the kind inquiry."

And they fell down again with their faces to the pavement.

"Enough of this bowing and bending," he said, "too much in fact. Let me see. Is that your youngest brother you told me about?" he asked in rather clumsy Canaanitish, for he was really out of practice, and he went up to Benjamin. The benedict, standing there in his fine garb, respectfully raised his clear grey eyes, with their usual expression of gentle sadness, to Joseph's face.

"God be gracious to you, my son," Joseph said, and laid his hand on the other's shoulder. "Have you always had such good eyes, and

such a fine shining helmet of hair even when you were a little urchin
and ran about in the meadows?"

He swallowed.

"I will come back in a moment," he said. "I will just — " and went
out quickly, probably to his own sleeping-chamber. He came back
presently, with his eyes fresh-washed.

"I am neglecting all my duties," he said, "and not making my guests
acquainted with each other. Gentlemen, these are merchants from
Canaan, of distinguished parentage, all sons of one remarkable man."

And he told the Egyptians the names of Jacob's sons, in the order
of their age, very fluently and rhythmically: after every third name
he dropped his voice, omitted his own, of course, making a little
pause after Zebulon, and then finished: "and Benjamin." The brothers, certainly, were vastly surprised to have him know all this, and
they marvelled among themselves.

Then he named the names of the Egyptian dignitaries, who behaved so stiffly that it made Joseph smile. Then he commanded the
meal to be served, rubbing his hands as one who goes to table. But
his steward pointed to the presents spread out on the buffet, and he
praised and admired them warmly.

"From the old man your father?" he asked. "That is a touching
attention. You must take him my best thanks."

It was a trifle, they told him: a few of the good things their country boasted.

"It is not a trifle, it is a great deal," he demurred. "And more than
that, the quality is very fine. I have never seen such fine tragacanth.
Or such pistache nuts. You can tell the wonderful taste of the oil
from here. Only in your home do they grow like that. I can hardly
keep my eyes off them. But now we must sit down."

Mai-Sachme showed them all to their places; and the brothers
found fresh matter for wonder; for they were seated exactly in order
of age, only in reverse, for the youngest sat next the master of the
house, then Zebulon, Issachar, and Asher and so on to big Reuben.
The feast was laid so that the dishes stood in an open triangle between
the columns running round the hall; and the apex of the triangle was
the host's seat. On his right were the Egyptian notables, on his left the
Asiatic foreigners, so that he presided over both, with Benjamin
on his left hand and the prophet of Ptah on his right. In hearty and
hospitable spirit he exhorted them all to fall to and not to spare the
food and drink.

The meal that followed is world-famous for being "merry." The
early stiffness of the Egyptian guests was put to rout; they soon
thawed out and forgot that it was an abomination to break bread
with the Hebrews. The King's Champion, Colonel Entef-oker, was

the first to relax, after several deep draughts of Syrian wine. He picked out the forthright Gad as the most likable of the sand-dwellers, and made the room ring by shouting across the table to him.

We must not be put off by the fact that tradition makes no mention of the presence of Joseph's wife, the daughter of the sun-priest; but represents the banquet as being entirely masculine — though it was Egyptian practice for married couples to eat together and the mistress of the house was regularly present at banquets. But the description that has been handed down is correct: Asenath was not present at the meal. That might be explained by recalling the terms of the marriage contract and concluding that the maiden was visiting her parents at the time. However, the true explanation lies in the routine of Joseph's days, which seldom permitted the exalted one to eat with his wife and children. This meal with the brothers and the resident honourables, however lively and enjoyable it was, was not a social but a business function, and Pharaoh's friend had to perform it nearly every day. Thus he usually took only the evening meal with his wife, in the women's wing of the house, after spending a little time playing with his charming half-breed sons, Manasseh and Ephraim. At midday, then, he took his meal in male society, either with the ranking and upper officials of the office or with important travelling dignitaries or emissaries or plenipotentiaries of foreign powers; the present feast was no exception in the house of the friend of the harvest of God. That is, it was outwardly no exception; for its actual significance, its place in the structure and development of a marvellous God-story and recurrent feast; or the reason why the exalted host was so uncommonly and infectiously hilarious — none of the guests knew aught of all this at the time.

None of the guests? Can we bear out that comprehensive statement? Mai-Sachme, standing stockily in the open side of the triangle and pointing the nimble cup-bearers and dapifers hither and thither with a white pointer, he knew; but he was not a guest. Was there any other for whom the disguise had a disturbing, delicious, uncanny, unconfessed semi-transparence? The question must certainly refer to little Turturra-Benoni, sitting at the left of the host; but it must as certainly remain unanswered. Benjamin's feelings were indescribable, they have never been described, and this narrative will not attempt what has never been attempted: will not put into words the faint intuition, with its accompanying mingled sweetness and terror, for a long time not even daring to be a conscious intuition but always stopping short at a sudden brief dreamlike attack of memory, which made the heart beat fast, but was after all only a recognition of this or that point of likeness between two quite different and remote phenomena: one of them from childhood days long gone and one here present in the flesh. Let us try to imagine what it was like.

They sat at ease in comfortable chairs with footstools, each had a table at his side, laden with delights for the eye and the appetite: fruit, cakes, vegetables, pastries, cucumbers and melons, cornucopias with flowers and spun-sugar ornaments. At the other side of each chair was a dainty washing-stand with amphora and copper refuse basin. Each person had the same. Aproned servants supervised by the wine steward kept the beakers full; others received the main dishes, veal, mutton, fish, fowl, and game, from the steward of the buffet and brought them to the guests, who, because of the high rank of the host, did not have precedence over him. For Adon not only was served first but also received the best and in greater quantity than the rest — to the end, indeed, that he could share with others; it is written: "Food was given them from his own dish." In other words, he sent with his compliments to various guests now a roast duck, now a quince jelly or a gilded bone trimmed with delicious ringlets of crust. He sent to the Egyptians, he sent to the stranger guests. But to the youngest of the Asiatics, his neighbour on the left, he gave over and over from his own plate. Such proofs of favour meant a great deal and were watched and counted by the Egyptians. They reckoned it up to each other and related it afterwards, so that it has come down to us, that the young Bedouin actually had five times as much as anyone else at the master's table.

Benjamin was embarrassed; he begged to be excused from all these gifts and looked round apologetically at the Egyptians as well as at his own brothers. He could not have eaten all he got even if he had felt like eating. He was possessed by a dazed and uneasy feeling; it sought, found, lost, and then so suddenly and unmistakably found again that his heart would give a quick, heavy, irregular throb. He looked into the beardless face of his host, framed in the hieratic winged cap, this man who had demanded him in evidence, this great Egyptian, a somewhat heavy figure, in the white garment with glittering jewels on his breast. He looked at the mouth moving after its own fashion as it smiled and spoke. He looked into the black eyes, which met his own sparkling with fun but then grew veiled as though in retreat; they looked most grave and forbidding at just those moments when Benjamin's own had widened with terror and incredulous joy. He looked at the hand as it gave him something or lifted the cup to drink: at its articulation and at the sky-blue stone that adorned it. And he was pervaded by an old, familiar, childhood air: pungent, sun-warmed, spicy, the essential aroma of all the love and trust, security and adoration, all the childlike bewildered sympathy, intuition, and half-knowledge Benoni had ever known. It was the scent of myrtle. The memory-fragrance was identical with what went on inside him as he faithfully, anxiously, trustingly tried to explore this bewitching riddle, this alarming and blissful possibility of a point where two things met: the jolly, friendly present and something far higher, something of the divine — ah, that was why Turturra's blunt little nose sniffed the spicy scent of childhood! For it was now as it had been then, only the other way on — but what did that matter? — and in the high and unknown presence here the familiar tried to make itself known in flashes that brought his heart into his mouth.

The lord of the grain chatted delightfully with him during the meal — five times as much with him as with the Egyptian dignitaries on his right. He asked Benoni about his life at home, his father, wives, and children; the oldest was named Belah, the youngest — youngest for the present — Muppim. "Muppim," said the lord of the grain. "Give him a kiss from me when you get home. I find it exquisite that the youngest son should have a youngest son. But what is the one next youngest? He is called Rosh? Bravo! Has he the same mother as the other — yes? And do they ramble about together through a green and flowery world? I hope the older lad does not frighten the little urchin with all sorts of God-stories and far-flung fancies unsuitable for small ears. You must look out for that, Father Benjamin!" Then he talked about Manasseh and Ephraim, his own sons, borne to him by the daughter of the sun. How did Benjamin like the names? "Very much," said Benjamin and was on the point of asking why he had chosen such significant ones; but hesitated and just sat there, wide-eyed. So the prince in the land of Egypt began to tell anecdotes about Manasseh and Ephraim, the funny things they said and the mischief they did. Benjamin was reminded of some nursery tale of his own; and the two were seen to be rocking with laughter over their stories.

As they talked and laughed Benjamin took heart to say:

"Would Your Excellency perhaps answer a question which puzzles me?"

"To the best of my ability," the other replied.

"It is only," said the little man, "that you should gratify my curiosity about the knowledge of us which you show in your arrangements. You have our names by heart, my brothers' and mine, also our ages in their right order, so you could reel them off — the way our father says all the children in the world will have to know them, because we are a chosen people of God. How do you know and how is it your steward could seat us in order of age from first-born to last?"

"Ah," answered the keeper of the market, "you are surprised at that? It is quite simple. Do you see this cup here? Silver, with a cuneiform inscription. I drink out of it, but I can see things in it too. Of course, I have a good intelligence; it may be above the average, for I am what I am, and Pharaoh himself wished to be higher than I only by the height of the royal throne. But even so I could scarcely get on without my cup. The King of Babylon presented it to Pharaoh's father — I do not mean myself, though you might think so because of my title, Father of Pharaoh (Pharaoh by the bye calls me uncle), I mean his real earthly father — not divine — Pharaoh's predecessor, King Neb-ma-re. The King of Babylon sent the cup to him as a present and so it came to my lord and master, who deigned to pleasure me with it. It is a thing I can really use, its properties are most helpful to me. I can read the past and future in it, penetrate the mysteries of the world, and lay open the relationships between them. Take for instance the order of your birth: I read it out of my cup with no trouble at all. A good part of my cleverness, pretty much all that is above the average, comes from this cup. I don't give this away to all and sundry, of course; but as you are my guest and my neighbour at table I don't mind telling you. You would not believe it; but when I hold the cup in the right way I can see pictures of distant places and things that happened there. Shall I describe your mother's grave to you?"

"You know she is dead?"

"Your brothers told me that she had gone westwards early in life; a lovely one whose cheeks smelled like rose leaves. I do not pretend to have got this knowledge by supernatural means. But now I need only put the magic cup to my forehead, like this, and I see your mother's grave, so clearly that it surprises even me. The clearness of the picture comes from the brightness of the morning sun; there are mountains; there is your own town on a slope, not far away at all, not more than a furlong. There are small ploughed fields in among the shingle, vineyards on the right and a dry masonry wall in the foreground. And there is a mulberry tree growing on the wall, old and partly hollow, the trunk leans over and is propped up with stones. No one has ever seen a tree more clearly than I see that mulberry tree with the morning breeze playing in its leaves. Near the tree is the grave with a stone marker. And lo, someone is kneeling at the spot; he has brought food and water and unleavened bread — he must be the rider of the ass waiting under the tree — what a nice animal, white with sensitive ears and a curly forelock growing down into its friendly eyes. I would never have thought the cup could make me see all that so plainly. Is that your mother's grave?"

"Yes, it is hers," said Benjamin. "But tell me, my lord, can you see the ass so clearly and not the rider?"

"Him I see, if possible, even more clearly. But there is not much to see. He is just a young chap, seventeen at most, kneeling with his offering. He has got some kind of bright-coloured finery draped round him, the silly youth, with figures woven in it. He must be foolish in his head, for he thinks he is just going a ride, but actually he is riding to his destruction. Only a day or so away from this grave his own awaits him."

"That is my brother Joseph," said Benjamin, and his grey eyes brimmed over with tears.

"Oh, forgive me," his neighbour begged in dismay and put down the cup. "I would not have spoken so lightly if I had known it was your lost brother. And what I said about the grave, I mean his grave, you must not take that too seriously. I mean do not exaggerate. Certainly the grave is serious enough, a deep dark pit; but its power to hold fast is not so great after all. Its nature is to be empty, you must know that — empty is the hollow when it awaits the prey, and if you come when it has taken it in, lo, it is empty again — the stone is rolled away. I do not say it is worth no weeping, the grave; one must even wail shrilly in its honour, for it is there, a fact, a profoundly melancholy dispensation throughout the world; and part of the story of the feast in all its hours. I would go so far as to say that out of reverence for the grave one should not betray one's knowledge of its inherent emptiness and impotence. That would be treating a serious matter far too lightly. So shall we weep and wail, aloud and shrilly; but privately we may tell ourselves that there is no descent whatever upon which a rising does not follow. The two belong together, else how fragmentary would everything be: the feast would be only half a feast which got as far as the grave and knew no more to follow. No, the world is not half but whole; the feast too is a whole, and in the whole lies comfort that cannot be taken away. So do not let your heart be troubled by what I said about your brother's grave, but be of good cheer."

And he took Benjamin's hand by the wrist and waved it in the air like a little fan.

Benoni was aghast. His situation had reached a pitch of singularity impossible to describe. His breath left him, his brows were fiercely drawn, tears stood in his eyes, and through them he looked into the face of the master of the corn — the mixture making an impossible conflict of expressions. His mouth stood open as though he would cry out, but he did not; for instead his head drooped somewhat to one side, the mouth closed, and the whole expression of his tearful face became one heartfelt, urgent prayer. Before it the other's eyes went on the defensive, they shrouded themselves once more; it would be a bold man who dared to say there might be something like assent in the drooping lid.

Ah, yes, let anyone try to think or say what was now going on in Benjamin's breast, the breast of a man near to belief.

"Let us get up now," he heard his neighbour say. "I hope you have all eaten well and enjoyed yourselves. Unfortunately I must now go to the office and be there until the evening. Your brothers will probably set out for home early tomorrow morning, after picking up the grain I will assign to you: food for twelve houses this time, yours and your father's. And I will gladly take pay for it for Pharaoh's treasury — what would you have? I am the god's man of business. Farewell, in case I do not see you again. But by the bye and in all friendliness, why do you not take heart and exchange your own country for this one: migrate into Egypt, father, sons, wives, and children, all seventy of you, or however many there are, and graze on Pharaoh's land? That is a proposal from me to you; think it over, it would not be the most foolish thing you could do! They would show you the most suitable grazing-ground, it would take only a word from me, for whatever I say here goes. I know that Canaan means a good deal to you, but after all, Egypt is the great world and Canaan a provincial hole, where they do not know how to live. You are a migrant folk, not a people of walled dwellings. Here there is a good living, you could trade and make profit freely through the country. Well, there is my advice to you, take it or not as you see fit. I must be off to hear the pleas of the improvident."

A servant had poured water on his hands as he talked in this man-of-the-world vein with the brothers. He got up, said good-bye to all the guests, and broke up the table. The tradition suggests that his brothers were drunken with Joseph at this meal. But that is a mistake, they were no more than merry. No one would have dared to get actually drunk, not even the wild twins. Only Benjamin was drunk — but not even he with wine.

THE CRY KEPT BACK

In definitely better spirits, this time, did the brothers take the road from Menfe towards the Bitter Lakes and the fortified frontier. Everything had gone off so well that it could not have gone better. The lord of the land had been unequivocally charming, Benjamin was safe, Simeon freed, and they were honourably acquitted of the charge of espionage; so honourably, indeed, that they had even broken bread with the all-powerful lord and his courtiers. It put them in a jovial frame, made their hearts light and prideful. For so is man: when he has been found innocent and pronounced blameless in some one connection, he straightway thinks he is innocent in all, oblivious of anything else he might have on his conscience. We can easily pardon the brothers. They had been wrongfully accused, and involuntarily they had associated the accusation with their ancient guilt. No wonder, then, that when they were cleared they promptly assumed that their former guilt was of no importance whatever.

They were soon to learn that they would not get off so cheaply or blithely, their sacks full to bursting with food for twelve houses, all duly paid for. Too soon they would learn that they were dragging a chain which would pull them back to fresh disaster. At first their spirits were so high they could have shouted and sung for joy in their new-found innocence. When the grain was given out they had been feasted again; Mai-Sachme had quietly supervised everything, and made them all presents as they took their leave. All that could give them credit in the father's eyes they had as they moved off: Benjamin, Simeon, provisions for twelve houses, even though Joseph was no longer there. They were still only eleven; but thanks to their proven innocence, they were still that.

Such was the colour of the brothers' minds — at least the minds of Leah's sons and the sons of the maids. No trouble to describe. But the mental state of Rachel's second son remains quite indescribable. Enough, the little man had scarcely slept, that night at the inn, or else with wild, confused, anomalous dreams — anomalous yet not nameless, for they did have a name, a dear and precious name, impossible and mad, for they were called Joseph. Benoni had seen a man in whom was Joseph. How could that possibly be described? It has happened that men have encountered gods who have chosen to assume a familiar human form and behaved accordingly though not willing to be so addressed. Here it was the other way round: the humanly familiar was not semi-transparent for the divine, but the high and divine semi-transparent for the long-familiar childhood, the memory being metamorphosed into this unknown, exalted shape. It would not let itself be addressed, it kept withdrawing behind its eyelids. Yet the disguised is not that behind which he disguises himself and from behind which he looks. They remain two. To recognize the one in the other does not mean to make one out of two, to relieve one's breast with the cry: "It is he!" It is impossible to produce the one out of the other, however desperately the mind struggles to do it. The cry was dammed back in Benjamin's breast though his heart nearly burst to contain it. Or rather it is not quite right to say it was dammed back, for it was not yet there, it had no voice or body — and therein precisely lay the indescribable thing. Its only refuge was in mad, dissolving dreams, which in the morning melted into pure distress which was not existence at all and had no other relation to outward circumstances than just this: that Benjamin could not understand how the brothers could now do their business and go, leaving the situation as it was behind them. "By the Eternal!" he swore to himself, "it is impossible for us to go! We must stay here and watch this, this man and vice-god, Pharaoh's great keeper of the market. There is still a cry due that is not yet: with it still in our breasts we cannot just leave and go home to our father and live as though nothing had happened. This cry is just on the point of bursting out and filling the whole world with the sound of it. For indeed it is so great a cry that it will crack my heart!"

In his distress Benjamin turned to big Reuben. Large-eyed he put the question: did Reuben think they should now leave for home, or did it seem to him, perhaps, that they were not quite finished here, or rather not finished at all; that there were good and sound reasons for stopping?

"What do you mean?" Reuben asked in his turn. "What are the good and sound reasons? Everything has been done and accomplished and the man dismissed us graciously when we produced you. Now the thing is to get back with all speed to the father, waiting and fearing there on your account, that we may bring him what we have bought and he can have bread again for the offering. Do you remember how angry the man was when he heard Jacob's complaint that his lamp went out and he had to sleep in the dark?"

"Yes," Benjamin said, "I remember." And he looked up urgently into the big brother's beardless, muscular face. Suddenly he saw — or was it an illusion? — that the red Leah-eyes retreated before his gaze behind the blinking lids. Only yesterday he had had that same defensive, half-assenting motion from other eyes. He said no more. Perhaps he only thought he saw it because he had seen it yesterday, and by night in his dreams. The plans were not changed, they took their leave — there being no words in which to suggest that they should stay. But Benjamin's distress was great. Their gracious dismissal by the keeper of the market was the sorest point of all. They could not go — not at any price — but on the other hand, if he himself sent them, then what else could they do? They set out.

Benjamin rode beside Reuben. In one way they made a pair: not only as the oldest and the youngest of a family, the big boy and the little boy; but also because they had something like the same relation to him that was gone and to the reason why he was gone. We remember Reuben's weakness — rather grumpy, to be sure — for the father's lamb, and his behaviour at the time of the mangling and burial. To all appearance he had shared in the brothers' feelings and their deed; and with them he had taken the frightful oath the ten had bound themselves by, never by word or deed, by sign or sound to betray that it had not been Joseph's blood but the blood of an animal or the remnants of his clothing which they had brought to the father. But Reuben had had no part in the sale, he had not been present, and his ideas about what had become of Joseph were vaguer than the brothers' — and theirs were hazy enough, though even so not hazy enough for their own comfort. They knew they had sold the boy to the Ishmaelites; even that was too much. Reuben had the advantage of not knowing it: while they were selling Joseph he had been at the pit; and the feelings of one standing by an empty grave must be quite different from those the brothers had, who had sold the sacrifice out into the wide, wide world.

In short, big Reuben, whether he knew it or not, had nourished the seed of expectation all these years; and by this measure he was closer than any of the others to Benjamin the blameless, who had shared not at all, and by whom the absence of his adored brother had never been accepted as final. It is long, long ago, but we can still hear his childish words to the broken old man: "He will come back. Or he will send for us to come." A good twenty years ago, that was; but the sound is still in our ears, and the hope still in Benjamin's heart. He had not the brothers' knowledge of the sale, nor yet Reuben's knowledge of the pit. Like the father, he knew only that Joseph had died, a fact which left no ground for either hope or faith. But faith actually seems to find lodgement best where there is no room for it.

Benjamin rode with Reuben; and on the way Reuben asked him what the man had talked about during the meal, he himself as the eldest having sat at the other end of the table.

"All sorts of things," answered the youngest. "We told each other funny stories about our children."

"Yes, and you laughed," said Reuben. "We all saw you rocking with laughter. I think the Egyptians were surprised."

"Of course, you know he is charming," went on the little man. "He knows how to talk with everybody to put them at their ease."

"But he can be otherwise too," replied Reuben. "He can be very awkward, we know that."

"Of course," said Benjamin, "you know all about that. And yet he wishes us well, I am certain of it. The last thing he said to me was that we should come and settle in Egypt, no matter how many of us; he invited us to migrate down here with the father and pasture our flocks."

"Did he say that?" asked Reuben. "Yes, a man like that knows a lot about us and our father, doesn't he! Especially about the father! And he always knows just what to say, does he? First he makes him send you on a journey to clear us and to fetch bread; then he invites Jacob himself to come down into the land of mud! A lot he knows about Jacob!"

"Are you mocking at him," asked Benjamin, "or at the father? I don't care for either, Reuben, for I am very sad. Reuben, listen to me, for my heart is heavy because we are leaving."

"Yes," said Reuben, "one cannot break bread every day with the lord of Egypt and jest with him. That is a treat, of course. But now you must remember that you are no longer a child but the head of a house, and your children are crying for bread."

BENJAMIN HAS IT

Soon they came to the spot where they thought to take their midday rest and wait till it was cooler. On their first return journey they had reached the place at night; but now it was only midday. We recognize the spot by the palm tree, the spring, and the hut; and see it as clearly as the man, thanks to his magic cup, had seen Rachel's grave. They rejoiced to have reached the pleasant spot. It had indeed some unpleasant memories, but that ghost was laid; it had dissolved in harmony and peace; they might enjoy their rest without a care.

They were still standing, looking about them; they had not put hand to their packs. There came a noise from the direction from which they had come, it grew and spread, they heard shouting and hallooing. Was it for them? They stood rooted to the spot to listen, so surprised that they did not even turn round. Only Benjamin did; then he flung up his arms and his stumpy hands and gave a cry, a single cry. After that he was silent — silent for a long time.

It was Mai-Sachme, approaching with chariot and steed, attended by several wagons full of armed men. They jumped out and barred off the opening in the rocky circle. The steward stolidly advanced.

His face was grim. He had drawn his heavy brows together and was biting one corner of his mouth, only one corner, which gave him an unusual, sinister look. He said:

"So I have found you and overtaken you. I rushed after you with all speed at my master's command and caught you where you thought you would camp and hide yourself. How do you feel now that you see me?"

The dazed group answered that they did not know. They saw that everything was beginning all over again. That the hand had once more reached out to drag them to judgment; that all the sweet harmony had turned into discord.

"We do not know how," they said. "We rejoiced to see you again so soon but we had not hoped to see you."

"You may not have hoped, but you must have feared. Why have you repaid good with evil, so that we had to come after you and stop you? Your position is very serious, my man."

"Explain yourself," said they. "What are you talking about?"

"Do you need to ask?" he answered. "I am talking about my master's drinking-cup out of which he divines. It has been missed. The master had it yesterday at table. It has been taken."

"You are speaking of a winecup?"

"I am. Of Pharaoh's silver beaker, my master's own. He drank out of it yesterday noon. It is gone. Clearly it has been filched. Somebody has got away with it. Who? Unfortunately there can be no doubt. Men, you have done very ill."

They were silent.

"You are suggesting," asked Judah, Leah's son, in a slightly unsteady voice, "your words mean that we have taken a dish from your master's table and made off with it like thieves?"

"Unfortunately there is no other name for your behaviour. The thing is gone since yesterday; obviously it has been bagged. Who can have done it? There is only one answer, alas. I can only repeat that you men have done very ill and are in a very serious case."

They were silent again, with their arms akimbo, puffing and blowing.

"Listen, my dear sir," said Judah. "How would it be if you gave heed to your words and considered before you spoke? The thing is unheard of. We ask you in all politeness but in all seriousness as well, what do you take us for? Do we look to you like vagabonds and thieves? Or what sort of impression may you have of us that you try to make it appear that we have taken a valuable piece from your master's table, a cup, apparently, and been light-fingered with it? That is what I mean when I say unheard of, speaking in the name of all eleven of us. For we are all faithfully sons of one man and our whole number was twelve. One is no longer with us, otherwise I would call it unheard of in his name as well. You say we have done ill. Well, I do not claim that we brothers are saints, having never done ill, but come through the rough and tumble of life without ever taking a fall. I do not say we are innocents, that would be sacrilege. But there is guilt and guilt; and maybe guilt is prouder than innocence is; anyhow, to nab silver cups is not in our line. We have cleared ourselves before your master and showed him that we walk in truth, by bringing our eleventh brother to witness. We have cleared ourselves before you, for the purchase money we found in our feedbags we brought back out of the land of Canaan and offered it to you again but you would not take it. After these experiences will you not stop and consider before you accuse us of taking silver or gold from your master's table?"

But Reuben was boiling over; he spirted out:

"Why do you not answer, steward, this convincing speech of my brother Jahudah? And why do you bite deeper in the corner of your mouth in that offensive way? Here we are. Search us! And with whomever it is found, your wretched silver cup, let him die! Search! If you find it, the rest of us, all of us, will be your slaves for life!"

"Reuben," said Judah, "do not burst out like that. Our complete innocence needs not such oaths."

And Mai-Sachme spoke: "You are right, there is no need of hasty words. We too know how to be moderate. He in whose sack we find the cup, he becomes our slave and remains in our hands. The rest of you will go free. Be pleased to open your sacks."

They were already at it. They had run to their sacks, they could not take them down fast enough from their asses and tear them open. "Laban!" they cried with laughter, "Laban, searching on the Mount of Gilead! Ha, ha! Let him sweat and swear! Here, master steward, come and search mine first!"

"Quietly, quietly," said Mai-Sachme. "Everything in order and in turn, the way my master knew your names. We will begin with the big hothead."

As he searched they mocked, their triumph mounting as he went on. They called him Laban and jeered at him for a sweating clod, as he moved from sack to sack, stooped and looked with his hands on his hips, shook his head and shrugged his shoulders, then went on to the next. He searched Asher and Issachar and came to Zebulon. Nothing there. He was almost at the end of his search, only Benjamin was left. They jeered yet more loudly.

"Now he is looking in Benjamin's," they cried. "What luck with the most innocent of all — not only in this but in all other respects, for he has never done ill in his life! Watch how he searches in the last bag, listen to what he will say next to justify — "

All at once they were still. They saw it shining in the steward's hand. Out of Benjamin's feed-bag, from not very far down, he had drawn the silver cup.

"Here it is," he said. "Found in the youngest's sack. I should have begun at the other end and spared myself trouble and abuse. So young and already so thievish! Of course, I am glad to have found the cup; but my pleasure is marred by the knowledge of such early corruption and ingratitude. Young one, you are in a bad fix."

And the others? They held their heads, staring at the cup till their eyes bulged out. They whistled through lips so puffed out that they could not speak but only whistle.

"Benoni!" they cried, their voices shrill to breaking. "Defend yourself! Open your mouth. How did you come by the cup?"

But Benjamin was silent. He dropped his chin on his chest so that no one could see his eyes, and was dumb. They tore their clothing. Some of them actually seized the hem of their smocks and with one pull rent them from bottom to top.

"We are shamed!" they wailed. "Shamed by our youngest! Benjamin, for the last time open your mouth and justify yourself!"

But Benjamin was silent. He did not lift his head, he spoke no word. His silence was quite impossible to describe.

"He did cry out at first," shouted Bilhah's Dan, "now I remember he gave a great cry when this man came up. Terror tore the shriek out of him, he knew why the man came after us!"

Then they fell on Benjamin with loud railing and reviling and called him a thief and the son of a thief, reminding him how his mother had stolen her father's teraphim. "It is inherited, he has it in his blood. Oh, thief's blood, did you have to apply your inheritance just here, to bring us all to shame with you, us and our whole stock, the father and all of us and our children?"

"Now you are exaggerating," said Mai-Sachme. "That is not our way. The rest of you are all cleared and free. We do not assume your guilt, but rather that your youngest stole on his own account. You can freely go home to your honourable father. Only he who took the cup, he falls to us."

But Judah answered him: "There can be no talk of that, steward, for I will speak with your master, he shall hear the words of Judah, I am resolved upon it. We all go back with you before his face and he shall judge us all. For we are all liable in this matter and are as one with respect to what has happened. Lo, our youngest was innocent all his years, for he was at home. But we others were out in the world and became guilty. We are not minded to play the guiltless and leave him in the lurch because he became guilty on his travels while we in this one respect are innocent. Up with us all, lead us together with him before the throne of the keeper of the market!"

"Be it so," said Mai-Sachme. "As you will."

So they went back to the city, surrounded with the troop of lancers, taking the road they had lately covered so free from care. But Benjamin said no word.

I AM HE

IT was already the latter part of the afternoon when they came before Joseph's house, for the steward led them thither and not to the great office where they had first bowed and bent their knees. Joseph was not there, he was in his own house.

"He was yet there," the story says, and it is correct. After the merry meeting of the day before, Pharaoh's friend had gone back to his office, but today he could not have left his house. He knew that his steward was at his task; and he waited with extreme impatience. The feast was nearing its climax and it rested with the ten whether they would be on the scene or only hear what happened at second hand. Would they make the youngest come back alone with Mai-Sachme? Or would they all stick together? Joseph's suspense was great: on this point depended his future relations with the brothers. We, of course, are in no suspense: in the first place we know all the phases of the story by heart; moreover we have just been present at the search for the cup and have seen that the brothers did not forsake Benjamin in his guilt, whereas the fact was still hidden from Joseph. So in our wisdom we may smile at him as he wandered up and down and to and fro, from the book-room to the reception-hall, thence to the banqueting-hall, back through all the rooms into his sleeping-chamber, where he feverishly gave this or that last touch to his toilette, like an actor nervously adjusting his make-up before the curtain goes up.

He went to see his wife Asenath, in the women's quarters; they sat together watching Manasseh and Ephraim at their play, and he could not disguise his stage fright.

"My husband and dear lord," said she, "what is the matter? You are nervous, you keep shuffling your feet and listening for something. What have you on your mind? Shall we have a game to divert you, or shall some of my women dance before you?"

"No, my girl," he replied. "Thank you, not now. I have other moves in my head from those in the game, and I cannot watch the dancing, I have too much jigging and juggling to do myself, while God and the world look on. I must get back nearer to the hall, that is the theatre. But for your maids I know a better task than dancing; for I came to tell them to make you beautiful even beyond your beauty, and dress and adorn you; and the nurses must wash Manasseh's and Ephraim's hands and put on their embroidered smocks, for I am expecting very special guests and will present you all as my family so soon as the word has been spoken and they know who I am and whose you are. Yes, you are making big eyes, my shield-maid with the tiny waist! But just do as I say and make yourselves fine, and you shall hear from me!"

With that he was off again into the other part of the house. He would gladly have luxuriated in pure waiting and the pleasure of suspense; but as always there was business to transact: officials to see, accounts and papers to examine and sign, brought to him in his bookroom by his reader and his acting scribe. He cursed them mentally, yet welcomed them for their company too.

The sun declined as he sat over his papers, with one ear cocked. At last he heard a confusion of sounds in front of the house: the hour had come, the brothers were here. Mai-Sachme entered, the corner of his mouth drawn tighter than ever, the cup in his hand. He handed it to his master. "The youngest had it," said he. "After a long search. They are in the hall, awaiting your sentence."

"All of them?" Joseph asked.

"All of them," Mai-Sachme replied.

"You see that I am busy," said Joseph. "These gentlemen here are not here for fun, we are occupied with the business of the crown. You have been my steward long enough to know whether I can take time from pressing official business for such petty matters. You and your men can wait."

And he bent again over the roll held open for him by an official. But as he could see nothing that was written there, he said after a pause:

"We might as well get that little matter over with first. It is a case of criminal ingratitude, and I must pass judgment. Gentlemen, follow me to the hall, where the evil-doers are awaiting sentence."

They attended him as he went up three steps and through a hanging out on to the raised dais of the hall, where stood his chair. With the cup in his hand he sat down. Servants straightway held fans over his head, for he was always thus protected the moment he sat down.

A slanting ray full of dancing motes shone from one of the left-hand upper openings between the columns and the sphinxes and the red sandstone crouching lions with Pharaoh-heads. It fell upon the group of sinners who had flung themselves down a few paces from Joseph's chair with their foreheads to the ground. Spears guarded them on either side. A host of the curious, cooks and waiting-boys, sprinklers and flower-table stewards, crowded round the doors.

"Brothers, stand up," said Joseph. "I should not have thought to see you again, and on such an occasion. But there are many things I should not have thought. I should not have thought you could do as you have done, when I had treated you like gentlemen. I am glad, of course, to have my cup back again, out of which I drink and from which I divine. But I am greatly cast down by your gross behaviour. It is incomprehensible to me. How could you bring yourselves so crudely to repay good with evil, to offend a man like me by taking away something he is fond of and which is useful to him? The deed was as stupid as it was hateful, for you might have guessed that a man like me would miss so valuable a piece at once and know everything. Did you imagine that when I saw I had been robbed I could not divine where it had gone? And now I assume that you have admitted your guilt?"

It was Judah who answered. He became the spokesman for them all this day, for he had passed through trials in life which they had been spared; he had familiar knowledge of sin and guilt, and therefore he could fitly represent the brothers. On their way back to Menfe this had been settled among them and he had considered what to say. Now, with his garments rent, he stood among his brothers and spoke:

"What shall we say unto my lord, and what sense would there be in trying to clear ourselves before him? We are guilty before you, O lord, guilty in the sense that your cup was found among us, with one of us and that means with all. How the cup came into the sack of the youngest and most innocent of us all, who was always safe at home, I do not know. We do not know. We are powerless to speculate about it before your seat. You are a mighty one of earth, you are good and evil, you raise up and cast down. We are your servants. No defence of ours has any worth before you, and foolish is the sinner who presumes upon present innocence when the avenger demands pay for all misdeeds. Not for nothing did our old father lament that we would make him childless in his old age. Lo, he was right. We and he with whom the cup was found are fallen to my lord as slaves."

In this opening speech of Judah's, which was not yet the one for

which he is famous, there were points which Joseph preferred to ignore. He therefore answered only the one touching on their slavery,
to reject it.

"No, not so," he said. "Far from it. There is no behaviour so bad
that it can make a man like me behave inhumanly. You have bought
food for the old man your father in the land of Egypt and he is waiting for it. I am Pharaoh's great man of business: no one shall say I
took advantage of your crime to keep the money, the goods, and the
buyers too. Whether only one of you sinned or all of you together
I will not inquire. To your youngest I talked familiarly at table, we
were merry together and I told him the virtues of my beloved cup and
by its means showed him his mother's grave. It may be he prattled to
you about it and all of you concerted the ungrateful plot of stealing
the treasure. I assume it was not for the sake of the silver you took it.
You wanted to use its magic for yourselves, perhaps to find out what
became of your missing brother, the one who left home — how can
I tell? But again, maybe your youngest committed the crime on his
own, told you nothing and took the cup. I do not wish to hear. The
booty was found with the thief. He shall be my servant. But the rest
of you may go home in peace to your father, the old man, that he
may not be childless and may have food to eat."

Thus the exalted; and for a while there was silence. Then Judah,
the man of afflictions, to whom they had given the word, strode out
of the group. He trod before the throne, close up to Joseph, took a
long breath, and spoke:

"Hear me now, my lord, for I will hold speech before your ears and
relate how it all came about and what you did and how it stands with
these and with me, with us brothers all. My words will make clear
beyond peradventure that you cannot and may not separate our
youngest from us and you may not keep him to belong to you. And
further, that we others, and in particular I, Judah, fourth among
us, cannot possibly ever return home to our father without our
youngest. And thirdly I will make my lord an offer and propose to
you how you will receive your due in a possible and not in an impossible way. This will be the order of my speech. Therefore let not your
anger burn against your servant and stop him not, I beg you, in the
speech which I shall make as the spirit gives it to me, and my own
guilt. You are as Pharaoh. Now I begin at the beginning and as you
began it, for it was thus:

"When we came down hither, sent by our father that we might
get us bread from this granary like thousands of others, we did not
fare like the other thousands, but were segregated and specially dealt
with and led down to your city and before my lord's face. And even
there we were unusually treated, for my lord too was strange, I mean
he was rough and smooth, soft and hard, in other words he showed

two faces. He questioned us particularly about our family. Have you,
asked my lord, a father at home or a brother? We have, we replied, a
father, he is old, and we have certainly a young brother too, the
youngest, late born to him and whom he cherishes as the apple of his
eye and keeps him by the hand because his brother fell away untimely and is gone. Only this one son of his mother remains to our
father, so that he clings to him beyond measure. Answered my lord:
bring him down here to me. Not a hair of his head shall be harmed.
It cannot be, we said, for the reason we have given. To snatch away
his youngest from the father will be his death. But you replied harshly
to your servants: By the life of Pharaoh! if ye come not with your
youngest brother, surviving from the lovely mother, so shall you not
see my face again."

And Judah continued and said:

"I ask my lord whether it was so and so begun or whether it was
not so but began otherwise than that my lord asked after the boy and
insisted on his coming, despite our warning. For it pleased my lord
to put it that we should clear ourselves from the accusation of spying
by bringing him down and thereby showing evidence that we deal
in truth. But what sort of clearing is that and what sort of accusation?
No man can take us for spies, we brothers in Jacob do not look like
spies and it does not clear us to produce our youngest, it is only an
arbitrary decision and only because my lord happens to be bent on
seeing our brother with his own eyes — why? On that point I may
not speak, it rests with God." And Jehudah went on in his speech,
flung up his leonine head, put out his hand and spoke:

"Lo, this your servant believes in the God of his fathers and that
all knowledge is with Him. But what he does not believe is that our
God smuggles valuables into the packs of his servants, so that they
have their purchase money back as well as the goods — that has never
been, and we have no tradition whatever of this kind. Not Abram nor
Isaac nor Jacob, our father, has ever found God-silver in his pack that
the Lord slipped him. What is not is not; all that happened was from
arbitrary choice and has its source in one single mystery.

"But can you now, my lord — can you, after we worked on our
father with the famine to our aid and got him to lend us his little one
for this journey — can you, who relentlessly forced his coming, for
without that extraordinary demand he would never have set foot
in the land, can you, who said: No harm shall come to him here below — can you hold him as a bondsman because they found your
cup in his bag?

"That you cannot!

"But we on our side and especially your servant Judah who here
holds speech, we cannot come before our father's face without his
youngest — nevermore. We can do it as little as without him we could

have come before yours — and not on grounds of personal whim but
on grounds most potent and compelling. Your servant, our father,
had spoken to us again and said: Go yet once more and buy us a little
food; and we answered him: We cannot go down unless you give us
our youngest brother, for the man down there who is lord in the
land said we must bring him or we shall not see his face. Then the
grey-haired one set up his lament, a song well known and which cut
us to the heart, like the flute that sobs in the gorges, for he launched
into song and said:

"'Rachel, the lovely and willing, for whom my young years
served Laban, the black moon, seven years; heart of my heart, who
died on the way and left me, only a furlong from the inn; she was my
wife and she gave me to my loving desire two sons, one in life and
one in death, Dumuzi-Absu, the lamb, Joseph, the brilliant one, who
knew how to get round me so that I gave him all that I had; and
Benoni, the little son of death, whom I still have at hand. For the
other went out from me, as I willed him to, and all the universe was
filled with the cry: Mangled is he, the lovely one mangled! Then fell
I on my back, and ever since I have been stiff. But with my stiffened
hand I hold this little one who is all I have left, for mangled, mangled
and torn in pieces, was the true son. If now you take from me my
only one, that the boar mayhap may tread him down, then you will
bring down my grey hairs to the grave in such sorrow that it would
be too much for the world and it could not bear it. Full to the outermost rim is the world with the cry: Mangled, mangled is the beloved;
and were this one given too, the world must be rent asunder and be
naught.'

"Has my lord heard this cry of the flutes, this father-lament? Then
let him judge after his own understanding if we brothers can come
before the old man without our youngest, the little man, and confess:
We have lost him, he is missing; whether we could hold out before
the soul that hangs on Benjamin's soul, and before the world which
is full of affliction and cannot bear more, for it would receive its
death-blow in this blow. And above all whether I, Judah, his fourth
son who speak, can so come before my father, that you shall judge.
For not yet all does my lord know, but far from all; the heart of your
servant feels that his word must mount to quite another theme at this
hour of our need: it must deal with this mystery here, and can only
do so through the revelation of another mystery."

A murmuring rose from among the troop of brothers. They stirred
uneasily. But Judah the lion raised his voice against it, spoke on and
said:

"I took the responsibility before my father and made myself surety
for the little one. Just as now I came close up to your seat to hold
this speech, so then I went close up to the father and took my oath

before him in these words: Give him into my hand, I vouch for him; if I bring him not again I will bear the blame before you for ever. Such my vow; now judge, O strange man, whether I can go back to my father without the little one, lest peradventure I see an evil too great for me and for the world to bear. Accept my offer! Me shall you keep for your bondman instead of the lad, that you may receive your due in a possible and not an impossible way. I myself will expiate for us all. Here before you, strange man, I take the frightful oath we brothers swore — with both hands I take that oath and I break it in two across my knee. Our eleventh brother, the father's ewe lamb, first son of the true wife, him the beast did not rend; but we his brothers sold him into the world."

Thus did Judah end his famous speech, thus and not otherwise. He stood there weaving to and fro. The brothers had gone pale; yet they were deeply relieved that the secret was out at last. For it is not impossible to go pale and yet feel relieved at the same time. But two of them cried out, and they were the oldest and the youngest. Reuben shouted: "What do I hear?" And Benjamin did just as he had done before when the steward overtook them: he flung up his arms and gave an indescribable cry. And Joseph? He had got up from his seat and glittering tears ran down his cheeks. For it happened that the shaft of light which had been falling aslant upon the group of brothers had now moved round and was coming through an opening at the end of the hall. It fell directly on Joseph's face and in it his tears glittered like jewels.

"All that is Egyptian go out from me!" said he. "Out with you, go! For I invited God and the world to this play, but now shall God alone be witness."

Reluctantly they obeyed. Mai-Sachme put his hands on the backs of the scribes on the platform, urged them towards the door with nods and gestures, and helped them out. The crowds vanished from the entrance — though it is not likely they moved very far; they all stood in and out of the book-room with their heads cocked in the direction of the hall. Some even held their hands to their ears.

And Joseph, heedless of the tears on his face, stretched out his arms and made himself known. Often before now he had done the same and made people stare, giving them to think that some higher power moved in him other than what he was himself and mingled in his single person with a dreamy and seductive charm. But now quite simply — and despite the outstretched arms with a deprecating little laugh — he said:

"Children, here I am, I am your brother Joseph!"

"Of course he is, of course he is!" shouted Benjamin, almost choking with joy. He stumbled forwards and up the steps, fell on his knees, and stormily embraced the new-found brother's knees.

"Jashup, Joseph-el, Jehosiph!" he sobbed, with his head tipped
back to look up in his brother's face. "You are, you are, of course
you are! You are not dead, you have overturned the great abode of the
shadow of death, you have risen up to the seventh threshold, you are
set as metatron and inner prince — I knew it, I knew it, you are lifted
up on high, the Lord has made you a seat like to his own! But me you
know still, your mother's son, and you fanned the air with my hand!"

"Little one!" said Joseph. "Little one!" He raised Benjamin up
and put their heads together. "Do not talk, it is none of it so great
nor so remote and I have no such glory and the great thing of all is
that we are twelve once more."

WRANGLE NOT

HE put his arm around Benoni's shoulders and went down with him
to the brothers — ah yes, the brothers: how was it with them as they
stood there? Some stood with legs apart and arms dangling awkwardly down almost to their knees. They stared open-mouthed into
space. Some held their clenched fists upon breasts that heaved up and
down with the fury of their panting. All of them had gone pale at
Judah's confession; now they were crimson, a deep dark red like the
colour of pine-trunks, red as that time when squatting on their hands
they had seen Joseph coming towards them in the coat of many
colours. Without Benoni's rapturous cry they would not have believed or even grasped what the man said. But now the sons of Rachel
came with their arms about each other to stand among them; and a
mere association — for all of them had long since felt that this man
had something or other to do with Joseph — swelled and changed
into an identification, and what wonder that their brains felt as though
they would burst? At one moment they would succeed in putting
together the sacrificed lamb yonder and the lord here in his glory; the
next moment the two ideas fell apart again. They had work to hold
them together, and that was because their chagrin and horror were
so great.

"Come here to me," said Joseph as he approached. "Yes, yes, I am
your brother Joseph whom you sold down into Egypt; but never
mind about that, for you did me no harm. Tell me, my father is truly
alive? — Speak to me, don't be afraid. Judah, that was a great speech
you made. You made it for ever and ever. I dearly embrace and congratulate you, I greet you and kiss your lion's head. See, it is the kiss
you gave me in front of the Minæans; today I give it back, my brother,
and it is all blotted out. I kiss you all in one, never think I am angry
that you sold me down here. That all had to be, God did it, not you.
El Shaddei estranged me early from my father's house, He separated me according to His plan. He sent me on ahead of you to be

your provider — and in His beautiful providence He brought it about
that I should feed Israel together with all strangers in time of dearth.
That was a perfectly simple, practical matter — though physically
important, of course; but nothing to make a shout about. For your
brother is no god-hero, no harbinger of spiritual salvation. He is just
a farmer and manager. Remember how your sheaves bowed down
to mine in the dream I prattled about when I was a young brat, and
the stars that made curtsies? Well, that has turned out to mean nothing so very extraordinary: just that my fathers and brothers would
thank me for what I could give them. When a man receives bread, he
says, not 'Hosannah in the highest,' but just 'Thank you very much.'
However, bread there has to be. Bread comes first, before all the
hosannahs. Now do you understand how simple the thing was that
the Lord meant, and will you not believe that I am alive? You know
yourselves that I did not stay in the pit, because the children of Ishmael drew me up out of it and you sold me to them. Put your hands
on me, take hold of me, feel and see that I am your brother Joseph and
I am alive!"

Two or three of them actually did touch him. They cautiously ran
their hands down his garment and timidly grinned.

"Then it was only a joke and you just behaved like a prince?" asked
Issachar. "And you are really only our brother Joseph?"

"Only?" he answered. "That is the best that I am. But you must
try to understand that I am both. I am Joseph, whom the Lord
Pharaoh has set as father and prince in all Egypt. Joseph I am, arrayed
in the splendour of this world."

"Then," said Zebulon, "we must not say you are only the one and
not the other, for actually you are both in one. We had a glimmering of it all along. And it is good that you are not the lord of the
market all the way through, else it would go hard with us. But under
your fine raiment you are our brother Joseph, who will protect us
from the wrath of the keeper of the market. But you must understand,
my lord —"

"Will you drop it, stupid, just leave off this lord business, once
and for all —"

"You must see that we have to seek the protection of the keeper
of the market against our brother, for in time past we did him ill."

"That you did," said Reuben, with the muscles of his jaw standing
out. "It is unheard of, Jehosiph, what I have been ignorant of up till
now! They sold you behind my back and never gave me a hint and
all these years I did not know that they got rid of you and took money
for you —"

"That will do, Reuben," said Bilhah's Dan. "You did this and that
behind our backs too and went secretly to the pit meaning to steal the
boy. As for the purchase price, it was no great sum, as Joseph's grace

well knows. Twenty shekels Phœnician, that was all, thanks to the old man's bargaining powers, and we can settle it any time and you can get your due."

"Wrangle not, men," said Joseph, "don't dispute about what one of you did without the other knowing. For God has put all right. I thank you, Reuben, my big brother, that you came to the pit with your rope to pull me out and give me back to the father. But I was not there. And that was good, for it was not to be so and would not have been right. But now it is right. Now we must all of us think of nothing but the father — "

"Yes, yes," nodded Naphtali, and his tongue went like a clapper and his legs twitched. "What our exalted brother said is quite right, for it must not be that Jacob sits far away in his house of hair or outside it without the dimmest idea of what has happened here: that Joseph is alive and has got high up in the world and has a glittering post among the heathen. Only think, there he sits, Jacob, wrapped in ignorance that we stand here talking face to face with the lost one and touch his garment to convince ourselves. Everything was misunderstanding and wrong information and the father's high-flown lament is as naught and as naught the worm that has gnawn us all our lives. All that is so thrilling it is enough to make a man jump out of his skin — everything in the world is so unbearably awry that we are here and know and he does not know only because he is there and great and foolish distances divide his knowledge from ours; so that the truth can only get a few paces ahead and then lies still and can no more. Oh, if I could just put my hands to my mouth and shout across seventeen days' distance and say: 'Father, halloo! Joseph is alive and he is as Pharaoh in the land of Egypt, that is the latest news.' But however loud one might shout, there he sits unhearing and unmoved. Or if one could loose a dove whose wings had the speed of lightning, with a screed under its wing: 'Know all men by these presents!' — that the awryness might be gone out of the world and everybody here and there know the same thing! No, I can stay here no longer, I cannot stand it. Send me, send me! I will do it; I will run, defying the fleet stag, to give him good account. For could any account be better than that which tells the latest news?"

Joseph applauded his zeal, but he said: "Let well alone, Naphtali, do not be precipitate, for you may not run off alone and no one has a right to say to our father what I will have said to him and what I planned to say long ago when I lay at night and mused on this story. You shall all stay with me seven days and share all my honours and I will set you before my wife the sun-maid and my sons shall bow before you. After that you shall load your animals and go up together with Benjamin and tell him: Joseph your son is not dead but lives, and speaks to you with his living voice and says: 'God gave me rank

among strangers, and folk I know not are subject to me. Come down
here to me, delay not nor fear, dear Father, fear not the land of tombs
whither Abram too came in time of famine. As for the scarcity, and
that for two years now there is no ploughing nor harvest in the
world, that will certainly go on either three or five years more. But I
will look out for you, and you shall settle here in rich pasture. If you
ask me whether Pharaoh permits it, I answer you: him your son
twists round his finger. And if His Majesty desire that you should
settle in the land of Goshen and on the plains of Zoan, towards
Arabia, I will see to it, you and your children and your children's
children, your flocks and herds and fowl and all that is yours. For the
land of Goshen, also called Gosem, or Gosen, is the place I had long
since chosen for you when you should be sent for, because it is not
yet quite Egypt, not quite so Egyptian, and you could live there on
the fish of the delta and the fat of the land and you need not have
much to do with the children of Egypt, and their old-man cleverness
and your own native ways need not clash. And you would be near
to me.' You must speak so to my father in my name and do it cleverly
and skilfully to bring it home to him in his rigid old age, first that I
am alive and then that you are all to come down here. Oh, if I could
only go up with you all and coax him into it, I certainly would. But
I cannot, I cannot get away for a day. So you must do it for me: very
lovingly and with great guile, and break these things to him about my
being alive and his coming down. Don't say to him all at once: 'Joseph
is alive'; begin by asking: 'Suppose it were true that Joseph had not
died, how would our lord and father feel?' So he could come on to
it gradually. And then do not blurt out that you are all to come down
and settle down below in the land of the corpse gods; say in the neighbourhood of Goshen. Can you do it like that without me, sly and
loving at once? In these next days we can talk about how it should
be done. Now I will show you my wife, the sun-maid, and my boys,
Manasseh and Ephraim. And we shall eat and drink all twelve of us
together and be merry. And recall old times, yet forgetting much. But
while I think of it: when you get home to our father, tell him all
that you have seen and stint not your description of my glory here
below. For his heart has been sorely bruised, and it must be healed
by the sweet music of his son's magnificence."

PHARAOH WRITES TO JOSEPH

It would be a pity if now, having heard all these things, our audience
were to disperse, or to turn away its ears, thinking: Well, that was
that; the great revelation has been made, the climax reached, nothing
better can be coming, there is only the end of the tale, and we know
how it turned out already, we cannot get excited. Take my word for

it, you are wrong. The author of this tale, by whom I mean Him who has made all tales, has given it many climaxes, and He knows how to get its effects one through the other. With Him it is always: "The best is still to come"; He always gives us something to look forward to. That was a lovely place where Joseph heard that his father was alive. But where Jacob, the old man, rigid with suffering in body and brain, slowly opens his senses to the song of spring and resurrection and girds himself to go down and embrace his living son — there is nothing thrilling in that? Some who still stay to listen might tell the others how thrilling it was; then they will be sorry all their lives for not having been there when Jacob blessed his Egyptian grandchildren with his hands crossed, and when the venerable man encountered his last hour. We know already! But that is a foolish thought. Anybody can know the story. To have been there is the thing. But it seems the injunction was needless: nobody has stirred.

So, then, when Joseph had thus spoken with the eleven, they went out thence together from where he had revealed himself, to Asenath the maiden, his wife, to bow before her. And they saw their nephews Manasseh and Ephraim with the Egyptian youth-lock on their heads. Through the whole great house there was a bustling and much joyous laughter, for all the household staff had listened at the doors and Joseph needed to make no announcement, no, for everybody knew and one shouted to another that the provider's brothers were come and the sons of his father had found their way hither from Zahi-land. It was the greatest fun for them all, especially because they could count on cakes and ale being given out to celebrate the event. But the scribes from the office had also listened and spread the news throughout the city, and it would have rejoiced the nimble Naphtali's heart to see it run like a forest fire throughout all Menfe so that everybody was quickly on an equal footing of knowledge; they all knew something at the same time: that the troop of brothers of Pharaoh's universal friend had arrived at his house. There was much jumping for joy in the streets and a crowd in front of Joseph's house in the best suburb of Menfe shouting hurrahs and demanding the sight of him surrounded by his Asiatic kin. They were finally gratified: the twelve showed themselves on the terrace. What a pity Menfe's folk knew not how to manipulate light-rays as we do, so that the group could be perpetuated in a photograph! They were satisfied with their own natural lenses and did not miss anything, because they could not even conceive of such an idea.

The titillating news did not long stop within the walls of the metropolis of tombs. It flew like a dove out into the land, and first to get wind of it was Pharaoh, who, and his whole court with him, was, of course, greatly delighted. Pharaoh was now called Ikhnaton, having laid aside the harsh Amun name and assumed one which contained

that of his Father in heaven. Some years before, he had moved nearer
to the city of his minister and favourite. He had ceased to reside in
Thebes, the house of Amun-Re and gone down further north into
the Upper Egyptian hare district. There after long search he had
found a spot suitable for the erection of a new city entirely dedicated
to his beloved deity. The site was a little south of Khnunu, the house
of Thoth, at a place where a little island rose from the stream that
simply cried out for the erection of elegant little pleasure-pavilions.
The rocks on the left bank retreated in a curve affording space for
laying out temples, palaces, and terraces, adequate to a thinker on
God who had a hard time in life and ought also to have an easy one.
The lord of the sweet breath had found a place after his own heart,
needing no counsel save his own thoughts and him who dwelt
therein, to whom alone in this sweet spot the songs of praise should
swell. The gracious command of His Majesty went forth to his artists and stone-masons to build here with the greatest speed a city, the
city of his father, the city of the horizon Akhetaton. It was a severe
blow for Nowet-Amun, hundred-gated Thebes, for with the departure of the court it ran the risk of sinking to the level of a provincial
city; moreover the move boldly served notice on the God of the
empire at Karnak, with whose domineering priesthood Pharaoh's
tender enthusiasm for the beloved all-in-one had during the fat years
come into ever increasing conflict.

Pharaoh's delicate constitution could not stand these recurrent
bouts with the might of the warlike national god, armed in the full
panoply of tradition. He suffered more and more from the contradiction between the placability of his own soul and the necessity of
doing offensive battle for his own higher God-concept. To flee from
this necessity was fortunately also the means of doing the enemy the
most harm. Thus he resolved for his own consecrated person to shake
Wese's dust from off his sandals, even though his little Mama, partly
for the sake of keeping watch of Amun, partly out of loyalty towards
the residence of King Neb-ma-re, her deceased husband, might stop
behind in her old palace. For two years Ikhnaton had had to control
his impatience to escape from Amun's jurisdiction, for it took that
long to build the city despite ruthless drafting of flogged slave labour.
And even when the King shifted thither with great pomp and ceremony and offerings of bread and beer, of horned and hornless cattle,
fowl, birds, wine, incense, and all fine herbs, it was as yet no city,
only an improvised residence of half-finished luxury, consisting of
a palace for him and the great consort Nefernefruaton-Nefertiti and
the royal princesses, wherein they might sleep but not properly live,
because painters and decorators were still everywhere at work. There
was further a temple for God the Lord, very bright and gay and
flower-scented, with floating and flapping red streamers, with seven

courts, splendid pylons, and magnificent pillared halls; and simply marvellous parks and ingenious sheltered nooks, artificial ponds, trees and shrubbery transplanted into the desert in clumps of earth from their habitat in the fertile region of the Nile. White quays shimmered along the shore and there were a dozen brand-new dwelling-houses for the Aton-worshipping royal retinue; as well as a whole row of conveniently placed rock tombs in the surrounding hills. Of the whole, these were the most nearly ready for occupation.

This, for the moment, was all there was of Akhetaton, but it was expected that the court would quickly draw hither in its train a growing population and the embellishment of the city would go zealously on, since Pharaoh was already there on his throne, serving his Father in heaven, holding feasts of tribute, and getting daughters to enlarge the state of his women's quarters; the third, Ankhsenpaaton, had already arrived.

Joseph had sent a special messenger to make formal announcement to the god of the arrival of his brothers, from whom he had been separated since early youth. But even before the messenger reached the new-smelling palace, the news had spread thither by word of mouth and been much and excitedly discussed by Pharaoh, his queen Nefertiti, her sister Nezemmut, his own sister Baketaton, and his courtiers and staff of artists. He answered the letter straightway. It was superscribed:

> *Command to the administrator of that which the heavens give, actual overseer of operations, vice-spender of the King and his universal friend; my Uncle:*
> Know that My Majesty regards your letter as one which he reads with sincere joy. Lo, Pharaoh has shed many joyful tears over the news which he has received from you; the great consort Nefernefruaton, also the sweet princesses Baketaton and Nezemut, have mingled their tears with those of the beloved son of my Father in heaven. All that you tell me is extraordinarily splendid and what you announce makes my heart to leap up. As for what you write, that your brothers have come to you, and your father is still alive, at this news the heavens are joyful, the earth exults, and the hearts of good men frolic, while even those of evil folk are doubtless softened thereby. Know herewith that the lovely child of Aton, Nefer-Kheperu-Re, lord of the two lands, in consequence of your letter finds himself in extraordinarily gracious mood. The wishes which you link with your enclosures were granted beforehand, even before you set them down. It is my beautiful will, and I give my gracious consent, that all of yours, however many, should come to Egypt where you are as myself, and you may allot them room wherein to settle according

to your best opinion, whose richness shall nourish them. Say to
your brothers: Thus shall you do and thus Pharaoh commands,
in whose heart is the love of his father Aton. Lade your beasts
and take wagons with you out of the stores of the king for your
little ones and your wives and your father and come. Look not
to your household goods, for you shall be provided in the land
with all that you need. Pharaoh knows indeed that your culture
does not stand very high and your wants are easy to satisfy. And
when you come into your land, take your father and his people
and his whole house and bring them down to me that you graze
near your brother, the steward of the whole land, for the land
shall lie open to you. Thus far the direction of Pharaoh to your
brothers, given amid tears. Did not many and important affairs
keep me at Akhetaton, the only capital of the lands, my residential city, I would mount my great car, made of electrum, and
hasten to Men-nefru-Mire that I might see you among your
brothers and you would set your brothers before me. But when
they are returned you must bring some of them before me. Not
all of them, for that would be too fatiguing for Pharaoh; but a
chosen group, that I may question them; and also the old man
your father shall you bring before me that I may show him favour by my words and he shall live in honour for that Pharaoh
has spoken with him. Farewell!

This letter Joseph received by running messenger in his house at
Menfe and showed it to the eleven, who kissed their fingertips. One
quarter of the moon they stayed in his house. It was twenty years
that the father had believed him mangled; a day or so more did not
matter, nor the exact moment when he should learn that Joseph was
alive. And Joseph's servants served them, and his wife the daughter
of the sun spoke them friendly words and they talked with their
aristocratic little nephews in the youth-lock, Manasseh and Ephraim,
who could speak to them in their tongue. The younger, Ephraim,
looked more like Joseph and Rachel than did Manasseh, who took
after the mother's, the Egyptian side, so that Judah said: "You will
see, Jacob will favour Ephraim and in his mouth it will be not Manasseh and Ephraim but Ephraim and Manasseh." And he advised his
brother to cut off the Egyptian youth-lock above the boys' ears before
Jacob came, as it would be an offence to him.
    Then, at the end of the week, they packed up and girded themselves
for the journey. For there was to be a trade caravan from the kingdom, from Menfe, balance of the lands, up through the land of
Canaan to Mitanniland, and the brothers were to join it, with wagons
from the royal stores, two- and four-wheeled carts, given them with
mules and drivers. Considering the ten asses, laden with all sorts of

luxurious specialties of Egypt, exclusive and costly specimens of a lofty culture and fastidious taste, presented by Joseph to Jacob; and the ten she-asses, likewise for Jacob, whose loads consisted of grain, wine, preserves, smoked meats, and unguents — considering all this, it is clear that the brothers' own train was a stately one even by itself, swollen as their possessions were in addition by presents from their brother. It is well known that he gave to each man a change of raiment; but to Benjamin he gave three hundred silver deben and no less than five feast-day garments, one for each of the five extra days in the year. That might have been the reason why he said to them as they took their leave: "Do not fall out on the way!" but he really meant that they should not dwell on old times and reproach each other for what one had done behind each other's back. For it never entered his head or theirs that they could be jealous of Benjamin because he had given so much more lavishly to his own little brother. They were like lambs, they found everything in the best of order. When they were young and unruly they had rebelled against injustice; now it had turned out that they had come to terms with injustice and nevermore had aught to object to in the great "I favour whom I favour and show mercy to whom I show mercy."

HOW SHALL WE TELL HIM?

THE MIND dwells pleasantly upon the marvellous correspondencies which history shows: it loves to contemplate the way in which one part is balanced by another part and one scene has its pendant in the next. As once the brothers, seven days after Jacob had received the sign of Joseph's death, had returned from Dothan to mourn with their father and they had been sick with dread, how they should find him and how dwell with him under the half false yet partly true suspicion that they were the lad's slayers: so now, with white hairs among their dark, they were returning again to Hebron, with the news that Joseph had not died at all, was not dead now, but living in great glory; and they were almost as weighed down with the task of telling the old man. For uncanny is uncanny and overwhelming overwhelming — whether the content be life or death. They were sore afraid that Jacob would fall on his back as before; and this time, since he had got twenty years older in the meantime, he might quite simply "die of joy," in other words of shock, so that Joseph's life would be the cause of his death and he would no longer see the living with his eyes nor the living him with his. Besides, the truth must now almost inevitably come out that they had not indeed slain the lad as Jacob all the time had half believed, but yet that they had half slain him and only by chance not quite, thanks to the enterprise of the Ishmaelites who had taken him down to Egypt. The thought added to their pangs of conflicting joy and dread. But they drew some comfort from the thought that Jacob would be impressed, seeing they had been saved from murder by His messengers, the Midianites; this favour which God had shown the brothers would prevent Jacob from quarreling with or cursing them.

They discussed all this during the whole seventeen-day journey; with all their impatience to bring it to an end they even found it too short a time in which to decide how to tell Jacob in the least dangerous way and how they would stand in his eyes once they had done so.

"Children," they said to each other — for since Joseph had said "Children, I am your brother," they often used the word to each other, though it could never have been their habit before — "children, you will see, we shall have him falling on his back when we tell him, unless we go about it very tactfully and cautiously. But whether well or ill told, do you think he will believe what we say? The chances are he will not. For in so many years the idea of death fixes itself firmly in head and heart and is not easily dislodged or exchanged for the thought of life — it is not welcome to the mind, for the mind clings to habit. Brother Joseph thinks it will be a great joy to the old man and so, of course, it will be, a tremendous joy, but let us hope not too tremendous for his strength. But does a man know how to take hold of a joy straight off, when sorrow was his portion for years on end, and does he want to be told that he spent his life in a delusion and his days in error? For his affliction was all his life and now it is all bitterness. It is passing strange that we shall have to talk him out of something we once talked him into by means of the bloodstained garment, so that he clings to it now. And in the end we shall suffer more because we take it away than because we did it to him in the first place. Certainly he will close his mind and not believe us, and that is all for the best. For some time he must and may not believe us, for if he grasped it all at once it would lay him out. The question is, how to tell him so that the joy shall not be too abrupt and we do not suddenly thwart his settled sorrow. The best thing would be if we did not need to say anything, but could just take him down to Egypt and set him before Joseph his son, so he could see him with his own eyes and make all words superfluous. But it will be hard enough to get him down to Mizraim on to the fat feeding-grounds even when he knows that Joseph lives there; he has to know it beforehand or he surely will not go. But truth has not only words, it has also signs, such as the presents of the exalted ones and Pharaoh's wagons at our disposal. We will show him them, perhaps first of all before we say anything, and then explain the signs. But by the signs he will see how kindly the exalted one means by us and how we are one heart and soul with him we sold; so when it comes out, the old man will not be able to scold us for long, neither curse us — for can he then curse Israel, ten out of twelve? That he cannot, for it would be to kick against God's plan, who sent Joseph down thither before us as quartermaster in Egypt. Therefore, children, let us not be too fearful. The hour will come, and the moment whisper us how we shall use it. First we will spread out the gifts before him, the pride of Egypt, and ask: Where do you suppose they come from, Father, and from whom? Guess! Well, they come from the great keeper of the market down yonder, he sent them to you. But then it must be he loves you very much? He must love you almost as a son loves his father? But when we have got as far as the little word 'son,' then we are more than half-way, we are past the worst. And then we play for a while on the word and finally, instead of saying the keeper of the market sent it, we say: Your son sent it, Joseph sent it to you, for he is still alive and is a lord over all Egypt."

Thus the eleven planned and took counsel together under their nightly tent, and almost too swiftly for their misgivings the now familiar road lay behind them: from Menfe up to the frontier fortress, through the wilderness, and then towards the land of the Philistines and Gaza the seaport Khadati, where they separated from the merchant caravan they had marched with and struck inland into the hills towards Hebron in short day-marches and mainly by night; for it was flowery spring when they came and the nights were beautiful, silvered by an almost full moon. Moreover, they found very troublesome the curiosity they excited everywhere by reason of their train, swollen as it was by the Egyptian wagons, the mules and mule-boys, and a herd of almost fifty asses. So they regularly rested by day and by nightly stages pushed nearer home to the terebinths of the grove of Mamre, where stood the father's house of hair and the huts of nearly all the tribe.

But the last day they set out early in the morning and by five in the afternoon were close to the goal, though it was still hidden by the familiar hills as they climbed the last slope. They had left the luggage a little distance back and they rode on before it, eleven silent donkey-riders who had left off talking, for their hearts were pounding in their chests, and despite all their previous planning none of them was clear how to begin to break the news to the father without upsetting him. Now they had come to the point, all the plans misliked them, they found them stupid and unsuitable; in particular such foolishness as "Just guess!" and "Who could it be?" seemed to them frightfully out of place. Each one of them privately rejected it with scorn, and some at the very last minute tried to think of another idea. Perhaps they ought to send one of them on ahead, for instance Naphtali the runner, to tell Jacob they were all close at hand with Benjamin and brought great, incredible news: incredible partly in the sense that one

could not believe it, partly because it went so counter to all their
habits of thought that perhaps one could not even wish to believe it —
and yet it was the living truth of God. So, thought some of them, the
father's heart would best be attuned to receive the news and be best
prepared for it by a forerunner before the others came up. They
rode at a foot pace.

TELLING THE NEWS

It was a rough, stony slope where their animals were picking their
way, but strewn thickly with spring flowers. There was larger-sized
rubble as well as small; but wherever there was any soil, or even, it
seemed, out of the stones themselves, wild flowers gushed, blossoms
far and wide, white, yellow, sky-blue, purple, and rose; low bushes,
mats and tussocks of bloom, a riot of gaiety and charm. The spring
had summoned them and they had blossomed at their due hour. Even
in the absence of the winter rains, it seemed they drew moisture
enough from the morning dew if only for a fleeting, soon fading
splendour. Even the bushes here and there bloomed in their season,
rose-coloured and white. Only the merest flaky cloudlets gathered
high up in the heavenly blue.

On a little rock, against which a foam of blossoms beat like surf on
a cliff, sat a figure almost, as seen from afar, like a flower itself. Soon
they could tell it was a little maid, alone under the wide sky, in red
smock with daisies in her hair. On her arm she held a zither and her
slender brown fingers travelled up and down the strings. It was
Serah, Asher's child; her father was the first to recognize her and
with fatherly pride he said:

"That is my little Serah, sitting there on a stone, playing herself a
little tune on her zither. The little wench is like that, she loves to sit
alone and practise herself in psalmody. She belongs to the tribe of
whistlers and fiddlers, God knows where she gets it, but she has had
it ever since she was born, she has to make psalter and psalm; she
can play on the strings till they ring and mingle her voice in songs
of praise, clearer and stronger than you could believe, seeing her
wisp of a body. Some day she will be famous in Israel, the little monkey. Look, she sees us, she flings up her arms and runs toward us.
Halloo, Serah! Here is your father Asher coming with your uncles."

The child was already there; she ran barefoot through blossoms
and rubble till the silver rings on wrists and ankles clashed and the
yellow and white wreath bobbed up and down on her head. She
laughed for pleasure and panted out breathless words of greeting;
but even the gasping sounds she made had something sonorous about
them, though one would not have known whence it came, her body
being so frail.

She was a proper little maid; no longer a child and not yet a maiden, at most twelve years old. Asher's wife was supposed to be a great-grandchild of Ishmael. Had Serah something in her of Isaac's wild and beautiful half-brother that made her sing? Or — since men's traits do undergo the strangest transformations in their posterity — did Father Asher's moist and sensual lips and eyes, his greedy love of sensation and feeling combined become a musical quality in little Serah? Perhaps it is too bold and far-fetched to trace back to the father's sweet-tooth the child's love of the art of song. But some explanation there must be — so why not that? — for little Serah's strange gift.

The eleven looked down from their long-legged asses upon the little maid, gave her greeting, caressed her, and their eyes grew speculative. Most of them dismounted and stood round Serah, their hands on their backs, nodding and wagging their heads, saying "Well, well!" and "Now, now!" and "So, little music-lips, have you run out to meet us and be the first to greet us, sitting here and playing on your zither like this?" But finally Dan, nicknamed snake and adder, said:

"Listen, children, I see by your eyes that we all have the same idea and it is Asher who should be saying what I now say; but being her father he does not think of it. Now, I have often shown that I am a good judge, and my native shrewdness tells me this is not just chance that the little monkey, Serah the song-maker, should meet us here before any of the others. God has sent her as a sign, to show what we should do. For the things we were planning about how to tell the father and hint to him so as not to harm him — that was all nonsense. Serah shall tell him, in her own way, so that the truth speaks to him in song, which is always the gentlest, whether sweet or bitter or bitter-sweet in one. Serah shall go on before us and sing to him, and even if he does not believe it, at least we shall have softened the soil of his soul and shall find it prepared for the seed of truth when we follow it up with chapter and verse and he will be forced to believe that song and truth are the same; just as we had to believe, however hard, that Pharaoh's keeper of the market was the same as our brother Joseph. Now have I spoken truly and put on solid ground what hung in the air in front of all your eyes when you saw Serah's childish little head dreaming into space?"

Yes, they said, he had, and he judged correctly. So it should be, it was the hand of heaven and a great relief. And then they took the child to instruct her and to stamp the truth on her mind. It was not easy, for they all talked at once and one would not let another speak, and Serah looked with darting, delighted eyes at their excited faces and their waving hands.

"Serah," said they, "it is thus and so. Believe it or not, just sing it and then we will come and prove it. But it would be better if you

believed it, for you would sing the better, and it is true, however unlikely it sounds; after all, you will believe your father and all your
uncles together? Look now, you did not know your uncle Jehosiph
who was lost and gone, the son of the true wife, Rachel's son, who
was called the star-virgin, but he was called Dumuzi. Well, he was
lost to your grandfather long before you were born, and the world
swallowed him up so that he was no more here, and in Jacob's heart
was he dead all these years. But now it turns out, though hard to believe, that the truth is quite different — "

> "Oh wondrous strange, for now the truth is plain
> That quite, quite otherwise it came to pass,"

Serah began, going off half-cocked, singing and laughing so loud and
musically that the gruff voices of her uncles were drowned out.

"Be quiet, little prodigy!" they cried. "You can't start singing until
you know what to say. Listen and learn before you warble: your
uncle Joseph has arisen, in other words he was never dead, he is alive,
and not only alive but lives in this and this way. He lives in Mizraim
and is this and this person. It was all a mistake, you see, the bloody
garment was a mistake, God has turned all to good in ways we knew
not of. Have you got that? We were with him in Egypt, and he made
himself known to us beyond the shadow of a doubt, saying: 'I am
he, I am your brother.' And spoke after such fashion to us that he
would have us all come down there, and you too, little Serah. Have
you taken all that in, so you could give it out again in song? Then
you are to sing it to Jacob. Our Serah is a clever maid, she will do it.
Take your zither and go on ahead of us, and sing loud and resound-
ingly that Joseph lives. Go in among the hills straight to Israel's camp,
look neither right nor left, but just keep on singing. If anyone meets
you and asks what you mean and what you are playing and singing,
make no reply, just run and sing and sing and ring: 'He is alive!' And
when you get to where Jacob your grandfather is, sit down at his feet
and sing as sweetly as you know how: 'Joseph is not dead, he is alive.'
He too will ask you what that means and what you are so rash as to
say in your singing. But you must not answer him either; just keep
on twanging your zither and singing away. Then all of us will come
up and explain it to him in proper words. Will you be our good clever
song-bird and do all this?"

"Gladly will I," answered Serah in her ringing tones. "Never before
have I had such words to string on my strings, perhaps now I can
show what they can do. Many sing, in tribe and town, but now I have
better matter than they and will sing them out of the field."

So saying she took her instrument from the stone where she had
sat and held it on one arm and spread her tapering brown fingers

across the strings, the thumb here, the four fingers there. She began
to move steadily through the flowers, now fast, now slow according
to the measure of her song:

> "Oh let my soul sing a new song as it goeth,
> For a fine chant on eight strings my heart knoweth.
> Of what it is full let it run over in rhyme
> More precious than gold and fine gold from the mine,
> Sweeter than purest honey in the comb,
> For the spring's message I bring home.

> "Hearken all people to my harp-tone sweet,
> Listen and mark what I may here repeat,
> For upon me the lovely lot doth fall,
> And I am chosen out among the daughters all,
> For given am I the strangest matter yet
> Singer ever fell on to his harp to set,
> Now on my eight my little fingers string
> To Grandfather old the golden news to bring.

> "Lovely notes in order ringing,
> Balsam to all worldly woes,
> Sweeter when to lofty silence bringing
> Singing voice in words the meaning shows.
> How all that is then exalted,
> Full of sense the sweetest sound,
> Over all is praise allotted
> To song and psalter in combined round."

Thus she sang as she went on across pastures toward the hills and
the opening between the hills; struck till they rang at the strings and
picked them till they thrilled and sang:

> "Burden worthy of the music,
> Tone and word together strive,
> Each combining other's beauty,
> For they sing: the lad's alive!

> "Yea, O Beneficent, what has here been wrought,
> And what have the ears of me little one caught,
> And what open-mouthed just now have I learned
> From men who were in Egypt and returned,
> From Father dear and high uncles mine
> Who show me words to make a song so fine.
> And they gave me matter of splendour unmeasured,
> For who was it in Egypt they discovered?

Little Grandfather dear at first you will not follow,
But in the end you will have it to swallow.
Lovely as a dream yet true withal,
And just as real as it is wonderful.

"Rarest wonder past believing
That in one should be the two,
That all poesy is living
And the beautiful the true.
Now for once is here achieved
That for which the soul doth strive,
Let my burden be believed,
True and beautiful, thy son's alive.

"Still 'twere better if you think it
Beautiful awhile but yet not true,
Lest the cup if suddenly you drink it
Fling you on your back and lay you low.
As when once the worthless bloody token,
Lying in their throats, they brought you home,
Night fell on your soul for ever unbroken,
Straight a pillar of salt you would become.

"Ah, what pangs you bore in thinking
Nevermore to see him with your eyes,
Dead he lay within your heart and buried,
Now therein he sweetly doth arise."

Here a man sought to question her, a shepherd in a shady hat standing on the hill. He had been watching her for a long time, listening
in wonder to her song. Now he came down to her, set his pace to
hers, and asked:

"Maiden, what is it you sing as you go? It sounds so strange. I have
often heard you praising and psaltering and I know you can play
right soundingly on the strings, but never before so teasingly and
riddlingly as this. And then the way you keep the time and set the
pace as you go! Are you going to Jacob the master, and has what you
sing to do with him? It seems to me so. But what do you mean by
beautiful and true, and what with your refrain: 'the lad's alive'?"

But Serah as she walked looked not at him, she only smiling shook
her head. She took her hand a moment from the strings to lay her
finger on her lips, then she went on:

"Sing, Serah, Asher's child, what thou hast learned
From the eleven now out of Egypt returned.

Sing how that God in His mercy has blessed them
That to the man down below they addressed them.
Who then the man, who but Joseph is he,
My uncle as tall and as fine as can be.
Old one, look up, it is thy dear son,
Greater is Pharaoh only by his throne.
Lord of the lands his name they call,
The state's first servant they name him all,
Kings of the earth his praises sing,
Stranger folk kneeling to him tribute bring.
Over uncounted lands is he set,
To all the people he giveth their meat,
From thousands of barns he spendeth them bread
To carry them over their hunger and need.
For he it was in foresight wisely hoarded
And therefore is his name o'er all belauded.
His garments in myrrh and in aloes are pressed,
In ivory palaces he sets up his rest,
Forth from them like a bridegroom doth he come —
Lo, old one, behold what has come of thy lamb!"

The man went along with her and listened with growing amazement to the words of her song. Seeing other folk at a distance, man or maid, he beckoned them up, to listen with him. Serah was soon the centre of a little troop of men, women, and children, which grew as they came nearer the camp. The children danced to the rhythm, the elders walked in the time of it; all their faces were turned to her, and she went on singing:

"Whiles thou believedst him mangled and dead,
And with tears hast watered thy daily bread,
Twenty measured years have sped,
Mourning him with ashes on thy head —
Lo, now, old one, behold and see,
God He can scourge and can heal;
How marvellous all His Ways can be
For human children's weal!

"Past understanding is His rule,
Great all the work of His hands;
He dealt with His servant as a fool
And laid thee under bands.
Creation laughs at the lordly jest,
Tabor and Hermon leap:
He snatched away thy dearest and best,
But now thou shalt have him to keep.

Thou hast writhen, old man, in thy pain,
And found thyself in it again;
But now he is returned to you,
Still lovely, though rather stouter to view.

"Thou knowest not his face,
Nor yet his name canst guess;
Stammering you will greet
Nor know who shall fall at whose feet.
Thus God went about at His ease
My dear little grandfather to tease."

By this time she had drawn with her train quite close to her home
under Mamre's terebinths. She saw Jacob, the man of the blessing,
sitting stately on his mat before the curtains of his dwelling. Now
she lifted her instrument and held it higher and more firmly in her
arm; up till then she had been picking and twanging the strings in
well-tried scherzos and dissonances; but now she drew from it sounding chords of sweeping harmony, to which she sang in her full-
throated voice:

"For a word of beauteous rareness
In my music interweaves,
Matching all it hath of fairness,
And it says: Thy darling lives!
Match, O soul, in exultation
Golden music of the strings;
For the grave no longer hath him —
Heart, he is arisen — sing!
Heart, it is the sorely missed,
For whom the earth its anguish bore,
Whom they lured into the coffin,
Whom the boar's vile tushes tore.
Ah, he was no longer present,
Desolate the barren earth,
Till we heard: He is arisen —
Dear old Father, pray have faith!
Godlike in his steps he paces,
Round his head bright summer birds do reel,
As across the flowery spaces
Lo, he greets thee with a smile!
Wintry grief and deathly anguish
From his kiss away have flown;
On his lips and cheeks and forehead
Hath the Eternal favour strewn.

Read it in his laughing features
All was but a godlike jest;
And in late-believing raptures
Take him to thy father-breast!"

Jacob had long since seen his grandchild, his little music-lips, coming towards him, and listened well pleased to her voice. He even clapped his hands benevolently, just like the audience at a play. When she reached him the maid, without other greeting than her song, sat down on the mat at his feet; her troop of followers stayed at some distance away. The old man listened, and his applauding hands slowly fell; his nodding as slowly turned into a doubtful head-shaking. When she came to an end of her verse he said:

"Good and charming, my granddaughter, so far. It is sweet of you, Serah, and thoughtful, to come and give a little pleasure to the lonely old man. You see, I know you well by name, as I do not all of my grandchildren, for there are too many. But you stand out for your gift of song; it makes a real person of you, so that one remembers your name. But listen now, my gifted one, while I say I have heard with pleasure the music and the poetry, but yet not without some misgiving the sense. For poesy, dear little one, poesy is always an alluring, seductive, dangerous thing. Sense and senses lie close together, and song rhymes all too easily with wrong; grace and charm are prone to gracelessness and harm, if they are not bridled by concern with God. Lovely is the play of thought; but holy the spirit alone. Poesy is play of heart and mind; willingly I applaud it, so long as it loses not sight of spirit but remains in the end concern with God. Now what was it you were saying in your warbling and trilling; and what can I make of a man like a god tripping across the fields with birds flitting about him and laughing at his own jest? He sounds to me like one of these nature-gods hereabouts, whom I hold in great suspicion: the folk of the countryside call him lord, and darken the counsels of the children of Abraham with their folly. We too speak of the Lord, of course; but our meaning is altogether different. Never can I be sufficiently concerned for Israel's soul, nor preach enough under the tree of wisdom, that this 'lord' is not the Lord; our people are always on the point of confusing the two and relapsing into idolatry. For God is a high and difficult task; but 'the gods' are a pleasant sin. Can I then, dear child, applaud, when you lend your gift to pleasant psaltery after the loose ways of the land?"

But Serah only shook her head with a smile, plucked her strings anew, and sang:

"Who then do I sing, O Grandfather mine,
Who but my uncle so tall and so fine?
Look up, old man, it is thy dear son,

Greater is Pharaoh only by his throne.
Grandfather, at first you cannot follow,
But in the end you will have it to swallow.
For a word of wonder-rareness
In my music interweaves,
Matching all it hath of fairness,
And it says: Thy darling lives!"

"Child," said Jacob, greatly moved, "truly it is lovely and pleasant
that you come before me and sing of my son Joseph, whom you never
knew, and devote your gift to divert me. But your song is riddling:
the rhymes are well enough but not the reason, and so it hath neither
rhyme nor reason. I cannot let it pass; for how can you sing 'The lad's
alive'? Such words can give me no joy, they are but lying flourishes,
for Joseph died long since. Mangled is he, mangled and dead."

But Serah answered him in ringing chords:

"Match, O soul, with exaltation
Golden music of the strings,
For the grave no longer hath him,
Heart, he is arisen — sing!
Ah, he was no longer present,
Desolate the barren earth —
Till we heard: He is arisen.
Dear old Father, pray have faith!
From thousands of barns he spendeth them bread
To carry them over their hunger and need;
For he like Noah wisely hath provided,
And therefore is his name o'er all beloved.
His garments in myrrh and in aloes are pressed,
In ivory palaces he sets up his rest,
And issueth like bridegroom forth from them —
Old one, behold what hath come of thy lamb!"

"Serah, my grandchild, reckless little one," said Jacob impressively,
"what shall I think of your loose-mouthed song? I have let much pass
as poetic licence, though I find it little respectful that you address me
as 'old man.' But poetic licence is not the only licence in your song, it
is altogether a string of disrespectful and cheating make-believe. You
may think to please me by it; but pleasure founded on falseness is no
true pleasure, nor can it profit the soul. Dare poesy lend itself to such,
is that its province? Are you not abusing your gift from God to dress
in it such untrue and unreasonable things? Verily there must be some
reason allied to the beauty, else it only mocks the heart."

"Rarest wonder,"
sang Serah, unheeding:

"Rarest wonder, past believing,
That in one should be the two:
That all poesy is living,
And the beautiful the true.
Here for once is now achieved
That for which the soul doth strive,
Let my burden be believed,
True and beautiful, thy son's alive!"

"Child," said Jacob, and his head was shaking on his shoulders, "dearest child . . ."

But her voice soared and revelled, borne on the leaping, exulting music of the strings:

"Lo, now, old one, behold and see,
God He can scourge and can heal,
How marvellous all His ways can be
For His human children's weal!
He snatched away thy dearest and best,
But thou shalt take him again to thy breast.
Thou hast writhen, old one, in thy pain,
Yet found thyself in it again;
But now he returneth to you,
Still lovely, though rather stouter to view.
So God goes about as He pleases
And dear little Grandfather teases."

Jacob, with his head turned away, for the brown eyes were full of tears, put out one hand as though to stop her. "Child!" he said again, and only that. He seemed not to hear the sudden bustle and movement among the tents; nor paid any heed to the joyous announcement now made him. For the group who had come up with Serah was increased by others approaching to bring glad tidings; servants and other folk came round Jacob from all sides and two of them addressed him:

"Israel, the eleven are back from Egypt, your sons with men and carts and many more asses than they set out with!"

But even as the men spoke, here were the brothers already. They dismounted and came up, with Benjamin in their midst and the rest pulling and pushing him forward, each one zealous to be the one to bring him before the father.

"Peace and good health," they said, "to our father and dear lord! Here is Benjamin. We have kept him safe for you, though he was at one time in some danger. But now you can have him once more at your apron-strings. And here is your hero Simeon. Furthermore, we bring abundance of food and rich presents from the giver of bread.

Lo, we are all well and happily returned — happily, in truth, is a word nowhere near strong enough for it."

"Boys," answered Jacob, who had got to his feet, "boys — yes, of course, I am glad to see you."

He put his hand possessively on Benjamin's arm, yet half absently too, and his gaze was bewildered. "You are here again," said he, "safe home again after perilous journey — under other circumstances this would be a great moment and quite fill my soul if it were not taken up with other matters. Yes, you find me greatly taken up, I mean by this little maid here — Asher, she is your child — who came and sat by me and played on her zither, singing so sweetly, yet harping upon such folly about my son Joseph that I know not how to defend my reason from her. I am tempted to welcome your coming solely because I count on you to protect me from this child and the lying tongue her music has, since I know you would not allow my grey hairs to be mocked."

"Never will we do so," responded Judah, "so far as we can prevent it. But in the opinion of all of us, Father, and it is a well-founded opinion, you would do better — even though at first afar off — to consider whether there might not be some truth in her harping."

"Some truth," repeated the old man. He stood up very straight. "You dare come to me with such cowardly advice and speak to Israel of half-measures and half-truths? Where should we be, and where God, if we had ever let ourselves in to be half and half? For the truth is one and indivisible. Three times this child has sung to me: 'Thy son's alive!' There can be nothing true in her words unless it were the truth. So what is it?"

"The truth!" said the eleven in chorus, raising their palms to the sky. And:

"The truth!" came back the amazed and exultant chorus from the gathered host. Men's, women's, and children's voices echoed triumphantly: "She sang the truth!"

"Dear little Father," said Benjamin, embracing Jacob. "As now you hear, so believe, for we too had to, first one of us and then another. The man down there who asked about me, and kept on asking: 'Does your father still live?' — that is Joseph, he and Joseph are one. Never was he dead, my mother's son. Roving men tore him from the claws of the ravening beast and took him down to Egypt, where he has flourished as by a spring and become the first among the men of the land below. The sons of strangers flatter him, for without him they would pine and die. Would you have tokens of this miracle? Look at our train! Twenty asses he sent you, whose load is the food and the riches of Egypt, and the wagons out of Pharaoh's stores shall carry us all down to your son. For from the beginning it was his plan that you should come and I guessed that it was so. He would have us to feed on fat pastures, not far from him, but where it is not too Egyptian, in the land of Goshen."

Jacob had preserved complete, almost severe composure.

"God will dispose," he said in a firm voice. "Only from Him does Israel take instructions and not from the great ones of this earth. — My Damu, my child!" broke from his lips. He had clasped his hands on his breast and stood with his brow raised to the clouds, slowly shaking his old head. Then he dropped it again.

"Boys," said he, "this little maid, whom I now bless and who shall not taste death but go living into the kingdom of heaven if God shall hear me — she sang to me that the Lord vouchsafes me Rachel's first-born back again, still handsome but somewhat heavy. That probably means he is already quite fat with the years and the fleshpots of Egypt?"

"Not really fat, dear Father, not very," answered Judah soothingly. "Only within the bounds of dignity. You must consider that not death gives him back to you, but life. Death, if that were thinkable, would give him back to you as he was; but since it is life at whose hand you receive him back, he is no more the faun of other days but a royal stag of four points. And you must be prepared to find him a little strange and worldly in his ways and wearing a pleated byssus, like Hermon's driven snow."

"I will go down and see him before I die," said Jacob. "If he had not lived he would not be living. Blessed be the name of the Lord!"

"Blessed!" cried they all, and rushed forward in a wave to congratulate him and the brothers and kiss the hem of Jacob's garment. He did not look down on their heads; his eyes were raised again and he kept shaking his head as he held it turned up to the sky. But Serah, the song-lips, sat on the mat and sang:

> "Read it in his laughing features,
> All was but a Godlike jest;
> And in late-believing raptures
> Take him to thy father-breast!"

Chapter VII

THE LOST IS FOUND

I WILL GO AND SEE HIM

AND so the refractory cow heard the voice of her calf when the crafty farmer brought it to the field that was to be ploughed, so that the cow would be contented there; and the cow yielded her neck to the yoke and ploughed. Hard enough it was for her still, with her considerable dislike of the field, which she thought of as a death-acre. Jacob's deliberate and declared intention was not easier to him than submission was to the cow; indeed, he was glad that at least he had time to think it over. Actually to carry it out, to part from all that was his by ingrained habit, to transport the tribe bag and baggage to the lowland, that took much time; and by the same token it gave him time. The Bene Yisrael were not the people to take literally Pharaoh's words, not to regard their stuff, for that they should be provided withal in the land of Goshen, and they were simply to leave everything where it was. "Not to regard their stuff," that meant at most not to take everything they had — which was impossible anyhow. Not all their tools and equipment and not all the cattle and fowl. On the other hand it certainly did not mean that they were to travel light and leave everything behind for the first comer. They sold off quantities of goods, and certainly not in unseemly haste or without very stiff bargaining. But Jacob let them go ahead and sell. Which proves that he kept to his resolve in its main lines although the way he talked about it might be open to various interpretations.

"I will go down thither and see him," he would say. That might mean: "I will visit him to see his face before I die and then come back." But it was clear to all of them, even to Jacob himself, that it really could not mean that. If it had been a matter of just a visit to behold his face, then certainly it would be his high-and-mightiness Joseph who owed his little father the visit in order to spare him the great inconvenience of a journey to Mizraim. But on the other hand such a thought ran counter to the motif of the sending after, and Jacob perfectly understood that the stars in their courses had so ruled in the matter. Joseph had not been separated and snatched away for that; Jacob's face had not to that end been swollen with weeping, only in order that they should now visit each other. No, the high purpose was that Joseph should have Israel come after him; and Jacob was far too much of an expert in God-knowledge not to know that the snatching away of the lovely one, his magnification down below, the obstinate famine which had driven the brothers down to Egypt – that all these were arrangements in a comprehensive plan, to ignore which would have been the crassest stupidity. One might find Jacob self-centred and arrogant in that a calamity like the present prolonged drought, so wide-spread, affecting so many people and causing such wholesale economic changes, was seen by him merely in the light of a plan for the furtherance of his own tribal history. Quite obviously it was his idea that where he and his house were in question the rest of the world would have to like it or lump it. But arrogance and egoism are only negative words for a highly positive and fruitful attitude which we might call by the more sympathetic name of piety. There are probably no virtues which cannot be called by unsympathetic names; none without inward contradictions, such as, in the present case, humility and arrogance. Piety is the subjectivation of the outer world, its concentration upon the self and its salvation; without the conviction, exaggerated to the point of offensiveness, of God's especial, yes, all-embracing concern, without the fixation of the self and its salvation in the very centre of all things, there is no piety. Piety, in short, is the name we give to that great virtue. Its opposite is the low esteem of the self and its relegation to the unimportant periphery, out of which nothing good can come. He who does not take himself seriously is soon lost, but he who thinks of himself as Abram did when he resolved that he, and in him man, might serve only the highest, he does, of course, behave presumptuously. But this presumption will be a blessing to many. For here is manifest the connection between the dignity of the self and the dignity of humanity. The claim of the human ego to central importance was the precondition for the discovery of God; and only together, with the consequence of the utter destruction of a humanity which does not take itself seriously, can both discoveries be lost sight of again.

But we must go on from here: for subjectivation does not mean subjection, nor esteem of self disesteem of others. It does not mean isolation or a callous disregard of the general, the exterior and suprapersonal; in short, of all that reaches beyond the self. On the contrary it therein solemnly recognizes itself. In other words, if piety is the being penetrated with the importance of the self, then worship is piety's extension and assimilation into the eternalness of being, which returns in it and wherein it recognizes itself. That is to depart from all singleness and limitation, yet with no violence to its own dignity, which it even enhances to the point of consecration.

In such a light, then, we may consider Jacob's mood at this time of the break-up; and we can scarcely think of it as more solemn than it actually was. He was about to carry out quite literally what he had dreamed of at the peak of his affliction and feverishly prattled in Eliezer's ear: he was going down to his dead son in the underworld. That was a cosmic procedure; and where the ego opens its borders to the cosmic and loses itself therein, even until its own identity is blurred, can there be any thought of narrowness or isolation? The very thought of the break-up was full of contrary-tending factors: the factor of abiding, the factor of the return — they elevated the moment above and beyond the episodic and atomic. Jacob the greybeard was Jacob the youth again; he who, after the deception that put things right, had departed from Beersheba to Naharaim. He was Jacob the man who with wives and flocks had got free from Harran after a stay of twenty-five years. But he was not only Jacob, the man in whose life-spiral the break-up repeated itself. He was also Isaac, who went to Gerar, to Abimelech in the land of the Philistines. Again and still further back, he was seeing repeat itself the primeval break-up, Abram the wanderer's exodus from Ur of the Chaldees — and even that was not the first form, but only the earthly reflection and imitation of a celestial wandering: the wandering of the moon, who took her way and freed herself from one station to the next: Bel Harran, the Lord of the Way. But Abram, the first earthly wanderer, had made pause at Harran; so it was plain that Beersheba was to represent it and that Jacob would there make his first moon-station.

He took comfort in the thought of Abram: how during a famine he too had gone to Egypt, to dwell there as a stranger. And Jacob had need of comfort. True, he was looking forward to a joy so keen that it was almost pain; after that he might depart in peace, since nothing to compare with it remained to look for. True, the migration to Egypt, there by Pharaoh's consent to pasture on fat land, was an enviable lot, and so esteemed by many. But when all was said and done, the decision was hard for Jacob. It was hard for him to adapt himself to God's command to void the land of his fathers and exchange it for the offensive land of the animal gods, the land of mud, the land of the children of Ham. He had settled in the land whither Abram had wandered; had done it provisionally, as it were, and like his forefathers had always been half a stranger there. Still he had thought to die as they had in this spot. He had always considered to refer to this land where he was born and where his dead rested the prophecy made to Abram that his seed would be strange in the land. But now it turned out that the prophecy which, not for nothing, was bound up with thoughts of terror and great darkness actually pointed to the land whither he was now going: to Mizraim, the Egyptian house of bondage. That, we know, had always been Jacob's mistrustful name for the strictly administered land down south. Certainly he had never contemplated its becoming a house of bondage for his own seed — as now became painfully clear to him. His leave-taking was burdened with the insight that God's pronouncement: "And they shall afflict them four hundred years," referred to the country whither he was going. It was in all probability the forced labour of many generations to which he was leading his people. The plan of salvation might be altogether good; or good and bad might be wholly cancelled out in the great concept of destiny and the future. But notwithstanding all that, this was uncontestably a break-up fraught with destiny, to which Jacob now committed himself in God, and as such he felt it.

Yes, they were going to the land of tombs, and that was bad enough. But actually it was the tombs he was leaving behind that he thought of with the keenest pain. Rachel's wayside grave, and Machpelach, the double hollow, which Abram had bought as a burial place with the field it stood in from Ephron the Hittite for four hundred silver shekels by weight according to custom. Israel like all shepherds was free-footed; still he did possess that much real estate, the field with the cave; and his it should remain. The emigrants disposed of many movables, but just this immovable, the field with the tomb, that was inalienable. To Jacob it was the guarantee of his return. For however many generations were to rot in Egypt's soil while his house increased, he was resolved to lay it upon God and man that when the remnant of his own days was lived out, he himself was to be brought back to the permanent home which he, the shepherd and wanderer, possessed on earth: that he might lie where lay his father and the mothers of his sons, all save only the beloved and untimely cut off, who lay by the wayside, mother of his darling taken hence, who summoned him now.

So it was good that Jacob had time to consider his departure down thither to the snatched one. For it was a heavy task, this of understanding God's purposes in the strange destiny of the set-apart darling. Jacob's conclusion on this subject can best be heard from himself. When he spoke of Joseph now he spoke of him not otherwise than as "his lordship my son." "I intend," he would say, "to travel down to his lordship my son in Egypt. He holds high office there." People to whom he said that probably smiled behind the old man's back and made merry over the paternal vanity. They did not know how much deadly serious effort after objectivity, how much renunciation and stern resolve lay behind Jacob's turn of phrase.

SEVENTY OF THEM

THE FLOWERY spring had become late summer before Israel had his affairs wound up and the train got under way from the grove of Mamre by Hebron. Beersheba was their nearest goal and some days of ceremonial sojourn were to be spent in this border place where Jacob and his father were born and where the resolute mother Rebecca had once readied the thief of the blessing for the journey into Mesopotamia.

Jacob departed from his own place and set forth with flocks and possessions, with sons and sons' sons, with daughters and daughters' sons. Or, as the story also says: with their little ones and their wives, a limited reckoning since by wives was meant the wives of the sons and by daughters the same thing with addition of the daughters of the sons, for instance the singing Serah. They left seventy strong — that is, they reckoned themselves seventy, but it was not by actual count, merely a feeling of a count, a sort of mental conclusion, in which there prevailed that lunar degree of exactness of which we well know that it was not like our own yet entirely right and justifiable in its time and place. Seventy was the number of the peoples of the earth listed in the tables of God. Consequently nothing in black and white was required in order to prove that seventy was the number of descendants from forefather's loins. But when it came to Jacob's loins, surely the wives of the sons ought not to have been counted in? And accordingly they were not. For where there is no counting at all there can be no counting in; the sum arrived at was not a matter of counting at all, resting as it did on a foregone conclusion; thus it is idle to ask what was counted and what not. We do not even know whether Jacob himself was one of the seventy, or whether they reckoned him separately as the seventy-first. We must be content to think that the age permitted both possibilities at the same time. Much later, for instance, a descendant of Judah, or more precisely of his son Perez, with whom Tamar had deliberately presented him — this descendant, a man named Isaiah, had seven sons, *and* a youngest son who tended the sheep, upon whom the horn of anointing was lifted up. What does this *and* mean? Was he included as the youngest of seven or did Isaiah have eight sons? The former is more likely, for it is much finer and more orthodox to have seven sons than eight. But it is more than likely, in fact it is certain, that the figure seven as the number of Isaiah's sons did not change to eight when the youngest came along and that the youngest succeeded in being included in the seven even though he was actually one over the count. And once there was another man who had full seventy sons, for he had many wives. One son of these mothers killed all his brothers, the whole seventy sons on one same stone. By our prosaic reckoning he can only, being their brother, have killed sixty-nine. Or rather sixty-eight, since another brother, whose name is given, Jotham, remained alive. The statement is hard to swallow. Yet here one of seventy did kill all seventy and yet left himself and another brother alive — a striking and instructive instance of "counting in" and "not counting in" at the same time.

Jacob, then, actually was the seventy-first among the seventy wanderers — in so far as this figure itself can stand the light of day. For in prosaic truth the number was less rather than more — a fresh contradiction, but unfortunately an unavoidable one. Jacob the father was the seventieth and not the seventy-first on the basis of the fact that the males of the seed came to sixty-nine. However, it did so by including Joseph, who was in Egypt, and his two sons who were even born there. These three males of the stock were certainly not in the train that went down; accordingly we must subtract them even although they belong in the figure seventy. Again, even this deduction leaves too many; for the figure seventy reckoned in a number of souls as yet unborn. We might let pass the case of Jochebed, a daughter of Levi, whose mother was already heavy with her at the time of the journey, she being born "between the walls," probably the walls of the border fortress on their entry into Egypt. But there is more to it than that. For the sum total counts in grandchildren who are neither born nor begot, not present but only foreseen. They came to Egypt, as pious scholars put it, *in lumbis patrum* and took part in the journey only in a metaphysical sense.

So much for the necessary subtractions. But there are equally compelling reasons for increasing the sum total. The male seed of Jacob came to that sum by itself; but if — or rather since — all his immediate descendants must be counted in, then, if certainly not the sons' wives, yet their daughters must be included, for example Serah, quite decidedly, to mention only one. It would be entirely wrong not to count the little maid who brought the good news about Joseph. Her fame was great in Israel and there was never any doubt about the fulfilment of the blessing which Jacob had gratefully conferred on her, that she should not taste death but go up living into heaven. Nobody in fact knows when she died: her life-story has every appearance of continuing on and on. There is the tale that generations later the man Moses, going about hunting for Joseph's grave, had the spot — in the middle of the Nile — pointed out to him by Serah. Vastly later than that even, she seems to have pursued her existence among the people of Abram, under the name of the "wise woman." However that may be, whether it was the same Serah all the time or whether other little maids assumed the name and nature of the first little herald and harbinger, in any event she must be included. No objecting voice will be raised, no matter how her inclusion affects the count.

But we cannot be so thoroughgoing about the wives of the sons — in other words, the mothers of Jacob's grandchildren. The word "mothers" is better than "wives" in this connection, on account of Tamar, who, conformably to the "whither thou goest I will go" made one in the train with her two stout Judah sons. Mostly she went on foot, leaning on a long staff, taking for a woman very long strides; tall and dark, with round nostrils and proud mouth, and that strange distant-dwelling look of hers. This resolute woman, who would not at any price be counted out, should she not be counted in? As for her two husbands, Er and Onan, they could not be counted — neither by moon nor by daylight reckoning, for they were dead; and even if Israel counted unborn souls, surely he did not count dead ones! Shelah, on the other hand, the husband whom she did not get, but whom she no longer needed, since she had given him two fine stout half-brothers, went along, being one among Leah's thirty-two grandchildren.

CARRY HIM

To the agreed number, then, of seventy, Israel pulled out of the grove of Mamre the Amorite. Counting everything not counted in, shepherds, drovers, drivers, baggage men, and slaves, the train was all of a hundred persons and more — a highly-coloured, noisy caterpillar of a migrating tribe, slow-moving, enveloped in clouds of dust raised by the trotting flocks. Its members got forward by various means — and between ourselves, the host of Egyptian conveyances sent by Joseph were of very little use. This does not apply to the so-called *agolt*, whose value should be acknowledged. These were heavy two-wheeled ox-carts, wonderful for household goods, leather water-bottles, and forage, as well as for the women and children. But the actual travelling carriages, such as the light *merkobt*, some of them very luxuriously equipped and drawn by a team of horses or mules, with the shapely wagon-box covered with stamped purple leather; open behind and often consisting simply of a curved wooden railing, gilded in every possible place: these elegant toys, however well-meaning Joseph and his royal master had been in sending them, proved impracticable and went back to Egypt mostly as empty as they had come. Nobody had any good of the fact that some of them were covered inside and out with linen and stucco and in the stucco delightful little reliefs of court and peasant life; or that the nails on the wheels were in the form of Moors' heads, exquisitely modelled. Only two persons could stand in these chariots, or three if they were crowded; they had no springs and were tiring in the long run, over ungentle roads. Or if you sat down you had to sit backwards on the floor with your legs dangling out. Some, like Tamar, chose the time-honoured way of the pilgrim and went on foot with a staff. Most of them, however, rode: on splay-footed camels, bony mules, white or grey asses, all of them decorated with big glass beads, embroidered saddle-cloths, and dangling mullen-stalks. Those were the saddle animals, who stirred up the dust in the roads. On them rode Jacob's people, whom Joseph had sent for: a gay, high-coloured tribe, in garments of woven wool, the bearded men in their heavy desert cloaks, with head-cloths often held in place by a felt ring on top. The women had black braids hanging on their shoulders, silver and bronze bracelets on their wrists, their foreheads were hung with coins, their nails reddened with henna they carried sucklings in their arms, swaddled in great soft wrappings with brocaded borders. They all munched as they rode along: roasted onions, sour bread, and olives. They mostly took the ridge road going down from Jerusalem and the heights of Hebron to the deeper southland, called Negeb, the arid land to Kirjath Sepher, the book city, and to Beersheba.

Our chief concern, of course, is the comfort of Jacob the father. How was he accommodated? Had Joseph, when he sent his wagons, thought that the venerable man would make the journey standing in one of those decorated chariots, behind a gilt railing? Not he. Not even Pharaoh his master thought that. The directions issued by the beautiful child of Aton from his new-smelling palace had said: "Take your father and carry him." The patriarch was to be borne as though in triumph, that was the word used; and among the mostly useless vehicles sent by Joseph was a single conveyance of a different kind, destined for precisely this solemn service, the carrying of Jacob. It was an Egyptian litter, such as the upper classes of Keme used on the streets and when they travelled: an exceptionally elegant specimen too, with a woven reed back-rest, the sides adorned with fine writings, with rich hangings and bronze carrying-poles; it was even provided with a light gaily painted wooden hood at the back for protection against dust and wind. This chair could be carried by boys or on the back of animals by means of cross-poles. Jacob was very comfortable in it, once he had made up his mind to use it. He did so only from Beersheba on, that being in his mind the boundary-line between home and foreign land. Up to that point he was carried by a dromedary, a wise, slow-gazing beast, on a saddle with a sunshade fastened to it.

The old man was a very fine and dignified sight, and he knew it too, as surrounded by his sons he swayed along on his high perch at the rocking gait of his clever beast. The fine wool of his *kofia* was fringed unevenly across his forehead; it lay in folds about neck and shoulder and fell softly on the dark red garment open at the front to reveal the embroidered under-garment. The breezes played in his

silver beard. The inward gaze of his gentle shepherd eyes showed that
he was musing on his tales, both past and future, and nobody ventured to disturb him; at most they inquired respectfully now and
again after his comfort. Foremost in his mind was the expected sight
of the sacred tree at Beersheba, planted by Abram, beneath which he
meant to sacrifice, to give instruction, and to sleep.

JACOB TEACHES AND DREAMS

THE GIANT tamarisk stood on a hill of medium height near the populated settlement of Beersheba, which our travellers passed by on one
side. Beneath its shade stood a primitive stone table and an upright
stone column or *massebe*. The tree had, strictly speaking, probably
not been planted by Jacob's father's father, but taken over by him
from the children of the land and changed from a Baal shrine into a
tree of God and *êlôn môreh* or oracle tree, the central point of a
shrine and cult of the highest and only God. Jacob might easily know
this without being shaken in his belief that the tree was planted by
Abram. In a symbolic sense it was, and the mental processes of the
father were broader and gentler than ours, which know only one
thing or else the other, and are prone to shout, banging on the table:
"If that had been a Baal tree, then Abram did not plant it!" Such zeal
for the truth is more peppery and thickheaded than wise, and there
is far more dignity in the quiet reconciliation of both points of view,
as Jacob achieved it.

But the forms in which Israel worshipped the eternal God under
the tree did not after all differ much from the cult of the children
of Canaan — aside from all the offensive sporting and unseemliness
in which the worship of those children used inevitably to wind up.
At the foot of the sacred hill, round about, the rest-tents were set up
and preparations for the slaughtering got under way at once, to be
performed on the dolmen, the primitive stone table, and afterwards
partaken of in common, the sacrificial meal. Had the children of Baal
done otherwise? Had not they too let the blood of sheep and goats
run down upon the altar and struck the caked side-posts with the
blood? Surely they had. But the children of Israel did it in a different spirit and in more enlightened wise, as is clear from the fact that
after the sacred meal they did not sport with each other in pairs, at
least not publicly.

And Jacob instructed them in God, too, under the tree. And it did
not bore them; even the young found his words most interesting and
important, because they were all more or less gifted in that way and
eagerly seized even on the subtleties of his remarks. He showed them
the difference between the many-namedness of Baal and that of their
Father the highest and only. The many-named Baal was a true plural-

ity; there was no one Baal but many — the occupants, possessors, and patrons of cult sites, groves, shrines, springs, trees: a host of gods of dwelling and soil who worked singly and locally, had in their collectivity no face, no person, no proper name, and at most were called Melkart, city king, if they were that sort of deity, as for instance him of Tyre. One was called Baal Peor after his site, or Baal Hermon or Baal Meon; one was Baal of the Bond, of course, which had been useful in Abram's work on God. There was even one called, quite absurdly, Dance-Baal. There was not much dignity about this and very little collective majesty. Quite otherwise was it with the many names of God the Father, which did no violence whatsoever to his personal oneness. He was called El-Elyon, the highest; El ro'i, the God that sees one; El Olam, God of the æons, or, after Jacob's great vision sprung from his humiliation, El Bethel, the God of Luz. But all these were only interchangeable designations for one and the same highest existing personal God; not localized, existing in everything, like the labelled multiplicity of the Baal gods of town and country, the single proprietorship of which was ascribed to them, the fertility they bestowed, the springs they guarded, the trees wherein they dwelt and murmured, the tempest they raged in, the burgeoning spring, the parching east wind — He was all this that they singly were, to Him it all belonged, He was the All-God of all of it, for from Him it came, in Himself He comprehended it, saying I, the Being of all being, Elohim, the many as one.

On the subject of this name Jacob exhausted himself. He spoke most engrossingly for his audience and not without subtlety. It was clear whence Dan, his fifth son, got his type of mind, though it was only a poor second-generation derivative from his father's much higher qualities. The question Jacob discussed was whether one was to regard Elohim as singular or plural: to say "Elohim wills it" or "the Elohim will it." If you admitted the importance of correct syntax, you must make the distinction, and Jacob seemed to make it correctly in deciding for the singular. God was One, and he who thought that Elohim was the plural of El or God involved himself in grave error. The plural of God would be Elim. Elohim was something quite different. It did not mean a multiplicity any more than the name Abram. The man from Ur had been named Abram and then had the honour of having his name expanded into Abraham. The same was true of Elohim. It was an honorific expansion, nothing else — certainly it had no taint of what one condemned as polytheism. The teacher stressed the point. Elohim was One. But then again it transpired that there were several of Him, some three. Three men came to Abraham in the grove of Mamre, as he sat at the door of his house in the heat of the day. And the three men were, as the hasting Abraham soon saw, God the Lord. "Lord," he had said, bowing to the earth; "Lord," and "thou." But also now and then "Lords" and "you." And had prayed them to sit down in the shade and strengthen themselves with milk and the flesh of cows. And they ate. And then they said: "I will come to you in a year." That was God. He was One, but He was explicitly threefold. He practised manifoldness, but always and on principle said "I," whereas Abraham had addressed him by turns in the singular and the plural. The use of the name Elohim as a plural, his audience heard Jacob further say, had, despite all the above stress to the contrary, something in its favour after all. Yes, as they heard him go on, they got a glimmer of an idea that his experience of God, like Abram's, had been threefold, and comprised three men. Three independent and yet again coincident persons. He spoke, that is, first of all of the Father-God, or God the Father, second of a Good Shepherd who fed His flocks, and third of one whom he called the Angel, of whom the seventy got the impression that He overshadowed as with the wings of doves. All together they were Elohim, the threefold unity.

I cannot tell whether all that goes home to you; but for Jacob's hearers under the tree it was vastly interesting and exciting — they had taste and gifts for such things. As they dispersed, and afterwards in their tents before they slept, they discussed what they had heard, long and eagerly. The honorific expansion and Abram's threefold guest, the avoidance of polytheism enjoined upon them in view of a God out of whose manifold existence there yet went a certain temptation in that direction — all that being like a test of their capacity for God-thoughts: a test to which all of Jacob's people, even the youngest, felt blithely adequate.

Their head and chief had his place spread under the sacred tree all the three nights he spent at Beersheba. The first two nights he did not dream, but the third brought him the vision to receive which he slept and which he needed for consolement and strength. He was afraid of Egypt, he urgently needed the assurance that he need not fear to go down thither, since the God of his fathers was not a local deity and would be with him in the lower world as he had been with him in Laban's land. He had need to his heart's depths of the confirmation that God did not only go down with him but after he had made them a multitude would lead him (or at least his seed) back into the land of his fathers. That was the land between Nimrod's kingdoms; an ignorant land indeed, and full of foolish aborigines, but yet no Nimrod kingdom: there better than anywhere else one might serve a spiritual God. In short, what he so thirsted for was the assurance that the promise of the great dream of the ladder that had come to him in Gilgal of Bethel should not be cancelled by his going hence, but that God the King stood by His word which He had sung to the sound of harps. It was to hear this that he slept and in sleep he heard it. God spoke to him in a solemn voice and promised that of which his soul had need. But sweetest of all was the promise that Joseph should "put his hands upon thine eyes" — a profound and meaningful expression which might signify that the all-powerful son would protect him and care for his old age among the heathen; but also that his darling would one day close his eyes — a dream in which for so long now Jacob had not let himself indulge.

Now he let himself dream both this and the other and his sleeping eyes were wet beneath their lids. But when he woke he was strengthened and reassured, and anxious to proceed onwards with all the seventy. He mounted the fine Egyptian carrying-chair, which was slung across the backs of two white asses adorned with mullen stalks; in it he looked even finer and more stately than on the camel.

OF WITHHOLDING LOVE

A TRADE route ran from the north-east of the delta through the arid southland of Canaan via Beersheba to Hebron. The children of Israel travelled on it, thus taking a somewhat different route from the one the brothers had used on their trips to buy corn. The region was at first well peopled, with many settlements large and small. Then as the days increased, the road ran through stretches where not a grassblade grew, places accurst, quite empty save for flitting figures afar off, assuredly bent on no good — the armed men of the train scarce let their bows from their hands. Yet even at the very worst, civilization did not quite forsake them. It went with them as God went with them, though with some dreadful gaps where it seemed there was no more trust save in God alone. Most of the time, however, it was visible in the shape of protected desert springs, signposts, spy-towers, and rest-places set up and kept in repair by the spirit of commerce, up to their goal — that is to say, to the region where the priceless land of Egypt had already pushed its guards and wards a good piece into the wilderness. After that came the actual border and the definite place of entry, the walls of the fortress Thel.

They reached it in seventeen days or perhaps a few more. Anyhow they considered it to be seventeen and would have scorned to reckon it up. Certainly it was something resembling seventeen, maybe less, maybe more — it might easily have been a bit more, at least if one counted in the days at Beersheba; for the summer sun still had power and for the sake of sparing the father they only got forward morning and evening. Yes, it was fully seventeen days since they had left Mamre and set out, in other words given themselves over for some time to a life of wandering and tenting. And now the days in their hours had brought them to Thel, the fortress, through which their way led to Joseph's kingdom.

Lest anyone be concerned about the difficulties of our travellers
at the forbidding border stronghold, let him be reassured. For, good
heavens! they had passes, papers, and official escort; certainly no
people of the wretched lands, knocking at the gates of Egypt, had
ever travelled so accompanied. For them there were no gates, no
walls, no gratings; the outworks and towers of Thel were thin air,
there was nothing but smiling politeness in lieu of the usual control.
Pharaoh's officers had their orders, of course, touching these travellers, orders to which they bowed. The children of Israel were invited
into the land by no less a person than Menfe's lord of bread, the
shadow-dispenser of the King, Djepnuteefonech, Pharaoh's universal
friend; invited to pasture and settle! Difficulties? Trouble? The very
litter in which they carried their old chieftain within the walls spoke
for itself and its occupant, for it bore the uræus, it came from Pharaoh's storehouses. And he who sat in it, the gentle, solemn, tired old
man, they were bearing him to the near-by rendezvous with his son,
a pretty highly placed personage, who could put in corpse-colour
anyone who even asked these children of Israel any questions, however politely.

It is impossible to picture the officer's bearing as more flattering
and obsequious than it was. The bronze gratings swung open, the
Jacob-people passed through rows of upstretched hands across the
drawbridge with luggage and trotting flocks, into a swampy marshy
pastureland with scattered clumps of trees, dams, ditches, and ham-
lets. This was Pharaoh's land, this was Gosen, also called Kosen,
Kesem, Gosem, and Goshen.

Thus varied were the pronunciations of the little people working
on a strip of land beside the towing-path, bordered by ditches and
reeds. The travellers' route led them along this path and they inquired of the cultivators whether they were on the right road. If they
went on westwards for one short day's travel, they were told, they
would reach the Per-Bastet arm of the Nile and the city of that name,
the abode of the she-cat. But nearer still lay the substantial little city
of Pa-Kos, market and county seat, which probably gave its name to
the district. For looking abroad over the land with its meadows and
marshes, its mirrorlike ponds, its islets of shrubbery and soggy flat-
lands, they saw the pylon of Pa-Koses temple against the morning
sky. It was early when Israel entered into Egypt, having camped before the fort the night before. And they went on for a couple of
hours towards the monument on the horizon. Then they halted and
Jacob's litter was let down from the asses' backs; for somewhere near
the market of Pa-Kos, not far from here, was the place Joseph had
appointed for the meeting, whither he had said he would come to
greet his family.

There is no doubt that this was a definite arrangement. The story says: "He sent Judah on before him to Joseph, to direct his face unto Goshen." But it would be a mistake to conclude that Judah went on to the house of the swaddled one and only thereupon did Joseph make ready his escort and set out to meet his father at Goshen. No, the exalted one was already close at hand and had been for a couple of days. Judah was merely sent out into the neighbourhood to seek him and take him to their father. "Here will Israel wait on his lordship and son," said Jacob. "Put me down. And thou, Jehudah, my son, take three servants and ride hence and find me out thy brother, Rahel's first-born, and tell him where we are." And Judah obeyed.

Certainly he was not long gone, only an hour or so, and came back after he had found Joseph. That he did not come with Joseph is clear from the question which Jacob, as we shall hear, asked as Joseph approached.

It was a charming spot where Jacob waited: three palm trees, growing, it seemed, from one root, shaded his seat, and coolness came from a little pool with tall papyrus and blue- and rose-coloured lotos blossoms. There he sat, surrounded by his sons, the ten, who were eleven as soon as Judah got back. In front of Jacob lay the open meadow and pastureland, with birds flying across and across. His old eyes could look far out to where the twelfth should appear.

Now he saw Judah posting up with his three servants; they nodded and motioned behind them across the land, without saying a word. So he looked where they pointed; and out there afar off something was stirring. There was a glittering and a flashing, a shimmer of colour; it rolled on swiftly and turned into chariots with prancing steeds and shining harness, gay with feathers. Runners were in front and rear and at the sides. They all fixed their eyes on the foremost car, above which were poles with fans. On it came, it grew to full size, and they could see distinct figures in it. Jacob gazed too, his old hands shading his eyes. Now he said to one of his sons who stood beside him:

"Judah!"

"Here am I, Father," he answered.

"Who is the fairly thickset man," asked Jacob, "arrayed in all the splendour of this world, just getting down from his car and the gilded basket of his car, and his neck-ornament is like the rainbow and his garment altogether like the brightness of heaven?"

"That is your son Joseph, Father," replied Judah.

"If it is indeed he," said Jacob, "then I will get up and go to meet him."

And although Benjamin and the others at first tried to prevent him, he rose from the litter with their help in laboured stateliness, limping from the hip more than ever, for he purposely exaggerated his lameness. Alone he went up to the other, who hastened his steps to shorten the distance between them. The man's smiling lips shaped the word "Father" and he held his arms open before him. But Jacob had his own stretched out like a blind man groping; his hands moved as though beckoning, yet partly too as though to protect himself. For as they came close he did not allow Joseph to fall on his neck and hide his face on his shoulder as his son would have done. Instead he peered and searched with his tired old eyes, his head laid back and sideways; peered long and urgently into the Egyptian's face with love and sorrow painted on his own, and did not recognize his son. But it came to pass that Joseph's eyes slowly filled with tears under Jacob's gaze. Their blackness swam in moisture, they overflowed; and lo, they were Rachel's eyes, Rachel's dewy cheeks where Jacob in life's dreamy long-ago had kissed away the tears. Now he knew his son. He let his head fall on the stranger's shoulder and wept bitter tears.

They stood there alone, for the brothers kept back and so did Joseph's train, his marshal, his écuyer, his runners and fan-bearers. And likewise all the curious from the near-by little city held aloof.

"Father, do you forgive me?" asked the son. And in that question he begged forgiveness for much: for playing fast and loose and for deceit; for childish arrogance and incorrigible naughtiness, for self-esteem and blind conceit, for a hundred follies, for which he had atoned with the silence of the dead, living behind the back of the old man who suffered with him. "Father, can you forgive me?"

Jacob straightened himself and stood erect, his self-control restored.

"God has forgiven us," he answered. "You see He has, for He has given you back to me, and Israel can die happy since you have come back."

"And you to me," Joseph said. "Little Father — may I call you that again?"

"If it is agreeable to you, my son," answered Jacob with formality — and old and dignified as he was, he bowed a little before the young man — "I should prefer to have you call me just Father. That the heart may compose itself in seriousness and not jest."

Joseph understood perfectly.

"I hear and obey," said he, and bowed in his turn. "But no more nonsense about dying," he added gaily. "Live, Father! We shall live together, the penance being performed and the long lack made good."

"It was bitterly long," the old man nodded, "for His anger is mighty and His wrath the wrath of a great and mighty God. He is so great and mighty that He can have no other kind of anger, no lesser kind, and He punishes us weaklings that our cries pour out like water."

"It would be understandable," said Joseph conversably, "if He could not in His greatness quite measure, and could not, He who has not His like, quite put Himself in the place of the likes of us. It may be He has a somewhat heavy hand, so that the weight of it is almost crushing even though He does not mean it so and would only prick us and stroke us."

Jacob could not forbear to smile.

"I see," he rejoined, "my son still has his old delightful keenness of perception in God-matters, even of stranger gods. What it has pleased you to say may have some truth in it. Even Abraham in his time often reproached Him for His intemperance, and I know I myself once spoke to Him in the same sense: 'Gently, gently, Lord, not so hasty!' But He is as He is and cannot make Himself more moderate for the sake of our weak hearts."

"A friendly restraining hand," Joseph responded, "as of one whom He loves, can do no harm. But now we will praise His mercy and His forgiving spirit, even though it has taken Him such a long time! For His greatness is like only to His wisdom, I mean the fullness of His thought and the rich meaning of His acts. Always there is added manifold action to His decrees, that is the admirable thing. When He punishes, He indeed means punishment, and this serious purpose is both for His own sake and as means to the furtherance of great events. You, my father, and me he had seized upon roughly and torn us apart so that I died to you. He meant it and He did it so. But at the same time He meant to bring me hither before you in order to save you, that I should provide for your needs, yours and the brothers' and your whole house in the famine, which He designed in manifold meaning and which in its turn was a means to much, but above all that we should come together again. All that is highly admirable in all its interweavings. We blow hot or cold, but His passion is providence and His anger far-seeing goodness. Has your son come somewhere near to fit expression about God the Father?"

"Somewhere near," Jacob confirmed him. "He is the God of life, and life, of course, one only gets somewhere near. This to praise and excuse you. But you need no praise of mine, for you are praised of kings. May your life which you have led in the place whither you were snatched be not all too much in need of excuse."

He said this while his mistrustful gaze travelled down the figure of the Egyptian Joseph, from the striped green and yellow head-dress, the gleaming ornaments, the costly fashionable costume, the rich jewelled tools in his girdle and his hand, on down to the gold buckles of his sandal-shoes.

"Child," he said earnestly, "have you kept your purity among a people whose lust is like the lust of the ass and the stallion?"

"Oh, dear little Father — I mean Father," answered Joseph in some embarrassment, "why does my dear lord trouble so? Let be: the children of Egypt are as other children, not essentially better or worse. Believe me, only Sodom in its time was especially distinguished in evil. Since it was swallowed up in fire and brimstone, things are pretty much the same everywhere in this respect, in other words they are so-so. You yourself once warned God and said to him: 'Not so hasty.' So it will not be a sin if now I, your child, warn you and would like in my love to advise you that since you are here, do not let the people of this country see what you think of them. Do not sit in judgment on their behaviour in the light of your own spirit; rather forget not that we are strangers and Gerim here and Pharaoh has made me great among these children; therefore take a position among them according to God's will."

"I know, my son, I know," answered Jacob and again he made a little bow. "Do not doubt of my respect for the world. — You say you have sons?" he added.

"Yes indeed, Father. From my maiden, the daughter of the sun, a very aristocratic woman. Their names — "

"Maiden? Daughter of the sun? That does not put me off. I have grandchildren from Shechem, and grandchildren from Moab, and have grandchildren from Midian. Why not grandchildren from a daughter of On? After all, it is myself from whom they descend. What are the boys called?"

"Manasseh, Father, and Ephraim."

"Ephraim and Manasseh. Good, my son, my lamb, it is very good that you have sons, two of them, and have given them such names. I will see them. As soon as possible you will bring them before me, if you will."

"At your command, Father," said Joseph.

"And do you know, dear child," Jacob went on softly and wet-eyed, "why it is so good and so fitting before the Lord?"

He laid his arm about Joseph's neck and spoke in his ear, which the son bent to his mouth by turning his face aside.

"Jehosiph, once I let you have the coat of many colours and gave it to you when you begged for it. You know that it did not mean the first-born and the inheritance?"

"I know," answered Joseph as softly.

"But I meant it so, I suppose, or more or less, in my heart," Jacob said; "for my heart loved you and will always love you, whether you live or are dead, more than your brothers. But God tore your garment and admonished me with mighty hand, against which is no rebelling. He separated you and sent you away from my house; the branch He took away from the trunk and planted it out in the world — there is only submission left. Submission of purpose and deed, for the heart knows not submission. He cannot take my heart from me or its election without taking my life. But if this heart neither purposes nor acts according to its love, that is submission. You understand?"

Joseph turned his head towards his father and nodded. He saw tears in the old brown eyes and his own too were wet.

"I hear and know," he whispered, and again turned his ear to listen.

"God has given and has taken you," murmured Jacob, "and He has given you back, but yet not quite, for He has kept you too. He did let the blood of the beast count for that of the son; yet you are not like Isaac, a saved sacrifice. You have spoken of the fullness of His thought and the high double meaning of His counsel and you have spoken wisely. For wisdom is His, but shrewdness is man's, to think himself carefully into the knowledge of wisdom. He has elevated and rejected you both in one, I say it in your ear, beloved child, and you are wise enough to be able to hear it. He has raised you above your brothers just as in your dream — and I have, my darling, ever held your dreams in my heart. But He has raised you in a worldly way, not in the sense of salvation and the inheritance of the blessing. You know that?"

"I hear and know," repeated Joseph, as for a moment he took his ear away and turned his whispering mouth instead.

"You are blessed, my dear one," went on Jacob, "blessed from the heavens above downward and from the depths that lie beneath, blessed with blitheness and with destiny, with wit and with dreams. Still, it is a worldly blessing, not a spiritual one. Have you ever heard the voice of self-denying love? Then you hear it now in your ear, in all submissiveness. God too loves you, child, though at the same time he denies you the inheritance and has punished me because secretly I wanted you to have it. The first-born you are, in earthly things, and a benefactor, as to strangers, so to your own. But through you salvation is not to reach the peoples and the leadership is denied you. You know it?"

"I know," answered Joseph.

"It is well," said Jacob. "It is well to look at fate with cheerful admiring eyes, one's own as well. But I will do as did God, who granted to you in denying to you. You are the set-apart, severed from your stem, you are and shall be no stem. But I will exalt you in the father-rank so that your sons, the first-born, shall be as my sons. Those you are still to get shall be yours, but these mine, for I will take them as sons. You are not like the fathers, my child, for you are no spiritual prince, but a worldly one. Yet you shall sit at my side, at the side of the progenitor, as a father of tribes. Are you content?"

"I thank you as low as your feet," answered Joseph softly, as once more he turned his ear away and put his mouth to Jacob's ear. Then Israel loosed him from his embrace.

THE RECEPTION

THE BYSTANDERS, Joseph's train at a distance on one side and the Jacob-people on the other, had respectfully looked on at the intimate converse between the two. Now they saw that it was over and that Pharaoh's friend was inviting his father to drive on. He turned towards the brothers and went to greet them. They on their side hastened to greet him and all bowed before him and he took to his heart Benjamin, his mother's son.

"Now I will see your wives and children, Turturra," he said to the little man. "The wives and children of all of you I will see and get acquainted with. You must present them before the father and me and I will sit at his side. I have had a tent set up near by to receive you, it was there my brother Judah found me and I came hither from there. Take our father again and carry him, and mount, all of you, and follow me. I will go ahead in my car, but if one of you will drive with me, for instance Judah, who was so kind as to come and meet me, there is room enough for us both and the driver. Judah, it is you whom I invite. Will you come with me?"

And Judah thanked him and mounted into the car that Joseph beckoned up; he drove in the car of the exalted one and stood with him in the gilded basket of the car with the prancing steeds in front with their gay feathers and purple leather harness. Joseph's people followed and then the children of Israel, at their head Jacob in his swaying sedan. The people from the market-place of Pa-Kos ran alongside, for they were eager to see all that went on.

So they came to a fine and spacious tent gaily painted and carpeted, with servants inside; along the walls were garlanded wine-jugs in reed holders; there were cushions and mats, drinking-vessels and water-basins and all sorts of cakes and fruits. Joseph ushered his father and brothers inside, welcomed them again, and offered them refreshments, assisted by his steward, Mai-Sachme, who was already known to the brothers. They were all very merry. He drank with them from golden beakers into which servants strained the wine. Afterwards he sat down with Jacob his father on two campstools at the door of the tent and Jacob's "wives, daughters, and sons and the wives of his sons" passed before him — that is to say, the wives of Joseph's brothers and their children, in short Israel — that he might see them and make their acquaintance. Reuben, his eldest brother, named their names and he spoke cordially to them all. But Jacob was recalling another such scene out of the depth of the past: the day after the night of the wrestling at Peni-el, when he presented his family to Esau, the hairy one: the maids first with their children, then

Leah with her six, and last Rachel, together with him who now sat beside him, whose head had been so lifted up in the world.

"They are seventy," he said proudly to Joseph. His son did not ask whether he meant seventy with or without Jacob and with or without himself; he did not ask for a count, just looked blithely at them as they walked before him, drew Benjamin's youngest sons, Muppim and Rosh, to his knee to stand beside him, and was most interested and pleased when Serah, Asher's child, was set before him and he learned that it was she who had first sung to Jacob the news that Joseph was alive. He thanked the little maid and said as soon as possible, as soon as he had time, she must sing the song to him too upon her eight strings, so that he might hear it. Among the brothers' wives Tamar passed over with her two sons from Judah. Reuben, naming their names, forbore to tell her story; it was too long and would have to go over to a more suitable time. Tall and dark, Tamar strode past, a son on either hand, and bowed haughtily to the shadow-dispenser. For to herself she was saying: "I am in the line of descent and you are not, no matter how much you glitter."

When they had all been introduced, the wives and the sons of the daughters and the daughters of the wives were all served to refreshments in the tent. But Joseph gathered the heads of houses about him and his father and with worldly foresight and circumspection instructed them in the details of his arrangements.

"You are now in the land of Goshen, Pharaoh's beautiful pastureland," he said. "And I will so arrange that you will stay here, where things are still not too Egyptian, and you shall live here as Gerim, free-footed and at will as you did in Canaan. Graze your flocks only on these meadows, build huts and sustain yourselves. Father, for you I have already set up a house, carefully copied from yours at Mamre, so that you may find everything as you are used to it — a little distance from here, nearer the market-place of Pa-Kos, for it is best to live in the country but yet not too far from a town. So did our fathers do, they lived under trees and not between walls but near to Beersheba and Hebron. At Pa-Kos, Per-Sopd, and Per-Bastet on this branch of the Nile you can market your wares; it will be pleasing to Pharaoh my master that you graze, trade, and transact your business. For I will petition His Majesty for an audience and speak before him about you. I will tell him that you are in Goshen and your staying here is clearly desirable, since you have always been shepherds of sheep and goats as were your fathers before you. I must explain to you that keepers of sheep have always been looked at a little askance by the children of Egypt — not so much as swineherds, not that; but they have a slight distaste, which you must not mind, on the contrary we must take advantage of it, so that you can stay here, somewhat apart from the Egyptians, for shepherds belong in the land of Goshen. After all, Pharaoh's flocks graze here, the god's own sheep and goats. So, as you brothers are experienced shepherds and breeders, it is a natural thought and I will suggest it to His Majesty so that he comes upon it by himself, as it were, that he should appoint you, or some of you, as overseers over his flocks. He is very charming and easy to get on with, and you know he has already given orders that I introduce some of you — a few of you, for the whole family would be too many — before him, so he can ask you questions and you can answer. But when he asks about your living and your occupation you will know that that is just for form's sake and that he already knows from me what you do, and I have already hinted at the idea of putting you over his flocks. That will be the idea behind his formal question. So you must back up what I have told him, saying: 'Your servants are people having to do with flocks from our youth up, and our fathers before us.' Then he will arrange that your abode shall be Goshen, the lowland region, and then he will come on the idea that I shall do well to set the most capable of you over his flocks. Which of you it shall be you must decide amongst yourselves, or perhaps our father and dear lord will decide. When all this has been seen to, I will also arrange a private audience for you, my dear father, with the son of the god; for it is fitting he should see you in all the dignity and weightiness of your God-stories and you should see him, who is so tenderly concerned and very much on the right way if not quite the right one for the way. He has himself already commanded in a letter to me that he will see and talk to you. I cannot say how much I look forward to presenting you to him, that he may behold Abram's grandson, the man of the blessing, in all his solemn greatness. He already knows something about you, for instance the story of the peeled wands. But when you stand before him, you will for my sake remember that I have a position among the children of Egypt and you will not criticize these children before Pharaoh their King because of the way their customs appear to you; for that would be a mistake."

"Certainly not, have no fear, my lord son and dear child," answered Jacob. "Your old father knows how to have consideration before the greatness of the world, for it too is from God. Our thanks for the house and dwelling you have made ready in the land of Goshen. Thither will Israel now go and muse upon all this to embody it into his tales."

ISRAEL STANDS BEFORE PHARAOH

WITH amazement we note that this story nears its end. Who would have thought that it would ever be finished or the well run dry? The truth is, it is ending just as little as it ever began. It is only that it cannot go on for ever; at some point it must make its adieux and the lips of the teller must close. It must in all common sense set a limit to itself, since end it has none. Faced by the infinite it is the part of reason to yield — indeed, it is proverbial that the more reasonable party always does.

The story, then, despite certain previously made statements about its immoderate character, does preserve a sound sense of proportion; and hence begins to fix its eye on its last little hour, just as Jacob did, when the seventeen years he had still to live were coming to an end and he set about putting his house in order. Seventeen years, that is the limit which is likewise fixed for our story, or rather the story fixes for itself by reason of its innate sense of proportion. Never, in its most expansive days, did it contemplate living longer than Jacob did — or at least only so much longer as would take to recount his death. Its proportions in space and time are patriarchal enough already. Old and satiated with life, satisfied that there should be a limit to all things, it will then set its feet together and be still.

But as long as it lasts it will not falter or tire but fill out its time and sturdily record what everybody already knows, that Joseph kept his word and brought before Pharaoh's face a group of his brothers, five in number. After that he formally presented Jacob, his father, to the lovely son of Aton, and the patriarch conducted himself with great dignity, if by worldly standards a thought too condescend-ingly. Of that anon. Joseph himself personally asked for the audience with the lord of the breath of sweetness, and it is worth while to notice how familiar tradition shows itself with the usage concerning the conceptions "up" and "down." One went down to Egypt: the children of Israel had come down to Goshen's meadows. But if you went down farther in the same direction you went up, that is to say upstream, towards Upper Egypt, and the story says quite correctly that Joseph betook himself up to Akhetaton, the city of the horizon in the hare district, the only capital of the land, to show Hor in the Palace that the brothers and the family of his father had come to him and to suggest that one could not do a cleverer thing than to set these experienced shepherds over the royal flocks in the land of Goshen. Pharaoh took pleasure in the thought which had come to him, and when the five brothers stood before him he talked of it to them and appointed them for his shepherds.

This happened not many days after Israel's arrival in Egypt, as soon as Pharaoh next visited On, his beloved city, and gleamed in the horizon of his palace as he had done when Joseph was first brought before him to interpret his dreams. This little pause had been made for Jacob's sake, the man of many days, that he need not have a long journey to Pharaoh's seat. At this time he was in Joseph's house at Menfe together with the five selected brothers, the two sons of Leah,

Reuben and Judah; one of Bilhah, Naphtali; one of Zilpah's, Gaddiel; and Benoni-Benjamin, Rachel's son. They had come up with their father to the city of the swaddled one on the west bank and were at the house of their exalted brother. There Asenath the maid greeted the father of her abductor and the Egyptian grandsons were brought before him, that he might try them and bless them. The old man was deeply moved. "The Lord's kindness is overpowering," said he; "He has let me to see your face, my son which I had not thought to see, and lo, God has showed me also your seed." And he asked the bigger boy his name.

"Manasseh," he replied.

"And what is your name?" he next asked the smaller one.

"Ephraim," was the reply.

"Ephraim and Manasseh," repeated the old man, naming first the name he had last heard. Then he held Ephraim at his right knee and Manasseh at the other, caressed them, and corrected their Hebrew pronunciation.

"How often have I told you both," Joseph chid them, "to say it like that?"

"Ephraim and Manasseh cannot help it," said the old man. "Your own mouth, my son, is already a little wry. Do you want to grow into a multitude in the name of your father?" he asked the two.

"We should like to," answered Ephraim, who had remarked that he was the favourite. And Jacob blessed them both for the time being.

Next it was reported that Pharaoh had come to the dwelling of Re-Horakhte at On, and Joseph drove down to him, followed by the five chosen brethren. But Jacob was carried. Should anyone ask why he, the man of years and stateliness, was not the first to be received in audience by Pharaoh, instead of the brothers, as we are told was the case, the answer is: for the sake of heightening the interest. In the ordering of any festal occasion, the best feature is seldom put first. It begins as a rule with some minor attraction, then comes something a bit better, and only at the end does true excellence and honour come swaying up, while the crescendo of applause and shouting rises to its climax. That is an old dispute, the struggle for precedence. But from the ceremonial point of view it was always an idle one. The poorer attraction has the *pas;* when it insists, its betters will always give way with a smile.

Furthermore, the audience with the brothers had something practical in view, it was a business appointment, with a certain matter to discuss and settle. Whereas Jacob's presentation to the young god was merely a graceful formality, with so little content indeed that Pharaoh was gravelled for lack of subject-matter and hit on nothing better than to ask the patriarch how old he was. His talk with the sons had more sense; on the other hand it was quite stereotyped, being like all the King's audiences, arranged beforehand by his ministers.

The five brothers were ushered by the mincing chamberlain into the council- and audience-chamber; young Pharaoh sat there surrounded by a ring of standing palace officials. He bore the crook, the scourge, and a life-symbol and sat under a beribboned baldachin, on a carved chair of the ancient and traditional uncomfortableness, yet he somehow contrived to relax and sit at ease in it, for he did not approve of the hieratic posture of the limbs, the stiffness of which he felt was out of harmony with the lovely naturalness of his god. His first mouthpiece, the lord of the bread, Djepnuteefonech, the provider, stood at the right forepost and saw to it that the interview, which was conducted through an interpreter, ran off according to plan. The newcomers duly brought their foreheads into contact with the pavement of the hall; then they mumbled a pæan of adulation, not too long a one, having been drilled by Joseph, who had so composed it that it answered the court requirements without offending their own beliefs. It was not translated, being a mere introductory flourish; Pharaoh thanked them for it at once, in his shy treble, and added that His Majesty was sincerely glad to welcome before his throne the worthy relatives of his faithful shadow-dispenser and uncle. "What is your occupation?" he next inquired.

It was Judah who answered, saying that they were shepherds, both they and also their fathers, and they understood every sort of cattle-breeding from the ground up. They had come hither to this country because there was no longer pasture for their flocks, the famine being sore in the land of Canaan. If they might venture a request before Pharaoh's countenance, it was this: that they might dwell in the land of Goshen, where they had for the time pitched their tent.

Ikhnaton's sensitive face betrayed a faint distaste when the interpreter pronounced the word for shepherd. He turned to Joseph, with the prescribed words: "Your kin have come unto you. The land of Egypt is before you and before them; in the best of the land make your father and your brethren to dwell; in the land of Goshen they can dwell, it will be very agreeable to My Majesty." Joseph prompted him by a glance, and he added: "My Father who is in heaven has also given My Majesty an idea which the heart of Pharaoh rejoices in: you, my friend, know your brothers and their activities better than anyone else; you shall set them according to their activities over my flocks and make them rulers over my cattle. My Majesty graciously and cordially commands that the indentures be written out. I have been very much gratified."

And next it was Jacob's turn. His entrance was most stately and labouring. He deliberately exaggerated his age and infirmities, that they might weigh down the balance against any Nimrod impressiveness and strengthen his God not to give ground. He was perfectly aware that his courtier son was uneasy lest the father behave with condescension to Pharaoh or begin talking about the ram Bindidi; with filial concern he had explicitly warned him against it. Jacob had no idea of doing so; on the other hand he was determined to give no ground, and so set up as a defence this overpowering impression of great age. He had been dispensed from any genuflections, being presumably too stiff; and also it had been decided to make the audience very brief to spare the old man long standing.

They looked at each other for a while in silence: the luxurious young modern and dreamer of dreams about God, curiously rising a little out of his gilt and adorned little box and his over-easy posture, and Yitzchak's son, the father of twelve. They looked at each other, all lapped in together as they were in this single hour, yet ages apart: the sickly boy, heir to an immemorial crown, striving with his feeble might to distil from millennial accumulations of religious thought the attar of a tender and sentimental religion of love; and the wise, experienced old man, whose position in time was at the very source and fount of widely developing being. Pharaoh soon became embarrassed. He was used to begin with the greeting hymn, according to protocol, and not to addressing the person who stood before him. But neither, we are told, was Jacob wholly unmindful of the opening formula; for on entering as on leaving he solemnly "blessed" Pharaoh. This must be taken quite literally: the patriarch substituted the blessing for the routine jingle of adulation; not lifting both hands, as he always did before his God, but only the right, stretching it straight out towards Pharaoh — it shook in the most impressive manner as he did it — as though from this distance he was putting a fatherly hand upon the young man's head.

"May the Lord bless you, King over Egypt," he said, in the voice of advanced old age. Pharaoh was greatly impressed.

"And how old might you be, little grandfather?" he inquired in amazement.

And here again Jacob exaggerated. We are told that he reckoned his age at a hundred and thirty years — an entirely arbitrary figure, for in the first place he did not know with any exactness; even today, in his part of the world, people are not very clear on the point of age, and aside from that, we know that he was to live a hundred and six years in all, an age within the bounds of the possible, if close to its extreme limit. And according to this reckoning he had by now not yet reached ninety, though very well preserved for so considerable an age. But the question gave him a chance to clothe himself in the uttermost solemnity before Pharaoh. His gesture was that of a blind prophet, his speech deliberately measured: "The days of the years of my pilgrimage are an hundred and thirty years," he said, and added: "few and evil have the days of the years of my life been and have not attained unto the days of the years of the life of my fathers in the days of their pilgrimage."

Pharaoh shuddered. He was destined to die young, and his sensitive nature was attuned to the idea; so that the mere thought of all that mass of life seemed to horrify him.

"Ye heavenly powers!" said he, in something like alarm. "And have you always lived at Hebron, little grandfather, in the wretched Retenu?"

"Mostly, my child," answered Jacob, so that it went through the pleated one at the side of the canopy like a stroke. And Joseph shook his head warningly at his father. Jacob saw him but pretended not to see. Obstinately continuing to bear down with all the oppressive evidence of age, he added:

"Two thousand and three hundred, according to the wise men, are the years of Hebron, and even Mempi, the city of tombs, does not go back so far."

Again Joseph hastily shook his head. But the old man paid not the least heed, and Pharaoh behaved with great compliance.

"It may be so, grandfather, it may be so," he hastened to say. "But how can you call your lifetime evil when you begot a son whom Pharaoh loves as the apple of his eye, so that none is greater in the two lands save only the lord of the double crown?"

"I begot twelve sons," answered Jacob, "and he was one of their number. Among them is cursing as well as blessing, and blessing as well as cursing. Some have been rejected and remain the chosen. But as one has been chosen, he remains rejected in love. As I lost him, so should I find him, and as I found him, so was he lost to me. Upon a pedestal was he lifted up, and withdrew from among the number of those I begot; but in his stead there come in those whom he raised up to me, before the one the other."

Pharaoh listened with his mouth open to these sibylline remarks, which had become even more obscure by the time the interpreter finished with them. He looked imploringly at Joseph, but the latter kept his eyes cast down.

"Yes, yes," said he. "Of course, little grandfather, that is quite clear. Well and wisely said, as Pharaoh loves to have it. But now you must not tire yourself with standing longer before My Majesty. Go in peace, and live, so long as you have joy of it, years without number added to your hundred and thirty!"

And Jacob blessed Pharaoh again with lifted hand and then, having given ground by not even the thickness of a hair, he went hence out of his presence, with the same majestic formality and the same labouring gait as before.

OF THE TWINKLING EYE

It may be in place here to set down a faithful account of Joseph's stewardship, in order once for all to take the ground from under the feet of the half-instructed chatterers whom we have always with us, very ready with their harsh judgment and abuse. The responsibility for these censures, which several times went so far as to use the word "atrocious" to describe Joseph's conduct of his office, must rest —the statement may not be shirked — first of all upon the earliest narration of the story, whose laconic style so little approaches the way in which it first told itself, I mean in the happening realism of "once upon a time."

They are hard dry facts, to which the first written account of the activities of Pharaoh's great man of business goes back; they give neither an idea of the general admiration which his measures originally called forth, nor any explanation of it, though it often came close to idolatry. Some of Joseph's titles — such as Provider and Lord of Bread — were taken quite literally by great masses of the people; who hazily thought of him as a sort of Nile deity, yes, an incarnation of Hapi himself, the preserver and life-giver.

This legendary popularity which Joseph achieved — he had probably counted on it from the beginning — rested most of all on the mixed and changeable character of his technique; which operated as it were on two planes, and in a way quite peculiar to him. In short, he used the magic of his wit to reconcile conflicting aims. I use the word "wit" because this principle has its place in the little cosmos of our tale, and quite early on it was said that wit is of the nature of a messenger to and fro and of a go-between betwixt opposed spheres and influences: for instance between the power of the sun and of the moon, between father- and mother-inheritance, between the blessing of the day and the blessing of the night, yes, to put it directly and succinctly, between life and death. This spirit of mediation, brisk, blithe, and nimble at its reconciling task, was not represented by any deity in the pantheon of Joseph's adopted country, the land of the black earth. Thoth, the scribe and guide of the dead, inventor of manifold skills, comes closest to it. Pharaoh only, before whom information about the divine was borne from distant lands, Pharaoh had inklings of a more consummate development of this god-nature. In fact the favour Joseph found in his eyes was due preponderantly to the circumstance that Pharaoh had recognized in him traits of the adroit child of the cave, the master of pranks, and rightly said to himself that no king could wish better for himself than to have as his minister a manifestation and incarnation of this most happy god-nature.

It was in the form of Joseph himself that the children of Egypt got acquainted with the winged figure; if they did not take it into their pantheon it was only because the place was occupied by Djehuti, the white ape. However, the experience meant for them an enrichment of their religion in a certain field and a highly diverting experience as well: I mean in the field of magic, and the change their legendary conception of it underwent to their own great amazement. To the children of Egypt magic was a serious and solemn business and gave them much concern. Its office was to build up walls against the dragon of evil, walls as thick as possible in order to fend it off and prevent its penetration. That was all the meaning the word had for them, and in that light they saw Joseph's preparations against famine, his hoarding of grain, the host of bins he built. But now for the first time they were seeing magic as a conjunction of evil and foresight. I mean this: that the shadow-dispenser, thanks to his foresight, led the dragon by the nose, made it serve their profit and advantage in purposes which the dragon, bent only on destruction, could never have thought of. This was magic married to enlightenment and good cheer, it made the children of Egypt laugh instead of cry.

In fact there was much laughter among the people, admiring laughter, at the way in which Joseph coolly exploited the price situation in dealing with the rich and great to the advantage of his master, Hor in the Palace, making him gold and silver by pouring vast sums into Pharaoh's treasury in exchange for the corn he gave the property-owners. He was displaying therein a shrewd loyalty to the divine, which is the essence of all dutiful, devoted, and rewarding service. But hand in hand with this service went the free distribution of grain among the hungry little people of the cities, in the name of young Pharaoh, the god-dreamer, to whom thus accrued as much and even more profit than to Joseph by his gilding. It was a combination of crown politics and concern for the little man, a novel, ingenious, an invigorating policy, the attractiveness of which can be gathered from the original narrator only by those who study his style with some care and know how to read between the lines. The relation of our source to its own original (I mean the self-narrating events themselves) is betrayed by certain crude phrases of comic relief, which seem like survivals of a popular farce; through these the character of the original events faintly glimmers. For instance, when the famished folk cried before Joseph: "Give us bread; for why should we die in your presence for that the money faileth?" A very poor way of talking, which does not occur elsewhere in the Pentateuch. But Joseph answered in the same style: namely, with the words: "Give your cattle and I will give you for your cattle, if money fail." Of course the needy folk and Pharaoh's great keeper of the market did not treat in this key, rather the style is reminiscent of the mood in which the people experienced the actual event — a farcical mood quite devoid of moral self-pity.

Still, the venerable document has not been able to stand aloof from the reproach of exploitation and harshness in Joseph's proceedings; indeed, it has evoked the moral condemnation of serious minds, and quite naturally. We learn that Joseph, in the course of the years of the lean ears, first gathered all the money in the country unto himself — that is, into Pharaoh's treasury — then took the people's cattle in pawn and then their lands; and finally drove them from hearth and home, sent them to work on strange soil as servants of the state. It is an unpleasant hearing. But the actual situation was quite different, as we can glean from certain remarkable turns of phrase. One reads: "He gave them bread in exchange for horses and for the flocks and for the cattle of the herds and for the asses; and he fed them with bread for all the cattle of that year." But the translation is inexact and makes us miss a certain reference which the original does not neglect to give. For instead of "fed" there is a word which means led: "and led them," it says, "with bread for all their cattle for that year." It is an odd expression and was deliberately chosen. For it is taken from shepherd's language and means protect or pasture, the gentle and careful tendance of helpless creatures, especially of an easily frightened flock of sheep. For an ear practised in mythology, the rôle and quality of the good shepherd is ascribed to the son of Jacob in these striking and traditional words: the shepherd who guards the sheep and leads them upon green meadows and to fresh waters. Here, as in the conventional comedy phrase quoted above, the colour of the original happening strikes through; this strange word, "led," which has as it were slipped out of reality into the narrative text, betrays the light in which the people saw Pharaoh's great favourite. Their judgment is quite distinct from that which state moralists think today to pass upon him; for cherishing, feeding, and leading are the activities of a god known as "lord of the under-earthly sheepfold."

There is no shaking the factual statements of the text. Joseph sold to those who had property, that is to the haughty district barons and owners of large estates, at the highest price the market would bear; and "put money," that is to say exchange, into the royal treasury; so that soon there was no money in the narrower sense of the word, that is to say precious metal in any form, among the people. Money in the sense of coin there was none; and all sorts of cattle had always been among the exchange values given for corn. That was not cause and effect, nor was it any rise of prices; any picture suggesting that Joseph used the scarcity of currency to take away the inhabitants' horses, oxen, and sheep is only a partial picture. Cattle are money too; they are money in the most definite sense, as is clear from our modern word "pecuniary"; and even before the well-to-do paid with their gold and silver vessels they paid with their flocks and herds. There is, however, no mention of their passing over the last cow to Pharaoh's stables and pens. It was not stalls and sheepfolds that Joseph had built for seven years on end, but granaries; and he would not have had space or use for all that cattle-money. If one is ignorant of the methods of money-lenders certainly one cannot follow a story like this. The cattle were loaned — or pawned, whichever you prefer. They remained for the most part on the estates and farmyards, but they ceased to belong to the occupants in the old sense of the word. That is, they were their property and yet they were not; it was only conditionally and as a lien on the property; and if our first authority fails us anywhere, it is here: it does not give the clear impression, which nevertheless it is so important to get, that Joseph's proceedings had as their consistent goal the dislocation of the property concept and its transformation into a state which was neither ownership nor not-ownership, but a conditioned feudal tenure.

For as one year of drought and low water was added to another; as the face of the harvest queen remained averted, no grass grew nor any grain; as the womb of mother earth was closed and she let no child of hers to prosper; then great parts of the black earth which up till now had been in private hands passed to the crown. For the text has it: "And Joseph bought all the land of Egypt for Pharaoh, for the Egyptians sold every man his field." For what? For seed-corn. Scholars agree that this must have been towards the end of the succession of hungry years, when the bonds of infertility began to loosen, the rainfall returned to more or less normal, and the fields would have been capable of yield if one could have sown them. Hence the words of the petitioners: "Wherefore shall we die before your eyes, both we and our land? Buy us and our land for bread and we and our land will be servants unto Pharaoh; and give us seed that we may live and not die, that the land be not desolate." Who is it speaking? These are spoken words, not a cry from the people. It is a proposal, an offer, made by individuals, a group, a class of men up till then very untractable and antagonistic, the great estate-owners and district princes, on whom Pharaoh Akhmose, at the beginning of the dynasty, had had to confer great titles, like First King's Son of the Goddess Nekhbet, and great independent landed possessions as well. They were old-fashioned recalcitrant feudal lords, whose out-of-date methods, injurious to the general weal, had long been a thorn in the flesh of the modern state. Joseph the statesman exploited the crisis to force these arrogant gentlemen into compliance with the spirit of the times. It was they with whom in the first instance the exploitations and migrations we hear of had to do; what happened under this wise and resolute minister was the breaking up of the still existing large estates and the settling of peasant owners on the smaller ones, farmers who became responsible to the state for an up-to-date management, improvement of the canals, and irrigation of the soil. The result was a more even distribution of the land among the people and an improvement of agriculture under crown supervision. Many "first sons of the king" became such tenant peasants or moved into the town, many a farmer was taken from the soil he had worked and put on one of the newly divided small properties, while his own passed into stranger hands. And if these shifts were practised in other cases, if one hears that the lord of bread parcelled out the people "by cities," that is to say in districts lying roundabout cities, and from one soil to another, Joseph did this in accordance with a deliberate policy of education involving that very remodelling of the property concept into something which was both preservation and abrogation.

The essential condition for all state requisition of state property was the continuation of the levy of the fifth part, the same tax by means of which, during the fat years, Joseph had amassed the magic store into which he now dipped; it was the promulgation of this tax in permanence, its confirmation to everlasting time. Note that this imposition, without the shifting of populations, would have been the only form in which the "sale" of the lands, together with their occupants — for the occupants were included in the bargain — could have expressed itself. It has never been sufficiently emphasized that Joseph made only nominal use of this feature (the sale of themselves by the small farmers, to which they had consented in order not to be ruined). Nobody has pointed out that for his own part Joseph never used the word "slavery" or "villeinage," which for easily understood reasons he did not like. The imposition of the tax meant in itself that land and people were no longer free in the old sense; it received no stronger emphasis, but in actual practice it meant that those who were provided with seed-corn no longer worked exclusively for themselves, but partly for Pharaoh, in other words for the state, the public land. To this extent their labour was the forced labour of serfs — every friend of humanity is free to use the word if at the same time he is ready to apply it to himself as well.

And yet if we observe the measure of serfdom which Joseph laid upon those who submitted to it, we shall feel that it can scarcely be called by that name without exaggeration. If he had forced them to surrender three quarters or even a half of their crops, that would have made them more sensible of the fact that they themselves and their fields no longer belonged to them. But twenty out of a hundred — malice itself must concede that that was keeping the exploitation within bounds. Four fifths of their harvest remained to the people for the new sowing and their own and their children's food. In view of this it is allowable to speak of the serfdom as nominal. Down the centuries ring the words of gratitude with which those under the yoke greeted their oppressor: "Thou hast saved our lives; let us find grace in the sight of my lord and we will be Pharaoh's servants." What more do we want? But if anyone does want more, let me tell him that Jacob himself, with whom Joseph repeatedly discussed the matter, expressly approved the tax, that is as to its amount if not as to its destination. If, said he, he had now increased to a multitude of people, for whom a constitution was to be laid down, then the people ought to regard themselves only as factors of their soil, and would have to pay the tax of the fifth — but not to any Hor-in-the-Palace, rather to Jahwe, the only King and Lord, to whom all fields belong and who grants all possession. But of course he understood that his lord son, the set-apart one, governing a heathen world, must deal in these things after his own way. And Joseph smiled.

But there was little realization of the actual state of things among those submitting to the tax, so long as they remained in the dwelling-places which were no longer theirs. Probably the imposition was too mild for that. Hence the measures of migration: they were the neces-sary complement to the tribute, which was not enough by itself to make the farmers realize the "sale" of their lands and establish the fact of their new relation to it. A husbandman who stopped on the same soil he had farmed for years would easily remain confused by obsolete conceptions and some day, out of forgetfulness, might lift his head against the claims of the crown. But if he was obliged to leave his own place and receive another from Pharaoh's hand, the lien character of his ownership was made much more perceptible to him.

But the remarkable thing was that the ownership still remained ownership. The criterion of free and personal property is the right of sale and inheritance; and these Joseph permitted to continue. In the whole of Egypt from that time on, all the land belonged to Phar-aoh; at the same time it could be sold and inherited. Not idly have we spoken of the way Joseph dealt with the property concept, spiriting it away and putting in its place an equivocal, double-faced picture; so that when the average man tried to fix it in his eye, it turned into a dissolving view. Nothing had been destroyed or cancelled; but there was a general feeling of neither here nor there, exceedingly confusing until one got used to it. Joseph's economic system, in short, was an astonishing mixture of socialization and freehold occupancy by the individual — a mixture which the children of Egypt thought of as "magic," a manifestation of a divinity benign and cunning at once.

The tradition emphasizes that the reform did not extend to the landed possessions of the church: the priesthoods of the numerous shrines endowed by the state, especially the landed property of Amun-Re, remain unmolested and tax-free. "Only the land of the

priests bought he not." That too was wise — if wisdom is a shrewdness amounting to guile, which knows how to disarm its antagonist
while yielding him all outward respect. This consideration for Amun
and the lesser local *lumina* was certainly not to Pharaoh's mind. He
would have liked to see the god of Karnak cropped and plundered,
and grumbled boyishly to his shadow-dispenser. But little Mama, the
mother of the god, agreed with Joseph; with her backing he stood
out for sparing the belief of the little man in the old gods of the
country, though Pharaoh would gladly have destroyed them root and
branch in favour of the doctrine of his Father in heaven. He tried
to gain his end by other means with which Joseph could not cope;
for he was too jealous to understand that the people would be much
more accessible to the new if they were allowed to keep their traditional habits of faith and form. And as for Amun himself, Joseph considered it altogether a mistake to give the ram-headed one the impression that the whole agrarian reform was directed against him and
intended as a means to diminish his power. That would only have made
him stir up the people against it. It was better to keep him quiet with
a polite gesture. The events of all these years, the plenty, the abundance, the preparation, and the saving of the people from famine,
were quite enough to weigh down the scale for Pharaoh and the
prestige of his teaching; while the riches his sale of corn got and went
on getting for the great house meant indirectly such a heavy loss to
the state god that the bowing before his anciently sacred right of
freedom from taxation looked like sheer irony. It was another case
of the same kind of blithe double-dealing which the children of
Israel were so ready to admire in their good shepherd.

Pharaoh's pacifism, his unwillingness to wage war, put a tool in the
hands of him of Karnak. But it was taken away again, at least deprived
of much of its keenness, by Joseph's system of grants and mortgages,
which, at least for a time, could restrain the arrogance aroused in our
common humanity by a rule grown fastidious and unwilling to use
force. Great were the dangers invoked upon the realm of Thutmose
the conqueror by the amiable nature of his successor far on in time.
The word had everywhere gone round, and was known in all the
chancelleries, that in Egypt the key was no longer set by the iron-
hearted Amun-Re but by a temperamental deity of flowery spring
and twittering birds: a god who at no price whatever would dye his
sword in blood. Not to make a fool of such a god would have been
asking too much of any ordinary common sense. A tendency to disrespect, to defection and betrayal, gained ground. The tributary
eastern provinces from Seir to Karmel were in a state of ferment.
There was an unmistakable movement towards independence among
the Syrian princes, in which they were supported by the warlike
Hatti, pressing southwards. At the same time the desert Bedouins of

the east and south had also heard of the reign of sweetness and light. They set fire to Pharaoh's cities and even to some extent took possession of them. Amun's daily summons to vigorous measures, though probably chiefly domestic politics directed against the "teaching," were in foreign affairs only too well justified. The heroic old here aligned itself effectively and convincingly against the effeminate new; and Pharaoh felt greatly stressed, on account of his Father in heaven. But the famine and Joseph together came to his rescue; they deprived Amun's war-cry of much of its force, by putting the wavering little kings of Asia under economic bonds. True, the mildness of Aton was not literally preserved in the process; but what harshness there was amounted to little compared to the fact that it saved Pharaoh from fleshing his sword. The outcry from those thus bound with golden chains to Pharaoh's throne was often so shrill that we can still hear it today; but we are not likely to dissolve in pity at the sound. It is true that to get grain not only silver and wood had to be delivered; actually the youth had to be sent down to Egypt as hostages and pledges. That was a hardship no doubt; but it need not break our hearts, for we know that the children of Asiatic princes were wonderfully well taken care of in elegant pensions at Thebes and Menfe and enjoyed a better upbringing than they would have had at home. "Hence," we hear, "are their sons, their daughters and the wooden furniture of their houses," but of whom is that said? Of Milkili, for instance, the city King of Ashdod; and of him it is hinted that his love for Pharaoh was not of the most reliable, and might very well need strengthening by the presence of his wife and children in Egypt.

In short, I cannot bring myself to see in all this any trustworthy evidence of signal cruelty, which moreover was not in Joseph's character. I am more inclined to agree with the people whom he "led," and to see in it a little trick performed with a twinkle in the eye by a shrewd and skilful servant deity. This was the general view of Joseph's conduct of business far beyond the confines of Egypt. It aroused laughter and admiration — and what is there better that a man can get among men than the kind of admiration which, while it binds hearts together, at the same time lightens them, so that they may laugh.

SUBMISSION

IN what remains of our narrative it will be well to turn a realistic eye upon the ages of the characters involved in it; for there has been much confusion and error on the subject, and the arts of painting and poetry have not helped to clear it up, but rather the reverse. I am not referring to Jacob. He is always represented, in his last period, as weighed down with years and almost blind (in fact his eyesight got much worse at the end and he exploited the weakness, taking as his model Isaac, the blind giver of the blessing, in order to heighten the impression of solemnity). But in the case of Joseph and his brothers and sons, tradition has inclined to keep them all more or less at a fixed age and perennially youthful, so that there is a great gap between them and the weight of years on the father's head.

It is necessary to correct this legendary vagueness and the resulting false impression, and to point out that it is only death — that is to say, the opposite of all happenings — which can arrest the flow of time and preserve a character as in amber. Life, on the contrary, that is to say a living character in a story, cannot stop as it is, the man must grow older as the story goes on. We ourselves have all got older as we told and listened to this tale; and that is another reason why we should be clear in the matter. I myself confess that I have found it more enjoyable to talk about the charming seventeen-year-old lad or even about the thirty-year-old man than about one hovering round fifty-five. But still we all owe it to life and the processes of life to accept and even insist upon the truth. Jacob, living in the land of Goshen, honoured and cherished by his children and his children's children, was increasing his age by another seventeen years to round them out to the venerable but still possible limit of one hundred and six; the while his set-apart darling, Pharaoh's universal friend, changed from a mature man to an elderly one, whose hair and beard — if the one had not been shorn and covered with an elaborate wig, the other kept smooth-shaven by the custom of the country — would have shown much white among the dark. True, the black Rachel-eyes preserved the friendly sparkle which had always made them a joy to mankind. All in all, despite natural change, the Tammuz-attribute of beauty remained to him, thanks to the double blessing whose child he had ever been and which was a blessing not only from above and in the nature of wit, but also a blessing of the deep which lies under and imparts maternal favour to the bodily form. Not seldom such a nature even experiences a second youth, which gives back to the figure something of its youthful lines. There are some misleading representations which depict Joseph standing by Jacob's death-bed; the violence they do to the truth is the less in that Rachel's first-born, some lustrums earlier, had grown heavier and more fleshy but by this time had got distinctly thinner again and looked more like his twenty-year-old than his forty-year-old self.

But it is certainly quite irresponsible and fantastic to depict the young Egyptian gentlemen Ephraim and Manasseh as curly haired children of seven or eight at the scene of their blessing by their departing grandfather. It is clear that they were then princely young cavaliers at the beginning of the twenties, in dandified belaced and beribboned court-costumes, with buckled sandals and chamberlains' fans; and the otherwise incomprehensible thoughtlessness of these portrayals can only be explained by a few unrealistic phrases in the early text, which says that Jacob put his grandsons on his knees, or rather that Joseph "brought them out from between his knees" after the old man had "kissed them and embraced them." Such treatment would have been most offensive to the young people; it is regrettable that the tradition countenances such nonsense; it can only be due to the desire to make time stand still for most of the people in the story and let Jacob alone grow old, out of all reason, even to a hundred and forty-seven years!

Let us see what actually happened on the visit in question, the second of three visits which Joseph paid his father in the latter end of his life. But first it will be well to cast a brief glance upon the foregoing seventeen years, during which the children of Israel settled down in the land of Goshen, grazed and sheared and milked, transacted their affairs, presented Jacob with great-grandsons, and addressed themselves to becoming a multitude of folk. It can never be said quite definitely how many of these seventeen years fell in the famine time, because it is not clear whether there were seven or "only" five of these (the quotation-marks are ironical, for the figure five is just as rich in associations as the figure seven). As I have pointed out before, the uncertainty was due to the variation in the degree of the affliction from year to year. In the sixth year the provider swelled at Menfe not less than fifteen ells in the season of increase. It went red and green by turns, as is its way when things are going well, and deposited a plenty of fertilizer. But in the next year it was undernourished and under-nourishing past all belief. So it was a matter of opinion whether these two years were to be counted with the five lean-ribbed ones, as the sixth and seventh, or not. In any case, round the time that this question was being discussed in all the temples and on all the street-corners, Joseph's work of agrarian reform was finished and he continued to govern on its foundation as Pharaoh's first mouthpiece and to feed his sheep while shearing them of a fifth.

It cannot be said that he saw his father and brothers very often. They had their tents close by compared with the distance that had once been between them; but even so it was a good journey between their place and Joseph's residence in the city of the swaddled one; and moreover, between his administrative duties and his court functions he was overworked. They saw much less of him than one would have gathered from the last three visits he made to his father in quick succession. But Jacob and his people took no offence, their silence was not only consent but also recognition of the existing obstacles. We, who overheard that murmured conversation between Jacob and Rachel's first-born at their meeting, as they stood alone with the seventy on one side and Joseph's train on the other, we know how to give to that mutual reserve — for it was mutual — its true and somewhat melancholy meaning. It meant submission and renunciation. Joseph was the one set apart, at once lifted up and withdrawn. He was severed from the tribe and was not to be a tribe. The fate of his lovely mother, "rejected despite goodwill," was, with appropriate variation, also her son's fate; its individual formula being "denying love." The truth was understood and accepted; far more than distance or preoccupation it was the reason for the reserve.

And how clearly, how chillingly the reserve is expressed in the phrase used by Jacob when he made a certain request of his son; I mean the rhetorical flourish: "if now I have found grace in thy sight." It is proof, it is almost shamefaced evidence of the distance between father and son, between Joseph and Israel. It reminds us, as it reminded Jacob, of that early dream, the dream of the threshing-floor, when the eleven Kokabim together with sun and moon had bowed down before the dreamer. Joseph's dream had stirred the brothers up to a fiery mortal hatred and ravished them to the evil deed for which they had suffered. How strange it is to think — as they too thought among themselves without saying so — that their misdeed had achieved its purpose and brought them to their desired goal! True, it had turned out, contrary to all reasonable expectation, that they had actually lain on their bellies before him. Yet they had not sold him in vain into the world and also to the world; for he had lost and they had won. The inheritance which the man of feeling had in his wilfulness wanted to give to Joseph was lost to him forever; from Rachel the beloved it had passed to Leah the rejected. Was that not worth a little bowing and scraping?

"If now I have found grace in thy sight." It was on the first of the three visits that Jacob so spoke to the beloved and lost one; at the time when he felt his life fast waning and knew that it was far on in its last quarter, rising low and late and red and wearily over the horizon before the final darkness. He was not ill; he could tell that there was no question of a sudden decline. For he had good control over his life and his powers, he reckoned shrewdly what was left and knew that the end was not quite yet. Still it was fully time to impress on him who alone had power to fulfil it a wish he had at heart, a wish which quite personally concerned him, Jacob.

So he sent to Joseph and begged him to come. Whom did he send? Naphtali, of course, Bilhah's son, the nimble one, for Naphtali was still nimble of limbs and tongue, despite his years. We must speak of this matter of the brothers' ages because here too the tradition is careless and blurred. If we stop to consider we must conclude that the whole span covered a period between forty-seven and seventy-eight years. For Benjamin, the little man, was not less than twenty-one years younger than Zebulon, who was the third youngest before Joseph, and he was sixty-eight years old. I speak of this in order that when Jacob gathers his sons about him in his last hours for cursing and blessing, we shall not picture the tent as full of young men in the prime of life. I repeat that Naphtali despite his five-and-seventy years still rejoiced in the same sinewy long legs and the same tongue like a bell-clapper; nor had he abated in his craving to equalize a state of knowledge among the kingdoms of the earth.

"Boy," said Jacob to this sinewy old man, "go down from here to the great city where my son lives, Pharaoh's friend, and speak before him and say: 'Jacob, our father, would speak to your grace on an important matter.' You must not alarm him or make him think I am dying. You are to tell him: 'Our father, the old man, finds himself in good health at Goshen considering his years and thinks not now to depart hence. But he judges the hour is come to speak with you concerning himself, though the matter reaches out beyond his own life. Therefore in your kindness come to his dwelling-place, which he mostly keeps, although not yet bedridden, in the house which you made for him.' Go, boy, go, step out and tell him that!"

Naphtali glibly repeated the message and betook himself to his heels. He went afoot and took several days for the journey, otherwise Joseph would have been there at once, for he travelled in his chariot with a small retinue, among them Mai-Sachme, his steward, who laid too great stress on being in this story to stop at home when Joseph went abroad. But Mai-Sachme waited outside with the others of Joseph's house while the exalted one was alone with his father in the tent, that well-garnished living- and sleeping-room which is the theatre to which our far-flung scene has now shrunk. For there on his bed in the background or not far from it Jacob spent the last days of his life, waited on by Damasek, Eliezer's son, himself now called Eliezer, a man in a white-belted smock, still youthful in the face, though bald on top with a fringe of grey hair.

In reality the man was a nephew of Jacob; for Eliezer, Joseph's teacher, was the half-brother of the man of the blessing, born of a maid. His position, however, was that of a servant, though higher than the others round the house. Like his father he called himself Jacob's eldest servant and was over his house as Joseph was over Pharaoh's house and Captain Mai-Sachme over Joseph's. He went out to the captain after announcing Joseph and conversed with him on an equal footing.

The Regent of Egypt knelt down when he entered the chamber and touched with his forehead the felt and the carpet of the floor.

"Not so, not so, my son," Jacob demurred. He sat on his bed at the back of the room, a skin drawn over his knees; on either side of him were earthenware lamps on wooden consoles. "We are in the world and the man of years and religion too much respects its greatness to acquiesce in your action. Welcome, welcome to me in my

weakness and age, on account of which I may be pardoned for not
coming in respect and fatherly feeling to greet you, my lifted-up
lamb! Take a stool here beside me, my dear one; Eliezer, my eldest
servant, might have drawn one up when he let you in — he is not what
his father was, the wooer of the bride, towards whom the earth
sprang; nor would he have been to me what his father was in the
time of my shedding tears of blood. What time do I mean? The time
when you were lost. He wiped my face with a damp cloth and tenderly reproved me for some refractory feeling that burst out of me
against my God. But you were alive. Thank you for asking, I am
well. Bilhah's boy, Naphtali, was to tell you that I was not calling
you to my death-bed. Or rather this will of course be my death-bed,
it is beginning by degrees to take on that character, but does not yet
possess it in fullness, for there is yet some life in me. I do not think
to die at once and you will return hence twice or thrice to your
Egyptian house and your affairs of state before I depart. Indeed, I
am minded and resolved to economize the strength I yet have with
measure and caution, for I shall still need them for various occasions,
especially at the very end, and I must save my strength and my words.
Therefore, my son, this our talk will be brief and confine itself to
the necessary and important matter in hand, for it were against God
to exhaust myself in a superfluity of words. It may even be that I
have already talked more than is necessary. When I have said what
is needful and put it to you in the form of an urgent plea, you may,
if you have time, sit with me a little while in silence on my future
death-bed, only for the sake of our being together without making
me use my strength in speaking. I will silently lean my head on your
shoulder and remember that it is you who are here and how my one
true wife bore you to me in Mesopotamia with more than natural
pangs; how I lost you and then to some extent got you back through
the extraordinary goodness of God. But when you were born with
the sun at his height and you lay in your swinging cradle beside the
maid who sang and gasped her weariness in song, there was something
like a dazzling sweetness about you and I knew, of course, how to
recognize it for what it was; and your eyes, as you opened them
when I touched you, were as blue as heaven's light and only later got
black with a twinkle of mischief in their blackness, which is why I
turned over to you the pictured bride-veil here in the house, out
at the front. I will perhaps come to speak about it at the very last,
but now it is probably unnecessary and does violence to economy. It
is very hard for the heart to distinguish between necessary and unnecessary talk. See, you stroke me soothingly in sign of your love
and your good faith. There will I begin — on your love and good
faith I will base the plea I have to make to you and I will build upon
it in the practical request I wish to make while avoiding unnecessary

words. For, Joseph-el, my uplifted lamb, the time has come that I am to die, and though I am by no means yet at the final stage, Jacob has come to the time of his departing and to the time of the last will and testament. But when I do put my feet together and am gathered to my fathers, I would like not to be buried in the land of Egypt, take it not amiss of me, I would like it not at all. And also to lie in the land of Goshen where we now are, even though it is not all too Egyptian, would be against my wishes. I know full well that a man when he is dead has no more wishes and it is all the same to him where he lies. But so long as he lives and has wishes it does matter to him that it shall happen to the dead according to the wishes of the living. Again I well know that very many of us, thousands in their number, will be buried in Egypt whether they were born here or in the land of the fathers. But I, the father of them all and of you, I cannot bring myself to give them an example in this matter. With them I came into your kingdom and into the country of your King for that God sent you on ahead as the opener of the way. But in death it is my wish to part from them. If now I have found grace in your sight, put your hand under my thigh, as Eliezer did to Abram, and swear to deal kindly and truly with me and not to bury me in the land of the dead. For I will lie with my fathers and be gathered unto them. Therefore you shall carry my bones out of Egypt and lay them in their tomb, which is called Machpelach or the double cave at Hebron in the land of Canaan. Abraham lies there, whose seed has been multiplied in honour; who in the cave of his birth was suckled by an angel in the form of a goat; he lies there by Sarai, the heroine and heaven-highest queen. Yitzchak lies there, the late-conceived, with Rebecca, the wise and resolute mother of Jacob and Esau, who put all things to rights. And Leah lies there too, whom I first knew, the mother of six. Beside them all will I lie and well see that you are meeting my wish with filial respect and readiness to obey, even though a shadow of doubt and silent questioning may cross your brow. My eyes are no more of the best, for I have entered upon my time of death and my gaze is shrouded in darkness. But the shadow that crosses your face, that I see clearly; because I knew that it would come, for why should it not? There is a grave by the way, only a little piece towards Ephrath, which now they call Bethlehem, where I put to her last sleep that which was dearest to me on God's earth. Will I not lie by her side when you bring me home as I command and lie with her, set apart, by the way? No, my son, I will not. I loved her, I loved her too dearly; but things do not go according to feeling and the luxurious softness of the heart but according to their importance and according to duty. It is not suitable that I lie by the way, rather with his fathers will Jacob lie and by Leah his first wife, from whom came the heir. Lo, now your black eyes are full of tears, that too I clearly

see. They look so much like the eyes of the dearly beloved as to make
me not believe my own. It is lovely, my son, that you are so like her,
when you now in your mercy put your hand under my thigh in token
that according to importance and duty you will bury me in Machpelach, the double cave."

Joseph swore the oath. And when he had done so, Israel bowed
himself upon the bed's head and gave thanks. Then the set-apart one
sat awhile in silence beside his father's couch, and the old man leaned
his head on his shoulder and saved his strength for what should come.

EPHRAIM AND MANASSEH

A FEW weeks later he fell ill. His old cheeks were flushed with a
slight fever, his breath came short, and he kept his bed, half sitting,
propped up in cushions to ease his breathing. It was not necessary for
Naphtali to run and tell Joseph, for Joseph had set up a messenger
service between Goshen and Menfe, and daily or twice daily had
news of the old man. Now he was told: "Your father is ill, with slight
fever," and he called his two sons and said in the Canaanitish tongue:

"Get ready, we shall be going down into the lowlands to visit your
grandfather on my side."

They answered: "But we have an engagement, Father and lord,
to hunt gazelles in the desert."

"Have you heard what I said," he asked in Egyptian, "or have you
not?"

"We rejoice greatly to make our grandfather a visit," they answered, and sent word to their friends, the rich young exquisites of
Menfe, that for family reasons they could not join in the gazelle-
hunt. They were exquisites themselves, products of the highest culture, manicured, curled, perfumed, and touched up, with mother-of-
pearl toe-nails, corseted waists, and coloured ribbons flowing down
their aprons at front, back, and sides. They were not bad, either of
them, and their dandyism was a result of the society they lived in,
they cannot be blamed for it. Manasseh, the elder, was very supercilious, of course; he prided himself less on his father's renown than on
his sun-priest blood from his mother's side. Ephraim, on the other
hand, with his Rachel-eyes, we may picture as harmless, jolly, and
rather modest — on the theory that a modest nature is more prone
to jollity than a supercilious one.

They stood behind their father in the bouncing car, steadying
themselves with their bebanded arms around each other's shoulders,
and drove northwards towards the delta region. Mai-Sachme was
with them, in the hope that his physicianly skill might be of some
service to the ailing one.

Jacob was dozing in his cushions when Damasek-Eliezer announced the approach of his son Joseph. The old man pulled himself together, had his ever present servant lift him up in bed, and showed extraordinary presence of mind. "If we have found grace," he said, "in the eyes of his lordship, my son, that he visits us, then we must not relax on account of a slight degree of fever." And he took up his silver beard and spread it out on his chest.

"The young gentlemen are with him too," said Eliezer.

"Good, good, that is right," said Jacob, and sat erect, ready to receive them.

Joseph presently entered with his young heirs. Manasseh and Ephraim greeted their grandfather gracefully and remained at the door while Joseph approached the bed and tenderly took the wan hands in his.

"Dear and sainted Father," said he, "I have come with my sons because I was told you were slightly ailing."

"It is only slight," answered Jacob, "as the illnesses of the aged are. Severe illness and high fever belong to youth and vigorous manhood. They attack with violence and dance recklessly with their victims to the grave — that would not be fitting for age. The man of full years has but a light finger laid upon him, the fever itself is weak that comes to quench his fire. But I am not yet quenched, my son. This fever is weaker than I, it has been deceived by my great years and it is not strong enough. You will go home again from this, your second visit to my dying bed, which has not yet become my death-bed. The first time I had you sent for; I begged you to come. This time you came of yourself, but yet once more will I summon you, for the third and last time and to the service for the dead."

"May it be far distant from my lord — yet many a jubilee!"

"How could it, child? Enough that its hour has not yet come, the hour of gathering together. It is courtly politeness that speaks in your words; but I am nigh my day of death, to which no flowers of speech are suited, only sternness and truth. And when we come to the hour of assembly they will be the only subject-matter. I tell you so beforehand."

Joseph bowed.

"Is it well with you, my child, before the Lord and before the gods of the land?" asked Jacob. "You see, my illness is so much weaker than I that I can permit myself to ask after another's health. At least that of those whom I love. Are you getting in your tax properly from the children of the land? It is not right, Yehosiph, for to the Lord alone should the fifth belong and not to any king. But I know, I well know, my exalted one. Do you probably burn incense to the sun and the stars as is due to your station in life?"

"Dear Father — "

"I know, my snatched-away lamb, I know so well! And how lovely

it is of you to come of your own free will between the first time and
the third to see the old man, despite the demand upon you with all
your affairs and your incense-burning! I will avail myself of your
visit to come back to a matter we have not spoken of since you appeared to me again at the plain, sore missed and found again. Then I
said in your ear, my darling, that I will divide you up in Jacob and
disperse you in Israel and split you up into the tribes of the grandsons that the sons of the sons of the true wife may become like Leah's
sons, but you shall be one of us and rise into the rank of the fathers
in order that the words may be fulfilled: He is the exalted one."
    Joseph bent his head.
    "Lo, there is a place in Canaan," Jacob began to give voice, his
eyes lifted up. He was excited by the fever and most grateful to it
for the stronger pulse of his blood. "A place once called Luz, where
they make a wonderful blue for dyeing wool. It is no longer called
Luz but Beth-el and E-sagila, the house of the lifting up of the head.
For there Almighty God appeared to me in a dream when I slept in
Gilgal with my head propped on a stone — for there above on the
ramp, the navel cord between heaven and earth, where the starry
angels streamed up and down amid harmonies, He appeared to me
in kingly guise, blessed me with the sign of life, and cried out abundance of consolation to the sound of the harps, for He promised me
His mighty favour and that He would make me to wax and increase
to a great multitude and to countless children of His election. Therefore now, Yehosiph, shall your two sons who were born to you in
Egypt before I came to you, Ephraim and Manasseh, they shall be
mine, just like Reuben and Simeon, and shall be called after my name;
but those whom you will have begot later on, they shall be yours
and called after their brothers' name that they shall be like their sons.
For you have been exiled from your seat in the circle of the twelve,
but with so much love that the fourth seat is there prepared for you
next the three most important ones."
    Here Joseph got ready to present the heirs to him. But now the
old man began to speak of Rachel. Once more he told how she had
died and left him when he came out of Mesopotamia, in the land of
Canaan — it was on the way, only a little way towards Ephrath; and
how he had buried her just there on the way to Ephrath, which was
now called Bethlehem. All this was in passing as it were, it had not
much to do with the matter in hand. Perhaps he wanted to invoke
the presence of his dear one at this hour. Perhaps his idea was to point
out to the descendants of Rachel their own special shrine; since
Machpelah, the double cave, was the place of pilgrimage for the
rest of the brothers. It is possible that he was thinking of the little
sleight-of-hand trick he had long had in mind and was trying to
justify it. Our teachers disagree about his intentions in the matter;

but most likely he simply had none at all, and talked about the lovely one because he was in his solemn mood and thinking of his tales. Anyhow, he simply loved to speak of her, even where there was no point at all — just as he loved to speak of God. Perhaps he talked about Rachel because he feared he might never have a chance to do it again.

And now, after he had buried her for the very last time in her wayside grave, he looked about him, laid his hand over his eyes, and asked:

"And who are these?"

"These are my sons, dear and reverend Father," answered Joseph, "the ones God gave me, as you know, here in this country."

"If they are, then bring them here to me, that I may bless them."

What was there to bring? The heirs came forward of themselves, bowing from the hips with exaggerated good form.

The old man wagged his head and made clucking noises with his tongue.

"Lovely youth, so far as I can see," said he. "Fine and charming before God, both of them. Bend down to me, treasures, that I may caress the young blood in your cheeks with my hundred-years-old mouth. Is this Ephraim I am kissing, or Manasseh? No matter. If it was Manasseh before, it is Ephraim now whom I kiss on the cheeks and on the eyes. Lo, I have seen your face again," he turned to Joseph, still holding Ephraim embraced, "that I thought not to see, and not only that, but God has now showed me your seed. Is it too much to call Him the source of infinite goodness?"

"By no means," Joseph answered, rather absently; for he was concerned that his sons should stand in the right order before Jacob, who plainly did not distinguish between them.

"Manasseh," he said in an undertone to the elder, "take care! Come here, and stand in your right order. Ephraim, stand there!"

And he took Ephraim by his right hand and pushed him towards Israel's left; and with his left he took Manasseh and put him at Israel's right, so that everything should be in order. But what, with surprise and annoyance, if with suppressed laughter at the same time, did he see? He saw this: the father, his blind face uplifted, laid his left hand upon Manasseh's bowed head, and crossing his arms, put his right hand over upon Ephraim's. With his blind eyes staring into space, he began, before Joseph could interrupt him, to speak and to bless. He invoked the threefold God, the Father, the Good Shepherd, and the Angel, who should bless the lads, and see that his name and the names of his fathers should be named upon them; and that they should grow into a multitude, like to a multitude of fishes in number. "Yea, so be it. Stream, blessing, sacred gift, out of my heart, through my hands, upon your heads, into your flesh and your blood. Amen."

It was quite impossible for Joseph to interrupt the blessing, and his sons did not notice what was happening. They were rather distrait, and a little out of sorts, particularly Manasseh, because this ceremony had made them miss the gazelle-hunt in the desert. Each of them felt the blessing hand on his head, but even if they could have seen that the hands were crossed and the right hand lay on the younger brother's head, the left on the elder's, they would have made nothing of it and simply thought it had to be that way on account of the outlandish customs of their foreign grandfather. They would not have been so far wrong. For Jacob, brother of the hairy one, was of course repeating a pattern. He was copying his own father, the blind man in the tent, who had given him the blessing before the red one. And to his way of thinking, the blessing did not work unless there was a trick in it. There must be an exchange; therefore he changed at least his hands so that the right one rested on the younger's head and he became the right one. Ephraim had Rachel's eyes and was obviously the more agreeable of the two: that very likely influenced him. But more important still was the fact that Ephraim was the younger, as he himself, Jacob, had been, and had been exchanged through the skin and through the fell of the beast. As he shifted his hands, there were humming in his ears the incantations which his stern-willed mother had muttered as she got him ready, but which themselves echoed hither from much further off, and were, in their beginnings, much older than his own experience: "I cover the child, I cover the stone, let the master eat, let the father eat, at thy feet must fall the brethren of the deeps!"

Joseph, as I said, was both amused and annoyed. His sense of humour was strong; but the statesman in him felt bound to come to the rescue of such order and justice as could still be saved. So soon as the old man had exhausted himself and his blessing, Joseph said:

"Father, forgive me; but I had placed the lads in their right order before you. If I had known you meant to cross your hands I would have placed them differently. May I call your attention to the fact that you put your left hand on Manasseh, my elder son, the right on Ephraim, the later-born? The bad light here is to blame for your having misblessed, so to speak. Will you not quickly correct it, change your hands back again, and perhaps just say Amen? For the right hand is not the right hand for Ephraim, it belongs to Manasseh."

And as he spoke he even took the old man's hands, which still lay upon the young heads, and would have respectfully changed them. But Jacob held them as they were.

"I know it, my son, I know it," said he. "And let it be so! You rule in Egypt and take your fifth; but in these things I govern and I know what I do. Do not grieve. This one — " he raised his left hand slightly — "will also become a people, and he also shall be great. But truly his younger brother shall be greater than he, and his seed shall become a multitude of nations. As I have done it I have done it; and indeed it is my will that it become a saying in Israel, so that when a man will bless anyone he shall say: 'God make thee as Ephraim and Manasseh.' Mark it, Israel!"

"As you command," said Joseph.

The young men drew their heads away from under the hands of blessing, adjusted their waists, smoothed their hair and were glad to stand up straight again. They were not much moved by the incident; and they were right, in so far as the time-honoured fiction which made them the sons of Jacob and at the same time descendants of Leah had no effect upon their individual destinies. They passed their lives as Egyptian nobility; it was only their children or, more correctly, some of their grandchildren who gradually, by marriage, intercourse, and religious adherence, went over to the Hebraic side. Finally some of them moved from Keme to Canaan; and in the end there was a posterity descended from Ephraim and Manasseh. But there was also another point on which the indifference of the young men was justified. For our researches indicate that at the height of their increase the tribe of Manasseh counted a good twenty thousand more souls than Ephraim's tribe. However, Jacob had had his little game with the blessing.

He was really exhausted after the ceremony, and not quite clear in his head. Joseph begged him to lie down; but he still sat up straight in his bed and talked to his favourite about a parcel of land he was making over to him, as a portion apart from his brothers, which he had "taken out of the hands of the Amorites with his sword and with his bow." That could only be the piece of cornland before Shechem, by the gate of the city, which Jacob had once acquired of the gouty Hamor or Hemor for a hundred pieces of silver, certainly not by his sword and his bow. And anyhow, how did Jacob, the man of tents and of peace, come by a sword or a bow? He had never cared for nor used such tools, and never ceased to take it ill of his sons that they had laid about them so savagely at Shechem — indeed, by reason of their conduct it was doubtful whether the purchase was still valid and Jacob could still dispose of the triangle of land.

At all events, he did so, feebly, and Joseph thanked him, with his forehead on his father's hands, for this special gift. He was touched by this token of Jacob's love, and at the same time by the strange phenomenon that it was precisely the old man's feebleness which made him see himself in the heroic role of a warrior. Joseph judged that it betokened the nearness of the end, and decided not to go back to Menfe, but to await at Pa-Kos the summons to the final gathering.

THE LAST ASSEMBLY

"GATHER yourselves together, ye children of Jacob! Come in your
hosts and assemble together round Israel your father, that he may
tell you who you are and what shall befall you in future times!"

That was the call which Jacob made to go forth out of the tent to
his sons when he judged the hour to have come when he should hold
his dying speech. For he held his life in his own hands and precisely
knew what strength he had left, that he might expend it in his last
words and so die. Through Eliezer, the old young man his head servant, he sent out the call; he told it to him, and then had him repeat
it several times, so that Damasek might have it not only more or less
right, but letter-perfect. "Not 'Come hither,' but 'Come in your
hosts'; and not 'present yourselves before Israel,' but 'assemble together.' Now say it all again and forget not the two things: 'who you
are,' and 'what shall befall you.' There, at last, that is right. I fear
I have spent too much strength instructing you. Now be off!"

And Damasek kilted his garment and ran in all directions, so fast
that the earth seemed to spring towards him. He put his hands round
his mouth and cried: "Assemble ye together, ye sons of Israel, and
gather together as you are, that good may come to you from day to
day!" He ran to all the settlements, to the fields, to the herds and
flocks, the royal ones over which the five were set, and to the others;
ran to and fro through moor and fen, with muddy water splashing his
lean legs, for it was ebb-time, the fifth day of the first month of the
winter season, what we should call the beginning of October; and in
the delta, after a long spell of late heat, it had rained a good deal. He
kept shouting aloud with his hands round his mouth, into the open
country and into the dwelling-houses: "Whoever you are, assemble,
sons of Jacob, and meet in your hosts about him for future times!"

He ran into Pa-Kos close by; Joseph was stopping there with the
magistrate and there were guards before the door. Damasek, with
disgraceful inaccuracy, shouted out the words which Jacob had so
carefully composed and designed for posterity. But it did not matter,
their effect was the same, and they were straightway obeyed in haste
by all who heard them. Pharaoh's friend hurried to his father's house,
with him Mai-Sachme, his major-domo; and many curious outsiders
heard the call and came to hang about.

The eleven awaited their brother at the entrance to the curtained
tent. He greeted them in a suitably grave and weighty manner, kissed
Benjamin, the little man of forty-seven, and talked with them all a
short time in low tones about their father's condition and the probability that he thought to hold his last speech and depart. They answered him with their eyes cast down, and rather tight-lipped; for

as usual they were afraid of the old man's tongue and knew that the stern old father-tyrant would probably spare them nothing in this final hour. Each one was privately telling himself, as human beings do: "Good lord, probably it will turn out all right!" Reuben, the seventy-eight-year-old shepherd tower, was clenching his jaw until his facial muscles were taut. He had behaved badly with Bilhah, he would certainly get to hear most explicitly about that on this solemn occasion, and he armed himself accordingly. Simeon and Levi, who in their young days had laid about them like savages at Shechem on their sister's account — that was long, long ago, but they could count on getting it dished up again, with due solemnity; they too braced themselves for the ordeal. There was Jehudah, who had had an affair with his daughter-in-law, by mistake. He had no manner of doubt that the old man would be harsh and cruel enough to hold it against him, even on his death-bed — the more so because he had been a little in love with Tamar himself. There they all were; and all of them but Benjamin, the stay-at-home, had once sold Dumuzi down into Egypt. Jacob on this occasion would be quite capable of making a song about it — they all expected it, and set their teeth accordingly. Particularly the sons of Leah did, for none of them had forgiven their father for choosing, after Rachel's death, not Leah their mother but Bilhah, Rachel's maid, for his first and favourite wife. Jacob had had his failings, and all his life he had been arbitrary in his exercise of feeling. They thought defiantly that he had been just as guilty as they were in the Joseph affair; he ought to remember that, before he used the occasion of his grand dying harangue to take them to task. In short, dread of the coming scene made them all awkward; they were putting on hurt faces beforehand. Joseph saw it, and spoke in the most friendly way. He went from one to another putting out his hand and saying:

"Let us go in to him, brothers, and let us in all humility bear the judgment which our dear one inflicts on us, each one his own. Let us hear him, if necessary, with forbearance. For forbearance, indeed, ought to descend from God to man and from father to child; but if it does not, then the child must practise reverent forbearance and be great in pardon towards the greater for that he is weak in pardon. Let us go in; he will judge us with a feeling for truth, and we shall all get what is coming to us, myself too, believe me!"

They went quietly into the tent, the Egyptian Joseph with them. He did not go first, although they would have had him lead them; he went with Benjamin behind the sons of Leah and only in front of the children of the maids. Mai-Sachme, his steward, went in too; partly with the justification that he had long been in the story and played his part in its embellishment; but partly too because the gathering was to a large extent public, and it turned out that everybody might go in who chose. It was very full in the room of death when

the twelve were inside, for besides Damask the crier there stood round
the master's couch a number of under-servants of his household staff,
and many of his descendants either stood or lay on their faces farther
off. There were even women with children, some giving them the
breast. Boys sat on the chests along the walls, and their conduct was
not always seemly; but all incorrectness was quickly suppressed. The
hangings before the tent had been flung wide open; the courtyard
folk and the little people from the hamlet of Pa-Kos, a great host in
all, had a clear view and were in a way included in the gathering. The
sun declined, and the crowd outside was outlined against an orange-
tinted evening sky, a shadowy mass with indistinguishable forms and
faces. But the two oil-lamps, flaring on high stands at the head and
foot of the bed, sent their rays from within to pick out a striking
figure: a gaunt matron in black, between two very broad-shouldered
men. Her grey hair was covered with a veil. She was Tamar, the resolute woman, with her doughty sons. She had not entered, she kept
outside; for it might be that Jacob in his dying speech would come
to speak of Judah's sin with her. But she was here, present and on the
spot—and *how* was she present, now that the time had come for
Jacob to hand down the blessing to him with whom she had sported
by the way and brought herself into the succession! Even without the
lamplight that proud profile would have been unmistakable against
the sallow rainy sky.

He who had once instructed her in the world, and in the great history into which she had wormed her way, he who had summoned
this death-bed gathering: Jaakob ben Yitzchak, blest before Esau, lay
propped on his cushions, under a sheepskin, on his death-bed at the
back of the tent, in just so much command of his powers as he needed
to be. The waxen pallor of his skin was faintly tinged by the tinted
twilight and the glow from the charcoal in the basin near by. The
look on his face was exalted and mild. A white band which he usually
wore when he sacrificed was round his forehead; the white locks
came out under it on the temples and ran down in even width into the
patriarchal beard that covered all his chest, thick and white beneath
the chin, farther down sparse and grey; through it showed the fine,
witty, rather bitter mouth. He had not moved his head; but the soft
eyes with the swollen ducts beneath were rolled sidewise so that they
showed much yellowish-white eyeball. His gaze sought his sons as
they entered and a lane quickly opened for them to the bedside.
Damasek and the servants drew back; and those begot across the
Euphrates, together with the little one whose mother had died of him
in Abram's land, bowed down on their foreheads and then stood
drawn up round their father and head. Complete silence had fallen,
all eyes were fixed upon Jacob's ashen lips.

They parted in an effort to speak, several times before they shaped any words. Painfully, in a low voice, his speech began. Later he got more freedom and his voice a fuller ring; only at the very last, when he blessed Benjamin, did it die away in weakness.

"Welcome, Israel," he said, "girdle of the earth, zone of your courses, stronghold and dike of the skies, ordered in sacred pictures! Lo, obediently you came in your host and stoutly gathered yourselves full-numbered round the bed of my death, that I may judge you according to the truth and foretell to you out of the wisdom of my last hour. Praise be yours, my ring of sons, for your readiness, and commendation for your courage. Blessed be ye all together by the hand of the dying and glorified altogether. Be blessed by my well-saved strength and blest to eternity! Mark now: what I have to say to you, each by himself in your order, is said within the bond of the general blessing."

Here he paused in his speech and only moved his lips awhile to himself, without any sound. Then his features became concentrated, the skin of his forehead wrinkled with strain as he drew his brows together to fight his weakness.

"Reuben!" came the summons from his lips.

The shepherd tower strode out on his girded legs like strong columns. He was quite grey-headed, and his red, smooth-shaven face worked like that of a chidden child about to cry. The eyes with their inflamed lids kept up a blinking beneath the white brows; the corners of his mouth were drawn down in such bitterness, so violently, that they made thick ridges of muscle at the sides. He knelt at the bed's edge and bowed himself over it.

"Reuben, my eldest son," Jacob began, "you are the beginning of my strength, the firstling of my manhood, yours was the right of the first-born, and a mighty pre-eminence. In the circle you were the highest, the nearest to the sacrificing and the nearest to the kingship. But it was all wrong. A heathen god showed it to me on the field in a dream, a biting beast, a dog-boy of the desert with beautiful legs, sitting on a stone. Begot by a mistake, begot with the wrong one in the blind night to which everything is the same and knows naught of distinctions in love. So I begot you, my eldest, in the windy night with the wrong one, the strong one, begot you in my delusion. I gave her the flower, but there had been an exchange, the veil was exchanged, and daylight taught me that I had only begot where I falsely thought to love — and my heart and my bowels turned over and I despaired of my soul."

Now there was a time when they did not understand what he said; he moved his lips and soundlessly talked to himself. Then his voice came back, stronger than before, and part of the time he spoke of Reuben in the third person, no longer to him.

"He shot away like water," said he. "Like water bubbling over out of a pot. Not he shall be the head, not he the king-post of the house, he shall have no pre-eminence. For he went up to his father's bed, and has defiled his father's bed with his going up. He has bared and mocked his father's shame and come near him with the sickle and committed naughtiness with his mother. Ham is he, black of face, and goes bare with naked shame, for as the dragon of the slime has he borne him and after the ways of the hippopotamus. Hear you, my early strength, what I say of you? May you be accursed, my son — that is, accurst within the scope of the blessing. For the first-born right is taken away from you, the priesthood revoked and the kingly headship recalled. For you are not worthy of the leadership and your first-born right is done away. Beyond the Salt Sea shall you live and border on Moab. Your deeds are weakly and your fruits are poor. Thank you, my eldest son, that you so stout-heartedly came to the gathering and boldly put yourself in the way of judgment. You are like a shepherd tower, and move on your legs like moving columns of a temple, because I scattered my first strength and manhood so mightily in the madness of the night. Receive a father's curse and so farewell!"

He ceased, and the aging Reuben stepped back among the ranks, all the muscles of his face grim with dignity and his eyes cast down just as his mother used to cast hers down to hide her squinting.

"The brothers!" Jacob next commanded. "The twin sons, inseparable in the skies!"

And Simeon and Levi bent and bowed down before him. They were seventy-five and seventy-six years old (for of course they were not twins, only inseparables); but they had astonishingly preserved their rough and blustering outward appearance.

"Oh, oh, how scored and scarred with ingrained savagery!" exclaimed their father. He even started back as though in fear. "They kiss the instruments of cruelty, I will know naught of them. For I love it not, ye savage ones, may my soul come not in their counsels nor my honour have any part with theirs. Their anger slew a man and their self-will mutilated the cattle. Therefore the curse of the injured struck them down and they were appointed for destruction. What have I said to them? Cursed be their anger that it was so fierce and their wrath for that it was stubborn. That have I said to you. Be accursed, my dear ones, accurst within the blessing. Ye shall be divided and scattered that ye commit not misdoing together for ever. Be dispersed in Jacob, my Levi! Yours be a lot and land none the less, stout Simeon, but I see it stands not alone but is consumed in Israel. Take your place in the background, double star, having heard the death-bed second-sight of the blessing one. Step back!"

They did so, not vastly upset by the judgment. They had long known it and expected nothing better. Having it once more expressly served up in open meeting did not cut them up, for everybody knew it before — and they still remained "Israel." Their rejection was only within the scope of the general blessing. Besides, they and the whole audience espoused the view that rejection is a destiny like any other, with a dignity of its own. Every condition is a condition of honour: such was their view, and the view of all the others. After all, it was pretty plain that part of what their father had said did not refer to them, but to the constellation of the Twin Brethren. Partly out of his native weakness for the allusive, partly in the mental confusion of his state, to which, on the same ground, he solemnly gave way, he had mixed them up with Gemini and brought in Babylonian allusions well known to them all, even to the lads sitting on the chests along the walls. Deliberately and blatantly he had at times confused them with Gilgamesh and Eabani in the song, so enraged about their sister that they had cut in pieces the heavenly steer and for this blasphemy been cursed by Ishtar. But they had not paid particular attention to any steer at Shechem, the city of Sichem, the scene of the butchery; nor did they recall having mutilated any. Jacob, however, had had this fixed idea about a steer from the beginning, and always brought it up when they came back to the subject. But can anyone be more honourably cursed than to be confused with the Dioscuri and the sun and moon? That is a rejection one can take, even in public: it is only half personal; the other half is spun out of the dream fancies of a dying man.

It is necessary to emphasize here that many astral allusions were thus mixed into these pronouncements of Jacob to his sons. They gave elevation to his discourse and also imparted a certain touch of human fallibility. That was both weakness and wilfulness — with a good deal of wilfulness in the weakness. There was a hint of Aquarius in what he had said to Reuben. Now it was Judah's turn. And Jacob so nearly expended himself in the decisive and tremendous blessing he now bestowed that after it he had repeatedly to call on God for help, fearing he might not last out, and particularly that he might not get round to Joseph. Judah had always been called the lion. But Jacob's dying words to him played so untiringly on the epithet and showed him so explicitly lionlike, that Judah writhed in torment and nobody present could possibly fail to recognize the heavenly phenomenon. A great deal of Cancer came out in Issachar — the constellation of the little asses, which stands in this sign of the zodiac, was brought into cosmic connection with his everyday nickname of the bony ass. In Dan everybody made out the scales, the metaphor of law and justice, though the adder in the path came out as well. And Naphtali's stag-and-hind passed over, intelligibly to most of the audience, into the Ram. Joseph himself was no exception. On the contrary, in his judgment the astral implication was double: the Virgin and the Bull alternated therein. Benjamin's judgment seemed to be conditioned by Scorpio, for the good little man was pronounced a ravening wolf, only because Lupus stands near by, south of the sign with a sting in its tail.

Here the mythological coloration and the divorce from the personal became clearest of all — it was that which made it so much easier for the big twins to take their condemnation with equanimity. They lived in an earlier time, but also in a time that was already a later one; in some directions they possessed a good deal of insight — for instance, into the not absolutely reliable character of death-bed prophecies. The gaze which the departing one sends into the future is impressive and hallowed; much faith may be put in it. Yet not too much, for it has not always been entirely justified; and it seems that the already unearthly state of the dying which produces it can also be a source of error. Jacob solemnly made some solemn misfires — along with some prophecies that amazingly hit the mark. Reuben's descendants never did amount to much, and Simeon's stock was never independent and was absorbed into Judah's. But that the blood of Levi would in time attain to the highest honour and achieve permanent election to the priesthood — as we who are in the story but also outside it already know — that was obviously hidden from Jacob's parting gaze. In this respect and in some others his dying prophecies were a dignified failure. Of Zebulon he said that he would dwell at the haven of the sea and before an haven of ships; his border should be unto Sidon. That was a natural guess, on account of Zebulon's well-known fondness for the sea and the smell of pitch. But the location of his tribe was not to be by green water at all nor did it ever border on Sidon. It lay between Sidon and the sea of Galilee, separated from the latter by Naphtali's portion and from the sea by Asher's.

For us such errors are valuable. For are there not clever people who assert that Jacob's blessing-speech was composed after the time of Joshua and should be regarded as prophecy after the event? We may shrug our shoulders at this: not only because we are present at the death-bed and hear the dying man's words with our own ears, but also because prophecies which are given out with history to go upon, back-dated prophecies, so to speak, have no trouble in being correct. The best evidence for the genuineness of a prophecy is its incorrectness.

And now Jacob summoned up Judah. It was a great moment. Deep stillness reigned in and without the tent. It is seldom that such a large assemblage preserves such a profound, motionless, and breathless stillness. The ancient raised his pallid hand towards his fourth son and Judah stood there ashamed to his very depth and bending low his seventy-five-year-old head. Jacob lifted his finger and pointed to him and spoke:

"Judah, you are the one!"

Yes, it was he, the tortured one, the man utterly unworthy in his own mind; the slave of the mistress, who had no lust to lust, but she to him: sinner and religious man in one. It might be supposed that at seventy-five years this slavery to desire cannot be so abject. But to suppose so would be wrong. That lasts to the last breath. A little blunter the spear may become, but that ever the mistress frees her slave is unheard of, it does not happen. Deeply abased, Judah bowed himself for the blessing. And now a strange thing came to pass: in proportion as the flood gushed out over him and the oil of the promise poured out upon his head, so his tumultuous feelings were calmed, he listened and in waxing pride he told himself: "Well, well, in spite of everything! Then it was not so bad after all, and apparently it does not affect the blessing! Perhaps it is not taken so seriously — maybe the purity I so craved was not so indispensable to salvation; maybe it is all taken in together, even hell itself is taken in — who would have thought it? For the oil is trickling down on my head, God have mercy on me, for I am the one!"

It did not trickle, it poured and roared. Jacob expended himself almost recklessly in blessing Judah; several of the brothers were cut off with a hasty mention and Jacob's voice quavered with weakness as he gave it.

"Judah, you are the one! Your hand will be in the neck of your enemies, your brethren shall praise you. Your father's children and the children of all the mothers shall praise in you the anointed one!" — Then came the lion. For some time there were only lions, and powerful lion metaphors. Judah was a lion's whelp, from the litter of a lioness, a veritable king of beasts, from the prey he went up ravening, he purred, he mewed, he roared. Upon his desert mountain he withdrew, there he couched and stretched like a maned king and like the son of a fierce lioness. Who shall dare to rouse him up? No one shall dare. It was surprising to have the father praise as ravening beasts those sons whom he blessed while those whom he did not bless he blamed unmercifully precisely because the instruments of cruelty were their familiars. As he himself in his dying weakness had seen himself in the rôle of a hero with sword and bow, so now he lauded his sons, first the tormented Judah and then little Benjamin, as savage warriors and beasts of prey rejoicing in blood. Remarkably enough, the foible of the mild and intellectual type is a weakness for the heroic.

But Jacob did not end his Judah-scene on the beast-of-prey note. The hero he had in view, whom he had sought out long since, was not the kind to make weakness forget itself in hero-worship. Shiloh was his name. From lions to him was a long way; therefore the old man made a transition in his blessing; he introduced a great king. The king sat on his throne and the sceptre leaned between his feet and should not move from there nor be taken from him until "the hero" appeared, until Shiloh came. To Judah, the king with the sceptre between his legs, this promise-name was quite new — indeed, it was a surprise to the whole gathering. They listened amazed. One only among them all knew it and had waited eagerly to hear it. Our gaze turns involuntarily out to the shadowy profile: she stood there erect, in darkling pride, to hear Jacob pronounce the seed of the woman. From Judah favour should not pass, he should not die, his eyes not close until his greatness should wax immense, for that out of him should come one upon whom all the people should depend, the bringer of peace, the man of the star.

Thus it went on beyond all expectation above Judah's abashed head. His own figure, or rather his tribe, mingled — whether intentionally or out of mental confusion or perhaps out of both, that is to say, the confusion being used to heighten the high-flown poetic effect — it mingled and melted in with Shiloh's figure so that in this vision of the fullness of the blessing and the grace no one knew whether Jacob was talking about Judah or about the promised one. Everything swam in wine — everything shone red with the red sparkle of the wine before the eyes of the host as they listened. It was a land, the kingdom of this king, where one bound his foal to the vine and his ass's colt to the choice vine. Were they the vineyards of Hebron, the wine-clad hills of Engedi? Into his city "he" rode on an ass and on a colt the foal of an ass — there was nothing but drunken desire as of red wine at the sight of him, and he himself was like a drunken wine-god treading the press, high-kilted, exalted; the blood of the wine sprinkled his apron and the red juice of the grape his garment. Lovely was he as he trod, wading and dancing the dance of the winepress — lovely above all mankind: as white as snow, as red as blood and as black as ebony.

Jacob's voice died away. His head bobbed down, his eyes rolled up from below. He had expended himself very much, almost too much, in this blessing. He seemed to be praying for a renewal of strength. Judah, finding his blessing blessed out, stepped back, amazed and abashed because it had turned out that impurity was no hindrance. The uproar in the assemblage at the appearance of Shiloh and the entirely new revelation and declarations brought out in this blessing were almost uncontrolled. A loud whispering went round both within and without the tent. Outside it was even vocal, voices were heard excitedly repeating the name of Shiloh. But all movement ceased again as Jacob once more raised his head and his hand. The name of Zebulon came from his lips.

The man of sixty-eight years put his head under the old hand. Since his name actually meant dwelling and habitation, it surprised no one that Jacob should point out his dwelling and his habitation: he should dwell at the haven of the sea and live near the treasures of ships and should border on Sidon. Very good: he had always wanted it, so now he got it — in a tired, perfunctory voice. Issachar. . . .

Issachar would be like a strong ass crouching down between the folds. The little asses in Cancer were his sponsors, but despite this connection Jacob seemed not to expect much of him. He spoke only briefly of him and in the past tense, which meant the future. Issachar saw that rest was good and the land that it was pleasant. He was strong and phlegmatic. He thought nothing of lending his bones as a beast of burden. To serve came easy to him and he bowed his shoulders to be laden. So much of Issachar. He touched the Jordan, so Jacob claimed to be able to see. Enough of him. Now for Dan.

Dan guided the scale and judged with wisdom. So subtle was he of mind and tongue that he was like a biting adder. Jacob took occasion here, lifting his finger to give his audience a little lesson in zoology: in the beginning, when God was creating the animals, He had crossed the hedgehog with the lizard and so produced the adder. Dan was an adder-serpent. A snake he was by the way and an horned adder in the path, not easy to see in the sand and very tricky. In him the heroic took the form of knavery. The enemy's horse he bit in the heels so that the rider fell backwards. Thus Dan, Bilhah's son. "I have waited for thy salvation, O Lord!"

In his exhaustion Jacob gave his sigh and ejaculated his prayer, distressed lest he should not get to the end before his end. He had begotten so may sons that in his last hour the number of them was almost beyond his strength. But with God's help he would win through.

He summoned the stocky Gad, whose clothes were besewn with bronze.

"Gaddiel, a troop shall overcome you, but you will overcome at the last. Stoutly, my stout one! Now Asher."

Asher, the sweet-tooth, had fat land from the mountain to near Tyre. The lowlands were full of waving corn and dripped with oil, that his bread should be fat and he should make fine ointment such as kings send each other for their pleasure. From him came pleasure and the love of bodily pleasure, which amounts to something too. "Asher, you will also be somebody. And since song came from you and joyous tidings, be praised for it before your brother Naphtali, whom I now summon beneath my hand."

Naphtali was a hind who leaps over ditches and a springing doe. His was the nimble gait, he was a running he-goat when he draws in his horns and leaps. His tongue too was nimble, it gave glib information and the fruits of the plain Gennesareth ripened apace. "Of quickly ripened fruits, Naphtali, may your trees be full, and quick success, if not too great, be your judgment and lot."

Then this son too, having been blessed, stepped back into the ranks. The old man rested, with closed eyes, in a deep silence, his chin on his breast. And after a little he smiled. They all saw and were touched, for they knew what summons it meant. It was a happy, yes, an artful smile and somewhat sad withal, though it was artful too, for the love and tenderness within overcame the sadness and renunciation. "Joseph!" said the old man. And a fifty-six-year-old man, who had been thirty and seventeen and nine, and lain in the cradle as a lamb of the mother sheep, a child of the time, beautiful of face, in Egyptian white, Pharaoh's sky-blue ring on his finger, fortune's minion, bowed beneath the ashen blessing-hand.

"Joseph, my scion and seed, son of the virgin, son of the dearest, son of the fruit tree by the spring, fruitful bough whose branches overhang the wall, I greet you! Who is the heart of the spring, firstborn bull in his adornment, greeting!"

Jacob had spoken loud and clear, a solemn address, to be heard by all. But then he dropped his voice almost to a whisper, obviously minded, if not to shut out the public, at least to limit its numbers during this blessing. Only the nearest heard his words of farewell to the set-apart one; those farther off only got a word here and there and those outside for the moment nothing at all. But afterwards it was all repeated over and over, reported and discussed.

"Most dearly beloved," came from the painfully smiling lips. "Chosen and preferred by the daring heart for the sake of the only beloved, who lived in you and with whose eyes she looks, just as once she first looked at me at the well, when she appeared among Laban's sheep and I rolled away the lid for her — I was allowed to kiss her and the shepherds shouted in delight: 'Lu, lu, lu!' In you I kept her, my darling, when the almighty tore her from me, in your loveliness she lived, and what is sweeter than the double and the doubtful? Well I know that the double is not of the spirit, for which we stand, but is the folly of the peoples. And still I yielded to that ancient mighty spell. Can one be ever and entirely of the spirit and avoid folly? Lo, I am double now myself, I am Jacob and Rachel. She am I, who went so hardly away from you into the summoning land, for me too it summons today away from you — it summons us all. You too, my joy and my care, have already made half the journey towards that land and yet you were once little and then young and were all that my heart understood of loveliness and charm. Serious was my heart but soft, therefore was it soft before beauty. Called to the heights and to the sight of diamond-sharp steeps, secretly I loved the gentle hills."

His voice failed for some minutes and he lay smiling with closed eyes as though his spirit wandered in the charming rolling landscape which had risen to his eyes as he gave Joseph his blessing.

When he began to speak again he seemed to have forgotten that Joseph's head was under his hand, for he spoke of him awhile as of a third person.

"Seventeen years he lived with me and another seventeen by God's mercy he lived: between them lay my stiffness and the destiny of the set-apart one. They lay in wait for his loveliness and that was folly; for with loveliness wisdom was ever one. On that their strong desire was wrecked. More alluring than has ever been seen are the women who climb up to look after him from house-tops and towers and windows, but they had not their desire. So it was made bitter to him and they attacked him with arrows of ill report. But his bow abode in strength, the arms of his hands were made strong and the hands of the Everlasting held him up. Not without rapture will his name be remembered, for he succeeded as few succeeded in finding favour before God and man. That is a rare blessing, for mostly one has the choice of pleasing either God or the world; but the spirit of charm and mediation gave it to him that he pleased them both. Be not proud, my child — have I need to warn you? No, I know your shrewdness saves you from presumption. For it is a charming blessing but not the highest and sternest. Lo, thy dear life lies open in its truth before the dying gaze. Play and playing it was, familiar, friendly appealingness, approaching salvation yet not quite seriously a calling or a gift. Love pierces my heart at sight of that mingled gladness and sadness; not so can anyone else love you, my child, who see, not as the father-heart can the sadness, but only the brilliance of your life. And so I bless you, blessed one, with all the strength of my heart in the name of the Eternal who gave you and took you and gave you again and now takes me from you. Higher shall my blessing mount than the blessings of my fathers upon my own head. Be blessed, as you are blessed, with the blessing of heaven above, blessings of the deep that lieth under, with blessings gushing from the breast of heaven and the womb of earth! Blessings, blessings on Joseph's head, and in your name shall they sun themselves who come from you. Songs shall stream far and wide singing the story of your life, ever anew, for after all it was a sacred play and you suffered and could forgive. So I too forgive you that you made me suffer. And God forgive us all!"

He finished and drew his hand back, slowly, from this head. So one life parts from another and must go hence; but in a little the other goes too.

Joseph stepped back among the brothers. He had not said too much in saying that he would receive his share and be judged with the truthfulness of the dying. He took Benjamin by both hands, since the old man failed to summon him, and brought him forward. Clearly Jacob was at the end of his strength and Joseph had to guide the blessing hand upon the little brother's head, for it would no longer have found the way. That it was the youngest who awaited his judgment he probably knew, but what his failing lips murmured had little to do with the little man. Possibly it would fit his descendants better. Benjamin, so they heard, was a ravening wolf, in the morning he would devour his prey and at night divide the spoil. He was vexed at what he heard.

Jacob's last thought went back to the cave, the double cave on the field of Ephrath, son of Zohar, and his wish that he be buried there among his fathers. "I enjoin upon you," he breathed, "it is paid for, paid by Abraham to the children of Heth with four hundred shekels in silver by weight, as it . . ." Here death interrupted him, he stretched out his feet, sank deeper into his bed, and his life stood still.

They all held their breath and their lives stopped a little too, when it came. Then Mai-Sachme, Joseph's steward, who was also a physician, stepped up quietly to the couch. He laid his ear to the quiet heart, watched with serious pursed mouth a feather he had laid on the muted lips — it did not stir — and struck a little blaze before the pupil, which gave no sign. So then he turned to Joseph, his master, and announced to him:

"He is gathered to his fathers."

But Joseph motioned him with his head to Judah, to whom, not to himself he should make the announcement. And as the good man went up to Judah and repeated: "He is gathered up," Joseph stepped to the death-bed and closed the eyes of the dead; for to that end he had motioned Mai-Sachme towards Judah. Then he laid his forehead on his father's brow and wept for Jacob.

Judah, the heir, made the necessary arrangements: the mourners, male and female, were ordered and male and female singers and flute-players; and the body was washed, anointed, and wrapped up. Dama-zek-Eliezer kindled an offering of incense in the chamber: stacte, neat's-foot oil from the Red Sea, galbanum and olibanum, mixed with salt. And as the spicy clouds floated round the dead, the guests streamed out, mingled with those outside, and moved away, eagerly discussing the judgment and the pronouncement that Jacob had made to the twelve.

JACOB IS SWADDLED

AND so now the story, grain of sand by grain of sand, has run steadily and silently through the neck in the glass; it lies below in a little heap, only a few grains are left to run. Nothing remains of all the happenings except what happens to a dead man. But that is not a little: you will be well advised to look reverently on as the last grains run through and fall gently on the heap beneath. For what happened to Jacob's husk was extraordinary, an honorific expenditure of an almost unique kind. No king has ever been borne to the grave as was Jacob, the man of years and dignity, by his son Joseph's command and disposition.

Joseph, of course, after his father's death left to Judah, the heir of the blessing, the first and immediate arrangements; after that he took matters in hand himself, since only he could attend to them, and embarked on certain measures, empowered by a quickly assenting council of the brothers. The measures followed upon the circumstances: upon Jacob's command and last wishes; and that they did so was dear to Joseph's heart. For the set-apart one thought as an Egyptian, and his ardent desire to do honour to his father in the best and most expensive way followed quite naturally an Egyptian train of thought.

Jacob had not wanted to be buried in the country of the dead gods. He had exacted a pledge that he be gathered to his fathers at home in the cave. That meant a far journey, for which Joseph had extravagant plans, very large in their scope and requiring time to carry out: time, that is, for the transportation itself, a period of at least seventeen days. To that end the body must be preserved, preserved by the art of Egypt, pickled and embalmed; and if he who had gone hence would have rejected the idea, then he should have forborne insisting upon being carried home. For it followed from his own stipulation that he should not be buried in Egypt that he had to be buried in the Egyptian way, magnificently dried and stuffed into an Osiris-mummy. The idea may be unpleasant to some of us. But we have not, as his son Joseph had, lived forty years in Egypt and been soaked in the sap and the spirit of that strange land till they were his pith and marrow. To him it was a joy, a consolation in the midst of grief, that his father's command allowed him to deal with the beloved shell after the most honourable and exquisite customs of the country and give it a permanence only imparted by the most costly methods.

Accordingly, as soon as he got back to his house in Menfe, where he spent the period of mourning, he sent to Goshen men whom the brothers called his "physicians." Actually they were not physicians but professional embalmers, masters of the technique of making the dead undying; the most sought-out and skilled in their line, who lived — not at all by chance — in the city of Menfe. With them came masons and carpenters, goldsmiths and engravers, and these set up their workshop next the house of hair and death, while within it the "physicians" did upon the body what the brothers called anointing

But that was not the right word. They drew his brains out through his nostrils with a bent iron and filled the empty skull with spices. They had an Ethiopian knife, made of obsidian and extremely sharp; they wielded it with great elegance, their fingers spread out, to open the left side of the abdomen in order to remove the entrails. These were preserved in special albaster jars with the likeness of the deceased's head on the lid. The cavity they thoroughly washed out with date wine and in place of the mesenteron put the very best materials inside: myrrh and spice-bark from the shoots of a laurel. They took professional pride in their work, for death was their province and they enjoyed making a man's body so much cleaner and more attractive than when he was alive.

Then they carefully sewed up the cut and put the corpse into a bath of saltpetre for a full seventy days. During that period they made holiday, ate and drank, and were paid high wages by the hour. When the time was up and the body salted, the bandaging could begin; and that was a considerable labour. Byssus bandages four hundred ells long daubed with gum, endless strips of linen, the finest of which came next the body: these they wound round Jacob, round and round, now alongside, now on top of one another, and among them on the shrunken neck they laid a gold collar and on the breast another ornament, a vulture with outspread wings, made of flat hammered gold. For during the seventy days the other artists had got on with their task and now contributed these ornaments; likewise ribbons wrought out of sheet gold, inscribed with the name of the dead and with laudatory phrases. These were drawn round the bandages, round the shoulders, the middle, and the knees and fastened to other gold bands running vertically front and back. Not content with this, that which had once been Jacob and was now in death an adorned and durable doll, purified from all corruption, was wrapped from head to foot in thin flexible plates of purest gold and then lifted into an *aron*, the chest which the cabinet-makers, jewelers, and sculptors had meantime made to measure: in human form, richly decorated with precious stones and vitreous paste. The figure fitted into the figure; the outside head was carved out of wood and covered with a mask of thick sheet gold; it had the Usir beard on its chin. Thus it went with Jacob, in all honour and splendour if not just according to his wishes but rather those of his transplanted son. However, it is probably right to have things done according to the feelings of him who still has his living entrails in his body; to the other it cannot matter.

To honour his father in death, to make his last wish the occasion of exceeding pomp: such was Joseph's dearest wish, the mainspring of all his actions. While the corpse was being got ready for the journey, the exalted one had taken steps to make the expedition an occasion to remember and marvel at, a tremendous triumph. To that end he needed Pharaoh's consent; but the mourning ritual and prescribed neglect of his person prevented him from speaking before the King. Instead he sent up an embassy to him to the city of the horizon in the hare district, and begged the lovely child of Áton for permission to accompany his father's body over the border into the land of his last resting-place. It was Mai-Sachme, his steward, whom Joseph entrusted with this mission, to give the good man the chance of being in the story up to its end. Indeed, he might confide in Mai's loyalty and poise for the accomplishment of the diplomatic mission which in fact it was; for it meant getting commands from Pharaoh which could only be suggested to, not asked of him. It meant procuring his consent for a highly solemn state funeral for the begetter of his first servant, or, in other words, to bring him to the point of ordering a so-called "great progress."

Again we see how much the thoughts of Rachel's lamb had got used to going Egyptian ways. The great progress was a peculiarly Egyptian concept, a favourite festival and ceremonial of Keme's people. Joseph had derived from Jacob's command not only the embalming in the highest price-range, but also the design of having a great procession which should be talked about beyond the Euphrates and the islands of the sea. It should vie with the most famous embassy ever sent out, to Babel, Mitanniland or to the great King Hattushilish of the Hittite lands and be worthy to be entered in the annals of the realm for posterity to read. It was necessary that Pharaoh should grant him official leave for seventy days in order that he with his eleven brothers, his sons, and his brothers' sons should take their father across the border to his grave on the route of honour which he had chosen for him. But that was only a part, it was even the least part of the programme. For so far it constituted no great procession, no royal progress; and Jacob's worldly son designed to bear his father to his grave not otherwise than as a king is borne. Pharaoh must be brought to consent and to direct; state, court, and military must he command as retinue; and that meant a considerable force of troops to cover the long desert route. And Pharaoh so thought and so ordered, after the steward had spoken before him. He so arranged partly out of feeling and the wish to show love and favour to his most deserving servant, who had done so much for him. But it was also out of the fear lest Joseph, if left uncovered by the power of Egypt to go into the country of his origin, might end by not coming back. That Meni seriously feared this, and also that Joseph reckoned with this fear, shows in the words which the basic tradition puts into his mouth in his dealings with the court: "Let me go up, I pray thee, and bury my father and I will come again." It may be that he made the promise voluntarily in advance; it may also be that Pharaoh asked it of him. But it is clear that the suspicion was present and it must have been a satisfaction to Pharaoh that he could combine favour with foresight and by means of a very heavy Egyptian escort secure himself against the loss of the irreplaceable.

The lord of the two crowns was no longer of the youngest; the years of his life were more than forty and that life was precarious and sad. He was already familiar with death: one of his daughters, the second of six, Meketaton, the most anaemic of them all, had died at nine years old; and Ikhnaton, the father of daughters, was far more dissolved in tears at the loss than was Nefernefruaton, his Queen. He wept much; tears came easy to him on all occasions, for he was lonely and unhappy and the preciousness of his life, the soft refinements among which he lived, made him more and more sensitive to loneliness and misunderstanding. He liked to say that a man who suffered much should live well. And in his case the good living went hand in hand with the tears; he lived too well to bear to suffer much; and he wept a great deal over himself. His dawn-cloud, golden-seamed, the Queen, and his transparent daughters had constantly to dry with fine batiste handkerchiefs the tears on his already elderly childish face.

It was his great pleasure to make offerings of flowers and choral services in the splendid court of the magnificent temple he had erected at Akhetaton, his only capital, to his Father in heaven, that mild friend of nature, whom he conceived as weeping a good deal too. But his pleasure was embittered by mistrust of his courtiers, whose sincerity he doubted. They lived on him, and they had accepted the "teaching." But all the evidence showed that they neither understood nor were capable of understanding it. Nobody was in the very least capable of understanding the teaching of his Father in heaven, who was infinitely distant yet tenderly concerned for every little mouse and worm; that Father of whom the sun's disk in heaven was only a symbol and a parable and who whispered the truth about his nature and essence into the ears of Ikhnaton, his beloved child. Nobody — he did not conceal the fact from himself — nobody had the least or faintest idea about it. He was remote from the people and afraid of contact with them. With the state religion of his country — the temples, the priesthood, not only with Amun but also with the rest of the ancient and traditionally honoured deities, the house of the sun at On being the only exception — between them all and him was hopeless strife. In his anguished zeal for his own revelation he had even gone so far as to take measures for their suppression and dissolution — again not only against Amun-Re but also against Usir, Lord of the West, and Eset, the mother, against Anup and Khnum, Thoth, Setekh, and even Ptah, the master of the arts. Thus the gulf widened between him and his people, a people profoundly practised in ideas and profoundly bent on loyalty to the old and its preservation everywhere. It made of him, shut off in his royal luxury, a stranger in their midst.

What wonder that his narrow grey eyes, the eyes of a dreamer, were almost always red with weeping! When Mai came before him to ask in Joseph's name for leave and to bring him the news of Jacob's death, he wept at once — he was always just about to weep and his tears found the occasion not one to miss.

"How frightfully sad!" he said. "So he is dead, that old, old man. That is a shock to My Majesty. He paid me a visit, I remember, when he was alive and made no little impression on me. He was a great wretch in his youth, I know some pranks he played, with his skins and his wands — My Majesty could still laugh till I cried at them. So now a term has been set to his years and my little uncle, who administers all the gifts of heaven, is bereaved? How infinitely sad! Is he sitting and weeping, my universal friend? I know he is no stranger to tears, that he is easy to weep, and my heart goes out to him, for it is always a good sign in a man. I know that when he revealed himself to his brothers and said to them: 'I am he!' he wept too. And he is asking for leave? Leave for seventy days? That is a long time to bury a father, however great a wretch he was! Does it have to be seventy days? It is so hard to spare him! Easier now, of course, than in the times of the fat and the lean kine, but even in these more equable years it will be very hard for me to lack him, who is over the kingdom of the blackness, for My Majesty has little understanding for such things. My field has always been the upper one and the light. Ah, it is a thankless task; human beings understand better a man who brings dark tidings than they do one who is the herald of the light. Do not think I am envious of your dear master. He shall be as Pharaoh to the very end of his life, for he has helped my poor Majesty beyond my power to thank him — in so far, that is, as I could be helped."

He wept again a little, and then he said:

"Of course he must bury his reverend father, the prankish old man, with explicit honours and carry him abroad with his sons and brothers and the sons of his brothers and all the male seed of the house — it will be a whole procession; it will be like a progress, and to the people it will look as though he went out of Egypt with all his family thither whence he came. Such a misleading impression should be avoided. It might cause unrest in the land and lead to scenes and disorder if the people thought the provider was departing — I think they would feel it much less if My Majesty departed and forsook the land out of grief over its ingratitude. Hearken, friend! What sort of retinue would that be, of only the children and the children's children? In my opinion there is nothing else to do, and this conveyance is a perfectly good occasion for it, but to make a great progress.

It must be one of the biggest that ever went abroad from Egypt and
in equal pomp returned again. What should I be if I granted a favour
to my universal friend and did not make the granting of it far out-
bid the favour asked? Say to him: Pharaoh grants you five and seventy
days and covers you with kisses, that you may convey your father
to Asia, and not only your family and their entourage shall attend you
and the corpse but Pharaoh will command a whole great progress,
a journey of state, and the cream of Egypt shall bring your father
to his grave; I will order my whole court, Ikhnaton sends word to
you, the highest of my servants and the most aristocratic in all the
land, the heads of state with their retinues, wagons and armed men
in very great strength. They shall all go with you, O apple of my
eye! and follow the bier in front and behind and on both sides, and
then just so escort you back to me, when you have deposited your
dear burden in the place where he would lie.

THE GREAT PROGRESS

SUCH was the answer which Mai-Sachme brought back from Akhetaton to Joseph, and all was arranged and put in train accordingly. Invitations which were of course commands were issued by a high palace official called privy councillor of the levee and of the privy
council and sent out by running footmen; and the day was fixed when
the participants were to come from all parts of the country and assemble in the desert outside Menfe. It was a burdensome honour that
was thus bestowed on Pharaoh's servants and the great ones of his
house and of the land of Egypt. But there were none who would
not have taken care not to refuse; yes, some notabilities who were not
bidden had to listen to the taunts of the favoured ones and were like
to fall ill with chagrin. It was no small undertaking to organize the
huge procession which assembled together in the desert by members
and groups; it fell to a captain of troops whose regular title was
"Charioteer of the King, high in the Army." For this occasion, however, and for the duration of the progress he received another title:
"Organizer of the great funeral train of the Osiris Jaacob ben Yitzchak, father of the great vice-spender of the King." It was this field
officer who drew up the order of the procession with the list of particulars in his hand, and reduced to order the confusion of wagons
and litters, riding animals and beasts of burden, into a properly
graded procession of regularity and beauty. He also had charge of
the military taken along for protection.

The order was this: A host of soldiers, trumpeters, and drummers
came first, then Nubian bowmen, Libyans armed with sickle-shaped
swords, and Egyptian lance-bearers. Then followed the pride of Pharaoh's court, as many as could be spared from his entourage without

derogation to the person of the god: friends and unique friends of the King, fan-bearers on the right hand, palace officials of the rank of the head of the privy council and privy councillors of the royal commands; highly placed personages such as His Majesty's chief baker and chief butler, the lord high steward, the keeper of the King's wardrobe, the head of the Fullers of the Great House, Pharaoh's sandal-bearer, his head wigmaker, who was also a privy councillor of the two kingdoms, and so on and so forth.

These elegant toadies formed the advance guard before the catafalque, which was taken into the procession when they reached Goshen and thereafter towered above it in glittering splendour. Jacob's coffin, shaped like a man, sparkled with gems and with the gold mask and beard it wore. It lay on a bier which in its turn rested on a gilded sledge and this again on a car with draped wheels drawn by twelve white oxen. The lofty vehicle swayed along, frequently accompanied by the wailing of flutes and the song of the professional mourners. It passed the houses of the dead and his connection, who now joined the train. There was Joseph with his sons and his household staff, of which Mai-Sachme was the eldest servant and head; there were Joseph's eleven brothers with their sons and the sons of their sons — all that bore male names in Israel followed Israel's bier, with the closest attendants of the dead, foremost among them Eliezer, his oldest servant, and a very long and numerous train. But what a host now followed after it!

For now came the administrative bureaucracy of the two lands: the Viziers of Upper and Lower Egypt, Joseph's immediate subordinates, the head book-keeper of the office of supply; such people as the inspector of the King's bulls and of all the cattle in the land (he had also the title of steward of all horned and clawed and feathered creatures), the head of the fleet, the actual steward of the privy chamber, the warden of the scales of the treasure-house, the general overseer of horses, and numerous actual judges and head scribes. Who could set down all the titles and offices whose wearers were honoured by the command to accompany to foreign parts the mummy of the father of the provider? Military, with standards and cornets, followed the officers of the state. And after that came the baggage train with luggage and tents and the forage wagons with mules and drivers — for what immense quantities of food and drink in the desert did not such a train require!

A very great company, as the tradition rightly says; one can only try to picture this long-drawn-out caravan of splendid riding-horses and luggage-carts, of bright feathers and glittering weapons; all the snorting and rolling and marching, the whinnying of steeds, the braying of donkeys and bellowing of bulls; the crashing of trumpets, the throbbing of drums, the wailing of the professional mourners —

and out of the midst of it all the amazing, towering structure of the
hearse with the mummied corpse inside. Joseph might be well pleased:
into Egypt the father-heart had once lost him; now all Egypt must
pay tribute to that agony and bear the dead Jacob on its shoulders
to his grave.

The amazing host wound its way eastward to the border, stared at
everywhere on its way. Now it entered the desolate stretches which
had to be covered in going from the bottom-land of Hapi in Pharaoh's eastern provinces to the land of Haru and Emor. It went along
the upper edge of the desert tableland of Sinai; but then it took a
direction which would have surprised anyone who knew its goal;
for it did not go by the usual and shortest way, to Gaza on the sea,
through the land of the Philistines and via Beersheba to Hebron; it
followed the fall of the land which runs south of the port of Khadati
eastwards, to Amalek and towards Edom to the southern end of
the Salt Sea. It skirted this and went along its eastern shore to the
mouth of the Jordan and a little way up the river valley, and thence
— that is, from Gilead and from the east — across the river and into
the land of Canaan.

A long detour for Jacob's great funeral procession! It made a
journey of twice seventeen days and was the reason why Joseph
had asked for seventy days' leave. Even so he had not asked
enough and overstepped the seventy-five that Pharaoh in his love
for his favourite had granted. But he had early decided on this
long way round and disclosed his intention to the officer who organized the procession and he had at once approved. For he had been
doubtful of the effect of an Egyptian irruption in such strength, with
so many soldiers, from Gaza up on the military highway, lest it make
difficulties and arouse excitement and mistrust. He had himself preferred to go around through more tranquil country. But in Joseph's
mind the long detour meant greater honour for the progress. The
solemn convoy could not be too extravagant in time and trouble
to please him; no distances were too far through which the pride
of Egypt should carry his father on its shoulders. That was the
thought which had determined him to make this detour.

When they had circled the Sea of the Plain and gone a piece
upstream along the Jordan, they came to a place near its bank called
Goren Atad. In olden times there had been nothing but a threshing-
floor there, grown round with thorns; but now it was a populous market. Near by, on the river, was a great grassy place; there they
spread out and made camp, watched curiously by the people of the
neighbourhood. They stopped seven days and held a wailing, renewed every day, a seven days' service of mourning and lamentations, very shrill and bitter, so that the children of the land were
much impressed — as was indeed the intention, since even the ani-

mals were in mourning. "A very important encampment," said the inhabitants, with their eyebrows raised, "and a grievous mourning to the Egyptians is this!" So they called the meadow thenceforward nothing but Abel-Mizraim or the Wailing Meadow of Egypt.

After this ceremonial pause the procession formed again and crossed the Jordan by a ford, which the children of the land had made easier for their own use by laying stones and sinking tree-trunks. The sledge with Jacob's mummy was taken from the wagon for the crossing and the twelve sons together bore it over the river on poles.

Now they were in their own country and went up from the steaming river valley to the fresher heights. On the ridge they followed the well-kept roads and came on the third day before Hebron. Kirjath Arba lay surrounded on the slope and a multitude of folk hurried down it to see the splendour which was moving in with its sacred burden and taking its place in the valley where the walled hollow was, the double cave, the ancestral burial place. Adapted by nature but enlarged and built up by the hand of man, it was not double on the outside and had only one door. But if you opened up the masonry, as they now did, a round shaft was revealed, leading downwards, and from it right and left two passages, closed by stone slabs, branched off and led into the two barrel-vaulted tomb cells which gave the place its name of the double hollow. But if one thinks of how many and who had found their eternal home in this hillside chamber, one pales with fear, as the brothers paled when they opened it. The Egyptians were not affected; some of them might even have stuck up their noses at such a home-made affair. But all that was Israel went pale.

Shaft and passages were very low and narrow. Only two people of Jacob's house, his eldest servant and his second eldest, one in front and one behind, could enter, and even they could hardly squeeze in to carry the mummy down and lay it in the chamber — whether the right or the left one is no longer known. If dust and bones could be surprised certainly there must have been great astonishment in the hollow when the newcomer arrived decked out in his foreign folly. But absolute indifference reigned and the two bearers hastened out of that ban of corruption and stooped through the shaft into the sweet air of the living world. There slave artisans stood ready with mortar and trowel and in a trice the lodging was closed again, for it should receive no one else after Jacob.

The father bestowed, his house closed after him, the ten stared as the workmen filled the last hole. What were they thinking? They looked so sallow; and they bit their lips. They stole glances at the eleventh and cast down their eyes. To be quite frank, they were afraid. They felt lost, forsaken and forlorn. The father is gone, the hundred-year-old father of these seventy-year-old sons. Till this moment he had been present, if only as a mummy — but now he was walled away and their hearts sank. Suddenly they felt that he had been their shield, he alone; he had stood where now nothing and nobody stood, between them and the payment.

They stuck close together and whispered in the fading light of day. The moon rose, the everlasting pictures hung themselves in the sky, the dampness of the mountain regions rose in a mist among the huts of Jacob's train. Then they called the twelfth, Benjamin, Rachel's son.

"Benjamin," said they, stiff-lipped, "listen to this. We have a message from the departed to Joseph your brother, and you are the best one to give it to him. For shortly before his death, in his last days, when Joseph was not there, the father summoned us and said: 'When I am dead, you are to say to your brother Joseph from me: Forgive your brothers their misdeed and their sin that they did so evilly by you. For between you and him will I be, in death as in life and I lay it upon you as my last wish and command that you do them no ill and forbear to take revenge for things gone by, even when I seem not to be there. Leave them to shear their sheep, unshorn.'"

"Is that so?" queried Benjamin. "I was not by when he said it."

"You were never by at anything," they answered, "you cannot talk. A little chap like you does not have to be by at everything. But you will not refuse to give his grace your brother Joseph the father's last wish and command. Go to him at once; we will follow you and wait to hear what he says."

So Benjamin went into the tent, to the exalted one, and said hesitatingly:

"Joseph-el, forgive me if I disturb you; but the brothers desire to say to you through me that on his death-bed our father solemnly adjured you not to do them harm after he was dead and gone, for what happened years ago, for even after death he would stand between you to protect them and forbid you your revenge."

"Is that so?" asked Joseph, and his eyes got wet.

"So particularly true it most likely is not," answered Benjamin.

"No, because he knew there was no need of it," added Joseph, and two tears rolled down from under his lashes.

"They are probably outside now and have followed you?" he asked.

"They are out there," the little man answered.

"Then let us go out to them," said Joseph. And he went out into the starlight and beneath the weaving beams of the moon. There they were. They fell down before him and said:

"Here we are, servants of your father's God, and we are your servants. So forgive us our trespasses, as your brother here has said to you, and repay us not according to your power. As you have forgiven us while Jacob lived, so forgive us likewise after his death."

"But brothers, my dear old brothers!" he answered, and bent down to them with his arms stretched out. "What are you saying, as though you were afraid — you talk as though you were and want me to forgive you! Am I then as God? Down in Egypt they say I am as Pharaoh and he is called god; but really he is just a sweet pathetic thing. When you talk to me about forgiveness it seems to me you have missed the meaning of the whole story we are in. I do not blame you for that. One can easily be in a story and not understand it. Perhaps that is the way it ought to be and I am to blame myself for always knowing far too well what was being played. Did you not hear from the father's own lips, when he gave me my blessing, that my life has always been only a play and a pattern? Did he remember, when he pronounced judgment on you, the bad things which happened between you and me? No, he kept quiet about them, because he too was in the play, God's play. I was protected by him when I had to rub you all the wrong way and provoke you to evil in my crude childishness that cried to heaven. God turned it all to good, for I came to feed many people and so I was forced to mature somewhat. But if it is a question of pardon between us human beings, then it is I myself must beg for it, for you had perforce to be cast in the villain's part so that things might turn out as they did. So now am I to use the might of Pharaoh simply because I command it, to avenge myself for three days' discipline in the well and so make ill again what God has made good? I could laugh at the thought! For a man who uses power only because he has it, against right and reason, he is absurd. If he is not today, he will be. And it is the future we are interested in. Sleep in peace! Tomorrow in God's good providence we shall take our way back into that quaint and comic land of Egypt."

Thus he spoke to them and they laughed and wept together and stretched out their hands as he stood among them and touched him, and he too caressed them with his hands. And so endeth the beautiful story and God-invention of

JOSEPH AND HIS BROTHERS

The Principal Works of Thomas Mann

First Editions in German

DER KLEINE HERR FRIEDEMANN
[Little Herr Friedemann]. Tales
Berlin, S. Fischer Verlag. 1898

BUDDENBROOKS
Novel
Berlin, S. Fischer Verlag. 1901

TRISTAN
Contains *Tonio Kröger*. Tales   Berlin, S. Fischer Verlag. 1903

FIORENZA
Drama
Berlin, S. Fischer Verlag. 1905

KÖNIGLICHE HOHEIT
[Royal Highness]. Novel   Berlin, S. Fischer Verlag. 1909

DER TOD IN VENEDIG
[Death in Venice]. Short novel   Berlin, S. Fischer Verlag. 1913

DAS WUNDERKIND
[The Infant Prodigy]. Tales   Berlin, S. Fischer Verlag. 1914

BETRACHTUNGEN EINES UNPOLITISCHEN
Autobiographical reflections   Berlin, S. Fischer Verlag. 1918

HERR UND HUND
[A Man and His Dog]. Idyll
Contains also *Gesang vom Kindchen,* an idyll in verse
Berlin, S. Fischer Verlag. 1919

WÄLSUNGENBLUT
Tale   München, Phantasus Verlag. 1921

BEKENNTNISSE DES HOCHSTAPLERS FELIX KRULL
Fragment of a novel   Stuttgart, Deutsche Verlags-Anstalt.

BEMÜHUNGEN
Essays
Berlin, S. Fischer Verlag. 1922

REDE UND ANTWORT
Essays
Berlin, S. Fischer Verlag. 1922

DER ZAUBERBERG
[The Magic Mountain]. Novel *Berlin, S. Fischer Verlag.* 1924

UNORDNUNG UND FRÜHES LEID
[Disorder and Early Sorrow]. Short novel
                                        Berlin, S. Fischer Verlag. 1926
KINO
   Fragment of a novel *Berlin, S. Fischer Verlag.* 1926

PARISER RECHENSCHAFT
   Travelogue *Berlin, S. Fischer Verlag.* 1926

DEUTSCHE ANSPRACHE
   Ein Appell an die Vernunft *Berlin, S. Fischer Verlag.* 1930

DIE FORDERUNG DES TAGES
   Essays *Berlin, S. Fischer Verlag.* 1930

MARIO UND DER ZAUBERER
   [Mario and the Magician]. Short novel
                                          Berlin, S. Fischer Verlag. 1930
GOETHE ALS REPRÄSENTANT DES
   BÜRGERLICHEN ZEITALTERS
   Lecture *Berlin, S. Fischer Verlag.* 1932

JOSEPH UND SEINE BRÜDER
   [Joseph and His Brothers]. Novel
   I. Die Geschichten Jaakobs. 1933.
   II. Der junge Joseph. 1934.
   III. Joseph in Ägypten. 1936.
   IV. Joseph, der Ernährer. 1943.
           I, II, Berlin, S. Fischer Verlag.
           III, Vienna, Bermann-Fischer Verlag.
           IV, Stockholm, Bermann-Fischer Verlag.

LEIDEN UND GRÖSSE DER MEISTER
   Essays *Berlin, S. Fischer Verlag.* 1935

FREUD UND DIE ZUKUNFT
   Lecture *Vienna, Bermann-Fischer Verlag.* 1936

EIN BRIEFWECHSEL
   [An Exchange of Letters]
           Zürich, Dr. Oprecht & Helbling AG. 1937

DAS PROBLEM DER FREIHEIT
   Essay *Stockholm, Bermann-Fischer Verlag.*

SCHOPENHAUER
   Essay *Stockholm, Bermann-Fischer Verlag.*

ACHTUNG, EUROPA!
  Manifesto   *Stockholm, Bermann-Fischer Verlag.*

DIE SCHÖNSTEN ERZÄHLUNGEN
  Contains *Tonio Kröger, Der Tod in Venedig, Unordnung
  und frühes Leid, Mario und der Zauberer*
                          Stockholm, Bermann-Fischer Verlag.   1938
LOTTE IN WEIMAR
  [The Beloved Returns]. Novel
                          Stockholm, Bermann-Fischer Verlag.   1939

DIE VERTAUSCHTEN KÖPFE
  Eine indische Legende [The Transposed Heads]
                          Stockholm, Bermann-Fischer Verlag.   1940
DEUTSCHE HÖRER
  [Listen, Germany!] Broadcasts
                          Stockholm, Bermann-Fischer Verlag.   1942
DAS GESETZ
  [The Tables of the Law]
                          Stockholm, Bermann-Fischer Verlag.   1944

DOKTOR FAUSTUS: DAS LEBEN DES DEUTSCHEN TONSETZERS
  ADRIAN LEVERKÜHN, ERZÄHLT VON EINEM FREUNDE
  Novel   *Stockholm, Bermann-Fischer Verlag.*   1947

DER ERWÄHLTE
  [The Holy Sinner]. Novel
                          Frankfurt am Main, S. Fischer Verlag.   1951
DIE BETROGENE
  [The Black Swan]. Short Novel
                          Frankfurt am Main, S. Fischer Verlag.   1953

BEKENNTNISSE DES HOCHSTAPLERS FELIX KRULL: DER MEMOIREN
  ERSTER TEIL [Confessions of Felix Krull]. Novel
                          Frankfurt am Main, S. Fischer Verlag.   1954

English Translation

ROYAL HIGHNESS: A NOVEL OF GERMAN COURT LIFE
  Translated by A. Cecil Curtis   1916

BUDDENBROOKS
  Translated by H. T. Lowe-Porter   1924

THE PRINCIPAL WORKS OF THOMAS MANN

DEATH IN VENICE AND OTHER STORIES
Translated by Kenneth Burke. Contains Der Tod in Venedig, Tristan, *and* Tonio Kröger *(out of print)* *   1925

THE MAGIC MOUNTAIN
Translated by H. T. Lowe-Porter. Two volumes   1927

CHILDREN AND FOOLS
Translated by Herman George Scheffauer. Nine stories, including translations of Der kleine Herr Friedemann *and* Unordnung und frühes Leid *(out of print)* *   1928

THREE ESSAYS
Translated by H. T. Lowe-Porter. Contains translations of Friedrich und die grosse Koalition *from* Rede und Antwort, *and of* Goethe und Tolstoi *and* Okkulte Erlebnisse *from* Bemühungen   1929

EARLY SORROW
Translated by Herman George Scheffauer (out of print) *   1930

A MAN AND HIS DOG
Translated by Herman George Scheffauer (out of print) *   1930

DEATH IN VENICE
A new translation by H. T. Lowe-Porter, with an Introduction by Ludwig Lewisohn.   1930

MARIO AND THE MAGICIAN
Translated by H. T. Lowe-Porter (out of print) *   1931

PAST MASTERS AND OTHER PAPERS
Translated by H. T. Lowe-Porter (out of print)   1933

JOSEPH AND HIS BROTHERS
   I. Joseph and His Brothers (The Tales of Jacob)   1934
  II. Young Joseph   1935
 III. Joseph in Egypt   1938
 IV. Joseph the Provider   1944
The complete work in 1 volume   1948
Translated by H. T. Lowe-Porter

STORIES OF THREE DECADES
Translated by H. T. Lowe-Porter. Contains all of Thomas Mann's fiction prior to 1940 except the long novels   1936

---

* Included in *Stories of Three Decades,* translated by H. T. Lowe-Porter.

THE PRINCIPAL WORKS OF THOMAS MANN

An Exchange of Letters
    Translated by H. T. Lowe-Porter †   1937

Freud, Goethe, Wagner
    Translated by H. T. Lowe-Porter and Rita Matthias-
    Reil. Three essays   1937

The Coming Victory of Democracy
    Translated by Agnes E. Meyer †   1938

This Peace
    Translated by H. T. Lowe-Porter †   1938

This War
    Translated by Eric Sutton †   1940

The Beloved Returns
    [Lotte in Weimar]
    Translated by H. T. Lowe-Porter   1940

The Transposed Heads
    Translated by H. T. Lowe-Porter   1941

Order of the Day
    Political Essays and Speeches of Two Decades
    Translated by H. T. Lowe-Porter, Agnes E. Meyer, and
    Eric Sutton   1942

Listen, Germany!
    Twenty-five Radio Messages to the German People over
    BBC   1943

The Tables of the Law
    Translated by H. T. Lowe-Porter   1945

Essays of Three Decades
    Translated by H. T. Lowe-Porter   1947

Doctor Faustus: The Life of the German Composer Adrian
    Leverkühn as Told by a Friend
    Translated by H. T. Lowe-Porter   1948

The Holy Sinner
    Translated by H. T. Lowe-Porter   1951

The Black Swan
    Translated by Willard R. Trask   1954

Confessions of Felix Krull, Confidence Man: The Early
    Years
    Translated by Denver Lindley   1955

———————

† Also included in *Order of the Day.*